A NEW AND TERRIBLE AGE IS DAWNING . . .

Weak and shivering, Galdar ~~~~~~~~~~~~~~~~~~~~~~~~~ voice
shaking with awe and won~~~~~~~~~~~~~~~~~~~~~~~~~ how
you did it, but I am in your ~~~~~~~~~~~~~~~~~~~~~~ you
want of me, I grant you."

"Swear to me by your swo~~~~~~~~~~~~~~~~~~ grant me what I ask,"
Mina said.

"I swear!" Galdar said harshly.

"Make me your commander," said Mina.

Galdar's jaw sagged. His mouth opened and closed. He swallowed.
"I . . . will recommend you to my superiors . . ."

"Make me your commander," she said, her voice hard as the ground,
dark as monoliths. "I do not fight for greed. I do not fight for gain. I
do not fight for power. I fight for one cause, and that is glory. Not for
myself, but for my god."

"Who is your god?" Galdar asked, awed.

Mina smiled, a fell smile, pale and cold. "The name may not be
spoken. My god is the One God. My god is the One God who made
your flesh whole. Swear your loyalty to me. Follow me to victory."

* * *

Praise for **The War of Souls Trilogy**

"Bestselling authors Weis and Hickman have made another admirable
addition to the history, lore and ways of Krynn."
—Publisher's Weekly on *Dragons of a Vanished Moon*

"*Dragons of a Fallen Sun* intertwines a multitude of threads into one
solid cord that is impossible to put down . . . For those who say there
is nothing new under the sun in the fantasy genre, this book will
make you eager for more Dragonlance."
—*Realms of Fantasy*

"Enjoyable fantasy written by professionals who know how
to make the pages turn."
—*West County Times*

"A must read."
—*Cinescape*

OMNIBUSES

THE WAR OF SOULS
Margaret Weis & Tracy Hickman

As the swelling army of Mina heads toward Sanction,
bringing entire nations under her god's banner, a group
of heroes holds out, knowing all too well the machinations
of dragons and gods have doomed Krynn before.

Dragons of a Fallen Sun
Dragons of a Lost Star
Dragons of a Vanished Moon

THE DRAGONLANCE CHRONICLES
Margaret Weis & Tracy Hickman

In the world of Krynn, the dragon minions of Takhisis,
the Dark Queen, have returned. An unlikely group of heroes
are given the power to save the world, but first they must learn
to understand themselves—and each other.

Dragons of Autumn Twilight
Dragons of Winter Night
Dragons of Spring Dawning

RAISTLIN CHRONICLES
Margaret Weis & Don Perrin

An ambitious young man sacrifices all he has to gain
the powers of a wizard. What happens will change him
in ways he never expected.

The Soulforge
Brothers at Arms

MARGARET
WEIS & TRACY
HICKMAN

THE WAR OF SOULS

DRAGONS
FALLEN
SUN

DRAGONS
LOST
STAR

DRAGONS
VANISHED
MOON

The War of Souls

©2010 Wizards of the Coast LLC

Published by Wizards of the Coast LLC

Printed in the U.S.A.

Cover art by Matthew Stawicki

Dragons of a Fallen Sun originally published April 2000
Dragons of a Lost Star originally published April 2001
Dragons of a Vanished Moon originally published January 2002

This Edition First Printing: November 2010

9 8 7 6 5 4 3 2 1

ISBN: 978-0-7869-5715-6
620- 26412000-001-EN

U.S., CANADA,
ASIA, PACIFIC, & LATIN AMERICA
Wizards of the Coast LLC
P.O. Box 707
Renton, WA 98057-0707
+1-800-324-6496

EUROPEAN HEADQUARTERS
Hasbro UK Ltd
Caswell Way
Newport, Gwent NP9 0YH
GREAT BRITAIN
Save this address for your records.

Visit our web site at www.wizards.com

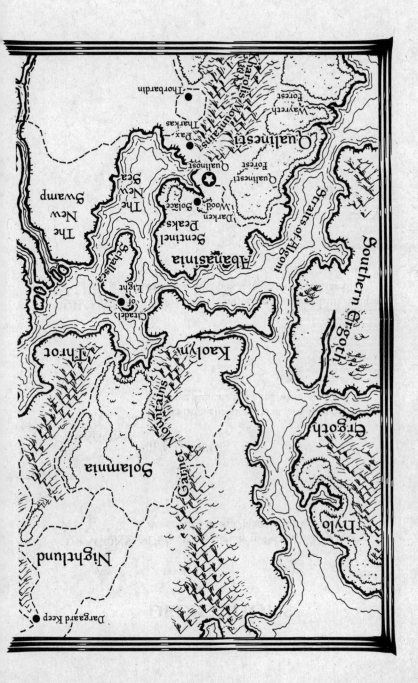

DEDICATIONS

DRAGONS
FALLEN
SUN

Dedicated gratefully to Peter Adkison, who made magic happen in Dragonlance again.

DRAGONS
LOST
STAR

To Laura Hickman

For her help, encouragement, and support over the years, we dedicate this book with much love.

DRAGONS
VANISHED
MOON

To those who fight the never ending battle against the darkness, this book is respectfully dedicated.

VOLUME

I

DRAGONS OF A

FALLEN
SUN

MINA'S SONG

The day has passed beyond our power.
The petals close upon the flower.
The light is failing in this hour
Of day's last waning breath.

The blackness of the night surrounds
The distant souls of stars now found,
Far from this world to which we're bound,
Of sorrow, fear and death.

Sleep, love; forever sleep.
Your soul the night will keep.
Embrace the darkness deep.
Sleep, love; forever sleep.

The gathering darkness takes our souls,
Embracing us in chilling folds,
Deep in a Mistress's void that holds
Our fate within her hands.

Dream, warriors, of the dark above
And feel the sweet redemption of
The Night's Consort, and of her love
For those within her bands.

Sleep, love; forever sleep.
Your soul the night will keep.
Embrace the darkness deep.
Sleep, love; forever sleep.

We close our eyes, our minds at rest,
Submit our wills to her behest,
Our weaknesses to her confessed,
And to her will we bend.

The strength of silence fills the sky,
Its depth beyond both you and I.
Into its arms our souls will fly,
Where fear and sorrows end.

Sleep, love; forever sleep.
Your soul the night will keep.
Embrace the darkness deep.
Sleep, love; forever sleep.

BOOK
1

BOOK
1

I   THE SONG OF DEATH

The dwarves named the valley *Gamashinoch*—the Song of Death. None of the living walked here of their own free will. Those who entered did so out of desperation, dire need, or because they had been ordered to do so by their commanding officer.

They had been listening to the "song" for several hours as their advance brought them nearer and nearer the desolate valley. The song was eerie, terrible. Its words, which were never clearly heard, never quite distinguishable—at least not with the ears—spoke of death and worse than death. The song spoke of entrapment, bitter frustration, unending torment. The song was a lament, a song of longing for a place the soul remembered, a haven of peace and bliss now unattainable.

On first hearing the mournful song, the Knights had reined in their steeds, hands reaching for their swords as they stared about them in unease, crying "what is that?" and "who goes there?"

But no one went there. No one of the living. The Knights looked at their commander, who stood up in his stirrups, inspecting the cliffs that soared above them on their right and the left.

"It is nothing," he said at last. "The wind among the rocks. Proceed."

He urged his horse forward along the road, which ran, turning and twisting, through the mountains known as the Lords of Doom. The men under his command followed single file, the pass was too narrow for the mounted patrol to ride abreast.

"I have heard the wind before, my lord," said one Knight gruffly, "and it has yet to have a human voice. It warns us to stay away. We would do well to heed it."

"Nonsense!" Talon Leader Ernst Magit swung around in his saddle to glare at his scout and second-in-command, who walked behind him. "Superstitious claptrap! But then you minotaurs are noted for clinging to old, outmoded ways and ideas. It is time you entered the modern era. The gods are gone, and good riddance, I say. We humans rule the world."

A single voice, a woman's voice, had first sung the Song of Death. Now her voice was joined by a fearful chorus of men, women, and children raised in a dreadful chant of hopeless loss and misery that echoed among the mountains.

At the doleful sound, several of the horses balked, refused to go farther, and, truth told, their masters did little to urge them.

Magit's horse shied and danced. He dug his spurs into the horse's flanks, leaving great bloody gouges, and the horse sulked forward, head lowered, ears twitching. Talon Leader Magit rode about half a mile when it occurred to him that he did not hear other hoof beats. Glancing around, he saw that he was proceeding alone. None of his men had followed.

Furious, Magit turned and galloped back to his command. He found half of his patrol dismounted, the other half looking very ill at ease, sitting astride horses that stood shivering on the road.

"The dumb beasts have more brains than their masters," said the minotaur from his place on the ground. Few horses will allow a minotaur to sit upon their backs and fewer still have the strength and girth to carry one of the huge minotaurs. Galdar was seven feet tall, counting his horns. He kept up with the patrol, running easily alongside the stirrup of his commander.

Magit sat upon his horse, his hands on the pommel, facing his men. He was a tall, excessively thin man, the type whose bones seem to be strung together with steel wire, for he was far stronger than he looked. His eyes were flat and watery blue, without intelligence, without depth. He was noted for his cruelty, his inflexible—many would say mindless—discipline, and his complete and total devotion to a single cause: Ernst Magit.

"You will mount your horses and you will ride after me," said Talon Leader Magit coldly, "or I will report each and every one of you to the groupcommander. I will accuse you of cowardice and betrayal of the Vision and mutiny. As you know, the penalty for even one of those counts is death."

"Can he do that?" whispered a newly made Knight on his first assignment.

"He can," returned the veterans grimly, "and he will."

The Knights remounted and urged their steeds forward, using their spurs. They were forced to circle around the minotaur, Galdar, who remained standing in the center of the road.

"Do you refuse to obey my command, minotaur?" demanded Magit angrily. "Think well before you do so. You may be the protege of the Protector of the Skull, but I doubt if even he could save you if I denounce you to the Council as a coward and an oath-breaker."

Leaning over his horse's neck, Magit spoke in mock confidentiality. "And from what I hear, Galdar, your master might not be too keen on protecting you anymore. A one-armed minotaur. A minotaur whose own kind view him with pity and with scorn. A minotaur who has been reduced to the position of 'scout.' And we all know that they assigned you to that post only because they had to do something with you. Although I did hear it suggested that they turn you out to pasture with the rest of the cows."

Galdar clenched his fist, his remaining fist, driving the sharp nails into his flesh. He knew very well that Magit was baiting him, goading him into a fight. Here, where there would be few witnesses. Here where Magit could kill the crippled minotaur and return home to claim that the fight had been a fair and glorious one. Galdar was not particularly attached to life, not since the loss of his sword arm had transformed him from fearsome warrior to plodding scout. But he'd be damned if he was going to die at the hands of Ernst Magit. Galdar wouldn't give his commander the satisfaction.

The minotaur shouldered his way past Ernst Magit, who watched him with a sneer of contempt upon his thin lips.

The patrol continued toward their destination, hoping to reach it while there was yet sunlight—if one could term the chill gray light that warmed nothing it touched sunlight. The Song of Death wailed and mourned. One of the new recruits rode with tears streaming down his cheeks. The veterans rode hunkered down, shoulders hunched up around their ears, as if they would block out the sound. But even if they had stuffed their ears with tow, even if they had blown out their eardrums, they would have still heard the terrible song.

The Song of Death sang in the heart.

The patrol rode into the valley that was called Neraka.

In a time past memory, the goddess Takhisis, Queen of Darkness, laid in the southern end of the valley a foundation stone, rescued from the blasted temple of the Kingpriest of Istar. The foundation stone began to grow, drawing upon the evil in the world to give it life. The stone grew into a temple, vast and awful; a temple of magnificent, hideous darkness.

Takhisis planned to use this temple to return to the world from which she'd been driven by Huma Dragonbane, but her way was blocked by love and self-sacrifice. Nevertheless she had great power, and she launched a war upon the world that came near to destroying it. Her evil commanders, like a pack of wild dogs, fell to fighting among themselves. A band of heroes rose up. Looking into their hearts, they found the power to thwart her, defeat her, and cast her down. Her temple at Neraka was destroyed, blasted apart in her rage at her downfall.

The temple's walls exploded and rained down from the skies on that terrible day, huge black boulders that crushed the city of Neraka. Cleansing fires destroyed the buildings of the cursed city, burned down its markets and its slave pens, its numerous guard houses, filling its twisted, mazelike streets with ash.

Over fifty years later, no trace of the original city remained. The splinters of the temple's bones littered the floor of the southern portion of the valley of Neraka. The ash had long since blown away. Nothing would grow in this part of the valley. All sign of life had long been covered up by the swirling sands.

Only the black boulders, remnants of the temple, remained in the valley. They were an awful sight, and even Talon Leader Magit, gazing upon them for the first time, wondered privately if his decision to ride into this part of the valley had been a smart one. He could have taken the long route around, but that would have added two days to his travel, and he was late as it was, having spent a few extra nights with a new whore who had arrived at his favorite bawdyhouse. He needed to make up time, and he'd chosen as his shortcut this route through the southern end of the valley.

Perhaps due to the force of the explosion, the black rock that had formed the outer walls of the temple had taken on a crystalline structure. Jutting up from the sand, the boulders were not craggy, not lumpy. They were smooth-sided, with sharply defined planes culminating in faceted points. Imagine black quartz crystals jutting up from gray sand, some four times the height of a man. Such a man could see his reflection in those glossy black planes, a reflection that was distorted, twisted, yet completely recognizable as being a reflection of himself.

These men had willingly joined up with the army of the Knights of Takhisis, tempted by the promises of loot and slaves won in battle, by their own delight in killing and bullying, by their hatred of elves or kender or dwarves or anyone different from themselves. These men, long since hardened against every good feeling, looked into the shining black plane of the crystals and were appalled by the faces that looked back. For on those faces they could see their mouths opening to sing the terrible song.

Most looked and shuddered and quickly averted their gaze. Galdar took care not to look. At first sight of the black crystals rising from the ground, he had lowered his eyes, and he kept them lowered out of reverence and respect. Call it superstition, as Ernst Magit most certainly would. The gods themselves were not in this valley. Galdar knew that to be impossible; the gods had been driven from Krynn more than thirty years ago. But the ghosts of the gods lingered here, of that Galdar was certain.

Ernst Magit looked at his reflection in the rocks, and simply because he shrank from it inwardly, he forced himself to stare at it until he had stared it down.

"I will not be *cowed* by the sight of my own shadow!" he said with a meaningful glance at Galdar. Magit had only recently thought up this bovine humor. He considered it extremely funny and highly original, and he lost no opportunity to use it. "Cowed. Do you get it, minotaur?" Ernst Magit laughed.

The death song swept up the man's laughter and gave it melody and tone—dark, off key, discordant, opposing the rhythm of the other voices of the song. The sound was so horrible that Magit was shaken. He coughed, swallowed his laughter, much to the relief of his men.

"You have brought us here, Talon Leader," said Galdar. "We have seen that this part of the valley is uninhabited, that no force of Solamnics hides here, prepared to sweep down on us. We may proceed toward our objective safe in the knowledge that we have nothing *from the land of the living* to fear from this direction. Let us now leave this place, and swiftly. Let us turn back and make our report."

The horses had entered the southern valley with such reluctance that in some cases their riders had been forced to dismount again and cover their eyes and guide them, as if from a burning building. Both man and beast were clearly eager to be gone. The horses edged their way back toward the road by which they'd arrived, their riders sidling along with them.

Ernst Magit wanted to leave this place as much as any of them. It was for precisely that reason that he decided they would stay. He was a coward at heart. He knew he was a coward. All his life, he'd done deeds to prove to himself that he wasn't. Nothing truly heroic. Magit avoided danger when at all possible, one reason he was riding patrol duty and not joining with the other Knights of Neraka to lay siege to the Solamnic-controlled city of Sanction. He undertook to perform cheap, petty actions and deeds that involved no risk to himself but that would prove to himself and to his men he wasn't afraid. A deed such as spending the night in this cursed valley.

Magit made a show of squinting up at the sky, which was a pale and unwholesome yellow, a peculiar shade, such as none of the Knights had ever before seen.

"It is now twilight," he announced sententiously. "I do not want to find myself benighted in the mountains. We will make camp here and ride out in the morning."

The Knights stared at their commander incredulously, appalled. The wind had ceased to blow. The song no longer sang in their hearts. Silence settled over the valley, a silence that was at first a welcome change but that they were growing to loathe the longer it lasted. The silence weighed on them, oppressed them, smothered them. None spoke. They waited for their commander to tell them he'd been playing a little joke on them.

Talon Leader Magit dismounted his horse. "We will set up camp here. Pitch my command tent near the tallest of those monoliths. Galdar, you're in charge of setting up camp. I trust you can handle that simple task?"

His words seemed unnaturally loud, his voice shrill and raucous. A breath of air, cold and sharp, hissed through the valley, swept the sand into dust devils that swirled across the barren ground and whispered away.

"You are making a mistake, sir," said Galdar in a soft undertone, to disturb the silence as little as possible. "We are not wanted here."

"Who does not want us, Galdar?" Talon Leader Magit sneered. "These rocks?" He slapped the side of a black crystal monolith. "Ha! What a thick-skulled, superstitious cow!" Magit's voice hardened. "You men. Dismount and begin setting up camp. That is an order."

Ernst Magit stretched his limbs, making a show of being relaxed. He bent double at the waist, did a few limbering exercises. The Knights, sullen and unhappy, did as he commanded. They unpacked their saddle rolls, began setting up the small, two-man tents carried by half the patrol. The others unpacked food and water.

The tents were a failure. No amount of hammering could drive the iron spikes into the hard ground. Every blow of the hammer reverberated among the mountains, came back to them amplified a hundred times, until it seemed as if the mountains were hammering on them.

Galdar threw down his mallet, which he had been awkwardly wielding with his remaining hand.

"What's the matter, minotaur?" Magit demanded. "Are you so weak you can't drive a tent stake?"

"Try it yourself, sir," said Galdar.

The other men tossed down their mallets and stood staring at their commander in sullen defiance.

Magit was pale with anger. "You men can sleep in the open if you are too stupid to pitch a simple tent!"

He did not, however, choose to try to hammer the tent stakes into the rocky floor. He searched around until he located four of the black, crystal monoliths that formed a rough, irregular square.

"Tie my tent to four of these boulders," he ordered. "At least *I* will sleep well this night."

Galdar did as he was commanded. He wrapped the ropes around the bases of the monoliths, all the while muttering a minotaur incantation meant to propitiate the spirits of the restless dead.

The men also endeavored to tie their horses to the monoliths, but the beasts plunged and bucked in panicked terror. Finally, the Knights strung a line between two of the monoliths and tied the horses up there. The horses huddled together, restive and nervous, rolling their eyes and keeping as far from the black rocks as possible.

While the men worked, Ernst Magit drew a map from his saddlebags and, with a final glare around to remind them of their duty, spread the map open and began studying it with a studious and unconcerned air that fooled no one. He was sweating, and he'd done no work.

Long shadows were stealing over the valley of Neraka, making the valley far darker than the sky, which was lit with a flame-yellow afterglow. The air was hot, hotter than when they'd entered, but sometimes eddies of cold wind swirled down from the west, chilling the bones to the marrow. The Knights had brought no wood with them. They ate cold rations, or tried to eat them. Every mouthful was polluted with sand, everything they ate tasted of ashes. They eventually threw most of their food away. Seated upon the hard ground, they constantly looked over their shoulders, peering intently into the shadows. Each man had his sword drawn. No need to set the watch. No man intended to sleep.

"Ho! Look at this!" Ernst Magit called out with triumph. "I have made an important discovery! It is well that we spent some time here." He pointed at his map and then to the west. "See that mountain range there. It is not marked upon the map. It must be newly formed. I shall certainly bring this to the attention of the Protector. Perhaps the range will be named in my honor."

Galdar looked at the mountain range. He rose slowly to his feet, staring hard into the western sky. Certainly at first glance the formation of iron gray and sullen blue looked very much as if a new mountain had thrust up from the ground. But as Galdar watched, he noticed something that the talon leader, in his eagerness, had missed. This mountain was growing, expanding, at an alarming rate.

"Sir!" Galdar cried. "That is no mountain! Those are storm clouds!"

"You are already a cow, don't be an ass as well," Magit said. He had picked up a bit of black rock and was using it like chalk to add Mount Magit to the wonders of the world.

"Sir, I spent ten years at sea when I was a youth," said Galdar. "I know a storm when I see one. Yet even I have never seen anything like that!"

Now the cloud bank reared up with incredible speed, solid black at its heart, roiling and churning like some many-headed devouring monster, biting off the tops of the mountains as it overtook them, crawling over them to consume them whole. The chill wind strengthened, whipping the sand from the ground into eyes and mouths, tearing at the command tent, which flapped wildly and strained against its bonds.

The wind began to sing again that same terrible song, keening, wailing in despair, shrieking in anguished torment.

Buffeted by the wind, the men struggled to their feet. "Commander! We should leave!" Galdar roared. "Now! Before the storm breaks!"

"Yes," said Ernst Magit, pale and shaken. He licked his lips, spit out sand. "Yes, you are right. We should leave immediately. Never mind the tent! Bring me my horse!"

A bolt of lightning flashed out from the blackness, speared the ground near where the horses were tethered. Thunder exploded. The concussion knocked some of the men flat. The horses screamed, reared, lashed out with their hooves. The men who were still standing tried to calm them, but the horses would have none of it. Tearing free of the rope that held them, the horses galloped away in mad panic.

"Catch them!" Ernst screamed, but the men had all they could do to stand upright against the pummeling wind. One or two took a few staggering steps after the horses, but it was obvious that the chase was a futile one.

The storm clouds raced across the sky, battling the sunlight, defeating it handily. The sun fell, overcome by darkness.

Night was upon them, a night thick with swirling sand. Galdar could see nothing at all, not even his own single hand. The next second all around him was illuminated by another devastating lightning bolt.

"Lie down!" he bellowed, flinging himself to the ground. "Lie flat! Keep away from the monoliths!"

Rain slashed sideways, coming at them like arrows fired from a million bowstrings. Hail pounded on them like iron-tipped flails, cutting and bruising. Galdar's hide was tough, the hail was like stinging ant bites to him. The other men cried out in pain and terror. Lightning walked among them, casting its flaming spears. Thunder shook the ground and boomed and roared.

Galdar lay sprawled on his stomach, fighting against the impulse to tear at the ground with his hand, to burrow into the depths of the world. He was astounded to see, in the next lightning flash, his commander trying to stand up.

"Sir, keep down!" Galdar roared and made a grab for him.

Magit snarled a curse and kicked at Galdar's hand. Head down against the wind, the talon leader lurched over to one of the monoliths. He crouched behind it, used its great bulk to shield him from the lancing rain and the hammering hail. Laughing at the rest of his men, he sat on the ground, placed his back against the stone and stretched out his legs.

The lightning flash blinded Galdar. The blast deafened him. The force of the thunderbolt lifted him up off the ground, slammed him back down. The bolt had struck so close that he had heard it sizzle the air, could smell the phosphorous and the sulphur. He could also smell something else—burned flesh. He rubbed his eyes to try to see through the jagged glare. When his sight was restored, he looked in the direction of the commander. In the next lightning flash, he saw a misshapen mass huddled at the foot of the monolith.

Magit's flesh glowed red beneath a black crust, like a hunk of overcooked meat. Smoke rose from it; the wind whipped it away, along with flecks of charred flesh. The skin of the man's face had burned away, revealing a mouthful of hideously grinning teeth.

"Glad to see you're still laughing, Talon Leader," Galdar muttered. "You were warned."

Galdar scrunched down even closer to the ground, cursed his ribs for being in the way.

The rain fell harder, if that were possible. He wondered how long the raging storm could last. It seemed to have lasted a lifetime, seemed to him that he had been born into this storm and that he would grow old and die in this storm. A hand grabbed hold of his arm, shook him.

"Sir! Look there!" One of the Knights had crawled across the ground, was right next to him. "Sir!" The Knight put his mouth to Galdar's ear, shouted hoarsely to make himself heard over the lashing rain and pounding hail, the constant thunder and, worse than rain or hail or thunder, the song of death. "I saw something move out there!"

Galdar lifted his head, peered in the direction the Knight pointed, peered into the very heart of the valley of Neraka.

"Wait until the next lightning flash!" the Knight yelled. "There! There it is!"

The next lightning flash was not a bolt but a sheet of flame that lit the sky and the ground and the mountains with a purple white radiance. Silhouetted against the awful glow, a figure moved toward them, walking calmly through the raging storm, seeming untouched by the gale, unmoved by the lightning, unafraid of the thunder.

"Is it one of ours?" Galdar asked, thinking at first that one of the men might have gone mad and bolted like the horses.

But he knew the moment he asked the question that this was not the case. The figure was walking, not running. The figure was not fleeing, it was approaching.

The lightning flared out. Darkness fell, and the figure was lost. Galdar waited impatiently for the next lightning flash to show him this insane being who braved the fury of the storm. The next flash lit the ground, the mountains, the sky. The person was still there, still moving toward them. And it seemed to Galdar that the song of death had transformed into a paean of celebration.

Darkness again. The wind died. The rain softened to a steady downpour. The hail ceased altogether. Thunder rumbled a drumroll, which seemed to mark time with the pace of the strange figure of darkness drawing steadily nearer with each illuminating flare. The storm carried the battle to the other side of the mountains, to other parts of the world. Galdar rose to his feet.

Soaking wet, the Knights wiped water and muck from their eyes, looked ruefully at sodden blankets. The wind was cold and crisp and chill, and they were shivering except Galdar, whose thick hide and fur pelt protected him from all but the most severe cold. He shook the rain water from his horns and waited for the figure to come within hailing distance.

Stars, glittering cold and deadly as spear points, appeared in the west. The ragged edges of the storm's rear echelon seemed to uncover the stars as they passed. The single moon had risen in defiance of the thunder. The figure was no more than twenty feet away now, and by the moon's argent light Galdar could see the person clearly.

Human, a youth, to judge by the slender, well-knit body and the smooth skin of the face. Dark hair had been shaved close to the skull, leaving only a red stubble. The absence of hair accentuated the features of the face and thrust into prominence the high cheekbones, the sharp chin, the mouth in its bow curve. The youth wore the shirt and tunic of a common foot knight and leather boots, carried no sword upon his hip nor any sort of weapon that Galdar could see.

"Halt and be recognized!" he shouted harshly. "Stop right there. At the edge of camp."

The youth obligingly halted, his hands raised, palms outward to show they were empty.

Galdar drew his sword. In this strange night, he was taking no chances. He held the sword awkwardly in his left hand. The weapon was almost useless to him. Unlike some other amputees, he had never learned to fight with his opposite hand. He had been a skilled swordsman before his injury, now he was clumsy and inept, as likely to do damage to himself as to a foe. Many were the times Ernst Magit had watched Galdar practice, watched him fumble, and laughed uproariously.

Magit wouldn't be doing much laughing now.

Galdar advanced, sword in hand. The hilt was wet and slippery, he hoped he wouldn't drop it. The youth could not know that Galdar was a washed-up warrior, a has-been. The minotaur looked intimidating, and Galdar was somewhat surprised that the youth did not quail before him, did not even really look all that impressed.

"I am unarmed," said the youth in a deep voice that did not match the youthful appearance. The voice had an odd timbre to it, sweet, musical, reminding Galdar strangely of one of the voices he'd heard in the song, the song now hushed and murmuring, as if in reverence. The voice was not the voice of a man.

Galdar looked closely at the youth, at the slender neck that was like the long stem of a lily, supporting the skull, which was perfectly smooth beneath its red down of hair, marvelously formed. The minotaur looked closely at the lithe body. The arms were muscular, as were the legs in their woolen stockings. The wet shirt, which was too big, hung loosely from the slender shoulders. Galdar could see nothing beneath its wet folds, could not ascertain yet whether this human was male or female.

The other knights gathered around him, all of them staring at the wet youth; wet and glistening as a newborn child. The men were frowning, uneasy, wary. Small blame to them. Everyone was asking the same question as Galdar. What in the name of the great horned god who had died and left his people bereft was this human doing in this accursed valley on this accursed night?

"What are you called?" Galdar demanded.

"My name is Mina."

A girl. A slip of a girl. She could be no more than seventeen . . . if that. Yet even though she had spoken her name, a feminine name popular among humans, even though he could trace her sex in the smooth lines of her neck and the grace of her movements, he still doubted. There was something very unwomanly about her.

Mina smiled slightly, as if she could hear his unspoken doubts, and said, "I *am* female." She shrugged. "Though it makes little difference."

"Come closer," Galdar ordered harshly.

The girl obeyed, took a step forward.

Galdar looked into her eyes, and his breath very nearly stopped. He had seen humans of all shapes and sizes during his lifetime, but he'd never seen one, never seen any living being with eyes like these.

Unnaturally large, deep-set, the eyes were the color of amber, the pupils black, the irises encircled by a ring of shadow. The absence of hair made the eyes appear larger still. Mina seemed all eyes, and those eyes absorbed Galdar and imprisoned him, as golden amber holds imprisoned the carcasses of small insects.

"Are you the commander?" she asked.

Galdar flicked a glance in the direction of the charred body lying at the base of the monolith. "I am now," he said.

Mina followed his gaze, regarded the corpse with cool detachment. She turned the amber eyes back to Galdar, who could have sworn he saw the body of Magit locked inside.

"What are you doing here, girl?" the minotaur asked harshly. "Did you lose your way in the storm?"

"No. I found my way in the storm," said Mina. The amber eyes were luminous, unblinking. "I found you. I have been called, and I have answered. You are Knights of Takhisis, are you not?"

"We were once," said Galdar dryly. "We waited long for Takhisis's return, but now the commanders admit what most of us knew long before. She is not coming back. Therefore we have come to term ourselves Knights of Neraka."

Mina listened, considered this. She seemed to like it, for she nodded gravely. "I understand. I have come to join the Knights of Neraka."

At any other time, in any other place, the Knights might have snickered or made rude remarks. But the men were in no mood for levity. Neither was Galdar. The storm had been terrifying, unlike any he'd ever experienced, and he had lived in this world forty years. Their talon leader was dead. They had a long walk ahead of them, unless by some miracle they could recover the horses. They had no food—the horses had run away with their supplies. No water except what they could wring out of their sodden blankets.

"Tell the silly chit to run back home to mama," said one Knight impatiently. "What do *we* do, Subcommander?"

"I say we get out of here," said another. "I'll walk all night if I have to." The others muttered their assent.

Galdar looked to the heavens. The sky was clear. Thunder rumbled, but in the distance. Far away, lightning flashed purple on the western horizon. The moon gave light enough to travel. Galdar was tired, unusually tired. The men were hollow-cheeked and gaunt, all of them near exhaustion. Yet he knew how they felt.

"We're moving out," he said. "But first we need to do something with that." He jerked a thumb at the smoldering body of Ernst Magit.

"Leave it," said one of the Knights.

Galdar shook his horned head. He was conscious, all the while, of the girl watching him intently with those strange eyes of hers.

"Do you want to be haunted by his spirit the rest of your days?" Galdar demanded.

The others eyed each other, eyed the body. They would have guffawed at the thought of Magit's ghost haunting them the day before. Not now.

"What do we do with him?" demanded one plaintively. "We can't bury the bastard. The ground's too hard. We don't have any wood for a fire."

"Wrap the body in that tent," said Mina. "Take those rocks and build a cairn over him. He is not the first to die in the valley of Neraka," she added coolly, "nor will he be the last."

Galdar glanced over his shoulder. The tent they had strung between the monoliths remained intact, though it sagged with an accumulation of rainwater.

"The girl's idea is a good one," he said. "Cut down the tent and use it for a shroud. And be quick about it. The quicker we're finished, the quicker we're away. Strip off his armor," he added. "We're required to take it back to headquarters as proof of his death."

"How?" asked one of the Knights, grimacing. "His flesh is stuck to the metal like a steak seared on a gridiron."

"Cut it off," said Galdar. "Clean it up as best you can. I wasn't that fond of him that I want to be hauling bits of him around."

The men went about their grisly task with a will, eager to be done and away.

Galdar turned back to Mina, found those amber eyes, large, intent upon him.

"You had best go back to your family, girl," he said gruffly. "We'll be traveling hard and fast. We won't have time to coddle you. Besides, you're a female. These men are not very great respecters of women's virtues. You run along home."

"I am home," said Mina with a glance around the valley. The black monoliths reflected the cold light of the stars, summoned the stars to shine pale and chill among them. "And I have found my family. I will become a Knight. That is my calling."

Galdar was exasperated, uncertain what to say. The last thing he wanted was this fey woman-child traveling with them. But she was so self-possessed, so completely in control of herself and in control of the situation that he could not come up with any rational argument.

Thinking the matter over, he made to return his sword to its sheath. The hilt was wet and slippery, his grip on it awkward. He fumbled, nearly dropped the sword. Managing to hang onto it by a desperate effort, he looked up fiercely, glowering, daring her to so much as smile with either derision or pity.

She watched his struggles, said nothing, her face expressionless.

Galdar shoved the sword into the sheath. "As to joining the Knighthood, the best thing to do is go to your local headquarters and put in your name."

He continued with a recitation of the recruitment policies, the training involved. He launched into a discourse about the years of dedication and self-sacrifice, all the while thinking of Ernst Magit, who had bought his way into the Knighthood, and suddenly Galdar realized that he'd lost her.

The girl was not listening to him. She seemed to be listening to another voice, a voice he could not hear. Her gaze was abstracted, her face smooth, without expression.

His words trailed off.

"Do you not find it difficult to fight one handed?" she asked.

He regarded her grimly. "I may be awkward," he said caustically, "but I can handle a sword well enough to strike your shorn head from your body!"

She smiled. "What are you called?"

He turned away. This conversation was at an end. He looked to see that the men had managed to separate Magit from his armor, were rolling the still-smoking lump of a corpse onto the tent.

"Galdar, I believe," Mina continued.

He turned back to stare at her in astonishment, wondering how she knew his name.

Of course, he thought, one of the men must have spoken it. But he could not recall any of them having done so.

"Give me your hand, Galdar," Mina said to him.

He glowered at her. "Leave this place while you have a chance, girl! We are in no mood for silly games. My commander's dead. These men are my responsibility. We have no mounts, no food."

"Give me your hand, Galdar," said Mina softly.

At the sound of her voice, rough, sweet, he heard again the song singing among the rocks. He felt his hackles rise. A shudder went through him, a thrill flashed along his spine. He meant to turn away from her, but he found himself raising his left hand.

"No, Galdar," said Mina. "Your right hand. Give me your right hand."

"I have no right hand!" Galdar cried out in rage and anguish.

The cry rattled in his throat. The men turned, alarmed, at the strangled sound.

Galdar stared in disbelief. The arm had been cut off at the shoulder. Extending outward from the stump was a ghostly image of what had once been his right arm. The image wavered in the wind, as if his arm were made of smoke and ash, yet he could see it clearly, could see it reflected in the smooth black plane of the monolith. He could feel the phantom arm, but then he'd always felt the arm even when it wasn't there. Now he watched his arm, his right arm, lift; watched his hand, his right hand, reach out trembling fingers.

Mina extended her hand, touched the phantom hand of the minotaur.

"Your sword arm is restored," she said to him.

Galdar stared in boundless astoundment.

His arm. His right arm was once again . . .

His right arm.

No longer a phantom arm. No longer an arm of smoke and ash, an arm of dreams to be lost in the despair of waking. Galdar closed his eyes, closed them tight, and then opened them.

The arm remained.

The other Knights were struck dumb and motionless. Their faces dead white in the moonlight, they stared at Galdar, stared at the arm, stared at Mina.

Galdar ordered his fingers to open and clench, and they obeyed. He reached out with his left hand, trembling, and touched the arm.

The skin was warm, the fur was soft, the arm was flesh and bone and blood. The arm was real.

Galdar reached down the hand and drew his sword. His fingers closed over the hilt lovingly. He was suddenly blinded by tears.

Weak and shivering, Galdar sank to his knees. "Lady," he said, his voice shaking with awe and wonder, "I do not know what you did or how you did it, but I am in your debt for the rest of my days. Whatever you want of me, I grant you."

"Swear to me by your sword arm that you will grant me what I ask," Mina said.

"I swear!" Galdar said harshly.

"Make me your commander," said Mina.

Galdar's jaw sagged. His mouth opened and closed. He swallowed. "I . . . I will recommend you to my superiors . . ."

"Make me your commander," she said, her voice hard as the ground, dark as the monoliths. "I do not fight for greed. I do not fight for gain. I do not fight for power. I fight for one cause, and that is glory. Not for myself, but for my god."

"Who is your god?" Galdar asked, awed.

Mina smiled, a fell smile, pale and cold. "The name may not be spoken. My god is the One God. The One who rides the storm, the One who rules the night. My god is the One God who made your flesh whole. Swear your loyalty to me, Galdar. Follow me to victory."

Galdar thought of all the commanders under whom he'd served. Commanders such as Ernst Magit, who rolled their eyes when the Vision of Neraka was mentioned. The Vision was fake, phony, most of the upper echelon knew it. Commanders such as the Master of the Lily, Galdar's patron, who yawned openly during the recitation of the Blood Oath, who had brought the minotaur into the Knighthood as a joke. Commanders such as the current Lord of the Night, Targonne, whom everyone knew was skimming funds from the knightly coffers to enrich himself.

Galdar raised his head, looked into the amber eyes. "You are my commander, Mina," he said. "I swear fealty to you and to no other."

Mina touched his hand again. Her touch was painful, scalded his blood. He reveled in the sensation. The pain was welcome. For too long now, he'd felt the pain of an arm that wasn't there.

"You will be my second in command, Galdar." Mina turned the amber gaze upon the other Knights. "Will the rest of you follow me?"

Some of the men had been with Galdar when he had lost his arm, had seen the blood spurt from the shattered limb. Four of these men had held him down when the surgeon cut off his arm. They had heard his pleas for death, a death they'd refused to grant him, a death that he could not, in honor, grant himself. These men looked at the new arm, saw Galdar holding a sword again. They had seen the girl walk through the murderous, unnatural storm, walk unscathed.

These men were in their thirties, some of them. Veterans of brutal wars and tough campaigns. It was all very well for Galdar to swear allegiance to this strange woman-child. She had made him whole. But for themselves . . .

Mina did not press them, she did not cajole or argue. She appeared to take their agreement for granted. Walking over to where the corpse of the talon leader lay on the ground beneath the monolith, the body partially wrapped in the tent, Mina picked up Magit's breastplate. She looked at it, studied it, and then, sliding her arms through the straps, she put on the breastplate over her wet shirt. The breastplate was too big for her and heavy. Galdar expected to see her bowed down under the weight.

He gaped to see instead the metal glow red, reform, mold itself to her slender body, embrace her like a lover.

The breastplate had been black with the image of a skull upon it. The armor had been hit by the lightning strike, apparently, though the damage the strike had done was exceedingly strange. The skull adorning the breastplate was split in twain. A lightning bolt of steel sliced through it.

"This will be my standard," said Mina, touching the skull.

She put on the rest of Magit's accoutrements, sliding the bracers over her arms, buckling the shin guards over her legs. Each piece of armor glowed red when it touched her as if newly come from the forge. Each piece, when cooled, fit her as if it had been fashioned for her.

She lifted the helm, but did not put it on her head. She handed the helm to Galdar. "Hold that for me, Subcommander," she said.

He received the helm proudly, reverently, as if it were an artifact for which he had quested all his life.

Mina knelt down beside the body of Ernst Magit. Lifting the dead, charred hand in her own, she bowed her head and began to pray.

None could hear her words, none could hear what she said or to whom she said it. The song of death keened among the stones. The stars vanished, the moon disappeared. Darkness enveloped them. She prayed, her whispered words bringing comfort.

Mina arose from her prayers to find all the Knights on their knees before her. In the darkness, they could see nothing, not each other, not even themselves. They saw only her.

"You are my commander, Mina," said one, gazing upon her as the starving gaze upon bread, the thirsty gaze upon cool water. "I pledge my life to you."

"Not to me," she said. "To the One God."

"The One God!" Their voices lifted and were swept up in the song that was no longer frightening but was exalting, stirring, a call to arms. "Mina and the One God!"

The stars shone in the monoliths. The moonlight gleamed in the jagged lightning bolt of Mina's armor. Thunder rumbled again, but this time it was not from the sky.

"The horses!" shouted one of the knights. "The horses have returned."

Leading the horses was a steed the likes of which none of them had ever seen. Red as wine, red as blood, the horse left the others far behind. The horse came straight to Mina and nuzzled her, rested its head over her shoulder.

"I sent Foxfire for the mounts. We will have need of them," said Mina, stroking the black mane of the blood-colored roan. "We ride south this night and ride hard. We must be in Sanction in three days' time."

"Sanction!" Galdar gaped. "But, girl—I mean, Talon Leader—the Solamnics control Sanction! The city is under siege. Our posting is in Khur. Our orders—"

"We ride this night to Sanction," said Mina. Her gaze turned southward and never looked back.

"But, why, Talon Leader?" Galdar asked.

"Because we are called," Mina answered.

2   SILVANOSHEI

The strange and unnatural storm laid siege to all of Ansalon. Lightning walked the land; gigantic, ground-shaking warriors who hurled bolts of fire. Ancient trees—huge oaks that had withstood both Cataclysms—burst into flame and were reduced to smoldering ruin in an instant. Whirlwinds raged behind the thundering warriors, ripping apart homes, flinging boards, brick, and stone and mortar into the air with lethal abandon. Torrential cloudbursts caused rivers to swell and overflow their banks, washing away the young green shoots of grain struggling up from the darkness to bask in the early summer sun.

In Sanction, besieger and besieged alike abandoned the ongoing struggle to seek refuge from the terrible storm. Ships on the high seas tried to ride it out, with the result that some went under, never to be seen or heard from again. Others would later limp home with jury-rigged masts, telling tales of sailors swept overboard, the pumps at work day and night.

In Palanthas, innumerable cracks appeared in the roof of the Great Library. The rain poured inside, sending Bertrem and the monks into a mad scramble to staunch the flow, mop the floor and move precious volumes to safety. In Tarsis, the rain was so heavy that the sea which had vanished during the Cataclysm returned, to the wonder and astonishment of all inhabitants. The sea was gone a few days later, leaving behind gasping fish and an ungodly smell.

The storm struck the island of Schallsea a particularly devastating blow. The winds blew out every single window in the Cozy Hearth. Ships that rode at anchor in the harbor were dashed against the cliffs or smashed into the docks. A tidal surge washed away many buildings and homes built near the shoreline. Countless people died, countless others were left homeless. Refugees stormed the Citadel of Light, pleading for the mystics to come to their aid.

The Citadel was a beacon of hope in Krynn's dark night. Trying to fill the void left by the absence of the gods, Goldmoon had discovered the mystical power of the heart, had brought healing back to the world. She was living proof that although Paladine and Mishakal were gone, their power for good lived on in the hearts of those who had loved them.

Yet Goldmoon was growing old. The memories of the gods were fading. And so, it seemed, was the power of the heart. One after another, the mystics felt their power recede, a tide that went out but never returned. Still the mystics of the Citadel were glad to open their doors and their hearts to the storm's victims, provide shelter and succor, and work to heal the injured as best they could.

Solamnic Knights, who had established a fortress on Schallsea, rode forth to do battle with the storm—one of the most fearsome enemies these valiant Knights had ever faced. At risk of their own lives, the Knights plucked people from the raging water and dragged them from beneath smashed buildings, working in the wind and rain and lightning-shattered darkness to save the lives of those they were sworn by Oath and Measure to protect.

The Citadel of Light withstood the storm's rage, although its buildings were buffeted by fierce winds and lancing rain. As if in a last ditch attempt to make its wrath felt, the storm hurled hailstones the size of a man's head upon the citadel's crystal walls. Everywhere the hailstones struck, tiny cracks appeared in the crystalline walls. Rainwater seeped through these cracks, trickled like tears down the walls.

One particularly loud crash came from the vicinity of the chambers of Goldmoon, founder and mistress of the Citadel. The mystics heard the sound of breaking glass and ran in fear to see if the elderly woman was safe. To their astonishment, they found the door to her rooms locked. They beat upon it, called upon her to let them inside.

A voice, low and awful to hear, a voice that was Goldmoon's beloved voice and yet was not, ordered them to leave her in peace, to go about their duties. Others needed their aid, she said. She did not. Baffled, uneasy, most did as they were told. Those who lingered behind reported hearing the sound of sobbing, heartbroken and despairing.

"She, too, has lost her power," said those outside her door. Thinking that they understood, they left her alone.

When morning finally came and the sun rose to shine a lurid red in the sky, people stood about in dazed horror, looking upon the destruction wrought during the terrible night. The mystics went to Goldmoon's chamber to ask for her counsel, but no answer came. The door to Goldmoon's chamber remained closed and barred.

The storm also swept through Qualinesti, an elven kingdom, but one that was separated from its cousins by distance that could be measured both in hundreds of miles and in ancient hatred and distrust. In Qualinesti, whirling winds uprooted giant trees and flung them about like the slender sticks used in *Quin Thalasi*, a popular elven game. The storm shook the fabled Tower of the Speaker of the Sun on its foundation, sent the beautiful stained glass of its storied windows raining down upon the floor. Rising water flooded the lower chambers of the newly constructed fortress of the Dark Knights at Newport, forcing them to do what an enemy army could not—abandon their posts.

The storm woke even the great dragons, slumbering, bloated and fat, in their lairs that were rich with tribute. The storm shook the Peak of Malys, lair of Malystryx, the enormous red dragon who now fashioned herself the Queen of Ansalon, soon to become Goddess of Ansalon, if she had her way. The rain formed rushing rivers that invaded Malys's volcanic home. Rainwater flowed into the lava pools, creating enormous clouds of a noxious-smelling steam that filled the corridors and halls. Wet, half-blind, choking in the fumes, Malys roared her indignation and flew from lair to lair, trying to find one that was dry enough for her to return to sleep.

Finally she was driven to seek the lower levels of her mountain home. Malys was an ancient dragon with a malevolent wisdom. She sensed something unnatural about this storm, and it made her uneasy. Grumbling and muttering to herself, she entered the Chamber of the Totem. Here, on an outcropping of black rock, Malys had piled the skulls of all the lesser dragons she had consumed when she first came to the world. Silver skulls and gold, red skulls and blue stood one atop the other, a monument to her greatness. Malys was comforted by the sight of the skulls. Each brought a memory of a battle won, a foe defeated and devoured. The rain could not penetrate this far down in her mountain home. She could not hear the wind howl. The flashes of lightning did not disturb her slumbers.

Malys gazed upon the empty eyes of the skulls with pleasure, and perhaps she dozed, because suddenly it seemed to her that the eyes of skulls were alive and they were watching her. She snorted, reared her head. She stared closely at the skulls, at the eyes. The lava pool at the heart of the mountain cast a lurid light upon the skulls, sent shadows winking and blinking in the empty eye sockets. Berating herself for an overactive imagination, Malys coiled her body comfortably around the totem and fell asleep.

Another of the great dragons, a Green known grandiosely as Beryllinthranox was also not able to sleep through the storm. Beryl's lair was formed of living trees—ironwoods and redwoods—and enormous, twining vines. The vines and branches of the trees were so thickly interwoven that no raindrop had ever managed to wriggle its way through. But the rain that fell from the roiling black clouds of this storm seemed to make it a personal mission to find a way to penetrate the leaves. Once one had managed to sneak inside, it opened the way for thousands of its fellows. Beryl woke in surprise at the unaccustomed feel of water splashing on her nose. One of the great redwoods that formed a pillar of her lair was struck by a lightning bolt. The tree burst into flames, flames that spread quickly, feeding on rainwater as if it were lamp oil.

Beryl's roar of alarm brought her minions scrambling to douse the flames. Dragons, Reds and Blues who had joined Beryl rather than be consumed by her, dared the flames to pluck out the burning trees and cast them into the sea. Draconians pulled down blazing vines, smothered the flames with dirt and mud. Hostages and prisoners were put to work fighting the fires. Many died doing so, but eventually Beryl's lair was saved. She was in a terrible humor for days afterward, however, convincing herself that the storm had been an attack waged magically by her cousin Malys. Beryl meant to rule someday in Malys's stead. Using her magic to rebuild—a magical power that had lately been dwindling, something else Beryl blamed on Malys—the Green nursed her wrongs and plotted revenge.

Khellendros the Blue (he had abandoned the name Skie for this more magnificent title, which meant Storm over Ansalon), was one of the few of the dragons native to Krynn to have emerged from the Dragon Purge. He was now ruler of Solamnia and all its environs. He was overseer of Schallsea and the Citadel of Light, which he allowed to remain because—according to him—he found it amusing to watch the petty humans struggle futilely against the growing darkness. In truth, the real reason he permitted the citadel to thrive in safety was the citadel's guardian, a silver dragon named Mirror. Mirror and Skie were longtime foes and now, in their mutual detestation of the new, great dragons from afar who had killed so many of their brethren, they had become not friends, but not quite enemies either.

Khellendros was bothered by the storm far more than either of the great dragons, although—strangely enough—the storm did not do his lair much damage. He paced restively about his enormous cave high in the Vingaard mountains, watched the lightning warriors strike viciously at the ramparts of the High Clerist's Tower, and he thought he heard a voice in the wind, a voice that sang of death. Khellendros did not sleep but watched the storm to its end.

The storm lost none of its power as it roared down upon the ancient elven kingdom of Silvanesti. The elves had erected a magical shield over their kingdom, a shield that had thus far kept the marauding dragons from conquering their lands, a shield that also kept out all other races. The elves had finally succeeded in their historic goal of isolating themselves from the troubles of the rest of the world. But the shield did not keep out the thunder and rain, wind and lightning.

Trees burned, houses were torn apart by the fierce winds. The Than-Thalas River flooded, sending those who lived on its banks scrambling to reach higher ground. Water seeped into the palace garden, the Garden of Astarin, where grew the magical tree that was, many believed, responsible for keeping the shield in place. The tree's magic kept it safe. Indeed, when the storm was ended, the soil around the tree was found to be bone dry. Everything else in the garden was drowned or washed away. The elf gardeners and Woodshapers, who bore for their plants and flowers, ornamental trees, herbs, and rose bushes the same love they bore their own children, were heartbroken, devastated to view the destruction.

They replanted after the storm, bringing plants from their own gardens to fill the once wondrous Garden of Astarin. Ever since the raising of the shield, the plants in the garden had not done well, and now they rotted in the muddy soil which could never, it seemed, soak up enough sunlight to dry out.

The strange and terrible storm eventually left the continent, marched away from the war, a victorious army abandoning the field of battle, leaving devastation and destruction behind. The next morning, the people of Ansalon would go dazedly to view the damage, to comfort the bereaved, to bury the dead, and to wonder at the dreadful night's ominous portent.

And yet, there was, after all, one person that night who enjoyed himself. His name was Silvanoshei, a young elf, and he exulted in the storm. The clash of the lightning warriors, the bolts that fell like sparks struck from swords of thunder, beat in his blood like crashing drums. Silvanoshei did not seek shelter from the storm but went out into it. He stood in a clearing in the forest, his face raised to the tumult, the rain drenching him, cooling the burning of vaguely felt wants and desires. He watched the dazzling display of lightning, marveled at the ground-shaking thunder, laughed at the blasts of wind that bent the great trees, making them bow their proud heads.

Silvanoshei's father was Porthios, once proud ruler of the Qualinesti, now cast out by them, termed a "dark elf," one cursed to live outside the light of elven society. Silvanoshei's mother was Alhana Starbreeze, exiled leader of the Silvanesti nation that had cast her out too when she married Porthios. They had meant, by their marriage, to at last reunite the two elven nations, bring them together as one nation, a nation that would have probably been strong enough to fight the cursed dragons and maintain itself in freedom.

Instead, their marriage had only deepened the hatred and mistrust. Now Beryl ruled Qualinesti, which was an occupied land, held in subjugation by the Knights of Neraka. Silvanesti was a land cut off, isolated, its inhabitants cowering under its shield like children hiding beneath a blanket, hoping it will protect them from the monsters who lurk in the darkness.

Silvanoshei was the only child of Porthios and Alhana.

"Silvan was born the year of the Chaos War," Alhana was wont to say. "His father and I were on the run, a target for every elven assassin who wanted to ingratiate himself with either the Qualinesti or the Silvanesti rulers. He was born the day they buried two of the sons of Caramon Majere. Chaos was Silvan's nursemaid, Death his midwife."

Silvan had been raised in an armed camp. Alhana's marriage to Porthios had been a marriage of politics that had deepened to one of love and friend- ship and utmost respect. Together she and her husband had waged a ceaseless, thankless battle, first against the Dark Knights who were now the overlords of Qualinest, then against the terrible domination of Beryl, the dragon who had laid claim to the Qualinesti lands and who now demanded tribute from the Qualinesti elves in return for allowing them to live.

When word had first reached Alhana and Porthios that the elves of Silvanesti had managed to raise a magical shield over their kingdom, a shield that would protect them from the ravages of the dragons, both had seen this as a possible salvation for their people. Alhana had traveled south with her own forces, leaving Porthios to continue the fight for Qualinesti.

She had tried to send an emissary to the Silvanesti elves, asking permission to pass through the shield. The emissary had not even been able to enter. She attacked the shield with steel and with magic, trying every way possible of breaking through it, without success. The more she studied the shield, the more she was appalled that her people could permit themselves to live beneath it.

Whatever the shield touched died. Woodlands near the shield's boundaries were filled with dead and dying trees. Grasslands near the shield were gray and barren. Flowers wilted, withered, decomposed into a fine gray dust that covered the dead like a shroud.

The shield's magic is responsible for this! Alhana had written to her husband. *The shield is not protecting the land. It is killing it!*

The Silvanesti do not care, Porthios had written in reply. *They are subsumed by fear. Fear of the ogres, fear of the humans, fear of the dragons, fear of terrors they can not even name. The shield is but the outward manifestation of their fear. No wonder anything that comes in contact with it withers and dies!*

These were the last words she had heard from him. For years Alhana had kept in contact with her husband through the messages carried between them by the swift and tireless elven runners. She knew of his increasingly futile efforts to defeat Beryl. Then came the day the runner from her husband did not return. She had sent another, and another vanished. Now weeks had passed and still no word from Porthios. Finally, unable to expend any more of her dwindling manpower, Alhana had ceased sending the runners.

The storm had caught Alhana and her army in the woods near the border of Silvanesti, after yet another futile attempt to penetrate the shield. Alhana took refuge from the storm in an ancient burial mound near the border of Silvanesti. She had discovered this mound long ago, when she had first begun her battle to wrest control of her homeland from the hands of those who seemed intent upon leading her people to disaster.

In other, happier circumstances, the elves would not have disturbed the rest of the dead, but they were being pursued by ogres, their ancient enemy, and were desperately seeking a defensible position. Even so, Alhana had entered the mound with prayers of propitiation, asking the spirits of the dead for understanding.

The elves had discovered the mound to be empty. They found no mummified corpses, no bones, no indication that anyone had ever been buried here. The elves who accompanied Alhana took this for a sign that their cause was just. She did not argue, though she felt the bitter irony that she—the true and rightful Queen of the Silvanesti—was forced to take refuge in a hole in the ground even the dead had abandoned.

The burial mound was now Alhana's headquarters. Her knights, her own personal bodyguard, were inside with her. The rest of the army was camped in the woods around her. A perimeter of elven runners kept watch for ogres, known to be rampaging in this area. The runners, lightly armed, wearing no armor, would not engage the enemy in battle, if they spotted them, but would race back to the picket lines to alert the army of an enemy's presence.

The elves of House Woodshaper had worked long to magically raise from the ground a barricade of thorn bushes surrounding the burial mound. The bushes had wicked barbs that could pierce even an ogre's tough hide. Within the barricade, the soldiers of the elven army found what shelter they could when the torrential storm came. Tents almost immediately collapsed, leaving the elves to hunker down behind boulders or crawl into ditches, avoiding, if possible, the tall trees—targets of the vicious lightning.

Wet to the bone, chilled and awed by the storm, the likes of which not even the longest lived among the elves had ever before seen, the soldiers looked at Silvanoshei, cavorting in the storm like a moonstruck fool, and shook their heads.

He was the son of their beloved queen. They would not say one word against him. They would give their lives defending him, for he was the hope of the elven nation. The elven soldiers liked him well enough, even if they neither admired nor respected him. Silvanoshei was handsome and charming, winning by nature, a boon companion, with a voice so sweet and melodious that he could talk the songbirds out of the trees and into his hand.

In this, Silvanoshei was like neither of his parents. He had none of his father's grim, dour, and resolute nature, and some might have whispered that he was not his father's child, but Silvanoshei so closely resembled Porthios there could be no mistaking the relationship. Silvanoshei, or Silvan, as his mother called him, did not inherit the regal bearing of Alhana Starbreeze. He had something of her pride but little of her compassion. He cared about his people, but he lacked her undying love and loyalty. He considered her battle to penetrate the shield a hopeless waste of time. He could not understand why she was expending so much energy to return to a people who clearly did not want her.

Alhana doted on her son, more so now that his father appeared to be lost. Silvan's feelings toward his mother were more complex, although he had but an imperfect understanding of them. Had anyone asked him, he would have said that he loved her and idolized her, and this was true. Yet that love was an oil floating upon the surface of troubled water. Sometimes Silvan felt an anger toward his parents, an anger that frightened him in its fury and intensity. They had robbed him of his childhood, they had robbed him of comfort, they had robbed him of his rightful standing among his people.

The burial mound remained relatively dry during the downpour. Alhana stood at the entrance, watching the storm, her attention divided between worry for her son—standing bareheaded in the rain, exposed to the murderous lightning and savage winds—and in thinking bitterly that the rain drops could penetrate the shield that surrounded Silvanesti and she, with all the might of her army, could not.

One particularly close lightning strike half-blinded her, its thunderclap shook the cave. Fearful for her son, she ventured a short distance outside the mound's entrance and endeavored to see through the driving rain. Another flash, overspreading the sky with a flame of purple white, revealed him staring upward, his mouth open, roaring back at the thunder in laughing defiance.

"Silvan!" she cried. "It is not safe out there! Come inside with me!"

He did not hear her. Thunder smashed her words, the wind blew them away. But perhaps sensing her concern, he turned his head. "Isn't it glorious, Mother?" he shouted, and the wind that had blown away his mother's words brought his own to her with perfect clarity.

"Do you want me to go out and drag him inside, my queen," asked a voice at her shoulder.

Alhana started, half-turned. "Samar! You frightened me!"

The elf bowed. "I am sorry, Your Majesty. I did not mean to alarm you."

She had not heard him approach, but that was not surprising. Even if there had been no deafening thunder, she would not have heard the elf if he did not want her to hear. He was from House Protector, had been assigned to her by Porthios, and had been faithful to his calling throughout thirty years of war and exile.

Samar was now her second in command, the leader of her armies. That he loved her, she knew well, though he had never spoken a word of it, for he was loyal to her husband Porthios as friend and ruler. Samar knew that she did not love him, that she was faithful to her husband, though they had heard no word of Porthios or from him for months. Samar's love for her was a gift he gave her daily, expecting nothing in return. He walked at her side, his love for her a torch to guide her footsteps along the dark path she walked.

Samar had no love for Silvanoshei, whom he took to be a spoilt dandy. Samar viewed life as a battle that had to be fought and won on a daily basis. Levity and laughter, jokes and pranks, would have been acceptable in an elf prince whose realm was at peace—an elf prince who, like elf princes of happier times, had nothing to do all day long but learn to play the lute and contemplate the perfection of a rose bud. The ebullient spirits of youth were out of place in this world where the elves struggled simply to survive. Slivanoshei's father was lost and probably dead. His mother expended her life hurling herself against fate, her body and spirit growing more bruised and battered every day. Samar considered Silvan's laughter and high spirits an affront to both, an insult to himself.

The only good Samar saw in the young man was that Silvanoshei could coax a smile from his mother's lips when nothing and no one else could cheer her.

Alhana laid her hand upon Samar's arm. "Tell him that I am anxious. A mother's foolish fears. Or not so foolish," she added to herself, for Samar had already departed. "There is something dire about this storm."

Samar was instantly drenched to the skin when he walked into the storm, as soaked as if he had stepped beneath a waterfall. The wind gusts staggered him. Putting his head down against the blinding torrent, cursing Silvan's heedless foolery, Samar forged ahead.

Silvan stood with his head back, his eyes closed, his lips parted. His arms were spread, his chest bare, his loose-woven shirt so wet that it had fallen from his shoulders. The rainwater poured over his half-naked body.

"Silvan!" Samar shouted into the young man's ear. Grabbing his arm roughly, Samar gave the young elf a good shake. "You are making a spectacle of yourself!" Samar said, his tone low and fierce. He shook Silvan again. "Your mother has worries enough without you adding to them! Get inside with her where you belong!"

Silvan opened his eyes a slit. His eyes were purple, like his mother's, only not as dark; more like wine than blood. The winelike eyes were alight with ecstasy, his lips parted in smile.

"The lightning, Samar! I've never seen anything like it! I can feel it as well as see it. It touches my body and raises the hair on my arms. It wraps me in sheets of flame that lick my skin and set me ablaze. The thunder shakes me to the core of my being, the ground moves beneath my feet. My blood burns, and the rain, the stinging rain, cools my fever. I am in no danger, Samar." Silvan's smile widened, the rain sleeked his face and hair. "I am in no more danger than if I were in bed with a lover—"

"Such talk is unseemly, Prince Silvan," Samar admonished in stern anger. "You should—"

Hunting horns, blowing wildly, frantically, interrupted him. Silvan's ecstatic dream shattered, dashed away by the blasting horns, a sound that was one of the first sounds he remembered hearing as a little child. The sound of warning, the sound of danger.

Silvan's eyes opened fully. He could not tell from what direction the horn calls came, they seemed to come from all directions at once. Alhana stood at the entrance of the mound, surrounded by her knights, peering into the storm.

An elven runner came crashing through the brush. No time for stealth. No need.

"What is it?" Silvan cried.

The soldier ignored him, raced to his commander. "Ogres, sir!" he cried.

"Where?" Samar demanded.

The soldier sucked in a breath. "All around us, sir! They have us surrounded. We didn't hear them. They used the storm to cover their movements. The pickets have retreated back behind the barricade, but the barricade . . ."

The elf could not continue, he was out of breath. He pointed to the north.

A strange glow lit the night purple white, the color of the lightning. But this glow did not strike and then depart. This glow grew brighter.

"What is it?" Silvan shouted, above the drumming of the thunder. "What does that mean?"

"The barricade the Woodshapers created is burning," Samar answered grimly. "Surely the rain will douse the fire—"

"No, sir." The runner had caught his breath. "The barricade was struck by lightning. Not only in one place, but in many."

He pointed again, this time to the east and to the west. The fires could be seen springing up in every direction now, every direction except due south.

"The lightning starts them. The rain has no effect on them. Indeed, the rain seems to fuel them, as if it were oil pouring down from the heavens."

"Tell the Woodshapers to use their magic to put the fire out."

The runner looked helpless. "Sir, the Woodshapers are exhausted. The spell they cast to create the barricade took all their strength."

"How can that be?" Samar demanded angrily. "It is a simple spell— No, never mind!"

He knew the answer, though he continually struggled against it. Of late, in the past two years, the elven sorcerers had felt their power to cast spells ebbing. The loss was gradual, barely felt at first, attributed to illness or exhaustion, but the sorcerers were at last forced to admit that their magical power was slipping away like grains of sand from between clutching fingers. They could hold onto some, but not all. The elves were not alone. They had reports that the same loss was being felt among humans, but this was little comfort.

Using the storm to conceal their movements, the ogres had slipped unseen past the runners and overwhelmed the sentries. The briar-wall barricade was burning furiously in several places at the base of the hill. Beyond the flames stood the tree line, where officers were forming the elven archers into ranks behind the barricade. The tips of their arrows glittered like sparks.

The fire would keep the ogres at bay temporarily, but when it died down, the monsters would come surging across. In the darkness and the slashing rain and the howling wind, the archers would stand little chance of hitting their targets before they were overrun. And when they were overrun, the carnage would be horrible. Ogres hate all other races on Krynn, but their hatred for elves goes back to the beginning of time, when the ogres were once beautiful, the favored of the gods. When the ogres fell, the elves became the favored, the pampered. The ogres had never forgiven them.

"Officers to me!" Samar shouted. "Fieldmaster! Bring your archers into a line behind the lancers at the barrier, and tell them to hold their volley until directed to loose it."

He ran back inside the mound. Silvan followed him, the excitement of the storm replaced by the tense, fierce excitement of the attack. Alhana cast her son a worried glance. Seeing he was unharmed, she turned her complete attention to Samar, as other elven officers crowded inside.

"Ogres?" she asked.

"Yes, my queen. They used the storm for cover. The runner believes that they have us surrounded. I am not certain. I think that the way south may still be open."

"You suggest?"

"That we fall back to the fortress of the Legion of Steel, Your Majesty. A fighting retreat. Your meetings with the human knights went well. It was my thought that—"

Plans and plots, strategy and tactics. Silvan was sick of them, sick of the sound of them. He took the opportunity to slip away. The prince hurried to the back of the mound, where he had laid out his bedroll. Reaching beneath his blanket, he grasped the hilt of a sword, the sword he had purchased in Solace. Silvan was delighted with the weapon, with its shiny newness. The sword had an ornately carved hilt with a griffon's beak. The hilt was admittedly difficult to hold—the beak dug into his flesh—but the sword looked splendid.

Silvanoshei was not a soldier. He had never been trained as a soldier. Small blame to him. Alhana had forbidden it.

"Unlike my hands, these hands"—his mother would take her son's hands in her own, hold them fast—"will not be stained with the blood of his own kind. These hands will heal the wounds that his father and I, against our will, have been forced to inflict. The hands of my son will never spill elven blood."

But this was not elven blood they were talking about spilling. It was ogre blood. His mother could not very well keep him out of this battle. Growing up unarmed and untrained for soldiering in a camp of soldiers, Silvan imagined that the others looked down upon him, that deep inside they thought him a coward. He had purchased the sword in secret, taken a few lessons—until he grew bored with them—and had been looking forward for some time for the chance to show off his prowess.

Pleased to have the opportunity, Silvan buckled the belt around his slender waist and returned to the officers, the sword clanking and banging against his thigh.

Elven runners continued to arrive with reports. The unnatural fire was consuming the barricade at an alarming rate. A few ogres had attempted to cross it. Illuminated by the flames, they had provided excellent targets for the archers. Unfortunately, any arrow that came within range of the fire was consumed by the flames before it could strike its target.

The strategy for retreat settled—Silvan didn't catch much of it, something about pulling back to the south where they would meet up with a force from the Legion of Steel—the officers returned to their commands. Samar and Alhana remained standing together, speaking in low, urgent tones.

Drawing his sword from his sheath with a ringing sound, Silvan gave it a flourish and very nearly sliced off Samar's arm.

"What the—" Samar glared at the bloody gash in his sleeve, glared at Silvan. "Give me that!" He reached out and before Silvan could react, snatched the sword from his grasp.

"Silvanoshei!" Alhana was angry, as angry as he had ever seen her. "This is no time for such nonsense!" She turned her back on him, an indication of her displeasure.

"It is not nonsense, Mother," Silvan retorted. "No, don't turn away from me! This time you will not take refuge behind a wall of silence. This time you will hear me and listen to what I have to say!"

Slowly Alhana turned around. She regarded him intently, her eyes large in her pale face.

The other elves, shocked and embarrassed, did not know where to look. No one defied the queen, no one contradicted her, not even her willful, headstrong son. Silvan himself was amazed at his courage.

"I am a prince of Silvanesti and of Qualinesti," he continued. "It is my privilege, it is my duty to join in the defense of my people. You have no right to try to stop me!"

"I have every right, my son," Alhana returned. She grasped his wrist, her nails pierced his flesh. "You are the heir, the only heir. You are all I have left. . . ." Alhana fell silent, regretting her words. "I am sorry. I did not mean that. A queen has nothing of her own. Everything she has and is belongs to the people. You are all your people have left, Silvan. Now go collect your things," she ordered, her voice tight with the need to control herself. "The knights will take you deeper into the woods—"

"No, Mother, I will not hide anymore," Silvan said, taking care to speak firmly, calmly, respectfully. His cause was lost if he sounded like petulant child. "All my life, whenever danger threatened, you whisked me away, stashed me in some cave, stuffed me under some bed. It is no wonder my people have small respect for me." His gaze shifted to Samar, who was watching the young man with grave attention. "I want to do my part for a change, Mother."

"Well spoken, Prince Silvanoshei," said Samar. "Yet the elves have a saying. 'A sword in the hand of an untrained friend is more dangerous than the sword in the hand of my foe.' One does not learn to fight on the eve of battle, young man. However, if you are serious about this pursuit, I will be pleased to instruct you at some later date. In the meanwhile, there is something you can do, a mission you can undertake."

He knew the response this would bring and he was not wrong. Alhana's arrow-sharp anger found a new target.

"Samar, I would speak with you!" Alhana said, her voice cold, biting, imperious. She turned on her heel, stalked with rigid back and uplifted chin to the rear of the burial mound. Samar, deferential, accompanied her.

Outside were cries and shouts, horns blasting, the deep and terrible ogre war chant sounding like war drums beneath it. The storm raged, unabated, giving succor to the enemy. Silvan stood near the entrance to the burial mound, amazed at himself, proud but appalled, sorry, yet defiant, fearless and terrified all at the same time. The jumble of his emotions confused him. He tried to see what was happening, but the smoke from the burning hedge had settled over the clearing. The shouts and screams grew muted, muffled. He wished he could eavesdrop on the conversation, might have lingered near where he could hear, but he considered that childish and beneath his pride. He could imagine what they were saying anyway. He'd heard the same conversation often enough.

In reality, he was probably not far wrong.

"Samar, you know my wishes for Silvanoshei," Alhana said, when they were out of earshot of the others. "Yet you defy me and encourage him in this wild behavior. I am deeply disappointed in you, Samar."

Her words, her anger were piercing, struck Samar to the heart and drew blood. But as Alhana was queen and responsible to her people, so Samar was also responsible to the people as a soldier. He was committed to providing his people with a present and a future. In that future, the elven nations would need a strong heir, not a milksop like Gilthas, the son of Tanis Half-Elven, who currently played at ruling Qualinesti.

Samar did not speak his true thoughts, however. He did *not* say, "Your Majesty, this is the first sign of spirit I've seen in your son, we should encourage it." He was diplomat as well as soldier.

"Your Majesty," he said, "Silvan is thirty years old—"

"A child—" Alhana interrupted.

Silvan bowed. "Perhaps by Silvanesti standards, my queen. Not by Qualinesti. Under Qualinesti law, he would have attained ranking as a youth. If he were in Qualinesti, he would already be participating in military training. Silvanoshei may be young in years, Alhana," Samar added, dropping the formal title as he did sometimes when they were alone together, "but think of the extraordinary life he has led! His lullabies were war chants, his cradle a shield. He has never known a home. Rarely have his parents been both together in the same room at the same time since the day of his birth. When battle called, you kissed him and rode forth, perhaps to your death. He knew that you might never come back to him, Alhana. I could see it in his eyes!"

"I tried to protect him from all that," she said, her gaze going to her son. He looked so like his father at that moment that her pain overwhelmed her. "If I lose him, Samar, what reason do I have to prolong this bleak and hopeless existence?"

"You cannot protect him from life, Alhana," Samar countered gently. "Nor from the role he is destined to play in life. Prince Silvanoshei is right. He has a duty to his people. We will let him fulfill that duty *and*"—he laid emphasis on the word—"we will take him out of harm's way at the same time."

Alhana said nothing, but by her look, she gave him reluctant permission to speak further.

"Only one of the runners has returned to camp," Samar continued. "The others are either dead or are fighting for their lives. You said yourself, Your Majesty, that we must send word to the Legion of Steel, warning them of this attack. I propose that we send Silvan to apprise the knights of our desperate need for help. We have only just returned from the fortress, he remembers the way. The main road is not far from the camp and easy to find and follow.

"The danger to him is small. The ogres have not encircled us. He will be safer away from camp than here." Samar smiled. "If I had my way, my Queen, you would go back to the fortress with him."

Alhana smiled, her anger dissipated. "My place is with my soldiers, Samar. I brought them here. They fight my cause. They would lose all trust and respect if I deserted them. Yes, I concede that you are right about Silvan," she added ruefully. "No need to rub salt in my many wounds."

"My queen, I never meant—"

"Yes, you did, Samar," Alhana said, "but you spoke from the heart, and you spoke the truth. We will send the prince upon this mission. He will carry word of our need to the Legion of Steel."

"We will sing his praises when we return to the fortress," said Samar. "And I will purchase him a sword suited to a prince, not a clown."

"No, Samar," said Alhana. "He may carry messages, but he will never carry a sword. On the day he was born, I made my vow to the gods that he would never bear arms against his people. Elven blood would never be spilled because of him."

Samar bowed, wisely remained silent. A skilled commander, he knew when to bring his advance to a halt, dig in, and wait. Alhana walked with stiff back and regal mien to the front of the cave.

"My son," Alhana said and there no emotion in her voice, no feeling. "I have made my decision."

Silvanoshei turned to face his mother. Daughter of Lorac, ill-fated king of the Silvanesti, who had very nearly been his people's downfall, Alhana Starbreeze had undertaken to pay for her father's misdeeds, to redeem her people. Because she had sought to unite them with their cousins, the Qualinesti, because she had advocated alliances with the humans and the dwarves, she was repudiated, cast out by those among the Silvanesti who maintained that only by keeping themselves aloof and isolated from the rest of the world could they and their culture survive.

She was in mature adulthood for the elves, not yet nearing her elder years, incredibly beautiful, more beautiful than at any other time of her life. Her hair was black as the depths of the sea, sunk far below where sunbeams can reach. Her eyes, once amethyst, had deepened and darkened as if colored by the despair and pain which was all they saw. Her beauty was a heartbreak to those around her, not a blessing. Like the legendary dragonlance, whose rediscovery helped bring victory to a beleaguered world, she might have been encased in a pillar of ice. Shatter the ice, shatter the protective barrier she had erected around her, and shatter the woman inside.

Only her son, only Silvan had the power to thaw the ice, to reach inside and touch the living warmth of the woman who was mother, not queen. But that woman was gone. Mother was gone. The woman who stood before him, cold and stern, was his queen. Awed, humbled, aware that he had behaved foolishly, he fell to his knees before her.

"I am sorry, Mother," he said. "I will obey you. I will leave—"

"Prince Silvanoshei," said the queen in a voice he recognized as being her court voice, one she had never used to him. He did not know whether to feel glad or to weep for something irrevocably lost. "Commander Samar has need of a messenger to run with all haste to the outpost of the Legion of Steel. There you will apprise them of our desperate situation. Tell the Lord Knight that we plan to retreat fighting. He should assemble his forces, ride out to meet us at the crossroads, attack the ogres on their right flank. At the moment his knights attack we will halt our retreat and stand our ground. You will need to travel swiftly through the night and the storm. Let nothing deter you, Silvan, for this message must get through."

"I understand, my queen," said Silvan. He rose to his feet, flushed with victory, the thrill of danger flashing like the lightning through his blood. "I will not fail you or my people. I thank you for your trust in me."

Alhana took his face in her hands, hands that were so cold that he could not repress a shiver. She placed her lips upon his forehead. Her kiss burned like ice, the chill struck through to his heart. He would always feel that kiss, from that moment after. He wondered if her pallid lips had left an indelible mark.

Samar's crisp professionalism came as a relief.

"You know the route, Prince Silvan," Samar said. "You rode it only two days before. The road lies about a mile and a half due south of here. You will have no stars to guide you, but the wind blows from the north. Keep the wind at your back and you will be heading in the right direction. The road runs east and west, straight and true. You must eventually cross it. Once you are on the road, travel westward. The storm wind will be on your right cheek. You should make good time. There is no need for stealth. The sound of battle will mask your movements. Good luck, Prince Silvanoshei."

"Thank you, Samar," said Silvan, touched and pleased. For the first time in his life, the elf had spoken to him as an equal, with even a modicum of respect. "I will not fail you or my mother."

"Do not fail your people, Prince," said Samar.

With a final glance and a smile for his mother, a smile she did not return, Silvan turned and left the burial mound, striking out in the direction of the forest. He had not gone far, when he heard Samar's voice raised in a bellowing cry.

"General Aranoshah! Take two orders of swordsmen off to the left flank and send two more to the right. We'll need to keep four units here with Her Majesty in reserve in case they breach the line and break through."

Break through! That was impossible. The line would hold. The line must hold. Silvan halted and looked back. The elves had raised their battle song, its music sweet and uplifting, soaring above the brutish chant of the ogres. He was cheered by the sight and started on, when a ball of fire, blue-white and blinding, exploded on the left side of the hill. The fireball hurtled down the hillside, heading for the burial mounds.

"Shift fire to your left!" Samar called down the slope.

The archers were momentarily confused, not understanding their targets, but their officers managed to turn them in the right direction. The ball of flame struck another portion of the barrier, ignited the thicket, and continued to blaze onward. At first Silvan thought the balls of flame were magical, and he wondered what good archers would do against sorcery, but then he saw that the fireballs were actually huge bundles of hay being pushed and shoved down the hillside by the ogres. He could see their hulking bodies silhouetted black against the leaping flames. The ogres carried long sticks that they used to shove the burning hay stacks.

"Wait for my order!" Samar cried, but the elves were nervous and several arrows were loosed in the direction of the blazing hay.

"No, damn it!" Samar yelled with rage down the slope. "They're not in range yet! Wait for the order!"

A crash of thunder drowned out his voice. Seeing their comrades fire, the remainder of the archer line loosed their first volley. The arrows arched through the smoke-filled night. Three of the ogres pushing the flaming haystacks fell under the withering fire, but the rest of the arrows landed far short of their marks.

"Still," Silvan told himself, "they will soon stop them."

A baying howl as of a thousand wolves converging on their prey cried from the woods close to the elven archers. Silvan stared, startled, thinking that the trees themselves had come alive.

"Shift fire forward!" Samar cried desperately.

The archers could not hear him over the roar of the approaching flames. Too late, their officers noticed the sudden rushing movement in the trees at the foot of the hill. A line of ogres surged into the open, charging the thicket wall that protected the archers. The flames had weakened the barrier. The huge ogres charged into the smoldering mass of burned sticks and logs, shouldering their way through. Cinders fell on their matted hair and sparked in their beards, but the ogres, in a battle rage, ignored the pain of their burns and lurched forward.

Now being attacked from the front and on their flank, the elven archers grappled desperately for their arrows, tried to loose another volley before the ogres closed. The flaming haystacks thundered down on them. The elves did not know which enemy to fight first. Some lost their heads in the chaos. Samar roared orders. The officers struggled to bring their troops under control. The elves fired a second volley, some into the burning hay bales, others into the ogres charging them on the flank.

More ogres fell, an immense number, and Silvan thought that they must retreat. He was amazed and appalled to see the ogres continue forward, undaunted.

"Samar, where are the reserves?" Alhana called out.

"I think they have been cut off," Samar returned grimly. "You should not be out here, Your Majesty. Go back inside where you are safe."

Silvan could see his mother now. She had left the burial mound. She was clad in silver armor, carried a sword at her side.

"I led my people here," Alhana returned. "Will you have me skulk in a cave while my people are dying, Samar?"

"Yes," he growled.

She smiled at him, a tight strained smile, but still a smile. She gripped the hilt of her sword. "Will they break through, do you think?"

"I don't see much stopping them, Your Majesty," Samar said grimly.

The elven archers loosed another volley. The officers had regained control of the troops. Every shot told. The ogres charging from the front fell by the score. Half the line disappeared. Still the ogres continued their advance, the living trampling the bodies of the fallen. In moments they would be within striking range of the archers' position.

"Launch the assault!" Samar roared.

Elven swordsmen rose up from their positions behind the left barricades. Shouting their battle cries, they charged the ogre line. Steel rang against steel. The flaming haystacks burst into the center of the camp, crushing men, setting fire to trees and grass and clothing. Suddenly, without warning, the ogre line turned. One of their number had caught sight of Alhana's silver armor, reflecting the firelight. With guttural cries, they pointed at her and were now charging toward the burial mound.

"Mother!" Silvan gasped, his heart tangled up with his stomach. He had to bring help. They were counting on him, but he was paralyzed, mesmerized by the terrible sight. He couldn't run to her. He couldn't run away. He couldn't move.

"Where are those reserves?" Samar shouted furiously. "Aranosha! You bastard! Where are Her Majesty's swordsmen!"

"Here, Samar!" cried a warrior. "We had to fight our way to you, but we are here!"

"Take them down there, Samar," said Alhana calmly.

"Your Majesty!" He started to protest. "I will not leave you without guards."

"If we don't halt the advance, Samar," Alhana returned. "It won't much matter whether I have guards or not. Go now. Quickly!"

Samar wanted to argue, but he knew by the remote and resolute expression on his queen's face that he would be wasting his breath. Gathering the reserves around him, Samar charged down into the advancing ogres.

Alhana stood alone, her silver armor burning with the reflected flames.

"Make haste, Silvan, my son. Make haste. Our lives rest on you."

She spoke to herself, but she spoke, unknowingly, to her son.

Her words impelled Silvan to action. He had been given an order and he would carry it out. Bitterly regretting the wasted time, his heart swelling with fear for his mother, he turned and plunged into the forest.

Adrenaline pumped in Silvan's veins. He shoved his way through the underbrush, thrusting aside tree limbs, trampling seedlings. Sticks snapped beneath his boots. The wind was cold and strong on his right cheek. He did not feel the pelting rain. He welcomed the lightning that lit his path.

He was prudent enough to keep careful watch for any signs of the enemy and constantly sniffed the air, for the filthy, flesh-eating ogre is usually smelt long before he is seen. Silvan kept his hearing alert, too, for though he himself made what an elf would consider to be an unconscionable amount of noise, he was a deer gliding through the forest compared to the smashing and cracking, ripping and tearing of an ogre.

Silvan traveled swiftly, encountering not so much as a nocturnal animal out hunting, and soon the sounds of battle dwindled behind him. Then it was that he realized he was alone in the forest in the night in the storm. The adrenaline started to ebb. A sliver of fear and doubt pierced his heart. What if he arrived too late? What if the humans—known for their vagaries and their changeable natures—refused to act? What if the attack overwhelmed his people? What if he had left them to die? None of this looked familiar to him. He had taken a wrong turning, he was lost. . . .

Resolutely Silvan pushed forward, running through the forest with the ease of one who has been born and raised in the woodlands. He was cheered by the sight of a ravine on his left hand; he remembered that ravine from his earlier travels to the fortress. His fear of being lost vanished. He took care to keep clear of the rocky edge of the ravine, which cut a large gash across the forest floor.

Silvan was young, strong. He banished his doubts that were a drag on his heart, and concentrated on his mission. A lightning flash revealed the road straight ahead. The sight renewed his strength and his determination. Once he reached the road, he could increase his pace. He was an excellent runner, often running long distances for the sheer pleasure of the feel of the muscles expanding and contracting, the sweat on his body, the wind in his face and the warm suffusing glow that eased all pain.

He imagined himself speaking to the Lord Knight, pleading their cause, urging him to haste. Silvan saw himself leading the rescue, saw his mother's face alight with pride. . . .

In reality, Silvan saw his way blocked. Annoyed, he slid to a halt on the muddy path to study this obstacle.

A gigantic tree limb, fallen from an ancient oak, lay across the path. Leaves and branches blocked his way. Silvan would be forced to circle around it, a move that would bring him close to the edge of the ravine. He was sure on his feet, however. The lightning lit his way. He edged around the end of the severed limb with a good few feet to spare. He was climbing over a single branch, reaching out his hand to steady himself on a nearby pine tree, when a single bolt of lightning streaked out of the darkness and struck the pine.

The tree exploded in a ball of white fire. The concussive force of the blast knocked Silvan over the edge of the ravine. Rolling and tumbling down its rock-strewn wall, he slammed against the stump of a broken tree at the bottom.

Pain seared his body, worse pain seared his heart. He had failed. He would not reach the fortress. The knights would never receive the message. His people could not fight alone against the ogres. They would die. His mother would die with the belief that he had let her down.

He tried to move, to rise, but the pain flashed through him, white hot, so horrible that when he felt consciousness slipping away, he was glad to think he was going to die. Glad to think that he would join his people in death, since he could do nothing else for them.

Despair and grief rose in a great, dark wave, crashed down upon Silvan and dragged him under.

3 AN UNEXPECTED VISITOR

The storm disappeared. A strange storm, it had burst upon Ansalon like an invading army, striking all parts of that vast continent at the same time, attacking throughout the night, only to retreat with the coming of dawn. The sun crawled out from the dark lightning-shot cloudbank to blaze triumphantly in the blue sky. Light and warmth cheered the inhabitants of Solace, who crept out of their homes to see what destruction the tempest had wrought.

Solace did not fare as badly as some other parts of Ansalon, although the storm appeared to have targeted that hamlet with particular hatred. The mighty vallenwoods proved stubbornly resistant to the devastating lightning that struck them time and again. The tops of the trees caught fire and burned, but the fire did not spread to the branches below. The trees' strong arms tossed in the whirling winds but held fast the homes built there, homes that were in their care. Creeks rose and fields flooded, but homes and barns were spared.

The Tomb of the Last Heroes, a beautiful structure of white and black stone that stood in a clearing on the outskirts of town, had sustained severe damage. Lightning had hit one of the spires, splitting it asunder, sending large chunks of marble crashing down to the lawn.

But the worst damage was done to the crude and makeshift homes of the refugees fleeing the lands to the west and south, lands which had been free only a year ago but which were now falling under control of the green dragon Beryl.

Three years ago, the great dragons who had fought for control of Ansalon had come to an uneasy truce. Realizing that their bloody battles were weakening them, the dragons agreed to be satisfied with the territory each had conquered, they would not wage war against each other to try to gain more. The dragons had kept this pact, until a year ago. It was then that Beryl had noticed her magical powers starting to decline. At first, she had thought she was imagining this, but as time passed, she became convinced that something was wrong.

Beryl blamed the red dragon Malys for the loss of her magic—this was some foul scheme being perpetrated by her larger and stronger cousin. Beryl also blamed the human mages, who were hiding the Tower of High Sorcery of Wayreth from her. Consequently, Beryl had begun ever so gradually to expand her control over human lands. She moved slowly, not wanting to draw Malys's attention. Malys would not care if here and there a town was burned or a village plundered. The city of Haven was one such, recently fallen to Beryl's might. Solace remained untouched, for the time being. But Beryl's eye was upon Solace. She had ordered closed the main roads leading into Solace, letting them feel the pressure as she bided her time.

The refugees who had managed to escape Haven and surrounding lands before the roads were closed had swelled Solace's population to three times its normal size. Arriving with their belongings tied up in bundles or piled on the back of carts, the refugees were being housed in what the town fathers designated "temporary housing." The hovels were truly meant only to be temporary, but the flood of refugees arriving daily overwhelmed good intentions. The temporary shelters had become, unfortunately, permanent.

The first person to reach the refugee camps the morning after the storm was Caramon Majere, driving a wagon loaded with sacks of food, lumber for rebuilding, dry firewood, and blankets.

Caramon was over eighty—just how far over no one really knew, for he himself had lost track of the years. He was what they term in Solamnia a "grand old man." Age had come to him as an honorable foe, facing him and saluting him, not creeping up to stab him in the back or rob him of his wits. Hale and hearty, his big frame corpulent but unbowed ("I can't grow stooped, my gut won't let me," he was wont to say with a roaring laugh), Caramon was the first of his household to rise, was out every morning chopping wood for the kitchen fires or hauling the heavy ale barrels up the stairs.

His two daughters saw to the day-to-day workings of the Inn of the Last Home—this was the only concession Caramon made to his age—but he still tended the bar, still told his stories. Laura ran the Inn, while Dezra, who had a taste for adventure, traveled to markets in Haven and elsewhere, searching out the very best in hops for the Inn's ale, honey for the Inn's legendary mead, and even hauling dwarf spirits back from Thorbardin. The moment Caramon went outdoors he was swarmed over by the children of Solace, who one and all called him "Grampy" and who vied for rides on his broad shoulders or begged to hear him tell tales of long-ago heroes. He was a friend to the refugees who would have likely had no housing at all had not Caramon donated the wood and supervised the construction. He was currently overseeing a project to build permanent dwellings on the outskirts of Solace, pushing, cajoling, and browbeating the recalcitrant authorities into taking action. Caramon Majere never walked the streets of Solace but that he heard his name spoken and blessed.

Once the refugees were assisted, Caramon traveled about the rest of Solace, making certain that everyone was safe, raising hearts and spirits oppressed by the terrible night. This done, he went to his own breakfast, a breakfast he had come to share, of late, with a Knight of Solamnia, a man who reminded Caramon of his own two sons who had died in the Chaos War.

In the days immediately following the Chaos War, the Solamnic Knights had established a garrison in Solace. The garrison had been a small one in the early days, intended only to provide Knights to stand honor guard for the Tomb of the Last Heroes. The garrison had been expanded to counter the threat of the great dragons, who were now the acknowledged, if hated, rulers of much of Ansalon.

So long as the humans of Solace and other cities and lands under her control continued to pay Beryl tribute, she allowed the people to continue on with their lives, allowed them to continue to generate more wealth so that they could pay even more tribute. Unlike the evil dragons of earlier ages, who had delighted in burning and looting and killing, Beryl had discovered that burned-out cities did not generate profit. Dead people did not pay taxes.

There were many who wondered why Beryl and her cousins with their wondrous and terrible magicks should covet wealth, should demand tribute. Beryl and Malys were cunning creatures. If they were rapaciously and wantonly cruel, indulging in wholesale slaughter of entire populations, the people of Ansalon would rise up out of desperation and march to destroy them. As it was, most humans found life under the dragon rule to be relatively comfortable. They were content to let well enough alone.

Bad things happened to some people, people who no doubt deserved their fate. If hundreds of kender were killed or driven from their homes, if rebellious Qualinesti elves were being tortured and imprisoned, what did this matter to humans? Beryl and Malys had minions and spies in every human town and village, placed there to foment discord and hatred and suspicion, as well as to make certain that no one was trying to hide so much as a cracked copper from the dragons.

Caramon Majere was one of the few outspoken in his hatred of paying tribute to the dragons and actually refused to do so.

"Not one drop of ale will I give to those fiends," he said heatedly whenever anyone asked, which they rarely did, knowing that one of Beryl's spies was probably taking down names.

He was staunch in his refusal, though much worried by it. Solace was a wealthy town, now larger than Haven. The tribute demanded from Solace was quite high. Caramon's wife Tika had pointed out that their share was being made up by the other citizens of Solace and that this was putting a hardship on the rest. Caramon could see the wisdom of Tika's argument. At length he came up with the novel idea of levying a special tax against himself, a tax that only the Inn paid, a tax whose monies were on no account to be sent to the dragon but that would be used to assist those who suffered unduly from having to pay what was come to be known as "the dragon tax."

The people of Solace paid extra tax, the city fathers refunded them a portion out of Caramon's contribution, and the tribute went to the dragon as demanded.

If they could have found a way to silence Caramon on the volatile subject, they would have done so, for he continued to be loud in his hatred of the dragons, continued to express his views that "if we just all got together we could poke out Beryl's eye with a dragonlance." Indeed, when the city of Haven was attacked by Beryl just a few weeks earlier—ostensibly for defaulting on its payments—the Solace town fathers actually came to Caramon and begged him on bended knee to cease his rabble-rousing remarks.

Impressed by their obvious fear and distress, Caramon agreed to tone down his rhetoric, and the town fathers left happy. Caramon did actually comply, expressing his views in a moderate tone of voice as opposed to the booming outrage he'd used previously.

He reiterated his unorthodox views that morning to his breakfast companion, the young Solamnic.

"A terrible storm, sir," said the Knight, seating himself opposite Caramon.

A group of his fellow Knights were breakfasting in another part of the Inn, but Gerard uth Mondar paid them scant attention. They, in their turn, paid him no attention at all.

"It bodes dark days to come, to my mind," Caramon agreed, settling his bulk into the high-backed wooden booth, a booth whose seat had been rubbed shiny by the old man's backside. "But all in all I found it exhilarating."

"Father!" Laura was scandalized. She slapped down a plate of beefsteak and eggs for her father, a bowl of porridge for the Knight. "How can you say such things? With so many people hurt. Whole houses blown, from what I hear."

"I didn't mean that," Caramon protested, contrite. "I'm sorry for the people who were hurt, of course, but, you know, it came to me in the night that this storm must be shaking Beryl's lair about pretty good. Maybe even burned the evil old bitch out. *That's* what I was thinking." He looked worriedly at the young Knight's bowl of porridge. "Are you certain that's enough to eat, Gerard? I can have Laura fry you up some potatoes—"

"Thank you, sir, this is all I am accustomed to eat for breakfast," Gerard said as he said every day in response to the same question.

Caramon sighed. Much as he had come to like this young man, Caramon could not understand any one who did not enjoy food. A person who did not relish Otik's famous spiced potatoes was a person who did not relish life. Only one time in his own life had Caramon ever ceased to enjoy his dinner and that was following the death several months earlier of his beloved wife Tika. Caramon had refused to eat a mouthful for days after that, to the terrible worry and consternation of the entire town, which went on a cooking frenzy to try to come up with something that would tempt him.

He would eat nothing, do nothing, say nothing. He either roamed aimlessly about the town or sat staring dry-eyed out the stained glass windows of the

Inn, the Inn where he had first met the red-haired and annoying little brat who had been his comrade in arms, his lover, his friend, his salvation. He shed no tears for her, he would not visit her grave beneath the vallenwoods. He would not sleep in their bed. He would not hear the messages of condolence that came from Laurana and Gilthas in Qualinesti, from Goldmoon in the Citadel of Light.

Caramon lost weight, his flesh sagged, his skin took on a gray hue.

"He will follow Tika soon," said the townsfolk.

He might have, too, had not one day a child, one of the refugee children, happened across Caramon in his dismal roamings. The child placed his small body squarely in front of the old man and held out a hunk of bread.

"Here, sir," said the child. "My mother says that if you don't eat you will die, and then what will become of us?"

Caramon gazed down at the child in wonder. Then he knelt down, gathered the child into his arms, and began to sob uncontrollably. Caramon ate the bread, every crumb, and that night he slept in the bed he had shared with Tika. He placed flowers on her grave the next morning and ate a breakfast that would have fed three men. He smiled again and laughed, but there was something in his smile and in his laughter that had not been there before. Not sorrow, but a wistful impatience.

Sometimes, when the door to the Inn opened, he would look out into the sunlit blue sky beyond and he would say, very softly, "I'm coming, my dear. Don't fret. I won't be long."

Gerard uth Mondar ate his porridge with dispatch, not really tasting it. He ate his porridge plain, refusing to flavor it with brown sugar or cinnamon, did not even add salt. Food fueled his body, and that was all it was good for. He ate his porridge, washing down the congealed mass with a mug of tar-bean tea, and listened to Caramon talk about the awful wonders of the storm.

The other Knights paid their bill and left, bidding Caramon a polite good-day as they passed, but saying nothing to his companion. Gerard appeared not to notice, but steadfastly spooned porridge from bowl to mouth.

Caramon watched the Knights depart and interrupted his story in mid-lightning bolt. "I appreciate the fact that you share your time with an old geezer like me, Gerard, but if you want to have breakfast with your friends—"

"They are not my friends," said Gerard without bitterness or rancor, simply making a statement of fact. "I much prefer dining with a man of wisdom and good, common sense." He raised his mug to Caramon in salute.

"It's just that you seem . . ." Caramon paused, chewed steak vigorously. "Lonely," he finished in a mumble, his mouth full. He swallowed, forked another piece. "You should have a girlfriend or . . . or a wife or something."

Gerard snorted. "What woman would look twice at a man with a face like this?" He eyed with dissatisfaction his own reflection in the highly polished pewter mug.

Gerard was ugly; there was no denying that fact. A childhood illness had left his face cragged and scarred. His nose had been broken in a fight with a neighbor when he was ten and had healed slightly askew. He had yellow hair—not blond, not fair, just plain, straw yellow. It was the consistency of straw, too, and would not lie flat, but stuck up at all sorts of odd angles if allowed. To avoid looking like a scarecrow, which had been his nickname when he was young, Gerard kept his hair cut as short as possible.

His only good feature were his eyes, which were of a startling, one might almost say, alarming blue. Because there was rarely any warmth behind these eyes and because these eyes always focused upon their objective with unblinking intensity, Gerard's blue eyes tended to repel more people than they attracted.

"Bah!" Caramon dismissed beauty and comeliness with a wave of his fork. "Women don't care about a man's looks. They want a man of honor, of courage. A young Knight your age . . . How old are you?"

"I have seen twenty-eight years, sir," Gerard replied. Finishing his porridge, he shoved the bowl to one side. "Twenty-eight boring and thoroughly wasted years."

"Boring?" Caramon was skeptical. "And you a Knight? I was in quite a few wars myself. Battles were lots of things, as I recall, but boring wasn't one of them—"

"I have never been in battle, sir," said Gerard and now his tone was bitter. He rose to his feet, placed a coin upon the table. "If you will excuse me, I am on duty at the tomb this morning. This being Midyear Day, and consequently a holiday, we expect an influx of rowdy and destructive kender. I have been ordered to report to my post an hour early. I wish you joy of the day, sir, and I thank you for your company."

He bowed stiffly, turned on his heel as if he were already performing the slow and stately march before the tomb, and walked out the door of the Inn. Caramon could hear his booted feet ringing on the long staircase that led down from the Inn, perched high in the branches of Solace's largest vallenwood.

Caramon leaned back comfortably in the booth. The sunshine streamed in through the red and green windows, warming him. His belly full, he was content. Outside, people were cleaning up after the storm, gathering up the branches that had fallen from the vallenwoods, airing out their damp houses, spreading straw over the muddy streets. In the afternoon, the people would dress in their best clothes, adorn their hair with flowers, and celebrate the longest day of the year with dancing and feasting. Caramon could see Gerard stalking stiff-backed and stiff-necked through the mud, paying no heed to anything going on around him, making his way to the Tomb of the Last Heroes. Caramon watched as long as he could see the Knight, before finally losing sight of him in the crowd.

"He's a strange one," said Laura, whipping away the empty bowl and pocketing the coin. "I wonder how you can eat alongside him, Father. His face curdles the milk."

"He cannot help his face, Daughter," Caramon returned sternly. "Are there any more eggs?"

"I'll bring you some. You've no idea what a pleasure it is to see you eating again." Laura paused in her work to kiss her father tenderly on his forehead. "As for that young man, it's not his face that makes him ugly. I've loved far uglier in looks in my time. It's his arrogance, his pride that drives people away. Thinks he's better than all the rest of us, so he does. Did you know that he comes from one of the wealthiest families in all of Palanthas? His father practically funds the Knighthood, they say. And he pays well for his son to be posted here in Solace, away from the fighting in Sanction and other places. It's small wonder the other Knights have no respect for him."

Laura flounced off to the kitchen to refill her father's plate.

Caramon stared after his daughter in astonishment. He'd been eating breakfast with this young man every day for the past two months, and he had no notion of any of this. They'd developed what he considered a close relationship, and here was Laura, who'd never said anything to the young Knight beyond, "Sugar for your tea?" knowing his life's history.

"Women," Caramon said to himself, basking in the sunlight. "Eighty years old and I might as well be sixteen again. I didn't understand them then, and I don't understand them now."

Laura returned with a plate of eggs piled high with spiced potatoes on the side. She gave her father another kiss and went about her day.

"She's so much like her mother, though," Caramon said fondly and ate his second plate of eggs with relish.

Gerard uth Mondar was thinking about women, as well, as he waded through the ankle-deep mud. Gerard would have agreed with Caramon that women were creatures not to be understood by men. Caramon liked women, however. Gerard neither liked them nor trusted them. Once when he had been fourteen and newly recovered from the illness that had destroyed his looks, a neighbor girl had laughed at him and called him "pock face."

Discovered in gulping tears by his mother, he was comforted by his mother, who said, "Pay no attention to the stupid chit, my son. Women will love you one day." And then she had added, in a vague afterthought, "You are very rich, after all."

Fourteen years later, he would wake in the night to hear the girl's shrill, mocking laughter, and his soul would cringe in shame and embarrassment. He would hear his mother's counsel and his embarrassment would burn away in anger, an anger that burned all the hotter because his mother had proved a prophetess. The "stupid chit" had thrown herself at Gerard when they were both eighteen and she had come to realize that money could make the ugliest weed beautiful as a rose. He had taken great pleasure in scornfully snubbing her. Ever since that day, he had suspected that any woman who looked at him with any interest whatsoever was secretly calculating his worth, all the while masking her disgust for him with sweet smiles and fluttering lashes.

Mindful of the precept that the best offense is a good defense, Gerard had built a most excellent fortress around himself, a fortress bristling with sharp barbs, its walls stocked with buckets of acidic comments, its high towers hidden in a cloud of dark humors, the entire fortress surrounded by a moat of sullen resentment.

His fortress proved extremely good at keeping out men, as well. Laura's gossip was more accurate than most. Gerard uth Mondar did indeed come from one of the wealthiest families in Palanthas, probably one of the wealthiest in all of Ansalon. Prior to the Chaos War, Gerard's father, Mondar uth Alfric, had been the owner of the most successful shipyard in Palanthas. Foreseeing the rise of the Dark Knights, Sir Mondar had wisely converted as much of his property into good solid steel as possible and moved his family to Southern Ergoth, where he started his shipbuilding and repairing business anew, a business which was now thriving.

Sir Mondar was a powerful force among the Knights of Solamnia. He contributed more money than any other Knight to the support and maintenance of the Knighthood. He had seen to it that his son became a Knight, had seen to it that his son had the very best, the safest posting available. Mondar had never asked Gerard what he wanted from life. The elder Knight took it for granted that his son wanted to be a Knight and the son had taken it for granted himself until the very night he was holding vigil before the ceremony of knighthood. In that night, a vision came to him, not a vision of glory and honor won on the battlefield, but a vision of a sword rusting away in its scabbard, a vision of running errands and posting guard detail over dust and ashes that didn't need guarding.

Too late to back out. To do so would break a family tradition that supposedly extended back to Vinas Solamnus. His father would renounce him, hate him forever. His mother, who had sent out hundreds of invitations to a celebratory party, would take to her bed for a month. Gerard had gone through with the ceremony. He had taken his vow, a vow he considered meaningless. He had donned the armor that had become his prison.

He had served in the Knighthood now for seven years, one of which had been spent in the "honorary" duty of guarding a bunch of corpses. Before that, he'd brewed tar-bean tea and written letters for his commanding officer in Southern Ergoth. He had requested posting to Sanction and had been on the verge of leaving, when the city was attacked by the armies of the Knights of Neraka and his father had seen to it that his son was sent instead to Solace. Returning to the fortress, Gerard cleaned the mud from his boots and left to join the fellow of his watch, taking up his hated and detested position of honor before the Tomb of the Last Heroes.

The tomb was a simple structure of elegant design, built by dwarves of white marble and black obsidian. The tomb was surrounded by trees, that had been planted by the elves, and which bore fragrant flowers all year long. Inside lay the bodies of Tanis Half-elven, fallen hero of the battle of the High Clerist's Tower, and Steel Brightblade, son of Sturm Brightblade and the hero of the final battle against Chaos. Here also were the bodies of the knights who had fought the Chaos god. Above the door of the tomb was written a single name, Tasslehoff Burrfoot, the kender hero of the Chaos war.

Kender came from all over Ansalon to pay tribute to their hero, feasting and picnicking on the lawns, singing songs of Uncle Tas and telling stories about his brave deeds. Unfortunately, some years after the tomb had been built, the kender took it into their heads to each come away with a piece of the tomb for luck. To this end, they began to attack the tomb with chisels and hammers, forcing the Solamnic knights to erect a wrought-iron fence around the tomb that was starting to have the appearance of being nibbled by mice.

The sun blazing down on him, his armor baking him slowly as Laura was slowly baking her beef roast, Gerard marched with slow and solemn step the one hundred paces that took him from the left of the tomb to the center. Here he met his fellow who had marched an equal distance. They saluted one another. Turning, they saluted the fallen heroes. Turning, they marched back, each guard's motions mirroring exactly the motions of the guard opposite.

One hundred paces back. One hundred paces forth.

Over and over and over.

An honor to some, such as the Knight who stood watch this day with Gerard. This Knight had purchased this posting with blood, not with money. The veteran Knight walked his beat with a slight limp, but he walked it proudly. Small blame to him that every time he came face to face with Gerard, he regarded him with lip-curling enmity.

Gerard marched back and forth. As the day progressed, crowds gathered, many having traveled to Solace especially for this holiday. Kender arrived in droves, spreading lunches on the lawn, eating and drinking, dancing and playing games of goblin ball and kender-keep-away. The kender loved to watch the Knights, loved to annoy them. The kender danced around the Knights, tried to make them smile, tickled them, rapped on their armor, called them "Kettle Head" and "Canned Meat," offered them food, thinking they might be hungry.

Gerard uth Mondar disliked humans. He distrusted elves. He hated kender. Actively hated them. Detested them. He hated all kender equally, including the so-called "afflicted" kender, whom most people now viewed with pity. These kender were survivors of an attack by the great dragon Malys on their homeland. They were said to have seen such acts of violence and cruelty that their merry, innocent natures had been forever altered, leaving them much like humans: suspicious, cautious, and vindictive. Gerard didn't believe this "afflicted" act. To his mind, it was just another sneaky way for kender to get their grubby little hands into a man's pockets.

Kender were like vermin. They could flatten their boneless little bodies and crawl into any structure made by man or dwarf. Of this Gerard was firmly convinced, and so he was only a little surprised when, sometime nearing the end of his watch, drawing on late afternoon, he heard a shrill voice hallooing and hollering. The voice came from inside the tomb.

"I say!" cried the voice. "Could someone let me out? It's extremely dark in here, and I can't find the door handle."

The partner of Gerard's watch actually missed a step. Halting, he turned to stare. "Did you hear that?" he demanded, regarding the tomb with frowning concern. "It sounded like someone was in there."

"Hear what?" Gerard said, though he himself had heard it plainly. "You're imagining things."

But they weren't. The noise grew louder. Knocking and pounding were now added to the hallooing and hollering.

"Hey, I heard a voice inside the tomb!" shouted a kender child, who had dashed forward to retrieve a ball that had bounced off Gerard's left foot. The kender put his face to the fence, pointed inside at the tomb's massive and sealed doors. "There's someone trapped in the tomb! And it *wants out!*"

The crowd of kender and other residents of Solace who had come to pay their respects to the dead by swilling ale and munching cold chicken forgot their suppers and their games. Gasping in wonder, they crowded around the fence, nearly overrunning the Knights.

"They buried someone alive in there!" a girl screamed.

The crowd surged forward.

"Keep back!" Gerard shouted, drawing his sword. "This is holy ground! Any who desecrates it will be arrested! Randolph, go and get reinforcements! We need to clear this area."

"I suppose it could be a ghost," his fellow Knight speculated, his eyes glowing with awe. "A ghost of one of the fallen Heroes come back to warn us of dire peril."

Gerard snorted. "You've been listening to too many bards' tales! It's nothing more than one of these filthy little vermin who's got himself inside there and can't get out. I have the key to the fence, but I have no idea how to open the tomb."

The banging on the door was growing louder.

The Knight cast Gerard a disgusted glance. "I will go fetch the provost. He'll know what to do."

Randolph pelted off, holding his sword to his side to keep it from clanking against his armor.

"Get away! Move aside!" Gerard ordered in firm tones.

He drew out the key and, putting his back against the gate, keeping his face to the crowd, he fumbled around behind his back until he managed to fit the key into the lock. Hearing it click, he opened the gate, much to the delight of the crowd, several of whom endeavored to push through. Gerard walloped the boldest with the flat of his sword, drove them back a few moments, time enough for him to hastily dodge inside the fence gate and slam it shut behind him.

The crowd of humans and kender pressed in around the fence. Children poked their heads through the bars, promptly got their heads stuck, and began to wail. Some climbed the bars in a futile attempt to crawl over, while others thrust their hands and arms and legs inside for no logical reason that Gerard could see, which only went to prove what he'd long suspected—that his fellow mortals were ninnies.

The Knight made certain the gate was locked and secure and then walked over to the tomb, intending to post himself at the entrance until the Provost came with some means of breaking the seal.

He was climbing the marble and obsidian stairs when he heard the voice say cheerfully, "Oh, never mind. I've got it!"

A loud snick, as of a lock being tripped, and the doors to the tomb began to slowly creak open.

The crowd gasped in thrilled horror and crowded nearer the fence, each trying to get the best view possible of the Knight being ripped apart by hordes of skeletal warriors.

A figure emerged from the tomb. It was dusty, dirty, its hair windswept, its clothes in disarray and singed, its pouches rather mangled and worse for wear. But it wasn't a skeleton. It wasn't a blood-sucking vampire or an emaciated ghoul.

It was a kender.

The crowd groaned in disappointment.

The kender peered out into the bright sunlight and blinked, half-blinded. "Hullo," he said. "I'm—" The kender paused to sneeze. "Sorry. It's extremely dusty in there. Someone should really do something about that. Do you have a handkerchief? I seem to have mislaid mine. Well, it actually belonged to Tanis, but I don't suppose he'll be wanting it back now that he's dead. Where am I?"

"Under arrest," said Gerard. Laying firm hands upon the kender, the Knight hauled him down the stairs.

Understandably disappointed that they weren't going to witness a battle between the Knight and the undead, the crowd returned to their picnics and playing goblin ball.

"I recognize this place," said the kender, staring about instead of watching where he was going and consequently tripping himself. "I'm in Solace. Good! That's where I meant to come. My name is Tasslehoff Burrfoot, and I'm here to speak at the funeral of Caramon Majere, so if you could just take me to the Inn quickly, I really do have to get back. You see, there's this giant foot about to come down—blam! right on top of me, and that's something I don't want to miss, and now then—"

Gerard put the key into the gate lock, turned it, and opened the gate. He gave the kender a shove that sent him sprawling. "The only place you're going is off to jail. You've done enough mischief already."

The kender picked himself up cheerfully, not at all angry or disconcerted. "Awfully nice of you to find me a place to spend the night. Not that I'll be here that long. I've come to speak . . ." He paused. "Did I mention that I was Tasslehoff Burrfoot?"

Gerard grunted, not interested. He took firm hold of the kender and stood waiting with him until someone came to take the little bastard off his hands.

"*The* Tasslehoff," said the kender.

Gerard cast a weary glance out over the crowd and shouted, "Everyone named Tasslehoff Burrfoot raise his hand!"

Thirty-seven hands shot up in the air, and two dogs barked.

"Oh, my!" said the kender, clearly taken aback.

"You can see why I'm not impressed," said Gerard and searched hopefully for some sign that relief was on the way.

"I don't suppose it would matter if I told you that I was the original Tasslehoff . . . No, I guess not." The kender sighed and stood fidgeting in the hot sun. His hand, strictly out of boredom, found its way into Gerard's money pouch, but Gerard was prepared for that and gave the kender a swift and nasty crack across the knuckles.

The kender sucked his bruised hand. "What's all this?" He looked around at the people larking and frolicking upon the lawn. "What are these people doing here? Why aren't they attending Caramon's funeral? It's the biggest event Solace has ever seen!"

"Probably because Caramon Majere is not dead yet," said Gerard caustically. "Where *is* that good-for-nothing provost?"

"Not dead?" The kender stared. "Are you sure?"

"I had breakfast with him myself this very morning," Gerard replied.

"Oh, no!" The kender gave a heartbroken wail and slapped himself on the forehead. "I've gone and goofed it up *again!* And I don't suppose that now I've got time to try it a third time. What with the giant foot and all." He began to rummage about in his pouch. "Still, I guess I had better try. Now, where did I put that device—"

Gerard glowered around as he tightened his grip on the collar of the kender's dusty jacket. The thirty-seven kender named Tasslehoff had all come over to meet number thirty-eight.

"The rest of you, clear out!" Gerard waved his hand as if he were shooing chickens.

Naturally, the kender ignored him. Though extremely disappointed that Tasslehoff hadn't turned out to be a shambling zombie, the kender were interested to hear where he'd been, what he'd seen and what he had in his pouches.

"Want some Midyear Day's cake?" asked a pretty female kender.

"Why, thank you. This is quite good. I—" The kender's eyes opened wide. He tried to say something, couldn't speak for the cake in his mouth, and ended up half choking himself. His fellow kender obligingly pounded him on the back. He bolted the cake, coughed, and gasped out, *"What* day is this?"

"Midyear's Day!" cried everyone.

"Then I haven't missed it!" the kender shouted triumphantly. "In fact, this is better than I could have hoped! I'll get to tell Caramon what I'm going to say at his funeral tomorrow! He'll probably find it extremely interesting."

The kender looked up into the sky. Spotting the position of the sun, which was about half-way down, heading for the horizon, he said, "Oh, dear. I don't have all that much time. If you'll just excuse me, I had best be running."

And run he did, leaving Gerard standing flat-footed on the grassy lawn, a kender jacket in his hand.

Gerard spent one baffled moment wondering how the imp had managed to wriggle out of his jacket, yet still retain all his pouches, which were jouncing and bouncing as he ran, spilling their contents to the delight of the thirty-seven Tasslehoffs. Concluding that this was a phenomenon that, much like the departure of the gods, he would never understand, Gerard was about to run after the errant kender, when he remembered that he could not leave his post unguarded.

At this juncture, the provost came into sight, accompanied by an entire detail of Solamnic Knights solemnly arrayed in their best armor to welcome back the returning Heroes, for this is what they had understood they were going to be meeting.

"Just a kender, sir," Gerard explained. "Somehow he managed to get himself locked inside the tomb. He let himself out. He got away from me, but I think I know where he's headed."

The provost, a stout man who loved his ale, turned very red in the face. The Knights looked extremely foolish—the kender were now dancing around them in a circle—and all looked very black at Gerard, whom they clearly blamed for the entire incident.

"Let them," Gerard muttered, and dashed off after his prisoner.

The kender had a good head start. He was quick and nimble and accustomed to fleeing pursuit. Gerard was strong and a swift runner, but he was encumbered by his heavy, ceremonial armor, which clanked and rattled and jabbed him uncomfortably in several tender areas. He would likely have never even caught sight of the felon had not the kender stopped at several junctures to look around in amazement, demanding loudly to know, "Where did *this* come from?" staring at a newly built garrison, and, a little farther on, "What are all these doing here?" This in reference to the refugee housing. And "Who put *that* there?" This to a large sign posted by the town fathers proclaiming that Solace was a town in good standing and had paid its tribute to the dragon and was therefore a safe place to visit.

The kender seemed extremely disconcerted by the sign. He stood before it, eyeing it severely. "That can't stay there," he said loudly. "It will block the path of the funeral procession."

Gerard thought he had him at this point, but the kender gave a bound and a leap and dashed off again. Gerard was forced to halt to catch his breath. Running in the heavy armor in the heat caused his head to swim and sent little shooting stars bursting across his vision. He was close to the Inn, however, and he had the grim satisfaction of seeing the kender dash up the stairs and through the front door.

"Good," Gerard thought grimly. "I have him."

Removing his helm, he tossed it to the ground, and leaned back against the signpost until his breathing returned to normal, while he watched the stairs to make certain the kender didn't depart. Acting completely against regulations, Gerard divested himself of the pieces of armor that were chafing him the worst, wrapped them in his cloak, and stashed the bundle in a dark corner of the Inn's woodshed. He then walked over to the community water barrel and plunged the gourd deep into the water. The barrel stood in a shady spot beneath one of the vallenwoods. The water was cool and sweet. Gerard kept one eye on the door of the Inn and, lifting the dipper, dumped the water over his head.

The water trickled down his neck and breast, wonderfully refreshing. He took a long drink, slicked back his hair, wiped his face, picked up his helm and, tucking it beneath his arm, made the long ascent up the stairs to the

Inn. He could hear the kender's voice quite clearly. Judging by his formal tones and unnaturally deep voice, the kender appeared to be making a speech.

" 'Caramon Majere was a very great hero. He fought dragons and undead and goblins and hobgoblins and ogres and draconians and lots of others I can't remember. He traveled back in time with this very device—right here, this very device—' " The kender resumed normal speech for a moment to say, "Then I show the crowd the device, Caramon. I'd show you that part, but I can't quite seem to find it right now. Don't worry, I won't let anyone touch it. Now, where was I?"

A pause and the sound of paper rustling.

Gerard continued climbing the stairs. He had never truly noticed just how many stairs there were before. His legs, already aching and stiff from running, burned, his breath came short. He wished he'd taken off all his armor. He was chagrined to see how far he'd let himself go. His formerly strong athlete's body was soft as a maiden's. He stopped on the landing to rest and heard the kender launch back into his speech.

" 'Caramon Majere traveled back in time. He saved Lady Crysania from the Abyss.' She'll be here, Caramon. She'll fly here on the back of a silver dragon. Goldmoon will be here, too, and Riverwind will come and their beautiful daughters and Silvanoshei, the king of the United Elven Nations, will be here, along with Gilthas, the new ambassador to the United Human Nations, and, of course, Laurana. Even Dalamar will be here! Think of that, Caramon! The Head of the Conclave coming to your funeral. He'll be standing right over there next to Palin, who's head of the White Robes, but then I guess you already know that, him being your son and all. At least, I think that's where they were standing. The last time I was here for your funeral I came after it was all over and everyone was going home. I heard about it later from Palin, who said that they were sorry. If they'd known I was coming they would have waited. I felt a bit insulted, but Palin said that they all thought I was dead, which I am, of course, only not at the moment. And because I missed your funeral the first time, that's why I had to try to hit it again."

Gerard groaned. Not only did he have to deal with a kender, he had to deal with a mad kender. Probably one of those who claimed to be "afflicted." He felt badly for Caramon, hoped the old man wasn't too upset by this incident. Caramon would probably be understanding. For reasons passing Gerard's comprehension, Caramon seemed to have a soft spot for the little nuisances.

"So anyway my speech goes on," the kender said. " 'Caramon Majere did all these things and more. He was a great hero and a great warrior, but do you know what he did best?' " The kender's voice softened. " 'He was a great friend. He was my friend, my very best friend in all of the world. I came back—or rather I came forward—to say this because I think it's important, and Fizban thought it was important, too, which is why he let me come. It seems to me that being a great friend is more important than being a great hero or a great warrior. Being a good friend is the most important thing there is. Just think, if everyone in the world were great friends, then we wouldn't be such terrible enemies. Some of you here are enemies now—' I look at Dalamar at this point,

Caramon. I look at him very sternly, for he's done some things that haven't been at all nice. And then I go on and say, 'But you people are here today because you were friends with this one man and he was your friend, just like he was mine. And so maybe when we lay Caramon Majere to rest, we will each leave his grave with friendlier feelings toward everyone. And maybe that will be the beginning of peace.' And then I bow and that's the end. What do you think?"

Gerard arrived in the doorway in time to see the kender jump down off a table, from which vantage point he'd been delivering his speech, and run over to stand in front of Caramon. Laura was wiping her eyes on the corners of her apron. Her gully dwarf helper blubbered shamelessly in a corner, while the Inn's patrons were applauding wildly and banging their mugs on the table, shouting, "Hear, hear!"

Caramon Majere sat in one of the high-backed booths. He was smiling, a smile touched by the last golden rays of the sun, rays that seem to have slipped into the Inn on purpose just to say goodnight.

"I'm sorry this had to happen, sir," said Gerard, walking inside. "I didn't realize he would trouble you. I'll take him away now."

Caramon reached out his hand and stroked the kender's topknot, the hair of which was standing straight up, like the fur of a startled cat.

"He's not bothering me. I'm glad to see him again. That part about friend-ship was wonderful, Tas. Truly wonderful. Thank you."

Caramon frowned, shook his head. "But I don't understand the rest of what you said, Tas. All about the United Elven Nations and Riverwind coming to the Inn when he's been dead these many years. Something's peculiar here. I'll have to think about it." Caramon stood up from the booth and headed toward the door. "I'll just be taking my evening walk, now, Laura."

"Your dinner will be waiting when you come back, Father," she said. Smoothing her apron, she shook the gully dwarf, ordered him to pull himself together and get back to work.

"Don't think about it too long, Caramon," Tas called out. "Because of . . . well, you know."

He looked up at Gerard, who had laid a firm hand on the kender's shoulder, getting a good grip on flesh and bone this time.

"It's because he's going to be dead pretty soon," Tas said in a loud whisper. "I didn't like to mention that. It would have been rude, don't you think?"

"I think you're going to spend the next year in prison," said Gerard sternly.

Caramon Majere stood at the top of the stairs. "Yes, Tika, dear. I'm coming," he said. Putting his hand over his heart, he pitched forward, headfirst.

The kender tore himself free of Gerard, flung himself to the floor, and burst into tears.

Gerard moved swiftly, but he was too late to halt Caramon's fall. The big man tumbled and rolled down the stairs of his beloved Inn. Laura screamed. The patrons cried out in shock and alarm. People in the street, seeing Caramon falling, began to run toward the Inn.

Gerard dashed down the stairs as fast as ever he could and was the first to reach Caramon. He feared to find the big man in terrible pain, for he must have broken every bone in his body. Caramon did not appear to be suffering however. He had already left mortal cares and pain behind, his spirit lingering only long enough to say good-bye. Laura threw herself beside him on the ground. Taking hold of his hand, she held it pressed to her lips.

"Don't cry, my dear," he said softly, smiling. "Your mother's here with me. She'll take good care of me. I'll be fine."

"Oh, Daddy!" Laura sobbed. "Don't leave me yet!"

Caramon's eyes glanced around at the townspeople who had gathered. He smiled and gave a little nod. He continued to search through the crowd and he frowned.

"But where's Raistlin?" he asked.

Laura looked startled, but said, brokenly, "Father, your brother's been dead a long, long time—"

"He said he would wait for me," Caramon said, his voice beginning strong, but growing fainter. "He should be here. Tika's here. I don't understand. This is not right. Tas . . . What Tas said . . . A different future . . ."

His gaze came to Gerard. He beckoned the Knight to come near.

"There's something you must . . . do," said Caramon, his breath rasping in his chest.

Gerard knelt beside him, more touched by this man's death than he could have imagined possible. "Yes, sir," he said. "What is it?"

"Promise me . . ." Caramon whispered. "On your honor . . . as a Knight."

"I promise," said Gerard. He supposed that the old man was going to ask him to watch over his daughters or to take care of his grandchildren, one of whom was also a Solamnic Knight. "What would you have me do, sir?"

"Dalamar will know. . . . Take Tasslehoff to Dalamar," Caramon said and his voice was suddenly strong and firm. He looked intently at Gerard. "Do you promise? Do you swear that you will do this?"

"But, sir," Gerard faltered, "what you ask of me is impossible! No one has seen Dalamar for years. Most believe that he is dead. And as for this kender who calls himself Tasslehoff . . ."

Caramon reached out his hand, a hand that was bloody from his fall. He grasped hold of Gerard's most unwilling hand and gripped it tightly.

"I promise, sir," said Gerard.

Caramon smiled. He let out his breath and did not draw another. His eyes fixed in death, fixed on Gerard. The hand, even in death, did not relinquish its grip. Gerard had to pry the old man's fingers loose and was left with a smear of blood on his palm.

"I'll be happy to go with you to see Dalamar, Sir Knight, but I can't go tomorrow," said the kender, snuffling and wiping his tear-grimed face with the sleeve of his shirt. "I have to speak at Caramon's funeral."

4 A STRANGE AWAKENING

Silvan's arm was on fire. He couldn't put out the blaze, and no one would come help him. He called out for Samar and for his mother, but his calls went unanswered. He was angry, deeply angry, angry and hurt that they would not come, that they were ignoring him. Then he realized that the reason they were not coming was that they were angry with him. He had failed them. He had let them down, and they would come to him no more. . . .

With a great cry, Silvan woke himself. He opened his eyes to see above him a canopy of gray. His vision was slightly blurred, and he mistook the gray mass above him for the gray ceiling of the burial mound. His arm pained him, and he remembered the fire. Gasping, he shifted to put out the flames. Pain lanced through his arm and hammered in his head. He saw no flames, and he realized dazedly that the fire had been a dream. The pain in his left arm was not a dream, however. The pain was real. He examined the arm as best he could, though every movement of his head cost him a gasp.

Not much doubt. The arm was broken just above the wrist. The flesh was swollen so that it looked like a monster arm, a strange color of greenish purple. He lay back down and stared around him, feeling sorry for himself, and wondered very much that his mother did not come to him when he was in such agony. . . .

"Mother!" Silvan sat up so suddenly that the pain coiled round his gut and caused him to vomit.

He had no idea how he came to be here or even where here was. He knew where he was supposed to be, knew he had been dispatched to bring help to his beleagured people. He looked around, trying to gain some sense of the time. Night had passed. The sun shone in the sky. He had mistaken a canopy of gray leaves for the ceiling of the burial mound. Dead gray leaves, hanging listlessly from dead branches. Death had not come naturally, as with the fall of the year, causing them to release their hold on life and drift in a dream of reds and golds upon the crisp air. The life had been sucked from leaves and branches, trunk and roots, leaving them desicated, mummified but still standing, a husk, an empty mockery of life.

Silvan had never seen a blight of this kind attack so many trees before, and his soul shrank from the sight. He could not take time to consider it, however. He had to complete his mission.

The sky above was a pearl gray with a strange kind of shimmer that he put down to the aftereffects of the storm. Not so many hours have passed, he told himself. The army could hold out this long. I have not failed them utterly. I can still bring help.

He needed to splint his arm, and he searched through the forest undergrowth for a strong stick. Thinking he'd found what he sought, he put out his hand to grasp it. The stick disintegrated beneath his fingers, turned to dust. He stared, startled. The ash was wet and had a greasy feel to it. Repulsed, he wiped his hand on his shirt, wet from the rain.

All around him were gray trees. Gray and dying or gray and dead. The grass was gray, the weeds gray, the fallen branches gray, all with that look of having been sucked dry.

He'd seen something like this before or heard of something like this. . . . He didn't recall what, and he had no time to think. He searched with increasingly frantic urgency among the gray-covered undergrowth for a stick and found one eventually, a stick that was covered with dust but had not been struck with the strange blight. Placing the stick on his arm, gasping at the pain, he gritted his teeth against it. He ripped off a shred of his shirttail and tied the splint in place. He could hear the broken ends of the bone grind together. The pain and the hideous sound combined to nearly make him pass out. He sat hunched over, his head down, fighting the nausea, the sudden heat that swept over his body.

Finally, the star bursts cleared from his vision. The pain eased somewhat. Holding his injured left arm close to his body, Silvan staggered to his feet. The wind had died. He could no longer feel its guiding touch upon his face. He could not see the sun itself for the pearl gray clouds, but the light shone brightest in one portion of the sky, which meant that way must be east. Silvan put his back to the light and looked to the west.

He did not remember his fall or what had occurred just prior to the fall. He began to talk to himself, finding the sound of his voice comforting.

"The last thing I remember, I was within sight of the road I needed to take to reach Sithelnost," he said. He spoke in Silvanesti, the language of his childhood, the language his mother favored.

A hill rose up above him. He was standing in the bottom of a ravine, a ravine he vaguely remembered from the night before.

"Someone either climbed or fell down into the ravine," he said, eyeing a crooked trail left in the gray ash that covered the hillside. He smiled ruefully. "My guess would be that someone was me. I must have taken a misstep in the darkness, tumbled down the ravine. Which means," he added, heartened, "the road must lie right up there. I do not have far to go."

He began to climb back up the steep sides of the ravine, but this proved more difficult than he'd supposed. The gray ash had formed a silt with the rain and was slippery as goose grease. He slid down the hill twice, jarring his injured arm, causing him almost to lose consciousness.

"This will never do," Silvan muttered.

He stayed at the bottom of the ravine where the walking was easier, always keeping the top of the hill in sight, hoping to find an outcropping of rock that would act as a staircase up the slippery slope.

He stumbled over the uneven ground in a haze of pain and fear. Every step brought a jolt of pain to his arm. He pushed himself on, however, trudging through the gray mud that seemed to try to drag him down among the dead vegetation, searching for a way out of this gray vale of death that he grew to loathe as a prisoner loathes his cell.

He was parched with thirst. The taste of ash filled his mouth, and he longed for a drink of water to wash it away. He found a puddle once, but it was covered with a gray film, and he could not bring himself to drink from it. He staggered on.

"I have to reach the road," he said and repeated it many times like a mantra, matching his footfalls to its rhythm. "I have to go on," he said to himself dreamily, "because if I die down here, I will turn into one of the gray mummies like the trees and no one will ever find me."

The ravine came to a sudden end in a jumble of rock and fallen trees. Silvan straightened, drew in a deep breath and wiped chill sweat from his forehead. He rested a moment, then began to climb, his feet slipping on the rocks, sending him scrabbling backward more than once. Grimly, he pressed on, determined to escape the ravine if it proved to be the last act of his life. He drew nearer and nearer the top, up to the point where he thought he should have been able to see the road.

He peered out through the boles of the gray trees, certain the road must be there but unable to see it due to some sort of strange distortion of the air, a distortion that caused the trees to waver in his sight.

Silvan continued to climb.

"A mirage," he said. "Like seeing water in the middle of the road on a hot day. It will disappear when I come near it."

He reached the top of the hill and tried to see through the trees to the road he knew must lie beyond. In order to keep moving, moving through the pain, he had concentrated his focus upon the road until the road had become his one goal.

"I have to reach the road," he mumbled, picking up the mantra. "The road is the end of pain, the road will save me, save my people. Once I reach the road, I am certain to run into a band of elven scouts from my mother's army.

I will turn over my mission to them. Then I will lie down upon the road and my pain will end and the gray ash will cover me . . ."

He slipped, nearly fell. Fear jolted him out of his terrible reverie. Silvan stood trembling, staring about, prodding his mind to return from whatever comforting place it had been trying to find refuge. He was only a few feet from the road. Here, he was thankful to see, the trees were not dead, though they appeared to be suffering from some sort of blight. The leaves were still green, though they drooped, wilting. The bark of the trunks had an unhealthy look to it, was staring to drop off in places.

He looked past them. He could see the road, but he could not see it clearly. The road wavered in his vision until he grew dizzy to look at it. He wondered uneasily if this was due to his fall.

"Perhaps I am going blind," he said to himself.

·Frightened, he turned his head and looked behind him. His vision cleared. The gray trees stood straight, did not shimmer. Relieved, he looked back to the road. The distortion returned.

"Strange," he muttered. "I wonder what is causing this?"

His walk slowed involuntarily. He studied the distortion closely. He had the oddest impression that the distortion was like a cobweb spun by some horrific spider strung between him and the road, and he was reluctant to come near the shimmer. The disquieting feeling came over him that the shimmering web would seize him and hold him and suck him dry as it had sucked dry the trees. Yet beyond the distortion was the road, his goal, his hope.

He took a step toward the road and came to a sudden halt. He could not go on. Yet there lay the road, only a few steps away. Gritting his teeth, he shoved forward, cringing as if he expected to feel sticky web cling to his face.

Silvan's way was blocked. He felt nothing. No physical presence halted him, but he could not move. Rather, he could not move forward. He could move sideways, he could move backward. He could not move ahead.

"An invisible barrier. Gray ash. Trees dead and dying," he murmured.

He reached into the swirling depths of pain and fear and despair and brought forth the answer.

"The shield. This is the shield!" he repeated, aghast.

The magical shield that the Silvanesti had dropped over their homeland. He had never seen it, but he'd heard his mother describe it often enough. He had heard others describe the strange shimmer, the distortion in the air produced by the shield.

"It can't be," Silvan cried in frustration. "The shield cannot be here. It is south of my position! I was on the road, traveling west. The shield was south of me." He twisted, looked up to find the sun, but the clouds had thickened, and he could not see it.

The answer came to him and with it bitter despair. "I'm turned around," he said. "I've come all this way . . . and it's been the wrong way!"

Tears stung his eyelids. The thought of descending this hill, of going back down into the ravine, of retracing his steps, each step that had cost him so dearly in pain, was almost too much to bear. He sank down to the ground, gave way to his misery.

"Alhana! Mother," he said in agony, "forgive me! I have failed you! What have I ever done in life but fail you . . . ?"

"Who are you who speaks the name that is forbidden to speak?" said a voice. "Who are you who speaks the name Alhana?"

Silvan leaped to his feet. He dashed the tears from his eyes with a backhand smear, looked about, startled, to see who had spoken.

At first he saw only a patch of vibrant, living green, and he thought that he had discovered a portion of the forest untouched by the disease that had stricken the rest. But then the patch moved and shifted and revealed a face and eyes and mouth and hands, revealed itself to be an elf.

The elf's eyes were gray as the forest around him, but they were only reflecting the death he saw, revealing the grief he felt for the loss.

"Who am I who speaks my mother's name?" Silvan asked impatiently. "Her son, of course." He took a lurching step forward, hand outstretched. "But the battle . . . Tell me how the battle went! How did we fare?"

The elf drew back, away from Silvan's touch. "What battle?" he asked.

Silvan stared at the man. As he did so, he noted movement behind him. Three more elves emerged from the woods. He would have never seen them had they not stirred, and he wondered how long they had been there. Silvan did not recognize them, but that wasn't unusual. He did not venture out much among the common soldiers of his mother's forces. She did not encourage such companionship for her son, who was someday destined to be king, would one day be their ruler.

"The battle!" Silvan repeated impatiently. "We were attacked by ogres in the night! Surely, you must . . . ?"

Realization dawned on him. These elves were not dressed for warfare. They were clad in clothes meant for traveling. They might well not know of any battle.

"You must be part of the long-range patrol. You've come back in good time." Silvan paused, concentrated his thoughts, trying to penetrate the smothering fog of pain and despair. "We were attacked last night, during the storm. An army of ogres. I . . . ." He paused, bit his lip, reluctant to reveal his failure. "I was sent to fetch aid. The Legion of Steel has a fortress near Sithelnost. Down that road." He made a feeble gesture. "I must have fallen. My arm is broken. I came the wrong way and now I must backtrack, and I don't have the strength. I can't make it, but you can. Take this message to the commander of the legion. Tell him that Alhana Starbreeze is under attack. . . ."

He stopped speaking. One of the elves had made a sound, a slight exclamation. The elf in the lead, the first to approach Silvan, raised his hand to impose silence.

Silvan was growing increasingly exasperated. He was mortifyingly aware that he cut but a poor figure, clutching his wounded arm to his side like a hurt bird dragging a wing. But he was desperate. The time must be midmorning now. He could not go on. He was very close to collapse. He drew himself up, draped in the cloak of his title and the dignity it lent him.

"You are in the service of my mother, Alhana Starbreeze," he said, his voice imperious. "She is not here, but her son, Silvanoshei, your prince, stands before you. In her name and in my own, I command you to bear her message calling for deliverance to the Legion of Steel. Make haste! I am losing patience!"

He was also rapidly losing his grip on consciousness, but he didn't want these soldiers to think him weak. Wavering on his feet, he reached out a hand to steady himself on a tree trunk. The elves had not moved. They were staring at him now in wary astonishment that widened their almond eyes. They shifted their gazes to the road that lay beyond the shield, looked back at him.

"Why do you stand there staring at me?" Silvan cried. "Do as you are commanded! I am your prince!" A thought came to him. "You need have no fear of leaving me," he said. "I'll be all right." He waved his hand. "Just go! Go! Save our people!"

The lead elf moved closer, his gray eyes intent upon Silvan, looking through him, sifting, sorting.

"What do you mean that you went the wrong way upon the road?"

"Why do you waste time with foolish questions?" Silvan returned angrily. "I will report you to Samar! I will have you demoted!" He glowered at the elf, who continued to regard him steadily. "The shield lies to the south of the road. I was traveling to Sithelnost. I must have gotten turned around when I fell! Because the shield . . . the road . . ."

He turned around to stare behind him. He tried to think this through, but his head was too muzzy from the pain.

"It can't be," he whispered.

No matter what direction he would have taken, he must have still been able to reach the road, which lay outside the shield.

The road still lay outside the shield. *He* was the one who was inside it.

"Where am I?" he asked.

"You are in Silvanesti," answered the elf.

Silvan closed his eyes. All was lost. His failure was complete. He sank to his knees and pitched forward to lie face down in the gray ash. He heard voices but they were far away and receding rapidly.

"Do you think it is truly him?"

"Yes. It is."

"How can you be sure, Rolan? Perhaps it is a trick!"

"You saw him. You heard him. You heard the anguish in his voice, you saw the desperation in his eyes. His arm is broken. Look at the bruises on his face, his torn and muddy clothes. We found the trail in ash left by his fall. We heard him talking to himself when he did not know we were close by. We saw him try to reach the road. How can you possibly doubt?"

Silence, then, in a piercing hiss, "But how did he come through the shield?"

"Some god sent him to us," said the lead elf, and Silvan felt a gentle hand touch his cheek.

"What god?" The other was bitter, skeptical. "There are no gods."

Silvan woke to find his vision clear, his senses restored. A dull ache in his head made thinking difficult, and at first he was content to lie quite still, take in his surroundings, while his brain scrambled to make sense of what was happening. He remembered the road . . .

Silvan struggled to sit up.

A firm hand on his chest arrested his movement.

"Do not move too hastily. I have set your arm and wrapped it in a poultice that will speed the healing. But you must take care not to jar it."

Silvan looked at his surroundings. He had the thought at first that it had all been a dream, that he would wake to find himself once again in the burial mound. He had not been dreaming, however. The boles of the trees were the same as he remembered—ugly gray, diseased, dying. The bed of leaves on which he lay was a deathbed of rotting vegetation. The young trees and plants and flowers that carpeted the forest floor drooped and languished.

Silvanoshei took the elf's counsel and lay back down, more to give himself time to sort out the confusion over what had happened to him than because he needed the rest.

"How do you feel?" The elf's tone was respectful.

"My head hurts a little," Silvan replied. "But the pain in my arm is gone."

"Good," said the elf. "You may sit up then. Slowly, slowly. Otherwise you will pass out."

A strong arm assisted Silvan to a seated position. He felt a brief flash of dizziness and nausea, but he closed his eyes until the sick feeling passed.

The elf held a wooden bowl to Silvan's lips.

"What's this?" he asked, eying with suspicion the brown liquid the bowl contained.

"An herbal potion," replied the elf. "I believe that you have suffered a mild concussion. This will ease the pain in your head and promote the healing. Come, drink it. Why do you refuse?"

"I have been taught never to eat or drink anything unless I know who prepared it and I have seen others taste it first," Silvanoshei replied.

The elf was amazed. "Even from another elf?"

"*Especially* from another elf," Silvanoshei replied grimly.

"Ah," said the elf, regarding him with sorrow. "Yes, of course. I understand."

Silvan attempted to rise to his feet, but the dizziness assailed him again. The elf put the bowl to his own lips and drank several mouthfuls. Then, politely wiping the edge of the bowl, he offered it again to Silvanoshei.

"Consider this, young man. If I wanted you dead, I could have slain you while you were unconscious. Or I could have simply left you here." He cast a glance around at the gray and withered trees. "Your death would be slower and more painful, but it would come to you as it has come to too many of us."

Silvanoshei thought this over as best he could through the throbbing of his head. What the elf said made sense. He took the bowl in unsteady hands and lifted it to his lips. The liquid was bitter, smelled and tasted of tree bark. The potion suffused his body with a pleasant warmth. The pain in his head eased, the dizziness passed.

Silvanoshei saw that he had been a fool to think this elf was a member of his mother's army. This elf wore a cloak strange to Silvan, a cloak made of leather that had the appearance of leaves and sunlight and grass and brush and flowers. Unless the elf moved, he would blend into his forest surroundings so perfectly that he would never be detected. Here in the midst of death, he stood out; his cloak retaining the green memory of the living forest, as if in defiance.

"How long have I been unconscious?" Silvan asked.

"Several hours from when we found you this morning. It is Midyear's Day, if that helps you in your reckoning."

Silvan glanced around. "Where are the others?" He had the thought that they might be in hiding.

"Where they need to be," the elf answered.

"I thank you for helping me. You have business elsewhere, and so do I." Silvan rose to his feet. "I must go. It may be too late. . . ." He tasted bitter gall in his mouth, took a moment to choke it down. "I must still fulfill my mission. If you will show me the place I can use to pass back through the shield . . ."

The elf regarded him with that same strange intensity. "There is no way through the shield."

"But there has to be!" Silvan retorted angrily. "I came through, didn't I?" He glanced back at the trees standing near the road, saw the strange distortion. "I'll go back to the point where I fell. I'll pass through there."

Grimly, he started off, retracing his steps. The elf said no word to halt him but accompanied him, following after him in silence.

Could his mother and her army have held out against the ogres this long? Silvan had seen the army perform some incredible feats. He had to believe the answer was yes. He had to believe there was still time.

Silvan found the place where he must have entered the shield, found the trail his body had left as it rolled down the ravine. The gray ash had been slippery when he'd first tried to climb back up, but it had dried now. The way was easier. Taking care not to jar his injured arm, Silvan clambored up the hill. The elf waited in the bottom of the ravine, watching in silence.

Silvan reached the shield. As before, he was loathe to touch it. Yet here, this place, was where he'd entered it before, however unknowingly. He could see the gouge his boot heel had made in the mud. He could see the fallen tree crossing the path. Some dim memory of attempting to circumvent it returned.

The shield itself was not visible, except as a barely perceptible shimmer when the sun struck it at exactly the correct angle. Other than that, the only way he could tell the shield was before him was by its effect on his view of the trees and plants beyond it. He was reminded of heat waves rising from a sun-baked road, causing everything visible behind the waves to ripple in a mockery of water.

Gritting his teeth, Silvan walked straight into the shield.

The barrier would not let him pass. Worse, wherever he touched the shield, he felt a sickening sensation, as if the shield had pressed gray lips against his flesh and was seeking to suck him dry.

Shuddering, Silvan backed away. He would not try that again. He glared at the shield in impotent fury. His mother had worked for months to penetrate that barrier and for months she had failed. She had thrown armies against it, only to see them flung back. At peril to her own life, she had ridden her griffon into it without success. What could he do against it, one elf.

"Yet," Silvan argued in frustration, "I am inside it! The shield let me in. It will let me out! There must be a way. The elf. It must have something to do with the elf. He and his cohorts have entrapped me, imprisoned me."

Silvan whipped around to find the elf still standing at the bottom of the ravine. Silvan scrambled down the slope, half-falling, slipping and sliding on the rain-wet grass. The sun was sinking. Midyear's Day was the longest day of the year, but it must eventually give way to night. He reached the bottom of the ravine.

"You brought me in here!" Silvan said, so angry that he had to suck in a huge breath to even force the words out. "You *will* let me out. You *have* to let me out!"

"That was the bravest thing I ever saw a man do." The elf cast a dark glance at the shield. "I myself cannot bear to come near it, and I am no coward. Brave, yet hopeless. You cannot pass. None can pass."

"You lie!" Silvan raged. "You dragged me inside here. Let me out!"

Without really knowing what he was doing, he reached out his hand to seize the elf by the throat and choke him, force him to obey, frighten him into obeying.

The elf caught hold of Silvan's wrist, gave it an expert twist, and before he knew what was happening, Silvan found himself on his knees on the ground. The elf immediately released him.

"You are young, and you are in trouble. You do not know me. I make allowances. My name is Rolan. I am one of the kirath. My companions and I found you lying at the bottom of the ravine. That is the truth. If you know of the kirath, you know that we do not lie. I do not know how you came through the shield."

Silvan had heard his parents speak of the kirath, a band of elves who patrolled the borders of Silvanesti. The kirath's duty was to prevent the entrance of outsiders into Silvanesti.

Silvan sighed and lowered his head to his hands.

"I have failed them! Failed them, and now they will die!"

Rolan came near, put his hand upon the young elf's shoulder. "You spoke your name before when we first found you, but I would ask that you give it to me again. There is no need to fear and no reason to keep your identity a secret, unless, of course," he added delicately, "you bear a name of which you are ashamed."

Silvan looked up, stung. "I bear my name proudly. I speak it proudly. If my name brings about my death, so be it." His voice faltered, trembled. "The rest of my people are dead, by now. Dead or dying. Why should I be spared?"

He blinked the tears from his eyes, looked at his captor. "I am the son of those you term 'dark elves' but who are, in truth, the only elves to see clearly in the darkness that covers us all. I am the son of Alhana Starbreeze and Porthios of the Qualinesti. My name is Silvanoshei."

He expected laughter. Disbelief, certainly.

"And why do you think your name would bring death to you, Silvanoshei of the House of Caldaron?" Rolan asked calmly.

"Because my parents are dark elves. Because elven assassins have tried more than once to kill them," Silvan returned.

"Yet Alhana Starbreeze and her armies have tried many times to penetrate the shield, to enter into this land where she is outlaw. I have myself seen her, as I and my fellows walked the border lands."

"I thought you were forbidden to speak her name," Silvan muttered sullenly.

"We are forbidden to do many things in Silvanesti," Rolan added. "The list grows daily, it seems. Why does Alhana Starbreeze want to return to a land that does not want her?

"This is her home," Silvan answered. "Where else would she come?"

"And where else would her son come?" Rolan asked gently.

"Then you believe me?" Silvan asked.

"I knew your mother and your father, Your Highness," Rolan replied. "I was a gardener for the unfortunate King Lorac before the war. I knew your mother when she was a child. I fought with your father Porthios against the dream. You favor him in looks, but there is something of her inside you that brings her closer to the mind. Only the faithless do not believe. The miracle has occurred. You have returned to us. It does not surprise me that, for you, Your Highness, the shield would part."

"Yet it will not let me out," said Silvan dryly.

"Perhaps because you are where you are supposed to be, Your Highness. Your people need you."

"If that is true, then why don't you lift the shield and let my mother return to her kingdom?" Silvanoshei demanded. "Why keep her out? Why keep your own people out? The elves who fight for her are in peril. My mother would not now be battling ogres, would not be trapped—"

Rolan's face darkened. "Believe me, Your Majesty. If we, the kirath, could take down this accursed shield, we would. The shield casts a pall of despair on those who venture near it. It kills every living thing it touches. Look! Look at this, Your Majesty."

Rolan pointed to the corpse of a squirrel lying on the ground, her young lying dead around her. He pointed to golden birds buried in the ash, their song forever silenced.

"Thus our people are slowly dying," he said sadly.

"What is this you say?" Silvan was shocked. "Dying?"

"Many people, young and old, contract a wasting sickness for which there is no cure. Their skin turns gray as the skin of these poor trees, their limbs wither, their eyes dull. First they cannot run without tiring, then they cannot walk, then they cannot stand or sit. They waste away until death claims them."

"Then why don't you take down the shield?" Silvan demanded.

"We have tried to convince the people to unite and stand against General Konnal and the Heads of House, who decided to raise the shield. But most refuse to heed our words. They say the sickness is a plague brought to us from the outside. The shield is all that stands between them and the evils of the world. If it is removed, we all will die."

"Perhaps they are right," Silvan said, glancing back through the shield, thinking of the ogres attacking in the night. "There is no plague striking down elves, at least none that I have heard of. But there are other enemies. The world is fraught with danger. In here, at least you are safe."

"Your father said that we elves had to join the world, become a part of it," Rolan replied with a grim smile. "Otherwise we would wither away and die, like a branch that is cut from the tree or the—"

"—rose stripped from the bush," Silvan said and smiled in remembrance. "We haven't heard from my father in a long time," he added, looking down at the gray ash and smoothing it with the toe of his boot. "He was fighting the great dragon Beryl near Qualinesti, a land she holds in thrall. Some believe he is dead—my mother among them, although she refuses to admit it."

"If he died, he died fighting for a cause he believed in," Rolan said. "His death has meaning. Though it may seem pointless now, his sacrifice will help destroy the evil, bring back the light to drive away the darkness. He died a living man! Defiant, courageous. When our people die," Rolan continued, his voice taking on increasing bitterness, "one hardly notices their passing. The feather flutters and falls limp."

He looked at Silvan. "You are young, vibrant, alive. I feel the life radiate from you, as once I felt it radiate from the sun. Contrast yourself with me. You see it, don't you: the fact that I am withering away? That we are all slowly being drained of life? Look at me, Your Highness. You can see I am dying."

Silvan did not know what to say. Certainly the elf was paler than normal, his skin had a gray tinge to it, but Silvan had put that down to age, perhaps, or to the gray dust. He recalled now that the other elves he had seen bore the same gaunt, hollow-eyed look.

"Our people will see you, and they will see by contrast what they have lost," Rolan pursued. "This is the reason you have been sent to us. To show them that there is no plague in the world outside. The only plague is within." Rolan laid his hand on his heart. "Within us! You will tell the people that if we rid ourselves of this shield, we will restore our land and ourselves to life."

Though my own has ended, Silvan said to himself. The pain returned. His head ached. His armed throbbed. Rolan regarded him with concern.

"You do not look well, Your Highness. We should leave this place. We have lingered near the shield too long already. You must come away before the sickness strikes you, as well."

Silvanoshei shook his head. "Thank you, Rolan, but I cannot leave. The Shield may yet open and let me out as it has let me in."

"If you stay here, you will die, Your Majesty," said Rolan. "Your mother would not want that. She would want you to come to Silvanost and to claim your rightful place upon the throne."

You will someday sit upon the throne of the United Elven Nations, Silvanoshei. On that day, you will right the wrongs of the past. You will purge our people of the sins we elves have committed, the sin of pride, the sin of prejudice, the sin of hatred. These sins have brought about our ruin. You will be our redemption.

His mother's words, He remembered the very first time she had spoken them. He had been five or six. They were camping in the wilderness near Qualinesti. It was night. Silvan was asleep. Suddenly a cry pierced his dreams, brought him wide awake. The fire burned low, but by its light he could see his father grappling with what seemed a shadow. More shadows surrounded them. He saw nothing else because his mother flung her body over his, pressed him to the ground. He could not see, he could not breathe, he could not cry out. Her fear, her warmth, her weight crushed and smothered him.

And then it was all over. His mother's warm, dark weight was lifted from him. Alhana held him in her arms, cradling him, weeping and kissing him and asking him to forgive her if she hurt him. She had a bloody gash on her thigh. His father bore a deep knife wound in his shoulder, just missing the heart. The bodies of three elves, clad all in black, lay around the fire. Years later Silvanoshei woke suddenly in the night with the cold realization that one of those assassins had been sent to murder him.

They dragged away the bodies, left them to the wolves, not considering them worthy of proper burial rites. His mother rocked him to sleep, and she spoke those words to him to comfort him. He would hear them often, again and again.

Perhaps now she was dead. His father dead. Their dream lived, however, lived in him.

He turned away from the shield. "I will come with you," he said to Rolan of the kirath.

5   THE HOLY FIRE

In the old days, the glory days, before the War of the Lance, the road that led from Neraka to the port city of Sanction had been well maintained, for that road was the only route through the mountains known as the Lords of Doom. The road—known as the Hundred Mile Road, for it was almost one hundred miles long, give or take a furlong or two—was paved with crushed rock. Thousands of feet had marched over the crushed rock during the intervening years; booted human feet, hairy goblin feet, clawed draconian feet. So many thousand that the rock had been pounded into the ground and was now deeply embedded.

During the height of the War of the Lance, the Hundred Mile Road had been clogged with men, beasts, and supply wagons. Anyone who had need of speed took to the air, riding on the backs of the swift-flying blue dragons or traversing the skies in floating citadels. Those forced to move along the road could be delayed for days, blocked by the hundreds of foot soldiers who slogged along its torturous route, either marching to the city of Neraka or marching away from it. Wagons lurched and jolted along the road. The grade was steep, descending from the high mountain valley all the way to sea level, making the journey a perilous one.

Wagons loaded with gold, silver, and steel, boxes of stolen jewels, booty looted from people the armies had conquered, were hauled by fearsome beasts known as mammoths, the only creatures strong enough to drag the heavily laden wagons up the mountain road. Occasionally one of the wagons would tip over and spill its contents or lose a wheel, or one of the mammoths would run berserk and trample its keepers and any one else unfortunate enough to be in its path. At these times, the road was shut down completely, bringing everything to a halt while officers tried to keep their men in order and fumed and fretted at the delay.

The mammoths were gone, died out. The men were gone too. Most of them now old. Some of them now dead. All of them now forgotten. The road was empty, deserted. Only the wind's whistling breath blew across the road, which, with its smooth, inlaid gravel surface, was considered one of the man-made wonders of Krynn.

The wind was at the backs of the Dark Knights as they galloped down the winding, twisting snake's back that was the Hundred Mile Road. The wind, a remnant of the storm, howled among the mountain tops, an echo of the Song of Death they had heard in Neraka, but only an echo, not as terrible, not as frightening. The Knights rode hard, rode in a daze, rode without any clear idea of why they rode or where they were heading. They rode in an ecstasy, an excitement that was unlike anything they had ever before experienced.

Certainly Galdar had felt nothing like it. He loped along at Mina's side, running with new-found strength. He could have run from here to Ice Wall without pause. He might have credited his energy to pure joy at regaining his severed limb, but he saw his awe and fervor reflected in the faces of the men who made that exhilarating, mad dash alongside him. It was as if they brought the storm with them—hooves thundering among the mountain walls, the iron shoes of the horses striking lightning bolts from the rock surface.

Mina rode at their head, urging them on when they would have stopped from fatigue, forcing them to look into themselves to find just a bit more strength than they knew they possessed. They rode through the night, their way lit by lightning flashes. They rode through the day, halting only to water the horses and eat a quick bite standing.

When it seemed the horses must founder, Mina called a halt. The Knights had traversed well over half the distance. As it was, her own roan, Foxfire, could have continued on. He appeared to actually resent the stop, for the horse stamped and snorted in displeasure, his irritated protests splitting the air and bouncing back from the mountain tops.

Foxfire was fiercely loyal to his mistress and to her alone. He had no use for any other being. During their first brief rest stop, Galdar had made the mistake of approaching the horse to hold Mina's stirrup as she dismounted, as he had been trained to do for his commander and with much better grace than he'd used for Ernst Magit. Foxfire's lip curled back over his teeth, his eyes gleamed with a wild, wicked light that gave Galdar some idea of how the beast had come by his name. Galdar hastily backed away.

Many horses are frightened by minotaurs. Thinking this might be the problem, Galdar ordered one of the others to attend the commander.

Mina countermanded his order. "Stay back, all of you. Foxfire has no love for any being other than myself. He obeys only my commands and then only when my commands agree with his own instincts. He is very protective of his rider, and I could not prevent him from lashing out at you if you came too near."

She dismounted nimbly, without aid. Removing her own saddle and bridle, she led Foxfire to drink. She fed him and brushed him down with her own hands. The rest of the soldiers tended to their own weary mounts, saw them safely settled for the night. Mina would not allow them to build a campfire. Solamnic eyes might be watching, she said. The fire would be visible a long distance.

The men were as tired as the horses. They'd had no sleep for two days and a night. The terror of the storm had drained them, the forced march left them all shaking with fatigue. The excitement that had carried them this far began to ebb. They looked like prisoners who have wakened from a wonderful dream of freedom to find that they still wear their shackles and their chains.

No longer crowned by lightning and robed with thunder, Mina looked like any other girl, and not even a very attractive girl, more like a scrawny youth. The Knights sat hunched over their food in the moonlit darkness, muttering that they'd been led on a fool's errand, casting Mina dark looks and angry glances. One man even went so far as to say that any of the dark mystics could have restored Galdar's arm, nothing so special in that.

Galdar could have silenced them by pointing out that no dark mystic had restored his arm, though he had begged them often enough. Whether they refused because their powers were not strong or because he lacked the steel to pay them, it was all the same to him. The dark mystics of the Knights of Neraka had not given him an arm. This strange girl had and he was dedicated to her for life. He kept quiet, however. He was ready to defend Mina with his life, should that become necessary, but he was curious to see how she would handle the increasingly tense situation.

Mina did not appear to notice that her command was slowly slipping away. She sat apart from the men, sat above them, perched on an enormous boulder. From her vantage point, she could look out across the mountain range, jagged black teeth taking a bite out of the starry sky. Here and there, fires from the active volcanoes were blots of orange against the black. Withdrawn, abstracted, she was absorbed in her thoughts to the point that she seemed totally unaware of the rising tide of mutiny at her back.

"I'll be damned if I'm riding to Sanction!" said one of the Knights. "You know what's waiting for us there. A thousand of the cursed Solamnics, that's what!"

"I'm off to Khur with the first light," said another. "I must have been thunderstruck to have come this far!"

"I'll not stand first watch," a third grumbled. "She won't let us have a fire to dry out our clothes or cook a decent meal. Let her stand first watch."

"Aye, let her stand first watch!" The others agreed.

"I intend to," said Mina calmly. Rising from her seat, she descended to the road. She stood astride it, her feet planted firmly. Arms crossed over her chest, she faced the men. "I will stand all the watches this night. You will need your rest for the morrow. You should sleep."

She was not angry. She was not sympathetic. She was certainly not pandering to them, did not seem to be agreeing with them in hope of gaining their favor. She was making a statement of fact, presenting a logical and rational argument. The men would need their rest for the morrow.

The Knights were mollified, but still angry, behaving like children who've been made the butt of a joke and don't like it. Mina ordered them to make up their beds and lie down.

The Knights did as they were told, grumbling that their blankets were still wet and how could she expect them to sleep on the hard rock? They vowed, one and all, to leave with the dawn.

Mina returned to her seat upon the boulder and looked out again at the stars and the rising moon. She began to sing.

The song was not like the Song of Death, the terrible dirge sung to them by the ghosts of Neraka. Mina's song was a battle song. A song sung by the brave as they march upon the foe, a song meant to stir the hearts of those who sing it, a song meant to strike terror into the hearts of their enemies.

> Glory calls us
> With trumpet's tongue,
> calls us do great deeds
> on the field of valor,
> calls us to give our blood
> to the flame,
> to the ground,
> the thirsty ground,
> the holy fire.

The song continued, a paean sung by the victors in their moment of triumph, a song of reminiscence sung by the old soldier telling his tale of valor.

Closing his eyes, Galdar saw deeds of courage and bravery, and he saw, thrilling with pride, that he was the one performing these heroic feats. His sword flared with the purple white of the lightning, he drank the blood of his enemies. He marched from one glorious battle to the next, this song of victory on his lips. Always Mina rode before him, leading him, inspiring him, urging him to follow her into the heart of the battle. The purple white glow that emanated from her shone on him.

The song ended. Galdar blinked, realized, to his astonishment and chagrin, that he had fallen asleep. He had not meant to, he had intended to stand watch with her. He rubbed his eyes, wished she would start singing again. The night was cold and empty without the song. He looked around to see if the others felt the same.

They slumbered deeply and peacefully, smiles on their lips. They had laid their swords within reach on the ground beside them. Their hands closed over the hilts as if they would leap up and race off to the fray in an instant. They were sharing Galdar's dream, the dream of the song.

Marveling, he looked at Mina to find her looking at him.

He rose to his feet, went to join her upon her rock.

"Do you know what I saw, Commander?" he asked.

Her amber eyes had caught the moon, encased it. "I know," she replied.

"Will you do that for me, for us? Will you lead us to victory?"

The amber eyes, holding the moon captive, turned upon him. "I will."

"Is it your god who promises you this?"

"It is," she replied gravely.

"Tell me the name of this god, that I may worship him," said Galdar.

Mina shook her head slowly, emphatically. Her gaze left the minotaur, went back to the sky, which was unusually dark, now that she had captured the moon. The light, the only light, was in her eyes. "It is not the right time."

"When will it be the right time?" Galdar pursued.

"Mortals have no faith in anything anymore. They are like men lost in a fog who can see no farther than their own noses, and so that is what they follow, if they follow anything at all. Some are so paralyzed with fear that they are afraid to move. The people must acquire faith in themselves before they are ready to believe in anything beyond themselves."

"Will you do this, Commander? Will you make this happen."

"Tomorrow, you will see a miracle," she said.

Galdar settled himself upon the rock. "Who are you, Commander?" he asked. "Where do you come from?"

Mina turned her gaze upon him and said, with a half-smile, "Who are you, Subcommander? Where do you come from?"

"Why, I'm a minotaur. I was born in—"

"No." She shook her head gently. "Where before that?"

"Before I was born?" Galdar was confused. "I don't know. No person does."

"Precisely," said Mina and turned away.

Galdar scratched his horned head, shrugged in his turn. Obviously she did not want to tell him, and why should she? It was none of his business. It made no difference to him. She was right. He had not believed in anything before this moment. Now he had found something in which to believe. He had found Mina.

She confronted him again, said abruptly, "Are you still tired?"

"No, Talon Leader, I am not," Galdar replied. He had slept only a few hours, but the sleep had left him unusually refreshed.

Mina shook her head. "Do not call me 'Talon Leader.' I want you to call me 'Mina.'"

"That is not right, Talon Leader," he protested. "Calling you by your name does not show proper respect."

"If the men have no respect for me, will it matter what they call me?" she returned. "Besides," she added with calm conviction, "the rank I hold does not yet exist."

Galdar really thought she was getting a bit above herself now, needed taking down a notch or two. "Perhaps you think you should be the 'Lord of the Night,'" he suggested by way of a joke, naming the highest rank that could be held by the Knights of Neraka.

Mina did not laugh. "Someday, the Lord of the Night will kneel down before me."

Galdar knew Lord Targonne well, had difficulty imagining the greedy, grasping, ambitious man kneeling to do anything unless it might be to scoop up a dropped copper. Galdar didn't quite know what to say to such a ludicrous concept and so fell silent, returning in his mind to the dream of glory, reaching for it as a parched man reaches out to water. He wanted so much to believe in it, wanted to believe it was more than mirage.

"If you are certain you are not tired, Galdar," Mina continued, "I want to ask a boon of you."

"Anything, Tal— Mina," he said, faltering.

"Tomorrow we ride into battle." A little frown line marred Mina's smooth complexion. "I have no weapon, nor have I ever been trained in the use of one. Have we time to do so tonight, do you think?"

Galdar's jaw went slack. He wondered if he'd heard correctly. He was so stunned, he could at first make no reply. "You . . . you've never wielded a weapon?"

Mina shook her head calmly.

"Have you ever been in battle, Mina?"

She shook her head again.

"Have you ever seen a battle?" Galdar was feeling desperate.

"No, Galdar." Mina smiled at him. "That is why I am asking for your help. We will go a little ways down the road to practice, so that we will not disturb the others. Do not worry. They will be safe. Foxfire would warn me if an enemy approached. Bring along whatever weapon you think would be easiest for me to learn."

Mina walked off down the road to find a suitable practice field, leaving an amazed Galdar to search through the weapons he and the others carried, to find one suitable for her, a girl who had never before held a weapon and who was, tomorrow, going to lead them into battle.

Galdar cudgeled his brain, tried to knock some common sense back into his head. A dream seemed reality, reality seemed a dream. Drawing his dagger, he stared at it a moment, watched the moonlight flow like quicksilver along the blade. He jabbed the point of the dagger into his arm, the arm Mina had restored to him. Stinging pain and the warm flow of blood indicated that the arm was real, confirmed that he was indeed awake.

Galdar had given his promise, and if he had one thing left to him in this life that he hadn't sold, battered, or flung away, it was his honor. He slid the dagger back into its sheath upon his belt and looked over the stock of weapons.

A sword was out of the question. There was no time to train her properly in its use, she would do more damage to herself or those around than to a foe. He could find nothing that he deemed suitable, and then he noticed the moonlight shining on one weapon in particular, as if it were trying to bring it to his attention—the weapon known as a morning star. Galdar eyed it. Frowning thoughtfully, he hefted it in his hand. The morning star is a battlehammer adorned with spikes on the end, spikes the fanciful said give it the look of a star, hence its name. The morning star was not heavy, took relatively little skill to learn to use, and was particularly effective against knights in armor. One simply bashed one's opponent with the morning star until his armor cracked like a nutshell. Of course, one had to avoid the enemy's own weapon while one was doing the bashing. Galdar picked up a small shield and, armed with these, trudged off down the road, leaving a horse to stand watch.

"I've gone mad," he muttered. "Stark, staring mad."

Mina had located an open space among the rocks, probably used as a wayside camping place for those long-ago armies that had marched along the road. She took hold of the morning star, eyed it critically, hefted it to test its weight and balance. Galdar showed her how to hold the shield, where to position it for best advantage. He instructed her in the use of the morning star, then gave her some simple exercises so that she could accustom herself to the feel of the weapon.

He was gratified (and relieved) to learn that Mina was a quick study. Though her frame was thin, she was well-muscled. Her balance was good, her movements were graceful and fluid. Galdar raised his own shield, let her take a few practice blows. Her first strike was impressive, her second drove him backward, her third put a great dent in his shield and jarred his arm to the marrow.

"I like this weapon, Galdar," she said approvingly. "You have chosen well."

Galdar grunted, rubbed his aching arm, and laid down his shield. Drawing his broadsword from its sheathe, he wrapped the sword in a cloak, bound the cloth around it tightly with rope, and took up a fighting stance.

"Now we go to work," he said.

At the end of two hours, Galdar was astonished at his pupil's progress.

"Are you certain you have never trained as a soldier?" he asked, pausing to catch his breath.

"I have never done so," said Mina. "Look, I will show you." Dropping her weapon, she held out the hand that had been wielding the morning star to the moonlight. "Judge my truthfulness."

Her soft palm was raw and bloody from opened blisters. Yet she had never once complained, never flinched in her strikes, though the pain of her wounds must have been excruciating.

Galdar regarded her with undisguised admiration. If there is one virtue the minotaurs prize, it is the ability to bear pain in stoic silence. "The spirit of some great warrior must live in you, Mina. My people believe that such a thing is possible. When one of our warriors dies courageously in battle, it is the custom in my tribe to cut out his heart and eat it, hoping that his spirit will enter our own."

"The only hearts I will eat will be those of my enemies," said Mina. "My strength and my skill are given to me by my god." She bent to pick up the morning star.

"No, no more practice this night," said Galdar, snatching it out from under her fingers. "We must tend to those blisters. Too bad," he said, eyeing her. "I fear that you will not be able to even set your hand to your horses' reins in the morning, much less hold a weapon. Perhaps we should wait here a few days until you are healed."

"We must reach Sanction tomorrow," said Mina. "So it is ordered. If we arrive a day late, the battle will be finished. Our troops will have suffered a terrible defeat."

"Sanction has long been besieged," Galdar said, disbelieving. "Ever since the foul Solamnics made a pact with that bastard who rules the city, Hogan Bight. We cannot dislodge them, and they do not have the strength to drive us back. The battle is at a stalemate. We attack the walls every day and they defend. Civilians are killed. Parts of the city catch fire. Eventually they'll grow weary of this and surrender. The siege has lasted for well over a year now. I don't see that a single day will make any difference. Stay here and rest."

"You do not see because your eyes are not yet fully open," Mina said. "Bring me some water to wash my hands and some cloth to wipe them clean of blood. Have no fear. I will be able to ride and to fight."

"Why not heal yourself, Mina?" Galdar suggested, testing her, hoping to see another miracle. "Heal yourself as you healed me."

Her amber eyes caught the light of the coming dawn, just starting to brighten the sky. She looked into the dawn and the thought came to his mind that she was already seeing tomorrow's sunset.

"Many hundreds will die in terrible agony," she said in a soft voice. "The pain I bear, I bear in tribute to them. I give it as gift to my god. Rouse the others, Galdar. It is time."

Galdar expected more than half the soldiers to depart, as they had threatened to do in the night. He found on his return to camp that the men were already up and stirring. They were in excellent spirits, confident, excited, speaking of the bold deeds they would do this day. Deeds that they said had come to them in dreams more real than waking.

Mina appeared among them, carrying her shield and her morning star in hands that still bled. Galdar watched her with concern. She was weary from her exercise and from the previous day's hard ride. Standing upon the road, isolated, alone, she seemed suddenly mortal, fragile. Her head drooped, her shoulders sagged. Her hands must burn and sting, her muscles ache. She sighed deeply and looked heavenward, as if questioning whether or not she truly had the strength to carry on.

At sight of her, the Knights lifted their swords, clashed them against their shields in salute.

"Mina! Mina!" they chanted and their chants bounded back from the mountains with the stirring sound of a clarion's call.

Mina lifted her head. The salute was wine to her flagging spirits. Her lips parted, she drank it in. Weariness fell from her like cast-off rags. Her armor shone red in the lurid light of the rising sun.

"Ride hard. We ride this day to glory," she told them, and the Knights cheered wildly.

Foxfire came at her command. She mounted and grasped the reins firmly in her bleeding, blistered hands. It was then that Galdar, taking his place alongside her, running at her stirrup, noted that she wore around her neck a silver medallion upon a silver chain. He looked at it closely, to see what the medallion might have engraved upon its surface.

The medallion was blank. Plain silver, without mark. Strange. Why should anyone wear a blank medallion? He had no chance to ask her, for at that instant Mina struck her spurs to her horse's flank.

Foxfire galloped down the road.

Mina's Knights rode behind her.

6 THE FUNERAL OF CARAMON MAJERE

At the rising of the sun—a splendid dawn of gold and purple with a heart of deep, vibrant red—the people of Solace gathered outside the Inn of the Last Home in silent vigil, offering their love and their respect for the brave, good and gentle man who lay inside.

There was little talk. The people stood in silence presaging the great silence that will fall eventually upon us all. Mothers quieted fretful children, who stared at the Inn, ablaze with lights, not understanding what had happened, only sensing that it was something great and awful, a sensation that impressed itself upon their unformed minds, one they would remember to the end of their own days.

"I'm truly sorry, Laura," Tas said to her in the quiet hour before dawn.

Laura stood beside the booth where Caramon was accustomed to have his breakfast. She stood there doing nothing, staring at nothing, her face pale and drawn.

"Caramon was my very best friend in all the world," Tas told her.

"Thank you." She smiled, though her smile trembled. Her eyes were red from weeping.

"Tasslehoff," the kender reminded her, thinking she had forgotten his name.

"Yes." Laura appeared uneasy. "Er . . . Tasslehoff."

"I *am* Tasslehoff Burrfoot. The original," the kender added, recalling his thirty-seven namesakes—thirty-nine counting the dogs. "Caramon recognized me. He gave me a hug and said he was glad to see me."

Laura regarded him uncertainly. "You certainly do *look* like Tasslehoff. But then I was just a little girl the last time I remember seeing him, and all kender look alike anyway, and it just doesn't make sense! Tasslehoff Burrfoot's been dead these thirty years!"

Tas would have explained—all about the Device of Time Journeying and Fizban having set the device wrong the first time so that Tas had arrived at Caramon's first funeral too late to give his speech, but there was a lump of sadness caught in the kender's gullet, a lump so very big that it prevented the words from coming out.

Laura's gaze went to the stairs of the Inn. Her eyes filled again with tears. She put her head in her hands.

"There, there," Tas said, patting her shoulder. "Palin will be here soon. He knows who I am, and he'll be able to explain everything."

"Palin won't be here," Laura sobbed. "I can't get word to him. It's too dangerous! His own father dead and him not able to come to the burial. His wife and my dear sister trapped in Haven, since the dragon's closed the roads. Only me here to say good-bye to father. It's too hard! Too hard to bear!"

"Why, of course, Palin will be here," Tas stated, wondering what dragon had closed the roads and why. He meant to ask, but with all the other thoughts in his mind, this one couldn't battle its way to the front. "There's that young wizard staying here in the Inn. Room Seventeen. His name is . . . well, I forget his name, but you'll send him to the Tower of High Sorcery in Wayreth, where Palin is Head of the Order of White Robes."

"What tower in Wayreth?" Laura said. She had stopped crying and was looking puzzled. "The tower's gone, disappeared, just like the tower in Palanthas. Palin was head of the Academy of Sorcery, but he doesn't even have that, anymore. The dragon Beryl destroyed the academy a year ago, almost to this date. And there is no Room Seventeen. Not since the Inn was rebuilt the second time."

Tas, busy with remembering, wasn't listening. "Palin will come right away and he'll bring Dalamar, too, and Jenna. Palin will send the messengers to Lady Crysania in the Temple of Paladine and to Goldmoon and Riverwind in Que-shu and Laurana and Gilthas and Silvanoshei in Silvanesti. They'll all be here soon so we . . . we . . ."

Tas's voice trailed off.

Laura was staring at him as if he'd suddenly sprouted two heads. Tas knew because he'd felt that same expression on his own face when he'd been in the presence of a troll who had done that very thing. Slowly, keeping her eyes on Tas, Laura edged away from him.

"You sit right down here," she said, and her voice was very soft and very gentle. "Sit right here, and I'll . . . I'll bring you a big plate of—"

"Spiced potatoes?" Tas asked brightly. If anything could get rid of the lump in his throat, it was Otik's spiced potatoes.

"Yes, a big, heaping dish of spiced potatoes. We haven't lit the cook fires yet this morning, and Cook was so upset I gave her the day off, so it may take me awhile. You sit down and promise you won't go anywhere," Laura said, backing away from the table. She slid a chair in between her and Tas.

"Oh, I won't go anywhere at all," Tas promised, plopping himself down. "I have to speak at the funeral, you know."

"Yes, that's right." Laura pressed her lips tightly together with the result that she wasn't able to say anything for a few moments. Drawing in a deep breath, she added, "You have to speak at the funeral. Stay here, that's a good kender."

"Good" and "kender" being two words that were rarely, if ever, linked, Tasslehoff spent the time sitting at the table, thinking about what a good kender might be and wondering if he was one himself. He assumed he probably was, since he was a hero and all that. Having settled this question to his satisfaction, he took out his notes and went over his speech, humming a little tune to keep himself company and to help the sadness work its way down his windpipe.

He heard Laura talking to a young man, perhaps the wizard in Room Seventeen, but Tas didn't really pay much attention to what she was saying, since it seemed to involve a poor person who was afflicted, a person who had gone crazy and might be dangerous. At any other time, Tas would have been interested to see a dangerous, afflicted, crazy person, but he had his speech to worry about, and since that was the reason he'd made this trip in the first place—or rather, in the second place—he concentrated on that.

He was still concentrating on it, along with a plate of potatoes and a mug of ale, when he became aware that a tall person was standing over him wearing a grim expression.

"Oh, hullo," Tas said, looking up smiling to see that the tall person was actually his extremely good friend, the Knight who'd arrested him yesterday. Since the Knight was an extremely good friend, it was a pity Tas couldn't recall his name. "Please, sit down. Would you like some potatoes? Maybe some eggs?"

The Knight refused all offers of anything to eat or drink. He took a seat opposite Tas, regarded the kender with a stern expression.

"I understand that you have been causing trouble," the Knight said in a cold and nasty flat tone of voice.

It just so happened that at that moment Tasslehoff was rather proud of himself for *not* causing any trouble. He'd been sitting quietly at the table, thinking sad thoughts of Caramon's being gone and happy thoughts of the wonderful time they'd spent together. He hadn't once looked to see if there might be something interesting in the wood box. He had foregone his usual inspection of the silver chest, and he had only acquired one strange purse, and while he didn't exactly remember how he had come by that, he had to assume that someone had dropped it. He'd be sure to return it after the funeral.

Tas was therefore justifiably resentful of the Knight's implication. He fixed the Knight with a stern eye—dueling stern eyes, as it were. "I'm sure you don't mean to be ugly," Tas said. "You're upset. I understand."

The young Knight's face took on a very peculiar color, going extremely red, almost purple. He tried to say something, but he was so angry that when he opened his mouth, only sputters came out.

"I see the problem," Tas said, correcting himself. "No wonder you didn't understand me. I didn't mean 'ugly' as in 'ugly.' I was referring to your disposition, not your face, which is, however, a remarkably ugly one. I don't know when I've seen one uglier. Still, I know you can't mend your face, and perhaps you can't mend your disposition either, being a Solamnic Knight and all, but you have made a mistake. I have *not* been causing trouble. I have been sitting at this table eating potatoes—they're really quite good, are you sure you won't have some? Well, if you won't, I'll just finish up these last few. Where was I? Oh, yes. I've been sitting here eating and working on my speech. For the funeral."

When the Knight was finally able to speak without sputters, his tone was even colder and nastier, if such a thing were possible. "Mistress Laura sent word through one of the customers that you were scaring her with your outlandish and irrational statements. My superiors sent me to bring you back to jail. They would also like to know," he added, his tone grim, "how you managed to get out of jail this morning."

"I'll be very happy to come back to the jail with you. It was a very nice jail," Tas answered politely. "I've never seen one that was kender-proof before. I'll go back with you right after the funeral. I missed the funeral once, you see. I can't miss it again. Oops! No, I forgot." Tas sighed. "I can't go back to the jail with you." He really wished he could remember the Knight's name. He didn't like to ask. It wasn't polite. "I have to return to my own time right away. I promised Fizban I wouldn't go gallivanting. Perhaps I could visit your jail another time."

"Maybe you should let him stay, Sir Gerard," Laura said, coming up to stand beside them, twisting her apron in her hands. "He seems very determined, and I wouldn't want him to cause any trouble. Besides"—her tears started to flow— "maybe he's telling the truth! After all, Father thought he was Tasslehoff."

Gerard! Tas was vastly relieved. Gerard was the knight's name.

"He did?" Gerard was skeptical. "He said so?"

"Yes," Laura said, wiping her eyes with her apron. "The kender walked into the Inn. Daddy was sitting here in his usual place. The kender walked right up to him and said, 'Hullo, Caramon! I've come to speak at your funeral. I'm a little bit early, so I thought you might like to hear what I'm going to say,' and Daddy looked at him in surprise. At first I don't think he believed him, but then he looked at him closer and cried out, 'Tas!' And he gave him a big hug."

"He did." Tas felt a snuffle coming on. "He hugged me, and he said he was glad to see me and where had I been all this time? I said that it was a very long story and time was the one thing he didn't have a lot of so I should really let him hear the speech first." Giving way to the snuffle, Tas mopped his dribbling nose with his sleeve.

"Perhaps we could let him stay for the funeral," Laura urged. "I think it would have pleased Daddy. If you could . . . well . . . just keep an eye on him."

Gerard was clearly dubious. He even ventured to argue with her, but Laura had made up her mind, and she was very much like her mother. When her mind was made up, an army of dragons would not move her.

Laura opened the doors to the Inn to let in the sunshine, to let in life and to let in the living who came to pay their respects to the dead. Caramon Majere lay in a simple wooden casket in front of the great fireplace of the Inn he loved. No fire burned, only ashes filled the grate. The people of Solace filed past, each pausing to offer something to the dead—a silent farewell, a quiet blessing, a favorite toy, fresh-picked flowers.

The mourners noted that his expression was peaceful, even cheerful, more cheerful than they had seen him since his beloved Tika died. "Somewhere, they're together," people said and smiled through their tears.

Laura stood near the door, accepting condolences. She was dressed in the clothes she wore for work—a snowy white blouse, a clean fresh apron, a pretty skirt of royal blue with white petticoats. People wondered that she wasn't draped head to toe in black.

"Father would not have wanted me to," was her simple reply.

People said it was sad that Laura was the only member of the family to be present to lay their father to rest. Dezra, her sister, had been in Haven purchasing hops for the Inn's famous ale, only to be trapped there when the dragon Beryl attacked the city. Dezra had managed to smuggle word to her sister that she was safe and well, but she dared not try to return; the roads were not safe for travelers.

As for Caramon's son, Palin, he was gone from Solace on yet another of his mysterious journeys. If Laura knew where he was, she didn't say. His wife, Usha, a portrait painter of some renown, had traveled to Haven as company for Dezra. Since Usha had painted the portraits of families of some of the commanders of the Knights of Neraka, she was involved in negotiations to try to win a guarantee of safe passage for herself and for Dezra. Usha's children, Ulin and Linsha, were off on adventures of their own. Linsha, a Solamnic Knight, had not been heard from in many months. Ulin had gone away after hearing a report of some magical artifact and was believed to be in Palanthas.

Tas sat in a booth, under guard, the Knight Gerard at his side. Watching the people file in, the kender shook his head.

"But I tell you this isn't the way Caramon's funeral's supposed to be," Tasslehoff repeated insistently.

"Shut your mouth, you little fiend," Gerard ordered in a low, harsh tone. "This is hard enough on Laura and her father's friends without you making matters worse with your foolish chatter." To emphasize his words, he gripped the kender's shoulder hard, gave him a good shake.

"You're hurting me," Tas protested.

"Good," Gerard growled. "Now just keep quiet, and do as you're told."

Tas kept quiet, a remarkable feat for him, but one that was easier at this moment than any of his friends might have had reason to expect. His unaccustomed silence was due to the lump of sadness that was still stuck in his throat and that he could not seem to swallow. The sadness was all mixed up with the confusion that was muddling his mind and making it hard to think.

Caramon's funeral was not going at all the way it was meant to go. Tas knew this quite well because he'd been to Caramon's funeral once already and remembered how it went. This wasn't it. Consequently, Tas wasn't enjoying himself nearly as much as he'd expected.

Things were wrong. All wrong. Utterly wrong. Completely and irretrievably wrong. None of the dignitaries were here who were supposed to be here. Palin hadn't arrived, and Tas began to think that perhaps Laura was right and he wasn't going to arrive. Lady Crysania did not come. Goldmoon and Riverwind were missing. Dalamar did not suddenly appear, materializing out of the shadows and giving everyone a good scare. Tas discovered that he couldn't give his speech. The lump was too big and wouldn't let him. Just one more thing that was wrong.

The crowds were large—the entire population of Solace and surrounding communities came to pay their final respects and to extol the memory of the beloved man. But the crowds were not as large as they had been at Caramon's first funeral.

Caramon was buried near the Inn he loved, next to the graves of his wife and sons. The vallenwood sapling Caramon had planted in honor of Tika was young and thriving. The vallenwoods he had planted for his fallen sons were full-grown trees, standing tall and proud as the guard provided by the Knights of Solamnia, who accorded Caramon the honor rarely performed for a man who was not a Knight: escorting his coffin to the burial site. Laura planted the vallenwood in her father's memory, planted the tree in the very heart of Solace, near the tree she had planted for her mother. The couple had been the heart of Solace for many years, and everyone felt it was fitting.

The sapling stood uneasily in the fresh-turned earth, looking lost and forlorn. The people said what was in their hearts, paid their tribute. The Knights sheathed their swords with solemn faces, and the funeral was over. Everyone went home to dinner.

The Inn was closed for the first time since the red dragon had picked it up and hurled it out of its tree during the War of the Lance. Laura's friends offered to spend the first lonely nights with her, but she refused, saying that she wanted to have her cry in private. She sent home Cook, who was in such a state that when she finally did come back to work, she did not need to use any salt in the food for the tears she dripped into it. As for the gully dwarf, he had not moved from the corner into which he'd collapsed the moment he heard of Caramon's death. He lay in a huddled heap wailing and howling dismally until, to everyone's relief, he cried himself to sleep.

"Good-bye, Laura," said Tas, reaching out his hand. He and Gerard were the last to leave; the kender having refused to budge until everyone was gone and he was quite certain that nothing was going to happen the way it was intended to happen. "The funeral was very nice. Not as nice as the other funeral, but then I guess you couldn't help that. I really do *not* understand what is going on. Perhaps that's why Caramon told Sir Gerard to take me to see Dalamar, which I would, except that I think Fizban might consider that to be gallivanting. But, anyway, good-bye and thank you."

Laura looked down at the kender, who was no longer jaunty and cheerful but looking very forlorn and bereft and downcast. Suddenly, Laura knelt beside him and enfolded him in her arms.

"I do believe you're Tasslehoff!" she said to him softly, fiercely. "Thank you for coming." She hugged the breath from his small body and then turned and ran through the door leading to the family's private quarters. "Lock up, will you, Sir Gerard?" she called out over her shoulder and shut and locked the door behind her.

The Inn was quiet. The only sound that could be heard was the rustling of the leaves of the vallenwood tree and the creaking of the branches. The rustling had a weepy sound to it, and it seemed that the branches were lamenting. Tas had never seen the Inn empty before. Looking around, he remembered the night they had all met here after their five-year separation. He could see Flint's face and hear his gruff complaining, he could see Caramon standing protectively near his twin brother, he could see Raistlin's sharp eyes keeping watch over everything. He could almost hear Goldmoon's song again.

> The staff flares in blue light
> And both of them vanish;
> The grasslands are faded, and autumn is here.

"Everyone's vanished," Tas said to himself softly, and felt another snuffle coming on.

"Let's go," said Gerard.

Hand on the kender's shoulder, the Knight steered Tas toward the door, where he brought the kender to a halt to remove several articles of a valuable nature, which had happened to tumble into his pouches. Gerard left them on the bar for their owners to reclaim. This done, he took down the key that hung from a hook on the wall near the door, and locked the door. He hung the key on a hook outside the Inn, placed there in case anyone needed a room after hours, and then marched the kender down the stairs.

"Where are we going?" Tas asked. "What's that bundle you're carrying? Can I look inside? Are you going to take me to see Dalamar? I haven't seen him in a long time. Did you ever hear the story of how I met Dalamar? Caramon and I were—"

"Just shut up, will you?" Gerard said in a nasty, snapping sort of way. "Your chatter is giving me a headache. As to where we're going, we're returning to the garrison. And speaking of the bundle I'm carrying, if you touch it I'll run you through with my sword."

The Knight would say nothing more than that, although Tas asked and asked and tried to guess and then asked if he'd guessed right and if not, could Gerard give him a clue. Was what was in the bundle bigger than a breadbox? Was it a cat? Was it a cat in a breadbox? All to no avail. The Knight said nothing. His grip on the kender was firm.

The two of them arrived at the Solamnic garrison. The guards on duty greeted the Knight distantly. Sir Gerard did not return their greetings but said that he needed to see the Lord of Shields. The guards, who were members of the Lord of Shield's own personal retinue, replied that his lordship had just returned from the funeral and left orders not to be disturbed. They wanted to know the nature of Gerard's request.

"The matter is personal," the knight said. "Tell his lordship that I seek a ruling on the Measure. My need is urgent."

A guardsman departed. He returned a moment later to say, grudgingly, that Sir Gerard was to go in.

Gerard started to enter with Tasslehoff in tow.

"Not so fast, sir," the guard said, blocking their way with his halberd. "The Lord of Shields said nothing about a kender."

"The kender is in my custody," said Gerard, "as ordered by the lord himself. I have not been given leave to release him from my care. I would, however, be willing to leave him here with you if you will guarantee that he does no harm during the time I am with His Lordship—which may be several hours, my dilemma is complex—and that he will be here when I return."

The Knight hesitated.

"He will be pleased to tell you his story of how he first met the wizard Dalamar," Gerard added dryly.

"Take him," said the Knight.

Tas and his escort entered the garrison, passing through the gate that stood in the center of a tall fence made of wooden poles, each planed to a sharp point at the top. Inside the garrison were stables for the horses, a small training field with a target set up for archery practice, and several buildings. The garrison was not a large one. Having been established to house those who guarded the Tomb of the Heroes, it had been expanded to accommodate the Knights who would make what would probably be a last-stand defence of Solace if the dragon Beryl attacked.

Gerard had been thinking with some elation that his days of guarding a tomb might be drawing to a close, that battle with the dragon was imminent, though he and all the Knights were under orders not mention this to anyone. The Knights had no proof that Beryl was preparing to sweep down on Solace and they did not want to provoke her into attacking. But the Solamnic commanders were quietly making plans.

Inside the stockade, a long, low building provided sleeping quarters for the Knights and the soldiers under their command. In addition, there were several outbuildings used for storage and an administrative building, where the head of the garrison had his own lodgings. These doubled as his office.

His lordship's aide-de-camp met Gerard and ushered him inside. "His lordship will be with you shortly, Sir Gerard," said the aide.

"Gerard!" called out a woman's voice. "How good to see you! I thought I heard your name."

Lady Warren was a handsome woman of about sixty years with white hair and a complexion the color of warm tea. Throughout their forty years of marriage, she had accompanied her husband on all his journeys. As gruff and bluff as any soldier, she presently wore an apron covered with flour. She kissed Gerard on his cheek—he stood stiffly at attention, his helm beneath his arm—and glanced askance at the kender.

"Oh, dear," she said. "Midge!" she called to the back of the house in a voice that might have rung across the battlefield, "lock up my jewels!"

"Tasslehoff Burrfoot, ma'am," said Tas, offering his hand.

"Who isn't these days?" Lady Warren returned and promptly thrust her flour-covered hands that sparkled with several interesting looking rings beneath her apron. "And how are your dear father and mother, Gerard?"

"Quite well, I thank you, ma'am," said Gerard.

"You naughty boy." Lady Warren scolded, shaking her finger at him. "You know nothing about their health at all. You haven't written to your dear mother in two months. She writes to my husband to complain and asks him, most pathetically, if you are well and keeping your feet dry. For shame. To worry your good mother so! His lordship has promised that you shall write to her this very day. I wouldn't be surprised if he didn't sit you down and have you compose the letter while you are in there with him."

"Yes, ma'am," said Gerard.

"Now I must go finish the baking. Midge and I are taking one hundred loaves of bread to Laura to help keep the Inn going, poor thing. Ah, it's a sad day for Solace." Lady Warren wiped her face with her hand, leaving a smear of flour behind.

"Yes, ma'am," said Gerard.

"You may go in now," said the aide and opened a door leading from the main lodging to the lord's personal quarters.

Lady Warren took her leave, asking to be remembered to Gerard's dear mother. Gerard promised, his voice expressionless, that he would do so. Bowing, he left to follow the aide.

A large man of middle years with the black skin common to the people of Southern Ergoth greeted the young man warmly, a greeting the young Knight returned with equal and unusual warmth.

"I'm glad you stopped by, Gerard!" said Lord Warren. "Come and sit down. So this is the kender, is it?"

"Yes, sir. Thank you, sir. I'll be with you in a moment." Gerard led Tas to a chair, plunked him down, and took out a length of rope. Acting so swiftly that Tas did not have time to protest, the Knight tied the kender's wrists to the chair's arms. He then brought out a gag and wrapped it around Tas's mouth.

"Is that necessary?" Lord Warren asked mildly.

"If we want to have any semblance of a rational conversation, it is, sir," Gerard replied, drawing up a chair. He placed the mysterious bundle on the floor at his feet. "Otherwise you would hear stories about how this was the second time Caramon Majere had died. The kender would tell you how this funeral differed from Caramon Majere's first funeral. You would hear a recitation of who attended the first time and who wasn't at this one."

"Indeed." Lord Warren's face took on a softened, pitying look. "He must be one of the afflicted ones. Poor thing."

"What's an afflicted one?" Tas asked, except that due to the gag the words came out all gruff and grumbly, sounding as if he were speaking dwarven with a touch of gnome thrown in for good measure. Consequently no one understood him, and no one bothered to answer.

Gerard and Lord Warren began to discuss the funeral. Lord Warren spoke in such warm tones about Caramon that the lump of sadness returned to Tas's throat with the result that he didn't need the gag at all.

"And now, Gerard, what can I do for you?" Lord Warren asked, when the subject of the funeral was exhausted. He regarded the young Knight intently. "My aide said you had a question about the Measure."

"Yes, my lord. I require a ruling."

"You, Gerard?" Lord Warren raised a graying eyebrow. "Since when do you give a damn about the dictates of the Measure?"

Gerard flushed, looked uncomfortable.

Lord Warren smiled at the Knight's discomfiture. "I've heard you express yourself quite clearly regarding what you consider to be the 'old-fashioned, hidebound' way of doing things—"

Gerard shifted in his chair. "Sir, I may have, on occasion, expressed my doubts about certain precepts of the Measure—"

Lord Warren's eyebrow twitched even higher.

Gerard considered that it was time to change the subject. "My lord, an incident occurred yesterday. There were several civilians present. There will be questions asked."

Lord Warren looked grave. "Will this require a Knight's Council?"

"No, my lord. I hold you in the highest esteem, and I will respect your decision concerning this matter. A task has been given me, and I need to know whether or not I should pursue it or if I may, in honor, refuse."

"Who gave you this task? Another Knight?" Lord Warren appeared uneasy. He knew of the rancor that existed between Gerard and the rest of the Knights in the garrison. He had long feared that some quarrel would break out, perhaps resulting in some foolish challenge on the field of honor.

"No, sir," Gerard answered evenly. "The task was given to me by a dying man."

"Ah!" said Lord Warren. "Caramon Majere."

"Yes, my lord."

"A last request?"

"Not so much a request, my lord," said Gerard. "An assignment. I would almost say an order, but Majere was not of the Knighthood."

"Not by birth, perhaps," said Lord Warren gently, "but in spirit there was no better Knight living."

"Yes, my lord." Gerard was silent a moment, and Tas saw, for the first time, that the young man was truly grieved at Caramon's death.

"The last wishes of the dying are sacred to the Measure, which states such wishes must be fulfilled if it be mortally possible. The Measure makes no distinction if the dying person be of the Knighthood, if it be male or female, human, elf, dwarf, gnome, or kender. You are honor bound to take this task, Gerard."

"If it be mortally possible," Gerard countered.

"Yes," said Lord Warren. "So reads the Measure. Son, I see you are deeply troubled by this. If you break no confidence, tell me the nature of Caramon's last wish."

"I break no confidence, sir. I must tell you in any case, for if I am to undertake it I will need your permission to be absent from my post. Caramon Majere asked me to take this kender I have here with me, a kender who claims to be Tasslehoff Burrfoot, dead these thirty years, to Dalamar."

"The wizard Dalamar?" Lord Warren was incredulous.

"Yes, my lord. This is what happened. As he lay dying, Caramon spoke of being reunited with his dead wife. Then he appeared to be searching for someone in the crowd of people gathered around him. He said, 'But where's Raistlin?' "

"That would be his twin brother," Lord Warren interrupted.

"Yes, sir. Caramon added, 'He said he would wait for me'—meaning Raistlin had agreed to wait for him before leaving this world for the next, or so Laura told me. Caramon often said that since they were twins, one could not enter into the blessed realm without the other."

"I would not think that Raistlin Majere would be permitted to enter a 'blessed realm' at all," Lord Warren said dryly.

"True, sir." Gerard gave a wry smile. "If there is even a blessed realm, which I doubt, then . . ."

He paused, coughed in embarrassment. Lord Warren was frowning and looking very stern. Gerard apparently decided to skip the philosophical discussion and continue with his story.

"Caramon added something to effect that 'Raistlin should be here. With Tika. I don't understand. This is not right. Tas . . . What Tas said . . . A different future . . . Dalamar will know. . . . Take Tasslehoff to Dalamar.' He was very upset, and it seemed to me that he would not die in peace unless I promised to do as he asked. So I promised."

"The wizard Raistlin has been dead over fifty years!" Lord Warren exclaimed.

"Yes, sir. The so-called hero Burrfoot has been dead over thirty years, so this cannot possibly be him. And the wizard Dalamar has disappeared. No one has seen or heard of him since the Tower of High Sorcery vanished. It is rumored that he has been declared legally dead by the members of the Last Conclave."

"The rumors are true. I had it as fact from Palin Majere. But we have no proof of that, and we have a man's dying wish to consider. I am not certain how to rule."

Gerard was silent. Tas would have spoken up but for the gag and the realization that nothing he said could or would or should make a difference. To be quite truthful, Tasslehoff himself didn't know what to do. He had been given strict orders by Fizban to go to the funeral and to hurry right back. "Don't go gallivanting!" had been the old wizard's exact words, and he'd looked very fierce when he'd said them. Tas sat in the chair, chewing reflectively on the gag and pondering the exact meaning of the word, "gallivanting."

"I have something to show you, my lord," Gerard said. "With your permission . . ."

Lifting the bundle, Gerard placed it on Lord Warren's desk and began to untie the string at the top.

In the interim, Tas managed to wriggle his hands free of their bonds. He could remove the gag now, and he could go off to explore this truly interesting room, which had several very fine swords hanging on the wall, a shield, and a whole case of maps. Tas looked longingly at the maps, and his feet very nearly carried him that direction, but he was extremely curious to see what was in the Knight's bundle.

Gerard was taking a long time to open it; he seemed to be having difficulty with the knots.

Tas would have offered to help but thus far every time he had offered to be of help, Gerard had not seemed to appreciate it much. Tas occupied himself by watching the grains of sand fall from the top of an hourglass into the bottom and trying to count them as they fell. This proved a challenge, for the sand grains fell quite rapidly and just when he had them sorted out, one after the other, two or three would fall all in a heap and ruin his calculations.

Tas was somewhere between five thousand seven hundred and thirty-six and five thousand seven hundred and thirty-eight when the sands ran out. Gerard was still fumbling with the knots. Lord Warren reached over and turned the glass. Tas began to count again. "One, two, threefourfive . . ."

"Finally!" Gerard muttered and released the ties of the bundle.

Tas left off counting sand grains and sat up as straight as he possibly could in order to get a good view.

Gerard pressed the folds of the sack down around the object, taking care—Tas saw—not to touch the object itself. Jewels flashed and sparkled in the rays of the setting sun. Tas was so excited that he jumped out of his chair and tore the gag from his mouth.

"Hey!" he cried, reaching for the object. "That's just like mine! Where did you get it? Say!" he said, taking a good, close look. "That *is* mine!"

Gerard closed his hand over the kender's hand that was just inches away from the bejeweled object. Lord Warren stared at the object, openmouthed.

"I found this in the kender's pouch, sir," said Gerard. "Last night, when we searched him before locking him up in our prison. A prison that, I might add, is not as kender-proof as we thought. I'm not certain—I am no mage, my lord—but the device appears to be to be to be magical. *Quite* magical."

"It *is* magical," Tasslehoff said proudly. "That's the way I came here. It used to belong to Caramon, but he was always worried for fear someone would steal it and misuse it—I can't imagine who would do such a thing, myself. I offered to take care of it for him, but Caramon said, no, he thought it should go somewhere where it would be truly safe, and Dalamar said he'd take it, so Caramon gave it to him and he . . ." Tas quit talking because he didn't have an audience.

Lord Warren had withdrawn his hands from the desk. The object was about the size of an egg, encrusted with jewels that sparkled and glowed. Close examination revealed it to be made up of a myriad small parts that looked as if they could be manipulated, moved about. Lord Warren eyed it warily. Gerard kept fast hold of the kender.

The sun sank down toward the horizon and now shone brightly through the window. The office was cool and shadowed. The object glittered and gleamed, its own small sun.

"I have never seen the like of it," said Lord Warren, awed.

"Nor have I, sir," said Gerard. "But Laura has."

Lord Warren looked up, startled.

"She said that her father had an object like this. He kept it locked in a secret place in a room in the Inn that is dedicated to the memory of his twin brother Raistlin. She remembers well the day, some months prior to the Chaos War, when he removed the object from its secret hiding place and gave it to . . ." Gerard paused.

"Dalamar?" said Lord Warren, astounded. He stared at the device again. "Did her father say what it did? What magic it possessed?"

"He said that the object had been given to him by Par-Salian and that he had traveled back in time by means of its magic."

"He did, too," Tasslehoff offered. "I went with him. That's how I knew how the device worked. You see, it occurred to me that I might not outlive Caramon—"

Lord Warren said a single word, said it with emphasis and sincerity. Tas was impressed. Knights didn't usually say words like that.

"Do you think it's possible?" Lord Warren had shifted his gaze. He began staring at Tas as if he'd sprouted two heads.

Obviously he's never seen a troll. These people should really get out more, Tas thought.

"Do you think this is the real Tasslehoff Burrfoot?"

"Caramon Majere believed it was, my lord."

Lord Warren looked back at the strange device. "It is obviously an ancient artifact. No wizard has the ability to make magical objects like this these days. Even I can feel its power, and I'm certainly no mage, for which I thank fate." He looked back at Tas. "No, I don't believe it's possible. This kender stole it, and he has devised this outlandish tale to conceal his crime.

"We must return the artifact to the wizards, of course, though not, I would say, to the wizard Dalamar." Lord Warren frowned. "At the very least the device should be kept out of the hands of the kender. Where is Palin Majere? It seems to me that he is the one to consult."

"But you can't stop the device from coming back to my hands," Tas pointed out. "It's meant to always come back to me, and it will, sooner or later. Par-Salian—the great Par-Salian, I met him once, you know. He was very respectful to kender. Very." Tas fixed Gerard with a stern eye, hoping the Knight would take the hint. "Anyhow, Par-Salian told Caramon that the device was magically designed to always return to the person who used it. That's a safety precaution, so that you don't end up stranded back in time with no way of going back home. It's come in quite handy, since I have a tendency to lose things. I once lost a woolly mammoth. The way it happened was—"

"I agree, my lord," Gerard said loudly. "Be silent, kender. Speak when you are spoken to."

"Excuse me," said Tas, beginning to be bored. "But if you're not going to listen to me, may I go look at your maps? I'm very fond of maps."

Lord Warren waved his hand. Tas wandered off and was soon absorbed in reading the maps, which were really lovely, but which, the more he looked at them, he found very puzzling.

Gerard dropped his voice so low that Tas had a difficult time hearing him. "Unfortunately, my lord, Palin Majere is on a secret mission to the elven kingdom of Qualinesti, to consult with the elven sorcerers. Such meetings have been banned by the dragon Beryl, and if his whereabouts became known to her, she would exact terrible retribution."

"Yet, it seems to me that he must know of this immediately!" Lord Warren argued.

"He must also know of his father's death. If you will grant me leave, my lord, I will undertake to escort the kender and this device to Qualinesti, there to put both of them in the hands of Palin Majere and also to impart the sad news about his father. I will relate to Palin his father's dying request and ask him to judge whether or not it may undertaken. I have little doubt but that he will absolve me of it."

Lord Warren's troubled expression eased. "You are right. We should put the matter into the hands of the son. If he declares his father's last request impossible to fulfill, you may, with honor, decline it. I wish you didn't have to go to Qualinesti, however. Wouldn't it be more prudent to wait until the wizard returns?"

"There is no telling when that will be, my lord. Especially now that Beryl has closed the roads. I believe this matter to be of the utmost urgency. Also"—Gerard lowered his voice—"we would have difficulty keeping the kender here indefinitely."

"Fizban told me to come right back to my own time," Tas informed them. "I'm not to go gallivanting. But I *would* like to see Palin and ask him why the funeral was all wrong. Do you think that could be considered 'gallivanting'?"

"Qualinesti lies deep in Beryl's territory," Lord Warren was saying. "The land is ruled by the Knights of Neraka, who would be only too pleased to lay their hands on one of our order. And if the Knights of Neraka don't seize you and execute you as a spy, the elves will. An army of our Knights could not enter that realm and survive."

"I do not ask for an army, my lord. I do not ask for any escort," Gerard said firmly. "I would prefer to travel on my own. *Much* prefer it," he added with emphasis. "I ask you for leave from my duties for a time, my lord."

"Granted, certainly." Lord Warren shook his head. "Though I don't know what your father will say."

"He will say that he is proud of his son, for you will tell him that I am undertaking a mission of the utmost importance, that I do it to fulfill the last request of a dying man."

"You are putting yourself in danger," said Lord Warren. "He would not like that at all. And as for your mother—" He frowned ominously.

Gerard stood straight and tall. "I have been ten years a Knight, my lord, and all I have to show for it is the dust of a tomb on my boots. I have earned this, my lord."

Lord Warren rose to his feet. "Here is my ruling. The Measure holds the final wishes of the dying to be sacred. We are bound in honor to fulfill them if it be mortally possible. You will go to Qualinesti and consult with the sorcerer Palin. I have found him to be a man of good judgment and common sense—for a mage, that is. One must not expect too much. Still, I believe that you can rely on him to help you determine what is right. Or, at the very least, to take the kender and this stolen magical artifact off our hands."

"Thank you, my lord." Gerard looked extremely happy.

Of course he's happy, Tasslehoff thought. He gets to travel to a land ruled by a dragon who's closed all the roads, and maybe he'll be captured by Dark Knights who'll think he's a spy, and if that doesn't work out he gets to go to the elven kingdom and see Palin and Laurana and Gilthas.

The pleasant tingle so well known to kender, a tingle to which they are seriously addicted, began in the vicinity of Tasslehoff's spine. The tingle burned its way right down to his feet, which started to itch, shot through his arms into his fingers, which started to wriggle, and up into his head. He could feel his hair beginning to curl from the excitement.

The tingle wound up in Tasslehoff's ears and, due to the rushing of the blood in his head, he noticed that Fizban's admonition to return *soon* was starting to get lost amidst thoughts of Dark Knights and spies and, most important of all, The Road.

Besides, Tas realized suddenly, Sir Gerard is counting on me to go with him! I can't let a Knight down. And then there's Caramon. I can't let him down either, even if he did hit his head one too many times on the stairs on the way down.

"I'll go with you, Sir Gerard," Tas announced magnanimously. "I've thought it over quite seriously, and it doesn't seem to me to be gallivanting. It seems to me to be a quest. And I'm sure Fizban won't mind if I went on a little quest."

"I will think of something to tell your father to placate him," Lord Warren was saying. "Is there any thing I can provide you for this mission? How will you travel? You know that according to the Measure you may not disguise your true identity."

"I will travel as a Knight, my lord," Gerard replied with a slight quirk of his eyebrow. "I give you my word on that."

Lord Warren eyed him speculatively. "You're up to something. No, don't tell me. The less I know about this the better." He glanced down at the device, glittering on the table, and heaved a sigh. "Magic and kender. It seems to me to be a fatal combination. My blessing go with you."

Gerard wrapped the device carefully in the bundle. Lord Warren left his desk to accompany Gerard to the door of the office, collecting Tasslehoff on the way. Gerard removed several of the smaller maps that had just happened to find their way down the front of the kender's shirt.

"I was taking them to be fixed," said Tas, looking at Lord Warren accusingly. "You really hire very poor mapmakers. They've made several serious mistakes. The Dark Knights aren't in Palanthas any more. We drove them out two years after the Chaos War. And why's that funny little circle like a bubble drawn around Silvanesti?"

The Knights were deep in a private discussion of their own, a discussion that had something to do with Gerard's mission, and they paid no attention. Tas pulled out another map that he had managed somehow to stuff itself down his trousers and that was at the moment pinching a sensitive portion of his anatomy. He transferred the map from his pants to his pouch and, while doing so, his knuckles brushed across something hard and sharp and egg-shaped.

The Device of Time Journeying. The device that would take him back to his own time. The device had come back to him, as it was bound to do. It was once more in his possession. Fizban's stern command seemed to ring loudly in his ears.

Tas looked at the device, thought about Fizban, and considered the promise he'd made to the old wizard. There was obviously only one thing to be done.

Taking firm hold of the device, careful not to accidentally activate it, Tasslehoff crept up behind Gerard, who was engrossed in his conversation with Lord Warren, and by dint of working loose a corner of the bundle, working nimbly and quietly as only a kender can work, Tasslehoff slipped the device back inside.

"And stay there!" he told it firmly.

7   BECKARD'S CUT

Located on the shore of New Sea, Sanction was the major port city for the northeastern part of Ansalon.

The city was an ancient one, established long before the Cataclysm. Nothing much is known for certain about its history except that prior to the Cataclysm, Sanction had been a pleasant place to live.

Many have wondered how it came by its odd name. Legend has it that there was once in the small village a human woman of advanced years whose opinions were well-known and respected far and wide. Disputes and disagreements over everything from ownership of boats to marriage contracts were brought before the old woman. She listened to all parties and then rendered her verdict, verdicts noted for being fair and impartial, wise and judicious. "The old 'un sanctioned it," was the response to her judgments, and thus the small village in which she resided became known as a place of authority and law.

When the gods in their wrath hurled the fiery mountain at the world, the mountain struck the continent of Ansalon and broke it asunder. The water of the Sirrion Ocean poured into the newly formed cracks and crevices creating a new sea, aptly named, by the pragmatic, New Sea. The volcanoes of the Doom Range flared into furious life, sending rivers of lava flowing into Sanction.

Mankind being ever resilient, quick to turn disaster to advantage, those who had once tilled the soil harvesting crops of beans and barley turned from the plow to the net, harvested the fruit of the sea. Small fishing villages sprang up along the coast of New Sea.

The people of Sanction moved to the beaches, where the offshore breeze blew away the fumes of the volcanoes. The town prospered, but it did not grow significantly until the tall ships arrived. Adventurous sailors out of Palanthas took their ships into New Sea, hoping to find quick and easy passage to the other side of the continent, avoiding the long and treacherous journey through the Sirrion Sea to the north. The explorers' hopes were dashed. No such passage existed. What they did discover, however, was a natural port in Sanction, an overland passage that was not too difficult, and markets waiting for their goods on the other side of the Khalkhist Mountains.

The town began to thrive, to expand, and, like any growing child, to dream. Sanction saw itself another Palanthas: famous, staid, stolid, and wealthy. Those dreams did not materialize, however. Solamnic Knights watched over Palanthas, guarded the city, ruled it with the Oath and the Measure. Sanction belonged to whoever had the might and the power to hold onto it. The city grew up headstrong and spoiled, with no codes, no laws, and plenty of money.

Sanction was not choosy about its companions. The city welcomed the greedy, the rapacious, the unscrupulous. Thieves and brigands, con men and whores, sell-swords and assassins called Sanction home.

The time came when Takhisis, Queen of Darkness, tried to return to the world. She raised up armies to conquer Ansalon in her name. Ariakas, general of these armies, recognized the strategic value of Sanction to the Queen's holy city of Neraka and the military outpost of Khur. Lord Ariakas marched his troops into Sanction, conquered the city, which put up little resistance. He built temples to his Queen in Sanction and made his headquarters there.

The Lords of Doom, the volcanoes that ringed Sanction, felt the heat of the Queen's ambition stirring beneath them and came again to life. Streams of lava flowed from the volcanoes, lighting Sanction with a lurid glow by night. The ground shook and shivered from tremors. The inns of Sanction lost a fortune in broken crockery and began to serve food on tin plates and drink in wooden mugs. The air was poisonous, thick with sulphurous fumes. Black-robed wizards worked constantly to keep the city fit for habitation.

Takhisis set out to conquer the world, but in the end she could not overcome herself. Her generals quarreled, turned on each other. Love and self-sacrifice, loyalty and honor won the day. The stones of Neraka lay blasted and cursed in the shadowed valley leading to Sanction.

The Solamnic Knights marched on Sanction. They seized the city after a pitched battle with its inhabitants. Recognizing Sanction's strategic as well as financial importance to this part of Ansalon, the Knights established a strong garrison in the city. They tore down the temples of evil, set fire to the slave markets, razed the brothels. The Conclave of Wizards sent mages to continue to cleanse the poisonous air.

When the Knights of Takhisis began to accumulate power, some twenty years later, Sanction was high on the list of priorities. The Knights might well have captured it. Years of peace had made the Solamnic Knights sleepy and bored. They dozed at their posts. But before the Dark Knights could attack Sanction, the Chaos War diverted the attention of the Dark Knights and woke up the Solamnics.

The Chaos War ended. The gods departed. The residents of Sanction came to realize that the gods were gone. Magic—as they had known it—was gone. The people who had survived the war now faced death by asphyxiation from the noxious fumes. They fled the city, ran to the beaches to breathe the clean sea air. And so for a time, Sanction returned to where it had begun.

A strange and mysterious wizard named Hogan Bight not only restored Sanction to its former glory but helped the city surpass itself. He did what no other wizard had been able to do: He not only cleansed the air, he diverted the lava away from the city. Water, cool and pure, flowed from the snowy mountain tops. A person could actually step outside and take a deep breath and not double over coughing and choking.

Older and wiser, Sanction became prosperous, wealthy, and respectable. Under Bight's protection and encouragement, good and honest merchants moved into the city. Both the Solamnic Knights and the Knights of Neraka approached Bight, each side offering to move into Sanction and provide protection from the other.

Bight trusted neither side, refused to allow either to enter. Angry, the Knights of Neraka argued that Sanction was part of the land given to them by the Council in return for their service during the Chaos War. The Knights of Solamnia continued to try to negotiate with Bight, who continued to refuse all their offers of aid.

Meanwhile the Dark Knights, now calling themselves Knights of Neraka, were growing in strength, in wealth, and in power—for it was they who collected the tribute due the dragons. They watched Sanction as the cat watches the mouse hole. The Knights of Neraka had long coveted the port that would allow them a base of operations from which they could sail forth and gain a firm hold on all the lands surrounding New Sea. Seeing that the mice were busy biting and clawing each other, the cat pounced.

The Knights of Neraka laid siege to Sanction. They expected the siege to be a long one. As soon as the Dark Knights attacked the city, its fractured elements would unite in its defense. The Knights were patient, however. They could not starve the city into submission; blockade runners continued to bring supplies into Sanction. But the Knights of Neraka could shut down all overland trade routes. Thus the Knights of Neraka effectively strangled the merchants and brought Sanction's economy to ruin.

Pressured by the demands of the citizens, Hogan Bight had agreed within the last year to permit the Solamnic Knights to send in a force to bolster the city's flagging defenses. At first, the Knights were welcomed as saviors. The people of Sanction expected the Knights would put an immediate end to the siege. The Solamnics replied that they had to study the situation. After months of watching the Knights study, the people again urged the Solamnics to break the siege. The Knights replied that their numbers were too few. They needed reinforcements.

Nightly the besiegers bombarded the city with boulders and fiery bales of hay flung from catapults. The burning hay bales started blazes, the boulders knocked holes in buildings. People died, property was destroyed. No one could get a good night's sleep. As the leadership of the Knights of Neraka had calculated, the excitement and fervor of Sanction's residents, which had burned hot when first defending their city against the foe, cooled as the siege dragged out month after month. They found fault with the Solamnics, called them cowards. The Knights retorted that the citizens were hot-heads who would have them all die for nothing. Hearing reports from their spies that the unity was starting to crack, the Knights of Neraka began to build up their forces for an all-out, major assault. Their leadership waited only for a sign that the cracks had penetrated to the enemy's heart.

A large valley known as Zhakar Valley lay to the east of Sanction. Early in the siege, the Knights of Neraka had gained control of this valley and all of the passes that led from Sanction into the valley. Hidden in the foothills of the Zhakar Mountains, the valley was being used by the Knights as a staging area for their armies.

"The Zhakar Valley is our destination," Mina told her Knights. But when asked why, what they would do there, she would say nothing other than, "We are called."

Mina and her forces arrived at noon. The sun was high in a cloudless sky, seeming to stare down upon all below with avid expectation, an expectation that sucked up the wind, left the air still and hot.

Mina brought her small command to a halt at the entrance to the valley. Directly opposite them, across the valley, was a pass known as Beckard's Cut. Through the cut, the Knights could see the besieged city, see a small portion of the wall that surrounded Sanction. Between the Knights and Sanction lay their own army. Another city had sprung up in the valley, a city of tents and campfires, wagons and draft animals, soldiers and camp followers.

Mina and her Knights had arrived at a propitious time, seemingly. The camp of the Knights of Neraka rang with cheers. Trumpets blared, officers bellowed, companies formed on the road. Already the lead forces were marching through the cut, heading toward Sanction. Others were quickly following.

"Good," said Mina. "We are in time."

She galloped her horse down the steep road, her Knights followed after. They heard in the trumpets the melody of the song they had heard in their sleep. Hearts pounded, pulses quickened, yet they had no idea why.

"Find out what is going on," Mina instructed Galdar.

The minotaur nabbed the first officer he could locate, questioned the man. Returning to Mina, the minotaur grinned and rubbed his hands.

"The cursed Solamnics have left the city!" he reported. "The wizard who runs Sanction has thrown the Solamnic Knights out on their ears. Kicked them in the ass. Sent them packing. If you look"—Galdar turned, pointed through Beckard's Cut—"you can see their ships, those little black dots on the horizon."

The Knights under Mina's command began to cheer. Mina looked at the distant ships, but she did not smile. Foxfire stirred restlessly, shook his mane and pawed the ground.

"You brought us here in good time, Mina," Galdar continued with enthusiasm. "They are preparing to launch the final assault. This day, we'll drink Sanction's blood. This night, we'll drink Sanction ale!"

The men laughed. Mina said nothing, her expression indicated neither elation nor joy. Her amber eyes roved the army camp, seeking something and not finding what she wanted, apparently, for a small frown line appeared between her brows. Her lips pursed in displeasure. She continued her search and finally, her expression cleared. She nodded to herself and patted Foxfire's neck, calming him.

"Galdar, do you see that company of archers over there?"

Galdar looked, found them, indicated that he did.

"They do not wear the livery of the Knights of Neraka."

"They are a mercenary company," Galdar explained. "In our pay, but they fight under their own officers."

"Excellent. Bring their commander to me."

"But, Mina, why—"

"Do as I have ordered, Galdar," said Mina.

Her Knights, gathered behind her, exchanged startled glances, shrugging, wondering. Galdar was about to argue. He was about to urge Mina to let him join in the final drive toward victory instead of sending him off on some fool's errand. A jarring, tingling sensation numbed his right arm, felt as if he'd struck his "funny bone." For one terrifying moment, he could not move his fingers. Nerves tingled and jangled. The feeling went away in a moment, leaving him shaken. Probably nothing more than a pinched nerve, but the tingling reminded him of what he owed her. Galdar swallowed his arguments and departed on his assignment.

He returned with the archer company's commander, an older human, in his forties, with the inordinately strong arms of a bowman. The mercenary officer's expression was sullen, hostile. He would not have come at all, but it is difficult to say no to a minotaur who towers over you head, shoulders, and horns and who is insistent upon your coming.

Mina wore her helm with the visor raised. A wise move, Galdar thought. The helm shadowed her youthful, girl's face, kept it hidden.

"What are you orders, Talon Leader?" Mina asked. Her voice resonated from within the visor, cold and hard as the metal.

The commander looked up at the Knight with a certain amount of scorn, not the least intimidated.

"I'm no blasted 'talon leader,' Sir Knight," he said and he laid a nasty, sarcastic emphasis on the word 'sir.' "I hold my rank as captain of my own command, and we don't take orders from your kind. Just money. We do whatever we damn well please."

"Speak politely to the talon leader," Galdar growled and gave the officer a shove that staggered him.

The man wheeled, glowered, reached for his short sword. Galdar grasped his own sword. His fellow soldiers drew their blades with a ringing sound. Mina did not move.

"What are your orders, Captain?" she asked again.

Seeing he was outnumbered, the officer slid his sword back into its sheath, his movement slow and deliberate, to show that he was still defiant, just not stupid.

"To wait until the assault is launched and then to fire at the guards on the walls. Sir," he said sulkily, adding in sullen tones, "We'll be the last ones into the city, which means all the choice pickings will already be gone."

Mina regarded him speculatively. "You have little respect for the Knights of Neraka or our cause."

"What cause?" The office gave a brief, barking laugh. "To fill your own coffers? That's all you care about. You and your foolish visions." He spat on the ground.

"Yet you were once one of us, Captain Samuval. You were once a Knight of Takhisis," Mina said. "You quit because the cause for which you joined was gone. You quit because you no longer believed."

The captain's eyes widened, his face muscles went slack. "How did—" He snapped his mouth shut. "What if I was?" he growled. "I didn't desert, if that's what you're thinking. I bought my way out. I have my papers—"

"If you do not believe in our cause, why do you continue to fight for us, Captain?" Mina asked.

Samuval snorted. "Oh, I believe in your cause now, all right," he said with a leer. "I believe in money, same as the rest of you."

Mina sat her horse, who was still and calm beneath her hand, and gazed through Beckard's Cut, gazed at the city of Sanction. Galdar had a sudden, strange impression that she could see through the walls of the city, see through the armor of those defending the city, see through their flesh and their bones to their very hearts and minds, just as she had seen through him. Just as she had seen through the captain.

"No one will enter Sanction this day, Captain Samuval," said Mina softly. "The carrion birds will be the ones who find 'choice pickings.' The ships that you see sailing away are not filled with Solamnic Knights. The troops that line their decks are in reality straw dummies wearing the armor of Solamnics Knights. It is a trap."

Galdar stared, aghast. He believed her. Believed as surely as if he had seen inside the ships, seen inside the walls to the enemy army hiding there, ready to spring.

"How do you know this?" the captain demanded.

"What if I gave you something to believe in, Captain Samuval?" she asked instead of answering. "What if I make you the hero of this battle? Would you pledge your loyalty to me?" She smiled slightly. "I have no money to offer you. I have only this sure knowledge that I freely share with you—fight for me and on this day you will come to know the one true god."

Captain Samuval gazed up at her in wordless astonishment. He looked dazed, lightning-struck.

Mina held out her raw and bleeding hands, palms open. "You are offered a choice, Captain Samuval. I hold death in one hand. Glory in the other. Which will it be?"

Samuval scratched his beard. "You're a strange one, Talon Leader. Not like any of your kind I've ever met before."

He looked back through Beckard's Cut.

"Rumor has spread among the men that the city is abandoned," Mina said. "They have heard it will open its gates in surrender. They have become a mob. They run to their own destruction."

She spoke truly. Ignoring the shouts of the officers, who were vainly endeavoring to maintain some semblance of order, the foot soldiers had broken ranks. Galdar watched the army disintegrate, become in an instant an undisciplined horde rampaging through the cut. Eager for the kill, eager for spoils. Captain Samuval spat again in disgust. His expression dark, he looked back at Mina.

"What would you have me do, Talon Leader?"

"Take your company of archers and post them on that ridge there. Do you see it?" Mina pointed to a foothill overlooking Beckard's Cut.

"I see it," he said, glancing over his shoulder. "And what do we do once we're there?"

"My Knights and I will take up our positions there. Once arrived, you will await my orders," Mina replied. "When I give those orders, you will obey my commands without question."

She held out her hand, her blood-smeared hand. Was it the hand that held death or the hand that held life? Galdar wondered.

Perhaps Captain Samuval wondered as well, for he hesitated before he finally took her hand into his own. His hand was large, callused from the bowstring, brown and grimy. Her hand was small, its touch light. Her palm was blistered, rimed with dried blood. Yet it was the captain who winced slightly.

He looked down at his hand when she released him, rubbed it on his leather corselet, as if rubbing away the pain of sting or burn.

"Make haste, Captain. We don't have much time," Mina ordered.

"And just who are you, Sir Knight?" Captain Samuval asked. He was still rubbing his hand.

"I am Mina," she said.

Grasping the reins, she pulled sharply. Foxfire wheeled. Mina dug in her spurs, galloped straight for the ridge above Beckard's Cut. Her Knights rode alongside her. Galdar ran at her stirrup, legs pumping to keep up.

"How do you know that Captain Samuval will obey you, Mina?" the minotaur roared over the pounding of horses' hooves.

She looked down on him and smiled. Her amber eyes were bright in the shadow of the helm.

"He will obey," she said, "if for no other reason now than to demonstrate his disdain for his superiors and their foolish commands. But the captain is a man who hungers, Galdar. He yearns for food. They have given him clay to fill his belly. I will give him meat. Meat to nourish his soul."

Mina leaned over her horse's head and urged the animal to gallop even faster.

Captain Samuval's Archer Company took up position on the ridgeline overlooking Beckard's Cut. They were several hundred strong, well-trained professional bowmen who had fought in many of Neraka's wars before now. They used the elven long bow, so highly prized among archers. Taking up their places, they stood foot to foot, packed tightly together, with not much room to maneuver, for the ridgeline was not long. The archers were in a foul mood. Watching the army of the Knights of Neraka sweep down on Sanction, the men muttered that there would be nothing left for them—the finest women carried off, the richest houses plundered. They might as well go home.

Above them clouds thickened; roiling gray clouds that bubbled up over the Zhakar Mountains and began to slide down the mountain's side.

The army camp was empty, now, except for the tents and supply wagons and a few wounded who had been unable to go with their brethren and were cursing their ill luck. The clamor of the battle moved away from them. The surrounding mountains and the lowering clouds deflected the sounds of the attacking army. The valley was eerily silent.

The archers looked sullenly to their captain, who looked impatiently to Mina.

"What are your orders, Talon Leader?" he asked.

"Wait," she said.

They waited. The army washed up against the walls of Sanction, pounded against the gate. The noise and commotion was far away, a distant rumbling. Mina removed her helm, ran her hand over her shorn head with its down of dark red hair. She sat straight-backed upon her horse, her chin lifted. Her gaze was not on Sanction but on the blue sky above them, blue sky that was rapidly darkening.

The archers stared, astounded at her youth, amazed at her strange beauty. She did not heed their stares, did not hear their coarse remarks that were swallowed by the silence welling up out of the valley. The men felt something ominous about the silence. Those who continued to make remarks did so out of bravado and were almost immediately hushed by their uneasy comrades.

An explosion rocked the ground around Sanction, shattered the silence. The clouds boiled, the sunlight vanished. The Neraka army's gloating roars of victory were abruptly cut off. Shouts of triumph shrilled to screams of panic.

"What is happening?" demanded the archers, their tongues loosed. Everyone talked at once. "Can you see?"

"Silence in the ranks!" Captain Samuval bellowed.

One of the Knights, who had been posted as observer near the cut, came galloping toward them.

"It was a trap!" He began to yell when he was still some distance away. "The gates of Sanction opened to our forces, but only to spew forth the Solamnics! There must be a thousand of them. Sorcerers ride at their head, dealing death with their cursed magicks!"

The Knight reined in his excited horse. "You spoke truly, Mina!" His voice was awed, reverent. "A huge blast of magical power killed hundreds of our troops at the outset. Their bodies lie smoldering on the field. Our soldiers are fleeing! They are running this way, retreating through the cut. It is a rout!"

"All is lost, then," said Captain Samuval, though he looked at Mina strangely. "The Solamnic forces will drive the army into the valley. We will be caught between the anvil of the mountains and the hammer of the Solamnics."

His words proved true. Those in the rear echelons were already streaming back through Beckard's Cut. Many had no idea where they were going, only that they wanted to be far away from the blood and the death. A few of the less confused and more calculating were making for the narrow road that ran through the mountains to Khur.

"A standard!" Mina said urgently. "Find me a standard!"

Captain Samuval took hold of the grimy white scarf he wore around his neck and handed it up to her. "Take this and welcome, Mina."

Mina took the scarf in her hands, bowed her head. Whispering words no one could hear, she kissed the scarf and handed it to Galdar. The white fabric was stained red with blood from the raw blisters on her hand. One of Mina's Knights offered his lance. Galdar tied the bloody scarf onto the lance, handed the lance back to Mina.

Wheeling Foxfire, she rode him up the rocks to a high promontory and held the standard aloft.

"To me, men!" she shouted. "To Mina!"

The clouds parted. A mote of sunlight jabbed from the heavens, touched only Mina as she sat astride her horse on the ridgeline. Her black armor blazed as if dipped in flame, her amber eyes gleamed, lit from behind with the light of battle. Her redound, a clarion call, brought the fleeing soldiers to a halt. They looked to see from whence the call came and saw Mina outlined in flame, blazing like a beacon fire upon the hillside.

The fleeing soldiers halted in their mad dash, looked up, dazzled.

"To me!" Mina yelled again. "Glory is ours this day!"

The soldiers hesitated, then one ran toward her, scrambling, slipping and sliding up the hillside. Another followed and another, glad to have purpose and direction once again.

"Bring those men over there to me," Mina ordered Galdar, pointing to another group of soldiers in full retreat. "As many as you can gather. See that they are armed. Draw them up in battle formation there on the rocks below."

Galdar did as he was commanded. He and the other Knights blocked the path of the retreating soldiers, ordered them to join their comrades who were starting to form a dark pool at Mina's feet. More and more soldiers were pouring through the cut, the Knights of Neraka riding among them, some of the officers making valiant attempts to halt the retreat, others joining the footmen in a run for their lives. Behind them rode Solamnic Knights in their gleaming silver armor, their white-feathered crests. Deadly, silver light flashed, and everywhere that light appeared, men withered and died in its magical heat. The Solamnic Knights entered the cut, driving the forces of the Knights of Neraka like cattle before them, driving them to slaughter.

"Captain Samuval," cried Mina, riding her horse down the hill, her standard streaming behind her. "Order your men to fire."

"The Solamnics are not in bow range," he said to her, shaking his head at her foolishness. "Any fool can see that."

"The Solamnics are not your target, Captain," Mina returned coolly. She pointed to the forces of the Knights of Neraka streaming through the cut. "Those are your targets."

"Our own men?" Captain Samuval stared at her. "You are mad!"

"Look upon the field of battle, Captain," Mina said. "It is the only way."

Captain Samuval looked. He wiped his face with his hand, then he gave the command. "Bowmen, fire."

"What target?" demanded one.

"You heard Mina!" said the captain harshly. Grabbing a bow from one of his men, he nocked an arrow and fired.

The arrow pierced the throat of one of the fleeing Knights of Neraka. He fell backward off his horse and was trampled in the rush of his retreating comrades.

Archer Company fired. Hundreds of arrows—each shot with deliberate, careful aim at point-blank range—filled the air with a deadly buzz. Most found their targets. Foot soldiers clutched their chests and dropped. The feathered shafts struck through the raised visors of the helmed Knights or took them in the throat.

"Continue firing, Captain," Mina commanded.

More arrows flew. More bodies fell. The panic-stricken soldiers realized that the arrows were coming from in front of them now. They faltered, halted, trying to discover the location of this new enemy. Their comrades crashed into them from behind, driven mad by the approaching Solamnic Knights. The steep walls of Beckard's Cut prevented any escape.

"Fire!" Captain Samuval shouted wildly, caught up in the fervor of death-dealing. "For Mina!"

"For Mina!" cried the archers and fired.

Arrows hummed with deadly accuracy, thunked into their targets. Men screamed and fell. The dying were starting to pile up like hideous cordwood in the cut, forming a blood-soaked barricade.

An officer came raging toward them, his sword in his hand. "You fool!" he screamed at Captain Samuval. "Who gave you your orders? You're firing on your own men!"

"I gave him the order," said Mina calmly.

Furious, the Knight accosted her. "Traitor!" He raised his blade.

Mina sat unmoving on her horse. She paid no attention to the Knight, she was intent upon the carnage below. Galdar brought down a crushing fist on the Knight's helm. The Knight, his neck broken, went rolling and tumbling down the hillside. Galdar sucked bruised knuckles and looked up at Mina.

He was astounded to see tears flowing unchecked down her cheeks. Her hand clasped the medallion around her neck. Her lips moved, she might have been praying.

Attacked from in front, attacked from behind, the soldiers inside Beckard's Cut began milling about in confusion. Behind them, their comrades faced a terrible choice. They could either be speared in the back by the Solamnics or they could turn and fight. They wheeled to face the enemy, battling with the ferocity of the desperate, the cornered.

The Solamnics continued to fight, but their charge was slowed and, at length, ground to a halt.

"Cease fire!" Mina ordered. She handed her standard to Galdar. Drawing her morning star, she held it high over her head. "Knights of Neraka! Our hour has come! We ride this day to glory!"

Foxfire gave a great leap and galloped down the hillside, carrying Mina straight at the vanguard of the Solamnic Knights. So swift was Foxfire, so sudden Mina's move, that she left her own Knights behind. They watched, open-mouthed, as Mina rode to what must be her doom. Then Galdar raised the white standard.

"Death is certain!" the minotaur thundered. "But so is glory! For Mina!"

"For Mina!" cried the Knights in grim, deep voices and they rode their horses down the hill.

"For Mina!" yelled Captain Samuval, dropping his bow and drawing his short sword. He and the entire Archer Company charged into the fray.

"For Mina!" shouted the soldiers, who had gathered around her standard. Rallying to her cause, they dashed after her, a dark cascade of death rumbling down the hillside.

Galdar raced down the hillside, desperate to catch up to Mina, to protect and defend her. She had never been in a battle. She was unskilled, untrained. She must surely die. Enemy faces loomed up before him. Their swords slashed at him, their spears jabbed at him, their arrows stung him. He struck their swords aside, broke their spears, ignored their arrows. The enemy was an irritant, keeping him from his goal. He lost her and then he found her, found her completely surrounded by the enemy.

Galdar saw one knight try to impale Mina on his sword. She turned the blow, struck at him with the morning star. Her first blow split open his helm. Her next blow split open his head. But while she fought him, another was coming to attack her from behind. Galdar bellowed a warning, though he knew with despair that she could not hear him. He battled ferociously to reach her, cutting down those who stood between him and his commander, no longer seeing their faces, only the bloody streaks of his slashing sword.

He kept his gaze fixed on her, and his fury blazed, and his heart stopped beating when he saw her pulled from her horse. He fought more furiously than ever, frantic to save her. A blow struck from behind stunned him. He fell to his knees. He tried to rise, but blow after savage blow rained down on him, and he knew nothing more.

The battle ended sometime near twilight. The Knights of Neraka held, the valley was secure. The Solamnics and soldiers of Sanction were forced to retreat back into the walled city, a city that was shocked and devastated by the crushing defeat. They had felt the victory wreath upon their heads, and then the wreath had been savagely snatched away, trampled in the mud. Devastated, disheartened, the Solamnic Knights dressed their wounds and burned the bodies of their dead. They had spent months working on this plan, deemed it their only chance to break the siege of Sanction. They wondered over and over how they could have failed.

One Solamnic Knight spoke of a warrior who had come upon him, so he said, like the wrath of the departed gods. Another had seen this warrior, too, and another and another after that. Some claimed it was a youth, but others said that no, it was a girl, a girl with a face for which a man might die. She had ridden in the front of the charge, smote their ranks like a thunderclap, battling without helm or shield, her weapon a morning star that dripped with blood.

Pulled from her horse, she fought alone on foot.

"She must be dead," said one angrily. "I saw her fall."

"True, she fell, but her horse stood guard over her," said another, "and struck out with lashing hooves at any who dared approach."

But whether the beautiful destructor had perished or survived, none could tell. The tide of battle turned, came to meet her, swept around her, and rolled over the heads of the Solamnic Knights, carried them in a confused heap back into their city.

"Mina!" Galdar called hoarsely. "Mina!"

There came no answer.

Desperate, despairing, Galdar searched on.

The smoke from the fires of the funeral pyres hung over the valley. Night had not yet fallen, the twilight was gray and thick with smoke and orange cinders. The minotaur went to the tents of the dark mystics, who were treating the wounded, and he could not find her. He looked through the bodies that were being lined up for the burning, an arduous task. Lifting one body, he rolled it over, looked closely at the face, shook his head, and moved on to the next.

He did not find her among the dead, at least, not those who had been brought back to camp thus far. The work of removing the bodies from that blood-soaked cut would last all night and into the morrow. Galdar's shoulders sagged. He was wounded, exhausted, but he was determined to keep searching. He carried with him, in his right hand, Mina's standard. The white cloth was white no longer. It was brownish red, stiff with dried blood.

He blamed himself. He should have been at her side. Then at least if he had not been able to protect her, he could have died with her. He had failed, struck down from behind. When he had finally regained consciousness, he found that the battle was over. He was told that their side had won.

Hurt and dizzy, Galdar staggered over to the place he had last glimpsed her. Bodies of her foes lay heaped on the ground, but she was nowhere to be found.

She was not among the living. She was not among the dead. Galdar was starting to think that he had dreamed her, created her out of his own hunger to believe in someone or something when he felt a touch upon his arm.

"Minotaur," said the man. "Sorry, I never did catch your name."

Galdar could not place the soldier for a moment—the face was almost completely obscured by a bloody bandage. Then he recognized the captain of Archer Company.

"You're searching for her, aren't you?" Captain Samuval asked. "For Mina?"

For Mina! The cry echoed in his heart. Galdar nodded. He was too tired, too dispirited to speak.

"Come with me," said Samuval. "I have something to show you."

The two trudged across the floor of the valley, heading for the battlefield. Those soldiers who had escaped the battle uninjured were busy rebuilding the camp, which had been wrecked during the chaos of the retreat. The men worked with a fervor unusual to see, worked without the incentive of the whip or the bullying cries of the masters-at-arms. Galdar had seen these same men in past battles crouched sullenly over their cooking fires, licking their wounds, swilling dwarf spirits, and boasting and bragging of their bravery in butchering the enemy's wounded.

Now, as he passed the groups of men hammering in tent stakes or pounding the dents out of breastplate and shield or picking up spent arrows or tending to countless other chores, he listened to them talk. Their talk was not of themselves, but of her, the blessed, the charmed. Mina.

Her name was on every soldier's lips, her deeds recounted time and again. A new spirit infused the camp, as if the lightning storm out of which Mina had walked had sent jolts of energy flashing from man to man.

Galdar listened and marveled but said nothing. He accompanied Captain Samuval, who appeared disinclined to talk about anything, refused to answer all Galdar's questions. In another time, the frustrated minotaur might have smashed the human's skull into his shoulders, but not now. They had shared in a moment of triumph and exaltation, the likes of which neither had ever before experienced in battle. They had both been carried out of themselves, done deeds of bravery and heroism they had never thought themselves capable of doing. They had fought for a cause, fought together for a cause, and against all odds they had won.

When Captain Samuval stumbled, Galdar reached out a steadying arm. When Galdar slipped in a pool of blood, Captain Samuval supported him. The two arrived at the edge of the battlefield. Captain Samuval peered through the smoke that hung over the valley. The sun had disappeared behind the mountains. Its afterglow filled the sky with a smear of pale red.

"There," said the captain, and he pointed.

The wind had lifted with the setting of the sun, blowing the smoke to rags that swirled and eddied like silken scarves. These were suddenly whisked away to reveal a horse the color of blood and a figure kneeling on the field of battle only a few feet away from him.

"Mina!" Galdar breathed. Relief weakened all the muscles in his body. A burning stung his eyes, a burning he attributed to the smoke, for minotaurs never wept, could not weep. He wiped his eyes. "What is she doing?" he asked after a moment.

"Praying," said Captain Samuval. "She is praying."

Mina knelt beside the body of a soldier. The arrow that had killed him had gone clean through his breast, pinned him to the ground. Mina lifted the hand of the dead man, placed the hand to her breast, bent her head. If she spoke, Galdar could not hear what she said, but he knew Samuval was right. She was praying to this god of hers, this one, true god. This god who had foreseen the trap, this god who had led her here to turn defeat into glorious victory.

Her prayers finished, Mina laid the man's hand atop the terrible wound. Bending over him, she pressed her lips to the cold forehead, kissed it, then rose to her feet.

She had barely strength to walk. She was covered with blood, some of it her own. She halted, her head drooped, her body sagged. Then she lifted her head to the heavens, where she seemed to find strength, for she straightened her shoulders and with strong step walked on.

"Ever since the battle was assured, she has been going from corpse to corpse," said Captain Samuval. "In particular, she finds those who fell by our own arrows. She stops and kneels in the blood-soaked mud and offers prayer. I have never seen the like."

"It is right that she honors them," Galdar said harshly. "Those men bought us victory with their blood."

"*She* bought us victory with their blood," Captain Samuval returned with a quirk of the only eyebrow visible through the bandage.

A sound rose behind Galdar. He was reminded of the *Gamashinoch,* the Song of Death. This song came from living throats, however; starting low and quiet, sung by only a few. More voices caught it up and began to carry it forward, as they had caught up their dropped swords and run forward into battle.

"Mina . . . Mina . . ."

The song swelled. Begun as a soft, reverent chant, it was now a triumphal march, a celebratory paean accompanied by a timpani of sword clashing against shield, of stomping feet and clapping hands.

"Mina! Mina! Mina!"

Galdar turned to see the remnants of the army gathering at the edge of the battlefield. The wounded who could not walk under their own power were being supported by those who could. Bloody, ragged, the soldiers chanted her name.

Galdar lifted his voice in a thunderous shout and raised Mina's standard. The chanting became a cheer that rolled among the mountains like thunder and shook the ground mounded high with the bodies of the dead.

Mina had started to kneel down again. The song arrested her. She paused, turned slowly to face the cheering throng. Her face was pale as bone. Her amber eyes were ringed with ash-like smudges of fatigue. Her lips were parched and cracked, stained with the kisses of the dead. She gazed upon the hundreds of living who were shouting, singing, chanting her name.

Mina raised her hands.

The voices ceased in an instant. Even the groans and screams of the wounded hushed. The only sound was her name echoing from the mountainside, and eventually that died away as silence settled over the valley.

Mina mounted her horse, so that all the multitude who had gathered at the edge of the field of the battle, now being called "Mina's Glory," could better see and hear her.

"You do wrong to honor me!" she told them. "I am only the vessel. The honor and the glory of this day belong to the god who guides me along the path I walk."

"Mina's path is a path for us all!" shouted someone.

The cheering began again.

"Listen to me!" Mina shouted, her voice ringing with authority and power. "The old gods are gone! They abandoned you. They will never return! One god has come in their place. One god to rule the world. One god only. To that one god, we owe our allegiance!"

"What is the name of this god?" one cried.

"I may not pronounce it," Mina replied. "The name is too holy, too powerful."

"Mina!" said one. "Mina, Mina!"

The crowd picked up the chant and, once started, they would not be stopped.

Mina looked exasperated for a moment, even angry. Lifting her hand, she clasped her fingers over the medallion she wore round her neck. Her face softened, cleared.

"Go forth! Speak my name," she cried. "But know that you speak it in the name of my god."

The cheers were deafening, jarred rocks from the mountain sides.

His own pain forgotten, Galdar shouted lustily. He looked down to see his companion grimly silent, his gaze turned elsewhere.

"What?" Galdar bellowed over the tumult. "What's wrong?"

"Look there," said Captain Samuval. "At the command tent."

Not everyone in camp was cheering. A group of Knights of Neraka were gathered around their leader, a Lord of the Skull. They looked on with black gazes and scowls, arms crossed over their chests.

"Who is that?" Galdar asked.

"Lord Milles," Samuval replied. "The one who ordered this disaster. As you see, he came well out of the fray. Not a speck of blood on his fine, shiny armor."

Lord Milles was attempting to gain the soldiers' attention. He waved his arms, shouted out words no one could hear. No one paid him any heed. Eventually he gave it up as a bad job.

Galdar grinned. "I wonder how this Milles likes seeing his command pissing away down the privy hole."

"Not well, I should imagine," said Samuval.

"He and the other Knights consider themselves well rid of the gods," Galdar said. "They ceased to speak of Takhisis's return long ago. Two years past, Lord of the Night Targonne changed the official name to Knights of Neraka. In times past, when a Knight was granted the Vision, he was given to know his place in the goddess's grand plan. After Takhisis fled the world, the leadership tried for some time to maintain the Vision through various mystical means. Knights still undergo the Vision, but now they can only be certain of what Targonne and his ilk plant in their minds."

"One reason I left," said Samuval. "Targonne and officers like this Milles enjoy being the ones in charge for a change, and they will not be pleased to hear that they are in danger of being knocked off the top of the mountain. You may be certain Milles will send news of this upstart to headquarters."

Mina climbed down from her horse. Leading Foxfire by the reins, she left the field of battle, walked into the camp. The men cheered and shouted until she reached them, and then, as she came near, moved by something they did not understand, they ceased their clamor and dropped to their knees. Some reached out their hands to touch her as she passed, others cried for her to look upon them and grant them her blessing.

Lord Milles watched this triumphant procession, his face twisted in disgust. Turning on his heel, he reentered his command tent.

"Bah! Let them skulk and plot!" Galdar said, elated. "She has an army now. What can they do to her?"

"Something treacherous and underhanded, you can be sure," said Samuval. He cast a glance heavenward. "It may be true that there is One who watches over her from above. But she needs friends to watch over her here below."

"You speak wisely," said Galdar. "Are you with her then, Captain?"

"To the end of my time or the world's, whichever comes first," said Samuval. "My men as well. And you?"

"I have been with her always," said Galdar, and it truly seemed to him that he had.

Minotaur and human shook hands. Galdar proudly raised Mina's standard and fell in beside her as she made her victory march through the camp. Captain Samuval walked behind Mina, his hand on his sword, guarding her back. Mina's Knights rode to her standard. Every one of those who had followed her from Neraka had suffered some wound, but none had perished. Already, they were telling stories of miracles.

"An arrow came straight toward me," said one. "I knew I was dead. I spoke Mina's name, and the arrow dropped to the ground at my feet."

"One of the cursed Solamnics held his sword to my throat," said another. "I called upon Mina, and the enemy's blade broke in twain."

Soldiers offered her food. They brought her wine, brought her water. Several soldiers seized the tent of one of Milles's officers, turned him out, and prepared it for Mina. Snatching up burning brands from the campfires, the soldiers held them aloft, lighting Mina's progress through the darkness. As she passed, they spoke her name as if it were an incantation that could work magic.

"Mina," cried the men and the wind and the darkness. "Mina!"

8 UNDER THE SHIELD

The Silvanesti elves have always revered the night.

The Qualinesti delight in the sunlight. Their ruler is the Speaker of the Sun. They fill their homes with sunlight, all business is conducted in the daylight hours, all important ceremonies such as marriage are held in the day so that they may be blessed by the light of the sun.

The Silvanesti are in love with the star-lit night.

The Silvanesti's leader is the Speaker of the Stars. Night had once been a blessed time in Silvanost, the capital of the elven state. Night brought the stars and sweet sleep and dreams of the beauty of their beloved land. But then came the War of the Lance. The wings of evil dragons blotted out the stars. One dragon in particular, a green dragon known as Cyan Bloodbane, laid claim to the realm of Silvanesti. He had long hated the elves and he wanted to see them suffer. He could have slaughtered them by the thousands, but he was cruel and clever. The dying suffer, that is true, but the pain is fleeting and is soon forgotten as the dead move from this reality to the next. Cyan wanted to inflict a pain that nothing could ease, a pain that would endure for centuries.

The ruler of Silvanesti at the time was an elf highly skilled in magic. Lorac Caladon foresaw the coming of evil to Ansalon. He sent his people into exile, telling them he had the power to keep their realm safe from the dragons. Unbeknownst to anyone, Lorac had stolen one of the magical dragon orbs from the Tower of High Sorcery. He had been warned that an attempt to use the orb by one who was not strong enough to control its magic could result in doom. In his arrogance, Lorac believed that he was strong enough to wrest the orb to his will. He looked into the orb and saw a dragon looking back. Lorac was caught and held in thrall.

Cyan Bloodbane had his chance. He found Lorac in the Tower of the Stars, as he sat upon his throne, his hand held fast by the orb. Cyan whispered into Lorac's ear a dream of Silvanesti, a terrible dream in which lovely trees became hideous, deformed monstrosities that attacked those who had once loved them. A dream in which Lorac saw his people die, one by one, each death painful and terrible to witness. A dream in which the Thon-Thalas river ran red with blood.

The War of the Lance ended. Queen Takhisis was defeated. Cyan Bloodbane was forced to flee Silvanesti, but he left smugly satisfied with the knowledge that he had accomplished his goal. He had inflicted upon the Silvanesti a tortured dream from which they would never awaken. When the elves returned to their land after the war was over, they discovered to their shock and horror that the nightmare was reality. Lorac's dream, given to him by Cyan Bloodbane, had hideously altered their once beautiful land.

The Silvanesti fought the dream and, under the leadership of a Qualinesti general, Porthios, the elves eventually managed to defeat it. The cost was dear, however. Many elves fell victim to the dream, and even when it was finally cast out of the land, the trees and plants and animals remained horribly deformed. Slowly, the elves coaxed their forests back to beauty, using newly discovered magicks to heal the wounds left by the dream, to cover over the scars.

Then came the need to forget. Porthios, who had risked his life more than once to wrest their land from the clutches of the dream, became a reminder of the dream. He was no longer a savior. He was a stranger, an interloper, a threat to the Silvanesti who wanted to return to their life of isolation and seclusion. Porthios wanted to take the elves into the world, to make them one with the world, to unify them with their cousins, the Qualinesti. He had married Alhana Starbreeze, daughter of Lorac, with this hope in mind. Thus if war came again, the elves would not struggle alone. They would have allies to fight on their side.

The elves did not want allies. Allies who might decide to gobble up Silvanesti land in return for their help. Allies who might want to marry Silvanesti sons and daughters and dilute the pure Silvanesti blood. These isolationists had declared Porthios and his wife, Alhana, "dark elves" who could never, under penalty of death, return to their homelands.

Porthios was driven out. General Konnal took control of the nation and placed it under martial law "until such time as a true king can be found to rule the Silvanesti." The Silvanesti ignored the pleas of their cousins, the Qualinesti, for help to free them from the rule of the great dragon Beryl and the Knights of Neraka. The Silvanesti ignored the pleas of those who fought the great dragons and who begged the elves for their help. The Silvanesti wanted no part of the world. Absorbed in their own affairs, their eyes looked at the mirror of life and saw only themselves. Thus it was that while they gazed with pride at their own reflections, Cyan Bloodbane, the green dragon who had been their bane, came back to the land he had once nearly destroyed. Or so at least, it was reported by the kirath, who kept watch on the borders.

"Do not raise the shield!" the kirath warned. "You will trap us inside with our worst enemy!"

The elves did not listen. They did not believe the rumors. Cyan Bloodbane was a figure out of the dark past. He had died in the Dragon Purge. He must have died. If he had returned, why had he not attacked them? So fearful were the elves of the world outside that the Heads of House were unanimous in their approval of the magical shield. The people of Silvanesti could now be said to have gained their dearest wish. Under the magical shield, they were truly isolated, cut off from everyone. They were safe, protected from the evil of the outside world.

"And yet, it seems to me that we have not so much as shut the evil out," Rolan said to Silvan, "as that we have locked the evil in."

Night had come to Silvanesti. The darkness was welcome to Silvan, even as it was a grief to him. They had traveled by day through the forest, covering many miles until Rolan deemed they were far enough from the ill effects of the shield to stop and rest. The day had been a day of wonder to Silvanoshei.

He had heard his mother speak with longing, regret, and sorrow of the beauty of her homeland. He remembered as a child when he and his exiled parents were hiding in some cave with danger all about them, his mother would tell him tales of Silvanesti to quiet his fears. He would close his eyes and see, not the darkness, but the emerald, silver and gold of the forest. He would hear not the howls of wolf or goblin but the melodious chime of the bell flower or the sweetly sorrowful music of the flute tree.

His imagination paled before the reality, however. He could not believe that such beauty existed. He had spent the day as in a waking dream, stumbling over rocks, tree roots, and his own feet as wonders on every side brought tears to his eyes and joy to his heart.

Trees whose bark was tipped with silver lifted their branches to the sky in graceful arcs, their silver-edged leaves shining in the sunlight. A profusion of broad-leafed bushes lined the path, every bush ablaze with flame-colored flowers that scented the air with sweetness. He had the impression he did not walk through a forest so much as through a garden, for there were no fallen branches, no straggling weeds, no thickets of brambles. The Woodshapers permitted only the beautiful, the fruitful, and the beneficial to grow in their forests. The Woodshapers' magical influence extended throughout the land, with the exception of the borders, where the shield cast upon their handiwork a killing frost.

The darkness brought rest to Silvan's dazzled eyes. Yet the night had its own heart-piercing beauty. The stars blazed with fierce brilliance, as if defying the shield to try to shut them out. Night flowers opened their petals to the starlight, scented the warm darkness with exotic perfumes, while their luminescent glow filled the forest with a soft silvery white light.

"What do you mean?" Silvan asked. He could not equate evil with the beauty he'd witnessed.

"The cruel punishment we inflicted on your parents, for one, Your Majesty," said Rolan. "Our way of thanking your father for his aid was to try to stab him in the back. I was ashamed to be Silvanesti when I heard of this. But there has come a reckoning. We are being made to pay for our shame and our dishonor, for cutting ourselves off from the rest of the world, for living beneath the shield, protected from the dragons while others suffer. We pay for such protection with our lives."

They had stopped to rest in a clearing near a swift-flowing stream. Silvan was thankful for the respite. His injuries had started to pain him once more, though he had not liked to say anything. The excitement and shock of the sudden change in his life had drained him, depleted his energy.

Rolan found fruit and water with a sweetness like nectar for their dinner. He tended to Silvan's wounds with a respectful, solicitous care that the young man found quite pleasant.

Samar would have tossed me a rag and told me to make the best of it, Silvanoshei thought.

"Perhaps Your Majesty would like to sleep for a few hours," Rolan suggested after their supper.

Silvan had thought he was dropping from fatigue but found that he felt much better after eating, refreshed and renewed.

"I would like to know more about my homeland," he said. "My mother has told me some, but, of course, she could not know what has been happening since she . . . she left. You spoke of the shield." Silvan glanced about him. The beauty took his breath away. "I can understand why you would want to protect this"—he gestured to the trees whose boles shone with an iridescent light, to the star flowers that sparkled in the grass—"from the ravages of our enemies."

"Yes, Your Majesty," said Rolan and his tone softened. "There are some who say that no price is too high to pay for such protection, not even the price of our own lives. But if all of us are dead, who will be left to appreciate the beauty? And if we die, I believe that eventually the forests will die, too, for the souls of the elves are bound up in all things living."

"Our people number as the stars," said Silvan, amused, thinking that Rolan was being overly dramatic.

Rolan glanced up at the heavens. "Erase half those stars, Your Majesty, and you will find the light considerably diminished."

"Half!" Silvanoshei was shocked. "Surely not *half!*"

"Half the population of Silvanost alone has perished from the wasting sickness, Your Majesty." He paused a moment, then said, "What I am about to tell you would be considered treason, for which I would be severely punished."

"By punished, you mean cast out?" Silvan was troubled. "Exiled? Sent into darkness?"

"No, we do not do that anymore, Your Majesty," Rolan replied. "We cannot very well cast people out, for they could not pass through the shield. Now people who speak against Governor General Konnal simply disappear. No one knows what happens to them."

"If this is true, why don't the people rebel?" Silvan asked, bewildered. "Why don't they overthrow Konnal and demand that the shield be brought down?"

"Because only a few know the truth. And those of us who do have no evidence. We could stand in the Tower of the Stars and say that Konnal has gone mad, that he is so fearful of the world outside that he would rather see us all dead than be a part of that world. We could say all that, and then Konnal would stand up and say, 'You lie! Lower the shield and the Dark Knights will enter our beloved woods with their axes, the ogres will break and maim the living trees, the Great Dragons will descend upon us and devour us.' That is what he will say, and the people will cry, 'Save us! Protect us, dear Governor General Konnal! We have no one else to turn to!' and that will be that."

"I see," said Silvan thoughtfully. He glanced at Rolan, who was gazing intently into the darkness.

"Now the people will have someone else to turn to, Your Majesty," said Rolan. "The rightful heir to the Silvanesti throne. But we must proceed carefully, cautiously." He smiled sadly. "Else you, too, might 'disappear.' "

The lovely song of the nightingale throbbed in the darkness. Rolan pursed his lips and whistled back. Three elves materialized, emerging from the shadows. Silvan recognized them as the three who had first accosted him near the shield this morning.

This morning! Silvan marveled. Was it only this morning? Days, months, years had gone by since then.

Rolan stood to greet the three, clasping the elves by the hand and exchanging the ritual kiss on the cheek.

The elves wore the same cloak as did Rolan, and even though Silvan knew that they had entered the clearing, he was having a difficult time seeing them, for they seemed to be wrapped in darkness and starlight.

Rolan questioned them about their patrol. They reported that the border along the Shield was quiet, "deathly quiet" one said with terrible irony. The three turned their attention back to Silvan.

"So have you questioned him, Rolan?" asked one, turning a stern gaze upon Silvanoshei. "Is he what he claims?"

Silvan scrambled to his feet, feeling awkward and embarrassed. He started to bow politely to his elders, as he had been taught, but then the thought came to him that he was king, after all. It was they who should bow to him. He looked at Rolan in some confusion.

"I did not 'question' him," Rolan said sternly. "We discussed certain things. And yes, I believe him to be Silvanoshei, the rightful Speaker of the Stars, son of Alhana and Porthios. Our king has returned to us. The day for which we have been waiting has arrived."

The three elves looked at Silvan, studied him up and down, then turned back to Rolan.

"He could be an imposter," said one.

"I am certain he is not," Rolan returned with firm conviction. "I knew his mother when she was his age. I fought with his father against the dreaming. He has the likeness of them both, though he favors his father. You, Drinel. You fought with Porthios. Look at this young man. You will see the father's image engraven on the son's."

The elf stared intently at Silvanoshei, who met his gaze and held it.

"See with your heart, Drinel," Rolan urged. "Eyes can be blinded. The heart cannot. You heard him when we followed him, when he had no idea we were spying on him. You heard what he said to us when he believed us to be soldiers of his mother's army. He was not dissembling. I stake my life on it."

"I grant you that he favors his father and that there is something of his mother in his eyes. By what miracle does the son of our exiled queen walk beneath the shield?" Drinel asked.

"I don't know how I came to be inside the shield," Silvan said, embarrassed. "I must have fallen through it. I don't remember. But when I sought to leave, the shield would not let me."

"He threw himself against the shield," Rolan said. "He tried to go back, tried to leave Silvanesti. Would an imposter do that when he had gone to so much trouble to enter? Would an imposter admit that he did not know how he came through the shield? No, an imposter would have a tale to hand us, logical and easy to believe."

"You spoke of seeing with my heart," said Drinel. He glanced back at the other elves. "We are agreed. We want to try the truth-seek on him."

"You disgrace us with your distrust!" Rolan said, highly displeased. "What will he think of us?"

"That we are wise and prudent," Drinel answered dryly. "If he has nothing to hide, he will not object."

"It is up to Silvanoshei," Rolan replied. "Though I would refuse, if I were him."

"What is it?" Silvan looked from one to another, puzzled. "What is this truth-seek?"

"It is a magical spell, Your Majesty," Rolan answered and his tone grew sad. "Once there was a time when the elves could trust each other. Trust each other implicitly. Once there was a time when no elf could possibly lie to another of our people. That time came to an end during Lorac's dream. The dream created phantasms of our people, false images of fellow elves that yet seemed very real to those who looked on them and touched them and spoke to them. These phantasms could lure those who believed in them to ruin and destruction. A husband might see his wife beckoning to him and plunge headlong over a cliff in an effort to reach her. A mother might see a child perishing in flames and rush into the fire, only to find the child vanished.

"We kirath developed the truth-seek to determine if these phantasms were real or if they were a part of the dream. The phantasms were empty inside, hollow. They had no memories, no thoughts, no feelings. A touch of a hand upon the heart and we would know if we dealt with living person or the dream.

"When the dream ended, the need for the truth-seek ended, as well," Rolan said. "Or so we hoped. A hope that proved forlorn. When the dream ended, the twisted, bleeding trees were gone, the ugliness that perverted our land departed. But the ugliness had entered the hearts of some of our people, turned them as hollow as the hearts of those created by the dream. Now elf can lie to elf and does so. New words have crept into the elven vocabulary. Human words. Words like distrust, dishonest, dishonor. We use the truth-seek on each other now and it seems to me that the more we use it, the more the need to use it." He looked very darkly upon Drinel, who remained resolute, defiant.

"I have nothing to hide," said Silvan. "You may use this truth-seek on me and welcome. Though it would grieve my mother deeply to hear that her people have come to such a pass. She would never think to question the loyalty of those who follow her, as they would never think to question her care of them."

"You see, Drinel," said Rolan, flushing. "You see how you shame us!"

"Nevertheless, I will know the truth," Drinel said stubbornly.

"Will you?" Rolan demanded. "What if the magic fails you again?"

Drinel's eyes flashed. He cast a dark glance at his fellow. "Curb your tongue, Rolan. I remind you that as yet we know nothing about this young man."

Silvanoshei said nothing. It was not his place to interject himself into this dispute. But he stored up the words for future thought. Perhaps the elf sorcerers of his mother's army were not the only people who had found their magical power starting to wane.

Drinel approached Silvan, who stood stiffly, eyeing the elf askance. Drinel reached out his left hand, his heart hand, for that is the hand closest to the heart, and rested his hand upon Silvan's breast. The elf's touch was light, yet Silvan could feel it strike through to his soul, or so it seemed.

Memory flowed from the font of his soul, good memories and bad, bubbling up from beneath surface feelings and thoughts and pouring into Drinel's hand. Memories of his father, a stern and implacable figure who rarely smiled and never laughed. Who never made any outward show of his affection, never spoke approval of his son's actions, rarely seemed to notice his son at all. Yet within that glittering flow of memory, Silvanoshei recalled one night, when he and his mother had narrowly escaped death at the hands of someone or other. Porthios had clasped them both in his arms, had held his small son close to his breast, had whispered a prayer over them in Elvish, an ancient prayer to gods who were no longer there to hear it. Silvanoshei remembered cold wet tears touching his cheek, remembered thinking to himself that these tears were not his. They were his father's.

This memory and others Drinel came to hold in his mind, as he might have held sparkling water in his cupped hands.

Drinel's expression altered. He looked at Silvan with new regard, new respect.

"Are you satisfied?" Silvan asked coldly. The memories had opened a bleeding gash in his being.

"I see his father in his face, his mother in his heart," Drinel replied. "I pledge you my allegiance, Silvanoshei. I urge others to do the same."

Drinel bowed deeply, his hand over his breast. The other two elves added their words of acceptance and allegiance. Silvan returned gracious thanks, all the while wondering a bit cynically just what all this kowtowing was truly worth to him. Elves had pledged allegiance to his mother, as well, and Alhana Starbreeze was little better than a bandit skulking in the woods.

If being the rightful Speaker of the Stars meant more nights hiding in burial mounds and more days dodging assassins, Silvan could do without it. He was sick of that sort of life, sick to death of it. He had never fully admitted that until now. For the first time he admitted to himself that he was angry—hotly, bitterly angry—at his parents for having forced that sort of life upon him.

He was ashamed of his anger the next moment. He reminded himself that perhaps his mother was either dead or captive, but, irrationally, his grief and worry increased his anger. The conflicting emotions, complicated further by guilt, confused and exhausted him. He needed time to think, and he couldn't do that with these elves staring at him like some sort of stuffed curiosity in a mageware shop.

The elves remained standing, and Silvan eventually realized that they were waiting for him to sit down and rest themselves. He had been raised in an elven court, albeit a rustic one, and he was experienced at courtly maneuverings. He urged the other elves to be seated, saying that they must be weary, and he invited them to eat some of the fruit and water. Then Silvan excused himself from their company, explaining that he needed to make his ablutions.

He was surprised when Rolan warned him to be careful, offered him the sword he wore.

"Why?" Silvan was incredulous. "What is there to fear? I thought the shield kept out all our enemies."

"With one exception," Rolan answered dryly. "There are reports that the great green dragon, Cyan Bloodbane, was—by a 'miscalculation' on the part of General Konnal—trapped inside the shield."

"Bah! That is nothing but a story Konnal puts about in order to distract us," Drinel asserted. "Name me one person who has seen this monster! No one. The dragon is rumored to be here. He is rumored to be there. We go here and we go there and never find a trace of him. I think it odd, Rolan, that this Cyan Bloodbane is always sighted just when Konnal feels himself under pressure to answer to the leaders of the Households about the state of his rule."

"True, no one has seen Cyan Bloodbane," Rolan agreed. "Nevertheless, I confess I believe that the dragon is in Silvanesti somewhere. I once saw tracks I found very difficult to explain otherwise. Be careful, therefore, Your Majesty. And take my sword. Just in case."

Silvan refused the sword. Thinking back to how he had almost skewered Samar, Silvan was ashamed to let the others know he could not handle a weapon, ashamed to let them know that he was completely untrained in its use. He assured Rolan that he would keep careful watch and walked into the glittering forest. His mother, he recalled, would have sent an armed guard with him.

For the first time in my life, Silvan thought suddenly, I am free. Truly free.

He washed his face and hands in a clear, cold stream, raked his fingers through his long hair, and looked long at his reflection in the rippling water. He could see nothing of his father in his face, and he was always somewhat irritated by those who claimed that they could. Silvan's memories of Porthios were of a stern, steel-hard warrior who, if he had ever known how to smile, had long since abandoned the practice. The only tenderness Silvan ever saw in his father's eyes was when they turned their gaze to his mother.

"You are king of the elves," Silvan said to his reflection. "You have accomplished in a day what your parents could not accomplish in thirty years. Could not . . . or would not."

He sat down on the bank. His reflection stirred and shimmered in the light of the newly risen moon. "The prize they sought is within your grasp. You didn't particularly want it before, but now that it is offered, why not take it?"

Silvan's reflection rippled as a breath of wind passed over the surface of the water. Then the wind stilled, the water smoothed, and his reflection was clear and unwavering.

"You must walk carefully. You must think before you speak, think of the consequences of every word. You must consider your actions. You must not be distracted by the least little thing.

"My mother is dead," he said, and he waited for the pain.

Tears welled up inside him, tears for his mother, tears for his father, tears for himself, alone and bereft of their comfort and support. Yet, a tiny voice whispered deep inside, when did your parents ever support you? When did they ever trust you to do anything? They kept you wrapped in cotton wool, afraid you'd break. Fate has offered you this chance to prove yourself. Take it!

A bush grew near the stream, a bush with fragrant white flowers shaped like tiny hearts. Silvan picked a cluster of flowers, stripped the blossoms from the leafy stems. "Honor to my father, who is dead," he said and scattered the blossoms in the stream. They fell upon the reflection that broke apart in the spreading ripples. "Honor to my mother, who is dead."

He scattered the last of the blossoms. Then, feeling cleansed, empty of tears and empty of emotion, he returned to the camp.

The elves started to rise, but he asked them to remain seated and not disturb themselves on his account. The elves appeared pleased with his modesty.

"I hope my long absence did not worry you," he said, knowing well that it had. He could tell they had been talking about him. "These changes have all been so drastic, so sudden. I needed time to think."

The elves bowed in acquiescence.

"We have been discussing how best to advance Your Majesty's cause," said Rolan.

"You have the full support of the kirath, Your Majesty," Drinel added.

Silvan acknowledged this with a nod. He thought on where he wanted this conversation to go and how best to take it there and asked mildly, "What is the 'kirath'? My mother spoke of many things in her homeland but not of this."

"There is no reason why she should," Rolan replied. "Your father created our order to fight the dream. We kirath were the ones who entered the forest, searching for the parts that were still held in thrall by the dream. The work took its toll on body and on mind, for we had to enter the dream in order to defeat it.

"Other kirath served to defend the Woodshapers and clerics who came into the forest to heal it. For twenty years we fought together to restore our homeland, and eventually we succeeded. When the dream was defeated we were no longer needed, and so we disbanded, returned to the lives we had led before the war. But those of us in the kirath had forged a bond closer than brothers and sisters. We kept in touch, passing news and information.

"Then the Dark Knights of Takhisis came to try to conquer the continent of Ansalon, and after that came the Chaos War. It was during this time that General Konnal took control of Silvanesti, saying that only the military could save us from the forces of evil at work in the world.

"We won the Chaos War, but at a great cost. We lost the gods, who, so it is said, made the ultimate sacrifice—withdrawing from the world so that Krynn and its people might continue on. With them went the magic of Solinari and healing powers. We grieved long for the gods, for Paladine and Mishakal, but we had to go on with our lives.

"We worked to continue to rebuild Silvanesti. Magic came to us again, a magic of the land, of living things. Though the war was over, General Konnal did not relinquish control. He said that now the threat came from Alhana and Porthios, dark elves who wanted only to avenge themselves on their people."

"Did you believe this?" Silvan asked indignantly.

"Of course not. We knew Porthios. We knew the great sacrifices he had made for this land. We knew Alhana and how much she loved her people. We did not believe him."

"And so you supported my father and mother?" Silvan asked.

"We did," Rolan replied.

"Then why didn't you aid them?" Silvan demanded, his tone sharpening. "You were armed and skilled in the use of arms. You were, as you have said, in close contact with one another. My mother and father waited on the borders, expecting confidently that the Silvanesti people would rise up and protest the injustice that had been done to them. They did not. You did nothing. My parents waited in vain."

"I could offer you many excuses, Your Majesty," Rolan said quietly. "We were weary of fighting. We did not want to start a civil war. We believed that over time this breach could all be made right by peaceful means. In other words"—he smiled faintly, sadly—"we pulled the blankets over our heads and went back to sleep."

"If it is any comfort to you, Your Majesty, we have paid for our sins," Drinel added. "Paid most grievously. We realized this when the magical shield was erected, but by that time it was too late. We could not go out. Your parents could not come within."

Understanding came to Silvan in a flash, dazzling and shocking as the lightning bolt that had struck right in front of him. All had been darkness before and in the next thudding heartbeat all was lit brighter than day, every detail clear cut and stark in the white-hot light.

His mother claimed to hate the shield. In truth the shield was her excuse, keeping her from leading her army into Silvanesti. She could have done so anytime during the years before the shield was raised. She and her father could have marched an army into Silvanesti, they would have found support among the people. Why hadn't they?

The spilling of elven blood. That was the excuse they gave then. They did not want to see elf killing elf. The truth was that Alhana had expected her people to come to her and lay the crown of Silvanesti at her feet. They had not done so. As Rolan had said, they wanted only to go back to sleep, wanted to forget Lorac's nightmare in more pleasant dreams. Alhana had been the cat yowling beneath the window, disturbing their rest.

His mother had refused to admit this to herself and thus, though she railed against the raising of the shield, in reality the shield had been a relief to her. Oh, she had done all she could to try to destroy it. She had done all she could to prove to herself that she wanted desperately to penetrate the barrier. She had thrown her armies against the shield, thrown herself against it. But all the while, secretly, in her heart, she did not want to enter and perhaps that was the reason the shield had been successful in keeping her out.

Drinel and Rolan and the rest of the elves were inside it for the very same reason. The shield was in place, the shield existed, because the elves wanted it. The Silvanesti had always yearned to be kept safe from the world, safe from the contamination of the crude and undisciplined humans, safe from the dangers of ogre and goblin and minotaur, safe from the dragons, safe amidst ease and luxury and beauty. That was why his mother had wanted to find a way inside—so that she too could finally sleep in warmth and in safety, not in burial mounds.

He said nothing, but he realized now what he had to do.

"You pledge your allegiance to me. How do I know that when the path grows dark you will not abandon me as you abandoned my parents?"

Rolan paled. Drinel's eyes flashed in anger. He started to speak, but his friend laid a calming hand on his arm.

"Silvanoshei is right to rebuke us, my friend. His Majesty is right to ask this question of us." Rolan turned to face Silvan. "Hand and heart, I pledge myself and my family to Your Majesty's cause. May my soul be held in thrall on this plane of existence if I fail."

Silvan nodded gravely. It was a terrible oath. He shifted his gaze to Drinel and the other two members of the kirath. Drinel was hesitant.

"You are very young," he said harshly. "How old are you? Thirty years? You are considered an adolescent among our people."

"But not among the Qualinesti," Silvanoshei returned. "And I ask you to think of this," he added, knowing that the Silvanesti were not likely to be impressed by comparisons with their more worldly (and therefore more corrupt) cousins. "I have not been raised in a pampered, sheltered Silvanesti household. I have been raised in caves, in shacks, in hovels—wherever my parents could find safe shelter. I can count on my two hands the number of nights I have slept in a room in a bed. I have been twice wounded in battles. I bear the scars upon my body."

Silvan did not add that he had not received his wounds while fighting in those battles. He did not mention that he had been injured while his body guards were hustling him off to a place of safety. He would have fought, he thought to himself, if anyone had given him a chance. He was prepared to fight now.

"I make the same pledge to you that I ask of you," Silvan said proudly. "Heart and hand, I pledge to do everything in my power to regain the throne that is mine by right. I pledge to bring wealth, peace, and prosperity back to our people. May my soul be held in thrall on this plane of existence if I fail."

Drinel's eyes sifted, searched that soul. The elder elf appeared satisfied with he saw. "I make my pledge to you, Silvanoshei, son of Porthios and Alhana. By aiding the son, may we make restitution for our failures in regard to the parents."

"And now," said Rolan. "We must make plans. We must find a suitable hiding place for His Majesty—"

"No," said Silvan firmly. "The time for hiding is past. I am the rightful heir to the throne. I have a lawful claim. I have nothing to fear. If I go sneaking and skulking about like a criminal, then I will be perceived as a criminal. If I arrive in Silvanost as a king, I will be perceived as a king."

"Yet, the danger—" Rolan began.

"His Majesty is right, my friend," Drinel said, regarding Silvan with now marked respect. "He will be in less danger by making a great stir than he would be if he were to go into hiding. In order to placate those who question his rule, Konnal has stated many times that he would gladly see the son of Alhana take his rightful place upon the throne. He could make such a promise easily enough, for he knew—or thought he knew—that with the shield in place, the son could not possibly enter.

"If Your Majesty arrives triumphantly in the capital, with the people cheering on all sides, Konnal will be forced to make some show of keeping his promise. He will find it difficult to make the rightful heir disappear, as have others in the past. The people would not stand for it."

"What you say has merit. Yet we must never underestimate Konnal," said Rolan. "Some believe he is mad, but if so, his is a cunning, calculating madness. He is dangerous."

"So am I," said Silvan. "As he will soon discover."

He sketched out his plan. The others listened, voiced their approval, offered changes he accepted, for they knew his people best. He listened gravely to the discussion of possible danger, but in truth, he paid little heed.

Silvanoshei was young, and the young know they will live forever.

9 GALLIVANTING

The same night that Silvanoshei accepted the rulership of the Silvanesti, Tasslehoff Burrfoot slept soundly and peacefully—much to his disappointment.

The kender was deposited for safekeeping in a room inside the Solamnic garrison in Solace. Tas had offered to return to the wonderful kender-proof Solace jail, but his request was firmly denied. The garrison room was clean and neat, with no windows, no furniture except a stern-looking bed with iron railings and a mattress so stiff and rigid that it could have stood at attention with the best of the Knights. The door had no lock at all, which might have provided some light after-dinner amusement but was held in place by a wooden bar across the outside.

"All in all," Tas said to himself as he sat disconsolately on his bed, kicking his feet against the iron railings and looking wistfully about, "this room is the single most boring place I've ever been in my life with the possible exception of the Abyss."

Gerard had even taken away his candle, leaving Tas alone in the dark. There seemed nothing to do but go to sleep.

Tasslehoff had long thought that someone would do a very good service to mankind by abolishing sleep. Tas had mentioned this to Raistlin once, remarking that a wizard of his expertise could probably find a way around sleep, which took up a good portion of one's time with very little benefit that Tas could see. Raistlin had replied that the kender should be thankful someone had invented sleep for this meant that Tasslehoff was quiet and comatose for eight hours out of a day and this was the sole reason that Raistlin had not yet strangled him.

Sleep had one benefit and that was dreams, but this benefit was almost completely nullified by the fact that one woke from a dream and was immediately faced with the crushing disappointment that it had been a dream, that the dragon chasing one with the intent of biting off one's head was not a real dragon, that the ogre trying to bash one into pulp with a club was not a real ogre. Add to this the fact that one always woke up at the most interesting and exciting part of the dream—when the dragon had one's head in his mouth, for example, or the ogre had hold of the back of one's collar. Sleep, as far as Tas was concerned, was a complete waste of time. Every night saw him determined to fight sleep off, and every morning found him waking up to discover that sleep had sneaked up on him unawares and run away with him.

Tasslehoff didn't offer sleep much of a fight this night. Worn out from the rigors of travel and the excitement and snuffles occasioned by Caramon's funeral, Tas lost the battle without a struggle. He woke to find that not only had sleep stolen in on him but that Gerard had done the same. The Knight stood over him, glaring down with his customary grim expression, which looked considerably grimmer by lantern light.

"Get up," said the Knight. "Put these on."

Gerard handed Tas some clothes that were clean and well-made, drab, dull and—the kender shuddered—serviceable.

"Thank you," said Tas, rubbing his eyes. "I know you mean well, but I have my own clothes—"

"I won't travel with someone who looks as if he had been in a fight with a Maypole and lost," Gerard countered. "A blind gully dwarf could see you from six miles off. Put these on, and be quick about it."

"A fight with a Maypole," Tas giggled. "I actually saw one of those once. It was at this Mayday celebration in Solace. Caramon put on a wig and petticoats and went out to dance with the young virgins, only his wig slipped over his eye—"

Gerard held up a stern finger. "Rule number one. No talking."

Tas opened his mouth to explain that he wasn't really talking, not talking as in talking, but talking as in telling a story, which was quite a different thing altogether. Before Tas was able to get a word out, Gerard displayed the gag.

Tasslehoff sighed. He enjoyed traveling, and he was truly looking forward to this adventure, but he did feel that he might have been granted a more congenial traveling companion. He sadly relinquished his colorful clothes, laying them on the bed with a fond pat, and dressed himself in the brown knickers, the brown wool socks, the brown shirt, and brown vest Gerard had laid out for him. Tas, looking down at himself, thought sadly that he looked exactly like a tree stump. He started to put his hands in his pockets when he discovered there weren't any.

"No pouches, either," said Gerard, picking up Tasslehoff's bags and pouches and preparing to add them to the pile of discarded clothing.

"Now, see here—" Tas began sternly.

One of the pouches fell open. The light from the lantern glittered merrily on the gleaming, winking jewels of the Device of Time Journeying.

"Oops," said Tasslehoff as innocently as ever he could and indeed he was innocent, this time at least.

"How did you get this away from me?" Gerard demanded.

Tasslehoff shrugged and, pointing to his sealed lips, shook his head.

"If I ask you a question, you may answer," Gerard stated, glowering. "When did you steal this from me?"

"I didn't steal it," Tas replied with dignity. "Stealing is extremely bad. I told you. The device keeps coming back to me. It's not my fault. *I* don't want it. I had a stern talk with it last night, in fact, but it doesn't seem to listen."

Gerard glared, then, muttering beneath his breath—something to the effect that he didn't know why he bothered—he thrust the magical device in a leather pouch he wore at his side. "And it had better *stay* there," he said grimly.

"Yes, you'd better do what the Knight says!" Tas added loudly, shaking his finger at the device. He was rewarded for his help by having the gag tied around his mouth.

The gag in place, Gerard snapped a pair of manacles over Tas's wrists. Tas would have slipped right out of ordinary manacles, but these manacles were specially made for a kender's slender wrists, or so it appeared. Tas worked and worked and couldn't free himself. Gerard laid a heavy hand on the kender's shoulder and marched him out of the room and down the hall.

The sun had not yet made an appearance. The garrison was dark and quiet. Gerard allowed Tas time to wash his face and hands—he had to wash around the gag—and do whatever else he needed to do, keeping close watch on him all the time and not allowing the kender a moment's privacy. He then escorted him out of the building.

Gerard wore a long, enveloping cloak over his armor. Tas couldn't see the armor beneath the cloak, and he knew the Knight was wearing armor only because he heard it clank and rattle. Gerard did not wear a helm or carry a sword. He walked the kender back to the Knights' quarters, where Gerard picked up a large knapsack and what could have been a sword wrapped up in a blanket tied with rope.

Gerard then marched Tasslehoff, bound and gagged, to the front of the garrison. The sun was a tiny sliver of light on the horizon and then it was swallowed by a cloudbank, so that it seemed as if the sun were starting to rise and had suddenly changed its mind and gone back to bed.

Gerard handed a paper to the Captain of the Guard. "As you can see, sir, I have Lord Warren's permission to remove the prisoner."

The captain glanced at it and then at the kender. Gerard, Tas noticed, was careful to keep out of the light of the flaring torches mounted on the wooden posts on either side of the gate. Instantly the idea came to Tas that Gerard was trying to hide something. The kender's curiosity was aroused, an occurrence that often proves fatal to the kender and also to those who happen to be a kender's companions. Tas stared with all his might, trying to see what was so interesting beneath the cloak.

He was in luck. The morning breeze came up. The cloak fluttered slightly. Gerard caught it quickly, held it fastened in front of him, but not before Tasslehoff had seen the torchlight shine on armor that was gleaming black.

Under normal circumstances Tas would have demanded loudly and excitedly to know why a Solamnic Knight was wearing black armor. The kender probably would have tugged on the cloak in order to obtain a better view and pointed out this odd and interesting fact to the captain of the guard. The gag prevented Tas from saying any of this except in muffled and incoherent squeaks and "*mfrts*," which was all he could manage.

On second thought—and it was due solely to the gag that Tasslehoff actually had a second thought—the kender realized that perhaps Gerard might not want anyone to know he was wearing black armor. Thus, the cloak.

Quite charmed by this new twist to the adventure, Tasslehoff kept silent, merely letting Gerard know with several cunning winks that he, the kender, was in on the secret.

"Where are you taking the little weasel?" the captain asked, handing the paper back to Gerard. "And what's wrong with his eye? He hasn't got pink eye, has he?"

"Not to my knowledge, sir. Begging the captain's pardon, but I can't tell you where I'm ordered to deliver the kender, sir. That information is secret," Gerard replied respectfully. Lowering his voice, he added, "He's the one who was caught desecrating the tomb, sir."

The captain nodded in understanding. He glanced askance at the bundles the Knight was carrying. "What's that?"

"Evidence, sir," Gerard replied.

The captain looked very grim. "Did a lot of damage, did he? I trust they'll make an example of him."

"I should think they might, sir," Gerard replied evenly.

The captain waved Gerard and Tas through the gate, paid no further attention to them. Gerard hustled the kender away from the garrison and out onto the main road. Although the morning itself wasn't quite awake yet, many people were. Farmers were bringing in their goods to market. Wagons were rolling out to the logging camps in the mountains. Anglers were heading for Crystalmir Lake. People cast a few curious glances at the cloaked Knight—the morning was already quite warm. Busy with their own cares, they passed by without comment. If he wanted to swelter, that was his concern. None of them so much as looked twice at Tasslehoff. The sight of a bound and gagged kender was nothing new.

Gerard and Tas took the road south out of Solace, a road that meandered alongside the Sentinel range of mountains and would eventually deposit them in South Pass. The sun had finally decided to crawl out of bed. Pink light spread in a colorful wash across the sky. Gold gilded the tree leaves, and diamonds of dew sparkled on the grass. A fine day for adventuring, and Tas would have enjoyed himself immensely but for the fact that he was hustled along and harried and not permitted to stop to look at anything along the road.

Although encumbered with the knapsack, which appeared quite heavy, and the sword in a blanket, Gerard set a fast pace. He carried both objects in one hand, keeping the other to prod Tasslehoff in the back if he started to slow down or to grab hold of his collar if he started to wander off or jerk him backward if he made a sudden dart across the road.

One would not have guessed it from looking at him, but Gerard, for all that he was of average height and medium build, was extremely strong.

The Knight was a grim and silent companion. He did not return the cheerful "good mornings" of those heading into Solace, and he coldly rebuffed a traveling tinker who was going in their direction and offered them a seat on his wagon.

He did at least remove the gag from the kender's mouth. Tas was thankful. Not as young as he used to be—something he would freely admit—he found that between the fast pace set by the Knight and the constant prodding, tugging, and jerking, he was doing more breathing than his nose alone could manage.

Tas immediately asked all the questions he had been storing up, starting with, "Why is your armor black? I've never seen black armor before. Well, yes, I have but it wasn't on a Knight of Solamnia," and ending with, "Are we going to walk all the way to Qualinesti, and if we are would you mind not seizing hold of my shirt collar in that very energetic way you have because it's starting to rub off all my skin."

Tas soon found out that he could ask all the questions he liked, just so long as he didn't expect any answers. Sir Gerard made no response except, "Keep moving."

The Knight was young, after all. Tas felt compelled to point out to him the mistake he was making.

"The very best part of questing," the kender said, "is seeing the sights along the way. Taking time to enjoy the view and investigating all the interesting things you find along the road and talking to all the people. If you stop to think about it, the goal of the quest, such as fighting the dragon or rescuing the woolly mammoth, takes up only a small bit of time, and although it's always very exciting, there's a whole lot more time stacked up in front of it and behind it—the getting there and the coming back—which can be very dull if you don't work at it."

"I am not interested in excitement," said Gerard. "I want simply to be done with this and to be done with you. The sooner I am finished the sooner I can do something to achieve my goal."

"And what's that?" Tas asked, delighted that the Knight was finally talking to him.

"To join the fighting in defense of Sanction," Gerard answered, "and when that is done, to free Palanthas from the scourge of the Knights of Neraka."

"Who are they?" Tas asked, interested.

"They used to be known as the Knights of Takhisis, but they changed their name when it grew clear to them that Takhisis wasn't coming back anymore."

"What do you mean, not coming back. Where did she go?" Tas asked.

Gerard shrugged. "With the other gods, if you believe what people say. Personally I think claiming that the bad times are a result of the gods leaving us is just an excuse for our own failures."

"The gods left!" Tas's jaw dropped. "When?"

Gerard snorted. "I'm not playing games with you, kender."

Tas pondered all that Gerard had told him.

"Don't you have this whole Knight business backward?" Tas asked finally. "Isn't Sanction being held by the Dark Knights and Palanthas by your Knights?"

"No, I do not have it backward. More's the pity," Gerard said.

Tas sighed deeply. "I'm extremely confused."

Gerard grunted and prodded the kender, who was slowing down a bit, his legs not being as young as they used to be either. "Hurry up," he said. "We don't have much farther."

"We don't?" Tas said meekly. "Did they move Qualinesti, too?"

"If you must know, kender, I have two mounts waiting for us at the Solace bridge. And before you can ask yet another question, the reason we walked from the garrison and did not ride is that the horse I am using is not my customary mount. The animal would have occasioned comment, would have required explanation."

"I have a horse? A horse of my own! How thrilling! I haven't ridden a horse in ever so long." Tasslehoff came to a halt, looked up at the Knight. "I'm terribly sorry I misjudged you. I guess you do understand about adventuring, after all."

"Keep moving." Gerard gave him a shove.

A thought occurred to the kender—a truly astonishing thought that took away what little breath he had remaining. He paused to find his breath again and then used it to ask the question the thought had produced.

"You don't like me, do you, Sir Gerard?" Tas said. He wasn't angry or accusing, just surprised.

"No," said Gerard, "I do not." He took a drink of water from a waterskin and handed the skin to Tas. "If it is any consolation, there is nothing personal in my dislike. I feel this way about all your kind."

Tas considered this as he drank the water, which was quite tepid and tasted of the waterskin. "Maybe I'm wrong, but it seems to me that I'd much rather be disliked for being me than to be disliked just because I'm a kender. I can do something about me, you see, but I can't do much about being a kender because my mother was a kender and so was my father and that seems to have a lot to do with me being a kender.

"I might have wanted to be a Knight," Tas continued, warming to his subject. "In fact, I'm pretty sure I probably did, but the gods must have figured that my mother, being small, couldn't very well give birth to someone as big as you, not without considerable inconvenience to herself, and so I came out a kender. Actually, no offense, but I take that back about being a Knight. I think what I really wanted to be was a draconian—they are so very fierce and scaly, and they have wings. I've always wanted wings. But, of course, that would have been *extremely* difficult for my mother to have managed."

"Keep moving," was all Gerard said in reply.

"I could help you carry that bundle if you'd take off these manacles," Tas offered, thinking that if he made himself useful, the Knight might come to like him.

"No," Gerard returned, and that was that. Not even a thank you.

"*Why* don't you like kender?" Tas pursued. "Flint always said he didn't like kender, but I know deep down he did. I don't think Raistlin liked kender much. He tried to murder me once, which gave me sort of a hint as to his true feelings. But I forgave him for that, although I'll never forgive him for murdering poor Gnimsh, but that's another story. I'll tell you that later. Where was I? Oh, yes. I was about to add that Sturm Brightblade was a Knight, and he liked kender, so I was just wondering what you have against us."

"Your people are frivolous and heedless," said Gerard, his voice hard. "These are dark days. Life is serious business and should be taken seriously. We do not have the luxury for joy and merriment."

"But if there's no joy and merriment, then of course the days will be dark," Tas argued. "What else do you expect?"

"How much joy did you feel, kender, when you heard the news that hundreds of your people in Kendermore had been slaughtered by the great dragon Malystryx?" Gerard asked grimly, "and that those who survived were driven from their homes and now seem to be under some sort of curse and are called afflicted because they now know fear and they carry swords, not pouches. Did you laugh when you heard that news, kender, and sing 'tra la, how merry we are this day'?"

Tasslehoff came to a stop and rounded so suddenly that the Knight very nearly tripped over him.

"Hundreds? Killed by a dragon?" Tas was aghast. "What do you mean hundreds of kender died in Kendermore? I never heard that. I never heard anything like that! It's not true. You're lying. . . . No," he added miserably. "I take that back. You can't lie. You're a Knight, and while you may not like me you're honor bound not to lie to me."

Gerard said nothing. Putting his hand on Tas's shoulder, he turned the kender around bodily and started him, once again, on his way.

Tas noticed a queer feeling in the vicinity of his heart, a constricting kind of feeling, as if he'd swallowed one of the more ferocious constricting snakes. The feeling was uncomfortable and not at all pleasant. Tas knew in that moment that the Knight had indeed spoken truly. That hundreds of his people had died most horribly and painfully. He did not know how this had happened, but he knew it was true, as true as the grass growing along the side of the road or the tree branches overhead or the sun gleaming down through the green leaves.

It was true in this world where Caramon's funeral had been different from what he remembered. But it hadn't been true in that other world, the world of Caramon's first funeral.

"I feel sort of strange," Tas said in a small voice. "Kind of dizzy. Like I might throw up. If you don't mind, I think I'm going to be quiet for awhile."

"Praise be," said the Knight, adding, with another shove. "Keep walking."

They walked in silence and eventually, about mid-morning, reached Solace Bridge. The bridge spanned Solace Stream, an easy-going, meandering brook that wandered around the foothills of the Sentinel Mountains and then tumbled blithely through South Pass until it reached the White Rage River. The bridge was wide in order to accommodate wagons and teams of horses as well as foot traffic.

In the old days, the bridge had been free for the use of the traveler, but as traffic increased over the bridge, so did the maintenance and the upkeep of the span. The Solace city fathers grew weary of spending tax money to keep the bridge in operation and so they erected a tollgate and added a toll-taker. The fee required was modest. Solace Stream was shallow, you could walk across it in places, and travelers could always cross at other fords along the route. However, the banks through which the stream ran were steep and slippery. More than one wagon load of valuable merchandise had ended up in the water. Most travelers elected to pay the toll.

The Knight and the kender were the only ones crossing this time of day. The toll-taker was eating breakfast in his booth. Two horses were tied up beneath a stand of cottonwood trees that grew along the bank. A young lad who looked and smelled like a stable hand dozed on the grass. One of the horses was glossy black, his coat gleamed in the sunlight. He was restive, pawed the ground and occasionally gave a jerk on the reins as a test to see if he could free himself. The other mount was a small pony, dapple gray, with a bright eye and twitching ears and nose. Her hooves were almost completely covered by long strands of fur.

The constricting snake around Tas's heart eased up a good deal at the sight of the pony, who seemed to regard the kender with a friendly, if somewhat mischievous, eye.

"Is she mine?" Tas asked, thrilled beyond belief.

"No," said Gerard. "The horses have been hired for the journey, that is all."

He kicked at the stable hand, who woke up and, yawning and scratching at himself, said that they owed him thirty steel for the horses, saddles, and blankets, ten of which would be given back to them upon the animals' safe return. Gerard took out his money purse and counted out the coin. The stable hand—keeping as far from Tasslehoff as possible—counted the money over again distrustfully, deposited it in a sack and stuffed the sack in his straw-covered shirt.

"What's the pony's name?" asked Tasslehoff, delighted.

"Little Gray," said the stable hand.

Tas frowned. "That doesn't show much imagination. I think you could have come up with something more original than that. What's the black horse's name?"

"Blackie," replied the stable hand, picking his teeth with a straw.

Tasslehoff sighed deeply.

The tollbooth keeper emerged from his little house. Gerard handed him the amount of the toll. The keeper raised the gate. This done, he eyed the Knight and kender with intense curiosity and seemed prepared to spend the rest of the morning discussing where the two were headed and why.

Gerard answered shortly, "yay" or "nay" as might be required. He hoisted Tasslehoff onto the pony, who swiveled her head to look back at him and winked at him as if they shared some wonderful secret. Gerard placed the mysterious bundle and the sword wrapped in the blanket on the back of his own horse, tied them securely. He took hold of the reins of Tas's pony and mounted his own horse, then rode off, leaving the toll-taker standing on the bridge talking to himself.

The Knight rode in front, keeping hold of the pony's reins. Tas rode behind, his manacled hands holding tight to the pommel of the saddle. Blackie didn't seem to like the gray pony much better than Gerard liked the kender. Perhaps Blackie was resentful of the slow pace he was forced to set to accommodate the pony or perhaps he was a horse of a stern and serious nature who took umbrage at a certain friskiness exhibited by the pony. Whatever the reason, if the black horse caught the gray pony doing a little sideways shuffle for the sheer fun of it, or if he thought she might be tempted to stop and nibble at some buttercups on the side of the road, he would turn his head and regard her and her rider with a cold eye.

They had ridden about five miles when Gerard called a halt. He stood in his saddle, looked up and down the road. They had not met any travelers since they had left the bridge, and now the road was completely empty. Dismounting, Gerard removed his cloak and rolling it up, he stuffed it in his bedroll. He was wearing the black breastplate decorated with skulls and the death lily of a Dark Knight.

"What a great disguise!" Tas exclaimed, charmed. "You told Lord Warren you were going to be a Knight and you didn't lie. You just didn't tell him what sort of Knight you were going to become. Do I get to be disguised as a Dark Knight? I mean a Neraka Knight? Oh, no, I get it! Don't tell me. I'm going to be your prisoner!" Tasslehoff was quite proud of himself for having figured this out. "This is going to be more fun—er, interesting—than I'd expected."

Gerard did not smile. "This is not a joy ride, kender," he said and his voice was stern and grim. "You hold my life and your own in your hands, as well as the fate of our mission. I must be a fool, to trust something so important to one of your kind, but I have no choice. We will soon be entering the territory controlled by the Knights of Neraka. If you breathe a word about my being a Solamnic Knight, I will be arrested and executed as a spy. But first, before they kill me, they will torture me to find out what I know. They use the rack to torture people. Have you ever seen a man stretched upon the rack, kender?"

"No, but I saw Caramon do calisthenics once, and he said that was torture. . . ."

Gerard ignored him. "They tie your hands and feet to the rack and then pull them in opposite directions. Your arms and legs, wrists and elbows, knees and ankles are pulled from their sockets. The pain is excruciating, but the beauty of the torture is that though the victim suffers terribly, he doesn't die. They can keep a man on the rack for days. The bones never return to their proper place. When they take a man off the rack, he is a cripple. They have to carry him to the scaffold, put him in a chair in order to hang him. That will be my fate if you betray me, kender. Do you understand?"

"Yes, Sir Gerard," said Tasslehoff. "And even though you don't like me, which I have to tell you really hurts my feelings, I wouldn't want to see you stretched on the rack. Maybe someone else—because I never saw anyone's arm pulled out of its socket before—but not you."

Gerard did not appear impressed by this magnanimous offer. "Keep a curb on your tongue for your sake as well as mine."

"I promise," said Tas, putting his hand to his topknot and giving it a painful yank that brought tears to his eyes. "I *can* keep a secret, you know. I've kept any number of secrets—important secrets, too. I'll keep this one. You can depend on me or my name's not Tasslehoff Burrfoot."

This appeared to impress Gerard even less. Looking very dour, he returned to his horse, remounted and rode forward—a Dark Knight leading his prisoner.

"How long will it take us to reach Qualinesti?" Tas asked.

"At this pace, four days," Gerard replied.

Four days. Gerard paid no more attention to the kender. The Knight refused to answer a single question. He was deaf to Tasslehoff's very best and most wonderful stories, and did not bother to respond when Tas suggested that he knew a most exciting short cut through Darken Wood.

"Four days of this! I don't like to complain," Tas said, talking to himself and the pony since the Knight wasn't listening, "but this adventure is turning out to be dull and boring. Not really an adventure at all, more of a drudge, if that is a word, which whether it is or not certainly fits the situation."

He and the pony plodded along, looking forward to four days with no one to talk to, nothing to do, nothing to see except trees and mountains, which would have been interesting if Tas could have spent some time exploring them, but, as he couldn't, he'd seen plenty of trees and mountains at a distance before. So bored was the kender that the next time the magical device came back to him, appearing suddenly in his manacled hands, Tasslehoff was tempted to use it. Anything, even getting squished by a giant, would be better than this. If it hadn't been for the pony ride, he would have.

At that moment, the black horse looked around to regard the pony balefully and perhaps some sort of communication passed between horse and rider for Gerard turned around too.

Grinning sheepishly and shrugging, Tas held up the Device of Time Journeying.

His face fixed and cold as that of the skull on his black breastplate, Gerard halted, waited for the pony to plod up beside him. He reached out his hand, snatched the magical device from Tas's hands, and, without a word, thrust the device in a saddlebag.

Tasslehoff sighed again. It was going to be a long four days.

10   LORD OF THE NIGHT

The Order of the Knights of Takhisis was born in a dream of darkness and founded upon a remote and secret island in Krynn's far north, an island known as Storm's Keep. But the island headquarters had been severely damaged during the Chaos War. Boiling seas completely submerged the fortress—some said due to the sea goddess Zeboim's grief at the death of her son, the Knights' founder, Lord Ariakan. Although the waters receded, no one ever returned to it. The fortress was now deemed too remote to be of practical use to the Knights of Takhisis, who had emerged from the Chaos War battered and bruised, bereft of their Queen and her Vision, but with a sizeable force, a force to be reckoned with.

Thus it was that a Knight of the Skull, Mirielle Abrena, attending the first Council of the Last Heroes, felt confident enough to demand that the remnant of the Knighthood that remained be granted land on the continent of Ansalon in return for their heroic deeds during the war. The council allowed the Knights to keep territory they had captured, mainly Qualinesti (as usual, few humans cared much about the elves) and also the land in the northeastern part of Ansalon that included Neraka and its environs. The Dark Knights accepted this region, blasted and cursed though parts of it were, and set about building up their Order.

Many on that first council hoped the Knights would suffocate and perish in the sulphur-laden air of Neraka. The Dark Knights not only survived, but thrived. This was due in part to the leadership of Abrena, Lord of the Night, who added to that military title the political title of governor-general of Neraka. Abrena instituted a new recruitment policy, a policy that was not so choosy as the old policy, not so nice, not so restrictive. The Knights had little problem filling their ranks. In the dark days following the Chaos War, the people felt alone and abandoned. What might be called the Ideal of the Great "I" arose on Ansalon. Its main precept: "No one else matters. Only I."

Embracing this precept, the Dark Knights were clever in their rule. They did not permit much in the way of personal freedoms, but they did encourage trade and promote business. When Khellendros, the great blue dragon, captured the city of Palanthas, he placed the Dark Knights in charge. Terrified at the thought of these cruel overlords ravishing their city, the people of Palanthas were amazed to find that they actually prospered under the rulership of the Dark Knights. And although the Palanthians were taxed for the privilege, they were able to keep enough of their profits to believe that life under the dictatorial rule of the Dark Knights wasn't all that bad. The knights kept law and order, they waged continuous war against the Thieves Guild, and they sought to rid the city of the gully dwarves residing in the sewers.

The dragon purge that followed the arrival of the great dragons at first appalled and angered the Knights of Takhisis, who lost many of their own dragons in the slaughter. In vain the Knights fought against the great Red, Malys, and her cousins. Many of the Knights' order died, as did many of their chromatic dragons. Mirielle's cunning leadership managed to turn even this near disaster into a triumph. The Dark Knights made secret pacts with the dragons, agreeing to work for them to collect tribute and maintain law and order in lands ruled by the dragons. In return, the dragons would give the Dark Knights a free hand and cease preying upon their surviving dragons.

The people of Palanthas, Neraka, and Qualinesti knew nothing of the pact made between the Knights and the Dragons. The people saw only that once again the Dark Knights had defended them against a terrible foe. The Knights of Solamnia and the mystics of the Citadel of Light knew or guessed of these pacts but could not prove anything.

Although there were some within the ranks of the Dark Knights who still held to the beliefs of honor and self-sacrifice expounded by the late Ariakan, they were mostly the older members, who were considered out of touch with the ways of the modern world. A new Vision had come to replace the old. This new Vision was based on the mystical powers of the heart developed by Goldmoon in the Citadel of Light and stolen by several Skull Knights, who disguised themselves and secretly entered the Citadel to learn how to use these powers for their own ambitious ends. The Dark Knight mystics came away with healing skills and, more frightening, the ability to manipulate their followers' thoughts.

Armed with the ability to control not only the bodies of those who entered the Knighthood but their minds as well, the Skull Knights rose to prominence within the ranks of the Dark Knights. Although the Dark Knights had long and loudly maintained that Queen Takhisis was going to return, they had ceased to believe it. They had ceased to believe in anything except their own power and might, and this was reflected in the new Vision. The Skull Knights who administered the new Vision were adept at probing a candidate's mind, finding his most secret terrors and playing upon those, while at the same time promising him his heart's desire—all in return for strict obedience.

So powerful did the Skull Knights grow through the use of the new Vision that those closest to Mirielle Abrena began to look upon the Skull Knights with distrust. In particular, they warned Abrena against the leader, the Adjudicator, a man named Morham Targonne.

Abrena scoffed at these warnings. "Targonne is an able administrator," she said. "I grant him that much. But, when all is said and done, what *is* an able administrator? Nothing more than a glorified clerk. And that is Targonne. He would never challenge me for leadership. The man grows queasy at the sight of blood! He refuses to attend the jousts or tourneys but keeps himself locked up in his dingy little cabinet, absorbed in his debits and his credits. He has no stomach for battle."

Abrena spoke truly. Targonne had no stomach for battle. He would have never dreamed of challenging Abrena for the leadership in honorable combat. The sight of blood really did make him sick. And so he had her poisoned.

As Lord of the Skull Knights, Targonne announced at Abrena's funeral that he was the rightful successor. No one stood to challenge him. Those who might have done so, friends and supporters of Abrena's, kept their mouths shut, lest they ingest the same "tainted meat" that had killed their leader. Eventually Targonne killed them too, so that by now he was firmly entrenched in power. He and those Knights who were trained in mentalism used their powers to delve into the minds of their followers to ferret out traitors and malcontents.

Targonne came from a wealthy family with extensive holdings in Neraka. The family's roots were in Jelek, a city north of what had formerly been the capital city of Neraka. The Targonne family's motto was the Great "I," which could have been entwined with the Great "P" for profit. They had risen to wealth and power with the rise of Queen Takhisis, first by supplying arms and weapons to the leaders of her armies, then, when it appeared that their side was losing, by supplying arms and weapons to the armies of Takhisis's enemies. Using the wealth obtained from the sale of weapons, the Targonnes bought up land, particularly the scarce and valuable agricultural land in Neraka.

The scion of the Targonne family had even had the incredible good fortune (he claimed it was foresight) to pull his money out of the city of Neraka only days before the Temple exploded. After the War of the Lance, during the days when Neraka was a defeated land, with roving bands of disenfranchised soldiers, goblins, and draconians, he was in sole possession of the two things people needed desperately: grain and steel.

It had been Abrena's ambition to build a fortress for the Dark Knights in southern Neraka, near the location of the old temple. She had the plans drawn up and sent in crews to start building. Such was the terror inspired by the accursed valley and its eerie and haunting Song of Death that the crews immediately fled. The capital city was shifted to the northern part of the Neraka valley, a site still too close to the southern part for the comfort of some.

One of Targonne's first orders of business was to move the capital city. The second was to change the name of the Knighthood. He established the headquarters of the Knights of Neraka in Jelek, close to the family business. Much closer to the family business than most of the Neraka Knights ever knew.

Jelek was now a highly prosperous and bustling city located at the intersection of the two major highways that ran through Neraka. Either by great good fortune or crafty dealing the city had escaped the ravages of the great dragons. Merchants from all over Neraka, even as far south as Khur, hastened to Jelek to start new businesses or to expand existing ones. So long as they made certain to stop by to pay the requisite fees to the Knights of Neraka and offer their respects to Lord of the Night and Governor-General Targonne, the merchants were welcome.

If respect for Targonne had a cold, substantial feel to it and made a fine clinking sound when deposited together with other demonstrations of respect in the Lord of the Night's large money box, the merchants knew better than to complain. Those who did complain or those who considered that verbal marks of respect were sufficient found that their businesses suffered severe and sudden reverses of fortune. If they persisted in their misguided notions, they were generally found dead in the street, having accidentally slipped and fallen backward onto a dagger.

Targonne personally designed the Neraka Knights' fortress that loomed large over the city of Jelek. He had the fortress built on the city's highest promontory with a commanding view of the city and the surrounding valley.

The fortress was practical in shape and design—innumerable squares and rectangles stacked one on top of the other, with squared-off towers. What windows there were—and there weren't many—were arrow-slits. The exterior and interior walls of the fortress were plain and unadorned. So stark and grim was the fortress that it was often mistaken by visitors for either a prison or a countinghouse. The sight of black-armored figures patrolling the walls soon corrected their first impression, which wasn't, after all, so very far wrong. The below-ground level of the fortress housed an extensive dungeon and, two levels below that and more heavily guarded, was the Knights' Treasury.

Lord of the Night Targonne had his headquarters and his living quarters in the fortress. Both were economical in design, strictly functional, and if the fortress was mistaken for a countinghouse, its commander was often mistaken for a clerk. A visitor to the Lord of the Night was led into a small, cramped office with bare walls and a sparse scattering of furniture, there to wait while a small, bald, bespectacled man dressed in somber, though well-made clothes, completed his work of copying figures in a great leather-bound ledger.

Thinking that he was in the presence of some minor functionary, who would eventually take him to the Lord of the Night, the visitor would often roam restlessly about the room, his thoughts wandering here and there. Those thoughts were snagged in midair, like butterflies in a web, by the man behind the desk. This man used his mentalist powers to delve into every portion of the visitor's mind. After a suitable length of time had passed, during which the spider had sucked his captive dry, the man would raise his bald head, peer through his spectacles, and acquaint the appalled visitor with the fact that he was in the presence of Lord of the Night Targonne.

The visitor who sat in the lord's presence this day knew very well that the mild looking man seated across from him was his lord and governor. The visitor was second in command to Lord Milles and, although Sir Roderick had not yet met Targonne, he had seen him in attendance at certain formal functions of the Knighthood. The Knight stood at attention, holding himself straight and stiff until his presence should be acknowledged. Having been warned about Targonne's mentalist capabilities, the Knight attempted to keep his thoughts stiffly in line as well, with less success. Before Sir Roderick even spoke, Lord Targonne knew a great deal of what had happened at the siege of Sanction. He never liked to exhibit his powers, however. He asked the Knight, in a mild voice, to be seated.

Sir Roderick, who was tall and brawny and could have lifted Targonne off the floor by the coat collar with very little exertion, took a seat in the only other chair in the office and sat on the chair's edge, tense, rigid.

Perhaps due to the fact that he had come to resemble what he most loved, the eyes of Morham Targonne resembled nothing so much as two steel coins—flat, shining, and cold. One looked into those eyes and saw not a soul, but numbers and figures in the ledger of Targonne's mind. Everything he looked upon was reduced to debits and credits, profits and loss, all weighed in the balance, counted to the penny, and chalked up into one column or another.

Sir Roderick saw himself reflected in the shining steel of those cold eyes and felt himself being moved into a column of unnecessary expenditures. He wondered if it was true that the spectacles were artifacts salvaged from the ruins of Neraka and that they gave the wearer the ability to see into one's brain. Roderick began to sweat in his armor, though the fortress with its massive stone and concrete walls was always cool, even during the warmest months of the summer.

"My aide tells me you have come from Sanction, Sir Roderick," said Targonne, his voice the voice of a clerk, mild and pleasant and unassuming. "How goes our siege of the city?"

It should be noted here that the Targonne family had extensive holdings in the city of Sanction, holdings they had lost when the Knights of Neraka lost Sanction. Targonne had made the taking of Sanction one of the top priorities for the Knighthood.

Sir Roderick had rehearsed his speech on the two-day ride from Sanction to Jelek and he was prepared with his answer.

"Excellency, I am here to report that on the day after Midyear Day, an attempt was made by the accursed Solamnics to break the siege of Sanction and to try to drive off our armies. The foul Knights endeavored to trick my commander, Lord Milles, into attacking by making him think they had abandoned the city. Lord Milles saw through their plot and he, in turn, led them into a trap. By launching an attack against the city of Sanction, Lord Milles lured the Knights out of hiding. He then faked a retreat. The Knights took the bait and pursued our forces. At Beckard's Cut, Lord Milles ordered our troops to turn and make a stand. The Solamnics were summarily defeated, many of their number killed or wounded. They were forced to retreat back inside Sanction. Lord Milles is pleased to report, Excellency, that the valley in which our armies are encamped remains safe and secure."

Sir Roderick's words went into Targonne's ears. Sir Roderick's thoughts went into Targonne's mind. Sir Roderick was recalling quite vividly fleeing for his life in front of the rampaging Solamnics, alongside Lord Milles who, commanding from the rear, had been caught up in the retreating stampede. And elsewhere in the mind of the Knight was a picture Targonne found very interesting, also rather disturbing. That picture was that of a young woman in black armor, exhausted and stained with blood, receiving the homage and accolades of Lord Milles's troops. Targonne heard her name resound in Roderick's mind: "Mina! Mina!"

With the tip of his pen the Lord of the Night scratched the thin mustache that covered his upper lip. "Indeed. It sounds a great victory. Lord Milles is to be congratulated."

"Yes, Excellency." Sir Roderick smiled, pleased. "Thank you, Excellency."

"It would have been a greater victory if Lord Milles had actually captured the city of Sanction as he has been ordered, but I suppose he will attend to that little matter when he finds it convenient."

Sir Roderick was no longer smiling. He started to speak, coughed, and spent a moment clearing his throat. "In point of fact, Excellency, we most likely would have been able to capture Sanction were it not for the mutinous actions of one of our junior officers. Completely contrary to Lord Milles's command, this officer pulled an entire company of archers from the fray, so that we had no covering fire necessary for us to launch an attack upon Sanction's walls. Not only that, but in her panic, this officer ordered the archers to shoot their arrows while our own soldiers were yet in the line of fire. The casualties we sustained were due completely to this officer's incompetence. Therefore Lord Milles felt it would not be wise to proceed with the attack."

"Dear, dear," Targonne murmured. "I trust this young officer has been dealt with summarily."

Sir Roderick licked his lips. This was the tricky part. "Lord Milles would have done so, Excellency, but he felt it would be best to consult with you first. A situation has arisen that makes it difficult for his lordship to know how to proceed. The young woman exerts some sort of magical and uncanny influence over the men, Excellency."

"Indeed?" Targonne appeared surprised. He spoke somewhat dryly. "The last I heard, the magical powers of our wizards were failing. I did not know any of our mages were this talented."

"She is not a magic-user, Excellency. Or at least, so she says. She claims to be a messenger sent by a god—the One, True God."

"And what is the name of this god?" Targonne asked.

"Ah, there she is quite clever, Excellency. She maintains that the name of the god is too holy to pronounce."

"Gods have come, and gods have gone," Targonne said impatiently. He was seeing a most astonishing and disquieting sight in Sir Roderick's mind, and he wanted to hear it from the man's lips. "Our soldiers would not be sucked in by such claptrap."

"Excellency, the woman does not make use of words alone. She performs miracles—miracles of healing the likes of which we have not seen in recent years due to the weakening of our mystics. This girl restores limbs that have been hacked off. She places her hands upon a man's chest, and the gaping hole in it closes over. She tells a man with a broken back that he can stand up, and he stands up! The only miracle she does not perform is raising the dead. Those she prays over."

Sir Roderick heard the creaking of a chair, looked up to see Targonne's steel eyes gleaming unpleasantly.

"Of course"—Sir Roderick hastened to correct his mistake—"Lord Milles knows that these are not miracles, Excellency. *He* knows that she is a charlatan. It's just that we can't seem to figure out how she does it," he added lamely. "And the men are quite taken with her."

Targonne understood with alarm that all of the foot soldiers and most of the Knights had mutinied, were refusing to obey Milles. They had transferred their allegiance to some shaven-headed chit in black armor.

"How old is this girl?" Targonne asked, frowning.

"She is reputed to be no more than seventeen, Excellency," Sir Roderick replied.

"Seventeen!" Targonne was aghast. "Whatever induced Milles to make her an officer in the first place?"

"He did not, Excellency," said Sir Roderick. "She is not part of our wing. None of us had ever seen her before her arrival in the valley just prior to the battle."

"Could she be a Solamnic in disguise?" Targonne wondered.

"I doubt that, Excellency. It was due to her that the Solamnics lost the battle," Sir Roderick replied, completely unconscious that the truth he had just now spoken accorded ill with the fabrications he'd pronounced earlier.

Targonne noted the inconsistency but was too absorbed in the clicking abacus of his mind to pay any attention to them, beyond marking down that Milles was an incompetent bungler who should be replaced as speedily as possible. Targonne rang a silver bell that stood upon his desk. The door to the office opened, and his aide entered.

"Look through the rolls of the Knighthood," Targonne ordered. "Locate a—What is her name?" he asked Roderick, though he could hear it echo in the Knight's mind.

"Mina, Excellency."

"Meenaa," Targonne repeated, holding the name in his mouth as if he were tasting it. "Nothing else? No surname?"

"Not to my knowledge, Excellency."

The aide departed, dispatched several clerks to undertake the task. The two Knights sat in silence while the search was being conducted. Targonne took advantage of the time to continue to sift through Roderick's mind, which affirmed his surmise that the siege against Sanction was being handled by a nincompoop. If it hadn't been for this girl, the siege might well have been broken, the Dark Knights defeated, annihilated, the Solamnics in triumphant and unhindered possession of Sanction.

The aide returned. "We find no knight named 'Mina' on the rolls, Excellency. Nothing even close."

Targonne made a dismissive gesture, and the aide departed.

"Brilliant, Excellency!" Sir Roderick exclaimed. "She is an imposter. We can have her arrested and executed."

"Hunh." Targonne grunted. "And just what do you think your soldiers will do in that instance, Sir Roderick? Those she has healed? Those she has led to victory against the detested foe? The morale among Milles's troops was not that good to begin with." Targonne flipped a hand at a stack of ledgers. "I've read the reports. The desertion rate is five times higher among Milles's troops than with any other commander in the army.

"Tell me this"—Targonne eyed the other Knight shrewdly—"are you capable of having this Mina girl arrested? Do you have guards who will obey your order? Or will they most likely arrest Lord Milles instead?"

Sir Roderick opened his mouth and shut it again without replying. He looked around the room, looked at the ceiling, looked anywhere but into those steel eyes, horribly magnified by the thick glass of the spectacles, but still he seemed to see them boring into his skull.

Targonne clicked the beads upon his mental abacus. The girl was an imposter, masquerading as a Knight. She had arrived at the moment she was most needed. In the face of terrible defeat, she had achieved stunning victory. She performed "miracles" in the name of a nameless god.

Was she an asset or a liability?

If liability, could she be turned into an asset?

Targonne abhorred waste. An excellent administrator and a shrewd bargainer, he knew where and how every steel coin was spent. He was not a miser. He made certain that the Knighthood had the best quality weapons and armor, he made certain that the recruits and mercenaries were paid well. He was adamant that his officers keep accurate records of monies paid out to them.

The soldiers wanted to follow this Mina. Very well. Let them follow her. Targonne had that very morning received a message from the great dragon Malystryx wanting to know why he permitted the Silvanesti elves to defy her edicts by maintaining a magical shield over their land and refusing to pay her tribute. Targonne had prepared a letter to send in return explaining to the dragon that attacking Silvanesti would be a waste of time and manpower that could be used elsewhere to more profit. Scouts sent to investigate the magical shield had reported that the shield was impossible to penetrate, that no weapon—be it steel or sorcery—had the slightest effect on the shield. One might hurl an entire army at it—so said his scouts—and one would achieve nothing.

Add to this the fact that an army heading into Silvanesti must first travel through Blöde, the homeland of the ogres. Former allies of the Dark Knights, the ogres had been infuriated when the Knights of Neraka expanded south-ward, taking over the ogres' best land and driving them into the mountains, killing hundreds in the process. Reports indicated that the ogres were currently hounding the dark elf Alhana Starbreeze and her forces somewhere near the shield. But if the Knights advanced into ogre lands, the ogres would be quite happy to leave off attacking elves—something they could do any time—to take vengeance on the ally who had betrayed them.

The letter was on his desk, awaiting his signature. It had been on his desk for several days. Targonne was fully aware that this letter of refusal would infuriate the dragon, but he was much better prepared to face Malys's fury than throw away valuable resources in a hopeless cause. Reaching for the letter, Targonne picked it up and slowly and thoughtfully tore it into small pieces.

The only god Targonne believed in was a small, round god that could stacked up in neat piles in his treasure room. He did not believe for a moment that this girl was a messenger from the gods. He did not believe in her miracles of healing or in the miracle of her generalship. Unlike the wretched and imbecilic Sir Roderick, Targonne didn't feel a need to explain how she had done what she had done. All he needed to know was that she was doing it for the benefit of the Knights of Neraka—and that which benefitted the Knights benefitted Morham Targonne.

He would give her a chance to perform a "miracle." He would send this imposter Knight and her addle-pated followers to attack and capture Silvanesti. By making a small investment of a handful of soldiers, Targonne would please the dragon, keep Malys happy. The dangerous Mina girl and her forces would be wiped out, but the loss would be offset by the gain. Let her die in the wilderness somewhere, let some ogre munch on her bones for his supper. That would be an end to the chit and her "nameless" god.

Targonne smiled upon Sir Roderick and even left his desk to walk the Knight to the door. He watched until the black-armored figure had marched down the echoing, empty hallways of the fortress, then summoned his aide to his office.

He dictated a letter to Malystryx, explaining his plan for the capture of Silvanesti. He issued an order to the commander of the Knights of Neraka in Khur to march his forces west to join the siege of Sanction, take over command from Lord Milles. He issued an order commanding Talon Leader Mina and a company of hand-picked soldiers to march south, there to attack and capture the great elven nation of Silvanesti.

"And what of Lord Milles, Excellency?" his aide asked. "Is he to be reassigned? Where is he to be sent?"

Targonne considered the matter. He was in an excellent humor, a feeling which normally came with the closing of an extremely good business deal.

"Send Milles to report in person to Malystryx. He can tell her the story of his great 'victory' over the Solamnics. I'm sure she will be very interested to hear how he fell into an enemy trap and in so doing came close to losing all that we have fought so hard to gain."

"Yes, Excellency." The aide gathered up his papers and prepared to return to his desk to execute the documents. "Shall I take Lord Milles off the rolls?" he asked, as an afterthought.

Targonne had returned to his ledger. He adjusted the spectacles carefully on his nose, picked up his pen, waved a negligent hand in acquiescence, and returned to his credits and debits, his additions and subtractions.

11   THE SONG OF LORAC

While Tasslehoff was near dying of boredom on the road to Qualinesti and while Sir Roderick was returning to Sanction, blissfully unaware that he had just delivered his commander into the jaws of the dragon, Silvanoshei and Rolan of the kirath began their journey to place Silvanoshei upon the throne of Silvanesti. Rolan's plan was to move close to the capital city of Silvanost, but not to enter it until word spread through the city that the true head of House Royal was returning to claim his rightful place as Speaker of the Stars.

"How long will that take?" Silvan asked with the impatience and impetuosity of youth.

"The news will travel faster than we will, Your Majesty," Rolan replied. "Drinel and the other kirath who were with us two nights ago have already left to spread it. They will tell every other kirath they meet and any of the Wildrunners they feel that they can trust. Most of the soldiers are loyal to General Konnal, but there are a few who are starting to doubt him. They do not openly state their opposition yet, but Your Majesty's arrival should do much to change that. The Wildrunners have always sworn allegiance to House Royal. As Konnal himself will be obliged to do—or at least make a show of doing."

"How long will it take us to reach Silvanost, then?" Silvanoshei asked.

"We will leave the trail and travel the Thon-Thalas by boat," Rolan responded. "I plan to take you to my house, which is located on the outskirts of the city. We should arrive in two days time. We will take a third day to rest and to receive the reports that will be coming in by then. Four days from now, Your Majesty, if all goes well, you will enter the capital in triumph."

"Four days!" Silvan was skeptical. "Can so much be accomplished that fast?"

"In the days when we fought the dream, we kirath could send a message from the north of Silvanesti into the far reaches of the south in a single day. I am not exaggerating, Your Majesty," Rolan said, smiling at Silvanoshei's obvious skepticism. "We accomplished such a feat many times over. We were highly organized then, and there were many more of us than there are now. But I believe that Your Majesty will be impressed, nevertheless."

"I am already impressed, Rolan," Silvanoshei replied. "I am deeply indebted to you and the others of the kirath. I will find some way of repaying you."

"Free our people from this dreadful scourge, Your Majesty," Rolan answered, his eyes shadowed with sorrow, "and that will be payment enough."

Despite his praise, Silvanoshei still harbored doubts, though he kept them to himself. His mother's army was well organized, yet even she would make plans, only to see them go awry. Ill luck, miscommunication, bad weather, any one of these or a host of other misfortunes could turn a day that had seemed meant for victory into disaster.

"No plan ever survives contact with the enemy," was one of Samar's dictums, a dictum that had proven tragically true.

Silvan anticipated disasters, delays. If the boat Rolan promised even existed, it would have a hole in it or it would have been burned to cinders. The river would be too low or too high, run too swift or too slow. Winds would blow them upstream instead of down or down when they wanted to travel up.

Silvan was vastly astonished to find the small boat at the river landing where Rolan had said it would be, perfectly sound and in good repair. Not only that, but the boat had been filled with food packed in waterproof sacks and stowed neatly in the prow.

"As you see, Your Majesty," Rolan said, "the kirath have been here ahead of us."

The Thon-Thalas River was calm and meandering this time of year. The boat, made of tree bark, was small and light and so well balanced that one would have to actively work to tip it over. Well knowing that Rolan would never think of asking the future Speaker of the Stars to help row, Silvan volunteered his assistance. Rolan at first demurred, but he could not argue with his future ruler and so at last he agreed and handed Silvanoshei a paddle. Silvan saw that he had earned the elder elf's respect by this act, a pleasant change for the young man, who, it seemed, had always earned Samar's disrespect.

Silvan enjoyed the exercise that burned away some of his pent-up energy. The river was placid, the forests through which it flowed were green and verdant. The weather was fine, but Silvan could not say that the day was beautiful. The sun shone through the shield. He could see blue sky through the shield. But the sun that shone on Silvanesti was not the same fiercely burning orb of orange fire that shone on the rest of Ansalon. The sun Silvan looked upon was a pale and sickly yellow, the yellow of jaundiced skin, the yellow of an ugly bruise. It was as if he were looking at a reflection of the sun, floating facedown, drowned in a pool of stagnant, oily water. The yellow sun altered the color of the sky from azure blue to a hard metallic blue-green. Silvan did not look long at the sun but instead shifted his gaze to the forest.

"Do you know a song to ease our labors?" he called out to Rolan who was seated in the front of the boat.

The kirath paddled with quick, strong strokes, digging his paddle deep into the water. The far-younger Silvan was hard pressed to keep pace with his elder.

Rolan hesitated, glanced back over his shoulder. "There is a song that is a favorite of the kirath, but I fear it may displease His Majesty. It is a song that tells the story of your honored grandfather, King Lorac."

"Does it start out, 'The Age of Might it was, the Age of the Kingpriest and his minions?' " Silvan asked, singing the melody tentatively. He had only heard the song once before.

"That is the beginning, Your Majesty," Rolan replied.

"Sing it for me," Silvan said. "My mother sang it once to me on the day I turned thirty. That was the first time I had ever heard the story of my grandfather. My mother never spoke of him before, nor has she spoken of him since. To honor her, none of the other elves speak of him either."

"I, too, honor your mother, who gathered roses in the Garden of Astarin when she was your age. And I understand her pain. We share in that pain every time we sing this song, for as Lorac was snared by his own hubris into betraying his country, so we who took the easy way out, who fled our land and left him to do battle alone, were also at fault.

"If all our people had stayed to fight, if all our people—those of House Royal to House Servitor, those of House Protector, House Mystic, House Mason—if we had all joined together and stood shoulder to shoulder, regardless of caste, against the dragonarmies, then I believe that we could have saved our land.

"But you shall hear the full tale in the song.

SONG OF LORAC

The Age of Might it was,
the Age of the Kingpriest and
his minions.
Jealous of the wizards, the Kingpriest
said, "You will hand over your high Towers
to me and you will fear me and obey me."
The wizards gave over their High Towers, the last
the Tower of Palanthas.

Comes to the Tower Lorac Caladon, King of the Silvanesti,
to take his Test in magic before the closing of the Tower.
In his Test, one of the dragon orbs,
fearful of falling into the hands
of the Kingpriest and his minions,
speaks to Lorac.

"You must not leave me here in Istar.
If you do, I will be lost and the world will perish."
Lorac obeys the voice of the dragon orb,
hides the orb away.
carries it with him from the Tower,
carries the orb back to Silvanesti,
holds the orb in secret, hugging his secret to him,
never telling anyone.

Comes the Cataclysm. Comes Takhisis, Queen of Darkness,
with her dragons, mighty and powerful.
Comes war. War to Silvanesti.
Lorac summons all his people, orders them to flee their homelands
Orders them away.
Says to them,
"I alone will be the savior of the people."
"I alone will stop the Queen of Darkness."

Away the people.
Away the loved daughter, Alhana Starbreeze.
Alone, Lorac hears the voice of the dragon orb,
calling his name, calling to him to come to the darkness.
Lorac heeds the call.
Descends into darkness.
Puts his hands upon the dragon orb and
the dragon orb puts its hands upon Lorac.
Comes the dream.
Comes the dream to Silvanesti,
dream of horror,
dream of fear,
dream of trees that bleed the blood of elvenkind,
dream of tears forming rivers,
dream of death.

Comes a dragon,
Cyan Bloodbane,
minion of Takhisis,
to hiss into Lorac's ear the terrors of the dream.
To hiss the words, "I alone have the power to save the people.
I alone." To mock the words, "I alone have the power to save."
The dream enters the land,
kills the land,
twists the trees, trees that bleed,
fills the rivers with the tears of the people,
the tears of Lorac,
held in thrall by the orb and by Cyan Bloodbane,

minion of Queen Takhisis,
minion of evil,
who alone has the power.

"I can understand why my mother does not like to hear that song," Silvan said when the last long-held, sweet, sad note drifted over the water, to be echoed by a sparrow. "And why our people do not like to remember it."

"Yet, they should remember it," said Rolan. "The song would be sung daily, if I had my way. Who knows but that the song of our own days will be just as tragic, just as terrible? We have not changed. Lorac Caladon believed that he was strong enough to wield the dragon orb, though he had been warned against it by all the wise. Thus he was snared, and thus he fell. Our people, in their fear, chose to flee rather than to stand and fight. And thus in fear today we cower under this shield, sacrificing the lives of some of our people in order to save a dream."

"A dream?" Silvan asked. He was thinking of Lorac's dream, the dream of the song.

"I do not refer to the whispers of the dragon," said Rolan. "That dream is gone, but the sleeper refuses to wake and thus another dream has come to take its place. A dream of the past. A dream of the glories of days that have gone. I do not blame them," Rolan added, sighing. "I, too, love to think upon what has gone and long to regain it. But those of us who fought alongside your father know that the past can never be recovered, nor should it be. The world has changed, and we must change with it. We must become a part of it, else we will sicken and die in the prison house in which we have locked ourselves."

Rolan ceased paddling for a moment. He turned in the boat to face Silvan. "Do you understand what I am saying, Your Majesty?"

"I think so," said Silvan cautiously. "I am of the world, so to speak. I come from the outside. I am the one who can lead our people out into the world."

"Yes, Your Majesty." Rolan smiled.

"So long as I avoid the sin of hubris," Silvan said, ceasing his paddling, thankful for the rest. He grinned when he said it for he meant it teasingly, but on reflection, he became more serious. "Pride, the family failing," Silvan said, half to himself. "I am forewarned, and that is forearmed, they say."

Picking up his paddle, he fell to work with a will.

The pallid sun sank down behind the trees. Day languished, as if it too was one of the victims of the wasting sickness. Rolan watched the bank, searching for a suitable site to moor for the night. Silvan watched the opposite shore and so he saw first what the kirath missed.

"Rolan!" Silvan whispered urgently. "Pull for the western shore! Quickly!"

"What is it, Your Majesty?" Rolan was quick to take alarm. "What do you see?"

"There! On the eastern bank! Don't you see them? Hurry! We are nearly within arrow range!"

Rolan halted his rapid stroking. He turned around to smile sympathetically at Silvan. "You are no longer among the hunted, Your Majesty. Those people you see gathered on that bank are your own. They have come to look upon you and do you honor."

Silvan was astonished. "But . . . how do they know?"

"The kirath have been here, Your Majesty."

"So soon?"

"I told Your Majesty that we would spread the word rapidly."

Silvan blushed. "I am sorry, Rolan. I did not mean to doubt you. It's just that . . . My mother uses runners. They travel in secret, carrying messages between my mother and her sister by marriage, Laurana, in Qualinesti. Thus we are kept apprised of what is happening with our people in that realm. But it would take them many days to cover the same number of miles. . . . I had thought—"

"You thought I was exaggerating. You need make no apology for that, Your Majesty. You are accustomed to the world beyond the shield, a world that is large and filled with dangers that wax and wane daily, like the moon. Here in Silvanesti, we kirath know every path, every tree that stands on that path, every flower that grows beside it, ever squirrel that crosses it, every bird that sings in every branch, so many times have we run them. If that bird sings one false note, if that squirrel twitches its ears in alarm, we are aware of it. Nothing can surprise us. Nothing can stop us."

Rolan frowned. "That is why we of the kirath find it troubling that the dragon Cyan Bloodbane has so long eluded us. It is not possible that he should. And yet it is possible that he has."

The river carried them within sight of the elves standing on the western shoreline. Their houses were in the trees, houses a human would have probably never seen, for they were made of the living tree, whose branches had been lovingly coaxed into forming walls and roofs. Their nets were spread out upon the ground to dry, their boats pulled up onto the shore. There were not many elves, this was only a small fishing village, and yet it was apparent that the entire population had turned out. The sick had even been carried to the river's edge, where they lay wrapped in blankets and propped up with pillows.

Self-conscious, Silvan ceased paddling and rested his oar at the bottom of the boat.

"What do I do, Rolan?" he asked nervously.

Rolan looked back, smiled reassuringly. "You need only be yourself, Your Majesty. That is what they expect."

Rolan steered closer to the bank. The river seemed to run faster here, rushed Silvan toward the people before he was quite ready. He had ridden on parade with his mother to review the troops and had experienced the same uneasiness and sense of unworthiness that assailed him now.

The river brought him level with his people. He looked at them and nodded slightly and raised his hand in a shy wave. No one waved back. No one cheered, as he had been half-expecting. They watched him float upon the river in silence, a silence that was poignant and touched Silvan more deeply than the wildest cheering. He saw in their eyes, he heard in their silence, a wistful hopefulness, a hope in which they did not want to believe, for they had felt hope before and been betrayed.

Profoundly moved, Silvan ceased his waving and stretched out his hand to them, as if he saw them sinking and he could keep them above the water. The river bore him away from them, took him around a hill, and they were lost to his sight.

Humbled, he huddled in the stern and did not move nor speak. For the first time, he came to the full realization of the crushing burden he had taken upon himself. What could he do to help them? What did they expect of him? Too much, perhaps. Much too much.

Rolan glanced back every now and again in concern, but he said nothing, made no comment. He continued to paddle alone until he found a suitable place to beach the boat. Silvan roused himself and jumped into the water, helped to drag the boat up onto the bank. The water was icy cold and came as a pleasant shock. He submerged his worries and fears of his own inadequacies in the Thon-Thalas, was glad to have something to do to keep himself busy.

Accustomed to living out of doors, Silvan knew what needed to be done to set up camp. He unloaded the supplies, spread out the bedrolls, and began to prepare their light supper of fruit and flatbread, while Rolan secured the boat. They ate for the most part in silence, Silvan still subdued by the enormity of the responsibility he had accepted so blithely just two nights before and Rolan respecting his ruler's wish for quiet. The two made an early night of it. Wrapping themselves in their blankets, they left the woodland animals and night birds to stand watch over their slumbers.

Silvan fell asleep much sooner than he'd anticipated. He was wakened in the night by the hooting of an owl and sat up in fear, but Rolan, stirring, said the owl was merely calling to a neighbor, sharing the gossip of the darkness.

Silvan lay awake, listening to the mournful, haunting call and its answer, a solemn echo in some distant part of the forest. He lay awake long, staring up at the stars that shimmered uneasily above the shield, the Song of Lorac running swift like the river water through his mind.

> The tears of Lorac,
> held in thrall by the orb and by Cyan Bloodbane,
> minion of Queen Takhisis,
> minion of evil,
> who alone has the power.

The words and melody of the song were at this moment being echoed by a minstrel singing to entertain guests at a party in the captial city of Silvanost.

The party was being held in the Garden of Astarin on the grounds of the Tower of the Stars, where the Speaker of the Stars would live had there been a Speaker. The setting was beautiful. The Tower of the Stars was magically shaped of marble, for the elves will not cut or otherwise harm any part of the land, and thus the Tower had a fluid, organic feel to it, looking almost as if someone had formed it of melted wax. During Lorac's dream, the Tower had been hideously transformed, as were all the other structures in Silvanost. Elven mages worked long years to reshape the dwelling. They replaced the myriad jewels in the walls of the tall building, jewels which had once captured the light of the silver moon, Solinari, and the red moon, Lunitari, and used their blessed moonlight to illuminate the Tower's interior so that it seemed bathed in silver and in flame. The moons were gone now. A single moon only shone on Krynn and for some reason that the wise among the elves could not explain, the pale light of this single moon glittered in each jewel like a staring eye, bringing no light at all to the Tower, so that the elves were forced to resort to candles and torches.

Chairs had been placed among the plants in the Garden of Astarin. The plants appeared to be flourishing. They filled the air with their fragrance. Only Konnal and his gardeners knew that the plants in the garden had not grown there but had been carried there by the Woodshapers from their own private gardens, for no plants lived long now in the Garden of Astarin. No plants except one, a tree. A tree surrounded by a magical shield. A tree known as the Shield Tree, for from its root was said to have sprung the magical shield that protected Silvanesti.

The minstrel was singing the Song of Lorac in answer to a request from a guest at the party. The minstrel finished, ending the song on its sad note, her hand brushing lightly the strings of her lute.

"Bravo! Well sung! Let the song be sung again," came a lilting voice from the back row of seats.

The minstrel looked uncertainly at her host. The elven audience was much too polite and too well bred to indicate overt shock at the request, but a performer comes to know the mood of the audience by various subtle signs. The minstrel noted faintly flushed cheeks and sidelong embarrassed glances cast at their host. Once around for this song was quite enough.

"Who said that?" General Reyl Konnal, military governor of Silvanesti, twisted in his seat.

"Whom do you suppose, Uncle?" his nephew replied with a dark glance for the seats behind them. "The person who requested it be sung in the first place. Your friend, Glaucous."

General Konnal rose abruptly to his feet, a move that ended the evening's musical entertainment. The minstrel bowed, thankful to be spared so arduous a task as singing that song again. The audience applauded politely but without enthusiasm. A sigh that might have been expressive of relief joined the night breeze in rustling the trees whose intertwined branches formed a barren canopy above them, for many of the leaves had dropped off. Lanterns of silver filigree hung from the boughs, lighting the night. The guests left the small amphitheater, moved to a table that had been set up beside a reflecting pool, there to dine on sugared fruits and buttery shortbreads and to drink chilled wine.

Konnal invited the minstrel to partake of a late night morsel and personally escorted the woman to the table. The elf named Glaucous who had requested the song was already there, a cup of wine in his hand. Raising a toast to the minstrel, he was lavish in her praise.

"A pity you were not permitted to sing the song again," he said, glancing in the general's direction. "I never tire of that particular melody. And the poetry! My favorite part is when—"

"Might I offer you food and drink, Madame?" the nephew asked, responding to a nudge from his uncle.

The minstrel cast him a grateful glance and accepted his invitation. He led her to the table, where she was graciously received by the other guests. The grassy area on which Glaucous and the general stood was soon empty. Although many of the guests would have been pleased to bask in the the presence of the charming and attractive Glaucous and pay their share of flattery to General Konnal, they could tell at a glance that the general was angry.

"I don't know why I invite you to these parties, Glaucous," Konnal said, seething. "You always do something to embarrass me. It was bad enough you requested she sing that piece, and then to ask for it a second time!"

"Considered in light of the rumors I heard today," Glaucous returned languidly, "I thought the song of Lorac Caladon most appropriate."

Konnal shot his friend a sharp glance from beneath lowered brows. "I heard . . ." He paused, glanced at his guests. "Come, walk with me around the pond."

The two moved away from the other guests. Now free of the constraint of the general's presence, the elves gathered in small groups, their voices sibilant with suppressed excitement, eager to discuss the rumors that were the talk of the capital.

"We need not have left," Glaucous observed, looking back upon the refreshment table. "Everyone has heard the same thing."

"Yes, but they speak of it as rumor. I have confirmation," Konnal said grimly.

Glaucous halted. "You know this for a fact?"

"I have my sources among the kirath. The man saw him, spoke to him. The young man is said to be the image of his father. He is Silvanoshei Caladon, son of Alhana Starbreeze, grandson of the late and unlamented King Lorac."

"But that is impossible!" Glaucous stated. "The last we heard of the whereabouts of that accursed witch, his mother, she was lurking about outside the shield and her son was with her. He could not have come through the shield. Nothing and no one can penetrate the shield." Glaucous was quite firm on that point.

"Then his arrival must be a miracle, as they are claiming," Konnal said dryly, with a wave of his hand at his whispering guests.

"Bah! It is some imposter. You shake your head." Glaucous regarded the governor in disbelief. "You have actually swallowed this!"

"My source is Drinel. As you know, he has the skill of truth-seek," Konnal replied. "There can be no doubt. The young man passed the test. Drinel saw into his heart. He knows more about what happened to him than the young man does, apparently."

"So what *did* happen to him?" Glaucous asked with a slight lift of a delicate eyebrow.

"The night of that terrible storm, Alhana and her rebels were preparing to launch an all-out assault on the shield when their camp was overrun by ogres.

The young man went running to the Legion of Steel to beg the help of the humans—witness how low this woman has sunk—when he was dazzled by a lightning bolt. He slipped and fell down an embankment. He lost consciousness. Apparently, when he awoke, he was inside the shield."

Glaucous stroked his chin with his hand. The chin was well-formed, the face handsome. His almond eyes were large and penetrating. He could make no move that was not graceful. His complexion was flawless, his skin smooth and pale. His features were perfectly molded.

To human eyes, all elves are beautiful. The wise say this accounts for the animosity between the two races. Humans—even the most beautiful among them—cannot help but feel that they are ugly by comparison. The elves, who worship beauty, see gradations of beauty among their own kind, but they always see beauty. In a land of beauty, Glaucous was the most beautiful.

At this moment, Glaucous's beauty, his perfection, irritated Konnal beyond measure.

The general shifted his gaze to his pond. Two new swans glided over its mirrorlike surface. He wondered how long these two would live, hoped it would be longer than the last pair. He was spending a fortune in swans, but the pond was bleak and empty without them.

Glaucous was a favorite at court, which was odd considering that he was responsible for many members of the elven court losing their positions, influence, and power. But then, no one ever blamed Glaucous. They blamed Konnal, the one responsible for their dismissal.

Yet, what choice do I have? Konnal would ask himself. These people were untrustworthy. Some of them even plotting against me! If it hadn't been for Glaucous, I might have never known.

Upon first being introduced into the general's retinue, Glaucous had ferreted out something bad about every person Konnal had ever trusted. One minister had been heard defending Porthios. Another was said to have once, when she was a youth, been in love with Dalamar the Dark. Still another was called to account because he had disagreed with Konnal over a matter of taxation. Then came the day when Konnal woke to the realization that he had only one advisor left and that advisor was Glaucous.

The exception was Konnal's nephew Kiryn. Glaucous made no secret of his affection for Kiryn. Glaucous flattered the young man, brought him little gifts, laughed heartily at his jokes, and was effusive in his attention to him. Courtiers who courted Glaucous's favor were intensely jealous of the young man. Kiryn himself would have much preferred Glaucous's dislike. Kiryn distrusted Glaucous, though the young man could give no reason why.

Kiryn dared say no word against Glaucous, however. No one dared say anything against him. Glaucous was a powerful wizard, the most powerful wizard the Silvanesti had ever known among their kind, even counting the dark elf Dalamar.

Glaucous had arrived in Silvanost one day shortly after the dragon purge began. He was, he said, a representative of those elves who served in the Tower of Shalost, a monument in western Silvanesti, where lay the body of the druid Waylorn Wyvernsbane. Although the gods of magic had departed, the enchantment remained around the crystal bier on which the hero of the elves lay enshrined. Careful not to disturb the rest of the dead, the elven sorcerers, desperate to regain their magic, had attempted to capture and use some of the enchantment.

"We succeeded," Glaucous had reported to the general. "That is," he had added with becoming modesty, "I succeeded."

Fearing the great dragons that were decimating the rest of Ansalon, Glaucous had worked with the Woodshapers to devise a means by which Silvanesti could be protected from the ravages of the dragons. The Woodshapers, acting under Glaucous's direction, had grown the tree now known as the Shield Tree. Surrounded by its own magical barrier through which nothing could penetrate to do it harm, the tree was planted in the Garden of Astarin and was much admired.

When Glaucous had proposed to the governor-general that he could raise a magical shield over all of Silvanesti, Konnal had experienced an overwhelming sense of thankfulness and relief. He had felt a weight lifted from his shoulders. Silvanesti would be safe, truly safe. Safe from dragons, safe from ogres, safe from humans, dark elves, safe from the rest of the world. He had put the matter to a vote by the Heads of House. The vote had been unanimous.

Glaucous had raised the shield and become the hero of the elves, some of whom were already talking about building him his own monument. Then plants in the Garden of Astarin began to die. Reports came that trees and plants and animals that lived within the borders touched by the magical shield were also dying. People in Silvanost and other elven villages started to die of a strange wasting sickness. The kirath and other rebels said it was the shield. Glaucous said it was a plague brought to their land by humans before the raising of the shield and that only the shield kept the rest of the populace from dying.

Konnal could not do without Glaucous now. Glaucous was his friend, his trusted adviser, his only trusted adviser. Glaucous's magic was responsible for placing the shield over Silvanesti and Glaucous could use his magic to remove the shield anytime he wanted. Remove the shield and leave the Silvanesti open to the terrors of the world beyond.

"Mmmm? I beg your pardon? What were you saying?" General Konnal tore his attention from his swans, returned it to Glaucous, who had been speaking all this time.

"I said, 'You are not listening to me,'" Glaucous repeated with a sweet smile.

"No, I am sorry. There is one thing I want to know, Glaucous. How did this young man come through the shield?" He lowered his voice to a whisper, though there was no one within earshot. "Is the shield's magic failing, too?"

Glaucous's expression darkened. "No," he replied.

"How can you be certain?" Konnal demanded. "Tell me honestly—have you not felt a weakening of your power over the past year? All other wizards have."

"That may be. *I* have not," Glaucous said coldly.

Konnal gazed at his friend intently. Glaucous refused to meet his gaze and Konnal guessed that the wizard was lying.

"Then what explanation do we have for this phenomenon?"

"A very simple one," Glaucous returned, unperturbed. "I brought him through."

"You?" Konnal was so shocked he shouted the word. Many in the crowd halted their conversations to turn and stare.

Glaucous smiled at them reassuringly and took hold of his friend's arm, led him to a more secluded area of the garden.

"Why would you do this? What do you plan to do with this young man, Glaucous?" Konnal demanded.

"I will do what you should have done," Glaucous said, smoothing back the flowing sleeves of his white robes. "I will put a Caladon on the throne. I remind you, my friend, that if you had proclaimed your nephew Speaker as I recommended there would be no problem with Silvanoshei."

"You know perfectly well that Kiryn refused to accept the position," Konnal returned.

"Due to misguided loyalty to his Aunt Alhana." Glaucous sighed. "I have tried to counsel him on this matter. He refuses to listen to me."

"He will not listen to me, either, if that is what you are implying, my friend," Konnal said. "And might I point out that it is your insistence on maintaining the right of the Caladon family to rule Silvanesti that has landed us in this stew. I am of House Royal myself—"

"You are not a Caladon, Reyl," Glaucous murmured.

"I can trace my lineage back beyond the Caladons!" Konnal said indignantly. "Back to Quinari, wife of Silvanos! I have as much right to rule as the Caladons. Perhaps more."

"I know that, my dear friend," said Glaucous softly, placing a soothing hand upon Konnal's arm. "But you would have a difficult time persuading the Heads of House."

"Lorac Caladon plunged this nation into ruin," Konnal continued bitterly. "His daughter Alhana Starbreeze took us from ruination to near destruction with her marriage to Porthios, a Qualinesti. If we had not acted quickly to rid ourselves of both these vipers, we would have found Silvanesti under the heel of that half-breed, dim-witted Speaker of Suns Gilthas, son of Tanis. Yet the people continue to argue that a Caladon should sit upon the throne! I do not understand it!"

"My friend," Glaucous said gently, "that bloodline has ruled Silvanesti for hundreds of years. The people would be content to accept another Caladon as ruler without a murmur. But if you put yourself forward as a ruler, there would be months or even years of endless arguments and jealousies, researchings of family histories, perhaps even rival claims to the throne. Who knows but that some powerful figure might arise who would oust you and seize control for himself? No, no. This is the best possible solution. I remind you again that your nephew is a Caladon and that he would be the perfect choice. The people would be quite willing to see your nephew take the position. His mother, your sister, married into the Caladon family. It is a compromise the Heads of House would accept.

"But this is all water beneath the bridge. In two days time, Silvanoshei Caladon will be in Silvanost. You have proclaimed publicly that you would support a member of the Caladon family as Speaker of the Stars."

"Because you advised that I do so!" Konnal returned.

"I have my reasons," Glaucous said. He glanced at the guests, who continued to talk, their voices rising in their excitement. The name "Silvanoshei" could be heard now, coming to them through the starlit darkness. "Reasons that will become clear to you someday, my friend. You must trust me."

"Very well, what do you recommend that I do about Silvanoshei?"

"You will make him Speaker of the Stars."

"What are you saying?" Konnal was thunderstruck. "This . . . this son of dark elves . . . Speaker of the Stars . . ."

"Calm yourself, my dear friend," Glaucous admonished in placating tones. "We will borrow a leaf out of the book of the Qualinesti. Silvanoshei will rule in name only. You will remain the general of the Wildrunners. You will retain control over all the military. You will be the true ruler of Silvanesti. And in the interim, Silvanesti will have a Speaker of the Stars. The people will be joyful. Silvanoshei's ascension to the throne will put a stop to the unrest that has developed of late. Once their goal is achieved, the militant factions among our people—most notably the kirath—will cease to cause trouble."

"I cannot believe you are serious, Glaucous." Konnal was shaking his head.

"Never more serious in my life, dear friend. The people will bring their cares and woes to the king now instead of you. You will be free to accomplish the real work of ruling Silvanesti. Someone must be proclaimed regent, of course. Silvanoshei is young, very young for such a vast responsibility."

"Ah!" Konnal looked quite knowing. "I begin to see what you have in mind. I suppose that I—"

He stopped. Glaucous was shaking his head.

"You cannot be regent and general of the Wildrunners," he said.

"And whom do *you* suggest?" Konnal asked.

Glaucous bowed with graceful humility. "I offer myself. I will undertake to counsel the young king. You have found my advice useful from time to time, I believe."

"But you have no qualifications!" Konnal protested. "You are not of House Royal. You have not served in the Senate. Before this you were a wizard serving in the Tower of Shalost," he stated brusquely.

"Oh, but you yourself will recommend me," said Glaucous, resting his hand on Konnal's arm.

"And what am I to say by way of recommendation?"

"Only this—you will remind them that the Shield Tree grows in the Garden of Astarin, a garden that I oversee. You will remind them that I am the one who helped plant the Shield Tree. You will remind them that I am the one currently responsible for keeping the shield in place."

"A threat?" Konnal glowered.

Glaucous gazed long at the general, who began to feel uncomfortable. "It is my fate never to be trusted," Glaucous said at last. "To have my motives questioned. I accept that, a sacrifice I make to serve my people."

"I am sorry," Konnal said gruffly. "It's just that—"

"Apology accepted. And now," Glaucous continued, "we should make preparations to welcome the young king to Silvanost. You will declare a national holiday. We will spare no expense. The people need something to celebrate. We will have that minstrel who sang tonight sing something in honor of our new Speaker. What a lovely voice she has."

"Yes," Konnal agreed absently, abstracted. He was beginning to think that this plan of Glaucous's wasn't a bad plan after all.

"Ah, how very sad, my friend," Glaucous said, pointing to the pond. "One of your swans is dying."

12 MARCHING ORDERS

The first day after the siege of Sanction, Mina tried to leave her tent to go stand in line with the other soldiers waiting for food. She was mobbed, surrounded by soldiers and camp followers who wanted to touch her for luck or who wanted her to touch them. The soldiers were respectful, awed in her presence. Mina spoke to each one, always in the name of the One, True God. But the press of men, women and children was overwhelming. Seeing that Mina was about to drop from exhaustion, her Knights, led by Galdar, drove the people away. Mina returned to her tent. Her Knights stood guard over her rest. Galdar brought her food and drink.

The next day, Mina held a formal audience. Galdar ordered the soldiers to form ranks. She passed among them, speaking to many by name, recalling their bravery in battle. They left her presence dazzled, her name upon their lips.

After the review, she visited the tents of the dark mystics. Her Knights had spread the story of how Mina had restored Galdar's arm. Miracles of healing such as this had once been common in the Fourth Age, but not anymore.

The mystic healers of the Knights of Neraka, healers who had stolen the means of healing from the Citadel of Light, had in years past been able to perform healing miracles that rivaled those the gods themselves had granted in the Fourth Age. But recently, the healers had noticed that they were losing some of their mystical powers. They could still heal, but even simple spells drained them of energy to the point where they found themselves near collapse.

No one could explain this strange and dire occurrence. At first, the healers blamed the mystics of the Citadel of Light, saying that they had found a way to prevent the Knights of Neraka from healing their soldiers. But they soon heard reports from their spies within the Citadel that the mystics on Schallsea and in other locations throughout Ansalon were encountering the very same phenomena. They, too, sought answers, but thus far, in vain.

Overwhelmed by the number of casualties, forced to conserve their energy, the healers had aided Lord Milles and his staff first, for the army needed its commanders. Even then, they could do nothing for critical wounds. They could not restore hacked off limbs, they could not stop internal bleeding, they could not mend a cracked skull.

The eyes of the wounded fixed on Mina the moment she entered the healers' tent. Even those who had been blinded, whose eyes were covered with bloody bandages, turned their sightless gaze instinctively in her direction, as a plant languishing in shadow seeks the sunlight.

The healers continued their work, pretending not to notice Mina's entry. One did pause, however, to look up. He seemed about to order her out, then saw Galdar, who stood behind her and who had placed his hand upon the hilt of his sword.

"We are busy. What do you want?" the healer demanded churlishly.

"To help," Mina replied. Her amber-eyed gaze roved swiftly about the tent. "What is that area back there? The place you have screened off?"

The healer cast a glance in that direction. Groans and moaning sounds came from behind the blanket which had been hastily strung up in the back end of the large hospital tent.

"The dying," he said, cold, casual. "We can do nothing for them."

"You do not give them anything for the pain?" Mina asked.

The healer shrugged. "They are of no more use to us. Our supplies are limited and must go to help those who have a chance to return to the battle."

"You will not mind, then, if I give them my prayers?"

The healer sniffed. "By all means, go 'pray' over them. I'm sure they'll appreciate it."

"I'm sure they will," she said gravely.

She walked to the back of the tent, passing along the rows of cots where lay the wounded. Many stretched out their hands to her or called out her name, begging her to notice them. She smiled upon them and promised to return. Reaching the blankets behind which lay the dying, Mina reached out her hand, parted the blankets and let them fall behind her.

Galdar took his place in front of the blankets, turned, hand on his sword, to keep an eye on the healers. They made a fine show of paying no attention, but they cast sidelong glances in the direction of the blankets and then exchanged those glances with each other.

Galdar listened to what was happening behind him. He could smell the stench of death. A look cast back through the curtain showed him seven men and two women. Some lay on cots, but others lay on the crude stretchers, which had been used to carry them from the battle field. Their wounds were horrendous, at least so Galdar perceived in that quick glance. Flesh cleaved open, organs and bone exposed. Blood dripped on the floor, forming gruesome pools. One man's intentestines spewed out of him like a string of grotesque sausages. A woman Knight was missing half her face, the eyeball dangling hideously from beneath a blood-soaked bandage.

Mina came to the first of the dying, the woman who had lost her face. Her one good eye was closed. Her breathing was labored. She seemed to have already started on her long journey. Mina rested her hand on the horrible wound.

"I saw you fight in the battle, Durya," Mina said softly. "You fought bravely, held your ground though those around you panicked and retreated. You must stay your journey, Durya. The One God has need of you."

The woman breathed easier. Her mangled face moved slowly toward Mina, who bent and kissed her.

Galdar heard murmuring behind him, turned back quickly. The healer's tent had grown quiet. All had heard Mina's words. The healers made no more pretense of working. Everyone was watching, waiting.

Galdar felt a hand touch him on the shoulder. Thinking it was Mina, he turned. He saw instead the woman, Durya, who had lain dying. Her face was covered with blood, she would always bear a hideous scar, but the flesh was whole, the eye back in its place. She walked, she smiled, she drew a tremulous breath.

"Mina brought me back," Durya said, her tone awed, wondering. "She brought me back to serve her. And I will. I will serve her all her days."

Exalted, her face radiant, Durya left the tent. The wounded cheered and began to chant, "Mina, Mina!" The healers started after Durya in shocked disbelief.

"What is she doing in there?" demanded one, seeking to enter.

"Praying," Galdar said gruffly, blocking the way. "You gave her permission, remember?"

The healer glowered and swiftly departed. Galdar saw the man hot-footing his way to Lord Milles's tent.

"Yes, you tell Lord Milles what you've witnessed," Galdar advised the man silently, gleefully. "Tell him and add yet another twist of the knife that rankles in his chest."

Mina healed them all, healed every one of the dying. She healed a Talon commander who had taken a Solamnic spear in his gut. She healed a foot soldier who had been trampled by the slashing hooves of a battle horse. One by one, the dying rose from their beds and walked out to cheers from the other wounded. They thanked her and praised her, but Mina turned all their gratitude aside.

"Offer your thanks and your loyalty to the One True God," she told them. "It is by the god's power that you are restored."

Indeed, it seemed that she was given divine assistance, for she did not grow weary or faint, no matter how many of the injured she treated. And that was many. When she came from helping the dying, she moved from one of the wounded to another, laying her hands upon them, kissing them, praising their deeds in battle.

"The power of healing does not come from me," she told them. "It comes from the God who has returned to care for you."

By midnight, the healer's tent was empty.

Under orders from Lord Milles, the dark mystics kept close watch on Mina, trying to figure out her secret so as to discredit her, denounce her as a charlatan. They said that she must be resorting to tricks or sleight-of-hand. They poked pins into limbs she had restored, trying to prove they were illusion, only to see real blood flow. They sent patients to her suffering from horrible contagious diseases, patients the healers themselves feared to approach. Mina sat beside these sufferers, laid her hands upon their open sores and oozing pustules and bid them be well in the name of the One God.

The grizzled veterans whispered that she was like the clerics of old, who were given wondrous powers by the gods. Such clerics, they said, had once been able to raise the dead. But that miracle, Mina either would not or could not perform. The dead received special attention from her, but she did not restore them to life, though she was often begged to do so.

"We are brought into this world to serve the One True God," Mina said. "As we serve the True God in this world, the dead do important service in the next. It would be wrong to bring them back."

By her command, the soldiers had carried all the bodies from the field—bodies of friend and foe alike—and arranged them in long rows on the bloodstained grass. Mina knelt beside each corpse, prayed over each no matter which side the person had fought on, commended the spirit of each to the nameless god. Then she ordered them to be buried in a mass grave.

At Galdar's insistence, the third day after the siege Mina held counsel with the Neraka Knights' commanders. They now included almost all the officers who had formerly reported to Lord Milles, and to a man these officers urged Mina to take up the siege of Sanction, to lead them to what must be a resounding victory over the Solamnics.

Mina refused their entreaties.

"Why?" Galdar demanded this morning, the morning of the fifth day, when he and Mina were alone. He was frustrated at her refusal. "Why will you not launch an attack? If you conquer Sanction, Lord Targonne will not be able to touch you! He will be forced to recognize you as one of his most valued Knights!"

Mina was seated at a large table she had ordered be brought into her tent. Maps of Ansalon were spread out upon it. She had studied the maps every day, moving her lips as she went over them, speaking silently the names of the towns and cities and villages to herself, memorizing their locations. Ceasing her work, she looked up at the minotaur.

"What do you fear, Galdar?" she asked mildly.

The minotaur scowled, the skin between his eyes, above his snout, creased into folds. "My fear is for you, Mina. Those who are deemed a threat to Targonne disappear from time to time. No one is safe from him. Not even our former leader, Mirielle Abrena. It was put about that she died after eating spoiled meat, but everyone knows the truth."

"And that truth is?" Mina asked in abstracted tones. She was looking again at the map.

"He had her poisoned, of course," Galdar returned. "Ask him yourself if you ever chance to meet him. He will not deny it."

Mina sighed. "Mirielle is fortunate. She is with her God. Though the Vision she proclaimed was false, she now knows the truth. She has been punished for her presumption and is now performing great deeds in the name of the One who shall be nameless. As for Targonne"—Mina lifted her gaze again—"he serves the One True God in this world, and so he will be permitted to remain for the time being."

"Targonne?" Galdar gave a tremendous snort. "He serves a god all right, the god of currency."

Mina smiled a secret, inward smile. "I did not say that Targonne knows he is serving the One, Galdar. But serve he does. That is why I will not attack Sanction. Others will fight that battle. Sanction is not our concern. We are called to greater glory."

"Greater glory?" Galdar was astonished. "You do not know what you are saying, Mina! What could be greater than seizing Sanction? Then the people would see that the Knights of Neraka are once again a powerful force in this world!"

Mina traced a line on the map with her finger, a line that came to rest near the southern portion of the map. "What about the conquering of the great elven kingdom of Silvanesti?"

"Hah! Hah!" Galdar roared his laughter. "You have me there, Mina. I concede. Yes, that would be a magnificent victory. And it would be magnificent to see the moon drop out of the sky and land on my breakfast plate, which is just about as likely to happen."

"You will see, Galdar," Mina said quietly. "Bring me word the moment the messenger arrives. Oh, and Galdar . . ."

"Yes, Mina?" The minotaur had turned to go.

"Take care," she said to him, her amber eyes piercing him through, as if they had been sharpened to arrow points. "Your mockery offends the God. Do not make that mistake again."

Galdar felt a throbbing pain in his sword arm. The fingers went numb.

"Yes, Mina," he mumbled. Massaging the arm, he ducked out of the tent, leaving Mina to study her map.

Galdar calculated it would take two days for one of Lord Milles's flunkies to ride to the Knights' headquarters in Jelek, a day to report to Lord of the Night Targonne, two days to ride back. They should hear something today. After he left Mina's tent, the minotaur roamed about the outskirts of camp, watching the road for riders.

He was not alone. Captain Samuval and his Archer Company were there, as well as many of the soldiers of Milles's command. They stood with weapons ready. They had sworn among themselves that they would stop anyone who tried to take Mina from them.

All eyes were on the road. The pickets who were supposed to be watching Sanction kept looking behind them, instead of ahead at the besieged city. Lord Milles, who had made one experimental foray out of his tent following the siege and who had been harried back inside by a barrage of horse turds, cat-calls and jeers, parted the tent flaps to glare impatiently up that road, never doubting but that Targonne would come to his commander's aide by sending troops to help him put down the mutiny.

The only eyes in camp who did not turn to the road were Mina's. She remained in her tent, absorbed in studying her maps.

"And that is the reason she gave for not attacking Sanction? That we are going to attack Silvanesti?" Captain Samuval said to Galdar as the two stood in the road, awaiting the arrival of the messenger. The captain frowned. "What nonsense! You don't suppose she could be afraid, do you?"

Galdar glowered. Placing his hand on the hilt of his sword, he drew it halfway from its sheath. "I should cut out your tongue for saying such a thing! You saw her ride alone into the front ranks of the enemy! Where was her fear then?"

"Peace, Minotaur," Samuval said. "Put away your sword. I meant no disrespect. You know as well as I that when the blood burns hot in battle, a man thinks himself invincible and he does deeds he would never dream of doing in cold blood. It is only natural she should be a little frightened now that she has taken a good long look at the situation and realized the enormity of the task."

"There is no fear in her," Galdar growled, sheathing his blade. "How can there be fear in one who speaks of death with a wistful, impatient look in her eyes, as if she would rush to embrace it if she could and is constrained to continue living against her will."

"A man may fear many things besides death," Samuval argued. "Failure, for one. Perhaps she fears that if she leads these worshipers of hers into battle and fails, they will turn against her as they did against Lord Milles."

Galdar twisted his horned head, looked back over his shoulder, back to where Mina's tent stood by itself upon a small rise, the bloody standard hanging before it. The tent was surrounded by people standing silent vigil, waiting, watching, hoping to catch a glimpse of her or hear her voice.

"Would you leave her now, Captain?" Galdar asked.

Captain Samuval followed the minotaur's gaze. "No, I would not," he said at last. "I don't know why. Perhaps she has bewitched me."

"I'll tell you why," Galdar said. "It's because she offers us something to believe in. Something besides ourselves. I mocked that something just now," he added humbly, rubbing his arm, which still tingled unpleasantly. "And I am sorry I did so."

A trumpet call rang out. The pickets placed at the entrance to the valley were letting those in camp know that the expected messenger approached. Every person in camp stopped what they were doing and looked up, ears pricked to hear, necks craned to see. A large crowd blocked the road. They parted to let the messenger on his steaming horse gallop past. Galdar hastened to take the news to Mina.

Lord Milles emerged from his command tent at precisely the same moment Mina left hers. Confident that the messenger was here to bring word of Targonne's anger and the promise of a force of armed Knights to seize and execute the imposter, Lord Milles glared triumphantly at Mina. He felt certain that her downfall was imminent.

She did not so much as glance at him. She stood outside her tent, awaiting developments with calm detachment, as if she already knew the outcome.

The messenger slid down from his horse. He looked in some astonishment at the crowd of people gathered around Mina's tent, was alarmed to see them regarding him with a baleful and threatening air. The messenger kept glancing backward at them over his shoulder as he went to deliver a scroll case to Lord Milles. Mina's followers did not take their eyes from him, nor did they take their hands from the hilts of their swords.

Lord Milles snatched the scroll case from the messenger's hand. So certain was he of its contents that he did not bother to retreat to the privacy of his tent to read it. He opened the plain and unadorned leather-bound case, removed the scroll, broke the seal and unfurled it with a snap. He had even filled his lungs to make the announcement that would cause the upstart female to be arrested.

The breath whistled from him as from a deflated pig's bladder. His complexion went sallow, then livid. Sweat beaded his forehead, his tongue passed several times over his lips. He crumpled the missive in his hand and, stumbling as one blind, he fumbled at the tent flaps, trying vainly to open them. An aide stepped forward. Lord Milles shoved the man aside with a savage snarl and entered the tent, closing the flaps behind him and tying them shut.

The messenger turned to face the crowd.

"I seek a Talon leader named 'Mina,'" he said, his voice loud and carrying.

"What is your business with her?" roared a gigantic minotaur, who stepped out of the crowd and confronted the messenger.

"I bear orders for her from Lord of the Night Targonne," the messenger replied.

"Let him come forward," called Mina.

The minotaur acted as escort. The crowd that had barred the messenger's way cleared a path leading from Lord Milles's tent to Mina's.

The messenger walked along the path that was bounded by soldiers, all keeping their weapons to hand, regarding him with not very friendly looks. He kept his gaze forward, though that was not very comfortable for him since he stared squarely at the back, shoulders, and bull neck of the enormous minotaur. The messenger continued on his way, mindful of his duty.

"I am sent to find a *knight officer* called 'Mina,'" the messenger repeated laying emphasis on the words. He stared at the young girl who confronted him in some confusion. "You are nothing but a child!"

"A child of battle. A child of war. A child of death. I am Mina," said the girl, and there was no doubting her air of authority, the calm consciousness of command.

The messenger bowed and handed over a second scroll case. This one was bound in elegant black leather, the seal of a skull and lily graven upon it in silver. Mina opened the case and drew forth the scroll. The crowd hushed, seemed to have stopped breathing. The messenger looked about, his astonishment growing. He would later report to Targonne that he felt as if he were in a temple, not a military camp.

Mina read the missive, her face expressionless. When she finished, she handed it to Galdar. He read it. His jaw dropped so that his sharp teeth glistened in the sun, his tongue lolled. He read and reread the message, turned his amazed gaze upon Mina.

"Forgive me, Mina," he said softly, handing the piece of parchment back to her.

"Do not ask my forgiveness, Galdar," she said. "I am not the one you doubted."

"What does the message say, Galdar?" Captain Samuval demanded impatiently, and his question was echoed by the crowd.

Mina raised her hand and the soldiers obeyed her unspoken command instantly. The templelike hush fell over them again.

"My orders are to march south, invade, seize, and hold the elven land of Silvanesti."

A low and angry rumble, like the rumble of thunder from an approaching storm, sounded in the throats of the soldiers.

"No!" several shouted, incensed. "They can't do this! Come with us, Mina! To the Abyss with Targonne! We'll march on Jelek! Yes, that's what we'll do! We'll march on Jelek!"

"Hear me!" Mina shouted above the clamor. "These orders do not come from General Targonne! His is but the hand that writes them. The orders come from the One God. It is our God's will that we attack Silvanesti in order to prove the God's return to all the world. We will march on Silvanesti!" Mina's voice raised in a stirring cry. "And we will be victorious!"

"Hurrah!" The soldiers cheered and began to chant, "Mina! Mina! Mina!"

The messenger stared about him in dazed astoundment. The entire camp, a thousand voices, were chanting this girl's name. The chant echoed off the mountains and thundered to the heavens. The chant was heard in the town of Sanction, whose residents trembled and whose Knights grimly gripped their weapons, thinking this portended some terrible doom for their besieged city.

A horrible, bubbling cry rose above the chanting, halting some of it, though those on the outskirts of the crowd continued on, unhearing. The cry came from the tent of Lord Milles. So awful was that cry that those standing near the tent backed away, regarded it in alarm.

"Go and see what has happened," Mina ordered.

Galdar did as commanded. The messenger accompanied him, knowing that Targonne would be interested in the outcome. Drawing his sword, Galdar sliced through the leather strings that held the flap shut. He went inside and came back out a instant later.

"His lordship is dead," he reported, "by his own hand."

The soldiers began to cheer again, and many jeered and laughed.

Mina rounded upon those near her in anger that lit the amber eyes with a pale fire. The soldiers ceased their cheering, quailed before her. Mina said no word but walked past them, her chin set, her back rigid. She came to the entrance of the tent.

"Mina," said Galdar, holding up the bloodstained message. "This wretch tried to have you hanged. The proof is here 'in Targonne's response."

"Lord Milles stands before the One God, now, Galdar," Mina said, "where we will all stand one day. It is not for us to judge him."

She took the bloody bit of paper, tucked it into her belt, and walked inside the tent. When Galdar started to go with her, she ordered him away, closed the tent flaps behind her.

Galdar put an eye to the flap. Shaking his head, he turned and mounted guard upon the entrance.

"Go about your business," the minotaur commanded the soldiers who were milling about in front of the tent. "There's work to be done if we're marching to Silvanesti."

"What is she doing in there?" asked the messenger.

"Praying," Galdar said shortly.

"Praying!" the messenger repeated to himself in wonder. Mounting his horse, he rode off, anxious not to lose a moment in reporting the day's astonishing events to the Lord of the Night.

"So what happened?" Captain Samuval asked, coming to stand next to Galdar.

"To Milles?" Galdar grunted. "He fell on his sword." He handed over the message. "I found this in his hand. As we guessed he would, he sent a pack of lies to Targonne, all about how Mina nearly lost the battle and Milles saved it. Targonne may be a murdering, conniving bastard, but he's not stupid." Galdar spoke with grudging admiration. "He saw through Milles's lies and ordered him to report word of his 'victory' directly to the great dragon Malystryx."

"No wonder he chose this way out," Samuval commented. "But why send Mina south to Silvanesti? What happens to Sanction?"

"Targonne has ordered General Dogah to leave Khur. He will take over the siege of Sanction. As I said, Targonne's not stupid. He knows that Mina and her talk of One True God is a threat to him and the phony 'Visions' he's been handing out. But he also knows that he will start a rebellion among the troops if he tries to have her arrested. The great dragon Malystryx has long been annoyed by Silvanesti and the fact that the elves have found a way to thwart her by hiding beneath their magical shield. Targonne can placate Malystryx on the one hand by telling her he has sent a force to attack Silvanesti, and he can rid himself of a dangerous threat to his authority at the same time."

"Does Mina know that in order to reach Silvanesti we must march through Blöde?" Captain Samuval demanded. "A realm held by the ogres? They are already angry that we have taken some of their land. They will resent any further incursion into their territory." Samuval shook his head. "This is suicidal! We will never even see Silvanesti. We must try to talk her out of this act of folly, Galdar."

"It is not my place to question her," said the minotaur. "She knew we were going to Silvanost this morning before the messenger arrived. Remember, Captain? I told you of it myself."

"Did you?" Captain Samuval mused. "In all the excitement, I had forgotten. I wonder how she found out?"

Mina emerged from Milles's tent. She was very pale.

"His crimes have been forgiven. His soul has been accepted." She sighed, glanced about, appeared disappointed to find herself back among mortals. "How I envy him!"

"Mina, what are your orders?" Galdar asked.

Mina looked at him without recognition for a moment, the amber still seeing wondrous sights not given to other mortals. Then she smiled bleakly, sighed again, and came back to her surroundings.

"Assemble the troops. Captain Samuval, you will address them. You will tell them truthfully that the assignment is dangerous one. Some might say 'suicidal.' " She smiled at Samuval. "I will order no man to make this march. Any who come do so of their own free will."

"They will all come, Mina," said Galdar softly.

Mina gazed at him, her eyes luminous, radiant. "If that be true, then the force will be too large, too unwieldy. We must move fast and we must keep our movement secret. My own Knights will accompany me, of course. You will select five hundred of the best of the foot soldiers, Galdar. The remainder will stay behind with my blessing. They must continue to besiege Sanction."

Galdar blinked. "But, Mina, didn't you hear? Targonne has given orders that General Dogah is to take over the siege of Sanction."

Mina smiled. "General Dogah will receive new orders telling him that he is to turn his forces south and march with all possible haste upon Silvanesti."

"But . . . where will these orders come from?" Galdar asked, gaping. "Not Targonne. He is ordering us to Silvanesti simply to get rid of us, Mina!"

"As I told you, Galdar, Targonne acts for the One God, whether he knows it or not." Mina reached into her belt, where she had tucked the orders Milles had received from Targonne. She held the parchment to the sunlight. Targonne's name loomed large and black at the bottom, his seal gleamed red. Mina pointed her finger to the words on the page, a page that was stained with Milles's blood.

"What does it say, Galdar?"

Mystified, Galdar looked at the words and began to read them, read exactly what he had read before.

Lord Milles is hereby commanded . . .

The words suddenly began to writhe and twist in his vision. Galdar closed his eyes, rubbed them, opened them. The words continued to writhe and now they began to crawl over the page, the black of the ink mingling with the red of Milles's blood.

"What does it say, Galdar?" Mina asked again.

Galdar felt his breath catch in his throat. He tried to speak, could only whisper huskily, "General Dogah is hereby commanded to shift his forces south and march with all possible speed to Silvanesti. Signed in Targonne's name."

The handwriting was Targonne's. There could be no doubt. His signature was in place, as was his seal.

Mina rolled the parchment neatly and tucked it back into the scroll case.

"I want you to deliver these orders yourself, Galdar. Then catch up with us on the road south. I will show you the route of our march. Samuval, you will be second in command until Galdar rejoins us."

"You can count on me and on my men, Mina," said Captain Samuval. "We would follow you into the Abyss."

Mina regarded him thoughtfully. "The Abyss is no more, Captain. She who ruled there has left, never to return. The dead have their own realm now—a realm in which they are permitted to continue their service to the One God."

Her gaze shifted focus, encompassed the mountains, the valley, the soldiers who were even now busy striking camp. "We will depart in the morning. The march will take us two weeks. Issue the necessary commands. I'll want two supply wagons to accompany us. Let me know when we are ready."

Galdar ordered his officers to call the men to assembly. Entering Mina's tent, he found her bent over one of her maps, placing small pebbles upon it at various locations. Galdar looked to see that the pebbles were all concentrated in an area designated "Blöde."

"You will meet us here," she said, indicating a place on the map marked with a pebble. "I calculate that it will take you two days to meet up with General Dogah and another three days to rejoin us. The One God speed you, Galdar."

"The One God be with you until we meet again, Mina," said Galdar.

He meant to leave. He could yet cover many miles before daylight waned. But he found the leaving difficult. He could not imagine a day going by without seeing her amber eyes, hearing her voice. He felt as bereft as if he were suddenly shorn of all his fur, left in the world shivering and weak as a newborn calf.

Mina laid her hand upon his, upon the hand she had given him. "I will be with you wherever you go, Galdar," she said.

He fell to one knee, pressed her hand to his forehead. Keeping the memory of her touch an amulet in his mind, he turned and ran from the tent.

Captain Samuval entered next, coming to report that, as he had foreseen, every single soldier in the camp had volunteered to come. He had chosen the five hundred he considered the best. These soldiers were now the envy of the rest.

"I fear that those left behind may desert to follow you, Mina," Captain Samuval said.

"I will speak to them," she said. "I will explain to them that they must continue to hold Sanction without any expectation of reinforcements. I will explain to them how it can be done. They will see their duty."

She continued to put the small stones upon the map.

"What is that?" Samuval asked curiously.

"The location of the ogre forces," Mina replied. "Look, Captain, if we march this way, directly east out of the Khalkist Mountains, we can make much better time heading southward across the Plains of Khur. We will avoid the largest concentration of their troops, which are down here in the southern end of the mountain range, fighting the Legion of Steel and the forces of the elf-witch, Alhana Starbreeze. We will attempt to steal a march on them by traveling along this route, the Thon-Thalas River. I fear that at some point we must fight the ogres, but if my plan works, we will fight only a diminished force. With the God's blessing, most of us will reach our destination."

And what happened when that destination was reached? How did she intend to break through a magical shield that had thus far baffled all attempts to enter it? Samuval did not ask her. Nor did he ask how she knew the position of the ogre forces or how she knew they were fighting the Legion of Steel and the dark elves. The Knights of Neraka had sent scouts into ogre lands but none had ever returned alive to tell what they saw. Captain Samuval did not ask Mina how she intended to hold Silvanesti with such a small force, a force that would be decimated by the time they reached their destination. Samuval asked her none of this.

He had faith. If not necessarily in this One God, he had faith in Mina.

13 THE SCOURGE OF ANSALON

The odd occurrence that befell Tasslehoff Burrfoot on the fifth night of his journey to Qualinesti in the custody of Sir Gerard can best be explained by the fact that although the days had been sunny and warm and fine for traveling, the nights had been cloudy and overcast, with a drizzly rain. Up until this night. This night the sky was clear, the air was soft and warm and alive with the sounds of the forest, crickets and owls and the occasional wolf howling.

Far north, near Sanction, the minotaur Galdar ran along the road that led to Khur. Far south, in Silvanesti, Silvanoshei entered Silvanost as he had planned, in triumph and with fanfare. The entire population of Silvanost came out to welcome him and stare at him and marvel over him. Silvanoshei was shocked and troubled by how few elves remained in the city. He said nothing to anyone however and was greeted with appropriate ceremony by General Konnal and a white-robed elven wizard whose charming manners endeared him to Silvanoshei at once.

While Silvanoshei dined on elven delicaces off plates of gold and drank sparkling wine from goblets of crystal, and while Galdar munched on dried peas as he marched, Tas and Gerard ate their customary boring and tasteless meal of flatbread and dried beef washed down with nothing more interesting than plain, ordinary water. They had ridden south as far as Gateway, where they passed several inns, whose innkeepers were standing in the doors with pinched faces. These innkeepers would have barred the door against a kender before the roads were closed by the dragon. Now they had come running out to offer them lodging and a meal for the unheard-of price of a single steel.

Sir Gerard had paid no attention to them. He had ridden past without a glance. Tasslehoff had sighed deeply and looked back longingly at the inns dwindling in the distance. When he had hinted that a mug of cold ale and a plate of hot food would be a welcome change, Gerard had said no, the less attention they called to themselves the better for all concerned.

So they continued on south, traveling along a new road that ran near the river, a road Gerard said had been built by the Knights of Neraka to maintain their supply lines into Qualinesti. Tas wondered at the time why the Knights of Neraka were interested in supplying the elves of Qualinesti, but he assumed that this must be some new project the elven king Gilthas had instituted.

Tas and Gerard had slept outdoors in a drizzling rain for the last four nights. This fifth night was fine. As usual, sleep sneaked up on the kender before he was quite ready for it. He woke up in the night, jolted from his slumbers by a light shining in his eyes.

"Hey! What's that?" he demanded in a loud voice. Throwing off his blanket, he leaped to his feet and grabbed Gerard by the shoulder, shaking him and pummeling him.

"Sir Gerard! Wake up!" Tasslehoff shouted. "Sir Gerard!"

The Knight was up and awake in an instant, his sword in his hand. "What?" He stared around, alert for danger. "What is it? Did you hear something? See something? What?"

"That! That right there!" Tasslehoff clutched the Knight's shirt and pointed.

Sir Gerard regarded the kender with an extremely grim look. "Is this your idea of a joke?"

"Oh, no," Tas stated. "My idea of a joke is this, I say, 'Knock, knock,' and you say, 'Who's there?' and I say, 'Minotaur,' and you say 'Minotaur who,' and I say, 'So *that's* what you stepped in.' That's my idea of a joke. This has to do with that strange light in the sky."

"That's the moon," said Sir Gerard through gritted teeth.

"No!" Tasslehoff was astonished. "Really? The moon?"

He looked back at it. The thing did appear to have certain moonlike qualities: it was orb-shaped, and it was in the sky alongside the stars, and it glowed. But that was where the resemblance ended.

"If that's Solinari," Tas said, eyeing the moon skeptically. "Then what happened to him? Is he sick?"

Sir Gerard did not answer. He lay back down on his blanket, placed his sword within hand's reach, and, grabbing hold of a corner of his blanket, rolled himself up in it. "Go to sleep," he said coldly, "and stay that way until morning."

"But I want to know about the moon!" Tas persisted, hunkering down beside the Knight, nothing daunted by the fact that Gerard's back was turned and his head covered up by the blanket and that he was still obviously extremely irate at having been violently wakened for nothing. Even his back looked angry. "What happened to make Solinari look so pale and sickly? And where's lovely red Lunitari? I guess I'd wonder where Nuitari was if I'd been able to see the black moon in the first place, which I couldn't, so it might be there and I just wouldn't know it—"

Sir Gerard flipped over quite suddenly. His head emerged from the blanket, revealing a stern and unfriendly eye. "You know perfectly well that Solinari has not been seen in the skies these past thirty-odd years, ever since the end of the Chaos War. Lunitari either. So you can stop this ridiculous nonsense. I am now going to sleep. I am to be awakened for nothing less than an invasion of hobgoblins. Is that clear?"

"But the moon!" Tas argued. "I remember when I came to Caramon's first funeral Solinari shown so very brightly that it was like day only it was night. Palin said this was Solinari's way of honoring his father and—"

Gerard flipped over again and covered his head.

Tas continued talking until he heard the Knight start to snore. Tas gave the Knight an experimental poke in the shoulder, to no avail. The kender thought that he might try prying open one of Gerard's eyelids to see if he was really asleep or just shamming, a trick which had never been known to fail with Flint, although it usually ended with the irate dwarf chasing the kender around the room with the poker.

Tas had other things to think about, however, and so he left the Knight alone and returned to his own blanket. Lying down, he put his hands beneath his head and gazed at the strange moon, which gazed back at him without the slightest hint of recognition. This gave Tas an idea. Abandoning the moon, he shifted his gaze to the stars, searched for his favorite constellations.

They were gone, as well. The stars he looked at now were cold and distant and unfamiliar. The only understanding star in the night sky was a single red star burning brightly not far from the strange moon. The star had a warm and comforting glow about it, which made up for the empty cold feeling in the pit of Tas's stomach, a feeling he had once thought, when he was a young kender, meant he needed something to eat but that he now knew, after years of adventuring, was his inside's way of telling him that something was wrong. In fact, he'd felt pretty much this same way just about the time the giant's foot had been poised over his head.

Tas kept his gaze on the red star, and after awhile the cold, empty feeling didn't hurt so much anymore. Just when he was feeling more comfortable and had put the thoughts of the strange moon and the unfriendly stars and the looming giant out of his mind, and just when he was starting to enjoy the night, sleep crept up and nabbed him again.

The kender wanted to discuss the moon the next day, and discuss it he did, but only with himself. Sir Gerard never responded to any of Tasslehoff's innumerable questions, never turned around, just rode along at a slow pace, the reins of Tas's pony in his hands.

The Knight rode in silence, though he was watchful and alert, constantly scanning the horizon. The entire world seemed to be riding in silence today, as well, once Tasslehoff quit talking, which he did after a couple of hours. It wasn't so much that he was bored with talking to himself, it was the answering himself that grew old fast. They met no one on the road, and now even the sounds of other living creatures came to an end. No bird sang. No squirrel scampered across the path. No deer walked among the shadows or ran from them, white tail flashing an alarm.

"Where are the animals?" Tas asked Gerard.

"They are in hiding," the Knight answered, the first words he'd spoken all morning. "They are afraid."

The air was hushed and still, as if the world held its breath, fearful of being heard. Not even the trees rustled and Tas had the feeling that if they had been able to make the choice, they would have dragged their roots out of the ground and run away.

"What are they afraid of?" Tasslehoff asked with interest, looking around in excitement, hoping for a haunted castle or a crumbling manor or, at the very least, a spooky cave.

"They fear the great green dragon. Beryl. We are in the West Plains now. We have crossed over into her realm."

"You keep talking about this green dragon. I've never heard of her. The only green dragon I knew was named Cyan Bloodbane. Who is Beryl? Where did she come from?"

"Who knows?" Gerard said impatiently. "From across the sea, I suppose, along with the great red dragon Malystryx and others of their foul kind."

"Well, if she isn't from around these parts, why doesn't some hero just go stick a lance into her?" Tas asked cheerfully.

Gerard halted his horse. He tugged on the reins of Tasslehoff's pony, who had been trudging behind, her head down, every bit as bored as the kender. She came plodding up level with the black, shaking her mane and eyeing a patch of grass hopefully.

"Keep your voice down!" Gerard said in a low voice. He looked as grim and stern as the kender had ever seen him. "Beryl's spies are everywhere, though we do not see them. Nothing moves in her realm but she is aware of it. Nothing moves here without her permission. We crossed into her realm an hour ago," he added. "I will be very surprised if someone doesn't come to take a look at us— Ah, there. What did I tell you?"

He had shifted in his saddle, to gaze intently to the east. A large speck of black in the sky was growing steadily larger and larger and larger with every passing moment. As Tas watched, he saw the speck develop wings and a long tail, saw a massive body—a massive green body.

Tasslehoff had seen dragons before, he'd ridden dragons before, he'd fought dragons before. But he had never seen or hoped to see a dragon this immense. Her tail seemed as long as the road they traveled; her teeth, set in slavering jaws, could have served as the high, crenellated walls of a formidable fortress. Her wicked red eyes burned with a hotter fire than the sun and seemed to illuminate all they looked upon with a glaring light.

"As you have any regard for your life or mine, kender," Gerard said in a fierce whisper, "do or say nothing!"

The dragon flew directly over them, her head swiveling to study them from all angles. The dragonfear slid over them like the dragon's shadow, blotting out the sunshine, blotting out reason and hope and sanity. The pony shook and whimpered. The black whinnied in terror and kicked and plunged. Gerard clung to the bucking horse's back, unable to calm the animal, prey to the same fear himself. Tasslehoff stared upward in open-mouthed astonishment. He felt a most unpleasant sensation come over him, a stomach-shriveling, spine-watering, knee-buckling, hand-sweating sort of feeling. As feelings went, he didn't much like it. For making a person miserable, it ranked right up there with a bad, sniffly cold in the head.

Beryl circled them twice and, seeing nothing more interesting than one of her own Knight allies with a kender prisoner in tow, she left them alone, flying lazily and unhurriedly back to her lair, her sharp eyes taking note of everything that moved upon her ground.

Gerard slid off his horse. He stood next to the shivering animal, leaned his head against its heaving flanks. He was exceedingly pale and sweating, a tremor shook his body. He opened and shut his mouth several times and at one point looked as if he might be sick, but he recovered himself. At length his breathing evened out.

"I have shamed myself," he said. "I did not know I could experience fear like that."

"*I* wasn't afraid," Tas announced in voice that seemed to have developed the same shakiness as his body. "I wasn't afraid one bit."

"If you had any sense, you would have been," Gerard said dourly.

"It's just that while I've seen some hideous dragons in my time I've never seen one quite that . . ."

Tasslehoff's words shriveled under Gerard's baleful stare.

"That . . . imposing," the kender said loudly, just in case any of the dragon's spies were listening. "Imposing," he whispered to Gerard. "That's a sort of compliment, isn't it?"

The Knight did not reply. Having calmed himself and his horse, he retrieved the reins to Tasslehoff's pony and, holding them in his hand, remounted the black. He did not set off immediately, but continued to sit some time in the middle of the road, gazing out to the west.

"I had never seen one of the great dragons before," he said quietly. "I did not think it would be that bad."

He sat quite still for several more moments, then, with a set jaw and pale face, he rode forward.

Tasslehoff followed along behind because he couldn't do anything else except follow along behind, what with the Knight holding onto the pony's reins.

"Was that the same dragon who killed all the kender?" Tasslehoff asked in a small voice.

"No," Gerard replied. "That was an even bigger dragon. A red dragon named Malys."

"Oh," said Tas. "Oh, my."

An even bigger dragon. He couldn't imagine it, and he very nearly said that he would like to see an even bigger dragon when it came to him quite forcibly that, in all honesty, he wouldn't.

"What is the matter with me?" Tasslehoff wailed in dismay. "I must be coming down with something. I'm *not* curious! I don't *want* to see a red dragon that might be bigger than Palanthas. This is just not like me."

Which led to an astounding thought, a thought so astounding Tas almost tumbled off the pony.

"Maybe I'm not me!"

Tasslehoff considered this. After all, no one else believed he was him except Caramon, and he was pretty old and almost dead at the time so perhaps he didn't count. Laura had *said* that she thought Tasslehoff was Tasslehoff but she was probably only being polite, so he couldn't count on that either. Sir Gerard had said that he couldn't possibly be Tasslehoff Burrfoot and Lord Warren had said the same thing, and they were Solamnic Knights, which meant that they were smart and most likely knew what they were talking about.

"That would explain everything," said Tasslehoff to himself, growing cheerier the more he thought about it. "That would explain why nothing that happened to me the first time I went to Caramon's funeral happened the second time, because it wasn't me it was happening to. It was someone else entirely. But if that's the case," he added, becoming rather muddled, "if I'm not me, I wonder who I am?"

He pondered on this for a good half-mile.

"One thing is certain," he said. "I can't keep calling myself Tasslehoff Burrfoot. If I meet the real one, he would be highly annoyed that I'd taken his name. Just the way I felt when I found out that there were thirty-seven other Tasslehoff Burrfoots in Solace—thirty-nine counting the dogs. I suppose I'll have to give him back the Device of Time Journeying, too. I wonder how I came to have it? Ah, of course. He must have dropped it."

Tas kicked his pony in the flanks. The pony perked up and trotted forward until Tas had caught up with the knight.

"Excuse me, Sir Gerard," Tas said.

The Knight glanced at him and frowned. "What?" he asked coldly.

"I just wanted to tell you that I made a mistake," Tas said meekly. "I'm not the person I said was."

"Ah, now there's a surprise!" Gerard grunted. "You mean you're not Tasslehoff Burrfoot, who's been dead for over thirty years?"

"I thought I was," Tas said wistfully. He found the notion more difficult to give up than he'd imagined. "But I can't be. You see, Tasslehoff Burrfoot was a hero. He wasn't afraid of anything. And I don't think he would have felt all strange the way I felt when that dragon flew over us. But I know what's wrong with me."

He waited for the Knight to ask politely but the Knight didn't. Tas volunteered the information.

"I have magnesia," he said solemnly.

This time Gerard said, "What?" only he didn't say it very politely.

Tas put his hand to his forehead, to see if he could feel it. "Magnesia. I'm not sure how a person gets magnesia. I think it has something to do with milk. But I remember that Raistlin said he knew someone with it once and that person couldn't remember who he was or why he was or where he'd left his spectacles or anything. So I must have magnesia, because that's my situation entirely."

This solved, Tasslehoff—or rather, the kender who used to think he was Tasslehoff—felt extremely proud to know he had come down with something so important.

"Of course," he added with a sigh, "a lot of people like you who expect me to be Tasslehoff are going to be in for a sad disappointment when they find out I'm not. But they'll just have to come to grips with it."

"I'll try to bear up," Gerard said dryly. "Now why don't you think really hard and see if you can 'remember' the truth about who you are."

"I wouldn't mind remembering the truth," Tas said. "I have the feeling that the truth doesn't want to remember me."

The two rode on in silence through a silent world until at last, to Tasslehoff's relief, he heard a sound, the sound of water, angry water of a river that foamed and seethed as if it resented being held prisoner within its rocky banks. Humans named the river the White-rage River. It marked the northern border of the elven land of Qualinesti.

Gerard slowed his horse. Rounding a bend in the road, they came within sight of the river, a broad expanse of white foaming water falling over and around glistening black rocks.

They had arrived at the end of the day. The forest was shadowed with the coming of darkness. The river held the light still, the water shining in the afterglow, and by that light they could see in the distance a narrow bridge spanning the river. The bridge was guarded by a lowered gate and guards wearing the same black armor as Gerard.

"Those are Dark Knights," said Tasslehoff in astonishment.

"Keep your voice down!" Gerard ordered sternly. Dismounting, he removed the gag from his belt and approached the kender. "Remember, the only way we're going to be able to see your alleged friend Palin Majere is if they let us past."

"But why are there Dark Knights here in Qualinesti?" Tas asked, talking quickly before Gerard had time to put the gag in place.

"The dragon Beryl rules the realm. These Knights are her overseers. They enforce her laws, collect the taxes and the tribute the elves pay to stay alive."

"Oh, no," said Tas, shaking his head. "There must be some mistake. The Dark Knights were driven out by the combined forces of Porthios and Gilthas in the year— Ulp!"

Gerard stuffed the gag in the kender's mouth, fastened it securely in a knot at the back of his head. "Keep saying things like that and I won't have to gag you. Everyone will just think you're crazy."

"If you'd tell me what has happened," Tas said, pulling the gag from his mouth and peering around at Gerard, "then I wouldn't have to ask questions."

Gerard, exasperated, put the gag back in place. "Very well," he said crossly. "The Knights of Neraka took Qualinesti during the Chaos War and they have never relinquished their hold on it," he said as he tied the knot. "They were prepared to go to war against the dragon, when she demanded that they cede the land to her. Beryl was clever enough to realize that she didn't need to fight. The Knights could be of use to her. She formed an alliance with them. The elves pay tribute, the Knights collect it and turn over a percentage—a large percentage—to the dragon. The Knights keep the rest. They prosper. The dragon prospers. It's the elves who are out of luck."

"I guess that must have happened when I had magnesia," Tas said, tugging one corner of the gag loose.

Gerard fastened the knot even tighter and added, irritably, "The word is 'amnesia,' damn it. And just keep quiet!"

He remounted his horse, and the two rode toward the gate. The guards were alert and had probably been on the watch for them, warned of their coming by the dragon, for they did not appear surprised to see the two emerge from the shadows. Knights armed with halberds stood guard at the gate, but it was an elf, clad all in green cloth and glittering chain mail, who walked up to question them. He was followed by an officer of the Knights of Neraka, who stood behind the elf, observing.

The elf regarded the two, particularly the kender, with disdain.

"The elven realm of Qualinesti is closed to all travelers by orders of Gilthas, Speaker of the Sun," said the elf, speaking Common. "What is your business here?"

Gerard smiled to indicate that he appreciated the joke. "I have urgent news for Marshal Medan," he said, and reaching into his black leather gauntlet he brought out a well-worn paper which he handed over with bored air of one who has done this many times before.

The elf did not even glance at the paper, but passed it to the officer of the Neraka Knights. The officer paid more attention to it. He studied it closely and then studied Gerard. The officer returned the paper to Gerard, who retrieved it and placed it back inside his glove.

"What business have you with Marshal Medan, Captain?" the officer inquired.

"I have something he wants, sir," Gerard replied. He jerked a thumb. "This kender."

The officer raised his eyebrows. "What does Marshal Medan want with a kender?"

"There is a warrant for the little thief, sir. He stole an important artifact from the Knights of the Thorn. A magical artifact that once purportedly belonged to Raistlin Majere."

The elf's eyes flickered at this. He regarded them with more interest.

"I've heard nothing of any bounty," the officer stated, frowning. "Or any robbery, for that matter."

"That is not surprising, sir, considering the Gray Robes," Gerard said with a wry smile and a covert glance around.

The officer nodded and twitched an eyebrow. The Gray Robes were sorcerers. They worked in secret, reporting to their own officers, working to forward their own goals and ambitions, which might or might not coincide with the rest of the Knighthood. As such, they were widely distrusted by the warrior

Knights, who viewed the Knights of the Thorn with the same suspicion that men of the sword have viewed men of the staff for centuries.

"Tell me of this crime," the officer said. "When and where was it committed?"

"As you know, the Gray Robes have been combing the Forest of Wayreth, searching for the magical and elusive Tower of High Sorcery. It was during this search that they uncovered this artifact. I do not know how or where, sir. That information was not provided to me. The Gray Robes were transporting the artifact to Palanthas for further study, when they stopped at an inn for some refreshment along the way. It was there the artifact was stolen. The Gray Robes missed it the next morning when they awoke," Gerard added with a meaningful roll of his eyes. "This kender had stolen it."

"So that's how I got it!" Tas said to himself, fascinated. "What a perfectly wonderful adventure. Too bad I can't remember it."

The officer nodded his head. "Damn Gray Robes. Dead drunk, no doubt. Carrying a valuable artifact. Just like their arrogance."

"Yes, sir. The criminal fled with his booty to Palanthas. We were told to be on the lookout for a kender who might try to fence stolen artifacts. We watched the mageware shops, and that was how we caught him. And a weary journey I've had of it to bring him back here, guarding the little fiend day and night."

Tas attempted to look quite fierce.

"I can imagine." The officer was sympathetic. "Was the artifact recovered?"

"I am afraid not, sir. He claims to have 'lost' it, but the fact that he was discovered in the mageware shop led us to believe that he has stashed it somewhere with the intent to produce it when he had closed a bargain. The Thorn Knights plan to question him regarding its whereabouts. Otherwise, of course"—Gerard shrugged—"we could have spared ourselves the trouble. We would have simply hung the thieving nit."

"The headquarters for the Thorns is down south. They're still looking for that damned tower. A waste of time, if you ask me. Magic is gone from the world again and I say good riddance."

"Yes, sir," Gerard replied. "I was instructed to report to Marshal Medan first, this being under his jurisdiction, but if you think I should proceed directly—"

"Report to Medan, by all means. If nothing else, he will get a good laugh out of the story. Do you need help with the kender? I have a man I could spare—"

"Thank you, sir. As you can see, he is well-secured. I anticipate no trouble."

"Ride on, then, Captain," said the officer, indicating with a wave of his hand that the gate was to be lifted. "Once you've delivered the vermin, ride back this way. We'll open a bottle of dwarf spirits, and you will tell me of the news from Palanthas."

"I will do that, sir," said Gerard, saluting.

He rode through the gate. Tasslehoff, bound and gagged, followed. The kender would have waved his manacled hands in a friendly good-bye, but he considered that this might not be in keeping with his new identity— Highwayman, Stealer of Valuable Magical Artifacts. He quite liked this new persona and decided he should try to be worthy of it. Therefore, instead of waving, he scowled defiantly at the knight as they rode past.

The elf had been standing in the road all this time, maintaining a deferential and bored silence. He did not even wait until the gate was lowered to go back to the gatehouse. The twilight had deepened to night and torches were being lit. Tasslehoff, peering over his shoulder as the pony clattered across the wooden bridge, saw the elf squat down beneath a torch and draw out a leather bag. A couple of the Knights knelt down in the dirt and they began a game of dice. The last Tas saw of them, the officer had joined them, bringing with him a bottle. Few travelers passed this way since the dragon now patrolled the roads. Their watch was a lonely one.

Tasslehoff indicated by various grunts and squeaks that he would be interested in talking about their successful adventure at the gate—in particular he wanted to hear more details about his daring theft—but Gerard paid no attention to the kender. He did not ride off at a gallop, but, once he was out of sight of the bridge he urged Blackie to increase his pace markedly.

Tasslehoff assumed that they would ride all night. They were not far from Qualinost, or at least so he remembered from his previous journeys to the elven capital. A couple of hours would find them in the city. Tas was eager to see his friends once again, eager to ask them if they had any idea who he was, if he wasn't himself. If anyone could cure magnesia, it would be Palin. Tasslehoff was extremely surprised when Gerard suddenly reined in his horse and, professing himself exhausted by the long day, announced that they would spend the night in the forest.

They made camp, building a fire, much to the kender's astonishment, for the Knight had refused to build a fire prior to this, saying that it was too dangerous.

"I guess he figures we're safe now that we're inside the borders of Qualinesti." Tasslehoff spoke to himself, for he was still wearing the gag. "I wonder why we stopped though? Maybe he doesn't know how close we are."

The Knight fried some salt pork. The aroma spread throughout the forest. He removed Tasslehoff's gag so that the kender could eat and was instantly sorry he'd done so.

"How did I steal the artifact?" Tas asked eagerly. "That's so exciting. I've never stolen anything before, you know. Stealing is extremely wrong. But I guess in this case it would be all right, since the Dark Knights are bad people. What inn was it? There are quite a few on the road to Palanthas. Was it the Dirty Duck? That's a great place. Everyone stops there. Or maybe the Fox and the Unicorn? They don't much like kender, so probably not."

Tasslehoff talked on, but he couldn't induce the Knight to tell him anything. That didn't really matter much to Tas, who was perfectly capable of making up the entire incident himself. By the time they had finished eating and Gerard had gone to wash the pan and the wooden bowls in a nearby stream, the bold kender had stolen not one but a host of wondrous magical artifacts, snatching them out from under the very noses of six Thorn Knights, who had threatened him with six powerful magicks, but who had, all six, been dispatched by a skilled blow from the kender's hoopak.

"And that must have been how I came down with magnesia!" Tas concluded. "One of the Thorn Knights struck me severely on the headbone! I was unconscious for several days. But, no," he added in disappointment. "That couldn't be true for otherwise I wouldn't have escaped." He pondered on this for a considerable time. "I have it," he said at last, looking with triumph at Gerard. "You hit me on the head when you arrested me!"

"Don't tempt me," Gerard said. "Now shut up and get some sleep." He spread out his blanket near the fire, which had been reduced to a pile of glowing embers. Pulling the blanket over himself, he turned his back to the kender.

Tasslehoff relaxed on his blanket, gazed up at the stars. Sleep wasn't going to catch him tonight. He was much too busy reliving his life as the Scourge of Ansalon, the Menace of Morgash, the Thug of Thorbardin. He was quite a wicked fellow. Women would faint and strong men would blanch at the mere sound of his name. He wasn't certain exactly what blanching entailed, but he had heard that strong men were subject to it when faced with a terrible foe, so it seemed suitable in this instance. He was just picturing his arrival in a town to find all the women passed out in their laundry tubs and the strong men blanching left and right when he heard a noise. A small noise, a twig snapping, nothing more.

Tas would not have noticed it except that he was used to not hearing any noises at all from the forest. He reached out his hand and tugged on the sleeve of Gerard's shirt.

"Gerard!" Tas said in a loud whisper. "I think someone's out there!"

Gerard snuffled and snorted, but didn't wake up. He hunched down deeper in his blanket.

Tasslehoff lay quite still, his ears stretched. He couldn't hear anything for a moment, then he heard another sound, a sound that might have been made by a boot slipping on a loose rock.

"Gerard!" said Tasslehoff. "I don't think it's the moon this time." He wished he had his hoopak.

Gerard rolled over at that moment and faced Tasslehoff, who was quite amazed to see by the dying fire that the Knight was not asleep. He was only playing possum.

"Keep quiet!" Gerard said in a hissing whisper. "Pretend you're asleep!" He shut his eyes.

Tasslehoff obediently shut his eyes, though he opened them again the next instant so as to be sure not to miss anything. Which was good, otherwise he would have never seen the elves creeping up on them from the darkness.

"Gerard, look out!" Tas started to shout, but a hand clapped down over his mouth and cold steel poked him in the neck before he could stammer out more than "Ger—"

"What?" Gerard mumbled sleepily. "What's—"

He was wide awake the next moment, trying to grab the sword that lay nearby.

One elf stomped down hard on Gerard's hand—Tas could hear bones crunch and he winced in sympathy. A second elf picked up the sword and moved it out of the Knight's reach. Gerard tried to stand up, but the elf who had stomped on his hand now kicked him viciously in the head. Gerard groaned and rolled over on his back, unconscious.

"We have them both, Master," said one of the elves, speaking to the shadows. "What are your orders?"

"Don't kill the kender, Kalindas," said a voice from the darkness, a human's voice, a man's voice, muffled, as if he were speaking from the depths of a hood. "I need him alive. He must tell us what he knows."

The human was not very woods-crafty apparently. Although Tas couldn't see him—the human had remained in the shadows—Tas could hear his booted feet mashing dry leaves and breaking sticks. The elves, by contrast, were as quiet as the night air.

"What about the Dark Knight?" the elf asked.

"Slay him," said the human indifferently.

The elf placed a knife at the Knight's throat.

"No!" Tas squeaked and wriggled. "You can't! He's not really a Dark—ulp!"

"Keep silent, kender," said the elf, who held onto Tas. He shifted the point of his knife from the kender's throat to his head. "Make another sound and I will cut off your ears. That will not affect your usefulness to us."

"I wish you wouldn't cut off my ears," said Tas, talking desperately, despite feeling the knife blade nick his skin. "They keep my hair from falling off my head. But if you have to, you have to, I guess. It's just that you're about to make a terrible mistake. We've come from Solace, Gerard's not a Dark Knight, you see. He's a Solamnic—"

"Gerard?" said the human suddenly from the darkness. "Hold your hand, Kellevandros! Don't kill him yet. I know a Solamnic named Gerard from Solace. Let me take a look."

The strange moon had risen again. Its light was intermittent, coming and going as dark clouds glided across its empty, vacuous face. Tas tried to catch a glimpse of the human, who was apparently in charge of this operation, for the elves deferred to him in all that was done. The kender was curious to see him, because he had a feeling he'd heard that voice before, although he couldn't quite place it.

Tas was doomed to disappointment. The human was heavily cloaked and hooded. He knelt beside Gerard. The Knight's head lolled to one side. Blood covered his face. His breathing was raspy. The human studied his face.

"Bring him along," he ordered.

"But, Master—" The elf called Kellevandros started to protest.

"You can always kill him later," said the human. Rising, he turned on his heel and walked back into the forest.

One of the elves doused the fire. Another elf went to calm the horses, particularly the black, who had reared in alarm at the sight of the intruders. A third elf put a gag in Tas's mouth, pricking Tas's right ear with the tip of the knife the moment the kender even looked as if he might protest.

The elves handled the Knight with efficiency and dispatch. They tied his hands and feet with leather cord, thrust a gag into his mouth, and fixed a blindfold around his eyes. Lifting the comatose Knight from the ground, they carried him to his horse and threw him over the saddle. Blackie had been alarmed by the sudden invasion of the camp, but he now stood quite calm and placid under an elf's soothing hand, his head over the elf's shoulder, nuzzling his ear. The elves tied Gerard's hands to his feet, passing the rope underneath the horse's belly, securing the Knight firmly to the saddle.

The human looked at the kender, but Tas couldn't get a glimpse of his face because at that moment an elf popped a gunny sack over his head and he couldn't see anything except gunny sack. The elves bound his feet together. Strong hands lifted him, tossed him headfirst over the saddle, and the Scourge of Ansalon, his head in a sack, was carried off into the night.

14 THE MASQUERADE

As the Scourge of Ansalon was being hauled off in ignominy and a sack, only a few miles away in Qualinost the Speaker of the Sun, ruler of the Qualinesti people, was hosting a masquerade ball. The masquerade was something relatively new to the elves—a human custom, brought to them by their Speaker, who had some share of human blood in him, a curse passed on by his father, Tanis Half-Elven. The elves generally disdained human customs as they disdained humans, but they had taken to the masquerade, which had been introduced by Gilthas in the year 21 to celebrate his ascension to the throne twenty years previously. Each year on this date he had given a masquerade, and it was now the social highlight of the season.

Invitations to this important event were coveted. The members of House Royal, the Heads of Household, the Thalas-Enthia—the elven Senate—were invited, as well as the top ranking leaders of the Dark Knights, Qualinesti's true rulers. In addition, twenty elf maidens were chosen to attend, handpicked by Prefect Palthainon, a former member of the elven Senate and now the chief magistrate newly appointed by the Knights of Neraka to oversee Qualinesti. Palthainon was nominally Gilthas's advisor and counselor. Around the capital he was jocularly referred to as the "Puppeteer."

The young ruler Gilthas was not yet married. There was no heir to the throne nor any prospect of one. Gilthas had no particular aversion to being married, but he simply could not quite make up his mind to go through with it. Marriage was an immense decision, he told his courtiers, and should not be entered into without due consideration. What if he made a mistake and chose the wrong person? His entire life could be ruined, as well as the life of the unfortunate woman. Nothing was ever said of love. It was not expected that the king should be in love with his wife. His marriage would be for political purposes only; this had been determined by Prefect Palthainon, who had chosen several eligible candidates from among the most prominent (and the most wealthy) elven families in Qualinesti.

Every year for the past five years, Palthainon had gathered together twenty of these hand-chosen elven women and presented them to the Speaker of the Sun for his approbation. Gilthas danced with them all, professed to like them all, saw good qualities in them all, but could not make up his mind. The prefect controlled much of the life of the Speaker—disparagingly termed "the puppet king" by his subjects—but Palthainon could not force his majesty to take a wife.

Now the time was an hour past midnight. The Speaker of the Sun had danced with each of the twenty in deference to the prefect, but Gilthas had not danced with any one of the elven maidens more than once—for a second dance would be seen as making a choice. After the close of every dance, the king retired to his chair and sat looking upon the festivities with a brooding air, as if the decision over which of the lovely women to dance with next was a weight upon him that was completely destroying his pleasure in the party.

The twenty maidens glanced at him out of the corners of their eyes, each hoping for some sign that he favored her above all the others. Gilthas was handsome to look upon. The human blood was not much apparent in his features, except, as he had matured, to give him a squareness of jaw and chin not usually seen in the male elf. His hair, of which he was said to be vain, was shoulder-length and honey-colored. His eyes were large and almond-shaped. His face was pale; it was known that he was in ill health much of the time. He rarely smiled and no one could fault him for that for everyone knew that the life he led was that of a caged bird. He was taught words to speak, was told when to speak them. His cage was covered up with a cloth when the bird was to be silent.

Small wonder then that Gilthas was known to be indecisive, vacillating, fond of solitude and of reading and writing poetry, an art he had taken up about three years previous and in which he showed undeniable talent. Seated on his throne, a chair of ancient make and design, the back of which was carved into the image of a sun and gilded with gold, Gilthas watched the dancers with a restive air and looked as if he could not wait to escape back to the privacy of his quarters and the happiness of his rhymes.

"His Majesty seems in unusually high spirits tonight," observed Prefect Palthainon. "Did you notice the way he favored the eldest daughter of the guildmaster of the Silversmiths?"

"Not particularly," returned Marshal Medan, leader of the occupation forces of the Knights of Neraka.

"Yes, I assure you, it is so," Palthainon argued testily. "See how he follows her with his eyes."

"His Majesty appears to me to be staring either at the floor or his shoes," Medan remarked. "If you are going to ever see an heir to the throne, Palthainon, you will have to make the marriage yourself."

"I would," Palthainon said, grumbling, "but elven law dictates that only the family may arrange a marriage, and his mother adamantly refuses to become involved unless and until the king makes up his mind."

"Then you had better hope His Majesty lives a long, long time," said Medan. "I should think he would, since you watch over him so closely and attend to his needs so assiduously. You can't really fault the king, Palthainon," the marshal added, "His Majesty is, after all, exactly what you and the late Senator Rashas have made him—a young man who dares not even take a piss without looking to you for permission."

"His Majesty's health is fragile," Palthainon returned stiffly. "It is my duty to remove from him from the burden of the cares and responsibilities of the ruler of the elven nation. Poor young man. He can't help dithering. The human blood, you know, Marshal. Notoriously weak. And now, if you will excuse me, I will go pay my respects to His Majesty."

The marshal, who was human, bowed wordlessly as the prefect, whose mask was, most appropriately, that of a stylized bird of prey, went over to peck at the young king. Politically, Medan found Prefect Palthainon extremely useful. Personally, Medan thought Palthainon utterly detestable.

Marshal Alexius Medan was fifty-five years old. He had joined the Knights of Takhisis under the leadership of Lord Ariakan prior to the Chaos War that had ended the Fourth Age of Krynn and brought in the Fifth. Medan had been the commander responsible for attacking Qualinesti over thirty years ago. He had been the one to accept the surrender of the Qualinesti people and had remained in charge ever since. Medan's rule was strict, harsh where it needed to be harsh, but he was not wantonly cruel. True, the elves had few personal freedoms anymore, but Medan did not view this lack as a hardship. To his mind, freedom was a dangerous notion, one that led to chaos, anarchy, the disruption of society.

Discipline, order, and honor—these were Medan's gods, now that Takhisis, with a complete lack of discipline and of honor, had turned traitor and run away, leaving her loyal Knights looking like utter fools. Medan imposed discipline and order on the Qualinesti. He imposed discipline and order on his Knights. Above all, he imposed these qualities on himself.

Medan watched with disgust as Palthainon bowed before the king. Well knowing that Palthainon's humility was all for show, Medan turned away. He could almost pity the young man Gilthas.

The dancers swirled about the marshal, elves dressed as swans and bears and every other variety of bird or woodland creature. Jesters and clowns clad in gay motley were in abundance. Medan attended the masquerade because protocol required it, but he refused to wear a mask or a costume. Years ago, the marshal had adopted the elven dress of loose flowing robes draped gracefully over the body as being most comfortable and practicable in the warm and temperate climate of Qualinesti. Since he was the only person in elven dress attending the masquerade, the human had the odd distinction of looking more like an elf than any other elf in the room.

The marshal left the hot and noisy dance floor and escaped, with relief, into the garden. He brought no body guards with him. Medan disliked being trailed about by Knights in clanking armor. He was not overly fearful for his safety. The Qualinesti had no love for him, but he had outlived a score of assassination attempts. He could take care of himself, probably better care than any of his Knights. Medan had no use for the men being taken into the Knighthood these days, considering them to be an undisciplined and surly lot of thieves, killers, and thugs. In truth, Medan trusted elves at his back far more than his own men.

The night air was soft and perfumed with the scents of roses and gardenias and orange blossoms. Nightingales sang in the trees, their melodies blending with the music of harp and lute. He recognized the music. Behind him, in the Hall of the Sky, lovely elf maidens were performing a traditional dance. He paused and half-turned, tempted to go back by the beauty of the music. The maidens were performing the *Quanisho*, the Awakening Promenade, a dance said to drive elf men wild with passion. He wondered if it would have any effect on the king. Perhaps he might be moved to a write a poem.

"Marshal Medan," said a voice at his elbow.

Medan turned. "Honored Mother of our Speaker," he said and bowed.

Laurana extended her hand, a hand that was white and soft and fragrant as the flower of the camellia. Medan took her hand, brought the hand to his lips.

"Come now," she said to him, "we are by ourselves. Such formal titles need not be observed between those of us who are—how should I describe us? 'Old enemies'?"

"Respected opponents," said Medan, smiling. He relinquished her hand, not without some reluctance.

Marshal Medan was not married, except to his duty. He did not believe in love, considered love a flaw in a man's armor, a flaw that left him vulnerable, open to attack. Medan admired Laurana and respected her. He thought her beautiful, as he thought his garden beautiful. He found her useful in assisting him to find his way through the sticky mass of fine-spun cobweb that was the elven version of government. He used her and he was well aware that in return she used him. A satisfactory and natural arrangement.

"Believe me, madam," he said quietly, "I find your dislike of me much preferable to other people's friendship."

He glanced meaningfully back into the palace, where Palthainon was standing at the young king's side, whispering into his ear.

Laurana followed his gaze. "I understand you, Marshal," she replied. "You are a representative of an organization I believe to be wholly given over to evil. You are the conqueror of my people, our subjugator. You are allied with our worst enemy, a dragon who is intent upon our total destruction. Yet, I trust you far more than I trust that man."

She turned away abruptly. "I do not like this view, sir. Would you mind if we walked to the arboretum?"

Medan was quite willing to spend a lovely moonlit night in the most enchanting land on Ansalon in company with the land's most enchanting woman. They walked side by side in companionable silence along a walkway of crushed marble that glittered and sparkled as if it would mimic the stars. The scent of orchids was intoxicating.

The Royal Arboretum was a house made of crystal, filled with plants whose fragile and delicate natures could not survive even the relatively mild winters of Qualinesti. The arboretum was some distance from the palace. Laurana did not speak during their long walk. Medan did not feel that it was his place to break this peaceful silence, and so he said nothing. In silence, the two approached the crystal building, its many facets reflecting the moon so that it seemed there must be a hundred moons in the sky instead of just one.

They entered through a crystal door. The air was heavy with the breath of the plants, which stirred and rustled as if in welcome.

The sound of the music and the laughter was completely shut out. Laurana sighed deeply, breathed deeply of the perfume that scented the warm, moist air.

She placed her hand upon an orchid, turning it to the moonlight.

"Exquisite," said Medan, admiring the plant. "My orchids thrive—especially those you have given me—but I cannot produce such magnificent blossoms."

"Time and patience," Laurana said. "As in all things. To continue our earlier conversation, Marshal, I will tell you why I respect you more than Palthainon. Though your words are not easy for me to hear sometimes I know that when you speak, you speak from your heart. You have never lied to me, even when a lie might have served your purpose better than the truth. Palthainon's words slide out of his mouth and fall to the ground, then slither away into the darkness."

Medan bowed to acknowledge the compliment, but he would not enter into further disparagement of the man who helped him keep Qualinesti under control. He changed the subject.

"You have left the revelries at an early hour, madam. I hope you are not unwell," he said politely.

"The heat and the noise were too much to bear," Laurana replied. "I came out into the garden for some quiet."

"Have you dined?" the marshal asked. "Could I send the servants for food or wine?"

"No, thank you, Marshal. I find I have very little appetite these days. You can serve me best by keeping me company for a while, if your duties do not call you away."

"With such a charming companion, I do not think that death himself could call me away," the Marshal returned.

Laurana glanced at him from beneath lowered lashes, smiled slightly. "Humans are not generally given to such pretty speeches. You have been around elves much too long, Marshal. In fact, I believe you are more elf than human now. You wear our clothes, you speak our language flawlessly, you enjoy our music and our poetry. You have issued laws that protect our woodlands, laws stronger than those we might have passed ourselves. Perhaps

I was wrong," she added lightly. "Perhaps you are the conquered and we are, in truth, your conquerors."

"You make sport of me, madam," Medan returned, "and you will probably laugh when I say that you are not far wrong. I was blind to nature before I came to Qualinesti. A tree was a thing I used to build a wall for a fortress or a handle for my battle-axe. The only music I enjoyed was the martial beating of the war drum. The only reading in which I took pleasure were dispatches from headquarters. I freely admit that I laughed when I first entered this land to see an elf speaking respectfully to a tree or talking gently to a flower. And then, one spring, after I had been living here about seven years, I was amazed to find myself eagerly awaiting the return of the flowers to my garden, wondering which would blossom first, wondering if the new rosebush the gardener had planted last year would bloom. At about the same time, I discovered the songs of the harpist running through my mind. I began to study the poetry to learn the words.

"In truth, Madam Lauralanthalasa, I do love your land. That is why," Medan added, his expression darkening, "I do my best to keep this land safe from the wrath of the dragon. That is why I must harshly punish those of your people who rebel against my authority. Beryl wants only an excuse to destroy you and your land. By persisting in resistance, by committing acts of terror and sabotage against my forces, the misguided rebels among your people threaten to bring destruction down upon you all."

Medan had no idea how old Laurana must be. Hundreds of years, perhaps. Yet she was as beautiful and youthful as the days when she had been the Golden General, leading the armies of light against the forces of Queen Takhisis during the War of the Lance. He had met old soldiers who spoke still of her courage in battle, her spirit that rallied the flagging spirits of the crumbling armies and led them to victory. He wished he could have known her then, though they would have been on opposite sides. He wished he could have seen her riding to battle on the back of her dragon, her golden hair a shining banner for her troops to follow.

"You say that you trust in my honor, madam," he continued and he took hold of her hand in his earnestness. "Then you must believe me when I tell you that I am working day and night to try to save Qualinesti. These rebels do not make my task easy. The dragon hears of their attacks and their defiance and grows extremely angry. She wonders aloud why she wastes her time and money ruling over such troublesome subjects. I do my best to placate her, but she is fast losing patience."

"Why do you tell me this, Marshal Medan?" Laurana asked. "What has this to do with me?"

"Madam, if you have any influence over these rebels, please stop them. Tell them that while their acts of terror may do some harm to myself and my troops, in the long run, the rebels are harming only their own people."

"And what makes you think that I, the Queen Mother, have anything to do with rebels?" Laurana asked. A flush came to her cheeks. Her eyes glittered.

Medan regarded her in silent admiration for a moment, then replied, "Let us say that I find it difficult to believe that someone who fought the Dark Queen and her minions so tenaciously over fifty years ago during the War of the Lance has ceased to do battle."

"You are wrong, Marshal," Laurana protested. "I am old, too old for such matters. No, Sir"—she forestalled his speaking—"I know what you are going to say. You are going to say that I look as young as a maiden at her first dance. Save your pretty compliments for those who desire to hear them. I do not. I have no heart left for battle, for defiance. My heart is in the tomb where my dear husband, Tanis, lies buried. My family is all that matters to me now. I want to see my son happily married, I want to hold grandchildren in my arms. I want our land to be at peace and I am willing to pay tribute to the dragon for our land to remain at peace."

Medan regarded her skeptically. He heard the ring of truth in her voice, but she was not telling him the entire truth. Laurana had been a skilled diplomat in the days following the war. She was accustomed to telling people what they wanted to hear while subtly swaying them to believe what she wanted them to believe. Still, it would have been extremely impolite to openly doubt her words. And if she meant them, Medan pitied her. The son on whom she doted was a spineless jellyfish who took hours to decide whether to have strawberries or blueberries for luncheon. Gilthas was not likely to ever take such an important step as making up his mind to wed. Unless, of course, someone else picked out his bride for him.

Laurana averted her head but not before Medan had seen the tears welling in her almond eyes. He changed the subject back to orchids. He was attempting to grow some in his own garden and was having minimal success. He discussed orchids for a long while, giving Laurana a chance to regain her composure. A quick touch of her hand to her eyes and she was once more in control. She recommended her own gardener, a master with orchids.

Medan accepted the offer with pleasure. The two of them lingered another hour in the arboretum, discussing strong roots and waxen flowers.

"Where is my honored mother, Palthainon?" Gilthas, Speaker of the Sun, asked. "I have not seen her this past half-hour."

The king was dressed in the costume of an elven ranger, all in greens and browns, colors that were becoming to him. Gilthas looked quite impressive, though few elven rangers were likely to go about their duties attired in the finest silken hose and shirts, or a hand-tooled and gold-embossed leather vest with matching boots. He held a cup of wine in his hand, but he only sipped at it out of politeness. Wine gave him a headache, everyone knew.

"I believe that your mother is walking in the garden, Your Majesty," said Prefect Palthainon, who missed nothing of the comings and goings of the House Royal. "She spoke of needing air. Would you have me send for her? Your Majesty does not look well."

"I am not well," Gilthas said. "Thank you for your kind offer, Palthainon, but do not disturb her." His eyes darkened, he looked out upon the throng of dancers with sadness and wistful envy. "Do you think anyone would take it amiss if I were to retire to my room, Prefect?" he asked in a low voice.

"Perhaps a dance would cheer Your Majesty," Palthainon said. "There, look at how the lovely Amiara smiles at you." The prefect leaned near the king to whisper, "Her father is one of the wealthiest elves in all of Qualinesti. Silversmith, you know. And she is perfectly charming—"

"Yes, she is," said Gilthas in disinterested agreement. "But I do not feel equal to dancing. I am feeling faint and nauseated. I believe that I really must retire."

"By all means, if Your Majesty is truly not well," said Palthainon reluctantly. Medan was right. Having robbed the king of a spine, the prefect could not very well fault the young man for crawling about on his hands and knees. "Your Majesty should rest in bed tomorrow. I will take care of the affairs of state."

"Thank you, Palthainon," Gilthas said quietly. "If I am not needed, I will spend the day working on the twelfth canto in my new poem."

He rose to his feet. The music came to a sudden halt. The dancers ceased in mid-whirl. Elven men bowed, elven women curtsied. The elven maidens looked up in expectation. Gilthas seemed embarrassed by the sight of them. Ducking his head, he stepped down off the dais and walked quickly toward the door that led to his private chambers. His personal servant accompanied him, walking ahead of the king, bearing a glowing candelabra to light His Majesty's way. The elven maidens shrugged and glanced about demurely for new partners. The music began again. The dancing continued.

Prefect Palthainon, muttering imprecations, headed for the refreshment table.

Gilthas, glancing back before he left the room, smiled to himself. Turning, he followed the soft glow of the candlelight through the darkened hallways of his palace. Here no courtiers flattered and fawned, here no one was permitted to enter without first obtaining permission from Palthainon, who lived in constant fear that some day someone else might wrest away the marionette's strings. Kagonesti guards stood at every entrance.

Freed from the music and the lights, the twittering laughter and the whispering conversations, Gilthas breathed a sigh of relief as he walked the well-guarded corridors. The newly built palace of the Speaker of the Sun was a large and airy dwelling of living trees that had been magically altered and lovingly transformed into ceilings and walls. The tapestries were made of flowers and plants coaxed to form beautiful works of art that changed daily depending on what was in bloom. The floors of some of the rooms of the palace, such as the dancing room and the audience chambers, were made of marble. Most of the private rooms and the hallways that wound among the boles of the trees were carpeted with fragrant plants.

The palace was considered something of a marvel among the Qualinesti people. Gilthas had insisted that all the trees standing on the land be utilized in the shapes and positions in which the trees had grown naturally. He would not permit the Woodshapers to coax them into bending themselves into unnatural poses to accommodate a staircase or shifting their branches to provide more light. Gilthas intended this as a sign of honor to the trees, who were pleased, it seemed, for they flourished and thrived. The result was, however, an irregular maze of leafy corridors, where those new to the palace would often lose themselves for hours on end.

The king did not speak, but walked with his head bowed and his hands clasped behind him. He was often to be seen in this attitude, roaming restlessly the halls of the palace. It was known that at these times he was mulling over some rhyme or trying to work out the rhythm of a stanza. The servants knew better than to interrupt him. Those who passed bowed low and said nothing.

The palace was quiet this night. The music of the dance could be heard, but it was soft and muted by the gentle rustling of the thickly entangled leaves that formed the high ceiling of the corridor through which they walked. The king lifted his head, glanced about. Seeing no one, Gilthas moved a step closer to his servant.

"Planchet," said Gilthas in a low voice, speaking the human language which few elves spoke, "where is Marshal Medan? I thought I saw him go into the garden."

"He did, Your Majesty," his servant replied, answering in the same language, soft and low, not turning around to look at the king lest someone should be watching them. Palthainon's spies were everywhere.

"That's unfortunate," said Gilthas, frowning. "What if he's still hanging about out there?"

"Your mother noticed and followed after him immediately, Your Majesty. She will keep him occupied."

"You are right," said Gilthas with a smile, a smile only a trusted few ever saw. "Medan will not bother us this night. Is everything ready?"

"I have packed food enough for a day's journeying, Your Majesty. The knapsack is hidden in the grotto."

"And Kerian? Does she know where to meet me?"

"Yes, Your Majesty. I left the message in the usual spot. It was gone the next morning when I went to check. A red rose was in its place."

"You have done well, as always, Planchet," Gilthas said. "I do not know what I would do without you. I want that rose, by the way."

"The rose is with Your Majesty's knapsack," said Planchet.

The two ceased talking. They had arrived at the Speaker's personal chambers. The king's Kagonesti guards—ostensibly body guards, but in reality, prison guards—saluted as His Majesty approached. Gilthas paid them no heed. The guards were in Palthainon's pay, they reported every movement the king made to the prefect. Servants waited in the king's bedroom to assist His Majesty in undressing and preparing for bed.

"His Majesty is not feeling well," Planchet announced to the servants as he placed the candelabra upon a table. "I will attend him. You have leave to go."

Gilthas, pale and languishing, dabbed his lips with his lace handkerchief and went immediately to lie down upon his bed, not even bothering to take off his boots. Planchet would see to that for him. The servants, who were accustomed to the king's ill health and his desire for solitude, had expected nothing else after the rigors of a party. They bowed and departed.

"No one is to disturb His Majesty," Planchet said, shutting the door and locking it. The guards also had keys, but they rarely used them now. In the past, they had checked upon the young king on a frequent basis. They always found him where he was supposed to be, sick in bed or dreaming over his pen and paper, and at last they'd stopped checking.

Planchet listened at the door a moment, waited to hear the guards relax and return to their games of chance with which they whiled away the long and boring hours. Satisfied, he crossed the room, threw open the doors that led to the balcony, and looked out into the night.

"All is well, Your Majesty."

Gilthas jumped from the bed and headed for the window. "You know what to do?"

"Yes, Your Majesty. The pillows are prepared that will take your place in the bed. I am to keep up the pretense that you are in the room. I will not permit anyone to visit you."

"Very good. You need not worry about Palthainon. He will not put in an appearance until tomorrow morning. He will be too busy signing my name and affixing my seal to important documents."

Gilthas stood by the balustrade of the balcony. Planchet affixed a rope to the balustrade, held it fast. "A profitable journey, Your Majesty. When do you return?"

"If all goes well, Planchet, I will be back by midnight tomorrow night."

"All will go well," said the elf. He was several years older than Gilthas, hand-picked by Laurana to serve her son. Prefect Palthainon had approved the choice. Had the prefect bothered to check Planchet's background, which included many years of loyal service to the dark elf Porthios, the prefect might not have. "Fate smiles upon Your Majesty."

Gilthas had been looking into the garden, searching for signs of movement. He glanced back quickly. "There was a time I could have argued with that statement, Planchet. I used to believe myself the unluckiest person in this world, snared by my own vanity and conceit, imprisoned by my own fear. There was a time I used to see death as my only escape."

Impulsively, he reached out and grasped the hand of his servant. "You forced me to look away from the mirror, Planchet. You forced me to stop staring into my own reflection, to turn and look upon the world. When I did, I saw my people suffering, crushed beneath the heel of black boots, living in the shadows of dark wings, facing a future of despair and certain destruction."

"No longer do they live without hope," said Planchet, gently withdrawing his hand, embarrassed by the king's regard. "Your Majesty's plan will succeed."

Gilthas sighed. "Let us hope so, Planchet. Let us hope that Fate smiles on more than me. Let us hope she smiles upon our people."

He descended the rope nimbly, hand over hand, and dropped lightly into the garden. Planchet watched from the balcony until the king had disappeared into the night. Planchet then shut the doors and walked back over to the bed. He placed the pillows on it and arranged the coverlet convincingly about them so that if anyone looked, they would see what appeared to be a body in the bed.

"And now, Your Majesty," Planchet said loudly, picking up a small harp and running his hands over the strings, "take your sleeping draught and I will play some soft music to lull you into slumber."

15   TASSLEHOFF, THE ONE AND ONLY

Despite being in pain and extreme discomfort, Sir Gerard was satified with the way things were going thus far. He had a throbbing head-ache from where the elf had kicked him. He was tied to his horse, dangling head down over the saddle. The blood pounded in his temples, his breastplate jabbed into his stomach and constricted his breathing, leather cords cut into his flesh, and he had lost all feeling in his feet. He did not know his captors, he'd been unable to see them in the darkness, and now, blindfolded, he could see nothing at all. They had very nearly killed him. He had the kender to thank for keeping him alive.

Yes, things were going as planned.

They traveled for a considerable distance. The journey seemed endless to Gerard, who began to think after awhile that they had been riding for decades, long enough to have circumnavigated Krynn itself at least six times. He had no idea how the kender was faring, but judging by the occasional indignant squeaks emanating from somewhere behind him Gerard assumed that Tasslehoff was relatively intact. Gerard must have dozed, either that or he'd passed out, for he woke suddenly when the horse came to a halt.

The human was speaking, the human whom Gerard took to be the leader. He was speaking in Elvish, a language Gerard did not understand. But it seemed that they had reached their destination for the elves were cutting loose the bindings holding him on the saddle. One of the elves grabbed him by the back of the breastplate, pulled him off the horse's back and dumped him on the ground.

"Get up, swine!" the elf said harshly in Common. "We are not going to carry you." The elf removed the Knight's blindfold. "Into that cave over there. March."

They had traveled through the night. The sky was pink with the coming of dawn. Gerard saw no cave, only thick and impenetrable forest, until one of the elves picked up what appeared to be a stand of young trees and moved it. A dark cavern in the side of a rock wall came into view. The elf placed the screen of trees to one side.

Staggering to his feet, Gerard limped forward. The sky was growing brighter, now fiery orange and sea-blue. He looked about for his companion, saw the kender's feet sticking out of a sack that was a bulky shape on the pony's back. The human leader stood near the cave entrance, keeping watch. He was cloaked and hooded, but Gerard caught a glimpse of dark robes beneath the cloak, robes such as a magic-user might wear. The Knight was becoming more and more certain that his plan had worked. Now he just had to hope that the elves would not kill him before he had a chance to explain himself.

The cave was set in a small hill in a heavily forested area. Gerard had the impression that they were not in some isolated patch of wilderness but close to a community. He could hear on the distant breeze the sound of the bell flowers elves liked to plant around the windows of their dwellings, flowers whose blossoms rang musically when the wind's breath touched them. He could also smell the scent of fresh-baked bread. Glancing in the direction of the rising sun, he confirmed that they had traveled due west during the night. If he was not actually in the city of Qualinost, he must be very close by.

The human entered the cavern. Two of the elves followed, one of them carrying the squirming kender trussed up in his sack, the other walking behind Gerard, prodding him in the back with a sword. The other elves who had accompanied them did not enter the cave but vanished into the woods, taking the pony and the Knight's horse with them. Gerard hesitated a moment before stepping into the cave. The elf shoved him in the back and he stumbled forward.

A dark, narrow passage opened up into a smallish chamber lit by a flame floating on a bowl of sweet-smelling oil. The elf carrying the kender dropped the sack to the floor, where the kender began to squeak and squeal and wriggle inside the sack. The elf gave the sack a nudge with his foot, told the kender to be silent; they would let him out in good time, and then only if he behaved himself. The elf guarding Gerard prodded him again in the back.

"On your knees, swine," said the elf.

Gerard sank to his knees and lifted his head. Now he had a good view of the human's face, for he could look up into it. The man in the cloak looked down grimly at Gerard.

"Palin Majere," said Gerard with a sigh of relief. "I have come a long way in search of you."

Palin brought the torch close. "Gerard uth Mondar. I thought that was you. But since when did you become a Knight of Neraka? You had best explain and quickly." He frowned. "As you know, I have no love for that accursed Knighthood."

"Yes, sir." Gerard glanced uncertainly at the elves. "Do they speak the human language, sir?"

"And Dwarvish and Common," Palin answered. "I can order them to kill you in any number of languages. I say again, explain yourself. You have one minute."

"Very well, sir," Gerard replied. "I wear this armor of necessity, not by choice. I bear important news for you and, finding out from your sister Laura that you were in Qualinesti, I disguised myself as one of the enemy so that I could safely reach you."

"What news?" Palin asked. He had not removed the dark hood, but spoke from its shadowy depths. Gerard could not see his face. His voice was deep and stern and cold.

Gerard thought of what people in Solace were saying about Palin Majere these days. He was changed since the Academy had been destroyed. He had changed and not for the better. He had veered off the sunlit road to walk a dark path, a path his uncle Raistlin had walked before him.

"Sir," said Gerard, "your honored father is dead."

Palin said nothing. His expression did not alter.

"He did not suffer," the Knight hastened to assure Palin. "Death took your father swiftly. He walked out the door of the Inn, looked into the sunset, spoke your mother's name, pressed his hand over his heart, and fell. I was with him when he died. He was at peace, in no pain. We held his funeral the next day. He was laid to rest at your mother's side."

"Did he say anything?" Palin asked at last.

"He made a request of me, which I will tell you about in due time."

Palin regarded Gerard in silence for long moments. Then he said, "And how is everything else in Solace?"

"Sir?" Gerard was astonished, appalled.

The kender in the sack gave a wail, but no one paid any attention.

"Did you not hear—?" Gerard began.

"My father is dead. I heard," Palin replied. He threw back his cowl, regarded Gerard with an unwavering gaze. "He was an old man. He missed my mother. Death is a part of life. Some might say"—his voice hardened—"the best part."

Gerard stared. He had last seen Palin Majere a few months ago, when he had attended the funeral of his mother, Tika. Palin had not remained in Solace long. He had left almost immediately on yet another search for ancient magical artifacts. With the Academy destroyed, Solace held nothing for Palin anymore. And with rumors running rife that wizards all over the world were losing their magical powers, people guessed that Palin was no different. It seemed, so they whispered, that life held nothing more for him. His marriage was not the happiest. He had grown careless, reckless of his safety, especially if the slightest chance offered of obtaining a magical artifact from the Fourth Age. For these artifacts had not lost their power and such power could be leeched by a skilled wizard.

Gerard had thought Palin looked unwell at the funeral. This trip had done nothing to improve the mage's health. If anything, he was more gaunt, more pallid, his manner more restive, his gaze furtive, distrustful.

Gerard knew a great deal about Palin. Caramon had been fond of talking about his only surviving son, and he had been a topic of conversation at almost every breakfast.

Palin Majere, the youngest son of Caramon and Tika, had been a promising young mage when the gods left Krynn, taking magic with them. Although he grieved the loss of the godly magic, Palin had not given up, as did so many wizards of his generation. He had brought together mages from all over Ansalon in an effort to learn to use the magic he believed remained in the world, wild magic that was of the world itself. Such magic had been part of the world before the coming of the gods, and, so he had supposed, would remain in the world even after the departure of the gods. His efforts had been successful. He had established the Academy of Sorcery in Solace, a center of learning for magic. The Academy had grown and prospered. He had used his skills to fight the great dragons and was renowed throughout Abanasinia as a hero.

Then the tapestry of his life had begun to unravel.

Extraordinarily sensitive to the wild magic, he had been among the first, two years ago, to notice that its powers were starting to weaken. At first, Palin thought this might be nothing more than a symptom of advancing age. He was past fifty, after all. But then his students began to report similar problems. Even the young were finding spell-casting more difficult. Obviously age was not a factor.

The spells would work, but they required more and more effort on the part of the magic-user to cast them. Palin compared it once to putting a jar over a lighted candle. The flame will burn only so long as there is air trapped within the jar. When the air is gone, the flame will falter, flicker, and die.

Was magic finite, as some were saying? Could it dry up like a pond in the desert? Palin didn't think so. The magic was there. He could feel it, see it. But it was as if the desert pond was being drunk dry by a vast multitude.

Who or what was draining the magic? Palin suspected the great dragons. He was forced to change his mind when the great green dragon Beryl grew more threatening, became more aggressive, sent her armies to seize more territory. Qualinesti spies reported that this was happening because the dragon was feeling her own magical powers on the decrease. Beryl had long sought to find the Tower of High Sorcery at Wayreth. The magical forest had kept the Tower hidden from her and from the Knights of the Thorn who had been searching for it. Her need for the Tower and its magic became more urgent. Angry and uneasy, she began to extend her reach over as much of Abanasinia as was possible without drawing down on herself the wrath of her cousin Malys.

The Knights of the Thorn, the magic-wielding arm of the Knights of Neraka, were also feeling their magical powers on the wane. They blamed Palin and his mages of the Academy of Sorcery. In a daring raid on the Academy, they kidnapped Palin, while Beryl's dragon minions destroyed it.

After months of "questioning," the Gray Robes had released Palin. Caramon had not wanted to go into details about the torment his son had endured, and Gerard had not pressed him. The residents of Solace discussed the matter at length, however. In their opinion, the enemy had not only twisted Palin's Majere's fingers, they had twisted his soul as well.

Palin's face was haggard, hollow-cheeked, with dark splotches beneath the eyes as if he slept little. He had few wrinkles; the skin was pulled taut, stretched over the fine bones. The deep lines around his mouth, which had marked the track of smiles, were beginning to fade away from disuse. His auburn hair had gone completely gray. The fingers of his hands, once supple and slender, were now twisted, cruelly deformed.

"Cut his bindings," Palin ordered the elves. "He is a Solamnic Knight, as he claims."

The two elves were dubious, but they did as they were told, though they continued to keep a close watch on him. Gerard rose to his feet, flexed his arms, and stretched his aching muscles.

"So you came all this way, disguised, risking your life to bring me this news," said Palin. "I must confess that I fail to see the need for the kender. Unless the story I heard is true, that this kender really did steal a powerful magical artifact. Let us have a look at him."

Palin knelt down beside the sack where the kender wriggled. He stretched out his hand, started to try to untie the knots, but his deformed fingers could not manage. Gerard looked at the wizard's fingers, looked quickly away, not wanting to seem to pity him.

"Does the sight distress you?" Palin asked with a sneer. Standing up, he covered his hands with the sleeves of his robes. "I'll take care not to trouble you."

"It does distress me, sir," Gerard said quietly. "It distresses me to see any good man suffer as you have suffered."

"Suffered, yes! I was a prisoner of the Thorn Knights for three months. Three months! And not a day passed when they did not torment me in some way. Do you know why? Do you know what they wanted? They wanted to know why their magical power was waning! They thought *I* had something to do with it!" Palin gave a bitter laugh. "And do you want to know why they let me go? Because they realized I was not a threat! Just a broken old man who could do nothing to harm them or hinder them."

"They might have killed you, sir," Gerard said.

"It would have been better if they had," Palin returned.

The two were silent. Gerard looked down at the floor. Even the kender was quiet, subdued. He had quit wrigglng.

Palin gave a soft sigh. Reaching out his broken hand, he touched Gerard's arm.

"Forgive me, Sir Knight," he said in a quieter tone. "Pay no heed to what I said. I am quick to take offense these days. And I have not yet even thanked you for bringing me news of my father. I do thank you. I am sorry for his death, but I cannot grieve for him. As I said, he has gone to a better place.

"And now," Palin added with a shrewd look at the young Knight, "I am beginning to think that this sad news alone has not brought you all this way. Wearing this disguise puts you in great danger, Gerard. If the Dark Knights were to discover the truth, you would endure torment far worse than what I suffered, and then you would be executed."

Palin's thin lips formed a bitter smile. "What other news do you have for me? It can't be good. No one would risk his life to bring me good news. And how could you know that you would find me?"

"I did not find you, sir," Gerard said. "You found me."

Palin looked puzzled, at first, then he nodded. "Ah, I understand. The mention of the artifact that once belonged to my Uncle Raistlin. You knew that would pique my interest."

"I hoped it would do so, sir," said Gerard. "My guess was that either the elf posted at the bridge would be part of the resistance movement or the bridge itself would be under observation. I trusted that the mention of an artifact coupled with the name Majere would be carried to you."

"You ran a great risk in trusting yourself to the elves. As you found out, there are those who would have no compunction in slaying one of your kind."

Gerard glanced at the two elves, Kalindas and Kelevandros, if he had heard the names right. They had not shifted their eyes from him once, kept their hands on the hilts of their swords.

"I am aware of that, sir," said Gerard. "But this seemed the only way to reach you."

"So I take it there is no artifact?" Palin said, adding in a tone of bitter disappointment. "It was all a ruse."

"On the contrary, sir, there *is* an artifact. That is part of the reason I came."

At this, the kender's squeaks started up again, louder and more insistent. He began to drum his feet on the floor, and he rolled about wildly in his sack.

"For mercy's sake, shut him up," Palin ordered irritably. "His screeching will summon every Dark Knight in Qualinesti. Carry him inside."

"We should leave him in the sack, Master," said Kalindas. "We do not want him finding his way back here."

"Very well," Palin agreed.

One of the elves picked up the kender, sack and all. The other elf glared sternly at Gerard and asked a question.

"No," Palin answered. "We do not need to blindfold him. He belongs to the old school of Knights: those who still believe in honor."

The elf carrying the kender walked toward the back of the cave and, to Gerard's intense astonishment, continued right through solid stone. Palin followed, placing his hand on Gerard's arm and propelling the Knight forward. The illusion of stone was so convincing that it was all Gerard could do to keep from wincing as he walked into what looked like a wall of sharp and jagged rocks.

"Some magic still works apparently," Gerard said, impressed.

"Some," Palin said. "But it is erratic. The spell can fail at any moment and must be constantly renewed."

Gerard emerged from the wall to find himself in a garden of wondrous beauty, shaded by trees whose branches and thick leaves formed a solid curtain above and around them. Kalindas carried the bagged kender through the wall, deposited him on the flagstone walk of the garden. Chairs made of bent willow branches and a table made of crystal stood beside a shining pool of clear water.

Palin said something to Kelevandros. Gerard caught the name, "Laurana." The elf departed, running lightly through the garden.

"You have loyal guardians, sir," said Gerard, looking after the elf.

"They belong to the household of the Queen Mother," Palin replied. "They have been in Laurana's service for years, ever since her husband died. Sit down."

He made a motion with his crooked hands and a fall of water began, streaming down in front of the illusionary wall to splash into the pool below.

"I have sent to inform the Queen Mother of your arrival. You are now a guest in her house. Or rather, one of the gardens in her house. Here, you are safe, as safe as anyone is in these dark times."

Thankfully, Gerard removed the heavy breastplate and rubbed his bruised ribs. He laved his face with the cool water and drank deeply.

"Let the kender out now," Palin ordered.

Kalindas untied the sack and the kender emerged, flushed and indignant, his long hair covering his face. He sucked in a huge breath and wiped his forehead.

"Whew! I was getting really sick of smelling nothing but sack."

Flipping his topknot back over his head, the kender looked around with interest.

"My," he said. "This garden is pretty. Are there fish in that pool? Could I catch one, do you think? It was certainly stuffy in that sack, and I much prefer riding a horse sitting up on the saddle instead of lying down. I have a sort of pain here in my side where something poked me. I would introduce myself," he said contritely, apparently realizing that he wasn't conforming to the mores of polite society, "but I'm suffering from"—he caught Gerard's eye and said, with emphasis, "I am suffering *from a severe bump on the head* and I'm not quite certain who I am. You look awfully familiar to me. Have we met?"

Palin Majere had said nothing through this diatribe. His face had gone livid. He opened his mouth, but no words came out.

"Sir." Gerard reached out a supporting hand. "Sir, you should sit down. You don't look well."

"I have no need of your support," Palin snapped, shoving aside Gerard's hand. He stared at the kender.

"Quit the nonsense," he said coldly. "Who are you?"

"Who do you think I am?" the kender parried.

Palin seemed about to make an angry rejoinder, but he closed his lips over the words and, after drawing in a deep breath, he said tightly, "You look like a kender I once knew named Tasslehoff Burrfoot."

"And you look sort of like a friend of mine named Palin Majere." The kender was gazing at Palin with interest.

"I am Palin Majere. Who are—"

"Really?" The kender's eyes opened wide. "You're Palin? What *happened* to you? You look *terrible!* Have you been sick? And your poor hands. Let me see them. You said the Dark Knights did that to you? How? Did they smash your finger bones with a hammer, 'cause that's what it looks like—"

Palin drew his sleeves over his hands, moved away from the kender. "You say you know me, kender? How?"

"I just saw you at Caramon's *first* funeral. You and I had a nice long chat, all about the Tower of High Sorcery at Wayreth and you being head of the White Robes, and Dalamar was there, and he was Head of the Conclave, and his girl friend Jenna was Head of the Red Robes, and—"

Palin frowned, looked at Gerard. "What is he talking about?"

"Don't pay any attention to him, sir. He's been acting crazy ever since I found him." Gerard looked strangely at Palin. "You said he resembled 'Tasslehoff.' That's who he claimed to be, until he started all this nonsense about having amnesia. I know it sounds odd, but your father also thought he was Tasslehoff."

"My father was an old man," Palin said, "and like many old men, he was probably reliving the days of his youth. And yet," he added softly, almost to himself, "he certainly does look like Tasslehoff!"

"Palin?" A voice called to him from the far end of the garden. "What is this Kelevandros tells me?"

Gerard turned to see an elven woman, beautiful as a winter's twilight, walking toward them along the flagstones. Her hair was long and the color of honey mingled with sunlight. She was dressed in robes of a pearly diaphanous material, so that she seemed to be clothed in mist. Catching sight of Gerard, she regarded him in disbelief, too outraged at first to pay any attention to the kender, who was jumping up and down and waving his hand in excitement.

Gerard, confused and awe-struck, made an awkward bow.

"You have brought a Dark Knight *here,* Palin!" Laurana turned on him in anger. "To our hidden garden! What is the reason for this?"

"He is not a Dark Knight, Laurana," Palin explained tersely, "as I told Kelevandros. Apparently, he doubts me. This man is Gerard uth Mondar, Knight of Solamnia, a friend of my father's from Solace."

Laurana looked at Gerard skeptically. "Are you certain, Palin? Then why is he wearing that foul armor?"

"I wear the armor for disguise only, my lady," Gerard said. "And, as you see, I have taken the first opportunity I could to cast it aside."

"This was the only way he could enter Qualinesti," Palin added.

"I beg your pardon, Sir Knight," Laurana said, extending a hand that was white and delicate. Yet, when he took it, he felt the calluses on her palm from her days when she had carried a shield and wielded a sword, the days when she had been the Golden General. "Forgive me. Welcome to my home."

Gerard bowed again in profound respect. He wanted to say something graceful and correct, but his tongue felt too big for his mouth, just as his hands and feet felt big and clumsy. He flushed deeply and stammered something that died away in a muddle.

"Me, Laurana! Look at me!" The kender called out.

Laurana turned now to take a good look at the kender and appeared astonished at what she saw. Her lips parted, her jaw went slack. Putting her hand to her heart, she fell back a step, staring all the while at the kender.

"*Alshana, Quenesti-Pah!*" she whispered. "It cannot be!"

Palin was watching her closely. "You recognize him, as well."

"Why, yes! It's Tasslehoff!" Laurana cried dazedly. "But how—Where—"

"I am Tasslehoff?" The kender looked anxious. "Are you certain?"

"What makes you think you're not?" Laurana asked.

"I always thought I was," Tas said solemnly. "But no one else did, and so I thought perhaps I'd made a mistake. But if you say I am Tasslehoff, Laurana, I suppose that settles it. You of all people wouldn't be likely to make a mistake. Would you mind if I gave you a hug?"

Tas flung his arms around Laurana's waist. She looked confusedly over his head from Palin back to Gerard, asking silently for an explanation.

"Are you in earnest?" Gerard demanded. "Begging your pardon, my lady," he added, flushing, realizing he'd come close to calling the Queen Mother a liar, "but Tasslehoff Burrfoot has been dead for over thirty years. How could this be possible? Unless—"

"Unless what?" Palin asked sharply.

"Unless his whole wild tale is somehow true." Gerard fell silent, pondering this unforeseen development.

"But, Tas, where have you been?" Laurana asked, removing one of her rings from his hand just as the ring was disappearing down his shirt front. "As Sir Gerard said, we thought you were dead!"

"I know. I saw the tomb. Very nice." Tas nodded. "That's where I met Sir Gerard. I do think you might work to keep the grounds cleaner—all the dogs you know—and the tomb itself is not in good repair. It was hit by lightning when I was inside it. I heard the most tremendous boom, and some of the marble fell off. And it was awfully dark inside. A few windows would sort of brighten the place—"

"We should go somewhere to talk, Palin," Gerard interrupted urgently. "Some place private."

"I agree. Laurana, the Knight has brought other sad news. My father is dead."

"Oh!" Laurana put her hand to her mouth. Tears filled her eyes. "Oh, I am sorry, Palin. My heart grieves for him, yet grief seems wrong. He is happy now," she added in wistful envy. "He and Tika are together. Come inside," she added, glancing about the garden where Tasslehoff was now wading in the ornamental pond, displacing the water lilies and terrorizing the fish. "We should not discuss this out here." She sighed. "I fear that even my garden is not safe anymore."

"What happened, Laurana?" Palin demanded. "What do you mean the garden is not safe?"

Laurana sighed, a line marred her smooth forehead. "I spoke to Marshal Medan at the masquerade last night. He suspects me of having dealings with the rebels. He urged me to use my influence to make them cease their acts of terror and disruption. The dragon Beryl is grown paranoid lately. She threatenes to send her armies to attack us. We are not yet prepared if she should."

"Pay no heed to Medan, Laurana. He is concerned only with saving his own precious skin," said Palin.

"I believe that he means well, Palin," Laurana returned. "Medan has no love for the dragon."

"He has no love for anyone except himself. Don't be fooled by his show of concern. Medan avoids trouble for Medan, that is all. He is caught in a quandary. If the attacks and sabotage continue, his superiors will relieve him of his command, and from what I've heard of their new Lord of the Night Targonne, Medan might well be relieved of his head. Now, if you will excuse me, I will go divest myself of this heavy cloak. I will meet you in the atrium."

Palin departed, the folds of his black traveling cloak sweeping behind him. His stance was straight, his walk quick and firm. Laurana looked after him, troubled.

"Madam," said Gerard, finding his tongue at last. "I agree with Palin. You must not trust this Marshal Medan. He is a Dark Knight, and although they speak of honor and sacrifice their words are empty and hollow as their souls."

"I know you are right," Laurana said. "Still, I have seen the seed of good fall in the darkest swamp to grow strong and beautiful though it was poisoned by the most noxious miasma. And I have seen the same seed, nurtured by the softest rains and the brightest sunshine, grow twisted and ugly, to bear a bitter fruit."

She continued to gaze after Palin. Sighing, she shook her head and turned around. "Come along, Tas. I would like you and Gerard to see the rest of the wonders I have in my house."

Cheerfully dripping, Tasslehoff climbed out of the pond. "You go ahead, Gerard. I want to talk to Laurana alone for a moment. It's a secret," he added.

Laurana smiled at the kender. "Very well, Tas. Tell me your secret. Kalindas," she said to the elf who had been waiting silently all this time, "escort Gerard to the house. Show him to one of the guest rooms."

Kalindas did as commanded. As he showed Gerard the way to the house, the elf's tone was gracious, but he kept his hand on the hilt of his sword.

When they were alone, Laurana turned to the kender.

"Yes, Tas," she said. "What is it?"

Tas looked extremely anxious. "This is very important, Laurana. Are you *sure* I'm Tasslehoff? Are you extremely sure?"

"Yes, Tas, I'm sure," Laurana said, smiling indulgently. "I don't know how or why, but I am quite certain you are Tasslehoff."

"It's just that I don't *feel* like Tasslehoff," Tas continued earnestly.

"You don't seem yourself, Tas, that is true," Laurana replied. "You are not as joyful as I remember you to be. Perhaps you are grieving for Caramon. He led a full life, Tas, a life of love and wonder and joy. He had his share of sorrow and trouble, but the dark days only made the days of light shine brighter. You were his good friend. He loved you. Don't be sad. He wouldn't want you to be unhappy."

"That's not what's making me unhappy," Tas protested. "That is, I was unhappy when Caramon died because it was so unexpected, even though I was expecting it. And I still sometimes have a lump of unhappiness right here in my throat when I think about him being gone, but I can manage a lump. It's the other feeling I can't manage, because I never felt anything like it before."

"I see. Perhaps we could talk about this later, Tas," Laurana said and started toward the house.

Tas caught hold of her sleeve, hung on for dear life. "It's the feeling that came to me when I saw the dragon!"

"What dragon?" Laurana stopped, turned back. "When did you see a dragon?"

"While Gerard and I were riding into Qualinesti. The dragon came around to take a look at us. I was . . ." Tas paused, then said in a awful whisper, "I think I was . . . scared." He gazed at Laurana with round eyes, expecting to see her reel backward into the pond, stunned with the shock and horror of this unnatural occurrence.

"You were wise to be scared, Tas," Laurana replied, taking the terrible news quite calmly. "The dragon Beryl is a loathsome, fearsome beast. Her claws are stained with blood. She is a cruel tyrant, and you are not the first to be afraid in her presence. Now, we should not keep the others waiting."

"But it's *me*, Laurana! Tasslehoff Burrfoot! Hero of the Lance!" Tas pounded himself frantically on his chest. "I'm not afraid of anything. There's a giant in the other time who's about to step on me and probably squash me flat, and that gives me a sort of squirmy feeling in my stomach when I think about it, but this is different." He sighed deeply. "You must be mistaken. I *can't* be Tasslehoff and be afraid."

The kender was truly upset, that much was obvious. Laurana regarded him thoughtfully. "Yes, this is different. This is very strange. You have been around dragons before, Tas."

"All sorts of dragons," Tas said proudly. "Blues and reds and greens and blacks, bronze and copper and silver and gold. I even flew on the back of one. It was glorious."

"And you never felt dragonfear?"

"I remember thinking that dragons were beautiful in an awful kind of way. And I felt afraid, but that was for my friends, never for myself. Much."

"This must have been true of the other kender, as well," Laurana mused, "the kender we now call 'afflicted.' Some of them must have experienced dragonfear years ago, during the War of the Lance and after. Why would these experiences be different? I never thought about it."

"Lots of times people don't think about us," Tas said in an understanding tone. "Don't feel bad."

"But I do feel badly," Laurana sighed. "We should have done something to help the kender. It's just that there's been so much happening that was more important. Or at least it seemed more important. If this fear is different from dragonfear, I wonder what it could be? A spell, perhaps?"

"That's it!" Tas shouted. "A spell! A curse!" He was thrilled. "I'm under a curse from the dragon. Do you truly think so?"

"I really don't know—" Laurana began, but the kender was no longer listening.

"A curse! I'm cursed!" Tasslehoff gave a blissful sigh. "Dragons have done lots of things to me but I've never before had one curse me! This is almost as good as the time Raistlin magicked me into a duck pond. Thank you, Laurana," he said, fervently shaking her hand and accidently removing the last of her rings. "You have no idea what a weight you have taken off my mind. I can be Tasslehoff now. A *cursed* Tasslehoff! Let's go tell Palin!

"Say, speaking of Palin," Tas added in a piercing whisper, "when did he become a Black Robe? The last I saw him, he was Head of the Order of White Robes! What made him change? Was it like Raistlin? Is someone else inhabit—habitat—habitating Palin's body?"

"Black robes, white robes, red robes, the distinction between one and the other is now gone, Tas," Laurana said. "Palin wore black robes because he wanted to blend in with the night." She looked at the kender oddly. "Palin was never Head of the Order of White Robes. What made you think that?"

"I'm beginning to wonder," Tasslehoff said. "I don't mind telling you, Laurana, but I'm *extremely confused*. Maybe someone's inhabiting my body," he added, but without much hope.

With all the strange feelings and lumps, there just didn't seem to be room for anyone else in there.

16 TASSLEHOFF'S TALE

The Queen Mother's house was built on the side of a cliff overlooking Qualinesti. Like all elven structures, the house blended with nature, seemed a part of the landscape, as, indeed, much of it was. The elven builders had constructed the house so as to utilize the cliff-face in the design. Seen from a distance, the house appeared to be a grove of trees growing on a broad ledge that jutted out from the cliff. Only when one drew closer, did one see the path leading up to the house and then one could tell that the trees were in reality walls, their branches the roof and that cliff was also used for many of the walls of the house.

The north wall of the atrium was made of the rocky slope of the cliff face. Flowers and small trees blossomed, birds sang in the trees. A stream of water ran down the cliff, splashing into many small pools along the way. As each pool varied in depth, the sound of the falling water differed from pool to pool, producing a wondrous harmony of musical sound.

Tasslehoff was quite enchanted with the fact that there was a real waterfall inside the house and he climbed upon the rocks, slipping perilously on the slippery surface. He loudly exclaimed over the wonder of every bird's nest, uprooted a rare plant while trying to pick its flower and was forcibly removed by Kalindas when the kender insisted on trying to climb clear up to the ceiling.

This *was* Tasslehoff. The more Palin watched, the more he remembered and the more he became convinced that this kender was the kender he had known well over thirty years ago. He noted that Laurana watched Tas, as well. She watched him with a bewilderment tinged with wonder. Palin supposed it was perfectly plausible that Tasslehoff could have been wandering the world for thirty-eight years and had finally taken it into his head to drop by for a chat with Caramon.

Palin discarded the notion. Another kender might have done so, but not Tasslehoff. He was a unique kender, as Caramon liked to say. Or perhaps, not so unique as all that. Perhaps if they had taken time to come to know another kender, they might have discovered that they were all loyal and compassionate friends. But if Tas had not been roaming the world for almost forty years, than where had he been?

Palin listened attentively to the Knight's story of Tas's appearance in the tomb the night of the storm (most remarkable, Palin made a mental note of this occurrence), Caramon's recognition, his subsequent death and his last words to Sir Gerard.

"Your father was upset that he could not find his brother Raistlin. He said that Raistlin had promised to wait for him. And then came your father's dying request, sir," said Gerard in conclusion. "He asked me to take Tasslehoff to Dalamar. I would have to assume that to be the wizard, Dalamar, of infamous repute?"

"I suppose so," said Palin evasively, determined to betray nothing of his thoughts.

"According to the Measure, sir, I am honor bound to fulfill a request made by the dying. But since the wizard Dalamar has disappeared and no one has heard from him in many years, I'm not quite certain what to do."

"Nor am I," Palin said.

His father's final words intrigued Palin. He was well aware of his father's firmly held belief that Raistlin would not depart this mortal plane until his twin had joined him.

"We're twins, Raist and I," Caramon would say. "And because we're twins, one of us can't leave this world and move on to the next without the other. The gods granted Raist peace in sleep, but then they woke him up during the Chaos War and it was then that he told me he would wait for me."

Raistlin had indeed returned from the dead during the Chaos War. He had gone to the Inn of the Last Home and had spent some time with Caramon. During that time, Raistlin had, according to Caramon, sought his brother's forgiveness. Palin had never questioned his father's faith in his faithless brother, though he had privately thought that Caramon was indulging in wishful thinking.

Still Palin did not feel he had the right to try to dissuade Caramon of his belief. After all, none could say for certain what happened to the souls of those who died.

"The kender maintains that he traveled forward in time and that he came here with the help of the magical device." Gerard shook his head, smiled. "At least it's the most original excuse I've heard from one of the little thieves."

"It's not an excuse," Tas said loudly. He had attempted to interrupt Gerard at several key points in the story, until finally the knight had threatened to gag him again if he wasn't quiet. "I *didn't* steal the device. Fizban gave it to me. And I *did* travel forward in time. Twice. The first time I was late and the second time I . . . don't know what happened."

"Let me see the magical artifact, Sir Gerard," Palin said. "Perhaps that will help us arrive at an answer."

"I'll show you!" Tas offered eagerly. He fumbled about in his pockets, looked down his shirtfront, felt all about his pant legs. "I know it's here somewhere . . ."

Palin looked accusingly at the knight. "If this artifact is as valuable as you describe, sir, why did you allow it to remain in the kender's possession? If it is still *in* his possession—"

"I didn't, sir," Gerard said defensively. "I've taken it away from him I don't know how many times. The artifact keeps going back to him. He says that's how it works."

Palin's heartbeat quickened. His blood warmed. His hands, that seemed always cold and numb, tingled with life. Laurana had risen involuntarily to her feet.

"Palin! You don't suppose . . ." she began.

"I found it!" Tas announced in triumph. He dragged the artifact out of his boot. "Would you like to hold it, Palin? It won't hurt you or anything."

The artifact had been small enough to fit inside the kender's small boot. Yet as Tas held it out, the kender had to hold the device with both hands. Yet Palin had not seen it change shape or enlarge. It was as if it was always the shape and size it was meant to be, no matter what the circumstances. If anything changed, it was the viewer's perception of the artifact, not the artifact itself.

Jewels of antiquity—rubies, sapphires, diamonds and emeralds—sparkled and glittered in the sunlight, catching the sunbeams and transforming them into smears of rainbow light splashed on the walls and the floor and shining up from the kender's cupped hands.

Palin started to reach out his own crippled hands to hold the device, then he hesitated. He was suddenly afraid. He did not fear that the artifact might do him some harm. He knew perfectly well it wouldn't. He had seen the artifact when he was a boy. His father had shown it off proudly to his children. In addition, Palin recognized the device from his studies when he was a youth. He had seen drawings of it in the books in the Tower of High Sorcery. This was the Device of Time Journeying, one of the greatest and most powerful of all the artifacts ever created by the masters of the Towers. It would not harm him, yet it would do him terrible, irrevocable damage.

Palin knew from experience the pleasure he would feel when he touched the artifact: he would sense the old magic, the pure magic, the loved magic, the magic that came to him untainted, freely given, a gift of faith, a blessing from the gods. He would sense the magic, but only faintly, as one senses the smell of rose leaves, pressed between the pages of a book, their sweet fragrance only a memory. And because it was only a memory, after the pleasure would come the pain—the aching, searing pain of loss.

But he could not help himself. He said to himself, "Perhaps this time I will be able to hold onto it. Perhaps this time with this artifact, the magic will come back to me."

Palin touched the artifact with trembling, twisted fingers.

Glory . . . brilliance . . . surrender . . .

Palin cried out, his broken fingers clenched over the artifact. The jewels cut into the flesh of his hand.

Truth . . . beauty . . . art . . . life . . .

Tears burned his eyelids, slid down his cheeks.

Death . . . loss . . . emptiness . . .

Palin sobbed harshly, bitterly for what was lost. He wept for his father's death, wept for the three moons that had vanished from the sky, wept for his broken hands, wept for his own betrayal of all that he had believed in, wept for his own inconstancy, his own desperate need to try to find the ecstasy again.

"He is ill. Should we do something?" Gerard asked uneasily.

"No, Sir Knight. Leave him be," Laurana admonished gently. "There is nothing we can do for him. There is nothing we *should* do for him. This is necessary to him. Though he suffers now, he will be better for this release."

"I'm sorry, Palin," Tasslehoff cried remorsefully. "I didn't think it would hurt you. Honestly, I didn't! It never hurt me."

"Of course it would not hurt you, wretched kender!" Palin returned, the pain a living thing inside him, twisting and coiling around his heart so that it fluttered in his chest like a frantic bird caught by the snake. "To you it is nothing but a pretty toy! To me it is an opiate that brings blissful, wondrous dreams." His voice cracked. "Until the effect wears off. The dreams end and I must wake again to drudgery and despair, wake to the bitter, mundane reality."

He clenched his hand over the device, quenched the light of its jewels. "Once," he said, his voice tight, "I might have crafted a marvelous and powerful artifact such as this. Once I might have been what you claim I was—Head of the Order of White Robes. Once I might have had the future my uncle foresaw for me. Once I might have been a wizard, gifted, puissant, powerful. I look at this device and that is what I see. But I look into a mirror and I see something far different."

He opened his hand. He could not see the device for his bitter tears. He could see only the light of its magic, glinting and winking, mocking. "My magic dwindles, my powers grow weaker every day. Without the magic, there is one hope left for us—to hope that death is better than this dismal life!"

"Palin, you must not speak like that!" Laurana said sternly. "So we thought in the dark days before the War of the Lance. I remember Raistlin saying something to the effect that hope was the carrot dangled before the nose of the cart horse to fool him into plodding forward. Yet we did plod forward and, in the end, we were rewarded."

"We were," said Tas. "I ate the carrot."

"We were rewarded all right," Palin said, sneering. "With this wretched world in which we find ourselves!"

The artifact was painful to his touch—indeed, he had clutched so tightly that the sharp-edged jewels had cut him. But still he held it fast, carressing it covetously. The pain was so much preferable to the feeling of numbness.

Gerard cleared his throat, looked embarrassed.

"I take it, sir, that I was right," he said diffidently. "This is a powerful artifact of the Fourth Age?"

"It is," Palin answered.

They waited for him to say more, but he refused to indulge them. He wanted them to leave. He wanted to be alone. He wanted to sort out his thoughts that were running hither and yon like rats in a cave when someone lights a torch. Scuttling down dark holes, crawling into crevices and some staring with glittering, fascinated eyes at the blazing fire. He had to endure them, their foolishness, their inane questions. He had to hear the rest of Tasslehoff's tale.

"Tell me what happened, Tas," Palin said. "None of your woolly mammoth stories. This is very important."

"I understand," Tas said, impressed. "I'll tell the truth. I promise. It all started one day when I was attending the funeral of an extremely good kender friend I'd met the day before. She'd had an unfortunate encounter with a bugbear. What happened was—er—"— Tas caught sight of Palin's brows constricting—"never mind, as the gnomes say. I'll tell you that story later. Anyhow during her funeral, it occurred to me that very few kender ever live long enough to be what you might call old. I've already lived a lot longer than most kender I know and I suddenly realized that Caramon was likely to live a lot longer than I was. The one thing I really, really wanted to do before I was dead was to tell everyone what a good friend Caramon had been to me. It seemed to me that the best time to do this would be at his funeral. But if Caramon outlived me, then me going to his funeral would be something of a problem.

"Anyway, I was talking to Fizban one day and I explained this and he said that he thought what I wanted to do was a fine and noble thing and he could fix it up. I could speak at Caramon's funeral by traveling to the time when the funeral was taking place. And he gave me this device and told me how it worked and gave me strict instructions to just jump ahead, talk at the funeral, and come straight back. 'No gallivanting,' he said. By the way," Tas asked anxiously, "you don't think he'd consider this trip 'gallivanting,' do you? Because I'm finding that I really am enjoying seeing all my friends again. It's much more fun than being stepped on by a giant."

"Go on with the story, Tas," Palin said tersely. "We'll discuss that later."

"Yes, right. So I used the device and I jumped forward in time, but, well, you know that Fizban gets things a bit muddled now and then. He's always forgetting his name or where his hat is when it's right on his head or forgetting how to cast a fireball spell and so I guess he just miscalculated. Because when I jumped forward in time the first time, Caramon's funeral was over. I'd missed it. I arrived just in time for refreshments. And while I did have a nice visit visiting with everyone and the cream cheese puffs Jenna made were truly scrumptious, I wasn't able to do what I'd meant to do all along. Remembering that I'd promised Fizban no gallivanting, I went back.

"And, to be honest"—Tas hung his head and shuffled his foot—"after that, I forgot all about speaking at Caramon's funeral. I had a really good reason. The Chaos War came and we were fighting shadow wights and I met Dougan and

Usha, your wife, you know, Palin. It was all immensely interesting and exciting. And now the world is about to come to an end and there's this horrible giant about to smash me flat and it was at that precise moment that I remembered that I hadn't spoken at Caramon's funeral. So I activated the device really quickly and came here to say what a good friend Caramon was before the giant steps on me."

Gerard was shaking his head. "This is ridiculous."

"Excuse me," said Tas, stern in his turn. "It's not polite to interrupt. So anyway I came here and ended up in the Tomb and Gerard found me and took me to see Caramon. And I was able to tell him what I was going to say about him at the funeral, which he enjoyed immensely, only nothing was like I remembered it the first time. I told that to Caramon, too, and he seemed really worried, but he dropped dead before he had time to do anything about it. And then he couldn't find Raistlin when he knew that Raistlin would never go on to the next life without his twin. Which is why I think he said I was to talk to Dalamar." Tas drew in a deep breath, having expended most of his air on his tale. "And that's why I'm here."

"Do you believe this, my lady?" Gerard demanded.

"I don't know what to believe," Laurana said softly. She glanced at Palin, but he carefully avoided her gaze, pretended to be absorbed in examining the device, almost as if he expected to find the answers engraved upon the shining metal.

"Tas," he said mildly, not wanting to reveal the direction of his thoughts, "tell me everything you remember about the first time you came to my father's funeral."

Tasslehoff did so, talking about how Dalamar attended and Lady Crysania and Riverwind and Goldmoon, how the Solamnic Knights sent a representative who traveled all the way from the High Clerist's Tower and Gilthas came from the elven kingdom of Qualinesti and Silvanoshei from his kingdom of Silvanesti and Porthios and Alhana came and she was as beautiful as ever. "And you were there, Laurana, and you were so happy because you said you'd lived to see your dearest dream come true, the elven kingdoms united in peace and brotherhood."

"It's just a story he's made up," Gerard said impatiently. "One of those tales of 'what might have been.' "

"What might have been," Palin said, watching the sunlight sparkle on the jewels. "My father had a story of what might have been." He looked at Tas. "You and my father traveled forward in time together once, didn't you?"

"It wasn't my fault," Tas said quickly. "We overshot our mark. You see, we were trying to go back to our own time which was 356 but due to a miscalculation we ended up in 358. Not the 358 which was 358, but a really horrible 358 where we found Tika's tomb and poor Bupu dead in the dust and Caramon's corpse, a 358 which thank goodness never happened because Caramon and I went back in time to make sure that Raistlin didn't become a god."

"Caramon once told me that story," Gerard said. "I thought—Well, he was getting on in years and he did like to tell tales, so I never really took him seriously."

"My father believed that it happened," Palin said and that was all he said.

"Do you believe it, Palin?" Laurana asked insistently. "More important, do you believe that Tas's story is true. That he really did travel through time? Is that what you are thinking?"

"What I am thinking is that I need to know much more about this device," he replied. "Which is, of course, why my father urged that the device be taken to Dalamar. He is the only person in this world who was actually present during the time my father worked the magic of the device."

"I was there!" Tas reminded them. "And now I'm here."

"Yes," said Palin with a cool, appraising glance. "So you are."

In his mind, an idea was forming. It was only a spark, a tiny flash of flame in a vast and empty darkness. Yet it had been enough to send the rats scurrying.

"You cannot ask Dalamar," Laurana said practically. "No one's seen him since his return from the Chaos War."

"No, Laurana, you are wrong," Palin said. "One person saw him before his mysterious disappearance—his lover, Jenna. She always claimed that she had no idea where he went, but I never believed her. And she would be the one person who might know something about this artifact."

"Where does this Jenna live?" Gerard asked. "Your father gave me the task of taking the kender and the device to Dalamar. I may not be able to do that, but I could at least escort you, sir, and the kender—"

Palin was shaking his head. "That will not be possible, Sir Knight. Mistress Jenna lives in Palanthas, a city under the control of the Dark Knights."

"So is Qualinesti, sir," Gerard pointed out, with a slight smile.

"Slipping unnoticed across the heavily wooded borders of Qualinesti is one thing," Palin observed. "Entering the walled and heavily guarded city of Palanthas is quite another. Besides the journey would take far too long. It would be easier to meet Jenna half way. Perhaps in Solace."

"But can Jenna leave Palanthas?" Laurana asked. "I thought the Dark Knights had restricted travel out of the city as well as into it."

"Such restrictions may apply to ordinary people," Palin said drily. "Not to Mistress Jenna. She made it her business to get on well with the knights when they took over the city. Very well, if you take my meaning. Youth is lost to her, but she is still an attractive woman. She is also the wealthiest woman in Solamnia and one of the most powerful mages. No, Laurana, Jenna will have no difficulty traveling to Solace." He rose to his feet. He needed to be alone, to think.

"But aren't her powers abating like yours, Palin?" Laurana asked.

He pressed his lips together in displeasure. He did not like speaking of his loss, as another might not like speaking of a cancerous growth. "Jenna has certain artifacts which continue to work for her, as I have some which continue to work for me. It is not much," he added caustically, "but we make do."

"Perhaps this is the best plan," Laurana agreed. "But how will you return to Solace? The roads are closed—"

Palin bit his lip, bit back bitter words. Would they never quit yammering at him?

"Not to one of the Dark Knights," Gerard was saying. "I offer myself as escort, sir. I came here with a kender prisoner. I will leave with a human one."

"Yes, yes, a good plan, Sir Knight," Palin said impatiently. "You work out the details." He started to walk off, eager to escape to the silence of his room, but he thought of one more important question. Pausing, he turned to ask it. "Does anyone else know of the discovery of this artifact?"

"Probably half of Solace by now, sir," Gerard answered dourly. "The kender was not very secretive."

"Then we must not waste time," Palin said tersely. "I will contact Jenna."

"How will you do that?" Laurana asked him.

"I have my ways," he said, adding, with a curl of his lip, "Not much, but I make do."

He left the room, left abruptly, without looking back. He had no need. He could feel her hurt and her sorrow accompany him like a gentle spirit. He was momentarily ashamed, half-turned to go back to apologize. He was her guest, after all. She was putting her very life in danger to host him. He hesitated, and then he kept walking.

No, he thought grimly. Laurana can't understand. Usha doesn't understand. That brash and arrogant knight doesn't understand. They can't any of them understand. They don't know what I've been through, what I've suffered. They don't know my loss.

Once, he cried in silent anguish, once I touched the minds of gods!

He paused, listening in the stillness, to see if he could by chance hear a faint voice answering his grieving cry.

He heard, as he always heard, only the empty echo.

They think I've been freed from prison. They think my torment is ended. They are wrong.

My confinement endures day after dreary day. The torture goes on indefintely. Gray walls surround me. I squat in my own filth. The bones of my spirit are cracked and splintered. My hunger is so great that I devour myself. My thirst so great that I drink my own waste. This is what I've become.

Reaching the sanctuary of his room, he shut the door and then dragged a chair across to lean against it. No elf would dream of disturbing the privacy of one who has shut himself away, but Palin didn't trust them. He didn't trust any of them.

He sat down at a writing desk, but he did not write to Jenna. He placed his hand on a small silver earring he wore in his ear lobe. He spoke the words to the spell, words that perhaps didn't matter anymore, for there was no one to hear them. Sometimes artifacts worked without the ritual words, sometimes they only worked with the words, sometimes they didn't work at all under any circumstances. That was happening more and more often these days.

He repeated the words and added "Jenna" to them.

A hungry wizard had sold her the six silver earrings. He was evasive about where he had found them, mumbled something to the effect that they had been left to him by a dead uncle.

Jenna had told Palin, "Certainly, the dead once owned these earrings. But they were not willed to him. He stole them."

She did not pursue the matter. Many once respectable wizards—including Palin himself—had turned to grave robbery in their desperate search for magic. The wizard had described what the earrings did, said he would not have sold them but that dire necessity drove him to it. She had paid him a handsome sum and, instead of placing the earrings in her shop, she had given one to Palin and one to Ulin, his son. She had not told Palin who wore the others.

He had not asked. Once there had been a time when the mages of the Conclave had trusted each other. In these dark days, with the magic dwindling, each now looked sidelong at the others wondering, "Does he have more than I do? Has he found something I have not? Has the power been given to him and not to me?"

Palin heard no response. Sighing, he repeated the words and rubbed the metal with his finger. When he was first given the earrings, the spell had worked immediately. Now it would take him three or four tries and there was always the nagging fear that this might be the time it would fail altogether.

"Jenna!" he whispered urgently.

Something wispy and delicate brushed across his face, like the touch of a fly's wings. Annoyed, he waved it away hurriedly, his concentration broken. He looked for the insect, to shoo it off, but couldn't find it. He was settling down to try the magic once again, when Jenna's thoughts answered his.

"Palin . . ."

He focused his thoughts, keeping the message short, in case the magic failed midway. "Urgent need. Meet me in Solace. Immediately."

"I will come at once." Jenna said nothing more, did not waste time or the her own magic with questions. She trusted him. He would not send for her unless he had good reason.

Palin looked down at the device that he cherished in his broken hands.

Is this the key to my cell? he asked himself. Or nothing but another lash of the whip?

"He is very changed," said Gerard, after Palin had left the atrium. "I would not have recognized him. And the way he spoke of his father . . ." He shook his head.

"Wherever Caramon is, I am certain he understands," Laurana said. "Palin is changed, yes, but then who would not be changed after such a terrible experience. I don't think any of us will ever know what torment he endured at the hands of the Gray Robes. Speaking of them, how do you plan to travel to Solace?" she asked, skillfully turning the subject away from Palin to more practical considerations.

"I have my horse, the black one. I thought that perhaps Palin could ride the smaller horse I brought for the kender."

"And then I could ride the black horse with you!" Tas announced, pleased. "Although I'm not sure Little Gray will really like Palin, but perhaps if I talk to her—"

"You are not going," Gerard said flatly.

"Not going!" Tas repeated, stunned. "But you need me!"

Gerard ignored this statement, which, of all statements ever made in the course of history, could be ranked as most likely to be ignored. "The journey will take many days, but that can't be helped. It seems the only course—"

"I have another suggestion," Laurana said. "Griffons could fly you to Solace. They brought Palin here and they will carry him back and you along with them. My falcon Brightwing will take a message to them. The griffons could be here the day after tomorrow. You and Palin will be in Solace by that evening."

Gerard had a brief, vivid image of flying on griffon back or perhaps it would be more accurate to say he had a brief vivid image of falling off a griffon's back and smashing headfirst into the ground. He flushed and fumbled for an answer that didn't make him out to be a craven coward.

"I couldn't possibly impose . . . We should leave at once . . ."

"Nonsense. The rest will do you good," Laurana replied, smiling as if she understood the real reason behind his reluctance. "This will save you over a week's time and, as Palin said, we must move swiftly before Beryl discovers such a valuable magical device is in her lands. Tomorrow night, after dark, Kalindas will guide you to the meeting place."

"I've never ridden a griffon," Tas said, hinting. "At least, not that I can remember. Uncle Trapspringer did once. He said . . ."

"No," Gerard cut in firmly. "Absolutely not. You will stay with the Queen Mother, if she'll have you. This is already dangerous enough without—" His words died away.

The magical device was once again in the kender's possession. Tasslehoff was, even now, stuffing the device down the front of his shirt.

Far from Qualinesti, but not so far that she couldn't keep an eye watching and an ear listening, the great green dragon Beryl lay in her tangled, overgrown, vine-ridden bower and chafed at the wrongs which had been done to her. Wrongs which itched and stung her like a parasitic infestation and, like a parasite, she could scratch here and scratch there, but the itch seemed to move so that she was never quite rid of it.

At the heart of all her trouble was a great red dragon, a monstrous wyrm that Beryl feared more than anything else in this world, though she would have allowed her green wings to be pulled off and her enormous green tail to be tied up in knots before she admitted it. This fear was the main reason Beryl had agreed to the pact three years ago. She had seen in her mind her own skull adorning Malys's totem. Besides the fact that she wanted to keep her skull, Beryl had resolved that she would never give her bloated red cousin that satisfaction.

The pact of peace between the dragons had seemed a good idea at the time. It ended the bloody Dragon Purge, during which the dragons had fought and killed not only mortals, but each other, as well. The dragons who had emerged alive and powerful divided up parts of Ansalon, each claiming a portion to rule and leaving some previously disputed lands, such as Abanasinia, untouched.

The peace had lasted about a year before it started to crumble. When Beryl felt her magical powers start to seep away, she blamed the elves, she blamed the humans, but in her heart she knew full well where the real blame lay. Malys was stealing her magic. No wonder her red cousin had no more need to kill her own kind! She had found some way to drain the other dragons of their power. Beryl's magic had been a major defense against her stronger cousin. Without that magic, the green dragon would be as helpless as a gully dwarf.

Night fell while Beryl was musing. Darkness wrapped around her bower like another, larger vine. She fell asleep, lulled by the lullaby of her scheming and plotting. She was dreaming that she had found at last the legendary Tower of High Sorcery at Wayreth. She wrapped her huge body around the tower and felt the magic flow into her, warm and sweet as the blood of a gold dragon. . . .

"Exalted One!" A hissing voice woke her from her pleasant dream.

Beryl blinked and snorted, sending fumes of poisonous gas roiling among the leaves. "Yes, what is it?" she demanded, focusing her eyes on the source of the hiss. She could see quite well in the darkness, had no need of light.

"A messenger from Qualinost," said her draconian servant. "He claims his news is urgent, else I would not have disturbed you."

"Send him in."

The draconian bowed and departed. Another draconian appeared in his place. A baaz named Groul, he was one of Beryl's favorites, a trusted messenger who traveled between her lair and Qualinesti. Draconians were created during the War of the Lance when black robed wizards and evil clerics loyal to Takhisis stole the eggs of good dragons and gave them hideous life in the form of these winged lizard-men. Like all his kind, the baaz walked upright on two powerful legs, but he could run on all fours, using his wings to increase his movement over the ground. His body was covered with scales that had a dull metallic sheen. He wore little in the way of clothing, which would have hampered his movements. He was a messenger and so he was armed only lightly, with a short sword that he wore strapped to his back, in between his wings.

Beryl wakened more fully. Normally a laconic creature, who rarely evinced any type of emotion, Groul appeared quite pleased with himself this night. His lizard eyes glittered with excitement, his fangs were prominent in a wide grin. The tip of his flickered in his mouth.

Beryl shifted and rolled her huge body, wallowing deeper in the muck to increase her comfort, gathering her vines around her like a writhing blanket.

"News from Qualinost?" Beryl asked casually. She did not want to seem too eager.

"Yes, Exalted One," said Groul, moving forward to stand near one of the gigantic claws of her front foot. "Most interesting news involving the Queen Mother, Laurana."

"Indeed? Is that fool knight Medan still enamored of her?"

"Of course." Groul dismissed this as old news. "According to our spy, he shields and protects her. But that is not such a bad thing, Mistress. The Queen Mother believes herself to be invulnerable and thus we are able to discover what the elves are plotting."

"True," Beryl agreed. "So long as Medan remembers where his true loyalties lie, I permit his little flirtation. He has served me well thus far and he is easily removed. What else? There is something else, I believe . . ."

Beryl rested her head on the ground, to put herself level with the draconian, gazed intently at him. His excitement was catching. She could feel it quiver through her. Her tail twitched, her claws dug deep into the oozing mud.

Groul drew closer still. "I reported to you several days ago that the human mage, Palin Majere, was hiding out in the Queen Mother's house. We wondered at the reason for this visit. You suspected he was there searching for magical artifacts."

"Yes," Beryl said. "Go on."

"I am pleased to report, Exalted One, that he found one."

"Indeed?" Beryl's eyes gleamed, casting an eerie green light over the draconian. "And what is the artifact he found? What does it do?"

"According to our elven spy, the artifact may have something to do with traveling through time. The artifact is in the possession of a kender, who claims that he came from another time, a time prior to the Chaos War."

Beryl snorted, filling her lair with noxious fumes. The draconian choked and coughed.

"Those vermin will say anything. If this is all—"

"No, no, Exalted One," Groul hastened to add when he could speak. "The elven spy reports that Palin Majere was tremendously excited over this find. So excited that he has made arrangements to leave Qualinost with the artifact immediately, in order to study it."

"Is that so?" Beryl relaxed, settled herself more comfortably. "He was excited by it. The artifact *must* be powerful, then. He has a nose for these things, as I said to the Gray Robes when they would have slain him. 'Let him go,' I told them. 'He will lead us to magic as a pig to truffles.' How may we acquire this?"

"The day after this day, Exalted One, the mage and the kender will depart Qualinesti. They will be met by a griffon who will fly them from there to Solace. That would be the best time to capture them."

"Return to Qualinost. Inform Medan—"

"Pardon me, Exalted One. I am not permitted into the marshal's presence. He finds me and my kind distasteful."

"He is becoming more like an elf every day," Beryl growled. "Some morning he will wake with pointed ears."

"I can send my spy to report to him. That is the way I usually operate. Thus my spy keeps me informed of what is going on in Medan's household as well."

"Very well. Here are my orders. Have your spy tell Marshal Medan that I want this mage captured and delivered alive. He is to be brought to *me*, mind you. Not those worthless Gray Robes."

"Yes, Exalted One." Groul started to leave, then turned back. "Do you trust the marshal with a matter of this importance?"

"Certainly not," Beryl said disdainfully. "But I will make my own arrangements. Now go!"

Marshal Medan was taking his breakfast in his garden, where he liked to watch the sun rise. He had placed his table and chair on a rock ledge beside a pond so covered with water lilies that he could barely see the water. A nearby snowfall bush filled the air with tiny white blossoms. Having finished his meal, he read the morning dispatches, which had just arrived, and wrote out his orders for the day. Every so often he paused in his work to toss bread crumbs to the fish who were so accustomed to his routine that every morning at this time they came to the surface in anticipation of his arrival.

"Sir." Medan's aide approached, irritably brushing the falling blossoms from his black tunic. "An elf to see you, sir. From the household of the Queen Mother."

"Our traitor?"

"Yes, sir."

"Bring him to me at once."

The aide sneezed, gave a sullen response and departed.

Medan drew his knife from the sheath he wore on a belt around his waist, placed the knife on the table, and sipped at his wine. He would not ordinarily have taken such precautions. There had been one assassination attempt against him long ago, when he had first arrived to take charge of Qualinesti. Nothing had come of it. The perpetrators had been caught and hanged, drawn and quartered; the pieces of their bodies fed to the carrion birds.

Recently, however, the rebel groups were becoming bolder, more desperate. He was concerned about one in particular, a female warrior whose personal beauty, courage in battle and daring exploits were making her a heroine to the subjugated elves. They called her "Lioness," for her mane of shining hair. She and her band of rebels attacked supply trains, harried patrols, ambushed messengers and generally made Medan's formerly quiet and peaceful life among the Qualinesti elves increasingly difficult.

Someone was feeding the rebels information on troop movements, the timing of patrols, the locations of baggage trains. Medan had clamped down tightly on security, removing all elves (except his gardener) from his staff and urging Prefect Palthainon and the other elven officials who were known to collaborate with the knights to watch what they said and where they said it. But security was difficult in a land where a squirrel sitting eating nuts on your windowsill might be taking a look at your maps, noting down the disposition of your forces.

Medan's aide returned, still sneezing, with the elf following along behind, bearing a slip of a branch in his hand.

Medan dismissed his aide with a recommendation that he drink some catnip tea to help his cold. The Marshal sipped his morning wine slowly, enjoying it. He loved the flavor of elven wine, could taste the flowers and the honey from which it was made.

"Marshal Medan, my mistress sends this lilac cutting to you for your garden. She says that your gardener will know how to plant it."

"Put it here," said Medan, indicating the table. He did not look at the elf, but continued to toss crumbs to the fish. "If that is all, you have leave to go."

The elf coughed, cleared his throat.

"Something more?" Medan asked casually.

The elf cast a furtive glance all around the garden.

"Speak. We are alone," Medan said.

"Sir, I have been ordered to relay information to you. I told you previously that the mage, Palin Majere, was visiting my mistress."

Medan nodded. "Yes, you were assigned to keep watch on him and report to me what he does. I must assume from the fact that you are here that he has done something."

"Palin Majere has recently come into possession of an extremely valuable artifact, a magical artifact from the Fourth Age. He is going to transport that artifact out of Qualinost. His plan is to take it to Solace."

"And you reported the discovery of this artifact to Groul who reported it to the dragon," said Medan with an inward sigh. More trouble. "And, of course, Beryl wants it."

"Majere will be traveling by griffon. He is to meet the griffin tomorrow morning at dawn in a clearing located about twenty miles north of Qualinost. He travels in company with a kender and a Solamnic Knight—"

"A Solamnic Knight?" Medan was amazed, more interested in the knight than in the magic-user. "How did a Solamnic Knight manage to enter Qualinesti without being discovered?"

"He disguised himself as one of your knights, my lord. He pretended that the kender was his prisoner, that he had stolen a magical artifact and that he was taking the prisoner to the Gray Robes. Word reached Majere of the artifact and he waylaid the knight and the kender, as the Knight had planned, and brought them to the home of the queen mother."

"Intelligent, courageous, resourceful." Medan threw crumbs to the fish. "I look forward to meeting this paragon."

"Yes, my lord. As I said, the Knight will be with Majere in the forest, along with the kender. I can provide you with a map—"

"I am certain you can," said Medan. He made a dismissive gesture. "Give the details to my aide. And remove your treacherous carcass from my garden. You poison the air."

"Excuse me, sir," the elf said boldly. "But there is the matter of payment. According to Groul, the dragon was extremely pleased with the information. That makes it worth a considerable amount. More than usual. Shall we say, double what I usually receive?"

Medan cast the elf a contemptuous glance, then reached for quill and paper.

"Give this to my aide. He will see that you are paid." Medan wrote slowly and deliberately, taking his time. He hated this business, considered the use of spies sordid and demeaning. "What are you doing with all this money we have paid you to betray your mistress, Elf?" He would not dignify the wretch with a name. "Do you plan to enter the Senate? Perhaps take over from Prefect Palthainon, that other monument to treachery."

The elf hovered near, his eyes on the paper and the figures the Marshal was writing, his hand waiting to pluck it away. "It is easy for you to talk, Human," the elf said bitterly. "You were not born a servant as I was, given no chance to better myself. 'You should be honored with your lot in life,' they tell me. 'After all, your father was a servant to the House Royal. Your grandfather was a servant in that household as was his grandfather before him. If you try to leave or raise yourself, you will bring about the downfall of elven society!' Hah!

"Let my brother demean himself. Let him bow and scrape and grovel to the mistress. Let him fetch and carry for her. Let him wait to die with her on the day the dragon attacks and destroys them all. I mean to do something better with my life. As soon as I have saved money enough, I will leave this place and make my own way in the world."

Medan signed the note, dripped melted wax beneath his signature, and pressed his seal ring into the wax. "Here, take this. I am pleased to be able to contribute to your departure."

The elf snatched the note, read the amount, smiled and, bowing, departed in haste.

Medan tossed the remainder of the bread into the pond and rose to his feet. His enjoyment of the day had been ruined by that contemptible creature, who, out of greed, was now informing on the woman he served, a woman who trusted him.

At least, Medan thought, I will capture this Palin Majere outside of Qualinost. There will be no need to bring Laurana into it. Had I been forced to apprehend Majere in the queen mother's house, I would have had to arrest the queen mother for harboring a fugitive.

He could imagine the uproar over such an arrest. The queen mother was immensely popular; her people having apparently forgiven her for marrying a half-human and for having a brother who was in exile, termed a "dark elf," one who is cast from the light. The Senate would be in a clamor. The population, already in an excited state, would be incensed. There was even the remote possibility that news of his mother's arrest would cause her worthless son to grow a backbone.

Much better this way. Medan had been waiting for just such an opportunity. He would turn Majere and his artifact over to Beryl and be done with it.

The marshal left the garden to put his lilac slip into water, so that it would not dry out.

17 GILTHAS AND THE LIONESS

Gilthas, Laurana's "worthless son," was at that moment resting his quite adequate backbone against a chair in an underground room of a tavern owned and run by gully dwarves. The tavern was called the Gulp and Belch—this being, as near as the gully dwarves could ascertain, the only thing humans did in a tavern.

The Gulp and Belch was located in a small habitation of gully dwarves (one could not dignify it by terming it a "village") located near the fortress of Pax Tharkas. The tavern was the only building in the habitation. The gully dwarves who ran the tavern lived in caves in the hills behind the tavern, caves that could be reached only by tunnels located beneath the tavern.

The gully dwarf community was located some eighty miles straight as the griffon flies from Qualinost, longer—far longer—if one traveled by road. Gilthas had flown here on the back of a griffon, one whose family was in the service of House Royal. The beast had landed the king and his guide in the forest and was now awaiting their return with less impatience than might have been expected. Kerian had made certain to provide the griffon with a freshly killed deer to make the long hours of waiting pass pleasantly and to ensure that the beast didn't dine on any of their hosts.

The Gulp and Belch was surprisingly popular. Or perhaps not surprising, considering that the prices were the lowest in Ansalon. Two coppers could buy anything. The business had been started by the same gully dwarf who had been a cook in the household of the late Dragon Highlord, Verminaard.

People who know gully dwarves, but who have never tasted gully dwarf cooking, find it impossible to even imagine eating anything a gully dwarf might prepare. Considering that a favorite delicacy of gully dwarf is rat meat, some equate the idea of having a gully dwarf for a cook with a death wish.

Gully dwarves are the outcasts of dwarfdom. Although they are dwarves, the dwarves do not claim them and will go to great lengths to explain why gully dwarves are dwarves in name only. Gully dwarves are extremely stupid, or so most people believe. Gully dwarves cannot count past two, their system of numbering being "one", "two." The very smartest gully dwarf, a legend among gully dwarves, whose name was Bupu, actually once counted past two, coming up with the term "a whole bunch."

Gully dwarves are not noted for their interest in higher mathematics. They are noted for their cowardice, for their filth, their love of squalor and—oddly enough—their cooking. Gully dwarves make extremely good cooks, so long as the diner sets down rules about what may and may not be served at the table and refrains from entering the kitchen to see how the food is prepared.

The Gulp and Belch served up an excellent roast haunch of venison smothered in onions and swimming in rich brown gravy. The ale was adequate—not as good as in many establishments, but the price was right. The dwarf spirits made the tavern's reputation. They were truly remarkable. The gully dwarves distilled their own from mushrooms cultivated in their bedrooms. Those drinking the brew are advised not to dwell on that fact for too long.

The tavern was frequented mainly by humans who could afford no better, by kender who were glad to find a tavernkeeper who did not immediately toss them out into the street, and by the lawless, who were quick to discover that the Knights of Neraka rarely patrolled the wagon ruts termed a road leading to the tavern.

The Gulp and Belch was also the hideout and headquarters for the warrior known as the Lioness, a woman who was also, had anyone known it, queen of Qualinesti, secret wife of the Speaker of the Sun, Gilthas.

The elven king sat in the chair in the semidarkness of the tavern's back room, trying to curb his impatience. Elves are never impatient. Elves, who live for hundreds of years, know that the water will boil, the bread will rise, the acorn will sprout, the oak will grow and that all the fuming and watching and attempts to hurry it make only for an upset stomach. Gilthas had inherited impatience from his half-human father, and although he did his best to hide it, his fingers drummed on the table and his foot tapped the floor.

Kerian glanced over at him, smiled. A single candle stood on the table between them. The candle's flame was reflected in her brown eyes, shone warmly on smooth, brown skin, glinted in the burnished gold of her mane of hair. Kerian was a Kagonesti, a Wilder elf, a race of elves who, unlike their city-dwelling cousins, the Qualinesti and the Silvanesti, live with nature. Since they do not try to alter nature or shape it, the Wilder elves are looked upon as barbarians by their more sophisticated cousins, who have also gone so far as to enslave the Kagonesti and force them to serve in wealthy elven households—all for the Kagonesti's own good, of course.

Kerian had been a slave in the household of Senator Rashas. She had been present when Gilthas was first brought to that house, ostensibly as a guest, in reality a prisoner. The two had fallen in love the first moment they had seen each other, although it was months, even years, before they actually spoke of their feelings, exchanged their secret vows.

Only two other people, Planchet and Gilthas's mother, Laurana, knew of the king's marriage to the girl who had once been a slave and who was now known as the Lioness, fearless leader of the Khansari, the Night People.

Catching Kerian's eye, Gilthas realized immediately what he was doing. He clenched the tapping fingers to a fist and crossed his booted feet to keep them quiet. "There," he said ruefully. "Is that better?"

"You will fret yourself into a sickness if you're not careful," Kerian scolded, smiling. "The dwarf will come. He gave his word."

"So much depends on this," said Gilthas. He stretched out his legs to ease the kinks of the unaccustomed exercise "Perhaps our very survival as a—" He halted, stared down at the floor. "Did you feel that?"

"The shaking? Yes. I've felt it the last couple of hours. It's probably just the gully dwarves adding to their tunnels. They love to dig in the dirt. As to what you were saying, there is no 'perhaps' about our ultimate destruction," Kerian returned crisply.

Her voice with its accent that civilized elves considered uncouth was like the song of the sparrow, of piercing sweetness with a note of melancholy.

"The Qualinesti have given the dragon everything she has demanded. They have sacrificed their freedom, their pride, their honor. They have, in some instances, even sacrificed their own—all in return for the dragon's permission to live. But the time will come when Beryl will make a demand your people will find impossible to fulfill. When that day comes and she finds her will thwarted, she will destroy the Qualinesti."

"Sometimes I wonder why you care," Gilthas said, looking gravely at his wife. "The Qualinesti enslaved you, took you from your family. You have every right to feel vengeful. You have every right to steal away into the wilderness and leave those who hurt you to the fate they so richly deserve. Yet you do not. You risk your life on a daily basis fighting to force our people to look at the truth, no matter how ugly, to hear it, no matter how unpleasant."

"That is the problem," she returned. "We must stop thinking of the elven people as 'yours' and 'mine.' Such division and isolation is what has brought us to this pass. Such division gives strength to our enemies."

"I don't see it changing," Gilthas said grimly. "Not unless some great calamity befalls us and forces us to change, and perhaps not even then. The Chaos War, which might have brought us closer, did nothing but further fragment our people. Not a day goes by but that some senator makes a speech telling of how our cousins the Silvanesti have shut us out of their safe haven beneath the shield, how they want us all to die so that they can take over our lands. Or someone starts a tirade against the Kagonesti, how their barbaric ways will bring down all that we have worked over the centuries to build. There are actually those who approve of the fact that the dragon has closed the roads. We will do better without contact with the humans, they say. The Knights of Neraka urge them on, of course. They love such rantings. It makes their task far easier."

"From the rumors I hear, the Silvanesti may be finding that their vaunted magical shield is in reality a tomb."

Gilthas looked startled, sat upright. "Where did you hear this? You have not told me."

"I have not seen you in a month," Kerian replied with a touch of bitterness. "I only heard this a few days ago, from the runner Kelevandros your mother sends regularly to keep in touch with your aunt Alhana Starbreeze. Alhana and her forces have settled on the border of Silvanesti, near the shield. They are allied with the humans who belong to the Legion of Steel. Alhana reports that the land around the shield is barren, trees sicken and die. A horrible gray dust settles over everything. She fears that this same malaise may be infecting all of Silvanesti."

"Then why do our cousins maintain the shield?" Gilthas wondered.

"They are afraid of the world beyond. Unfortunately, they are right in some instances. Alhana and her forces fought a pitched battle with ogres only a short time ago, the night of that terrible thunderstorm. The Legion of Steel came to their rescue or they would have been wiped out. As it was, Alhana's son Silvanoshei was captured by ogres, or so she believes. She could find no trace of him when the battle was ended. Alhana grieves for him as for the dead."

"My mother has said nothing of this to me," Gilthas stated, frowning.

"According to Kelevandros, Laurana fears Marshal Medan's heightened watchfulness. She trusts only those in her household. She dare not trust anyone outside it. Whenever the two of you are together, she is certain that you are spied upon. She does not want the Dark Knights to find out that she is in constant contact with Alhana."

"Mother is probably right," Gilthas admitted. "My servant Planchet is the only person I trust and that is because he has proven his loyalty to me time and again. So Silvanoshei is dead, killed by ogres. Poor young man. His death must have been a cruel one. Let us hope he passed swiftly."

"Did you ever meet him?"

Gilthas shook his head. "He was born in the Inn of the Last Home in Solace during the time Alhana was exiled. I never saw her after that. My mother told me that the boy favored my Uncle Porthios in looks."

"His death makes you heir to both kingdoms," Kerian observed. "The Speaker of the Sun and Stars."

"Which Senator Rashas always wanted," Gilthas said caustically. "In reality, it seems I will be nothing more than the Speaker of the Dead."

"Speak no words of ill omen!" Kerian said and made the sign against evil with her hand, drawing a circle in the air to encompass the words and keep them trapped. "You— Yes, what is it, Silverwing?"

She turned to speak to an elf who had entered the secret room. The elf started to say something but was interrupted by a gully dwarf, who appeared to be in a state of extreme excitement, to judge by the smell.

"Me tell!" the gully dwarf cried indignantly, jostling the elf. "Me lookout! Her say so!" He pointed at Kerian.

"Your Majesty." The elf made a hurried bow to Gilthas, before he turned to Kerian, his commander, with his information. "The high king of Thorbardin has arrived."

"Him here," the gully dwarf announced loudly. Although he did not speak Elvish, he could guess at what was being said. "Me bring in?"

"Thank you, Ponce." Kerian rose to her feet, adjusted the sword she wore at her waist. "I will come to meet him. It would be better if you remained here, Your Majesty," she added. Their marriage was a secret, even from the elves under Kerian's command.

"Big muckity-muck dwarf. Him wear hat!" Ponce was impressed. "Him wear shoes!" The gully dwarf was doubly impressed. "Me never see dwarf wear shoes."

"The high king has brought four guards with him," the elf told Kerian. "As you ordered, we have watched their movements ever since they left Thorbardin."

"For their safety, as well as ours, Your Majesty," Kerian was quick to add, seeing Gilthas's expression darken.

"They met with no one," the elf continued, "and they were not followed—"

"Except by us," Gilthas said sardonically.

"It never hurts to be cautious, Your Majesty," Kerian said. "Tarn Bellowgranite is the new high king of the clans of Thorbardin. His rule is secure among his people, but dwarves have traitors living among them, as do we elves."

Gilthas sighed deeply. "I wish the day would come when this was not so. I trust the dwarves did not notice that we were dogging them?"

"They saw the starlight, Your Majesty," said the elf proudly. "They heard the wind in the trees. They did not see or hear us."

"Him say he like our dwarf spirits," Ponce said importantly, his face shining, though this might have been due to the fact that it was smeared with grease from the goose he had been basting. "Him say we make fine dwarf spirits. You want try?" he asked Gilthas. "Put hair up your nose."

Kerian and the elf departed, taking the gully dwarf with them. Gilthas sat watching the candle flame flicker with the stirring of the air. Beneath his feet came that strange shivering in the ground, as if the very world trembled. All around him was darkness. The candle's flame was the only light, and it could be extinguished in a breath. So much could go wrong. Even now, Marshal Medan might be entering Gilthas's bedroom. The Marshal might be ripping up the pillows from the bed, arresting Planchet, demanding to know the whereabouts of the king.

Gilthas was suddenly very tired. He was tired of this duplicitous life, tired of the lies and the deceptions, tired of the fact that he was constantly performing. He was always on stage, never allowed a moment to rest in the wings. He could not even sleep well at night, for he was afraid he might say something in his sleep that would bring about his downfall.

Not that he would be the one to suffer. Prefect Palthainon would see to that. So would Medan. They needed Gilthas on the throne, jerking and twitching to the strings they pulled. If they found out that he'd cut those strings, they would simply reattach them. He would remain on the throne. He would remain alive. Planchet would die, tortured until he was forced to reveal all he knew. Laurana might not be executed but she would certainly be exiled, deemed a dark elf like her brother. Kerian might well be captured, and Medan had proclaimed publicly the terrible death the Lioness would suffer should she ever fall into his hands.

Gilthas would not suffer, except that he would be forced to watch those he loved most in the world suffer and know he was powerless to help them. That would be, perhaps, the greatest torment of all.

Out of the darkness crept his old companions: fear, self-doubt, self-hatred, self-loathing. He felt them lay their cold hands upon him and reach inside and twist his gut and wring the icy sweat from his shivering body. He heard their wailing voices cry to him warnings of doom, shout prophecies of death and destruction. He was not equal to this task. He dared not continue this course of action. It was foolhardy. He was putting his people at risk. He was certain they had been discovered. Medan knew everything. Perhaps if Gilthas went back now, he could make it all right. He would crawl into his bed and they would never know he had been gone. . . .

"Gilthas," said a stern voice.

Gilthas started. He looked wildly into a face he did not know.

"My husband," Kerian said gently.

Gilthas shut his eyes, a shudder passed through his body. Slowly he unclenched the hands that had tightened to fists. He made himself relax, forced the tension to ease from his body, forced himself to quit shaking. The darkness that had momentarily blinded him retreated. The candle's flame that was Kerian burned brightly, steadily. He drew in a deep, shivering breath.

"I am well, now," he said.

"Are you certain?" Kerian asked. "The thane waits in the adjacent room. Should I stall him?"

"No, the attack has passed," Gilthas said, swallowing to rid his mouth of the taste of bile. "You drove away the demons. Give me a moment to make myself presentable. How do I look?"

"As if you had seen a wraith," said Kerian. "But the dwarf will not notice anything amiss. All elves seem pasty-faced to them."

Gilthas caught hold of his wife, held her close.

"Stop it!" she protested, half-laughing and half in earnest. "There's no time for this now. What if someone saw us?"

"Let them," he said, casting caution aside. "I am tired of lying to the world. You are my strength, my salvation. You saved my life, my sanity. When I think back to what I was, a prisoner to those same demons, I wonder how you ever came to love me."

"I looked through the cell bars and saw the man locked inside," Kerian replied, relaxing in her husband's arms, if only for a moment. "I saw his love for his people. I saw how he suffered because they suffered and he felt helpless to prevent their pain. Love was the key. All I did was put it into the door and turn the lock. You have done all the rest."

She slid out of his embrace and was, once again, the warrior queen. "Are you ready? We should not keep the high king waiting longer."

"I am ready," Gilthas said.

He took in another deep breath, shook back his hair and, walking straight and tall, entered the room.

"His Majesty, Speaker of the Sun, Gilthas of the House of Solostaran," Kerian announced formally.

The dwarf, who was enjoying a mug of dwarf spirits, placed the mug on a table and lowered his head in a gesture of respect. He was tall for a dwarf and looked far older than his true age, for his hair had gone prematurely gray, his beard was gray streaked with white. His eyes were bright and clear and youthful, his gaze sharp and penetrating. He kept his gaze fixed on Gilthas, seemed to bore through the elf's breastbone as if he would see straight into his heart.

"He has heard rumors of me," Gilthas said to himself. "He wonders what to believe. Am I a weak dish rag to be wrung out by every hand? Or am I truly the ruler of my people as he is the ruler of his?"

"The High King of the Eight Clans," said Kerian, "Tarn Bellowgranite."

The dwarf was himself a half-breed. Much as Gilthas, who had human blood in his veins, Tarn was a product of a liaison between a Hylar dwarf—the nobles of dwarfdom—and a Daergar, the dark dwarves. After the Chaos War, the Thorbardin dwarves had worked with humans to rebuild the fortress of Pax Tharkas. It seemed that the Thorbardin dwarves might actually once more begin to interact with the other races, including their brethren, the hill dwarves, who, due to a feud that dated back to the Cataclysm, had long been shut out of the great dwarven kingdom beneath the mountain.

But with the coming of the great dragons and the death and destruction they brought, the dwarves had gone back underground. They had sealed up the gates of Thorbardin once again, and the world had lost contact with them. The Daergar had taken advantage of the turmoil to try to seize the rulership of Thorbardin, plunging that nation into a bloody civil war. Tarn Bellowgranite was a hero of the war, and when it came time to pick up the pieces, the thanes had turned to him for leadership. He had found a people divided, a kingdom tottering on the edge of ruin when he came to his rule. He had placed that kingdom upon a firm foundation. He had united the warring clans behind his leadership. Now he was about to contemplate another step that would be something new in the annals of the dwarves of Thorbardin.

Gilthas stepped forward and bowed deeply, with sincere respect. "High King," he said speaking flawless Dwarvish, a language he had learned from his father. "I am honored to meet you at last. I know you do not like to leave your home beneath the mountain. Your journey was a long one and perilous, as are all journeys made in the world during these dark times. I thank you for making the journey, for undertaking to meet me here this day to close and formally seal our agreement."

The high king nodded his head, tugging on his beard, a sign that he was pleased with the words. The fact that the elf spoke Dwarvish had already impressed Tarn. Gilthas had been right. The dwarf king had heard stories of the elf king's weak and indecisive nature. But Tarn had learned over the years that it was never wise to judge a man until, as the dwarves would say, you had seen the color of his beard.

"The journey was pleasant. It is good to breathe the air above the ground for a change," Tarn replied. "And now, let us get down to business." He looked at Gilthas shrewdly. "I know how you elves love to palaver. I believe that we can dispense with the niceties."

"I am part human," Gilthas replied with a smile. "The impatient part, or so they tell me. I must be back in Qualinost before tomorrow's dawning. Therefore I will begin. This matter has been under negotiation for a month. We know where we stand, I believe? Nothing has changed?"

"Nothing has changed with us," said Tarn. "Has anything changed with you?"

"No, it has not. We are in agreement then." Gilthas dropped the formal tone. "You have refused to accept any payment, sir. I would not permit this, but that I know there is not wealth enough in all of Qualinesti to compensate you and your people for what you are doing. I know the risks that you run. I know that this agreement has caused controversy among your people. I guess that it has even threatened your rule. And I can give you nothing in return except for our thanks—our eternal and undying thanks."

"Nay, lad," said Tarn, flushing in embarrassment. Dwarves dislike being praised. "What I do will bring good to my people as well as yours. Not all of them can see that at this point, but they will. Too long we have lived hidden away from the world beneath the mountain. The notion came to me when civil war erupted in Thorbardin, that we dwarves might well kill each other off and who would ever know? Who would grieve for us? None in this world. The caverns of Thorbardin might fall silent in death, darkness overtake us, and there would be none to speak a word to fill that silence, none to light a lamp. The shadows would close over us, and we would be forgotten.

"I determined I would not allow that to happen. We dwarves would return to the world. The world would enter Thorbardin. Of course," Tarn said, with a wink and sip of dwarf spirits, "I could not thrust such change upon my people overnight. It has taken me long years to bring them around to my way of thinking, and even then many are still wagging their beards and stamping their feet over it. But we are doing the right thing. Of that I am convinced. We have already started work on the tunnels," he added complacently.

"Have you? Before the papers were signed?" Gilthas asked amazed.

Tarn took a long gulp, belched contentedly, and grinned. "Bah! What are papers? What are signatures? Give me your hand, King Gilthas. That will seal our bargain."

"I give you my hand, King Tarn, and I am honored to do so," Gilthas replied, deeply touched. "Is there any point on which I can reassure you? Do you have any questions to ask of me?"

"Just one, lad," said Tarn, putting down his mug and wiping his chin with his sleeve. "Some of the thanes, most notably the Neidar—a suspicious lot if I do say so—have said repeatedly that if we allow elves to enter Thorbardin, they will turn on us and seize our realm and make it their new home. You and I know that will not happen," Tarn added, raising his hand to forestall Gilthas's quick protest, "but what would you say to my people to convince them that this tragedy would not come about?"

"I would ask the thanes of the Neidar," said Gilthas, smiling, "if they would build their homes in trees. What would be their answer, do you think, sir?"

"Hah, hah! They would as soon think of hanging themselves by their beards," Tarn said, chuckling.

"Then, by the same token, we elves would as soon think of hanging ourselves by our *ears* as to live in a hole in the ground. No insult to Thorbardin intended," Gilthas added politely.

"None taken, lad. I will tell the Neidar exactly what you have said. That should blow the foam off their ale!" Tarn continued to chuckle.

"To speak more clearly, I vow on my honor and my life that the Qualinesti will use the tunnels only for the purpose of removing those in peril from the dragon's wrath. We have made arrangements with the Plains people to shelter the refugees until such time as we can welcome them back to their own homeland."

"May that day be quick to dawn," said Tarn gravely, no longer laughing. He regarded Gilthas intently. "I would ask why you do not send your refugees to the land of your cousins, the realm of Silvanesti, but I hear that it is closed and barred to you. The elves there have placed some sort of magical fortress around it."

"The forces of Alhana Starbreeze continue to try to find some way to enter the shield," Gilthas said. "We must hope that they will eventually find a way, not only for our sakes, but for the sake of our cousins, as well. How long do you believe the work will take for the tunnel to reach Qualinost?"

"A fortnight, not more," said Tarn easily.

"A fortnight, sir! To dig a tunnel over sixty-five miles through solid rock? I know the dwarves are master stonecutters," Gilthas said, "but I must confess that this astounds me."

"As I said, we had already started working. And we have help," said Tarn. "Have you ever heard of the Urkhan? No? I'm not surprised. Few outsiders know anything about them. The Urkhan are gigantic worms that eat rock. We harness them up, and they gnaw through granite as if it were fresh-baked bread. Who do you think built the thousands of miles of tunnels in Thorbardin?" Tarn grinned. "The Urkhan, of course. The worm does all the work, and we dwarves take all the credit!"

Gilthas expressed his admiration for the remarkable worms and listened politely to a discussion of the Urkhan's habits, its docile nature, and what happened to the rock after it passed through the worm's system.

"But enough of this. Would you like to see them in action?" Tarn asked suddenly.

"I would, sir," Gilthas said, "but perhaps some other time. As I mentioned earlier, I must return to Qualinost by morning light—"

"You shall, lad, you shall," the dwarf replied, grinning hugely. "Watch this." He stomped his booted foot twice on the floor.

A momentary pause and then two thumps resonated loudly, coming from the ground.

Gilthas looked at Kerian, who was looking angered and alarmed. Angry that she had not thought to investigate the strange rumblings, alarmed because, if this was a trap, they had just fallen neatly into it.

Tarn laughed loudly at their discomfiture.

"The Urkhan!" he said by way of explanation. "They're right beneath us!"

"Here? Is that true?" Gilthas gasped. "They have come so far? I know that I felt the ground shake—"

Tarn was nodding his head, his beard wagging. "And we have gone farther. Would you come below?"

Gilthas looked at his wife. "In all the rest of Qualinesti I am king, but the Lioness is in charge here," he said, smiling. "What do you say, madam? Shall we go see these wonderful worms?"

Kerian made no objection, although this unforeseen turn of events had made her wary. She said nothing outright that might offend the dwarves, but Gilthas noted that every time she encountered one of her Wilder elves, she gave him a signal with either a look, a tilt of the head, or a slight gesture of her hand. The elves disappeared, but Gilthas guessed that they had not gone far, were watching and waiting, their hands on their weapons.

They left the Gulp and Belch, some of Tarn's escort departing with every show of reluctance, wiping their lips and heaving sighs laced with the pungent smell of dwarf spirits. Tarn walked no trail but shouldered and trampled his way through the brush, thrusting or pushing aside anything that happened to be in his path. Gilthas, looking back, saw the dwarves had cut a large swath through the woods, a trail of broken limbs, trampled grass, dangling vines, and crushed grass.

Kerian cast a glance at Gilthas and rolled her eyes. He knew exactly what she was thinking. No need to worry about the dwarves hearing some trace of sound from shadowing elves. The dwarves would have been hard put to hear a thunderclap over their stomping and crashing. Tarn slowed his pace. He appeared to be searching for something. He said something in Dwarvish to his companions, who also began to search.

"He's looking for the tunnel entrance," Gilthas said softly to Kerian. "He says that his people were supposed to have left one here, but he can't find it."

"He won't, either," Kerian stated grimly. She was still irritated over being hoodwinked by the dwarves. "I know this land. Every inch of it. If there had been any sort of—"

She stopped, stared.

"Tunnel entrance," Gilthas finished, teasing. "You would have discovered it?"

They had come to a large outcropping of granite some thirty feet high jutting up through the forest floor. The striations on the rock ran sideways. Small trees and patches of wild flowers and grass grew between the layers. A large mass of boulders, parts of the outcropping that had broken off and tumbled down the side, lay at the foot of the outcropping. The boulders were huge, some came to Gilthas's waist, many were larger than the dwarves. He watched in astonishment as Tarn walked up to one of these boulders, placed his hand on it, and give it a shove. The boulder rolled aside as if it were hollow.

Which, in fact, it was.

Tarn and his fellows cleared the boulder fall, revealing a large and gaping hole in the outcropping.

"This way!" Tarn bellowed, waving his hand.

Gilthas looked at Kerian, who simply shook her head and gave a wry smile. She stopped to investigate the boulder, the inside of which had been hollowed out like a melon at a feast.

"The worms did this?" she asked, awed.

"The Urkhan," said Tarn proudly, gesturing with his hand. "The little ones," he added. "They nibble. The bigger ones would have gulped down the boulder whole. They're not very bright, I'm afraid. And they're always very hungry."

"Look at it this way, my dear," said Gilthas to Kerian as the passed from the moonlit night into the coolness of the dwarf-made cavern. "If the dwarves managed to hide the tunnel entrance from you and your people, they will have no trouble at all hiding it from the cursed Knights."

"True," Kerian admitted.

Inside the cavern, Tarn stomped twice again on what appeared to be nothing but a dirt floor. Two knocks greeted him from below. Cracks formed in the dirt, and a trapdoor, cunningly hidden, popped open. The head of dwarf poked out. Light streamed upward.

"Visitors," said Tarn in Dwarvish.

The dwarf nodded, and his head vanished. They could hear his thick boots clumping down the rungs of a ladder.

"Your Majesty," said Tarn, gesturing politely.

Gilthas went immediately. To hesitate would imply that he did not trust the high thane and Gilthas had no intention of alienating this new ally. He climbed nimbly down the sturdy ladder, descending about fifteen feet and coming to rest on a smooth surface. The tunnel was well-lit by what Gilthas first took to be lanterns.

Strange lanterns, though, he thought, drawing close to one. They gave off no heat. He looked closer and saw to his amazement that the light came not from burning oil but from the body of what appeared to be a large insect larvae. The larva lay curled up in a ball at the bottom of an iron cage that hung from a hook on the tunnel wall. A cage hung every few feet. The glow from the body of the slumbering larva lit the tunnels as bright as day.

"Even the offspring of the Urkhan work for us," Tarn said, arriving at the bottom of the ladder. "The larva glow like this for a month, and then they go dark. By that time, they are too big to fit into the cages anyway, and so we replace them. Fortunately, there is always a new crop of Urkhan to be harvested. But you must see them. This way. This way."

He led them along the tunnels. Rounding a bend, they came upon an astonishing sight. An enormous, undulating, slime-covered body, reddish brown in color, took up about half the tunnel. Dwarven handlers walked alongside the worm, guiding it by reins attached to straps wrapped around its body, slapping it with their hands or with sticks if the body of the worm started to veer off course or perhaps roll over and crush the handlers. Half the tunnel had been cleared already by a worm up ahead, so Tarn told them. This second worm came behind, widening what had already been built.

The huge worm moved incredibly fast. Gilthas and Kerian marveled at its size. The worm's body was as big around as Gilthas was tall and, according to Tarn, this worm was thirty feet in length. Piles of chewed and half-digested rock littered the floor behind the worm. Dwarves came along to shovel it to one side, keeping a sharp eye out for gold nuggets or unrefined gemstones as they cleared the rubble.

Gilthas walked the worm's length, finally reaching its head. It had no eyes, for it had no need of eyes, spending its life burrowing beneath the ground. Two horns protruded from the top of its head. The dwarves had placed a leather harness over these horns. Reins extended from the harness back to a dwarf who sat in a large basket strapped to the worm's body. The dwarf guided the worm from the basket, pulling the head in the direction he wanted to go.

The worm seemed not to even know the dwarf was there. Its one thought was to eat. It spewed liquid onto the solid rock in front of it, liquid that must have been some sort of acid, for it hissed when it hit the rock, which immediately started to bubble and sizzle. Several large chunks of rock split apart. The worm's maw opened, seized a chunk, and gulped it down.

"Most impressive!" Gilthas said with such utter sincerity that the high thane was immensely pleased, while the other dwarves looked gratified.

There was only one drawback. As the worm gnawed its way through the rock, its body heaved and undulated, causing the ground to shake. Being accustomed to it, the dwarves paid no attention to the motion but walked with the ease of sailors on a canting deck. Gilthas and Kerian had slightly more difficulty, stumbling into each other or falling against the wall.

"The Dark Knights will notice this!" Kerian observed, shouting to be heard over the worm's rending of the rock and the dwarven handlers' yelling and cursing. "When Medan's bed starts to bounce across the room and he hears shouts coming from beneath his floor, he's going to be suspicious."

"Tarn, this shaking and rumbling," Gilthas said, speaking directly into the dwarf's ear. "Can anything be done to quiet it? The Dark Knights are sure to hear it or at least feel it."

Tarn shook his head. "Impossible!" he bellowed. "Look at it this way, lad, the worms are far quieter than a work force of dwarves going at it with hammer and pick."

Gilthas looked dubious. Tarn motioned, and they followed him back down the tunnel, leaving the worms and the worst of the commotion behind.

Climbing the ladder, they emerged out into a night that was far less dark than it had been when they went underground. Dawn was coming. Gilthas would have to leave soon.

"My thought was that we would not tunnel under Qualinost itself," Tarn explained, as they walked back to the Gulp and Belch. "We're about forty miles away now. We will run our tunnels to within five miles of the city limits. That should be far enough so that the Neraka Knights have no idea what we are about. Also they'll be less likely to discover the entrances."

"What would happen if they did discover it?" Gilthas asked. "They could use the tunnels to invade Thorbardin."

"We'd collapse it first," Tarn said bluntly. "Bring it down on top of them and, likely, on top of a few of us, too."

"More and more I understand the risks you run for us," Gilthas said. "There is no way to thank you."

Tarn Bellowgranite waved aside the words, looked uncomfortable and embarrassed. Gilthas thought it best to change the subject.

"How many tunnels will there be altogether, sir?"

"Given time enough, we can build three fine ones," the dwarf replied. "As it is, we have one this far. You can begin to evacuate some of your people soon. Not many, for the walls are not completely shored up yet, but we can manage a few. As for the other two tunnels, we will need at least two months."

"Let us hope we have that long," Gilthas said quietly. "In the meanwhile, there are people in Qualinost who have run afoul of the Neraka Knights. The punishment of the Knights for lawbreakers is swift and cruel. The smallest infraction of one of their many laws can result in imprisonment or death. With this tunnel, we will be able to save some who otherwise would have perished.

"Tell me, Thane," Gilthas asked, knowing the answer, but needing to hear it for himself, "would it be possible to evacuate the entire city of Qualinost through that one tunnel?"

"Yes, I think so," said the High Thane, "given a fortnight to do it."

A fortnight. If the dragon and the Neraka Knights attacked, they would have hours at most to evacuate the people. At the end of a fortnight, there would be no one left alive to evacuate. Gilthas sighed deeply.

Kerian drew closer, put her hand on his arm. Her fingers were strong and cool, and their touch reassured him. He had been granted more than he had ever expected. He was not a baby, to cry for the stars when he had been given the moon.

He looked meaningfully at Kerian. "We will have to lay low and not antagonize the dragon for at least a month."

"My warriors will not roll over and play dead!" Kerian returned sharply, "if that is what you have in mind. Besides, if we suddenly ceased all our attacks, the Knights would grow suspicious that we were up to something, and they would start searching for it. This way, we will keep them distracted."

"A month," Gilthas said softly, silently, praying to whatever was out there, if anything was out there. "Just give me a month. Give my people a month."

18 DAWN IN A TIME OF DARKNESS

Morning came to Ansalon, too fast for some, too slow for others. The sun was a red slit in the sky, as if someone had drawn a knife across the throat of the darkness. Gilthas slipped hurriedly through the shadowy garden that surrounded his prison palace, returning somewhat late to take up the dangerous role he must continue to play.

Planchet was lurking upon the balcony, watching anxiously for the young king, when a knock on the door announced Prefect Palthainon, come for his morning string-jerking. Planchet could not plead His Majesty's indisposition this day as he had the last. Palthainon, an early riser, was here to bully the king, exercise his power over the young man, make a show of his puppeteering to the rest of the court.

"Just a moment, Prefect!" Planchet shouted. "His Majesty is using the chamber pot." The elf caught sight of movement in the garden. "Your Majesty!" he hissed as loudly as he dared. "Make haste!"

Gilthas stood under the balcony. Planchet lowered the rope. The king grasped it, climbed up nimbly, hand over hand.

The knocking resumed, louder and more impatient.

"I insist upon seeing His Majesty!" Palthainon demanded.

Gilthas clambered over the balcony. He made a dive for his bed, climbed in between the sheets fully dressed. Planchet tossed the blankets over the king's head and answered the door with his finger on his lips.

"His Majesty was ill all night. This morning he is unable to keep down so much as a bit of dry toast," Planchet whispered. "I had to help him back to bed."

The prefect peered over Planchet's shoulder. He saw the king raise his head, peering at the senator with bleary eyes.

"I am sorry His Majesty has been ill," said the prefect, frowning, "but he would be better up and doing instead of lying about feeling sorry himself. I will be back in an hour. I trust His Majesty will be dressed to receive me."

Palthainon departed. Planchet closed the door. Gilthas smiled, stretched his arms over his head, and sighed. His parting from Kerian had been wrenching. He could still smell the scent of the wood smoke that clung to her clothing, the rose oil she rubbed on her skin. He could smell the crushed grass on which they had lain, wrapped in each others arms, loathe to say good-bye. He sighed again and then climbed out of bed, going to his bath, reluctantly washing away all traces of his clandestine meeting with his wife.

When the prefect entered an hour later, he found the king busy writing a poem, a poem—if one could believe it—about a dwarf. Palthainon sniffed and told the young man to leave off such foolishness and return to business.

Clouds rolled in over Qualinesti, blotting out the sun. A light drizzle began to fall.

The same morning sunshine that had gleamed down upon Gilthas shone on his cousin, Silvanoshei, who had also been awake all night. He was not dreading the morning, as was Gilthas. Silvanoshei waited for the morning with an impatience and a joy that still left him dazed and disbelieving.

This day, Silvanoshei was to be crowned Speaker of the Stars. This day, beyond all hope, beyond all expectation, he was to be proclaimed ruler of his people. He would succeed in doing what his mother and his father had tried to do and failed.

Events had happened so fast, Silvanoshei was still dazed by it all. Closing his eyes, he relived it all again.

He and Rolan, arriving yesterday on the outskirts of Silvanost, were confronted by a group of elf soldiers.

"So much for my kingship," Silvanoshei thought, more disappointed than afraid. When the elf soldiers drew their swords, Silvan expected to die. He waited, braced, weaponless. At least he would meet his end with dignity. He would not fight his people. He would be true to what his mother wanted from him.

To Silvan's amazement, the elf soldiers lifted their swords to the sunlight and began to cheer, proclaiming him Speaker of the Stars, proclaiming him king. This was not an execution squad, Silvan realized. It was an honor guard.

They brought him a horse to ride, a beautiful white stallion. He mounted and rode into Silvanost in triumph. Elves lined the streets, cheering and throwing flowers so that the street was covered with them. Their perfume scented the air.

The soldiers marched on either side, keeping the crowd back. Silvan waved graciously. He thought of his mother and father. Alhana had wanted this more than anything in the world. She had been willing to give her life to attain it. Perhaps she was watching from wherever the dead go, perhaps she was smiling to see her son fulfill her dearest dream. He hoped so. He was no longer angry at his mother. He had forgiven her, and he hoped that she had forgiven him.

The parade ended at the Tower of the Stars. Here a tall and stern-looking elf with graying hair met them. He introduced himself as General Konnal. He introduced his nephew, Kiryn, who—Silvan was delighted to discover—was a cousin. Konnal then introduced the Heads of House, who would have to determine if Silvanoshei was indeed the grandson of Lorac Caladon (his mother's name was not mentioned) and therefore rightful heir to the Silvanesti throne. This, Konnal assured Silvanoshei in an aside, was a mere formality.

"The people want a king," Konnal said. "The Heads of House are quite ready to believe you are a Caladon, as you claim to be."

"I *am* a Caladon," Silvanoshei said, offended by the implication that whether he was or he wasn't, the Heads would approve him anyhow. "I am the grandson of Lorac Caladon and the son of Alhana Starbreeze." He spoke her name loudly, knowing quite well that he wasn't supposed to speak the name of one deemed a dark elf.

And then an elf had walked up to him, one of the most beautiful of his people that Silvanoshei had ever seen. This elf, who was dressed in white robes, stood looking at him intently.

"I knew Lorac," the elf said at last. His voice was gentle and musical. "This is indeed his grandson. There can be no doubt." Leaning forward, he kissed Silvanoshei on both cheeks. He looked at General Konnal and said again, "There can be no doubt."

"Who are you, sir?" Silvan asked, dazzled.

"My name is Glaucous," said the elf, bowing low. "I have been named regent to aid you in the coming days. If General Konnal approves, I will make arrangements for your coronation to be held tomorrow. The people have waited long years for this joyful day. We will not make them wait longer."

Silvan lay in bed, a bed that had once belonged to his grandfather, Lorac. The bedposts were made of gold and of silver twined together to resemble vines, decorated with flowers formed of sparkling jewels. Fine sheets scented with lavender covered the mattress that was stuffed with swan's down. A silken coverlet of scarlet kept the night's chill from him. The ceiling above him was crystal. He could lie in his bed and give audience every night to the moon and the stars, come to pay homage.

Silvanoshei laughed softly to himself for the delight of it all. He thought that he should pinch his flesh to wake himself from this wonderful dream, but he decided not to risk it. If he were dreaming, let him never wake. Let him never wake to find himself shivering in some dank cave, eating dried berries and waybread, drinking brackish water. Let him never wake to see elf warriors drop dead at his feet, pierced by ogre arrows. Let him never wake. Let this dream last the remainder of his life.

He was hungry, wonderfully hungry, a hunger he could enjoy because he knew it would be satiated. He imagined what he would order for breakfast. Honeyed cakes, perhaps. Sugared rose petals. Cream laced with nutmeg and cinnamon. He could have anything he wanted, and if he didn't like it, he would send it away and ask for something else.

Reaching out his hand lazily for the silver bell that stood on an ornate gold and silver nightstand, Silvanoshei rang for his servants. He lay back to await the deluge of elf attendants to flood the room, wash him out of his bed to be bathed and dressed and combed and brushed and perfumed and bejeweled, made ready for his coronation.

The face of Alhana Starbreeze, his mother's face, came to Silvan's mind. He wished her well, but this was his dream, a dream in which she had no part. He had succeeded where she had failed. He would make whole what she had broken.

"Your Majesty. Your Majesty. Your Majesty."

The elves of House Servitor bowed low before him. He acknowledged them with a charming smile, allowed them to fluff up his pillows and smooth the coverlet. He sat up in bed and waited languidly to see what they would bring him for breakfast.

"Your Majesty," said an elf who had been chosen by the Regent Glaucous to serve in the capacity of chamberlain, "Prince Kiryn waits without to pay you honor on this day."

Silvanoshei turned from the mirror in which he'd been admiring his new finery. Seamstresses had worked all yesterday and all today in a frantic hurry to stitch the young king's robes and cape he would wear for the ceremony.

"My cousin! Please, let him enter without delay."

"Your Majesty should never say, 'Please,' the chamberlain chided with a smile. "When Your Majesty wants something done, speak it and it will be done."

"Yes, I will. Thank you." Silvan saw his second mistake and flushed. "I guess I'm not supposed to say, 'Thank you' either, am I?"

The chamberlain shook his head and departed. He returned with an elf youth, several years older than Silvan. They had met only briefly the day before. This was the first time they had been alone together. Both young men regarded each other intently, searching for some sign of relationship and, pleasing to both, finding it.

"How do you like all this, Cousin?" Kiryn asked, after the many niceties and polite nothings had been given and received. "Excuse me. I meant to say, 'Your Majesty.' " He bowed.

"Please, call me 'cousin,' " Silvan said warmly. "I never had a cousin before. That is, I never knew my cousin. He is the king of Qualinesti, you know. At least, that's what they call him."

"Your cousin Gilthas. The son of Lauralanthalasa and the half-human, Tanis. I know of him. Porthios spoke of him. He said that Speaker Gilthas was in poor health."

"You needn't be polite, Cousin. All of us know that he is melancholy mad. Not his fault, but there you have it. Is it proper for me to call you 'cousin'?"

"Perhaps not in public, Your Majesty," Kiryn replied with a smile. "As you may have noted, we in Silvanesti love formalities. But in private, I would be honored." He paused a moment, then added quietly, "I heard of the deaths of your father and mother. I want to say how deeply grieved I am. I admired both of them very much."

"Thank you," Silvan said and, after a decent interval, he changed the subject. "To answer your earlier question, I must admit that I find all this rather daunting. Wonderful, but daunting. A month ago I was living in a cave and sleeping on the ground. Now I have this bed, this beautiful bed, a bed in which my grandfather slept. The Regent Glaucous arranged for the bed to be brought to this chamber, thinking it would please me. I have these clothes. I have whatever I want to eat and drink. It all seems a dream."

Silvan turned back to regarding himself again in the mirror. He was enchanted with his new clothing, his new appearance. He was clean, his hair perfumed and brushed, his fingers adorned with jewels. He was not flea bitten, he was not stiff from sleeping with a rock for a pillow. He vowed, in his heart, never again. He did not notice that Kiryn appeared grave when Silvan spoke of the regent.

His cousin's gravity deepened as Silvan continued speaking. "Talking of Glaucous, what an estimable man he is! I am quite pleased with him as regent. So polite and condescending. Asking my opinion about everything. At first, I don't mind telling you, Cousin, I was a little put out at General Konnal for suggesting to the Heads of House that a regent be appointed to guide me until I am of age. I am already considered of age by Qualinesti standards, you see."

Silvan's expression hardened. "And I am determined not to be a puppet king like my poor cousin Gilthas. However, the Regent Glaucous gave me to understand that he will not be the ruler. He will be the person to smooth the way so that my wishes and commands are carried out."

Kiryn was silent, made no answer. He looked around the room as if making up his mind to something. Drawing a step nearer Silvan, he said, in a low voice, "May I suggest that Your Majesty dismiss the servants?"

Silvan regarded Kiryn in troubled astonishment, suddenly wary, suspicious. Glaucous had told him that Kiryn himself had designs upon the throne. What if this were a ploy to catch him alone and helpless. . . .

Silvan looked at Kiryn, who was slender and delicate of build, with the soft, smooth hands of the scholar. Silvan compared his cousin to himself, whose body was hardened, well-muscled. Kiryn was unarmed. He could hardly represent a threat.

"Very well," Silvan said and sent away the servants, who had been tidying the room and laying out the clothes he would wear at the formal dance given in his honor this evening.

"There, Cousin. We are alone, What is it you have to say to me?" Silvan's voice and manner were cool.

"Your Majesty, Cousin," Kiryn spoke earnestly, keeping his voice low, despite the fact that the two of them were alone in the large and echoing room, "I came here today with one fixed purpose and that is to warn you against this Glaucous."

"Ah," said Silvan, with a knowing air. "I see."

"You don't seem surprised, Your Majesty."

"I am not, Cousin. Disappointed, I confess, but not surprised. Glaucous himself warned me that you might be jealous of both him and of me. He told me quite candidly that you seemed to dislike him. The feeling is not mutual. Glaucous speaks of you with the highest regard and is deeply saddened that the two of you cannot be friends."

"I am afraid I cannot return the compliment," Kiryn said. "The man is not worthy to be regent, Your Majesty. He is not of House Royal. He is . . . or was . . . a wizard who tended the Tower of Shalost. I know that my Uncle Konnal suggested him, but . . ."

He stopped talking, as if he found it difficult to proceed. "I tell you what I have never told anyone else, Your Majesty. I believe that Glaucous has some sort of strange hold upon my uncle.

"My uncle is a good man, Your Majesty. He fought bravely during the War of the Lance. He fought the dream alongside Porthios, your father. What he saw during those awful times has caused him to live in constant fear, unreasoning fear. He is terrified of the evil days returning. He believes that this shield will save the Silvanesti from the coming darkness. Glaucous controls the magic of the shield and through threats of lowering it, he controls my uncle. I would not want to see Glaucous control you in the same way."

"Perhaps you think, Cousin, that I am already under his control. Perhaps you think that you would be a better Speaker of Stars?" Silvan asked with mounting anger.

"I could have been Speaker, Cousin," Kiryn said with quiet dignity. "Glaucous sought to make me Speaker. I refused. I knew your mother and your father. I loved them both. The throne is yours by right. I would not usurp it."

Silvan felt he deserved the rebuke. "Forgive me, Cousin. I spoke before my brain had time to guide my tongue. But I believe that you are mistaken about Glaucous. He has only the best interests of the Silvanesti at heart. The fact that he has risen to his high estate from a low one is to his credit and to the credit of your uncle for seeing his true worth and not being blinded by class as we elves have been in the past. My mother said often that we have harmed ourselves by keeping people of talent from fulfilling their true potential by judging a person only by birth and not by ability. One of my mother's most trusted advisers was Samar, who began life as a soldier in the ranks."

"If Glaucous had come to us with expertise in the governing of our people, I would be the first to support him, no matter what his background. But all he has done is to plant a magical tree," Kiryn said wryly, "and cause a shield to be raised over us."

"The shield is for our protection," Silvanoshei argued.

"Just as prisoners in their jail cells are protected," Kiryn returned.

Silvan was thoughtful. He could not doubt his cousin's sincerity and his earnestness. Silvan did not want to hear anything against the regent. Quite honestly, Silvan was overwhelmed by the new responsibilities that had been thrust so suddenly upon him. He found it comforting to think that someone like Glaucous was there to advise and counsel him. Someone as formal and polite and charming as Glaucous.

"Let us not quarrel over this, Cousin," Silvan said. "I will consider your words, and I thank you for speaking from your heart, for I know that this cannot have been an easy task for you." He extended his hand.

Kiryn took his cousin's hand with true goodwill and pressed it warmly. The two talked of other matters, of the ceremonies of the forthcoming coronation, of the current fashions in elven dancing. Kiryn then took his leave, promising to return to escort his cousin to his crowning.

"I will be wearing the crown that last graced the head of my grandfather," said Silvan.

"May it bring you better fortune than it brought him, Your Majesty," said Kiryn. With a grave expression, he took his departure.

Silvan was sorry to see his cousin leave, for he was very pleased with Kiryn's warm friendliness and lively nature, even though he felt rather resentful at Kiryn for spoiling the morning. On this day of all days, a new king should experience nothing but joy.

"He is just envious," Silvan said to himself. "Perfectly natural. I am sure I would feel the same."

"Your Majesty," said one of his servants, "I grieve to report that it is starting to rain."

"Well, and what do you think of our new king?" General Konnal asked his companion as they ascended the stairs of the royal palace to pay homage to His Majesty on the morning of his coronation. The rain was steady and heavy now, had drawn a curtain of gray over the sun.

"I find him to be intelligent, modest, unaffected," Glaucous replied, smiling. "I am extremely pleased with him. You?"

"He is an adolescent puppy," said Konnal, shrugging. "He will give us no trouble." His tone softened. "Your advice was right, my friend. We did well to place him on the throne. The people adore him. I have not seen them so happy in a long time. The entire city has turned out to celebrate. The streets are decked with flowers, everyone is dressed in his or her finest clothes. There will be parties that last for days. They are calling his coming a miracle. It is being said that those afflicted with the wasting sickness feel life restored to their limbs. There will be no more talk of lifting the shield. No reason to do so now."

"Yes, we have uprooted the weed of rebellion the kirath were attempting to plant in our lovely garden," Glaucous replied. "The kirath imagine they have defeated you by placing Lorac's grandson on the throne. Do nothing to disillusion them. Let them celebrate. They have their king. They will trouble us no more."

"And if by some unfortunate chance the shield should fail us," Konnal stated with a meaningful look at the wizard, "we have settled his mother, as well. She will rush in with her troops, armed to the teeth, to save her country and find it in the hands of her very own son. It would almost be worth it just to see the expression on her face."

"Yes, well, perhaps." Glaucous did not seem to find this idea all that amusing. "I, for one, can do very well without ever seeing the witch's face again. I do not believe for a moment that she would let her son remain on the throne. She wants that prize for herself. Fortunately," he said smiling, his good humor restored, "she is unlikely to ever find her way inside. The shield will keep her out."

"Yet the shield admitted her son," said Konnal.

"Because I wanted it to do so," Glaucous reminded the general.

"So you say."

"Do you doubt me, my friend?"

Glaucous halted, turned to face the general. The wizard's white robes rippled around him.

"Yes," Konnal replied evenly. "Because I sense that you doubt yourself."

Glaucous started to reply, closed his mouth on his words. Clasping his hands behind him, he walked on.

"I am sorry," Konnal began.

"No, my friend." Glaucous halted, turned. "I am not angry. I am hurt, that is all. Saddened."

"It's just that—"

"I will explain myself. Perhaps then you will believe me."

Konnal sighed. "You purposefully misunderstand me. But, very well, I will hear your explanation."

"I will tell you how it came about. But not here. Too many people." Glaucous indicated a servant carrying a large wreath of laurel leaves. "Come into the library where we may talk privately."

A large room lined with shelves of dark, polished wood filled with books and scrolls, the library was quiet, the books seeming to absorb the sounds of anyone who spoke, as if noting them down for future reference.

"When I said that the shield acted according to my wishes," Glaucous explained, "I did not mean that I gave the shield a specific command to admit this young man. The magic of the shield emanates from the tree in the Garden of Astarin. Acting on my direction, the Woodshapers planted and nurtured the Shield Tree. I instructed them in the magic that caused the tree to grow. The magic is very much a part of me. I devote an immense amount of my strength and energy to maintaining the magic and keeping the shield in place. I feel sometimes," Glaucous added softly, "as if I *am* the shield. The shield that keeps our people safe."

Konnal said nothing, waited to hear more.

"I have suspected before now that the shield has been reacting to my unspoken wishes," Glaucous continued, "wishes I did not even know I was making. I have long wanted a king to sit upon the throne. The shield knew that unconscious desire of mine. Thus when Silvanoshei happened to be near it, the shield embraced him."

The general wanted to believe this, but his doubts lingered. Why has Glaucous said nothing of this before? Konnal wondered. Why do his eyes avoid mine when he speaks of it? He knows something. He is keeping something from me.

Konnal turned to Glaucous. "Can you assure me that no one else will enter the shield?"

"I can assure you of that, my dear General," Glaucous answered. "I stake my life upon it."

19 THE BLIND BEGGAR

Mina's troops left Sanction in good spirits, roaring out songs to keep the cadence of the march and speaking of the bold deeds they would do in Silvanesti in the name of their idolized commander. Whenever Mina came in sight, riding her blood-red horse, the soldiers cheered wildly, often breaking ranks (braving the ire of their commanding officers) to cluster round her and touch her for luck.

Galdar was gone. He had left several days earlier for Khur, bearing Mina's orders to General Dogah. Captain Samuval was in command in the minotaur's absence. His command was easy at this point. The sun shone. The summer days were warm. The marching at this stage was safe and easy, for the Knights were only a few days out of Sanction and still in friendly territory. Soon they would enter the land of the ogres—once allies and now bitter enemies. The thought of fighting even those savage monsters could not cloud their spirits. Mina lit their shadows like a cold, pale sun.

A veteran campaigner, Samuval knew that when the weather broke and the rain set in, when the road narrowed, the wind howled and the enemy nipped at their heels, the soldiers would begin to have second thoughts about this venture. They would start to grouse and grumble, and a few might take it into their heads to start trouble. But, for now, his duties were light. He marched at Mina's side—the envy of all in the column. He stood next to her as she sat on her horse reviewing the troops as they passed by. He was in her tent every night, studying the map and marking out the next day's route. He slept near her tent, wrapped in his cloak, his hand on his sword hilt, ready to rush to her defense should she have need of him.

He did not fear any of the men would try to harm her. Lying on his cloak one night, he stared into the stars in the clear sky and wondered about that. She was a young woman—a very attractive young woman. He was a man who loved women, all kinds of women. He could not begin to count the number he had bedded. Usually the sight of a young slip of a maid as pretty as Mina would have had his blood bubbling, his loins aching. But he felt no twinge of desire in Mina's presence and, listening to the talk around the campfires, he knew the other men in the ranks felt the same. They loved her, they adored her. They were awestruck, reverent. But he did not want her and he could not name anyone who did.

The next morning's march began the same as those before it. Samuval calculated that if all went well with Galdar's business in Khur, the minotaur would catch up to them in another two days. Prior to this, Samuval had never had much use for minotaurs, but he was actually looking forward to seeing Galdar again. . . .

"Sir! Stop the men!" a scout shouted.

Samuval halted the column's march and walked forward to meet the scout. "What is it?" the captain demanded. "Ogres?"

"No, sir." The scout saluted. "There's a blind beggar on the path ahead, sir." Samuval was irate. "You called a halt for a blasted beggar?"

"Well, sir"—the scout was discomfited—"he's blocking the path."

"Shove him out of the way then!" Samuval said, infuriated.

"There's something strange about him, sir." The scout was uneasy. "He's no ordinary beggar. I think you should come talk to him, sir. He said . . . he said he is waiting for Mina." The soldier's eyes were round.

Samuval rubbed his chin. He was not surprised to hear that word of Mina had spread abroad, but he was considerably surprised and not particularly pleased to hear that knowledge of their march and the route they were taking had also apparently traveled ahead of them.

"I'll see to this," he said and started to leave with the scout. Samuval planned to question this beggar to find out what else he knew and how he knew it. Hopefully, he would be able to deal with the man before Mina heard about it.

He had taken about three steps when he heard Mina's voice behind him.

"Captain Samuval," she said, riding up on Foxfire, "what is the problem? Why have we stopped?"

Samuval was about to say that the road ahead was blocked by a boulder, but, before he could open his mouth, the scout had blurted out the truth in a loud voice that could be heard up and down the column.

"Mina! There's a blind beggar up ahead. He says he's waiting for you."

The men were pleased, nodding and thinking it only natural that Mina should rate such attention. Fools! One would think they were parading through the streets of Jelek!

Samuval could envision the road ahead lined with the poxed and the lame from every measly village on their route, begging Mina to cure them.

"Captain," said Mina, "bring the man to me."

Samuval went to stand by her stirrup. "Listen a moment, Mina," he argued. "I know you mean well, but if you stop to heal every wretched cripple between here and Silvanost, we'll arrive in the elf kingdom in time to celebrate Yule with 'em. That is if we arrive at all. Every moment we waste is another moment the ogres have to gather their forces to come meet us."

"The man asks for me. I will see him," Mina said and slid down off her horse. "We have marched long. The men could do with a rest. Where he is, Rolof?"

"He's right up ahead," said the scout, pointing. "About half a mile. At the top of the hill."

"Samuval, come with me," Mina said. "The rest of you, wait here."

Samuval saw the man before they reached him. The road they were following led up and down small hillocks and, as the scout had said, the beggar was waiting for them at the top of one of these. He sat on the ground, his back against a boulder; a long, stout staff in his hand. Hearing their approach, he rose to his feet and turned slowly and sightlessly to face them.

The man was younger than the captain had expected. Long hair that shimmered with a silver sheen in the morning sunshine fell over his shoulders. His face was smooth and youthful. Once it might have been handsome. He was dressed in robes that were pearl gray in color, travel-worn and frayed at the hem, but clean. All this, Samuval noted later. For now, all he could do was stare at the hideous scar that disfigured the man's face.

The scar looked to be a burn mark. The hair on the right side of the man's head had been singed off. The scar slanted across the man's face from the right side of his head to below the left side of his chin. He wore a rag tied around his right eye socket. Samuval wondered with morbid curiosity if the eye was still there or if it was destroyed, melted in the terrible heat that had seared the flesh and burned away the hair to the roots. The left eye remained, but it was useless seemingly, for it held no light. The horrible wound was fresh, not a month old. The man must be in pain from the injury, but if so he did not reveal it. He stood waiting for them silently and, though he could not see her, his face turned toward Mina. He must have picked out the sound of her lighter steps from Samuval's heavier footfalls.

Mina paused, just a moment, and Samuval saw her stiffen, as if she were taken by surprise. Then, shrugging, she continued to walk toward the beggar. Samuval came behind, his hand on his sword hilt. Despite the fact that the man was blind, Samuval sensed him to be a threat. As the scout had said, there was something strange about this blind beggar.

"You know me, then," the man said, his sightless eye gazing over her head.

"Yes, I know you," she replied.

Samuval found it hard to look at the beggar's horrid wounds. Yellow puss oozed from beneath the rag. The skin around the burn was fiery red, swollen and inflamed. The captain could smell the stink of putrefying flesh.

"When did this happen to you?" Mina asked.

"The night of the storm," he replied.

She nodded gravely, as if she had expected that answer. "Why did you venture out into the storm?"

"I heard a voice," he replied. "I wanted to investigate."

"The voice of the One God," Mina said.

The beggar shook his head, disbelieving. "I could hear the voice over the roaring of the wind and the crashing thunder, but I could not hear the words it spoke. I traveled far through rain and the hail in search of the voice, and I was near the source, I think. I was almost in Neraka when a lightning bolt struck me. I remember nothing after that."

"You take this human form," she said abruptly. "Why?"

"Can you blame me, Mina?" he asked, his tone rueful. "I am forced to walk through the land of my enemies." He gestured with his staff. "This is the only way I am able to travel now—on two feet, with my stick to guide me."

"Mina"—Samuval spoke to her, but he kept his eyes on the blind man—"we have many more miles to march this day. Say the word and I will rid both the path and the world of this fellow."

"Easy, Captain," Mina said quietly, resting her hand on his arm. "This is an old acquaintance. I will be only a moment longer. How did you find me?" she asked the blind man.

"I have heard the stories of your deeds everywhere I go," the beggar answered. "I knew the name, and I recognized the description. Could there be another Mina with eyes the color of amber? No, I said to myself. Only one—the orphan girl who, years ago, washed up on the shores of Schallsea. The orphan girl who was taken in by Goldmoon and who won the First Master's heart. She grieves for you, Mina. Grieves for you these three years as for one dead. Why did you run away from her and the rest of us who loved you?"

"Because she could not answer my questions," Mina replied. "None of you could."

"And have you found the answer, Mina?" the man asked and his voice was stern.

"I have," she said steadily.

The beggar shook his head. He did not seem angry, only sorrowful.

"I could heal you," Mina offered, and she took a step toward him, her hand outstretched.

Swiftly the beggar stepped backward. In the same movement, he shifted the staff from one hand to two and held it out in front of his body, barring her way. "No!" he cried. "As much as my wound pains me now, that pain is physical. It does not strike to my soul as would the pain of your so-called healing touch. And though I walk in darkness, my darkness is not so deep as the darkness in which you now walk, Mina."

She smiled at him, her smile calm, radiant.

"You heard the voice, Solomirathnius," she said. "You hear it still. Don't you?"

He did not reply. He lowered his staff slowly, stared at her long moments. He stared so long that Samuval wondered suspiciously if the man could see out of that one milky white eye.

"Don't you?" she pressed him.

Abruptly, angrily, the man turned away from her. Tapping the ground with his staff, he left the path and entered the woods. The end of his staff knocked brutally against the boles of trees and thrust savagely into bushes. His hand groped to feel his way.

"I don't trust him," Samuval said. "He has the stink of a Solamnic about him. Let me skewer him."

Mina turned away. "You could do him no harm, Captain. He may look feeble, but he is not."

"What is he then? A wizard?" Samuval asked with a slight sneer.

"No, he is much more powerful than any wizard," Mina replied. "In his true form, he is the silver dragon known to most as Mirror. He is the Guardian of the Citadel of Light."

"A dragon!" Samuval stopped dead in the path, stared back into the brush. He could no longer see the blind beggar, and that worried him more now than ever. "Mina," he said urgently, "let me take a squadron of men after him! He will surely try to kill us all!"

Mina smiled slightly at Samuval's fears. "We are safe, Captain. Order the men to resume the march. The path ahead is clear. Mirror will not trouble us."

"Why not?" Samuval was frowning, doubtful.

"Because once, many years ago, every night, Goldmoon, the First Master of the Citadel of Light, brushed my hair," Mina said softly.

Reaching up her hand, she touched, very lightly, her shaven head.

20 BETRAYED

The days of waiting had passed pleasantly for Gerard. The queen mother's house was a sanctuary of peace and serenity. Every room was a bower of green and growing plants and flowers. The sounds of falling water soothed and relaxed. He was not in possession of the supposed time travel device, yet he had the feeling that here time was suspended. The sunlit hours melted into dusk that melted into night and back to sunlight again with no one seeming to notice the change of one day to next. No hourglass dropped its sands into elven lives, or so Gerard imagined. He was jolted back into harsh reality when, on the afternoon of the day they were to leave, he walked in the garden and saw, quite by chance, sunlight flash off shining black armor.

The Neraka Knight was distant, but he was plainly keeping watch on the house. Gerard ducked back into the doorway, his idyll of peace shattered. He waited tensely for the Neraka Knights to come beating on the door, but hours passed and no one disturbed them. He trusted, at last, that he had not been seen. He took care not to venture outside after that, not until nightfall, when they were ready to depart.

Gerard had seen little of Palin Majere, for which he was not sorry. He deplored the mage's rudeness to everyone in the household, but most particularly to Laurana. Gerard tried to make allowances. Palin Majere had suffered a great deal, the Knight reminded himself. But the mage's dark moods cast a shadow that dimmed the brightest sunlight. Even the two servant elves tiptoed around, afraid of making a sound that would bring down on them the mage's irrational anger. When Gerard mentioned this to Laurana, making some comment on what he considered boorish human behavior, she smiled and urged him to be patient.

"I was a prisoner once," she said, her eyes dark with memory, "a prisoner of the Dark Queen. Unless you have been a prisoner, Sir Knight; until you have been shut away in darkness, alone in pain and in fear, I don't believe you can understand."

Gerard accepted the gentle rebuke and said nothing more.

He had seen little of the kender, as well, for which the Knight was extremely grateful. Palin Majere kept Tasslehoff closeted away for hours at a time, having the kender relate in detail his ridiculous stories over and over. No torture devised by the cruelest Neraka Knight could match being forced to endure the kender's shrill voice for hours on end.

The night they were to leave Qualinesti came all too soon. The world beyond, the world of humans, seemed a hurried, grasping, sordid sort of place. Gerard was sorry to be returning to it. He had come to understand why the elves were loathe to travel outside their beautiful, serene realm.

Their elven guide stood waiting. Laurana kissed Tas, who, feeling a snuffle coming on, was quiet for all of three minutes. She thanked Gerard graciously for his help and gave him her hand to kiss, which he did with respect and admiration and a true feeling of loss. She spoke last to Palin, who had remained aloof, off to one side. He was obviously impatient to be gone.

"My friend," she said to him, placing her hand on his arm, "I believe that I know something of what you are thinking."

He frowned at this and shook his head slightly.

Laurana continued, "Be careful, Palin. Think long and well before you act."

He made no answer but kissed her as was the elven custom between old friends and told her, rather curtly, not to worry. He knew what he was about.

As he followed their elven guide into the night, Gerard looked back at the house on the cliff. Its lights shone brilliant as stars, but, like the stars, they were too small to bring day to night.

"Yet without the darkness," said Palin suddenly, "we would never be aware that the stars exist."

So that's how you rationalize evil, Gerard thought. He made no comment, and Palin did not speak again. The mage's morose silence was more than made up for by Tasslehoff.

"One would think that a cursed kender would talk less," Gerard grumbled.

"The curse isn't on my tongue," Tasslehoff pointed out. "It's on my insides. It made them go all squirmy. Have you ever been cursed like that?"

"Yes, the moment I set eyes on you," Gerard retorted.

"You are all making noise enough to wake a drunken gully dwarf!" their elven guide said irritably, speaking Common. Gerard had no idea if this was Kalindas or Kelevandros. He could never keep the two brothers straight. They were as alike as twins, although one was older than the other, or so he had been told. Their elven names, both beginning with K, blurred in his mind. He might have asked Palin, but the mage was disinclined to talk, appeared absorbed in his own dark thoughts.

"The kender's chatter is like the twittering of birds compared to the rattle and clank of your armor, Sir Knight," the elf added. "Not that it would be much different if you were naked. You humans cannot even draw a breath without making noise. I could hear the huffing and bellowing of your breathing a mile distant."

"We've been on the move through this forest for hours," Gerard countered. "Are we anywhere near our destination?"

"Quite near," the elf replied. "The clearing where you will meet the griffon is straight ahead at the end of this trail. If you had elven sight you could see it from here. In fact, this would be a good place to halt, if you would like to rest. We should keep under cover until the last possible moment."

"Don't worry. I'm not going anywhere," Gerard said gratefully. Dropping his pack, he sank down at the base of a tall aspen tree, leaned his back against it, closed his eyes and stretched his legs. "How long until morning?"

"An hour. And now I must leave you for a while to go hunting. We should be prepared to offer the griffons fresh meat. They will be hungry from their long flight and will appreciate the courtesy. You should be safe here, provided none of you wander off." The elf looked at the kender as he spoke.

"We will be fine," Palin said the first words he had spoken in hours. He did not sit down, but paced beneath the trees, restless and impatient. "No, Tas. You stay here with us. Where is the device? You still have it, don't you? No, don't bring it out. I just want to know it's safe."

"Oh, it's safe," the kender said. "It couldn't be unsafe, if you know what I mean."

"Damn funny time to go hunting," Gerard observed, watching the elf slip off into the darkness.

"He leaves on my orders," Palin said. "The griffons will be in a much better humor when they have eaten, and we will have a safer ride. I was once on the back of a griffon who decided that her empty belly was more important than her rider. Spying a deer on the ground, she swooped down upon it. I could do nothing but cling to her in terror. Fortunately we all came out of it alive, including the deer, who heard my cries to the griffon to stop and dashed off into the forest. The griffon was in a foul mood, however, and refused to carry me farther. Since then, I have always made certain that I brought a gift of food."

"Then why didn't the elf do that before we left instead of waiting to go hunting now?"

"Probably because he did not want to walk for miles lugging a deer carcass over his shoulder," Palin said sardonically. "You must take into account the fact that the smell of fresh-killed meat makes many elves sick to their stomachs."

Gerard said nothing, fearing to say too much. By the mage's tone, Palin took the Knight for an idiot. Perhaps he had not meant it that way, but that was how Gerard understood it.

"By the way, Sir Gerard," Palin said stiffly, "I want you to know that I consider that you have done your part in fulfilling my father's dying request. I will take up the matter from here. You need no longer concern yourself with it."

"As you wish, sir," Gerard returned.

"I want to thank you for what you have done," Palin added after a pause during which the chill in the air could have caused snow to start falling in midsummer. "You have performed a great service at the risk of your own life. A great service," he repeated softly. "I will recommend to Lord Warren that you be given a commendation."

"Thank you, sir," Gerard said. "But I'm only doing my duty by your father, a man I much admired."

"As opposed to his son, is that it?" Palin asked. He turned and walked off a few paces, his head bowed, his arms folded in the sleeves of his dark-colored robes. He obviously considered their conversation at an end.

Tasslehoff settled himself down beside Gerard, and because a kender's hands must always be busy doing something, he turned out all the pockets in the new shirt he'd persuaded Laurana to sew for him. The shirt was a riot of color and gave Gerard eyestrain just to look it. By the lambent light of a half-moon and many thousand stars, Tas sorted through the interesting things he'd picked up while in Laurana's house.

No doubt about it. Gerard would be extremely glad to deposit the mage and the kender in Solace and be done with them both.

The sky above them gradually grew lighter, the stars faded away, the moon paled, but the elf did not return.

Marshal Medan and his escort reached the rendezvous appointed by the elf about an hour before dawn. He and the two Knights with him reined in their horses. Medan did not dismount. Rebel elves were known to inhabit this part of the forest. He looked intently into the shadows and the swirling mists and thought that this would make an excellent place for an ambush.

"Subcommander," Medan said. "Go see if you can find our traitor. He said he would be waiting by those three white rocks over there."

The subcommander dismounted. Keeping his hand on his sword, half-drawing it from its scabbard, he moved slowly forward, making as little noise as possible. He wore only his breastplate, no other metal armor.

The marshal's horse was restive. The animal snorted and blew and pricked his ears. Medan patted the horse on the neck. "What is it, boy?" he asked softly. "What's out there?"

The subcommander disappeared in the shadows, reappeared again as a shadowy silhouette against the backdrop of the three large white boulders. Medan could hear the man's harsh whisper. He could not hear if there was a reply but assumed there must have been, for the subcommander nodded and returned to make his report.

"The traitor says the three are not far from here, near a clearing, where they are to meet the griffon. He will lead us there. We should walk, he says. The horses make too much noise."

The marshal dismounted and dropped the reins with a single spoken word of command. The horse would remain where it was, would not move from the spot until ordered. The other Knight dismounted, taking from his saddle a short bow and a quiver of arrows.

Medan and his escorts crept through the forest.

"And this is what I've been reduced to," Medan muttered to himself, shoving aside tree branches, stepping carefully through the undergrowth. He could barely see the man in front of him. Only the three white rocks showed up clearly and they were sometimes obscured by the dank mists. "Skulking about the woods at night like a blasted thief. Relying on the word of an elf who thinks nothing of betraying his mistress for a handful of steel. And all for what? To ambush some wretch of a wizard!"

"Did you say something, sir?" the subcommander whispered.

"Yes," Medan returned. "I said I would rather be on the field of honorable battle lying dead with a spear through my heart than here at this moment. What about you, Subcommander?"

"Sir?" The subcommander stared at him. The man had no clue what his marshal was talking about.

"Never mind," Medan grated. "Just keep going." He waved his hand.

The traitor elf appeared, a glimmer of a pale face in the darkness. He raised a pallid hand, motioned for Medan to join him. The marshal drew forward, eyed the elf grimly.

"Well? Where are they?" Medan did not use the elf's name. In Medan's mind, the elf was not worthy of a name.

"There!" The elf pointed. "Beneath that tree. You cannot see it from here, but there is a clearing a hundred paces beyond. They plan to meet the griffon there."

The sky was graying with the dawn. Medan could see nothing at first and then the mists swirled apart, revealing three shadowy figures. One appeared to be wearing dark armor, for though Medan could not see it clearly, he could hear it rattle and clank.

"Sir," said the traitor, sounding nervous, "have you further need of me? If not, I should be going. My absence may be noted."

"Leave, by all means," said Medan.

The elf slipped away into the woods.

The marshal motioned for the knight with the bow to come forward.

"Remember, the dragon wants them alive," Medan said. "Aim high. Shoot to cripple. Fire on my order. Not before."

The Knight nodded and took his place in the brush. He fit an arrow to his bow string and looked to the marshal.

Medan watched and waited.

Gerard heard a flapping sound, as of immense wings. He'd never before seen a griffon, but this sounded like what he expected a griffon would sound like. He jumped to his feet.

"What is it?" Palin lifted his head, startled by the Knight's sudden movement.

"I think I hear the griffon, sir," Gerard replied.

Palin drew back his hood to hear better, looked toward the clearing. They could not see the griffon yet. The beast was still among the treetops, but the wind from its wings was starting to scatter dead leaves and kick up dust.

"Where? Where?" Tasslehoff cried, hastily gathering up all his valuables and stuffing them into whatever location presented itself.

The griffon came into view, huge wings stilled now, floating on the air currents to a smooth landing. Gerard forgot his irritation with the mage and his annoyance at the kender in wonder at the sight of the strange beast. Elves ride griffons as humans ride horses, but few humans did. Griffons have always had a distrust of humans, who were known to hunt and kill them.

Gerard had tried not to dwell on the fact that he would soon be trusting his life to a beast that had little reason to love him, but now he was forced to confront the idea of actually riding on the back of one of these creatures, riding it not over a road but into the air. High in the air, so that any mischance would send him plummeting to a horrible death.

Gerard steeled himself, faced this as he faced any other daunting task. He noted the proud eagle head with its white feathers, the shining black eyes, and the hooked beak that could, or so he'd heard, snap a man's spine in two or rip his head from his neck. The front legs were those of an eagle, with rending talons; the back legs and body were those of a lion, covered in a soft brown fur. The wings were large and snow white underneath, brown on top. The griffon was taller than Gerard by at least head and shoulders.

"There is only one of them," Gerard reported coolly, as if meeting one were an everyday occurrence with him. "At least so far. And no sign of the elf."

"Strange," Palin said, glancing about. "I wonder where he went? This is not like him."

The griffon flapped its wings and turned its head, searching for its riders. The wind of the enormous wings whipped up a gale that sent wisps of morning fog swirling and lashed the tree branches. They waited another few moments, but no other griffon appeared.

"It seems there is to be only one, sir," Gerard said, trying not to sound relieved. "You and the kender go ahead. I'll see you off safely. Don't worry about me. I'll find my own way out of Qualinesti. I have my horse. . . ."

"Nonsense," said Palin crisply, displeased at any change in plans. "The griffon can carry all three of us. The kender counts as nothing."

"I do, too, count for something!" Tasslehoff stated, offended.

"Sir, I really don't mind," Gerard began.

An arrow thunked into the tree beside him. Another arrow whizzed over his head. Gerard dropped to the ground, grabbing hold of the kender on the way down.

"Sir! Take cover!" he yelled at Palin.

"Rebel elves," Palin said, peering through the shadows. "They have seen your armor. We are friends!" he called out in elven and lifted his hand to wave.

An arrow tore through the sleeve of his robe. He stared at the hole in angry astonishment. Gerard leaped to his feet, caught hold of the mage and pulled him to cover behind a large oak tree.

"They're not elves, sir!" he said and he pointed grimly to one of the arrows. The tip was steel and the arrow was fletched in black feathers. "They're Knights of Neraka."

"But so are you," said Palin, eyeing Gerard's breastplate, adorned with the skull and the death lily. "At least for all they know."

"Oh, they know all right," Gerard answered grimly. "You notice the elf never returned. I think we've been betrayed."

"It's not possible—" Palin began.

"I see them!" Tasslehoff cried, pointing. "Over there in those bushes. Three of them. They're wearing black armor."

"You have sharp eyes, kender," Gerard conceded. He couldn't see a thing in the shadows and mists of early dawn.

"We cannot stay here. We must make a run for the griffon!" Palin said, and started to stand up.

Gerard pulled the mage back down.

"Those archers rarely miss, sir. You'll never make it alive!"

"True, they don't miss," Palin retorted. "And yet they have fired three arrows at us and we live. If we have been betrayed, they know we carry the artifact! That's what they want. They mean to capture us alive and interrogate us." He gripped Gerard's arm hard, his cruelly deformed fingers driving the chain mail painfully into the knight's flesh. "I won't give up the device. And I won't be taken alive! Not again! Do you hear me? I won't!"

Two more arrows thudded into the tree, causing the kender, who had poked his head up to see, to duck back down.

"Whew!" he said, feeling his top-knot anxiously. "That was close! Do I still have my hair?"

Gerard looked at Palin. The mage's face was pale, his lips a thin, tight line. Laurana's words came back to Gerard. *Until you have been a prisoner, you cannot understand.*

"You go on, sir. You and the kender."

"Don't be a fool," said Palin. "We leave together. They want me alive. They have a use for me. They don't need you at all. You will be tortured and killed."

Behind them, the griffon's harsh cry sounded loud and raucous and impatient.

"I am not the fool, sir," Gerard said, looking the mage in the eye. "You are, if you don't listen to me. I can distract them, and I can defend myself properly. You cannot, unless you have some magical spell at your fingertips?"

He knew by Majere's pale, pinched face that he did not.

"Very well," said Gerard. "Take the kender and your precious magical artifact and get out of here!"

Palin hesitated a moment, staring at the direction of the enemy. His face was set, rigid, corpselike. Slowly, he withdrew his hand from Gerard's arm. "This is what I have become," he said. "Useless. Wretched. Forced to run instead of facing my enemies . . ."

"Sir, if you're going, go now," Gerard said, drawing his sword with a ringing sound. "Keep low and use the trees for cover. Fast!"

He rose from his hiding position. Brandishing his sword, he charged unhesitatingly at the Knights crouched in the brush, shouting his battle challenge, drawing their fire.

Palin rose to his feet. Crouching low, he grabbed hold of Tasslehoff's shirt collar, jerked the kender to a standing position. "You're coming with me," he ordered.

"But what about Gerard?" Tas hung back.

"You heard him," Palin said, dragging the kender forward. "He can take care of himself. Besides, the Knights must not capture the artifact!"

"But they *can't* take the device away from me!" Tas protested, tugging at his shirt to free it from Palin's grasp. "It will always come back to me!"

"Not if you're dead," Palin said harshly, biting the words.

Tas stopped suddenly and turned around. His eyes went wide.

"Do . . . do you see a dragon anywhere?" he asked nervously.

"Quit stalling!" Palin seized hold of the kender by the arm this time and, using strength borne of adrenaline, hauled Tasslehoff bodily through the trees toward the griffon.

"I'm not stalling. I feel sick," Tas asserted. "I think the curse is working on me again."

Palin paid no attention to the kender's whining. He could hear Gerard yelling, shouting challenges to his enemies. Another arrow whistled past, but it fell spent about a yard away from Palin. His dark robes blended into the forest, he was a running target moving through the mists and dim light, keeping low, as Gerard had recommended, and putting the trunks of the trees between him and the enemy whenever possible.

Behind him, Palin heard steel clash against steel. The arrows ceased. Gerard was fighting the Knights. Alone.

Palin plunged grimly ahead, dragging the protesting kender along with him. The mage was not proud of himself. His fear and his shame rankled in him, more painful than one of the arrows if it had happened to hit. He risked a glance backward but could see nothing for the shadows and the fog.

He was near the griffon. He was near escape. His steps slowed. He hesitated, half-turned . . .

A blackness came over him. He was once again in the prison cell in the Gray Robes' encampment on the border of Qualinesti. He crouched at the bottom of a deep, narrow pit dug into the ground. The walls of the pit were smooth. He could not climb up them. An iron grating was placed over the top. A few holes in the grate permitted the air to filter down into the pit, along with the rain that dripped monotonously and filled the bottom of the pit with water.

He was alone, forced to live in his own filth. Forced to eat whatever scraps they tossed down to him. No one spoke to him. He had no guards. None were necessary. He was trapped, and they knew it. He rarely even heard the sound of a human voice for days on end. He almost came to welcome those times when his captors threw down a ladder and brought him up for "questioning."

Almost.

The bright blazing pain seared through him again. Breaking his fingers, slowly, one by one. Ripping out his fingernails. Flailing his back with leather cords that cut through his flesh to the bone.

A shudder ran through him. He bit his tongue, tasted blood and bile that surged up from his clenching stomach. Sweat trickled down his face.

"I'm sorry, Gerard!" he gasped. "I'm sorry!"

Catching hold of Tasslehoff by the scruff of his neck, Palin lifted the kender and tossed him bodily onto the griffon's back. "Hold on tightly!" he ordered the kender.

"I think I'm going to throw up," Tas cried, squirming. "Let's wait for Gerard!"

Palin had no time for any kender ploys. "Leave at once!" he ordered the griffon. Palin pulled himself into the saddle that was strapped onto the griffon's back, between the feathery wings. "The Knights of Neraka surround us. Our guard is holding them off, but I doubt he can last for long."

The griffon glared back at the mage with bright, black eyes.

"Do we leave him behind, then?" the griffon asked.

"Yes," said Palin evenly. "We leave him behind."

The griffon did not argue. He had his orders. The strange habits of humans were not his concern. The beast lifted his great wings and leaped into the air, his powerful lion legs driving into the ground. He circled the clearing, striving to gain altitude and avoid the trees. Palin peered down, trying to find Gerard. The sun had cleared the horizon, was burning away the mists and lighting the shadows. Palin could see flashes of steel and hear ringing blows.

Miraculously, the Knight was still alive.

Palin turned away. He faced into the rushing wind. The sun vanished suddenly, overtaken by huge, rolling gray storm clouds that boiled up over the horizon. Lightning flickered amid the churning clouds. Thunder rumbled. A chill wind, blowing from the storm, cooled the sweat that had drenched his robes and left his hair wringing wet. He shivered slightly and drew his dark cloak close around him. He did not look back again.

The griffon rose high above the trees. Feeling the air currents beneath his wings, the beast soared into the blue sky.

"Palin!" Tasslehoff cried, tugging urgently on the back of his robes. "There's something flying behind us!"

Palin twisted to look.

The green dragon was distant, but it was moving at great speed, its wings slicing the air, its clawed feet pressed up against its body, its green tail streaming out behind. It was not Beryl. One of her minions, out doing her bidding.

Of course. She would not trust the Knights of Neraka to bring her this prize. She would send one of her own kind to fetch it. He leaned over the griffon's shoulder.

"A dragon!" he shouted. "East of us!"

"I see it!" the griffon snarled.

Palin shaded his eyes to view the dragon, trying not to blink in case he should miss a single beat of the immense wings.

"The dragon has spotted us," he reported. "It is coming straight for us."

"Hang on!" The griffon veered sharply, made a steep, banking turn. "I'm going to fly into the storm. The ride will be rough!"

Tall, spiring clouds formed a wall of gray and purple-black on the horizon. The clouds had the look of a fortress, massive and impenetrable. Lightning flared from breaks in the clouds, like torchlight through windows. Thunder rolled and boomed.

"I do not like the looks of that storm!" Palin cried out to the griffon.

"Do you like the insides of the dragon's belly better?" the griffon demanded. "The beast gains on us. We cannot outfly it."

Palin looked back, hoping that the griffon might have misjudged. Huge wings beat the air, the dragon's jaws parted. Palin met the dragon's eyes, saw the single-minded purpose in them, saw them intent on him.

Grasping the reins with one hand and taking firm hold of a shouting Tas with the other, Palin bent low over the griffon's neck, keeping his head and body down so that the rushing wind did not blow him off the griffon's back. The first few drops of rain pelted his face, stinging.

The clouds rose to immense heights, towering spires of lightning-shot gray-black, taller than the mighty fortress of Pax Tharkas. Palin looked up in awe, his head bent so that his neck ached and still he could not see the top. The griffon swooped nearer. Tasslehoff was still shouting something, but the wind took his words and whipped them away behind him, as it whipped his topknot.

Palin looked back. The dragon was almost on them. The claws of the dragon twitched now in anticipation of the capture. She would breathe her lethal gas on them, then seize them all three in one of her huge clawed feet and hurl them to the ground. With luck, the fall would kill them. The dragon would devour the griffon and then, at her leisure, she would rip their bodies apart, searching for the device.

Palin averted his eyes, stared ahead into the storm and urged the griffon to fly faster.

The cloud fortress rose before them. A flash of lightning blinded him. Thunder rolled, sounding like enormous cables turning a gigantic cog wheel. A solid bank of clouds suddenly parted, revealing a dark, lightning-lit hallway curtained by driving rain.

The griffon plunged into the cloud bank. Rain lashed at them in stinging torrents, deluged them. Wiping the water from his eyes, Palin stared in awe. Row after row of columns of gray cloud rose from a mottled gray floor to support a ceiling of boiling black.

Clouds shrouded them, wrapped around them. Palin could see nothing for the woolly grayness. He could not even see the griffon's head. Lightning sizzled near him. He could smell the brimstone, thunder crashed, nearly stopping his heart.

The griffon flew a zigzag course among the columns, soaring up and diving down, rounding and circling, then doubling back. Sheets of rain hung like silver tapestries, drenching them as they flew beneath. Palin could not see the dragon, though he could hear the discordant horn blast of its frustration as it tried desperately to find them.

The griffon left the cavernous halls of the fortress of storm clouds and flew out into the sunshine. Palin looked back, waited tensely for the dragon to appear. The griffon chortled, pleased. The dragon was lost somewhere in the storm clouds.

Palin told himself that he'd had no choice in the matter, he had acted logically in escaping. He had to protect the magical artifact. Gerard had practically ordered the mage to leave. If he had stayed, he could have accomplished nothing. They would have all died, and the artifact would have been in Beryl's possession.

The artifact was safe. Gerard was either dead or a prisoner. There was nothing that could be done to save him now.

"Best to forget it," Palin said to himself. "Put it out of my mind. What's done is done and can't be undone."

He dropped remorse and guilt into a dark pit, a deep pit in his soul and covered them with the iron grating of necessity.

"Sir," reported Medan's subcommander, "the Knight is attacking—alone. The magic-user and the kender are escaping. What are your orders?"

"Attacking alone. So he is," Medan replied, astonished.

The Solamnic came crashing through the underbrush, brandishing his sword and shouting the Solamnic battle-cry, a cry Marshal Medan had not heard in many years. The sight took the marshal back to the days when knights in shining silver and gleaming black clashed headlong on the field of battle; when champions came forward to duel to the death while armies looked on, their fates in the hands of heroes; when combatants saluted each other with honor before commencing with the deadly business at hand.

Here was Medan, crouched in a bush, safely ensconced behind a large tree stump, taking potshots at a washed-up mage and a kender.

"Can I sink any lower?" he muttered to himself.

The archer was drawing his bow. Having lost sight of the mage, he shifted his aim to the Knight, going for the legs, hoping for a crippling shot.

"Belay that," Medan snapped, resting his hand on the bowman's arm.

The subcommander looked around. "Sir? Your orders?"

The Solamnic was closing in. The magic-user and the kender were out of range, lost in the trees and the mists.

"Sir, should we pursue them?" the subcommander asked.

"No," Medan answered and saw a look of amazement cross the man's face.

"But our orders," he ventured.

"I know our orders," Medan snapped. "Do you want to be remembered in song as the Knight who slew a kender and a broken-down old mage, or as a Knight who fought a battle with an equal?"

The subcommander evidently did not want to be remembered in song. "But our orders," he persisted.

Damn the man for a thick-headed lout! Medan glowered at him.

"You *have* your orders, Subcommander. Don't make me repeat them."

The forest grew dark again. The sun had risen only to have its warmth and light cut off by storm clouds. Thunder rumbled in the distance, a few drops of rain pelted down. The kender and the mage had disappeared. They were on the back of the griffon and heading away from Qualinesti. Away from Laurana. Now, with luck, he could shield her from any involvement with the mage.

"Go meet the Knight," Medan said, waving his hand. "He challenges you to combat. Fight him."

The subcommander rose from his place, sword drawn. The archer dropped his bow. He held a dagger in his hand, ready to strike from behind while the subcommander attacked from the front.

"Single combat," Medan added, holding the bowman back. "Face him one on one, Subcommander."

"Sir?" The man was incredulous. He looked back to see if the marshal was joking.

What had the subcommander been before he became a Knight? Sell-sword? Thief? Thug? Well, this day, he would have a lesson in honor.

"You heard me," Medan said.

The subcommander exchanged dour glances with his fellow, then walked forward without enthusiasm to meet the Solamnic's crashing charge. Medan rose to his feet. Crossing his arms over his chest, he leaned back against one of the white boulders to watch the encounter.

The subcommander was a powerfully built man with a bull neck, thick shoulders and muscular arms. He was accustomed to relying on his strength and low cunning in battle, hacking and slashing at his opponent until either a lucky cut or sheer brute force wore the enemy down.

The subcommander charged head-on like a snorting bison, swinging his sword with murderous strength. The Solamnic parried the blow, met it with such force that sparks glittered on the steel blades. The subcommander held on, swords locked, trying to drive his opponent into the ground. The Solamnic was no match for such strength. He recognized this and changed tactics. He staggered backward, leaving himself temptingly open.

The subcommander fell for the ruse. He leaped to the attack, slashing with his blade, thinking to make a quick kill. He managed to wound the knight in the left upper arm, cutting through the leather armor to open a great bleeding gash.

The Solamnic took the blow and never winced. He held his ground, watched for his opportunity and coolly drove his sword into the subcommander's belly.

The subcommander dropped his sword and doubled over with a horrible, gurgling cry, clutching himself, trying to hold his insides in. The Solamnic yanked his sword free. Blood gushed from the man's mouth. He toppled over.

Before Medan could stop him, the bowman had lifted his bow, shot an arrow at the Solamnic. The arrow plunged deep into the Knight's thigh. He cried out in agony, stumbled, off-balance.

"You cowardly bastard!" Medan swore. Snatching the bow, he slammed it against the rock, smashing it.

The archer then drew his sword and ran to engage the wounded Solamnic. Medan considered halting the battle, but he was interested to see how the Solamnic handled this new challenge. He watched dispassionately, glorying in a battle-to-the-death contest such as he had not witnessed in years.

The archer was a shorter, lighter man, a cagier fighter than the subcommander. He took his time, testing his opponent with jabbing strikes of his short sword, searching for weaknesses, wearing him down. He caught the Solamnic a glancing blow to the face beneath the raised visor. The wound was not serious, but blood poured from it, running into the Solamnic's eye, partially blinding him. The Solamnic blinked the blood out of his eye and fought on. Crippled and bleeding, he grimaced every time he was forced to put weight on his leg. The arrow remained lodged in his thigh. He had not had time to yank it out. Now he was on the offensive. He had to end this fight soon, or he would not have any strength to pursue it.

Lightning flashed. The rain fell harder. The men struggled together over the corpse of the subcommander. The Solamnic jabbed and slashed, his sword seeming to be everywhere like a striking snake. Now it was the archer who was hard-pressed. He had all he could do to keep that snake's fang from biting.

"Well struck, Solamnic," Medan said softly more than once, watching with pleasure the sight of such skill, such excellent training.

The archer slipped in the rain-wet grass. The Solamnic lunged forward on his wounded leg and drove his sword into the man's breast. The archer fell, and so did the Solamnic, collapsing on his knees onto the forest floor, gasping for breath.

Medan left his boulder, walked out into the open. The Solamnic, hearing him coming, staggered to his feet with a wrenching cry of pain. His wounded leg gave out beneath him. Limping, the Solamnic placed his back against a tree trunk to provide stability and raised his sword. He looked at death. He knew he could not win this last battle, but at least he would die upright, not on his knees.

"I thought the flame had gone out in the hearts of the Knighthood, but it lives on in one man seemingly," said Medan, facing the Solamnic. The marshal rested his hand on the hilt of his sword, but he did not draw it.

The Solamnic's face was a mask of blood. Eyes of a startling, arresting blue color regarded Medan without hope, but without fear.

He waited for Medan to strike.

The marshal stood in the mud and the rain, straddling the bodies of his two dead subordinates, and waited.

The Solamnic's defiance began to waver. He realized suddenly what Medan was doing, realized that he was waiting for the Solamnic to collapse, waiting to capture him alive.

"Fight, damn you!" The Solamnic lurched forward, lashed out with his sword.

Medan stepped to one side.

The Solamnic forgot, put his weight on his bad leg. The leg gave way. He lost his balance, fell to the forest floor. Even then, he made one last opportunity to try to struggle to his feet, but he was too weak. He had lost too much blood. His eyes closed. He lay face down in the muck alongside the bodies of his foes.

Medan rolled the Knight over. Placing his hand on the Knight's thigh for leverage, the marshal took hold of the arrow and yanked it out. The Knight groaned with the pain, but did not regain consciousness. Medan took off his cloak, cut the material into strips with his sword, and made a battlefield tourniquet to staunch the bleeding. He then wrapped the Knight warmly in what remained of the cloak.

"You have lost a lot of blood," Medan said, returning his sword to its sheath, "but you are young and strong. We will see what the healers can do for you."

Rounding up the two horses of his subordinates, Medan threw the bodies unceremoniously over their saddles, tied them securely. Then the marshal whistled to his own horse. The animal came trotting over in response to his master's summons to stand quietly at Medan's side.

Medan lifted the Solamnic in his arms, eased the wounded Knight into the saddle. He examined the wound, was pleased to see that the tourniquet had stopped the flow of blood. He relaxed the tourniquet a notch, not wanting to cut off the blood flow to the leg completely, then climbed into the saddle. Seating himself behind the injured Knight, Medan put his arm around the man and held him gently but firmly in the saddle. He took hold of the reins of the other two horses and, leading them behind, began the long ride back to Qualinost.

21 THE DEVICE OF TIME JOURNEYING

The wild and terrifying flight from the dragon ended in blue sky and sunshine. The flight took longer than usual, for the griffon had been blown off course by the storm. The beast made landfall somewhere in the wilds of the Kharolis Mountains to feed on a deer, a delay Palin chafed at, but all his pleas for haste went unheeded. After dining, the griffon took a nap, while Palin paced back and forth, keeping a firm grip on Tasslehoff. When night fell, the creature stated that it would not fly after dark. The griffon and Tasslehoff slept. Palin sat fuming and waiting for the sun to rise.

They continued their journey the next day. The griffon landed Palin and Tasslehoff at midmorning in an empty field not far from what had once been the Academy of Sorcery. The stone walls of the academy still stood, but they were black and crumbling. The roof was a skeleton of charred beams. The tower that had once been a symbol of hope to the world, hope that magic had returned, was nothing but a pile of rubble, demolished by the blast that had torn out its heart.

Palin had once planned to rebuild the academy, if for no other reason than to show his defiance for Beryl. When he began to lose the magic, began to feel it slip away from him like water falling from cupped palms, he discarded the idea. It was a waste of time and effort. Better far to spend his energies searching for artifacts of the Fourth Age, artifacts that still held the magic inside and could still be used by those who knew how.

"What is that place?" Tasslehoff asked, sliding down from the griffon's back. He stared with interest at the destroyed walls with their gaping, empty windows. "And what happened to it?"

"Nothing. Never mind," Palin said, not wanting to enter into long explanations involving the death of a dream. "Come along. We have no time to was—"

"Look!" Tas cried, pointing. "Someone's walking around there. I'm going to go look!"

He was off, his bright shirt tail fluttering behind him, his topknot bouncing with glee.

"Come back—" Palin began and then realized he might as well save his breath.

Tas was right. Someone was indeed walking around the ruins of the academy and Palin wondered who it might be. The residents of Solace considered the place cursed and never went there for any reason. The person was wearing long robes; Palin caught a glimpse of crimson fabric beneath a gold-trimmed beige cloak. This could, of course, be some former student, come back to gaze in nostalgia at his wrecked place of learning, but Palin doubted it. By the graceful walk and the rich dress, he realized that this was Jenna.

Mistress Jenna of Palanthas had been a powerful red-robed wizardess in the days before the Chaos War. An extraordinarily beautiful woman, she was reputed to have been the lover of Dalamar the Dark, pupil of Raistlin Majere and once Master of the Tower of High Sorcery at Palanthas. Jenna had earned her living by running a mageware shop in Palanthas. Her shop had done moderately well during the Fourth Age, when magic had been a gift granted to people by the three gods, Solinari, Lunitari, and Nuitari. She carried the usual assorted spell components: bat guano, butterfly wings, sulphur, rose leaves (whole and crushed), spider eggs, and so forth. She had a good supply of potions and was known to have the best collection of spell scrolls and books outside the Tower of Wayreth, all to be had for a price. She was particularly renowned for her collection of magical artifacts: rings, bracers, daggers, swords, pendants, charms, amulets. These were the artifacts on display. She had other, more potent, more dangerous, more powerful artifacts, which she kept hidden away, to be shown only to serious customers and that by appointment.

When the Chaos War came, Jenna had joined Dalamar and a white-robed mage on a perilous mission to help defeat the rampaging Father of the Gods. She never spoke of what befell them on that terrible journey. All Palin knew was that on their return Dalamar had been critically wounded. He had lain near death in his tower for many long weeks.

Jenna had been his constant companion and nurse until the day when she walked out of the tower, never to return. For on that night, the Tower of High Sorcery at Palanthas was destroyed in a magical blast. No one ever saw Dalamar again. After many years had passed and he had not returned, the Conclave pronounced him officially dead. Mistress Jenna reopened her mageware shop and discovered that she was sitting on a treasure trove.

With the magic of the gods vanished, desperate mages had sought ways to hold onto their power. They discovered that magical artifacts crafted in the Fourth Age retained their power. The only drawback was that sometimes this power was erratic, did not act as expected. A magical sword, once an artifact of good, suddenly began to slay those it was meant to protect. A ring of invisibility failed its owner at a critical moment, landing the thief five years in a Sanction dungeon. No one knew the reason. Some said the unreliability was due to the fact that the gods no longer had influence over them, others said that it had nothing to do with the gods. Artifacts were always known to be tricky objects to handle.

Buyers were more than willing to take the risk, however, and the demand for Fourth Age artifacts soared higher than a gnomish steam-driven mechanical flapjack-flipping device. Mistress Jenna's prices rose to match. She was now, at the age of sixty-something, one of the wealthiest women in Ansalon. Still beautiful, though her beauty had ripened, she had retained her influence and power even under the rule of the Knights of Neraka, whose commanders found her charming, fascinating, mysterious, and accommodating. She paid no attention to those who termed her "collaborator." Jenna had long been accustomed to playing both ends against the middle, knew how to fool the middle and the ends into thinking each was getting the best of the bargain.

Mistress Jenna was also the acknowledged expert in Ansalon on Fourth Age magical artifacts.

Palin could not go immediately to greet her. The griffon complained again of hunger. The beast was, in fact, eyeing the kender avariciously, obviously considering Tas a toothsome morsel. Palin promised he would send back a haunch of venison. This satisfied the griffon, who began to preen herself, pleased at having reached her destination.

Palin went off in pursuit of Tasslehoff, who was happily picking his way through the rubble, turning over rocks to see what was underneath and exclaiming over every find.

Jenna had been strolling around the grounds of the ruined academy. Curious herself to see what the kender had discovered, she walked over to look.

Tas lifted his head, stared at the mage for long moments and then, with a glad cry, he jumped up and ran straight for her with arms outstretched.

Jenna quickly extended both hands, palms outward. Light flashed from one of several rings she wore, and Tas stumbled backward as if he'd run headlong into a brick wall.

"Keep your distance, Kender," she said calmly.

"But, Jenna!" Tas cried, rubbing his nose and eyeing the rings with interest, "don't you recognize me? It's Tasslehoff! Tasslehoff Burrfoot. We met in Palanthas during the Chaos War, only a few days ago for me, but I guess for you it's been years and years 'cause you're a lot older now. A *lot* older," he added with emphasis. "I came to your mageware shop and . . ." Tas prattled on.

Jenna kept her hands stretched outward, regarding the kender with amusement—a pleasant distraction. She obviously did not believe a word he was saying.

Hearing footsteps crunch on rock, Jenna turned her head quickly. "Palin!" She smiled to see him.

"Jenna." He bowed in respect. "I am pleased you could find the time to come."

"My dear, if what you intimated to me is true, I would not have missed this for all the treasure in Istar. You will excuse me if I do not shake hands, but I am keeping this kender at bay."

"How was your journey?"

"Long." She rolled her eyes. "My ring of teleportation"—she indicated a large ring of sparkling amethyst set in silver that she wore on her thumb— "used to take me from one end of the continent to another in a flash. Now it takes me two days to travel from Palanthas to Solace."

"And what are you doing here at the academy?" Palin asked, glancing around. "If you're looking for artifacts, don't bother. We salvaged what we could."

Jenna shook her head. "No, I was just taking a walk. I stopped by your house," she added with an arch glance. "Your wife was there, and she was not overly pleased to see me. Finding the reception a bit chilly indoors, I decided I would prefer a walk in the sunshine." She looked around in her turn, shook her head sadly. "I had not been here since the destruction. They did a thorough job. You're not going to rebuild?"

"Why should I?" Palin shrugged. His tone was bitter. "What use does anyone have for an Academy of Sorcery if there is no more sorcery? Tas," he said abruptly, "Usha is at home. Why don't you go surprise her?" Turning, he pointed to a large house which could barely be seen for the tall trees surrounding it. "There is our house—"

"I know!" Tasslehoff said excitedly. "I was there the first time I went to Caramon's funeral. Does Usha paint wonderful pictures like she did then?"

"Why don't you go ask her yourself?" Palin said irritably.

Tas glanced at the rubble and appeared undecided.

"Usha would be very hurt if you didn't go to see her," Palin added.

"Yes, you're right," Tas replied, making up his mind. "I wouldn't do anything to hurt her. We are *great* friends. Besides, I can always come back here later. Good-bye, Jenna!" He started to extend his hand, thought better of it. "And thanks for magicking me. That hasn't happened to me in a long time. I really enjoyed it."

"Odd little fellow," remarked Jenna, gazing after Tas, who was running pell-mell down the hillside. "He looks and talks very much like the kender I knew as Tasslehoff Burrfoot. One would almost think he *is* Tasslehoff."

"He is," said Palin.

Jenna shifted her gaze to him. "Oh, come now." She scrutinized him more closely. "By the lost gods, I believe that you are serious. Tasslehoff Burrfoot died—"

"I know!" Palin said impatiently. "Thirty-odd years ago. Or thereabouts. I'm sorry, Jenna." He sighed. "It's been a long night. Beryl found out about the artifact. We were ambushed by Neraka Knights. The kender and I barely escaped with our lives, and the Solamnic who brought Tas to me didn't escape at all. Then we were attacked in the air by one of Beryl's greens. We escaped the dragon only by making a harrowing flight into a thunderstorm."

"You should get some sleep," Jenna advised, regarding him with concern.

"I can't sleep," Palin returned, rubbing his eyes, which were red-rimmed and burning. "My thoughts are in turmoil, they give me no rest. We need to talk!" he added in a kind of frantic desperation.

"That's why I am here, my friend," Jenna said. "But you should at least eat something. Let us go to your house and drink a glass of wine. Say hello to your wife, who has just returned herself from what I gather was a very harrowing journey herself."

Palin grew calmer. He smiled at her wanly. "Yes, you are right, as usual. It's just . . ." He paused, thinking what to say and how to say it. "That is the real Tasslehoff, Jenna. I'm convinced of it. And he has been to a future that is not ours, a future in which the great dragons do not exist. A future where the world is at peace. He has brought with him the device he used to travel to that future."

Jenna gazed at him searchingly and intently. Seeing that he was in earnest, utterly serious, her eyes darkened, narrowed with interest.

"Yes," she said at last. "We do need to talk." She took his arm, they walked side by side.

"Tell me everything, Palin," she said.

The Majeres' house was a large structure that had once belonged to a Master Theobald, the man who had taught Raistlin Majere magic. Caramon had purchased the house at the master's death, in memory of his brother, and had given the house as gift to Palin and Usha when they were married. Here their children had been born and grown up, going off on adventures of their own. Palin had transformed the classroom where the young Raistlin had once droned through his lessons into a studio for his wife, a portrait painter of some renown throughout Solamnia and Abanasinia. He continued to use the master's old laboratory for his studies.

Tasslehoff had spoken truly when he told Palin that he remembered the house from Caramon's first funeral. He did remember the house—*it* hadn't changed. But Palin certainly had.

"I suppose having your fingers all mangled would give you a mangled view of life," Tas was saying to Usha as he sat with her in the kitchen, eating a large bowl of oatmeal. "That must be the reason, because at Caramon's first funeral, Palin's fingers were just fine and so was he. He was cheerful and happy. Well, maybe not happy, because poor Caramon had just died and no one could feel truly happy. But Palin was happy underneath. So that when he was over being sad, I knew he would be happy again. But now he's terribly unhappy, so unhappy that he can't even be sad."

"I . . . I suppose so," Usha murmured.

The kitchen was a large one with a high, beamed ceiling and an enormous stone fireplace, charred and blackened with years of use. A pot hung from a black chain in the center of the fireplace. Usha sat across from the kender at a large, butcher-block table used for chopping the heads off chickens and such, or so Tas supposed. Right now it was washed clean, no headless chickens lying about. But then it was only midmorning. Dinnertime was a long way off.

Usha was staring at him just like all the rest of them—as if he'd grown two heads or maybe was headless altogether, like the chickens. She had been staring at him that way ever since his arrival, when he had thrown open the front door (remembering to knock afterward), and cried out, "Usha! It's me, Tas! I haven't been stepped on by the giant yet!"

Usha Majere had been a lovely young woman. Age had enhanced her good looks, although, Tas thought, *she doesn't have quite the same prettiness she had when I came back here for Caramon's funeral the first time*. Her hair shone with the same silver sheen, her eyes glinted with the same gold, but the gold lacked warmth, the silver was dull and tarnished. She looked faded and tired.

She's unhappy, too, Tas realized suddenly. *It must be catching. Like measles.*

"That will be Palin now!" Usha said, hearing the front door open and close. She sounded relieved.

"And Jenna," Tas mumbled, his mouth full.

"Yes. Jenna," Usha repeated, her voice cool. "You can stay here, if you like, er . . . Tas. Finish your oatmeal. There's more in the pot."

She rose to her feet and left the kitchen. The door swung shut behind her. Tas ate his oatmeal and eavesdropped with interest on the conversation being held in the entry hall. Ordinarily he would not have listened in on someone else's conversation, because that wasn't polite, but they were talking about him when he wasn't there, which wasn't polite, either, and so he felt justified.

Besides, Tas was starting not to like Palin very much. The kender felt badly about this, but he couldn't help the feeling. He'd spent a considerable amount of time with the mage when they were at Laurana's, relating over and over everything he could remember about Caramon's first funeral. The kender added the usual embellishments, of course, without which no kender tale is considered complete. Unfortunately, instead of entertaining Palin, these embellishments—which shifted from story to story—appeared to irritate him to no end. Palin had a way of looking at him—Tas—not as if he had two heads, but more as if the mage would like to rip off the kender's single head and open it up to see what was inside.

"Not even Raistlin looked at me like that," Tas said to himself, scraping the oatmeal out of the bowl with his finger. "He looked at me as if he'd like to kill me sometimes, but never like he wanted to turn me inside out first."

Usha's voice came floating through the door ". . . *claims* he's Tasslehoff . . ."

"He *is* Tasslehoff, my dear," Palin returned. "You know Mistress Jenna, I believe, Usha? Mistress Jenna will be spending a few days with us. Will you make up the guest room?"

There was a silence that sounded as if it had been mashed through a sieve, then Usha's voice, cold as the oatmeal had grown by now. "Palin, may I see you in the kitchen?"

Palin's voice, colder than the oatmeal. "Please excuse us, Mistress Jenna."

Tasslehoff sighed and, thinking he should look as if he hadn't been listening, began to hum loudly to himself and started to rummage through the pantry, searching for something else to eat.

Fortunately, neither Palin nor Usha paid any attention to the kender at all, except for Palin to snap at him to stop that infernal racket.

"What is *she* doing here?" Usha demanded, her hands on her hips.

"We have important matters to discuss," Palin answered evasively.

Usha fixed him with a look. "Palin, you promised me! This trip to Qualinesti would be your last! You know how dangerous this search for artifacts has become—"

"Yes, my dear, I do know," Palin interrupted, his tone cool. "That is why I think it would be best if you left Solace."

"Left!" Usha repeated, astonished. "I've just come back home after being away for three months! Your sister and I were virtual prisoners in Haven. Did you know that?"

"Yes, I knew—"

"You knew! And you didn't say anything? You weren't worried? You didn't ask how we escaped—"

"My dear, I haven't had time—"

"We couldn't even come back for your father's funeral!" Usha continued. "We were permitted to leave only because I agreed to paint a portrait of the magistrate's wife. She has a face that would have been ugly on a hobgoblin. Now you want me to leave again."

"It's for your own safety."

"What about your safety?" she demanded.

"I can take care of myself."

"Can you, Palin?" Usha asked. Her voice was suddenly gentle. She reached out, tried to take hold of his hands in her own.

"Yes," he snapped and snatched his crippled hands away, folded them in the sleeves of his robes.

Tasslehoff, feeling extremely uncomfortable, wished he could crawl inside the pantry and shut the door. Unfortunately, there was no room, not even after he'd cleared out a space by stashing several interesting-looking objects in his pockets.

"Very well, if that's how you feel. I'm not to touch you apparently"—Usha folded her arms across her chest—"but I do think you owe me an explanation. What is going on? Why did you send this kender here claiming to be Tas! What are you up to?"

"We're keeping Mistress Jenna waiting—"

"I'm sure she won't mind. I am your wife, in case you've forgotten!" Usha tossed her silver hair. "I wouldn't be surprised if you had. We never see each other anymore."

"Don't start that again!" he shouted angrily and turned away toward the door.

"Palin!" Usha reached out her hand impulsively. "I love you! I want to help you!"

"You can't help me!" he cried, rounding on her. "No one can." He lifted his hands, held them to the light, the fingers crooked and turned inward like the claws of a bird. "No one can," he repeated.

More silence. Tas recalled the time he'd been a prisoner in the Abyss. He had felt very alone then, desolate and unhappy. Strangely, he was feeling the same now sitting in his friends' kitchen. He lacked the spirit to even give the lock on the silver cabinet a second glance.

"I am sorry, Usha," Palin said stiffly. "You are right. You deserve an explanation. This kender *is* Tasslehoff."

Usha shook her head.

"Do you remember my father telling the story about how he and Tas traveled back in time?" Palin continued.

"Yes," she answered, her voice tight.

"They did so by means of a magical artifact. Tasslehoff used that same device to jump forward in time so he could speak at Caramon's funeral. He was here once, but he overshot the mark. He arrived too late. The funeral was over, so he came back a second time. In this instance, he was on time. Only everything was different. The other future he saw was a future of hope and happiness. The gods had not gone away. I was head of the Order of White Robes. The elven kingdoms were united—"

"And you *believe* all this?" Usha asked, amazed.

"I do," Palin said stubbornly. "I believe it because I have seen the device, Usha. I've held it in my hands. I've felt its power. That's why Mistress Jenna is here. I need her advice. And that's why it's not safe for you to stay in Solace. The dragon knows I have the device. I'm not sure how she found out, but I fear someone in Laurana's household may be a traitor. If so, Beryl may already be aware that I have brought the device to Solace. She'll send her people to try to—"

"You're going to use it!" Usha gasped, pointed her finger at Palin.

He made no response

"I know you, Palin Majere," Usha said. "You're planning to use the device yourself! To try to go back in time and . . . and . . . who knows what else!"

"I've only been thinking about it," he returned, uneasily. "I haven't made up my mind. That's why I needed to speak to Mistress Jenna."

"You planned to speak to her and not to me? Your wife?"

"I was going to tell you," Palin said.

"*Tell* me? Not ask me? Not ask me what I thought about this insanity? Not ask my opinion? No." She answered her own question. "You intend to do this whether I want you to or not. No matter how dangerous. No matter that you could be killed!"

"Usha," he said, after a moment, "it's so very important. The magic . . . if I could . . ." He shook his head, unable to explain. His voice trailed away.

"The magic is dead, Palin," Usha cried, her voice choked with tears. "Good riddance, I say. What did it ever do for you? Nothing except destroy you and ruin our marriage."

He reached out his hand, but this time she was the one who pulled away.

"I'm going to the Inn," she said, not looking at him. "Let me know if . . . if you want me to come home."

Turning away from him, she walked over to Tas. Usha looked him over long and hard. "You really are Tas, aren't you?" she said, awed.

"Yes, Usha," Tas said miserably. "But I wish right now I wasn't."

She leaned down, kissed him on the forehead. He could see the unshed tears shimmer in her golden eyes.

"Good-bye, Tas. It was nice to see you again."

"I'm sorry, Usha," he wailed. "I didn't mean to make a mess of things. I just came back to speak at Caramon's funeral."

"It's not your fault, Tas. Things were a mess long before you came."

Usha left the kitchen, walking past Palin without glancing at him. He stood where she had left him, staring at nothing, his expression dark, his face pale. Tas heard Usha say something to Jenna, something he couldn't quite catch. He heard Jenna respond, but he couldn't catch that either. Usha left the house. The front door shut with a bang. The house was silent, except for Jenna's restive pacing. Still Palin did not move.

Tas reached into several of his pockets and at last located the device. He removed some string that had become tangled around it, dusted off the lint from his pocket and some crumbs from a biscuit he'd meant to eat two days ago.

"Here, Palin," Tas said, holding out the device. "You can have it."

Palin stared at him, uncomprehending.

"Go on," Tas said, pushing the device at him. "If you want to use it, like Usha said you did, I'll let you. Especially if you can go back and make things the way they're supposed to be. That's what you're thinking, isn't it? Here," Tas said insistently and he gave the device a shake, which caused its jewels to wink.

"Take it!" Jenna said.

Tas was startled. He had been so intent on Palin, he hadn't heard Jenna come into the kitchen. She stood in the doorway, the door partially ajar.

"Take it!" she repeated urgently. "Palin, you were worried about overcoming the geas laid on the device, the spell that would always return the device to the person who uses it. Such a geas would protect the owner if the device was ever stolen or lost, but if the device is *freely given*, this act may break the geas!"

"I don't know anything about gewgaws," said Tas, "but I know that I'll let you use the device if you want to."

Palin lowered his head. His gray hair fell forward, covering his face, but not before Tas had seen the pain that contorted and twisted it into a face he did not recognize. Reaching out, Palin took hold of the device, his crooked fingers wrapping around it lovingly.

Tas watched the device go with something akin to relief. Whenever the device was in his possession, he could always hear Fizban's voice reminding him in irritable tones that he wasn't supposed to be off having adventures. He was supposed to go back to his own time. And while this adventure certainly left a lot to be desired as far as adventures go—what with being cursed and having to see Usha cry and discovering that he didn't like Palin anymore—Tas was starting to think that even a bad adventure was probably better than being stepped on by a giant.

"I can tell you how it works," Tas offered.

Palin placed the device on the kitchen table. He sat there staring at it, not saying a word.

"There's a rhyme that goes with it and stuff you have to do to it," Tas added, "but it's pretty easy to learn. Fizban said I had to know it so that I could recite it standing on my head and I could, so I'm sure you probably can, too."

Palin was only half-listening. He looked up at Jenna. "What do you think?"

"It is the Device of Time Journeying," she said. "I saw it at the Tower of High Sorcery when your father brought it to Dalamar for safekeeping. He studied it, of course. I believe he had some of your uncle's notes regarding it. He never used it that I know of, but he has more knowledge about it than anyone now living. I never heard that the device went missing. However, as I recall, we *did* find Tasslehoff in the Tower right before the Chaos War. He might have taken it then."

Jenna eyed the kender quite sternly.

"I did not take it!" Tas said, insulted. "Fizban gave it to me! He told me—"

"Hush, Tas." Palin leaned across the table, lowered his voice. "I don't suppose there is any way you could contact Dalamar."

"I do not practice necromancy," Jenna returned coolly.

Palin's eyes narrowed. "Come now, you don't believe he's dead. Do you?"

Jenna relaxed back in her chair. "Perhaps I don't. But he might as well be. I have not heard a word from him in more than thirty years. I don't know where he may have gone."

Palin looked dubious, as if he did not quite believe her. Jenna spread her bejeweled hands on the table's surface, fingers apart. "Listen to me, Palin. You do not know him. No one knows him as I know him. You did not see him at the end, when he came back from the Chaos War. I did. I was with him. Day and night. I nursed him to health. If you could call it that."

She sat back, her expression dark and frowning.

"I am sorry if I offended you," Palin said. "I never heard. . . . You never told me."

"It is not something I enjoy talking about," Jenna said tersely. "You know that Dalamar was gravely wounded during our battle against Chaos. I brought him back to the Tower. For weeks he hovered between the realm of the living and that of the dead. I left my home and my shop and moved into the Tower to care for him. He survived. But the loss of the gods, the loss of godly magic, was a terrible blow, one from which he never truly recovered. He changed, Palin. Do you remember how he used to be?"

"I didn't know him very well. He supervised my Test in the Tower, the Test during which my Uncle Raistlin took him by surprise, turning what Dalamar had intended as illusion into reality. I'll never forget the look on his face when he saw I had been given my uncle's staff." Palin sighed deeply, regretfully. The memories were sweet, yet painful. "All I remember of Dalamar is that I thought him sharp-tongued and sarcastic, self-centered and arrogant.

I know that my father had a better opinion of him. My father said Dalamar was a very complicated man, whose loyalty was to magic, rather than to the Dark Queen. From what little I knew of Dalamar, I believe that to be true."

"He was excitable," Tas chimed in. "He used to get very excited when I started to touch anything that belonged to him. Jumpy, too."

"Yes, he was all that. But he could also be charming, soft-spoken, wise . . ." Jenna smiled and sighed. "I loved him, Palin. I still do, I suppose. I have never met any other man to equal him." She was quiet a moment, then she shrugged and said, "But that was long ago."

"What happened between you two?" Palin asked.

She shook her head. "After his illness, he withdrew into himself, became sullen and silent, morose and isolated. I have never been a particularly patient person," Jenna admitted. "I couldn't stomach his self-pity and I told him so. We quarreled, I walked out, and that was the last I saw of him."

"I can understand how he felt," Palin said. "I know how lost I felt when I realized the gods were gone. Dalamar had practiced the arcane art far longer than I. He had sacrificed so much for it. He must have been devastated."

"We all were," Jenna said bluntly, "but we dealt with it. You went on with your life, and so did I. Dalamar could not. He fretted and fumed until I feared that his frustration would do what his wounds could not. I honestly thought he would die of it. He could not eat or sleep. He spent hours locked up in his laboratory searching desperately for what had been lost. He had the key to it, he once told me during one of the rare times he actually spoke to me. He said the key had come to him during his sickness. Now he had only to find the door. It's my belief," Jenna added wryly, "that he found it."

"So you do not think he destroyed himself when he destroyed the Tower," Palin said.

"The Tower's gone?" Tas was stunned. "That great big Tower of High Sorcery in Palanthas? What happened to it?"

"I am not even convinced he blew up the Tower," Jenna said, continuing the conversation as if the kender wasn't there. "Oh, I know what people say. That he destroyed the Tower for fear the dragon Khellendros would seize it and use its magic. I saw the pile of rubble that was left. People found all sorts of magical artifacts in the ruins. I bought many of them and resold them later for five times what I paid for them. But I know something I've never told anyone. The truly valuable artifacts that were in the Tower were never found. Not a trace. The scrollbooks, the spellbooks, those belonging to Raistlin and Fistandantilus, Dalamar's own spellbooks—those were gone, too. People thought they were destroyed in the blast. If so," she added with fine irony, "the blast was extremely selective. It took only what was valuable and important, left the trinkets behind."

She eyed Palin speculatively. "Tell me, my friend, would you take this device to Dalamar if you had the chance?"

Palin stirred restlessly. "Probably not, now that I think of it. If he knew I had it, the device would not remain long in my possession."

"Do you truly intend to use it?" she asked.

"I don't know." Palin was evasive. "What do you think? Would it be dangerous?"

"Yes, very," she answered.

"But the kender used it—"

"*If* you believe him, he used it in his own time," she said. "And that was the time of the gods. The artifact is now in *this* time. You know as well as I do that the magic of the artifacts from the Fourth Age is erratic in nature. Some artifacts behave perfectly predictably and others go haywire."

"So I won't really find out until I try," Palin said. "What do you suppose *could* happen?"

"Who knows!" Jenna lifted her hands, the jewels on her fingers glittered. "The journey alone might kill you. You might be stranded back in time, unable to return. You might accidently do something to change the past and, in so doing, obliterate the present. You might blow up this house and everything around it for a twenty-mile radius. I would not risk it. Not for a kender tale."

"Yet I would like to go back to before the Chaos War. Go back simply to look. Perhaps I could see the moment where destiny veered off the path it should have taken. Then we would know how to steer it back on the right course."

Jenna snorted. "You speak of time as if it were a horse and cart. For all you know, this kender has made up this nonsensical story of a future in which the gods never left us. He is a kender, after all."

"But he is an unusual kender. My father believed him, and Caramon knew something about traveling through time."

"Your father also said the kender and the device were to be given to Dalamar," Jenna reminded him.

Palin frowned. "I think we have to find out the truth for ourselves," he argued. "I believe that it is worth the risk. Consider this, Jenna. If there is another future, a better future for our world, a future in which the gods did not depart, no price would be too great to pay for it."

"Even your life?" she asked.

"My life!" Palin was bitter. "Of what value is my life to me now? My wife is right. The old magic is gone, the new magic is dead. I am nothing without the magic!"

"I do not believe that the new magic is dead," Jenna said gravely. "Nor do I believe those who say that we 'used it all up.' Does one use up water? Does one use up air? The magic is a part of this world. We could not consume it."

"Then what has happened to it?" Palin demanded impatiently. "Why do our spells fail? Why do even simple spells require so much energy that one has to go to bed for a week after casting them?"

"Do you remember that old test they used to give us in school?" Jenna asked. "The one where they put an object on the table and tell you to move it without touching it. You do, and then they put the object on a table behind a brick wall and tell you to move it. Suddenly, it's much more difficult. Since you can't see the object, it's difficult to focus your magic on it. I feel the same when I try to cast a spell—as if something is in the way. A brick wall, if you will. Goldmoon told me her healers were experiencing similar feelings—"

"Goldmoon!" Tas cried eagerly. "Where is Goldmoon? If anyone could fix things around here, it's Goldmoon." He was on his feet, as if he would run out the door that instant. "She'll know what to do. Where is she?"

"Goldmoon? Who brought up Goldmoon? What does she have to do with anything?" Palin glowered at the kender. "Please sit down and be quiet! You've interrupted my thoughts!"

"I'd really like to see Goldmoon," Tas said, but he said it quietly, under his breath, so as not to disturb Palin.

The mage lifted the device carefully in his hand, turned it over, examined it, caressed it.

"Your wife was right," Jenna stated. "You're going to use the device, aren't you, Palin?"

"Yes, I am," he replied, closing his hands over it.

"No matter what I say?"

"No matter what anyone says." He glanced at her, appeared embarrased. "Thank you for your help. I'm certain my sister can find you a room at the Inn. I'll send word."

"Did you really think I would leave and miss this?" Jenna asked, amused.

"It's dangerous. You said—"

"These days, walking across the street is dangerous." Jenna shrugged. "Besides, you will need a witness. Or at the very least," she added lightly, "you'll need someone to identify your body."

"Thank you very much," Palin said, but he managed a smile, the first Tas had seen the mage wear. Palin drew in a deep breath, let it out slowly. His hands holding the device trembled.

"When should we try this?" he asked

"No *time* like the present," Jenna said and grinned.

22 THE JOURNEY BACK

And that's the rhyme," said Tasslehoff. "Do you want me to repeat it again?"

"No, I have it memorized," Palin said.

"Are you sure?" Tas was anxious. "You'll need to recite it to return to this time. Unless you want to take me with you?" he added excitedly. "Then I could bring us."

"I am quite sure I have the spell memorized," Palin said firmly. And, indeed, the words were emblazoned in his mind. It seemed to him that he could see their fiery images on the backs of his eyes. "And, no, I'm *not* taking you with me. Someone needs to stay here and keep Mistress Jenna company."

"And to identify the body," Tas said, nodding and settling down in his chair, kicking his feet against the rungs. "Sorry, I forgot about that. I'll stay here. You won't be gone long anyway. Unless you don't come back at all," he mentioned, as an afterthought. Twisting in his chair, he looked at Jenna, who had dragged her chair to a far corner in the kitchen. "Do you really think he'll blow up?"

Palin carefully ignored the kender.

"I will chant the magic that activates the device. If the spell works, I believe that I will vanish from your sight. As the kender says, I should not be gone long. I do not plan to stay in the past. I am going to my father's first funeral where, hopefully, I will be able talk to Dalamar. Perhaps I'll even talk to myself." He smiled grimly. "I'll try to find out what went wrong—"

"Take no action, Palin," Jenna warned. "If you do find out anything useful, return and report. We will need to think long and hard before acting upon it."

"Who is 'we'?" Palin demanded, frowning.

"I suggest a gathering of the wise," Jenna said. "The elven king Gilthas, his mother Laurana, Goldmoon, Lady Crysania—"

"And while we are spreading the word of what we've found far and wide and waiting for all these people to come together, Beryl murders us and steals the device," Palin said acerbically. "She uses it, and we're all dead."

"Palin, you are talking about altering the past," Jenna said in stern rebuke. "We have no idea what the ramifications would be to those of us living in the present."

"I know," he said, after a moment. "I understand. I will return and report. But we must be prepared to act rapidly after that."

"We will. How long do you think you will be gone?"

"According to Tasslehoff, hundreds of days will pass for me for each second of time that passes for you. I estimate that I may be gone an hour or two marked by our time."

"Good fortune on your journey," Jenna said quietly. "Kender, come over here and stand beside me."

Palin took hold of the device, moved to the center of the kitchen. The jewels glinted and sparkled in the sunshine.

He closed his eyes. He stood for long moments in deep thought and concentration. His hands cherished the device. He delighted in the feel of the magic. He began to give himself to the magic, let it cherish him, caress him. The dark years slipped away like receding waves, leaving memory's shoreline smooth and clean. Palin was, for a moment, young and filled with hope and promise. Tears blurred his vision.

"Holding the pendant in my hand, I repeat the first verse, turning the face of the device up toward myself." Palin recited the first words of the spell: " 'Thy time is thy own.' " Acting as he had been instructed, he twisted the face plate of the device.

"Next, at the second verse, I move the face plate from the right to the left." He moved the face of the device in the direction indicated and recited the second verse of the chant: " 'Though across it you travel.' "

"At the recitation of the third verse, the back plate drops to form two spheres connected by rods. " 'Its expanses you see.' "

Palin gave the device another twist and smiled with pleasure when it performed as designed. He no longer held an egg-shaped bauble in his hand but something that resembled a scepter. "At the fourth verse, twist the top clockwise—a chain will drop down."

Palin repeated the fourth verse: " 'Whirling across forever.' "

The chain dropped as Tas had foretold. Palin's heartbeat increased with excitement and exultation. The spell was working.

"The fifth verse warns me to make certain that the chain is clear of the mechanism. As the sixth verse instructs, I hold the device by each sphere and rotate the spheres forward, while reciting the seventh verse. The chain will wind itself into the body. I hold the device over my head, repeating the final verse, and summon a clear vision of where I want to be and the time I want to be there."

Palin drew in a deep breath. Manipulating the device as instructed, he recited the rest of the chant: " 'Obstruct not its flow. Grasp firmly the end and the beginning. Turn them forward upon themselves. All that is loose shall be secure. Destiny will be over your own head.' "

He held the device over his head and brought to mind a vision of the Chaos War, his own part in it. His part and Tasslehoff's.

Closing his eyes, Palin focused on the vision and gave himself to the magic. He surrendered himself to his longtime mistress. She proved faithful to him.

The floor of the kitchen elongated, scrolled up into the air. The ceiling slid underneath the floor, the dishes on the shelves melted and trickled down the walls, the walls merged with the floor and the ceiling, and all began to roll into themselves, forming an enormous spiral. The spiral sucked in the house and then the woods beyond. Trees and grass wrapped around Palin, then the blue sky, and the ball in which he was the center started to revolve, faster and faster.

His feet left the floor. He was suspended in the center of a whirling, spinning kaleidoscope of places and people and events. He saw Jenna and Tas whirl past, saw the blur of their faces, and then they disappeared. He was moving very slowly but the people around him were moving fast, or perhaps he was the one speeding past them while they walked by him as slowly if they were walking under water.

He saw forests and mountains. He saw villages and cities. He saw the ocean and ships on the ocean, and all of them were drawn up to form part of the great ball in the middle of which he drifted.

The spiral wound down. The spinning slowed, slowed . . . he could see people, objects more clearly . . .

He saw Chaos, the Father of All and of Nothing, a fearsome giant with beard and hair of flame, standing taller than the tallest mountain, the top of his head brushing eternity, his feet extending to the deepest part of the Abyss. Chaos had just smashed his foot down on the ground, presumably killing Tasslehoff but inflicting his death blow upon himself, for Usha would catch a drop of his blood in the Chaos jewel and banish him.

The spinning continued, carrying Palin on past that moment into . . .

Blackness. Utter darkness. A darkness so vast and deep that Palin feared he'd been struck blind. And then he saw light behind him, blazing firelight.

He glanced back into fire, looked ahead into darkness. Looked into nothing.

Panic-stricken, he closed his eyes. "Go back beyond the Chaos War!" he said, half-suffocated with fear. "Go back to my childhood! Go back to my father's childhood! Go back to Istar! Go back to the Kingpriest! Go back to Huma! Go back . . . go back . . ."

He opened his eyes.

Darkness, emptiness, nothing.

He took another step and realized that he had taken a step too far. He had stepped off the precipice.

He screamed, but no sound came from his throat. Time's rushing wind carried it away from. He experienced the sickening sensation of falling that one feels in a dream. His stomach dropped. Cold sweat bathed him. He tried desperately to wake himself, but then came the horrible knowledge that he would never wake.

Fear seized him, paralyzed him. He was falling, and he would continue to fall and fall and keep falling into time's well of darkness.

Time's empty well.

Having been the one using the device to travel back through time, Tasslehoff had never actually seen what happened to himself when he used it. He had always rather regretted this and had once tried to go back to watch himself going back, but that hadn't worked. He was extremely gratified, therefore, to watch Palin using the device and quite charmed to see the mage disappear before his very eyes.

All that was interesting and exciting, but it lasted only a few moments. Then Palin was gone, and Tasslehoff and Jenna were alone in the Majere's kitchen.

"We didn't explode," Tas observed.

"No, we didn't," Jenna agreed. "Disappointed?"

"A little. I've never seen anything explode before, not counting the time Fizban tried to boil water to cook an egg. Speaking of eggs, would you like something to eat while we wait? I could heat up some oatmeal." Tas felt it incumbent upon himself to act as host in Usha's and Palin's absence.

"Thank you," Jenna replied, glancing at the remains of the congealed oatmeal in the pot and making a slight grimace, "but I think not. If you could find some brandy, now, I believe I could use a drink—"

Palin materialized in the room. He was ashen, disheveled, and he clutched the device in a hand that shook so he could barely hold it.

"Palin!" Jenna cried, rising from her chair in amazement and consternation. "Are you hurt?"

He stared at her wildly, without recognition. Then he shuddered, gave a gasping sigh of relief. Staggering, he very nearly fell. His hand went limp. The device tumbled to the floor and bounced away in a flash of jewels. Tas chased after it, caught it before it rolled into the fireplace.

"Palin, what went wrong?" Jenna ran to him. "What happened? Tas, help me!"

Palin started to crumple. Between the two of them, Tas and Jenna eased the mage to the floor.

"Go fetch blankets," Jenna ordered.

Tasslehoff dashed out of the kitchen, pausing only a moment to deposit the device in a pocket. He returned moments later, tottering under a load of several blankets, three pillows, and a feather mattress that he had dragged off the master bed.

Palin lay on the floor, his eyes closed. He was too weak to move or speak. Jenna put her hand on his wrist, felt his pulse racing. His breathing was rapid, rasping, his body chilled. He was shivering so that his teeth clicked together. She wrapped two of the blankets snugly around him.

"Palin!" she called urgently.

He opened his eyes, stared at her. "Darkness. All darkness."

"Palin, what do you mean? What did you see in the past?"

He grasped her hand, hard, hurting her. He held fast to her as if he were being swept away by a raging river and she was his only salvation.

"There is no past!" he whispered through pallid lips. He sank back, exhausted.

"Darkness," he murmured. "Only darkness."

Jenna sat back on her heels, frowning.

"That doesn't make any sense. Brandy," she said to Tas.

She held the flask to Palin's lips. He drank a little, and some color came to his pale cheeks. The shivering eased. Jenna took a swallow of the brandy herself, then handed the flask to the kender. Tas helped himself, just to be sociable.

"Put it back on the table," Jenna ordered.

Tas removed the flask from his pocket and, after several more sociable gulps, he placed it on the table.

The kender looked down at Palin in remorseful concern. "What's wrong? Was this my fault? I didn't mean it, if it was."

Palin's eyes flared open again. "Your fault!" he cried hoarsely. Flinging off the blankets, he sat up. "Yes, it's your fault!"

"Palin, keep calm," Jenna said, alarmed. "You'll make yourself ill again. Tell me what you saw."

"I'll tell you what I saw, Jenna." Palin said, his voice hollow. "I saw nothing. Nothing!"

"I don't understand," Jenna said.

"I don't either." Palin sighed, concentrated, tried to order his thoughts. "I traveled back in time and as I did so, time unrolled before me, like a vast parchment. I saw all that has passed in the Fifth Age. I saw the coming of the great dragons. I saw the dragon purge. I saw the building of this Citadel. I saw the raising of the shield over Silvanesti. I saw the dedication of the Tomb of the Last Heroes. I saw the defeat of Chaos, and that is where it all ends. Or begins."

"Ends? Begins?" Jenna repeated, baffled. "But that can't be, Palin. What of the Fourth Age? What of the War of the Lance? What of the Cataclysm?"

"Gone. All of it. I stood amidst the ether and saw the battle with Chaos, but when I tried to see beyond, when I looked into the past, I saw only darkness. I took a step and . . ." He shuddered. "I fell into the darkness. A void where no light shines, no light has ever shone. Darkness that is eternal, everlasting. I had the feeling that I was falling through centuries of time and that I would continue to fall until death took me, and then my corpse would keep falling. . . ."

"If that is true, what does it mean?" Jenna pondered.

"I'll tell you what it means," Palin said raggedly. He pointed at Tasslehoff. "This is Tas's fault. Everything that has happened is his fault."

"Why? What does he have to do with it?"

"Because *he's not dead!*" Palin said, hissing the words through clenched teeth. "He changed time by *not* dying! The future he saw was the future that happened because he died and by his death, we were able to defeat Chaos.

But he's not dead! We didn't defeat Chaos. The Father of All and Nothing banished his children, the gods, and these past forty years of death and turmoil have been the result!"

Jenna looked at Tas. Palin was looking at Tas, this time as if he'd grown five heads, wings and a tail.

"Let's all have another drink of brandy," Tas suggested, taking his own advice. "Just to make us feel better. *Clear our heads,*" he added pointedly.

"You could be right, Palin," Jenna said thoughtfully.

"I know I'm right!" he said grimly.

"And we all know that two rights make a wrong," Tas observed helpfully. "Would anyone like oatmeal?"

"What other explanation could there be?" Palin continued, ignoring the kender.

"I'm not sure," said Tas, backing up a few steps toward the kitchen door, "but if you give me a moment, I'll bet I could think of several."

Palin threw off the blanket and rose to his feet. "We have to send Tas back to die."

"Palin, I'm not so sure . . ." Jenna began, but he wasn't listening to her.

"Where's the device?" he demanded feverishly. "What happened to it?"

"While it is true," Tas said, "that I had promised Fizban I would go back in time for the giant to step on me, the more I think about that part of it, the less I like it. For while being stepped on by a giant might be extremely interesting, it would be interesting for only a few seconds at most, and then as you said I would be dead."

Tas bumped up against the kitchen door.

"And while I've never been dead," he continued, "I've seen people being dead before, and I must say that it looks like about the most uninteresting thing that could happen to a person."

"Where is the device?" Palin demanded.

"It rolled into the ashes!" Tas cried and pointed at the fireplace. He took another gulp of brandy.

"I'll look," Jenna offered. Seizing the poker, she began to sift through the ashes.

Palin peered over her shoulder. "We *must* find it!"

Tasslehoff put his hand in his pocket and, taking hold of the Device of Time Journeying, he began to turn it and twist it and slide it, all the while speaking the rhyme under his breath.

" 'Thy time is thy own, though across it you travel . . .' "

"Are you sure it went under here, Tas?" Jenna asked. "Because I can't see anything except cinders—"

Tas spoke faster, his nimble fingers working swiftly.

" 'Whirling across forever. Obstruct not its flow,' " he whispered.

This was going to be the tricky part.

Palin's head jerked up. Turning around, he made a diving leap for the kender.

Tas whipped the device out of his pocket and held it up. "Destiny be over your own head!" he cried, and he was pleased to realize, as time rolled up the kitchen, the brandy flask, and him along with it, that he had just made a very pithy remark.

"The little weasel," said Jenna, looking at the empty place on the floor where the kender had once been standing. "So he had the device all along."

"My gods!" Palin gasped. "What have I done?"

"Scared the oatmeal out of him, unless I'm much mistaken," Jenna returned. "Which is quite an accomplishment, considering he's a kender. I don't blame him," she added, scrubbing her soot-covered hands vigorously on a towel. "If you had shouted at me like that, I would have run, too."

"I'm not a monster," Palin said, exasperated. "I am scared! I don't mind admitting it." He pressed his hand over his heart. "The fear is here, worse than anything I've ever known, even during the dark days of my captivity. Something strange and terrible has happened to the world, Jenna, and I don't understand what!" His fists clenched. "The kender is the cause. I'm sure of it!"

"If so, we better find him," said Jenna practically. "Where do you think he would have gone? Not back in time?"

"If he has, we'll never locate him. But I don't think he would," Palin said, pondering. "He wouldn't go back because if he did, he'd wind up exactly where he doesn't want to be—dead. I believe he's still in the present. Then where would he go?"

"To someone who would protect him from you," said Jenna bluntly.

"Goldmoon," said Palin. "He talked about wanting to see her only moments before he left. Or Laurana. He's already been to see Laurana. Knowing Tas, though, he'd want some new adventure. I will travel to the Citadel of Light. I would like to discuss what I have seen with Goldmoon anyhow."

"I'll loan you one of my magical rings to speed you across the miles," Jenna said, tugging the ring off her finger. "Meanwhile, I will send a message to Laurana, warning her to watch for the kender and if he shows up on her doorstep, to hang onto him."

Palin accepted the ring. "Warn her to be cautious of what she says and does," he added, his expression troubled. "I believe that there may be a traitor in her household. Either that or the Neraka Knights have found some way to spy on her. Will you . . ." He paused, swallowed. "Will you stop by the Inn and tell Usha . . . tell her . . ."

"I'll tell her you're not a monster," said Jenna, patting his arm with a smile. She looked at him intently, frowning in anxiety. "Are you certain you are well enough for this?"

"I was not injured. Only shocked. I can't say that's wearing off, but I'll be well enough to make the journey." He looked curiously at the ring. "How does this work?"

"Not all that well anymore," Jenna wryly. "It will take you two or three jumps to reach your destination. Place the ring on the middle finger of your left hand. That's close enough," she added, seeing Palin struggle to ease it over a swollen joint. "Put your right hand over the ring and conjure up the image of where you want to be. Keep that image in your mind, repeat it to yourself over and over again. I want that ring back, by the way."

"Certainly." He smiled at her wanly. "Farewell, Jenna. Thank you for your help. I'll keep you informed."

He placed his hand over the ring and began to picture in his mind the crytal rainbow domes of the Citadel of Light.

"Palin," Jenna said suddenly, "I haven't been entirely honest with you. I may have an idea where to find Dalamar."

"Good," Palin replied. "My father was right. We need him."

23 THE HEDGE MAZE

The gnome was lost in the hedge maze.

This was nothing unusual. The gnome was frequently lost in the hedge maze. In fact, whenever anyone in the Citadel of Light wanted the gnome (which wasn't often) and asked where he was, the response was invariably, "Lost in the hedge maze."

The gnome did not wander the hedge maze aimlessly. Far from it. He entered the hedge maze daily with a set purpose, a mission, and that was to make a map of the maze. The gnome, who belonged to the Guild of PuzzlesRiddles EnigmasRebusLogogriphsMonogramsAnagramsAcrosticsCrosswordsMazes LabyrinthsParadoxesScrabbleFeminineLogicandPoliticians, otherwise known as P3 for short, knew of a certainty that if he could map the hedge maze, he would find in that map the key to the Great Mysteries of Life, among these being: Why Is It That When You Wash Two Socks You Only End Up With One? Is There Life After Death? and Where Did The Other Sock Go? The gnome was convinced that if you found the answer to the second question you would also find the answer to the third.

In vain the mystics of the Citadel attempted to explain to him that the hedge maze was magical. Those who entered it with minds troubled or sad found their cares eased, their burdens lifted. Those who entered it seeking solitude and peace were not disturbed, no matter how many other people walked the fragrant hedgerows at the same moment. Those who entered seeking a solution to a problem found that their thoughts grew centered, their minds cleared of clutter. Those who entered on their mystical journey to climb the Silver Stair that stood in the center of the maze found that they did not journey through a maze of shrubbery, but through the maze of their hearts.

Those who entered the hedge maze with the firm resolve to map out the hedge maze, to try to define it in terms of X number of rows and left and right turnings and longitudes and latitudes and degrees of angles and radiuses and circumferences discovered that here mathematics need not apply. The hedge maze shifted beneath the compass, skittered out from underneath the ruler, defied all calculation.

The gnome, whose name (the short version) was Conundrum, refused to listen. He entered the hedge maze every day, convinced that this would be the day he solved the mystery. This would be the day he would achieve his Life Quest and produce the definitive map of the hedge maze, a map he would then copy and sell to tour groups.

With one quill pen stuck behind his ear and another through the bosom of his robe, rather as if he'd been stabbed, the gnome would enter the hedge maze in the morning and work feverishly all during the hours of sunlight. He would measure and count his steps, note down the elevation of the hedge at Point A, indicate where Point A converged with Point B, and cover himself in ink and perspiration. He would emerge at the end of the day glowing with pride, with bits of the hedge stuck in his hair and beard, and produce for the edification of any poor unfortunate he could coerce into viewing his project an ink-spattered and sweat-stained map of the hedge maze.

He would then spend the night copying the map so that it was perfect, absolutely perfect, not a twig missing. Next morning he would take the map into the hedge maze and become immediately and hopelessly lost. He would manage to find his way out about noontime, which just gave him daylight enough to redraw his map—and so forth and so on daily for about a year now.

On this day Conundrum had worked his way through the hedge maze to about the halfway point. He was down on his knees, tape in hand, measuring the angle between a zig and a zag when he noted a foot blocking his way. The foot was encased in a boot that was attached to a leg that was attached—on looking up—to a kender.

"Excuse me," said the kender politely, "but I'm lost and I was wondering—"

"Lost! Lost!" Conundrum scrambled to his feet, overturning his ink jar, which left a large purple stain on the grassy path. Sobbing, the gnome flung his arms around the kender. "How gratifying! I'm so glad! So glad! You can't know!"

"There, there," said the kender, patting the gnome on the back. "I'm certain that whatever it is, it will be all right. Have you a hankie? Here, borrow mine. Actually, it's Palin's, but I don't suppose he'd care."

"Thank you," said the gnome, blowing his nose.

Generally gnomes talk extremely fast and mash all their words together, one on top of the other, in the belief that if you don't reach the end of a sentence quickly you might never reach it all. Conundrum had lived among humans long enough to have learned to slow his speech pattern. He now talked very slowly and haltingly, which led other gnomes he encountered to consider him quite stupid.

"I'm sorry I fell apart like that." The gnome sniffed. "It's just, I've been working so long, and no one has been kind enough to get lost before . . ." He started to weep again.

"Glad I could oblige," said the kender hurriedly. "Now that I am lost, I was wondering if you could show me the way out. You see, I have just arrived through magical means"—the kender was quite proud of this and repeated it to make certain the gnome was impressed—"magical means that are quite secret and mysterious, otherwise I'd tell you about them. Anyhow my business is extremely urgent. I'm looking for Goldmoon. I have a feeling she must be here because I thought about her very hard just as the magic happened. My name is Tasslehoff Burrfoot, by the way."

"Conundrum Solitaire," replied the gnome, and the two shook hands, after which Tasslehoff completed the ruin of Palin's handkerchief by using it to wipe the residual ink left on his fingers.

"I can show you the way out!" the gnome added eagerly. "I have drawn this map, you see."

Proudly, with a flourish of his hand, Conundrum presented the map to Tasslehoff's view. Drawn on an immense piece of parchment, the map lay on the ground, covering the path between the two hedge rows, overlapping on the edges. The map was bigger than the gnome, who was a smallish, misty-eyed, dimly smiling gnome with a nut-brown complexion and a long wispy beard that had probably once been white but was now stained purple due to the fact that the gnome invariably dragged his beard through the wet ink as he bent on hands and knees over the map.

The map was quite complicated, with Xs and Arrows and Do Not Enters and Turn Left Heres scrawled all over it in Common. Tasslehoff looked down at the map. Looking up, he saw the end of the row in which they were standing. The hedge opened up and he could see the sun shining on several very beautiful crystalline domed structures that caught the sunlight and turned it into rainbows. Two golden dragons formed an immense archway. The grounds were green and filled with flowers. People dressed in white robes strolled around, talking in low voices.

"Oh, that must be the way out!" said Tasslehoff. "Thanks all the same."

The gnome looked at his map and looked at what was undeniably the exit from the hedge maze.

"Drat," he said and began to stomp on the map.

"I'm extremely sorry," said Tas, feeling guilty. "It was a really nice map."

"Hah!" Conundrum jumped up and down on the map.

"Well, excuse me, but I've got to go," Tasslehoff said, inching toward the exit. "But once I have talked to Goldmoon, I'll be glad to come back and get lost again, if that will help."

"Bah!" cried the gnome, kicking the ink jar into the hedge.

The last Tasslehoff saw of Conundrum, he was back at the beginning of the hedge maze, measuring his foot with the tape in preparation to pace off the precise distance between the first turning and the second.

Tas walked a good distance, leaving the hedge maze far behind. He was about to wander into a lovely building made of sparkling crystal when he heard footsteps behind him and felt a hand on his shoulder.

"Have you business in the Citadel of Light, kender?" asked a voice, speaking Common.

"The where?" said Tasslehoff. "Oh, yes. Of course."

Quite accustomed to having the heavy hand of the law fall on his shoulder, he was not surprised to find himself in the custody of a tall young woman of stern expression wearing a helm of silver chain mail and a chain-mail shirt that glittered in the sun. She wore a long tabard marked with the symbol of the sun and carried a sword in a silver scabbard, girded around her waist.

"I'm here to see Goldmoon, ma'am," Tasslehoff said politely. "My business is urgent. Quite urgent. If you could just show me where—"

"What do you have here, Guardian?" asked another voice. "Trouble?"

Tasslehoff twisted his head to see another woman clad in armor, except that she was wearing the armor of a Solamnic Knight. Two more Solamnic Knights walked on either side of her as she proceeded up the walkway.

"I am not certain, Lady Camilla," replied the guard, saluting. "This kender has asked to see Goldmoon."

The two exchanged glances and it seemed to Tas that a shadow crossed the face of the lady Knight. "What does a kender want of the First Master?"

"The who?" Tas wondered.

"Goldmoon, the First Master."

"I'm an old friend of hers," Tas said. He held out his hand. "My name is . . ." He paused. He was growing extremely tired of people staring at him oddly whenever he said his name. He withdrew his hand. "It's not important. If you'll just tell me where to find Goldmoon . . ."

Neither of the women answered, but Tas, watching closely, saw the Solamnic Knight glance in the direction of the largest crystal dome. He guessed at once that this was where he needed to be.

"You both look very busy," he said, edging away. "I'm sorry to have bothered you. If you'll excuse me . . ." He made a dash for it.

"Should I go after him, sir?" he heard the guard ask the Knight.

"No, leave him be," Lady Camilla replied. "The First Master has a soft spot in her heart for kender."

"But he might disturb her solitude," the guard said.

"I would give him thirty steel pieces, if he could," Lady Camilla replied.

The lady Knight was fifty years old, a handsome woman, hale and hearty, though her black hair was streaked with silver. Stern of countenance, grim and stoic, she did not appear to be the sort of person given to displays of emotion. Yet, Tas heard her say this with a sigh.

Tas reached to the door of the crystal dome and halted, fully expecting someone to come out and tell him he shouldn't be there. Two white-robed men did emerge, but they only smiled at him and wished him a good afternoon.

"And a good afternoon to you, sirs," Tas said, bowing. "By the way, I'm lost. What building is this?"

"The Grand Lyceum," said one.

"Oh," said Tas, looking wise, although he hadn't a clue what a lyceum was. "I'm so glad I've found it. Thank you."

Bidding the gentlemen good-bye, the kender entered the Grand Lyceum. After a thorough exploration of the area, an exploration involving opening doors and interrupting classes, asking innumerable questions, and eavesdropping on private conversations, the kender discovered that he was inside the Grand Hall, a popular meeting place for the people who lived and worked and studied in the Citadel of Light.

This being afternoon, the Grand Hall was quiet, with only a few people reading or talking together in small groups. At night, the Grand Hall would be crowded, for it served as the dining hall for the Citadel, and here everyone— teachers and students alike—gathered for their evening meal.

The rooms inside the crystal dome glowed with sunshine. Chairs were numerous and comfortable. Long wooden tables stood at one end of the enormous room. The smell of baking bread wafted from the kitchen that was located on a level below. The reception rooms were at the far end, some of them occupied by students and their masters.

Tasslehoff had no difficulty gathering information about Goldmoon. Every conversation he overheard and half those he interrupted were centered on the First Master. Everyone, it seemed, was very worried about her.

"I cannot believe that the Masters have allowed this to go on this long," one woman said to a visitor. "Permitting the First Master to remain sealed up in her room like this! She might be in danger. She might be ill."

"Has no one made any attempt to try to talk to her?"

"Of course, we have tried to talk to her!" The woman shook her head. "We are all of us worried about her. Ever since the night of the storm, she has refused to see or speak to anyone, even those closest to her. Food and water are left for her on a tray during the night. The tray is always found empty in the morning. She leaves us notes on the tray assuring us that she is well, but she begs that we will respect her privacy and not disturb her."

"I won't disturb her," Tasslehoff said to himself. "I'll tell her very quickly what's happened, and then I'll leave."

"What are we to do?" the woman continued. "The handwriting on the notes is her own. We are all agreed on that."

"That proves nothing. She may be a prisoner. She may be writing those notes under duress, especially if she fears she will bring down harm upon others in the Citadel."

"But with what motive? If she were taken hostage, we would expect a ransom request or that some demand be made in return for her well-being. Nothing has been asked of us. We have not been attacked. The island remains as peaceful as anywhere in this dark time. Ships come and go. Refugees arrive daily. Our lives continue apace."

"What of the silver dragon?" the second woman asked. "Mirror is one of the guardians of Schallsea Isle and of the Citadel of Light. I would think that the dragon, with his magic, would be able to discover if some evil had taken possession of the First Master."

"He undoubtedly could, but Mirror has vanished as well," her friend returned helplessly. "He took flight during the worst of the storm. No one has seen him since."

"I knew a silver dragon once," Tas said, barging in on the conversation. "Her name was Silvara. I couldn't help overhearing you talk about Goldmoon. She's a very good friend of mine. I'm deeply worried about her. Where did you say her rooms were?"

"At the very top of the Lyceum. Up those stairs," said one.

"Thank you," said Tas and turned that direction.

"But no one's allowed up there," the woman added sternly.

Tas turned back again. "Oh, sure. I understand. Thanks."

The two women walked off, continuing their conversation. Tasslehoff loitered in the area, admiring a large statue of a silver dragon that occupied an honored place in the center of the hall. When the women were gone, Tas glanced about. Seeing that one was watching him, he began to climb the stairs.

Goldmoon's chambers were located at the very top of the Grand Lyceum. A spiral staircase of many hundred steps led upward through the various levels. The climb was long, the stairs built for the tall legs of humans, not the short legs of kender. Tas had begun bounding up the stairs enthusiastically, but after stair number seventy-five, he was forced to sit down and take a brief rest.

"Whew!" he said, panting. "I wish I were a silver dragon. At least then I'd have wings."

The sun was starting to dip down into the sea, by the time Tasslehoff—after a few more rests—reached the top.

The staircase ended, so Tas presumed he'd arrived at the level where Goldmoon lived. The hallway was peaceful and quiet, or so it seemed at first. A door decorated with sheaves of wheat and vines and fruit and flowers stood at the end of the corridor. As Tas moved closer to the door, he detected the faint sound of someone weeping.

The tender-hearted kender forgot his own trouble. He knocked gently on the door. "Goldmoon," he called out. "It's me, Tasslehoff. Is anything wrong? Maybe I can help."

The sound of weeping ceased immediately, replaced by silence.

"Goldmoon," Tas began. "I really need to talk to—"

A hand grasped hold of his shoulder. Startled, Tas jumped and banged his head against the door. He looked wildly around.

Palin gazed down at him sternly.

"I thought I might find you here," he stated.

"I'm not going back," Tas said, rubbing his head. "Not yet. Not until I talk to Goldmoon." He looked up at Palin with suspicion. "Why are you here?"

"We were worried about you," Palin replied.

"I'll bet," Tas muttered. Sidling away from Palin, he turned back to the door. "Goldmoon!" He knocked again on the door. "Let me in! It's me, Tasslehoff!"

"First Master," Palin added, "I am here with Tas. Something very strange has happened. We would like your wise counsel."

A moment's silence, then a voice, muffled from crying, came back, "You must excuse me, Palin, but I am seeing no one at present."

"Goldmoon," Palin said, after a moment. "I have very sad news. My father is dead."

Another moment's silence, then the voice, strained and hushed. "Caramon dead?"

"He died several weeks ago. His end was peaceful."

"I came in time to speak at his funeral, Goldmoon," Tasslehoff added. "It's too bad you missed my speech. But I could give it again if you—"

A terrible cry burst from behind the door. "Oh, fortunate man! Oh, lucky, lucky man!"

Palin looked grim. "Goldmoon!" he called out. "Please let me in!"

Tasslehoff, very subdued and solemn, put his nose to the doorknob.

"Goldmoon," he said, speaking through the key hole, "I'm very sorry to hear that you've been sick. And I was sorry to hear that Riverwind was dead. But I heard he died being a hero and saving my people from the dragon when there were probably quite a few who said that we kender weren't worth saving. I want you to know that I'm grateful and that I was proud to call Riverwind my friend."

"This is a shabby trick you play upon me, Palin," said the voice angrily from inside. "You have inherited your uncle's gift of mimickry. Everyone knows that Tasslehoff Burrfoot is dead."

"No, I'm not," Tas returned. "And that's the problem. At least it is for *some* people." He gave Palin a stern look. "It's really me, Goldmoon," Tas continued. "If you put your eye to the keyhole you can see me."

He waved his hand.

A lock clicked. Slowly, the door opened. Goldmoon stood framed within. Her room was lit by many candles, their glow cast a halo of light around her. The corridor into which she stepped was dark, except for the light of a single red star. She was cloaked in shadows. Tas could not see her.

"First Master . . ." Palin stepped forward, his hand outstretched.

Goldmoon turned, allowed the light from her room to touch her face. "Now, you see . . ." she said softly.

The light of the candles gleamed on hair that was thick and golden and luxuriant, on a face that was soft and smooth, on eyes that, though red with weeping, were blue as the morning sky and shone with the luster of youth. Her body was strong as the days when the Chieftain's Daughter had first fallen in love with a young warrior named Riverwind. The years Goldmoon had lived in the world numbered ninety, but her body, her hair, her eyes, her voice, her lips and hands were those of the young woman who had carried the blue crystal staff into the Inn of the Last Home.

Beautiful, she stood sorrowfully before them, her head drooping like the bud of a cut rose.

"What miracle is this?" Palin cried, awed.

"No miracle," said Goldmoon bitterly. "A curse."

"Are you cursed?" said Tas with interest. "So am I!"

Goldmoon turned to the kender, looked him up and down. "It *is* you!" she murmured. "I recognized your voice. Why are you here? Where have you been? Why have you come?"

Tasslehoff extended his hand, shook hers politely. "I'd love to tell you all about everything, Goldmoon. All about Caramon's first funeral and then his second funeral and how I'm cursed. But right now Palin is trying to murder me. I came to see if you would tell him to stop. So if you'll just speak to him, I'll be going."

Tas made a break for it. He had very nearly reached the stairs and was just about to dash down them when Palin's hand snaked out and snagged him by the collar of his shirt.

Tas wriggled and writhed, trying various kender tricks developed through years of practice at escaping the long arm of irritated sheriffs and irate shop-keepers. He used the old Twist and Bite and the always effective Stomp and Kick, but Palin was proof against them. At last, truly desperate, Tas tried the Lizard. He endeavored to slide his arms out of his shirt sleeves, regretful at having to leave his shirt behind, but, like the lizard who leaves part of his tail in the hand of the would-be captor, he would be free. Unfortunately, the new shirt proved a bit snug, and this didn't work. Palin was thin, but he was strong and, in addition, he had a strong incentive to hold onto the kender.

"What is he talking about?" Goldmoon asked, staring at Tas in bewilder-ment. She shifted her gaze to Palin. "*Are* you trying to murder him?"

"Of course not," Palin said impatiently.

"Are too!" Tas muttered, squirming.

"Listen to me, Tas. I'm truly sorry about what happened back there," Palin said.

He seemed about to continue, then sighed and lowered his head. He looked old, older than Tas remembered, and he'd seen him only a few moments ago. The lines in his face had deepened, darkened, pulled taut; the skin stretched tight across the bones. He blinked his eyes too frequently and often rubbed them, as if trying to see through a film or mist covering them. Tas—who was set to run—was touched by Palin's obvious trouble. The kender decided he could at least stay to listen.

"I'm sorry, Tas," Palin said finally, and his voice was tight as the lines on his face. "I was upset. I was frightened. Jenna was quite angry with me. After you left, she said she didn't blame you for running. She was right. I should have explained things to you calmly and rationally. I shouldn't have yelled at you. After what I saw, I panicked."

He looked down at Tas and sighed deeply. "Tas, I wish there was some other way. You have to understand. I'll try to explain this as best I can. You were meant to die. And because you haven't died, it is possible that this is the reason all these terrible things that have happened to the world have happened. To put it another way, if you were dead, the world might be the world you saw the first time you came back to my father's funeral. Do you understand?"

"No," said Tas.

Palin regarded the kender with obvious disappoinment. "I'm afraid I can't explain it any better than that. Perhaps you and Goldmoon and I should discuss it. You don't need to run away again. I won't force you to go back."

"I don't want to hurt your feelings, Palin," Tas returned, "but you can't force me to do anything. I have the device, and you don't."

Palin regarded the kender with deepening gravity, then suddenly and unexpectedly he smiled. The smile was not quite a whole smile, more a quarter-smile, for it lifted the corners of his thin lips and didn't come anywhere near his unhappy eyes, but it was a start.

"That is true, Tas," he said. "You do have the device. You know yourself what is right. You know that you made a promise to Fizban and that he trusted you to keep that promise."

Palin paused, then said quietly. "Were you aware, Tas, that Caramon spoke at *your* funeral?"

"He did?" Tas was astonished. "I didn't even know I had a funeral! I just figured there probably wouldn't be much of me left, except a bit of goo between the giant's toes. What did Caramon say? Was there a big turnout? Did Jenna bring cheese puffs?"

"There was an immense turnout," Palin said. "People came from all over Ansalon to pay their respects to a heroic kender. As for my father, he called you 'a kender among kender.' He said that you exemplifed all that was best in the kender race: you were noble, self-sacrificing, brave, and, above all, honorable."

"Maybe Caramon was wrong about me," Tas said uneasily, glancing at Palin out of the corner of his eyes.

"Maybe he was," Palin said.

Tas didn't like the way Palin was looking at him, as if he were shriveling into something icky, like a squished cockroach. He didn't know what to do or say—an unusual feeling for him. He couldn't recall ever having had this feeling before, and he hoped he never would again. The silence grew stretched, until Tas was afraid that if one of them let loose, the silence would snap back and smack someone in the face. He was therefore quite thankful when a commotion sounded on the stairs, distracting Palin and easing the tense silence.

"First Master!" Lady Camilla called. "We thought we heard your voice. Someone said they saw a kender come up here—"

Reaching the head of the stairs, she caught sight of Goldmoon.

"First Master!" The Knight stopped dead in her tracks and stared. The Citadel guards bunched up behind her, staring and gaping.

This was Tas's opportunity to head for freedom again. No one would try to stop him. No one was paying the least attention to him. He could slip past them all and run away. Almost certainly the gnome Conundrum had some sort of sailing vessel. Gnomes always had sailing vessels. Sometimes they had flying vessels, as well, and sometimes they had vessels that both flew and sailed, although this generally resulted in an explosion.

Yes, thought Tas, eyeing the stairs and the people standing there with their mouths open. That's what I'll do. I'll go. Right now. I'm running. Any moment now. My feet will start to run.

But his feet had other ideas, apparently, because they stayed pretty much firmly attached to the floor.

Perhaps his feet were thinking the same thing as his head. His head was thinking about what Caramon had said. Those words were almost the very same words he'd heard people say about Sturm Brightblade, about Tanis Half-Elven. And they'd said those words about him! Tasslehoff Burrfoot! He felt a warm glow in the vicinity of his heart, and, at the same time, he felt another kind of glow around his stomach. A much more uncomfortable glow, a sort of gurgling glow, as if he'd eaten something that disagreed with him. He wondered if it could be the oatmeal.

"Excuse me, Goldmoon," Tas said, interrupting the gaping and staring and general stupidity that was taking place around him. "Do you think I could go inside your room and lie down? I'm not feeling very well."

Goldmoon drew herself up. Her face was pale, cold. Her voice was bitter. "I knew it would be like this. I knew you would look upon me as some sort of sideshow at a fair."

"Forgive me, First Master," Lady Camilla said, her own face crimson with shame. She lowered her gaze. "I beg your pardon. It's just . . . this miracle . . ."

"It is *not* a miracle!" Goldmoon said in sharp tones. She lifted her head and something of her regal presence, her noble spirit, flashed from her. "I am sorry for all the trouble I have caused, Lady Camilla. I know that I have brought pain to many. Please carry word to all in the Citadel that they need worry for me no longer. I am well. I will come among them presently, but first I want to speak to my friends in private."

"Of course, I will be happy to do whatever you ask, First Master," Lady Camilla said, and though she tried her best not to stare, she could not help but gaze with astonishment at the amazing change that had come over Goldmoon.

Palin coughed meaningfully.

Lady Camilla blinked. "I am sorry, First Master. It's just—"

She shook her head, helpless to put her confused thoughts into words. Turning away, yet with one more backward glance, as if to reassure herself that what she saw was real, she hastened down the spiral stairs. The Citadel guards, after a moment's hesitation, turned to run down after the Knight. Tas could hear their voices loudly exclaiming over the "miracle."

"They will all be like that," Goldmoon said in anguish, returning thoughtfully to her chambers. "They will all stare at me and exclaim and wonder." She shut the door swiftly behind them, leaned against it.

"You can hardly blame them, First Master," said Palin.

"Yes. I know. That's one reason I kept myself locked inside this room. I had hoped that when the change first happened it would be . . . temporary." Goldmoon gestured. "Please sit down. We have much to discuss, it seems."

Her chambers were plainly furnished, contained a bed made of a simple wood frame, a writing desk, handwoven rugs upon the floor, and a large number of soft cushions scattered about. A lute stood in one corner. The only other article of furniture—a tall standing mirror—lay toppled on the floor. The broken glass had been swept into a neat pile.

"What happened to you, First Master?" Palin asked. "Was this transformation magical in nature?"

"I don't know! I wish I could find an explanation!" she said helplessly. "The transformation occurred the night of the thunderstorm."

"The storm," Palin murmured and glanced at Tas. "Many strange things happened during that storm, seemingly. The kender arrived the night of the storm."

"The rain drummed on the roof," Goldmoon continued, as if she hadn't heard. "The wind howled and beat against the crystal as if it would smash it in. A brilliant lightning flash lit up the entire room more brightly than the brightest sunshine. It was so bright that it blinded me. For a time, I could see nothing at all. The blindness passed in a moment. I saw my reflection in the mirror.

"I . . . I thought a stranger was in the room. I turned, but there was no one there. It was then, when I turned back, that I recognized myself. Not as I had been, not gray and wrinkled and old, but young. Young as on my wedding day . . ."

She closed her eyes. Tears rolled down her cheeks.

"The crash they heard below," Palin said. "You broke the mirror."

"Yes!" Goldmoon cried, her fists clenched. "I was so close to reaching him, Palin! So near! Riverwind and I would have been together soon. He has waited so patiently. He knew that I had important tasks to perform, but my work is done now and I could hear him calling to me to join him. We would be together forever. I was going to walk again with my beloved at last and . . . and now . . . this!"

"You truly have no idea how this happened?" Palin hesitated, frowning. "Perhaps a secret wish of your heart . . . some potion . . . or magical artifact . . ."

"In other words, did I ask for this?" Goldmoon returned, her voice cool. "No, I did not. I was content. My work is finished. Others have the strength and heart and will to carry on. I want only to rest in my husband's arms again, Palin. I want to walk with him into the next stage of being. Riverwind and I used to speak of that next step on our great journey. I was given a glimpse of it during the time I was with Mishakal, the time she gave me the staff. The beauty of that far distant place . . . I can't describe it.

"I am tired. So very tired. I look young, but I don't feel young, Palin. This body is like a costume for the masquerade, the face a mask. Except that I can't take it off! I've tried and I can't!"

Goldmoon put her hands to her cheeks, pressed on them. Her face was scarred and now Tas, shocked, knew the cause. In her desperation, she had endeavored to claw away the smooth, supple flesh.

"Inside I am still old, Palin," Goldmoon said, her voice hollow and ragged. "I have lived my allotted life span. My husband has traveled on before me, my friends are gone. I am alone. Oh, I know." She raised her hand to forestall his objections. "I know that I have friends here. But they are not of my time. They . . . don't sing the same songs."

She turned to Tasslehoff with a smile that was sweet but so sad that the kender's eyes filled with tears.

"*Is* this my fault, Goldmoon?" Tas asked mournfully. "I didn't mean to make you unhappy! I didn't!"

"No, kenderken." Goldmoon soothed him with her gentle touch. "You have brought me cheer. And a puzzle." She turned to Palin. "How does he come to be here? Has he been roaming the world these thirty years when we thought him dead?"

"The kender came the night of the storm by using a magical device, Goldmoon," Palin said in a low voice. "The Device of Time Journeying. A device that once belonged to my father. Do you remember hearing the story of how Caramon traveled back in time with Lady Crysania—"

"Yes, I remember," Goldmoon said, flushing. "I must say that I found your father's story very difficult to believe. If it hadn't been for Lady Crysania's account—"

"There is no need to apologize," Palin said. "I admit that I myself found the story difficult to credit. I was able to speak to Dalamar about it years ago, before the Chaos War. And I talked to Tanis Half-Elven. Both confirmed my father's tale. In addition, I read Par-Salian's notes, which spoke of how the decision to send my father back into time came to be made. And I have a friend, Mistress Jenna, who was present in the Tower of High Sorcery when my father handed over the device to Dalamar for safekeeping. She had seen the device before and she recognized it. Above all, I have my account to serve as witness. Tasslehoff has with him the magical device my father used to transport himself through time. I know because I used it myself."

Goldmoon's eyes widened. She drew in a breath, soft as a sigh.

"Are you saying that the kender has come to us from the past? That he has traveled through time? That *you* traveled through time?"

"Tasslehoff," Palin said, "tell Goldmoon what you told me about Caramon's funeral. The first one. Be brief and concise as possible."

Since neither the word "brief" nor the word "concise" are in the kender vocabulary, Tasslehoff's story was considerably involved and extended, taking many little detours and side trips, and once losing himself completely in a morass of words from which he had to be patiently extricated. Goldmoon was a most attentive listener, however, seating herself next to him on the floor amongst the cushions and never saying a word.

When Tas spoke of how she and Riverwind had attended Caramon's first funeral together; her husband gray and stooped, the proud chieftain of the united tribes of the Plains, accompanied by his son and daughters, grandchildren and great-grandchildren, Goldmoon's tears flowed again. She wept silently, however, and never took her rapt gaze from the kender.

Tasslehoff came to a halt, mainly because his voice gave out. He was given a restorative glass of water and lay back down on the cushions.

"Well, what do you think of his tale, First Master?" Palin asked.

"A time in which Riverwind did *not* die," Goldmoon murmured. "A time in which we grow old together. Is it possible?"

"I used the device," Palin said. "I went back into the past, hoping to find the moment in time when we traded one future for the other. I had hoped to find such a moment, thinking that I might be able to effect a change."

"That would be very dangerous," Goldmoon said, her tone sharp-edged.

"Yes, well, it doesn't matter if it was or it wasn't," Palin returned, "because I did not find such a moment in our past."

"That is just as well," Goldmoon began.

Palin interrupted her. "First Master," he said, "I found no past at all."

"What do you mean? No past?"

"I went back in time," Palin said. "I saw the end of the Chaos War. I witnessed the departure of the gods. When I looked beyond that, when I tried to see the beginning of the Chaos War, when I tried to see events that had come before that, I saw nothing but a vast and empty darkness, like looking down into an enormous well."

"What does this mean?" Goldmoon asked.

"I don't know, First Master." Palin looked at Tasslehoff. "What I do know is this: Many years ago, Tasslehoff Burrfoot died. At least, he was supposed to die. As you see, here he sits, very much alive."

"That is why you wanted to send him back to die," Goldmoon murmured, looking sorrowfully at Tas.

"Perhaps I am wrong. Perhaps that wouldn't make any difference. I am the first to admit that I do not understand time journeying," Palin said ruefully. "Only one of our order does, and that is Dalamar. But none know if he is dead or alive or how to find him if he is alive."

"Dalamar!" Goldmoon's expression darkened. "When I heard of his disappearance and that of the Tower of High Sorcery, I remember thinking how wonderful it was that some good had come out of the evil of these times. I know others liked and trusted him—Tanis, for example, and your father. But every time I saw him, I saw that he walked in shadow, and more than that, that he liked the shadow. He wrapped it around him, hiding his deeds. I believe Tanis and Caramon were deceived by him and I, for one, hope he has left this world. Bad as things are, they are better than if he were here. I trust," she added sharply, "that you will have nothing to do with him, should he happen to reappear."

"There seems little likelihood Dalamar will enter into this at all," Palin returned impatiently. "If he is not dead, he is where we are not likely to ever find him. Now that I have spoken to you, First Master, what I find most singular is that all these strange events happened the night of the storm."

"There was a voice in that storm," Goldmoon said, shivering. "It filled me with terror, though I could not understand what it said." She looked again at Tas. "The question is, what do we do now?"

"That is up to Tas," Palin replied. "The fate of the world in the hands of a kender." He looked very grim.

Tas rose, with dignity, to his feet. "I'll give the matter serious thought," he announced. "The decision isn't easy. I have lots of things to consider. But before I go away to think and to help Conundrum map the hedge maze, which

I promised I would do before I left, I want to say one thing. If you people had left the fate of the world in the hands of kender all along, you probably wouldn't be in this mess."

Leaving that shot to rankle in Palin's bosom, Tasslehoff Burrfoot left the room.

24 SLEEP, LOVE; FOREVER SLEEP

Over a week had passed since Mina had received her orders to march on Silvanesti. During that time, Silvanoshei had been crowned king of the Silvanesti kingdom that slumbered beneath its protective shield, unaware of doom marching nearer.

Galdar had spent three days racing to Khur to deliver Mina's orders to General Dogah. He had spent another three days traveling south from Khur, eager to meet up with Mina and her troops, following the route she'd shown him on her map. Finding them was easy. He could see signs of their passing all along the way—wheel ruts, footprints, abandoned equipment. If he could find the army this easily, so could the ogres.

Galdar marched with bowed head, slogging through the mud, rain running into his eyes, dripping from his muzzle. The rain had been falling for two days straight now, ever since Galdar's return, with no letup in sight. Not a soft drizzly summer shower, either, but a lancing, wind-driven rain that chilled the spirit and cast a gloom over the soul.

The men were wet through, cold, and miserable. The trail was slick with mud that was either so slippery no man could stand on it or was so sticky that it nearly sucked the men's boots off their feet. The heavily laden supply wagons were mired in the mud at least thrice daily, requiring the men to put poles beneath the wheels and heave them out. Galdar's strength was called upon during these mishaps. The minotaur's back and shoulders ached with the strain, for he often had to lift the wagon to free the wheel.

The soldiers began to actively hate the rain, to view it as the enemy, never mind ogres. The rain beating on the soldiers' helms sounded like someone constantly drumming on a tin pot, or so one grumbled. Captain Samuval and his archers worried that the feathers with which the arrows were fletched were so wet and bedraggled that the arrows would not fly accurately.

Mina required the men to be up and marching with the dawn, always supposing there was a dawn, which there hadn't been for the last few days. They marched until the twilight grew so gloomy that the officers feared the wagon masters would drive off the road in the darkness. The wood was too wet for even the most experienced fire-builder to have any success. Their food tasted of mud. They slept in the mud, with mud for a pillow and rain for a blanket. The next morning they were up and marching again. Marching to glory with Mina. So all firmly believed. So all knew.

According to the mystics, the soldiers would have no chance to penetrate the magical shield. They would be caught between the anvil of the shield to their front and the hammer of the ogres to their back. They would perish ignominiously. The soldiers scoffed at the mystics. Mina could raise the shield, Mina could batter it down with a touch of her hand. They believed in her, and so they followed her. Not a man deserted during that long and arduous march.

They did complain—complained bitterly—about the mud and the rain and the poor food and the lack of sleep. Their grumblings grew louder. Mina could not help but hear them. "What I want to know is this," one man said loudly, his voice sounding above the squelching of boots in the mud. "If the God we follow wants us to win, then why doesn't the Nameless One send us sunshine and a dry road?"

Galdar marched in his accustomed place at Mina's side. He glanced up at her. She had heard the grumblings before now and had ignored them. But this was the first man who had dared question her god.

Mina reined in her horse, wheeled the animal. She galloped back along the column, searching for the man who had spoken. None of his comrades pointed him out, but Mina found him. She fixed the man with her amber eyes.

"Subcommander Paregin, is it not?" she said.

"Yes, Mina," he replied, defiant.

"You took an arrow in the chest. You were dying. I restored you to life," Mina said. She was angry. The men had never seen her angry. Galdar shivered, recalled suddenly the appalling storm of lightning and thunder that had given her birth.

Paregin's face went red with shame. He mumbled a reply, lowered his gaze before her.

"Listen to me, Subcommander," Mina said and her voice was cold and sharp. "If we marched in dry weather under the blazing sun, it would not be rain drops that pierce your armor but ogre lances. The gray gloom is a curtain that hides us from the sight of our enemy. The rain washes away all trace of our passing. Do not question the God's wisdom, Paregin, especially since it seems you have little of your own."

Paregin's face was pale. "Forgive me, Mina," he said through pallid lips. "I meant no disrespect. I honor the God. I honor you." He looked at her in adoration. "Would that I had a chance to prove it!"

Mina's expression softened. Her amber eyes glowed, the only color in the gray gloom. "You will have that chance, Paregin," she said gently, "I promise it to you."

Wheeling her horse, she galloped back to the head of the column, mud flying from the horse's hooves.

The men lowered their heads against the rain and prepared to march on.

"Mina!" a voice cried from the rear. A figure was slipping and sliding, hastening toward the front of the line.

Mina halted her steed, turned to see what was amiss. "One of the rearguard," Galdar reported.

"Mina!" The man arrived panting and out of breath. "Blue dragons!" he gasped. "From the north." He looked back, frowned. "I swear, Mina! I saw them. . . ."

"There!" Galdar said, pointing.

Blue dragons, five of them, emerged from the clouds, their scales glistening with the rain. The ragged column of men slowed and shuffled to a stop, all staring in alarm.

The dragons were immense creatures, beautiful, awful. The rain gleamed on scales that were blue as the ice of a frozen lake beneath a clear winter sky. They rode the storm winds without fear, their immense wings barely moving to keep the dragons aloft. They had no fear of the jagged lightning, for their breath was lightning, could blast a stone tower to rubble or kill a man as he stood on the ground far below.

Mina said nothing, gave no orders. She calmed her horse, who shied at the sight of the dragons, and gazed up at them in silence. The blue dragons flew nearer, and now Galdar could see riders clad in black armor. One by one, in formation, each of the blue dragons swooped low over the ragged column of marching men. The dragonriders and their mounts took a good long look, then the blue dragons flapped their wings and lifted back up among the gray clouds.

The dragons were lost to sight, but their presence could still be felt, oppressing the heart, sapping courage.

"What's going on?" Captain Samuval slogged through the mud. At the sight of the dragons, his archers had drawn their bows, fitted their arrows. "What was that all about?"

"Targonne's spies," Galdar growled. "By now he must know that you countermanded his order and sent General Dogah an order of your own, Mina. That's treason. He'll have you drawn and quartered, your head on a spike."

"Then why didn't he attack us?" Captain Samuval demanded, with a grim glance skyward. "His dragons could have incinerated us where we stood."

"Yes, but what would that gain him?" Mina answered. "He does not profit by killing us. He does profit if we succeed. He is a short-sighted, avaricious, grasping, covetous man. A man like Targonne has never been loyal to anyone in his life, cannot believe anyone else can be loyal. A man who believes in nothing except the clink of steel coins mounting one on top of the other cannot understand another's faith. Judging all people by himself, he cannot understand what is happening here, and consequently he does not know how to deal with it. I will give him what he wants. Our victory will earn him the wealth of the Silvanesti nation and Malystryx's favor."

"Are you so certain we will win, Mina?" Galdar asked. "It's not that I'm doubting," he added hastily. "But five hundred against the entire Silvanesti nation? And we have yet to march through ogre lands."

"Of course, we will win, Galdar," Mina replied. "The One God has decreed it."

Child of battle, child of war, child of death, she rode forward, and the men followed after her through the steadily falling rain.

Mina's army marched southward, following the Thon-Thalas River. The rain finally stopped. The sun returned, its heat welcome to the soldiers, though they had to pay for warmth and dry clothes by redoubling their patrols. They were deep in ogre lands now.

The ogres were now threatened from the south by the cursed elves and the Legion of Steel and from the north by their former allies. Finding they could not dislodge the Knights of Neraka from the north, the ogres had lately pulled their armies from that front and sent them south, concentrating their attacks against the Legion of Steel, believing that they were the weaker foe and would thus more readily fall.

Mina sent out scouting parties daily. Long-range scouts returned to report that a large army of ogres was gathering around the fortress of the Legion of Steel, near the border of Silvanesti. The Legion of Steel and an army of elves, believed to be under the leadership of the dark elf Alhana Starbreeze, were inside the fort preparing to stave off the ogre attack. The battle had not yet begun. The ogres were waiting for something—more manpower, perhaps, or favorable omens.

Mina heard the scouts' reports in the morning, prior to setting out on the day's march. The men were packing their gear, complaining as usual but in better spirits since the rain had quit. The blue dragons that dogged them kept their distance. Occasionally someone would catch sight of dark wings and the flash of sunlight off blue scales, but the dragons did not fly closer. The men ate their meager breakfast, waited for the orders to move out.

"You bring good news, gentlemen," Mina said to the scouts, "but we must not relax our vigilance. How close are we to the shield, Galdar?"

"The scouts report that we are within two days' march, Mina," he said.

Her amber eyes gazed past him, past the army, past the trees and the river, past the sky itself or so it seemed to him. "We are called, Galdar. I feel a great urgency. We must be at the border of Silvanesti by tonight."

Galdar gaped. He was loyal to his commander. He would have laid down his life for her and considered his death a privilege. Her strategies were unorthodox, but they had proven effective. But there were some things not even she could do. Or her god.

"We can't, Mina," Galdar said flatly. "The men have been marching ten hours a day already. They're exhausted. Besides, the supply wagons can't move that fast. Look at them." He waved his hand. Acting under the direction of the quartermaster, his men were digging out one of the wagons, which had sunk in the mud during the night. "They won't be ready to set out for another hour, at least. What you ask is impossible, Mina."

"Nothing is impossible to the One God, Galdar," said Mina. "We will camp beside the shield this night. You will see. I— What is that noise?"

A frantic horn call split the air, coming from behind them.

The long line of troops stretched along the road that ran over a hill, around a bend, down a valley, and over another hill. The men stood up, hearing the horn call, and looked back down the ranks. Those digging out the wagon ceased their work.

A single scout, riding hard, crested the hill. The troops scrambled to move off the road, out of his way. It seemed he shouted a question as he rode, for many of the men pointed to the front. Putting his head down, he dug his spurs into his horse's flanks and urged his steed forward.

Mina stepped out into the road to wait for him. The scout, reaching her, pulled up so hard on his horse that the animal reared on its hind legs.

"Mina!" The scout was breathless. "Ogres! In the hills behind us! Coming fast!"

"How many?" she asked.

"It's hard to tell. They're spread out all over the place, not in column or in any sort of order. But there's a lot of them. One hundred. Maybe more. Coming down out of the hills."

"A raiding party, most likely." Galdar grunted. "Probably heard about the big battle in the south and they're off to claim their fair share of the loot."

"They'll come together quick enough when they pick up our trail," Captain Samuval predicted. "They'll do that the moment they strike the river."

"They've done that now, seemingly," Galdar said.

Grinding shouts of rage and glee bounded like boulders among the hills. The raucous blasts of ram horns split the air. A few ogres had spotted them and were calling their fellows to battle.

The scout's report spread with the swiftness of wildfire along the line of Mina's troops. The soldiers scrambled to their feet, weariness and fatigue vanishing like dry leaves in the flames. Ogres are terrible enemies. Hulking, fierce, and savage, an ogre army, led by ogre mages, operates with a good notion of strategy and tactics. An ogre raiding party does not.

Ogre raiding parties have no leaders. Outcasts from their own brutal society, these ogres are extremely dangerous, will prey even upon their own kind. They do not bother with formations but will attack whenever the enemy is in sight, trusting to their strength, brute force, and ferocity to overwhelm the foe.

Ogres are fearless in battle and, due to thick and hairy hides, are difficult to kill. Pain maddens them, goads them to greater ferocity. Ogre raiders have no word for "mercy," they scorn the word "surrender," either with regard to themselves or an opponent. Ogre raiders take only a few prisoners, and these are saved to provide the evening's entertainment.

A disciplined, heavily armed, and well-organized army can turn back an ogre assault. Leaderless ogres are led easily into traps and completely vanquished by clever stratagems. They are not good archers, having no patience for the practice required to develop skill with bow and arrow. They wield enormous swords and battles-axes that they use to hack the enemy to pieces, or throw spears, which their strong arms can hurl long distances with deadly effect.

Hearing the ogres' fierce yells and the sound of their horns, Mina's officers began shouting orders. Her Knights turned their horses, ready to gallop back to face the foe. The wagon masters plied the whip, the draft horses snorted and strained.

"Pull those wagons forward!" Galdar bellowed out commands. "Footmen, form a line across the trail, anchor on the river. Captain Samuval, your men take positions behind—"

"No," said Mina and though she did not raise her voice, her single word sounded like a clarion and brought all action to a halt. The clamor and uproar fell silent. The men turned to look at her. "We are not going to fight the ogres. We're going to flee them."

"The ogres will chase after us, Mina," Samuval protested. "We'll never be able to outrun them. We have to stand and fight!"

"Wagon masters," Mina called, ignoring him, "cut free the horses!"

"But, Mina!" Galdar added his own protest, "we can't leave the supplies!"

"The wagons slow us down," Mina replied. "Instead, we will allow the wagons to slow down the ogres."

Galdar stared. At first he didn't comprehend, and then he saw her plan.

"It just might work," he said, mulling over her strategy in his mind.

"It will work," said Samuval jubilantly. "We'll toss the wagons to the ogres like you toss food to a ravening wolf pack at your heels. An ogre raiding party will not be able to resist such a prize."

"Footmen, form a double line, march column. Prepare to move out. You will run," Mina told the men, "but not in a panic. You will run until you have no more strength left to run and then you will run faster."

"Perhaps the dragons will come to our aid," said Samuval, glancing skyward. "If they're even still up there."

"They're up there," Galdar growled, "but they won't come to our rescue. If we're wiped out at the hands of ogres, Targonne will be spared the expense of executing us."

"We're not going to be wiped out," Mina said crisply. "Pass the word for Subcommander Paregin!"

"I am here, Mina!" The officer pushed his way forward through his men, who were hurriedly falling into position.

"Paregin, you are loyal to me?"

"Yes, Mina," he said firmly.

"You asked for a chance to prove that loyalty."

"Yes, Mina, I did," he said again, but this time his voice faltered.

"I saved your life," Mina said. The shouts and yells of the ogres were coming closer. The men glanced uneasily behind them. "That life is therefore mine."

"Yes, Mina," he replied.

"Subcommander Paregin, you and your men will remain here to defend the wagons. You will hold off the ogres as long as possible, thereby giving the rest of us the time we need to escape."

Paregin swallowed. "Yes, Mina," he said, but he said the words without a voice.

"I will pray for you, Paregin," Mina said softly. She extended her hand to him. "And for all those who stay behind. The One God blesses you and accepts your sacrifice. Take your positions."

Grasping her hand, Paregin reverently pressed her hand to his lips. He looked exalted, uplifted. When he returned to the lines, he spoke to his troops in excited tones as if she had conferred upon them a great reward. Galdar watched closely to see that Paregin's men obeyed him and did not try to skulk off in the face of orders that were essentially a death warrant. The men obeyed, some looking dazed, others grim, but all determined and resolved. They ranged themselves around the supply wagons that were filled with barrels of beef and ale, sacks of flour, the smith's equipment, swords, shields and armor, tents and rope.

"The ogres will think it is Yule come early," Samuval remarked.

Galdar nodded, but made no comment. He remembered back to Beckard's Cut, remembered Mina ordering him to pack extra supplies. A shiver ran along his spine, caused his fur to rise. Had she known all along? Had she been given knowledge that this would come to pass? Had she foreseen it all? Were their ends determined? Had she marked Paregin for death the day she saved his life? Galdar felt a moment's panic. He wanted suddenly to cut and run, just to prove to himself that he could. Prove that he was still the master of his own fate, that he was not trapped like a bug in her amber eyes.

"We will reach Silvanesti by nightfall," said Mina.

Galdar looked up at her, fear and awe constricting his heart.

"Give the order to move out, Galdar. I will set the pace."

She dismounted and handed the reins to one of her Knights. Taking her place at the front of the line, she raised her voice, and it was sweet and cold as the silver moonlight. "On to Silvanesti! On to victory!"

She began to march double-time, her strides long, starting out at swift but easy pace until her muscles warmed to the exercise. The men, hearing the ogres rampaging in the rear, needed no urging to keep up with her.

Galdar could escape into the hills. He could volunteer to remain with the doomed rear guard. He could follow her for as long as he lived. He fell into step beside her and was rewarded with her smile.

"For Mina," Subcommander Paregin shouted. He stood beside the loaded wagon, listening to the ogres raise their battle cry.

Gripping his sword, he waited for death.

Now that the troops no longer had the wagons to slow them, Mina's army made excellent time, especially with the howls and hoots of the ogres to spur them on. Each man could hear the sounds of the battle behind him, each man imagined what was happening, could tell the progress of the battle by the noise. Ogre shouts of rage, human death cries. Wild yelps of glee—the ogres discovered the wagons. Silence. The ogres were looting the wagons and hacking apart the bodies of those they had slaughtered.

The men ran as Mina had told them they would run. They ran until they were exhausted, and then she urged them to run faster. Those who fell were left behind. Mina permitted no one to assist them and this gave the men additional incentive for keeping their aching legs moving. Whenever a soldier thought he could no longer go on, he had only to look to the front of the line, to see the slender, fragile-looking girl, wearing plate and chain mail, leading the march, never flagging, never pausing to rest, never looking behind to see if anyone was following. Her gallant courage, her indomitable spirit, her faith was the standard that led her men on.

Mina permitted the soldiers only a brief rest, standing, to drink sparingly of water. She would not let them sit or lie down for fear their muscles would stiffen so that they would not be able to move. Those who collapsed were left where they fell, to straggle along behind when and if they recovered.

The sun's shadows grew longer. The men continued to run, officers setting the grueling pace with songs at first. Then no one had any breath left except for breathing. Yet with every step, they drew closer to their destination—the shield that protected the border of Silvanesti.

Galdar saw in growing alarm that Mina's own strength was flagging. She stumbled several times and then, at last, she fell.

Galdar leaped to her side.

"No," she gasped and shoved away his hand. She regained her feet, staggered forward several more steps and fell again.

"Mina," said Galdar, "your horse, Foxfire, is here, ready and able to carry you. There is no shame in riding."

"My soldiers run," she told Galdar faintly. "I will run with them. I will not ask them to do what I cannot!"

She tried to rise. Her legs would not support her. Her face grim, she began to crawl on her hands and knees along the trail. Some of the soldiers cheered, but many others wept.

Galdar lifted her in his arms. She protested, she ordered him to set her back on her feet.

"If I do, you will only fall again. You will be the one to slow us down, Mina," Galdar said. "The men would never leave you. We will never make the Silvanesti border by nightfall. The choice is yours."

"Very well," she said, after a moment's bitter struggle against her own weakness. "I will ride."

He helped her onto Foxfire. She slumped over the saddle, so tired that he feared for a moment she could not even remain in the saddle. Then she set her jaw, straightened her back, sat upright.

Mina looked down, her amber eyes cool.

"Do not ever defy my orders again, Galdar," she said. "You can serve the One God just as well dead as alive."

"Yes, Mina," he answered quietly.

Gripping the reins in her hands, she urged the horse forward at a gallop.

Mina's prediction proved correct. Her army reached the forested lands outside the Shield before sundown.

"Our march ends here for the night," Mina said and climbed down from her exhausted horse.

"What ails this place?" Galdar asked, eyeing the dead and dying trees, the decaying plants, the corpses of animals found lying along the trail. "Is it cursed?"

"In a way, yes. We are near the shield," Mina said, looking intently at everything around her. "The devastation you see is the mark of its passing."

"The shield brings death?" Galdar asked, alarmed.

"To all it touches," she replied.

"And we must break through it?"

"We cannot break through it." Mina was calm. "No weapon can penetrate it. No force—not even the magical force of the most powerful dragon—can shatter it. The elves under the leadership of their witch-queen have hurled themselves against it for months and it remains unyielding. The Legion of Steel has sent its knights to batter it to no effect.

"There." Mina pointed. "The shield lies directly before us. You can see it, Galdar. The shield and beyond the shield, Silvanesti and victory."

Galdar squinted against the glare. The water caught the setting sun's lurid red glow, turning the Thon-Thalas into a river of blood. He could see nothing at first, and then the trees in front of him rippled, as if they were reflected in the blood-tinged water. He rubbed his eyes, thinking fatigue was causing them to blur. He blinked and stared and saw the trees ripple again, and he realized then that what he was seeing was a distortion of the air created by the magic of the shield.

He drew closer, fascinated. Now that he knew where to look, he fancied he could see the shield itself. It was transparent, but its transparency had an oily quality to it, like a soap bubble. Everything inside it—trees and boulders, brush and grasses—looked wobbly and insubstantial.

Just like the elf army, he thought, and immediately took this as a good omen. But they still had to pass through the shield.

The officers brought the troops to a halt. Many of the men pitched forward face-first on the ground as soon as the order to cease march was given. Some lay sobbing for breath or sobbing from the pain of muscle spasms in their legs. Some lay quiet and still, as if the deadly curse that had touched the trees around them had claimed them as well.

"All in all," Galdar growled in an undertone to Captain Samuval, who stood gasping for breath beside him, "Given a choice between walking into that shield and facing ogres, I think I'd take the ogres. At least then you know what you're up against."

"You said a true word there, friend," Captain Samuval agreed when he had recaptured some of his breath and had enough left over to use for speech. "This place has an uncanny feel to it."

He nodded his head in the direction of the shimmering air. "Whatever we're going to do, we'd best be doing it soon. We may have slowed the ogres down a bit, but they'll catch up with us fast enough."

"By morning, I'd say," Galdar agreed, slumping to the ground. He lay on his back. He had never been so tired in all his life. "I know ogre raiding parties. Looting the wagons and butchering our men will occupy them for a while, but they'll be looking for more sport and more loot. They're on our trail right now. I'll bet money on it."

"And us too goddamn worn out to go anywhere, even if we had anywhere to go," Captain Samuval said, dropping wearily down alongside him. "I don't know about you, but I don't have energy enough to lift my hand to brush away a gnat, much less attack some blamed magical shield."

He cast a sidelong glance at Mina, who alone of all her army remained on her feet. She stood staring intently at the shield, or at least in the direction of the shield, for night was closing upon them fast, and its distortion could no longer be easily detected.

"I think this ends it, my friend," Captain Samuval said in a low voice to the minotaur. "We cannot get inside the magic of the shield. The ogres will catch us here in the morning. Ogres at our rear. The shield to our front. Us caught between. All that mad dash for naught."

Galdar didn't reply. He had not lost faith, though he was too tired to argue. Mina had a plan. She would not lead them into a blind alley to be caught and slaughtered by ogres. He didn't know what her plan might be, but he had seen enough of her and enough of the power of her God that he now believed her capable of doing the impossible.

Mina shoved her way through the gray and lifeless trees, walked toward the shield. Dead limbs fell around her. Dead, dry leaves crackled beneath her boots. Dust like ashes sifted down upon her shoulders and covered her shaved head with a pearl gray mantle. She walked until she could go no farther. She came up against an invisible wall.

Mina reached out her hand, pushed at the shield, and it seemed to Galdar that the insubstantial oily soap bubble must give way. She drew back her hand swiftly, as if she had touched a thistle and been stung. Galdar thought he saw a tiny ripple in the shield, but that might have been his imagination. Drawing her morning star, Mina struck it against the shield. The morning star fell from her hand, jarred out of her grasp by the blow. Shrugging, she bent down to pick up her weapon. Reports confirmed, she turned and made her way back through the forest of death to her command.

"What are your orders, Mina?" Galdar asked.

She looked around her army that lay scattered over the gray ground like so many corpses.

"The men have done well," she said. "They are exhausted. We will make camp here. This is close enough, I think," she added, looking back at the shield. "Yes, this should be close enough."

Galdar didn't ask, "Close enough for what?" He didn't have the energy. He staggered to his feet. "I'll go set the watch—"

"No," Mina countered. She laid her hand on his shoulder. "We will not set a watch this night. Everyone will sleep."

"Not set a watch!" Galdar protested. "But, Mina, the ogres are in pursuit—"

"They will be on us by morning," she said. "The men should eat if they are hungry and then they must sleep."

Eat what? Galdar wondered. Their food was now filling the bellies of the ogres. Those who had started out on that mad run carrying packs had long ago dropped them by the side of the road. He knew better than to question her.

Assembling the officers, he relayed Mina's orders. To Galdar's surprise, there was little protest or argument. The men were too tired. They didn't care anymore. As one soldier said, setting a watch wouldn't do much good anyhow. They'd all wake soon enough when the ogres arrived. Wake up in time to die.

Galdar's stomach rumbled, but he was too tired to go searching for food. He would not eat anything from this accursed forest, that much was certain. He wondered if the magic that had sucked the life from the trees would do the same for them in the night. He pictured the ogres arriving tomorrow morning to find nothing but desiccated husks. The thought brought a smile to his lips.

The night was dark as death. Tangled in the black branches of the skeleton trees, the stars looked small and meager. Galdar was too stupid with fatigue to remember if the moon would rise this night or not. He hoped it wouldn't. The less he saw of this ghastly forest, the better. He stumbled over limp bodies as he walked. A few groaned, and a few cursed him, and that was the only way he knew they were alive.

He returned to the place he had left Mina, but she was not there. He could not find her in the darkness, and his heart spasmed with a nameless fear, the fear a child feels on finding himself lost and alone in the night. He dare not call. The silence was a temple silence, had an awful quality he did not want to disturb. But he had to find her.

"Mina!" he hissed in a penetrating whisper.

"Here, Galdar," she replied.

He circled around a stand of dead trees, found her cradled in a severed arm that had fallen from an enormous oak. Her face glimmered pale, more luminous than the moonlight, and he wondered that he could have missed her.

He made his report. "Four hundred and fifty men, Mina," he said. He staggered as he spoke.

"Sit down," she ordered.

"Thirty left behind with the wagons. Twenty more fallen on the road. Some of those may catch up, if the ogres don't find them first."

She nodded silently. Galdar eased himself to the ground. His muscles ached. He would be sore and stiff tomorrow, and he wouldn't be the only one.

"Everyone's bedded down." He gave a cavernous yawn.

"You should sleep, too, Galdar."

"What about you?"

"I am wakeful. I will sit up for awhile. Not long. Don't worry about me."

He settled himself at her feet, his head pillowed on a pile of dead leaves that crackled every time he moved. During that hellish run, all he had been able to think about had been the blessed night when he would be able to lie down, to rest, to sleep. He stretched his limbs, closed his eyes, and saw the trail at his feet. The trail went on and on into forever. He ran and ran, and forever moved farther away from him. The trail undulated, twisted, wrapped around his legs like a snake. Tripped him, sent him plunging head first into a river of blood.

Galdar woke with a hoarse cry and a start.

"What is it?" Mina was still seated on the log. She hadn't moved.

"That damned run!" Galdar swore. "I see the road in my dreams! I can't sleep. It's no use."

He wasn't the only one. All around him came the sounds of breathing— heavy, panting—restless shifting, groans and coughs and whispers of fear, loss, despair. Mina listened, shook her head, and sighed.

"Lie down, Galdar," she said. "Lie down and I will sing you a lullaby. Then you will sleep."

"Mina . . ." Embarrassed for her, Galdar cleared his throat. "There is no need for that. I'm not a child."

"You are a child, Galdar," she said softly. "We are all children. Children of the One God. Lie down. Close your eyes."

Galdar did as he was told. He lay down and closed his eyes, and the road was ahead of him, and he was running, running for his life . . .

Mina began to sing. Her voice was low, untrained, raw and yet there was a sweetness and a clarity that struck through to the soul.

> The day has passed beyond our power.
> The petals close upon the flower.
> The light is failing in this hour
> Of day's last waning breath.
>
> The blackness of the night surrounds
> The distant souls of stars now found.
> Far from this world to which we're bound,
> Of sorrow, fear and death.
>
> Sleep, love; forever sleep.
> Your soul the night will keep.
> Embrace the darkness deep.
> Sleep, love; forever sleep.
>
> The gathering darkness takes our souls,
> Embracing us in a chilling folds,
> Deep in a Mistress's void that holds
> Our fate within her hands.

Dream, warriors, of the dark above,
And feel the sweet redemption of
The Night's Consort, and of her love
For those within her bands.

Sleep, love; forever sleep.
Your soul the night will keep.
Embrace the darkness deep.
Sleep, love; forever sleep.

Galdar felt a lethargy steal over him, a languor similar to that experienced by those who bleed to death. His limbs grew heavy, his body was dead weight, so heavy that he was sinking into the ground. Sinking into the soft dirt and the ash of the dead plants and the leaves that drifted down upon him, settling over him like a blanket of dirt thrown into his grave.

He was at peace. He knew no fear. Consciousness drained away from him. *Gamashinoch*, the dwarves called it. The Song of Death.

Targonne's dragon riders were up with the gray dawn, flying low over the forests of the ogre land of Blöde. They had watched from the heavens yesterday, watched the small army run before the ogre raiding party. The soldiers had fled before the ogres in near panic, so far as the dragon riders could see, abandoning their supply wagons, leaving them for the ogres. One of the riders noted grimly that Targonne would not be pleased to hear that several hundred steel worth of equipment was now adorning ogre bodies.

The ragtag army had run blindly, although they had managed to keep in formation. But their mad dash to safety had taken them nowhere. The army had run headlong into the magical shield surrounding Silvanesti. The army had come to a halt here at sundown. They were spent, they could go no farther, even if there had been any place for them to go, which there wasn't.

Looting the wagons had occupied the ogre raiding party for a couple of hours, but when there was nothing more to eat and they had stolen all there was to steal, the ogres moved south, following the trail of the humans, following their hated scent that drove them to fury and battle madness.

The dragon riders could have dealt with the ogres. The blues would have made short work of the raiding party. But the riders had their orders. They were to keep watch on this rebellious Knight and her army of fanatics. The dragon riders were not to interfere. Targonne could not be blamed if ogres destroyed the Silvanesti invasion force. He had told Malys many times that the ogres should be driven out of Blöde, exterminated like the kender. Maybe next time she would listen to him.

"There they are," said one of the riders, as his dragon circled low. "In the Dead Land. The same place where we left them last night. They haven't moved. Maybe they're dead themselves. They look it."

"If not, they soon will be," said his commander.

The ogres were a black mass, moving like sludge along the road that ran alongside what the Knight had termed the Dead Land, the gray zone of death that marked the edge of the shield, the border of Silvanesti.

The dragon riders watched with interest, looking forward with anticipation to the battle that would finally bring an end to this tiresome duty and allow them to return to their barracks in Khur.

The Knights settled themselves comfortably to watch.

"Do you see that?" said one suddenly, sitting forward.

"Circle lower," the commander ordered.

The dragons flew lower, wings making a gentle sweep, catching the pre-dawn breeze. The riders stared down at the astonishing sight below.

"I think, gentlemen," said the commander, after a moment spent watching in gaping wonder, "that we should fly to Jelek and report this to Targonne ourselves. Otherwise, we might not be believed."

A horn blast woke Galdar, brought him to his feet before he was fully conscious, fumbling for his sword.

"Ogres attacking! Fall in, men! Fall in!" Captain Samuval was shouting himself hoarse, kicking at the men of his company to rouse them from their slumbers.

"Mina!" Galdar searched for her, determined to protect her, or, if he could not do that, to kill her so that she should not fall alive into ogre hands. "Mina!"

He found her in the same place he had left her. Mina sat in the curl of the dead oak's arm. Her weapon, the morning star, lay across her lap.

"Mina," said Galdar, plunging through the gray ash and trampling the dead leaves, "hurry! There may yet be a chance for you to escape—"

Mina looked at him and began to laugh.

He stared, appalled. He had never heard her laugh. The laughter was sweet and merry, the laughter of a girl running to meet a lover. Mina climbed upon the stump of a dead tree.

"Put your weapons away, men!" she called out. "The ogres cannot touch us."

"She has gone mad!" Samuval said.

"No," said Galdar, staring, unbelieving. "Look."

Ogres had formed a battle line not ten feet away from them. The ogres danced along this line. They clamored, roared, gnashed their teeth, gibbered, and cursed. They were so close that their foul stench made his nostrils twitch. The ogres jumped up and down, kicked and hammered with their fists, wielded their weapons in murderous rage.

Murderous, frustrated rage. The enemy was in clear sight, yet he might as well have been playing among the stars in some distant part of the universe. The trees that stood between Galdar and the ogres shimmered in the half-light, rippled as Mina's laughter rippled through the gray dawn. The ogres beat their heads against a shield, an invisible shield, a magical shield. They could not pass.

Galdar watched the ogres, watched to make certain that they could not reach him or his comrades. It seemed impossible to him that they could not enter through this strange and unseen barrier, but at last he had to admit that what his mind at first disbelieved was true. Many of the ogres fell back away from the barrier, alarmed and frightened of the magic. A few seemed to have simply grown weary of beating their heads against nothing but air. One by one, the ogres turned their hairy backs upon the human army that they could see, but could not reach. Their clamor began to die down. With threats and rude gestures, the ogres straggled off, disappeared into the forest.

"We are *inside* the shield, men!" Mina called out in triumph. "You stand safe within the borders of the Silvanesti! Witness the might and power of the One True God!"

The men stood staring, unable at first to comprehend the miracle that had befallen them. They blinked and gaped, reminding Galdar of prisoners who have been locked in dark cells for most of their lives, suddenly released to walk in the bright sunshine. A few exclaimed, but they did so softly, as if fearful to break the spell. Some rubbed their eyes, some doubted their own sanity, but there was the unmistakable sight of ogre backsides—ogres in retreat—to tell the soldiers that they were in their right minds, that they were not seeing things. One by one, the men fell to their knees before Mina and pressed their faces into the gray ash. They did not chant her name in triumph, not this time. This moment was too holy, too sacred. They paid Mina homage in silent awe and reverence.

"On your feet, men!" Mina shouted. "Take up your arms. This day we march to Silvanost. And there is no force in the world that can stop us!"

25   FROM DAY TO NIGHT

Faces.

Faces floating over him. Bobbing and receding on a rippling surface of pain. When Gerard rose to the surface, the faces were very close to him—strange faces, with no expression, corpses, drowned in the dark sea in which he floundered. The pain was worse closest to the surface, and he didn't like the faceless faces so near his own. He let himself sink back into the darkness, and there was some part of him that whispered he should cease struggling and give himself to the sea and become one of the faceless himself.

Gerard might have done so, but for a firm hand that gripped his when the pain was very bad and kept him from sinking. He might have done so but for a voice which was calm and commanding and ordered him to stay afloat. Accustomed to obedience, Gerard obeyed the voice. He did not drown but floundered in the dark water, clinging to the hand that held him fast. Finally, he made his way to the shore, pulled himself out of the pain and, collapsing on the banks of consciousness, he slept deeply and peacefully.

He woke hungry and pleasantly drowsy to wonder where he was, how he came to be here, what had happened to him. The faces that had bobbed around in his delirium were real faces now, but they were not much more comforting than the drowned faces in his dreams. The faces were cold and inexpressive, passionless faces of men and women, humans, dressed in long, black robes trimmed in silver.

"How are you feeling, sir?" one of these faces asked, bending over him and placing a chill hand upon his neck to feel his pulse. The woman's arm was covered with black cloth that fell over his face, and Gerard understood the image of the dark water in which he'd believed himself to be drowning.

"Better," said Gerard cautiously. "I'm hungry."

"A good sign. Your pulse is still weak. I will have one of the acolytes bring you some beef broth. You have lost blood, and the beef will help restore it."

Gerard looked at his surroundings. He lay in a bed in a large room filled with beds, most of which were empty. Other black-robed figures drifted about the room, moving silently on slippered feet. Pungent smells of herbs scented the air.

"Where am I?" Gerard asked, puzzled. "What happened?"

"You are in a hospital of our order, Sir Knight," the healer replied. "In Qualinesti. You were ambushed by elves, seemingly. I do not know much more than that." Nor did she care, by her cold expression. "Marshal Medan found you. He brought you here the day before yesterday. He saved your life."

Gerard was baffled. "Elves attacked me?"

"I know nothing more," the healer told him. "You are not my only patient. You must ask the marshal. He will be here shortly. He has been here every morning since he brought you in, sitting by your side."

Gerard remembered the firm hand, the strong, commanding voice and presence. He turned his body, slowly, painfully. His wounds were tightly bound, his muscles weak from lying in bed. He looked to see his armor—black armor, cleaned and polished—placed carefully on a stand near his bed.

Gerard closed his eyes with a groan that must have made the healer think he had suffered a relapse. He remembered all, or at least most, of what had happened. He remembered fighting two Neraka Knights. He remembered the arrow, remembered a third Knight, remembered challenging the Knight to fight. . . .

He did not remember being attacked by elves.

A young man came carrying a tray on which was a bowl of broth, a bit of bread, and a mug.

"Shall I help you, sir?" the young man asked politely.

Gerard imagined being spoon-fed like a child. "No," he said, and, though it cost him considerable pain, he struggled to a seated position.

The young man placed the tray on Gerard's lap and sat down on a chair at his side to watch him eat.

Gerard dunked his bread in the broth. He drank the clear, cool water from the mug and wondered how to find out the truth.

"I take it I am a prisoner here," he said to the young man.

"Why, no, sir!" The acolyte appeared astonished. "Why should you think that? You were ambushed by a band of elves, sir!" The acolyte was regarding Gerard with obvious admiration. "Marshal Medan told everyone the story when he brought you to us. He carried you in his arms himself, sir. He was covered with your blood. He said you were a true hero and that you were to receive the very best care, to spare no effort. We have had seven dark mystics working on you. You! A prisoner!" The young man laughed and shook his head.

Gerard shoved the bowl of soup away, uneaten. He had lost his appetite. Mumbling something to the effect that he was weaker than he'd supposed, he lay back among his pillows. The acolyte fussed over him, adjusting his bandages and checking to see if any of his wounds had ripped open. He said that they were all almost healed, then left, telling Gerard he should sleep.

Gerard closed his eyes, pretended to be asleep, but sleep was far from coming. He had no idea what was going on. He could only guess that this Medan was playing some sort of sadistic game that would end in Gerard's torture and death.

This decided, he was at peace, and he slept.

"No, don't wake him," said a voice, deep and familiar. "I just came to see how he was doing this morning."

Gerard opened his eyes. A man wearing the armor of a Knight of Neraka, with a marshal's sash, stood by the side of the bed. The man was in his fifties. His face was sun-darkened, heavily lined, stern, and grim, but it was not a cruel face. It was the face of a commander who could order men to their deaths but who took no pleasure in it.

Gerard knew him immediately. Marshal Medan.

Laurana had spoken of the marshal with a certain grudging respect, and Gerard could now understand why. Medan had governed a hostile race for thirty years, and there had been no death camps established, no gallows set up in the marketplace, no burning and looting and wanton destruction of elven households and business. Medan saw to it that the dragon's tribute was collected and paid. He had learned to play elven politics and, according to Laurana, he played it well. He had his spies and his informers. He dealt harshly with rebels, but he did so to maintain order and stability. He kept tight hold on his troops. No small feat in these days when the Knights of Neraka were recruited from the dregs of society.

Gerard was forced to abandon the notion that this man would use him for sport, would make a mockery of him and of his death. But if that were true, then what was Medan's game? What was the tale of elves attacking?

Gerard pushed himself to a sitting position, made his salute as best he could with his chest and arm bound with bandages. The marshal might be the enemy, but he was a commander and Gerard was bound to give him the respect that was due his rank.

The marshal returned the salute and told Gerard to lie back, take care not to reopen his wounds. Gerard barely heard him. He was thinking of something else. He was thinking back to the attack.

Medan had ambushed them for a reason—to catch Palin and recover the artifact. That means Medan knew exactly where to find us, Gerard said to himself. Someone told him where we were going to be and when.

Someone had betrayed them, but who? Someone in Laurana's own household? That was hard to credit, yet Gerard thought of the elf who had left to go "hunting" and had not returned. Perhaps he had been killed by the Knights. Perhaps not.

His thoughts were in bubbling turmoil. What had happened to Palin and the kender? Had they managed to escape safely? Or were they being held prisoner, too?

"How do you feel, sir?" Medan asked, regarding Gerard with concern.

"I am much better, my lord, thank you," Gerard replied. "I want to tell you, sir, that there is no need to continue with this pretense, which, perhaps, you do out of concern for my health. I know I am your prisoner. There is no reason why you should believe me, but I want you to know that I am not a spy. I am—"

"—a Solamnic Knight." Medan finished, smiling. "Yes, I am aware of that, Sir—" He paused.

"Gerard uth Mondar, my lord," Gerard replied.

"And I am Marshal Alexius Medan. Yes, Sir Gerard, I know you are a Solamnic." Medan pulled up a chair, seated himself near Gerard's bed. "I know you are my prisoner. I want you to keep your voice down." He glanced at the dark mystics, who were moving about at the far end of the room. "These two pieces of information will be our little secret."

"My lord?" Gerard gaped. If the dragon Beryl had plummeted out of the skies and landed in his soup, he could not have been more astonished.

"Listen to me, Sir Gerard," Medan said, resting a firm hand on the Solamnic's arm. "You were captured wearing the armor of a Knight of Neraka. You claim that you are not a spy, but who will believe you, do you suppose? No one. Do you know the fate that would befall you, as a spy? You would be interrogated by men skilled in the art of making other men talk. We are quite modern and up to date here in Qualinesti. We have the rack, the wheel, red-hot pincers, bone-crackers. We have the iron maiden with her painful and deadly embrace. After a few weeks of such interrogation, you would, I think, be quite glad to tell your interrogators everything you know and a lot of things you didn't. Anything to end the torment."

Gerard opened his mouth, but Medan exerted painful pressure on his arm and Gerard kept silent.

"What would you tell them? You would tell them about the queen mother. You would tell them that Laurana was harboring a human mage who had discovered a valuable magical artifact. Because of Laurana's intervention, this mage and the artifact are now safely beyond Beryl's reach."

Gerard breathed an inward sigh. Medan was watching him closely. "Yes, I thought you might be glad to hear that," he said dryly. "The mage escaped. The dragon Beryl was thwarted in her desire for the magical artifact. You will die. You will be glad to die. Your death will not save Laurana."

Gerard was silent, taking this all in. He wriggled and squirmed in the grasp of Medan's logic. The Knight could see no way out. He would have liked to think he could withstand any torture, go to his death mute and silent, but he could not be certain. He'd heard of the effects of the rack—how it pulled the joints out of the socket, left a man crippled, for the injuries would never fully heal. He had heard stories of the other torments they could inflict on a man; he recalled Palin's twisted hands, deformed fingers. He pictured

Laurana's hands, white, slender, marred with the calluses where she had once held a sword.

Gerard cast another glance at the black-robed mystics. The Knight looked back at Medan. "What do you want me to do, my lord?" he asked quietly.

"You will go along with the tale I have concocted about the battle with the elves. In return for your heroic actions, I will take you on as my aide. I need someone I can trust," Medan said wryly. "I believe that the life of the queen mother is in danger. I do what I can to shield her, but it may not be enough. I need an assistant who has the same regard for the queen mother as I have myself."

"Yet, my lord," said Gerard, bewildered, "you yourself spy upon her."

"For her own protection," Medan returned. "Believe me, I do not enjoy it."

Gerard shook his head, looked up at the marshal. "My lord, here is my answer. I ask that you draw your sword and kill me. Here, where I lie in this bed. I cannot offer any resistance. I absolve you in advance of the crime of murder. My death here and now will solve all our problems."

Medan's grim face relaxed into a smile. "Perhaps not as many as you might think. I refuse, of course. I have taken a liking to you, Solamnic. I would not have missed seeing that fight you put up for all the jewels in Qualinesti! Most other Knights I know would have flung down their weapons and taken to their heels."

Medan's expression darkened, his tone grew bitter. "The days of glory for our order are long dead. Once we were led by a man of honor, a man of courage. A man who was the son of a dragonlord and Zeboim, Goddess of the Sea. Who is our leader now?" Medan's lip curled. "An accountant. A man who wears a money belt instead of sword belt. Those he makes Knights no longer win their places through valor in battle or by deeds of bravery. They buy their rank with cold cash."

Gerard thought of his own father and felt his skin grow flushed and hot. He had not bought his way into the Knighthood, at least he could credit himself there. But his father had certainly bought his son's way into every soft-cushioned assignment that came along. "The Solamnics are no better," he muttered, lowering his gaze, smoothing out the wrinkles in the sweat-soaked sheet.

"Indeed? I am sorry to hear that," Medan said and he did sound genuinely disappointed. "Perhaps, in these last days, the final battle will be fought by men who choose honor instead of choosing sides. I hope so," he added quietly, "or else I believe that we are all lost."

"Last days?" Gerard asked, uneasily. "What do you mean, my lord?"

Medan looked about the room. The mystics had departed. They were alone, the two of them.

"Beryl is going to attack Qualinesti," Medan said. "I don't know when, but she is gathering her armies. When she does, I will have a bitter choice to make." He looked at Gerard intently. "I do not want the queen mother to be part of that choice. I will need someone I can trust to help her escape."

This man is in love with Laurana! Gerard realized, amazed. Not so surprising, he supposed. He was a little bit in love with her himself. One could not be around her without becoming enchanted by her beauty and grace. Still Gerard hesitated.

"Have I mistaken you, sir?" Medan asked, and his voice was cold. He rose to his feet. "Perhaps you are as devoid of honor as the rest."

"No, my lord," Gerard said emphatically. Strange as it seemed, he wanted the marshal to think well of him. "I worked to become a Knight. I read books on the art of warfare. I studied strategy and tactics. I have held my place in tourney and joust. I became a Knight to defend the helpless, to find honor and glory in battle and instead, because of my father's influence"—Gerard paused, a shame-filled pause—"I guarded a tomb in Solace."

Medan said nothing, looked down at him, waited for his decision.

"I accept your offer, my lord," Gerard said. "I do not understand you, but I will do what I can to help the Qualinesti," he said pointedly, "and the queen mother."

"Fair enough," said the marshal. With a curt nod, Medan turned, started to walk away. Halting, he glanced back over his shoulder.

"I joined the Knighthood for the same reasons you did, young man," he said, and then strode to the door, his footsteps loud, his cloak sweeping behind him. "If the healers pronounce you well, you will move into my house tomorrow."

Gerard settled back into his bed.

I do not trust him, Gerard reflected. I will not allow myself to trust him or admire him. He could be lying about the dragon. This could all be a trick. To what end, I do not know, but I will remain watchful and on my guard.

At least, he thought, feeling a strange sort of contentment wash through him, I'll be doing more than freeing some damn kender who manages to lock himself in a tomb.

Medan left the hospital, well pleased with his interview. He did not trust the Solamnic, of course. Medan trusted no one these days. The marshal would watch the man closely over the next few days, see how he acquitted himself. He could always take the Solamnic up on his offer and run his sword through him.

At least, I do not doubt his courage or his loyalty to his friends, the marshal reflected. He has proven these to me already.

The marshal turned his steps toward Laurana's house. He enjoyed the walk. Qualinesti was beautiful in all seasons, but summer was his favorite, the season of festivals, with its myriad flowers, the soft air filled with exquisite perfumes, the silvery green of the leaves and the wondrous bird song.

He took his time, pausing to lean over garden walls to admire a flaming display of day lilies lifting their orange heads to the sunshine. He lingered in the walkway to watch a shower of white blossoms shaken from a snow-ball bush by a fluttering robin. Coming upon an elf from House Woodshaper, Medan stopped the man to discuss a blight he feared had overtaken one of his rose bushes. The Woodshaper was hostile, made it clear he talked to Medan only because he was forced to do so. Medan was polite, respectful, his questions were intelligent. Gradually the elf warmed to his topic and, in the end, promised to come to the marshal's house to treat the ailing rose.

Arriving at Laurana's house, Medan rang the silver chimes and stood listening with pleasure to their sweet song as he waited for a response.

An elf answered the door, bowed politely. Medan looked at him intently.

"Kelevandros, isn't it?" he asked.

"Yes, Marshal," the elf returned.

"I came to see—"

"Who is it, Kelevandros?" Laurana appeared, walking down the hallway. "Ah, Marshal Medan. Welcome to my home. Please come in. Will you take some refreshment?"

"Thank you, madam, but I cannot stay," Medan said politely. "We have had reports that a band of rebels are operating in the wilderness not far from here. One of my own men was savagely attacked." He eyed her closely. "The rebels have no love for the royal family, considering them to be collaborators. If, as you say, you have no influence over these rebels—"

"I live a quiet and retired life, Marshal," Laurana said. "I go nowhere except to the palace to visit my son. Yet I find myself constantly under suspicion. My first love and loyalty are to my homeland and my people."

"I am aware of that fact, madam," Medan said with a cool smile. "Therefore, madam, until we have caught these rebels, it is not safe for you to leave the confines of your house. I must ask that you and those you care about remain close to home. You have permission to visit the palace, naturally, but I must prohibit trips to other places in the realm."

"Am I a prisoner in my house, then, Marshal?" Laurana demanded.

"I do this for your own protection, madam," Medan said. He reached out his hand to draw near one of the purple blossoms, inhaled its sweet fragrance. "My commendations on this beautiful lilac bush. I have never known one to bloom so long past spring. Good-day to you, Queen Mother."

"And to you, Marshal Medan," Laurana said.

"How I detest this game," said Medan to himself. Making his solitary way back to his own dwelling, he could smell the lilac's perfume.

"How I hate this game," Laurana said, shutting the door and leaning her head with its crown of golden hair against it.

The waterfall played sweet and gentle music and Laurana listened to its song, let the melody soothe her, restore her to her customary hopefulness. She was not one to give way to despair. She had walked in darkness, the greatest darkness the world had known. She had come face-to-face with the dread goddess Takhisis. She had seen love surmount the darkness, love triumph. She believed that even the darkest night must eventually give way to the dawn.

She held fast to that belief through all the sorrows and travails of her life, through the loss of her son to the political machinations of her own people, through the death of her beloved husband, Tanis, who had died defending the High Clerist's Tower against the Dark Knights, died of a sword thrust in the back. She grieved his loss, she missed him sorely, she established a shrine to him in her heart, but his death did not bring about her own. She did not bury her heart in his grave. To do so would have been to deny his life, to undo all the good that he had done. She continued to fight for the causes both of them had championed.

Some people took exception to this. They thought she should have clothed herself in black and retired from the world. They took offense that she should laugh and smile, or listen with pleasure to the minstrel's song.

"It is so sad," they would say. "Your husband died such a senseless death."

"Tell me, sir," Laurana would reply, or, "Tell me, madam. Tell me what you consider to be a *sensible* death?"

Smiling to herself at their discomfiture, Laurana heard, in her heart, Tanis's laughter. There had been a time, shortly after his death, when she could hear his voice and sense his presence watching over her, not protectively, but supporting, reassuring. She had not felt his presence, however, in a long, long time. She could only assume that he had passed on to the next stage on life's journey. She was not saddened or sorrowful. She would meet him when it was time for her to depart this life. They would find each other, though all eternity might stand between them. Meanwhile, the dead did not need her. The living did.

"My lady," said Kelevandros softly, "do not let the marshal's threats upset you. We will outwit him. We have always done so."

Laurana lifted her head and smiled. "Yes, we will. How fortunate that you had returned from your mission, Kelevandros. Medan might have noted your absence, and that would have made things awkward. We must take extra precautions from now on. Gilthas reports that the dwarven tunnels are near completion. You will use that route now. It will take you out of your way, but it will be safer. Kalindas! You should not be out of bed!"

The elf stood swaying unsteadily in the doorway. His head was swathed in bandages, he was so pale that his skin had a translucent quality. Laurana could see the blue veins in his face. Kelevandros came to his brother's aide, put his arm around him, assisted him to a couch. He eased his brother down gently, all the while scolding Kalindas roundly for leaving his bed and causing their mistress concern.

"What happened to me?" Kalindas asked dazedly.

"You don't remember?" Laurana asked.

"Nothing!" He put his hand to his head.

"Kelevandros," Laurana said sharply, "go to the front door. Make certain that Marshal Medan remembered to leave."

"Birds sing in the trees," Kelevandros reported on his return. "The bees buzz among the flowers. No one is about."

"Now, Kalindas"—Laurana turned to him—"do you remember guiding Master Palin, Gerard, and the kender to the meeting with the griffon?"

Kalindas considered. "Vaguely, madam."

"You were attacked while you were in the wilderness," said Laurana, readjusting the bandages on the young elf's head. "We have been very worried about you. When you didn't return, I asked the Lioness to send her people to search for you. The rebels found you lying wounded in the forest. They brought you back yesterday. Why did you rise? Do you need anything?"

"No, madam, thank you," said Kalindas. "Forgive me for causing you alarm. I heard the marshal's voice and thought perhaps you might stand in need of me. I fancied myself well enough to leave my bed. I was mistaken, it seems."

Kelevandros eased his injured brother to a more comfortable position on the couch, while Laurana spread her own shawl over Kalindas to keep him warm.

"You have endured enough from Medan and his men," Laurana said, her voice cool with anger. "You are fortunate you weren't killed!"

"They had no need to kill me," Kalindas said bitterly. "They must have struck me from behind. Did Master Palin and the kender escape safely with the magical device?"

"We believe so. The rebels found no trace of them, and we have received no reports that they were captured."

"What about the Solamnic?"

"The Lioness reported signs of a fight. Two of the Neraka Knights were killed. They could not find Gerard's body and so they assume that he was made prisoner." Laurana sighed. "If that is true, I could almost wish him dead. The rebels have their spies in the army trying to discover information about him. He is not in prison, that much we know, and that is all we know.

"As for Palin, Kelevandros has just returned from a meeting with the griffons, who arrived bearing a message, which I hope is from Palin."

"I have it here, madam," said Kelevandros. He removed a roll of parchment from his boot, handed the roll to Laurana.

"Are you certain you are all right?" she asked Kalindas, accepting the scroll. "Shall I call for a glass of wine?"

"Please read your letter, Madam," Kalindas said. "Do not worry about me."

After another worried glance, Laurana went to her writing desk and sat down. Kelevandros lit a candle for her, brought it to her desk. She unrolled the parchment. It was covered with ink and smelled faintly of lemon. The words written in the letter were inconsequential. A former neighbor told Laurana of the crops that he had planted, how big his children were growing, how he'd recently purchased a fine horse at the Midyear Day's Fair. He inquired after her health, hoped she was well.

Laurana held the parchment above the candle's flame, taking care not to hold it too near, taking care not to burn the paper or singe it. Slowly, more writing began to appear on the parchment, words written in between the lines of words written in ink. She passed the paper back and forth above the flame until the hidden message written on the parchment was revealed.

Placing it on the desk, she read the missive silently, to herself. The handwriting was not Palin's. Laurana was puzzled as to who had written the letter, looked to see the signature on the bottom.

"Ah, Jenna," she murmured.

She read on, growing more amazed with each line.

"What is it, madam?" Kalindas asked, alarmed. "What has happened?"

"Strange," she murmured. "So very strange. I cannot believe this. Going back in time to find the past no longer exists. I don't understand."

She continued on. "Tasslehoff missing." She shook her head. "He did not come here."

She read on. The brothers exchanged glances. A dark line marred the smooth skin of her forehead. Her brows came together. She read to the end of the scroll, stared at it long moments, as if willing it to say something other than what it said, she slowly released the end. The scroll curled in upon itself, hung limply in her hand.

"We are being spied upon, it seems," Laurana said, and her tone was deliberatly even and calm. "Palin and Tasslehoff were chased by a dragon, one of Beryl's minions. Palin believes that the dragon was after the artifact. That means Beryl knows of the artifact's existence and where it is to be found. The Neraka Knights did not stumble across the four of you by accident, Kalindas. You walked into an ambush."

"A spy! In your own house. Perhaps one of us? That is impossible, madam," Kelevandros stated heatedly.

"Indeed, it is," said Kalindas.

"I hope you are right," Laurana said gravely. "An elf who would betray his own people . . ." She shook her head, her tone was sorrowful. "It is hard to believe that such evil could exist. Yet, it has happened before."

"You know that none of us would betray you," Kalindas reiterated, with emphasis.

Laurana sighed. "I don't know what to think. Mistress Jenna suggests that perhaps there is a mentalist among the Neraka Knights, one who has learned to see into our minds and gather our thoughts. What a bitter pass we are come to! We have to set a guard now upon what we think!"

She slipped the message into the girdle of gold she wore around her waist. "Kelevandros, bring me some lemon juice and then ready Brightwing to carry a message to the griffons."

The elf did as he was told, departing on his errands in silence. He exchanged a final glance with his brother before he left. Both noted that Laurana had not answered the question about Palin. She had taken care to change the subject. She did not trust even them, it seemed. A shadow had fallen over their peaceful dwelling place, a shadow that would not soon be lifted.

Laurana's answer to the letter was short.

Tasslehoff is not here. I will watch for him. Thank you for the warning about spies. I will be on my guard.

She rolled the message tightly so that it would fit in the small crystal tube that would be tied to the hawk's leg.

"Forgive me for disturbing you, madam," Kalindas said, "but the pain in my head has increased. Kelevandros told me that the healer spoke of poppy juice. I think that might help me, if my brother would bring it to me."

"I will send for the healer at once," Laurana said, concerned. "Lie here until your brother returns to fetch her for you."

Marshal Medan walked late in his garden. He enjoyed watching the miracle of the night-blooming flowers that shunned the sun and opened their blossoms to the pale moonlight. He was alone. He had dismissed his aide, ordered him to clear out his things. The Solamnic would arrive tomorrow, start upon his new duties.

Medan was pausing to admire a white orchid that seemed to glow in the moonlight, when he heard a voice hissing from the bushes.

"Marshal! It is I!"

"Indeed," said Medan, "and here I thought it was a snake. I am weary. Crawl back under your rock until morning."

"I have important information that cannot wait," the voice said. "Information Beryl will find most interesting. The mage Palin Majere has used the artifact to journey back in time. This is a powerful magical artifact, perhaps the most powerful yet discovered in this world."

"Perhaps." Medan was noncommittal. He had a very low opinion of mages and magic. "Where is this powerful artifact now?"

"I do not know for certain," said the elf. "His letter to my mistress said that the kender had run off with the artifact. Majere believes the kender has gone to the Citadel of Light. He travels there to attempt to recover it."

"At least he did not come back here," Medan said, breathing a sigh of relief. "Good riddance to him and the blasted artifact."

"This information is worth a great deal," the elf said.

"You will be paid. But in the morning," Medan said. "Now be gone before your mistress misses you."

"She will not." The elf sounded smug. "She sleeps soundly. Very soundly. I laced her evening tea with poppy juice."

"I told you to leave," Medan said coldly. "I will deduct a steel piece for every second you remain in my presence. You have lost one already."

He heard a scrabbling sound in the bushes. The marshal waited a moment longer, to be certain the elf was gone. The moon disappeared behind a cloud. The garden was submerged in darkness. The pale glowing orchid vanished from his sight.

It seemed a sign. A portent.

"Only a matter of time," he said to himself. "Days, maybe. Not longer. This night I have made my decision. I have chosen my course. I can do nothing now but wait."

His pleasure in the night destroyed, the marshal returned to his house, forced to fumble his way through the darkness for he could no longer see the path.

26 PAWN TO KING'S KNIGHT FOUR

This day, Gerard would meet with Marshal Medan and be coerced into serving the commander of the Knights of Neraka. This day, Laurana would discover that she harbored a spy, perhaps in her own home. This day, Tasslehoff would discover that it is difficult to live up to what people say about you after you are dead. This day, Mina's army would march deeper into Silvanesti. This day, Silvanoshei was playing a game with his cousin.

Silvanoshei was king of the Silvanesti. He was king of his people, just like the bejeweled and ornately carved bit of alabaster who was king of the *xadrez* board. A silly, inefffectual king, who could only move a single square at a time. A king who had to be protected by his knights and his ministers. Even his pawns had more important work to do than the king.

"My queen takes your rook," said Kiryn, sliding an ornate game piece across the green-and-white marble board. "Your king is doomed. This gives me the game, I think."

"Blast! So it does!" Silvan gave the board an irritated shove, scattering the pieces. "I used to be quite good at *xadrez*. My mother taught me to play. I could even beat Samar on occasion. You are a far worse player than he was. No offense, Cousin."

"None taken," said Kiryn, crawling on the floor to retrieve a foot soldier who had fled the field and taken refuge underneath the bed. "You are preoccupied, that is all. You're not giving the game your complete concentration."

"Here, let me do that," Silvan offered, remorseful. "I was the one who spilled them."

"I can manage—" Kiryn began.

"No, let me do something constructive, at least!" Silvan dived under the table to come up with a knight, a wizard and, after some searching, his beleaguered king, who had sought to escape defeat by hiding behind a curtain.

Silvan retrieved all the pieces, set the board up again.

"Do you want to play another?"

"No, I am sick to death of this game!" Silvan said irritably.

Leaving the gaming table, he walked to the window, stared out it for a few moments, then, restless, he turned away again. "You say I am preoccupied, Cousin. I don't know by what. I don't *do* anything."

He wandered over to a side table on which stood bowls of chilled fruit, nuts, cheese, and a decanter of wine. Cracking nuts, as if he had some grudge against them, he sorted through the shells to find the meats. "Want some?"

Kiryn shook his head. Silvan tossed the shells onto the table, wiped them from his hand.

"I hate nuts!" he said and walked back across the room to the window. "How long have I been king?" he asked.

"Some weeks, Cousin—"

"And during that time, what have I accomplished?"

"It is early days, yet, Cousin—"

"Nothing," Silvan said emphatically. "Not a damn thing. I am not allowed out of the palace for fear I will catch this wasting disease. I am not permitted to speak to my people for fear of assassins. I sign my name to orders and edicts, but I'm never permitted to read them for fear it will fatigue me. Your uncle does all the work."

"He will continue to do it so long as you let him," Kiryn said pointedly. "He and Glaucous."

"Glaucous!" Silvan repeated. Turning, he eyed his friend suspiciously. "You are always on me about Glaucous. I'll have you know that if it were not for Glaucous, I would not know the little I do know about what is happening in my very own kingdom. Look! Look there, now!" Silvan pointed out the window. "Here is an example of what I mean. Something is happening. Something is going on, and will I hear what it is? I will"—Silvan was bitter—"but only if I ask my servants!"

A man dressed in the garb of one of the kirath could be seen running pell-mell across the broad courtyard with its walkways and gardens that surrounded the palace. Once the elaborate gardens had been a favorite place for the citizens of Silvanost to walk, to meet, to have luncheons on the broad green swards beneath the willow trees. Lovers took boats fashioned in the shape of swans out upon the sparkling streams that ran through the garden. Students came with their masters to sit upon the grass and indulge in the philosophical discussions so dear to elves.

That was before the wasting sickness had come to Silvanost. Now many people were afraid to leave their homes, afraid to meet in groups, lest they catch the sickness. The gardens were almost empty, except for a few members of the military, who had just come off-duty and were returning to their barracks.

The soldiers looked in astonishment at the racing kirath, stood aside to let him pass. He paid no heed to them but hurried onward. He ran up the broad marble stairs that led to the palace and vanished from sight.

"There! What did I tell you, Kiryn? Something important has happened," said Silvan, gnawing his lower lip. "And will the messenger come to me? No, he will go straight to your uncle. I am king, not General Konnal!"

Silvan turned from the window, his expression dark and grim. "I am becoming what I most detest. I am becoming my cousin Gilthas. A puppet dancing on another's strings!"

"If you are a puppet, Silvan, then that is because you want to be a puppet," Kiryn said boldly. "The fault is yours, not my uncle's! You have shown no interest in the day-to-day business of the kingdom. You could have read those edicts, but you were too busy learning the newest dance steps."

Silvan looked at him, anger flaring. "How dare you speak to me like that. I am your—" He checked himself. He had been about to say, "your king!" but realized that in view of the conversation, that would sound ridiculous.

Besides, he admitted, Kiryn had spoken nothing more than the truth. Silvan had enjoyed playing at being king. He wore the crown upon his head, but he would not take up the mantle of responsibility and drape it around his shoulders. He drew in a deep breath, let it out. He had behaved like a child, and so he had been treated like a child. But no more.

"You are right, Cousin," Silvan said, his tone calm and even. "If your uncle has no respect for me, why should he? What have I done since I came here but skulk about in my room playing games and eating sweets. Respect must be earned. It cannot be dictated. I have done nothing to earn his regard. I have done nothing to prove to him and to my people that I am king. That ends. Today."

Silvan threw open the huge double doors that led to his chambers, threw them open with such force that they banged back against the walls. The sound startled the guards, who had been dozing on their feet in the quiet, drowsy afternoon. They clattered to attention as Silvan strode out the door and walked right past them.

"Your Majesty!" cried one. "Where are you going? Your Majesty, you should not be leaving your room. General Konnal has ordered . . . Your Majesty!" The guard found he was speaking to the king's back.

Silvan descended the long, broad marble staircase, walking rapidly, with Kiryn at his heels and the guards hastening along behind.

"Silvan!" Kiryn remonstrated, catching up, "I didn't intend that you should take charge this very moment. You have much to learn about Silvanesti and its people. You've never lived among us. You are very young."

Silvan had understood his cousin's intentions quite well. He paid him no heed, but kept walking.

"What I meant," Kiryn continued, dogging Silvan's footsteps, "was that you should take more interest in the daily business of the kingdom, ask questions. Visit the people in their homes. See how we live. There are many of the wise among our people who would be glad to help you learn. Rolan of the kirath is one. Why not seek his advice and counsel? You would find him far wiser than Glaucous, if less pleasing."

Silvan's lips tightened. He walked on. "I know what I am doing," he said.

"Yes, and so did your Grandfather Lorac. Listen to me, Silvan," Kiryn said earnestly. "Don't make the same mistake. Your grandfather's downfall was not the dragon Cyan Bloodbane. Pride and fear were Lorac's downfall. The dragon was the embodiment of his pride and his fear. Pride whispered to Lorac that he was wiser than the wise. Pride whispered that he could flout rules and laws. Fear urged him to act alone, to refuse help, to turn a deaf ear to advice and counsel."

Silvanoshei halted. "All my life, Cousin, I've heard that side of the story, and I have accepted it. I have been taught to be ashamed of my grandfather. But in recent days I've heard another side, a side no one mentions because they find it easy to blame my grandfather for their troubles. The Silvanesti people survived the War of the Lance. They are alive today *because* of my grandfather. If he had not sacrificed himself as he did, you and I would not be standing here discussing the matter. The welfare of the people was Lorac's responsibility. He accepted that responsibility. He saved them, and now instead of being blessed by them he is denigrated!"

"Who told you this, Cousin?" Kiryn asked.

Silvan saw no reason to answer this, and so he turned on his heel and continued walking. Glaucous had known his grandfather. He had been very close to Lorac. Who would know better the truth of the matter?

Kiryn guessed the name Silvan did not speak. He walked a few paces behind his king, said no more.

Silvan and his oddly assorted escort, consisting of his cousin and the clamoring guards, strode rapidly through the corridors of the palace. Silvan passed by magnificent paintings and wondrous tapestries without a glance. His boots rang loudly on the floor, expressive of his haste and his determination. Accustomed only to silence in this part of the palace, the servants came running to see what was amiss.

"Your Majesty, Your Majesty," they murmured, bowing in fluttered confusion and looking at each other askance when he had gone by, as much as to say, "The bird has flown the cage. The rabbit has escaped the warren. Well, well. Not surprising, considering that he is a Caladon."

The king left the royal quarters of the palace, entered the public areas, which were crowded with people: messengers coming and going, lords and ladies of House Royal standing in clusters talking among themselves, people bustling about with ledgers under their arms or scrolls in their hands. Here was the true heart of the kingdom. Here the business of the kingdom was accomplished. Here—on the side of the palace opposite the royal quarters where Silvan resided.

The courtiers heard the commotion, paused and turned to see what was going on, and when they saw it was their king, they were astonished. So astonished that some lords forgot to bow, remembered only belatedly and then because scandalized wives poked them in the ribs.

Silvan noted the difference between the two sides of the palace immediately. His lips tightened. He ignored the courtiers and brushed aside those who tried to speak. Rounding a corner, he approached another set of double doors. Guards stood here, but these guards were alert, not dozing. They came to attention when the king approached.

"Your Majesty," said one, moving as if to block his way. "Forgive me, Sire, but General Konnal has given orders that he is not to be disturbed."

Silvan gazed long at the man, then said, "Tell the general he will be disturbed. His king is here to disturb him."

Silvan enjoyed watching the struggle on the guard's face. The elf had his orders from Konnal, yet here stood his king before him. The guard had a choice to make. He looked at the pale eyes and set jaw of the young king and saw in them the blood line that had ruled Silvanesti for generations. This guard was an older man, perhaps he had served under Lorac. Perhaps he recognized that pale fire. The guard bowed with respect, and, throwing open the doors, announced in firm tones, "His Majesty, the King."

Konnal looked up in amazement. Glaucous's expression was one of astonishment at first, but that swiftly changed to secret pleasure. Perhaps he, too, had been waiting the day when the lion would tear free of his chains. Bowing, Glaucous cast a glance at Silvan that said plainly, "Forgive me, Your Majesty, but I am under the general's control."

"Your Majesty, to what do we owe this honor?" Konnal asked, highly irritated at the interruption. He had obviously received some unsettling news for his face was flushed, his brows contracted. He had to struggle to maintain a show of politeness, and then his voice was cold. Glaucous was disturbed by something as well. His face was grim, he seemed disturbed and anxious.

Silvan did not reply to the general's question. Instead, he turned to the elf of the kirath, who immediately bowed very low.

"You bring news, sir?" the king asked imperiously.

"I do, Your Majesty," said the kirath.

"News of importance to the kingdom?"

The kirath stole a glance at Konnal, who shrugged in response.

"Of the utmost importance, Your Majesty," the kirath replied.

"And you do not bring that news to your king!" Silvan was pale with anger.

The general intervened. "Your Majesty, I would have apprised you of the situation at the proper time. This matter is extremely serious. Immediate action must be taken—"

"So you thought you would tell me of the matter *after* you had taken the action," said Silvan. He looked back at the kirath. "What is your news, sir? No, don't look at him! Tell me! I am your king!"

"A force of Dark Knights has managed to penetrate the shield, Your Majesty. They are inside the borders of Silvanesti and marching toward Silvanost."

"Dark Knights?" Silvan repeated, astonished. "But how . . . ? Are you certain?"

"Yes, Your Majesty," the kirath replied. "I saw them myself. We had received reports of an army of ogres assembling outside the shield. We went to investigate these reports and it was then we discovered this force of about four hundred human soldiers *inside* the shield. The officers are those known to us as the Dark Knights of Takhisis. We recognized their armor. A company of archers, probably mercenaries, marches with them. They have among their number a minotaur, who is second in command."

"Who is their leader?" Silvan asked.

"There is not time for this—" Konnal began.

"I want to know all the details," Silvan stated coldly.

"The leader is very strange, Your Majesty," the kirath replied. "She is a human female. That in itself is not surprising, but this leader is a child, even among their kind. She cannot be more than eighteen human years, if she is that. Yet she is a Knight, and she is their commander. She wears the black armor, and the soldiers defer to her in everything."

"That is odd," said Silvan, frowning. "I can hardly believe it. I am familiar with the structure of the Dark Knights, who now call themselves Knights of Neraka. I have never heard of a person that young being made a Knight, much less an officer."

Silvan shifted his gaze to Konnal. "What do you plan to do about this threat, General?"

"We will mobilize the army, at once, Your Majesty," Konnal replied stiffly. "I have already given orders to do so. The kirath are following the enemy's progress through our land. We will march out to meet them, and we will repulse them and destroy them. Their force numbers only four hundred. They have no supplies, no means of acquiring supplies. They are cut off, isolated. The battle will not last long."

"Do you have any experience fighting against the Knights of Neraka, General Konnal?" Silvan asked.

Konnal's face darkened. He pursed his lips. "No, Your Majesty. I have not."

"Do you have any experience fighting against any foe other than a dream foe?" Silvan pursued.

Konnal was extremely angry. He went livid. Two bright flaring spots of red stained his cheeks. Jumping to his feet, he slammed his hands on the desk. "You young—"

"General!" Glaucous came back from wherever his thoughts had been wandering to hastily intervene. "He is your king."

Konnal muttered something that sounded like, "He is not *my* king . . ." but he said the words beneath his breath.

"I have fought against these Knights and their forces, General," Silvan continued. "My father and mother fought the Dark Knights in the forests around Qualinesti. I have fought ogres and human brigands. I have fought elves, as you may know, General."

The elves they had fought had been elven assassins sent out before the shield was put in place, sent to murder Porthios and Alhana, who had been declared dark elves, perhaps on the orders of General Konnal.

"Although I myself did not fight," Silvan said, bound to be truthful, "I have been witness to many of these battles. In addition, I have taken part in the meetings during which my father and mother and their officers planned their strategies."

"And yet, the Dark Knights managed to capture Qualinesti, despite your father's best efforts," Konnal said, with a slight curl of his lip.

"They did, sir," Silvan replied gravely, "and that is why I warn you not to underestimate them. I agree with your decision, General. We will send out a force to fight them. I would like to see a map of the area."

"Your Majesty—" Konnal began impatiently, but Silvanoshei was already spreading a map on the desk.

"Where are the Dark Knights, kirath?" Silvan asked.

The kirath stepped forward, indicated with his finger on the map the location of the troops. "As you can see, Your Majesty, by following the Thon-Thalas River, they entered the shield here at the Silvanesti border, where the two intersect. Our reports indicate that they are currently hugging the banks of the Thon-Thalas. We have no reason to believe that they will deviate from that course, which will lead them directly into Silvanost."

Silvan studied the map. "I agree with the kirath that they are not likely to abandon the road that runs alongside the river. To do so would be to risk losing themselves in unfamiliar wilderness. They know they have been seen. They have no reason to hide. They have every reason to move with haste. Their only hope is to attack us while we are presumably reeling from the shock of finding them inside our borders."

He glanced pointedly at Konnal as he said this. The general's face was stone hard, stone cold. He said nothing.

"I suggest that here"—Silvan placed his finger on the map— "would be an excellent location for us to engage them. The enemy will come down out of the hills to find our forces spread out in this valley. They will find themselves trapped between the river on one side and hills on the other, which will make it difficult for them to deploy their forces to best advantage. While the foot soldiers hit them from the front, a company of cavalry can circle around and hit them from the rear. We will gradually close the jaws of our army"—he moved his finger from the footmen in the front to the cavalry in the rear, forming a semicircle—"and swallow them."

Silvan looked up. Konnal stared down at the map, frowning, his hands clasped behind his back.

"That is a good plan, Your Majesty," Glaucous said, sounding impressed.

"General Konnal?" Silvan demanded.

"It might work," General Konnal conceded grudgingly.

"My only concern is that the Knights may hide in the wilderness," Silvan added. "If they do that, we will have a difficult time flushing them out."

"Bah! We will find them," Konnal stated.

"It seems your forces cannot find an immense green dragon, General," Silvan returned. "They've been searching for Cyan Bloodbane for thirty years. If this army of humans was to separate, scatter, we might search for them for a century."

Glaucous laughed, causing the general to cast him a baleful glance.

"I find nothing amusing in any of this," Konnal said. "How did this spawn of evil come through that precious shield of yours, Glaucous? Answer me that?"

"I assure you, General, I do not know," Glaucous said and his face was once again troubled, shadowed. "Not yet, at any rate. There is some fell magic at work here. I can smell it."

"All I smell is the stench of humans," Konnal said bitterly.

"I suggest that we try to capture alive this strange woman-child who leads them. I would like very much to speak to her. Very much indeed," Glaucous added, frowning.

"I agree with Glaucous, General." Silvanoshei turned to Konnal. "You will give the necessary orders. And you will arrange for me to join the army."

"Out of the question," Konnal said shortly.

"I *will* go," said Silvan imperiously, staring intently at the general, daring him to defiance. "You will make the arrangements, sir. Would you have me cower under the bed while my people ride to defend their homes?"

Konnal considered, then he made an ice-rimed bow to the king. "Very well. If your Majesty insists, I will see to it," he said.

Silvan turned on his heel. He left the room in a flurry of robes. Kiryn cast a thoughtful glance at Glaucous, then followed after the king. The guards closed the doors behind them, took up their posts.

"I would be interested to know why you changed your mind, General," Glaucous said quietly.

"Battles are chancy affairs," Konnal replied, shrugging. "No one knows how they will turn out. No one knows who may fall victim to the enemy. If His Majesty were to suffer some hurt—"

"—you would make him a martyr," said Glaucous, "as you made his parents martyrs. You will be blamed. Never doubt it. You should not permit him to go." The mage was grave, withdrawing into himself again. "I have a presentiment that, if he does, something awful will happen."

"Something awful has already happened, in case you hadn't noticed!" Konnal said angrily. "Your magic is failing, Glaucous! Like all the others! Admit it!"

"Your fear is talking, my friend," said Glaucous. "I understand that, and I forgive you for impugning my magical skills. I forgive you this time." His voice softened. "Consider well what I have said. I will endeavor to persuade His Majesty to reconsider riding to war. If I cannot do so, permit him to come, but keep him safe."

"Leave me!" Konnal said harshly. "I do not need a wizard telling me what to do."

"I will leave," said Glaucous, "but remember this, General. You need me. *I* stand between the Silvanesti and the world. Cast me aside, and you cast aside all hope. I am the only one who can save you."

Konnal spoke no word, did not look up.

27 THE TOUCH OF THE DEAD

This evening, while Silvanoshei prepared himself for his first battle, Goldmoon prepared herself as if for battle. For the first time in many long weeks, Goldmoon asked that a hand mirror be brought to her quarters. For the first time since the storm, she lifted the mirror and looked at her face.

Goldmoon had been vain as a girl. She was graced with a rare beauty, the only woman in her tribe to have hair that was like a shimmering tapestry woven of silken threads of sunshine and of moonlight. The chieftain's daughter, she was spoiled, pampered, brought up with an exalted opinion of herself. She spent long hours gazing into the water bowl just to see her own reflection. The young warriors of her tribe adored her. They came to blows for her smile. All except one.

One day, she looked into the eyes of a tall outcast, a young shepherd named Riverwind, and she saw herself in the mirror he held up to her. Looking into his eyes, she saw her vanity, her selfishness. She saw that she was ugly in his eyes, and she was shamed and despairing. For him, for Riverwind, Goldmoon wanted to be beautiful.

So she had come to be beautiful, but only after they had both gone through many trials and travails together, only after they had confronted death fearlessly, clasped in each other's arms. She had been given the blue crystal staff. She had been given the power of bringing the healing love of the gods back into the world.

Children were born to Goldmoon and Riverwind. They worked to unite the contentious tribes of the Plains people. They were happy in their lives and in their children and their friends, the companions of their journeying. They had looked forward to growing old together, to taking their final rest together, to leaving together this plane of existence and moving on to the next, whatever that might be. They were not afraid, for they would be together.

It had not happened that way.

When the gods left following the Chaos War, Goldmoon mourned their absence. She was not one who railed against them. She understood their sacrifice, or thought she did. The gods had left so that Chaos would leave, the world would be at peace. She did not understand, but she had faith in the gods, and so she did what she could to argue against the anger and bitterness that poisoned so many.

She believed in her heart that someday the gods would return. That belief dwindled with the coming of the monstrous dragons, who brought terror and death to Ansalon. Her belief vanished altogether when word came that her beloved Riverwind and one of her daughters had both been slain by the heinous dragon Malys. Goldmoon had longed to die herself. She had fully intended to end her life, but then Riverwind's spirit had come to her.

She must stay, he told her. She must continue her fight to keep hope alive in the world. If she left the world, the darkness would win.

She had not wanted to heed his words, but she had given way.

She had been rewarded. She had been given the gift of healing a second time. Not a blessing from the gods, but a mystical power of the heart which even she did not understand. She brought this gift to others and they had banded together to build the Citadel of Light in order to teach all people how to use the power.

Goldmoon had grown old in the Citadel. She had seen the spirit of her husband as a handsome youth once again. Though he curbed his impatience, she knew he was eager to be gone and that he waited only for her to complete her journey.

Goldmoon lifted the mirror and looked at her face.

Lines of age were gone. Her skin was smooth. Her once sunken cheeks were now plump, the pale skin rose colored. Her eyes had always been bright, shining with the indomitable courage and hope that had made her seem young to her devoted followers. Her lips, thin and gray, were full, tinged with coral. Her hair had remained her one vanity. Though her hair had turned silver white, it remained thick and luxuriant. She reached her hand to touch her hair, a hand that was young and smooth and strong again, and the fingers touched gold and silver strands. But her hair had an odd feel to it. Coarser than she remembered, not as fine.

She knew suddenly why she hated this unasked for, unlooked for, unwanted gift. The face in the mirror was not her face. The face was a memory of her face, and the memory was not her own. The memory was another's. The face was someone's idea of her face. This face was perfect, and her face had not been perfect.

The same was true of her body. Youthful, vigorous, strong, slender waist, full breasts, this body was not the body she remembered. This body was perfect. No aches, no pains, not so much as a torn nail or a blister on her heel.

Her old soul did not fit into this new young flesh. Her old soul had been light and airy, ready to take wing and soar into eternity. That soul had been content to leave behind mundane cares and woes. Now her soul was caged in a prison of flesh and bone and blood, a prison that was making its own demands on her. She did not understand how or why. She could not give reasons. All she knew was that the face in the mirror terrified her.

She laid the mirror down, facedown on the dressing table, and, sighing deeply, prepared to leave the one prison she could leave, desperately wishing all the while that she could leave the other.

Wonder and amazement greeted Goldmoon's appearance in the hall of the Grand Lyceum that night. As she had feared, her transformation was taken for a miracle, a good miracle, a blessed miracle.

"Wait until word spreads!" her pupils whispered. "Wait until the people hear! Goldmoon has conquered age. She has vanquished death! The people will come flocking to our cause now!"

Pupils and masters clustered around her and reached out to touch her. They fell to their knees and kissed her hand. They begged her to grant them her blessing, and they rose to their feet exalted. Only a few looked closely at Goldmoon to see the pain and anguish on the youthful, beautiful face, a face they recognized more by the light in her eyes than by any resemblance to the face of contentment and wisdom they had come to know and revere. Even that light seemed unhealthy, a luster that was the luster of a fever.

The evening was a trial to Goldmoon. They held a banquet in her honor, forced her to sit in a place of honor at the head of the hall. She felt everyone was looking at her, and she was right. Few seemed able to take their eyes off her, and they stared at her until it occurred to them that they were being rude, then they shifted their gazes pointedly in another direction. Goldmoon couldn't decide which was worse. She ate well, much better than usual. Her strange body demanded large quantities of food, but she did not taste any of it. She was doing nothing more than fueling a fire, a fire she feared must consume her.

"In a few days, they will be used to me," she said to herself drearily. "They will cease to notice that I am so terribly altered. *I* will know, however. If I could just understand why this has been done to me."

Palin sat at her right hand, but he was grim and cheerless. He picked at his food and finally pushed most of the meal away uneaten. He paid no attention to conversation but was wrapped in his own thoughts. He was, she guessed, making that journey back through time over and over again in his mind, searching for some clue to its strange conclusion.

Tasslehoff was also out of spirits. The kender sat beside Palin, who kept close watch on him. He kicked the chair rungs and occasionally heaved a doleful sigh. Most of his eating utensils, a salt cellar, and a pepper pot made their way into his pockets, but the borrowing was halfhearted at best, a reflexive action. He was clearly not enjoying himself.

"Will you help me map the hedge maze tomorrow?" asked his neighbor, the gnome. "I have come up with a scientific solution to my problem. My solution requires another person, however, and a pair of socks."

"Tomorrow?" said Tas.

"Yes, tomorrow," repeated the gnome.

Tas looked at Palin. The mage looked at Tas.

"I'll be glad to help," Tas said. He slid off his chair. "Come on, Conundrum. You were going to show me your ship."

"Ah, yes, my ship." The gnome tucked some bread into his pocket for later. "The *Indestructible XVIII*. It's tied up at the dock. At least it was. I'll never forget the surprise I had when I went to board its predecessor, the *Indestructible XVII*, only to discover that it had been woefully misnamed. The committee made sweeping changes to the design, however, and I am quite confident—"

Palin watched Tasslehoff walk away.

"You must talk to him, Goldmoon," the mage said in a low voice. "Convince him he has to go back."

"Go back to his death? How can I ask that of Tas? How could I ask that of anyone?"

"I know," Palin said, sighing and rubbing his temples as if they ached. "Believe me, First Master, I wish there were some other way. All I know is that he's supposed to be dead, and he's not, and the world has gone awry."

"Yet you admit yourself you are not certain that Tasslehoff, either dead or alive, has anything to do with the world's problems."

"You don't understand, First Master—" Palin began wearily.

"You are right. I don't understand. And therefore what would you have me say to him?" she asked sharply. "How can I offer counsel when I do not comprehend what is happening?" She shook her head. "The decision is his alone to make. I will not interfere."

Goldmoon rested her hand on her smooth cheek. She could feel her fingers against her skin, but her skin could not sense the touch of her fingers. She might have been placing her fingers on a waxen image.

The banquet ended, finally. Goldmoon rose to her feet and the others rose in respect. One of the acolytes, an exuberant youngster, gave a cheer. Others picked it up. Soon they were applauding and yelling lustily.

The cheering frightened Goldmoon. The noise will draw attention to us, was her first panicked thought. She wondered at herself a moment later. She'd had the strangest feeling that they were trapped in a house and that something evil was searching for them. The feeling passed, but the cheering continued to jar on her nerves. She lifted her hands to halt the shouting.

"I thank you, my friends. My dear friends," Goldmoon said, moistening lips that were stiff and dry. "I . . . I ask you to keep me in your hearts, to surround me with your good thoughts. I feel I need them."

The people glanced at each other, troubled. This wasn't what any of them had expected to hear her say. They wanted to hear her tell them about the wondrous miracle that had been wrought upon her. How she would perform the same miracles for them. Goldmoon made a gesture of dismissal. People filed out, returning to their work or their studies, glancing back at her often and talking in low voices.

"I beg your pardon for disturbing you, First Master," Lady Camilla said, approaching. Her eyes were cast down. She was trying very hard not to look at Goldmoon's face. "The patients in the hospital have missed you. I was wondering, if you are not too tired, if you would come . . ."

"Yes, assuredly," said Goldmoon readily, glad to have something to do. She would forget herself in her work. She was not in the least fatigued. The strange body was not, that is.

"Palin, would you care to accompany us?" she asked.

"What for? Your healers can do nothing for me," he returned irritably. "I know. They have tried."

"You speak to the First Master, sir," Lady Camilla said in rebuke.

"I am sorry, First Master," Palin said with a slight bow. "Please forgive my rudeness. I am very tired. I have not slept in a long time. I must find the kender, then I plan to go straight to my bed. I bid you a good night."

He bowed and turned and walked away.

"Palin!" Goldmoon called after him, but either he didn't hear or he was ignoring her.

Goldmoon accompanied Lady Camilla to the hospital—a separate building located on the Citadel grounds. The night was cool, unusually cool for this time of year. Goldmoon gazed up at the stars, at the pale moon to which she had never grown truly accustomed but always saw with a sense of shock and unease. This night, she looked at the stars, but they seemed small and distant. For the first time, she looked beyond them, to the vast and empty darkness that surrounded them.

"As it surrounds us," she said, chilled.

"I beg your pardon, First Master," Lady Camilla said. "Were you speaking to me?"

The two women had been antagonists at one point in their lives. When Goldmoon made the decision to build the Citadel of Light on Schallsea, Lady Camilla had been opposed. The Solamnic was loyal to the old gods, the departed gods. She was suspicious and distrustful of this new "power of the heart." Then she had come to witness the tireless efforts of the Citadel's mystics to do good in the world, to bring light to the darkness. She had come to love and to admire Goldmoon. She would do anything for the First Master, Lady Camilla was wont to say, and she had proved that statement, spending an inordinate amount of time and money on a fruitless search for a lost child, a child who had been dear to Goldmoon, but who had gone missing three years earlier, a child whose name no one mentioned, to avoid causing the First Master grief.

Goldmoon often thought of the child, especially whenever she walked along the seashore.

"It wasn't important," Goldmoon said, adding, "You must forgive me, Lady Camilla. I am poor company, I know."

"Not at all, First Master," said Lady Camilla. "You have much on your mind." The two continued their walk to the hospital in silence.

The hospital, located in one of the crystal domes that were the central structures of the Citadel of Light, consisted of a large room filled with beds that stood in straight rows up one side and down the other. Sweet herbs perfumed the air and sweet music added its own healing properties. The healers worked among the sick and injured, using the power of the heart to heal them, a power Goldmoon had discovered and first used to heal the dying dwarf, Jasper Fireforge.

She had performed many miracles since that time, or so people claimed. She had healed those thought to be past hope. She had mended broken bodies with the touch of her hands. She had restored life to paralyzed limbs, brought sight to the blind. Her miracles of healing were as wonderful as those she had performed as a cleric of Mishakal. She was glad and grateful to be able to ease the suffering of others. But the healing had not brought her the same joy she had experienced when the blessing of the healing art came to her as a gift from the god, when she and Mishakal worked in partnership.

A year or so ago, her healing powers had begun to wane. At first, she blamed the loss on her advancing age. But she was not the only one of her healers to experience the diminution of healing power.

"It is as if someone has hung a gauze curtain between me and my patient," one young healer had said in frustration. "I try to draw the curtain aside to reach the patient, but there is another and another. I don't feel as if I can come close to my patients anymore."

Reports had begun coming in from Citadel masters throughout Ansalon, all bearing witness to the same dread phenomenon. Some had blamed it on the dragons. Some had blamed it on the Knights of Neraka. Then they had heard rumors that the Knights' dark mystics were losing their powers, as well.

Goldmoon asked her counselor, Mirror, the silver dragon who was the Citadel's guardian, if he thought that Malys was responsible.

"No, First Master, I do not," Mirror replied. He was in his human form then, a handsome youth with silver hair. She saw sorrow and trouble in his eyes, eyes that held the wisdom of centuries in them. "I have felt my own magical powers start to wane. It is rumored among dragonkind that our enemies are also feeling their powers weaken."

"Then there is some good in this," Goldmoon said.

Mirror remained grave. "I fear not, First Master. The tyrant who feels power slipping away does not let loose. He tightens his grasp."

Goldmoon paused on the threshold of the hospital. The beds were filled with patients, some sleeping, some talking quietly, some reading. The atmosphere was restful, peaceful. Bereft of much of their mystical power, the healers had gone back to the herbal remedies once practiced by healers in the days following the Cataclysm. The smells of sage and rosemary, chamomille and mint spiced the air. Soft music played. Goldmoon felt the soothing influence of the restful solitude, and her heart was eased. Here, perhaps, the healer would herself be healed.

Catching sight of Goldmoon, one of the master healers came forward immediately to welcome her. The welcome was, of necessity, low-key, lest the patients be disturbed by undue commotion or excitement. The healer said how pleased she was that the First Master was returned to them and stared with all her might at Goldmoon's altered face.

Goldmoon said something pleasant and innocuous and turned her face from the amazed scrutiny to look around. She asked after the patients.

"The hospital is quiet this night, First Master," said the healer, leading the way into the ward. "We have many patients, but, fortunately, few who are really worrisome. We have a baby suffering from the croup, a Knight who received a broken leg during a joust, and a young fisherman who was rescued from drowning. The rest of our patients are convalescing."

"How is Sir Wilfer?" Lady Camilla asked.

"The leg is mended, my lady," the healer replied, "but it is still weak. He insists he is ready to be released, and I cannot convince him that he would do better to remain another few days to fully recover. I know that he finds it very dull here, but perhaps if you were to—"

"I will speak to him," said Lady Camilla.

She moved among the rows of beds. Most of the patients came from outside the Citadel, from villages and towns on Schallsea. They knew the elderly Goldmoon, for she often visited their homes. But they did not recognize this youthful Goldmoon. Most thought her a stranger and paid little attention to her, for which she was grateful. At the far end was the cradle with the baby, his watchful mother at his side. He coughed still and whimpered. His face was flushed with fever. The healers were preparing a bowl of herbs to which they would add boiling water. The steam would moisten the lungs and ease the child's cough. Goldmoon drew near, intending to say a few words of comfort to the mother.

As Goldmoon approached the cradle, she saw that another figure hovered over the fretful baby. At first, Goldmoon thought this to be one of the healers. She did not recognize the face, but then she had been absent from them for weeks. Probably this was a new student . . .

Goldmoon's steps slowed. She halted about three beds away from that of the sick child, put out a hand to steady herself upon the wooden bedpost.

The figure was not a healer. The figure was not a student. The figure was not alive. A ghost hovered over the child, the ghost of a young woman.

"If you will excuse me, First Master," said the healer, "I will go see what I can do for this sick child."

The healer walked over to the child. The healer laid her hands upon the baby, but at the same instant, the fleshless hands of the ghost intervened. The ghost grasped the healer's hands.

"Give me the blessed power," the ghost whispered. "I must have it, or I will be cast into oblivion!"

The baby's coughing grew worse. The mother hung over him worriedly. The healer, shaking her head, removed her hands. Her healing touch had failed the baby. The ghost had stolen the energy for herself.

"He should breathe in this steam," the healer said, sounding tired and defeated. "The steam will help keep his lungs clear."

The ghost of the woman drifted away. More insubstantial figures took her place, crowding around the sick baby, their burning eyes staring avidly at the healer. When the healer moved to another bed, they followed her, clinging to her like trailing cobweb. When she put out her hands to try to heal another patient, the dead grasped hold of her, crying and moaning.

"Mine! Mine! Give the power to me!"

Goldmoon staggered. If she had not been holding onto the bedpost, she would have fallen. She closed her eyes tightly shut, hoping the fearful apparitions would disappear. She opened her eyes to see more ghosts. Legions of the dead crowded and jostled each other as each sought to steal for his own the blessed life-giving power that flowed from the healers. Restless, the dead were in constant motion. They passed by Goldmoon like a vast and turbulent river, all flowing in the same direction—north. Those who gathered around the healers were not permitted to linger long. Some unheard voice ordered them away, some unseen hand pulled them back into the water.

The river of dead shifted course, swept around Goldmoon. The dead reached out to touch her, begged her to bless them in their hollow whisperings.

"No! Leave me alone!" she cried, cringing away. "I cannot help you!"

Some of the dead flowed past her, wailing in disappointment. Other ghosts pressed near her. Their breath was cold, their eyes burned. Their words were smoke, their touch like ashes falling on her skin.

Startled faces surrounded her. Faces of the living.

"Healer!" someone was calling. "Come quickly! The First Master!"

The healer was in a flutter. Had she done something to offend the First Master? She had not meant to.

Goldmoon recoiled from the healer in horror. The dead were all around her, pulling on her arm, tugging at her robes. Ghosts surged forward, rushing at her, trying to seize hold of her hands.

"Give us . . ." they pleaded in their terrible whisperings. "Give us what we crave . . . what we must have . . ."

"First Master!" Lady Camilla's voice boomed through the sibiliant hissings of the dead. She sounded panicked. "Please let us help you! Tell us what is wrong!"

"Can't you see them?" Goldmoon cried. "The dead!" She pointed. "There, with the baby! There, with the healer. Here, in front of me! The dead are draining us, stealing our power. Can't you see them?"

Voices clamored around Goldmoon, voices of the living. She could not understand them, they made no sense. Her own voice failed her. She felt herself falling and could do nothing to halt her fall.

She was lying in a bed in the hospital. The voices still clamored. Opening her eyes, she saw the faces of the dead surrounding her.

28 THE DRAGON'S EDICT

General Medan rarely visited his own headquarters in Qualinost. Constructed by humans, the fortress was ugly, purposefully ugly. Squat, square, made of gray sandstone, with barred windows and heavy, iron-bound doors, the fortress was intended to be ugly, intended as an insult to the elves, to impress upon them who was master. No elf would come near it of his own free will, though many had seen the inside of it, particularly the room located far below ground, the room to which they were taken when the order was given to "put them to the question."

Marshal Medan had developed an extreme dislike for this building, a dislike almost as great as that of the elves. He preferred to conduct most of his business from his home where his work area was a shady bower dappled with sunlight. He preferred listening to the song of the lark rather than to the sounds of screams of the tortured, preferred the scent of his roses to that of blood.

The infamous room was not much in use these days. Elves thought to be rebels or in league with the rebels vanished like shadows when the sun hides beneath a cloud before the Neraka Knights could arrest them. Medan knew very well that the elves were being spirited away somehow, probably through underground tunnels. In the old days, when he had first taken on the governing of an occupied land, he would have turned Qualinost upside down and inside out, excavated, probed, brought in Thorn Knights to look for magic, tortured hundreds. He did none of these things. He was just as glad that his Knights arrested so few. He had come to loathe the torturing, the death, as he had come to love Qualinesti.

Medan loved the land. He loved the beauty of the land, loved the peaceful serenity that meandered through Qualinesti as the stream wound its sparkling way through his garden. Alexius Medan did not love the elven people. Elves were beyond his ken, his understanding. He might as well have said that he loved the sun or the stars or the moon. He admired them, as he admired the beauty of an orchid, but he could not love them. He sometimes envied them their long life span and sometimes pitied them for it.

Medan did not love Laurana as a woman, Gerard had come to realize. He loved her as the embodiment of all that was beautiful in his adopted homeland.

Gerard was amazed, entranced, and astounded upon his first entrance into Marshal Medan's dwelling. His amazement increased when the marshal told him, proudly, that he had supervised the design of the house and had laid out the garden entirely to his own liking.

Elves would not have lived happily in the marshal's house, which was too ordered and structured for their tastes. He disliked the elven practice of using living trees as walls and trailing vines for curtains, nor did he want green grasses for his roof. Elves enjoy the murmur and whispers of living walls around them in the night. Medan preferred his walls to allow him to sleep. His house was built of rough-hewn stone. He took care not to cut living trees, an act the elves considered a grievous crime.

Ivy and morning glories clung to the surfaces of the rock walls. The house itself was practically hidden by a profusion of flowers. Gerard could not believe that such beauty could live in the soul of this man, an avowed follower of the precepts of darkness.

Gerard had moved into the house yesterday afternoon. Acting on Medan's orders, the healers of the Nereka Knights had pooled their dwindling energies to restore the Solamnic to almost complete health. His wounds had knit with astonishing rapidity. Gerard smiled to himself, imagining their ire if they knew they were expending their limited energies to heal the enemy.

He occupied one wing, a wing that had been vacant until now, for the marshal had not permitted his aides to live in his dwelling, ever since the last man Medan had retained had been discovered urinating in the fish pond. Medan had transferred the man to the very farthest outpost on the elven border, an outpost built on the edge of the desolate wasteland known as the Plains of Dust. He hoped the man's brain exploded from the heat.

Gerard's quarters were comfortable, if small. His duties thus far—after two days on the job—had been light. Marshal Medan was an early riser. He took his breakfast in the garden on sunny days, dined on the porch that overlooked the garden on days when it rained. Gerard was on hand to stand behind the marshal's chair, pour the marshal's tea, and commiserate with the marshal's concerns over those he considered his most implacable foes: aphids, spider mites, and bagworms. He handled Medan's correspondence, introduced and screened visitors and carried orders from the marshal's dwelling to the detested headquarters building. Here he was looked upon with envy and jealousy by the other knights, who had made crude remarks about the "upstart," the "toady," the "ass-licker."

Gerard was ill-at-ease and tense, at first. So much had happened so suddenly. Five days ago, he had been a guest in Laurana's house. Now he was a prisoner of the Knights of Neraka, permitted to remain alive so long as Medan considered Gerard might be useful to him.

Gerard resolved to stay with the marshal only as long as it took to find out the identity of the person who was spying on the queen mother. When this was accomplished, he would pass the information on to Laurana and attempt to escape. After he had made this decision, he relaxed and felt better.

After Medan's supper, Gerard was dispatched to headquarters again to receive the daily reports and the prisoner list—the record of those who had escaped and who were now wanted criminals. Gerard would also be given any dispatches that had arrived for the marshal from other parts of the continent. Usually, few came, Medan told him. The marshal had no interest in other parts of the continent and those parts had very little interest in him. This evening there was a dispatch, carried in the clawed hands of Beryl's draconian messenger.

Gerard had heard of the draconians—the spawn born years ago of the magically corrupted eggs of good dragons. He had never seen one, however. He decided, on viewing this one—a large Baaz—that he could have gone all his life without seeing one and never missed it.

The draconian stood on two legs like a man, but his body was covered with scales. His hands were large, scaly, the fingers ending in sharp claws. His face was that of a lizard or a snake, with sharp fangs that he revealed in a gaping grin, and a long, lolling tongue. His short, stubby wings, sprouting from his back, were constantly in gentle motion, fanning the air around him.

The draconian was waiting for Gerard inside the headquarters building. Gerard saw this creature the moment he entered, and for the life of him he could not help hesitating, pausing in the doorway, overcome by revulsion. The other Knights, lounging around the room, watched him with knowing smirks that broadened to smug grins when they saw his discomfiture.

Angry with himself, Gerard entered the headquarters building with firm strides. He marched past the draconian, who had risen to his feet with a scrape of his claws on the floor.

The officer in charge handed over the daily reports. Gerard took them and started to leave. The officer stopped him.

"That's for the marshal, too." He jerked a thumb at the draconian, who lifted his head with a leer. "Groul, here, has a dispatch for the marshal."

Gerard steeled himself. With an air of nonchalance, which he hoped didn't look as phony as it felt, he approached the foul creature.

"I am the marshal's aide. Give me the letter."

Groul snapped his teeth together with a disconcerting click and held up the scroll case but did not relinquish it to Gerard.

"My orders are to deliver it to the marshal in person," Groul stated.

Gerard had expected the reptile to be barely sentient, to speak gibberish or, at the best, a corrupt form of Common. He had not expected to find the creature so articulate and, therefore, intelligent. Gerard was forced to readjust his thinking about how to deal with the creature.

"I will give the dispatch to the marshal," Gerard replied. "There have been several attempts on the marshal's life. As a consequence, he does not permit strangers to enter his presence. You have my word of honor that I will deliver it directly into his hands."

"Honor! This is what I think of your honor." Groul's tongue slid out of his mouth, then slurped back, splashing Gerard with saliva. The draconian moved closer to Gerard, clawed feet scraping across the floor. "Listen, Knight," he hissed, "I am sent by the exalted Beryllinthranox. She has ordered me to hand this dispatch to Marshal Medan and to wait for his reply. The matter is one of utmost urgency. I will do as I am ordered. Take me to the marshal."

Gerard could have done as the draconian demanded and saved himself what was probably going to be a world of trouble. He had two reasons for not doing so. First, he fully intended to read the dispatch from the dragon before handing it over to Medan, and that would be difficult to manage with the dispatch clutched firmly in the draconian's claws. The second reason was more subtle. Gerard found this reason incomprehensible, but he felt oddly guided by it. He did not like the thought of the loathsome creature entering the marshal's beautiful house, his clawed feet ripping holes in the ground, tearing up the flower beds, trampling the plants, smashing furniture with his tail, leering and poking, sneering and slavering.

Groul held the scroll in his right hand. The creature wore his sword on his left hip. That meant the draco was right-handed, or so Gerard hoped, though there was always the possibility the creatures were ambidextrous. Resolving to himself that if he lived through this, he would take up a study of the draconian race, Gerard drew his sword with an overdone flourish and jumped at the draconian.

Startled, Groul reacted instinctively, dropping the scroll case to the floor and reaching with his right hand for his sword. Gerard pivoted, stooped down to the floor and snatched up the scroll case. Rising, he drove his shoulder and elbow, with the full weight of his armor, into the midriff of the draconian. Groul went down with a clatter of sword and sheath, his wings flapping wildly, his hands waving as he lost the struggle to retain his balance. He crashed into a bench, smashing it.

The sudden movement and attack on the draconian tore open several of Gerard's wounds. Sucking in his breath against the pain, he glared a moment at the creature floundering on the floor, then turned and, resisting the impulse to see how badly he'd injured himself, started to leave.

Hearing clawed feet scrabbling and a vicious cursing, Gerard wheeled, sword in hand, intending to finish the fight if the creature pursued it. To Gerard's astonishment, three of the Knights of Neraka had drawn their swords and now blocked the draconian's path.

"The marshal's aide is right," said one, an older man, who had served in Qualinesti many years and had even taken an elven wife. "We've heard stories of you, Groul. Perhaps you carry a dispatch from Beryl as you say. Or perhaps the dragon has given orders that you are to 'dispatch' our marshal. I advise you to sit down on what you've left of our bench and wait. If the marshal wants to see you, he'll come himself." ·

Groul hesitated, eyeing the Knights balefully. Two of the guards drew their swords and joined their officers. The draconian cursed, and, with a snarl, sheathed his sword. Muttering something about needing fresh air, he stalked over to the window and stood staring out of it.

"Go along," said the Knight to Gerard. "We'll keep an eye on him."

"Yes, sir. Thank you, sir."

The Knight grunted and returned to his duties.

Gerard left the headquarters with haste. The street on which the building stood was empty. The elves never came anywhere near it voluntarily. Most of the soldiers were either on duty or had just come off duty and were now asleep.

Leaving the street on which the headquarters building was located, Gerard entered the city proper, or rather the city's outskirts. He walked among the city's inhabitants now, and he faced another danger. Medan had advised him to wear his breastplate and helm, make his trip to headquarters before darkness fell. He was conscious of beautiful faces, of almond eyes either staring at him with open, avowed hatred, or purposefully averting their gaze, so as not to disturb the loveliness of the midsummer's twilight by adding his ugly human visage to it.

Gerard was likewise conscious of his strangeness. His body seemed thick and clumsy in comparison to the slender, delicate elven frames; his straw-colored hair, a color not usually seen among elves, was probably regarded as freakish. His scarred and lumpish features, considered ugly by human standards, must be looked upon as hideous by the elves.

Gerard could understand why some humans had come to hate the elves. He felt himself inferior to them in every way— in appearance, in culture, in wisdom, in manner. The only way in which some humans could feel superior to elves was to conquer them, subjugate them, torture and kill them.

Gerard turned onto the road leading to Medan's house. Part of him sighed when he left the streets where the elves lived and worked behind, as if he had awakened from a lovely dream to dreary reality. Part of him was relieved. He did not keep looking constantly over his shoulder to see if someone was sneaking up on him with a knife.

He had a walk of about a mile to reach the marshal's secluded house. The path wound among shimmering aspens, poplars, and rustling willows, whose arms overstretched a bubbling brook. The day was fine, the temperature unusually cool for this time of year, bringing with it the hint of an early fall. Reaching the halfway point, Gerard looked carefully up the path and down the path. He listened intently for the sound of other footfalls. Hearing nothing, seeing nobody, he stepped off the trail and walked to the brook. He squatted down on his haunches as if to drink and examined the scroll case.

It was sealed with wax, but that was easily managed. Removing his knife, he laid the blade upon a flat rock still hot from the afternoon sun. When the metal had heated, Gerard edged the knife blade carefully beneath the wax seal.

He removed the seal intact, placed it on a bit of bark to keep it safe. Gerard eyed the scroll case, started to open it, hesitated.

He was about to read a dispatch intended for his commander. True, Medan was the enemy, he was not really Gerard's commander, but the dispatch was private, meant for Medan only. No honorable man would read another's correspondence. Certainly no Solamnic Knight would stoop so low. The Measure did not countenance the use of spies upon the enemy, deeming them "dishonorable, treacherous." He recalled one paragraph in particular.

Some say that spies are useful, that the information they gather by low and sneaking means might lead us to victory. We knights answer that victory obtained by such means is no victory at all but the ultimate defeat, for if we abandon the principles of honor for which we fight, what makes us better than our enemy?

"What indeed?" Gerard asked himself, the scroll case unopened in his hand. "Nothing, I guess." With a quick twist, he opened the lid and, glancing about the forest one final time, he drew out the parchment, unrolled it, and began to read.

A weakness came over him. His body chilled. He sank down upon the bank, continued reading in disbelief. Completing his perusal, he considered what to do. His first thought was to burn the terrible missive so that it would never reach its destination. He dared not do that, however. Too many people had seen him take it. He thought of burning it and substituting another in its place, but he abandoned that wild idea immediately. He had no parchment, no pen, no ink. And perhaps Medan was familiar with the handwriting of the scribe who penned this message at the dragon's injunction.

No, Gerard reasoned, sick at heart, there was nothing he could do now but deliver the dispatch. To do otherwise would be to put himself in danger, and he might be the only means of thwarting the dragon's evil design.

Medan would be wondering what had become of him. Gerard had already been longer on his daily errand than usual. He hurriedly rolled up the dispatch, thrust it into the tube, carefully replaced the wax seal, and made sure that it was firmly stuck. Thrusting the foul thing in his belt, unwilling to touch it more than necessary, he continued on his way back to the marshal's at a run.

Gerard found the marshal strolling in his garden, taking his exercise after his evening meal. Hearing footsteps along the walkway, the marshal glanced around.

"Ah, Gerard. You are behind your time. I was starting to fear something might have happened to you." The marshal looked intently at Gerard's arm. "Something has happened to you. You are injured."

Gerard glanced down at his shirtsleeve, saw it wet with blood. In his distraction over the dispatch, he'd forgotten his wounds, forgotten the fight with the draconian.

"There was an altercation at headquarters," he said, knowing that Medan would come to hear what had happened. "Here are the daily reports." He placed those upon a table that stood beneath a trellis over which Medan had patiently trained grapevines to grow, forming a green and leafy bower. "And there is this dispatch, which comes from the dragon Beryl."

Medan took the dispatch with a grimace. He did not immediately open it. He was much more interested in hearing about the fight. "What was the altercation, Sir Gerard?"

"The draconian messenger insisted on bringing the dispatch to you himself. Your Knights did not think that this was necessary. They insisted he remain there to await your response."

"Your doing, I think, sir," said Medan with a smile. "You acted rightly. I am wary of Groul. Who knows what he is thinking in that lizard brain of his? He is not to be trusted."

He turned his attention to the dispatch. Gerard saluted, started to leave.

"No, no. You might as well wait. I will have to draft an answer. . . ." He fell silent, reading.

Gerard, who knew every line because he felt each one burned on his brain, could follow Medan's progress through the dispatch by watching the expression on his face. Medan's lips tightened, his jaw set. If he had appeared happy, overjoyed, Gerard had determined to kill the marshal where he stood, regardless of the consequences.

Medan was not overjoyed, however. Far from it. His face lost its color, took on a sallow, grayish hue. He completed reading the dispatch and then, with studied deliberation, read it through again. Finished, he crushed it in his hand and, with a curse, hurled it to the walkway.

Arms folded across his chest, he turned his back, stared grimly at nothing until he had regained some measure of his composure. Gerard stood in silence. Now might have been a politic time to absent himself, but he was desperate to know what Medan intended to do.

At length, the marshal turned around. He glanced down at the crumpled piece of parchment, glanced up at Gerard. "Read it," he said.

"Sir." Gerard flushed. "It's not meant for—"

"Read it, damn you!" Medan shouted. Calming himself with an effort, he added, "You might as well. I must think what to do, what to say to the dragon in reply and how to say it. Carefully," he admonished himself softly. "I must proceed carefully, or all is lost!"

Gerard picked up the dispatch and smoothed it out.

"Read it aloud," Medan ordered. "Perhaps I misread it. Perhaps there was some part of it I misunderstood." His tone was ironic.

Gerard skipped through the formal address, came to the body of the text.

" 'It has come to my attention,' " he read, " 'through one who is in sympathy with my interests, that the outlawed sorcerer Palin Majere has discovered a most valuable and wondrous magical artifact while he was unlawfully in my territory. I consider that the artifact is therefore mine. I must and I will have it.

" 'Informants tell me that Palin Majere and the kender have fled with the artifact to the Citadel of Light. I give the elf king, Gilthas, three days to recover the device and the culprits who carry it and another three days to deliver them up to me.

" 'In addition, the elf king will also send me the head of the elf woman, Lauranalanthalas, who harbored the sorcerer and the kender in her home and who aided and abetted them in their escape.

" 'If, at the end of six days, I have not received the head of this traitor elf woman and if the artifact and those who stole it are not in my hands, I will order the destruction of Qualinesti to commence. Every man, woman, and child in that wretched nation shall be put to sword or flame. None shall survive. As for those in the Citadel of Light who dare harbor these criminals, I will destroy them, burn their Citadel to the ground, and recover the magical device from amidst the bones and ashes.' "

Gerard was thankful he'd read this once. Had he not been prepared, he would not have been able to read it as calmly as he managed. As it was, his voice caught in his throat and he was forced to cover his emotions with a harsh cough. He finished reading and looked up to find Medan observing him closely.

"Well, what do you think of this?" Medan demanded.

Gerard cleared his throat. "I believe that it is presumptuous of the dragon to give you orders, my lord. The Knights of Neraka are not her personal army."

Medan's grim expression relaxed. He almost smiled. "That is an excellent argument, Gerard. Would it were true! Unfortunately, the High Command crawled on their bellies before the great dragons years ago."

"She can't mean this, my lord," Gerard said cautiously. "She wouldn't do this. Not an entire race of people—"

"She could and she will," Medan replied grimly. "Look what she did to Kenderhome. Slaughtered the little nuisances by the thousands. Not that kender are any great loss, but it goes to prove that she will do what she says."

Gerard had heard other Solamnic Knights say the same thing about the slaughter of the kender, and he recalled laughing with them. He knew some Solamnic Knights who would not be displeased to see the elves depart this world. We consider ourselves so much better, so much more moral and more honorable than the Dark Knights, Gerard said to himself. In reality, the only difference is the armor. Silver or black, it masks the same prejudices, the same intolerance, the same ignorance. Gerard felt suddenly, deeply ashamed.

Medan had begun to pace the walkway. "Damn the blasted elves! All these years I work to save them, and now it is for nothing! Damn the queen mother anyhow! If she had only listened to me! But, no. She must consort with rebels and the like, and now what comes of it? She has doomed herself and her people. Unless . . ."

He paused in his pacing, hands clasped behind his back, brooding, his thoughts turned inward. His robes, of elven make, elven cut, and elven design, fell loosely about his body. The hem, trimmed with silk ribbon, brushed his feet. Gerard remained silent, absorbed with his own thoughts—a confusion of sickening rage against the dragon for wanting to destroy the elves and rage at himself and his own kind for standing idly by and doing nothing all these years to stop her.

Medan raised his head. He had made a decision. "The day has arrived sooner than I anticipated. I will not be a party to genocide. I have no compunction about killing another warrior in battle, but I will not butcher helpless civilians who have no way to fight back. To do so is the height of cowardice, and such wanton slaughter would break the oath I swore when I became a Knight. Perhaps there is a way to stop the dragon. But I will require your help."

"You have it, my lord," said Gerard.

"You will have to trust me." Medan raised an eyebrow.

"And you will have to trust me, my lord," said Gerard, smiling.

Medan nodded. A man of quick and decisive actions, he did not waste breath in further talk but seated himself at the table. He reached for pen and ink. "We must stall for time," he said, writing rapidly. "You will deliver my answer to the draconian Groul, but he must never reach the dragon. Do you understand?"

"Yes, sir," said Gerard.

Medan completed his writing. He sprinkled sand on the paper, to help the ink dry, rolled it and handed it to Gerard. "Put that in the same scroll case. No need to seal it. The message states that I am the Exalted One's Obedient Servant and that I will do her bidding."

Medan rose to his feet. "When you have completed your task, go straight to the Royal Palace. I will leave orders that you are to be admitted. We must make haste. Beryl is a treacherous fiend, not to be trusted. She may have already decided to act on her own."

"Yes, my lord," Gerard said. "And where will you be, my lord? Where can I find you?"

Medan smiled grimly. "I will be arresting the queen mother."

Marshal Medan walked along the path that led through the garden to the main dwelling of Laurana's modest estate. Night had fallen. He had brought a torch to light his way. The flame singed the hanging flowers as he passed beneath them, caused leaves to blacken and curl. Bugs flew into the fire. He could hear them sizzle.

The marshal was not wearing his elven robes. He was accoutered in his full ceremonial armor. Kelevandros, who answered Medan's resounding knock upon the door, was quick to note the change. He eyed the marshal warily.

"Marshal Medan. Welcome. Please enter. I will inform madam that she has a visitor. She will see you in the arboretum, as usual."

"I prefer to remain where I am," said the marshal. "Tell your mistress to meet me here. Tell her," he added, his voice grating, "that she should be dressed for travel. She will need her cloak. The night air is chill. And tell her to make haste."

He looked intently and constantly about the garden, paying particular attention to the parts of the garden hidden in shadow.

"Madam will want to know why," Kelevandros said, hesitating.

Medan gave him a shove that sent him staggering across the room. "Go fetch your mistress," he ordered.

"Travel?" Laurana said, astonished. She had been sitting in the arboretum, pretending to listen to Kalindas read aloud from an ancient elven text. In reality, she had not heard a word. "Where am I going?"

Kelevandros shook his head. "The marshal will not tell me, Madam. He is acting very strangely."

"I don't like this, Madam," Kalindas stated, lowering the book. "First imprisonment in your house, now this. You should not go with the marshal."

"I agree with my brother, Madam," Kelevandros added. "I will tell him you are not well. We will do what we have talked about before. This night, we will smuggle you out in the tunnels."

"I will not," said Laurana determinedly. "Would you have me flee to safety while the rest of my people are forced to stay behind? Bring my cloak."

"Madam," Kelevandros dared to argue, "please—"

"Fetch me my cloak," Laurana stated. Her tone was gentle but firm, brooked no further debate.

Kelevandros bowed silently.

Kalindas went to fetch the cloak. Kelevandros returned with Laurana to the front door, where Marshal Medan had remained standing.

Sighting her, he straightened. "Lauranalanthalas of the House of Solostaran," he said formally, "you are under arrest. You will surrender yourself peacefully to me as my prisoner."

"Indeed?" Laurana was quite calm. "What is the charge? Or is there a charge?" she asked. She turned so that Kalindas could place the cloak about her shoulders.

The elf started to do so, but Medan took the cloak himself. The marshal, his expression grave, settled the cloak around Laurana's shoulders.

"The charges are numerous, Madam. Harboring a human sorcerer who is wanted by the Gray Robes, concealing your knowledge of a valuable magical artifact, which the sorcerer had in his possession when, by law, all magical artifacts located in Qualinesti are to be handed over to the dragon. Aiding and abetting the outlaw sorcerer in his escape from Qualinesti with the artifact."

"I see," said Laurana.

"I tried to warn you, madam, but you would not heed me," Medan said.

"Yes, you did try to warn me, marshal, and for that I am grateful." Laurana fastened the cloak around her neck with a jeweled pin. Her hands were steady, did not tremble. "And what is to be done with me, Marshal Medan?"

"My orders are to execute you, madam," said Medan. "I am to send your head to the dragon."

Kalindas gasped. Kelevandros gave a hoarse shout and lunged at Medan, grappling for his throat with his bare hands.

"Stop, Kelevandros!" Laurana ordered, throwing herself between the elf and the marshal. "This will not help! Stop this madness!"

Kelevandros fell back, panting, glaring at Medan with hatred. Kalindas took hold of his brother's arm, but Kelevandros angrily shook him off.

"Come, madam," said Marshal Medan. He offered Laurana his arm. The torch smoked and sputtered. Orchids, hanging over the door, shriveled in the heat.

Laurana rested her hand on the marshal's arm. She looked back at the two brothers, standing, white-faced with shadowed eyes, watching her being led away to her death.

Which one? she asked herself, sick at heart. Which one?

29 PRISON OF AMBER

The midsummer's morning dawned unusually cool in Silvanesti.

"A fine day for battle, gentlemen," said Mina to her assembled officers.

Galdar led the cheers, which shook the trees along the riverbank, caused the leaves of the aspens to tremble.

"So may our valor set the elves to trembling," said Captain Samuval. "A great victory will be ours this day, Mina! We cannot fail!"

"On the contrary," said Mina coolly. "This day we will be defeated."

Knights and officers stared at her blankly. They had seen her perform miracle after miracle, until the miracles were now stacked up one on top of the other like crockery in a neat housewife's cupboard. The idea that these miracles were to now come spilling out of the cupboard, come crashing down around their ears was a catastrophe not to be believed. So they did not believe it.

"She's joking," said Galdar, attempting to pass it off with a laugh.

Mina shook her head. "We will lose the battle this day. An army of a thousand elven warriors has come to test us. We are outnumbered over two to one. We cannot win this battle."

The Knights and officers looked at each other uneasily. They looked at Mina grimly, doubtfully.

"But though we lose the battle this day," Mina continued, smiling slightly, her amber eyes lit from behind with an eerie glow that made the faces captured in them glitter like tiny stars, "this day we will win the war. But only if you obey me without question. Only if you follow my orders exactly."

The men grinned, relaxed. "We will, Mina," several shouted, and the rest cheered.

Mina was no longer smiling. The amber of her eyes flowed over them, congealed around them, froze them where they stood. "You will obey my orders, though you do not understand them. You will obey my orders, though you do not like them. You will swear this to me on your knees, swear by the Nameless God who is witness to your oath and who will exact terrible revenge upon the oath breaker. Do you so swear?"

The Knights sank down on their knees in a semicircle around her. Removing their swords, they held them by the blade, beneath the hilt. They lifted their swords to Mina. Captain Samuval went down on his knees, bowed his head. Galdar remained standing. Mina turned her amber eyes on him.

"On you, Galdar, more than on anyone else rests the outcome of this battle. If you refuse to obey me, if you refuse to obey the God who gave you back your warrior's arm, we are lost. All of us. But you, most especially."

"What is your command, Mina?" Galdar asked harshly. "Tell me first, that I may know."

"No, Galdar," she said gently. "You either trust me or you do not. You put your faith in the God or you do not. Which will it be?"

Slowly, Galdar knelt down upon his knees before her. Slowly he drew his sword from its scabbard and slowly held it up as did the others. He held it in the hand the God had returned to him.

"I so swear, Mina!" he said.

The rest spoke as one.

"I so swear!"

The battleground was a large field located on the banks of the Thon-Thalas River. The elf soldiers trampled tender stalks of wheat beneath their soft leather boots. The elf archers took their places amid tall stands of green, tasseled corn. General Konnal set up his command tent in a peach orchard. The arms of a great windmill turned endlessly, creaking in the wind that had a taste of autumn's harvest in it.

There would be a harvest on this field, a dread harvest, a harvest of young lives. When it was over, the water that ran at the feet of the great windmill would run red.

The field stood between the approaching enemy army and the capital of Silvanost. The elves put themselves in harm's way, intending to stop the army of darkness before it could reach the heart of the elf kingdom. The Silvanesti were outraged, insulted, infuriated. In hundreds of years, no enemy had set foot on this sacred land. The only enemy they had fought had been one of their own making, the twisted dream of Lorac.

Their wonderful magical shield had failed them. They did not know how or why, but most of the elves were convinced that it had been penetrated by an evil machination of the Knights of Neraka.

"To that end, General," Glaucous was saying, "the capture of their leader is of the utmost importance. Bring this girl in for interrogation. She will tell me how she managed to thwart the shield's magic."

"What makes you think she will tell you?" Konnal asked, annoyed at the wizard and his harping on this subject alone.

"She may refuse, General," Glaucous assured him, "but she will not have any choice in the matter. I will use the truth-seek on her."

The two were in the general's command tent. They had met early that morning with the elf officers. Silvan had explained his strategy. The officers had agreed that the tactics were sound. Konnal had then dismissed them to deploy their men. The enemy was reported to be about five miles away. According to the scouts, the Knights of Neraka had halted to arm themselves and put on their armor. They were obviously preparing for battle.

"I cannot spare the men who would be required to seize a single officer, Glaucous," the general added, recording his orders in a large book. "If the girl is captured in battle, fine. If not . . ." He shrugged, continued writing.

"I will undertake her capture, General," Silvan offered.

"Absolutely not, Your Majesty," Glaucous said hurriedly.

"Give me a small detachment of mounted warriors," Silvan urged, coming to stand before the general. "We will circle around their flank, come in from behind. We will wait until the battle is fairly joined and then we will drive through the lines in a wedge, strike down her bodyguard, capture this commander of theirs and carry her back to our lines."

Konnal looked up from his work.

"You said yourself, Glaucous, that discovering the means by which these evil fiends came through the shield would be useful. I think His Majesty's plan is sound."

"His Majesty puts himself in too much danger," Glaucous protested.

"I will order members of my own bodyguard to ride with the king," Konnal said. "No harm will come to him."

"It had better not," Glaucous said softly.

Ignoring his adviser, Konnal walked over to the map, stared down at it. He laid his finger on a certain point. "My guess is that the enemy commander will take up her position here, on this rise. That is where you should look for her and her bodyguard. You can circle around the battle by riding through this stand of trees, emerging at this point. You will be practically on top of them. You will have the element of surprise, and you should be able to strike before they are aware of you. Does Your Majesty agree?"

"The plan is an excellent one, General," said Silvan with enthusiasm.

He was to wear new armor, beautifully made, wonderfully designed. The breastplate bore the pattern of a twelve-pointed star, his helm was formed in the likeness of two swan's wings done in shining steel. He carried a new sword, and he now knew how to use one, having spent many hours each day since his arrival in Silvanost studying with an expert elf swordsman, who had been most complimentary on His Majesty's progress. Silvan felt invincible. Victory would belong to the elves this day, and he was determined to play a glorious part, a part that would be celebrated in story and song for generations to come.

He left, ecstatic, to go prepare for battle.

Glaucous lingered behind.

Konnal had returned to his work. Glaucous made no sound, but Konnal sensed his presence, as one senses hungry eyes watching one in a dark forest.

"Begone. I have work to do."

"I am going. I only want to emphasize what I said earlier. The king must be kept safe."

Konnal sighed, looked up. "If he comes to harm, it will not be through me. I am not an ogre, to kill one of my own kind. I spoke in haste yesterday, without thinking. I will give my guards orders to watch over him as if he were my own son."

"Excellent, General," said Glaucous with his beautiful smile. "I am much relieved. My hopes for this land and its people depend on him. Silvanoshei Caladon must live to rule Silvanesti for many years. As did his grandfather before him."

"Are you certain you will not reconsider and ride with us, Kiryn? This will be a battle celebrated for generations to come!"

Silvan fidgeted under the ministrations of his squire, who was attempting to buckle the straps of the king's damascened armor and having a difficult time of it. The leather was stiff and new, the straps refused to ease into place. Silvan's constant shifting and moving did not help matters.

"If Your Majesty would please hold still!" the exasperated squire begged.

"Sorry," Silvan said and did as he was told, for a few seconds at any rate. Then he turned his head to look at Kiryn, who sat on a cot, watching the proceedings. "I could lend you some armor. I have another full suit."

Kiryn shook his head. "My uncle has given me my assignment. I am to carry dispatches and messages between the officers. No armor for me. I must travel light."

A trumpet call sounded, causing Silvan to give such a start of excitement that he undid a good quarter of an hour's worth of work. "The enemy is in sight! Hurry, you oaf!"

The squire sucked in a breath and held his tongue. Kiryn added his assistance, and between the two of them the king was readied for battle.

"I would embrace you for luck, Cousin," said Kiryn, "but I would be bruised for a week. I do wish you luck, though," he said more seriously as he clasped Silvan's hand in his, "though I hardly think you'll need it."

Silvan was grave, solemn for a moment. "Battles are chancy things, Samar used to say. One man's bravery may save the day. One man's cowardice may spoil it. That is what I fear most, Cousin. More than death. I fear that I will turn coward and flee the field. I've seen it happen. I've seen good men, brave men fall to their knees and tremble and weep like little children."

"Your mother's courage flows in your veins along with your father's fortitude," Kiryn reassured him. "You will not fail their memories. You will not fail your people. You will not fail yourself."

Silvan drew in a deep breath of the flower-scented air, let it out slowly. The sunshine was like warm honey spilling from the sky. All around him were familiar sounds and smells, sounds of battle and war, smells of leather and sweat, sounds and smells he had been born to, sounds and smells he had come to loathe but which, oddly, he had also come to miss. His playground had been a battlefield, a command tent his cradle. He was more at home here, he realized, than he was in his fine castle.

Smiling ruefully, he walked out of his tent, his armor of silver and gold gleaming brightly, to be greeted by the enthusiastic cheers of his people.

The battle plans for both sides were simple. The elves formed ranks across the field, with the archers in the rear. The army of the Knights of Neraka extended their thinner lines among the trees of the low hillside, hoping to tempt the elves into attacking rashly, attacking up hill.

Konnal was far too smart to fall for that. He was patient, if his troops were not, and he kept fast hold of them. He had time, all the time in the world. The army of the Knights of Neraka, running low on supplies, did not.

Toward midafternoon, a single braying trumpet sounded from the hills. The elves gripped their weapons. The army of darkness came out of the hills on the run, shouting insults and defiance to their foes. Arrows from both sides arced into the skies, forming a canopy of death above the heads of the armies, who came together with a resounding crash.

When battle was joined, Silvan and his mounted escort galloped into the woods on the west side of the battlefield. Their small force screened by the trees, they rode around the flank of their own army, crossed over enemy lines, and rode around the enemy's flank. No one noticed them. No one shouted or called out. Those fighting saw only the foe before them. Arriving at a point near the edge of the field, Silvan called a halt, raising his hand. He rode cautiously to the edge of the forest, taking the commander of the general's guard with him. The two looked out upon the field of battle.

"Send out the scouting party," Silvan ordered. "Bring back word the moment they have located the enemy commanders."

The scouts proceeded ahead through the woods, edging closer to the field of battle. Silvan waited, watching the progress of the war.

Combat was hand to hand. The archers on both sides were now effectively useless, with the armies locked together in a bloody embrace. At first, Silvan could make nothing of the confusion he looked upon, but after watching several moments, it seemed to him that the elf army was gaining ground.

"A glorious victory already, Your Majesty," his commander said in triumph. "The vermin are falling back!"

"Yes, you are right," Silvan replied, and he frowned.

"Your Majesty does not seem pleased. We are crushing the human insects!"

"So it would seem," said Silvan. "But if you look closely, Commander, you will note that the enemy is not running in panic. They are falling back, certainly, but their movements are calculated, disciplined. See how they hold their line? See how one man steps in to take the place if another falls? Our troops, on the other hand," he added with disgust, "have gone completely berserk!"

The elves, seeing the enemy in retreat, had broken ranks and were flailing at the enemy in a murderous rage, heedless of the shouts and cries of their commanders. Competing trumpet calls sounded over the screams of the wounded and dying, fighting their own battle. Silvan noted that the Dark Knights listened closely for their trumpet calls and responded immediately to the brayed commands, while the maddened elves were deaf to all.

"Still," Silvan said, "we cannot help but win, seeing that we outnumber them so greatly. The only way could possibly lose would be to turn our swords on ourselves. I will have a few words with General Konnal on my return, however. Samar would never permit such a lack of discipline."

"Your Majesty!" One of the scouts returned, riding at a full gallop. "We have located the officers!"

Silvan turned his horse's head, rode after the scout. They had advanced only a short way through the forest, before they met up with another scout, who had been left to keep watch.

He pointed. "There, Your Majesty. On that rise. They're easy to see."

So they were. A huge minotaur, the first Silvan had ever seen, stood upon the rise. The minotaur wore the regalia of a Knight of Neraka. A massive sword was buckled at his side. He was watching the progress of the battle intently. Twelve more Knights, mounted on horses, were also observing the battle. Beside them stood the standard-bearer, holding a flag that might have once been white, but was now a dirty brownish red color, as if it had been soaked in blood. An aide stood nearby, holding the reins of a magnificent red horse.

"Surely the minotaur is their commander," Silvan said. "We were misinformed."

"No, Your Majesty," the scout replied. "See there, behind the minotaur. That is the commander, the one with the blood-red sash."

Silvan could not see her, at first, and then the minotaur stepped to one side to confer with another of the Knights. Behind him, a slight, delicate human female stood on a knoll, her gaze fixed with rapt intensity upon the battle. She carried her helm beneath her arm. A morning star hung from a belt at her waist.

"*That* is their commander?" Silvan said, amazed. "She does not look old enough to be attending her first dance, much less leading seasoned troops into battle."

As if she had heard him, though that was impossible, for she was a good forty yards distant, she turned her face toward him. He felt himself suddenly exposed to her view, and he backed up hurriedly, keeping to the deep shadows of the dense woods.

She stared in his direction for long moments, and Silvan was certain that they had been seen. He was about to order his men forward, when she turned her head away. She said something to the minotaur, apparently, for he left his conference and walked over to her. Even from this distance, Silvan could see that the minotaur regarded the girl with the utmost respect, even reverence.

He listened intently to her orders, looked over his shoulder at the battle and nodded his horned head.

He turned and, with a wave of his hand, summoned the mounted Knights. With a roar, the minotaur ran forward toward the rear of his own lines. The Knights galloped after him, with what purpose Silvan could not tell. A countercharge, perhaps.

"Now is our chance, Your Majesty!" said the commander excitedly. "She stands alone."

This was beyond all possible luck, so far beyond that Silvan mistrusted his good fortune. He hesitated before ordering his men forward, fearing a trap.

"Your Majesty!" the commander urged. "What are you waiting for?"

Silvan looked and looked. He could see no troops lying in ambush. The mounted Knights of the enemy were riding away from their commander.

Silvan spurred his horse and galloped forward, the other soldiers streaming behind him. They rode with the swiftness of an arrow, with Silvan as the silver arrowhead, aiming straight at the enemy's heart. They were halfway to their destination before anyone was aware of them. The girl kept her gaze fixed on her forces. It was her standard-bearer who spotted them. He cried out and pointed. The red horse lifted its head, whinnied loud enough to rival the trumpets.

At the sound, the minotaur halted in his charge and turned around.

Silvan kept the minotaur in the corner of his eye as he rode, dug his spurs into his horse's flank, urging more speed. The mad race was exhilarating. A skilled rider, he outdistanced his bodyguard. He was not far from his objective now. She must have heard the pounding hooves, but still she did not turn her head.

A great and terrible roar sounded over the battlefield. A roar of grief and rage and fury. A roar so horrible that the sound caused Silvan's stomach to shrivel and brought beads of sweat to his forehead. He looked to see the minotaur rushing for him, a great sword raised to cleave him in twain. Silvan gritted his teeth and pressed the horse forward. If he could lay his hands on the girl, he would use her as both shield and hostage.

The minotaur was extraordinarily fast. Though he was on foot and Silvan was mounted, it seemed that the racing minotaur must reach Silvan before Silvan's horse could reach the enemy commander. Silvan looked from the minotaur to the girl. She had still taken no notice of him. She seemed completely unaware of her danger. Her gaze was fixed upon the minotaur.

"Galdar," she called, her voice beautifully clear, oddly deep. "Remember your oath."

Her voice resounded over the cries and screams and clashing steel. The call acted upon the minotaur like a spear to his heart. He ceased his furious rush. He stared at her, his gaze pleading.

She did not relent, or so it seemed. She shifted her gaze from him to the heavens. The minotaur gave another howl of rage and then plunged his sword into the ground, drove it into the cornfield with such force that he buried it halfway to the hilt.

Silvan galloped up the rise. At last the girl shifted her gaze from the heavens. She turned her eyes full upon Silvan.

Amber eyes. Silvan had never seen the like. Her eyes did not repel him but drew him forward. He rode toward her, and he could see nothing but her eyes. It seemed he was riding into them.

She clasped her morning star, hefted it in her hand, and stood awaiting him fearlessly.

Silvan dashed his horse up the small rise, came level with the girl. She struck at him with the morning star, a blow he deflected easily, kicking it aside with his foot. Another kick knocked the morning star from her hand and sent her staggering backward. She lost her balance, fell heavily to the ground. His guards surrounded her. The guards killed her standard-bearer and made an attempt to seize the horse, but the animal lashed out with its hooves. Breaking free of the holder, the horse charged straight for the rear lines, as if it would join the battle alone and riderless.

The girl lay stunned on the ground. She was covered with blood, but he could not tell if it was hers or that of her standard-bearer, who lay decapitated by her side.

Fearing she would be trampled, Silvan furiously ordered his guards to keep back. He slid from his horse, ran to the girl and lifted her in his arms. She moaned, her eyes fluttered. He breathed again. She was alive.

"I will take her, Your Majesty," offered his commander.

Silvan would not give her up. He placed her on his saddle, climbed up behind her. Clasping one arm around her tightly, he took hold of the reins in the other. Her head rested against his silver breastplate. He had never in his life seen any face so delicate, so perfectly formed, so beautiful. He cradled her tenderly, anxiously.

"Ride!" he ordered and he started for the woods, riding swiftly, but not so swiftly that he risked jarring her.

He rode past the minotaur, who was on his knees beside his buried sword, his horned head bowed in grief.

"What do you men think you are doing?" Silvan demanded. Several of the elves were starting to ride in the minotaur's direction, their swords raised. "He is not a threat to us. Leave him."

"He is a minotaur, Your Majesty. He is always a threat," protested the commander.

"Would you kill him unarmed and unresisting?" Silvan demanded sternly.

"He would have no compunction killing us, if the situation was reversed," the commander replied grimly.

"And so now we are reduced to the level of beasts," Silvan said coldly. "I said leave him, Commander. We have achieved our objective. Let us get out of here before we are overrun."

Indeed, that seemed likely. The army of the Knights of Neraka was falling back rapidly now. Their retreat was in good order, they were keeping their lines intact. Silvan and his Knights galloped from the field, Silvan bearing their prize proudly in his arms.

He reached the shadows of the trees. The girl stirred and moaned again and opened her eyes.

Silvan looked down into them, saw himself encased in amber.

The girl was a docile captive, causing no trouble, accepting her fate without complaint. When they arrived back in camp, she refused Silvan's offers of assistance. Sliding gracefully from Silvan's horse, she gave herself willingly into custody. The elves clapped iron manacles on her wrists and ankles and marched her into a tent that was furnished with nothing but a pallet of straw and a blanket.

Silvan followed her. He could not leave her.

"Are you wounded? Shall I send the healers to you?"

She shook her head. She had not spoken a word to him or to anyone. She refused his offer of food and drink.

He stood at the entrance to the prison tent, feeling helpless and foolish in his regal armor. She, by contrast, blood-covered and in chains, was calm and self-possessed. She sat down cross-legged on her blanket, stared unblinking into the darkness. Silvan left the tent with the uncomfortable feeling that he was the one who had been taken prisoner.

"Where is Glaucous?" Silvan demanded. "He wanted to question her."

But no one could say what had become of Glaucous. He had not been seen since the start of the battle.

"Let me know when he comes to interrogate her," Silvan commanded and went to his tent to remove his armor. He held still this time, still and unmoving, as his squire detached the buckles and lifted the armor from him piece by piece.

"Congratulations, Cousin!" Kiryn entered the tent, ducking through the tent flap. "You are a hero! I will not need to write your song, after all. Your people are already singing it!" He waited for a laughing response, and when it did not come, he looked at Silvan more closely. "Cousin? What is it? You don't look well. Are you wounded?"

"Did you see her, Kiryn?" Silvan asked. "Go away!" he shouted irritably at his squire. "Get out. I can finish this myself."

The squire bowed and left. Silvan sat down upon his cot, one boot on and one boot off.

"Did I see the prisoner? Only a glimpse," Kiryn said. "Why?"

"What did you think of her?"

"She is the first human I have ever seen, and I did not find her as ugly as I had been led to believe. Still, I thought her extremely strange. Bewitching. Uncanny." Kiryn grimaced. "And is it now the custom among human females to shave their heads?"

"What? Oh, no. Perhaps it is the custom of the Knights of Neraka." Silvan sat with his boot in his hand, staring at the darkness and seeing amber eyes. "I thought her beautiful. The most beautiful woman I have ever seen."

Kiryn sat down beside his cousin. "Silvan, she is the enemy. Because of her, hundreds of our people lie dead or dying in that blood-soaked field."

"I know. I know!" Silvan cried, standing up. He tossed the boot into the corner. Sitting down, he began to tug viciously on the other. "She wouldn't say a word to me. She wouldn't tell me her name. She just looked at me with those strange eyes."

"Your Majesty." An officer appeared at the entrance. "General Konnal has asked me to relate to you the news. The day is ours. We have won."

Silvan made no response. He had ceased to tug on the boot, was once again staring into the dark tent corner.

Kiryn rose, went outside. "His Majesty is fatigued," he said. "I'm certain he is overjoyed."

"Then he's the only one," said the officer wryly.

Victory belonged to the elves, but few in the elven camp that night rejoiced. They had halted the enemy's advance, driven him back, kept him from reaching Silvanost, but they had not destroyed him. They counted thirty human bodies upon the field of battle, not four hundred as they had anticipated. They laid the blame to a strange fog that had arisen from the river, a dank, chill, gray fog that hung low over the ground, a swirling, obfuscating fog that hid foe from foe, comrade from comrade. In this fog, the enemy had simply disappeared, vanished, as if the blood-soaked ground had opened up and swallowed him.

"Which is probably exactly what happened," said General Konnal to his officers. "They had their escape arranged in advance. They retreated, and when the fog came, they ran to their hideout. They are skulking about in the caves somewhere near here."

"To what purpose, General?" Silvan demanded impatiently.

The king was feeling irritable and out of sorts, restless and antsy. He left his tent that was suddenly cramped and confining, came to confer with the officers. Silvan's courage had been praised and lauded. He was undoubtedly the hero of the hour, as even General Konnal admitted. Silvan cared nothing for their praise. His gaze shifted constantly to the tent where the girl was being held prisoner.

"The humans have no food, no supplies," he continued, "and no way of obtaining any. They are cut off, isolated. They know that they can never take Silvanost now. Surely, if anything, they will attempt to retreat back to the borders."

"They know we would cut them down if they tried that," Konnal said. "Yet, you are right, Your Majesty, they cannot remain in hiding forever. Sooner or later they must come out, and then we will have them. I just wish I knew," he added, more to himself than to anyone else, "what they are planning. For there was a plan here as certain as I live and breathe."

His officers offered various theories: The humans had panicked and were now scattered to the four winds, the humans had descended below ground in hopes of finding tunnels that would lead them back north, and so on and so forth. Each theory had its opponents, and the elves argued among themselves. Growing weary of the debate, Silvan left abruptly, walked out into the night.

"There is one person who knows," he said to himself, "and she will tell me. She *will* talk to me!"

He strode purposefully toward her tent, past the bonfires where the elves sat disconsolately, reliving the battle. The soldiers were bitter and chagrined at their failure to annihilate the detested foe. They swore that when it was dawn they would search beneath every rock until they found the cowardly humans, who had run away to hide when it became clear defeat was imminent. The elves vowed to slay them, every one.

Silvan discovered that he wasn't the only one interested in the prisoner. Glaucous stood at the entrance to her tent, being cleared for admittance by the guard. Silvan was about to advance and make himself known when he realized that Glaucous had not seen him.

Silvan was suddenly interested to hear what Glaucous would ask her. He circled around to the rear of the prisoner's tent. The night was dark. No guard stood back here. Silvan crept close to the tent, being careful to make no sound. He quieted even his breathing.

A candle on the floor inside the tent flared, brought to life two dark silhouettes—the girl's with her smooth head and long, graceful neck and the elf, tall and straight, his white robes black against the light. The two stared at each other unspeaking for long moments and then, suddenly, Glaucous recoiled. He shrank back away from her, though she had done nothing to him, had not moved, had not raised her hand, had not said a word.

"Who *are* you?" he demanded and his voice was awed.

"I am called Mina," she replied.

"And I am—"

"No need to tell me," she said. "I know your name."

"How could you?" he asked, amazed. "You couldn't. You have never seen me before."

"But I know it," she replied calmly.

Glaucous had regained his self-possession. "Answer me one thing, witch. How did you pass through my shield? By what magic? What sorcery did you use?"

"No magic," she said. "No sorcery. The Hand of the God reached down and the shield was lifted."

"What hand?" Glaucous was angry, thinking she mocked him. "What god? There are no gods! Not anymore!"

"There is One God," Mina stated.

"And what is the name of this god?"

"The God has no name. The God needs no name. The God is the One God, the True God, the Only God."

"Lies! You will tell me what I want to know." Glaucous lifted his hand.

Silvanoshei expected Glaucous to use the truth-seek, as had been done to him.

"You feel your throat start to close," said Glaucous. "You gasp for air and find none. You begin to suffocate."

"This is not the truth-seek," Silvan said to himself. "What is he doing?"

"Your lungs burn and seem about to burst," Glaucous continued. "The magic tightens, tightens all the while until you lose consciousness. I will end the torment, when you agree to tell me the truth."

He began to chant strange words, words that Silvan did not understand, but which he guessed must be words to a magical spell. Alarmed for Mina's safety, Silvan was ready to rush to her rescue, to tear the fabric of the tent with his bare hands if need be to reach her.

Mina sat calmly on the cot. She did not gasp. She did not choke. She continued to breathe normally.

Glaucous ceased his chant. He stared at her in amazement. "You thwart me! How?"

"Your magic has no effect on me," Mina said, shrugging. The chains that bound her rang like silver bells. She looked up at him. "I know you. I know the truth."

Glaucous regarded her in silence, and though Silvan could see only Glaucous's silhouette, he could tell that the elf was enraged and, also, that he was afraid.

Glaucous left the tent abruptly.

Troubled, fascinated, Silvan came around to the front of the tent. He waited in the darkness until he saw Glaucous enter General Konnal's tent, then approached the guard.

"I will speak with the prisoner," he said.

"Yes, Your Majesty." The guard bowed, started to accompany the king.

"Alone," Silvan said. "You have leave to go."

The guard did not move.

"I am in no danger. She is chained and manacled! Go fetch yourself some dinner. I will take over your watch."

"Your Majesty, I have my orders—"

"I countermand them!" Silvan said angrily, thinking he was cutting a very poor figure in the sight of those amber eyes. "Go and take the fellow of your watch with you."

The guard hesitated a moment longer, but his king had spoken. He dared not disobey. He and his companion walked off toward the cooking fires. Silvan entered the tent. He stood looking at the prisoner, stood inside the amber of her eyes, warm and liquid around him.

"I want to know . . . if . . . if they are treating you well. . . ." What a stupid thing to say! Silvan thought, even as the words fumbled their way out of his mouth.

"Thank you, Silvanoshei Caladon," the girl said. "I need nothing. I am in the care of my God."

"You know who I am?" Silvan asked.

"Of course, you are Silvanoshei, son of Alhana Starbreeze, daughter of Lorac Caladon and of Porthios of the House of Solostaran."

"And you are . . . ?"

"Mina."

"Just Mina?"

She shrugged and when she shrugged, the chains on her manacles chimed. "Just Mina."

The amber began to congeal around Silvan. He felt short of breath, as if he were the one to fall victim to Glaucous's suffocating spell. He came closer to her, knelt on one knee before her to bring those lovely eyes level with his own.

"You mention your god. I would ask you a question. If the Knights of Neraka follow this god, then I must assume that this god is evil. Why does someone so young and so beautiful walk the ways of darkness?"

Mina smiled at him, the kind and pitying smile one bestows upon the blind or the feebleminded.

"There is no good, there is no evil. There is no light, there is no darkness. There is only one. One truth. All the rest is falsehood."

"But this god must be evil," Silvan argued. "Otherwise why attack our nation? We are peace-loving. We have done nothing to provoke this war. Yet now my people lie dead at the hands of their enemy."

"I do not come to conquer," Mina said. "I come to free you, to save you and your people. If some die, it is only that countless others may live. The dead understand their sacrifice."

"Perhaps *they* do," said Silvan with a wry shake of his head. "I confess that I do not. How could you—a human, single and alone—save the elven nation?"

Mina sat quite still for long moments, so still that her chains made no sound. Her amber eyes left him, shifted to stare into the candle's flame. He was content to sit and gaze at her. He could have been content to sit at her feet and gaze at her all night, perhaps all his life. He had never seen a human woman with such delicate features, such fine bone structure, such smooth skin. Every movement was graceful and fluid. He found his eyes drawn to her shaved head. The shape of the skull was perfect, the skin smooth with a faint shimmering red down upon it, which must be like feathery down to touch . . .

"I am permitted to tell you a secret, Silvanoshei," said Mina.

Silvan, lost in her, started at the sound of her voice. "Who gives you this permission?"

"You must swear that you will tell no one else."

"I swear," said Silvan.

"Truly swear," said Mina.

"I swear," Silvan said slowly, "on my mother's grave."

"An oath I cannot accept," Mina returned. "Your mother is not dead."

"What?" Silvan sank back, amazed. "What are you saying?"

"Your mother lives, and so does your father. The ogres did not kill your mother or her followers, as you feared. They were rescued by the Legion of Steel. But your parents' story is ended, they are in the past. Your story is just begun, Silvanoshei Caladon."

Mina reached out her hand, the chains ringing like altar bells. She touched Silvan's cheek. Exerting a gentle pressure, she drew him near. "Swear to me by the One True God that you will not reveal what I am about to tell you to anyone."

"But I don't believe in this god," Silvan faltered. Her touch was like the lightning bolt that had struck so near him, raised the hair on his neck and arms, sent prickles of desire through his bloodstream.

"The One God believes in *you*, Silvanoshei," Mina told him. "That is all that matters. The One God will accept your oath."

"I swear, then, by the . . . One God." He felt uncomfortable, saying the word, felt uncomfortable swearing the vow. He did not believe, not at all, but he had the strange and uneasy impression that his vow had been recorded by some immortal hand and that he would be held to it.

"How did *you* enter the shield?" Mina asked.

"Glaucous raised the shield so that I could—" Silvan began, but he stopped when he saw her smile. "What? Did this God lift it for me, as you told Glaucous?"

"I told him what he wanted to hear. In effect, you did not enter the shield. The shield captured you while you were helpless."

"Yes, I see what you are saying." Silvan remembered back to the night of the storm. "I was unconscious. I collapsed on one side of the Shield and when I woke, I was on the other. *I* did not move. The shield moved to cover me! Of course, that is the explanation!"

"The shield will stand firm against an attack, but it will try to apprehend the helpless, or so I was given to know. My soldiers and I slept and while we slept, the shield moved over us."

"But if the shield protects the elves," Silvan argued. "How could it admit our enemies?"

"The shield does not protect you," Mina replied. "The Shield keeps out those who would help you. In truth, the shield is your prison. Not only your prison, it is also your executioner."

Silvan drew back, away from her touch. Her nearness confused him, made thinking difficult. "What do you mean?"

"Your people are dying of a wasting sickness," she said. "Every day, many more succumb. Some believe the shield is causing this illness. They are partly right. What they do not know is that the lives of the elves are being drained to provide energy to the shield. The lives of your people keep the shield in place. The shield is now a prison. Soon it will be your tomb."

Silvan sank back on his heels. "I don't believe you."

"I have proof," Mina said. "What I speak is true. I swear by my God."

"Then give your proof to me," Silvan urged. "Let me consider it."

"I will tell you, Silvanoshei, and gladly. My God sent me here with that purpose. Glaucous—"

"Your Majesty," said a stern voice outside the tent.

Silvan cursed softly, turned swiftly.

"Remember, not a word!" Mina warned.

His hand trembling, Silvan opened the tent flap to see General Konnal, flanked by the two guards.

"Your Majesty," General Konnal repeated and his voice held a patronizing tone that grated on Silvan, "not even a king may dismiss those who guard such an important and dangerous prisoner. Your Majesty places himself in peril, and that cannot be allowed. Take up your positions," the general ordered.

The elf guard moved to stand in front of the prison tent.

Words of explanation clustered thick on Silvan's tongue, but he couldn't articulate any of them. He might have said that he was there to interrogate the prisoner about the shield, but that was coming too close to her secret, and he feared he could not mention one without revealing the other.

"I will escort Your Majesty back to his tent," said Konnal. "Even heroes must sleep."

Silvan maintained a silence that he hoped was the silence of injured dignity and misunderstood intentions. He fell into step beside the general, walked past campfires that were being allowed to die down. Those elves not out on patrol, searching for the humans, had wrapped themselves in their blankets and were already asleep. Elf healers tended to the wounded, made them comfortable. The camp was quiet and still.

"Good night, General," said Silvan coldly. "I give you joy on your victory this day." He started to enter his tent.

"I advise Your Majesty to go straight to bed," the General said. "You will need to be rested for tomorrow. To preside over the execution."

"What?" Silvan gasped. He caught hold of the tent post to steady himself. "What execution? Whose?"

"Tomorrow at noon, when the glorious sun stands high in the sky to serve as our witness, we will execute the human," said Konnal. He did not look at the king as he spoke, but stared straight into the night. "Glaucous has recommended it, and in this I agree with him."

"Glaucous!" Silvan repeated.

He remembered Glaucous in the tent, remembered the fear he had sensed in him. Mina had been about to tell Silvan something about Glaucous before they had been interrupted.

"You cannot kill her!" Silvan said firmly. "You will not. I forbid it."

"I am afraid that Your Majesty has no say in this matter," said Konnal. "The Heads of House have been apprised of the situation. They have voted, and their vote is unanimous."

"How will she be killed?" Silvan asked.

Konnal laid a kindly hand on the king's shoulder. "I know this is an onerous task, Your Majesty. You don't need to remain to watch. Just step out and say a few words, and then retire to your tent. No one will think the worse of you."

"Answer me, damn you!" Silvan cried, striking the man's hand away.

Konnal's face froze. "The human is to be taken to the field that is drenched in the blood of our people. She is to be tied to a stake. Seven of our best archers will be chosen. When the sun is directly overhead, when the human no longer casts a shadow, the archers will fire seven arrows into her body."

Silvan could not see the general for the blinding white rage that filled his being. He clenched his fist, dug his nails into his flesh. The pain helped him steady his voice. "Why does Glaucous say she must die?"

"His reasoning is sound. So long as she lives, the humans will remain in the area, hoping to rescue her. With her execution, they will lose all hope. They will be demoralized. Easier to locate, easier to destroy."

Silvan felt his gorge rise. He feared he would be sick, but he struggled to make one last argument. "We elves revere life. We do not by law take the life of any elf, no matter how terrible his or her crime. Elf assassins exist, but only outside the law."

"We do not take the life of an elf," Konnal answered. "We take the life of a human. Goodnight, Your Majesty. I will send a messenger to you before dawn."

Silvan entered his tent and shut the flap behind him. His servants awaited him.

"Leave me," Silvan ordered irritably, and the servants hurriedly departed.

Silvan threw himself on his bed, but he was up almost immediately. He flung himself into a chair and stared moodily into the darkness. He could not let this girl die. He loved her. Adored her. He had loved her from the moment he had seen her standing courageously, fearlessly, among her soldiers. He had stepped off the precipice of sanity and plummeted down on love's sharp rocks. They tore and mangled him. He gloried in the pain and wanted more.

A plan formed in his mind. What he was doing was wrong. He might well be placing his people in danger, but—he argued—what they were doing was wrong, and their wrong was greater than his. He was, in a way, saving them from themselves.

Silvan gave the general time to return to his tent, then wrapped himself in a dark cloak. He thrust a long, sharp knife into his boot. Peering out of the tent flap, he looked to see that no one was about. He left his tent, sneaked through the slumbering camp with quiet tread.

Two guards, alert and watchful, stood outside Mina's tent. Silvan did not go near them. He circled to the back of the tent where he had hidden to eavesdrop on Glaucous. Silvan looked carefully around. The woods were only a few paces away. They could reach them easily. They would find a cave. He would hide her there in safety, come to visit her in the night, bring her food, water, his love . . .

Removing the knife, Silvan placed its sharp point against the fabric of the tent and, working carefully and silently, cut a slit near the bottom. He crawled through the slit and inside the tent.

The candle still burned. Silvan was careful to keep his body from passing in front of it, afraid that the guards would see his shadow.

Mina had fallen asleep on her straw pallet. She slept on her side, her legs drawn up, her hands—still chained—curled up against her breast. She looked very fragile. Her slumbers were seemingly dreamless, and peaceful. Her breath came and went easily through her nose and her parted lips.

Silvan clapped his hand over her mouth to prevent any startled exclamation. "Mina!" he whispered urgently. "Mina."

Her eyes opened. She made no sound. The amber eyes gazed up at him, aware of him, cognizant of her surroundings.

"Don't be afraid," he said and realized as he said it that this girl had never known fear. She did not know fear now. "I've come to free you." He tried to speak calmly, but his voice and his hands trembled. "We can escape out the back of the tent into the woods. We have to get these manacles off."

He moved his hand away. "Call the guard. He has the key. Tell him you're ill. I'll wait in the shadows and—"

Mina put her fingers on his lips, stopped his words. "No," she said. "Thank you, but I will not leave."

"What was that?" one of the guards asked his fellow. "Did you hear something?"

"It came from inside the tent."

Silvan lifted his knife. Mina laid a restraining hand on his arm. She began to sing.

> Sleep, love; forever sleep.
> Your soul the night will keep.
> Embrace the darkness deep.
> Sleep, love; forever sleep.

The voices of the guards ceased.

"There," she said to Silvan. "The guards are asleep. We may talk without fear."

"Asleep . . ." Silvan lifted the tent flap. The guards remained standing at their posts, their heads bowed, their chins resting on their chests. Their eyes were closed.

"Are you a sorceress?" he asked, coming back to her.

"No, I am only a faithful follower," Mina replied. "The gifts I have are from my God."

"May your God keep you safe. Hurry, Mina! Out this way. We will find a path not far from here. The path runs through . . ," Silvan halted.

She was shaking her head.

"Mina," he said desperately, "we must escape! They're going to execute you at noon this very day. With the rising of the sun. Glaucous has convinced them. He fears you, Mina."

"He has good reason to fear me," she said sternly.

"Why, Mina?" Silvan asked. "You were going to tell me something about him. What is it?"

"Only that he is not what he appears and that by his magic, your people are dying. Tell me this"—she put her hand upon his cheek—"is it your desire to punish Glaucous? Reveal his intentions to your people and thereby reveal his murderous plan?"

"Yes, of course, but what—"

"Then do as I instruct you," Mina said. "Do exactly as I say. My life is in your keeping. If you fail me—"

"I will not fail you, Mina," Silvan whispered. Seizing her hand, he pressed it to his lips. "I am yours to command."

"You will attend my execution— Hush! Say nothing. You promised. Make certain that you are armed. Position yourself at Glaucous's side. Keep a large number of your bodyguards around you. Will you do that?"

"Yes, but what then? Must I watch you die?"

"You will know what to do and when to do it. Rest assured. The One God is with us. You must go now, Silvan. The general will send someone to your tent to check on you. He must not find you absent."

To leave her was to leave a part of himself. Silvan reached out his hand, ran his fingers over her head, felt the warmth of her skin, the softness of the downlike hair, the hardness of the bone beneath. She held perfectly still under his touch, did not warm to him, but did not move away from him either.

"What did your hair look like, Mina?" he asked.

"It was the color of flame, long and thick. The strands would curl around your finger and tug at your heart like a baby's hand."

"Your hair must have been beautiful," Silvan said. "Did you lose it in a fever?"

"I cut it," she told him. "I took a knife and I cut it off at the roots."

"Why?" He was aghast.

"My God required it of me. I cared too much for my looks," Mina replied. "I liked to be petted, admired, loved. My hair was my vanity, my pride. I sacrificed it to prove my faith. I have only one love, now. Only one loyalty. You must leave me now, Silvan."

Silvan stood up. Reluctantly, he moved to the back of the tent.

"You are my one love, Mina," he said softly.

"It is not me that you love," she said to him. "It is the God in me."

Silvan did not remember leaving her tent, but he found himself standing outside in the darkness.

30 TO YOUR HEALTH!

Night settled over the battlefield of Silvanesti, shrouding the bodies of the dead that were being ceremoniously prepared for burial. The same night wrapped like a winding cloth around the elven capital of Qualinost.

The night had a feel of doom about it, or so Gerard thought. He walked the streets of the elven capital with his hand on the hilt of his sword, his watchful gaze looking for the glint of steel in every shadowed corner, every dark doorway. He crossed the street to avoid passing in front of an alley. He scrutinized every second story window curtain to see if it fluttered, as it might if an archer stood behind it, ready with an assassin's arrow.

He was conscious, always, of eyes watching him, and once he felt so threatened that he whipped around, sword drawn, to defend against a knife in the back. He saw nothing, however, but he was certain someone had been there, someone who had perhaps been daunted by the Knight's heavy battle armor and his shining sword.

Gerard could not even breath a sigh of relief when he reached safely the Headquarters of the Knights of Neraka. Danger was no longer sneaking stealthily behind him. Danger was front and center.

He entered the headquarters to find a single officer on duty, the draconian asleep the floor.

"Here's the answer for Beryl from Marshal Medan," said Gerard, saluting.

"About time!" The officer grunted. "You can't believe how loudly that thing snores!"

Gerard walked over to the draconian, who was twitching in his sleep and making strange, guttural sounds.

"Groul," Gerard said and reached out a hand to shake the slumbering draconian.

A hiss, a snarl, a flapping of wings and scrabbling of feet. Clawed hands grappled for Gerard's throat.

"Hey!" Gerard yelled, fending off the draconian's attack. "Calm down, will you?"

Groul glared at him with squint lizard eyes. His tongue flicked. Lowering his hand from Gerard's neck, the draconian drew back. "Sorry," he muttered. "You startled me."

The marks of Groul's claws stung and burned on Gerard's skin. "My fault," he said stiffly. "I shouldn't have wakened you so suddenly." He held out the scroll case. "Here is the marshal's answer."

Groul took it, eyed it to make certain the seal was intact. Satisfied, he thrust it into the belt of his harness, turned and, with a grunt, headed for the door. The creature wasn't wearing armor, Gerard noted, thinking glumly to himself that the draco didn't need to wear armor. The thick, scaly hide was protection enough.

Gerard drew in a deep breath, sighed it out, and followed the draconian.

Groul turned. "What are you doing, Nerakan?"

"You are in a hostile land after nightfall. My orders are to accompany you safely to the border," Gerard said.

"You are going to protect me?" Groul gave a gurgle that might have been a laugh. "Bah! Go back to your soft bed, Nerakan. I am in no danger. I know how to deal with elf scum."

"I have my orders," said Gerard stubbornly. "If anything happened to you, the marshal would do the same to me."

Groul's lizard eyes glittered in anger.

"I have something with me that might shorten the journey for both of us," Gerard added. Drawing aside his cloak, he revealed a flask he wore on his hip.

The glitter of anger brightened to a gleam of desire, a gleam swiftly hooded.

"What is in the flask, Nerakan?" Groul asked, his tongue darting out between his sharp teeth.

"Dwarf spirits," said Gerard. "A gift from the marshal. He asks that once we are safe across the border, we join him in drinking to the downfall of the elves."

Groul made no more protest about Gerard's accompanying him. The two trudged off through the silent streets of Qualinost. Again, Gerard felt eyes watching them, but no one attacked. Gerard was not surprised. The draconian was a fearsome opponent.

Reaching the wilderness, the draconian followed one of the main trails leading into the woods. Then, with a suddenness that took Gerard by surprise, Groul plunged into the forest, taking a route known only to the draconian, or so Gerard guessed. The draconian had excellent night vision, to judge by the rapidity with which he moved through the tangled forest. The moon was waning, but the stars provided light, as did the glow of the lights of Qualinost.

The forest floor was a mass of brush and vines. Weighed down by his heavy armor, Gerard found the going hard. He had no need to feign fatigue when he called out for the draconian to halt.

"No need to kill ourselves," Gerard said, panting. "How about a moment's rest?"

"Humans!" Groul sneered. He was not even breathing hard, but he came to a halt, looked back at the Knight. To be more precise, the draconian looked at the flask. "Still, this walking is thirsty work. I could use a drink."

Gerard hesitated. "My orders—"

"To the Abyss with your orders!" Groul snarled.

"I don't suppose one little nip would hurt," Gerard said and removed the flask. He drew the cork, sniffed. The pungent, dark and musky odor of dwarf spirits burned his nostrils. Snorting, he held the flask at arm's length. "A good year," he said, his eyes tearing.

The draconian snatched the flask and brought it to his mouth. He took a long drink, then lowered the flask with a satisfied sigh. "Very good," he said in husky tones and burped.

"To your health," Gerard said and put the flask to his mouth. Keeping his tongue pressed against the opening, he pretended to swallow. "There," he said with seeming reluctance, putting the cork back in the flask, "that's enough. We should be on our way."

"Not so fast!" Groul seized the flask, drew out the cork and tossed it away. "Sit down, Nerakan."

"But your mission—"

"Beryl isn't going anywhere," Groul said, settling himself against the bole of a tree. "Whether she gets this message tomorrow or a year from tomorrow won't make any difference. Her plans for the elves are already in motion."

Gerard's heart lurched. "What do you mean?" he asked, trying to sound casual. He settled down beside the draconian and reached for the flask.

Groul handed it over with obvious reluctance. He kept his gaze fixed on Gerard, grudging every drop the Knight supposedly drank, and snatched it back the moment Gerard lowered it from his lips.

The liquid gurgled down the draconian's throat. Gerard was alarmed by how much the creature could drink, wondered if one flask would be enough.

Groul sighed, belched and wiped his mouth with the back of a clawed hand.

"You were telling me about Beryl," Gerard said.

"Ah, yes!" Groul held the flask to the moonlight. "Here's to my lady dragon, the lovely Beryl. And to the death of the elves."

He drank. Gerard pretended to drink.

"Yes," said Gerard. "The marshal told me. She has given the elves six days—"

"Ha, ha! Six days!" Groul's laugh bubbled in his throat. "The elves do not have six minutes! Beryl's army is probably crossing the border as we speak! It is a huge army, the largest seen on Ansalon since the Chaos War. Draconians, goblins, hobgoblins, ogres, human conscripts. We attack Qualinost from without. You Neraka Knights attack the elves from within. The Qualinesti are caught between fire and water with nowhere to run. At last, I will see the day dawn when not one of the pointy-eared scum are left alive."

Gerard's stomach twisted. Beryl's army crossing the border! Perhaps within a day's march on Qualinost!

"Will Beryl herself come to ensure her victory?" he asked, hoping that the catch in his throat would be mistaken for an aftereffect of the fiery liquor.

"No, no." Groul chuckled. "She leaves the elves to us. Beryl is flying off to Schallsea, to destroy the so-called Citadel of Light. And to capture some wretched mage. Here, Nerakan, stop hogging that flask!"

Groul grabbed the flask, slid his tongue over the rim.

Gerard's hand closed over the hilt of his knife. Slowly, quietly, he drew it from its sheath on his belt. He waited until Groul had lifted the flask one more time. The flask was almost empty. The draconian tilted back his head to retrieve every last drop.

Gerard struck, driving his knife with all his strength into the draconian's ribs, hoping to hit the heart.

He would have hit the heart on a human, but apparently a draconian's heart was in a different place. Either that or the creatures didn't possess hearts, which would not have surprised Gerard.

Realizing that his blow had not killed, Gerard yanked free the bloody knife. He scrambled to his feet, drawing his sword in the same motion.

Groul was injured but not critically. His grunt of pain rising to a howl of rage, he jumped up out of the brush, roaring in fury, his clawed hand grappling for his sword. The draconian attacked with a hacking blow, meant to split open his opponent's head.

Gerard parried the blow and managed to knock the sword from Groul's hand. The weapon fell into the brush at Gerard's feet. Frantically, he kicked it away as Groul sought to recover it. Gerard drove his booted foot into Groul's chin, knocking him back, but not felling him.

Drawing a curved-bladed dagger, Groul leaped into the air, using his wings to lift him well above Gerard. Slashing with his dagger, Groul launched himself bodily at the Knight.

The draconian's weight and the force of his blow drove Gerard to the ground. He fell heavily, landing on his back, with Groul on top, slavering and snarling and trying to stab Gerard with the dagger. The draconian's wings beat frantically, flapping in Gerard's face, stirring up dust that stung Gerard's eyes. He fought in panicked desperation, striking at Groul with his knife while trying to seize hold of the draconian's dagger.

The two rolled in the dust. Gerard felt his dagger hit home more than once. He was covered with blood, but whether the blood was his or Groul's, he could not tell. Still, Groul would not die, and Gerard's strength was giving out. Fear-pumped adrenaline was all that was keeping him going, and that was starting to recede.

Suddenly Groul choked, gagged. Blood spewed from the draconian, splashed over Gerard's face, blinding him. Groul stiffened, snarled in fury. He raised himself up off Gerard, lifted his dagger. The blade fell from the draconian's hand. Groul fell back onto Gerard, but this time, the draconian did not move. He was dead.

Gerard paused to draw a shuddering breath of relief, a pause that was his undoing. Too late, he remembered Medan's warning. A dead draconian is just as dangerous as a draconian living. Before Gerard could heave the carcass off him, the body of the Baaz draconian had changed into solid stone. Gerard felt as if he had the weight of a tomb on top of him. The stone carcass pressed him into the ground. He could not breathe. He was slowly suffocating. He fought to heave it off him, but it was too heavy. He drew in a ragged breath, planning to exert every last ounce of energy.

The stone statue crumbled to dust.

Gerard staggered to his feet, sank back against a tree. He wiped Groul's blood from his eyes, spit and retched until he had cleared it out of his mouth. He rested a few moments, waiting for his heart to quit trying to beat its way out from beneath his armor, waited until the battle rage had cleared from his eyes. When he could see, he fumbled at the draconian's harness, found the scroll case, and retrieved it.

Gerard took one last look at the heap of dust that had been Groul. Then, still spitting, still trying to rid himself of the foul taste in his mouth, the Knight turned and wearily made his way back through the darkness, back toward the flickering lights of Qualinost. Lights that were just starting to pale with the coming of dawn.

Sunshine streamed in through the crystal windows of the Palace of the Speaker of the Sun. Gilthas sat bathed in the sunlight, absorbed in his work. He was writing another poem, this one about his father's adventures during the War of the Lance, a poem that also contained encoded messages for two families of elves who had come under suspicion of being rebel sympathizers.

He had nearly completed it and was planning to send Planchet out to deliver the poem to those who took an interest in the king's literary pursuits, when Gilthas suddenly visibly shuddered. His fingers holding the quill pen shook. He left a blot upon his manuscript and laid down the pen hurriedly. Cold sweat beaded his brow.

"Your Majesty!" Planchet asked, alarmed. "What is wrong? Are you unwell?" He left his task of sorting the king's papers and hastened to his side.

"Your Majesty?" he repeated anxiously.

"I just had the strangest feeling," Gilthas said in a low voice. "As though a goose had walked on my grave."

"A goose, Your Majesty!" Planchet was baffled.

"It is a human saying, my friend." Gilthas smiled. "Did you never hear it? My father used to use it. The saying describes that feeling you get when for no reason that you can explain a chill causes your flesh to raise and your hair to prickle. That's exactly how I felt a moment ago. What is even stranger is that for an instant I had a very strong impression of my cousin's face! Silvanoshei. I could see him quite clearly, as clearly as I see you."

"Silvanoshei is dead, Your Majesty," Planchet reminded him. "Slain by ogres. Perhaps the goose was walking on his grave."

"I wonder," said Gilthas, thoughtfully. "My cousin did not look dead, I assure you. He wore silver armor, the kind worn by Silvanesti warriors. I saw smoke and blood, battle raged around him, but he was not touched by it. He stood at the edge of a precipice. I reached out my hand, but whether it was to pull him back or push him over, I don't know."

"I trust you were going to pull him back, Your Majesty," said Planchet, looking slightly shocked.

"I trust so, too." Gilthas frowned, shook his head. "I remember being quite angry and afraid. Strange." He shrugged. "Whatever it was, the feeling's gone now."

"Your Majesty must have dozed off. You have not been getting much sleep—"

Planchet suddenly ceased speaking. Making a sign to Gilthas to keep silent, his servant crept across the room and put his ear to the door.

"Someone is coming, Your Majesty," Planchet reported, speaking Common.

"At this hour in the morning? I am expecting no one. I hope it's not Palthainon," said Gilthas. "I have to finish this poem. Tell him I am not to be disturbed."

"Let me pass!" An elven voice outside the door spoke to the guards. The voice was calm but held an underlying note of tension and strain. "I have a message to the king from his mother."

One of the guards knocked loudly. Planchet cast a warning glance at Gilthas, who subsided back into his chair and resumed his writing.

"Hide those clothes!" he whispered urgently, with a gesture.

Gilthas's traveling clothes lay neatly folded on top of a chest, in preparation for another nightly journey. Planchet whisked the clothes back into the chest, which he closed and locked. He dropped the key into the bottom of a large vase of fresh-cut roses. This done, he walked over to answer the knock.

Gilthas played with his pen and took up a pensive attitude. Lounging back in his chair, he propped his feet up on a cushion, ran the tip of the feather over his lips, and stared at the ceiling.

"The Runner Kelevandros," announced the guard, "to see His Majesty."

"Let him enter," said Gilthas languidly.

Kelevandros came into the room in a bound. He was hooded and cloaked, the hood covering his face. Planchet shut the door behind him. Kelevandros threw back his hood. His face was deathly pale.

Gilthas rose involuntarily to his feet.

"What—"

"Your Majesty must not excite himself," Planchet remonstrated with a glance at the door, reminding the king that the guards could hear him.

"What has happened, Kelevandros?" Gilthas asked indolently. "You look as if you had seen a ghost."

"Your Majesty!" Kelevandros said in a low, quivering voice. "The queen mother has been arrested!"

"Arrested?" Gilthas repeated in astonishment. "Who has done this? Who would dare? And why? What is the charge?"

"Marshal Medan. Your Majesty." Kelevandros gulped. "I don't know how to say this—"

"Out with it, man!" Gilthas said sharply.

"Last night, Marshal Medan placed your honored mother under arrest. He has orders from the dragon Beryl to put . . . to put the queen mother to death."

Gilthas stared wordlessly. The blood drained from his face, as if someone had taken a knife and drawn it across his throat. He was so pale and shaken that Planchet left the door and hastened to the king's side, placed a firm and comforting hand on Gilthas's shoulder.

"I attempted to stop him, Your Majesty," Kelevandros said miserably. "I failed."

"Last night!" Gilthas cried, anguished. "Why didn't you come to me at once?"

"I tried, Your Majesty," Kelevandros said, "but the guards would not let me inside without orders from Palthainon."

"Where has Medan taken the queen mother?" Planchet asked. "What is the charge against her?"

"The charge is harboring the sorcerer Palin and helping him escape with the magical device brought by the kender. I don't know where Medan has taken my mistress. I went first to the Knight's headquarters, but if she is being held there, no one would tell me. I have had people searching for her all night. They are to report back to Kalindas, who has offered to remain in the house in case there is news. Finally, one of the guards who is a friend of our cause admitted me.

"I came next to you. You have heard nothing then?" Kelevandros looked anxiously at the king.

"No," said Gilthas. The word made no sound as it left his pallid lips.

"We are about to learn something more, I believe," said Planchet, his ear cocked. "That is Medan's heavy tread on the staircase. His footsteps shake the house. He comes quickly."

They could hear the stamp of the guards' feet as they came to attention, hear the thud of their spears strike the floor. One of the guards started to knock, but the knock was never finished. Medan, accompanied by one of his bodyguards—helmed and wearing black leather armor—thrust the door open, strode into the room.

"Your Majesty—"

Gilthas lunged from his chair. He covered the distance between himself and the marshal in two great bounds. Catching hold of the startled Medan by the throat, Gilthas slammed the human back against the wall, while Planchet accosted the bodyguard. Seizing hold of the man's arm, Planchet twisted it behind his back, held a knife to his ear.

"What have you done with my mother?" Gilthas demanded, his voice hard and grim. "Tell me!" He tightened his grip on Medan's throat. "Tell me!"

The marshal had been caught flat-footed by the king's sudden assault. Medan did not move. The young king's fingers were exceptionally strong, and he appeared to know precisely what he was doing.

The marshal was by no means afraid. He had his hand on the handle of his dirk and could at any moment draw the weapon and plunge it into the king's belly. That was not, however, what Medan had come here to accomplish.

He stared at Gilthas long moments without speaking, then said, as best he could for being choked, "Either the pup has grown into a wolf, or I am in the presence of a consummate actor." Noting the fearless determination in the young elf's eyes, the resolution in the jaw, the firmness of the fingers and the expertness of the hold, Medan had his answer.

"I tend to think the latter," he gasped.

"My mother, sir!" Gilthas said through clenched teeth. "Where is she?"

"I am here, Gilthas," Laurana replied, her voice echoing inside the helm of the Neraka Knights.

"Queen Mother!" Planchet gasped. He dropped the knife he had been holding and fell to his knees. "Forgive me! I had no idea . . ."

"You weren't supposed to, Planchet," Laurana said, removing the helm. "Let the marshal go, Gilthas. I am safe. For the moment. As safe as any of us."

Gilthas let loose of Medan, who stepped away from the wall, massaging his bruised throat.

"Mother, are you hurt?" Gilthas demanded. "Did he harm you? If he did, I swear—"

"No, my son, no!" Laurana reassured him. "The marshal has treated me with all possible respect. With great kindness, even. He took me to his house last night. This morning, he provided me with this disguise. The marshal fears my life may be in peril. He took me into custody for my own safety."

Gilthas frowned as if he found all this difficult to believe. "Mother, sit down. You look exhausted. Planchet, bring my mother some wine."

While Planchet went to fetch the wine, the marshal walked over to the door. Flinging it open, he stepped out into the hallway. The guards scrambled to attention.

"Guards, the rebel force has been reported within the city limits. His Majesty's life is in danger. Clear the household. Send all the servants home. Everyone. No one is to remain within the palace. Is that understood? I want guards posted at all the entrances. Admit no one, with the exception of my aide. Send him to king's chambers directly upon his arrival. Go!"

The guards departed, and soon their voices could be heard loudly ordering everyone to leave the palace. The voices of the servants rose in perplexity or consternation. It was early morning, breakfast was prepared but had not been served, the floors had yet to be swept. The guards were firm. There was a hubbub of voices, the household staff exclaiming loudly and fearfully, the scream of an overexcited maid. The guards herded everyone out the doors and took up their positions outside as ordered.

Within a few moments, the palace was strangely, unnaturally quiet.

Medan reentered the room. "Where do you think you are going?" he demanded, finding Kelevandros about to depart.

"I must take this news to my brother, my lord," Kelevandros said. "He is frantic with worry—"

"You are not taking this news to him or to anyone. Go sit down and keep quiet."

Laurana glanced up swiftly at this, looked searchingly at Kelevandros. The elf glanced at her uncertainly and then did as he was told.

Medan left the door open behind him. "I want to be able to hear what is going on outside. Are you all right, madam?"

"Yes, thank you, Marshal. Will you join me in a glass of wine?"

"With His Majesty's permission." The marshal made a slight bow.

"Planchet," Gilthas said, "pour the marshal some wine." The king continued to stand protectively beside his mother, continued to glower at the marshal.

Medan raised his glass in a toast. "I congratulate you, Your Majesty. I have been duped for the first and only time in my life. That weak, vacillating, poetry-loving act of yours took me in completely. I have long wondered how and why so many of my best plans were thwarted. I believe that I now have the answer. Your health, Your Majesty."

Medan drank the wine. Gilthas turned his back on the man.

"Mother, what is going on?"

"Sit down, Gilthas, and I will tell you," Laurana said. "Or better yet, you may read for yourself."

She looked to Medan. He reached inside his armor, produced the scroll sent by the dragon, and handed it, with a new and marked show of respect, to the king.

Gilthas walked to the window, unrolled the parchment. He held it to the waning twilight and read it slowly and carefully.

"The dragon cannot mean this," he said, his voice strained.

"She means it," said Medan grimly. "Erase all doubt from your mind, Your Majesty. Beryl has long been seeking an excuse to destroy Qualinesti. The rebel attacks grow bolder. She suspects the elves of keeping the Tower of Wayreth from her. The unfortunate fact that Palin Majere was discovered hiding in the house of the queen mother merely confirms the dragon's suspicions that the elves and the sorcerers are in collusion to rob her of her magic."

"We pay her tribute—" Gilthas began.

"Bah! What is money to her? She demands tribute only because it pleases her to think she is inflicting a hardship on you. Magic is what she lusts after, magic of the old world, magic of the gods. It is a pity this blasted device ever came into his land. A pity you sought to keep it from me, madam." The marshal's voice was stern. "Had you turned it over to me, this tragedy might have been averted."

Laurana sipped her wine, made no answer.

Medan shrugged. "But, you didn't. Spilled ale, as they said. Now you must fetch the device back. You must, madam," he reiterated. "I have done what I can to stall for time, but I have bought us only a few days. Send your griffon messenger to the Citadel. Instruct Palin Majere to turn over the device and the kender who bears it. I will take them to the dragon personally. I may be able to stave off this doom that hangs over us—"

"Us!" Gilthas cried in anger. "*You* hold the executioner's axe, Marshal! The axe hangs poised over our heads, not yours!"

"Forgive me, Your Majesty," Medan replied with a low bow. "I have lived in this land for so long that it has come to seem like my home."

"You are our conqueror," said Gilthas, speaking the words distinctly, separately them with bitter emphasis on each. "You are our master. You are our jailer. Qualinesti can never be your home, sir."

"I suppose not, Your Majesty," said Medan, after a moment's pause. "I should like you to consider, however, that I escorted your mother to the palace, when I might have escorted her to the block. I have come to warn you of the dragon's intent, when I might have been marching prisoners to the market place to serve as targets for my archers."

"What is all this generosity to cost us?" Gilthas demanded, his voice cold. "What is the price you set on our lives, Marshal Medan?"

Medan smiled slightly. "I should like to die in my garden, Your Majesty. Of old age, if that is possible." He poured himself another glass of wine.

"Do not trust him, Your Majesty," Planchet said softly, coming to pour wine for the king.

"Don't worry," said Gilthas, twisting the fragile stem of the glass in his fingers.

"And now, madam, we do not have much time," the Marshal said. "Here is paper and ink. Compose your letter to Majere."

"No, Marshal," Laurana said firmly. "I have been giving this matter a great deal of thought. Beryl must never come into possession of this device. I would die a hundred deaths first."

"You would die a hundred deaths, madam," said Medan grimly, "but what about thousands of deaths? What about your people? Will you sacrifice them to save some sorcerer's toy?"

Laurana was pale, resolute. "It is not a toy, Marshal Medan. If Palin is right, it is one of the most powerful magical artifacts ever made. Qualinesti could be burned to the ground before I would turn over the artifact to Beryl."

"Tell me the nature of this artifact, then," Medan said.

"I cannot, Marshal," Laurana replied. "It is bad enough that Beryl knows the artifact exists. I will not provide her with any more information." Calmly, she lifted her blue eyes to meet his irate gaze. "You see, sir, I have reason to believe that I am being spied upon."

Medan's face flushed. He seemed about to say something, changed his mind and turned abruptly to speak to the king.

"Your Majesty. What have you to say?"

"I agree with my mother. She told me of this device, described its powers to me. I will not give the device to the dragon. "

"Do you realize what you are doing? You sentence your nation to death! No magical artifact is worth this," Medan protested angrily.

"This one is, Marshal," Laurana said. "You must trust me."

Medan regarded her intently.

She met his gaze, held it, did not blink or flinch away.

"Hush!" Planchet warned. "Someone's coming."

They could hear footfalls on the stairs, taking them two at a time.

"My aide," Medan replied.

"Can he be trusted?" Laurana asked.

Medan gave a wry smile. "Judge for yourself, Madam."

A Knight entered the room. His black armor was covered in blood and gray dust. He stood still for some moments, breathing heavily, his head bowed, as if climbing those stairs had drained every last ounce of his energy. At length, he raised his head, lifted his hand, held out a scroll to the marshal.

"I have it, sir. Groul is dead."

"Well done, Sir Gerard," said the Marshal, accepting the scroll. He looked at the Knight, at the blood on his armor. "Are you wounded?" he asked.

"To be honest, my lord, I can't tell," Gerard said with a grimace. "There isn't one single part of me that doesn't hurt. But if I am, it's not serious, or else I'd be lying out there dead in the street."

Laurana was staring, amazed.

"Queen Mother," Gerard said, bowing.

Laurana seemed about to speak, but, glancing at Medan, she caught herself.

"I do not believe that we have met, sir," she said coolly.

Gerard's blood-masked face relaxed into a faint smile. "Thank you, madam, for trying to protect me, but the marshal knows I am a Solamnic Knight. I am the marshal's prisoner, in fact."

"A Solamnic?" Gilthas was startled.

"The one I told you about," Laurana said. "The Knight who accompanied Palin and the kender."

"I see. And so you are the marshal's prisoner. Did he do this to you?" Gilthas demanded angrily.

"No, Your Majesty," said Gerard. "A draconian did this to me. Beryl's messenger. Or rather, Beryl's former messenger." He sank down in a chair, sighed, and closed his eyes.

"Some wine here," Medan ordered. "The dragon won't be receiving any more information from Qualinesti," he added with satisfaction. "Beryl will wait at least a day to hear from me. When she does not, she will be forced to send another messenger. We have gained some time, at least."

He handed Gerard a glass of wine.

"No, my lord," said Gerard, accepting the wine, but not drinking it. "We haven't. The dragon deceived us. Beryl's forces are on the march. Groul figured that they might already be crossing the border. The largest army assembled since the Chaos War is marching on Qualinesti."

A silence as of death settled over the room. Each person listened unmoving, absorbing the news. No one's eyes sought another's. No one wanted to see the reflection of his own fear.

Marshal Medan smiled ruefully, shook his head.

"I am not to die of old age, after all, it seems," he said, and poured himself another glass of wine.

31 THE PALE RIVER OF THE DEAD

That night, Goldmoon left the hospital, ignoring the pleas of the Healers and Lady Camilla.

"I am well," Goldmoon said, fending off their attempts to keep her in bed. "I need rest, that is all, and I will not find rest here!"

Not with the dead.

She walked swiftly through the gardens and courtyards of the citadel complex, bright with lights. She looked neither to the left nor the right. She did not answer greetings. She kept her gaze fixed upon the path before her. If she looked anywhere else, she would see them. They were following her.

She heard their whispered beggings. She felt their touch, soft as milkweed, upon her hands, her face. They wrapped around her like silken scarves. She was afraid, if she looked at them, she would see Riverwind. Then she thought, perhaps this is why his spirit has not come to me. He is lost and foundering in this river, swept away. I will never find him.

Reaching the Grand Lyceum, she ran swiftly up the many stairs leading to her chambers. For the first time, she blessed this strange, young body, which was not only quick but was eager to meet the physical demands she now placed upon it. Brought to bay, Goldmoon turned to face them.

"Be gone. I have nothing for you."

The dead drew near, an old, old man, a thief, a warrior, a crippled child. Beggars all, their hands extended. Then, quite suddenly, they left—as if a voice had ordered them gone. But not her voice.

Goldmoon shut the door behind.

In her chamber, she was alone, truly alone. The dead were not here. Perhaps when she had refused to grant them what they sought, they had left her to seek other prey. She sank back against the door, overwhelmed by her vision. Standing in the darkness, she could see again, in her mind's eye, the dead draining the life-giving power from her followers. This was the reason healing was failing in the world. The dead were robbing the living. But why? What need had the dead for mystical power? What force constrained them? Where were they bound with such urgency?

"And why has it been given to me to see them?" Goldmoon murmured.

A knock sounded on her door. She ignored it and felt to make certain the door was locked. The knock was repeated several times. Voices—living voices—called to her. When she did not answer, they were perplexed. She could hear them wondering aloud what to do.

"Go away!" she ordered finally, wearily. "Go away, and leave me in peace."

And eventually, like the dead, the living also departed and left her alone.

Crossing her chambers, Goldmoon stood before the large windows that overlooked the sea and flung open the casement.

The waning moon cast a pallid light upon the ocean. The sea had a strange look to it. An oily film covered the water, and beneath this film, the water was smooth, still. No breeze stirred, not a breath. The air had a foul smell to it, tainted by the oil upon the water, perhaps. The night was clear. The stars bright. The sky empty.

Ships were putting out to sea, black against the moonlight waters. There was a smell of thunder in the air. Seasoned mariners were reading the signs and heading for the open waters, far safer for them than lying close to shore, where crashing waves could send them smashing up against the docks or the rocks of the island's coast. Goldmoon watched them from her window, looking like toy boats gliding across a dark mirror.

There, moving over the ocean, were the dead.

Goldmoon sank to her knees at the window. She placed her hands upon the window frame, rested her chin upon her hands, and watched the dead cross the sea. The moon sank beneath the horizon, drowned in dark water. The stars shone cold and bleak in the sky, and they also shone in the water, which was so still that Goldmoon could not perceive where the sky ended and the sea began. Small waves lapped gently upon the shore with a forlorn urgency, like a sick and fretful child trying to capture someone's attention. The dead were traveling north, a pallid stream, paying no attention to anything except to that call they alone could hear.

Yet not quite alone.

Goldmoon heard the song. The voice that sang the song was compelling, stirred Goldmoon to the depths of her soul.

"You will find him," said the voice. "He serves me. You will be together."

Goldmoon crouched at the window, head bowed, and shivered in awe and fear and an exaltation that made her cry out in longing, reach her hands out in longing for the singer of that song as the dead had reached out their hands to her in longing. She spent the night on her knees, her soul listening to the song with a thrill that was both pain and pleasure, watching the dead travel north, heeding the call, while the wavelets of the still sea clung as long as they could to the shore, then receded, leaving the sand smooth and empty in their going.

Day dawned. The sun slid out of the oily water. Its light seemed covered with the same film of oil, for it had a greenish sheen smeared across the yellow. The air was tainted, hot, and unsatisfying to breathe. Not a cloud marred the sky.

Goldmoon rose from kneeling. Her muscles were stiff and sore from the uncomfortable position, but usage warmed and limbered them. She picked up a cloak, thick and heavy, and wrapped it around her, though the early morning was already hot.

Opening her door, she found Palin standing outside, his hand raised to knock. "First Master," he said. "We have all been worried . . ."

The dead were all around him. They plucked at the sleeves of his robes. Their lips pressed against his broken fingers, their ragged hands clutched at the magical ring he wore, trying to pull it loose, but not succeeding, to judge by their wails of frustration.

"What?" Palin halted in the middle of his speech of concern, alarmed by the expression on her face. "What is it, First Master? Why do you stare at me like that?"

She pushed past him, shoving him out of her way with such force that he staggered backward. Goldmoon caught up the skirts of her white robes and ran down the stairs, her cloak billowing behind her. She arrived in the hall, startling masters and students. They called after her, some ran after her. The guards stood staring and helpless. Goldmoon ignored them all and kept running.

Past the crystal domes, past the gardens and the fountains, past the hedge maze and the silver stair, past Knights and guards, visitors and pupils, past the dead. She ran down to the harbor. She ran down to the still, smooth sea.

Tas and the gnome were mapping the hedge maze—successfully mapping the hedge maze, which must be considered a first in the long and inglorious history of gnomish science.

"Are we getting close, do you think?" Tasslehoff asked the gnome. "Because I think I'm losing all the feeling in my left foot."

"Hold still!" Conundrum ordered. "Don't move. I've almost got it. Drat this wind," he added irritably. "I wish it would stop. It keeps blowing away my map."

Tasslehoff endeavored to do as he was ordered, although not moving was extremely difficult. He stood on the path in the middle of the hedge maze, balanced precariously on his left foot. He held his right leg hoisted in a most uncomfortable position in the air, his foot attached to a branch of the hedge maze by the end of the thread of the unraveled right stocking. The stocking was considerably reduced in size, its cream-colored thread trailing along the path through the hedge maze.

The gnome's plan to use the socks had proved a brilliant success, though Conundrum sighed inwardly over the fact that the means by which he was going to finally succeed in mapping the hedge maze lacked the buttons, the gears, the pulleys, the spindles and the wheels, which are such a comfort to the scientific mind.

To have to describe the wondrous mechanism by which he had achieved his Life Quest as "two socks, wool" was a terrible blow. He had spent the night trying to think of some way to add steam power, with the result that he developed plans for snowshoes that not only went extremely fast but kept the feet warm as well. But that did nothing to advance his Life Quest.

At length Conundrum was forced to proceed with the simple plan he'd originally developed. He could always, he reflected, embellish the proceedings during the final report. They began early in the morning, up before the dawn. Conundrum posted Tasslehoff at the entry of the hedge maze, tied one end of the kender's sock to a branch, and marched Tasslehoff forward. The sock unraveled nicely, leaving a cream-colored track behind. Whenever Tasslehoff took a wrong turn and came to a dead end, he reversed direction, rolling up the thread, and proceeded down the path until he came to the right turn in the path, which was leading them deeper into the middle of the hedge maze.

Whenever they struck a correct turning, Conundrum would fall flat on his belly and mark the route on his map. By this means, he advanced farther than he'd ever been able to go. So long as Tasslehoff's supply of hosiery held out, the gnome felt certain that he would have the entire hedge maze well and truly mapped by day's end.

As for Tasslehoff, he was not feeling quite as cheery and pleased as one might expect for someone who was on the verge of wondrous scientific breakthrough. Every time he put his hand in a pocket he felt the prickly jewels and the cold, hard surface of the Device of Time Journeying. He more than half suspected the device of deliberately making a nuisance of itself by turning up in places and pockets where he knew for a fact it had not been ten minutes earlier. No matter where he put his hands, the Device was jabbing him or poking him.

Every time the device jabbed him or poked him, it was like Fizban's bony finger jabbing him or poking him, reminding him of his promise to come right back.

Of course, kender have traditionally considered promises to be about as binding as a silken strand of gossamer—good for holding butterflies, but not much more. Normally anyone relying on a kender's promise would be considered loony, unstable, incompetent and just plain daft, all of which descriptions fit Fizban to a tee. Tasslehoff would not have worried at all about breaking a promise he had really never intended to keep in the first place and that he had assumed Fizban knew he never meant to keep, but for what Palin had said about his—Tasslehoff's—funeral.

That funeral speech seemed to indicate that Fizban expected Tasslehoff to keep his promise. Fizban expected it because Tas was not an ordinary kender. He was a brave kender, a courageous kender, and—that dreadful word—an *honorable* kender.

Tasslehoff looked honor up and he looked it down. He looked it inside out and sideways, and there were just no two ways about it. Honorable people kept promises. Even promises that were terrible promises, promises that meant one had to go back in time to be stepped on by a giant and squashed flat and killed dead.

"Right! That's got it!" said the gnome briskly. "You can put your foot down. Now, just hop along around that corner. To your right. No, left. No, right . . ."

Tasslehoff hopped, feeling the sock unravel from around his leg. Rounding the corner, he came upon a staircase. A spiral staircase. A spiral staircase made all of silver. A silver spiral staircase in the middle of the hedge maze.

"We've done it!" The gnome shouted ecstatically.

"We have?" asked Tasslehoff, staring at the stair. "What have we done?"

"We've reached the very center of the hedge maze!" The gnome was capering about, flinging ink to the four winds.

"How beautiful!" said Tasslehoff and walked toward the silver stair.

"Stop! You're unraveling too fast!" the gnome cried. "We still have to map the exit."

At that moment, Tasslehoff's sock gave out. He barely noticed, he was so interested in the staircase. The stair seemed to rise up out of nothing. The stair had no supports, but hung suspended in the air, shining and fluid as quicksilver. The stair turned round and round upon itself, leading ever upward. Arriving at the bottom, he looked up to see the top.

He looked up and up and all he saw was sky, blue sky that seemed to go on and on like a bright and lovely summer's day, which is so bright and so lovely that you never want the day to end. You want it to go on and on forever. Yet you know, the sky seemed to say, that night must come, or else there will be no day tomorrow. And the night has its own blessing, its own beauty.

Tasslehoff began to climb the silver stair.

A few steps below, Conundrum was also starting to climb. "Strange construction," he remarked. "No pylons, no struts, no rivets, no balusters, no hand railings—safety hazard. Someone should be reported." The gnome paused about twenty steps up to look around. "My what a view. I can see the harbor—"

The gnome let out a shriek that might have been mistaken for the Mt. Nevermind noon whistle, which generally goes off at about three in the morning.

"My ship!"

Conundrum dropped his maps, he spilled his ink. He dashed down the stair, his wispy hair flying in the wind, tripped over Tasslehoff's stocking, which was tied to the end of the hedge, picked himself up and ran toward the harbor with a speed that the makers of the steam-powered, piston-driven snowshoes might have tried hard to emulate.

"Stop thief!" the gnome bellowed. "That's my ship!"

Tasslehoff glanced down to see what all the excitement was about, saw it was the gnome, and thought nothing more about it. Gnomes were always excitable.

Tasslehoff sat down on the stairs, put his small pointed chin in his hand and thought about promises.

Palin tried to catch up with Goldmoon, but a cramp in his leg had brought him up, gasping in pain. He massaged the leg and then, when he could walk, he limped down the stairs to find the hall in an uproar. Goldmoon had come running through like a madwoman. She had run out before any could stop her. The masters and healers had been taken by such surprise that only belatedly had some thought to chase after her. By that time, she had vanished. The entire Citadel was being turned upside down, searching for her.

Palin kept to himself what Goldmoon had said to him. The others were already speaking of her in tense whispers. Her wild talk about the dead feeding off him would only convince them—as it had convinced him—that the poor woman had been driven insane by her amazing transformation. He could still see her look of horror, still feel the powerful blow that had sent him falling back against the wall. He offered to search for her, but Lady Camilla told him curtly that both her Knights and the citadel guards had been sent to locate the First Master and that they were quite capable of handling the situation.

Not knowing what else to do, he returned to his rooms, telling Lady Camilla to be certain to notify him upon the First Master's return.

"In the meantime," he said to himself, sighing, "the best I can do is to leave Schallsea. I've made a mess of things. Tas won't come near me, and I can't blame him. I am only adding to Goldmoon's burdens. Perhaps I am the one responsible for her madness!"

His guest room in the Citadel was a spacious one, located on the second floor. He had a small bedroom, a study, and a parlor. One wall of the parlor was crystal, facing west, providing a magnificent view of sea and sky. Restless, exhausted, but too tense to sleep, he wandered into the parlor and stood gazing out across the sea. The water was like green glass, mirroring the sky. Except for a gray-green line on the horizon, he could not tell where one left off and the other began. The sight was strangely disquieting.

Leaving the parlor, Palin entered his study and sat down at his desk, thinking he would write a letter to Jenna. He picked up the pen, but the words scrambled in his head, made no sense. He rubbed his burning eyes. He had not been able to sleep all night. Every time he drifted off, he thought he heard a voice calling to him and he woke with a start to find that no one was there.

His head sank down, pillowed on his arms. He closed his eyes. The smooth crystal sea stole over him, the water warm and dark.

"Palin!" a voice cried, a hollow, whispering voice. "Palin! Wake up!"

"Just a moment more, father," Palin said, lost in a dream that he was a child again. "I'll be down—"

Caramon stood over him. Big of body, big of heart as when Palin had last seen him, except that he was wavering and insubstantial as the smoke from dying embers. His father was not alone. He was surrounded by ghosts, who reached out grasping hands to Palin.

"Father!" Palin cried. His head jerked up. He stared in amazement. He could say nothing more, only stare, gaping, at the phantasmic shapes that had gathered around him and seemed to be trying to seize hold of him.

"Get back!" Caramon shouted in that dreadful whisper. He glared around, and the ghosts shrank back, but they did not go far. They stared at Palin with hungry eyes.

"Father," Palin said—or tried to say. His throat was so dry that the words seemed to shred his flesh. "Father, what—"

"I've been searching for you!" Caramon said desperately. "Listen to me! Raistlin's not here! I can't find him! Something's wrong. . . ."

More ghosts appeared in the study. The ghosts surged past Caramon, over him and around him. They could not rest, could not remain long in one place. They seized Caramon and tried to carry him away, like a panicked mob that bears its members to destruction.

Exerting all his effort, Caramon broke free of the raging current and flung himself at Palin.

"Palin!" he shouted, a shout that made no sound. "Don't kill Tas! He's the—"

Caramon vanished suddenly. The ephemeral forms swirled a moment and then separated into ragged wisps, as if a hand had brushed through smoke. The wisps were wafted away on a soul-chilling wind.

"Father? I don't understand! Father!"

The sound of his own voice woke Palin. He sat upright with a start, gasping, as if he'd been splashed with cold water. He stared about wildly. "Father!"

The room was empty. Sunlight streamed in through the open window. The air was hot and fetid.

"A dream," Palin said, dazedly.

But a very real dream. Remembering the dead clustering around him, Palin felt horror thrilling through him, raising the hair on his arms and his neck. He still seemed to feel the clutching hands of the dead, plucking at his clothes, whispering and pleading. He brushed at his face, as if he'd run into a spider's web in the dark.

Just as Goldmoon had said. . . .

"Nonsense," he said to himself out loud, needing to hear a living voice after those terrible whispers. "She put the thought into my mind, that is all. No wonder I'm having nightmares. Tonight, I will take a sleeping potion."

Someone rattled the doorknob, trying to open the door, only to find that it was locked. Palin's heart was in his throat.

Then came the sound of metal—a lockpick—clicking and snicking in the door lock.

Not ghosts. Just a kender.

Palin, sighing, stood up and walked to the door, opened it.

"Good morning, Tas," said Palin.

"Oh, hullo," said Tasslehoff. The kender was bent double, a lockpick in his hand, peering intently at the place where the lock had been before the door swung open. Tas straightened, tucked the lockpick back in a front pocket.

"I thought you might be asleep. I didn't want to bother you. Do you have anything to eat?" The kender entered the room, making himself at home.

"Look, Tas," Palin said, trying hard to be patient, "this isn't a good time. I am very tired. I didn't sleep well—"

"Me neither," said Tas, marching into the parlor and plunking himself down on a chair. "I guess you don't have anything to eat. That's all right. I'm not really hungry."

He sat in silence, swinging his feet back and forth, looking out at the sky and the sea. The kender was silent for several whole minutes put together.

Palin, recognizing this as an extraordinarily unusual phenomenon, drew up another chair and sat down beside him.

"What is it, Tas?" he asked gently.

"I've decided to go back," Tas said, not looking at Palin, but still looking out at the empty sky. "I made a promise. I never thought about it before, but a promise isn't something you make with your mouth. You make a promise with your heart. Every time you break a promise, your heart breaks a little until pretty soon you have cracks running all through it. I think, all in all, it's better to be squished by a giant."

"You are very wise, Tas," said Palin, feeling ashamed of himself. "You are far wiser than I am."

He paused a moment. He could hear again his father's voice. *Don't kill Tas!* The vision was real, much more real than any dream. A mage learns to trust his instincts, to listen to the inner voices of heart and soul, for those are the voices that speak the language of magic. He wondered if, perhaps, this dream wasn't that inner voice cautioning him to slow down, take no drastic actions, do further study.

"Tas," said Palin slowly. "I've changed my mind. I don't want you to go back. At least not yet."

Tas leaped to his feet. "What? I don't have to die? Is that true? Do you mean it?"

"I said only that you didn't have to go back yet," Palin admonished. "Of course, you have to go back sometime."

His words were lost on the excited kender. Tas was skipping around the room, scattering the contents of his pouches every which way. "This is wonderful! Can we go sailing off in a boat like Goldmoon?"

"Goldmoon went off in a boat?" Palin repeated, amazed.

"Yes," said Tas cheerfully. "With the gnome. At least I guess Conundrum caught up with her. He was swimming awfully fast. I didn't know gnomes could swim so well."

"She has gone mad," Palin said to himself. He headed for the door. "We must alert the guards. Someone will have to go rescue her."

"Oh, they've gone after them," Tas said casually, "but I don't think they'll find them. You see, Conundrum told me that the *Destructible* can dive down under the water just like a dolphin. It's a sub—sup—soop—whatchamacallit. A boat that travels under water. Conundrum showed it to me last night. It looks exactly like a gigantic steel fish. Say, I wonder if we could see them from here?"

Tasslehoff ran to the window. Pressing his nose against the crystal, he peered out, searching for some sight of the boat. Palin forgot the strange vision in his amazement and consternation. He hoped very much that this was just another of Tasslehoff's tales and that Goldmoon had not sailed away in a gnomish contraption.

He was about to go downstairs, to find out the truth of the matter, and was heading for the door when the morning stillness was split by a trumpet blast. Bells rang out, loudly, insistently. In the hallway voices could be heard demanding to know what was going on. Other voices answered, sounding panicked.

"What's that?" Tas asked, still peering out the window.

"They're sounding the call to arms," Palin said. "I wonder why—"

"Maybe it has something to do with those dragons," Tasslehoff said, pointing.

Winged shapes, black against the morning sky, flew toward the citadel. One shape, flying in the center, was larger than the rest, so large that it seemed the green tinge in the sky was a reflection of the sunlight on the dragon's scales. Palin took one good look. Appalled, he drew back into the center of the room, into the shadows, as if, even at that distance, the dragon's red eyes might find him.

"That is Beryl!" he said, his throat constricting. "Beryl and her minions!"

Tas's eyes were round. "I thought it was finding out that I didn't have to go back to die that was making me feel all squirmy inside. It's the curse, isn't it?" He gazed at Palin. "Why is she coming here?"

A good question. Of course, Beryl might have decided to attack the citadel on a whim, but Palin doubted it. The Citadel of Light was in the territory of Khellendros, the blue dragon who ruled this part of the world. Beryl would not encroach on the Blue's territory unless she had desperate need. And he guessed what that need was.

"She wants the device," Palin said.

"The magical device?" Tasslehoff reached into a pocket and drew forth the magical artifact.

"Ugh!" He brushed his hand over his face. "You must have spiders in here. I feel all cobwebby." He clutched the device protectively. "Can the dragon sniff it out, Palin? How does she know we're here?"

"I don't know," Palin said grimly. He could see it all quite clearly. "It doesn't matter." He held out his hand. "Give me the device."

"What are we going to do?" Tas asked, hesitating. He was still a bit mistrustful.

"We're going to get out of here," Palin said. "The magical device must not come into her possession."

Palin could only imagine what the dragon might do with it. The magic of the device would make the dragon the undisputed ruler of Ansalon. Even if there was no longer past, she could go back to the point after the Chaos War when the great dragons had first come to Ansalon. She could go back to any point in time and change events so that she emerged victorious from any battle. At the very least, she could use the device to transport her great bloated body to circumnavigate the world. No place would be safe from her ravages.

"Give me the device," Palin repeated urgently, reaching for it. "We have to leave. Hurry, Tas!"

"Am I coming with you?" Tas asked, still hanging onto the device.

"Yes!" Palin almost shouted. He started to add that they didn't have much time—but time was the one thing they did have. "Just . . . give me the device."

Tas handed it over. "Where are we going?" he asked eagerly.

A good question. In all the turmoil, Palin had not given that important matter any thought.

"Solace," he said. "We will go back to Solace. We'll alert the Knights. The Solamnic Knights in the garrison ride silver dragons. They can come to the aid of the people here."

The dragons were closer now, much closer. The sun shone on green scales and red. Their broad wings cast shadows that glided over the oily water. Outside the door the bells clamored, urging people to seek shelter, to flee to the hills and forests. Trumpets sounded, blaring the call to arms. Feet pounded, steel clashed, voices shouted terse orders and commands.

He held the device in his hands. The magic warmed him, calmed him like a draught of fine brandy. He closed his eyes, called to mind the words of the spell, the manipulation of the device.

"Keep close to me!" he ordered Tas.

The kender obediently clamped his hand firmly onto the sleeve of Palin's robes.

Palin began to recite the spell.

" 'Thy time is thy own . . .' "

He tried to turn the jeweled face of the pendant upward. Something was not quite right. There was a catch in the mechanism. Palin applied a bit more force, and the face plate shifted.

" 'Though across it you travel . . .' "

Palin adjusted the face plate right to left. He felt something scrape, but the face plate moved.

" 'Its expanses you see . . .' "

Now the back plate was supposed to drop to form two spheres connected by rods. But quite astonishingly, the back plate dropped completely off. It fell to the floor with a clatter.

"Oops," said Tas, looking down at the spherical plate that lay rolling like a crazed top on the floor. "Did you mean for that to happen?"

"No!" Palin gasped. He stood holding in his hands a single sphere with a rod protruding from one end, staring down at the plate in horror.

"Here, I'll fix it!" Tas helpfully picked up the broken piece.

"Give it to me!" Palin snatched the plate. He stared helplessly at the plate, tried to fit the rod into it, but there was no place for the rod to go. A misty film of fear and frustration swam before his eyes, blinding him.

He spoke the verse again, terse, panicked. " 'Its expanses you see!' " He shook the sphere and the rod, shook the plate. "Work!" he commanded in anger and desperation. "Work, damn you!"

The chain dropped down, slithered out of Palin's grasping fingers to lie like a glittering silver snake on the floor. The rod separated from the sphere. Jewels winked and sparkled in the sunlight. And then the room went dark, the light of the jewels vanished. The dragons' wings blotted out the sun.

Palin Majere stood in the Citadel of Light holding the shattered remnants of the Device of Time Journeying in his crippled hands.

The dead! Goldmoon had told him. They are feeding off you!

He saw his father, saw the river of dead pouring around him. A dream. No, not a dream. Reality was the dream. Goldmoon had tried to tell him.

"This is what is wrong with the magic! This is why my spells go awry. The dead are leeching the magical power from me. They are all around me. Touching me with their hands, their lips. . . ."

He could feel them. Their touch was like cobwebs brushing across his skin. Or insect wings, such as he had felt at Laurana's home. So much was made clear now. The loss of the magic. It wasn't that he had lost his power. It was that the dead had sucked it from him.

"Well," said Tas, "at least the dragon won't have the artifact."

"No," said Palin quietly, "she'll have us."

Though he could not see them, he could feel the dead all around him, feeding.

32 THE EXECUTION

The candle that kept count of the hours stood beside Silvan's bed. He lay on his belly, watching the hours melt with the wax. One by one, the lines that marked the hours vanished until only a single line was left. The candle had been crafted to burn for twelve hours. Silvan had lit it at midnight. Eleven hours had been devoured by the flame. The time was nearly noon, the time set for Mina's execution.

Silvan extinguished the candle with a breath. He rose and dressed himself in his finest clothes, clothes he had brought to wear on the return march—the victory march—into Silvanost. Fashioned of soft pearl gray, the doublet was stitched with silver that had been twisted and spun into thread. His hose were gray, his boots gray. Touches of white lace were at his wrist and neck.

"Your Majesty?" a voice called from outside his tent, "it is Kiryn. May I come in?"

"If you want," said Silvan shortly, "but no one else."

"I was here earlier," Kiryn said, upon entering. "You didn't answer. You must have been asleep."

"I have not closed my eyes," Silvan said coldly, adjusting his collar.

Kiryn was silent a moment, an uncomfortable silence. "Have you had breakfast?" he asked.

Silvan cast a him a look that would have been a blow to anyone else. He did not even bother to respond.

"Cousin, I know how you feel," Kiryn said. "This act they contemplate is monstrous. Truly monstrous. I have argued with my uncle and the others until my throat is raw from talking, and nothing I say makes any difference. Glaucous feeds their fear. They are all gorging themselves on terror."

"Aren't you dining with them?" Silvan asked, half-turning.

"No, Cousin! Of course not!" Kiryn was astonished. "Could you imagine that I would? This is murder. Plain and simple. They may call it an 'execution' and try to dress it up so that it looks respectable, but they cannot hide the ugly truth. I do not care if this human is the worst, most reprehensible, most dangerous human who ever lived. Her blood will forever stain the ground upon which it falls, a stain that will spread like a blight among us."

Kiryn's voice dropped. He cast an apprehensive glance out the tent. "Already, Cousin, Glaucous speaks of traitors among our people, of meting out the same punishment to elves. My uncle and the Heads of House were all horrified and utterly opposed to the idea, but I fear that they will cease to feed on fear and start to feed on each other."

"Glaucous," Silvan repeated softly. He might have said more, but he remembered his promise to Mina. "Fetch my breastplate, will you, Cousin? And my sword. Help me on with them, will you?"

"I can call your attendants," Kiryn offered.

"No, I want no one." Silvan clenched his fist. "If one of my servants said something insulting about her I might . . . I might do something I would regret."

Kiryn helped with the leather buckles.

"I have heard that she is quite lovely. For a human," he remarked.

Silvan cast his cousin a sharp, suspicious glance.

Kiryn did not look up from his work. Muttering under his breath, he pretended to be preoccupied with a recalcitrant strap.

Reassured, Silvan relaxed. "She is the most beautiful woman I ever saw, Kiryn! So fragile and delicate. And her eyes! I have never seen such eyes!"

"And yet, Cousin," Kiryn rebuked gently, "she is a Knight of Neraka. One of those who have pledged our destruction."

"A mistake!" Silvan cried, going from ice to fire in a flash. "I am certain of it! She has been bewitched by the Knights or . . . or they hold her family hostage . . . or any number of reasons! In truth, she came here to save us."

"Bringing with her a troop of armed soldiers," Kiryn said dryly.

"You will see, Cousin," Silvan predicted. "You will see that I am right. I'll prove it to you." He rounded on Kiryn. "Do you know what I did? I went last night to set her free. I did! I cut a hole in her tent. I was going to unlock her chains. She refused to leave."

"You did what?" Kiryn gasped, appalled. "Cousin—"

"Never mind," said Silvan, turning away, the flame flaring out, the ice reforming. "I don't want to discuss it. I shouldn't have told you. You're as bad as the rest. Get out! Leave me alone."

Kiryn thought it best to obey. He put his hand on the tent flap and was halfway out when Silvan caught hold of him by the shoulder, gripped him hard.

"Are you going to run to tell Konnal what I told you? Because if you are—"

"I am not, Cousin," Kiryn said quietly. "I will keep what you have said in confidence. You need not threaten me."

Silvan appeared ashamed. Mumbling something, he let loose of Kiryn's sleeve, turned his back on him.

Grieved, worried, afraid, both for his people and for his cousin, Kiryn stood outside the king's tent and tried to think what to do. He did not trust the human girl. He did not know much about the Knights of Neraka, but he had to believe that they would not promote someone who served them reluctantly or unwillingly to the rank of commander. And though no elf could ever speak well of a human, the elven soldiers had talked grudgingly of the enemy's tenacity in battle, their discipline. Even General Konnal, who detested all humans, had admitted that these soldiers had fought well, and though they had retreated, they had done so in good order. They had followed the girl through the shield and into a well-defended realm, where surely they must have known they would march to their deaths. No, these men did not serve an unwilling, treacherous commander.

It was not the girl who was bewitched. It was the girl who had done the bewitching. Silvan was clearly enamored of her. He was of an age when elven men first begin to feel the stirrings of passion, the age when a man falls in love with love itself. An age when he may become drunk with adoration. "I love to love my love," was the first line of a chorus of a popular elven song. A pity that fortune had thrown the two of them together, had literally tossed the exotic and beautiful human girl into the young king's arms.

Silvan was plotting something. Kiryn could not imagine what, but he was sick at heart. Kiryn liked his cousin. He considered that Silvanoshei had the makings of a good king. This folly could ruin him. The fact that he had tried to free this girl, their mortal enemy, was enough to brand him a traitor if anyone came to know of it. The Heads of House would never forgive Silvan. They would declare him a "dark elf" and would exile him as they had exiled his mother and his father. General Konnal only wanted an excuse.

Kiryn did not for a moment consider breaking his vow to the king. He would not tell anyone what Silvan had told him. He wished very much that Silvan had never spoken of it. Kiryn wondered unhappily what his cousin planned, wondered what he could do to prevent Silvan from acting in some foolish, hotheaded, impulsive manner that would end in his ruin. The best, the only thing he could do would be to keep close to his cousin and be ready to try to stop him.

The sun hung directly overhead, its single eye glaring down through the gauzy curtain of the shield as if frustrated that it could not gain a clearer view. The watery eye shown upon the bloody field being readied for yet another wetting. The sun gazed unwinking upon the sowers of death, who were planting bodies in the ground, not seeds. The Thon-Thalas had run red with blood yesterday. None could drink of it.

The elves had searched the woodlands to find a fallen tree that would be suitable for use as a stake. The Woodshapers crafted it so that it was smooth and sturdy and straight. They thrust the stake deep into the ground, hammered it into the soil, drove it deeply so that it was stable and would not fall.

General Konnal, accompanied by Glaucous, took the field. He wore his armor, carried his sword. The general's face was stern and set. Glaucous was pleased, triumphant. Officers formed the elven army into ranks in the field, brought them to attention. Elf soldiers surrounded the field, forming a protective barrier, keeping a lookout for the humans, who might take it into their heads to try to rescue their leader. The Heads of House assembled. The wounded who could drag themselves from their beds lined up to watch.

Kiryn took his place beside his uncle. The young man looked so unwell that Konnal advised him in a low voice to return to his tent. Kiryn shook his head and remained where he was.

Seven archers had been chosen to make up the death squad. They formed a single line about twenty paces from the stake. They nocked their arrows, held their bows ready.

A trumpet sounded announcing the arrival of His Majesty the Speaker of the Stars. Silvanoshei walked alone, without escort, onto the field. He was extremely pale, so pale that the whispered rumor ran among the Heads of House that his majesty had suffered a wound in the battle, a wound that had drained his heart's blood.

Silvan halted at the edge of the field. He looked around at the disposition of the troops, looked at the stake, looked at the Heads of House, looked at Konnal and at Glaucous. A chair had been placed for the king on one side of the field, at a safe distance from where the prisoner must make her final walk. Silvan glanced at the chair, strode past it. He took up his place beside General Konnal, standing between Konnal and Glaucous.

Konnal was not pleased. "We have a chair for Your Majesty. In a place of safety."

"I stand at your side, General," Silvan said, turning his gaze full upon Konnal. "I can think of nowhere I would be safer. Can you?"

The general flushed, flustered. He cast a sidelong glance at Glaucous, who shrugged as much as to say, "Don't waste time arguing. What does it matter?"

"Let the prisoner be brought forth!" Konnal ordered.

Silvan held himself rigid, his hand on his sword hilt. His expression was fixed, set, gave away nothing of his inner thoughts or feelings.

Six elven guards with swords drawn, their blades flashing white in the sunlight, marched the prisoner onto the field. The guards were tall and accoutered in plate mail. The girl wore a white shift, a plain gown, unadorned, like a child's nightclothes. Her hands and feet were manacled. She looked small and frail, fragile and delicate, a waif surrounded by adults. Cruel adults.

A murmur swept among some of the Heads of House, a murmur of pity and dismay, a murmur of doubt. This was the dread commander! This girl! This child! The murmur was answered with an angry growl from the soldiers. She is human. She is our enemy.

Konnal turned his head, silenced the dismay and the anger with a single baleful glance.

"Bring the prisoner to me," Konnal called, "so that she may know the charges for which her life is forfeit."

The guards escorted the prisoner, who walked slowly, due to the manacles on her ankles, but who walked with regal bearing—straight back and lifted head and a strange, calm smile upon her lips. Her guards, by contrast, looked exceedingly uncomfortable. She stepped lightly over the ground, seemed to barely touch it. The guards slogged across the churned-up dirt as if it were rough going. They were winded and exhausted by the time they escorted their charge to stand before the general. The guards cast watchful, nervous glances at their prisoner, who never once looked at them.

Mina did not look at Silvanoshei, who was looking at her with all his heart and all his soul, willing her to give him the sign, ready to battle the entire elven army if she but said the word. Mina's amber-eyed gaze took in General Konnal, and though he appeared to struggle against it for a moment, he could not help himself. He joined the other insects, trapped inside the golden resin.

Konnal launched into a speech, explaining why it was necessary to go against elven custom and belief and rob this person of her most precious gift—her life. He was an effective speaker and produced many salient points. The speech would have gone over well if he had given it earlier, before the people were allowed to see the prisoner. As it was, he had now the look of a brutal father inflicting abusive punishment on a helpless child. He understood that he was losing his audience; many in the crowd were growing restless and uneasy, reconsidering their verdict. Konnal brought his speech to a swift, if somewhat abrupt, end.

"Prisoner, what is your name?" he barked, speaking Common. His voice, unnaturally loud, bounded back at him from the mountains.

"Mina," she replied, her voice cool as the blood-tinged Thon-Thalas and with the same hint of iron.

"Surname?" he asked. "For the record."

"Mina is the only name I bear," she said.

"Prisoner Mina," said General Konnal sternly, "you led an armed force into our lands without cause, for we are a peace-loving people. Because there exists no formal declaration of war between our peoples, we consider you to be nothing but a brigand, an outlaw, a murderer. You are therefore sentenced to death. Do you have aught to say in answer to these charges?"

"I do," Mina replied, serious and earnest. "I did not come here to make war upon the Qualinesti people. I came to save them."

Konnal gave a bitter, angry laugh. "We know full well that to the Knights of Neraka 'salvation' is another word for conquering and enslavement."

"I came to save your people," said Mina quietly, gently, "and I will do so."

"She makes a mockery of you, General," Glaucous whispered urgently into Konnal's left ear. "Get this over with!"

Konnal paid no attention to his adviser, except to shrug him off and move a step away from him.

"I have one more question, Prisoner," the General continued in portentous tones. "Your answer will not save you from death, but the arrows might fly a little straighter and hit their target a little quicker if you cooperate. How did you manage to enter the shield?"

"I will tell you and gladly," Mina said at once. "The hand of the God I follow, the Hand of the One True God of the world and all peoples in the world reached down from the heavens and raised the shield so that I and those who accompany me could enter."

A whisper like an icy wind blowing unexpectedly on a summer's day passed from elf to elf, repeating her words, though that was not necessary. All had heard her clearly.

"You speak falsely, Prisoner!" said Konnal in a hollow, furious voice. "The gods are gone and will not return."

"I warned you," Glaucous said, sighing. He eyed Mina uneasily. "Put her to death! Now!"

"I am not the one who speaks falsely," Mina said. "I am not the one who will die this day. I am not the one whose life is forfeit. Hear the words of the One True God."

She turned and looked directly at Glaucous. "Greedy, ambitious, you colluded with my enemies to rob me of what is rightfully mine. The penalty for faithlessness is death."

Mina raised her hands to the heavens. No cloud marred the sky, but the manacles that bound her wrists split apart as if struck by lightning and fell, ringing, to the ground. The chains that bound her melted, dissolved. Freed of her restraints, she pointed at Glaucous, pointed at his breast.

"Your spell is broken! The illusion ended! You can no longer hide your body on the plane of enchantment while your soul walks about in another form. Let them see you, Cyan Bloodbane. Let the elves see their 'savior.' "

A flash of light flared from the breast of the elf known as Glaucous. He cried out in pain, grappled for the magical amulet, but the silver rope that held it around his neck was broken, and with it broke the spell the amulet had cast.

The elves beheld an astonishing sight. The form of Glaucous grew and expanded so that for the span of a heartbeat his elven body was immense, hideous, contorted. The elf sprouted green wings. Green scales slid over the mouth that was twisted in hatred. Green scales rippled across the rapidly elongating nose. Fangs thrust up from the lengthening jaws, impeding the flow of vile curses that were spewing from his mouth, transforming the words into poisonous fumes. His arms became legs that ended in jabbing claws. His legs were now hind legs, strong and muscular. His great tail coiled, prepared to lash out with the deadly power of a whip or a striking snake.

"Cyan!" the elves cried in terror. "Cyan! Cyan!"

No one moved. No one could move. The dragonfear paralyzed their limbs, froze hands and hearts, seized them and shook them like a wolf shakes a rabbit to break its spine.

Yet Cyan Bloodbane was not yet truly among them. His soul and body were still joining, still coming together. He was in mid-transformation, vulnerable, and he knew it. He required seconds only to become one, but he had to have those few precious seconds.

He used the dragonfear to buy himself the time he needed, rendering the elves helpless, sending some of them wild with fear and despair. General Konnal, dazed by the overwhelming horror of the destruction he had brought down upon his own people, was like a man struck by a thunderbolt. He made a feeble attempt to draw his sword, but his right hand refused to obey his command.

Cyan ignored the general. He would deal with that wretch later. The dragon concentrated his fury and his ire upon the one, true danger—the creature who had unmasked him. The creature who had somehow managed to break the powerful spell of the amulet, an amulet that permitted body and soul to live apart, an amulet given to the dragon as a gift from his former master, the infamous wizard Raistlin Majere.

Mina shivered with the dragonfear. Not even her faith could guard her against it. She was unarmed, helpless. Cyan breathed his poisonous fumes, fumes that were weak, just as his crushing jaws were still weak. The lethal gas would immobilize this puny mortal, and then his jaws would be strong enough to tear the human's heart from her breast and rip her head from her body.

Silvan was also consumed with dragonfear—fear and astonishment, horror and a terrifying realization: Cyan Bloodbane, the dragon who had been the curse of the grandfather, was now the curse of the grandson. Silvan shuddered to think what he might have done at Glaucous's bidding if Mina had not opened his eyes to the truth.

Mina! He turned to find her, saw her stagger, clasp her throat, and fall backward to lie senseless on the ground in front of the dragon, whose slavering jaws were opening wide.

Fear for Mina, stronger and more powerful than the dragonfear, ran through Silvan's veins. Drawing his sword, he leaped to stand over her, placing his body between her and the striking dragon.

Cyan had not wanted this Caladon to die so swiftly. He had looked forward to years of tormenting him as he had tormented his grandfather. Such a disappointment, but it could not be helped. Cyan breathed his poisoned gas on the elf.

Silvan coughed and gagged. The fumes sickened him, he felt himself drowning in them. Weakening, he yet managed a single wild sword swipe at the hideous head.

The blade sank into the soft flesh beneath the jaw, doing little true damage but causing the dragon pain. Cyan reared his head, the sword still embedded in the jaw, jerking the blade from Silvan's limp hand. A shake of the dragon's head sent blood spattering and the sword flying across the field

The dragon was whole. He was powerful. He was furious. His hatred for the elves bubbled in his gut. He intended to unleash his poison upon them, watch them die in writhing, choking agony. Cyan spread his wings and bounded into the air.

"Look upon me!" the dragon roared. "Look upon me, Silvanesti! Look upon my might and my power, and look upon your own doom!"

General Konnal saw suddenly the full extent of Glaucous's deception. He had been duped by the dragon. He had been as much Cyan Bloodbane's pawn as the man Konnal had despised, Lorac Caladon. In those last moments, Konnal saw the truth. The shield was not protecting them. It was killing them. Horror-stricken at the thought of the terrible fate he had unwittingly brought down upon his people, Konnal stared up at the green dragon that had been his bane. He opened his mouth to give the order to attack, but at that moment, his heart, filled with fury and guilt, burst in his chest. He pitched forward on his face.

Kiryn ran to his uncle, but Konnal was dead.

The dragon soared higher, circling, beating the air with his great wings, letting the dragonfear settle over the elves like a thick, blinding fog.

Silvan, his vision dimming, sank to the ground beside Mina. He tried, even as he fell dying, to shield her body with his own.

"Mina," he whispered, the last words he would ever speak, "I love you!"

He collapsed. Darkness closed over him.

Mina heard his words. Her amber eyes opened. She looked to see Silvan lying beside her. His own eyes were closed. He was not breathing. She looked about and saw the dragon above the battlefield, preparing to launch his attack. The elves were helpless, paralzyed by the dragonfear that twisted inside them, squeezing their hearts until they could not breathe or move or think of anything except the coming pain and horror. The elven archers stood staring up at death, their arrows nocked and ready to fire, but their shaking hands were limp on the bow strings, barely able to hold the weapons.

Their general lay dead on the ground.

Mina bent over Silvanoshei. Kissing him, she whispered, "You must not die! I need you!"

He began to breathe, but he did not move.

"The archers, Silvanoshei!" she cried. "Tell them to fire! You are their king! They will obey you."

She shook him. "Silvanoshei!"

He stirred, groaned. His eyes flickered, but Mina was running out of time.

She leaped to her feet. "Archers!" she shouted in flawless Silvanesti Elvish. "*Sagasto!* Fire! Fire!"

Her clarion call penetrated the dragonfear of a single archer. He did not know who spoke. He heard only the one word that seemed to have been pounded into his brain with the force of an iron spike. He lifted his bow and aimed at the dragon.

"*Sagasto!*" Mina cried. "Slay him! He betrayed you!"

Another archer heard her words and obeyed, and then another and another after that. They let fly their arrows and, as they did so, they overcame the dragonfear within themselves. The elves saw only an enemy now, one who was mortal, and they reached swiftly to nock their arrows. The first shafts fired from fingers that still trembled flew none too straight, but their target was so immense that even the worst shot must hit its mark, though perhaps not the mark at which it had been aimed. Two arrows tore holes in the dragon's wings. One stuck in his lashing tail. One struck the green scales on his chest and bounced off, fell harmlessly to the ground.

Once the dragonfear was overcome, the elves would not be affected by it again. Now the archers aimed for the vulnerable parts of the dragon's body, aimed for the tender flesh the scales did not cover, under the front legs, so near the heart. They aimed for the joints where the wings attached to the dragon's main body. They aimed for the dragon's eyes.

The other elves lifted their heads now. Dozens at first, then hundreds shook off the dragonfear and grabbed up bow and arrow, spear and lance, and joined the battle. Cries of horror changed to fierce exultation. At last, they were able to face in combat the foe who had brought despair and ruin and death to their land and their people. The sky was dark with arrows and with the dragon's falling blood.

Maddened by the pain, Cyan Bloodbane made a mistake. He did not retreat from the fight. He could have withdrawn, even now, grievously hurt as he was, and flown away to one of his many lairs to nurse his wounds. But he could not believe that the puny people who had been subject to his will for so long could possibly do him mortal harm. One enormous breath of poison would settle them. One breath would end it.

Cyan sucked in that breath and let it out. But the breath that should have been a killing cloud came out a gasp. The poisonous gas was little more than a mist that dissipated in the morning's soft breeze. His next breath rattled in his chest. He felt the arrows sink deep into his bowels. He felt their points perilously close to his heart. He felt them puncture his lungs. Too late, he tried to break off the battle. Too late, he sought to flee his tormentors. His torn and broken wings would not hold the air. He could not maintain his altitude.

Cyan rolled over on his back. He was falling, and he could not stop his fall. Plummeting to the ground, he realized in a final moment of bitter despair that his last wrenching moves had carried him away from the battlefield, where his body crashing down on top of the elves might have taken many of his enemies with him. He was over the forest, above the trees.

With a last defiant roar of fury, Cyan Bloodbane fell onto the trees of Silvanesti, the trees that he had twisted and tormented during the dream. The trees were waiting to receive him. The aspens and the oaks, the cypress and the pines stood firm, like bold pikeman. They did not break beneath his weight but held strong and true as their enemy smashed into them. The trees punched through Cyan Bloodbane's scales, pierced his flesh, impaled him on their splintered limbs. The trees of Silvanesti took their own full measure of revenge.

Silvanoshei opened his eyes to see Mina standing protectively over him. He staggered to his feet, dazed and unsteady, but improving with each passing moment. Mina was watching the battle against the dragon. Her face held no expression, as she watched the arrows meant to pierce her own body penetrate the body of her foe.

Silvan barely noticed the battle. He could see and think only of Mina.

"You brought me back from death," Silvan whispered, his throat raw from the gas. "I was dying, dead. I felt my soul slipping away. I saw my own body lying on the ground. I saw you kiss me. You kissed me, and I could not leave you! And so I live!"

"The One God brought you back, Silvanoshei," said Mina calmly. "The One God has a purpose for you yet in this life."

"No, you!" he insisted. "You gave me life! Because you love me! My life is yours, now, Mina. My life and my heart."

Mina smiled, but she was intent on the fight. "Look there, Silvanoshei," she said, pointing, "This day you have defeated your most terrible enemy, Cyan Bloodbane, who put you on the throne, thinking you as weak as your grandfather. You have proved him wrong."

"We owe our victory to you, Mina," Silvan said, exultant. "You gave the order to fire. I heard your voice through the darkness."

"We have not achieved victory yet," she said, and her gaze was farseeing, abstracted. "Not yet. The battle has not ended. Your people remain in mortal danger. Cyan Bloodbane will die, but the shield he placed over you remains."

Silvan could barely hear her voice over the cheers of his people and the furious howls of the mortally wounded dragon. Putting his arm around her slender waist, he drew her near to him, to hear her words better.

"Tell me again, Mina," he said. "Tell me again what you told me earlier about the shield."

"I tell you nothing more than what Cyan Bloodbane told you," Mina replied. "He used the elves' fear of the world against them. They imagine the shield protects them, but in reality it is killing them. The magic of the shield draws upon the life-force of the elves to maintain its life. So long as it remains in place, your people will slowly die until at last there will be no one left for the shield to protect. Thus did Cyan Bloodbane mean to destroy every one of you, laughing all the while because your people imagined themselves to be safe and protected when, in reality, they were the means of their own destruction."

"If this is true, the shield must be destroyed," said Silvan. "But I doubt if even our strongest sorcerers could shatter its powerful magic."

"You don't need sorcerers, Silvan. You are the grandson of Lorac Caladon. You can end what your grandfather began. You have the power to bring down the shield. Come with me." Mina held out her hand to him. "I will show you what you must do."

Silvan took hold of her hand, small-boned, fine. He drew close to her, looked down into her eyes. He saw himself, shining in the amber.

"You must kiss me," she said and she lifted her lips.

Silvan was quick to obey. His lips touched hers, tasted the sweetness for which he hungered.

Not far distant, Kiryn kept watch beside the body of his uncle. He had seen Silvanoshei fall. He had known that his cousin was dead, for no one could not survive the dragon's poisoned breath. Kiryn grieved for them both, for his cousin, for his uncle. Both had been deluded by Glaucous. Both had paid the price. Kiryn had knelt beside his uncle to wait for his own death, wait for the dragon to slay them.

Kiryn watched, astonished, to see the human girl, Mina, lift her head and regain her feet. She was strong, alert, seemingly untouched by the poison. She looked down at Silvanoshei, lying at her side. She kissed the lifeless lips, and to Kiryn's amazement and unease, his cousin drew in a breath.

Kiryn saw Mina act to rally the flagging spirits of the elven archers. He heard her voice, crying out the order to fire in Elvish. He watched his people rally, watched them battle back against their foe. He watched the dragon die.

He watched all with boundless gladness, a gladness that brought tears to his eyes, but with a sense of unease in his heart.

Why had the human done this? What was her reason? Why had she watched her army kill elves one day and acted to save elves the next?

He watched her embrace Silvan. Kiryn wanted to run to them, to snatch his cousin away from the girl's touch. He wanted to shake him, shake some sense into him. But Silvan would not listen.

And why should he? Kiryn thought.

He himself was confused, stunned by the day's awful events. Why should his cousin listen to Kiryn's words of warning when the only proof he could offer of their veracity was a dark shadow that passed over his soul every time he looked upon the girl, Mina.

Kiryn turned away from them. Reaching down, he closed his uncle's staring eyes with a gentle touch. His duty, as a nephew, was to the dead.

"Come with me, Silvan," Mina urged him, her lips soft against his cheek. "Do this for your people."

"I do this for you, Mina," Silvan whispered. Closing his eyes, he placed his lips on hers.

Her kiss was honey, yet it stung him. He drank in the sweetness, flinched from the searing pain. She drew him into darkness, a darkness that was like the darkness of the storm cloud. Her kiss was like the lightning bolt, blinded him, sent him tumbling over the edge of a precipice. He could not stop his fall. He crashed against rocks, felt his bones breaking, his body bruised and aching. The pain was excruciating, and the pain was ecstasy. He wanted it to end so badly that he would have been glad for death. He wanted the pain to last beyond forever.

Her lips drew away from his, the spell was broken.

As though he had come back from the dead, Silvan opened his eyes and was amazed to see the sun, the blood-red sun of twilight. Yet it had been noontime when he had kissed her. Hours had passed, seemingly, but where had they gone? Lost in her, forgotten in her. All around him was still and quiet. The dragon had vanished. The armies were nowhere in sight. His cousin was gone. Silvan slowly realized that he no longer stood on the field of battle. He was in a garden, a garden he dimly recognized by the fading light of the waning sun.

I know this place, he thought dazedly. It seems familiar. Yet where am I?

And how do I come to be here? Mina! Mina! He was momentarily panicked, thinking he had lost her.

He felt her hand close over his, and he sighed deeply and clasped his hand over hers.

I stand in the Garden of Astarin, he realized. The palace garden. A garden I can see from my bedroom window. I came here once, and I hated it. The place made my flesh crawl. There—a dead plant. And another and another. A tree dying as I watch, its leaves curling and twisting as if in pain, turning gray, falling off. The only reason there are any living plants at all in this garden is because the palace gardeners and the Woodshapers replace the dead plants with living plants from their own personal gardens. Yet, to bring anything living into this garden is to sentence it to death.

Only one tree survives in this garden. The tree in the very heart of the garden. The tree they call the Shield Tree, because it was once surrounded by a luminous shield nothing could penetrate. Glaucous claimed the magic of the tree kept the shield in place. So it does, but the tree's roots do not draw nourishment from the soil. The tree's roots extend into the heart of every elf in Silvanesti.

He felt the tree's roots coiling inside him.

Taking hold of Mina by the hand, Silvanoshei led her through the dying garden to the tree that grew in the center. The Shield Tree lived. The Shield Tree thrived. The Shield tree's leaves were green and healthy, green as the scales of the green dragon. The Shield Tree's trunk was blood-colored, seemed to ooze blood, as they looked at it. Its limbs contorted, wriggled like snakes.

I must uproot the tree. I am the Grandson of Lorac. I must tear the tree's roots from the hearts of my people, and so I will free them. Yet I am loathe to touch the evil thing. I'll find an axe, chop it down.

Though you were to chop it down a hundred times, a voice whispered to him, *a hundred times it would grow back.*

It will die, now that Cyan Bloodbane is dead. He was the one who kept it alive.

You are the one keeping it alive. Mina spoke no word, but she laid her hand on his heart. *You and your people. Can't you feel its roots twisting and turning inside you, sapping your strength, sucking the very life from you?*

Silvan could feel something wringing his heart, but whether it was the evil of the tree or the touch of her hand, he could not tell.

He caught up her hand and kissed it. Leaving her standing on the path, among the dying plants, he walked toward the living tree. The tree sensed its danger. Gray vines twined around his ankles. Dead branches fell on him, struck him on the back and on his shoulder. He kicked at the vines and tossed the branches away from him.

As he drew near the tree, he felt the weakness. He felt it grow on him the closer he came. The tree sought to kill him as it had killed so many before him. Its sap ran red with the blood of his people. Every shining leaf was the soul of a murdered elf.

The tree was tall, but its trunk was spindly. Silvan could easily place his hands around it. He was weak and wobbly from the aftereffects of the poison and wondered if he would have the strength to pull it from the ground.

You have the strength. You alone.

Silvan wrapped his hands around the tree trunk. The trunk writhed in his grasp like a snake, and he shuddered at the horrible feeling.

He let loose, fell back. If the shield falls, he thought, suddenly assailed by doubt, our land will lie unprotected.

The Silvanesti nation has stood proudly for centuries protected by the courage and skill of its warriors. Those days of glory will return. The days when the world respected the elves and honored them and feared them. You will be king of a powerful nation, a powerful people.

I will be king, Silvan repeated to himself. She will see me puissant, noble, and she will love me.

He planted his feet on the ground. He took firm hold of the slithering tree trunk and, summoning strength from his excitement, his love, his ambition, his dreams, he gave a great heave.

A single root snapped. Perhaps it was the root that had tapped into his own heart for when it released, his strength and his will increased. He pulled and tugged, his shoulders straining. He felt more roots give, and he redoubled his efforts.

"For Mina!" he said beneath his breath.

The roots let go their hold so suddenly that Silvan toppled over backward. The tree came crashing down on top of him. He was unhurt, but he could see nothing for the leaves and twigs and branches that covered him.

Angry, feeling that he must look a fool, he crawled out from under. His face flushed with triumph and embarrassment, he wiped the dirt and the muck from his hands.

The sun shone hot on his face. Looking up, Silvan saw the sun, saw it shining with an angry red fire. No gauzy curtain obscured its rays, no shimmering aura filtered its light. He found he could not look directly at the blazing sun, could not look anywhere near it. The sight was painful, hurt his eyes. Blinking away tears, he could see nothing except a black spot where the sun had been.

"Mina!" he cried, shading his eyes, trying to see her. "Look, Mina! Your God was right. The shield is down!"

Silvan stumbled out onto the path. He could not yet see clearly. "Mina?" he cried. "Mina?"

Silvan called and called. He called long after the sun had fallen from the sky, called long into the darkness. He called her name until he had no voice left, and then he whispered it.

"Mina!"

No answer came.

33 FOR LOVE OF MINA

Galdar had not slept since the day of the battle. He kept watch all the long night, standing just inside the shadows of the caves where what remained of the forces of her Knights had taken refuge. He refused to relinquish his post to anyone, although several had offered to relieve him of his self-imposed duty. He shook his horned head to all proposals, sent the men away, and eventually they quit coming.

The men who had survived the battle lay in the caves, tired and frightened, speaking little. The wounded did their best to stifle their groans and cries, afraid that the noise would draw down the enemy upon them. Mostly they whispered a name, her name and wondered why she did not come to comfort them. Those who died did so with her name on their lips.

Galdar was not watching for the enemy. That duty was being handled by others. Pickets crouched in the thick foliage on watch for any elven scout who might happen to stumble upon their hiding place. Two elves did so, early this morning. The pickets dealt with them swiftly and silently, breaking their necks and throwing the bodies into the deep and swift-flowing Thon-Thalas.

Galdar was furious when he found out that his men had actually captured the two elves alive before killing them.

"I wanted to question them, you dolts!" he cried in a rage, raising his hand to strike one of the scouts.

"Relax, Galdar," Samuval admonished, placing his hand on the minotaur's fur-covered arm. "What good would torturing them have done? The elves would only refuse to talk, and their screams would be heard for miles."

"They would tell me what they have done with her," Galdar said, lowering his arm, but glowering viciously at the scouts, who beat a hasty retreat. "They would tell me where she was being held. I would see to that." He clenched and unclenched his fist.

"Mina left orders that no prisoners were to be taken, Galdar. She ordered that any elf we found was to be put immediately to death. You vowed to obey her orders. Would you be foresworn?" Samuval asked.

"I'll keep my vow." Galdar growled and took up his post again. "I promised her, and I will keep my promise. Didn't I keep it yesterday? I stood there and watched her taken captive by that bastard elven king. Captured alive by her most bitter enemy. Carried off in triumph to what terrible fate? To be made sport of, to be made a slave, to be tormented, killed. I promised her I would not interfere, and I kept my word. But I am sorry now that I did so," he added with a bitter oath.

"Remember what she said, my friend," Samuval said quietly. "Remember her words. 'They think they will make me their captive. But in so doing I will capture them, every single one.' Remember that, and do not lose your faith."

Galdar stood at the entrance to the cave all that morning. He saw the sun rise to its zenith, saw its angry eye glare through the shield, and he envied it fiercely, for the sun could see Mina and he could not.

He watched in wonder the fight with the green dragon, saw the sky rain blood and green scales. Galdar had no love for dragons, even those who fought on his side. An old minotaur adage, dating back from the time of their great hero, Kaz, maintained that dragons had only one side: their own. Galdar heard the dragon's death roar, felt the ground shake from the beast's fall, and wondered only what portent this held for them. For Mina.

Captain Samuval joined Galdar to watch the fight. He brought the minotaur food—rat, caught in the cave—and drink. Galdar drank the water, but he refused the rat meat. The men had little enough to eat as it was. Others needed it more than he did. Captain Samuval shrugged and ate the rat himself. Galdar continued his watch.

The hours passed. The wounded groaned quietly, died quietly. The sun started to fall, a blood-red sun, dropping behind its curtain of gauze. The sun was distorted and misshapen, looking like no sun Galdar had ever before seen. He shifted his gaze away. He did not like seeing the sun through the shield, wondered how the elves could stand it.

His eyes closed in spite of himself. He was nodding off, drowsing on his feet, when Captain Samuval's voice sounded right next to him, seemed to explode over the minotaur like a fireball.

"Would you look at that!"

Galdar's eyes flared open. He fumbled for his sword. "What? Where?"

"The sun!" Captain Samuval said. "No, don't look at it directly. It will blind you!" He shaded his eyes with his hand, peered out from beneath the shadow. "Damn!"

Galdar looked heavenward. The light was so bright it made his eyes water, and he had to look hurriedly away. He wiped the tears from his muzzle and squinted. The sun had burned away the gauze. It shone bright and fierce upon the world as if it were a new-made sun and was exulting in its power. He lowered his gaze, half-blinded.

Mina stood before him, bathed in the blood-red light of the new-born sun.

Galdar was about to raise a shout of joy, but she laid a finger on her lips, counseling silence. The minotaur settled for a huge grin. He did not tell her he was thankful to see her. She had promised she would return to them, and he did not want her to think he doubted. In truth, he had not doubted. Not in his heart. He jerked a thumb toward the horizon.

"What does it mean?" he asked.

"The shield is lowered," Mina replied. She was pale and weary to the point of falling. She reached out her hand, and Galdar was honored and proud to support her with his arm, his right arm. "The spell is broken. As we speak, the forces of General Dogah, many thousands strong, are marching across the border of Silvanesti."

Leaning on Galdar's strong arm, Mina entered the cave. The men would have cheered, but she cautioned them to silence.

The men gathered around her, reached out their hands to touch her. Tired as she was, she said a word to each one of them, calling each by name. She would not eat or drink or rest until she had visited the wounded and asked the God to heal them. She prayed over every one of the dead, as well, holding the cold hands in her own, her head bowed.

Then and only then would she drink water and sit down to rest. She summoned her Knights and officers to a council of war.

"We have only to continue a little while longer in hiding," she told them. "My plan is to meet up with the armies of General Dogah and join them in the capture of Silvanost."

"How soon can he be here?" Samuval asked.

"Dogah and his forces will be able to march rapidly," Mina replied. "He will meet no resistance. The elven border patrol was pulled back to deal with us. Their army is in disarray. Their general is dead. The shield has fallen."

"How, Mina?" Galdar asked and others echoed his wonder. "Tell us how you brought down the shield?"

"I told the king the truth," Mina said. "I told him that the shield was killing his people. Their king himself brought down the shield."

The Knights laughed, enjoying the fine irony. They were in excellent spirits, cheered and heartened by Mina's return and the miraculous lowering of the magical shield, which had for so long kept them from striking at their enemy.

Turning to ask Mina a question, Galdar saw that she had fallen asleep. Gently, he lifted her in his arms and carried her—she was a light as a child—to the bed he had made for her himself, a blanket spread over dried pine needles in a niche in the rock wall. He eased her down, covered her with a blanket. She never opened her eyes.

The minotaur settled himself near her, seated with his broad back against the rocky wall to guard her sleep.

Captain Samuval came to keep watch beside Galdar. The captain offered the minotaur more rat meat, and this time Galdar did not refuse.

"Why would the king lower the shield?" Galdar wondered, crunching the rat, bones and all. "Why would he bring down the elves' only defense? It doesn't make any sense. Elves are sneaky. Perhaps it is a trap."

"No trap," said Samuval. Bunching up a blanket, he shoved it beneath his head and stretched himself out on the cold cavern floor. "You will see, my friend. In a week's time, we'll be walking arm and arm down the streets of Silvanost."

"But why would he do such a thing?" Galdar persisted.

"Why else?" Samuval said, yawning until his jaws cracked. "You saw the way he looked at her. You saw her take him captive. He did it for love of her, of course."

Galdar settled himself. He considered the answer, decided that his comrade was right. Before he slept, he whispered the words softly to the night.

"For love of Mina."

EPILOGUE

Far from where Mina slept, guarded by her troops, Gilthas watched from a window of the Tower of the Speaker of the Sun as the sun lifted higher into the sky. He imagined its rays gilding the spears of the armies of Beryl as that army marched across the border into Qualinesti. The Solamnic, Gerard, had suggested a plan, a desperate plan, and now he and Marshal Medan waited for Gilthas to make a decision, a decision that would either mean salvation for his people or would end in their ultimate destruction. Gilthas would make that decision. He would make it because he was their king. But he would put off the decision for the moment. He would spend this moment watching the sun shimmer on the green leaves of the trees of his homeland.

On Schallsea, Tasslehoff and Palin watched Beryl and her minions fly closer and closer. They heard the trumpets blasting, heard people crying out in terror. They heard them cry for Goldmoon, but she was gone. The broken bits of the magical Device of Time Journeying lay scattered on the floor, the light of the jewels dimmed by the shadows of the wings of dragons.

Goldmoon did not see the sun. She did not see the dragons. She was far beneath the ocean, wrapped in its darkness. The gnome expostulated and sweated and raced here and dashed there, mopping up water, sopping up oil, cranking cranks and pumping bellows. Goldmoon paid no attention to him. She had been absorbed by the darkness. She traveled northward with the river of the dead.

Silvanoshei stood alone in the Garden of Astarin, beside the dying Shield Tree, and watched the new-made blazing sun wither the tree's roots.

Poised on the borders of Silvanesti, General Dogah of the Knights of Neraka watched the sun emerge from the crysallis of the fallen shield. The next morning, when the sun had mounted into the sky, when it shone clear and bright, General Dogah gave his army the order to march.

VOLUME
II

DRAGONS OF A
LOST
STAR

AN ACCOUNTING NIGHTMARE

Morham Targonne was having a bad day. His accounts would not balance. The difference in the totals was paltry, a matter of a few steel. He could have made it up with the spare change from his purse. But Targonne liked things to be neat, orderly. His rows of figures should add up. There should be no discrepancies. Yet here he was. He had the various accounts of moneys coming into the knights' coffers. He had the various accounts of moneys going out of the Knights' coffers, and there was a difference of twenty-seven steel, fourteen silver, and five coppers. Had it been a major sum, he might have suspected embezzlement. As it was, he was certain that some minor functionary had made a simple miscalculation. Targonne would have to go back through all the accounts, redo the calculations, track down the error.

An uninformed observer, seeing Morham Targonne seated at his desk, his fingers black with ink, his head bent over his accounts, would have said that he was looking on a loyal and dedicated clerk. The uninformed observer would have been wrong. Morham Targonne was the leader of the Dark Knights of Neraka and thereby, since the Dark Knights were in control of several major nations on the continent of Ansalon, Morham Targonne held the power of life and death over millions of people. Yet here he was, working into the night, looking with the diligence of the stodgiest clerk for twenty-seven steel, fourteen silver, and five coppers.

But although he was concentrating on his work to the extent that he had skipped supper to continue his perusal of the accounts, Lord Targonne was not absorbed in his work to the exclusion of all else. He had the ability to focus a part of his mental powers on a task and, at the same time, to be keenly alert, aware of what was going on around him. His mind was a desk constructed of innumerable compartments into which he sorted and slotted every occurrence, no matter how minor, placed it in its proper hole, available for his use at some later time.

Targonne knew, for example, when his aide left to go to his own supper, knew precisely how long the man was away from his desk, knew when he returned. Knowing approximately how long it would take a man to eat his supper, Targonne was able to say that his aide had not lingered over his tarbean tea but had returned to his work with alacrity. Targonne would remember this in the aide's favor someday, setting that against the opposite column in which he posted minor infractions of duty.

The aide was staying at work late this night. He would stay until Targonne discovered the twenty-seven steel, fourteen silver, and five coppers, even if they were both awake until the sun's rays crept through Targonne's freshly cleaned window. The aide had his own work to keep him occupied—Targonne saw to that. If there was one thing he hated, it was to see a man idling. The two worked late into the night, the aide sitting at a desk outside the office, trying to see by lamplight as he stifled his yawns, and Targonne sitting inside his sparsely furnished office, head bent over his bookkeeping, whispering the numbers to himself as he wrote them, a habit of his of which he was completely unconscious.

The aide was himself slipping toward unconsciousness when, fortunately for him, a loud commotion in the courtyard outside the fortress of the Dark Knights startled him from a brief nap.

A blast of wind set the window panes rattling. Voices shouted out harshly in irritation or warning. Booted feet came running. The aide left his desk and went to see what was happening at the same time as Targonne's voice called from his office, demanding to know what was going on and who in the Abyss was making all this blasted racket.

The aide returned almost immediately.

"My lord, a dragonrider has arrived from—"

"What does the fool mean, landing in the courtyard?"

Hearing the noise, Targonne had actually left his accounting long enough to turn to look out his window. He was infuriated to see the large blue dragon flapping about his courtyard. The large blue looked infuriated herself, for she had been forced to alight in an area that was much too small and cramped for her bulk. She had just missed a guard tower with her wing. Her tail had taken out a small portion of the battlements. Other than that, she had managed to land safely and now squatted in the courtyard, her wings folded tight at her sides, her tail twitching. She was hungry and thirsty. There were no dragon stables close by nor any sign that she was going to have anything to eat or drink anytime soon. She glared balefully at Targonne through the window, as though she blamed him for her troubles.

"My lord," said the aide, "the rider comes from Silvanesti—"

"My lord!" The dragonrider, a tall man, stood behind the aide, loomed over him. "Forgive the disruption, but I bring news of such dire urgency and importance that I felt I had to inform you immediately."

"Silvanesti." Targonne snorted. Returning to his desk, he continued writing. "Has the shield fallen?" he asked sarcastically.

"Yes, my lord!" The dragonrider gasped, out of breath.

Targonne dropped his pen. Lifting his head, he stared at the messenger in astonishment. "What? How?"

"The young officer named Mina—" The dragonrider was forced to interrupt himself with a fit of coughing. "Might I have something to drink, my lord? I have swallowed a vast quantity of dust between here and Silvanesti."

Targonne made a motion with his hand, and his aide left to fetch ale. While they waited, Targonne invited the rider to be seated and rest himself.

"Order your thoughts," Targonne instructed, and as the Knight did just that, Targonne used his powers as a mentalist to probe the Knight's mind, to eavesdrop on those thoughts, see what the Knight had seen, hear what the Knight had heard.

The images bombarded Targonne. For the first time in his career, he found himself at a loss to know what to think. Too much was happening too fast for him to comprehend. What was overwhelmingly clear to Morham Targonne was that too much of it was happening without his knowledge and outside his control. He was so disturbed by this that he actually for the moment forgot the twenty-seven steel, fourteen silver, and five coppers, although he wasn't so rattled but that he made a note to himself when he closed his books as to where he left off in his calculations.

The aide returned with a mug of cold ale. The Knight drank deeply and, by that time, Targonne had managed to compose himself to listen with every appearance of outward calm. Inside, he was seething.

"Tell me everything," Targonne instructed.

The Knight complied.

"My lord, the young Knight officer known as Mina was able, as we reported to you earlier, to penetrate the magical shield that had been raised around Silvanesti—"

"But not lower the shield," Targonne interrupted, seeking clarification.

"No, my lord. In fact, she used the shield to fend off pursuing ogres, who were unable to break the enchantment. Mina led her small force of Knights and foot soldiers into Silvanesti with the apparent design of attacking the capital, Silvanost."

Targonne sniffed in derision.

"They were intercepted by a large force of elves and were handily defeated. Mina was captured during the battle and made prisoner. The elves planned to execute her the following morning. However, just prior to her execution, Mina attacked the green dragon Cyan Bloodbane, who had, as you were no doubt aware, my lord, been masquerading as an elf."

Targonne had not known that, nor did he see how he should have known it, since not even he could have seen through the cursed magical shield the elves had raised over their land. He made no comment, however. He never minded appearing omniscient.

"Her attack forced Cyan to reveal to the elves the fact that he was a dragon. The elves were terrified. Cyan would have slaughtered thousands of them, but this Mina roused the elven army and ordered them to attack the green dragon."

"Help me understand the situation," said Targonne, who was starting to feel an aching behind his right temple. "One of our own officers rallied the army of our most bitter enemy, who in turn slew one of the mightiest of our green dragons?"

"Yes, my lord," said the Knight. "You see, my lord, as it turned out, it was the dragon Cyan Bloodbane who had raised the magical shield that had been keeping our armies out of Silvanesti. The shield, as it turns out, was killing the elves."

"Ah," said Targonne and rubbed his temple with a forefinger. He hadn't known that either. But he might have been able to deduce it, had he given it much thought. The green dragon Cyan Bloodbane, terrified of Malystryx, vengeful toward the elves, built a shield that protected him from one enemy and helped destroy another. Ingenious. Flawed, but ingenious. "Proceed."

The Knight hesitated. "What happened after that is rather confused, my lord. General Dogah had received your orders to halt his march to Sanction and proceed instead to Silvanesti."

Targonne had given no such orders, but he had already observed Dogah's march from the Knight's mental processes and let this comment pass unremarked. He would deal with that later.

"General Dogah arrived to find the shield prohibited him from entering. He was furious, thinking he'd been sent on a kender's errand. The land around the shield is a terrible place, my lord, filled with dead trees and animal corpses. The air is fetid and foul to breathe. The men were upset, claiming the place was haunted and that we ourselves would die from being so near it, when, suddenly, with the rising of the sun, the shield shattered. I was with General Dogah, and I saw it with my own eyes."

"Describe it," Targonne ordered, eyeing the man intently.

"I have been thinking about how to do so, my lord. Once when I was a child, I stepped on an ice-covered pond. The ice beneath my feet began to crack. The cracks spread across the ice with a snapping sound, then the ice gave way, and I plunged into the black water. This was much the same. I saw the shield shimmering like ice in the sunshine, and then it seemed to me that I saw a million, million infinitesimal cracks, as thin as the strands of a cobweb, spread across the shield with lightning speed. There was a shivering, tinkling sound as of a thousand glass goblets crashing onto a stone floor, and the shield was gone.

"We could not believe our senses. At first, General Dogah dared not enter the shield, fearing a cunning elven trap. Perhaps, he said, we shall march across and the shield will crash down behind us, and we will end up facing an army of ten thousand elves, yet have nowhere to go. Suddenly there appeared among us, as if by magic, one of Mina's Knights. Through the power of the

One God, he came to tell us that the shield had indeed fallen, brought down by the elven king himself, Silvanoshei, son of Alhana—"

"Yes, yes," said Targonne impatiently. "I know the whelp's pedigree. Dogah believed this chit, and he and his troops crossed the border."

"Yes, my lord. General Dogah ordered me to take my blue dragon and fly back to report to you that he is now marching on Silvanost, the capital."

"What of the ten-thousand-man elven army?" Targonne asked dryly.

"As to the army, my lord, they have not attacked us. According to Mina, the king, Silvanoshei, has told them that Mina has come to save the Silvanesti nation in the name of the One God. I must say, my lord, that the elves are in pitiable condition. When our advance troops entered an elven fishing village near the shield, we observed that most of the elves were sick or dying from the cursed magic of the shield. We thought to slay the wretches, but Mina forbade it. She performed miracles of healing on the dying elves and restored them to life. When we left, the elves were singing her praises and blessing the One God and vowing to worship this god in Mina's name.

"Yet not all elves trust her. Mina warned us that we might be attacked by those who call themselves 'the kirath.' But, according to her, their numbers are few, and they are disorganized. Alhana Starbreeze has forces on the border, but Mina does not fear them. She does not appear to fear anything," the Knight added with an admiration he could not conceal.

The One God! Ha! Targonne thought to himself, seeing far more in the messenger's mind than he was saying. Sorcery. This Mina is a witch. She has everyone ensorcelled—the elves, Dogah, and my Knights included. They are as smitten with this upstart chippy as the elves. What is she after?

The answer was obvious to Targonne.

She is after my position, of course. She is subverting the loyalty of my officers and winning the admiration of my troops. She plots against me. A dangerous game for such a little girl.

He mused, forgetting the weary messenger. Outside the room came the thud of booted feet and a loud voice demanding to see the Lord of the Night.

"My lord!" His aide hastened into the room, interrupting Targonne's dark thoughts. "Another messenger has arrived."

A second messenger entered the room, glanced askance at the first.

"Yes, what is *your* news?" Targonne demanded of the second.

"I have been contacted by Feur the Red, our agent in the service of the great green dragon overlord Beryl. The red reports that she and a host of dragons bearing draconian soldiers have been ordered to undertake an assault on the Citadel of Light."

"The citadel?" Targonne struck his fist on the desk, causing a neatly stacked pile of steel coins to topple. "Is that green bitch of a dragon insane? What does she mean, attacking the citadel?"

"According to the red, Beryl has sent a messenger to tell you and her cousin Malystryx that this is a private quarrel and that there is no need for Malys to get involved. Beryl seeks a sorcerer who sneaked into her lands and stole a valuable magical artifact. She learned that the sorcerer fled for safety to the citadel, and she has gone to fetch him. Once she has him and the artifact, she will withdraw."

"Magic!" Targonne swore viciously. "Beryl is obsessed with magic. She thinks of nothing else. I have gray-robed wizards who spend all their time hunting for some blamed magical Tower just to placate that bloated lizard. Assaulting the citadel! What of the pact of the dragons? 'Cousin Malystryx' will most certainly see this as a threat from Beryl. This could mean all-out war, and that would wreck the economy."

Targonne rose to his feet. He was about to give an order to have messengers standing by, ready to carry this news to Malys, who must certainly hear of this from him, when he heard more shouting in the hallway.

"Urgent message for the Lord of the Night."

Targonne's aide, looking slightly frazzled, entered the room.

"What is it now?" Targonne growled.

"A messenger brings word from Marshal Medan in Qualinost that Beryl's forces have crossed the border into Qualinesti, pillaging and looting as they march. Medan urgently requests orders. He believes that Beryl intends to destroy Qualinesti, burn the forests to the ground, tear down the cities, and exterminate the elves."

"Dead elves pay me no tribute!" Targonne exclaimed, cursing Beryl with all his heart and soul. He began to pace behind his desk. "I cannot cut timber in a burned-out forest. Beryl attacks Qualinesti *and* the citadel. She is lying to me and to Malys. Beryl intends to break the pact. She plans war against Malys and against the Knighthood. I must find some way to stop her. Leave me! All of you," he ordered peremptorily. "I have work to do."

The first messenger bowed and left to eat and take what rest he could before the return flight. The second left to await orders. The aide departed to dispatch runners to wake other messengers and alert the blue dragons who would carry them.

After the aide and the messengers had gone, Targonne continued to pace the room. He was angry, infuriated, frustrated. Only a few moments before, he had been working on his accounts, content in the knowledge that the world was going as it should, that he had everything under control. True, the dragon overlords imagined that they were the ones in charge, but Targonne knew better. Bloated, enormous, they were—or had been—content to slumber in their lairs, allowing the Dark Knights of Neraka to rule in their names. The Dark Knights controlled Palanthas and Qualinost, two of the wealthiest cities on the continent. They would soon break the siege of Sanction and seize that seaport city, giving them access to New Sea. They had taken Haven, and he was even now drawing up plans to attack the prosperous crossroads town of Solace.

Now, he watched his plans topple in a heap like the stack of steel coins. Returning to his desk, Targonne laid out several sheets of foolscap. He dipped his pen into the ink and, after several more moments of profound thought, began to write.

General Dogah

Congratulations on your victory over the Silvanesti elves. These people have defied us for many years. However, I must warn you, do not trust them. I have no need to tell you that we do not have the manpower to hold Silvanesti if the elves decide to rise up in a body and rebel against us. I understand that they are sick and weakened, their population decimated, but they are tricky. Especially this king of theirs—Silvanoshei. He is the son of a cunning, treacherous mother and an outlawed father. He is undoubtedly in league with them. I want you to bring to me for interrogation any elves you believe might be able to provide me with information regarding any subversive plots of the elves. Be discreet in this, Dogah. I do not want to rouse the elves' suspicions.

Lord of the Night,
Targonne

He read over this letter, dusted the wet ink with sand to hasten the drying process, and set it aside. After a moment's thought, he set about composing the next.

To Dragon Overlord Malystryx, Your Most Exalted Majesty etc., etc.

It is with great pleasure that I make known to Your Most Illustrious Majesty that the elven people of Silvanesti, who have long defied us, have been utterly vanquished by the armies of the Dark Knights of Neraka. Tribute from these rich lands will soon be flowing into your coffers. The Knights of Neraka will, as usual, handle all the financial dealings to relieve you of such a mundane burden.

During the battle, the green dragon, Cyan Bloodbane, was discovered to have been hiding in Silvanesti. Fearing your wrath, he sided with the elves. Indeed, it was he who raised the magical shield that has so long kept us out of that land. He was slain during the battle. If possible, I will have his head found and delivered to Your Grace.

You may hear certain wild rumors that your cousin, Beryllinthranox, has broken the pact of the dragons by attacking the Citadel of Light and marching her armies into Qualinesti. I hasten to assure Your Grace that such is not the case. Beryllinthranox is acting under my orders. We have evidence that the Mystics of the Citadel of Light have been causing our own Mystics to fail in their magic. I deemed these Mystics a threat, and Beryllinthranox graciously offered to destroy them for me. As to Qualinesti, Beryllinthranox's armies are marching in order to join up with the forces of Marshal Medan. His orders are to destroy the rebels under the leadership of an elf known as the Lioness, who has harassed our troops and disrupted the flow of tribute.

As you see, I have everything under control. You need have no cause for alarm.

Lord of the Night,
Morham Targonne

He dusted sand on that letter and immediately launched into the next, which was easier to write due to the fact that there was some truth to this one.

> To Khellendros the Blue Dragon, Most Esteemed, etc., etc.
> You have undoubtedly heard that the great green dragon Beryllinthranox has launched an attack against the Citadel of Light. Fearing that you may misunderstand this incursion into lands so close to your territory, I hasten to reassure your lordship that Beryllinthranox is acting under my orders in this. The Mystics of the Citadel of Light have been discovered to be the cause of the failure of our Mystics in their magic. I would have made the request of you, Magnificent Khellendros, but I know that you must be keeping a close eye on the gathering of accursed Solamnic Knights in the city of Solanthus. Not wanting to call you away at this critical time, I requested that Beryllinthranox deal with the problem.
> Lord of the Night,
> Morham Targonne
>
> Postscript: You are aware of the gathering of Solamnic Knights at Solanthus, are you not, Exalted One?

His last letter was easier still and took him very little thought.

> Marshal Medan,
>
> You are hereby ordered to hand over the capital city of Qualinost intact and undamaged to Her Grace, Beryllinthranox. You will arrest all members of the elven royal family, including King Gilthas and the Queen Mother, Laurana. They are to be given alive to Beryllinthranox, who may do with them what she pleases. In return for this, you will make clear to Beryllinthranox that her forces are to immediately cease their wanton destruction of forests, farms, buildings, etc. You will impress upon Beryllinthranox that although she, in her magnificence, does not need money, we poor unfortunate worms of mortals do. You have leave to make the following offer: Every human soldier in her army will be granted a gift of elven land, including all buildings and structures on the land. All high-ranking human officers in her armies will be given fine homes in Qualinost. This should curb the looting and destruction. Once matters have returned to normal, I will see to it that human settlers are moved in to take over the remainder of elven lands.
> Lord of the Night,
> Morham Targonne
>
> Postscript 1: This offer of land does not apply to goblins, hobgoblins, minotaurs, or draconians. Promise them the equivalent value in steel, to

be paid at a later date. I trust you will see to it that these creatures are in the vanguard of the army and that they will take the heaviest casualties.

Postscript 2: As to the elven residents of Qualinesti, it is probable that they will refuse to give up their ownership of their lands and property. Since by so doing they defy a direct order of the Knights of Neraka, they have broken the law and are hereby sentenced to death. Your soldiers are ordered to carry out the sentence on the spot.

Once the ink had dried, Targonne affixed his seal to each letter and, summoning his aide, dispatched them. As dawn broke, four blue dragonriders took to the skies.

This done, Targonne considered going to his bed. He knew, however, that he would not be able to rest with the specter of that accounting mistake haunting his otherwise pleasant dreams of neat charts and columns. He sat down doggedly to work, and as often happens when one has left a task upon which one has concentrated, he found the error almost immediately. The twenty-seven steel, fourteen silver, and five coppers were accounted for at last. Targonne made the correction with a precise pen stroke.

Pleased, he closed the book, tidied his desk, and left for a brief nap, confident that all was once more well with the world.

2 ATTACK ON
THE CITADEL OF LIGHT

Beryl and her dragon minions flew over the Citadel of Light. The dragonfear they generated crashed down upon the inhabitants, a tidal wave that drowned courage in despair and terror. Four large red dragons flew overhead. The black shadows cast by their wings were darker than the deepest night, and every person the shadow touched felt his heart wither and his blood chill.

Beryllinthranox was an enormous green dragon who had appeared on Krynn shortly after the Chaos War; no one knew how or from where. Upon arrival, she and other dragons of her kind—most notably her cousin Malystryx—had attacked the dragons inhabiting Krynn, metallic and chromatic alike, waging war upon their own kind. Her body bloated from feeding off the dragons she had killed, Beryl circled high in the sky, far above the reds, who were her minions and her subjects, observing, watching. She was pleased with what she saw, pleased with the progress of the battle.

The citadel was defenseless against her. Had the great silver dragon, Mirror, been present, he might have dared defy her, but he was gone, mysteriously vanished. The Solamnic Knights, who had a fortress on Schallsea Isle, would make an heroic stand, but their numbers were few, and they could not hope to survive a concentrated attack from Beryl and her followers. The great green dragon would never have to fly within range of their arrows. She had only to breathe on them. A single poisonous blast from Beryl would kill every defender in the fort.

The Solamnic Knights were not going lie down and die. She could count on them to give her servants a lively battle. Their archers lined the battlements as their commanders strove to keep up their courage, even as the dragonfear unmanned many and left them weak and trembling. Knights rode with haste through island villages and towns, trying to quell the panic of the inhabitants and help them flee inland to the caves that were stocked and provisioned against just such an attack.

In the citadel itself, the Citadel Guards had always planned to use their mystical powers to defend themselves against a dragon attack. These powers had mysteriously waned over the past year, and thus the Mystics were forced to flee their beautiful crystal buildings and leave them to the ravages of the dragons. The first to be evacuated were the orphans. The children were frightened and cried for Goldmoon, for she was much loved by the children, but she did not come to them. Students and masters lifted the smallest children in their arms and soothed them, as they hastened to carry them to safety, telling them that Goldmoon would certainly come to them, but that she was now busy and that they must be brave and make her proud of them. As they spoke, the Mystics glanced at each other in sorrow and dismay. Goldmoon had fled the citadel with the dawning. She had fled like one mad or possessed. None of the Mystics knew where she had gone.

The residents of Schallsea Isle left their homes and streamed inland, those debilitated by dragonfear urged and guided by those who had managed to overcome it. In the hills in the center of the island were large caves. The people had fondly believed that they would be safe from the ravages of the dragons inside these caves, but now that the attack had come, many were starting to realize how foolish such plans had been. The flames of the red dragons would destroy the forests and the buildings. As flames ravaged the surface, the noxious breath of the huge green would poison the air and the water. Nothing could survive. Schallsea would be an isle of corpses.

The people waited in terror for the attack to begin, waited for the flames to melt the crystal domes and the rock walls of the fortress, waited for the cloud of poison to choke the life from them. But the dragons did not attack. The reds circled overhead, watching the panic on the ground with gleeful satisfaction but making no move to kill. The people wondered what they were waiting for. Some of the foolish took hope, thinking that this might be nothing more than intimidation and that the dragons, having terrified everyone, would depart. The wise knew better.

In his room located high in the Lyceum, the main building of the crystal-domed Citadel of Light, Palin Majere watched through the enormous window—actually a wall of crystal—the coming of the dragons. He kept watch on the dragons while he desperately attempted to put back together the broken pieces of the magical artifact that was to have transported himself and Tasslehoff to the safety of Solace.

"Look at it this way," said Tas, with maddening kender cheerfulness, "at least the dragon won't get her claws on the artifact."

"No," said Palin shortly, "she'll get her claws on us."

"Maybe not," Tas argued, ferreting out a piece of the device that had rolled under the bed. "With the Device of Time Journeying being broken and its magic all gone—" He paused and sat up. "I guess its magic *is* all gone, isn't it, Palin?"

Palin didn't answer. He barely heard the kender's voice. He could see no way out of this. Fear shook him, despair gnawed at him until he was weak and limp. He was too exhausted to fight to stay alive, and why should he bother? It was the dead who were stealing the magic, siphoning it off for some unknown reason. He shivered, reminded of the feeling of those cold lips pressed against his flesh, of the voices crying, begging, pleading for the magic. They had taken it . . . and the Device of Time Journeying was now a hodgepodge of wheels, gears, rods, and sparkling jewels, lying scattered on the rug.

"As I was saying, with the magic gone"—Tas was still prattling—"Beryl won't be able to find us because she won't have the magic to guide her to us."

Palin lifted his head, looked at the kender.

"What did you say?"

"I said a lot of things. About the dragon not having the artifact and maybe not having us because if the magic is gone—"

"You may be right," Palin said.

"I am?" Tas was no end astonished.

"Hand me that," Palin instructed, pointing.

Appropriating one of the kender's pouches, Palin dumped out its contents and began to hastily gather up the bits and pieces of the artifact, stuffing them into the pouch.

"The guards will be evacuating people into the hills. We'll lose ourselves in the crowd. No, don't touch that!" he ordered sharply, slapping the kender's small hand that was reaching for the jeweled faceplate. "I must keep all the pieces together."

"I just wanted a memento," Tas explained, sucking on his red knuckles. "Something to remember Caramon by. Especially since I won't be using the artifact to go back in time now."

Palin grunted. His hands shook, and it was difficult for his twisted fingers to grasp some of the smaller pieces.

"I don't know why you want that old thing anyhow," Tas observed. "I doubt you can fix it. I doubt anyone can fix it. It looks to be *extremely* broken."

Palin shot the kender a baleful glance. "You said you had decided to use it to return to the past."

"That was then," said Tas. "Before things got really interesting here. What with Goldmoon sailing off in the gnome's submersible and now being attacked by dragons. Not to mention the dead people," he added, as an afterthought.

Palin didn't like the reminder. "Make yourself useful at least. Go out in the hallway and find out what's going on."

Tas did as he was told, heading for the door, although he continued to talk over his shoulder. "I told you about seeing the dead people. Right when the artifact busted. Didn't I? They were all over you, like leeches."

"Do you see any of them now?" Palin asked.

Tas glanced around. "No, not a one. But then," he pointed out helpfully, "the magic's gone, isn't it?"

"Yes." Palin snapped tight the strings on the bag that held the broken pieces. "The magic is gone."

Tas was reaching for the handle when a thundering knock nearly staved in the door.

"Master Majere!" a voice called. "Are you inside?"

"We're here!" Tasslehoff called.

"The citadel is under attack from Beryl and a host of red dragons," the voice said. "Master, you must make haste!"

Palin knew very well they were under attack. He expected death at any moment. He wanted nothing more than to run, and yet he remained on his knees, sweeping his broken hands over the rug, anxious to ascertain that he had not overlooked a single tiny jewel or small mechanism of the broken Device of Time Journeying.

Finding nothing, he rose to his feet as Lady Camilla, leader of the Solamnic Knights on Schallsea, strode into the room. She was a veteran with a veteran's calmness, thinking clearly and matter-of-factly. Her business was not to fight dragons. She could rely on her soldiers at the fortress to undertake that charge. Her business in the citadel was to safely evacuate as many people as possible. Like most Solamnics, Lady Camilla was highly suspicious of magic-users, and she regarded Palin with a grim look, as if she did not put it past him to be in league with the dragons.

"Master Majere, someone said they thought you were still here. Do you know what is happening outside?"

Palin looked out the window to see the dragons circling above them, the shadows of their wings floating over the surface of the flat, oily sea.

"I could not very well miss it," he answered coolly. He, for his part, did not much like Lady Camilla.

"What have you been doing?" Lady Camilla demanded angrily. "We need your help! I expected to find you working your magic to fight against these monsters, but one of the guards said he thought you were still in your room. I could not believe it, yet here you are, playing with a . . . a gewgaw!"

Palin wondered what Lady Camilla would say if she knew that the reason the dragons were attacking in the first place was to try to steal the "gewgaw."

"We were just leaving," Palin said, reaching out to grab the excited kender. "Come along, Tas."

"He's telling the truth, Lady Camilla," said Tasslehoff, noting the Knight's skepticism. "We *were* just leaving. We were heading for Solace but the magical device we were going to use for our escape broke—"

"That's enough, Tas." Palin shoved the kender out the door.

"Escape!" Lady Camilla repeated, her voice shaking in fury. "You planned to escape and leave the rest of us to die? I don't believe such cowardice. Not even of a wizard."

Palin kept firm hold of Tasslehoff's shoulder, pushed him roughly down the hallway toward the stairs.

"The kender is right, Lady Camilla," he said in caustic tones. "We *were* planning to escape. Something any *sensible* person would do in this situation, be he wizard or knight. As it turns out, we can't. We are stuck here with the rest of you. We will be heading for the hills with the rest of you. Or heading to our deaths, whichever the dragons decide. Move along, Tas! This is no time for your chatter!"

"But your magic—" Lady Camilla persisted.

Palin rounded on her. "I have no magic!" he said savagely. "I have no more power to fight these monsters than this kender! Less, perhaps, for his body is whole, whereas mine is broken."

He glared at her. She glared at him, her face pale and chill. They had reached the stairs that wound through the various levels of the Lyceum, stairs that had been crowded with people but were now empty. The residents of the Lyceum had joined the throngs fleeing the dragons, hoping to find shelter in the hills. Palin could see them streaming toward the island's interior. If the dragons attacked now and the reds breathed their flames upon these terrified masses, the slaughter would be horrific. Yet still the dragons circled above them, watching, waiting.

He knew very well why they were waiting. Beryl was trying to sense the artifact's magic. She was trying to determine which of these puny creatures fleeing from her carried the precious artifact. That is why she had not ordered her minions to kill. Not yet. He'd be damned if he was going to tell this to the Knight. She'd probably hand him over to the dragon.

"I assume you have duties elsewhere, Lady Camilla," Palin said, turning his back on her. "Do not concern yourself with us."

"Trust me," she retorted, "I will not!"

Shoving past him, she ran down the stairs, her sword clanking at her side, her armor rattling.

"Hurry up," Palin ordered Tas. "We'll lose ourselves in the crowd."

Kilting the skirts of his robes, Palin ran down the stairs. Tasslehoff followed, enjoying the excitement as only a kender can. The two exited the building, the last to do so. Just as Palin paused near the entryway to catch his breath and to determine which was the best way to go, one of the red dragons swooped low. People flung themselves screaming onto the ground. Palin shrank back against the crystal wall of the Lyceum, dragging Tas with him. The dragon flew by with a rush of wings, doing nothing except sending many running mad with terror.

Thinking the dragon might have seen him, Palin looked up into the sky, fearing the dragon might be planning to make another pass. What he saw perplexed and astonished him.

Large objects like enormous birds, filled the skies. At first Palin thought they were birds and then he saw glints of sunlight off metal.

"What in the Abyss is that?" he wondered.

Tasslehoff turned his face skyward, squinting against the sun. Another red dragon made a low swoop over the citadel.

"Draconian soldiers," said Tasslehoff calmly. "They're dropping off the backs of the dragons. I saw them do that in the War of the Lance." He gave an envious sigh. "I really do wish I'd been born a draconian sometimes."

"What did you say?" Palin gasped. "Draconians?"

"Oh, yes," said Tas. "Doesn't it look like fun? They ride on the backs of the dragons and then they jump off and—there, you can see them—see how they spread their wings to break their fall. Wouldn't it be wonderful, Palin? To be able to sail through the air like—"

"*That's* why Beryl hasn't let the dragons burn the place down!" Palin exclaimed in a rush of dismayed understanding. "She plans to use the draconians to find the magical artifact . . . to find us!"

Intelligent, strong, born to battle and bred to fight, draconians were the most feared of all the troops of the dragon overlords. Created during the War of the Lance by evil magicks from the eggs of metallic dragons, draconians are enormous lizardlike creatures who walk upright on two legs like humans. Draconians have wings, but these wings are short and will not lift their large and well-muscled bodies in sustained flight. The wings are suitable for allowing the creatures to float through the air, as they were doing now, enabling them to make a safe and gentle landing.

The moment the draconians hit the ground, they began to form into ranks in response to the shouted commands of their officers. The ranks of draconian soldiers spread out, seizing any person they could catch.

One group of draconians surrounded the Citadel Guards, ordered them to surrender. Outnumbered, the guards threw down their weapons. The draconians forced them to kneel on the ground, then cast magic spells on them, spells that entangled them in webs or sent them to sleep. Palin made a mental note to himself that the draconians were able to cast spells without apparent difficulty when every other mage on Ansalon could barely find enough magic to boil water. He found this fact ominous and would have liked to have had time to think about it further, but that didn't seem probable.

The draconians were not killing their prisoners. Not yet. Not until the prisoners had been questioned. They were left to lie where they had fallen, bound neatly in magic cobwebs. The draconian soldiers moved on, while other draconians began hauling the web-bound prisoners into the abandoned Lyceum.

Again, a red dragon flew overhead, slicing the air with its massive wings. Draconian troops leaped off the dragon's back. Their objective was now clear to Palin. The draconians were going to take and hold the Citadel of Light, use it as their base of operations. Once established, they would spread throughout the island, rounding up all civilians. Another force was probably attacking the Solamnic Knights, keeping them penned up in their fortress.

Do they have a description of Tas and me? Palin asked himself. Or have they been told to bring to Beryl any magic-user and kender they come across? Not that it matters, he realized bitterly. Either way, I'll soon be a prisoner again. Tormented and tortured. Chained up in the darkness, to rot in my own filth. I am helpless to save myself. I have no way to fight them. If I try to use my magic, the dead will siphon it off, take it for themselves, whatever good it does them.

He stood in the shadows of the crystal wall, his mind in turmoil, fear roiling inside him so that he was sick with it, thought he might die of it. He was not afraid of death. Dying was the easy part. Living as a prisoner . . . he could not face that. Not again.

"Palin," said Tas urgently. "I think they've seen us."

A draconian officer had indeed seen them. He pointed in their direction and issued orders. His troops started toward them. Palin wondered where Lady Camilla was and had a panicked notion to call for help. He discarded that immediately. Wherever she was, she had enough to do to help herself.

"Are we going to fight them?" Tas asked eagerly. "I have my special knife, Rabbit Slayer." He began to rummage inside his pouches, dumping out pieces of cutlery, bootlacings, an old sock. "Caramon named it that, because he said it would be good only for killing dangerous rabbits. I never met a dangerous rabbit, but it works pretty well against draconians. I just have to remember where I put it—"

I'll dash back inside the building, Palin thought, panic taking hold of him. I'll find a place to hide, any place to hide. He had an image of the draconians discovering him huddled, whimpering, in a closet. Dragging him forth . . .

Bitter gall filled Palin's mouth. If he ran away this time he would run away the next time and he would keep on running, leaving others to die for him. He was finished running. He would make his stand here.

I do not matter, Palin said to himself. I am expendable. Tasslehoff is the one who matters. The kender must not come to harm. Not in this time, not in this world. For if the kender dies, if he dies in a place and a time he is not meant to, the world and all of us on it—dragons, draconians, myself alike—will cease to exist.

"Tas," said Palin quietly, his voice steady, "I'm going to draw off these draconians, and while I'm doing that, you run into the hills. You'll be safe there. When the dragons leave—and I think they will, once they have captured me—I want you to go to Palanthas, find Jenna, and have her take you to Dalamar. When I say the word, you must run, Tas. Run as fast as ever you can."

The draconians were coming nearer. They were able to see him clearly now, and they had begun to talk loudly among themselves, pointing at him and jabbering. Judging by their excitement, one of his questions was answered. They had a description of him.

"I can't leave you, Palin!" Tas was protesting. "I admit that I was mad at you because you were trying to kill me by making me go back to be stepped on by a giant, but I'm mostly over that now and—"

"Run, Tas!" Palin ordered, angry with desperation. Opening the bag containing the pieces of the magical device, he took the faceplate of the device in his hand. "Run! My father was right. You must get to Dalamar! You must tell him—"

"I know!" Tas cried. He hadn't been listening. "We'll hide in the Hedge Maze. They'll never find us there. C'mon, Palin! Quickly!"

The draconians were shouting and calling out. Other draconians, hearing their yells, turned to look.

"Tas!" Palin rounded on him furiously. "Do as I tell you! Go!"

"Not without you," Tas said stubbornly. "What would Caramon say if he found out I left you here to die all by yourself? They're moving awfully fast, Palin," he added. "If we're going to try to make it to the Hedge Maze, I think we better go now."

Palin brought out the faceplate. With the Device of Time Journeying, his father had traveled back to the time of the First Cataclysm to try to save Lady Crysania and prevent his twin brother Raistlin from entering the Abyss. With this device, Tasslehoff had traveled here, bringing with him a mystery and a hope. With this device, Palin had gone back in time to find that time before the Second Cataclysm did not exist. The device was one of the most powerful and wondrous ever created by the wizards of Krynn. He was about to destroy it, and by destroying it, perhaps he was destroying them all. Yet, it was the only way.

He grasped the faceplate in his hand, gripped it so hard that the metal edges cut into his flesh. Crying out words of magic that he had not spoken since the gods had departed with the end of the Fourth Age, Palin hurled the faceplate at the advancing draconians. He had no idea what he hoped to accomplish. His was an act of despair.

Seeing the mage throwing something at them, the draconians skidded warily to a halt.

The faceplate struck the ground at their feet.

The draconians scrambled back, arms raised to protect their faces, expecting the device to explode.

The faceplate rolled on the ground, wobbled, and fell over. Some of the draconians started to laugh.

The faceplate began to glow. A jet of brilliant, blinding blue light streaked out, struck Palin in the chest.

The jolt shocked him, nearly stopping his heart. He feared for a horrible moment that the device was punishing him, exacting revenge upon him. Then he felt his body suffused with power. Magic, the old magic, burned inside him. The magic bubbled in his blood, intoxicating, exhilarating. The magic sang in his soul and thrilled his flesh. He cried out words to a spell, the first spell that came to mind, and marveled that he still remembered the words.

Not such a marvel, after all. Hadn't he recited them in a litany of grief, over and over to himself for all these many years?

Balls of fire flashed from his fingertips and struck the advancing draconians. The magic fire burned with such ferocity that the lizard-men burst into flame, became living torches. The blazing flames almost immediately consumed them, leaving them a mass of charred flesh, melted armor, piles of smoldering bones and teeth.

"You did it!" Tasslehoff shouted gleefully. "It worked."

Daunted by the horrific fate of their comrades, the other draconians were regarding Palin with hatred but also new and wary respect.

"Now will you run?" Palin shouted in exasperation.

"Are you coming?" Tas asked, balancing on his toes.

"Yes, damn it! Yes!" Palin assured him, and Tas dashed off.

Palin ran after him. He was a gray-headed, middle-aged man, who had once been in shape, but had not performed strenuous physical exertion like this in a long time. Casting the magic spell had drained him. He could already feel himself starting to weaken. He could not keep up this pace for long.

Behind him, an officer shouted furious orders. Palin glanced back to see the draconians once more in pursuit, their clawed feet tearing up the grassy lawns, sending divots of mud into the air. Draconians use their wings to help them run, and they were taking to the air, skimming over the ground at a rate that neither the middle-aged Palin nor the short-legged kender could ever hope to match.

The Hedge Maze was still some distance away. Palin's breath was coming in painful gasps. He had a sharp pain in his side, and his leg muscles burned. Tas ran gamely, but he was no longer a young kender. He stumbled and panted for air. The draconians were steadily gaining on them.

Halting, Palin turned to once again face his enemy. He sought the magic, felt it as a cold trickle in his blood, not a raging torrent. Reaching into the bag, he took hold of another piece of the Device of Time Journeying—the chain that was supposed to wind up inside the artifact. Shouting words that were more defiance than magic, Palin hurled the chain at the flapping-winged draconians.

The chain transformed, growing, lengthening, expanding until the links were as thick and strong as those of a chain attached to a ship's heavy anchor. The enormous chain struck the draconians in their midriffs. Writhing like an iron snake, it wrapped itself around and around the pursuing draconians. The links contracted, holding the monsters fast.

Palin could not take time to marvel. Catching hold of Tasslehoff's hand, he turned to run again, both of them racing frantically to reach the Hedge Maze ahead of their pursuers. For the moment the chase had ended. Wrapped in the chain, the draconians howled in pain and struggled desperately to escape its coils. No other draconians dared come after him.

Palin was exalted, thinking he had defeated his foes, then he caught movement out of the corner of his eyes. His elation evaporated. Now he knew why those draconians were not coming after him. They did not fear him. They were merely leaving the task of his capture to reinforcements, who were running to cut him off from the front.

An armed squadron of fifteen draconian soldiers took up positions between Palin, Tas, and the Hedge Maze.

"I hope . . . there's more of that device . . . left. . . ." Tas gasped with what breath he had available for talking.

Palin reached into the bag. His hand closed over a fistful of jewels that had once adorned the device. He saw the artifact again, saw its beauty and felt its power. His heart almost refused, but the hesitation lasted only a moment. He tossed the jewels at the draconians.

Sapphires, rubies, emeralds, and diamonds sparkled in the air as they rained down over the heads of the astonished draconians, falling around them like sand scattered by children playing at magic. The jewels shone in the sunlight. A few of the draconians, chortling in glee, bent to pick them up.

The jewels exploded, forming a thick cloud of glittering jewel dust that surrounded the draconians. Shouts of glee changed to curses and cries of pain as the gritty jewel dust clogged the eyes of those who had bent to grab them. Some had their mouths open, and the dust flew up their snouts, choking them. The fine dust penetrated beneath their scales, causing them to itch and scratch at themselves, yelping and howling.

While the draconians staggered around blindly bumping into each other, or rolled on the ground, or gasped for air, Palin and Tasslehoff circled around them. Another sprint and they both plunged into the green haven of the Hedge Maze.

The Hedge Maze had been constructed by Qualinesti Woodshapers, a gift from Laurana. The maze was designed to offer a place of beauty and solitude to all who entered, a place where people could walk, rest, meditate, study. A leafy embodiment of the maze that is man's heart, the Hedge Maze could never be mapped, as the gnome, Conundrum, had discovered to his immense frustration. Those who successfully walked the maze of their own hearts came at last to the Silver Stair located at the heart of the Hedge Maze, the culmination of the spiritual journey.

Palin did not have much hope that the draconians would lose him in the maze, but he did hope that the maze's own powerful magic would protect him and Tas, perhaps hide them from the eyes of the monsters. His hope was going to be put to the test. More draconians had joined in the pursuit, driven now by anger and the desire for revenge.

"Stop a moment," Palin said to Tas, who had no breath left to answer. He nodded and gulped air.

The two had reached the first bend in the Hedge Maze. No point in going farther unless Palin knew whether or not the draconians were going to be able to come after them. He turned to watch.

The first several draconians dashed inside the Hedge Maze and almost immediately came to a stop. Branches spread across the path, stems shot up from the ground. Foliage grew at an astonishing rate. Within moments, the path on which Palin and Tas had walked was overgrown with shrubbery so thick the mage could no longer see the draconians.

Palin breathed a sigh of relief. He had been right. The magic of the Hedge Maze would keep out those who entered with evil intent. He had a momentary fear that the draconians might use their wings to lift themselves over the maze, but, as he looked up, flowering vines twined overhead to form a canopy that would hide him from sight. For the moment, he and Tas were safe.

"Whew! That was close!" said Tasslehoff happily. "I thought we were goners there for a moment. You are a really good wizard, Palin. I saw Raistlin cast lots of spells, but I don't believe he ever caused draconians to sizzle up like bacon before, though I once saw him summon the Great Worm Catyrpelius. Did you ever hear about that one? Raistlin—"

A roar and a blast of flame interrupted Tasslehoff's tale. The bushes that had so recently grown to block the draconians burst into bright orange flame.

"The dragons!" Palin said with a bitter curse, coughing as the intense heat seared his lungs. "They're going to try to smoke us out."

In his elation at defeating the draconians, he had forgotten the dragons. The Hedge Maze could withstand almost all other attacks, but apparently it was not impervious to dragon fire. Another red breathed its fiery breath on the maze. Flames crackled, smoke filled the air. The way out was blocked off by a wall of flame. They had no choice but to run deeper into the maze.

Palin led the way down the aisle of green, made a right turn, and came to a halt when the hedgerow at the end of the path erupted up in a blaze of flame and smoke. Choking, Palin covered his mouth with his sleeve and searched for a way out. Another pathway opened in front of him, the bushes parting to let him and Tas through. They had only made it a short distance when, again, flames blocked their path. Still another path opened. Though the Hedge Maze itself was dying, it sought a way to save them. He had the impression that they were being led somewhere specific, but he had no idea where. The smoke made him dizzy and disoriented. His strength was starting to ebb. He staggered, more than ran. Tasslehoff, too, was falling prey to fatigue. His shoulders slumped, his breathing was ragged. His very topknot seemed to droop.

The red dragon that was attacking the maze did not want to kill them. The dragon could have done that long ago. The red was driving them like sheep, using fire to dog their footsteps, nip at their heels, try to force them out in the open. Still, the maze itself urged them on, revealing yet another path when their way was blocked.

Smoke swirled around them. Palin could barely see the kender right beside him. He coughed until his throat was raw, coughed until he retched. Whenever one of the hedge ways opened up, a flow of air would refresh him, but almost immediately the air became tainted with smoke and the smell of brimstone. They stumbled on.

A wall of flame burst in front of them. Palin fell back, looked frantically to the left to see another wall of flame. He turned to the right, and the maze crackled with fire. Heat seared his lungs. He could not breathe. Smoke swirled, stinging his eyes.

"Palin!" Tas pointed. "The stair!"

Palin wiped away the tears to see silver steps spiraling upward, vanishing in the smoke.

"Let's climb it!" Tas urged.

Palin shook his head. "It won't help. The stair doesn't lead anywhere, Tas," he croaked, his throat raw and bleeding, as a fit of coughing seized him.

"Yes, it does," Tas argued. "I'm not sure where, but I climbed it the last time I was here, when I decided that I should really go back and be stepped on by the giant. A decision I have since rethought," he added hastily. "Anyway I saw— Oh, look! There's Caramon! Hullo, Caramon!"

Palin raised his head, peered through the smoke. He was sick and faint, and when he saw his father, standing at the top of the Silver Stair, he did not wonder at the sight. Caramon had come to his son once before, in the Citadel of Light, come to him to urge him not to send Tasslehoff back to die. Caramon looked now as he had looked to his son before his death, old but still hearty and hale. His father's face was different, though. Caramon's face had always been quick to laughter, quick to smile. The eyes that had seen much sorrow and known much pain had always been light with hope. Caramon had changed. Now the eyes were different, lost, searching.

Tasslehoff was already clambering up the stairs, jabbering excitedly to Caramon, who said no word. There had been only a few stairs, when Tasslehoff began to climb. He was quite close to the top already. But when Palin placed his foot upon the first shining silver step, he looked up and saw the stairs appeared to be without number, never ending. He did not have the strength to climb all those stairs, and he feared he would be left behind. As his foot touched the stair, a breath of fresh air wafted over him. He gulped it eagerly. Lifting his face, he saw blue sky above him. He drew in another deep breath of fresh air and began to climb. The distance seemed short now.

Caramon stood at the top, waiting patiently. Lifting a ghostly hand, he beckoned to them.

Tasslehoff reached the top, only to find, as Palin had said, that the Silver Stair led nowhere. The staircase came to an abrupt end, his next step would carry him over the edge. Far below, the ugly black smoke of the dying hedge swirled like the waters of a maelstrom.

"What do I do now, Caramon?" Tas yelled.

Palin heard no reply, but apparently the kender did.

"How wonderful," Tas cried. "I'll fly just like the draconians!"

Palin shouted out in horror. He lunged, tried to grasp hold of the kender's shirttail, and missed.

With a cry of glee, Tasslehoff spread his arms like a bird and leaped straight off the final stair. He plunged downward and disappeared into the smoke.

Palin clung to the stair. In his desperate attempt to grab hold of Tas, he had almost toppled off. He waited, his heart in his throat, to hear the kender's death cry, but all he heard was the crackling of flame and the roaring of the dragons.

Palin looked into the swirling smoke and shuddered. He looked back at his father, but Caramon was not there. In his place flew the red dragon. Wings blotted out the patch of blue sky. The dragon reached out a talon, intending to pluck Palin from his stair and carry him back to his cell. He was tired, tired of being afraid. He wanted only to rest and to be rid of fear forever.

He knew now where the Silver Stair led.

Death.

Caramon was dead. His son would soon join him.

"At least," Palin said calmly, grimly, "I will nevermore be a prisoner."

He leaped off the stair—and fell heavily on his side on a hard stone floor.

The landing being completely unexpected, Palin made no attempt to break his fall. He rolled and tumbled, came up hard against a stone wall. Jolted by the impact, shocked and confused, he lay blinking at the ceiling and wondered that he was alive.

Tasslehoff bent over him.

"Are you all right?" he asked, but didn't wait for an answer. "Look, Palin! Isn't it wonderful? You told me to find Dalamar and I have! He's right here! But I can't find Caramon anymore. He's nowhere."

Palin eased himself carefully to a sitting position. He was bruised and battered, his throat hurt, and his lungs wheezed as though they were still filled with smoke, but he felt no stabbing pains, heard no bones crunch together. His astonishment and shock at the sight of the elf caused him to forget his minor injuries. Palin was shocked not only to see Dalamar—who had not been seen in this world for thirty years—he was shocked to see how Dalamar changed.

The long-lived elves do not appear to humans to age. Dalamar was an elf in the prime of manhood. He should have looked the same now as he had looked when Palin last saw him more than thirty years ago. He did not. So drastic was the change that Palin was not completely convinced that this apparition was Dalamar and not another ghost.

The elf's long hair that had once been as black as the wing of a raven was streaked with gray. His face, though still elegantly carved and beautifully proportioned, was wasted. The elf's pale skin was stretched tight over the bones of the skull, making it look as if his face were carved of ivory. The aquiline nose was beakish, the chin sharp. His robes hung loosely on an emaciated frame. His long-fingered, elegant hands were bony and chafed, the knuckles red and prominent. The veins on the backs of his hands traced a blue road map of illness and despair.

Palin had always liked and admired Dalamar, though he could not say why. Their philosophies were not remotely the same. Dalamar had been the servant of Nuitari, god of the Dark Moon and darker magicks. Palin had served Solinari, god of the Silver Moon, god of the magic of light. Both men had been devastated when the gods of magic had departed, taking the magic with them. Palin had gone into the world to seek out the magic they called "wild" magic. Dalamar had withdrawn from other magi, withdrawn from the world. He had gone seeking magic in dark places.

"Are you injured?" Dalamar asked. He sounded annoyed, not concerned for Palin's well-being, but only that Palin might require some sort of attention, an exertion of power on the part of the elf.

Palin struggled to stand. Speaking was painful. His throat hurt abominably.

"I am all right," he rasped, watching Dalamar as the elf watched him, wary, suspicious. "Thank you for helping us—"

Dalamar cut him off with a sharp, emphatic gesture of a pallid hand. The skin of the hand was so pale against the black robes that it seemed disembodied.

"I did what I had to do, considering the mess you had made of things." The pale hand snaked out, seized hold of Tas by the collar. "Come with me, kender."

"I'd be glad to come with you, Dalamar," Tas answered. "And, by the way, it really is me, Tasslehoff Burrfoot, so you needn't keep calling me 'kender' in that nasty tone. I'm very glad to see you again, except, you're pinching me. Actually you're hurting me quite a bit—"

"*In* silence," Dalamar said and gave the kender's collar an expert twist that effectively caused Tas to obey the order by half-choking him. Dragging the squirming kender with him, Dalamar crossed the small, narrow room to a heavy wooden door. He beckoned with a pale hand, and the door swung silently open.

Keeping a tight grasp on Tas, Dalamar paused in the doorway and turned to face Palin.

"You have much to answer for, Majere."

"Wait!" Palin croaked, wincing at the pain in his throat. "Where is my father? I saw him."

"Where?" Dalamar demanded, frowning.

"At the top of the Silver Stair," Tasslehoff volunteered. "We both saw him."

"I have no idea. I did not send him, if that is what you are thinking," said Dalamar. "Although, I appreciate his help."

He walked out, and the door slammed shut behind him. Alarmed, panicked, feeling himself start to suffocate, Palin hurled himself at the door.

"Dalamar!" he shouted, beating on the wood. "Don't leave me in here!"

Dalamar spoke, but it was only to chant words of magic.

Palin recognized the spell—a wizard lock.

His strength gone, he slid down the door and slumped to the cold, stone floor.

A prisoner.

3 SUN ARISE

In the dark hour before the dawn, Gilthas, the king of the Qualinesti stood on the balcony of his palace. Rather, his body stood on the balcony. His soul walked the streets of the silent city. His soul walked every street, paused at every doorway, looked in every window. His soul saw a newlywed couple asleep, clasped in each other arms. His soul saw a mother sitting in a rocking chair, nursing her babe, the babe sleeping, the mother dozing, gently rocking. His soul saw young elf brothers sharing the same bed with a large hound. The two boys slept with their arms flung around the neck of the dog, all three dreaming of playing catch in sunlit meadows. His soul saw an elderly elf sleeping in the same house that his father had slept in and his father before him. Above his bed, a portrait of the wife who had passed on. In the next room, the son who would inherit the house, his wife by his side.

"Sleep long this night," Gilthas's soul said softly to each one he touched. "Do not wake too early in the morning, for when you wake, it will not be the beginning of a new day but the end of all days. The sun you see in the sky is not the rising sun, but the setting sun. The daylight will be night and night the darkness of despair. Yet, for now, sleep in peace. Let me guard that peace while I can."

"Your Majesty," said a voice.

Gilthas was loath to pay heed. He knew that when he turned to listen, to answer, to respond, the spell would be shattered. His soul would return to his body. The people of Qualinesti would find their sleep disturbed by dreams of smoke and fire, blood and shining steel. He tried to pretend he had not heard, but even as he watched, he saw the bright silver of the stars start to fade, saw a faint, pale light in the sky.

"Your Majesty," said a voice, another voice.

Dawn. And with the dawn, death.

Gilthas turned around. "Marshal Medan," he said, a hint of coolness in his tone. He shifted his gaze from the leader of the Dark Knights of Neraka to the person standing next to him, his trusted servant. "Planchet. You both have news, by the looks of it. Marshal Medan, I'll hear yours first."

Alexius Medan was a human male in his fifties, and although he bowed deferentially to the king, the Marshal was the true ruler of Qualinesti and had been for more than thirty years, ever since the Dark Knights of Neraka seized Qualinesti during the Chaos War. Gilthas was known to all the world as the "Puppet King." The Dark Knights had left the young and apparently weak and sickly youth on the throne in order to placate the elven people and give them the illusion of elven control. In reality, it was Marshal Medan who held the strings that caused the arms of the puppet Gilthas to move, and Senator Palthainon, a powerful member of the Thalas-Enthia, who played the tune to which the puppet danced.

But as Marshal Medan had learned only yesterday, he had been deceived. Gilthas had not been a puppet but a most gifted actor. He had played the weak and vacillating king in order to mask his real persona, that of leader of the elven resistance movement. Gilthas had fooled Medan completely. The Puppet King had cut the strings, and the dances he performed were done to music of His Majesty's own choosing.

"You left us after dark and have been gone all night, Marshal," Gilthas stated, eyeing the man suspiciously. "Where have you been?"

"I have been at my headquarters, Your Majesty, as I told you before I left," Medan replied.

He was tall and well-built. Despite his fifty-five years—or perhaps because of them—he worked at keeping himself fighting fit. His gray eyes contrasted with his dark hair and dark brows and gave him an expression of perpetual gravity that did not lighten, even when he smiled. His face was deeply tan, weathered. He had been a dragonrider in his early days.

Gilthas cast a very slight glance at Planchet, who gave a discreet nod of his head. Both glance and nod were seen by the observant Medan, who looked more than usually grave.

"Your Majesty, I do not blame you for not trusting me. It has been said that kings cannot afford the luxury of trusting anyone—" the Marshal began.

"Especially the conqueror of our people, who has held us in his iron grasp for over thirty years," Gilthas interjected. Both elven and human blood ran in the young king's veins, though the elven dominated. "You release the grip on our throats to offer the same hand in friendship. You will understand me, sir, when I say that I still feel the bite of your fingers around my windpipe."

"Well put, Your Majesty," replied the Marshal with a hint of smile. "As I said, I approve your caution. I wish I had a year to prove my loyalty—"

"To me?" Gilthas said with a slight sneer. "To the 'puppet'?"

"No, Your Majesty," Marshal Medan said. "My loyalty to the land I have come to consider my home. My loyalty to a people I have come to respect. My loyalty to your mother." He did not add the words, "whom I have come to love," though he might have said them in his heart.

The Marshal had been awake all night the night before, removing the Queen Mother to a place of safety, out of reach of the hands of Beryl's approaching assassins. He had been awake all day yesterday, having taken Laurana in secret to the palace where they had both met with Gilthas. It had been Medan's unhappy task to inform Gilthas that Beryl's armies were marching on Qualinesti with the intent of destroying the land and its people. Medan had not slept this night, either. The only outward signs of weariness were on the Marshal's haggard face, however, not in his clear, alert eyes.

Gilthas's tension relaxed, his suspicions eased. "You are wise, Marshal. Your answer is the only answer I would ever accept from you. Had you sought to flatter me, I would have known you lied. As it is, my mother has told me of your garden, that you have worked to make it beautiful, that you take pleasure not only in the flowers themselves but in planting them and caring for them. However, I must say that I find it difficult to believe that such a man could have once sworn loyalty to the likes of Lord Ariakan."

"I find it difficult to understand how a young man could have been tricked into running away from parents who doted on him to fly into a web spun by a certain senator," said Marshal Medan coolly, "a web that nearly led to the young man's destruction, as well as that of his people."

Gilthas flushed, hearing his own story repeated back to him. "What I did was wrong. I was young."

"As was I, Your Majesty," said the Marshal. "Young enough to believe the lies of Queen Takhisis. I do not flatter you when I say, Gilthas, that I have come to respect you. The role you played of the indolent dreamer, who cared more for his poetry than his people, fooled me completely. Although," the Marshal added dryly, "I must say that you and your rebels have caused me no end of trouble."

"And I have come to respect you, Marshal, and even to trust you somewhat," said Gilthas. "Though not completely. Is that good enough?"

Medan extended his hand. "Good enough, Your Majesty."

Gilthas accepted the Marshal's hand. Their handshake was firm and brief, on both sides.

"Now," said Medan, "perhaps your servant will tell his spies to cease following me about. We need everyone focused on the task ahead."

"What is your news, Marshal?" said Gilthas, neither agreeing nor disagreeing.

"It is relatively good news, Your Majesty," Medan stated. "All things considered. The reports we heard yesterday are true. Beryl's forces have crossed the border into Qualinesti."

"What good news can there be in this?" Gilthas demanded.

"Beryl is not with them, Your Majesty," said the Marshal. "Nor are any of her minions. Where they are and why they are not with the army, I cannot imagine. Perhaps she is holding them back for some reason."

"To be in on the final kill," said Gilthas bitterly. "The attack on Qualinost."

"Perhaps, Your Majesty. At any rate, they are not with the army, and that has bought us time. Her army is large, burdened with supply wagons and siege towers, and they are finding it difficult going through the forest. From the reports coming from our garrisons on the border, not only are they being harassed by bands of elves operating under the Lioness, but the very trees and plants and even the animals themselves are battling the enemy."

"Yes, they would," said Gilthas quietly, "but all these forces are mortal, as are we, and can only withstand so much."

"Indeed, Your Majesty. They could not withstand dragon fire, that is certain. Until the dragons arrive, however, we have a breathing space. Even if the dragons were to set the forests aflame, I calculate that it will take ten days for the army to reach Qualinost. That should give you time to institute the plan you outlined for us last night."

Gilthas sighed deeply and turned his gaze from the Marshal to the brightening sky. He made no response, but silently watched the sun rise.

"Preparations for evacuation should have begun last night," Medan stated in stern tones.

"Please, Marshal," said Planchet in a low voice. "You do not understand."

"He speaks truly. You do not understand, Marshal Medan," Gilthas said, turning around. "You could not possibly understand. You love this land, you say, but you cannot love it as we do. Our blood runs in every leaf and flower. The blood of every aspen tree flows through our veins. You hear the song of the sparrow, but we understand the words of that song. The axes and flames that fell the trees cut us and scorch us. The poison that kills the birds causes a part of us to die. This morning I must tell my people that they have to leave their homes, homes that trembled in the Cataclysm and yet stood firm. They must leave their bowers and their gardens and their waterfalls and grottos. They must flee, and where will they go?"

"Your Majesty," said Planchet, "on that score I, too, have good news for you. I received word in the night from the messenger of Alhana Starbreeze. The shield has fallen. The borders of Silvanesti are once more open."

Gilthas stared in disbelief, not daring to hope. "Can this be possible? Are you certain? How? What happened?"

"The messenger had no details, my lord. He started on his glad journey to bring us the good tidings the moment the elves knew it to be true. The shield is indeed fallen. Alhana Starbreeze walked across the border herself. I am expecting another messenger with more information soon."

"This is wonderful news," Gilthas exclaimed, ecstatic. "Our people will go to Silvanesti. Our cousins cannot deny us entry. Once there, we will combine our forces and launch an attack to retake our homeland."

Seeing Planchet regard him gravely, Gilthas sighed.

"I know, I know. You needn't remind me. I am leaping ahead of myself. But this joyful news gives me the first hope I have known in weeks. Come,"

Gilthas added, leaving the balcony and walking inside his chambers, "we must tell Mother—"

"She sleeps still, Your Majesty," said Planchet in a low voice.

"No, I do not," said Laurana. "Or, if I was, I will gladly wake to hear good news. What is this you say? The shield has fallen?"

Exhausted after the flight from her home in the night and a day of hearing nothing but dire news, Laurana had at last been persuaded to sleep. She had her own room in the royal palace, but Medan, fearful of Beryl's assassins, had given orders that the palace be cleared of all servants, ladies-in-waiting, elven nobility, clerks, and cooks. He had posted elven guards around the palace with orders to allow no one to enter except for himself and his aide. Medan might not have even trusted his aide, except that he knew him to be a Solamnic Knight and loyal to Laurana. Medan had then insisted that Laurana sleep on a couch in Gilthas's sitting room where her slumbers could be guarded. When Medan had departed for his headquarters, he had left behind the Solamnic, Gerard, as well as her son to watch over her during the night.

"The news is true, Mother," said Gilthas, coming to stand beside her. "The shield has fallen."

"It *sounds* wonderful," said Laurana cautiously. "Hand me my dressing gown, Planchet, so that I do not further disturb the Marshal's sensibilities. I don't trust the news, however. I find the timing disquieting."

Laurana's gown was a soft lilac color with lace at the throat. Her hair poured over her shoulders like warm honey. Her almond-shaped eyes were luminous, as blue as forget-me-nots. She was older than Medan by many, many years and looked far younger than he did, for the elven summer of youth and beauty diminishes into the winter of old age far more slowly than it does with humans.

Watching the Marshal, Gilthas saw in the man's face not the cool reserve of chivalry, but the pain of love, a hopeless love that could never be returned, could never even be spoken. Gilthas still did not like the Marshal, but this look softened his feelings for the man and even led him to pity him. The Marshal remained staring out the window until he could regain his stern composure.

"Say that the timing is fortuitous, Mother," urged Gilthas. "The shield falls when we most need it to fall. If there were gods, I would suppose they watch over us."

"Yet there are no gods," Laurana replied, wrapping her dressing gown around her. "The gods have left us. So I do not know what to say to this news except be cautious and do not build your hopes upon it."

"I must tell the people something, Mother," Gilthas returned impatiently. "I have called a meeting of the Senate this very morning." He cast a glance at Medan. "You see, my lord, I have *not* been idle this night. We must begin the evacuation today if we are to have a hope of emptying the city of its thousands. What I must say to our people will be devastating, Mother. I need hope to offer them."

" 'Hope is the carrot they hang in front of the horse's nose to keep him plodding on,' " Laurana murmured.

"What did you say, Mother?" Gilthas asked. "You spoke so softly, I could not hear you."

"I was thinking of something someone said to me long ago. At the time I thought the person was embittered and cynical. Now I think perhaps he was wise." Laurana sighed, shook off her memories. "I am sorry, my son. I know this isn't helping."

A Knight, Medan's aide, entered the room. He stood respectfully silent, but it was clear from the tenseness of his posture that he was attempting to gain their attention. Medan was the first to notice him.

"Yes, Gerard, what is it?" Medan asked.

"A trivial matter. I do not want to disturb the Queen Mother," said Gerard with a bow. "Might we speak in private, my lord? If His Majesty will permit?"

"You have leave," said Gilthas, and turned back to try to persuade his mother.

Medan, with a bow, withdrew with Gerard, walking out on the balcony of the king's chamber, overlooking the garden.

Gerard wore the armor of a Dark Knight of Neraka, although he had removed the heavy breastplate for comfort's sake. He had washed away the blood and other traces of his recent battle with a draconian, but he still looked considerably the worse for wear. No one would have ever called the young Solamnic handsome. His hair was as yellow as corn, his face was scarred with pockmarks, and the addition of numerous fresh bruises, blue and green and purple, rising to the surface, did nothing to enhance his appearance. His eyes were his best feature, an intense, arresting blue. The blue eyes were serious, shadowed, and belied his words about the trivial nature of the interruption.

"One of the guards sent word that two people wait below, both demanding to enter the palace. One is a senator. . . ." He paused, frowning. "I can't recall the name—elven names are a muddle to me—but he is tall and had a way of looking down his nose at me as if I were an ant perched on the tip."

Medan's mouth twitched in amusement. "And has he the expression of someone who has just bitten into a bad fig?"

"Correct, my lord."

"Palthainon," said Medan. "The Puppet Master. I was wondering when he would turn up." Medan glanced through the glass-paned door at the king. "As the story goes in the old child's tale, Palthainon will find his puppet king has turned into a real one. Unlike the child's tale, I don't think this puppeteer will be pleased to lose his puppet."

"Should he be permitted to come up, my lord?"

"No," said Medan coolly. "The king is otherwise engaged. Let Palthainon await His Majesty's pleasure. Who else wants admittance?"

Gerard's expression darkened. He lowered his voice. "The elf Kalindas, my lord. He requests admittance. He has heard, he says, that the Queen Mother is here. He refuses to leave."

Medan frowned. "How did he find out the Queen Mother was in the palace?"

"I don't know, my lord," said Gerard. "He did not hear it from his brother. As you ordered, we did not permit Kelevandros to leave. When I was so weary I could not keep my eyes open anymore, Planchet kept watch to see that he did not try to slip out."

Medan cast a glance at Kelevandros. The elf, wrapped in his cloak, was still apparently sound asleep in a far corner of the room.

"My lord," said Gerard, "may I speak plainly?"

Medan gave a wry smile. "You've done nothing else since you entered my service, young man."

"I wouldn't exactly call it 'entering' your service, my lord," returned Gerard. "I am here because, as you must know or could have guessed, I deemed my remaining with you to be the best way to protect the Queen Mother. I know that one of those two elves is a traitor. I know that one of them has betrayed Laurana, the mistress who trusted them. That was how you knew to be waiting for Palin Majere that morning in the woods. One of those two told you. They were the only ones who knew. Am I right?" His voice was harsh, accusing.

Medan eyed him. "Yes, you are right. Believe me when I say, Sir Solamnic, that you do not look at me with more disgust than I look at myself. Yes, I used Kalindas. I had no choice. If the scum did not report to me, he would have reported directly to Beryl, and I would not have known what was going on. I did what I could to protect the Queen Mother. I knew well that she aided and abetted the rebels. Beryl would have killed Laurana long ago, if it hadn't been for me. So do not presume to judge me, young man."

"I am sorry, my lord," Gerard said, contrite. "I did not understand. What do we do? Should I send Kalindas away?"

"No, said Medan, rubbing his jaw that was gray and grizzled with a day's growth of stubble. "Better to have him here where I can keep an eye on him. There is no telling what mischief he might cause if he were wandering around loose."

"He could be . . . removed," Gerard suggested uncomfortably.

Medan shook his head. "Laurana might believe that one of her servants was a spy, but I doubt very much if her son would. Kelevandros would certainly not, and if we killed his brother he would raise such an outcry that we would have to kill him, as well. How will it look to the elven people, whose trust I must win, if they hear that I have started butchering elves on His Majesty's very doorstep? Besides, I need to ascertain if Kalindas has been in communication with Beryl's forces and what he told them."

"Very good, my lord," said Gerard. "I will keep close watch on him."

"*I* will keep watch on him, Gerard," the Marshal amended. "Kalindas knows you, or have you forgotten? He betrayed you, as well. If he finds you here with me, my trusted confidant, he will be immediately suspicious. He might do something desperate."

"You are right, my lord," Gerard said, frowning. "I had forgotten. Perhaps I could return to headquarters."

"You will return to headquarters, Sir Knight," Medan said. "Your own headquarters. I am sending you back to Solamnia."

"No, my lord," Gerard said stubbornly. "I refuse to go."

"Listen to me, Gerard," the Marshal said, resting his hand on the young man's shoulder, "I have not said this to His Majesty or the Queen Mother—although I think she already knows. The battle we are about to fight is the last desperate struggle of a drowning man going under for the third time. Qualinost cannot hope to stand against the might of Beryl's army. This fight is at best a delaying action to buy time for the refugees to flee."

"Then I will most certainly stay, my lord," Gerard said steadily, his tone defiant. "I could not in honor do otherwise."

"If I make this an order?" Medan asked.

"I would say you are not my commander and that I owe no allegiance to you," Gerard returned, his expression grim.

"And I would say you are a very selfish young man who has no concept of true honor," Medan replied.

"Selfish, my lord?" Gerard repeated, stung by the accusation. "How can it be selfish to offer my life for this cause?"

"You will be of more value to the cause alive than dead," Medan stated. "You did not hear me out. When I suggested that you return to Solamnia, I was not sending you to some safe haven. I had in mind that you will take word of our plight to the Knights' Council in Solanthus and ask for their aid."

Gerard regarded the Marshal skeptically. "You are asking for the aid of the Solamnics, my lord?"

"No," said Medan. "The Queen Mother is asking for the aid of the Solamnic Knights. You will be her representative."

Gerard was clearly still distrustful.

"I have calculated that we have ten days, Gerard," the Marshal continued. "Ten days until the army reaches Qualinost. If you leave immediately on dragonback, you could reach Solanthus the day after tomorrow at the latest. The Knights could not send an army, but mounted dragonriders could at least help guard the civilians." He smiled grimly. "Do not believe that I am sending you out of harm's way, sir. I expect you to come back with them, and then you and I will not fight each other, but side by side."

Gerard's face cleared. "I am sorry I questioned you, my lord. I will leave at once. I will need a swift mount."

"You will have one. My own Razor. You will ride him."

"I could not take your horse, sir," Gerard protested.

"Razor is not a horse," said Medan. "He is my dragon. A blue. He has been in my service since the Chaos War. What is the matter now?"

Gerard had gone extremely pale. "Sir," he said, clearing his throat, "I feel it only right that you know . . . I have never ridden a dragon. . . ." He swallowed, burning with shame. "I have never even seen one."

"It is high time you did," Medan said, clapping Gerard on the back. "A most exhilarating experience. I have always regretted that my duties as Marshal kept me from riding as much as I would have liked. Razor is stabled in a secret location outside Qualinost. I will give you directions and send written orders with my seal so that the stable master will know you come by my command.

I will also send a message to Razor. Do not worry. He will bear you swiftly and in safety. You are not fearful of heights, are you?"

"No, my lord," Gerard said, gulping. What else could he say?

"Excellent. I will draw up the orders at once," Medan said.

Returning to the main chamber, motioning for Gerard to accompany him, Medan sat down at Planchet's desk and began to write.

"What of Kalindas, my lord?" Gerard asked in a low undertone.

Medan glanced at Laurana and Gilthas, who were together on the opposite side of the room, still conferring.

"It will not hurt him to cool his heels for awhile."

Gerard stood in silence, watching the Marshal's hand flow over the paper. Medan wrote swiftly and concisely. The orders did not take long, not nearly long enough as far as Gerard was concerned. He had no doubt that he was going to die, and he would much rather die with a sword in his hand than by toppling off the back of a dragon, falling with sickening terror to a bone-shattering end. Deeming himself a coward, he reminded himself of the importance and urgency of his mission, and thus he was able to take Medan's sealed orders with a hand that did not shake.

"Farewell, Sir Gerard," Medan said, clasping the young man by the hand.

"Only for a time, my lord," said Gerard. "I will not fail you. I will return and bring aid."

"You should leave immediately. Beryl and her followers would think twice about attacking a blue dragon, especially one belonging to the Dark Knights, but it would be best for you to take advantage of the fact that for the moment Beryl's dragons are not around. Planchet will show you the way out the back, through the garden, so that Kalindas does not catch sight of you."

"Yes, my lord."

Gerard lifted his hand in a salute, the salute a Solamnic Knight gives his enemy.

"Very well, my son, I agree," Laurana's voice reached them from across the chamber. She stood near a window. The first rays of the morning sunshine touched her hair like the hand of the alchemist, changed the honey to gold. "You convince me. You have your father's own way about you, Gilthas. How proud he would have been of you. I wish he could be here to see you."

"I wish he were here to offer his wise counsel," said Gilthas, leaning forward to kiss his mother gently on the cheek. "Now, if you will excuse me, Mother, I must write down the words that I will shortly be called upon to speak. This is so important, I do not want to make a mistake."

"Your Majesty," said Gerard, stepping forward. "If I might have a moment of your time. I want to pay my respects before I go."

"Are you leaving us, Sir Gerard?" Laurana asked.

"Yes, Madam," said Gerard. "The Marshal has orders for me. He dispatches me to Solamnia, there to plead your cause before the Council of Knights and ask for their aid. If I might have a letter from you, Your Majesty, in your hand with your seal, vouching for my credentials as your messenger and also stating the dire nature of the situation—"

"The Solamnics have never cared for Qualinesti before," Gilthas interrupted, frowning. "I see no reason why they should start now."

"They did care, once," said Laurana gently, looking searchingly at Gerard. "There was a Knight called Sturm Brightblade who cared very much." She held out her hand to Gerard, who bent low to touch her soft skin with his lips. "Go safely in the memory of that brave and gentle knight, Sir Gerard."

The story of Sturm Brightblade had never meant two coppers to Gerard before now. He had heard the tale of his death at the High Clerist's Tower so many times that it had grown stale in the telling. Indeed, he had even expressed his doubts that the episode had truly happened. Yet now he recalled that here was the comrade who had stood over the body of the dead Knight, the comrade who had wept for him even as she lifted the fabled dragonlance to defy his killer. Receiving her blessing in Sturm Brightblade's name, Gerard was humbled and chastened. He bent his knee before her, accepted the blessing with bowed head.

"I will, Madam," he said. "Thank you."

He rose to his feet, exalted. His fears over riding the dragon seemed paltry and ignoble now, and he was ashamed of them.

The young king looked chastened as well and gave Gerard his hand to shake. "Ignore my words, Sir Knight. I spoke without thought. If the Solamnics have been careless of Qualinesti, then it might be truly said that the Qualinesti have been careless of the Solamnics. For one to help the other would be the beginning of a new and better relationship for both. You shall have your letter."

The king dipped his pen in ink, wrote a few paragraphs on a sheet of fine vellum, and signed his name. Beneath his name, he affixed his seal, pressing into soft wax a ring he wore on his index finger. The ring left behind the image of an aspen leaf. He waited for the wax to harden, then folded the letter and handed it to Gerard.

"So I will convey to them, Your Majesty," said Gerard, accepting the letter. He looked once more at Laurana, to take with him in his mind her beautiful image for inspiration. He was disquieted to see sorrow darken her eyes as she gazed at her son, to hear her sigh softly.

Planchet told him how to find his way out of the garden. Gerard departed, scrambling awkwardly over the balcony, dropping heavily to the garden below. He looked up for one final wave, one final glimpse, but Planchet had closed the doors behind him.

Gerard recalled Laurana's look, her sadness, and he had a sudden terrible fear that this would be the last time he ever saw her, the last time he ever saw Qualinost. The fear was overwhelming, and his earlier resolve to stay and help them fight resurfaced. But he could not very well return now, not without looking foolish, or—worse—a coward. Gripping the Marshal's orders in his hand, Gerard departed, running through the garden that was starting to come alive with the warm rays of the sun.

The sooner he reached the council, the sooner he would be back.

4 THE TRAITOR

The room was quiet. Gilthas sat at his desk, writing his speech, the pen moving swiftly across the page. He had spent the night thinking of what to say. The words came rapidly, so that the ink seemed to flow from the heart and not his pen. Planchet was laying out a light breakfast of fruit, bread, and honey, although it seemed unlikely anyone would have much appetite. Marshal Medan stood at the window, watched Gerard depart through the garden. The Marshal saw the young Knight pause, perhaps he even guessed what Gerard was thinking. When Gerard turned and left, Medan smiled to himself and nodded.

"That was good of you, Marshal Medan," said Laurana, coming to stand at his side. She kept her voice low so as not to interrupt Gilthas in his work. "To send the young man safely away. For you do not truly believe the Solamnic Knights will come to our aid, do you?"

"No, I do not," said the Marshal, equally quiet. "Not because they will not, but because they cannot." He looked out the window, across the garden to the distant hills to the north. "They have their own problems. Beryl's attack means that the so-called Pact of the Dragons is broken. Oh, I am certain that Lord Targonne is doing his best to try to placate Malys and the others, but his efforts will be for naught. Many believe that Khellendros the Blue plays a game of cat and mouse. He pretends to be oblivious to all that is going on around him, but that is only to lull Malys and the others into complacency. In fact, it is my belief that he has long had his eye on Solanthus. He held off attacking only for fear that Beryl would consider such an attack a threat to her own territory to the south. But now he will feel that he can seize Solanthus with impunity. And so it will go from there. We may be the first, but we will not be the last.

"As to Gerard," Medan continued, "I returned to the Solamnic Knighthood a good soldier. I hope his commanders have sense enough to realize that."

He paused a moment, watching Gilthas. When the king had reached the end of a sentence, Medan spoke. "I am sorry to interrupt Your Majesty's work, but a matter has arisen that must be dealt with swiftly. A matter of some unpleasantness, I fear."

Medan shifted his gaze to Laurana. "Gerard reported to me that your servant, Kalindas, waits downstairs. It seems that he heard you were in the palace and was worried for you."

Medan watched Laurana carefully as he spoke. He saw her color wane, saw her troubled gaze flash across the room to Kelevandros, who was still sleeping.

She knows, Medan said to himself. If she does not know which of them is the traitor, yet she knows that one of them is. Good. That will make this easier.

"I will send Kelevandros to fetch him," Laurana said through pallid lips.

"I do not believe that would be wise," Medan replied. "I suggest that you ask Planchet to take Kalindas to my headquarters. My second-in-command, Dumat, will look after him. Kalindas will not be harmed, I assure you, Madam, but he must be kept safe, where he cannot communicate with anyone."

Laurana looked at the Marshal with sorrow. "My lord, I don't think . . . Is this necessary?"

"It is, Madam," he said firmly.

"I don't understand," Gilthas said, his voice tinged with anger. He rose to his feet. "My mother's servant is to be thrown in prison! Why? What is his crime?"

Medan was about to answer, but Laurana forestalled him.

"Kalindas is a spy, my son."

"A spy?" Gilthas was astonished. "For whom?"

"The Dark Knights," Laurana replied. "He reports directly to Marshal Medan, unless I am much mistaken."

Gilthas cast the Marshal a look of unutterable disgust.

"I make no apology, Your Majesty," Medan said calmly. "Nor, do I expect you to make any apology for the spies you have planted in my household."

Gilthas flushed. "A dirty business," he muttered.

"Indeed, Your Majesty. This makes an end of it. I, for one, will be glad to wash my hands. Planchet, you will find Kalindas waiting downstairs. Remove him to—"

"No, Planchet," said Gilthas peremptorily. "Bring him here to me. Kalindas has the right to answer his accusor."

"Do not do this, Your Majesty," Medan said earnestly. "Once Kalindas sees me here with you, he will know he has been unmasked. He is a dangerous man, cornered and desperate. He has no care for anyone. He will stop at nothing. I cannot guarantee Your Majesty's safety."

"Nevertheless," said Gilthas steadily, "elven law provides that Kalindas have the chance to defend himself against these charges. For too long, we have lived under your law, Marshal Medan. The law of the tyrant is no law at all. If I am to be king, then I make this my first act."

"Madam?" Medan turned to Laurana.

"His Majesty is right," said Laurana. "You have made your accusations, and we have listened. Kalindas must have his turn to tell his story."

"You will not find it a pretty one. Very well," Medan said, shrugging. "But we must be prepared. If I might suggest a plan of action . . ."

"Kelevandros," Laurana said, shaking the slumbering elf by the shoulder. "Your brother waits downstairs."

"Kalindas is here?" Kelevandros jumped to his feet.

"The guards refuse to allow him to enter," Laurana continued. "Go down and tell the guards they have my permission to bring him here."

"Yes, Madam."

Kelevandros hastened out the door. Laurana looked back at Medan. Her face was very pale, but she was calm, composed.

"Was that satisfactory?"

"Perfect, Madam," said Medan. "He was not the least suspicious. Take your seat at the table. Your Majesty, you should return to your work."

Laurana sighed deeply and sat down at the dining table. Planchet selected the very best fruit for her repast and poured her a glass of wine.

Marshal Medan had never admired Laurana's courage more than now, as he watched her take bites of fruit, chew and swallow, though the food must have tasted like ashes in her mouth. Opening one of the doors that led to the balcony, Medan moved outside, leaving the door ajar, so that he could hear and see what took place in the room without being seen himself.

Kalindas entered at his brother's heels.

"Madam, I have been frantic with concern for your safety. When that loathsome Marshal took you away, I feared he meant your death!"

"Did you, Kalindas?" Laurana said gently. "I am sorry to have caused you so much concern. As you see, I am safe here. Safe for the time being, at least. We have reports that Beryl's armies are marching on Qualinesti."

"Indeed, Madam, I heard that terrible rumor," said Kalindas, advancing until he stood close to the table at which she sat. "You are not safe here, Madam. You must take flight immediately."

"Yes, Madam," said Kelevandros. "My brother has told me that you are in danger. You and the king."

Gilthas had completed his writing. The parchment in his hand, the king rose from his desk, preparing to leave.

"Planchet," he said, "bring me my cloak."

"You are right to act swiftly, Your Majesty," said Kalindas, mistaking Gilthas's intent. "Madam, I will take the liberty of fetching your cloak, as well—"

"No, Kalindas," said Gilthas. "That is not what I meant."

Planchet returned with the king's cloak. Holding the garment over his right hand and arm, he moved to stand next to Gilthas.

"I have no intention of fleeing," Gilthas was saying. "I go now to make a speech to the people. We begin immediately to evacuate the population of Qualinost and make plans for the defense of the city."

Kalindas bowed to the king. "I understand. Your Majesty will make his speech, and then I will take you and your honored mother to a place of safety. I have friends waiting."

"I'll wager you do, Kalindas," said Marshal Medan, stepping through the door. "Friends of Beryl's waiting to assassinate both His Majesty and the Queen Mother. Where would these friends of yours happen to be?"

Kalindas's eyes darted warily from the Marshal to Gilthas and back to the Marshal. The elf licked dry lips. His gaze slid to Laurana. "I don't know what has been said about me, Madam—"

Gilthas intervened. "I will tell you what has been said, Kalindas. The Marshal has made the accusation that you are a spy in his employ. We have evidence that appears to indicate that this is true. By elven law, you are granted the right to speak in your defense."

"You don't believe him, do you, Madam?" Kelevandros cried. Shocked and outraged, he came to stand stolidly beside his brother. "Whatever this human has told you about Kalindas is a lie! The Marshal is a Dark Knight, and he is human!"

"Indeed, I am both those," said Medan. "I am also the one who paid your brother to spy upon the Queen Mother. I'll wager that if you search his person, you will find on him a stash of steel coins with the head of Lord Targonne stamped upon them."

"I knew someone in my household had betrayed me," Laurana said. Her voice ached with sorrow. "I received a letter from Palin Majere, warning me. That was how the dragon knew to wait for him and for Tasslehoff. The only person who could have warned the dragon was someone in my house. No one else knew."

"You are mistaken, Madam," Kelevandros insisted desperately. "The Dark Knights were spying on us. That is how they came to know. Kalindas would never betray you, Madam. Never! He loves you too well."

"Does he?" Medan asked quietly. "Look at his face."

Kalindas was livid, his skin whiter than the fine linen of the bed sheets. His lips curled back from his teeth in a sneer. His blue eyes were pale and glittering.

"Yes, I have a bag of steel coins," he said, spittle flecking his lips. "Coins paid to me by this human pig who thinks that by betraying me he may win the chance to crawl into your bed. Perhaps he already has. You are known to enjoy rutting with humans. Love you, Madam? This is how much I love you!"

Kalindas's hand darted inside his tunic. The blade of a dagger flashed in the sunlight.

Gilthas cried out. Medan drew his sword, but he had placed himself to guard the king. Medan was too far across the room to save Laurana.

She snatched up a wine glass and flung the contents into Kalindas's face. Half-blinded by the wine stinging his eyes, he stabbed wildly. The blow aimed for Laurana's heart struck her shoulder.

Cursing, Kalindas lifted the knife to strike again.

He gave a terrible cry. The knife fell from his hand. The blade of a sword protruded from his stomach. Blood soaked his shirt front.

Kelevandros, tears streaming down his cheeks, jerked his sword out of his brother's body. Dropping the weapon, Kelevandros caught hold of Kalindas, lowered him to the ground, cradled his dying brother in his arms.

"Forgive me, Kalindas!" Kelevandros said softly. He looked up, pleading. "Forgive him, Queen Mother—"

"Forgive!" Kalindas's lips, flecked with blood, twisted. "No!" He choked. His last words were squeezed out. "I curse them! I curse them both!"

He stiffened in his brother's arms. His face contorted. He tried again to speak, but blood gushed from his mouth, and with it went his life. Even in death, his eyes continued to stare at Laurana. The eyes were dark, and when the light of life faded in them, the shadows were lit with the cold glitter of his hate.

"Mother!" Gilthas sprang to her side. "Mother, you are hurt! Come, lie down."

"I am all right," Laurana said, though her voice shook. "Don't fuss. . . ."

"That was quick thinking on your part, Madam. Throwing the wine at him. He caught the rest of us flat-footed. Let me see." Medan peeled back the fabric of the sleeve that was soaked with blood. His touch was as gentle as he could make it. "The wound does not appear to be serious," he reported, after a cursory examination. "The dagger glanced off the bone. You will have a scar there, I am afraid, Madam, but the wound is clean and should heal well."

"It would not be the first scar I've borne," Laurana said with a wan smile. She clasped her hands together, to try to stop the trembling. Her gaze went involuntarily to the corpse.

"Throw something over that!" Medan commanded harshly. "Cover it up."

Planchet grabbed hold of the cloak he had been holding, spread it over Kalindas. Kelevandros knelt beside his brother, one hand holding the dead hand, the other holding the sword that had slain him.

"Planchet, summon a healer—" Gilthas began.

"No," Laurana countermanded his order. "No one must know of this. You heard the Marshal. The wound is not serious. It has already stopped bleeding."

"Your Majesty," said Planchet. "The meeting of the Thalas-Enthia . . . it is past time."

As if to emphasize this statement, a voice came from below, querulous and demanding. "I tell you I will wait no longer! A servant is permitted to see His Majesty, and I am kept waiting? You do not intimidate me. You dare not lay a hand on me, a member of the Thalas-Enthia. I will see His Majesty, do you hear? I will not be kept out!"

"Palthainon," said Medan. "After the last act of the tragedy, they send in the clowns." The Marshal started toward the door. "I will stall him as long as possible. Get this mess cleaned up!"

Laurana rose hurriedly to her feet. "He should not see me wounded like this. He must not know anything is wrong. I will wait in my own chambers, my son."

Gilthas was obviously reluctant to leave, but he knew as well as she did the importance of his talk before the Senate. "I will go to the Thalas-Enthia," he said. "First, Mother, I have a question to ask Kelevandros, and I want you to be here to hear it. Kelevandros, did you know of your brother's foul scheming? Were you part of it?"

Kelevandros was deathly pale and covered with his brother's blood, yet he faced the king with dignity. "I knew he was ambitious, yet I never thought . . . I never . . ." He paused, swallowed, and said quietly, "No, Your Majesty. I did not."

"Then I grieve for you, Kelevandros," said Gilthas, his harsh tone softening. "For what you had to do."

"I loved him," said Kelevandros in a low voice. "He was all the family I had left. Yet I could not let him harm our mistress."

Blood was starting to seep through the cloak. Kelevandros knelt over his brother's body, wrapped the cloak around it more tightly.

"With your permission, Your Majesty," he said with quiet dignity, "I will take my brother away."

Planchet made as if to help, but Kelevandros refused his assistance.

"No, he is my brother. My responsibility."

Kelevandros lifted Kalindas's body in his arms and, after a brief struggle, managed to stand upright. "Madam," he said, not raising his eyes to meet hers, "your home was the only home we ever knew, but I fear it would be unseemly—"

"I understand, Kelevandros," she said. "Take him there."

"Thank you, Madam."

"Planchet," Gilthas said, "go with Kelevandros. Give him what help he needs. Explain matters to the guard."

Planchet hesitated. "Your Honored Mother is wise. We should keep this secret, Your Majesty. If the people were to discover that his brother had made an attempt on the Queen Mother's life, I fear they might do Kelevandros some harm. And if they heard that Marshal Medan had been using elves to spy . . ."

"You are right, Planchet," Gilthas said. "See to it. Kelevandros, you should use the servant's—"

Realizing what he had been about to say, he stopped the words.

"The servant's entrance around back," said Kelevandros finished. "Yes, Your Majesty. I understand."

Turning, he bore his heavy burden out the door.

Laurana looked after them. "The curses of the dead always come true, they say."

"Who says?" Gilthas demanded. "Toothless old grannies? Kalindas had no high and noble goals. He did what he did out of greed alone. He cared only for the money."

Laurana shook her head. Her hair was gummed with her own blood, stuck to the wound. Gilthas started to add comforting words, but they were interrupted by a commotion outside the door. Marshal Medan could be heard tromping heavily up the stairs. He had raised his voice, to let them know he was coming and that he had company.

Laurana kissed her son with lips that were as pale as her cheeks. "You must leave now. My blessings go with you—and those of your father."

She left hurriedly, hastening down the hall.

"Planchet, the blood—" Gilthas began, but Planchet had already whisked a small ornamental table over the stain and planted himself in front of it.

Senator Palthainon entered the room with fuss and bustle. Fire smoldered in his eyes, and he began talking the instant his foot crossed the threshold.

"Your Majesty, I was told that you convened the Thalas-Enthia without first asking my approval—"

The senator halted in midword, the speech he had been rehearsing all the way up the stairs driven clean from his head. He had expected to find his puppet lying limp on the floor, tangled in his own strings. Instead, the puppet was walking out the door.

"I convened the Senate because I am king," said Gilthas, brushing past the senator. "I did not consult you, Senator, for the same reason. I am king."

Palthainon stared, began to burble and sputter. "What— What— Your Majesty! Where are you going? We must discuss this."

Gilthas paid no attention. He continued out the door, slammed it shut behind him. The speech he had written so carefully lay on the desk. After all, he would speak the words from his heart.

Palthainon stared after him, confounded. Needing someone to blame, he rounded on Marshal Medan. "This is your doing, Marshal. You put the fool boy up to this. What are you plotting, Medan? What is going on?"

The Marshal was amused. "This is none of my doing, Senator. Gilthas is king, as he says, and he has been king for many years. Longer than you realize apparently. As for what is going on"—Medan shrugged—"I suggest you ask His Majesty. He *may* deign to tell you."

"Ask His Majesty, indeed!" returned the senator with a blustering sneer. "I do not *ask* His Majesty anything. I tell His Majesty what to think and what to say, just as I always have. You are blathering, Marshal. I do not understand you."

"No, but you will," Medan advised the senator's retreating back, as the elf picked up what shreds of dignity remained him and swept out of the chamber.

"Planchet," said Medan, after king and senator were gone and the palace was again quiet. "Bring water and bandages. I will attend to the Queen Mother. You should pull up the carpet. Take it out and burn it."

Armed with a wash basin and a roll of linen, Medan knocked at the door to Laurana's chambers. She bade him enter. He frowned to see her on her feet, looking out the window.

"You should lie down, Madam. Take this time to rest."

She turned to face him. "Palthainon will cause trouble in the Senate. You may be assured of that."

"Your son will skewer him, Madam," said the Marshal. "With words, not steel. He will let so much air out of that windbag I would not be surprised to see him come whizzing past the window. There," he added, "I made you smile."

Laurana did smile, but the next moment she swayed on her feet and reached to steady herself on the arm of a chair. Medan was at her side, helping her to sit down.

"Madam, you have lost a vast quantity of blood, and the wound continues to bleed. If I would not offend . . ." He paused, embarrassed. Coughing, he continued. "I could clean and dress the wound for you."

"We are both old soldiers, Marshal," said Laurana, sliding her arm out of the sleeve of her dressing gown. "I have lived and fought with men under circumstances where I could not afford to indulge in modesty. It is most kind of you to offer."

The Marshal reached to touch the warm skin and saw his hand—coarse, large, thick-fingered, and clumsy—in sharp contrast to the slender white shoulder of the elven woman, her own skin as smooth as the silken coverlet, the blood crimson and warm from the jagged cut. He snatched his hand back, the fingers clenched.

"I fear I hurt you, Madam," he said, feeling her flinch at his touch. "I am sorry. I am rough and clumsy. I know no other way."

Laurana clasped her hair with her hand, drew it over her shoulder, so that it was out of his way. "Marshal Medan, my son explained his plan for the defense of Qualinost to you. Do you think it will work?"

"The plan is a good one, Madam," said the Marshal, wrapping the bandage around her shoulder. "If the dwarves agree to it and do their part, it even has a chance of succeeding. I do not trust dwarves, however, as I warned His Majesty."

"A great many lives will be lost," said Laurana sadly.

"Yes, Madam. Those who remain to fight the rearguard action may not be able to escape in time. The battle will be a glorious one," he added, tying off the bandage with a knot. "Like the old days. I, for one, would not miss it."

"You would give your life for us, Marshal?" Laurana asked, turning to look him full in the face. "You, a human and our enemy, will die defending elves?"

He pretended to be preoccupied with the wound, in order not to meet her penetrating gaze. He did not answer the question immediately but thought about it for a long time.

"I do not regret my past, Madam," he said at last. "I do not regret past decisions. I was born of common stock, a serf's son. I would have been a serf myself, illiterate, unschooled, but then Lord Ariakan found me. He gave me knowledge, he gave me training. Most important, he gave me faith in a power greater than myself. Perhaps you cannot understand this, Madam, but I worshipped Her Dark Majesty with all my soul. The Vision she gave me comes to me still in my dreams, although I cannot understand why, since she is gone."

"I understand, Marshal," said Laurana softly. "I stood in the presence of Takhisis, Queen of Darkness. I still feel the awe and reverence I experienced then. Although I knew her power to be evil, it was awful to behold. Perhaps that was because when I dared try to look into her eyes, I saw myself. I saw her darkness inside me."

"You, Madam?" Medan shook his head.

"I was the Golden General, Marshal," Laurana said earnestly. "A fine title. People cheered me in the streets. Children gave me bouquets of flowers. Yet I ordered those same people into battle. I orphaned many of those children. Because of me thousands died, when they might have lived to lead happy and productive lives. Their blood is on my hands."

"Do not regret your actions, Madam. To do so is selfish. Your regret robs the dead of the honor that is theirs. You fought for a cause you knew to be just and right. They followed you into battle—into death, if you will—because they saw that cause shining in you. That is why you were called the Golden General," he added. "Not for your hair."

"Still," she said, "I would like to give something back to them."

She fell silent, absorbed in her own thoughts. He started to leave, thinking that she would like to rest, but she detained him.

"We were speaking of you, Marshal," she said, resting her hand light upon his arm. "Why you are prepared to give your life for elves."

Looking into her eyes, he could have said he was prepared to lay down his life for one elf, but he did not. His love would not be welcome to her, whereas his friendship was. Counting himself blessed, he did not seek for more.

"I fight for my homeland, Madam," he replied simply.

"One's homeland is where one is born, Marshal."

"Precisely, Madam. My homeland is here."

His response gave her pleasure. Her blue eyes were soft with sympathy, glimmered with sudden tears. She was warmth and sweetness and perfume, and she was low in her spirits, shaken and hurt. He rose to his feet quickly, so quickly that he clumsily overturned the bowl of water he had used to wash the wound.

"I am sorry, Madam." He bent to wipe up the spill, glad to have the chance to hide his face. He rose again, did not look at her. "The bandage is not too tight, is it, Madam?" he asked gruffly.

"No, not too tight," said Laurana.

"Good. Then if you will excuse me, Madam, I must return to headquarters, to see if there have been any further reports of the army's progress."

With a bow, he turned on his heel and departed in haste, leaving her to her thoughts.

Laurana drew the sleeve of her gown over her shoulder. She flexed her fingers, rubbed her fingers over old calluses on her palm.

"I will give something back," she said.

5 DRAGON FLIGHT

The stables of the Dark Knights were located a considerable distance from Qualinesti. Not surprising, Gerard considered, since the stables housed a blue dragon. He had never been there, never had occasion to go, and had only a vague idea where the stables were. Medan's directions were easy to follow, however, and guided Gerard unerringly.

Mindful of the necessity for haste, he advanced at a jogging run. Gerard was soon winded, however. His wounds from his battle with the draconian throbbed. He'd had very little sleep, and he was weighted down with his armor. The thought that at the end of all this toil he would confront a blue dragon did not bring ease to his sore muscles or lighten the weight of his armor. Just the reverse.

He smelled the stables before he could see them. They were surrounded by a stockade with guards at the entrance. Alert and wary, they hailed him the moment they heard his footsteps. He replied with the proper code word and handed over Medan's orders. The guards peered at these intently, looked closely at Gerard, whom they did not recognize. There was no mistaking Medan's seal, however, and they let him pass.

The stables housed horses, griffons, and dragons, although not in the same location. Low, sprawling wooden buildings housed the horses. The griffons had their nests atop a cliff. Griffons prefer the heights, and they had to be kept far from the horses so that the horses were not made nervous by the smell of the beasts. The blue dragon, Gerard learned, was stabled in a cave beneath the cliff.

One of the stable hands offered to take Gerard to the dragon, and, his heart sinking so low that he seemed to walk on it with every reluctant step, Gerard agreed. They were forced to wait, however, due to the arrival of another blue dragon bearing a rider. The blue landed in a clearing near the horse stables, sending the horses into a panic. Gerard's guide left him, ran to calm the horses. Other stable hands shouted imprecations at the dragonrider, telling him he'd landed in the wrong spot and shaking their fists at him.

The dragonrider ignored them. Sliding from his saddle, he brushed away their jeers.

"I am from Lord Targonne," he said brusquely. "I have urgent orders for Marshal Medan. Fetch down one of the griffons to take me to headquarters and then see to my dragon. I want him properly housed and fed for the return flight. I leave tomorrow."

At the mention of the name Targonne, the stable hands shut their mouths and scattered to obey the Knight's commands. Several led the blue dragon to the caves beneath the mountains, while others began the long process of trying to whistle down one of the griffons. The proceeding took some time, for griffons are notoriously ill-tempered and will pretend to be deaf to a command in the hope that their master will eventually give up and go away.

Gerard was interested to hear what news the Dark Knight was taking with such speed to Medan. Seeing the Knight wipe his mouth, Gerard removed the flask from his belt.

"You appear to thirst, sir," he said, holding out the flask.

"I don't suppose you have any brandy in there?" asked the Knight, eyeing the flask eagerly.

"Water, I'm sorry to say," said Gerard.

The Knight shrugged, seized the flask and drank. His thirst slaked, he handed the flask back to Gerard. "I'll drink the Marshal's brandy when I meet with him." He eyed Gerard curiously. "Are you coming or going?"

"Going," said Gerard. "A mission for Marshal Medan. I heard you say you've come from Lord Targonne. How has his lordship reacted to the news that Beryl is attacking Qualinesti?"

The Knight shrugged, looked around with disdain. "Marshal Medan is the ruler of a backwater province. Hardly surprising that he was caught off-guard by the dragon's actions. I assure you, sir, Lord Targonne was not."

Gerard sighed deeply. "You have no idea how hard this duty is. Stuck here among these filthy elves who think that just because they live for centuries that makes them better than us. Can't get a mug of good ale to save your soul. As to the women, they're all so blasted snooty and proud.

"I'll tell you the truth, though." Gerard edged closer, lowered his voice. "They really want us, you know. Elf women like us human men. They just pretend they don't. They lead a fellow on and then scream when he tries to take what's been offered."

"I hear the Marshal sides with the vermin." The Knight's lip curled.

Gerard snorted. "The Marshal—he's more elf than human, if you ask me. Won't let us have any fun. My guess is that's about to change."

The Knight gave Gerard a knowing look. "Let's just say that wherever you're going, you'd best hurry back, or you're going to miss out."

Gerard regarded the Knight with admiration and envy. "I'd give anything to be posted at headquarters. Must be really exciting, being around his lordship. I'll bet you know everything that's happening in the whole world."

"I know my share," the Knight stated, rocking back on his heels and regarding the very stars in the sky with proprietory interest. "Actually I'm considering moving here. There'll be land for the asking soon. Elf land and fancy elf houses. And elf women, if that's what you like." He gave Gerard a disparaging glance. "Personally I wouldn't want to touch one of the cold, clammy hags. Turns my stomach to think of it. You had best have your fun with one of them fast, though, or she might not be around for the taking."

Gerard was able now to guess the import of Targonne's orders to Medan. He saw quite clearly the plan the Lord of the Night had in mind, and he was sickened by it. Seize elven property and elven homes, murder the owners, and hand the wealth out as gifts to loyal members of the Knighthood. Gerard's hand tightened around his sword. He would have liked to turn this Knight's proud stomach—turn it inside out. He would have to forego the pleasure. Leave that to Marshal Medan.

The Knight slapped his gloves against his thigh and glanced over at the stable hands, who were yelling at the griffons, who were continuing to ignore them.

"Louts!" he said impatiently. "I suppose I must do this myself. Well, a good journey to you, sir."

"And to you, sir," said Gerard. He watched the Knight stalk off to bully the stable hands, striking them with his fist when they did not give him the answers he thought he deserved. The stable hands slunk away, leaving the Knight to yell for the griffons himself.

"Bastard," said one of the men, nursing a bruised cheek. "Now we'll be up all night tending to his blasted dragon."

"I wouldn't work too hard at it," said Gerard. "I think the Knight's errand will take longer than he anticipates. Far longer."

The stable hand cast Gerard a sulky glance and, rubbing his cheek, led Gerard to the cave of the Marshal's blue dragon.

Gerard prepared nervously to meet the blue by recalling every bit of information he'd ever heard about dragons. Of primary importance would be controlling the dragonfear, which he had heard could be extremely debilitating. He took a firm grip on his courage and hoped he would do nothing to disgrace himself.

The stable hands brought the dragon forth from his lair. Razor was a magnificent sight. The sunlight gleamed on his blue scales. His head was elegantly shaped, eyes keen, nostrils flared. He moved with sinuous grace. Gerard had never been this close to a dragon, any dragon. The dragonfear touched Gerard, but the dragon was not exerting his power to panic the human, and Gerard felt the fear as awe and wonder.

The dragon, aware that he was being admired, shook his crest and flexed his wings, lashed his tail about.

An elderly man left the dragon's side, walked over to Gerard. The old man was short and bowlegged and scrawny. Squinty eyes were almost lost in a web of wrinkles, and he peered at Gerard with intense curiosity and suspicion.

"I am Razor's trainer, sir," said the old man. "I've never known the Marshal to allow another person on his dragon's back. What's going on?"

Gerard handed over Medan's orders. The old man stared at them with equal intensity, held the seal close to his nose to see it with what was probably his single good eye. Gerard thought for a moment that the old man was going to keep him from leaving, and he didn't know whether to be glad or disappointed.

"Well, there's a first time for everything," the old man muttered and handed back the orders. He looked at Gerard's armor, raised an eyebrow. "You're not thinking of taking to the air in that, are you, sir?"

"I . . . I suppose . . ." Gerard stammered.

The old man was scandalized. "You'd freeze your privates off!" He shook his head. "Now if you was going into battle on dragonback, yes, you'd want all that there metal, but you're not. You're flying far and you're flying fast. I have some old leathers of the Marshal's that'll fit you. Might be a trifle big, but they'll do. Is there any special way you would like us to place the saddle, sir? The Marshal prefers it set just back of the shoulder blades, but I've known other riders who want it between the wings. They claim the flight is smoother."

"I . . . I don't really know. . . ." Gerard looked at the dragon, and the knowledge struck home that he was really going to have go through with this.

"By Our Queen," stated the old man, amazed. "You've never sat a dragon afore, have you?"

Gerard confessed, red-faced, that he had not. "I hope it is not difficult," he added, remembering vividly learning to ride a horse. If he fell off the dragon as many times as he fell off the horse . . .

"Razor is a veteran, Sir Knight," stated the old man proudly. "He is a thorough soldier. Disciplined, obeys orders. Not temperamental like some of these blues can be. He and the general fought together as a team during the Chaos War and after. But when those freakish, bloated dragons came and began killing their own kind, the Marshal kept Razor hidden away. Razor wasn't happy about that, mind you. The rows they had."

The old man shook his head. He squinted up at Gerard. "I think I'm beginning to understand after all." He nodded his wizened head. "I've heard the rumors that the Green Bitch was heading this way."

He leaned close to Gerard, spoke in a loud whisper. "Don't let on to Razor, though, sir. If he thought he'd have a chance at that green beast what killed his mate, he'd stay and fight, Marshal or no Marshal. You just take him safe away from here, Sir Knight. Good luck to the both of you."

Gerard opened his mouth to say that he and Razor would be returning to fight just as soon as he had delivered his message, but he shut it again, fearing to say too much. Let the old man think what he wanted.

"Will . . . Razor mind that I am not Marshal Medan?" Gerard asked hesitantly. "I wouldn't want to upset the dragon. He might refuse to carry me."

"Razor is dedicated to the Marshal, sir, but once he understands that Medan has sent you, he will serve you well. This way, sir. I'll introduce you."

Razor listened attentively as a nearly tongue-tied Gerard haltingly explained his mission and exhibited Medan's orders.

"Where is our destination?" Razor demanded.

"I am not permitted to reveal that, yet," Gerard said apologetically. "I am to tell you once we are airborne. The fewer who know, the better."

The dragon gave a shake of his head to indicate his readiness to obey. He was not the talkative sort, apparently, and after that single question, he lapsed into disciplined silence.

Saddling the dragon took some time, not because Razor in any way hindered the operation, but the act of positioning the saddle and the harness with its innumerable buckles and straps was a complex and time-consuming procedure. Gerard put on the "leathers," consisting of a padded leather tunic with long sleeves that he pulled on over a pair of thick leather breeches. Leather gloves protected the hands. A leather cap that resembled an executioner's hood fit over his head, protected both head and neck. The leather tunic was overlarge, the leather pants were stiff, the leather helm stifling. Gerard found it almost impossible to see out of the eye-slits and wondered why they even bothered. The insignia of the Dark Knights—the death lily and the skull—had been incorporated into the stitching of the padding.

Other than that and his sword, nothing else marked Gerard as a Dark Knight. He placed the precious letter safely in a leather pack, tied the pack tightly to the dragon's saddle.

The sun was high in the sky by the time both dragon and rider were ready to leave. Gerard mounted the dragon awkwardly, requiring assistance from the stable hands and the dragon, who bore his incompetence with exemplary patience. Red-faced and embarrassed, Gerard had barely grasped the reins in his hand when Razor gave a galvanized leap straight into the air, powering himself upward with the strong muscles of his hind legs.

The jolt drove Gerard's stomach down somewhere around his boots, and he held on so tightly his fingers lost all feeling and went numb. But when the dragon spread his wings and soared into the morning, Gerard's spirit soared with him.

He had never before understood why anyone would want to be a part of a dragon-wing. He understood then. The experience of flight was exhilarating as well as terrifying. Memories came to him of childish dreams of flying like the eagles. He had even attempted to do so himself by jumping off the barn roof with arms extended, only to crash into a hayrick, nearly breaking his neck. A thrill of excitement warmed his blood and diluted the fear in his belly.

Watching the ground fall away beneath him, he marveled at the strange feeling that it was the world that was leaving him, not the other way around. He was entranced by the silence, a silence that was whole and complete, not what is termed silence by the land-bound. That silence is made up of various small sounds that are so constant we no longer hear them: the chirping of birds, the rustling of the wind in the leaves, the sound of distant voices, the murmur of brook and stream.

Gerard could hear nothing except the creak of the tendons of the dragon's wings, and when the dragon floated on the thermals, he could not hear even that. The silence filled him with a sensation of peace, euphoria. He was no longer a part of the world. He floated above its cares, its woes, its problems. He felt weightless, as if he had shed his bulky flesh and bone. The thought of going back down, of gaining back the weight, of resuming the burden, was suddenly abhorrent. He could have flown forever, flown to the place the sun went when it set, flown to places where the moon hid.

The dragon cleared the treetops.

"What direction?" Razor shouted, his voice booming, shaking Gerard out of his reverie.

"North," Gerard shouted. The wind rushing past his head whipped the words from his mouth. The dragon turned his head to hear better. "Solanthus."

Razor's eye regarded him askance, and Gerard was afraid the dragon might refuse. Solanthus was in nominally free territory. The Solamnic Knights had transformed Solanthus into a heavily fortified city, probably the most heavily fortified in all of Ansalon. Razor might very well wonder why he was being ordered to fly into an enemy stronghold, and if he didn't like the answer he might decide to dump Gerard from the saddle.

Gerard was ready with an explanation, but the dragon explained the situation to himself.

"Ah, a reconnaissance mission," he said and adjusted his course.

Razor maintained silence during the flight. This suited Gerard, who was preoccupied with his own thoughts, dark thoughts that cast a shadow over the beautiful panorama of the landscape sliding away far beneath him. He had spoken hopefully, positively of being able to persuade the Solamnic Knights to come to Qualinesti's aid, but now that he was on his way, he began to doubt that he would be able to persuade them.

"Sir," said Razor, "look below."

Gerard looked, and his heart seemed to plummet to the ground.

"Drop down," he ordered the dragon. He didn't know if he could be heard, and he accompanied his words with a gesture of his gloved hand. "I want a better view."

The dragon swooped out of the clouds, circled slowly in a descending spiral.

"That's close enough," said Gerard, indicating with a gesture that the dragon was to remain stationary.

Gerard bent over the saddle, grasping it with his gloved hands, and looked out over the dragon's left wing.

A vast army swarmed across the land, its numbers so large that it stretched like a great black snake for as far as he could see. A ribbon of blue that wound through the green forests was surely the White-rage River that formed the border of Qualinesti. The head of the black snake had already crawled over the border, was well inland.

Gerard leaned forward. "Would it be possible for you to increase your speed?" he shouted and illustrated his question with a jabbing finger, pointing north.

Razor grunted. "I can fly faster," he shouted, "but you will not find it comfortable."

Gerard looked down, estimating numbers, counting companies, supply wagons, gaining all the information he could. He gritted his teeth, bent in the saddle and gave the nod to proceed.

The dragon's enormous wings began to beat. Razor lifted his head to the clouds, soared up to reach them.

The sudden acceleration pressed Gerard into the saddle. He blessed the designer of the leather helm, understood the need for the eye-slits. Even then, the rushing wind half-blinded him, brought tears to his eyes. The motion of the dragon's wings caused the saddle to rock back and forth. Gerard's stomach heaved. Grimly he hung on and prayed that somewhere there were gods to pray to.

6 THE MARCH ON SILVANOST

No one quite knew how word came to spread throughout the capital city of Silvanost that the hands of the human girl named Mina were the hands of a healer. The elves might have heard news of her from the outside world, except that they had been long cut off from the outside world, covered by the shield that had been presumably protecting them but had been, in reality, slowly killing them. No elf could say where he had first heard this rumor, but he credited it to neighbor, cousin, or passerby.

The rumor started with the fall of darkness. It spread through the night, whispered on the flower-scented night breeze, sung by the nightingale, mentioned by the owl. The rumor spread with excitement and joy among the young, yet there were those among the older elves who frowned to hear it and who cautioned against it.

Strong among these were the kirath, the elves who had long patrolled and guarded the borders of Silvanesti. These elves had watched with grief as the shield killed every living thing along the border. They had fought the cruel dream cast by the dragon Cyan Bloodbane many years ago during the War of the Lance. The kirath knew from their bitter experience with the dream that evil can come in lovely forms, only to grow hideous and murderous when confronted. The kirath warned against this human girl. They tried to halt the rumors that were spreading through the city, as fast and bright and slippery as quicksilver. But every time the rumor came to a house where a young elven mother held to her breast her dying child, the rumor was believed. The warnings of the kirath went unheeded.

That night, when the moon lifted high in the heavens, the single moon, the moon that the elves had never grown accustomed to seeing in a sky where once the silver and the red moons had swung among the stars, the guards on the gates of Silvanost looked out along the highway leading into their city, a highway of moondust, to see a force of humans marching on Silvanost. The force was small, twenty Knights clad in the black armor of the Knights of Neraka and several hundred foot soldiers marching behind. The army was a shabby one. The foot soldiers stumbled, they limped, footsore and weary. Even the Knights were afoot, their horses having died in battle or been eaten by their starving riders. Only one Knight rode, and that was their leader, a slender figure mounted on a horse the color of blood.

A thousand elven archers, armed with the storied elven longbow, legendary for its accuracy, looked down upon this advancing army, and each picked out his or her target. There were so many archers that had the order been given to fire, each one of those advancing soldiers would have been stuck full with as many arrows as there are quills on the porcupine.

The elven archers looked uncertainly to their commanders. The archers had heard the rumors, as had their commanders. The archers had sick at home: wives, husbands, mothers, fathers, children, all dying of the wasting disease. Many of the archers themselves were in the first stages of the illness and remained at their posts only through sheer effort of will. So too with their commanders. The kirath, who were not members of the elven army, stood among the archers, wrapped in their cloaks that could blend in with the leaves and trees of the forests they loved, and watched grimly.

Mina rode unerringly straight toward the silver gates, rode into arrow range unflinching, her horse carrying its head proudly, neck arched, tail flicking. At her side walked a giant minotaur. Her Knights came behind her, the foot soldiers followed after. Now within sight of the elves, the soldiers took some pains to dress their lines, straighten their backs, march upright and tall with the appearance of being unafraid, although many must have quaked and shivered at the sight of the arrow tips shining in the moonlight.

Mina halted her horse before the gate. She raised her voice, and it carried as clear and ringing as the notes of a silver bell.

"I am called Mina. I come to Silvanost in the name of the One God. I come to Silvanost to teach my elven brothers and sisters of the One God and to accept them into the service of the One God. I call upon you, the people of Silvanost, to open the gates, that I may enter in peace."

"Do not trust her," urged the kirath. "Do not believe her!"

No one listened, and when one of the kirath, a man named Rolan, lifted his bow and would have fired a shaft at the human girl, those standing around him struck him down so that he fell bloody and dazed to the pavement. Finding that no one paid them any heed, the kirath picked up their fallen comrade and left the city of Silvanost, retreated back to their woodlands.

A herald advanced and read aloud a proclamation.

"His Majesty the king orders that the gates of Silvanost be opened to Mina, whom His Majesty names Dragonslayer, Savior of the Silvanesti."

The elven archers flung down their bows and gave a ragged cheer. The elven gatekeepers hastened to the gates that were made of steel and silver and magic. Though these gates looked as frail and fragile as spun cobweb, they were so bound by ancient magicks that no force on Krynn could break them, unless it was the breath of a dragon. But Mina, it seemed, had only to set her hand to the gates, and they opened.

Mina rode slowly into Silvanost. The minotaur walked at her stirrup, glowering distrustfully at the elves, his hand on his sword. Her soldiers came after, nervous, watchful, wary. The elves, after their initial cheer, fell silent. Crowds of elves lined the highway that was chalk-white in the moonlight. No one spoke, and all that could be heard was the jingle of chain mail and the rattle of armor and sword, the steady shuffling march of booted feet.

Mina had gone only a short distance, and some of the army still remained outside the gate, when she drew her horse to a halt. She heard a sound, and now she looked out into the crowd.

Dismounting, she left the highway and walked straight into the crowd of elves. The huge minotaur drew his sword and would have followed to guard her back, but she raised her hand in a wordless command, and he halted as though she had struck him. Mina came to a young elven woman trying vainly to stifle the whimperings of fretful child of about three years. It was the child's wail that had caught Mina's ears.

The elves drew aside to let Mina pass, flinching from her as though her touch pained them. Yet, after she had passed, some of the younger reached out hesitatingly to touch her again. She paid them no heed.

Approaching the elf woman, Mina said, speaking in Elvish, "Your baby cries. She burns with fever. What is wrong with her?"

The mother held the child protectively in her arms, bowed her head over the little girl. Her tears fell on the child's hot forehead.

"She has the wasting sickness. She has been ill for days now. She grows worse all the time. I fear that . . . she is dying."

"Give me the child," said Mina, holding out her hands.

"No!" The elven woman clasped the child to her. "No, do not harm her!"

"Give me the child," said Mina gently.

The mother lifted fearful eyes and looked into Mina's. The warm liquid amber flowed around the mother and the child. The mother handed the baby to Mina.

The little girl weighed almost nothing. She was as light as a will-o'-the-wisp in Mina's arms.

"I bless you in the name of the One God," said Mina, "and I call you back to this life."

The child's whimpering ceased. She went limp in Mina's arms, and the elder elves drew in hissing breaths.

"She is well now," Mina said, handing back the child to the mother. "The fever has broken. Take her home and keep her warm. She will live."

The mother looked fearfully into the face of her child and gave a cry of joy. The child's whimpering had ceased, and she had gone limp because she now slept peacefully. Her forehead was cool to the touch, her breathing easy.

"Mina!" the elf woman cried, falling to her knees. "Bless you, Mina!"

"Not me," said Mina. "The One God."

"The One God," the mother cried. "I thank the One God."

"Lies!" cried an elf, thrusting his way forward through the crowd. "Lies and blasphemy. The only true god is Paladine."

"Paladine forsook you," Mina said. "Paladine left you. The One God is with you. The One God cares for you."

The elf opened his mouth to make an angry rejoinder. Before he could speak, Mina said to him, "Your beloved wife is not with you here this night."

The elf shut his mouth. Muttering, he started to turn away.

"She is sick at home," Mina told him. "She has not been well for a long, long time. Every day, you watch her sink closer to death. She lies in bed, unable to walk. This morning, she could not lift her head from the pillow."

"She is dying!" the elf said harshly, keeping his head turned away. "Many have died. We bear our suffering and go on."

"When you return home," said Mina, "your wife will meet you at the door. She will take you by the hands, and you will dance in the garden as you once used to."

The elf turned to face her. His face was streaked with tears, his expression was wary, disbelieving. "This is some trick."

"No, it is not," Mina returned, smiling. "I speak the truth, and you know it. Go to her. Go and see."

The elf stared at Mina, then, with a hollow cry, pushed his way through those who surrounded him and vanished into the crowd.

Mina extended her hand toward an elven couple. Father and mother each held a young boy by the hand. The boys were twins, thin and listless, their young faces so pinched with pain they looked like wizened old men.

Mina beckoned to the boys. "Come to me."

The boys shrank away from her. "You are human," said one. "You hate us."

"You will kill us," said his brother. "My father says so."

"To be human, elf, or minotaur makes no difference to the One God. We are all children of the One God, but we must be obedient children. Come to me. Come to the One God."

The boys looked up at their parents. The elves stared at Mina, saying nothing, making no sign. The crowd around them was hushed and still, watching the drama. Finally, one boy let loose his mother's hand and came forward, walking weakly and unsteadily. He took hold of Mina's hand.

"The One God has the power to heal one of you," said Mina. "Which will it be? You or your brother."

"My brother," the child said immediately.

Mina rested her hand on the boy's head. "The One God admires sacrifice. The One God is pleased. The One God heals you both."

Healthful color flooded the pallid cheeks. The listless eyes blazed with life and vigor. The weak legs no longer trembled, the bent spines straightened.

The other boy left his father and ran to join his twin, both flinging their arms around Mina.

"Bless you! Bless you, Mina!" some of the younger Silvanesti elves began to chant, and they gathered close to Mina, reaching out to seize hold of her, begging her to heal them, their wives, their husbands, their children. The crowd surged and heaved around her so that she was in danger of being adored to death.

The minotaur, Galdar, Mina's second-in-command and self-appointed guardian, waded into the mass. Catching hold of Mina, he bore her out of the press, thrusting aside the desperate elves with his strong arms.

Mounting her horse, Mina rose up in the stirrups and lifted her hand for silence. The elves hushed immediately, strained to hear her words.

"It has been given to me to tell you that all those who ask of the One God in humility and reverence will be healed of the sickness brought upon you by the dragon Cyan Bloodbane. The One God has freed you from this peril. Pray to the One God upon your knees, acknowledge the One God as the true god of the elves and you will be cured."

Some of the younger elves fell to their knees at once and began to pray. Others, the elder elves, refused. Never before had the elves prayed to any god except Paladine. Some began to mutter that the kirath had been right, but then those who had prayed lifted their heads to the moonlight and cried out in joy that the pain had left their bodies. At the sight of the miraculous healing, more elves dropped to their knees, raised their voices in praise. The elder elves, watching in dismay and disbelief, shook their heads. One in particular, who was dressed in the magical camouflaging cloak of the kirath, stared hard at Mina for long moments before vanishing among the shadows.

The blood-red horse proceeded forward at a walk. Mina's soldiers cleared her way through the press of bodies. The Tower of the Stars glimmered softly in the moonlight, pointing the way to heaven. Walking at her side, Galdar tried to breathe as little as possible. The stench of elf was overpowering, cloying, sickeningly sweet to the minotaur, like the scent of something long dead.

"Mina," said Galdar in a harsh growl, "these are *elves!*" He made no effort to conceal his disgust. "What does the One God want with elves?"

"The souls of all mortals are valuable to the One God, Galdar," Mina responded.

Galdar mulled this over but could not understand. Looking back at her, he saw, in the moonlight, the images of countless elves held prisoner in the warm golden amber of her eyes.

Mina continued through Silvanost as prayers to the One God, spoken in the Elvish language, rustled and whispered through the night.

Silvanoshei, son of Alhana Starbreeze and Porthios of the House of Solostaran, the heir to both kingdoms of the elves, the Qualinesti and the Silvanesti, stood with his face and hands pressed against the crystal window-pane, peering into the night.

"Where is she?" he demanded impatiently. "No, wait! I think I see her!" He stared long and then fell back with a sigh. "No, it is not her. I was mistaken. Why doesn't she come?" He turned around to demand in sudden fear, "You don't think anything has happened to her, Cousin?"

Kiryn opened his mouth to reply, but before he could say a word, Silvanoshei had spoken to a servant. "Find out what is happening at the gate. Return to me at once."

The servant bowed and departed, leaving the two alone in the room.

"Cousin," said Kiryn, keeping his voice carefully modulated, "that is the sixth servant you have sent this past half hour. He will return with the same message that they have all brought. The progress of the procession is slow, due to the fact that so many of our people want to see her."

Silvanoshei went back to the window, stared out again with an impatience he did not bother to hide. "It was a mistake. I should have been there to greet her." He cast a cold glance at his cousin. "I should not have listened to you."

"Your Majesty," said Kiryn with a sigh, "it would not have looked good. You, the king, welcoming in person the leader of our enemies. Bad enough that we have admitted her into the city in the first place," he added to himself, but Silvanoshei had sharp ears.

"Need I remind you, Cousin," said the king tersely, "that it was this same leader of our enemies who saved us from the machinations of the foul dragon Cyan Bloodbane? Because of her, I was brought back to life and given the chance to lower the shield he erected over us, the shield that was sucking out our very lives. Because of her, I was able to destroy the Shield Tree and save our people. If not for her, there would be no elves in the streets of Silvanost, only corpses."

"I am aware of that, Your Majesty," Kiryn said. "Yet I ask myself why? What are her motives?"

"I might ask the same of you, Cousin," Silvanoshei said coolly. "What are you motives?"

"I don't know what you mean," Kiryn said.

"Don't you? It has been brought to my attention that you are plotting behind my back. You have been seen meeting with members of the kirath."

"What of that, Cousin?" Kiryn asked mildly. "They are your loyal subjects."

"They are not my loyal subjects!" Silvanoshei said angrily. "They conspire against me!"

"They conspire against our enemies, the Dark Knights—"

"Mina, you mean. They conspire against Mina. That is the same as conspiring against me."

Kiryn sighed softly and said, "There is someone waiting to speak to Your Majesty."

"I will see no one," Silvanoshei said.

"I think you should see him," Kiryn continued. "He comes from your mother."

Silvanoshei turned away from the window and stared at Kiryn. "What are you saying? My mother is dead. She died the night the ogres raided our camp. The night I fell through the shield . . ."

"No, Cousin," said Kiryn. "Your mother, Alhana, lives. She and her forces have crossed the border. She has been in contact with the kirath. That is why . . . They tried to see you, Cousin, but were denied. They came to me."

Silvanoshei sank down into a chair. He lowered his head to his shaking hand to hide his sudden tears.

"Forgive me, Cousin," Kiryn said. "I should have found some better way to tell you—"

"No! You could have brought me no happier news!" Silvanoshei cried, lifting his face. "My mother's messenger is here?" He rose to his feet, walked impatiently toward the door. "Bring him in."

"He is not in the antechamber. He would be in danger here in the palace. I took the liberty—"

"Of course. I had forgotten. My mother is a dark elf," Silvanoshei said bitterly. "She is under penalty of death, as are those who follow her."

"Your Majesty now has the power to set that right," said Kiryn.

"By law, perhaps," said Silvanoshei. "But laws cannot erase years of hatred. Go and fetch him, then, wherever you have hidden him."

Kiryn left the room. Silvanoshei returned to the window, his thoughts a confused and joyous muddle. His mother alive. Mina returned to him. The two of them must meet. They would like each other. Well, perhaps not at first. . . .

He heard a scraping sound behind him, turned to see movement behind one of the heavy curtains. The curtain was drawn aside, revealing an opening in the wall, a secret passageway. Silvanoshei had heard stories from his mother about these passageways. As a lark, Silvanoshei had searched for the passages, but had found only this one. The passage led to the hidden garden, a garden now lifeless, its flowers having been killed by the blight of the shield.

Kiryn stepped out from behind the curtain. Another elf, cloaked and hooded, followed after him.

"Samar!" exclaimed Silvanoshei in a recognition that was both pleasurable and filled with pain.

His first impulse was to run forward, grasp Samar by the hand or perhaps even embrace him, so glad was he to see him and know he was alive and that his mother was alive. Kiryn was hoping for just such a reunion. He hoped that the news that his mother was near, that she and her forces had crossed the border would wrench Silvanoshei's mind away from Mina.

Kiryn's hopes were doomed to failure.

Samar did not see Silvanoshei the king. He saw Silvanoshei the spoiled child, dressed in fine clothes and glittering jewels, while his mother wore clothes she made of homespun and adorned herself in the cold metal of chain mail. He saw Silvanoshei residing in a grand palace with every comfort he could wish for, saw his mother shivering in a barren cave. Samar saw a vast bed with a thick down mattress and blankets of angora wool and sheets of silk, and he saw Alhana sleeping on the cold ground with her tattered cloak wrapped around her.

Anger pounded in Samar's veins, dimmed his vision, blurred his thinking. He blotted out Silvanoshei completely and saw only Alhana, who had been overcome with joy and emotion on hearing that Silvanoshei, whom she had believed to be dead, was alive. Not only alive but crowned king of Silvanesti—her dearest wish for him.

She had wanted to come immediately to see him, an act that would have placed in jeopardy not only her life but the lives of her people. Samar had pleaded long and hard to dissuade her from this course of action, and only the knowledge that she risked imperiling all for which she had labored so long had at last convinced her that he should go in her stead. He would take her love to her son, but he would not fawn or dote on the boy. Samar would remind Silvanoshei of a son's duty to a mother, be he king or commoner. Duty to his mother, duty to his people.

Samar's cold look halted Silvanoshei in midstep.

"Prince Silvanoshei," said Samar, with a very slight bow. "I trust I find you well. I certainly find you well-fed." He cast a scathing glance at the laden table. "That much food would feed your mother's army for a year!"

Silvanoshei's warm affection froze to solid ice in an instant. He forgot how much he owed Samar, remembered instead only that the man had never approved of him, perhaps never even liked him. Silvanoshei drew himself up to his full height.

"Undoubtedly you have not heard the news, Samar," Silvanoshei said with quiet dignity, "and so I forgive you. I am king of the Silvanesti, and you will address me as such."

"I will address you as what you are," Samar said, his voice shaking, "a spoiled brat!"

"How dare you—" Silvanoshei began hotly.

"Stop it! Both of you." Kiryn stared at them, aghast. "What are you two doing? Have you forgotten the terrible crisis that is at hand? Cousin Silvanoshei, you have known this man from childhood. You have told me many times that you admired and respected him as a second father. Samar risked his life to come to you. Is this how you repay him?"

Silvanoshei said nothing. He pressed his lips together, regarded Samar with an expression of injured dignity.

"And you, Samar," said Kiryn, turning to the elven warrior. "You are in the wrong. Silvanoshei is the crowned and anointed king of the Silvanesti people. You are Qualinesti. Perhaps the ways of your people are different. We Silvanesti revere our king. When you demean him, you demean us all."

Samar and the King were silent long moments, staring at each other—not as two friends who have been quick to quarrel and are glad to make up, but as two duelists who are sizing each other up even as they are forced to shake hands before the final contest. Kiryn was grieved to the heart.

"We have started out all wrong," he said. "Let us begin again."

"How is my mother, Samar?" Silvanoshei asked abruptly.

"Your mother is well . . . Your Majesty," Samar replied. He left a deliberate pause before the title, but he spoke it. "She sends her love."

Silvanoshei nodded. He was keeping a tight grip on himself. "The night of the storm. I thought . . . It seemed impossible that you could survive."

"As it turned out, the Legion of Steel had been keeping watch on the movements of the ogres, and so they came to our aid. It seems," Samar added, his voice gruff, "that you and your mother have been grieving together. When you did not return, we searched for you for days. We could only conclude that you had been captured by the ogres and dragged off to torment and death. When the shield fell and your mother crossed over into her homeland, we were met by the kirath. Her joy was boundless when she heard that not only were you alive, but that you were now king, Silvanoshei."

His tone hardened. "Then the reports of you and this human female—"

Silvanoshei flashed Kiryn an angry glance. "Now I understand the reason you brought him here, Cousin. To lecture me." He turned back to the window.

"Silvanoshei—" Kiryn began.

Samar strode forward, grabbed hold of Silvanoshei by the shoulder. "Yes, I am going to lecture you. You are behaving like a spoiled brat. Your honored mother did not believe the rumors. She told the kirath who spoke of this that they lied. What happens? I overhear you speaking of this human. I hear from your own lips that the rumors are true! You mope and whine for her, while a massive army of Dark Knights crosses the border. An army that was waiting at the border, prepared to cross when the shield came down.

"And, lo and behold, the shield fell! How did this army come to be there, Silvanoshei? Was it coincidence? Did the Dark Knights happen to arrive at the precise moment the shield happened to fall? No, Silvanoshei, the Dark Knights were there on the border because they *knew* the shield was going to fall. Now they march on Silvanost, five thousand strong, and you have opened the gates of the city to the female who brought them here."

"That is not true!" Silvanoshei returned heatedly, ignoring Kiryn's attempts to placate him. "Mina came to save us. She knew the truth about Cyan Bloodbane. She knew the dragon was the one responsible for raising the shield. She knew the shield was killing us. When I died at the hands of the dragon, she restored me to life. She—" Silvanoshei halted, his tongue cleaving to his palate.

"*She* told you to lower the shield," Samar said. "She told you *how* to lower the shield."

"Yes, I lowered the shield!" Silvanoshei returned defiantly. "I did what my mother has been striving to do for years! You know that to be true, Samar. My mother saw the shield for what it was. She knew it was not raised to protect us, and she was right. It was put in place to kill us. What would you have had me do, Samar? Leave the shield in place? Watch it suck the lives from my people?"

"You might have left it in place long enough to check to see if your enemy was massing on your border," Samar said caustically. "The kirath could have warned you, if you had taken time to listen to them, but no, you chose to listen to a human female, the leader of those who would see you and your people destroyed."

"The decision was mine alone to make," said Silvanoshei with dignity. "I acted on my own. I did what my mother would have done in my place. You know that, Samar. She herself told me of the time she flew on griffon-back straight into the shield in her efforts to shatter it. Time and again she tried and was flung back—"

"Enough!" Samar interrupted impatiently. "What's done is done." He had lost this round, and he knew it. He was quiet a moment, pondering. When he spoke again, there was a change in his voice, a note of apology in his tone. "You are young, Silvanoshei, and it is the province of youth to make mistakes, although this, I fear, may well prove fatal to our cause. However, we have not given up. We may yet be able to undo the damage you have—however well-meaning—caused."

Reaching beneath his cloak, Samar drew out another cloak and hood. "Dark Knights ride into our sacred city with impunity. I watched them enter. I saw this female. I saw our people, especially our young people, bewitched by her. They are blind to the truth. It will be our task to make them see again. Conceal yourself with this cloak, Silvanoshei. We will leave by the secret passage through which I entered, escape the city in the confusion."

"Leave?" Silvanoshei stared at Samar in astonishment. "Why should I leave?"

Samar would have spoken, but Kiryn interrupted, hoping to salvage his plan.

"Because you are in danger, Cousin," said Kiryn. "Do you think the Dark Knights will allow you to remain king? If they do, you will be no more than a puppet, like your cousin Gilthas. But, as king in exile, you will be a force to rally the people—"

Go? I cannot go, Silvanoshei said to himself. She is coming back to me. She draws closer every moment. This very night perhaps I will fold her in my arms. I would not leave though I knew death itself had come for me.

He looked at Kiryn and he looked at Samar and he saw not friends, but strangers, conspiring against him. He could not trust them. He could trust no one.

"You say that my people are in danger," said Silvanoshei. He turned his back, turned his gaze out the window, as if he were looking over the city below. In truth, he searched for her. "My people are in danger, and you would have me flee to safety and leave them to face the threat alone. What poor sort of king is that, Samar?"

"A live king, Your Majesty," Samar said dryly. "A king who thinks enough of his people to live for them instead of for himself. They will understand and honor you for your decision."

Silvanoshei glanced coolly over his shoulder. "You are wrong, Samar. My mother fled, and the people did not honor her for it. They despised her. I will not make the same mistake. I thank you for coming, Samar. You are dismissed."

Trembling, amazed at his own temerity, he turned back to the window, stared out unseeing.

"You ungrateful whelp!" Samar was half-choked with the gall of his rage, could barely speak. "You will come with me if I have to drag you!"

Kiryn stepped between Samar and the king.

"I think you had better leave, sir," Kiryn said, his voice calm, eyes level. He was angry with both of them, angry and disappointed. "Or I will be forced to summon the guards. His Majesty has made his decision."

Samar ignored Kiryn, glowered balefully at Silvanoshei. "I will leave. I will tell your mother that her son has made a noble, heroic sacrifice in the name of the people. I will *not* tell her the truth: that he stays for love of a human witch. I will not tell her, but others will. She will know, and her heart will break."

He tossed the cloak on the floor at Silvanoshei's feet. "You are a fool, young man. I would not mind if by your folly you brought ruin only on yourself, Silvanoshei, but you will bring ruin upon us all."

Samar left, stalking across the room to the secret passage. He flung the curtain aside with a violence that almost ripped it from its rings.

Silvanoshei cast a scathing glance at Kiryn. "Don't think I don't know what you were after. Remove me, and you ascend the throne!"

"You don't think that of me, Cousin," Kiryn said quietly, gently. "You can't think that."

Silvanoshei tried very hard to think it, but he failed. Of all the people he knew, Kiryn was the only one who seemed to have a true affection for him. For him alone. Not for the king. For Silvanoshei.

Leaving the window, he walked over, took Kiryn by the hand, pressed it warmly. "I'm sorry, Cousin. Forgive me. He makes me so angry, I don't know what I'm saying. I know you meant well." Silvanoshei looked after Samar. "I know that *he* means well, but he doesn't understand. No one understands."

Silvanoshei felt a great weariness come over him. He had not slept in a long time. He couldn't remember how long. Whenever he closed his eyes, he saw her face, heard her voice, felt the touch of her lips on his, and his heart leaped, his blood thrilled, and he lay awake, staring into the darkness, waiting for her to return to him.

"Go after Samar, Kiryn. Make certain he leaves the palace safely. I would not want any harm to come to him."

Kiryn gave his king a helpless glance, sighed, shook his head, and did as he was told.

Silvanoshei went back to the window.

7 SAILING THE RIVER OF THE DEAD

It is a sad truism that the misfortunes of others, no matter how terrible, always pale in comparison to our own. At this moment in his life, if someone had told Conundrum that armies of goblins and hobgoblins, draconians, hired thugs, and murderers were marching on the elves, the gnome would have laughed in derision and rolled his eyes.

"They think *they* have trouble?" he would have said. "Hah! They should be down beneath the ocean in a leaky submersible with a crazed human woman who keeps insisting that I follow a bunch of dead people. Now *that* is trouble."

If Conundrum had been told that his friend the kender, who had provided him with the means to finally be able to achieve his life quest and map the Hedge Maze, was being held prisoner by the most powerful mage in all the world in the Tower of High Sorcery, Conundrum would have sneered.

"The kender thinks *he* has trouble! Hah! He should try to operate the submersible all by himself when it requires a crew of twenty. There is trouble for you!"

In fact, the submersible worked far better with a crew of one, since the other nineteen simply added to the weight and got in the way and used up the air. The original voyage that left Mt. Nevermind and headed to the citadel had started with a crew of twenty, but the others had become lost, mislaid, or seriously burned along the way, leaving at last only Conundrum, who had been but a lowly passenger, in sole control. He knew nothing whatsoever about the complicated system of mechanics designed to power the MNS *Indestructible*, undoubtedly the reason the vessel had remained afloat as long as it had.

The vessel was designed in the shape of a large fish. It was made of wood, which made it light enough to float, and then covered with iron, which made it heavy enough to sink. Conundrum knew that there was a crank he had to crank in order to keep the vessel moving forward, another crank that made the vessel move up, and a third that made the vessel go down. He was somewhat vague on what the cranks actually did, although he recalled a gnome (perhaps the late captain) telling him that the rear crank caused the fins at the rear of the vessel to whirl about in a frenzied manner, stirring up the water and thus propelling the vessel forward. The crank at the bottom caused fins at the bottom to whirl, sending the vessel upward, while fins on the top reversed that process.

Conundrum knew that along with the cranking there were a good many gears that had to be constantly oiled. He knew this because all gnomes everywhere know that gears must be constantly oiled. He had been told that there were bellows that pumped air into the submersible, but he was unable to figure out how these worked and so concluded that it would be wisest, if less scientific, to bring the *Indestructible* up to the surface for air every few hours. Since the bellows did not work and had never worked, this proved to be sound reasoning on his part.

At the start of his enforced journey, Conundrum asked Goldmoon why she had stolen his submersible, where she planned to go with it, and what she intended to do once they got there. It was then she made the startling pronouncement that she was following the dead, that the dead guided her and protected her, and the dead were leading her across New Sea to where she must go. When he asked, quite logically, why the dead had seen fit to tell her to steal his boat, she had said that diving underwater was the only means by which they could escape the dragon.

Conundrum tried to interest Goldmoon in the workings of the submersible and to elicit her help in the cranking—which was wearing on the arms—or at least the help of the dead, since they appeared to be the ones in charge of this trip. She paid no attention to him. Conundrum found his passenger exasperating, and he would have turned the *Indestructible* around on the spot and sailed back to his Hedge Maze, dragon or no dragon, but for the lamentable fact that he did not have the faintest idea how to make the boat go in any direction other than up, down, and forward.

Nor, as it turned out, did the gnome know how to make the boat stop, thus giving a new and unfortunate meaning to the term "landfall."

Due to either fate or the guidance of the dead, the *Indestructible* did not smash headlong into a cliff or run aground on a reef. Instead it plowed into a sandy beach, its fins still flapping, sending up great spumes of sand and seawater, mangling jellyfish, and terrorizing the sea birds.

The final mad plunge up onto the beach was jouncing and uncomfortable but not fatal to the passengers. Goldmoon and Conundrum escaped with only minor cuts and bruises. The same could not be said of the *Indestructible*.

Goldmoon stood on the deserted beach and breathed the fresh sea air deeply. She paid no attention to the cuts on her arms or the bruise on her forehead. This strange new body of hers had the capacity to heal itself. Within moments, the blood would dry, the flesh close together, the bruises fade away. She would continue to feel the pain of the injuries, but only on her true body, the body that was the weak and frail body of an elderly human.

She did not like this new body that had been miraculously bestowed on her—an unwilling recipient—the night of the terrible storm, but she had come to realize that its strength and health were essential in order to take her to wherever it was the dead wanted her to go. The old body would not have made it this far. It was near death. The spirit that resided in the old body neared death as well. Perhaps that was the reason Goldmoon could see the dead when others could not. She was closer now to the dead than to the living.

The pale river of spirits flowed over the windswept dunes, heading north. The long greenish-brown grass that grew on the dunes rippled with the wind of their passing. Gathering up the hem of her long white robes, the robes that marked her a Mystic of the Citadel of Light, Goldmoon made ready to follow.

"Wait!" cried Conundrum, who had been staring open-mouthed at the destruction of the *Indestructible.* "What are you doing? Where are you going?"

Goldmoon did not reply but continued on. Walking was difficult. She sank into the soft sand with every step. Her robes hampered her movements.

"You can't leave me," Conundrum stated. He waved an oil-covered hand. "I've lost an immense amount of time ferrying you across the sea, and now you have broken my boat. How am I going to return to my life quest—mapping the Hedge Maze?"

Goldmoon halted and turned to look back at the gnome. He was not a savory sight, with his scraggly hair and untidy beard, his face flushed with righteous indignation and smeared with oil and blood.

"I thank you for bringing me," she said, raising her voice to be heard above the freshening wind and the crashing waves. "I am sorry for your loss, but I can do nothing to help you." She shifted her head, gazed northward. "I have a journey I must make. I cannot linger here or anywhere." Looking back at the gnome, she added, kindly, "I would not leave you stranded. You may come with me, if you choose."

Conundrum looked at her, then back at the *Indestructible,* which had certainly not lived up to its name. Even he, a passenger, could see that repairs were going to be long and costly, to say nothing of the fact that since he'd never understood how the contraption worked in the first place, making it work again would present certain problems.

"Besides," he said to himself, more brightly, "I'm certain the owner has it insured, and he will no doubt be compensated for the loss."

This was taking an optimistic view of the matter. One might say an optimistic and completely unrealistic view, since it was a well known fact that the Guild of InsurersEquityUnderandOverwritersCollisionAccidentalDismemb ermentFireFloodNotLiableforActsofGod had never paid out a single copper piece, although there were, following the Chaos War, innumerable lawsuits pending, contending that ActsofGod no longer counted, since there were no longer any gods. Due to the fact that the lawsuits had to go through the gnomish legal system, it was not expected that they would be settled during the litigants' lifetimes but would be handed down to the generations coming afterward, all of whom would be financially ruined by the accruing legal fees.

Conundrum had few belongings to retrieve from the wreckage. He had run off from the citadel so fast that he had left behind his most important belonging—the map of the Hedge Maze. The gnome was confident that the map would be found and, considering that it was a Marvel to end all Marvels, would naturally be placed in a most safe and secure part of the Citadel of Light.

The only thing salvaged from the wreckage was a knife that had belonged to the late captain. The knife was remarkable, for it had all sorts of tools attached to it and could do just about everything. It could open a bottle of wine, tell you which direction was north, and crack the shells of recalcitrant oysters. Its one drawback was that you couldn't cut anything with it, since it lacked a blade, the inventor having run out of room, but that was a minor inconvenience compared to the fact that you could use it to trim your nose hairs.

Thrusting the remarkable knife in the pocket of his ink-stained and oily robes, Conundrum floundered, sliding and stumbling along the beach. He paused once to turn and look back at the *Indestructible*. The submersible had the forlorn appearance of a beached whale and was already being covered over by drifting sand.

Conundrum set out after Goldmoon, who was following the river of the dead.

8 BALANCING ACCOUNTS

Five days after Beryl's attack on the Citadel of Light, five days after the fall of the shield in Silvanesti and five days after the first ranks of Beryl's army crossed the border into the realm of Qualinesti, Lord Targonne sat at his desk going over the reports that had been flooding in from various parts of the continent of Ansalon.

Targonne found the report from Malys pleasing, at first. The enormous red dragon Malystryx, the dragon whom everyone acknowledged to be the true ruler of Ansalon, had taken the news of her cousin Beryl's aggression far better than Targonne had dared hope. Malys had ranted and raved, to be sure, but in the end she had stated that any move by Beryl to annex lands beyond Qualinesti would be viewed as a most serious affront to Malys and would be dealt with summarily.

The more Targonne thought about it, however, the more he began to have second thoughts. Malystryx had been too accommodating. She had received the news too calmly. He had the feeling that the giant red was plotting something and that whatever she was plotting would be catastrophic. For the moment, however, she was keeping to her lair, apparently content to let him deal with the situation. That, he fully intended to do.

According to reports, Beryl had demolished the Citadel of Light, crushing the crystal domes in a fit of pique because, according to his agents, who had been on the scene and who had witnessed the destruction firsthand, she had not been able to locate the magical artifact that had been the reason for this misguided attack. The loss of life on the island might have been incalculable but for the fact that before she razed the buildings, Beryl had sent down squadrons of draconians to search for the artifact and the wizard who wielded it.

The delay provided time for the inhabitants to flee to safety inland. Targonne's agents, who had been attending the citadel in disguise, hoping to discover why their healing spells were going awry, had been among those who had fled to safety and were thus able to send back their reports. Beryl had departed early on in the battle, leaving her reds to finish the destruction for her. The draconians had gone after the refugees but had been fought off by the forces of the Solamnic Knights and some fierce tribal warriors who dwelt in the island's interior. The draconians had sustained heavy casualties.

Targonne, who did not like draconians, counted this as no great loss.

"Next report," he said to his aide.

The aide drew out a sheet of vellum. "A message from Marshal Medan, my lord. The Marshal apologizes for the delay in responding to your orders but says that your messenger met with a most unfortunate accident. He was flying to Qualinost when the griffon on which he was riding suddenly went berserk and attacked him. He was able to deliver his message, but he died of his injuries shortly thereafter. The Marshal states that he will comply fully with your orders and hand over the elven city of Qualinost to the dragon Beryl, along with the Queen Mother, both of whom he holds prisoner. The Marshal has disbanded the elven Senate, arrested the senators and the Heads of House. He was going to arrest the elven king, Gilthas, but the young man was smuggled out of the city and is now in hiding. The Marshal reports that Beryl's army is encountering attacks from elven forces and that these are slowing the army's march but otherwise doing little damage."

"That is good news, if it's true," Targonne said, frowning. "I have never quite trusted Medan. He was one of Ariakan's favorites, the main reason he was put in charge of Qualinesti. There were those stories Beryl put out that he had grown more elf than human, raising flowers and playing the lute."

"Thus far, he appears to have the situation under control, my lord," said the aide, glancing back over the neatly written page.

Targonne grunted. "We will see. Send a message to the great green bitch that she can have Qualinost and that I trust she will leave it intact and unspoiled. Include an account of the revenues we collected from Qualinost last year. That should convince her."

"Yes, my lord," said the aide, making a note.

"Anything new to report from Sanction?" Targonne asked in a resigned tone that indicated he would be shocked if there were.

The walled city of Sanction, located on the western shores of New Sea, controlled the only ports on New Sea for that part of Ansalon. During the War of the Lance, the city had been a stronghold of the dragon highlords, but it was now controlled by a mysterious and powerful wizard known as Hogan Bight. Thought to be acting independently, Bight had been wooed by the Dark Knights of Neraka, in hopes that he would ally with them and make the ports of Sanction available to them. Knowing that Bight was also being wooed by the Solamnics, the Dark Knights had laid siege to Sanction in order to hasten Bight's decision-making process. The siege had dragged on for long months now. The Solamnics had attempted to break it, but they had been routed by this very Mina who had now taken Silvanesti. Targonne supposed he should be grateful to Mina for having saved the day for him. He would have been a damn sight more grateful to her if he'd actually ordered her to do it.

"Sanction is still under siege, my lord," said the aide, after a moment's shuffle to the bottom of the pile. "The commanders complain they do not have enough men to take the city. They maintain that if General Dogah's forces had been allowed to march to Sanction instead of being diverted to Silvanesti, the city would now be in their hands."

"And I'm a gully dwarf," Targonne said with a snort. "Once Silvanesti is secure, we will deal with Sanction."

"Regarding Silvanesti, my lord." The aide returned to the top of the pile and extracted a sheet of paper. "I have here the report from the interrogation of the elven prisoners. The three—two males and a female—are members of what is known as the 'kirath,' a sort of border patrol, I believe."

He handed over the report. Immediately after hearing of the fall of Silvanesti, Targonne had ordered Dogah's troops to capture several elves alive and have them transported back to Jelek for interrogation. Targonne scanned the report briefly. His eyebrows lifted in astonishment, then came together in a frown. He could not believe what he was reading and started over at the beginning to see if he'd missed something.

Lifting his head, Targonne stared at his aide. "Have you read this?" he demanded.

"Yes, my lord," said the aide.

"The Mina girl is mad! Absolutely mad! Worse than that, I don't think she's even on our side! *Healing* the elves! She is *healing the bloody elves!*"

"So it would appear, my lord," said the aide.

Targonne picked up the paper to read aloud, " 'She has now a cult of young elven followers, who stand outside the palace where she has taken up residence, chanting her name.' And this. 'She has seduced the elven king Silvanoshei, who was publicly heard to say he is going to marry her. This news reportedly has greatly angered his mother, Alhana Starbreeze, who attempted to persuade her son to flee Silvanesti in advance of the arrival of the Dark Knights. Silvanoshei is said to be besotted with this Mina and refuses to leave her side.' "

Targonne threw down the report in anger. "This cannot go on. Mina is a threat, a danger. She must be stopped."

"That may prove difficult, my lord," said his aide. "You will see in Dogah's report that he approves and admires everything she does. He is infatuated by her. His men are loyal to her, as are her own. You will note that Dogah now signs his report, 'In the name of the One God.' "

"This Mina has bewitched them. Once she is gone and her spell is broken, they will return to their senses. But how to get rid of her? That is the problem. I don't want Dogah's forces turning on me. . . ."

Targonne picked up the report again, reread it. This time, he began to smile. He laid the report down, sat back, went over the plan in his mind. The numbers, he thought, added up nicely.

"Are the elven prisoners still alive?" he asked abruptly.

"Yes, my lord. It was thought you might have further need of them."

"You said there was a female among them?"

"One, my lord."

"Excellent. I have no further use for the males. Dispatch them in whatever way the executioner finds amusing. Have the female brought here to me. I will need a quill and ink—see to it that it's squeezed from berries or however the elves make it. And a scrollcase of elven design and manufacture."

"I believe there are some in the treasury room, my lord."

"Bring the least valuable. Finally, I want this." Targonne drew a diagram, handed it to the aide.

"Yes, my lord," the aide said, after a moment's perusal. "It will have to be specially made."

"Of course. Elven design. Emphasize that. And," Targonne added, "keep the cost to a minimum."

"Of course, my lord," said the aide.

"Once I have planted my instructions in the elf's mind, she is to be returned to Silvanesti and dropped off near the city of Silvanost. Have one of the messengers ready to depart this night."

"I understand, my lord," said the aide.

"One more thing," Targonne added, "I will be making a trip to Silvanesti myself sometime within the fortnight. I'm not sure when, so see to it that arrangements are made for me to leave whenever I have to."

"Why would you go there, my lord?" his aide asked, startled.

"Protocol will require my attendance at the funeral," Targonne replied.

9   THE RING OF TEARS

Silvanesti was an occupied land, Silvanost an occupied capital. The worst fears of the elves had been realized. It was to protect against this very disaster that they had authorized the creation of the magical shield. The embodiment of their fear and their distrust of the world, the shield had slowly drained them, drawing upon that fear to give itself unwholesome life. When the shield fell, the world, represented by the soldiers of the Dark Knights, marched into Silvanost, and sick and exhausted, the elves capitulated. They surrendered the city to their most feared foe.

The kirath predicted the worst. They spoke of slave camps, of looting and burning, of torment and torture. They urged the elves to fight until death had taken every one of them. Better to die free, said the kirath, than live as slaves.

A week passed and not a single elf male was dragged from his house and tortured. No elf babies were spitted on the ends of spears. No elf women were raped and left to die on dung heaps. The Dark Knights did not even enter the city of Silvanost. They camped outside the city on the battlefield where Mina's troops had fought and lost and Mina herself had been made prisoner. The first order given to the soldiers of the Dark Knights was not to set fire to Silvanost but to burn the carcass of the green dragon, Cyan Bloodbane. A detachment even fought and defeated a band of ogres who had been elated to discover the shield had fallen and attempted an invasion of their own. Many among the younger elves were calling the Dark Knights saviors.

Babies were healed and played upon the grass that grew green in the fierce bright sunlight. Women strolled in their gardens, finding joy in the flowers that had withered beneath the shield, but which were now starting to bloom. Men walked the streets free and unfettered. The elf king, Silvanoshei, remained the ruler. The Heads of House were consulted on all matters. A confused observer might have said it was the Dark Knights who had capitulated to the Silvanesti.

To say that the kirath were disappointed would be unfair. They were loyal to their people, and they were glad—and most were thankful—that thus far the bloodbath they had expected had not occurred. Some of the older members of the kirath claimed that what was happening to the elves was far worse. They did not like this talk of a One God. They mistrusted the Dark Knights, who, they suspected, were not as peace-loving as they appeared. The kirath had heard rumors of comrades ambushed and spirited away on the backs of blue dragons. Those who disappeared were never heard of again.

Alhana Starbreeze and her forces had crossed the border when the shield fell. They now occupied territory to the north of the capital, about halfway between Silvanost and the border. They never remained in one location long but shifted from camp to camp, covering their movements, blending into the forests that many of them, including Alhana herself, had once known and loved. Alhana did not have much fear that she and her troops would be discovered. The five thousand troops of Dark Knights would have all they could do to hold Silvanost. The commander would be a fool to divide his forces and send them into unfamiliar territory, searching for elves who had been born and bred to the forests. Nonetheless Alhana had survived this long by never taking chances, and so the elves remained on the move.

Not a day passed, but that Alhana did not long to see her son. She lay awake nights making plans to sneak into the city, where her life was forfeit, not only from the Dark Knights, but from her very own people. She knew Silvanost, she knew the palace, for it had been her home. In the night the plans seemed sound, and she was determined to follow through with them. In the morning she would tell Samar, and he would bring up every difficulty, present her with every opportunity for disaster. He always won the argument, not so much because she feared what might happen to her if she were caught, but because she feared what might happen to Silvanoshei. She kept in touch with what was happening in Silvanost through the kirath. She watched and waited and agonized, and like all the other elves, she wondered what the Knights of Neraka were plotting.

It appeared to the kirath, to men and women such as Rolan, Alhana Starbreeze, and Samar and their meager resistance forces, that their people had once more fallen under the spell of a dream such as had been cast on the land during the War of the Lance. Except that this dream was a waking dream and none of them could battle it, for to do so would be to battle the dreamers. The kirath and Alhana made what plans they could for the day when the dream must end and the dreamer wake to a nightmare reality.

General Dogah's troops camped outside Silvanost. Mina and her knights had moved into the Tower of the Stars. They had taken over one wing of the building, that which had previously belonged to the late Governor General

Konnal. All the elves knew that their young king was enamored of Mina. The story of how she had brought Silvanoshei back from death had been made into a song sung by the young people throughout Silvanesti.

Never before would the elves have countenanced a marriage between one of their own and a human. Alhana Starbreeze had been declared a dark elf for having married "outside her kind" by marrying a Qualinesti. Yet the young people—those who were near the same age as their king—had come to adore Mina. She could not walk the streets but that she was mobbed. The palace was surrounded, day and night, by young elves who sought to catch a glimpse of her. They were pleased and flattered to think that she loved their king, and they confidently expected to hear news of the marriage any day.

Silvanoshei expected it, too. He dreamed of her walking into the palace, being led to his throne room, where he would be seated in regal state. In his dreams, she flung herself eagerly, adoringly into his arms. That had been five days ago. She had not yet asked to see him. On her arrival, she had gone straight to her quarters and remained there.

Five days had passed, and he had neither seen nor spoken to her. He made excuses for her. She feared to see him, feared her troops might not understand. She would come to him at night and declare her love for him, then swear him to secrecy. He lay awake nights in anticipation, but she did not come, and Silvanoshei's dream began to wither, as did the bouquet of roses and violets he had handpicked from the royal garden to present to her.

Outside the Tower of the Stars, the young elves chanted "Mina! Mina!" The words that had been so sweet to his ears only days before now stabbed him like knives. Standing at the window, hearing that name echo in the bitter emptiness of his heart, he made his decision.

"I am going to her," he said.

"Cousin—" Kiryn began.

"No!" Silvanoshei said, cutting off the reprimand he knew was coming. "I have listened to you and those fools of advisers long enough! 'She should come to you,' they say. 'It would be undignified for you to go to her, Your Majesty.' 'It is you who do her the honor.' 'You put yourself in a false position.' You are wrong. All of you. I have thought this over. I believe that I know the problem. Mina wants to come to me, but her officers will not let her. That great, hulking minotaur and the rest. Who knows but that they are holding her against her will?"

"Cousin," said Kiryn gently, "she walks the streets of Silvanost, she comes and goes freely from the palace. She meets with her officers and, from what I have heard, even the highest ranking defer to her in all things. You must face it, Cousin, if she wanted to see you, she would."

Silvanoshei was dressing himself in his very finest garments, and either he was pretending not to hear, or he had truly not heard. Kiryn's heart ached for his cousin. He had witnessed with alarm Silvanoshei's obsession with this girl. He had guessed from the beginning that she was using Silvanoshei to her own ends, though what those ends might be, Kiryn could not tell. Part of the reason he had hoped Silvanoshei would seek safety in the forest with the resistance movement was to take him away from Mina, break the hold she had over him. Kiryn's plans had failed, and he was at his wit's end.

Silvanoshei had no appetite. He had lost weight. He could not sleep but roamed around his room at night, leaping out of bed at every sound, thinking it was her coming to him. His long hair had lost its sheen and hung limp and ragged. His nails were bitten almost to the quick. Mina was healing the elven people. She was bringing them back to life. Yet she was killing their king.

Dressed in his royal robes that hung from his wasted frame, Silvanoshei enveloped himself in his cloth of gold and made ready to leave his chambers.

Kiryn, greatly daring, knowing that he risked rebuke, made one last attempt to stop him.

"Cousin," he said, his voice soft with the affection he truly felt, "do not do this. Do not demean yourself. Try to forget about her."

"Forget her," Silvanoshei said with a hollow laugh. "I might as well try to forget to breathe!"

Thrusting aside his cousin's hand, Silvanoshei swept out the door, the cloth of gold fluttering behind him.

Kiryn followed him, heartsick. Elven courtiers bowed as the king passed, many attempting to catch his eye. He paid them no heed. He wended his way through the palace until he reached the wing occupied by Mina and her Knights. In contrast to his chambers that were filled with people, the part of the tower where Mina had set up her command post was quiet and empty. Two of her Knights stood guard outside a closed door. At the sight of Silvanoshei, the Knights came to respectful attention, but they did not stand aside.

Silvanoshei gave them a baleful look. "Open the door," he commanded.

The Knights made no move to comply.

"I gave you an order," said Silvanoshei, flushing, the red staining the unhealthy pallor of his skin as if he were cut and bleeding.

"I am sorry, Your Majesty," said one of the Knights, "but our orders are to admit no one."

"I am not *no one!*" Silvanoshei's voice shook. "I am king. This is my palace. All doors open to me. Do as I tell you!"

"Cousin," Kiryn urged softly, "please come away!"

The door opened at that moment, not from without. It opened from within. The huge minotaur stood in the door, his head level with the top of the gilded frame. He had to stoop to pass through.

"What is this commotion?" the minotaur demanded in his rumbling voice. "You disturb the commander."

"His Majesty begs an audience with Mina, Galdar," said one of the Knights.

"I do not beg!" said Silvanoshei angrily. He glowered at the minotaur blocking the door. "Stand aside. I *will* speak to Mina. You cannot keep her locked away from me!"

Kiryn was watching the minotaur closely, saw the monster's lips twitch in what might have been the beginning of a derisive smile, but at the last moment, the minotaur rearranged his expression to one of somber gravity. Bowing his horned head, he stood aside.

"Mina," he said, turning on his heel, "His Majesty, the king of Silvanesti, is here to see you."

Silvanoshei swept into the room.

"Mina!" he cried, his heart in his voice, on his lips, in his outstretched hands, in his eyes. "Mina, why have you not come to me?"

The girl sat behind a desk covered with what looked to be map rolls. One map was spread out upon the desk, the curling edges held down with a sword at one corner, a morning star on the other. Kiryn had last seen Mina the day of the battle with Cyan Bloodbane. He had seen her dressed in the coarse robes of a prisoner, he had seen her being led to her execution.

She had changed since then. Her head had been shaved to only a fine down of red. The hair had grown back some, was thick and curly and flamed in the sunlight streaming through the crystal panes of the window behind her. She wore the black tunic of a Knight of Neraka over black chain mail. The amber eyes that gazed at Silvanoshei were cool, preoccupied, held the markings of the map, held roads and cities, hills and mountains, rivers and valleys. The eyes did not hold him.

"Silvanoshei," Mina said after a moment, during which the roads and cities caught in the golden amber were slowly overlaid by the image of the young elf. "Forgive me for not coming to pay my respects sooner, Your Majesty, but I have been extremely busy."

Caught in the amber, Silvanoshei struggled. "Mina! Respect! How can you use such a word to me? I love you, Mina. I thought . . . I thought you loved me."

"I do love you, Silvanoshei," said Mina gently, as one speaks to a fretful child. "The One God loves you."

Silvanoshei's struggles availed him nothing. The amber absorbed him, hardened, held him fast.

"Mina!" he cried in agony and lurched toward her.

The minotaur sprang in front of her, drew his sword.

"Silvan!" Kiryn shouted in alarm, catching hold of him.

Silvanoshei's strength gave way. The shock was too much. He crumpled and fell to the floor, clutching Kiryn's arm, nearly dragging his cousin down with him.

"His Majesty is unwell. Take him back to his room," said Mina, adding in a voice soft with pity, "Tell him I will pray for him."

Kiryn, with the help of the servants, managed to assist Silvanoshei to his chambers. They took secret hallways and stairs, for it would never do for the courtiers to see their king in such a pitiable condition. Once in his chambers, Silvanoshei flung himself on his bed and refused to speak to anyone. Kiryn stayed with him, worried until he was almost ill himself. He waited until, finally, he saw with relief that Silvanoshei slept, his exhaustion eventually overcoming his grief.

Thinking Silvanoshei was likely to sleep for hours, Kiryn went to his own rest. He gave orders to the servants that His Majesty was unwell and that he was not to be disturbed. The curtains over the windows were closed and drawn, the room darkened. The servants stole out, softly shutting the door behind them. Musicians sat outside the king's bedchamber, playing soft music to soothe his slumbers.

Silvanoshei slept heavily, as though drugged, and when he woke some hours later, he was stupefied and groggy. He lay staring into the shadows, hearing Mina's voice. *I was busy, too busy to come to you. . . . I will pray for you. . . .* Her words were sharp steel and inflicted a fresh wound every time he repeated them. He repeated them over and over. The sharp blade struck his heart and struck his pride. *He* knew she had once loved him, but now no one would believe that. All believed that she had used him, and they pitied him, just as she pitied him.

Angry, restless, he threw off the silken sheets and the embroidered down coverlet and left his bed. A thousand plans came to mind so that his brain was fevered with them. Plans to win her back, plans to humiliate her, noble plans to do grand things in spite of her, degrading plans to cast himself at her feet and plead with her to love him again. He found that none of the plans spread soothing salve over the terrible wounds. None of them eased this horrible pain.

He walked the length of his room and back many times, passing by his writing desk, but he was so preoccupied that he did not notice the strange scrollcase until the twentieth or twenty-first turn, when a shaft of dusty sunlight filtered through a chink in the velvet curtains, struck the scrollcase, and illuminated it, bringing it to his attention.

He paused, stared at the case, wondering. The scrollcase had not been there this morning. Of that, he was certain. It did not belong to him. It did not bear upon it the royal crest, nor was it as richly decorated as those that bore his messages. The case had a battered appearance, as if it had been often used.

The wild thought came to him that the scrollcase belonged to Mina. This notion was completely irrational, but when one is in love, all things are possible. He reached out his hand to snatch it up, then paused.

Silvanoshei was a young man who felt desperately in love, but he was not deranged enough to have forgotten the lessons in caution learned from spending most of his life running from those who sought to take his life. He had heard tales of scrollcases that harbored venomous snakes or were magically enchanted and spewed forth poisonous gas. He should summon a guard and have the case removed.

"Yet, after all, what does it matter?" he asked himself bitterly. "If I die, I die. That at least would end this torment. And . . . it might be from her!"

Recklessly, he caught up the scrollcase. He did take time to examine the seal, but the wax impression was smudged, and he couldn't make it out. Breaking the seal, he tugged impatiently at the lid with trembling fingers and finally pulled it off with such force that an object flew out and landed on the carpet, where it lay sparkling in the single shaft of sunlight.

He bent down to stare at it in wonder, then picked it up. He held between his thumb and forefinger a small ring, a circlet of rubies that had all been cut in a teardrop shape—or perhaps blood drop would better describe them. The ring was of exquisite workmanship. Only elves do such fine work.

His heart beat fast. The ring came from Mina. He knew it! Looking back inside the scrollcase, he saw a rolled missive. Dropping the ring on the desk, he drew out the letter. The first words quenched the flicker of hope that had so briefly warmed his heart. *My cherished son . . .* the letter began. But as he read, hope returned, a ravening flame, all-consuming.

> *My cherished son,*
> *This letter will be brief as I have been very ill. I am recovered, but I am still very weak, too weak to write. One of my ladies acts as my scribe. The rumors that you are in love with a human girl have reached my ears. At first I was angry, but my illness carried me so close to death that it has taught me to think differently. I want only your happiness, Silvanoshei. This ring has magical properties. If you give it to one who loves you, it will ensure that her love for you will endure forever. If you give it to one who does not love you, the ring will cause her to love you with a passion equal to your own.*
> *Take the ring with a mother's blessing, my beloved son, and give it to the woman you love with a kiss from me.*

The letter was signed with his mother's name, though it was not her signature. The letter must have been written by one of the elven women who had once been Alhana's ladies-in-waiting but were now her friends, having chosen to share with her the harsh life of an outcast. He did not recognize the handwriting, but there was no reason he should. He felt a pang of worry over his mother's ill health, but was reassured to hear that she was better. His joy, as he looked at the ring and read once more of the ring's magical properties, was overwhelming. Joy overwhelmed reason, overwhelmed logic.

Cradling the precious ring in the palm of his hand, he brought it to his lips and kissed it. He began to make plans for a great banquet. Plans to show to all the world that Mina loved him and him alone.

10 THE BETROTHAL BANQUET

The Tower of the Stars was in a bustle of excitement and frantic preparation. His Majesty, the Speaker of the Stars, was giving a grand banquet in honor of Mina, the savior of the Silvanesti. Ordinarily, among the elves, such a banquet would have required months of preparation, days spent agonizing over guest lists, weeks of consultation with the cooks over the menu, more weeks spent arranging the table and deciding on the perfect choice for flowers. It was a mark of the king's youth, some said, and his impetuosity, that he had announced that the banquet would be held within twenty-four hours.

His minister of protocol wasted two of those twenty-four by attempting to remonstrate with His Majesty that such a feat was beyond the realm of possibility. His Majesty had been adamant, and so the minister had been forced to give way in despair and rush forth to marshal his forces.

The king's invitation was presented to Mina. She accepted in the name of herself and her officers. The minister was horrified. The elves had not intended to invite the officers of the Dark Knights of Neraka. So far as the longest lived among the elves could remember, no Silvanesti elf had ever shared a meal with a human on Silvanesti soil. Mina was different. The elves had begun to consider Mina as one of themselves. Rumors were circulating among her followers that she had elven blood in her; the fact that she was a commander in the army of the Dark Knights of Neraka having conveniently slipped their minds. Mina helped foster this belief, never appearing in public in her black armor, but always dressing in silvery white.

At this point, an argument arose. The aide to the minister of protocol maintained that during the War of the Lance, when the *daughter of Lorac* (who was Alhana Starbreeze, but since she was a dark elf and her name could not be mentioned, she was referred to in this manner) had returned to Silvanost, she had brought with her several human companions. There was no record of whether or not they had dined while on Silvanesti soil, but it was to be presumed they had. Thus a precedent had been set. The minister of protocol observed that they might have dined, but, if so, the dining was informal, due to the unfortunate circumstances of the time. Thus, such a dinner did not count.

As for the notion of the minotaur dining with elves, that was simply out of the question.

Flustered, the minister hinted to Mina that her officers would be bored with the proceedings, which they would find long and tedious, particularly since none of them spoke Elvish. They would not like the food, they would not like the wine. The minister was certain that her officers would be much happier dining as they were accustomed to dine in their camp outside of the walls of Silvanost. His Majesty would send food, wine, and so forth.

"My officers will attend me," Mina said to him, "or I will not come."

At the thought of delivering this message to His Majesty, the minister decided that eating dinner with humans would be less traumatic. General Dogah, Captain Samuval, the minotaur Galdar, and Mina's Knights would all attend. The minister could only hope fervently that the minotaur would not slurp his soup.

His Majesty was in a festive mood, and his gaiety affected the palace staff. Silvanoshei was a favorite among the servants and staff members, and all had noted his wan appearance and were anxious about him. The staff was pleased at the change in him and did not question it. If a banquet would lift him from the doldrums, they would throw the most lavish banquet that had ever been seen in Silvanesti.

Kiryn was less pleased at the change, viewed it with unease. He alone noted that Silvanoshei's gaiety had a frantic quality to it, that the color in his cheeks was not the rosy color of health but seemed to have been burned into the pale flesh. He could not question the king, for Silvanoshei was immersed in preparations for the grand event, overseeing everything to make certain all was perfect, down to personally selecting the flowers that were to grace the table. He claimed he had no time to talk.

"You will see, Cousin," Silvanoshei said, pausing a moment in his headlong rush to grasp Kiryn's hand and squeeze it. "She does love me. You will see."

Kiryn could only conclude that Silvanoshei and Mina had been in contact and that she had somehow reassured him. This was the only explanation for Silvanoshei's erratic behavior, although Kiryn, thinking over again all that Mina had said the day before, found it difficult to believe that those cruel words of hers had been an act. But she was human, and the ways of humans were never to be understood.

Elven royal banquets are always held outdoors, at midnight, beneath the stars. In the old days, before the War of the Lance, before the coming of Cyan Bloodbane and the casting of the dream, rows and rows of tables would have been set up in the tower's garden to accommodate all the elves of House Royal. Many nobles had died fighting the dream. Many more had died of the wasting sickness brought on them by the shield. Of those who had survived, most refused the invitation—a terrible affront to the young king. Rather it would have been an affront, if Silvanoshei had paid any heed to it. He said only, with a laugh, that the old fools would not be missed. As it was, only two long tables were required now, and the elder elves of House Servitor, who remembered the past glory of Silvanesti, let fall tears as they polished the delicate silver and set the fragile, eggshell-thin porcelain dishes upon the cobweb-fine lace table coverings.

Silvanoshei was dressed and ready long before midnight. The hours until the banquet appeared to him to have been mounted on the backs of snails, they crawled so slowly. He worried that all might not be right, although he had been to check the laying of the tables eight times already and was with difficulty dissuaded from going down a ninth. The discordant sound of the musicians tuning their instruments was sweetest music to him, for it meant that there was only a single hour remaining. He threatened to backhand the minister of protocol, who said that the king could not possibly make his regal appearance until all the guests had entered. Silvanoshei was the first to arrive and charmed and bewildered all his guests by greeting them personally.

He carried the ruby ring in a jeweled box in a velvet pouch inside his blue velvet doublet and beneath his silken shirt. He checked continuously to make certain the box was still there, pressing his hand over his breast so often that some of the guests took note and wondered uneasily if their young king suffered from some heart complaint. They had not seen His Majesty so joyful since his coronation, however, and they were soon caught up in his merriment and forgot their fears.

Mina came with the midnight, and Silvanoshei's joy was complete. She wore a gown of white silk, simple, with no ornamentation. Her only jewelry was the pendant that she always wore, a pendant round and plain with no decoration or design. She herself was in high spirits. Those elves she knew, she greeted by name, graciously accepting their blessings and their thanks for the miracles she had performed. She was as slender as any elf maid and almost as beautiful said the young elves, which was, for them, a high compliment, one rarely paid to any human.

"I thank you for the honor you do me this night, Your Majesty," said Mina when she came to make her bow to Silvanoshei.

He would not let her bow but took her hand and raised her up. "I wish I had time to do more," he said. "Someday you will see a true elven celebration." *Our wedding*, his heart sang to him.

"I do not mean this honor," she said, dismissing with a glance the beautifully decorated tables, the fragrant flowers and the myriad candles that illuminated the night. "I thank you for the honor you do me this night. The gift you intend to give me is one I have long wanted, one for which I have long prepared. I hope I may be worthy of it," she added quietly, almost reverently.

Silvanoshei was astonished and for a moment felt the pleasure in his gift—that was to have been a marvelous surprise—diminished. Then the import of her words struck him. *The honor he would do her. The gift she had long wanted. She hoped she may be worthy.* What could that mean except that she spoke of the gift of his love?

Ecstatic, he kissed fervently the hand she offered him. He promised himself that within hours he would kiss her lips.

The musicians ceased playing. Silver chimes rang out, announcing dinner. Silvanoshei took his place at the head table, leading Mina by the hand and seating her on his right. The other elves and the human officers took their places, or at least so Silvanoshei presumed. He could not have sworn to that, or the fact that there was anyone else present or that the stars were in the sky, or that the grass was beneath his feet.

He was aware of nothing except Mina. Kiryn, seated opposite Silvanoshei, tried to speak to his cousin, but Silvanoshei never heard a word. He did not drink wine. He drank Mina. He did not eat fruit or cake. He devoured Mina. The pale moon did not light the night. Mina lit the night. The music was harsh compared to Mina's voice. The amber of her eyes surrounded him. He existed in a golden stupor of happiness, and as if drunk on honey wine, he did not question anything. As for Mina, she spoke to her neighbors, enchanting them with her fluent Elvish and her talk of the One God and the miracles this god performed. She rarely spoke to Silvanoshei, but her amber gaze was often on him, and that gaze was not warm and loving but cool, expectant.

Silvanoshei might have been uneasy at this, but he touched the box over his heart for reassurance, brought to mind Mina's words to him, and his unease vanished.

Maidenly confusion, he told himself, and gazed at her as she talked of this One God, proud to watch her hold her own among the elven wise and scholars such as his cousin, Kiryn.

"You will forgive me if I ask a question about this One God, Mina," said Kiryn deferentially.

"I not only forgive you," Mina answered with a slight smile. "I encourage you. I do not fear questions, though some might fear the answers."

"You are an officer in the Dark Knights of Takhisis—"

"Neraka," Mina corrected. "We are the Dark Knights of Neraka."

"Yes, I heard your organization had made that change, Takhisis having departed—"

"As did the god of the elves, Paladine."

"True." Kiryn was grave. "Although the circumstances of their departures are known to be different. Still, that is not relevant to my question. In their brief history, the Dark Knights of whatever allegiance have held that the elves are their sworn and bitter enemies. They have never made secret their manifesto that they plan to purge the world of elves and seize their lands for their own."

"Kiryn," Silvanoshei intervened angrily, "this is hardly suitable—"

Mina rested her hand on his. Her touch was like fire licking his flesh. The flames both seared and cauterized.

"Let your cousin speak, Your Majesty," said Mina. "Please continue, sir."

"I do not understand, therefore, why now you conquer our lands and . . ." He paused, looked stern.

"And let you live," Mina finished for him.

"Not only that," said Kiryn, "but you heal our sick in the name of this One God. What care can this One God—a god of our enemies—have for elves?"

Mina sat back. Lifting a wineglass, she revolved the fragile crystal goblet in her hand, watching as the candles seemed to burn in the wine. "Let us say that I am the ruler of a large city. Inside the city's walls are thousands of people who look to me for protection. Now, within this city are two strong and powerful families. They hate and detest each other. They have sworn each other's destruction. They fight among themselves whenever they meet, creating strife and enmity in my city. Now, let us say that my city is suddenly threatened. It is under attack from powerful forces from the outside. What happens? If these two families continue to quarrel, the city will surely fall. But if the families agree to unite and battle this foe together, we have a chance to defeat our common enemy."

"That common enemy would be what—the ogres?" asked Kiryn. "They were once your allies, but I have heard since that they have turned on you—"

Mina was shaking her head. "The ogres will come to know the One God. They will come to join the battle. Be blunt, sir," she said, smiling with encouragement. "You elves are always so polite. You need not be fearful of hurting my feelings. You will not anger me. Ask the question that is in your heart."

"Very well," said Kiryn. "You are responsible for revealing the dragon to us. You are responsible for the dragon's death. You led us to know the truth about the shield. You have given us our lives when you could have taken them. Nothing for nothing, they say. Tit for tat. What do you expect us to give you in return? What is the price we must pay for all this?"

"Serve the One God," Mina said. "That is all that is required of you."

"And if we do not choose to serve this One God?" Kiryn said, frowning and grave. "What then?"

"The One God chooses us, Kiryn," said Mina, gazing at the wavering drop of flame flickering in the wine. "We do not choose the One. The living serve the One God. So do the dead. Especially the dead," she added in a voice so low and soft and wistful that only Silvanoshei heard her.

Her tone and her strange look frightened him.

"Come, Cousin," Silvanoshei said, flashing Kiryn a warning, irate glance. "Let us make an end to these philosophical discussions. They give me a headache." He gestured to the servants. "Pour more wine. Bring on the fruit and cake. Tell the musicians to resume playing. That we may drown him out," he said with a laugh to Mina.

Kiryn said no more, but sat regarding Silvanoshei with a troubled and worried expression.

Mina did not hear Silvanoshei. Her gaze was sifting through the crowd. Jealous of anyone who stole her attention from himself, Silvanoshei was quick to notice that she was searching for someone. He marked where her gaze roamed and saw that she was locating every one of her officers. One by one, her gaze touched each of them and one by one, each of them responded, either by a conscious look of understanding or, with the minotaur, a slight nod of the horned head.

"You need not worry, Mina," Silvanoshei said, an edge to his voice, to show he was displeased, "your men are behaving themselves well. Much better than I had hoped. The minotaur has only broken his wineglass, shattered a plate, torn a hole in the tablecloth, and belched loudly enough to be heard in Thorbardin. All in all, a most highly successful evening."

"Trivialities," she murmured. "So trivial. So meaningless."

Mina clasped Silvanoshei's hand suddenly, her grip tightening around his heart. She looked at him with the amber eyes. "I prepare them for what is to come, Your Majesty. You imagine that the danger has passed, but you are mistaken. Danger surrounds us. There are those who fear us. Those who seek our destruction. We must not be lulled into complacency by gentle music and fine wine. So I remind my officers of their duty."

"What danger?" asked Silvanoshei, now thoroughly alarmed. "Where?"

"Close," said Mina, drawing him into the amber. "Very close."

"Mina," said Silvanoshei, "I was going to wait to give this to you. I had a speech all prepared. . . ." He shook his head. "I've forgotten every word of it. Not that it matters. The words I truly want to say to you are in my heart, and you know them. You've heard them in my voice. You've seen them every time you see me."

Thrusting his trembling hand into the breast of his doublet, he drew forth the velvet bag. He reached inside, brought out the silver box and placed it on the table in front of Mina.

"Open it," he urged her. "It's for you."

Mina regarded the box for long moments. Her face was very pale. He heard her give a small, soft sigh.

"Don't worry," he said wretchedly. "I'm not going to ask anything of you in return. Not now. I hope that someday you might come to love me or at least think fondly of me. I think you might someday, if you will wear this ring."

Seeing that she made no move to touch the box, Silvanoshei seized hold of it and opened it.

The rubies in the ring glittered in the candlelight, each shining like a drop of blood—Silvanoshei's heart's blood.

"Will you take it, Mina?" he asked eagerly, desperately. "Will you take this ring and wear it for my sake?"

Mina reached out her hand, a hand that was cold and steady. "I will take the ring and I will wear it," she said. "For the sake of the One God."

She slipped the ring onto the index finger of her left hand.

Silvanoshei's joy was boundless. He was annoyed at first that she had dragged this god of hers into the matter, but perhaps she was merely asking the One God's blessing. Silvanoshei would be willing to ask that, too. He would be willing to fall onto his knees before this One God, if that would gain him Mina.

He watched her expectantly, waiting for the ring's magic to work on her, waiting for her to look at him with adoration.

She looked at the ring, twisted it on her finger to see the rubies sparkle. For Silvanoshei, no one else was present. No one except the two of them. The other people at the table, the other people at the banquet, the other people in the world were a blur of candlelight and music and the fragrance of gardenia and rose, and all of it was Mina.

"Now, Mina," he said, ecstatic. "You must kiss me."

She leaned near him. The magic of the ring was working. He could feel her love. His arms encircled her. But before their lips could touch, her lips parted in a gasp. Her body stiffened in his arms. Her eyes widened in shock.

"Mina!" he cried, terrified, "what is wrong?"

She screamed in agony. Her lips formed a word. She tried to speak it, but her throat closed, and she gagged. Frantic, she clutched at the ring and tried to drag it off her finger, but her body convulsed, painful spasms wracking her slender frame. She pitched forward onto the table, her arms thrust out, knocking over glasses, scattering the plates. She made an inarticulate, animal sound, terrible to hear. Her life rattled in her throat. Then she was still. Horribly still. Her eyes fixed in her head. Their amber gaze stared accusingly at Silvanoshei.

Kiryn rose to his feet. His action was involuntary. He had no immediate plan. His thoughts were a confusion. His first thought was for Silvanoshei, that he should try to somehow engineer his escape, but he immediately abandoned that idea. Impossible with all the Dark Knights around. At that moment, although he did not consciously know it, Kiryn abandoned Silvanoshei. The Silvanesti people were now Kiryn's, his care and his responsibility. He could do nothing to save his cousin. Kiryn had tried, and he had failed. But he might be able to save his people. The kirath must hear of this. They must be warned so they could be prepared to take whatever actions might be necessary.

The other elves who sat around them were rigid with shock, too stunned to move, unable to comprehend what had just occurred. Time slowed and stopped altogether. No one drew breath, no eye blinked, no heart beat—all were frozen in disbelief.

"Mina!" Silvanoshei cried in desperation and reached out to hold her.

Suddenly, all was turmoil. Mina's officers, crying out in rage, surged through the crowd, smashing chairs, overturning tables, knocking down anyone who impeded their progress. Elves cried out, screamed. Some of the more astute grabbed husband or wife and fled in haste. Among these was Kiryn. As the Dark Knights surrounded the table where Mina lay still and unmoving, Kiryn cast one last, aching glance at his unfortunate cousin and, with a heavy heart and deep foreboding, slipped away into the night.

An enormous hand, a hand covered in brown fur, seized the king's shoulder in a bone-crushing grasp. The minotaur, his hideous face monstrous with fury and with grief, lifted Silvanoshei from his chair and, snarling a curse, flung the young elf aside, as he might have flung away a piece of refuse.

Silvanoshei smashed through an ornamental trellis and tumbled backward into the hole where the Shield Tree had once stood. He lay dazed, breathless, then faces, grim, human faces, contorted in murderous rage, surrounded him. Rough hands seized him and hauled him from the pit. Pain shot through his body, and he moaned. The pain might have come from broken bones. Perhaps every bone in his body was broken. The true pain came from his shattered heart.

The knights hauled Silvanoshei to the banquet table. The minotaur had his hand on Mina's neck.

"The lifebeat is gone. She is dead," he said, his lips flecked with foam. Turning, he jabbed a shaking finger at Silvanoshei. "There is her murderer!"

"No!" Silvanoshei cried. "I loved her! I gave her my ring—"

The minotaur seized hold of Mina's lifeless hand. He gave the circlet of rubies a vicious tug, dragged it off her finger. Thrusting the ring under Silvanoshei's nose, the minotaur shook it.

"Yes, you gave her a ring. A poisoned ring! You gave her the ring that killed her!"

Jutting from one of the rubies was a tiny needle. On that needle glistened a drop of blood.

"The needle is operated by a spring," the minotaur announced, now holding the ring high for all to see. "When the victim touches the ring or turns it upon her finger, the needle activates and pierces the flesh, sending its deadly poison into the bloodstream. I'll wager," he added grimly, "that we discover the poison is a kind whose use is well known to elves."

"I didn't . . . " Silvanoshei cried from the agony of his grief. "It wasn't the ring. . . . It couldn't . . . "

His tongue cleaved to the roof of his mouth. He saw again Samar standing in his chambers. Samar, who knew all the secret passages in the palace. Samar, who had tried to force Silvanoshei to flee, who had made no secret of his hatred and distrust of Mina. Yet, the note had been written in a woman's hand. His mother . . .

A blow sent Silvanoshei reeling. The blow came from the minotaur's fist, but, in truth, Silvanoshei did not feel it, though it broke his jaw. The true blow was the knowledge of his guilt. He loved Mina, and he had slain her.

The minotaur's next blow brought darkness.

II   THE WAKE

The stars faded slowly with the coming of dawn, each bright, glittering pinprick of flame quenched by the brighter fire of Krynn's sun. Dawn brought no hope to the people of Silvanost. A day and a night had passed since the death of Mina. By orders of General Dogah, the city had been sealed off, the gates shut. The inhabitants were told to remain in their houses for their own safety, and the elves had no thought of doing otherwise. Patrols marched the streets. The only sounds that could be heard were the rhythmic tramp of booted feet and the occasional sharp command of an officer.

Outside Silvanost, in the encampment of the Dark Knights of Neraka, the three top officers came together in front of what had once been Mina's command tent. They had arranged a meeting for sunrise, and it was almost time. They arrived simultaneously and stood staring at one another uneasily, irresolutely. None wanted to enter that empty tent. Her spirit lingered there. She was present in every object, and that presence only made her absence more acutely felt. At last, Dogah, his face grim, thrust aside the tent flap and marched in. Samuval followed, and Galdar came, last of all.

Inside the tent, Captain Samuval lit an oil lamp, for night's shadows still held residence. The three looked bleakly about. Although Mina had taken quarters in the palace, she preferred to live and work among her troops. The original command tent and a few pieces of furniture had been lost to the ogres. This tent was elven in make, gaily colored. The humans considered that it looked more like a tent for harlequins than for military men, but they were grudgingly impressed by the fact that it was lightweight, easy to pack and to assemble, and kept out the elements far better than the tents supplied by the Dark Knights.

The tent was furnished with a table, borrowed from the palace, several chairs, and a cot, for Mina sometimes slept here if she worked late into the night. No one had been inside this tent since the banquet. Her belongings had not been touched. A map, marked in her handwriting, remained spread out upon the table. Small blocks and arrows indicated troop movements. Galdar glanced at it without interest, thinking it was a map of Silvanesti. When he saw that it wasn't, he sighed and shook his horned head. A battered tin cup, half-filled with cold tarbean tea, held down the eastern corner of the world. A guttered candle stood on the northwest. She had worked up until the time of departure for the banquet. A flow of melted wax had run down the side of the candle, streamed into the New Sea. A rumble sounded deep in Galdar's chest. He rubbed the side of his snout, looked away.

"What's that?" Samuval asked, moving closer to stare at the map. "I'll be damned," he said, after a moment. "Solamnia. Looks like we have a long march ahead of us."

The minotaur scowled. "March! Bah! Mina is dead. I felt for her lifebeat. It is not there. I think something went wrong!"

"Hush, the guards," Samuval warned, with a glance at the tent flap. He had closed and tied shut the opening, but two soldiers stood outside.

"Dismiss them," said Dogah.

Samuval stalked over to the tent flap, poked his head out. "Report to the mess tent. Return in an hour."

He paused briefly to look at a tent that stood beside the command tent. That tent had been the tent where Mina slept, and it was now where her body lay in state. They had placed her upon her cot. Dressed in her white robes, she lay with her hands at her sides. Her armor and weapons had been piled at her feet. The tent flaps had been rolled up, so that all could see her and come to pay her homage. The soldiers and Knights had not only come, they had stayed. Those who were not on duty had kept vigil throughout the day after her death and into the long night. When they had to go on duty, others took their places. The soldiers were silent. No one spoke.

The silence was not only the silence of grief but of anger. Elves had killed their Mina, and they wanted the elves to pay. They would have destroyed Silvanost the night when they first heard, but their officers had not permitted it. Dogah, Samuval, and Galdar had endured many bad hours following Mina's death trying to keep the troops in line. Only by repeating over and over the words, "By Mina's command," had they at last brought the enraged soldiers under control.

Dogah had put them to work, ordering them to cut down trees to make a funeral pyre. The soldiers, many with tears streaming down their faces, had performed their grim task with a fierce will, cutting down the trees of the Silvanesti forest with as much delight as if they were cutting down elves. The elves in Silvanost heard the death cries of their trees—the woods of Silvanesti had never before felt the blade of an axe—and they grieved deeply, even as they shuddered in fear. The soldiers had worked all day yesterday and all through the night. The pyre was now almost ready. But ready for what? Her three officers were not quite certain.

They took their seats around the table. Outside the tent, the camp was noisy with the thud of the axes and the crews hauling the giant logs to the growing pyre that stood in the center of the field where the elven army had defeated Mina's troops and had yet, in the end, fallen to her might. The noise had a strangely quiet quality to it. There was no laughing or bantering, no singing of work songs. The men carried out their duties in grim silence.

Dogah rolled up the map, stowed it away. General Dogah was a grim-faced, heavily bearded human of around forty. A short man, he appeared to be as wide as he was tall. He was not corpulent but stocky, with massive shoulders and a bull neck. His black beard was as thick and curly as a dwarf's, and this and his short stature gave him the nickname among his troops of Dwarf Dogah. He was not related to dwarves in any way, shape or form, as he was quick to emphasize with his fists if anyone dared suggest such a thing. He was most decidedly human, and he had been a member of the Dark Knights of Neraka for twenty of his forty years.

He was technically the highest-ranking officer among them, but, being the newest member of Mina's command group, he was at somewhat of a disadvantage in that her officers and troops did not know him and had been immediately distrustful of him. Dogah had been suspicious of them and, in particular, of this upstart wench who had, he discovered to his immense shock and outrage, sent him forged orders, had brought him to Silvanesti on what had appeared at first to be a kender's errand.

He had arrived at the border with several thousand troops, only to find that shield was up and they could not enter. Scouts reported that a huge ogre army was massing, ready to deal a death blow to the Dark Knights who had stolen their land. Dogah and his forces were trapped. They could not retreat, for to do so would have meant a march back through ogre lands. They could not advance. Dogah had cursed Mina's name loudly and viciously, and then the shield had fallen.

Dogah had received the report with astonishment. He had gone himself to look in disbelief. He had been loath to cross, fearing that elven warriors would suddenly spring up, as thick as the dust of the dead vegetation that coated the ground. But there on the other side, waving to him from horseback, was one of Mina's Knights.

"Mina bids you cross in safety, General Dogah!" the Knight had called. "The elven army is in Silvanost, and they have been considerably weakened both by their battle with the dragon, Cyan Bloodbane, and by the wasting effects of the shield. They do not pose a threat to you. You may proceed in safety."

Dogah had been dubious, but he had crossed the border, his hand on his sword, expecting at any moment to be ambushed by a thousand pointy-ears. His army had met with no resistance, none at all. Those elves they had encountered had been easily captured and were at first killed, but then they had been sent to Lord Targonne, as his lordship ordered.

Dogah had remained wary, however, his troops nervous and on alert. There was still the city of Silvanost. Then came the astonishing report that the city had fallen to a handful of soldiers. Mina had entered in triumph and was now ensconced in the Tower of the Stars. She awaited Dogah's arrival with impatience, and she bade him make haste.

It was not until Dogah had entered the city and strode its streets with impunity did he come finally to believe that the Dark Knights of Neraka had captured the elven nation of Silvanesti. The enormity of this feat overwhelmed him. The Dark Knights had accomplished what no other force in history had been able to do, not even the grand armies of Queen Takhisis during the War of the Lance. He had looked forward with intense curiosity to meeting this Mina. He had, in truth, not really believed that she could be the person responsible. He had guessed that perhaps it was some older, wiser officer who was truly in command, using the girl as a front to keep the troops happy.

Dogah had discovered his mistake immediately on first meeting her. Watching carefully, he had seen how every single officer deferred to her. Not only that, they regarded her with a respect that was close to worship. Her lightest word was a command. Her commands were obeyed instantly and without question. Dogah had been prepared to respect her, but after a few moments in her presence, he was both charmed and awed. He had joined wholeheartedly the ranks of those who adored her. When he had looked into Mina's amber eyes, he had been proud and pleased to see a tiny image of himself.

Those eyes were closed now, the warm fire that lit the amber quenched.

Galdar leaned across the table to hiss, "I say again, something has gone wrong." He sat back, scowling. The fur that covered his face was streaked with two dark furrows. "She looks dead. She feels dead. Her skin is cold. She does not breathe."

"She told us the potion would have that effect," said Samuval irritably. The fact that he was irritable was a certain sign of his nervousness.

"Keep your voices down," Dogah ordered.

"No one can hear us over that infernal racket," Samuval returned, referring to the erratic staccato of the axes.

"Still, it is best not to take chances. We are the only three who know Mina's secret, and we must guard the secret as we promised. If word got out, the news would spread like a grass fire in the dry season and that would ruin everything. The soldiers' grief must appear to be real."

"Perhaps they are wiser than we are," Galdar muttered. "Perhaps they know the truth, and *we* are the ones who have been deluded."

"What would you have us do, minotaur?" Dogah demanded, his black brows forming a solid bar across his thick nose. "Would you disobey her?"

"Even if she is . . ." Samuval paused, not wanting to speak aloud the ill-omened word. "Even if something did go wrong," he amended, "those commands she gave us would be her last commands. I, for one, will obey them."

"I also," said Dogah.

"I will not disobey her," said Galdar, choosing his words carefully, "but let us face it, her commands are contingent upon one thing happening, and thus far her prediction has not yet come to pass."

"She foretold an attempt on her life," argued Captain Samuval. "She foretold that the foolish elf would be the cat's paw. Both came true."

"Yet, she did *not* foretell the use of the poison ring," Galdar said, his voice harsh. "You saw the needle. You saw that it punctured her skin."

He drummed his fingers on the table, glanced at his comrades from beneath narrowed eyes. He had something on his mind, something unpleasant to judge by the frown, but he seemed uncertain whether to speak his thought or not.

"Come, Galdar," said Samuval finally. "Out with it."

"Very well." Galdar looked from one to the other. "You have both heard her say that even the dead serve the One God."

Dogah shifted his bulk in the chair that creaked beneath his weight. Samuval picked at the wax from the guttered candle. Neither made any response.

"She promised the One God would confound her enemies," Galdar continued, his tone heavy. "She never promised we should see her again alive—"

"Hail the command tent," a voice shouted. "I have a message from Lord Targonne. Permission to enter?"

The three officers exchanged glances. Dogah rose hastily to his feet and hurriedly untied the flaps. The messenger entered. He wore the armor of a dragonrider, and he was wind-blown and dust-covered. Saluting, he handed Dogah a scrollcase.

"No reply is expected, my lord," the messenger said.

"Very well. You are dismissed." Dogah eyed the seal on the scrollcase and again exchanged glances with his comrades.

When the messenger had gone, Dogah cracked the seal with a sharp rap on the table. The other two looked on expectantly as he opened the case and withdrew the scroll. He unfurled it, cast his gaze over it, and lifted his eyes, glittering black with triumph.

"He is coming," he said. "Mina was right."

"Praise the One God," said Captain Samuval, sighing with relief. He nudged Galdar. "What do you say now, friend?"

Galdar shrugged, nodded, said nothing aloud. When the others had gone, shouting for their aides, giving orders to make ready for his lordship's arrival, Galdar remained alone in the tent where Mina's spirit lingered.

"When I touch your hand and feel your flesh warm again, then I will praise the One God," he whispered to her. "Not before."

Lord Targonne arrived about an hour after sunrise, accompanied by six outriders. His lordship rode a blue dragon, as did the others. Unlike many high-ranking Knights of Neraka, Targonne did not keep a personal dragon but preferred to use one from the stables. This cut down on his own out-of-pocket expenditures, or so he always claimed. In truth, if he had wanted to keep his own dragon, he would have done so and charged the care and feeding to the Knighthood. As it was, Targonne did not keep a dragon because he neither liked nor trusted dragons. Perhaps this was because as a mentalist, Targonne knew perfectly well that dragons neither liked nor trusted him.

He took no pleasure in dragon flight and avoided it when possible, preferring to make his journeys on horseback. In this instance, however, the sooner this annoying girl went up in flames the better, as far as Targonne was concerned, and he was willing to sacrifice his own personal comfort to see this accomplished. He brought other dragonriders with him not so much because he wished to make a show or that he feared attack, but that he was convinced his dragon was going to do something to imperil him—either take it into its head to plummet from the skies or be struck by lightning or dump him off deliberately. He wanted additional riders around him so that they could rescue him.

His officers knew all this about Targonne. In fact, Dogah was laughing about this to Galdar and Captain Samuval as they watched the blue dragons fly in tight circles to a landing. Mina's army was drawn up in formation on the battlefield, with the exception of the few who were still at work on the pyre. Mina's funeral would be held at noon, the hour she herself had chosen.

"Do you think any of them would really risk their necks to save the mercenary old buzzard?" Samuval asked, watching the circling blues. "From what I've heard, most of his staff would just as soon see him bounce several times off sharp rocks while falling into a bottomless chasm."

Dogah grunted. "Targonne makes certain he will be saved. He takes along as escort only those officers to whom he owes large sums of money."

The blue dragons settled to the ground, their wings stirring up great clouds of dust. The dragonriders emerged from the cloud. Sighting the waiting honor guard, they headed in that direction. Mina's cadre of officers approached to greet his lordship.

"Which one is he?" asked Captain Samuval, who had never met the leader of the Knights of Neraka. The captain's curious gaze ranged over the tall, well-built, grim-faced Knights who were moving with rapid stride toward him.

"The little runt in the middle," said Galdar.

Thinking the minotaur was making sport of him, Captain Samuval chuckled in disbelief and looked to Dogah for the truth. Captain Samuval saw Dogah's gaze focus tensely on the short man who was almost bent double from coughing in the dust, waving his hand to clear the air. Galdar was also keeping close watch on the little man. The minotaur's hands clenched and unclenched.

Targonne did not cut a very prepossessing figure. He was short, squat and somewhat bowlegged. He did not like wearing full armor, for he found it chafed him, and he made concession to his rank by wearing only a breastplate. Expensive, hand-tooled, it was made of the finest steel, embossed in gold, and suited his exalted station. Due to the fact that Lord Targonne was stoop-shouldered, with a caved-in chest and slightly curved back, the breastplate did not fit well, but hung forward, giving the unfortunate impression of a bib tied around the neck of a child, rather than the armor of a valiant Knight.

Samuval was not impressed with Targonne's appearance, but nonetheless, he had heard stories about Targonne's ruthless and cold-blooded nature and thus did not find it at all strange that these two officers were so apprehensive of this meeting. All knew that Targonne had been responsible for the untimely death of the former leader of the Knights, Mirielle Abrena, and a great many of her followers, though no one ever mentioned such a thing aloud.

"Targonne is sly, cunning, and subtle, with an amazing ability to probe deeply into the minds of those he encounters," warned Dogah. "Some even claim that he uses this ability to infiltrate the minds of enemies and bend them to his will."

Small wonder, thought Samuval, that the mighty Galdar, who could have lifted Targonne and tossed him around like a child, was panting with nervousness. The rank bovine odor was so strong that Samuval edged upwind to keep from gagging.

"Be prepared," Galdar warned in a low rumble.

"Let him look into our minds. He will be surprised by what he finds there," Dogah said dryly, moving forward, saluting his superior.

"So, Galdar, it is good to see you again," Targonne said, speaking pleasantly. The last time Targonne had seen the minotaur, he had lost his right arm in battle. Unable to fight, Galdar had hung around Neraka, hoping for employment. Targonne might have rid himself of the useless creature, but he considered the minotaur a curiosity.

"You have come by a new arm. That bit of healing must have cost you a pretty steel piece or two. I wasn't aware that our officers were so highly paid. Or perhaps you found your own private stash. I suppose you are aware, Galdar, of the rule that states all treasure discovered by those in the service of the Knighthood is to be turned over to the Knighthood?"

"The arm was a gift, my lord," said Galdar, staring straight over Targonne's head. "A gift of the One God."

"The One God." Targonne marveled. "I see. Look at me, Galdar. I like eyes at a level."

Reluctantly, Galdar lowered his gaze to meet Targonne's. Immediately Targonne entered the minotaur's mind. He had a glimpse of roiling storm clouds, fierce winds, driving rain. A figure emerged from the storm and began to walk toward him. The figure was a girl with a shaved head and amber eyes. The eyes looked into Targonne's, and a bolt of lightning struck the ground in front of him. Dazzling, shattering white light flared. He could see nothing for long seconds and stood blinking his eyes to clear them. When he was able to see once more, Targonne saw the empty valley of Neraka, the rain-slick black monoliths, and the storm clouds vanishing over the mountains. Probe and pierce as he might, Targonne could not get past these mountains. He could not take himself out of the accursed valley. He withdrew his thought from Galdar's mind.

"How did you do that?" Targonne demanded, eyeing the minotaur and frowning.

"Do what, my lord?" Galdar protested, clearly astonished. The astonishment was real, he wasn't feigning. "I didn't do anything, sir. I've just been standing here."

Targonne grunted. The minotaur had always been a freak. He would gain more from a human. He turned to Captain Samuval. Targonne was not pleased to find this man among the officers greeting him. Samuval had once been a Knight, but he had either quit or been drummed out; Targonne couldn't remember the details. Most likely drummed out. Samuval was nothing but a draggle-tail mercenary leading his own company of archers.

"*Captain* Samuval," said Lord Targonne, laying nasty emphasis on the low rank. He sent his gaze into Samuval's brain.

Flight after flight of arrows arched through the air with the vicious whir of a thousand wasps. The arrows found their marks, piercing black armor and black chain mail. Black-fletched arrows struck through men's throats and brought down their horses. The dying screamed, horrible to hear, and still the arrows flew and the bodies began to mount, blocking the pass so that those behind were forced to turn and fight the enemy who had almost made it through the pass, almost ridden to glory.

An arrow was fired at him, at Targonne. It flew straight and true, aiming for his eye. He tried to duck, to flee, to escape, but he was held fast. The arrow pierced his eye, glanced through to the brain. Pain exploded so that he clutched at his head, fearing his skull might split apart. Blood poured down over his vision. He could see nothing except blood, no matter where he looked.

The pain ended swiftly, so swiftly that Targonne wondered if he had imagined it. Finding himself clutching at his head, he made as if to brush back his hair from his face and made another attempt to look into the mind of Captain Samuval. He saw only blood.

He tried to stanch the flow, to clear his vision, but the blood continued to pour down around him, and eventually he gave it up. Blinking, having the strange feeling that his eyelids were gummed together, he glared frowningly at this annoying captain, searching for some signs that the man was not what he appeared to be—not a bluff and ordinary soldier, but a wizard of high intelligence and cunning, a rogue Gray Robe or mystic in disguise. The captain's eyes were eyes that followed the arrow's flight until it hit its target. Nothing more.

Targonne was vastly puzzled and starting to grow frustrated and angry. Some force was at work here, thwarting him, and he was determined to ferret it out. He left the captain. Who cared about a blasted sell-sword anyway? Next to him stood Dogah, and Targonne relaxed. Dogah was Targonne's man. Dogah was to be trusted. Targonne had walked the length and breadth of Dogah's mind on previous occasions. Targonne knew all the dark secrets tucked away in shadowed corners, knew that he could count on Dogah's loyalty. Targonne had deliberately saved Dogah for last, knowing that if he had questions, Dogah would answer them.

"My lord," said General Dogah before Targonne could open his mouth, "let me first state for the record that I believed the orders I received telling me to march to Silvanesti came from you. I had no idea they had been forged by Mina."

Since the orders commanding Dogah to march to Silvanesti had provided the Dark Knights of Neraka with one of the greatest victories ever in the history of the Knighthood, Targonne did not like to be reminded of the fact that he was not the one who had given them.

"Well, well," he said, highly displeased, "perhaps I had more to do with those than you imagine, Dogah. The Knight Officer who issued those orders may have indicated that she was acting on her own, but the truth was that she was obeying my commands."

The girl was dead. Targonne could afford to play fast and loose with the truth. She was certainly not going to contradict him.

He continued blandly, "She and I agreed between us to keep this secret. The mission was so risky, so hazardous, so fraught with possibilities of failure, that I feared to mention it to anyone, lest word leak out to the elves and put them on their guard. And then, there is the dragon Malys to be considered. I did not want to raise her hopes, to give her expectations that might not come to pass. As it is, Malystryx is astonished at our great triumph and holds us in even higher regard than before."

All the while he was speaking, Targonne was attempting to probe Dogah's brain. Targonne could not manage it, however. A shield rose before his eyes, a shield that shimmered eerily in the light of a blazing sun. He could see beyond the shield, see dying trees and a land covered with gray ash, but he could not enter the shield nor cause it to be lifted.

Targonne grew increasingly angry, and thus he became more bland, more friendly. Those who knew him well were most terrified of him whenever he linked arms with them and spoke to them as chums.

Targonne linked arms with General Dogah.

"Our Mina was a gallant officer," he said in mournful tones. "Now the accursed elves have assassinated her. I am not surprised. That is like them. Skulking, sneaking, belly-crawling worms. They are too cowardly to attack face to face, and so they resort to this."

"Indeed, my lord," said Dogah, his voice grating, "it is a coward's act."

"They will pay for it, though," Targonne continued. "By my head, they will pay! So that's her funeral pyre, is it?"

He and Dogah had walked slowly, arm in arm, across the field of battle. The minotaur and the captain of archers followed slowly after.

"It's massive," said Targonne. "A bit too massive, don't you think? She was a gallant officer but only a junior officer. This pyre"—he indicated the immense stack of trees with a wave of his hand—"could well be the pyre of a leader of the Knighthood. A leader such as myself."

"Indeed it could, my lord," agreed Dogah quietly.

The base of the pyre was formed of six enormous trees. The work crews had wrapped chains around the logs, then dragged them into position in the center of the battlefield. The logs were soaked with any sort of inflammable liquid the men had been able find. The place reeked of oils, resins and spirits, and the fresh green blood of the trees. Atop this pile of logs, the men had thrown more logs, huge amounts of brush, and dead wood they had scavenged from the forest. The stack was now almost eight feet in height and ten feet in length. Climbing on ladders, they laid willow branches across the top, weaving them into a latticework of leaves. On this platform they would lay Mina's body.

"Where is the body? I would like to pay my last respects," said Targonne in dirgelike tones.

He was led to the tent where Mina lay in state, guarded by a group of silent soldiers, who parted to allow him to pass. Targonne stuck a mental needle in several as he walked among them, and their thoughts were only too clear, only too easy to read: loss, grief, sorrow, white-hot anger, vengeance. He was pleased. He could turn such thoughts as these to his own purposes.

He looked down at the corpse and was not in the least moved or touched beyond an annoyed wonder that this hoyden should have managed to garner such a loyal—one might say fanatical—following. He played to his audience, however, and saluted her and spoke the proper words. Perhaps the men noted some lack of sincerity in his voice, for they did not cheer him, as he considered he had the right to expect. They seemed to pay very little attention to him at all. They were Mina's men, and if they could have followed her into death to bring her back, they would have done so.

"Now, Dogah," said Targonne, when they were alone inside the command tent, "relate to me the circumstances of this tragic business. It was the elf king who murdered her, or so I understand. What have you done with him?"

Dogah related laconically the events of the previous night. "We questioned the young elf—his name is Silvanoshei. He is a sly one. He pretends to be almost mad with grief. A cunning actor, my lord. The ring came from his mother, the witch Starbreeze. We know from spies in the king's household that one of her agents, an elf named Samar, paid a secret visit to the king not long ago. We have no doubt that, between them, they plotted this murder. The elf made a show of being in love with Mina. She took pity on him and accepted the ring from his hand. The ring was poisoned, my lord. She died almost instantly.

"As to the elf king, we have him in chains. Galdar broke his jaw, and so it has been difficult to get much out of him, but we managed." Dogah smiled grimly. "Would your lordship like to see him?"

"Hanged, perhaps," said Targonne and gave a small, dry chuckle at his little pleasantry. "Drawn and quartered. No, no, I have no interest in the wretch. Do what you please with him. Give him to the men, if you like. His screams will help assuage their grief."

"Yes, my lord." General Dogah rose to his feet. "Now, I must attend to preparations for the funeral. Permission to withdraw?"

Targonne waved his hand. "Certainly. Let me know when all is made ready. I will make a speech. The men will like that, I know."

Dogah saluted and withdrew, leaving Targonne alone in the command tent. He rifled through Mina's papers, read her personal correspondence, and kept those that appeared to implicate various officers in plots against him. He perused the map of Solamnia and shook his head derisively. What he found only proved that she had been a traitor, a dangerous traitor and a fool.

Priding himself on the brilliance of his plan and its success, he settled back in his chair to take a short nap and recover from the rigors of the journey.

Outside the tent, the three officers conferred.

"What's he doing in there, do you suppose?" Samuval asked.

"Rummaging through Mina's things," Galdar said with a baleful glare back at the command tent.

"Much good may it do him," said Dogah.

The three eyed each other, ill at ease.

"This is not going as planned. What do we do now?" Galdar demanded.

"We do what we promised her we would do," Dogah replied gruffly. "We prepare for the funeral."

"But it wasn't supposed to happen like this!" Galdar growled, insistent. "It is time she ended it."

"I know, I know," Dogah muttered with a dark, sidelong glance at the tent where Mina lay, pale and still. "But she hasn't, and we have no choice to but to carry on."

"We could stall," suggested Captain Samuval, gnawing on his lower lip. "We could make some excuse—"

"Gentlemen." Lord Targonne appeared at the entrance to the tent. "I thought I heard you out here. I believe you have duties to attend to in regard to this funeral. This is no time to be standing around talking. I fly only in daylight, never at night. I must depart this afternoon. I cannot stay lollygagging around here. I expect the funeral to be held at noon as planned. Oh, by the way," he added, having ducked into the tent and then popped his head back out again, "if you think you might have trouble lighting the pyre, I would remind you that I have seven blue dragons at my command who will be most pleased to offer their assistance."

He withdrew, leaving the three to stare uneasily at one another.

"Go fetch her, Galdar," said Dogah.

"You don't mean to put her on that pyre?" Galdar hissed through clenched teeth. "No! I refuse!"

"You heard Targonne, Galdar," Samuval said grimly. "That was a threat, in case you misunderstood him. If we don't obey him, her funeral pyre won't be the only thing those blasted dragons set ablaze!"

"Listen to me, Galdar," Dogah added, "if we don't go through with this, Targonne will order his own officers to do so. I don't know what's gone wrong, but we have to play this out. Mina would want us to. You are second in command. It is your place to bring her to the pyre. Do you want one of us to take over?"

"No!" Galdar said with a vicious snap of his teeth. "I will carry her. No one else! I will do this!" He blinked, his eyes were red-rimmed. "But I do so only because she commanded it. Otherwise, I would let his dragons set fire to all the world and myself with it. If she *is* dead, I see no reason to go on living."

Inside the command tent, Targonne overheard this statement. He made a mental note to get rid of the minotaur at the first opportunity.

12 THE FUNERAL

Pacing slowly and solemnly, Galdar carried Mina's body in his arms to the funeral bier. Tears ran in rivulets down the minotaur's grief-ravaged face. He could not speak, his throat was choked with his sorrow. He held her cradled in his arms, her head resting on the right arm she had given to him. Her body was cold, her skin a ghastly white. Her lips were blue, her eyelids closed, the eyes behind them fixed and unmoving.

When he had arrived at the tent where her body lay, he had attempted, surreptitiously, to find some sign of life in her. He had held his steel bracer up to her lips, hoping to see the slight moistness of breath on the metal. He had hoped, when he picked her up in his arms, to be able to feel the faint beating of her heart.

No breath stirred. Her heart was still.

I will seem to be as one dead, she had told him. *Yet I live. The One God performs this deception that I may strike out at our enemies.*

She had said that, but she had also said that she would wake to accuse her murderer and call him to justice, and here she lay, in Galdar's arms, as cold and pale as a cut lily frozen in the snow. He was about to place that fragile lily on the top of a pile of wood that would blaze into a raging inferno with a single spark.

Mina's Knights formed a guard of honor, marching behind Galdar in the funeral procession. They wore their armor, polished to a black sheen, and kept their visors lowered, each hiding his own grief behind a mask of steel. Unbidden by their commanders, the troops formed a double line leading from the tent to the bier. Soldiers who had followed her for weeks stood side by side with those who had just newly arrived but who had already come to adore her. Galdar walked slowly between the rows of soldiers, never pausing as their hands reached out to touch her chill flesh for one last blessing. Young soldiers wept unashamedly. Scarred and grizzled veterans looked grim and stern and brushed hastily at their eyes.

Walking behind Galdar, Captain Samuval led Mina's horse, Foxfire. As was customary, her boots were reversed in the stirrups. Foxfire was edgy and restless, perhaps due to the proximity of the minotaur—the two had formed a grudging alliance, but neither truly liked the other—or perhaps the raw emotions of the soldiers affected the animal, or perhaps the horse, too, felt Mina's loss. Captain Samuval had his hands full controlling the beast, who snorted and shivered, bared his teeth, rolled his eyes until the whites showed, and made dangerous and unexpected lunges into the crowd.

The sun was near its zenith. The sky was a strange, cobalt blue, a winter sky in summer, with a winter sun that burned bright but gave no warmth, a sun that seemed lost in the empty blue vastness. The line of men came to an end. Galdar stood before the huge pyre. A litter wound round with ropes rested on the ground at the minotaur's feet. Men with tear-grimed faces stood atop the pyre, waiting to receive their Mina.

Galdar looked to his right. Lord Targonne stood at attention. He wore his grief mask, probably the same one he'd worn at the funeral of Mirielle Abrena. He was impatient for the end of the ceremony, however, and he permitted his gaze to shift often to watch the progress of the sun—a not-so-subtle reminder to Galdar to speed matters along.

General Dogah stood at Galdar's left. The minotaur shot the commander a speaking glance.

We have to stall! Galdar pleaded.

Dogah lifted his gaze to the sun that was almost directly overhead. Galdar looked up to see seven blue dragons circling, taking an unusual interest in the proceedings. As a rule, dragons find such ceremonies boring in the extreme. Humans are like bugs. They lead short and frantic lives, and like bugs, humans are constantly dying. Unless the human and the dragon have formed a particular bond, dragons little care what becomes of them. Yet, now Galdar watched them fly above Mina's funeral pyre. The shadows of their wings slid repeatedly over her still face.

If Targonne meant the dragons to intimidate, he was succeeding. Dogah felt the cringe of dragonfear twist his heart, already wrung by grief. He lowered his gaze in defeat. There was nothing to be done.

"Carry on, Galdar," Dogah said quietly.

Galdar knelt from his great height and with uncommon gentleness placed Mina's body on the litter. Somewhere someone had found a fine woven silk cloth of gold and of purple. Probably stolen from the elves. Galdar arranged Mina's body on the litter, her hands folded over her breast. He drew the cloth over her, as a father might lovingly cover a slumbering child.

"Good-bye, Mina," Galdar whispered.

Half-blinded by his tears that were rolling unchecked down his snout, he rose to his feet and made a fierce gesture. The soldiers atop the pyre pulled on the ropes. The ropes tightened, went taut, and the litter bearing Mina's body rose slowly to the top of the pyre. The soldiers settled the litter, rearranged the cloth over her. Each one stooped to kiss her cold forehead or kiss her chill hands. Then they climbed down from the top of the pyre.

Mina remained there, alone.

Captain Samuval brought Foxfire to a halt at the foot of the pyre. The horse, now seemingly aware that he was on show, stood quiet with dignity and pride.

Mina's Knights gathered around the pyre. Each held in his hand a lighted torch. The flames did not waver or flicker, but burned steadily. The smoke rose straight into the air.

"Let us get on with it," said Lord Targonne in annoyed tones. "What do you wait for?"

"A moment longer, my lord," said Dogah. Raising his voice, he shouted, "Bring the prisoner."

Targonne cast Dogah a baleful glance. "What do we need him for?"

Because it was Mina's command, Dogah might have said. He offered the first explanation that came into his mind.

"We plan to throw him onto the pyre, my lord," said Dogah.

"Ah," said Targonne, "a burnt offering." He chuckled at his little jest and was annoyed when no one else did.

Two guards led forth the elf king who had been responsible for Mina's death. The young man was festooned in chains—fetters on his wrists and ankles were attached to an iron belt around his waist, an iron collar had been locked around his neck. He could scarcely walk for the weight and had to be assisted by his captors. His face was bruised practically beyond recognition, one eye swollen shut. His fine clothes were covered with blood.

His guards brought him to a halt at the foot of the pyre. The young man lifted his head. He saw Mina's body resting atop the pyre. The elf went so white that he was paler than the corpse. He let out a low, wretched cry and lurched suddenly forward. His guards, thinking he was trying to escape, seized hold of him roughly.

Silvanoshei had no thought of escape, however. He heard them cursing him and talking of throwing him onto the fire. He didn't care. He hoped they would, that he might die and be with her. He stood with his head bowed, his long hair falling over his battered face.

"Now that we are finished with the histrionics," said Lord Targonne snappishly, "may we proceed?"

Galdar's lips curled back from his teeth. His huge fist clenched.

"By my beard, here come the elves," Dogah exclaimed in disbelief.

It had been Mina's command that all elves who wanted to attend the ceremony were to be permitted to do so, and they were not to be harassed or threatened or harmed, but welcomed in the name of the One God. Mina's officers had not expected any elves would come. Fearing retribution, most elves had locked themselves in their houses, preparing to defend their homes and families or, in some cases, making plans to flee into the wilderness.

Yet now out of the city gates came pouring a vast gathering of Silvanesti elves, mostly the young, who had been Mina's followers. They bore flowers in their hands—those flowers that had survived the ravaging touch of the shield—and they walked with slow and measured tread to the tune of the mournful music of muted harp and somber flute. The human soldiers had good reason to resent this appearance of their enemy, those they held responsible for their beloved commander's death. A muttering arose among the troops, hardening into a growl of anger and a warning to the elves to keep their distance.

Galdar took heart. Here was the perfect way to stall! If the men would decide to ignore their orders and take out their fury on these elves, Galdar and the other officers could not be expected to stop them. He glanced skyward. Blue dragons would not interfere with the slaughter of elves. After such an unseemly disruption, the funeral would certainly have to be postponed.

The elves proceeded toward the pyre. The shadows of the dragons' wings flowed over them. Many blanched and shuddered. The dragonfear that touched even Galdar must be horrible for these elves. For all they knew, they would be brutally attacked by the human soldiers who had good reason to hate them. Yet still they came to pay homage to the girl who had touched them and healed them.

Galdar could not help but pay grudging homage to their courage. So, too, did the men. Perhaps because Mina had touched them all, human and elf felt a bond that day. The growls of anger and muttered threats died away. The elves took their places a respectful distance from the pyre, as if they were aware they had no right to come closer. They lifted their hands. A soft breeze sprang up from the east, caught the flowers they bore, and carried them in a cloud of fragrance to the pyre, where the white petals floated down around Mina's body.

The chill sunlight illuminated the pyre, illuminated Mina's face, shimmered in the golden cloth so that it seemed to burn with its own fire.

"Are we expecting anyone else?" Targonne demanded sarcastically. "Dwarves, perhaps? A contingent of kender? If not, then get this over with, Dogah!"

"Certainly, my lord. First, you said you intended to speak her eulogy. As you said, my lord, the troops would appreciate hearing from you."

Targonne glowered. He was growing increasingly nervous, and he could not explain why. Perhaps it was the strange way these three officers stared at him, with hatred in their eyes. Not that this was particularly unusual. There were many people on Ansalon who had good reason to hate and fear the Lord of the Night. What made Targonne uneasy was the fact that he could not enter their minds to discover what they were thinking, what they were plotting.

Targonne felt suddenly threatened, and he could not understand why that should make him nervous. He was surrounded by his own bodyguard, Knights who had good reason to make certain that he remained alive. He had seven dragons at his command, dragons who would make short work of humans and elves alike, if the Lord of the Night ordered. Still he could not argue away the feeling of imminent peril.

The feeling made him irritated, annoyed, and sorry he had ever come. This hadn't turned out as he had planned. He had come to flaunt this victory as his own, to bask in the renewed adulation of the troops and their officers. Instead, he found himself overshadowed by a dead girl.

Clearing his throat, Targonne straightened. In a voice that was cold and flat, he said, "She did her duty."

The officers and men regarded him expectantly, waited for him to go on.

"That is her eulogy," Targonne said coldly. "A fitting eulogy for any soldier. Dogah, give the command to light the pyre."

Dogah said no word, but cast a helpless look at the other two officers. Captain Samuval was bleak, defeated. Galdar gazed with his soul in his eyes to the top of the pyre, where Mina lay still, unmoving.

Or did she move? Galdar saw a quiver in the cloth of gold that covered her. He saw color return to her wan cheek, and his heart leaped with hope. He stared enthralled, waiting for her to rise. She did not, and he came to the bitter realization that the stirring of the cloth was caused by the gentle breeze and the mockery of warmth was the pale light of the sun.

Lifting his voice in a ragged howl of grief and rage, Galdar snatched a torch from the hand of one of Mina's Knights and hurled it with all the might of his strong right arm onto the top of Mina's funeral pyre.

The flaming torch landed at Mina's feet, set the cloth that covered her ablaze.

Raising their own voices in hollow cries, the Knights under Mina's command flung their own torches onto the pyre. The oil-soaked wood burst into flame. The fires spread rapidly, flames reaching out like eager hands to join together and encircle the pyre. Galdar kept watch. He stared at the top to keep sight of her, blinking painfully as smoke stung his eyes and cinders landed in his fur. At last the heat was so intense that he was forced to retreat, but he did not do so until he lost sight of Mina's dear body in the thick smoke coiling around her.

Lord Targonne, coughing and flapping his hands at the smoke, backed away immediately. He waited long enough to make certain that the fire was blazing merrily, then turned to Dogah.

"Well," said his lordship, "I'll be off—"

A shadow blotted out the sun. Bright day darkened to night in the pause between one heartbeat and the next. Thinking it might be an eclipse—albeit a strange and sudden one—Galdar lifted amazed eyes, still stinging from the smoke, to the heavens.

A shadow blotted out the sun, but it was not the round shadow of the single moon. Silhouetted against tendrils of fire was a sinuous body, a curved tail, a dragon's head. Seen against the sun, the dragon appeared as black as time's ending. When it spread its massive wings, the sun vanished completely, only to reappear as a burst of flame in the dragon's eye.

Darkness deep and impenetrable fell upon Silvanost and, in that instant, the flames that consumed the pyre were doused by a breath that was neither heard nor felt.

Galdar gave a roar of triumph. Samuval dropped to his knees, his hands covering his face. Dogah gazed at the dragon with wonder. Mina's Knights stared upward in awe.

The darkness grew deeper, until Targonne could barely see those standing next to him.

"Get me out of here! Quick!" he ordered tersely.

No one obeyed his commands. His Knight escorts stared at the strange, immense dragon that had blotted out the sun, and they seemed, one and all, to have been changed to stone by the sight.

Now thoroughly frightened, feeling the darkness closing in around him, Targonne kicked at his Knights and swore at them. Fear shook him and shredded him and turned his bowels to water. One moment he threatened his officers he would see them flayed alive, the next he was promising them a fortune in steel to save him.

The darkness grew yet deeper. White lightning flared, splitting the unnatural night. Thunder crashed, shaking the ground. Targonne started to yell for his dragons to come rescue him.

The yell died in this throat.

The white lightning illuminated a figure standing atop the pyre, a figure wearing shining black armor and shrouded in a cloth of gold that was charred and burnt. The blue dragons flew above her, the lightning crackled around her. Swooping low over the ash-laden pyre, each blue dragon bowed its head to her.

"Mina!" The blue dragons sounded the paean. "Mina!"

"Mina!" Galdar sobbed and fell to his knees.

"Mina!" whispered General Dogah in relief.

"Mina!" Captain Samuval shouted in vindication.

Behind them, in the darkness, the elves took the word and made of it a song. "Mina . . . Mina . . ." The soldiers joined in, chanting, "Mina . . . Mina!"

The darkness lifted. The sun shone, and it was warm and dazzling to the eye. The strange dragon descended through the ethers. Such was the terror and the awe of its coming that few in the crowd could lift their shuddering gazes to look at it. Those who managed, and Galdar was one of them, saw a dragon such as they had never before beheld on Krynn. They were not able to look on it long, for the sight made their eyes water and burn, as if they stared into the sun.

The dragon was white, but not the white of those dragons who live in the lands of perpetual snow and frost. This dragon was the white of the flame of the forger's hottest fire. The white that is in direct opposition to black. The white that is not the absence of color but the blending together of all colors of the spectrum.

As the strange looking dragon drifted lower to the ground, its wings did not stir the air, nor did the ground shake from the impact when it landed. The blue dragons, all seven of them, lowered their heads and spread their wings in homage.

"Death!" they cried together in a single voice, fell and terrible. "The dead return!"

Now they could see that the dragon was not a living dragon. It was a ghostly dragon, a dragon formed of the souls of the chromatic dragons who had died during the Age of Mortals, killed by their own kind.

The death dragon lifted its front clawed foot and, turning it upward, placed that foot upon the top of the pyre. Mina stepped upon the upturned claw. The death dragon lowered her reverently to the charred, blackened, and ash-covered ground.

"Mina! Mina!" The soldiers were stamping their feet, clashing sword on shield, yelling until they were hoarse, and still the chant rang out. The elven voices had made of her name a madrigal whose beauty enchanted even the most obdurate and hardened human heart.

Mina gazed at them all in pleasure that warmed the amber eyes so that they shone purest gold. Overwhelmed by the love and the adoration, she seemed at a loss as to how to respond. At length, she acknowledged the tribute with an almost shy wave of her hand and a grateful smile.

She reached out and clasped the hands of Dogah and Captain Samuval, who could not speak for their joy. Then Mina walked over to stand in front of Galdar.

The minotaur fell on his knees, his head bent so low that the horns brushed the ground.

"Galdar," said Mina gently.

He lifted his head.

Mina held out her hand. "Take it, Galdar," she said.

He took hold of her hand, felt the flesh warm to the touch.

"Praise the One God, Galdar," Mina told him. "As you promised."

"Praise the One God!" Galdar whispered, choking.

"Will you always doubt, Galdar?" Mina asked him.

He looked at her fearfully, afraid of her anger, but he saw that her smile was fond and caring.

"Forgive me, Mina," he faltered. "I won't doubt anymore. I promise."

"Yes, you will, Galdar," Mina said, "but I am not angry. Without doubters, there would be no miracles."

He pressed her hand to his lips.

"Now arise, Galdar," said Mina, her voice hardening as the amber in her eyes hardened. "Arise and lay hands on the one who sought to kill me."

Mina pointed to the assassin.

She did not point at the wretched Silvanoshei, who was staring at her with dumb amazement and disbelief.

She pointed at Targonne.

13 AVENGING THE DEAD

Morham Targonne had no use for miracles. He had seen them all in his time, seen the smoke and seen the mirrors. Like everything else in this world, miracles could be bought and sold on the open market like fish and yesterday's fish at that, for most of them stunk to the heavens. He had to admit that the show he'd just witnessed was good, better than most. He couldn't explain it, but he was convinced that the explanation was there. He had to find it. He would find it in this girl's mind.

He sent a mental probe into Mina's red-crowned head, launched it as swift and straight as a steel-tipped arrow. When he found out the truth, he would denounce her to her addlepated believers. He would reveal to them how truly dangerous she was. They would thank him. . . .

In her mind, he saw eternity, that which no mortal is ever meant to see.

No mortal mind can encompass the smallness that holds the vastness.

No mortal eye can see that blinding light for the illuminating darkness.

Mortal flesh withers in the cooling fire of the burning ice.

Mortal ears cannot bear to hear the roaring silence of the thundering quiet.

Mortal spirits cannot comprehend the life that begins in death and the death that lives in life.

Certainly not a mortal mind like Targonne's. A mind that divides honor by ambition and multiplies gain by greed. The numbers that were the sum of his life were halved and halved again and halved again after that, and he was, in the end, a fraction.

The great are humbled by even a glimpse of eternity. The mean tremble in fear. Targonne was horrified. He was a rat in that immense vastness, a cornered rat who could not find a corner.

Yet, even at the end, the cornered rat is a cunning rat. Cunning was all Targonne had left to him. Looking about, he saw that he had no friends, no allies. All he had were those who served him out of fear or ambition or need, and every one of these petty concerns were so much dust swept away by an immortal hand. His guilt was plain for even the stupidest to see. He could deny it or embrace it.

Awkwardly, the bib of his ill-fitting breastplate thumping and banging against his bony knees, Targonne knelt before Mina in an attitude of the most abject humility.

"Yes, it is true," he blubbered, squeezing out a meager tear or two. "I sought to have you killed. I had no choice. I was ordered to do it." He kept his head humbly lowered, but managed to steal a glance to see how his speech was being received. "Malystryx ordered your death. She fears you, and with good reason!"

Now he thought it was time he could lift his head, and he arranged his face to match his words. "I was wrong. I admit it. I feared Malystryx. Now I see my fear is unfounded. This god of yours, this One God—a most wonderful and magnificent and powerful god." He clasped his hands. "Forgive me. Let me serve you, Mina. Let me serve your god!"

He looked into the amber eyes and saw himself, a tiny vermin, scurrying frantically until the amber flowed over him and held him immobile.

"I foretold that someday you would kneel before me," said Mina, and her tone was not smug, but gentle. "I forgive you. More important, the One God forgives you and accepts your service."

Targonne, grinning inside, started to rise.

"Galdar," Mina continued, "your sword."

Galdar drew a huge, curved-bladed sword, lifted it. He held it poised a moment over Targonne's head, long enough to allow the coward a moment to fully comprehend what was going to happen. Targonne's shriek of terror, the squeal of the dying rat, was cut off by the sweep of the blade that severed the man's head from his neck. Blood spattered on Mina. The head rolled to Mina's feet and lay there in a gruesome pool, facedown in the mud and the ash.

"Hail, Mina! Lord of the Night!" General Dogah shouted.

"Hail, Mina! Lord of the Night!" The soldiers picked up the cheer, and their voices carried it to heaven.

Amazed by what they had seen and heard, the elves were horrified by the brutal murder, even of one who had so richly deserved punishment. Their hymns of praise faded out discordantly. They stared to see that Mina did not even bother to wipe away the blood.

"What are your orders, Mina?" Dogah asked, saluting.

"You and the men under your command will remain here to hold the land of Silvanesti in the name of the Dark Knights of Neraka," Mina said. "You will send rich tribute to Dragon Overlord Malystryx in my name. That should placate her and keep her eye turned inward."

Dogah stroked his beard. "Where are we to find this rich tribute, Mina?"

She motioned Captain Samuval to release Foxfire. The horse danced up to her, nuzzled her. Mina stroked the horse's neck affectionately and began to remove the saddlebags.

"Where do you suppose you will find it, Dogah?" she asked. "In the Royal Treasury in the Tower of the Stars. In the homes of the members of House Royal and in the storerooms of the elven merchants. Even the poorest of these elves," she continued, tossing the saddlebags onto the ground, "have family heirlooms hidden away."

Dogah chuckled. "What of the elves themselves?"

Mina cast a glance at the headless corpse that was being rolled unceremoniously onto the base of the funeral pyre.

"They promised to serve the One God, and the One God needs them now," Mina said. "Let those who have pledged themselves to the One God fulfill that pledge by working with us to maintain control over the land."

"They won't do that, Mina," Dogah said grimly. "Their service won't extend that far."

"You will be surprised, Galdar," said Mina. "Like all of us, the elves have sought something beyond themselves, something in which to believe. The One God has given that to them, and many will come to the service of the One God. The Silvanesti who are faithful to the One will erect a Temple to the One in the heart of Silvanost. Elven priests of the One will be granted the power of healing and given the means to perform other miracles.

"First, though, Dogah, the One will expect them to prove that loyalty. They should be the first to hand over their riches, and they should be the ones who take the riches from those who prove recalcitrant. The elves who claim to be loyal to the One God will be expected to reveal to us all those who are enemies of the One God, even if those enemies are their own lovers, wives, fathers, or children. All this you will ask of them, and those who are truly faithful will make the sacrifice. If they do not, they may serve the One God dead as well as alive."

"I understand," said Dogah.

Mina knelt to unbuckle the straps of the saddle that encircled Foxfire's belly. Her Knights would have leaped to do this for her, but the moment one made a move toward the horse, Foxfire curled back his lip and halted the man with a jealous eye.

"I leave you in charge, Dogah. I ride this day with those under my command for Solamnia. We must be there in two days."

"Two days!" Galdar protested. "Mina, Solamnia is at the other end of the continent! A thousand miles away, across the New Sea. Such a feat is impossible—"

Mina straightened, looked the minotaur full in the eye.

Galdar gulped, swallowed. "Such a feat would be impossible," he amended contritely, "for anyone but you."

"The One God, Galdar," Mina corrected him. "The One God."

Removing the saddle from Foxfire, she placed it on the ground. Last, she took off the bridle and tossed it down next to the saddle. "Pack that with the rest of my things," she commanded.

Putting her arms around the horse's neck, Mina spoke softly to the animal. Foxfire listened attentively, head bowed, ears forward to catch the slightest whisper. At length Foxfire nodded his head. Mina kissed the horse and stroked him lovingly. "You are in the hands of the One God," she said. "The One God bring you safe to me at my need."

Foxfire lifted his head, shook his mane proudly, then wheeled and galloped off, heading for the forest. Those in his path were forced to jump and scramble to get out of his way, for he cared not whom he trampled.

Mina watched him depart, then, as if by accident, she noticed Silvanoshei.

The elf had witnessed all that had passed with the dazed look of one who walks in a dream and cannot wake. He watched the fire blaze in grief that approached madness. He witnessed Mina's triumphant return to life with disbelief that flared into joy. So convinced was Silvanoshei of his own guilt, that when he heard her accuse her assassin, he waited to die. Even now he could not comprehend what had happened. Silvanoshei knew only that his love was alive. He gazed at her in wonder and in despair, in hope and in dejection, seeing all, understanding nothing.

She walked over to him. He tried to rise, but the chains weighed him down and hobbled him so he found it difficult to move.

"Mina . . ." He tried to speak, but he could only mumble through the swelling and the pain of his broken jaw.

Mina touched his forehead, and the pain vanished, the jaw healed. The bruises disappeared, the swelling subsided. Seizing her hands, he pressed them passionately to his lips.

"I love you, Mina!"

"I am not worthy of your love," she said.

"You are, Mina! You are!" he gabbled. "I may be a king, but you are queen—"

"You misunderstand me, Silvanoshei,' Mina said softly. "Your love should not be for me but for the One God who guides and directs me."

She withdrew her hands from his grasp.

"Mina!" he cried in despair.

"Let your love for me lead you to the One God, Silvanoshei," Mina said to him. "The hand of the One God brought us together. The hand of the One God forces us to separate now, but if you allow the One God to guide you, we will be together again. You are the Chosen of the One God, Silvanoshei. Take this and keep it in faith."

She took from her finger the ruby ring, the poison ring. Dropping the ring in his trembling palm, she turned and walked away without a glance.

"Mina!" Silvanoshei cried, but she did not heed him.

His manacled hands hung listlessly before him. He paid no attention to anything going on around him. He continued to kneel on the bloody ground, clutching the ring, staring at Mina, his heart and his soul in his eyes.

"Why did you tell him that, Mina?" Galdar asked in a low voice as he hurried to accompany her. "You care nothing for the elf, that is obvious. Why lead him on? Why bother?"

"Because he could be a danger to us, Galdar," Mina replied. "I leave behind a small force of men to rule over a large nation. If the elves ever find a strong leader, they could unite and overthrow us. He has it within him to be such a leader."

Galdar glanced back, saw the elf groveling on the ground. "That sniveling wretch? Let me slay him." Galdar placed his hand on the hilt of his sword that was stained with Targonne's blood.

"And make of him a martyr?" Mina shook her head. "No, far better for us if he is seen to worship the One God, seen to ignore the cries of his people. For those cries will change to curses.

"Have no fear, Galdar," she added, drawing on a pair of soft leather riding gloves. "The One God has seen to it that Silvanoshei is no longer a threat."

"Do you mean the One God did this to him?" Galdar asked.

Mina flashed him a glance of amber. "Of course, Galdar. The One God guides all our destinies. His destiny. Yours. Mine."

She looked at him long, then said softly, almost to herself, "I know what you are feeling. I had difficulty accepting the will of the One as opposed to my own. I fought and struggled against it for a long time. Let me tell you a story, and perhaps you will understand.

"Once, when I was a little girl, a bird flew inside the place where I lived. The walls were made of crystal, and the bird could see outside, see the sun and the blue sky and freedom. The bird hurled itself at the crystal, trying frantically to escape back into the sunshine. We tried to catch it, but it would not let us near. At last, wounded and exhausted, the bird fell to the floor and lay there quivering. Goldmoon picked up the bird, smoothed its feathers with her hand, and healed its wounds. She carried it out into the sunlight and set it free.

"I was like that bird, Galdar. I flung myself against the crystal walls of my creation, and when I was battered and bruised, the One God lifted me and healed me and now guides me and carries me, as the One God guides and carries us all. Do you understand, Galdar?"

He was not sure he did. He was not sure he wanted to, but he said, "Yes, Mina," because he wanted to please her, to smooth the frown from her forehead and bring the light back to her amber eyes.

She looked at him long, then she turned away, saying briskly, "Summon the men. Have them collect their gear and make ready to depart for Solamnia."

"Yes, Mina," said Galdar.

She paused, looked back at him. A corner of her mouth twitched. "You do not ask how we will get there, Galdar," she said.

"No, Mina," he said. "If you tell me to fly, I trust that I will sprout wings."

Mina laughed gaily. She was in excellent spirits, sparkling and ebullient. She pointed to the horizon.

"There, Galdar," she said. "There is how a minotaur will fly."

The sun was falling toward night, sinking into a pool of blood and fire.

Galdar saw a spectacle thrilling in its terrible beauty. Dragons filled the sky. The sun gleamed on red wings and blue, shining through them like fire glowing through stained glass. The scales of the black dragons shimmered with dark iridescence, the scales of the green dragons were emeralds scattered against cobalt.

Red dragons—powerful and enormous, blue dragons—small and swift, black dragons—vicious and cruel, white dragons—cold and beautiful, green dragons—noxious and deadly. Dragons of all colors, male and female, old and young, they came at Mina's call. Many of these dragons had been hiding deep in their lairs, terrified of Malys and of Beryl, of Khellendros, one of their own who had turned on them. They had hidden away, afraid they would find their skulls upon one of the totems of the dragon overlords.

Then had come the great storm. Above the fearsome winds, blasting lightning, and booming thunder, these dragons had heard a voice telling them to prepare, to make ready, to come when summoned.

Tired of living in fear, longing for revenge for the deaths of their mates, their children, their comrades, they answered the call, and now they flew to Silvanesti, their many-colored scales forming a terrible rainbow over the ancient homeland of the elves.

The dragons' scales glittered in the sunshine so that each might have been encrusted with a wealth of jewels. The shadows of their passing rippled along the ground beneath them, flowing over hillock and farmhouse, lake and forest.

The swift-flying blues took the lead, wing tip to wing tip, keeping time with matching strokes, taking pride in their precision. The ponderous reds brought up the rear, their enormous wings moving a single sweeping flap to every four of the faster blues. Blacks and greens were scattered throughout.

The elves felt the terror of their coming. Many collapsed, senseless, and others fled in the madness of their fear. Dogah sent his men after them, bidding them to make certain no elf escaped into the wilderness.

Mina's men ran to collect their gear and any supplies that could be carried on dragonback. They brought Mina's maps to her, she said she needed nothing else. They were ready and waiting to mount by the time the first of the dragons began to circle down and land upon the battlefield. Galdar mounted a gigantic red. Captain Samuval chose a blue. Mina rode the strange dragon, the dragon she termed the "death dragon."

"We travel by darkness," said Mina. "The light of neither moon nor star will shine this night so our journey may remain secret."

"What is our destination?" Galdar asked.

"A place where the dead gather," she said. "A place called Nightlund."

Her dragon spread its ghastly wings and soared into the air effortlessly, as if it weighed no more than the ashes that drifted up from the pyre, where they were burning Targonne's body. The other dragons, bearing the soldiers of Mina's army upon their backs, took to the skies. Clouds foamed up from the west, blotting out the sun, gathering thick around the multitude of dragons.

Dogah returned to the command tent. He had work to do: comandeering storehouses to hold the loot, establishing slave-labor camps, interrogation centers and prisons, brothels to keep the men entertained. He had noted, when in Silvanost, a temple dedicated to an old god, Mishakal. He would establish the worship of the One God there, he decided. An appropriate place.

As he made his plans, he could hear the screams of elves who were probably, even now, being dispatched into the One God's service.

Out on the battlefield, Silvanoshei remained where Mina had left him. He had been unable to take his eyes from her. In despair, he had watched her depart, clinging to the rag of hope she had left him as a child clings to the tattered blanket he clutches to keep away the terrors of the night. He did not hear the cries of his people. He heard only Mina's voice.

The One God. Embrace the One God, and we will be together again.

14 THE CHOSEN OF THE ONE GOD

Ten members of the kirath and ten elves of Alhana's army were hiding in the forests outside Silvanost to watch the funeral. They were hiding there when the dragons came. Wearing the magical cloaks of the kirath that made them invisible to any who might be watching for them, the elves were able to creep within close proximity of the funeral pyre. They saw everything that happened but were helpless to intervene. They could do nothing to save their people. Their numbers were too small. Help would come later. These elves were here with one mission, one purpose, and that was to rescue their young king.

The elves heard death all around them. The stumps of dying trees cried out in agony. The ghost of Cyan Bloodbane hissed and howled in the wind. These elves had fought the dream with courage. They had fought ogres without blanching. Forced to listen to the song of death, they felt their palms sweat and their stomachs clench.

The elves hiding in the forest were reminded of the dream, yet this was worse, for the dream had been a dream of death, and this was real. They watched their brethren mourn the death of the strange human girl child, Mina. As the Knights cast their torches onto the pyre, the elves did not cheer, even in their hearts. They watched in wary silence.

Crouched among the boughs severed from a living aspen that had been left to wither and die, Alhana Starbreeze saw flames crackle on the pyre and smoke begin to rise to the heavens. She kept her gaze on her son, Silvanoshei, who had been dragged in chains and now appeared on the verge of collapse.

Beside her, Samar muttered something. He had not wanted her to come, he had argued against it, but this time she insisted on having her way.

"What did you say, Commander?" Kiryn whispered.

"Nothing," Samar returned, with a glance at Alhana.

He would not speak ill of Alhana's son to anyone but himself, especially not to Kiryn, who never ceased to defend Silvanoshei, to maintain that the king was in the grip of some strange power.

Samar liked Kiryn. He admired the young man for having had the wit, resourcefulness, and foresight to escape the calamitous banquet, to seek out the kirath, and alert them to what had happened. But Kiryn was a Silvanesti, and although he claimed he had remained loyal all these years to Alhana, Samar did not trust him.

A hand touched his arm, and in spite of himself, Samar started, unable to repress a shudder. He looked around, half-angry, though if he had heard the sounds of the elven scout approaching, he would have severely reprimanded such carelessness.

"Well," he growled, "what did you find out?"

"It is true, what we heard," the woman said, her voice softer than the ghostly whispers. "Silvanoshei was responsible for the human girl's death. He gave her a ring, a ring he told people came from his mother. The ring was poisoned. The human died almost instantly."

"I sent no such ring!" Alhana said, seeing the cold stares of the kirath. For years, they had been told Alhana Starbreeze was a dark elf. Perhaps some had even believed it. "I fight my enemies face to face. I do not poison them, especially when I know that it is my people who will suffer the consequences!"

"This smacks of treachery," Samar said. "Human treachery. This Lord Targonne is known to have made his way to the top by climbing a ladder of the corpses of his enemies. This girl was just one more rung—"

"Commander! Look!" The scout pointed.

The elves hiding amid the shadows of the death-singing forest watched in amazement to see the human girl rise whole and alive from the blazing pyre. The humans were proclaiming it a miracle. The elves were skeptical.

"Ah, I thought there would be some trick in this," Samar said.

Then came the strange death dragon, and the elves turned dark and shadowed eyes to each other.

"What is this?" Alhana wondered aloud. "What does it portend?"

Samar had no answer. In his hundreds of years, he had roamed almost every portion of Ansalon and had encountered nothing like this horrible creature.

The elves heard the girl accuse Targonne, and although many could not understand her language, they were able to guess the import of her words by the expression on the doomed human's face. They watched his headless corpse topple to the ground without comment or surprise. Such barbarous behavior was only to be expected of humans.

As the flight of many colored dragons formed a hideous rainbow in the skies above Silvanesti, the song of death rose to a shrieking paean. The elves shrank among the shadows and shivered as the dragonfear swept over them.

They flattened themselves among the dead trees. They were able to do nothing but think of death, to see nothing but the image of their own dying.

The dragons departed, bearing the strange girl away with them. The Dark Knights of Neraka swept down upon the Silvanesti people, carrying salvation in one hand, death in the other.

Alhana's heart hurt almost to breaking at the sound of the screams of those first to fall victim to the wrath of the Dark Knights. Smoke was already starting to rise from the beautiful city. Yet she reached out a hand to detain Rolan of the kirath, who was on his feet, sword in hand.

"Where do you think you are going?" Alhana demanded.

"To save them," Rolan said grimly. "To save them or die with them."

"A witless act. Would you throw away your life for nothing?"

"We must do something!" Rolan cried, his face livid. "We must help them!"

"We are thirty," Alhana answered. "The humans outnumber us dozens to one." She looked back grimly, pointed to the fleeing Silvanesti. "If our people would stand and fight, we might be able to help them, but—look at that! Look at them! Some flee in confusion and panic. Others stand and sing praises to this false god!"

"The human is clever," Samar said quietly. "With her trickery and her promises, she seduced your people as surely as she seduced that poor besotted boy out there. We can do nothing to help them. Not now—not until reason prevails. But we might be able to help him."

Tears streamed down Rolan's cheeks. Every elven death cry seemed to strike him, for his body shuddered at each. He stood irresolute, blinking his eyes and watching the gray tendrils of smoke rising from Silvanost. Alhana did not weep. She had no more tears left.

"Samar, look!" Kiryn pointed. "Silvanoshei. They are taking him away. If we're going to do something, we'd better do it fast, before they reach the city and lock him up in some dungeon."

The young man stood on the battlefield in the shadow of Mina's pyre and appeared stunned to the point of insensibility. He did not look to see what was happening to his people. He did not make any move at all. He stared as if transfixed at where she had stood. Four humans—soldiers, not Knights—had been left to guard him. Seizing hold of him, two began to drag him off. The other two followed along, swords drawn, keeping careful watch.

Only four of them. The rest of the Knights and soldiers had raced off to effect the subjugation and looting of Silvanost, about a mile distant. Their camp was empty, abandoned except for these four and the prince.

"We do what we came to do," Alhana said. "We rescue the prince. Now is our chance."

Samar rose up from his hiding place. He gave a piercing cry, that of a hawk, and the woods were alive with elven warriors, emerging from the shadows.

Samar motioned his warriors forward. Alhana rose too, but she remained behind a moment, placed her hand upon Rolan's shoulder.

"Forgive me, Rolan of the Kirath," Alhana said. "I know your pain, and I share it. I spoke in haste. There *is* something we can do."

Rolan looked at her, the tears still glimmering in his eyes.

"We can vow to return and avenge the dead," she said.

Rolan gave a fierce nod.

Gripping her weapon, Alhana caught up with Samar, and they soon joined the main body of the elven warriors, who ran silently, unseen, from out the whispering shadows.

Silvanoshei's captors hauled him back toward Silvanost. The four men were put out, grumbling that they were missing the fun of looting and burning the elven city.

Silvanoshei stumbled over the uneven ground, blind, deaf, oblivious to everything. He could not hear the cries, he could not smell the smoke of destruction nor see it rising from his city. He saw only Mina. He smelled only the smoke of her pyre. He heard only her voice chanting the litany of the One God. The god she worshiped. The god who had brought them together. *You are the Chosen.*

He remembered the night of the storm, the night the ogres had attacked their camp. He remembered how the storm had made his blood burn. He had likened it to a lover. He remembered the desperate run to try to save his people, and the lightning bolt that had sent him tumbling down the ravine and into the shield.

The Chosen.

How had he been able to pass through the shield, when no others could do so?

That same lightning bolt blazed through his mind.

Mina had passed through the shield.

The Chosen. The hand of the One God. An immortal hand that had touched him with a lover's caress. The same hand had thrown the bolt to block his path and raised the shield to let him enter. The immortal hand had pointed his way to Mina on the battlefield, had guided the arrows that felled Cyan Bloodbane. The hand had rested against his own hand and given him the strength to uproot the lethal Shield Tree.

The immortal hand cupped around him, held him, healed him, and he was comforted as he had been in his mother's arms the night the assassins had tried to slay him. He was the Chosen. Mina had told him so. He would give himself to the One God. He would allow that comforting hand to guide him along the chosen path. Mina would be there waiting for him at the end.

What did the One God want of him now? What was the plan for him? He was a prisoner, chained and manacled.

Silvanoshei had never prayed to any god. After the Chaos War, there had been no gods to answer prayers. His parents had told him that mortals were on their own. They had to make do in this world, rely on themselves. It seemed to him, looking back, that mortals had made a hash of things.

Perhaps Mina had been right when she told him that he did not love her, he loved the god in her. She was so confident, so certain, so self-possessed. She never doubted. She was never afraid. In a world of darkness where everyone else was stumbling blindly, she alone was granted the gift of sight.

Silvanoshei did not even know how to pray to a god. His parents had never spoken of the old religion. The subject was a painful one for them. They were hurt, but they were also angry. The gods, with their departure, had betrayed those who had put their faith in them.

But how did he know for certain that the One God cared for him? How did he know that he was truly the Chosen?

He determined to test the One God, a test to reassure himself, as a child assures himself by small tests that his parents really do love him.

Silvanoshei prayed, humbly, "If there is something you want me to do, I cannot do it if I am prisoner. Set me free, and I will obey your will."

"Sir!" shouted one of the soldiers who had been guarding the rear. "Behind—" Whatever he had been about to say ended in a shriek. The tip of a sword protruded from his gut. He had been stabbed in the back, the blow so fierce that it had pierced the chain mail shirt he wore. He fell forward and was trampled under a rush of elven warriors.

The guards holding Silvanoshei let loose as they turned to fight. One managed actually to draw his sword, but he could make no use of it, for Rolan sliced off his arm. Rolan's next cut was to the throat. The guard fell in a pool of his own gore. The other guard was dead before he could reach his weapon. Samar's blade swept the head from the man's neck. The fourth man was dispatched handily by Alhana Starbreeze, who thrust her sword in his throat.

So lost was he in religious fervor that Silvanoshei was barely aware of what was happening, of grunts of pain and stifled cries, the thud of bodies falling to the ground. First he was being hauled away by soldiers, then, looking up, he saw the face of his mother.

"My son!" Alhana cried softly. Dropping her bloody sword, she gathered Silvanoshei into her embrace and held him close.

"Mother?" Silvanoshei said dazedly. He could not understand, for at first, when the arms wrapped around him in maternal love, he had seen another face. "Mother . . ." he repeated, bewildered. "Where— How—"

"My Queen," said Samar warningly.

"Yes, I know," said Alhana. She reluctantly released her son. Wiping away her tears, she said, "I will tell you everything, my son. We will have a long talk, but now is not the time. Samar, can you remove his chains?"

"Keep watch," Samar ordered an elf. "Let me know if anyone has spotted us."

"Not likely, Commander," was the grim return. "They are too busy with their butchery."

Samar examined the manacles and the chains and shook his head. "There is no time to remove these, Silvanoshei, not until we are far from Silvanost and pursuit. We will do what we can to help you along the way, but you must be strong, Your Highness, and bear this burden awhile longer."

Samar looked and spoke doubtfully. He had seen Silvanoshei a sodden mess on the battlefield. He was prepared to find the young elf shattered, demoralized, uncaring whether he lived or died, unwilling to make an effort to do either.

Silvanoshei stood upright. He had been confused at first. His rescue had come too quickly. The sight of his mother had shaken him, but now that he had time to think, he saw with elation that the One God had been responsible. The One God had answered his prayer. He *was* the Chosen. The manacles cut his flesh so that it bled, but he bore the pain gladly as a testament to his love for Mina and his newfound faith in the One God.

"I do not need you or anyone to help me, Samar," Silvanoshei said with quiet calm. "I can bear this burden for as long and as far as necessary. Now, as you say, we must make haste. My mother is in danger."

Enjoying Samar's look of astonishment, Silvanoshei shoved past the startled warrior and began to hobble clumsily toward the forest.

"Help him, Samar," Alhana ordered, retrieving her sword. She watched her son with fondness and pride—and faint unease. He had changed, and although she told herself that his ordeal would have changed anyone, she found this change disturbing. It wasn't so much that he had grown from a boy to a man. It was that he had grown from her boy into a man she did not know.

Silvanoshei felt imbued with strength. The chains weighed nothing, were gossamer and silk. He began to run, awkwardly, occasionally tripping and stumbling, but he was doing as well for himself as he might have done with assistance. The elven warriors surrounded him, guarding him, but no one was there to stop them. The Knights of Neraka were acting swiftly to seize Silvanost and wrap the city in its own chains, forged of iron and fire and blood.

The elves and their freed captive traveled north for a short distance, far enough that they could not smell the smoke of destruction. They turned east and, under Rolan's guidance, came to the river, where the kirath had boats ready to carry the prince upstream, north to the camp of Alhana's forces. Here they would rest for a short time. They lit no fires, set careful watch.

Silvanoshei had managed to keep up with the rest, although by the end of the journey his breath was coming in painful gasps, his muscles burned, and his hands were covered with the blood that ran from his chafed wrists. He fell more than once, and at last, because his mother pleaded with him, he permitted the other elves to assist him. No word of complaint passed his lips. He held on with a grim determination that won even Samar's approval.

Once they reached the riverbank and relative safety, the elves hacked at his fetters with axes. Silvanoshei sat still, unflinching, though the axe blades sometimes came perilously close to cutting off a foot or slicing into his leg. Sparks flew, but the chains would not break, and eventually, after all the axe blades were notched, the elves were forced to give up. Without a key they could not remove the iron manacles round Silvanoshei's ankles and his wrists.

Alhana assured her son that once they arrived at his mother's camp, the blacksmith would be able to make a key that would fit the locks and so remove them.

"Until then, we travel by boat the rest of the way. The journey will not be nearly so difficult for you, my son."

Silvanoshei shrugged, unconcerned. He bore the pain and discomfort with quiet fortitude. Chains clanking, he wrapped himself in a blanket and lay down on the ground, again without complaint.

Alhana sat beside her son. The night was hushed, as if all living things held their breath in fear. Only the river continued to speak, the swift-flowing water rushing past them, talking to itself in a deep, sorrowful murmur, knowing what terrible sights it would see downstream, loath to continue on its journey, yet unable to halt the flow.

"You must be exhausted, my son," Alhana said, her own voice low, "and I will not keep you from your sleep long, but I want to tell you that I understand. You have lived through a difficult time. You have experienced events that might have overwhelmed the best and wisest of men, and you are only a youth. I must confess that I feared to find you crushed by what happened this day. I was afraid that you were so entangled in the snares of the human witch that you would never be free of her. Her tricks are impressive, but you must not be fooled by them. She is a witch and a charlatan and makes people see what they want to see. The power of the gods is gone in this world. I see no evidence that it has returned."

Alhana paused to allow Silvanoshei to comment. The young man was silent. His eyes, glittering with starlight, were wide open and gazing into the darkness.

"I know that you must grieve over what is now happening in Silvanost," Alhana continued, disappointed that he did not respond. "I promise you as I promised Rolan of the kirath that we will come back in strength to free the people and drive the legions of darkness from that fair city. You will be restored as king. That is my dearest wish. You have proven by the courage and strength I see in you this night that you are worthy to hold that holy trust, assume that great responsibility."

A pale smile flickered over Silvanoshei's lips. "So I have proven myself to you, have I, Mother? You think that at last I am worthy of my heritage?"

"You did not need to prove yourself to me, Silvanoshei," said Alhana, regretting her words the moment she had spoken them. She faltered, tried to explain. "If I gave you that impression, I never meant to. I love you, my son. I am proud of you. I think that the strange and terrible events of which you have been a part have forced you to grow up rapidly. You have grown, when you might have been crushed by them."

"I am glad to have earned your good opinion, Mother," Silvanoshei said.

Alhana was bewildered and hurt by his cool and detached demeanor. She did not understand but, after some thought, put it down to the fact that he had endured much and must be worn out. Silvanoshei's face was smooth and placid. His eyes were fixed on the night sky with such intensity that he might have been counting every single pinpoint of bright, white light.

"My father used to tell a story, Mother," said Silvanoshei, just as she was about to rise. The prince rolled over on his side, his chains clanking and rattling, a discordant sound in the still night. "A story of a human woman—I can't recall her name. She came to the Qualinesti elves during another time of turmoil and danger, bearing a blue crystal staff, saying that she was sent to them by the gods. Do you recall this story, Mother?"

"Her name was Goldmoon," said Alhana. "The story is a true one."

"Did the elves believe her when she said that she came bearing a gift of the gods?"

"No, they did not," Alhana said, troubled.

"She was termed a witch and a charlatan by many elves, among them my own father. Yet she did bring a gift from the gods, didn't she?"

"My son," Alhana began, "there is a difference—"

"I am very tired, Mother." Silvanoshei drew his blanket up over his shoulders and rolled over, so that his back was to her. "May your rest be blessed," he added.

"Peaceful rest, my son," said Alhana, bending down to kiss his cheek. "We will speak of this more in the morning, but I would remind you that the Dark Knights are killing elves in the name of this so-called One God."

There came no sound from the prince except the bitter music of the chains. Either he stirred in discomfort, or he was settling himself for sleep. Alhana had no way of telling, for Silvanoshei's face was hidden from her.

Alhana made the rounds of the camp, checking to see that those who stood guard duty were at their posts. Assured that all were watchful and alert, she sat down at the river's edge and thought with despair and anger of the terror that reigned in Silvanost this night.

The river mourned and lamented with her until she imagined that she began to hear words in its murmurings.

> Sleep, love; forever sleep
> Your soul the night will keep
> Embrace the darkness deep
> Sleep, love; forever sleep.

The river left its banks. Dark water overflowed, rose up, and drowned her.

Alhana woke with a start to find it was morning. The sun had lifted above the treetops. Drifting clouds raced past, hiding the sun from sight, then restoring it to view, so that it seemed as if the orb were winking at some shared joke.

Angry that she had been so undisciplined as to let herself slumber when danger was all around them, she jumped to her feet. To her dismay, she found that she was not the only one who had slept at her post. Those on guard duty slumbered standing up, their chins on their chests, their eyes closed, their weapons lying on the ground at their feet.

Samar lay beside her. His hand was outstretched, as if he had been about to speak to her. Sleep had felled him before he could say a word.

"Samar!" she said, shaking him. "Samar! Something strange has happened to us."

Samar woke immediately, flushed in shame to find that he had failed in his duty. He gave an angry roar that roused every elf.

"I am at fault," he said, bitterly chagrined. It is a wonder to me that our enemies did not take advantage of our weakness to slit our throats! I had intended to leave with the dawn. We have a long journey, and we have lost at least two hours of travel. We must make—"

"Samar!" Alhana cried, her voice piercing his heart. "Come quickly! My son!"

Alhana pointed to an empty blanket and four broken manacles—manacles no axe had been able to cut. In the dirt near the blanket were deep prints of two booted feet and prints of a horse's hooves.

"They have taken him," she said, frightened. "They have taken him away in the night!"

Samar tracked the hoof prints to the water's edge, and there they vanished. He recalled, with startling clarity, the red horse that had galloped riderless into the forest.

"No one took him, My Queen," Samar said. "One came to fetch him. He went eagerly, I fear."

Alhana stared across the sun-dappled river, saw it bright and sparkling on the surface, dark and wild and dangerous beneath. She recalled with a shudder the words she had heard the river sing last night.

Sleep, love. Forever sleep.

15 PRISONERS, GHOSTS, THE DEAD, AND THE LIVING

Palin Majere was no longer a prisoner in the Tower of High Sorcery. That is to say, he was and he was not. He was not a prisoner in that he was, not confined to a single room in the Tower. He was not chained or bound or physically restrained in any way. He could roam freely about the Tower but no farther. He could not leave the Tower. A single door at the lower level of the Tower permitted entry and egress, and that was enchanted, sealed shut by a wizard lock.

Palin had his own room with a bed but no chair and no desk. The room had a door but no window. The room had a fire grate, but no fire, and was chill and dank. For food, there were loaves of bread, stacked up in what had once been the Tower's pantry, along with crockery bowls—most of which were cracked and chipped—filled with dried fruit. Palin recognized bread that had been created by magic and not the baker, because it was tasteless and pale and had a spongy texture. For drink, there was water in pitchers that continually refilled themselves. The water was brackish and had an unpleasant odor.

Palin had been reluctant to drink it, but he could find nothing else, and after casting a spell on it to make certain it did not contain some sort of potion, he used it to wash down the knots of bread that stuck in his throat. He cast a spell and summoned a fire into existence, but it didn't help lift the atmosphere of gloom.

Ghosts haunted the Tower of High Sorcery. Not the ghosts of the dead who had stolen his magic. Some sort of warding spell kept them at bay. These ghosts were ghosts of his past. At this turning, he encountered the ghost of himself inside this Tower, arriving to take the dread Test of magic. At that turning, he imagined the ghost of his uncle, who had predicted a future of greatness for the young mage. Here he found the ghost of Usha when he had first met her: beautiful, mysterious, fond, and loving. The ghosts were sorrowful, shades of promise and hope, both dead. Ghosts of love, either dead or dying.

Most terrible was the ghost of the magic. It whispered to him from the cracks in the stone stairs, from the torn threads in the carpet, from the dust on the velvet curtains, from the lichen that had died years ago but had never been scraped off the wall.

Perhaps because of the presence of the ghosts, Palin was strangely at home in the Tower. He was more at home here than he was at his own light, airy, and comfortable home in Solace. He didn't enjoy admitting that to himself. He felt guilty because of it.

After days of wandering alone through the Tower, locked up with himself and the ghosts, he understood why this chill, dread place was home. Here in the Tower he had been a child, a child of the magic. Here the magic had watched over him, guided him, loved him, cared for him. Even now he could sometimes smell the scent of faded rose petals and would recall that time, that happy time. Here in the Tower all was quiet. Here no one had any claim on him. No one expected anything of him. No one looked at him with pity. He disappointed no one.

It was then he realized he had to leave. He had to escape from this place, or he would become just another ghost among many.

Having spent the greater portion of his four days as a prisoner roaming the Tower, much as a ghost might roam the place it was doomed to frequent, he was familiar with the physical layout of the Tower. It was similar to what he remembered, but with differences. Every Master of the Tower altered the building to suit his or her needs. Raistlin had made the Tower of High Sorcery his own when he was Master. He had shared it with no one except a single apprentice, Dalamar, the undead who served them, and the Live Ones, poor, twisted creatures who lived out their miserable, misbegotten lives below the surface of the ground in the Chamber of Seeing.

Upon Raistlin's death, Dalamar was made Master of the Tower of High Sorcery. The Tower had been located in the lord city of Palanthas, which considered itself the center of the known world. Previously the Tower of High Sorcery had been a sinister object, one of foreboding and terror. Dalamar was a forward-thinking mage, despite being an elf and a Black Robe (or perhaps because he was an elf and a Black Robe). He wanted to flaunt the power of mages, not hide it, and so he had opened the Tower to students, adding rooms in which his apprentices could live and study.

Fond of comfort and luxury as any elf, he had brought into the Tower many objects that he collected over his travels: the wondrous and the hideous, the beautiful and the awful, the plain and the curious. The objects were all gone, at least so far as Palin could discover. Dalamar might have stashed them in his chamber, which was also wizard-locked, but Palin doubted it. He had the impression that if he entered Dalamar's living quarters he would find them as bare and empty as the rest of the dark and silent rooms in the Tower. These things were part of the past. Either they had been broken in the cataclysmic upheaval of the Tower's move from Palanthas, or their owner had cast them off in pain and in anger. Palin guessed the latter.

He recalled very well when he had heard the news that Dalamar had destroyed the Tower, rather than permit the great blue dragon Khellendros to seize control of it. The citizens of Palanthas woke to a thundering blast that shook houses, cracked streets, broke windows. At first, the people thought they were under attack by dragons, but after that initial shock, nothing further happened.

The next morning, they were awestruck and astonished and generally pleased to find that the Tower of High Sorcery—long considered an eyesore and a haven of evil—had disappeared. In its place was a reflecting pool where, if one looked, it was said one could see the Tower in the dark waters. Thus many began to circulate rumors that the Tower had imploded and sunk into the ground. Palin had never believed those rumors, nor, as he had discussed with his longtime friend and fellow mage Jenna, did he believe Dalamar was dead or the Tower destroyed.

Jenna had agreed with him, and if anyone would know it would be she, for she had been Dalamar's lover for many years and was the last to see him prior to his departure more than thirty years ago.

"Perhaps not so long ago as that," Palin muttered to himself, staring in frustration and simmering anger out the window. "Dalamar knew exactly where to find us. Knew where to lay his hands on us. Only one person could have told him. Only one person knew: Jenna."

He probably should be glad the powerful wizard had rescued them. Otherwise he and Tasslehoff would be sitting in the dragon Beryl's prison cell under far less propitious circumstances. Palin's feelings of gratitude toward Dalamar had effectively evaporated by now. Once he might have shaken Dalamar's hand. Now, he wanted only to wring the elf's neck.

The Tower's relocation from Palanthas to wherever it was now—Palin hadn't the vaguest idea, he could see nothing but trees around it—had brought about other changes. Palin saw several large cracks in the walls, cracks that might have alarmed him for his own safety had he not been fairly certain (or at least hoped) that Dalamar had shored up the walls with magic. The spiral staircase had always been treacherous to walk, but now was doubly so, due to the fact that some of the stairs had not survived the move. Tasslehoff climbed nimbly up and down the stairs like a squirrel, but Palin held his breath every time.

Tasslehoff—who had explored every inch of the Tower during the first hour of his arrival—reported that the entrance to one of the minarets was completely blocked off by a caved-in wall and that the other minaret was missing half the roof. The fearful Shoikan Grove that had once so effectively guarded the Tower had been left behind in Palanthas, where it stood now as a sad curiosity. The Tower was surrounded by a new grove—a grove of immense cypress trees.

Having lived among the vallenwoods all his life, Palin was accustomed to gigantic trees, but he was impressed by the cypresses. Most of the trees stood far taller than the Tower, which was dwarfed by comparison. The cypresses held their enormous green-clothed arms protectively over the Tower, shielding it from the view of roaming dragons, particularly Beryl, who would have given her fangs and her claws and her green scaly tail thrown into the bargain for knowledge of the whereabouts of the Tower that had once reigned so proudly in Palanthas.

Peering out of one of the few upper-story windows still in existence in the Tower—many others that he had remembered had been sealed up—Palin looked out upon a thick forest of cypress that rolled in undulating waves of green to the horizon. No matter what direction he looked, he saw only those spreading green boughs, an ocean of limbs and branches, leaves and shadow. No path cut through these boughs, not even an animal path, for the forest was eerily quiet. No bird sang, no squirrel scolded, no owl hooted, no dove mourned. Nothing living roamed the forest. The Tower was not a ship bobbing upon this ocean. It was submerged in the depths, lost to the sight and knowledge of those who lived in the world beyond.

The forest was the province of the dead.

One of the remaining windows was located at the very bottom of the Tower, a few feet from the massive oaken door. The window looked out upon the forest floor, a floor that was thick with shadow, for sunlight very rarely managed to penetrate through the leaves that formed a canopy above.

Amid the shadows, the souls roamed. The aspect was not a pleasant one. Yet Palin found himself fascinated, and often he would stand here, shivering in the cold, his arms folded for warmth in the sleeves of his robes, gazing out upon the restless, ever-moving, ever-shifting congregation of the dead.

He would watch until he could stand it no more, then he would turn away, his own soul riven with pity and horror, only to be drawn back again.

The dead could not enter the Tower seemingly. Palin did not sense them near him as he had felt them in the citadel. He did not feel that strange tickling sensation when he used his magic to cast spells, a sensation he had set down as gnats or bits of cobweb or a straggling strand of hair or any of a hundred other ordinary occurrences. Now he knew that what he had felt had been the hands of the dead, stealing the magic from him.

Locked up in the Tower alone with Tasslehoff, Palin guessed that it was Dalamar who had been giving the dead their orders. Dalamar had been usurping the magic. Why? What was he doing with it? Certainly, Palin thought sardonically, Dalamar was not using the magic to redecorate.

Palin might have asked him, but he could not find Dalamar. Nor could Tasslehoff, who had been recruited to help in the search. Admittedly, there were many doors in the Tower that were magically locked to both Palin and the kender—especially the kender.

Tasslehoff put his ear to these doors, but not even the kender with his sharp hearing had been able to detect any sounds coming from behind any of them, including one that led to what Palin remembered were Dalamar's private chambers.

Palin had knocked at this door, knocked and shouted, but he had received no answer. Either Dalamar was deliberately ignoring him, or he was not there. Palin had first thought the former and was angry. Now he was starting to think the latter, and he was uneasy. The notion came to his mind that he and Tas had been brought here, then abandoned, to live out their days as prisoners in this Tower, surrounded and guarded by the dead.

"No," Palin amended, talking softly to himself as he stared out the window on the lower floor, "the dead are not guards. They, too, are prisoners."

The souls clogged the shadows beneath the trees, unable to find rest, unable to find peace, wandering in aimless, constant motion. Palin could not comprehend the numbers—thousands, thousands of thousands, and thousands more beyond that. He saw no one he recognized. At first, he had hoped to find his father again, hoped that Caramon could give him some answers to the myriad questions teeming in his son's fevered mind. Palin soon came to realize that his search for one soul among the countless many was as hopeless as searching for a single grain of sand on a beach. If Caramon had been free to come to Palin, his father would surely have done so.

Palin recalled vividly now the vision he had seen of his father in the Citadel of Light. In that vision, Caramon had fought his way to his son through a mass of dead pressing around Palin. Caramon had been trying to tell his son something, but before he could make himself understood, he had been seized by some unseen force and dragged away.

"I think it's awfully sad," said Tasslehoff. He stood with his forehead pressed against the window, peering out the glass. "Look, there's a kender. And another. And another. Hullo!" Tasslehoff tapped with his hands on the window. "Hullo, there! What have you got in your pouches?"

The spirits of the dead kender ignored this customary kender greeting—a question no living kender could have resisted—and were soon lost in the crowd, disappearing among the other souls: elves, dwarves, humans, minotaurs, centaurs, goblins, hobgoblins, draconians, gully dwarves, gnomes, and other races—races Palin had never before seen but had only read about. He saw what he thought were the souls of the Theiwar, the dark dwarves, a cursed race. He saw the souls of the Dimernesti, elves who live beneath the sea and whose very existence had long been disputed. He saw souls of the Thanoi, the strange and fearsome creatures of Ice Wall.

Friend and foe were here. Goblin souls passed shoulder to shoulder with human souls. Draconian souls drifted near elven souls. Minotaur and dwarf roamed side by side. No one soul paid attention to another. One was not aware of the other or seemed to know the other existed. Each ghostly soul went on his or her way, intent upon some quest—some hopeless quest by the looks of it, for on the face of every spirit Palin saw searching and longing, dejection and despair.

"I wonder what it is they're all looking for," Tasslehoff said.

"A way out," replied Palin.

He slung over his shoulder a pack containing several loaves of the magicked bread and a waterskin. Making up his mind, not taking time to think for fear he would argue himself out of his decision, he walked to the Tower's main door.

"Where are you going?" asked Tas.

"Out," said Palin.

"Are you taking me with you?"

"Of course."

Tas looked longingly at the door, but he held back, hovering near the stairs. "We're not going back to the citadel to look for the Device of Time Journeying, are we?"

"What's left of it?" Palin returned bitterly. "If any of it remained undamaged, which I doubt, the bits and pieces were probably picked up by Beryl's draconians and are now in her possession."

"That's good," Tas said, heaving a relieved sigh. Absorbed in arranging his pouches for the journey, he missed Palin's withering glare. "Very well, I'll go along. The Tower was an extremely interesting place to visit, and I'm glad we came here, but it does get boring after awhile. Where do you suppose Dalamar is? Why did he bring us here and then disappear?"

"To flaunt his power over me," said Palin, coming to stand in front of the door. "He imagines that I am finished. He wants to break my spirit, force me to grovel to him, beg him to release me. He will find that he has caught a shark in his net, not a minnow. I had once thought he might be of some help to us, but no more. I will not be a pawn in his khas game."

Palin looked very hard at the kender. "You don't have any magical objects on you? Nothing you've discovered here in the Tower?"

"No, Palin," said Tas with round-eyed innocence. "I haven't discovered anything. Like I said, it's been pretty boring."

Palin persisted. "Nothing you've found that you are intending to return to Dalamar, for example? Nothing that fell into your pouches when you weren't looking? Nothing that you picked up so that someone wouldn't trip over it?"

"Well . . ." Tas scratched his head. "Maybe . . ."

"This is very important, Tas," Palin said, his tone serious. He cast a glance out the window. "You see the dead out there? If we have anything magic, they will try to take it from us. Look, I have removed all my rings and my earring that Jenna gave me. I have left behind my pouches of spell components. Just to be safe, why don't you leave your pouches here, as well? Dalamar will take good care of them," he added in reassuring tones, for Tas was clutching his pouches next to his body and staring at him in horror.

"Leave my pouches?" Tas protested in agony. Palin might as well have asked the kender to leave his head or his topknot. "Will we come back for them?"

"Yes," said Palin. Lies told to a kender are not really lies, more akin to self-defense.

"I guess . . . in that case . . . since it is important . . . " Tas removed his pouches, gave each of them a fond, parting pat, then stowed them safely in a dark corner beneath the stair. "I hope no one steals them."

"I don't think that's likely. Stand over there by the stairs, Tas, where you will be out of the way, and do not interrupt me. I'm going to cast a spell. Alert me if you see anyone coming."

"I'm the rear guard? You're posting me as rear guard?" Tas was captivated and immediately forgot about the pouches. "No one ever posted me as rear guard before! Not even Tanis."

"Yes, you're the . . . er . . . rear guard. You must keep careful watch, and not bother me, no matter what you hear or see me doing."

"Yes, Palin. I will," Tasslehoff promised solemnly, and took up his position. He came bouncing back again. "Excuse me, Palin, but since we're alone here, who is it I'm supposed to be rear-guarding against?"

Palin counseled patience to himself, then said, "If, for example, the wizard-lock includes magical guards, casting a counterspell on the lock might cause these guardians to appear."

Tas sucked in a breath. "Do you mean like skeletons and wraiths and liches? Oh, I hope so—that is, no I don't," he amended quickly, catching sight of Palin's baleful expression. "I'll keep watch. I promise."

Tas retreated back to his post, but just as Palin was calling the words to the spell to his mind, he felt a tug on his sleeve.

"Yes, Tas?" Palin fought the temptation to toss the kender out the window. "What is it now?"

"Is it because you're afraid of the wraiths and liches that you haven't tried to escape before this?"

"No, Tas," said Palin quietly. "It was because I was afraid of myself."

Tas considered this. "I don't think I can rear guard you against yourself, Palin."

"You can't, Tas," Palin said. "Now return to your post."

Palin figured that he had about fifteen seconds of peace before the novelty of being rear guard wore off and Tasslehoff would again be pestering him. Approaching the door, he closed his eyes and extended his hands.

He did not touch the door. He touched the magic that enchanted the door. His broken fingers . . . He remembered a time they had been long and delicate and supple. He felt for the magic, groped for it like a blind man. Sensing a tingling in his fingertips, his soul thrilled. He had found a thread of magic. He smoothed the thread and found another thread and another until the spell rippled beneath his touch. The fabric of the magic was smooth and sheer, a piece of cloth cut from a bolt and hung over the door.

The spell was not simple, but it was certainly not that complex. One of his better students could have undone this spell. Palin's anger increased. Now his pride was hurt.

"You always did underestimate me," Palin muttered to the absent Dalamar. He plucked a thread, and the fabric of magic came apart in his hands.

The door swung open.

Cool air, crisp with the sharp smell of the cypress, breathed into the Tower, as one might try to breathe life through the lips of a drowned man. The souls in the shadows of the trees ceased their aimless roaming, and hundreds turned as one to stare with their shadowed eyes at the Tower. None moved toward it. None made any attempt to approach it. They hung, wavering, in the whispering air.

"I will use no magic," Palin told them. "I have only food in my pack, food and water. You will leave me alone." He motioned to Tas, an unnecessary gesture, since the kender was now dancing at his side. "Keep near me, Tas. This is no time to go off exploring. We must not get separated."

"I know," said Tas excitedly. "I'm still the rear guard. Where is it we're going, exactly?"

Palin looked out the door. Years ago, there had been stone stairs, a courtyard. Now his first step out of the Tower of High Sorcery would fall onto a bed of brown, dead cypress needles that surrounded the Tower like a dry moat. The cypress trees formed a wall around the brown moat, their branches serving as a canopy under which they would walk. Standing in the shadows of the trees, watching, were the souls of the dead.

"We're going to find a path, a trail. Anything to lead us out of this forest," Palin said.

Thrusting his hands in the sleeves of his robes, to emphasize the fact that he was not going to use them, he strode out the door and headed straight for the tree line. Tas followed after, discharging his role as rear guard by attempting to look backward while walking forward, a feat of agility that apparently took some practice, for Tas was having a difficult time of it.

"Stop that!" said Palin through clenched teeth the second time Tasslehoff bumbled into him. They were nearing the tree line. Palin removed his hand from his sleeve long enough to grasp Tas by the shoulder and forcibly turn him around. "Face forward."

"But I'm the rear—" Tas protested. He interrupted himself. "Oh, I see. It's what's in front of us you're worried about."

The dead had no bodies. These they had left behind, abandoning the shells of cold flesh as butterflies leave the cocoon. Once, like butterflies, these spirits might have flown free to whatever new destination awaited them. Now they were trapped as in an enormous jar, constrained to wander aimlessly, searching for the way out.

So many souls. A river of souls, swirling about the boles of the cypress trees, each one a drop of water in a mighty torrent. Palin could barely distinguish one from another. Faces flitted past, hands or arms or hair trailing like diaphanous silken scarves. The faces were the most terrible, for they all looked at him with a hunger that caused him to hesitate, his steps to slow. Whispered breath that he had mistaken for the wind touched his cheek. He heard words in the whispers and shivered.

The magic, they said. *Give us the magic.* They looked at him. They paid no attention to the kender. Tasslehoff was saying something. Palin could see his mouth moving and almost hear the words, but he couldn't hear. It was as if his ears were stuffed with the whispers of the dead.

"I have nothing to give you," he told the souls. His own voice sounded muffled and faraway. "I have no magical artifacts. Let us pass."

He came to the tree line. The whispering souls were a white, frothing pool among the shadows of the trees. He had hoped that the souls would part before him, like the early morning fog lifting from the valleys, but they remained, blocking his way. He could see dimly through them, see more trees with the eerie white mist of souls wavering beneath. He was reminded of the hordes of mendicants that crowded the streets of Palanthas, grimy hands outstretched, shrill voices begging.

He halted, cast a glance back at the Tower of High Sorcery, saw a broken, crumbling ruin. He faced forward.

They did not harm you in the past, he reminded himself. You know their touch. It is unpleasant but no worse than walking into a cobweb. If you go back there, you will never leave. Not until you are one of them.

He walked into the river of souls.

Chill, pale hands touched his hands, his arms. Chill, pale eyes stared at him. Chill, pale lips pressed against his lips, sucked the breath from him. He could not move for the swirling souls that had hold of him and were dragging him under. He could hear nothing except the whispered roar of their terrible voices. He turned, trying to find the way back, but all he saw were eyes, mouths, and hands. He turned and turned again, and now he was disoriented and confused, and there were more of them and still more.

He couldn't breathe, he couldn't speak, he couldn't cry out. He fell to the ground, gasping for air. They rose and ebbed around him, touching, pulling, yanking. He was shredded, torn asunder. They searched through the fibers of his being.

Magic . . . magic . . . give us the magic. . . .

He slipped beneath the awful surface and ceased to struggle.

Tasslehoff saw Palin walk into the shadows of the trees, but the kender did not immediately follow after him. Instead he attempted to gain the attention of several dead kender, who were standing beneath the trees, watching Palin.

"I say," said Tas very loudly, over the sound of buzzing in his ears, a sound that was starting to be annoying, "have you seen my friend, Caramon? He's one of you."

Tas had been about to tell them that Caramon was dead, like them, but he refrained, thinking that it might make them sad to be reminded of the fact.

"He's a really big human, and the last time I saw him alive he was very old, but now that he's dead—no offense—he looks young again. He has curly hair and a very friendly smile."

No use. The kender refused to pay the least bit of attention to him.

"I hate to tell you this, but you are extremely rude," Tas told the kender as he walked past. He might as well follow Palin, since no one was going to talk to him. "One would think you'd been raised by humans. You must not be from Kendermore. No Kendermore kender would act that— Now that's odd. Where did he go?"

Tas searched the forest ahead of him as well as he could, considering the poor ghosts, who were whirling about in a frenetic manner, enough to make a fellow dizzy.

"Palin! Where are you? I'm supposed to be the rear guard, and I can't be the rear guard if you're not in front."

He waited a bit to see if Palin answered his call, but if the sorcerer did, Tas probably wouldn't be able to hear it over the buzzing that was starting to give him a pain in the head. Putting his fingers in his ears to try to shut out the sound, Tas turned to look behind him, thinking that perhaps Palin had forgotten something and gone back to the Tower to fetch it. Tas could see the Tower, looking small beneath the cypress trees, but no sign of Palin.

"Drat it!" Tas took his fingers out of his ears to wave his hands, trying to disperse the dead who were really making a most frightful nuisance of themselves. "Get out of here. I can't see a thing. Palin!"

It was like walking through a thick fog, only worse, because fog didn't look at you with pleading eyes or try to grab hold of you with wispy hands. Tasslehoff groped his way forward. Tripping over something, probably a tree root, he fell headlong on the forest floor. Whatever he had fallen over jerked beneath his legs. It's not a tree root, he thought, or if it is, the root belongs to one of the more lively varieties of tree.

Tas recognized Palin's robes, and after a moment more, he recognized Palin. He hovered over his friend in consternation.

Palin's face was exceedingly white, more white than the spirits surrounding him. His eyes were closed. He gasped for air. One hand clutched at this throat, the other clawed at the dirt.

"Get away, you! Go! Leave him alone," Tas cried, endeavoring to drive away the dead souls, who seemed to be wrapping themselves around Palin like some evil web. "Stop it!" the kender shouted, jumping up and stamping his foot. He was starting to grow desperate. "You're killing him!"

The buzzing sound grew louder, as if hornets were flying into his ears and using his head for a hive. The sound was so awful that Tasslehoff couldn't think, but he realized he didn't have to think. He only had to rescue Palin before the dead turned him into one of themselves.

Tas glanced behind him again to get his bearings. He could see the Tower or catch glimpses of it, at any rate, through the ever-shifting mist of the souls. Running around to Palin's head, Tas took hold of the man by the shoulders. The kender dug his heels into the ground and gave a grunt and a heave. Palin was not large as humans went—Tas envisioned himself trying to drag Caramon—but he was a full-grown man and deadweight, at this point more dead than alive. Tas was a kender and an older kender at that. He dragged Palin over the rough, needle-strewn ground and managed to move him a couple of feet before he had to drop him and stop to catch his breath.

The dead did not try to stop Tas, but the buzzing noise grew so loud that he had to grit his teeth against it. He picked up Palin again, glanced behind once more to reassure himself that the Tower was still where he thought it was, and gave another tug. He pulled and panted and floundered, but he never lost his grip on Palin. With a final great heave that caused his feet to slip out from under him, he dragged Palin out of the forest onto the bed of brown needles that surrounded the Tower.

Keeping a wary eye on the dead, who hovered in the dark shadows beneath the trees, watching, waiting, Tas crawled around on all fours to look anxiously at his friend.

Palin no longer gasped for air. He gulped it down thankfully. His eyes blinked a few times, then opened wide with a look that was wild and terrified. He sat up suddenly with a cry, thrusting out his arms.

"It's all right, Palin!" Tas grabbed hold of one of Palin's flailing hands and clutching it tightly. "You're safe. At least I think you're safe. There seems to be some sort of barrier they can't cross."

Palin glanced over at the souls writhing in the darkness. Shuddering, he averted his gaze, looked back at the door to the Tower. His expression grew grim, he stood up, brushing brown needles from his robes.

"I saved your life, Palin," Tas said. "You might have died out there."

"Yes, Tas, I might have," Palin said. "Thank you." Stopping, he looked down at the kender, and his grim expression softened. He put a hand on Tas's shoulder. "Thank you very much."

He glanced again at the Tower, and the grimness returned. A frown caused the lines on his face to turn dark and jagged. He continued to stare fixedly at the Tower and, after drawing in a few more deep breaths, he walked toward it. He was very pale, almost paler than when he had been dying, and he looked extremely determined. As determined as Tas had ever seen anyone.

"Where are you going now?" Tas asked, game for another adventure, although he wouldn't have minded a brief rest.

"To find Dalamar."

"But we've looked and looked—"

"No, we haven't," Palin said. He was angry now, and he intended to act before his anger cooled. "Dalamar has no right to do this! He has no right to imprison these wretched souls."

Sweeping through the Tower door, Palin began to climb the spiral staircase that led into the upper levels of the building. He kept close to the wall that was on his right, for the stairs had no railing on his left. A misstep would send him plummeting down into darkness.

"Are we going to free them?" Tas asked, clambering up the staircase behind Palin. "Even after they tried to kill you?"

"They didn't mean to," Palin said. "They can't help themselves. They are being driven to seek out the magic. I know now who is behind it, and I intend to stop him."

"How will we do that?" Tas asked eagerly. Palin hadn't exactly included him in this adventure, but that was probably an oversight. "Stop him, I mean? We don't even know where he is."

"I'll stop him if I have to tear this Tower down stone by stone," was all Palin would say.

A long and perilous climb up the spiral staircase through the near darkness brought them to a door.

"I already tried this," Tas announced. Examining it, he gave it an experimental shove. "It won't budge."

"Oh, yes, it will," said Palin.

He raised his hands and spoke a word. Blue light began to glow, flames crackled from his fingers. He drew a breath and reached out toward the door. The flames burned brighter.

Suddenly, silently, the door swung open.

"Stop, Tas!" Palin ordered, as the kender was about to bound inside.

"But you opened it," Tas protested.

"No," said Palin, and his voice was harsh. The blue flames had died away. "No, I didn't."

He took a step forward, staring intently into the room. The few rays of sunlight that managed to struggle through the heavy, overhanging boughs of the cypress trees had to work to penetrate the years of silt and mud that covered the windows outside and the layer of dust that caked the inside. No sound came from within.

"You stay out in the hall, Tas."

"Do you want me to be rear guard again?" Tas asked.

"Yes, Tas," said Palin quietly. He took another step forward. His head cocked, he was listening for the slightest sound. He moved slowly into the room. "You be the rear guard. Let me know if you see anything coming."

"Like a wraith or a ghoul? Sure, Palin."

Tas stood in the hall, hopping from one foot to the other, trying to see what was happening in the room.

"Rear guard is a really important assignment," Tasslehoff reminded himself, fidgeting, unable to hear or see anything. "Sturm was always rear guard. Or Caramon. I never got to be rear guard because Tanis said kender don't make good rear guards, mainly because they never stay in the rear—

"Don't worry! I'm coming, Palin!" Tas called, giving up. He dashed into the room. "Nothing's sneaking up behind us. Our rears are safe. Oh!"

Tas came to a halt. He didn't have much choice in the matter. Palin's hand had a good, strong hold on his shoulder.

The room's interior was gray and chill, and even on the warmest, brightest summer day would always be gray and chill. The wintry light illuminated shelves containing innumerable books. Next to these were the scroll repositories, like honeycombs, a few filled, but most empty. Wooden chests stood on the floor, their ornate carvings almost obliterated by dust. The heavy curtains that covered the windows, the once-beautiful rugs on the floors, were dust-covered, the fabric rotting and frayed.

At the far end of the room was a desk. Someone was sitting behind the desk. Tas squinted, tried to see in the dim, gray light. The someone was an elf, with long, lank hair that had once been black but now had a gray, jagged streak that ran from the forehead back.

"Who's that?" he asked in a loud whisper.

The elf sat perfectly still. Tas, thinking he was asleep, didn't want to wake him.

"Dalamar," said Palin.

"Dalamar!" Tas repeated, stunned. He twisted his head to look up at Palin, thinking this might be a joke. If it was, Palin wasn't laughing. "But that can't be right! He's not here. I know because I banged on the door and shouted 'Dalamar' real loud, like that, and no one answered."

"Dalamar!" Tas raised his voice. "Hullo! Where have you been?"

"He can't hear, Tas," Palin said. "He can't see you or hear you."

Dalamar sat behind his desk, his thin hands folded before him, his eyes staring straight ahead. He had not moved as they entered. His eyes did not shift, as they surely must have, at the sound of the kender's shrill voice. His hands did not stir, his fingers did not twitch.

"Maybe he's dead," Tas said, a funny feeling squirming in his stomach. "He certainly looks dead, doesn't he, Palin?"

The elf sat unmoving in the chair.

"No," said Palin. "He is not dead."

"It's a funny way to take a nap, then," Tas remarked. "Sitting straight up. Maybe if I pinched him—"

"Don't touch him!" Palin warned sharply. "He is in stasis."

"I know where that is," Tas stated. "It's north of Flotsam, about fifty miles. But he's not in Stasis, Palin. He's right here."

The elf's eyes, which had been open and unseeing, suddenly closed. They remained closed for a long, long time. He was coming back from the stasis, back from the enchantment that had taken his spirit out into the world, leaving his body behind. He drew air in through his nose, keeping his lips pressed tightly shut. His fingers curled, and he winced, as if in pain. He curled them and uncurled them and began to rub them.

"The circulation stops," Dalamar said, opening his eyes and looking at Palin. "It is quite painful."

"My heart bleeds for you," said Palin.

Dalamar's gaze went to Palin's own broken, twisted fingers. He said nothing, continued to rub his hands.

"Hullo, Dalamar!" Tas said cheerfully, glad for a chance to be included in the conversation. "It's nice to see you again. Did I tell you how much you have changed from the time I saw you at Caramon's first funeral? Do you want to hear about it? I made a really good speech, and then it began to rain and everyone was already sad, and that made it sadder, but then you cast a magic spell, a wonderful spell that made the raindrops sparkle and the sky was filled with rainbows—"

"No!" Dalamar said, making a sharp, cutting motion with his hand.

Tas was about to go on to the other parts of the funeral, since Dalamar didn't want to talk about the rainbows, but the elf gave him a peculiar look, raised his hand, and pointed.

Perhaps I'm going to Stasis, Tas thought, and that was the last conscious thought he had for a good, long while.

16 A BORED KENDER

Palin placed the comatose kender in one of the shabby, dust-covered and mildewed chairs that stood at the far end of the library, a portion that was in shadow. Affecting to be settling Tas, Palin took the opportunity to look closely at Dalamar, who remained seated behind the desk, his head bowed into his hands.

Palin had seen the elf only briefly on first arriving. He had been shocked then at the ruinous alteration in the features of the once handsome and vain elven wizard: the gray-streaked black hair, the wasted features, the thin hands with their branching blue veins like rivers drawn on a map, rivers of blood, rivers of souls. And this, their master . . . Master of the Tower.

Struck by a new thought, Palin walked over to the window and looked down into the forest below, where the dead flowed still and silent among the boles of the cypress trees.

"The wizard-lock on the door below," Palin said abruptly. "It was not meant to keep us in, was it?"

No answer came from Dalamar. Palin was left to answer himself. "It was meant to keep them out. If that is true, you might want to replace it."

Dalamar, a grim look on his face, left the room. He returned long moments later. Palin had not moved. Dalamar came to stand beside him, looked into the mist of swirling souls.

"They gather around you," Dalamar said softly. "Their grave-cold hands clasp you. Their ice lips press against your flesh. Their chill arms embrace you, dead fingers clutch at you. You know!"

"Yes," said Palin. "I know." He shook off the remembered horror. "You can't leave, either."

"My body cannot leave," Dalamar corrected. "My spirit is free to roam. When I depart, I must always come back." He shrugged. "What is it the *Shalafi* used to say? 'Even wizards must suffer.' There is always a price." Dalamar lowered his gaze to Palin's broken fingers. "Isn't there?"

Palin thrust his hands into the sleeves of his robes. "Where has your spirit been?"

"Traveling Ansalon, investigating this fantastical time-traveling story of yours," Dalamar replied.

"Story? *I* told you no story," Palin returned crisply. "I haven't spoken one word to you. You've been to see Jenna. *She* was the one who told you. And she said that she hadn't seen you in years."

"She did not lie, Majere, if that's what you're insinuating, although I admit she did not tell you all the truth. She has not *seen* me, at least not my physical form. She has heard my voice, and that only recently. I arranged a meeting with her after the strange storm that swept over all Ansalon in a single night."

"I asked her if she knew where to find you."

"Again, she told you the truth. She does *not* know where to find me. I did not tell her. She has never been here. No one has been here. You are the first, and believe me"—Dalamar's brows constricted—"if you had not been in such dire straits, you would not be here now. I do not pine for company," he added with a dark glance.

Palin was silent, uncertain whether to believe him or not.

"For mercy's sake, don't sulk, Majere," Dalamar said, willfully misinterpreting Palin's silence. "It's undignified for a man of your age. How old are you anyway? Sixty, seventy, a hundred? I can never tell with humans. You look ancient enough to me. As for Jenna 'betraying' your confidence, it is well for you and the kender that she did, else I would have not taken an interest in you, and you would now be in Beryl's tender care."

"Do not try to taunt me by remarking on the fact that I am old," Palin said calmly. "I know I have aged. The process is natural in humans. In elves, it is not. Look in a mirror, Dalamar. If the years have taken a toll on me, they have taken a far more terrible toll on you. As for pride"—Palin shrugged in his turn—"I lost that a long time ago. It is hard to remain proud when you can no longer summon magic enough to heat my morning tea. I think you have reason to know that."

"Perhaps I do," Dalamar replied. "I know that I have changed. The battle I fought with Chaos stole hundreds of years from me, yet I could live with that. I was victorious, after all. Victor and loser, all at the same time. I won the war and was defeated by what came after. The loss of the magic.

"I risked my life for the sake of the magic," Dalamar continued, his voice low and hollow. "I would have given my life for the sake of the magic. What happened? The magic departed. The gods left. They left me bereft, powerless, helpless. They left me—ordinary!"

Dalamar breathed shallowly. "All that I gave up for the magic—my homeland, my nation, my people . . . I used to consider I had made a fair trade. My sacrifice—and it was a wrenching sacrifice, though only another elf would understand—had been rewarded. But the reward was gone, and I was left with nothing. Nothing. And everyone knew it.

"It was then I began to hear rumors—rumors that Khellendros the Blue was going to seize my Tower, rumors that the Dark Knights were going to attack it. My Tower!" Dalamar gave a vicious snarl. His thin fist clenched. Then, his hand relaxed, and he gave a grating laugh.

"I tell you, Majere, gully dwarves could have taken over my Tower, and I could have done nothing to stop them. I had once been the most powerful wizard in Ansalon, and now, as you said, I could not so much as boil water."

"You were not alone." Palin was unsympathetic. "All of us were affected the same way."

"No, you weren't," Dalamar retorted passionately. "You could not be. You had not sacrificed as I had sacrificed. You had your father and mother. You had a wife and children."

"Jenna loved you—" Palin began.

"Did she?" Dalamar grimaced. "Sometimes I think we only used each other. She could not understand me either. She was like you, with her damnable human hope and optimism. Why are you humans like that? Why do you go on hoping when it is obvious that all hope is lost? I could not stomach her platitudes. We quarreled. She left, and I was glad to see her leave. I had no need of her. I had no need of anyone. It was up to me to protect my Tower from those great, bloated wyrms, and I did what I had to do. The only way to save the Tower was to appear to destroy it. And I did so. My plan worked. No one knows the Tower is here. No one will, unless I want it to be found."

"Moving the Tower must have taken an immense amount of magical power—a bit more than would be required to boil water," Palin observed. "You must have had some of the old magic left to you."

"No, I assure you, I did not," Dalamar said, his passion cooling. "I was as barren as you."

He gave Palin a sharp and meaningful glance. "Like you, I understood magic was in the world, if one knew where to look for it."

Palin avoided Dalamar's intense gaze. "I do not know what you're implying. I discovered the wild magic—"

"Not alone. You had help. I know, because I had the same help. A strange personage known as the Shadow Sorcerer."

"Yes!" Palin was astonished. "Hooded and cloaked in gray. A voice that was as soft as shadow, might have belonged to either man or woman."

"You never saw a face—"

"But I did," Palin protested. "In that last terrible battle, I saw she was a woman. She was an agent of the dragon Malystryx—"

"Indeed?" Dalamar lifted an eyebrow. "In my last 'terrible' battle, I saw that the Shadow Sorcerer was a man, an agent for the dragon Khellendros who, according to my sources, had supposedly left this world in search of the soul of his late master, that demon-witch Kitiara."

"The Shadow Sorcerer taught you wild magic?"

"No," Dalamar replied. "The Shadow Sorcerer taught me death magic. Necromancy."

Palin looked back out the window to the roaming spirits. He looked around the shabby room with its books of magic that were so many ghosts, lined up on the shelves. He looked at the elf, who was thin and wasted, like a gnawed bone. "What went wrong?" he asked at last.

"I was duped," Dalamar returned. "I was given to believe I was master of the dead. Too late, I discovered I was not the master. I was the prisoner. A prisoner of my own ambition, my own lust for power.

"It is not easy for me to say these things about myself, Majere," Dalamar added. "It is especially hard for me to say them to you, the darling child of magic. Oh, yes. I knew. You were the gifted one, beloved of Solinari, beloved of your Uncle Raistlin. You would have been one of the great archmages of all time. I saw that. Was I jealous? A little. More than a little. Especially of Raistlin's care for you. You wouldn't think I would want that, would you? That I would hunger for his approval, his notice. But I did."

"All this time," said Palin, his gaze returning to the trapped souls, "I have been jealous of you."

The silence of the empty Tower twined around them.

"I wanted to talk to you," Palin said at last, almost loathe to break that binding silence. "To ask you about the Device of Time Journeying—"

"Rather late for that now," Dalamar interrupted, his tone caustic. "Since you destroyed it."

"I did what I had to do," Palin returned, stating it as fact, not apology. "I had to save Tasslehoff. If he dies in a time that is not his own, our time and all in it will end."

"Good riddance." Dalamar gave a wave of his hand, walked back to his desk. He walked slowly, his shoulders stooped and rounded. "Oblivion would be welcome."

"If you truly thought that you would be dead by now," Palin returned.

"No," said Dalamar, stopping to glance out another window. "No, I said oblivion. Not death." He returned to his desk, sank down into the chair. "*You* could leave. You have the magical earring that would carry you through the portals of magic back to your home. The earring will work here. The dead cannot interfere."

"The magic wouldn't carry Tasslehoff," Palin pointed out, "and I won't leave without him."

Dalamar regarded the slumbering kender with a speculative, thoughtful gaze. "He is not the key," he said musingly, "but perhaps he is the picklock."

Tasslehoff was bored.

Everyone on Krynn either knows, or should know, how dangerous a bored kender can be. Palin and Dalamar both knew, but unfortunately they both forgot. Their combined memory lapse is perhaps understandable, given their preoccupation with trying to find the answers to their innumerable questions. What was worse, not only did they forget that a bored kender is a dangerous kender, they forgot the kender completely. And that is well nigh inexcusable.

The reunion of these old friends had gotten off to a pretty good start, at least as far as Tas was concerned. He had been awakened from his unexpected nap in order to explain his role in the important events that had transpired of late. Perching on the edge of Dalamar's desk and kicking his heels against the wood—until Dalamar curtly told him to stop—Tasslehoff gleefully joined in the conversation.

He found this entertaining for a time. Palin described their visit to Laurana in Qualinesti, his discovery that Tasslehoff was really Tasslehoff and the revelation about the Device of Time Journeying, and his subsequent decision to travel back in time to try to find the other time Tasslehoff had told him about. Since Tasslehoff had been intimately involved in all this, he was called upon to provide certain details, which he was happy to do.

He would have been more happy had he been allowed to tell his complete tale without interruption, but Dalamar said he didn't have time to hear it. Having always been told when he was a small kender that one can't have everything (he had always wondered why one couldn't have everything but had at last arrived at the conclusion that his pouches weren't big enough to hold it all), Tas had to be content with telling the abbreviated version.

After he had described how he had come to Caramon's first funeral and found Dalamar head of the Black Robes, Palin head of the White Robes, and Silvanoshei king of the united elven nations, and the world mostly at peace and there were no—repeat—*no* humungous dragons running about killing kender in Kendermore, Tasslehoff was told that his observations were no longer required. In other words, he was supposed to go sit in a chair, keep still, and answer questions only when he was asked.

Going back to the chair that stood in a shadowy corner, Tasslehoff listened to Palin telling about how he had used the Device of Time Journeying to go back into the past, only to find that there wasn't a past. That was interesting, because Tasslehoff had been there to see that happen, and he could have provided eyewitness testimony if anyone had asked him, which no one did. When he volunteered, he was told to be quiet.

Then came the part where Palin said how the one thing he knew for a fact was that Tasslehoff should have died by being squished by Chaos and that Tasslehoff had not died, thus implying that everything from humungous dragons to the lost gods was all Tasslehoff's fault.

Palin described how he—Palin—had told him—Tasslehoff—that he had to use the Device of Time Journeying to return to die and that Tasslehoff had most strongly and—logically, Tas felt compelled to point out—refused to do this. Palin related how Tasslehoff had fled to the citadel to seek Goldmoon's protection by telling Goldmoon that Palin was trying to murder him. How Palin had arrived to say that, no, he was not and found Goldmoon growing younger, not older. That caused the conversation to take a bit of a detour, but they soon—too soon, as far as Tas was concerned—returned to the main highway.

Palin told Dalamar that Tasslehoff had finally come to the conclusion that going back in time was the only honorable thing to do—and here Palin most generously praised the kender for his courage. Then Palin explained that before Tas could go back, the dead had broken the Device of Time Journeying and they had been attacked by draconians. Palin had been forced to use the pieces of the device to fend off the draconians, and now pieces of the device were scattered over most of the Hedge Maze, and how were they going to send the kender back to die?

Tasslehoff rose to present the novel idea that perhaps the kender should *not* be sent back to die, but at this juncture Dalamar fixed Tas with a cold eye and said that in his opinion the most important thing they could do to help save the world, short of slaying the humungous dragons, was to send Tasslehoff back to die and that they would have to figure out some way to do it without the Device of Time Journeying.

Dalamar and Palin began snatching books from the shelves, paging through them, muttering and mumbling about rivers of time and Graygems and kender jumping in and mucking things up and a lot of other mind-numbing stuff. Dalamar magicked up a fire in the large fireplace, and the room that had been cold and dank, grew warm and stuffy, smelling of vellum, mildew, lamp oil, and dead roses. Since there was no longer anything of interest to see or hear, Tasslehoff's eyes decided to close. His ears agreed with his eyes, and his mind agreed with his ears, and all of them took another brief nap, this one of his own choosing.

Tas woke to something poking him uncomfortably in the posterior. His nap had apparently not been as brief as he thought, for it was dark outside the window—so dark that the darkness had overflowed from outside and was now inside. Tasslehoff could not see a thing. Not himself, not Dalamar, and not Palin.

Tasslehoff squirmed about in the chair in order to stop whatever was sticking him in a tender region from sticking him. It was then, after he woke up a bit, that he realized the reason he couldn't see either Palin or Dalamar was that they were no longer in the room. Or, if they were, they were playing at hide and seek, and while that was a charming and amusing game, the two of them didn't seem the type to go in for it.

Leaving his chair, Tasslehoff fumbled his way to Dalamar's desk, where he found the oil lamp. A few embers remained in the fireplace. Tas felt about on the desk until he discovered some paper. Hoping that the paper didn't have a magic spell written on it or if did, it was a spell that Dalamar didn't want anymore, Tas stuck the end of the paper in the fireplace, lit it, and lit the oil lamp.

Now that he could see, he reached into his back pocket to find out what had been poking him. Taking out the offending object, he held it to the oil lamp.

"Uh, oh!" Tas exclaimed.

"Oh, no!" he cried.

"How did *you* get here?" he wailed.

The thing that had been poking him was the chain from the Device of Time Journeying. Tas threw it onto the desk and reached back into his pocket. He pulled out another piece of the device, then another and another. He pulled out all the jewels, one by one. Spreading the pieces on the desk, he gazed at them sadly. He might have actually shaken his fist at them, but such a gesture would not have been worthy of a Hero of the Lance, and so we will say here that he did not.

As a Hero of the Lance, Tas knew what he should do. He should gather up all the pieces of the device in his handkerchief (make that Palin's handkerchief) take them straightway to wherever Palin and Dalamar were, and hand them over and say, quite bravely, that he was prepared to go back and die for the world. That would be a Noble Deed, and Tasslehoff had been ready once before to do a Noble Deed. But one had to be in the proper mood for being Noble, and Tas discovered he wasn't in that mood at all. He supposed that one also had to be in the proper mood to be stepped on by a giant, and he wasn't in that particular mood either. After seeing the dead people roaming about aimlessly outside—especially the dead kender, who didn't even care what they had in their pouches—Tasslehoff was in the mood to live and go on living.

He knew this was not likely to happen if Dalamar and Palin discovered that he had the magical device in his pocket, even if it was broken. Fearing that any moment Palin and Dalamar might remember they'd left him here and come back to check on him or offer him dinner, Tasslehoff hurriedly gathered up the pieces of the magical device, wrapped them in the handkerchief, and stuffed them in one of his pouches.

That was the easy part. Now came the hard part.

Far from being Noble, he was going to be Ignoble. He thought that was the right word. He was going to Escape.

Leaving by the front door was out. He had tried the windows already, and they were no help. You couldn't even break them by heaving a rock through the glass like you could an ordinary, respectable window. Tas had heaved, and the rock had bounced off and landed on his foot, smashing his toes.

"I have to consider this logically," Tas said to himself. It may be noted as a historical fact that this was the only time a kender ever said such a thing and only goes to show how truly dire was the situation in which he found himself. "Palin got out, but he's a wizard, and he had to use magic to do it. However, using logic, I say to myself—if nothing but a wizard can get out can anything other than a wizard get in? If so, what and how?"

Tas thought this over. While he thought, he watched the embers glow in the fireplace. Suddenly he let out a cry and immediately clapped his hand over his mouth, afraid that Palin and Dalamar would hear and remember him.

"I've got it!" he whispered. "Something does get in! Air gets in! And it goes out, too. And where it goes, I can go."

Tasslehoff kicked and stomped on the embers until they went out. Picking up the oil lamp, he walked into the fireplace and took a look around. It was a large fireplace, and he didn't have to stoop all that much to get inside. Holding the lamp high, he peered up into the darkness. He was almost immediately forced to lower his head and blink quite frantically until he dislodged the soot that had fallen into his eyes. Once he could see again, he was rewarded by a lovely sight—the wall of the chimney was not smooth. Instead it was nubbly, wonderfully nubbly, with the ends and fronts and sides of large stones sticking out every which way.

"Why, I could climb up that wall with one leg tied behind my back," Tasslehoff exclaimed.

This not being something he did on a regular basis, he decided that it would be far more efficient to use two legs. He couldn't very well climb and hang onto the oil lamp, so he left that on the desk, thoughtfully blowing out the flame first so that he wouldn't set anything on fire. Entering the chimney, he found a good foot- and handhold right off and began his climb.

He had gone only a short distance—moving slowly because he had to feel his way in the darkness and pausing occasionally to wipe gunk out of his eyes—when he heard voices coming from below. Tasslehoff froze, clinging like a spider to the wall of the chimney, afraid to move lest he send a shower of soot raining down into the fireplace. He did think, rather resentfully, that Dalamar might at least have spent some magic on a chimney sweep.

The voices were raised and heated.

"I tell you, Majere, your story makes no sense! From all we have read, you should have seen the past flow by you like a great river. In my opinion, you simply miscast the spell."

"And I tell you, Dalamar, that while I may not have your vaunted power in magic, I did *not* miscast the spell. The past was not there, and it all goes wrong at the very moment Tasslehoff was supposed to die."

"From what we have read in Raistlin's journal, the death of the kender should be a drop in time's vast river and should not affect time one way or the other."

"For the fourteenth time the fact that Chaos was involved alters matters completely. The kender's death becomes vitally important. What of this future he says he visited? A future in which everything is different?"

"Bah! You are gullible, Majere! The kender is a liar. He made it all up. Where is that blasted scroll? That should explain everything. I know it is here somewhere. Look over there in that cabinet."

Tasslehoff was understandably annoyed to hear himself referred to as a liar. He considered dropping down and giving Dalamar and Palin both a piece of his mind but reflected that, if he did so, it would be difficult to explain why exactly he'd gone up the chimney in the first place. He kept quiet.

"It would help if I knew what I was looking for."

"A scroll! I suppose you know a scroll when you see one."

"Just find the damn thing!" Tasslehoff muttered. He was growing quite weary of hanging onto the wall. His hands were starting to ache, and his legs to quiver, and he feared he wasn't going to be able to hold on much longer.

"I know what a scroll looks like, but—" A pause. "Speaking of Tasslehoff, where is he? Do you know?"

"I neither know nor care."

"When we left, he was asleep in the chair."

"Then he's probably gone to bed, or he's attempting to pick the lock of the door to the laboratory again."

"Still, don't you think we should—"

"Found it! This is it!" The sound of paper being unrolled. "*A Treatise on Time Journeying Dealing Specifically with the Unacceptability of Permitting Any Member of the Graygem Races to Journey Back in Time Due to the Unpredictability of Their Actions and How This Might Affect Not Only the Past but the Future.*"

"Who's the author?"

"Marwort."

"Marwort! Who termed himself Marwort the Illustrious? The Kingpriest's pet wizard? Everyone knows that when he wrote about the magic, the Kingpriest guided his hand. Of what use is this? You can't believe a word that traitor says."

"So the history of our Order has recorded, and therefore no one studies him. But I have often found what he has to say interesting—if one reads between the lines. For example, notice this paragraph. The third one down."

Tasslehoff's stiff fingers began to slip. He gulped and readjusted his hold on the stones and wished Palin and Dalamar and Marwort gone with all his heart and soul.

"I can't read by this light," Palin said. "My eyes are not what they used to be. And the fire has gone out."

"I could light the fire again," Dalamar offered.

Tasslehoff nearly lost his grip on the stones.

"No," said Palin. "I find this room depressing. Let us take it back where we can be comfortable."

They doused the light, leaving Tas in darkness. He heaved a sigh of relief. When he heard the door close, he began his climb once again.

He was not a young, agile kender anymore, and he soon found that climbing chimneys in the dark was wearing work. Fortunately, he had reached a point in the chimney where the walls started to narrow, so that at least he could lean his back against one wall while keeping himself from slipping by planting his feet firmly against the wall opposite.

He was hot and tired. He had grime in his eyes and soot up his nose and his mouth. His legs were scraped, his fingers rubbed raw, his clothes ripped and torn. He was bored of being in the dark, bored of the stones, bored of the whole business—and he didn't appear to be any closer to the way out than when he'd started.

"I really don't see why it is necessary to have this much chimney," Tasslehoff muttered, cursing the Tower's builder with every grimy foothold.

Just when he thought that his hands were going to refuse to clamp down on another stone and that his legs were going to drop off and fall to the bottom, something filled his nose, and for a change it wasn't soot.

"Fresh air!" Tasslehoff breathed deeply, and his spirits revived.

The whiff of fresh air wafting down from above lent strength to Tasslehoff's legs and banished the aches from his fingers. Peering upward in hope of seeing stars or maybe the sun—for he had the notion that he'd been climbing for the past six months or so—he was disappointed to see only more darkness. He'd had darkness enough to last a lifetime, maybe even two lifetimes. However, the air was fresh, and that meant outside air, so he clambered upward with renewed vigor.

At length, as all things must do, good or otherwise, the chimney came to an end.

The opening was covered with an iron grate to keep birds and squirrels and other undesirables from nesting in the chimney shaft. After what Tasslehoff had already been through, an iron grate was nothing more than a minor inconvenience. He gave it an experimental shove, not expecting anything to come of it. Luck was with him, however. The bolts holding the grate in place had long since rusted away—probably sometime prior to the First Cataclysm—and at the kender's enthusiastic push the gate popped off.

Tasslehoff was unprepared for its sudden departure. He made a desperate grab but missed, and the grate went sailing into the air. The kender froze again, squinched shut his eyes, hunched his shoulders, and waited for the grate to strike the ground at the bottom with what would undoubtedly be a clang loud enough to wake any of the dead who happened to be snoozing at the moment.

He waited and waited and kept on waiting. Considering the amount of chimney he'd had to climb, he supposed it must be a couple of hundred miles to the bottom of the Tower, but, after awhile, even he was forced to admit that if the grate had been going to clang it would have done so by now. He poked his head up out of the hole and was immediately struck in the face by the end of a tree branch, while the sharp pungent smell of cypress cleaned the soot from his nostrils.

He shoved aside the tree branch and looked around to get his bearings. The strange and unfamiliar moon of this strange and unfamiliar Krynn was very bright this night, and Tasslehoff was at last able to see something, although that something was only more tree branches. Tree branches to the left of him, tree branches to the right. Tree branches up, and tree branches down. Tree branches as far as the eye could see. He looked over the edge of the chimney and found the grate, perched in a branch about six feet below him.

Tasslehoff tried to determine how far he was from the ground, but the branches were in the way. He looked to the side and located the top of one of the Tower's two broken minarets. The top was about level with him. That gave him some idea of how far he had climbed and, more importantly, how far the ground was below.

That was not a problem, however, for here were all these handy trees.

Tasslehoff pulled himself out of the chimney. Finding a sturdy limb, he crawled carefully out on it, testing his weight as he went. The limb was strong and didn't so much as creak. After chimney climbing, tree climbing was simple. Tasslehoff shinnied down the trunk, lowered himself from limb to friendly and supportive limb, and finally, as he gave a sigh of exultation and relief, his feet touched firm and solid ground.

Down here, the moonlight was not very bright, hardly filtering through the thick leaves at all. Tas could make out the Tower but only because it was a black, hulking blot amongst the trees. He could see, very far up, a patch of light and figured that must be the window in Dalamar's private chamber.

"I've made it this far, but I'm not out of the woods yet," he said to himself. "Dalamar told Palin we were near Solanthus. I recall someone saying something about the Solamnic Knights having a headquarters at Solanthus, so that seems like a good place to go to find out what's become of Gerard. He may be dull, and he certainly is ugly, and he doesn't like kender, but he is a Solamnic Knight, and one thing you can say about Solamnic Knights is that they aren't the type to send a fellow back in time to be stepped on. I'll find Gerard and explain everything to him, and I'm sure he'll be on my side."

Tasslehoff remembered suddenly that the last time he'd seen Gerard, the Knight had been surrounded by Dark Knights firing arrows at him. Tas was rather downhearted at this thought, but then it occurred to him that Solamnic Knights were plentiful and if one was dead, you could always find another.

The question now was, how to find his way out of the forest.

All this time he'd been on the ground, the dead were flowing around him like fog with eyes and mouths and hands and feet, moving past him and over him, but he hadn't really taken any notice, he'd been too busy thinking. He noticed now. Although being surrounded by dead people with their sad faces and their hands that plucked at one of his pouches wasn't the most comfortable experience in the world, he thought perhaps they might make up for being so extremely cold and creepy by providing him with directions.

"I say, excuse me, sir— Madam, excuse me— Hobgoblin, old chum, could you tell me— I beg your pardon, but that's my pouch. Hey, kid, if I give you a copper would you show— Kender! Fellow kender! I need to find a way to reach— Drat," Tasslehoff said after several moments spent in a futile attempt to converse with the dead. "They don't seem to see me. They look right through me. I'd ask Caramon, but just when he might be useful, he isn't around. I don't mean to be insulting," he added in irritable tones, trying without success to find a path through the cypress trees that pressed thick around him, "but there really are a lot of you dead people! Far more than is necessary."

He continued searching for a path—any sort of a path— but without much luck. Walking in the dark was difficult, although the dead were lit with a soft white light that Tas thought was interesting at first but after awhile, seeing that the dead looked very lost, sorrowful, and terrified, he decided that darkness—any darkness—would be preferable.

At least, he could put some distance between himself and Palin and Dalamar. If he, a kender who was never lost, was lost in these trees, he had no doubt that a mere human and a dark elf—wizards though they might be—would be just as lost and that by losing himself he was also losing them.

He kept going, bashing into trees and knocking his head against low branches, until he took a nasty tumble over a tree root and fell down onto a bed of dead cypress needles. The needles were sweet-smelling, at least, and they were decently dead—all brown and crispy—not like some other dead he could mention.

His legs were pleased that he wasn't using them anymore. The brown needles were comfortable, after you got used to them sticking you in various places, and, all in all, Tasslehoff decided that since he was down here he might as well take this opportunity to rest.

He crawled to the base of the tree trunk, settled himself as comfortably as possible, pillowing his head on a bed of soft green moss. It was not surprising, therefore, that the last thing he thought of, as he was drifting off to sleep, was his father.

Not that his father was moss-covered.

It was his father telling him, "Moss always grows on the side of a tree facing—"

Facing . . .

Tas closed his eyes.

Now, if he could just remember what direction . . .

"North," he said and woke himself up.

Realizing that he now could tell what direction he was traveling, he was about to roll over and go back to sleep when he looked up and saw one of the ghosts standing over him, staring down at him.

The ghost was that of a kender, a kender who appeared vaguely familiar to Tas, but then most kender appear familiar to their fellow kender since the odds are quite likely that in all their ambulations, they must have run into each other sometime.

"Now, look," said Tasslehoff, sitting up. "I don't mean to be rude, but I have spent most of the day escaping from the Tower of High Sorcery, and—as I am certain you know—escaping from sorcerous towers makes a fellow extremely tired. So if you don't mind, I'm just going to go to sleep."

Tas shut his eyes, but he had the feeling the ghost of the kender was still there, still looking down at him. Not only that, but Tas continued to see the ghost of the kender on the backs of his eyelids, and the more he thought about it the more he was quite certain he had definitely met that kender somewhere before.

The kender was quite a handsome fellow with a taste in clothes that others might have considered garish and outlandish but that Tasslehoff considered charming. The kender was festooned with pouches, but that wasn't unusual. What was unusual was the expression on the kender's face—sad, lost, alone, seeking.

A cold chill shivered through Tasslehoff. Not a thrilling, excited chill, like you feel when you're about to pull the glittering ring off the bony finger of a skeleton and the finger twitches! This was a nasty, sickening kind of chill that scrunches up the stomach and squeezes the lungs, making it hard to breathe. Tas thought he would open his eyes, then he thought he wouldn't. He squinched them shut very hard so they wouldn't open by themselves and curled into an even tighter ball. He knew where he had seen that kender before.

"Go away," he said softly. "Please."

He knew quite well, though he couldn't see, that the ghost hadn't gone away.

"Go away, go away, go away!" Tas cried frantically, and when that didn't work, he opened his eyes and jumped to his feet and yelled angrily at the ghost, "Go away!"

The ghost stood staring at Tasslehoff.

Tasslehoff stood staring at himself.

"Tell me," Tas said, his voice quivering, "why are you here? What do you want? Are you . . . are you mad because I'm not dead yet?"

The ghost of himself said nothing. It stared at Tas a little longer, then turned and walked away, not as if it wanted to but because it couldn't help itself. Tas watched his own ghost join a milling throng of other restless spirits. He watched until he could no longer distinguish his ghost from any other.

Tears stung his eyes. Panic seized him. He turned and ran as he had never run before. He ran and ran, not looking where he was going, smashing into bushes, caroming off tree trunks, falling down, getting up, running some more, running and running until he fell down and couldn't get up because his legs wouldn't work anymore.

Exhausted, frightened, horrified, Tasslehoff did something he had never done.

He wept for himself.

17 MISTAKEN IDENTITY

While Tasslehoff was recalling with fond nostalgia his travels with Gerard, it may be truthfully stated that at this time Gerard was not thinking fond thoughts about the kender. He wasn't thinking any sort of thoughts about the kender at all. Gerard assumed, quite confidently, that he would never have anything more to do with kender and put Tasslehoff out of his mind. The Knight had far more important and worrisome matters to consider.

Gerard wanted desperately to be back in Qualinesti, assisting Marshal Medan and Gilthas to prepare the city for the battle with Beryl's forces. In his heart, he was there with the elves. In reality, he was on the back of the blue dragon, Razor, flying north—the exact opposite direction from Qualinesti, heading for Solanthus.

They were passing over the northern portion of Abanasinia—Gerard was able to see the vast shining expanse of New Sea from the air—when Razor started to descend. The dragon informed Gerard that he needed to rest and eat. The flight over New Sea was long, and once they started out over the water there would be nowhere to stop until they reached land on the other side.

Although he grudged the time, Gerard was in wholehearted agreement that the dragon should be well-rested before the flight. The blue extended his wings to slow his descent and began to circle around and around, dropping lower with every rotation, his destination a large expanse of sandy beach. The sea was entrancing seen from above. Sunlight striking the water made it blaze like molten fire. The dragon's flight seemed leisurely to Gerard until

Razor drew closer to the ground, or rather, when the ground came rushing up to meet them.

Gerard had never been so terrified in his life. He had to clamp his teeth tightly shut to keep from shrieking at the dragon to slow down. The last few yards, the ground leaped up, the dragon plummeted down, and Gerard knew he was finished. He considered himself as brave as the next man, but he couldn't help but shut his eyes until he felt a gentle bump that rocked him slightly forward in the saddle. The dragon settled his muscular body comfortably, folded his wings to his sides and tossed his head with pleasure.

Gerard opened his eyes and spent a moment recovering from the ordeal, then climbed stiffly from the saddle. He'd been afraid to move during much of the flight for fear he'd fall, and now his muscles were cramped and sore. He hobbled around for a bit, groaning and stretching out the kinks. Razor watched him with condescending, if respectful, amusement.

Razor lumbered off to find something to eat. The dragon looked clumsy on land, compared to the air. Trusting that the dragon would keep watch, Gerard wrapped himself in a blanket and lay down on the sun-warmed sand. He meant only to rest his eyes. . . .

Gerard woke from the sleep he had never meant to take to find the dragon basking in sunlight, gazing out across the water. At first, Gerard thought he had been napping only a few hours, then he noted that the sun was in a much different portion of the sky.

"How long have I been asleep?" he demanded, clambering to his feet and shaking the sand out of his leathers.

"All the night and much of the morning," the dragon replied.

Cursing the fact that he had wasted time sleeping, noting that he had left the dragon burdened with the saddle, which was now knocked askew, Gerard began to apologize, but Razor passed it off.

At that, the dragon appeared uneasy, as if something were preying on his mind. Razor looked often at Gerard as if about to speak and then seemingly decided against it. He snapped his mouth shut and twitched his tail moodily. Gerard would have liked to have encouraged the dragon's confidences, but he did not feel they knew each other that well, so he said nothing.

He had a bad several minutes tugging and pulling the saddle back into position and redoing some of the harness, all the while conscious of more precious time slipping by. At last he had the saddle positioned correctly, or at least so he hoped. He had visions of his grand plans ending in failure as the saddle slid off the dragon in midflight, dumping Gerard to an ignominious death.

Razor was reassuring, however, stating that the saddle felt secure to him, and Gerard trusted to the dragon's expertise, having none of his own. They flew off just as dusk was settling over the sea. Gerard was concerned about flying at night, but as Razor sensibly pointed out, night flying was much safer these days than flying by daylight.

The dusk had a strange smoky quality to it that caused the sun to blaze red as it sank below the smudged horizon line. The smell of burning in the air made Gerard's nose twitch. The smoke increased, and he wondered if there was a forest fire somewhere. He looked down below to see if he could spot it but could find nothing. The gloom deepened and blotted out the stars and the moon, so that they flew in a smoke-tinged fog.

"Can you find your way in this, Razor?" Gerard shouted.

"Strangely enough, I can, sir," Razor returned. He fell into one of the uncomfortable silences again, then said abruptly, "I feel obliged to tell you something, sir. I must confess to a dereliction of duty."

"Eh? What?" Gerard cried, hearing only about one word in three. "Duty? What about duty?"

"I was waiting for your return at about noon time yesterday when I heard a call, sir. The call was as a trumpet, summoning me to war. I had never heard the like, sir, not even in the old days. I . . . I almost followed it, sir. I came close to forgetting my duty and departing, leaving you stranded. I will turn myself in for disciplinary action upon our return."

If this had been another human talking, Gerard would have said comfortingly that the man must have been dreaming. He couldn't very well say that to a creature hundreds of years older and more experienced than himself, so all he ended up saying was that the dragon had remained and that was what counted. At least Gerard knew now why Razor had appeared so uneasy.

Talk ended between them. Gerard could see nothing and only hoped that they would not fly headlong into a mountain in the darkness. He had to trust Razor, however, who appeared to be able to see where he was going, for he flew confidently and swiftly. At length Gerard relaxed enough to be able to pry loose his fingers from the saddle horn.

Gerard had no notion of the passing of time. It seemed they had been flying for hours, and he even dozed off again, only to wake with a horrific start in a cold sweat from a dream that he was falling to find that the sun was rising.

"Sir," said Razor. "Solanthus is in sight."

He could see the towers of a large city just appearing over the horizon. Gerard ordered Razor to land some distance from Solanthus, find a place where the blue could rest, and remain safely in hiding, not only from the Solamnic Knights, but from Skie, otherwise known as Khellendros, the great blue dragon, who had held his own against Beryl and Malystryx.

Razor found what he considered a suitable location. Under the cover of a cloud bank, he made an easy landing, spiraling downward in wide sweeping circles onto a vast expanse of grasslands near a heavily wooded forest.

The dragon smashed and trampled the grass when he landed, digging gouges into the dirt with his clawed feet and thrashing the grass with his tail. Anyone who came upon the site would be able to guess at once that some mighty creature had walked here, but this area was remote. A few farms could be seen, carved out of the forest. A single road wound snakelike through the tall grass, but it was several miles distant.

Gerard had sighted a stream from the air, and he was looking forward to nothing so much as a swim in the cool water. His own stench was so bad that he came near making himself sick, and he was itchy from sand and dried sweat. He would bathe and change clothes—rid himself of the leather tunic, at least, that marked him a Dark Knight. He'd have to enter Solanthus dressed like a farm hand—shirtless, clad only in his breeches. He had no way to prove he was a Solamnic Knight, but Gerard was not worried. His father had friends in the Knighthood, and almost certainly Gerard would find someone who knew him.

As for Razor, if the dragon asked why they were here, Gerard was prepared to explain that he was under Medan's orders to spy upon the Solamnic Knighthood.

The dragon did not ask questions. Razor was far more interested in discovering a place to hide and rest. He was in the territory of the mighty Skie now. The enormous blue dragon had discovered that he could gain strength and power by preying on his own kind, and he was hated and feared by his brethren.

Gerard was anxious that Razor find a hiding place. The dragon was graceful in the air, his wings barely moving as he soared silently on the thermals. On the ground, the blue was a lumbering monster, his feet trampling and smashing, his tail knocking over small trees, sending animals fleeing in terror. He brought down a stag with a snap of his jaws, and, hauling the carcass by the broken neck in his teeth, brought it along with him to enjoy at his leisure.

This made conversation difficult, but he answered Gerard's questions concerning Skie with grunts and nods. Strange rumors had circulated about the mighty blue dragon, who was the nominal ruler of Palanthas and environs. Rumors had it that the dragon had vanished, that he'd handed over control to an underling. Razor had heard these rumors, but he discounted them.

Investigating a depression in a rocky cliff to see if it would make a suitable resting place, Razor dropped the deer carcass by the bank of the stream.

"I believe that Skie is involved in some deep plot that will result in his downfall," Razor told Gerard. "If so, it will be a punishment for slaying his own kind. If we even are his own kind," he added, as an afterthought.

"He's a blue dragon, isn't he?" Gerard asked, looking longingly at the creek and hoping the dragon settled himself soon.

"Yes, sir," said Razor. "But he has grown so that he is far larger than any blue ever seen on Krynn before. He is larger than the reds—except Malystryx—a great bloated monster. My brethren and I have often commented on it."

"Yet he fought in the War of the Lance," said Gerard. "Is this satisfactory? There don't appear to be any caves."

"True, sir. He was a loyal servant to our departed queen. But one has to wonder, sir."

Unable to find a cave large enough to hold him, Razor pronounced the depression a good start, declared his intention to widen it by blasting chunks of rock out of the side of the cliff. Gerard watched from a safe distance as the blue dragon spat bolts of lightning that blew huge holes in the solid rock, sending boulders splashing into the water and causing the ground to shake beneath his feet.

Certain that the noise of the splitting rock, the blasting explosions, and the concussive thunder must be heard in Solanthus, he feared a patrol would be sent out to investigate.

"If the Solanthians hear anything at all, sir," Razor said during a rest break, "they will think it is merely a coming storm."

Once he had created his cave and the dust had settled and the numerous small avalanches had stopped, Razor retired inside to rest and enjoy his meal.

Gerard removed the saddle from the dragon's back—a proceeding that took some time since he was not familiar with the complicated harness. Razor offered his assistance, and once this was done and Gerard had dragged the heavy saddle into a corner of the cave, out of the way, he left the dragon to his meal and his slumber.

Gerard traveled downstream a good distance until he found a place shallow enough for bathing. He stripped off his leathers and undergarments and waded, naked, into the rippling stream.

The water was deep and cold. He gasped, shivered, and, gritting his teeth, plunged in headfirst. He was not a particularly good swimmer, so he stayed clear of the deeper part of the stream where the current ran swift. The sun was warm, the cold tingled his skin, felt invigorating. He began to splash and leap about, at first to keep the blood flowing and then because he was enjoying himself.

For a few moments, at least, he was free. Free of all his worries and anxieties, free of responsibility, free of anyone telling him what to do. For a few moments, he let himself be a child again.

He tried to catch fish with his bare hands. He dog-paddled beneath the overhanging willow trees. He floated on his back, enjoying the warmth of the sun on his skin and the refreshing contrasting cold of the water. He scrubbed off the caked-on dirt and blood with a handful of grass, all the while wishing he had some of his mother's tallow soap.

Once he was clean, he could examine his wounds. They were inflamed but only slightly infected. He had treated them with a salve given to him by the Queen Mother, and they were healing well. Peering at his reflection in the water, he grimaced, ran his hand over his jaw. He had a stubbly growth of beard, dark brown, not yellow, like his hair. His face was ugly enough without the beard, which was patchy and splotchy and looked like some sort of malignant plant life crawling up his jaw.

He thought back to the time in his youth when he'd tried in vain to grow the silky flowing mustache that was the pride of the Solamnic Knighthood. His mustache proved to be rough and bristly, stuck out every which way like his recalcitrant hair. His father, whose own mustache was full and thick, had taken his son's failure as a personal affront, irrationally blaming whatever was rebellious inside Gerard for manifesting itself through his hair.

Gerard turned to wade back to where he had left his leathers and his pack, intending to retrieve his knife and shave off the stubble. A flash of sunlight off metal half-blinded him. Looking up on the bank, he saw a Solamnic Knight.

The Knight was clad in a leather vest, padded for protection, worn over a knee-length tunic that was belted at the waist. The flash of metal came from a half-helm that covered the head but had no visor. A red ribbon fluttered from the top of the half-helm, the padded vest was decorated with a red rose.

A long bow slung over the shoulders indicated that the Knight had been out hunting, as evidenced by the carcass of a stag hanging over the back of a pack mule. The Knight's horse was nearby, head down, grazing.

Gerard cursed himself for not having kept closer watch. Had he been paying attention, instead of larking about like a schoolboy, he would have heard horse and rider approaching.

The Knight's booted foot was planted firmly atop Gerard's sword belt and sword. The Knight held a long sword in one gloved hand. In the other, a coil of rope.

Gerard could not see the Knight's face, due to the shadows of the trees, but he had no doubt that the expression would be grim and stern and undoubtedly triumphant.

He stood in the middle of the stream that was growing colder by the second and pondered on the odd quirk in human nature that makes us feel we are far more vulnerable naked than when wearing clothes. Shirt and breeches will not stop arrow, knife, or sword, yet had he been dressed, Gerard would have been able to face this Knight with confidence. As it was, he stood in the stream and gaped at the Knight with about as much intelligence as the fish that were making darts at his bare legs.

"You are my prisoner," said the Solamnic, speaking Common. "Come forth slowly and keep your hands raised so that I may see them."

Gerard's discomfiture was complete. The Knight's voice was rich and mellow and unquestioningly feminine. At that moment, she turned her head to glance warily about her, and he saw two long thick braids of glossy blue-black hair streaming out from beneath the back of the half-helm.

Gerard felt his skin burn so hot that it was a wonder the water around him didn't steam.

"Lady Knight," he said when he could find his voice, "I concede readily that I am your prisoner, at least for the moment, until I can explain the unusual circumstances, and I would do as you command, but I am . . . as you can see . . . not dressed."

"Since your clothes are here on the bank, I did not think that you would be," the Knight returned. "Come out of the water now."

Gerard thought briefly of making a dash for it to the opposite bank, but the stream ran deep and swift, and he was not that good a swimmer. He doubted if he could manage it. He pictured himself floundering in the water, drowning, calling for help, destroying what shreds of dignity he might have left.

"I don't suppose you would turn your head, Lady, and allow me to dress myself?" he asked.

"And let you stab me in the back?" Laughing she leaned forward. "Do you know, Knight of Neraka, I find it amusing that you, a champion of evil, who has undoubtedly slaughtered any number of innocents, burned villages, robbed the dead, looted, and raped, are such a shrinking lily."

She was pleased with her joke. The emblem of the Dark Knights on which her foot rested, was the skull and the lily.

"If it makes you feel better," the Lady Knight continued, "I have served in the Knighthood for twelve years, I have held my own in battle and tourney. I have seen the male body not only unclothed but ripped open. Which is how I will view yours if you do not obey me." She raised her sword. "Either you come out or I will come in after you."

Gerard began to splash through the water toward the bank. He was angry now, angry at the mocking tone of the woman, and his anger in part alleviated his embarrassment. He looked forward to fetching his pack and exhibiting his letter from Gilthas, proving to this female jokester that he was a true Knight of Solamnia here on an urgent mission and that he probably outranked her.

She watched him carefully every step of the way, her face evincing further amusement at the sight of his nakedness—not surprising, since his skin was shriveled like a prune, and he was blue and shaking with the cold. Arriving at the bank, he cast one furious glance at her and reached for his clothes. She continued to stand with her foot on his sword, her own sword raised and at the ready.

He dressed himself in the leather trousers he'd brought with him. He was going to ignore the tunic, that lay crumpled on the bank, hoping that she might not notice the emblem stitched on the front. She lifted it with the tip of her sword, however, and tossed it at him.

"Wouldn't want you to get sunburned," she said. "Put it on. Did you have a nice flight?"

Gerard's heart sank, but he made a game try. "I don't know what you mean. I walked—"

"Give it up, Neraka," she said to him. "I saw the blue dragon. I saw the beast land. I marked its trail and followed it and found you." She regarded him with interest, all the while keeping the sword pointed at him and dangling the length of rope in her hands. "So what were you intending to do, Neraka? Spy on us, maybe? Pretend to be some loutish farm lad coming to the city for a good time? You appear to have the lout part down well."

"I am not a spy," he said through teeth clenched to keep them from chattering. "I know that you're not going to believe this, but I am not a Dark Knight of Neraka. I am a Solamnic, like yourself—"

"Oh, that is rich! A blue Solamnic riding a blue dragon." The Lady Knight laughed heartily, then flicked her hand and, with alacrity tossed the loop of rope over his head. "Don't worry. I won't hang you here, Neraka. I mean to take you back to Solanthus. You can tell your tale to an admiring audience. The inquisitor has been in low spirits these days. You'll cheer him right up, I'm sure."

She jerked the rope, grinned to see Gerard grab it to keep from choking. "Whether you arrive there alive, half-alive, or barely breathing is up to you."

"I'll prove it," Gerard stated. "Let me open my pack—"

He looked down on the ground. The pack was not there.

Gerard searched frantically along the riverbank. No pack. And then he remembered. He had left the pack with the letter hooked to the dragon's saddle. The saddle and the pack were back in the cave with the blue dragon.

He bowed his head that was dripping wet, too overwhelmed to swear. The hot words were in his heart but they couldn't make it past the lump in his throat to reach his tongue. Raising his head, he looked at the Lady Knight, looked her full in the eyes that, he noted, were tree-leaf green.

"I swear to you, Lady, on my honor as a true Knight that I am a Solamnic. My name is Gerard uth Mondar. I am stationed in Solace, where I am one of the honor guard for the Tomb of the Last Heroes. I can offer no proof of what I say, I admit that, but my father is well known among the Knighthood. I am certain there are Lord Knights in Solanthus who will recognize me. I have been sent to bring urgent news to the Council of Knights in Solanthus. In my pack, I have a letter from Gilthas, king of the elves—"

"Ah, yes," she said, "and in my pack I have a letter from Mulberry Miklebush, queen of the kender. Where is this pack with this wonderful letter?"

Gerard muttered something.

"I didn't catch that, Neraka?" She bent nearer.

"It's attached to the saddle of the . . . blue dragon," he said glumly. "I could go fetch it. I give you my word of honor that I would return and surrender myself."

She frowned slightly. "I don't, by any chance, have hay stuck in my hair, do I?"

Gerard glared at her.

"I thought I might," she said. "Because you obviously think I have just fallen out of the hay wagon. Yes, Sweet Neraka, I'll accept the word of honor of a blue dragonrider, and I'll let you run off and fetch your pack *and* your blue dragon. Then I'll wave my hankie to you as you both fly away."

She prodded him in the belly with her sword.

"Get on the horse."

"Listen, Lady," Gerard said, his anger and frustration growing. "I know that this looks bad, but if you'll use that steel-covered head of yours for thinking, you'll realize that I'm telling the truth! If I were a real dragonrider of Neraka, do you think you'd be standing here poking me with that sword of yours? You'd be food for my dragon about now. I am on an urgent mission. Thousands of lives are at stake— Stop that, damn you!"

She had been prodding him with her sword at every third word, steadily forcing him to fall back until he bumped into her horse. Furious, he thrust aside the sword with his bare hand, slicing open his palm.

"I do love to hear you talk, Neraka," she said. "I could listen to you all day, but, unfortunately, I go on duty in a few hours. So mount up, and let's be off."

Gerard was now so angry that he was seriously tempted to summon the dragon. Razor would make short work of this infuriating female, who had apparently been born with solid steel in her head instead of on top of it. He controlled his rage, however, and mounted the horse. Knowing full well what she intended to do with him, he put his hands behind his back, wrists together.

Sheathing her sword, keeping a firm grip on the rope that was around his neck, she tied his wrists together with the same length of rope, adjusting it so that if he moved his arms or any part of his body, he'd end up strangling himself. All the while, she kept up her jocular banter, calling him Neraka,

Sweet Neraka, and Neraka of Her Heart and other mocking endearments that were galling in the extreme.

When all was ready, she took her horse's reins and led the horse through the forest at a brisk walk.

"Aren't you going to gag me?" Gerard demanded.

She glanced over her shoulder. "Your words are music to my ears, Neraka. Speak on. Tell me more about the king of the elves. Does he dress in green gossamer and sprout wings from his back?"

"I could yet summon the dragon," Gerard stated. "I do not because I do not want to hurt you, Lady Knight. This proves what I have been telling you, if you'd only think about it."

"It might," she conceded. "You may well be telling the truth. But you may well not be telling the truth. You might not be summoning the dragon because the beasts are notoriously untrustworthy and unpredictable and would just as soon kill you as me. Right, Neraka?"

Gerard was beginning to understand why she had not gagged him. He could think of nothing to say that would not incriminate himself or make matters worse. Her argument about the evil nature of blue dragons was one he might have made himself before he had come to know Razor. Gerard had no doubt that if he summoned Razor to deal with this Knight, the dragon would make short work of her and leave Gerard untouched. But while Gerard would have preferred Razor to this annoying female as a traveling companion any day, he could not very well countenance the horrible death of a fellow Solamnic, no matter how obnoxious she might be.

"When I reach Solanthus, I will send a company to slay the dragon," she continued. "He cannot be far from here. Judging from the explosions I heard, we will have no trouble finding evidence of his hiding place."

Gerard was reasonably certain that Razor could take care of himself, and that left him concerned for the welfare of his fellow Knights. He decided that the best course of action he could take now was to wait until he came before the council. Once there, he could explain himself and his mission. He was confident the council would believe him, despite his lack of credentials. Undoubtedly there would be someone on the council who knew him or knew his father. If all went well, he would return to Razor and both he, the dragon, and a force of Knights would fly to Qualinesti. After this Knight had made her most abject and humble apologies.

They left the wooded stream bank behind, entered the grasslands not far from where the dragon had alighted. Gerard could see in the distance the road leading to Solanthus. The tops of the city's towers were just visible over the tips of the tall grass.

"There is Solanthus, Neraka," she said, pointing. "That tall building there on your left is—"

"My name is *not* Neraka. My name is Gerard uth Mondar. What are you called," he asked, adding in a muttered undertone, "besides godawful?"

"I heard that!" she sang out. She glanced at him over her shoulder. "My name is Odila Windlass."

"Windlass. Isn't that some sort of mechanical device on board a ship?"

"It is," she replied. "My people are seafaring.".

"Pirates, no doubt," he remarked caustically.

"Your wit is as small and shriveled as certain other parts of you, Neraka," she returned, grinning at his embarrasment.

They had reached the road by now, and their pace increased. Gerard had ample opportunity to study her as she walked alongside him, leading the horse and the pack mule. She was tall, considerably taller than he was, with a shapely, muscular build. She did not have the dark skin of the seafaring Ergothians. Her skin was the color of polished mahogany, indicating a blending of races somewhere in her past.

Her hair was long, falling in two braids to her waist. He had never seen such black hair, blue-black, like a crow's wing. Her brows were thick, her face square-jawed. Her lips were her best feature, being full, heart-shaped, crimson, and prone to laughter, as she had already proven.

Gerard would not concede that she had any good features. He had little use for women, considering them conniving, sneaking, and mercenary. Of the women he distrusted and disliked most, he decided that dark-haired, dark-complexioned female Knights who laughed at him ranked at the top of his list.

Odila continued to talk, pointing out the sights of Solanthus on the theory that he would get to see little of the city from his cell in the dungeons. Gerard ignored her. He went over in his mind what he was going to say to the Knights' Council, how best to portray the admittedly sinister-looking circumstances of his arrival. He rehearsed the eloquent words he would use to present the plight of the beleaguered elves. He hoped against hope that someone would know him. He was forced to concede that in the irritating female's place, he would not have believed him either. He had been a dolt for forgetting that pack.

Recalling the desperate situation of the elves, he wondered what they were doing, how they were faring. He thought back to Marshal Medan, Laurana, and Gilthas, and he forgot himself and his own troubles in his earnest concern for those who had come to be his friends. So lost in thought was he that he rode along without paying attention to his surroundings and was astonished to look up and realize that night had fallen while they were on the road and that they had reached the outer walls of Solanthus.

Gerard had heard that Solanthus was the best fortified city in all of Ansalon, even surpassing the lord city of Palanthas. Now, gazing up at the immense walls, black against the stars, walls that were only the outer ring of defenses, he could well believe it.

An outer curtain wall surrounded the city. The wall consisted of several layers of stone packed with sand, slathered over with mud and then covered with more stone. On the other side of the curtain wall was a moat. Gates in several locations pierced the curtain wall. Large drawbridges led over the moat. Beyond the moat was yet another wall, this one lined with murder holes and slits for archers. Large kettles that could be filled with boiling oil were positioned at intervals. On the other side of this wall, trees and bushes had been planted so that any enemy succeeding in taking this wall would not be able to leap down into the city unimpeded. Beyond that lay the streets of the city and its buildings, the vast majority of which were also constructed of stone.

Even at this late hour, people stood at the gatehouse waiting to enter the city. Each person was stopped and questioned by the gatehouse guards. Lady Odila was well known to the guards and did not have to stand in line, but was passed through with merry jests about her fine "catch" and the success of her hunting.

Gerard bore the jokes and crude comments in dignified silence. Odila kept up the mirth until one guard, at the last post, shouted, "I see you had to hog-tie this man to keep him, Lady Odila."

Odila's smile slipped. The green leaf eyes glittered emerald. She turned and gave the guard a look that caused him to flush red, sent him hastening back into the guardhouse.

"Dolt," she muttered. She tossed her black braids, affected to laugh, but Gerard could see that the verbal arrow had struck something vital in her, drawn blood.

Odila led the horse among the crowds in the city streets. People stared at Gerard curiously. When they saw the emblem on his chest, they jeered and spoke loudly of the executioner's blood-tipped axe.

A slight flutter of doubt caused Gerard a moment's unease, almost a moment's panic. What if he could not convince them of the truth? What if they did not believe him? He pictured himself being led to the block, protesting his innocence. The black bag being drawn over his head, the heavy hand pressing his head down on the bloodstained block. The final moments of terror waiting for the axe to fall.

Gerard shuddered. The images he conjured up were so vivid that he broke out into a cold sweat. Berating himself for giving way to his imagination, he forced himself to concentrate on the here and now.

He had presumed, for some reason, that Lady Odila would take him immediately before the Knights' Council. Instead, she led the horse down a dark and narrow alley. At the end stood an enormous stone building.

"Where are we?" he asked.

"The prison house," said Lady Odila.

Gerard was amazed. He had been so focused on speaking to the Knights' Council that the idea that she should take him anywhere else had never occurred to him.

"Why are you bringing me here?" he demanded.

"You have two guesses, Neraka. The first—we're attending a cotillion. You are going to be my dancing partner, and we're going to drink wine and make love to each other all night. Either that"— she smiled sweetly— "or you're going to lock you up in a cell."

She ordered the horse to halt. Torches burned on the walls. Firelight glowed yellow from a square, barred window. Guards, hearing her approach, came running to relieve her of her prisoner. The warden emerged, wiping the back of his hand across his mouth. They'd obviously interrupted his dinner.

"Given a choice," said Gerard acidly, "I'll take the cell."

"I'm glad," Odila said, with a fond pat on his leg. "I would so hate to see you disappointed. Now, alas, I must leave you, Sweet Neraka. I am on duty. Don't pine away, missing me."

"Please, Lady Odila," said Gerard, "if you can be serious for once, there must be someone here who knows the name uth Mondar. Ask around for me. Will you do that much?"

Lady Odila regarded him for a moment with quiet intensity. "It might prove amusing, at that." She turned away to speak to the warden. Gerard had the feeling he had made an impression on her, but whether good or bad, whether she would do what he had asked or not, he could not tell.

Before she left, Lady Odila gave a concise account of all of Gerard's crimes—how she'd seen him fly in on a blue dragon, how he had landed far outside the city, and how the dragon had taken pains to hide himself in a cave. The warden regarded Gerard with a baleful eye and said that he had an especially strong cell located in the basement that was tailor-made for blue dragonriders.

With a parting gibe and a wave of her hand, Lady Odila mounted her horse, grabbed the reins of the pack mule, and cantered out of the yard, leaving Gerard to the mercies of the warden and his guards.

In vain Gerard protested and argued and demanded to see the Knight Commander or some other officer. No one paid the least attention to him. Two guards hauled him inside with ruthless efficiency, while two other guards stood ready with huge spiked-tipped clubs should he make an attempt to escape. They cut loose his bonds, only to replace the rope with iron manacles.

The guards hustled him through the outer rooms where the warden had his office and the jailer his stool and table. The iron keys to the cells hung on hooks ranged in neat rows along the wall. Gerard caught only a glimpse of this, before he was shoved and dragged, stumbling, down a stair that ran straight and true to a narrow corridor below ground level. They led him to his cell with torches—he was the only prisoner down on this level, apparently—and tossed him inside. They gave him to know that there was a bucket for his waste and a straw mattress for sleeping. He would receive two meals a day, morning and night. The door, made of heavy oak with a small iron grate in the top, began to close. All this happened so fast that Gerard was left dazed, disbelieving.

The warden stood in the corridor outside his cell, watching to make certain to the last that his prisoner was safe.

Gerard flung himself forward, wedging his body between the wall and the door.

"Sir!"—he pleaded—"I must speak before the Knights' Council! Let them know Gerard uth Mondar is here! I have urgent news! Information—"

"Tell it to the inquisitor," said the warden coldly.

The guards gave Gerard a brutal shove that sent him staggering, manacles clanking, back into his cell. The cell door shut. He heard the sounds of their feet clomping up the stairs. The torch light diminished and was gone. Another door slammed at the top of the stairs.

Gerard was left alone in darkness so complete and silence so profound that he might have been cast off this world and left to float in the empty nothingness that was said to have existed long before the coming of the gods.

18 BERYL'S MESSENGER

Marshal Medan sat stolidly at his desk in his office that was located in the massive and ugly building the Knights of Neraka had constructed in Qualinost. The Marshal considered the building every bit as ugly as did the elves, who averted their eyes if they were forced to walk anywhere near its hulking, gray walls, and he rarely entered his own headquarters. He detested the barren, cold rooms. Due to the humid air, the stone walls accumulated moisture and always seemed to be sweating. He felt stifled whenever he had to remain here extended periods of time and the feeling was not in his imagination. For the greater protection of those inside, the building had no windows, and the smell of mold was all-pervasive.

Today was worse than ever. The smell clogged his nose and gave him a swelling pain behind his eyes. Due to the pain and the pressure, he was listless and lethargic, found it difficult to think.

"This will never do," he said to himself and was just about to leave the room to take a refreshing walk outside when his second-in-command, a Knight named Dumat, knocked at the wooden door.

The Marshal glowered, returned to seat himself behind the desk, and gave a horrific snort in an effort to clear his nose.

Taking the snort for permission to enter, Dumat came in, carefully shutting the door behind him.

"He's here," he said, with a jerk of his thumb over his shoulder.

"Who is it, Dumat?" Medan asked. "Another draco?"

"Yes, my lord. A bozak. A captain. He's got two baaz with him. Bodyguards, I'd say."

Medan gave another snort and rubbed his aching eyes.

"We can handle three dracos, my lord," said Dumat complacently.

Dumat was a strange man. Medan had given up trying to figure him out. Small, compact, dark-haired, Dumat was in his thirties, or so Medan supposed. He really knew very little about him. Dumat was quiet, reserved, rarely smiled, kept to himself. He had nothing to say of his past life, never joined the other soldiers in boasting of exploits either on the battlefield or between the sheets. He had come to the Knighthood only a few years earlier. He told his commander only what was necessary for the records and that, Medan had always guessed, was probably all lies. Medan had never been able to figure out why Dumat had joined the Knights of Neraka.

Dumat was not a soldier. He had no love for battle. He was not prone to quarreling. He was not sadistic. He was not particularly skilled at arms, although he had proven in a barracks brawl that he could handle himself in a fight. He was even-tempered, though there were smoldering embers in the dark eyes that told of fires burning somewhere deep inside. Medan had never been more astonished in his life than the day almost a year ago when Dumat had come to him and said that he had fallen in love with an elven woman and wanted to make her his wife.

Medan had done all he could to discourage relations between elves and humans. He was in a difficult situation, dealing with explosive racial tensions, trying to retain control of a populace that actively hated its human conquerors. He had to maintain discipline over his troops, as well. He laid down strict rules against rape and those who, in the early days of the elven occupation, broke the rules were given swift, harsh punishment.

But Medan was experienced enough in the strange ways of people to know that sometimes captive fell in love with captor and that not all elf women found human males repulsive.

He had interviewed the elf woman Dumat wanted to marry, to make certain she was not being coerced or threatened. He found that she was not some giddy maiden, but a grown woman, a seamstress by trade. She loved Dumat and wanted to be his wife. Medan represented to her that she would be ostracized from the elven community, cut off from family and friends. She had no family, she told him, and if her friends did not like her choice of husband, they were no true friends. He could not very well argue this point, and the two were married in a human ceremony, since the elves would not officially recognize such a heinous alliance.

The two lived happily, quietly, absorbed in each other. Dumat continued to serve as he had always done, obeying orders with strict discipline. Thus, when Medan had to decide which of his Knights and soldiers he could trust, he had chosen Dumat as among those few to remain with him to assist in the last defense of Qualinost. The rest were sent away south to assist the Gray Robes in their continuing fruitless and ludicrous search for the magical Tower of Wayreth. Medan had told Dumat plainly what he faced, for the

Marshal would not lie to any man, and had given him a choice. He could stay or take his wife and depart. Dumat had agreed to stay. His wife, he said, would remain with him.

"My lord," said Dumat, "is something wrong?"

Medan came to himself with a start. He had been woolgathering, staring at Dumat all the while so that the man must be wondering if his nose was on crooked.

"Three draconians, you said." Medan forced himself to concentrate. The danger was very great, and he could not afford any more mental lapses.

"Yes, my lord. We can deal with them." Dumat was not boastful. He was merely stating a fact.

Medan shook his head and was sorry he'd done so. The pain behind his eyes increased markedly. He gave another ineffectual snort. "No, we can't keep killing off Beryl's pet lizard men. She will eventually get suspicious. Besides, I need this messenger to report back to the great green bitch, assure her that all is proceeding according to plan."

"Yes, my lord."

Medan rose to his feet. He eyed Dumat. "If something goes wrong, be prepared to act on my command. Not before."

Dumat gave a nod and stepped aside to allow his commander to precede him, falling into step behind.

"Captain Nogga, my lord," said the draconian, saluting.

"Captain," said the Marshal, advancing to meet the draconian.

The bozak was enormous, topping Medan by a lizard head, massive shoulders and wing tips. The baaz bodyguards—shorter, but just as muscular—were attentive, alert, and armed to the teeth, of which they had a good many.

"Her Majesty Beryl has sent me," Captain Nogga announced. "I am to apprise you of the current military situation, answer any questions you might have, and take stock of the situation in Qualinost. Then I am to report back to Her Majesty."

Medan bowed his acknowledgment. "You must have had a perilous journey, Captain. Traveling through elven territory with only a small guard. It is a wonder you were not attacked."

"Yes, we heard that you were having difficulty maintaining order in this realm, Marshal Medan," Nogga returned. "That is one of the reasons Beryl is sending in her army. As to how we came, we flew here on dragonback. Not that I fear the pointy-ears," he added disparagingly, "but I wanted to take a look around."

"I hope you find everything to your satisfaction, Captain," Medan said, not bothering to hide his ire. He had been insulted, and the draconian would have thought it strange if he did not respond.

"Indeed, I was pleasantly surprised. I had been prepared to find the city in an uproar, with rioting in the streets. Instead I find the streets almost empty. I must ask you, Marshal Medan, where are the elves? Have they escaped? Her Majesty would be most unhappy to hear that."

"You flew over the roads," Medan said shortly. "Did you see hordes of refugees fleeing southward?"

"No, I did not," Nogga admitted. "However—"

"Did you see refugees heading east, perhaps?"

"No, Marshal, I saw nothing. Therefore I—"

"Did you notice, as you flew over Qualinost, on the outskirts of the city, a large plot of cleared land, freshly dug-up ground?"

"Yes, I saw it," Nogga replied impatiently. "What of it?"

"That is where you will find the elves, Captain," said Marshal Medan.

"I don't understand," Captain Nogga said.

"We had to do something with the bodies," Medan continued offhand-edly. "We couldn't leave them to rot in the streets. The elderly, the sickly, the children, and any who put up resistance were dispatched. The rest are being retained for the slave markets of Neraka."

The draconian scowled, his lips curled back. "Beryl gave no orders concerning slaves going to Neraka, Marshal."

"I respectfully remind you and Her Majesty that I receive my orders from Lord of the Night Targonne, not from Her Majesty. If Beryl wishes to take up the matter with Lord Targonne, she may do so. Until then, I follow my lord's commands."

Medan straightened his shoulders, a movement that brought his hand near his sword hilt. Dumat had his hand on his sword hilt, and he moved quietly, with seeming nonchalance, to stand near the two baaz. Nogga had no idea that his next words might be his last. If he demanded to see the mass grave or the slave pens, the only thing he would end up seeing would be Medan's sword sticking out of his scaly gut.

As it was, the draconian shrugged. "I am acting on orders myself, Marshal. I am an old soldier, as are you. Neither of us has any interest in politics. I will report back to my mistress and, as you so wisely suggest, urge her to talk it over with your Lord Targonne."

Medan eyed the draconian intently, but, of course, there was no way to read the expression on the lizard's face. He nodded and, removing his hand from his sword hilt, strode past the draconian to stand in the doorway, where he could take a breath of fresh, sweet-scented air.

"I have a complaint to register, Captain." Medan glanced over his shoulder at Nogga. "A complaint against a draconian. One called Groul."

"Groul?" Nogga was forced to clump over to where Medan stood. The draconian's eyes narrowed. "I intended to ask about Groul. He was sent here almost a fortnight ago, and he has not reported back."

"Nor will he," said Medan brusquely. He drew in another welcome breath of fresh air. "Groul is dead."

"Dead!" Nogga was grim. "How did he die? What is this about a complaint?"

"Not only was he foolish enough to get himself killed," Medan stated, "he killed one of my best agents, a spy I had planted in the house of the Queen Mother." He cast a scathing glance at Nogga. "In future, if you must send draconian messengers, make certain that they arrive sober."

Now it was Nogga's turn to bristle. "What happened?"

"We are not certain," Medan said, shrugging. "When we found the two of them—Groul and the spy—they were both dead. At least we have to assume that the pile of dust next to the elf's corpse was Groul. What we do know is that Groul came here and delivered to me the message sent by Beryl. He had already imbibed a fair quantity of dwarf spirits. He reeked of them. Presumably after he left me, he fell in with the agent, an elf named Kalindas. The elf had long complained over the amount of money he was being paid for his information. My guess is that Kalindas confronted Groul and demanded more money. Groul refused. The two fought and killed each other. Now I am short one spy, and you are short one draconian soldier."

Nogga's long, lizard tongue flicked from between his teeth. He fiddled with his sword hilt.

"Strange," said Nogga at last, his red-eyed gaze intent upon the Marshal, "that they should end up slaying each other."

"Not so strange," Medan returned dryly. "When you consider that one was soused and the other was slime."

Nogga's teeth clicked together. His tail twitched, scraping across the floor. He muttered something that Medan chose to ignore.

"If that is all, Captain," the Marshal said, turning his back yet again upon the draconian and walking toward his office, "I have a great deal of work to do. . . ."

"Just a moment!" Nogga rumbled. "The orders Groul carried stated that the Queen Mother was to be executed and her head given over to Beryl. I assume these orders have been carried out, Marshal. I will take the elf's head now. Or did yet another strange circumstance befall the Queen Mother?"

Pausing, Medan rounded on his heel. "Surely the dragon was not serious when she gave those orders?"

"Not serious!" Nogga scowled.

"Beryl's sense of humor is well known," said the Marshal. "I thought Her Majesty was having a jest with me."

"It was no jest, I assure you, my lord. Where is the Queen Mother?" Nogga demanded, teeth grating.

"In prison," Medan said coolly. "Alive. Waiting to be handed over to Beryl as my gift when the dragon enters Qualinost in triumph. Orders of Lord Targonne."

Nogga had opened his mouth, prepared to accuse Medan of treachery. The draconian snapped it shut again.

Medan knew what Nogga must be thinking. Beryl might consider herself the ruler of Qualinesti. She might consider the Knights to be acting under her auspices, and in many ways they were. But Lord Targonne was still in command of the Dark Knights. More importantly, he was known to be in high favor with Beryl's cousin, the great red dragon Malystryx. Medan had been wondering how Malys was reacting to Beryl's sudden decision to move troops into Qualinesti. In that snap of Nogga's jaws, Medan had his answer.

Beryl had no desire to antagonize Targonne, who would most certainly run tattling to Malys that he was being mistreated.

"I will see the elf bitch," Nogga said sullenly. "To make certain there are no tricks."

The Marshal gestured toward the stairs that led to the dungeons located below the main building. "The corridor is narrow," the Marshal said, when the baaz would have followed after their commander. "We will all be a tight fit."

"Wait here," Nogga growled to the baaz.

"Keep them company," said Medan to Dumat, who nodded and almost, but not quite, smiled.

The draconian stumped down the spiral stairs. Cut out of the bedrock, the stairs were rough and uneven. The dungeons were located far underground, and they soon lost the sunlight. Medan apologized for not having thought to bring a torch with him and hinted that perhaps they should go back.

Nogga brushed that aside. Draconians can see well in the darkness, and he was having no difficulty. Medan followed several paces after the captain, groping his way in the darkness. Once, quite by accident, he stepped hard on Nogga's tail. The draconian grunted in irritation. Medan apologized politely. They wound their way downward, finally arrived at the bottom of the stairs.

Here torches burned on the walls, but by some strange fluke they gave little light and created a great deal of smoke. Reaching the bottom of the stairs, Nogga blinked and grumbled, peering this way and that in the thick atmosphere. Medan shouted for the gaoler, who came to meet them. He wore a black hood over his head, in the manner of an executioner, and was a grim and ghostly figure in the smoke.

"The Queen Mother," Medan said.

The gaoler nodded and led them to a cell that was nothing more than an iron-barred cage set into a rock wall. He pointed silently inside.

An elf woman crouched on the floor of the cell. Her long golden hair was lank and filthy. Her clothes were rich, but torn and disheveled, stained with dark splotches that might have been blood. Hearing the Marshal's voice, she rose to meet them, stood facing them defiantly. Although there were six cells in the dungeon, the rest were empty. She was the only prisoner.

The draconian approached the cell. "So this is the famous Golden General. I saw the elf witch once long ago in Neraka at the time of the fall."

He looked her up, and he looked her down, slowly, insultingly.

Laurana stood at ease, calm and dignified. She regarded the draconian steadfastly, without flinching. Marshal Medan's hand clasped spasmodically over the hilt of his sword.

I need this lizard alive, he reminded himself.

"A pretty wench," said Nogga with a leer. "I remember thinking so at the time. A fine wench to bed, if one can stomach the stench of elf."

"A wench who proved something of a disaster to you and your kind," Medan could not refrain from observing, though he realized almost the moment the words were said that the remark had been made a mistake.

Nogga's eyes flared in anger. His lips curled back from his teeth, the tip of his long tongue flicked out. Staring at Laurana, he sucked his tongue in with a seething breath. "By the lost gods, elf, you will not look at me so smugly when I am through with you!"

The draconian seized hold of the iron-barred door. Muscles on his gigantic arms bunched. With a jerk and a pull, he wrenched the door free of its moorings and flung the door to one side, nearly crushing the gaoler, who had to make a nimble jump to save himself. Nogga bounded inside the cell.

Caught off guard by the draconian's sudden violent outburst, Medan cursed himself for a fool and leaped to stop him. The gaoler, Planchet, was closer to the draconian, but his way was impeded by the iron door that Nogga had tossed aside and that was now leaning at a crazy angle against one of the other cells.

"What are you doing, Captain?" Medan shouted. "Have you lost your senses? Leave her alone! Beryl will not want her prisoner damaged."

"Bah, I'm only having a little fun," Nogga growled, reaching out his hand. Steel flashed. From the folds of her dress, Laurana snatched a dagger. Nogga skidded to a halt, his clawed feet scraping against the stone floor. He stared down in astonishment to find the dagger pressed against his throat.

"Don't move," Laurana warned, speaking the draconian's own language.

Nogga chuckled. He had recovered from his initial amazement. Defiance added spice to his lust, and he knocked aside the dagger with his clawed hand. The blade slit his scaled skin, spattering blood, but he ignored the wound. He seized hold of Laurana. Still holding the dagger, she stabbed at him, while she struggled in his strong grasp.

"I said let her go, Lizard!"

Locking his fists together, Medan struck Nogga a solid thwack on the back of the head. The blow would have felled a human, but Nogga was barely distracted by it. His clawed hands tore at Laurana's dress.

Planchet finally managed to kick aside the cell door. Grabbing hold of a flaring torch, he brought it down on the draconian's head. Cinders flew, the torch broke in half.

"I'll be back to you in a moment," Nogga promised with a snarl and flung Laurana against the wall. Teeth bared, the draconian turned to face his assailants.

"Don't kill him!" Medan ordered in Elvish, and punched the draconian in the gut, a blow that doubled him over.

"Do you think there's a chance we might?" Planchet gasped, driving his knee into the draconian's chin, snapping his head back.

Nogga sank to his knees, but he was still trying to regain his feet. Laurana grabbed hold of a wooden stool and brought it down on the draconian's head. The stool smashed into splinters, and Nogga slumped to the floor. The draconian lay on his belly, legs spraddled, the fight gone out of him at last.

The three of them stood breathing heavily, eyeing the draconian.

"I am deeply sorry, Madam," said Medan, turning to Laurana.

Her dress was torn. Her face and hands were spattered with the draconian's blood. His claws had raked across the white skin of her breasts. Drops of blood oozed from the scratches, sparkled in the torchlight. She smiled, exultant, grimly triumphant.

Medan was enchanted. He had never seen her so beautiful, so strong and courageous, and at the same time so vulnerable. Before he quite knew what he was doing, he put his arms around her, drew her close.

"I should have known the creature would try something like this," Medan continued remorsefully. "I should never have put you at such risk, Laurana. Forgive me."

She lifted her gaze to meet his. She said a soft word of reassurance and then, ever so gently, she slipped out of his grasp, her hand drawing the tatters of her dress modestly over her breasts.

"No need to apologize, Marshal," she said, her eyes alight with mischief. "To be truthful, I found it quite exhilarating."

She looked down at the draconian. Her voice hardened, her hand clenched. "Many of my people have already given their lives in this battle. Many more will die in the last fight for Qualinost. At last I feel I am doing my share, small though that may be."

When she looked back up at him, the mischief sparkled. "But I fear we have damaged your messenger, Marshal."

Medan grunted something in response. He dared not look at Laurana, dared not remember her warmth as she had rested, just a moment, in his arms. All these years, he had been proof against love, or so he had convinced himself. In reality, he had fallen in love with her long ago, pierced through by love for her, for the elven nation. What bitter irony that only now, at the end, had he come to fully understand.

"What do we do with him, sir?" Planchet asked. The elf was limping, favoring a sore knee.

"I'll be damned if I'm going to haul that heavy carcass of his up the stairs," Medan said harshly. "Planchet, escort your mistress to my office. Bolt the door behind you and remain there until you receive word that it is safe to leave. On your way there, tell Dumat to come down here and bring those baaz with him."

Planchet removed his cloak and wrapped it around Laurana's shoulders. She held the cloak fast over her torn dress with one hand and placed her other hand on Medan's arm. She looked up into his eyes.

"Are you certain you will be all right, Marshal?" she asked softly.

She was not talking about leaving him alone with the draconian. She was talking about leaving him alone with his pain.

"Yes, Madam," Medan said, and he smiled in his turn. "Like you, I found it exhilarating."

She sighed, lowered her gaze, and for a moment it seemed as if she would say something else. He didn't want to hear it. He didn't want to hear her say that her heart was buried with her husband Tanis. He didn't want to hear that he was jealous of a ghost. It was enough for him to know that she respected him and trusted him. He took hold of her hand, as it lay on his arm. Lifting her fingers, he pressed them to his lips. She smiled tremulously, reassured, and allowed Planchet to lead her away.

Medan remained in the dungeons alone, glad of the quiet, glad of the smoke-tinged darkness. He massaged his aching hand and, when he was once more master of himself, he picked up the bucket of water that they used to douse the torches and flung the filthy liquid in Captain Nogga's face.

Nogga snuffled and spluttered. Shaking his head muzzily, he heaved himself up off the floor.

"You!" he snarled and swung round, waving his meaty fist. "I'll have you—"

Medan drew his sword. "I would like nothing better than to drive this steel into your vitals, Captain Nogga. So don't tempt me. You will go back to Beryl, and you will tell Her Majesty that in accord with the orders of my commander, Lord Targonne, I will turn over the elven capital of Qualinost to her. I will, at the same time, hand over the Queen Mother, alive and undamaged. Understood, Captain?"

Nogga glanced around, saw that Laurana was gone. His red eyes glinted in the darkness. He wiped a dribble of blood and saliva from his mouth, regarded Medan with a look of inveterate hatred.

"At that time, I will return," said the draconian, "and we will settle the score that lies between us."

"I look forward to it," said Medan politely. "You have no idea how much."

Dumat came running down the stairs. The baaz were right behind him, weapons in hand.

"Everything is under control," Medan stated, returning his sword to its sheath. "Captain Nogga forgot himself for a moment, but he has remembered again."

Nogga gave an incoherent snarl and slouched out of the cell, wiping away blood and spitting out a broken tooth. Motioning to the baaz, he made his way back up the stairs.

"Provide an honor guard for the captain," Medan ordered Dumat. "He is to be escorted safely to the dragon that brought him here."

Dumat saluted and accompanied the draconians up the stairs. Medan lingered a moment longer in the darkness. He saw a splotch of white on the floor, a tattered bit of Laurana's dress, torn off by the draconian. Medan reached down, picked it up. The fabric was as soft as gossamer. Smoothing it gently with his hand, he tucked it into the cuff of his shirt sleeve, and then went upstairs to see the Queen Mother safely home.

19 DESPERATE GAME

The great green dragon, Beryl, flew in wide circles over the forests of Qualinesti and tried to do away with her doubts by reassuring herself that all was proceeding as planned. As *she* planned. Events were moving forward at a rapid pace. Too rapid, to her mind. She had ordered these events. She. Beryl. No other. Therefore why the strange and nagging feeling that she was not in control, that she was being pushed, rushed? That someone at the gaming table had jostled her elbow, causing her to toss the dice before the other players had laid down their bets.

It had all started so innocently. She had wanted nothing more than what was rightfully hers—a magical artifact. A wondrous magical artifact that had no business being in the hands of the crippled, washed-up human mage who had acquired it—mistakenly at that, from some runt of a mewling kender. The artifact belonged to her. The artifact was in her territory, and everything in her territory belonged to her. All knew that. No one could dispute the point. In her quite rightful effort to acquire this artifact, she had somehow ended up sending her armies to war.

Beryl blamed her cousin Malystryx.

Two months ago, the green dragon had been happily wallowing in her leafy bower with never a thought of going to war against the elves. Well, perhaps that was not quite true. She had been building up her armies, using the vast wealth amassed from the elves and humans under her subjugation to buy the loyalties of legions of mercenaries, hordes of goblins and hobgoblins, and as many draconians as she could lure to her with promises of loot, rapine, and murder. She held these slavering dogs on a tight leash, tossing them bits of elf now and again to whet their appetites. Now she had unleashed them. She had no doubt that she would win.

Yet, she sensed that there was another player in the game, a player she could not see, a player watching from the shadows, one who was betting on another game: a bigger game with higher stakes. A player who was betting that she, Beryl, would lose.

Malystryx, of course.

Beryl did not watch the north for Solamnic Knights with their silver dragons or the mighty blue dragon Skie. The silvers had purportedly vanished, according to her spies, and it was common knowledge—again among her spies—that Skie had gone mad. Obsessed with a human master, he had disappeared for a time, only to return with some story of having been in a place he called the Gray.

Beryl did not watch the east where lived the black dragon Sable. The slimy creature was content with her foul miasma. Let her rot there. As to the white, Frost, the white dragon did not live who could challenge a green of Beryl's power and cunning. No, Beryl watched the northeast, watched for red eyes that remained constantly on the horizon of her fear.

Now it seemed Malystryx had made her move at last, a move that was both unexpected and cunning. The Green had discovered only days earlier that almost all her minion dragons—dragons native to Krynn, who had sworn allegiance to Beryl—had deserted her. Only two red dragons remained and she did not trust them. Had never trusted reds. No one could tell her for certain where the others had gone, but Beryl knew. These lesser dragons had switched sides. They had gone over to Malystryx. Her cousin was undoubtedly laughing at Beryl right now. Beryl gnashed her teeth and belched a cloud of noxious gas, spewed it forth as if she had her treacherous cousin in her claws.

Beryl saw Malys's game. The Red had tricked her. Malys had forced Beryl to enter into this war against the elves, forced her to commit her troops to the south, all the while building up her strength as Beryl expended hers. Malys had tricked Beryl into destroying the Citadel of Light—those Mystics had long been stinging parasites beneath Malys's scales. Beryl suspected now that Malys had been the one to plant the magical device where Beryl would hear of it.

Beryl had considered calling back her armies, but she immediately abandoned that plan. Once unleashed, the dogs would never return to her hand. They had the smell, the taste of elven blood, and they would not heed her call. Now she was glad that she had not.

From her vast height, Beryl looked down in pride to see the enormous snake that was her military might winding its way through the thick forests of Qualinesti. Its forward movement was slow. An army marches on its stomach, so the saying goes. The troops could move only as fast as the heavily laden supply wagons. Her forces dared not forage, dared not live off the land, as they might have done. The animals and even the vegetation of Qualinesti had entered the fray.

Apples poisoned those who ate them. Bread made from elven wheat sickened an entire division. Soldiers reported comrades strangled by vines or killed by trees that let fall huge limbs with crushing force. This was a foe easily defeated, however. This foe could be fought with fire. Clouds of smoke from the burning forests of Qualinesti turned day into night over much of Abanasinia. Beryl watched the smoke billowing into the air, watched the prevailing winds carry it westward. She breathed in the smoke of the dying trees in delight. As her armies moved slowly but inexorably forward, Beryl grew stronger daily.

As for Malys, she would smell the smoke of war, and she would sniff in it the stench of her own doom.

"For though you may have tricked me into acting, Cousin," Beryl told those wrathful red eyes glowering at her from the west, "you have done me a favor. Soon I will rule over a vast territory. Thousands of slaves will do my bidding. All of Ansalon will hear of my victory over the elves. Your armies will desert you and flock to my standard. The Tower of High Sorcery at Wayreth will be mine. No longer will the wizards be able to hide it and its powerful magicks from me. The longer you skulk in the shadows, waiting, the stronger I grow. Soon your great ugly skull will crown my totem, and I will be the ruler of Ansalon."

Thus Beryl began already to calculate her winnings. Still she could not rid herself of the disquieting feeling that from somewhere in the shadows, outside the circle, another player waited, another player watched.

Far, far below, eyes did watch Beryl, but they were not the eyes of a player in this game, or at least, he could not flatter himself that he was a player. His were the bones that rattled in the cup and were flung upon the table, to bounce about aimlessly until they came to rest ignominiously in a corner and the winner was declared.

Gilthas stood at the hidden entrance to one of the underground tunnels, keeping watch on Beryl. The dragon was enormous, huge, monstrous. Her scaled body, bloated, misshapen, was so ponderous that it seemed impossible her wings could lift the loathsome mass of flesh off the ground. Impossible until one noticed the thick and heavy musculature of the shoulders and the sheer width and breadth of the wingspan. Her shadow spread across the land, blotting out the haze-dimmed sun, turning bright day to horrid night.

Gilthas shivered as the shadow of the dragon's wings swept over him, chilling him. Although the wings were soon gone, he felt as if he remained in the black shadow of death.

"Is it safe, Your Majesty?" a quivering voice asked.

No, you foolish child! Gilthas wanted to rage. No it is not safe! Nowhere in this wide world is safe for us. The dragon keeps watch on us from the sky day and night. Her army, thousands strong, marches on the land, killing, burning. They have blotted out the very sun with the smoke of death. We may delay them, at the cost of precious lives, but we cannot stop them. Not this time. We run, but where do we run to? Where is the safe haven we seek? Death. Death is the only refuge. . . .

"Your Majesty," called the voice again.

Gilthas roused himself with an effort. "It is not safe," he cautioned in low tones, "but for the moment the dragon is gone. Come now quickly! Quickly."

This tunnel was one of many tunnels built by the dwarves who were helping hundreds of elven refugees escape the city of Qualinost and smaller settlements to the north, areas that had already fallen to Beryl's army. The tunnel's entrance was only a couple of miles south of the city proper—the dwarves had extended their tunnels to reach the city itself, and even now, as Gilthas spoke to these refugees, who had been caught above ground, other elves walked through the tunnel behind him.

The elves had begun to evacuate Qualinost six days ago, the day Gilthas had informed the people that their land was under attack by the forces of the dragon Beryl. He had told the elves the truth, the brutal truth. The only hope they had of surviving this war was to leave behind that which they loved most, their homeland. Even then, though they might survive as a people, Gilthas had not been able to give them any assurance that they would survive as a nation.

He had given the Qualinesti their orders. The children must leave. They were the hope of the race, and they should be protected. Caretakers for the children should go with them, be it mothers, fathers, grandparents, aunts, uncles, cousins. Those elves who were able to fight, those who were trained warriors, were asked to stay behind to fight the battle to defend Qualinost.

He had not promised the elves that they would escape to a safe haven for he could not promise that they would find such a haven. He would not tell his people comforting lies. Too long, the Qualinesti people had slept snugly beneath the blanket of comforting lies. He had told them the truth and, with quiet fortitude, they had accepted it.

He had been proud of his people in that moment and in the sorrowful moments that came after. Mates parted, one to go with the children, the other staying behind. Those remaining kissed their children lovingly, held them close, bade them be good and be obedient. As Gilthas told his people no lies, the elven parents told their children none. Those staying behind did not promise that they would see their loved ones again. They bade them do only one thing: Remember. Always remember.

At Gilthas's gesture, the elves who had been in hiding slipped out from the shadows of the trees, whose leafy boughs had provided them protection from Beryl's searching eyes. The forest had been quiet with the coming of the dragon, animal noises hushed, bird song silenced. All living things crouched, trembling, until Beryl had passed. Now that the dragon was gone, the forest came alive. The elves took their children by their hands, assisting the elderly and the infirm, and slid and slipped down the sides of a narrow ravine. The tunnel's entrance was at the bottom, concealed by a lean-to made of tree branches.

"Hurry!" Gilthas motioned, keeping watch for the dragon's return. "Hurry!"

The elves hastened past him and into the darkness of the tunnel beyond, where they were met by dwarves, who pointed out the way to go. One of those dwarves who was gesturing and saying in Elvish, "Left, left, keep to the left, mind that puddle there," was Tarn Bellowsgranite, King of the Dwarves. He was dressed as any dwarven laborer, his beard caked with dirt, and his boots covered in mud and crushed rock. The elves never guessed his royal stature.

The elves looked relieved at first when they reached the safety of the dark tunnel and they were glad to duck inside. As they confronted the line of dwarves, pointing and gesturing for them to move deeper below ground, relief changed to unease. Elves are not happy below ground. They do not like confined places. They like to see the sky above their heads and the branching trees and breathe the fresh air. Below ground, they feel stifled and closed in. The tunnels smelled of darkness, of black loam and the gigantic worms, the Urkhan, that burrowed through the rock. Some elves hesitated, glanced back outside, where the sun shone brightly. One older elf, whom Gilthas recognized as belonging to the Thon-Thalas, the elven Senate, turned around and started to go back.

"I can't do this, Your Majesty," the senator said to Gilthas in apology. He was gasping for breath, his face was pale. "I'm suffocating! I'll die down there!"

Gilthas started to reply, but Tarn Bellowsgranite stepped forward, blocked the senator's path.

"Good sir," said the dwarf, cocking one eye at the elf senator, "yes, it's dark down here and, yes, it smells bad, and, yes, the air is not the freshest. But, consider this, good sir." Tarn raised one grubby finger. "How dark will it be inside the dragon's belly? How bad will *that* smell?"

The senator looked down at the dwarf and managed a wan smile. "You are right, sir. I had not considered that particular argument. It is a cogent one, I admit."

The senator looked back down the corridor. He looked outside, drew a deep breath of fresh air. Reaching out, he touched Gilthas on the hand, a mark of respect. Bowing to the dwarf, the elf ducked his head, and plunged into the tunnel, holding his breath, as if he would hold it for the miles he would have to travel below ground.

Gilthas smiled. "You've said those words before, Thane, I'll wager."

"Many times," said the dwarf, stroking his beard and grinning. "Many times. If not me, then the others." He gestured to the dwarven helpers. "We use the same argument. It never fails." He shook his head. "Elves living below ground. Who would have thought it, eh, Your Majesty?"

"Someday," said Gilthas in reply, "we'll have to teach dwarves to climb trees."

Bellowsgranite snorted, laughed at the thought. Shaking his head, he went stomping down the tunnel, shouting encouragement to the dwarves who were working to keep the passageway clear of falling rock and to make certain the braces they used to shore up the tunnel were strong and secure.

The last elves to enter the tunnel were a group of twelve, members of a single family. The eldest daughter, who had almost come into her majority, had volunteered to take the children. Father and mother—both trained warriors—would remain to fight to save their city.

Gilthas recognized the girl, remembered her from the masquerade he had held not so long ago. He remembered her dancing, dressed in her finest silken gown, her hair adorned with flowers, her eyes shining with happiness and excitement. Now her hair was uncombed and unwashed, adorned with the dead leaves in which she had been hiding. Her dress was torn and travel-stained. She was frightened and pale, but resolute and firm, not giving way to her fear, for the younger children looked to her for courage.

The journey from Qualinost had been slow. Since the day Beryl had caught a group of elves on the road and killed them all with a blast of her poisonous breath, the elves had dared not travel in the open. The elves had kept to the forests for protection, holding as still as the rabbit in the presence of the fox when the green dragon swept overhead. Thus their progress was slow, heartbreakingly slow.

As Gilthas watched, the girl picked up a toddler from a nest of leaves and pine needles. Summoning the other children to her side, she ran toward the tunnel. The children followed her, the elder children carrying the younger on their backs.

Where was she going? Silvanesti. A land that was to this girl nothing more than a dream. A sad dream, for she had heard all her life that the Silvanesti disliked and distrusted their Qualinesti cousins. Yet now she was on her way to beg them for sanctuary. Before they could even reach Silvanesti, she and her siblings would have to travel miles below ground, then emerge to cross the arid, empty Plains of Dust.

"Quickly, quickly!" Gilthas urged, thinking he caught a glimpse of the dragon above the treetops.

When the last child was inside, he reached out, grabbed the tree-branch lean-to, and dragged it across the opening, concealing it from sight.

The girl paused inside the tunnel to take a quick head count. Satisfied all her brood were with her, she managed a smile for Gilthas and, lifting her head and adjusting the toddler to more comfortable position on her back, started to enter the tunnel proper.

One of the younger boys held back. "I don't want to go, 'Trina," he said, his voice quavering. "It's dark in here."

"No, no, it's not," said Gilthas. He pointed to a globe, hanging from the ceiling. A soft warm glow shone from inside the globe, illuminating the darkness. "You see that lantern?" Gilthas asked the child. "You'll find those lanterns all through the tunnel. Do you know what makes that light?"

"Fire?" asked the boy doubtfully.

"A baby worm," said Gilthas. "The adult worms dig the tunnels for us, and their young light our way. You're not afraid now, are you?"

"No," said the young elf. His sister cast him a scandalized look, and he flushed. "I mean, no, Your Majesty."

"Good," said Gilthas. "Then off you go."

A deep voice sang out in Dwarvish, repeating it in Elvish, "Make way! Worm a'coming! Make way!"

The dwarf spoke in Elvish but as if he had a mouthful of rocks. The children did not understand. Gilthas made a jump for the girl. "Get back!" he shouted to the other children. "Get back against the wall! Quickly!"

The floor of the tunnel began to shake.

Catching hold of the startled girl, he dragged her out of the center of the tunnel. She was terrified, and the child she carried began to wail in fear. Gilthas took the toddler in his arms, soothed her as best he could. The other children crowded around him, wide-eyed, staring. Some began to whimper.

"Watch this," he said, smiling at them. "No need to be afraid. These are our saviors."

The head of one of the gigantic worms the dwarves used for burrowing came into sight at the far end of the tunnel. The worm had no eyes, for it was accustomed to living in darkness below ground. Two horns protruded from the top of its head. A dwarf, seated in a large basket on the worm's back, held the reins of a leather harness in his hands. The harness wrapped around the two horns and allowed the wormrider to guide the Urkhan as an elf rider guided his horse.

The worm paid little attention to the dwarf on its back. The Urkhan was interested only in its dinner. The worm spewed liquid onto the solid rock at the side of the tunnel. The worm-spit hissed on the rock, began to bubble. Large chunks of rock split apart and fell to the tunnel floor. The Urkhan's maw opened, seized a chunk, and swallowed it.

The worm crawled nearer, a fearsome sight. Its enormous, undulating, slime-covered body was reddish brown in color and filled half the tunnel. The floor of the tunnel shook beneath the worm's weight. Urkhan wranglers, as they were called, helped the rider guide the worm by reins attached to straps wrapped around its body.

As the worm came closer to Gilthas and the children, it suddenly swung its blind head around, started to veer toward their side of the tunnel. For one moment, Gilthas feared they would be crushed. The girl clutched at him. He pressed her back against the wall, shielding her and as many of the children as he could with his body.

The wranglers knew their business and were quick to react. Bawling loud curses, the dwarves began to drag on the reins and beat on the Urkhan with their fists and sticks. The creature gave a great, snuffling snort and, shaking its huge head, turned back to its meal.

"There now, you see. That wasn't so bad," Gilthas said cheerfully.

The children did not look particularly reassured, but at a sharp word from their sister they fell back into line and began to straggle down the tunnel, keeping wary eyes on the worm as they crept past it.

Glithas remained behind, waiting. He had promised his wife that he would meet her at the entrance to the tunnel. He was starting to return to the entryway when felt her hand upon his shoulder.

"My love," she said.

Her touch was gentle, her voice soft and soothing. She must have entered the tunnel when he was helping the children. He smiled to see her, and the darkness of despair the dragon had brought down on him departed in the glow of the larva light that glistened in her mane of golden hair. A kiss or two was all they had time to share, for both had news to impart and urgent matters to discuss.

Both began speaking simultaneously.

"My husband, the news we heard is true. The shield has fallen!"

"My wife, the dwarves have agreed!"

They both stopped, looked at each other, and laughed.

Gilthas could not remember the last time he had laughed or heard his wife laugh. Thinking this a good omen, he said, "You first."

She was about to continue, then she glanced around, frowned. "Where is Planchet? Where are your guards?"

"Planchet remained behind to help the Marshal foil some draconians. As to my guards, I ordered them to return to Qualinost. Don't scold, my dear." Gilthas smiled. "They are needed there to help ready the defenses. Where are your guards, Madam Lioness?" he asked in mock severity.

"Around," she said, smiling. Her elf soldiers could be quite close at hand, and he would never see them or hear them, not unless they wanted him to. Her smile faded from her lips and eyes. "We came upon the young elf girl and the children. I offered to send one of my people with her, but she refused. She said she would not think of taking a warrior from the battle."

"A few weeks ago she danced at her first ball. Now, she cowers in a tunnel and runs for her life." He could not go on for a moment for the emotion choking him. "What courage our people have!" he said huskily.

The two stood in the tunnel. The floor shook beneath them. The dwarven wranglers bellowed and shouted. Dwarves crouched by the entrance, waiting to assist more refugees. Other elves, coming from farther down the tunnel, walked past them. Seeing their king, they nodded and smiled and acted as if this, escaping through a dark and shaking tunnel, guided by dwarves, were an everyday occurrence.

Clearing his throat, Gilthas said, more briskly, "You have verified the first reports we heard?"

The Lioness brushed a tangle of her shining hair from her face. "Yes, but what the fall of the shield means, whether this is good or bad, cannot be told."

"What happened? How did this come about? Did the Silvanesti lower it themselves?"

She shook her head, and the golden, curling, rampant mass of hair that gave her the nickname of the Lioness covered her face once more. Fondly, her husband smoothed the locks back with his hand. He loved to look upon her face. Some noble Qualinesti elven women, with their cream and rose-petal complexions, looked with disdain on the Kagonesti, whose skin was tanned a deep brown from days spent in the sunshine.

Unlike his face, wherein one could see traces of his human heritage in his square jaw and slightly more rounded eyes, her face was all elven: heart-shaped, with almond eyes. Her features were strong, not delicate, her gaze bold and decisive. Seeing him look at her with love and admiration, the Lioness captured his hand, kissed his palm.

"I have missed you," she said softly.

"And I, you." He sighed deeply, drew her close. "Will we ever be at peace, do you think, Beloved? Will there ever be a time when we can sleep until long,

long after sunrise, then wake and spend the rest of the day doing nothing except loving each other?"

She did not answer him. He kissed the mane of hair and held her close.

"What of the shield?" he said at last.

"I talked to a runner who saw it was down, but when he tried to find Alhana and her people, they had moved on. That is not unexpected. Alhana would have immediately crossed the border into Silvanesti. We may not hear anything more from her for some time."

"I had not let myself hope that this news was true," Gilthas said, "but you ease my care and lift my fear. By lowering the shield, the Silvanesti show they are willing to enter the world again. I will send emissaries immediately to tell them of our plight and ask for their aid. Our people will travel there and find food and rest and shelter. If our plans fail and Qualinost falls, with our cousins' help, we will build a large army. We will return to drive the dragon from our homeland."

The Lioness put her hand over his mouth. "Hush, Husband. You are spinning steel out of moonbeams. We have no idea what is happening in Silvanesti, why the shield was lowered, what this may portend. The runner reported that all living things that grew near the shield were either dead or dying. Perhaps this shield was not a blessing to the Silvanesti but a curse.

"There is also the fact," she added relentlessly, "that our cousins the Silvanesti have not acted very cousinly in the past. They named your Uncle Porthios a dark elf. They have no love for your father. They deem you a half-breed, your mother something worse."

"They cannot deny us entry," Gilthas said firmly. "They will not. You will not deprive me of my moonbeams, my dear. I believe the lowering of the shield is a sign of a change of heart among the Silvanesti. I have hope to offer our people. They will cross the Plains of Dust. They will reach Silvanesti, and once there our cousins will welcome them. The journey will not be easy, but you know better than anyone the courage that lives in the hearts of our people. Courage such as we saw in that young girl."

"Yes, the journey will be hard," the Lioness said, regarding her husband earnestly. "Our people will succeed, but they will need a leader: one who will urge us to keep going when we are tired and hungry and thirsty and there is no rest, no food, no water. If our king travels with us, we will follow him. When we arrive in Silvanesti, our king must be our emissary. Our king must speak for us, so that we do not seem a mob of beggars."

"The senators, the Heads of House—"

"—will squabble among themselves, Gilthas, you know that. One third will want to march west instead of east. Another third will want to march north instead of south. And the other third will not want to march at all. They will fight over this for months. If they ever did manage to reach Silvanesti, the first thing they would do is drag up all the quarrels for the past three centuries, and that will be an end to everything. You, Gilthas. You are the only one who has a hope of making this work. You are the only one who can unify the various factions and lead the people across the desert. You are the only one who can smooth the way with the Silvanesti."

"And yet," Gilthas argued, "I cannot be in two places at once. I cannot fight to defend Qualinost and lead our people into the Plains of Dust."

"No, you cannot," the Lioness agreed. "You must put someone else in charge of the defense of Qualinost."

"What sort of king flees to safety and leaves his people to die in his stead?" Gilthas demanded frowning.

"The sort of king who makes certain that the last sacrifice of those who stay behind will not be made in vain," said his wife. "Do not think that because you do not remain to fight the dragon that you will have the easier task. You are asking a people born to the woods, born to lush gardens and bountiful water, to venture into the Plains of Dust, an arid land of shifting sand dunes and blazing sun. Place me in charge of Qualinost—"

"No," he said shortly. "I will not hear of it."

"My love—"

"We will not discuss it. I have said no, and I mean it. How can I do what you tell me I must do, without you at my side?" Gilthas demanded, his voice rising in his passion.

She gazed at him in silence, and he grew calmer.

"We will not speak of this anymore," he told her.

"Yet we must speak of it sometime."

Gilthas shook his head. His lips compressed into a tight, grim line. "What other news?" he asked abruptly.

The Lioness, who knew her husband's moods, understood that continuing to argue would be fruitless. "Our forces harass Beryl's armies. Yet, their numbers are so great that we are as gnats attacking a pack of ravening wolves."

"Withdraw your people. Order them south. They will be needed to guard the survivors if Qualinost falls."

"I thought that would be your command," she said. "I have already done so. From now on, Beryl's troops will move unimpeded, looting and burning and killing."

Gilthas felt the hope that had warmed his blood seep away, leaving him once again despairing, chilled.

"Yet we will have our revenge upon her. You said that the dwarves have agreed to your plan." The Lioness, sorry she had spoken so harshly, tried to lift him from the dark mood she saw settling on him.

"Yes," he said. "I spoke to Tarn Bellowsgranite. Our meeting was fortuitous. I had not expected to find him in the tunnels. I had thought I would have to ride to Thorbardin to speak with him, but he has taken charge of the work himself, and thus we were able to settle the matter at once."

"He knows that perhaps some of his own people may die defending elves?"

"He knows better than I can tell him what the cost will be to the dwarves. Yet they are willing to make the sacrifice. 'If once the great green dragon swallows Qualinesti, she will next have an appetite for Thorbardin,' he told me."

"Where is the dwarven army?" the Lioness demanded. "Skulking underground, prepared to defend Thorbardin. An army of hundreds of thousands, doughty warriors. With them, we could withstand Beryl's assault—"

"My dear," said Gilthas, gently, "the dwarves have a right to defend their homeland. Would we elves rush to their aid if they were the ones attacked? They have done much for us. They have saved the lives of countless people, and they are prepared to sacrifice their lives for a cause that is not their own. They should be honored, not castigated."

The Lioness glared at him, defiant for a moment, then she said with a shrug and a rueful smile. "You are right, of course. You see both sides, whereas I see only one. This is why I say again, you must be the one to lead our people."

"I said we would speak of this later," Gilthas returned, his voice cool.

"I wonder," he said, changing the subject, "does that young girl cry when she is alone and wakeful in the night, her charges slumbering around her, trusting in her even when the darkness is deep?"

"No," the Lioness answered. "She does not cry, for one of them might wake and see her tears and lose faith."

Gilthas sighed deeply, held his wife close. "Beryl has crossed the border into our land. How many days before the army reaches Qualinost?"

"Four," the Lioness replied.

20 THE MARCH INTO NIGHTLUND

Mina's small army, only a few hundred in number, made up of the group of Knights who had followed her from the ghastly valley of Neraka to Sanction to Silvanesti, and now to this strange land.

The dragons flew through darkness so deep that Galdar could not see Captain Samuval flying on the dragon next to him. Galdar could not even see his own dragon's long tail or wings for the darkness that shrouded them. He saw one dragon only and that was the strange dragon Mina rode, the death dragon, for it shimmered with a ghostly iridescence that was both terrible and beautiful. Red, blue, green, white, red-blue, as two of the souls of the dead dragons combined, then white-green, constantly changing until he grew dizzy and was forced to look away.

But his gaze was drawn back to the death dragon, marveling, awed. He wondered how Mina found courage to ride a beast that seemed as insubstantial as the morning mist, for he could see through the dragon, see the darkness beyond it. Mina had no qualms apparently, and her faith was justified, for the dragon bore her safely through the skies of Ansalon and deposited her gently and reverently on the ground.

The other dragons landed on a vast plain, allowed their riders to dismount, then took to the air again.

"Listen for my call," Mina told the dragons. "I will have need of you."

The dragons—giant reds and fleet blues, sly blacks, aloof whites and cunning greens—bowed low their heads, spread their wings, and bent their proud necks before her. The death dragon circled once above her head and then vanished as if it had been absorbed into the darkness. The other dragons lifted their wings and flew away, heading different directions. Their departure created a great wind that nearly blew the men over. The dragons were gone, and they were left on foot, with no mounts, in a strange land, with no idea where they were.

It was then Mina told them.

"Nightlund," she said.

Once this land had been ruled by a Solamnic Knight named Soth. Given the chance by the gods to halt the Cataclysm, Lord Soth had failed and brought down a curse upon himself and the land. Since the time of the Cataclysm, other doomed souls, both living and dead, had found in Nightlund a place of refuge and they had come to dwell within its deep shadows. Hearing that the land had become a hideout for those fleeing the law, the Solamnic Knights, who ruled this land, had made several attempts to clean them out. These proved futile, and soon the Knights quit entering the forest, leaving it to Soth, the accursed knight, to rule. Nightlund was a no-man's-land, where none of the living came, if they could help it,

This land had an evil reputation, even among the Dark Knights of Neraka, for the dead had no allegiances to any government of the living. Mina's Knights and soldiers formed ranks and marched after her without a murmur of complaint. They were so confident of her now, they believed in her—and in the One God—so strongly, that they did not question her judgment.

Mina's soldiers entered Nightlund with impunity. They encountered no enemy—living or dead. They marched beneath huge cypress trees that had been old at the time of the forging of the Graygem. They saw no living creature, no squirrel or bird, mouse or chipmunk, no deer or bear. They saw no dead, either, for none of them possessed magic, and thus the dead took no interest in them. But the soldiers and knights sensed the dead around them, sensed it as one senses he is being watched by unseen eyes. After several days of marching through the eerie forest, the men who had followed Mina into Nightlund without hesitation were starting to have second thoughts.

The fur on the back of Galdar's neck prickled and twitched, and he was continually whipping his head around to see if something was creeping up on him. Captain Samuval complained—in low tones and only when Mina could not hear him—that he had "the horrors." When asked what malady this might be, he could not explain, except to say that it made his feet and hands cold so that no fire could warm them and gave him an ache in his belly. The sharp crack of a falling branch sent men diving to the ground, to lie quivering in terror until someone told them what it was. Shamefaced, they would rise and carry on.

The men doubled the watch at night, though Mina told them that they had no need to set a watch at all. She did not explain why, but Galdar guessed that they were being guarded by those who had no more need of sleep. He did not find this particularly reassuring, and he often woke from a dream of hundreds of people standing around him, staring down at him with eyes that were empty of all except pain.

Mina was strangely silent during this march. She walked in the front of the line, refused all company, said no word to any man, yet Galdar could sometimes see her lips moving, as though she were speaking. When he once ventured to ask to whom she spoke, she replied, "To them," and made a sweeping gesture with her hand that encompassed nothing.

"The dead, Mina?" Galdar asked hesitantly.

"The souls of the dead. They have no more need of the shells that once housed them."

"You can see them?"

"The One God gives me that power."

"But I can't."

"I could cause you to see them, Galdar," Mina said to him, "but you would find it most unpleasant and disconcerting."

"No, Mina, no, I don't want to see them," Galdar said hastily. "How . . . how many of them are there?"

"Thousands," she replied. "Thousands upon thousands and thousands more after that. The souls of all who have died in this world since the Chaos War, Galdar. That is how many. And more join their ranks daily. Elves dying in Silvanesti and Qualinesti, soldiers dying defending Sanction, mothers dying in childbirth, children dying of sickness, the elderly dying in their beds—all these souls are flowing into Nightlund in a vast river. Brought here by the One God, prepared to do the bidding of the One God."

"You said since the end of the Chaos War. Where did the souls go before that?"

"The blessed souls went to other realms beyond. Cursed souls were doomed to remain here, until they learned the lessons they were meant to learn in life. Then they, too, left for the next stage. The old gods encouraged the souls to leave. The old gods gave the souls no choice. The old gods ignored the fact that the souls did not want to depart. They longed to remain within the world and do what they could to assist the living. The One God saw this and granted the souls the gift that they could remain in the world and serve the One God. So they do, Galdar. And so they will."

Mina looked at him with her amber eyes. "You would not want to leave, would you, Galdar?"

"I would not want to leave you, Mina," he replied. "That is what I fear most about dying. That I would have to leave you."

"You never will, Galdar," Mina said to him, her voice gentle. The amber warmed. Her hand touched his arm, and her touch was as warm as the amber. "I promise you that. You never will."

Galdar was uneasy. He hesitated to say the next, for fear she would be displeased, but he was her second-in-command, and he was responsible not only to her but to those under his command.

"How long are we going to stay here, Mina? The men don't like it in this forest. I can't say that I blame them. The living have no place here. We're not wanted."

"Not long," she said. "I must pay a visit to someone who lives within this forest. Yes, he *lives*," she emphasized the word. "A wizard by the name of Dalamar. Perhaps you've heard of him?"

Galdar shook his head. He had as little to do with wizards as possible and took no interest in them or their business.

"After that," Mina continued, "I must leave for a brief time—"

"Leave?" Galdar repeated, involuntarily raising his voice.

"Leave?" Captain Samuval came hurrying over. "What is this? Who is leaving?"

"Mina," said Galdar, his throat constricting.

"Mina the only reason the troops stay is because of you," said Samuval. "If you go—"

"I will not be gone long," said Mina, frowning.

"Long or short, Mina, I'm not sure we can control the men," said Captain Samuval. He kept jerking his head about, constantly looking over his shoulder. "And I don't blame them. This land is cursed. Ghosts crawl all over it. I can feel them crawling all over me!"

He shivered and rubbed his arms and glanced fearfully about. "You can't see them except out of the corner of your eye. And when you look at them, they're gone. It's enough to drive a man stark, staring mad."

"I will speak to the men, Captain Samuval," Mina replied. "You and Galdar must speak to them, as well, and you must show them by example that you are not afraid."

"Even though we are," the minotaur growled.

"The dead will not harm you. They have been ordered to congregate here for one purpose and one purpose alone. The One God commands them. They serve the One God, and through the intercession of the One God, they serve me."

"What is this purpose, Mina? You keep saying that, but you tell us nothing."

"All will be revealed. You must be patient and have faith," Mina said. The amber eyes cooled and hardened.

Galdar and Samuval exchanged glances. Samuval held still, no longer jerked his head about or rubbed his arms, afraid of offending Mina.

"How long will you be gone?" Galdar asked.

"You will come with me to the wizard's Tower. Then I travel north, to speak to the dragon who rules Palanthas, the dragon known as Khellendros or, as I prefer to call him, Skie."

"Skie? He's not even around anymore. All know that he departed on some strange quest."

"The dragon is there," Mina said. "He waits for me, though he does not know it."

"Waits to attack you, maybe," said Samuval with a snort. "He's not like one of our blue dragons, Mina. This Skie is a butcher. He devours his own kind to gain power, just like Malystryx."

"You should not go alone, Mina," Galdar urged tersely. "Take some of us with you."

"The Hand of the One God brought down Cyan Bloodbane," Mina said sternly. "The Hand of the One God will bring down Skie, if he thwarts the God's commands. Skie will obey. He has no choice. He cannot help himself.

"You will obey me, too, Galdar, Captain Samuval," Mina added. "As will the men." Her tone and her look softened. "You have no need to fear. The One God rewards obedience. You will be safe in the forest of the dead. They guard you. They have no thought of harming you. Resume the march, Galdar. We must make haste. Events in the world move swiftly, and we are called."

"We are called," muttered Galdar, after Mina had departed, traveling deeper into the forest. "We are always called, it seems."

"Called to victory," observed Captain Samuval. "Called to glory. I don't mind that. Do you?"

"No, not that part," Galdar admitted.

"Then what's wrong—besides this place frightens the pudding out of us." Samuval glanced around the shadowed forest with a shudder.

"I guess I'd like to think I had some say in the matter," Galdar muttered. "Some choice."

"In the military?" Samuval chortled. "Your mama must have dropped you on your head when you were a calf if you think that!"

He looked down the path. Mina had passed beyond his sight. "Come on," he said uneasily. "Let's keep moving. The sooner we're out of this place, the better."

Galdar pondered this. Samuval was right, of course. In the military one obeyed orders. A soldier didn't get to vote on whether or not he'd like to storm a city, whether or not he'd like to face a barrage of arrows or have a cauldron of hot boiling oil poured on his head. A soldier did what he was told to do without question. Galdar knew that, and he accepted that. Why was this any different?

Galdar didn't know. Couldn't answer.

21 AN UNEXPECTED VISITOR

Palin looked up from the book he had been studying and rubbed his watery eyes and the back of his neck. His vision, once so clear and keen, had deteriorated with age. He could still see well at a distance, but he was forced to read through spectacles that magnified the text or—in their absence—(he was forever misplacing them)—he had to read with his head bent close to the page. Slamming shut the book in frustration, he shoved it across the stone table, there to reside with the other books that had been of no help.

Palin glanced with little hope at the other books he had found upon the shelves and had yet to read. He had chosen these simply because he recognized his uncle's handwriting on the covers and because they pertained to magical artifacts. He had no reason to suppose they referred specifically to the Device of Time Journeying.

To be truthful, he found them depressing. Their references to magic and the gods of magic filled him with memories, longings, desires. This room where he sat—his uncle's laboratory—was the same, depressing.

He thought back to his conversation with Dalamar yesterday, the day the kender had been discovered missing, the day Palin had insisted on entering his uncle's old laboratory, searching through Raistlin's books on magic in hopes of finding useful information on the Device of Time Journeying.

"I know that the Wizards' Council ordered Raistlin's laboratory shut," Palin said as they wended their way up the treacherous stairs that spiraled around the dark heart of the Tower of High Sorcery—a misnomer now, if ever there was one. "But they are gone, as the magic is gone. I doubt they'll come looking for us."

Dalamar glanced at him, seemed amused. "What a fool you are, Majere. Did you really think I would let rules laid down by Par-Salian stop me from entering? I broke the seal to the laboratory long ago."

"Why?"

"Can't you guess?" Dalamar asked caustically.

"You were hoping to find the magic."

"I thought . . . well, it doesn't matter what I thought." Dalamar shrugged. "The Portal to the Abyss . . . the spellbooks . . . something might be left. Perhaps I was hoping that some of the *Shalafi's* power might have lingered where he once walked. Or maybe I was hoping I would find the gods. . . ."

Dalamar spoke softly, gazing into the darkness, into the emptiness. "My mind was fevered. I wasn't well. Instead of the gods, I found death. I found necromancy. Or perhaps it found me."

They climbed the stairs, stood before the door that held so many memories. The door that had once looked so imposing, so forbidding, seemed now small and shabby. Palin reminded himself that many, many years had passed since he had last seen it.

"The undead that once guarded it are gone now," Dalamar remarked. "There is no longer any need for them."

"What of the Portal to the Abyss?" Palin asked.

"It leads to nowhere and to nothing," Dalamar answered.

"My uncle's spellbooks?"

"Jenna could fetch a high price for them at that shop of hers, but only as antiques, curiosities." Dalamar broke the wizard-lock. "I wouldn't have even locked the door if it hadn't been for the kender."

"Aren't you coming?" Palin asked.

Dalamar refused. "Hopeless as it may seem, I'm going to continue to search for the kender."

"He's been missing a day and a night. If Tas were here, he certainly could not go that long without popping up to annoy one of us. Face it, Dalamar, he has managed to escape."

"I have ringed this Tower round with magic," Dalamar stated grimly. "The kender could not have escaped."

"Famous last words," Palin remarked.

Palin felt a thrill of awe and excitement as he entered the laboratory that had been his Uncle Raistlin's, the place where his uncle had worked some of his most powerful and awful magic. Those feelings soon evaporated, to be replaced by the sadness and disappointment experienced by those of us who return to the home of our childhood to find that it is smaller than we remembered and that the current owners have let it fall into neglect.

The fabled stone table, a table so large a minotaur could lie down full length upon it, was dusty and covered in mouse dung. Jars that had once held the experiments of Raistlin's attempts to create life still stood upon the shelves, their contents dead and desiccated. The fabled spellbooks belonging not only to Raistlin Majere but to the archmage Fistandantilus, lay scattered about in disarray, their spines rotting, their pages grimy and covered in cobwebs.

Palin rose to stretch the kinks from his legs. Lifting the lamp that lighted his work, he walked to the very back of the lab to the Portal to the Abyss.

The dread Portal, created by the mages of Krynn to allow those with faith and courage and powerful magicks to enter the dark realm of Queen Takhisis. Raistlin Majere had done that, to his great cost. So potent was the evil of the Portal that Dalamar, as Master of the Tower, had sealed up the laboratory and everything inside.

The cloth that had once covered the Portal was rotted away, fell in rags about it. The carved heads of the five dragons that had glowed radiantly in homage to the Queen of Darkness were dark. Cobwebs covered their eyes, spiders crawled into their mouths. Once they had given the impression of silently screaming. Now they appeared to be gasping for air. Palin looked past the heads, looked inside the Portal.

Where once had been eternity was now only an empty room, not very large, covered with dust, populated by spiders.

Hearing the rustling of robes on the stairs leading to the laboratory, Palin hastily left the Portal. He returned to his seat, pretended to be absorbed in once more studying the ancient spellbooks.

"The kender has escaped," Dalamar reported, shoving open the door.

Taking one look at the elf's cold and angry expression, Palin bit his tongue on the "I told you so."

"I cast a spell that would reveal to me the presence of any living creature in the building," Dalamar continued. "The spell located you and myriad rodents but no kender."

"How did he get out?" Palin asked.

"Come with me to the library, and I will show you."

Palin was not sorry to leave the laboratory. He brought the books he had not yet read with him. He did not plan on coming back. He was sorry he had ever returned.

"Shortsighted of me, no doubt, but it never occurred to me to spellbind the chimney!" Dalamar stated. Bending down to peer into the fireplace, he made an irritated gesture. "Look, you can see a great quantity of soot in the grate, as well as several bits of broken stone that appear to have been dislodged. The chimney is narrow, and the climb long and arduous, but that would only encourage a kender, not stop him. Once he was outside, he could shinny down a tree trunk and so make his way into Nightlund."

"Nightlund is filled with the dead—" Palin began.

"An added inducement for a kender," Dalamar interjected dryly.

"It's my fault. I should have been keeping an eye on him. But, to be honest, I did not think there was any possible way he could escape."

"It's just like the perversity of the little beasts," said Dalamar. "When you *want* to lose one, you can't possibly. The one time we actually want to keep one, we can't hang onto him. No telling where he has gone. He could be halfway to Flotsam by now."

"The dead—"

"They would not bother him. It's magic they are after."

"To give to you?" Palin said bitterly.

"Only a pittance. What they do with the rest of it, I haven't been able to discover. I can almost see it out there, like a vast ocean, yet I receive but a trickle, barely enough to slake my thirst. Never enough to satisfy it. At first, when the Shadow Sorcerer led me to discover necromancy, I was given all I wanted. My power was immense. I thought to increase that power by removing to this location. I discovered, too late, that I had walked into my own prison cell.

"Then I heard from Jenna that you had come across the magical Device of Time Journeying. For the first time in years, I felt hope. At last, this would offer a way out."

"For you," Palin said coldly.

"For all of us!" Dalamar returned with a flash of his dark eyes. "Yet what do I find? You have broken it. Not only that, but you managed to scatter pieces of it throughout the Citadel of Light!"

"Better than Beryl having it!"

"Perhaps she has it already. Perhaps she had brains enough to gather up the bits and pieces—"

"She would not be able to put it back together. I'm not even sure *we* could put it back together." Palin gestured toward the books piled up on the desk. "I can find no reference to what to do if the artifact breaks."

"Because it was never meant to break. Its maker had no notion of the dead feeding off it. How could he? Such a thing never happened in the Krynn of the gods. The Krynn we knew."

"Why have the dead begun feeding now?" Palin wondered. "Why not five years ago or ten? The wild magic worked for me once, just as necromancy worked for you and healing worked for Goldmoon and the Mystics. The dead never interfered with us before."

"The wisest among us never really knew what happened to the souls of the dead," Dalamar said, musing. "We knew that some of the dead remained on this plane, those who had ties to this world, like your uncle, or those who were cursed to remain here. The god Chemosh ruled over these unquiet spirits. What of the rest? Where did they go? Because none ever returned to tell us, we never found out."

"The clerics of Paladine taught that the blessed spirits departed this stage of life to travel on to the next," Palin said. "That is what my father and mother believed. Yet—"

He glanced out the window, hopeful—and fearful—of seeing his father's spirit among those unhappy ghosts.

"I will tell you what I think," said Dalamar. "Mind you, this is only what I think, not what I know. If the dead were once allowed to depart, they are not being allowed to leave now. The night of the storm . . . Did you mark that terrible storm?"

"Yes," said Palin. "It was no ordinary storm. It was fraught with magic."

"There was a voice in the storm," Dalamar said. "A voice that boomed in the thunder and cracked in the lightning. Almost I could hear it and understand it. Almost, but not quite. The voice sent out a call that night, and it was then the dead began to congregate in Nightlund in force. I watched them from my window, flowing from all directions, an immense river of souls. They have been summoned here for a purpose. As to what the purpose is—"

"Hail the Tower!" a voice called out from below the laboratory window. Simultaneously, a battering knock sounded on the Tower door.

Astounded, Palin and Dalamar stared at one another.

"Who can that be?" Palin asked, but at the very moment he spoke the words, he saw that he was talking to himself.

Dalamar's body stood before him, but that body might have been a wax dummy on exhibit at some traveling fair. The eyes were open, stared straight at Palin, but they did not see him. The body breathed, but that was all it did.

Before Palin could react, Dalamar's eyes blinked. Life and light and intelligence returned.

"What is it?" Palin demanded.

"Two Knights of Neraka, as they are calling themselves these days. One is a minotaur, and the other is very strange."

As he talked, Dalamar began half-leading, half-dragging Palin across the room. Reaching a far wall, he pressed on a stone in certain way. Part of the wall slid aside, revealing a narrow opening and a staircase.

"They must not find you here!" Dalamar said, shoving Palin inside.

Palin had come to the same conclusion himself. "How did they travel through the forest? How did they find the Tower—"

"No time! Down those stairs!" Dalamar hissed. "They lead to a chamber located in the library. There is an opening in the wall. You'll be able to hear and to see. Go quickly! They will start to get suspicious."

The pounding on the door and the shouting had increased.

"The wizard Dalamar!" the deep voice of the minotaur rumbled. "We have come a long distance to talk to you!"

Palin ducked inside. Dalamar pressed his hand against the panel, and the wall slid noiselessly in place, leaving Palin in complete darkness.

He took a moment to calm himself after the alarm and the flurry, put a hand against the cold stone. He tried casting a light spell, uncertain of his success. To his relief, the spell worked perfectly. A flame like the flame of a candle burned in the palm of his hand.

Palin traversed the stairs quietly and swiftly, keeping one hand against the wall to steady his steps, the other lifted to light his way. The staircase spiraled down at such a steep angle that rounding the last turn in the stair, he came up against a blank wall with a suddenness that nearly caused him to bash his head against the stones.

He searched for the opening Dalamar had promised him but found nothing. The stones were set solidly in place. There was no chink or crack in the mortar. He might have feared that Dalamar had used this ruse to imprison him except that he could hear voices growing steadily louder.

Palin reached out his hand, began to touch each of the stones. The first several were solid—cold, hard, rough. He moved higher. Reaching over his head, he tried to touch one of the stones and saw his hand pass right through.

"Of course," he said to himself. "Dalamar is taller than I am by a head and shoulders. I should have made allowances."

The illusion of stone dispelled, Palin looked through it directly into the library. From his vantage point, he could see the desk, see the person seated at the desk, and observe any visitors. He could hear every word as clearly as if he were in the room, and he had to fight against an uneasy impression that those inside the library could see him as clearly as he could see them.

Perhaps the apprentice Dalamar had once hidden himself to spy upon Raistlin Majere, his *Shalafi*. The notion provided Palin some amusement, as he settled himself to watch—a rather uncomfortable proceeding, since he had to stand as tall as possible and stretch his neck to look through the opening in the stone wall. Recalling the fact that Raistlin had been aware that his apprentice had been spying on him did little to add to Palin's sense of well-being. He reminded himself that he had been in this very library and had undoubtedly looked at this very wall without any notion that a small portion was not real.

The door opened. Dalamar ushered his visitors inside. One was a mino-taur—hulkish and brutish with that gleam of intelligence in the animal eyes that was both disconcerting and dangerous. The other Dark Knight was, as Dalamar had said, "very strange."

"Why . . ." Palin whispered, shocked as he watched her walk into Dalamar's library, her armor gleaming in the light of the fire. "I know her! Or rather, I knew her. Mina!"

The girl entered the room and looked about her with what Palin at first took for childlike wonder. She looked at the shelves of books, the ornately carved and beautiful desk, the dusty velvet curtains, the frayed silk rugs of elven make that covered the stone floor. He knew teenage girls—he'd had them as pupils in his school—and expected the usual squeals at the sight of the more grisly objects, such as the skull of a baaz draconian. (Raistlin had once engaged on a study of these creatures, perhaps with the intent of recreating them himself. The full skeleton could be found in the old laboratory, along with some of the internal organs, kept in a solution in a jar.)

Mina remained silent and apparently unimpressed by anything she saw, including Dalamar.

She shifted her gaze around the room, taking in everything. She turned her face toward Palin. Eyes that were the color of amber focused on the place in the wall behind which he was hiding. Palin had the impression that they saw through the illusion, saw him as plainly as if he were standing in the room. He felt this so acutely that he recoiled, glanced about him to ascertain his route of escape, for he was certain that her next move would be to point him out, demand his capture.

The eyes fixed on him, absorbed him. The liquid amber surrounded him, solidified, passed on to continue the investigation of the room. She said nothing, made no mention of him, and Palin's fast-beating heart began to return to some semblance of normal.

Of course, she had not seen him. He berated himself. How could she? He thought back to the last time he had seen her, an orphan in the Citadel of Light. She had been a scrawny little girl with skinned knees and a mass of glorious red hair. Now she was a slender young woman, the red hair cut off, playing at dress-up in a Knight's armor. Yet she had a look on her face that was certainly not childlike. Resolute, purposeful, confident—all that and something more. Exalted . . .

"You are the wizard Dalamar," Mina said, turning the amber eyes on him. "I was told I would find you here."

"I am Dalamar, the Master of the Tower. I would be considerably interested to know who told you where to find me," said Dalamar, folding his hands in the sleeves of his robes and giving a graceful bow.

"The Master of the Tower . . ." Mina repeated softly with a half-smile, as if she knew the truth of the matter. "As to how I found you, the dead told me."

"Indeed?" Dalamar seemed to find this troubling. He tried to evade her eyes, slid out from beneath the amber gaze. "Who might you be, Lady Knight, that you are on such intimate terms with the dead?"

"I am Mina," she said. She raised the amber eyes, and this time she caught him. She gestured. "This is my second-in-command, Galdar."

The minotaur gave an abrupt nod of his horned head. He was not comfortable in the Tower. He kept glancing about darkly as if he expected something to spring out and attack at any moment. He was not worried about himself, however. His sole concern appeared to be for Mina. He was protective to the point of worship, adoration.

Palin was overcome by curiosity. Dalamar was wary.

"I am interested to know how you made your way unscathed through Nightlund, Lady Mina," Dalamar said. He sat down in the chair behind his desk, perhaps trying to break that entrancing gaze. "Will you be seated?"

"Thank you, no," Mina replied and continued to stand. She now gazed down upon him, putting Dalamar at an unexpected disadvantage. "Why does my being in Nightlund astonish you, Wizard?"

Dalamar shifted in his chair, not willing to stand up, for that would make him appear vacillating and weak, yet not enjoying being looked down upon.

"I am a necromancer. I sense magic about you," he said. "The dead drain magic, they feed off it. I am surprised that you were not mobbed."

"That which you sense about me is not magic," Mina replied, and her voice was unusually low and mature for one her age. "You feel the power of the God I serve, the One God. As to the dead, they do not touch me. The One God rules the dead. They see in me the One God, and they bow down before me."

Dalamar's lip twitched.

"It is true!" Galdar stated, growling in anger. "I saw it myself! Mina comes to lead—"

"—my army into Nightlund," Mina concluded. Resting her hand upon the minotaur's arm, she commanded silence.

"Lead your army against what?" Dalamar asked sarcastically. "The dead?"

"Against the living," Mina replied. "We plan to seize control of Solamnia."

"You must have a large army, Lady Knight," Dalamar said. "You must have brought along every soldier in the Dark Knighthood."

"My army is small," Mina admitted. "I was required to leave troops behind to guard Silvanesti, which fell to our might not long ago—"

"Silvanesti . . . fallen . . ." Dalamar was livid. He stared at her. "I don't believe it!"

Mina shrugged. "Your belief or disbelief is all one to me. Besides, what do you care? Your people cast you out, or so I have heard tell. I mentioned that only in passing. I have come to ask a favor of you, Master of the Tower."

Dalamar was shaken to the core of his being. Palin saw that despite claiming not to believe her, the dark elf realized she spoke the truth. It was impossible to hear that calm, resolute, confident voice and not believe whatever she said.

Dalamar struggled to regain at least outward control of himself. He would have liked to have asked questions, demanded answers, but he could not quite see how to do this without revealing an uncharacteristic concern. Dalamar's love for his people was a love that he constantly denied and in that denial constantly reaffirmed.

"You have heard correctly," he said with a tight smile. "They cast me out. What favor can I do for you, Lady Mina?"

"I have arranged to meet someone here," she began.

"Here? In the Tower?" Dalamar was astonished beyond words. "Out of the question. I am not running an inn, Lady Mina."

"I realize that, Wizard Dalamar," Mina replied, and her tone was gentle. "I realize that what I am asking will be an imposition, an inconvenience to you, an interruption to your studies. Rest assured that I would not ask this of you, but that there are certain requirements that must be met as to the location of this meeting. The Tower of High Sorcery fulfills all those requirements. Indeed, it is the only place on Krynn that fulfills the requirements. The meeting must take place here."

"I am to have no say in this? What are these requirements of which you speak?" Dalamar demanded, frowning.

"I am not permitted to reveal them. Not yet. As to your say in this, what you do or say matters not at all. The One God has decided this will be, and therefore this will be."

Dalamar's dark eyes flickered. His face smoothed.

"Your guest is welcome in the Tower, Lady. In order to make the guest's stay comfortable, it would help if I knew something about this person . . . male or female? A name, perhaps?"

"Thank you, Wizard," Mina said, and turned away.

"When will the guest arrive?" Dalamar pursued. "How will I know that the person who comes is the person you expect?"

"You will know," Mina replied. "We will leave now, Galdar."

The minotaur had already crossed the room and was reaching for the door handle.

"There is a favor you could do for me in return, Lady," Dalamar said mildly. Mina glanced back. "What is that, Wizard?"

"A kender I was using in an important experiment has escaped," Dalamar said, his tone casual, as if kender were like caged mice and were found or lost on a routine basis. "His loss would be of no importance to me, but the experiment was. I would like very much to recover him, and it occurs to me that perhaps, if you are bringing an army into Nightlund, you might come upon him. If you do, I would appreciate his return. He calls himself Tasslehoff," Dalamar added with an offhanded and charming smile, "as so many of them do these days."

"Tasslehoff!" Mina's attention was caught directly. A crease marred her forehead. "The Tasslehoff who carried with him the magical Device of Time Journeying? You had him here? You had him and the device, and you *lost* him?"

Dalamar stared, confounded. The elven wizard was older by hundreds of years than this girl. He had been deemed one of the great mages of his or any time. Though he worked in magic's shadows, he had gained the respect, if not the love, of those who worked in the light. Mina's amber-eyed gaze pinned the powerful wizard to the chair. Dalamar wriggled beneath her gaze, struggled, but she had caught him and held him fast.

Two bright spots of color stained Dalamar's pale cheeks. The elf's slender fingers nervously stroked a bit of carving on the desk, an oak leaf. The too-thin fingers traced its shape over and over until Palin longed to rush from his hiding place and seize that nervous hand to make it stop.

"Where is the device?" Mina demanded, advancing on him until she stood at his desk, gazing down at him. "Did he have it with him? Do you have it here?"

Dalamar had reached his limit. He rose from his chair, looked down at her, looked down the length of his aquiline nose, looked down from his greater height, looked down from the confidence of his own power.

"What business can this possibly be of yours, Lady Mina?"

"Not *my* business," Mina said, not at all intimidated. Indeed, it was Dalamar who seemed to shrink as she spoke. "The business of the One God. All that happens in this world is the business of the One God. The One God sees into your heart and into your mind and your soul, Wizard. Though you may hide the truth from my mortal eyes, you cannot hide the truth from the One God. We will search for this kender, and if we find him we will do with him what needs to be done."

She turned again and walked away calm, unruffled.

Dalamar remained standing at his desk, the hand that had nervously traced the oak leaf clenched tightly in a fist that he concealed beneath his robes.

Arriving at the door, Mina turned around. Her gaze passed over Dalamar, another insect in her display case, and fixed on Palin. In vain he told himself she could not see him. She caught him, held him.

"You believe the artifact was lost in the Citadel of Light. It was not. It came back to the kender. He has it in his possession. That is why he ran away."

Palin doused the magical light. In the darkness, he could see nothing but those amber eyes, hear nothing but her voice. He remained there so long that

Dalamar came searching for him. The elf's footsteps were soft upon the stone stairs, and Palin did not hear him until he sensed movement. He looked up in alarm, found Dalamar standing in front of him.

"What are you still doing here? Are you all right? I thought for certain something had happened to you," Dalamar said, irritated.

"Something did happen to me," Palin returned. "*She* happened to me. She saw me. She looked straight at me. The last words she spoke were to me!"

"Impossible," Dalamar said. "No eyes, not even amber eyes, can see through solid stone *and* magic."

Palin shook his head, unconvinced. "She spoke to me."

He expected a sarcastic rejoinder from Dalamar, but the dark elf was in no mood to banter, apparently, for he climbed the stairs leading back to the laboratory in silence.

"I know that girl, Dalamar," Palin said.

Dalamar halted on the staircase, turned to stare. "How?"

"I haven't seen her in a long time. Not since she ran away. She was an orphan. A fisherman found her washed upon the shore of Schallsea Isle. He brought her to the Citadel of Light, to the orphans' home. She became a favorite of Goldmoon's, almost a daughter to her. Three years ago she ran away. She was fourteen. Goldmoon was devastated. Mina had a good home. She was loved, pampered. She seemed happy, except I never knew a child to ask so many questions. None of us could understand why she ran off. And now . . . a Dark Knight. Goldmoon will be heartbroken."

"That is very odd," Dalamar said thoughtfully, and they resumed their climb. "So she was raised by Goldmoon. . . ."

"Do you suppose what she said about Tas and the device was true?" Palin asked, as they emerged from the hidden stairwell.

"Of course, it was true," Dalamar replied. He walked over to the window, stared down into the cypress trees below. "That explains why the kender ran away. He feared we would find it."

"We would have, if we had bothered to think through this rationally, instead of haring off in a panic. What ninnies we are! The device will always return to the one who owns it. Even in pieces, it will always return."

Palin was frustrated. He felt the urgent need to do something, yet there was nothing he could do.

"You could search for him, Dalamar. Your spirit can walk this world, at least—"

"And do what?" Dalamar demanded. "If I did find him—which would be a miracle to surpass all miracles—I could do nothing except frighten him into burrowing deeper into whatever hole he's dug."

Dalamar had been staring out the window. He stiffened. His body went rigid.

"What is it?" Palin asked, alarmed. "What's wrong?"

Dalamar made no answer, except to point out the window.

Mina walked through the forest, trod upon the brown pine needles. The dead gathered around her. The dead bowed to her.

22 REUNION OF OLD FRIENDS

$\mathbf{A}$ kender is never out of sorts for long, not even after encountering his own ghost. True, the sight had been a considerable shock, and Tasslehoff still experienced unpleasant qualms whenever he thought about it, but he knew how to handle a qualm. You held your breath and drank five sips of water, and the qualm would go away. This done, his next decision was that he had to leave this terrible place where ghosts went around giving one qualms. He had to leave it, leave it fast, and never, never come back.

Moss and his father proved to be of little help, since as far as Tas could see, moss had the bad habit of growing on all sides of rocks and trees, with apparently no regard for the fact that someone might be trying to use it to find north. Tasslehoff decided to turn instead to the time-honored techniques that have been developed by kender over centuries of Wanderlust, techniques guaranteed to find one's self after losing one's self. The best known and most favored of these involves the use of the body compass.

The theory behind the body compass is as follows. It is well-known that the body is made up of various elements, among these being iron. The reason that we know the body has iron in it is because we can taste the iron in our blood. Therefore, it stands to reason that the iron in our blood will be drawn to the north, just as the iron needle on the compass is drawn to the north. (Kender go so far to state that we would, all of us, be congregated at the north end of the world if we let our blood have its way. We fight a constant battle with our blood, otherwise we would all collect at the top of the world, thereby causing it to tip over.)

In order to make the body compass work, you must shut your eyes, so as not to confuse things, extend the right arm with the index finger pointing, then spin around three times to the left. When you stop, open your eyes, and you will discover that you are facing north.

Kender who use this technique almost never arrive at where they're going, but they will tell you that they always arrive at where they need to be. Thus it was that Tasslehoff wandered about in the forests of Nightlund for a good many hours (he was *not* lost), without finding either Solanthus or the way out, and he was just about to try the body compass one last time when he heard voices, real, live voices, not the tickling whispers of the poor souls.

Tasslehoff's natural instinct was to introduce himself to the voices, who were perhaps lost, and offer to show them which way was north. However, at this juncture, he heard yet another voice. This voice was inside his head and belonged to Tanis Half-Elven. Tasslehoff often heard Tanis's voice on occasions such as this, reminding him to stop and think if what he was doing was "conducive to self-preservation." Sometimes Tas listened to Tanis's voice in his head, and sometimes he did not, which was pretty much how their relationship had worked when Tanis had been alive.

This time, Tasslehoff recalled that he was running away from Dalamar and Palin, both of whom wanted to murder him, and that they might either be out hunting for him themselves or they might have sent out minions. Wizards, Tas recalled, were forever sending out minions. Tas wasn't sure what a minion was—he thought it some sort of small fish—but he decided that it would be conducive to his self-preservation if he climbed a tree and hid in the branches.

Tasslehoff climbed nimbly and swiftly and was soon settled comfortably high up amidst the pine needles. The three voices, with bodies attached, walked right underneath him.

Seeing that they were Knights of Takhisis or Neraka or whatever it was they were calling themselves these days, Tas congratulated himself on having listened to Tanis. An entire army, Knights and foot soldiers, marched beneath Tas's tree. They marched swiftly and did not appear to be in very good spirits. Some darted nervous glances left and right, as if searching for something, while others traveled with eyes facing forward, fearful that if they looked they might find it. There was little talking in the ranks. If they did speak, they kept their voices low. The tail end of the line of soldiers was just moving underneath Tasslehoff's tree, and he was just congratulating himself on having successfully avoided detection when the front of the line came to a halt, which meant the back of the line had to come to a halt, too.

The soldiers stopped, standing beneath Tas. They breathed heavily and looked tired to the point of dropping, but when the word came down the line that there was to be a fifteen-minute rest, none of them looked happy. A few squatted down on the ground, but they did not leave the trail, they did not throw off their packs.

"Let's get on with it, I say," said one. "I don't want to spend another night in this death's den."

"You're right, there," said another. "Let's march on Solanthus. This minute. I'd welcome a fight with an enemy who's got flesh and blood in him."

"Two hundred of us, and we're going to take Solanthus," said a third. "Rot! If there were two hundred thousand we couldn't take that city, even with the help of the One God. It's got walls the size of Mt. Nevermind. Infernal devices, too, or so I've heard. Giant ballista that can shoot dragons out of the skies."

"Like you said we'd never take the elf city," said one of his comrades irritably. "Remember, boys? 'It'll take two hundred thousand of us to whip those pointy-ears.' "

The others laughed, but it was nervous laughter, and no one laughed too long or too loudly.

"We're off again," said one, rising to his feet.

The others stood up, moved back into formation. Those in front turned to say something to those in back.

"Keep watch for the kender. Pass it on." The word came down the line. "Keep watch for the kender."

The soldiers in back waited impatiently for those in front to start moving. Finally, with a sluggish lurch, the line of men began to advance, and they were soon lost to Tasslehoff's eyes and ears.

" 'Keep watch for the kender,' " Tas repeated. "Hah! Those must be Dalamar's minions. I was wrong about the fish part. I'll just wait here until I'm sure they're gone. I wonder who this One God is? It must very dull, to have only one god. Unless, of course, it was Fizban, but then there probably wouldn't be any world, because he'd keep misplacing it, just like he misplaces his hat.

"Uh, oh!" The kender gave a stifled groan, noting that the troops were heading in the identical direction his finger had pointed. "They're going north. That means I have to go some other direction. The opposite direction, in fact."

Which was how Tasslehoff came at last to find his way out of Nightlund and on the road leading to Solanthus—proving yet again that the kender body compass works.

Arriving at the great walled fortress city of Solanthus, Tasslehoff walked around the walls until he came to the front entrance. There he stopped to rest himself a bit and to watch with interest the crowds of people coming and going. Those entering the city stood in a long line that moved very slowly. People stood in the road, fanning themselves and talking to their neighbors. Farmers dozed on their carts, their horses knowing enough to move forward as the line inched along. Soldiers posted outside the walls kept watch to make certain that the line continued to move, that no one grew impatient and attempted to shove his way to the front. No one seemed too upset by the delay but appeared to expect it and to take in stride.

Every person who entered the city was being questioned by the guards. Pouches were searched. Wagons were searched. If the wagon carried goods, the goods were examined by the guards, who loosened bags, pried up the tops of crates, and poked pitchforks into loads of hay. Once he was familiar with the rules, fully intending to comply with them, Tasslehoff took his place at the very end of the line.

"Hullo, how are you?" he said to a large matronly woman carrying an enormous basket of apples, who was gossiping with another large woman, carrying a basket of eggs. "My name is Tasslehoff Burrfoot. My, this is a long line. Is there any other way in?"

The two turned around to look at him. Both scowled at him fiercely, and one actually shook her fist at him.

"Keep away from me, you little vermin. You're wasting your time. Kender aren't allowed inside the city."

"What a very unfriendly place," Tasslehoff observed and walked off.

He did not go far, however, but sat down in the shade of a tree near the front entrance to enjoy his apple. As he ate, he observed that while no kender could be seen entering the city, two were seen leaving it, accompanied by city guards.

Tas waited until the kender had picked themselves up, dusted themselves off, and gathered up their pouches. Then he began to wave and shout. Pleased as always to see a fellow kender, the two came running over to greet him.

"Leafwort Thumbfloggin," said one, extending his hand.

"Merribell Hartshorn," said the other, extending her hand.

"Tasslehoff Burrfoot," said Tas.

"No, really?" said Merribell, highly pleased. "Why I met you just last week. You don't look the same though. Are you doing something different with your hair?"

"What have you got in your pouches?" asked Leafwort.

In the ensuing excitement of answering that interesting question, followed by Tas's asking them what they had in their pouches and a general round of pouch-dumping and object-trading, Tas explained that he wasn't one of the innumerable Tasslehoffs wandering about Ansalon, he was the original. He was particularly proud to show off the pieces of the Device of Time Journeying, complete with the story of how he and Caramon had used it to travel back to the past and how it had taken him inadvertently to the Abyss and how it had brought him forward to a future that wasn't this future but some other.

The two kender were impressed and quite happy to trade their most valuable objects for pieces of the device. Tas watched the pieces vanish into their pouches without much hope that they would stay there. Still it was worth a shot. Finally, when everything had been traded that could possibly be traded and all the stories told that could possibly be told, he told them why he was in Solanthus.

"I'm on a quest," Tas announced, and the other two kender appeared quite respectful. "I'm searching for a Solamnic Knight."

"You've come to the right place," said Leafwort, jerking a thumb behind him at the city walls. "There're more Knights in there than you can shake a stick at."

"What do you plan on doing once you've got one?" Merribell wondered. "They don't look like they'd be much fun to me."

"I'm searching for a specific Knight," Tas explained. "I had him once, you see, but I lost him, and I was hoping he might have come here, this being a place where Knights tend to congregate, or so I've heard. He's about so high"—Tas jumped to his feet, stood on his tiptoes and raised his arm—"and he's extremely ugly, even for a human, and he has hair the color of Tika's corn bread muffins."

The two kender shook their heads. They'd seen lots of Knights—they described several—but Tas didn't have any use for them.

"I have to find my own," he said, squatting down comfortably again. "He and I are great friends. I guess I'll just go look for myself. These ladies told me— I say, would anyone care for an apple? Anyhow two ladies told me that kender aren't allowed inside Solanthus."

"That's not true. They're really quite fond of kender in Solanthus," Merribell assured him.

"They just have to say that to keep up appearances," added Leafwort.

"They don't put kender in jail in Solanthus," Merribell continued enthusiastically. "Imagine that! The moment they catch—er—find you, they give you an armed escort through the town—"

"—so that you can see all the sights—"

"—and they throw you out the front gate. Just like a regular person."

Tasslehoff agreed that Solanthus sounded like a wonderful place. All he had to do was to find a way inside. His new friends provided him with several entrances that were not known to the general public, adding that it was best to have an alternate route in case the first he tried happened to have been shut down by the guards.

Bidding good-bye to his new friends, Tas went off to try his luck. The number-two location worked extraordinarily well (we have been asked not to reveal it) and after only an hour's work, Tasslehoff entered the city of Solanthus. He was hot and sweaty, grimy and torn, but all his pouches were intact and that, of course, was of paramount importance.

Fascinated by the immensity of the city, as well as by the large numbers of people, he wandered the streets until his feet were sore and the apples he'd had for lunch were just a distant memory. He saw lots of Knights, but none who resembled Gerard. Tas might have stopped to question a few, but he was afraid that they might treat him in the friendly fashion the other two kender had described, and while he would have liked to have been shown the sights of the city by armed guards and nothing would have made him happier than to be tossed bodily out the front gate, he was forced to put aside such pleasures in the more serious pursuit of his quest.

It was about sunset when Tas began to grow seriously annoyed with Gerard. Having decided that the Knight should be in Solanthus, the fact that he was not where he was supposed to be was highly provoking. Tired of tramping up and down the streets in search of him, weary of dodging city guards (fun at the beginning but old after awhile), Tas decided grumpily that he would sit down and let Gerard find *him* for a change. Tas planted himself in the shadows of a large statue near a fountain close to the main entrance on the main street, figuring that he would watch everyone coming in and out and that Gerard would be bound to find him eventually.

He was sitting with his chin in hand, trying to decide which inn he was going favor with his presence for dinner when he saw someone he knew enter the front gate. It wasn't Gerard, but someone even better. Tasslehoff jumped to his feet with a glad cry.

"Goldmoon!" he shouted, waving.

Respectful of Goldmoon's white robes that marked her a Mystic of the Citadel of Light, one of the city guards was providing her a personal escort into the city. He pointed in a certain direction. She nodded and thanked him. He touched his forehead to her, then returned to his duties. A small and dust-covered figure trotted along at Goldmoon's heels, hard-pressed to keep up with her long strides. Tas didn't pay much attention to this other person. He was so glad and so thankful to see Goldmoon that he didn't notice anyone else, and he forgot all about Gerard. If anyone could save him from Dalamar and Palin, it was Goldmoon.

Tas raced across the crowded highway. Bumping into people, and nimbly avoiding the long arm and grasping hands of the law, Tasslehoff was about to greet Goldmoon with his usual hug when he stopped short.

She was Goldmoon, but she wasn't. She was still in the youthful body that had been so detestable to her. She was still beautiful, with her shining silver-gold hair and her lovely eyes, but the hair was straggly and uncombed, and the eyes had a vague and distant look about them, as if she wasn't seeing anything close to her but was staring at something very far away. Her white robes were mud-stained, the hem frayed. She seemed tired to the point of falling, but she walked on determinedly, using a wooden staff to aid her steps. The small, dusty person kept up with her.

"Goldmoon?" Tasslehoff said, uncertain.

She did not pause, but she did glance down at him. "Hello, Tas," she said in a sort of distracted way and continued on.

Just that. Hello, Tas. Not, My gosh, I'm glad to see you, where have you been all this time, Tas? Just, Hello, Tas.

The small and dusty person *was* surprised to see him, however. Also very pleased.

"Burrfoot!"

"Conundrum!" Tas cried, at last recognizing the gnome through the dust. The two shook hands.

"What are you doing here?" Tas asked. "The last time I saw you, you were mapping the Hedge Maze at the Citadel of Light. By the way, the last time I saw the Hedge Maze it was on fire."

Tasslehoff realized too late that he shouldn't have sprung such terrible news on the gnome in so sudden a manner.

"Fire!" Conundrum gasped. "My life quest! On fire!"

Stricken to the heart, he collapsed against the side of a building, clutching his breast and gulping for breath. Tas paused to fan the gasping gnome with his hat, still keeping one eye on Goldmoon. Not noticing the gnome's distress, she kept on walking. When Conundrum showed signs of recovering, Tas grasped his arm and pulled him along down the street after her.

"Just think," Tas said soothingly, aiding the gnome's staggering steps, "when they start to rebuild, they'll come to you because you've got the only map."

"That's right!" Conundrum exclaimed on thinking this over. He perked up considerably. "You're absolutely right." He would have halted on the spot to drag the map out of his knapsack, but Tas said hurriedly that they didn't have time, they had to keep up with Goldmoon.

"How do you two come to be here in Solanthus, anyway?" Tasslehoff asked, to distract the gnome from thoughts of the blazing Hedge Maze.

Conundrum regaled Tas with the doleful tale of the wreck of the *Indestructible*, how he and Goldmoon had been cast up on strange shores, and how they had been walking ever since.

"You will not believe this," Conundrum said, lowering his voice to a fearful whisper, "but she is following *ghosts!*"

"Really?" said Tasslehoff. "I just left a forest filled with ghosts."

"Not you, too!" The gnome regarded Tas in disgust.

"I'm quite experienced around the undead," Tas said with a careless air. "Skeletal warriors, disembodied hands, chain-rattling ghouls . . . Never a problem for the experienced traveler. I have the Kender Spoon of Turning given to me by my Uncle Trapspringer. If you'd like to see it—"

He began to rummage in his pouch but stopped abruptly when he came across the bits and pieces of the Device of Time Journeying.

"Personally, I think the woman's mad, unhinged, loony, deranged, bricks missing, spilt marbles, that sort of thing," Conundrum was saying in low and solemn tones.

"Yes, I suspect you're right," said Tas, glancing at Goldmoon, sighing. "She certainly doesn't act like the Goldmoon I once knew. *That* Goldmoon was pleased to see a kender. *That* Goldmoon wouldn't have let evil wizards send a kender off to be squashed by a giant." Tas patted Conundrum's arm. "It's awfully good of you to stick with her, look out for her."

"I have to be honest with you," said Conundrum, "I wouldn't do it except for the money. Look at this, will you?"

Glancing around to make certain no pickpockets were lurking about, the gnome pulled from the very bottom of his knapsack a large purse that was bulging with coins. Tasslehoff expressed his admiration and reach out to take a look at the pouch. Conundrum cracked the kender's hand across the knuckles and stuffed the purse back in his sack.

"And don't you touch it!" the gnome warned with a scowl.

"I don't think much of money," Tas said, rubbing his bruised knuckles. "It's heavy to carry around, and what's the good of it? I have all these apples with me. Now, no one's going to clonk me over the head for these apples, but if I had a coin to buy the apples, they'd hit me over the head to steal the coin, and so it's much better to have the apples. Don't you agree?"

"Why are you talking about apples?" Conundrum shouted, waving his hands in the air. "What have apples got to do with anything? Or spoons for that matter?"

"You started it," Tas advised him. Knowing gnomes and how excitable they were, he decided it would be polite to change the subject. "How did you come by all that money anyway?"

"People give it to her," Conundrum replied, shifting the hand-waving in Goldmoon's general direction. "Wherever we go, people give her money or a bed for the night or food or wine. They're extremely kind to her. They're kind to me, too. No one's ever been kind to me before," the gnome added wistfully. "People always say nasty, stupid things to me like, 'Is it supposed to smoke like that?' and 'Who's going to pay for all the damage?' but when I'm with Goldmoon, people say kind things to me. They give *me* food and cold ale and a bed for the night and money. She doesn't want the money. She gives it to me. I'm keeping it, too." Conundrum looked quite fierce. "The repairs to *Indestructible* are going to cost a bundle. I think it was insured for liability only and not collision—"

Tas had a feeling the subject was veering off into a boring area, so he interrupted. "By the way, where are we going?"

"Something to do with Knights," Conundrum replied. "Live knights, I hope, although I wouldn't bet on it. You can't believe how sick I am of hearing about dead people all the time."

"Knights!" Tasslehoff cried joyfully. "I'm here for the same thing!"

At this juncture, Goldmoon halted. She looked up one street and down another and appeared to be lost. Tasslehoff left the gnome, who was still muttering to himself about insurance, and hastened over to see if Goldmoon required help.

Goldmoon ignored Tas and instead stopped a woman who, to judge by her tabard marked with a red rose, was a Solamnic Knight. The woman gave her directions and then asked what brought Goldmoon to Solanthus.

"I am Goldmoon, a Mystic of the Citadel of Light," she said, introducing herself. "I hope to be able to speak before the Knights' Council."

"I am Lady Odila, Knight of the Rose," the woman replied and bowed respectfully. "We have heard of Goldmoon of the Citadel of Light. A most highly revered woman. You must be her daughter."

Goldmoon looked suddenly very worn and weary, as if she had heard this many times before now.

"Yes," she said with a sigh. "I am her daughter."

Lady Odila bowed low again. "Welcome to Solanthus, Daughter of Goldmoon. The Knights' Council has many urgent matters before it, but they are always glad to hear from one of the Mystics of the Citadel of Light, particularly after the terrible news we received of the attack on the citadel."

"What attack?" Goldmoon went exceedingly pale, so pale that Tasslehoff took hold of her hand and gave a sympathetic squeeze.

"I can tell you—" Tas began.

"Merciful goodness, it's a kender," said Lady Odila in the same tone as she might have said, "Merciful goodness, it's a bugbear." The Knight detached Tasslehoff's hand, placed herself in between Tas and Goldmoon. "Don't worry, Healer. I'll deal with it. Guard! Another of the little beasts has broken in. Remove it—"

"I am *not* a little beast!" Tasslehoff stated indignantly. "I'm with Goldmoon . . . her daughter, that is. I'm a friend of her mother's."

"And I'm her business manager," said Conundrum, bustling up importantly. "If you'd care to contribute money—"

"What attack?" Goldmoon demanded desperately. "Is this true, Tas? When did it happen?"

"It all started when— Excuse me, but I'm talking to Goldmoon!" Tas said, wriggling in the grip of the City Guard.

"Please, leave him alone. He *is* with me," Goldmoon pleaded. "I take full responsibility."

The guard looked dubious, but he could not very well go against the express wishes of one of the revered Mystics of the citadel. He looked to Lady Odila, who shrugged and said in an undertone, "Don't worry. I will see to it that he is removed before nightfall."

Tas, meanwhile, was telling his tale.

"It all started when I went to Palin's room because I had decided that I would be noble and go back in time and let the giant squish me, only I've changed my mind about that now, Goldmoon. You see, I thought about it and—"

"Tas!" Goldmoon said sharply, giving him a little shake. "The attack!"

"Oh, right. Well, Palin and I were talking this over and I looked out the window and saw a big dragon flying toward the citadel."

"What dragon?" Goldmoon pressed her hand against her heart.

"Beryl. The same dragon who put the curse on me," Tasslehoff stated. "I know because I went squirmy and shivery all over, even my stomach. So did Palin. We tried to use the Device of Time Journeying to escape, but Palin broke it. By that time Beryl was there, and a lot of other dragons and draconians were jumping out of the skies, and people were running around screaming. Like that time in Tarsis. Do you remember that? When the red dragons attacked us, and the building fell on top of me, and we lost Tanis and Raistlin?"

"My people!" Goldmoon whispered, half-suffocated. She swayed unsteadily on her feet. "What about my people?"

"Healer, please, sit down," Lady Odila said gently. Putting her arms around Goldmoon, she led her to a low wall that encircled a splashing fountain.

"Can this be true?" Goldmoon asked the Knight.

"I am sorry to say that, strange as it may seem, the kender's tale is a true one. We received reports from our garrison stationed on Schallsea Isle that the Citadel was attacked by Beryl and her dragons. They did an immense amount of destruction, but most of the people were able to escape safely into the hills."

"Thank the One God," Goldmoon murmured.

"What, Healer?" Lady Odila asked, perplexed. "What did you say?"

"I'm not certain," Goldmoon faltered. "What *did* I say?"

"You said, 'Thank the One God.' We have heard of no god coming to Krynn." Lady Odila looked intrigued. "What do you mean?"

"I wish I knew," said Goldmoon softly. Her gaze grew abstracted. "I don't know why I said that. . . ."

"I escaped, too," Tas exclaimed loudly. "Along with Palin. It was quite exciting. Palin threw the pieces of the device at the draconians, and it made some truly spectacular magic, and we ran up the Silver Stair in the smoke of the burning Hedge Maze—"

At this further reminder of his life quest going up in smoke, Conundrum began to wheeze and sat down heavily beside Goldmoon.

"—and Dalamar saved us!" Tas announced. "One minute we were on the very edge of the Silver Stair, and then *whoosh!* we were in the Tower of High Sorcery in Palanthas, only it isn't anymore. In Palanthas. It's still a Tower of High Sorcery—"

"What a little liar you are," said Lady Odila. She sounded almost respectful, so Tas chose to take this as a compliment.

"Thank you," he said modestly, "but I'm not making this up. I really did find Dalamar and the Tower. I understand it's been lost for quite a while."

"I left them to face the danger alone," Goldmoon was saying distractedly, paying no attention to Tas. "I left my people to face the dragons alone, and yet what could I do? The voices of the dead called to me. . . . I had to follow!"

"Do you hear her?" asked Conundrum, prodding the Knight with his finger. "Ghosts. Ghouls. That's who she's talking to, you know. Mad. Quite mad." He rattled the money pouch. "If you'd like to make a donation . . . it's tax-deductible—"

Lady Odila regarded them as if they were all suitable candidates for a donation, but seeing Goldmoon's fatigue and distress, the Knight's expression softened. She put her arm around Goldmoon's thin shoulders.

"You have had a shock, Healer. You have traveled far, by the sounds of it, and in strange company. Come with me. I will take you to Starmaster Mikelis."

"Yes, I know him! Although," Goldmoon added, sighing deeply, "he will not know me."

Lady Odila rose to lead Goldmoon away. Tas and Conundrum rose, too, following right behind. Hearing their footsteps, the Knight turned around. She had that look on her face that Knights get when they are about to summon the City Guard and have someone dragged off to jail. Guessing that the someone might be him, Tasslehoff thought fast.

"Say, Lady Odila!" he said. "Do you know a Knight named Gerard uth Mondar? Because I'm looking for him."

The Lady Knight, who had indeed been about to shout for the guard, shut her mouth on the words and stared at him.

"What did you say?"

"Gerard uth Mondar. Do you know him?" Tas asked.

"Maybe I do. Excuse me a moment, Healer. This won't take long." Lady Odila squatted down in front of Tas, to look him in the eye. "Describe him to me."

"He has hair the color of Tika's corn bread and a face that looks ugly at first, until you get to know him, then for some reason, it doesn't seem all that ugly anymore, especially when he's rescuing you from Dark Knights. He has eyes that are—"

"Blue as cornflowers," said Lady Odila. "Corn bread and cornflowers. Yes, that pretty much describes him. How do you know him?"

"He's a great friend," said Tas. "We traveled to Qualinesti together—"

"Ah, so *that's* where he came from." Lady Odila regarded Tas intently, then she said, "Your friend Gerard is here in Solanthus. He is being brought up before the Knights' Council. They suspect him of espionage."

"Oh, dear! I'm sorry to hear he's sick," said Tas. "Where is he? I'm sure he'll be glad to see me."

"Actually such a meeting might prove extremely interesting," the lady returned. "Bring these two along, Guard. I suppose the gnome is in on this plot, too?"

"Oh, yes," said Tasslehoff, taking firm hold of Conundrum's hand. "He keeps the money."

"Don't mention the money!" Conundrum snapped, clutching his robes.

"Obviously some sort of mix-up," Tasslehoff whispered. "Don't worry, Conundrum. I'll fix everything."

Knowing that *I'll fix everything* has been emblazoned in the annals of Krynnish history as the last words many associates of kender ever hear, the gnome was not comforted.

23 COUNCIL OF THE KNIGHTS OF SOLAMNIA

Goldmoon was weary from her long journey, weary as if her body were the frail and elderly one that was rightfully her own, not this strange, youthful, strong body. She had come to use the body as she used the wooden staff, to take her to wherever strange destiny called. The body carried her long distances every day without tiring. It ate and drank. It was young and beautiful. People were entranced by it and were glad to help her. Farmers gave her lodging in their humble cottages and eased her weary way by providing rides in their farm carts. Noble lords and ladies took her into their castles and sent her forth on her journey in their fine carriages. Thus, because of the body, she had traveled to Solanthus far more swiftly than she had dared hope.

Goldmoon believed her beauty and youth charmed them, but in this she was wrong. The farmers and the noble lords saw first that she was beautiful, but then they looked into her eyes. They saw there a sorrow and a seeking that touched them deeply, touched the peasant who shared a loaf of bread with her and received her grateful thanks with bowed head, touched the wealthy lady who kissed her and asked for her blessing. They saw in Goldmoon's sorrow their own fears and anxieties. They saw in her seeking their own questing for something more, something better, something in which to believe.

Lady Odila, noting Goldmoon's pallor and her faltering steps, took her directly to the hall where the Knights' Council convened and found her a small, comfortable room in the main chamber with a warm fire. The Knight ordered servants to bring water for washing away the stains of the road, and food and drink. After assuring herself that she could do nothing more to make Goldmoon comfortable, Lady Odila departed. She sent a runner to the Temple of the Mystics with word of Goldmoon's arrival, while she herself saw to the disposition of her prisoners, Tasslehoff and Conundrum.

Goldmoon ate and drank without tasting the food or knowing that she had consumed it. The body demanded fuel to keep going, and she was forced to accede to its demands. She had to keep going, to follow the river of the dead, who called to her and swept her along in their chill, dread current. She sought among the ghostly faces that pressed around her for some among them that she knew: Riverwind, Tika, Caramon, her own beloved daughter . . . all the old friends who had departed this world, leaving her behind. She could not find them, but that was not surprising, for the numbers of the dead were like the drops in a river, bewildering, overwhelming.

The body was hale and strong, but she was tired, so very tired. She thought of herself as a candle flame burning inside an ornate lantern. The flame burned low, the wax had all melted, the wick was down to the last tiny portion. What she could not see was that as the flame dwindled, her light burned ever brighter.

The One God. Goldmoon did not remember having spoken of the One God. She had not said anything, but she had dreamed about the One God. Dreamed often, the same dream, over and over so that her sleep was almost as wearying as her waking hours.

In the dream, Goldmoon was once again in the Temple of the Gods in the ancient city of Xak Tsaroth. She held in her hands the blue crystal staff. Before her was the statue of the blessed Mishakal, goddess of healing. The statue's hand was curled as if to hold a staff, yet no staff was there. As Goldmoon had done once, so long ago, she gave the magical staff to the statue. That time, the statue had accepted it, and Goldmoon had come to understand the love the gods bore their children. In the dream, though, when she tried to give the staff to the goddess, the crystal staff shattered, cutting her hands that were soon covered in blood. Her joy changed to terror.

The dream ended with Goldmoon waking, trembling and confused.

She pondered the portent of this dream. First she thought it might mean one thing, then another. She dwelled on it until the images began to wheel in her mind, one chasing the other, like a snake swallowing its own tail. Shutting her eyes, she pressed her hands against them, trying to banish the wheel.

"Daughter of Goldmoon?" came a concerned voice.

She dropped her hands, startled, and looked into the kindly, anxious face of Starmaster Mikelis. She had met him before. He had studied at the Citadel of Light, where he had been an excellent student, a capable and gentle healer. A Solamnic by birth, he had returned to Solanthus and was now head of the Temple of Light in that city. Often they had spent hours talking together, and she sighed to see that he did not recognize her.

"I am sorry," he said gently. "I did not mean to frighten you, Daughter. I would not have entered without knocking, but Lady Odila said she feared you might be unwell, and she hoped you might be sleeping. Yet I am glad to see that you have eaten and drunk with good appetite."

He looked with some perplexity at the numerous plates and a basket that had been filled with bread. The strange body had eaten a dinner that would have fed two, and there was not a crumb left.

"Thank you, Starmaster," Goldmoon said. "You did not frighten me. I have traveled a long distance, and I am fatigued. I am distraught over this news that the citadel was attacked. I did not know. It was the first I had heard—"

"Some were killed," Mikelis said, taking a seat beside her. "We grieve for them and trust that their spirits wing their way from this world to the next. Daughter," he asked in sudden alarm, "are you ill? Is there something I can do?"

Goldmoon had started at this statement about the spirits and, shuddering, glanced around. Ghosts filled the room, some watching her, some roving about restlessly, some seeking to touch her, others paying no attention to her. They never stayed long. They were forced to keep moving, to join the river that flowed steadily north.

"No," she said confusedly. "It's this terrible news. . . ."

She knew better than to try to explain. Mikelis was a good man, a dedicated man, but he would not understand that the spirits could never wing their way anywhere, that they were trapped, prisoners.

"I regret to say," he added, "that we have received no news of your mother. We take this as a hopeful sign that Goldmoon was not injured in the attack."

"She was not," said Goldmoon briskly. Better to end this and tell the truth. She did not have much time. The river drew her onward. "Goldmoon was not hurt in the attack because she wasn't there. She fled. She left her people to face the dragons without her."

Starmaster Mikelis looked troubled. "Daughter, do not speak so disrespectfully of your mother."

"I know that she fled," Goldmoon continued relentlessly. "I am *not* Goldmoon's daughter, as you well know, Starmaster. You know that I have only two daughters, one of whom is . . . dead. *I* am Goldmoon. I have come to Solanthus to tell my story before the Knights' Council, to see if they can help me and also to give them a warning. Surely," she added, "you have heard rumors of my 'miraculous' transformation."

Starmaster Mikelis was clearly uncomfortable. He was obviously trying not to stare, yet he could not take his eyes from her. He looked at her, then looked quickly away, only to gaze back at her in bewilderment.

"Some of our young Mystics made a pilgrimage to the citadel not long ago," he conceded. "They returned with the tale that you had been the recipient of a miracle, that you had been given back your youth. I confess that I thought this an overabundance of youthful exuberance." He halted, now openly staring. "Can it be you, First Master? Forgive me," he added awkwardly, "but we have received reports that the Dark Knights have infiltrated the Orders of the Mystics. . . ."

"Do you remember the night we sat beneath the stars, Starmaster, and spoke of the gods you had known in your youth and how, even as a small boy, you felt drawn to be a cleric of Paladine?"

"First Master!" Mikelis cried. Taking hold of her hands, he pressed them to his lips. "This is truly you, and it is truly a miracle."

"No, it is not," said Goldmoon tiredly. "It is me, but it is not me. It is not a miracle, it is a curse. I don't expect you to understand. How could I, when I don't understand? I know that the Knights honor and revere you. I sent for you to ask you a favor. I must speak before the Knights' Council, and I cannot wait until next week or next month or whenever it is they might make room for me on their schedule. Can you gain me entry to see them now, this day?"

"I can!" Mikelis returned, smiling. "I am not the only Mystic they revere. When they hear that First Master Goldmoon is present, they will be only too glad to give you audience. The council has adjourned but only for supper. They are holding a special session to consider the fate of a spy, but that should not take long. Once that sordid business is concluded, you will come as a ray of light to the darkness."

"I fear that I come only to deepen the darkness, but that will be as it may." Goldmoon rose to her feet, gripping the wooden staff. "Take me to the council room."

"But, Master," Mikelis protested, rising in his turn, "the Knights will still be at table. They may be there some time. And there is this matter of the spy. You should remain here where you are comfortable—"

"I am never comfortable," she said, her voice crisp with anger and impatience, "so it does not matter whether I remain here or sit in a drafty chamber. I must speak before the council this day. Who knows but that this business with the spy might drag on, and they would send me word that I should return tomorrow."

"Master, I assure you—"

"No! I do *not* intend to be put off until tomorrow or whenever it may suit them. If I am present in the room, they cannot very well refuse to listen to me. And, you will make no mention to them of this so-called miracle."

"Certainly, Master, if that is what you wish," Mikelis said.

He looked and sounded hurt. He was disappointed in her. Here was a miracle, right before his eyes, and she would not permit him to glory in it.

In my hands, the blue crystal staff shattered.

She accompanied Starmaster Mikelis to the council chamber, where he persuaded the guards to permit her entry. Once they were inside, he started to ask if she was comfortable—she saw the words form on his lips—but he stammered and, with a stumbling apology, said that he would go to apprise the Lord Knight that she was here. Goldmoon took a seat in the large, echoing chamber decorated with roses. Their perfume scented the air.

She waited alone in the darkness, for the room faced away from the afternoon sunlight and the candles that lit it had been put out upon the Knights' departure. The servants offered to bring light, but Goldmoon preferred to sit in the darkness.

At the same moment Goldmoon was being led to the council chamber, Gerard was being escorted by Lady Odila from his prison cell to the meeting of the Knights' Council. He had not been treated harshly, not by the standards of the Dark Knights of Neraka. He had not been tied to the rack nor hung by his thumbs. He had been brought before the inquisitor and badgered with questions for days, the same questions, over and over, the man tossing them out at random, jumping forward in time, leapfrogging back, always hoping to catch him in a lie.

Gerard was faced with a choice. Either he could tell his story from beginning to end, starting with a time-traveling dead kender and ending with his inadvertently switching sides to become aide-de-camp to Marshal Medan, one of the most notorious of the Dark Knights of Neraka. Or he could state over and over that he was a Solamnic Knight who had been sent on a secret mission by Lord Warren and that he had a perfectly logical, reasonable and innocent explanation for why he came to be riding a blue dragon and wearing the leathers of a Dark Knight dragonrider, all of which he would explain in full before the Knights' Council.

Not, admittedly, the best of choices. Gerard had decided on the latter.

At length, after many weary hours of badgering, the inquisitor reported to his superiors that the prisoner was sticking by his story and that he would speak only to the Knights' Council. The inquisitor had also added that, in his opinion, the prisoner was either telling the truth, or he was one of the most cunning and clever spies of this age. Whichever was true, he should be brought before the Knights' Council and questioned.

As Lady Odila accompanied Gerard to the hall, she disconcerted him by staring quite often at his hair, which was probably standing straight up, since it would do nothing else.

"It's yellow," he said at last, put out. "And it needs trimming. I don't usually—"

"Tika's corn bread," said Lady Odila, her green-eyed gaze on his hair. "You have hair as yellow as Tika's corn bread."

"How do you know Tika?" Gerard demanded, astonished.

"How do *you* know Tika?" she returned.

"She was the proprietor of the Inn of the Last Home in Solace, where I was posted, as I stated, if you're trying to test me—"

"Ah," said Lady Odila. "That Tika."

"Where did you— Who said—"

Lady Odila, a thoughtful expression on her face, shook her head, refused to answer any of his questions. She held his arm in a pincerlike grip—she had uncommonly large, strong hands—and was absentmindedly urging him forward at her own long-strided pace, taking no notice that he was hampered by the manacles and chains on his ankles and was forced to keep up with her by means of a painful, hobbled trot.

He saw no reason to call her attention to this fact. He had no intention of saying anything further to this baffling female, who would only make a jest or a riddle of his words. He was going before the Knights' Council, appearing before lords who would hear him without prejudice. He had decided on which parts of his story he would tell without qualification and which he would keep to himself (such as the time-traveling dead kender). His tale, although strange, was believable.

They arrived at the Hall of Knights, the oldest building in Solanthus, dating back to the city's founding by, so legend had it, a son of the founder of the Knighthood, Vinus Solamnus. Made of granite faced with marble, the Hall of Knights had originally been a simple structure, resembling a block house. Additional levels had been added down through the ages—wings and towers and spires—so that now the simple block house had been transformed into a complex of buildings, surrounding an inner courtyard. A school had been established, instructing aspiring Knights not only in the art of warfare, but also the study of the Measure and how its laws were to be interpreted, for these Knights would spend only a small portion of their time fighting. Noble lords, they were leaders in their communities and would be expected to hear pleas, render judgment. Although the vast complex of structures had long outgrown the term "hall," the Knights continued to refer to it as that, in deference to the past.

Once, temples to Paladine and Kiri-Jolith, a god particularly honored by the Knights, had been a part of the complex. After the departure of the gods, the Knights had politely permitted the priests to remain, but—their power of prayer gone—the priests had felt useless and uncomfortable. The temples held such sorrowful memories that they had departed. The temples remained open. They had become a favorite place for Knights to go to study or to spend evenings in long philosophical discussions. The temples had a peace about them that was conducive to thought, or so it was said. Many of the younger students found them a curiosity.

Gerard had himself never visited Solanthus, but he had heard his father describe it, and recalling his father's descriptions, he tried to figure out which buildings were which. He knew the Great Hall, of course, with its sharply pointed roof and flying buttresses and ornate stonework.

Odila led him inside the Great Hall. He caught a glimpse of the enormous chamber, where town meetings were held. Odila escorted him up a winding stone stairway and down a long, echoing corridor. The corridor was lit with oil lamps mounted on tall, heavy pedestals carved from stone to resemble maidens holding lamps in their outstretched hands. The sculptures were extraordinary— each maiden was different, having been modeled from real life—but Gerard was so absorbed in his thoughts that he paid them scant attention.

The council, made up of three Knights, the heads of the three Orders of the Knighthood—Knights of the Sword, Knights of the Rose, Knights of the Crown—was just convening. The Knights stood together at the end of the hallway, apart from the noble lords and ladies and a few common folk who had come to witness the proceedings and who were now filing quietly into the chamber. A Knights' Council was a solemn procedure. Few spoke, or if they did, they kept their voices low. Lady Odila brought her prisoner to a halt and, leaving him in the care of guards, went to inform the herald the prisoner was present.

When those seated in the gallery had all entered, the Lord Knights walked into the room, preceded by several squires carrying the emblem of the Knights of Solamnia with its sword, rose, and kingfisher. Next came the flag of the city of Solanthus, and after that the banners of the Lord Knights who sat upon the council.

While waiting for them to take their places, Gerard scanned the crowd, searching for someone who might know either him or his father. He saw no signs of anyone he recognized, and his heart sank.

"There *is* someone here who claims to know you," said Lady Odila, returning. She had seen his scrutiny of the assembly, guessed what he was doing.

"There is?" he asked, relieved. "Who is it? Perhaps Lord Jeffrey of Lynchburg or perhaps Lord Grantus?"

Lady Odila shook her head, her mouth twitched. "No, no. None of those. Not a Knight at all, in fact. He's going to be called to testify on your behalf. Please accept my condolences."

"What—" Gerard began angrily, but she cut him off.

"Oh, and in case you were concerned about your blue dragon, you will be pleased to know that he has thus far escaped our attempts to slay him. We discovered the cave empty, but we know he is still in the vicinity. We have received reports of livestock disappearing."

Gerard knew that he should be on the Knights' side in this contest, but he found himself rooting for Razor, who had been a loyal and gallant mount. He was touched by the fact that the dragon was risking his own life to remain in the area, even though Razor must realize by now that something unfortunate had happened to Gerard.

"Bring forth the prisoner," cried the bailiff.

Lady Odila reached to take hold of Gerard, to lead him into the hall.

"I am sorry you must be manacled," she said to him quietly, "but that is the law."

He looked at her in astonishment. He could not, for the life of him, figure her out. Giving her a grudging nod, he evaded her grip and walked past her. He might have to enter the council room clanking and shackled, but he would enter on his own, carrying himself proudly, with his head high.

He hobbled into the room to the whispers and murmurs of those seated in the gallery. The Lord Knights sat behind a long wooden table placed at the front of the chamber. Gerard knew the custom. He had attended Knights' Councils as a spectator before, and he advanced to the center of the room, to make his obeisance to the three who would be sitting in judgment upon him. The Lord Knights watched him with grave countenances, but he guessed by their approving looks and nods that he was creating a favorable impression. He rose from his bow and was turning to take his place at the dock when he heard a voice that dashed all his hopes and expectations and caused him to think that he might as well call for the executioner and save everyone the trouble.

"Gerard!" cried the voice. "Over here, Gerard! It's me! Tasslehoff! Tasslehoff Burrfoot!"

The spectators were located at the far end of the large, rectangular room. The Lord Knights were seated at the front. The dock, holding the prisoners and their guards, was to their left. On the right, against the wall, were chairs for those who had business before the Knights' Council, petitions to present, or testimony to offer.

Goldmoon rested in one of these chairs. She had waited two hours for the council to convene. She had slept some during that time, her sleep disturbed as usual by the spinning wheel of whirling, multicolored forms and images. She woke when she heard the people filing in to take their seats at the gallery. They looked at her strangely, some staring, others painfully careful to avoid doing so. When the Lord Knights entered, each bowed low before her. One knelt to ask for her blessing.

Goldmoon understood by this that Starmaster Mikelis had spread the word of the miracle of her renewed youth.

At first she was annoyed and even angry with the Starmaster for having told people when she had specifically requested him not to do so. On reflection, she admitted that she was being unreasonable. He would have to offer some explanation for her altered appearance, and he had saved her the weary work of having to describe yet again what had happened to her, to relive the night of that terrible transformation. She accepted the Knights' homage and reverence with patience. The dead flitted around her, as well, but then the dead were always around her.

Starmaster Mikelis returned to sit protectively beside her, watching over her with a mixture of awe and pity and perplexity. Obviously he could not understand why she was not running through the streets displaying the wondrous gift she had been granted. None of them understood. They mistook her patience for humility, and they honored her for that, but they resented her for it as well. She had been given this great gift, a gift every one of them would have been glad to receive. The least she could do was enjoy it.

The Knights' Council convened with the ritual formalities the Solamnics love. Such formalities grace every important epoch in a Solamnic's life, from birth to death, and no function is considered to have truly happened without innumerable solemn pronouncements and readings and quotations from the Measure.

Goldmoon sank back against the wall, closed her eyes, and fell asleep. The trial of some Knight began, but Goldmoon was not consciously aware of it. The droning voices were an undercurrent to her dreams, and in her dreams she was back in Tarsis. The city was being attacked by an immense flight of dragons. She cowered in terror as the shadows of their many-colored wings turned bright day into darkest night. Tasslehoff was calling her name. He was telling her something, something important. . . .

"Tas!" she cried, sitting bolt upright. "Tas, fetch Tanis! I must speak to him—"

She blinked and looked around her in confusion.

"Goldmoon, First Master," Mikelis was saying softly, as he chafed her hands soothingly. "You were dreaming."

"Yes," she murmured, "I was dreaming. . . ."

She tried to recall the dream, for she had discovered something important, and she had been going to tell Tanis. But of course, Tanis was not there. None of them were there. She was alone, and she could not remember what it was she had been dreaming about.

Everyone in the hall was staring at her. Her outburst had interrupted the proceedings. Starmaster Mikelis made a sign that all was well. The Lord Knights turned their attention to the case at hand, calling forth the prisoner Knight to take his place before them.

Goldmoon's gaze roamed aimlessly about the room, watching the restless dead rove among the living. The voices of the Lord Knights droned, and she paid no attention to them until they called upon Tasslehoff to give testimony. He stood in the dock, a shabby and diminutive figure among the tall, splendidly accoutered guards.

Never daunted or intimidated by any show of either ceremony or force, the kender gave the Lord Knights an account of his arrival in Solace and told what had happened to him after that.

Goldmoon had heard this story before in the Citadel of Light. She recalled Tasslehoff talking about a Solamnic Knight who had accompanied him to Qualinesti in search of Palin. Listening to the kender, Goldmoon realized that the Knight on trial was the very Knight who had discovered the kender in the Tomb of the Last Heroes, the Knight who had been present at Caramon's death, who had stayed behind to fight the Dark Knights so that Palin could escape Qualinesti. The Knight who had forged the first link in a long chain of events.

She looked with interest now at the Knight. He had entered the room with an air of grim and injured dignity, but now that the kender began to defend him, he stood in a state of dejection. He slumped in the dock, his hands dangling before him, his head bowed, as if his fate had already been determined and he were being led to the block. Tasslehoff, needless to say, was enjoying himself.

"You state, kender, that you have attended a Knights' Council prior to this one," said Lord Ulrich, Knight of the Sword, who was apparently endeavoring to impress upon the kender the gravity of the situation.

"Oh, yes," Tas answered. "Sturm Brightblade's."

"I beg your pardon," said Lord Ulrich in bemused tones.

"Sturm Brightblade," said Tas, raising his voice. "You've heard of Sturm? One of the Heroes of the Lance. Like myself." Tasslehoff placed his hand modestly on his chest. Seeing the Knights regarding him with blank stares, he determined it was time to elaborate. "While I wasn't at the High Clerist's Tower when Sir Derek tried to have Sturm thrown out of the Knighthood for cowardice, I heard all about it from my friend Flint Fireforge when I came later, after I broke the dragon orb at the Council of Whitestone. The elves and the Knights were arguing about who should have the dragon orb—"

Lord Tasgall, Knight of the Rose, and head of the council, interrupted. "We are familiar with the story, kender. You could not possibly have been there, so dispense with your lies. Now, please tell us again how it was that you came to be in the tomb—"

"Oh, but he *was* there, my lords," said Goldmoon, rising to her feet. "If you know your history as you claim, then you know that Tasslehoff Burrfoot was at the Council of Whitestone and that he did break the dragon orb."

"I am aware that the heroic kender Tasslehoff Burrfoot did these things, Master," said Lord Tasgall, speaking to her in respectful, gentle tones. "Perhaps your confusion arises from the fact that this kender calls himself Tasslehoff Burrfoot, undoubtedly in honor of the heroic kender who bore the original name."

"I am *not* confused," Goldmoon stated sharply. "The so-called miracle that transformed my body did not affect my mind. I knew the kender you refer to. I knew him then, and I know him now. Haven't you been listening to his story?" she demanded impatiently.

The Knights stared at her. Gerard lifted his head, a flush of hope reddening his face.

"Are you saying that you affirm his story, First Master?" Lord Nigel, Knight of the Crown, asked, frowning.

"I do," said Goldmoon. "Palin Majere and Tasslehoff Burrfoot traveled to the Citadel of Light to meet me there. I recognized Tasslehoff. He is not an easy person to forget. Palin told me that Tasslehoff was in possession of a magical artifact that permitted him to travel through time. Tasslehoff came to the Tomb of the Last Heroes the night of the terrible storm. It was a night for miracles," she added with a touch of bitter irony.

"This kender"—Lord Tasgall glanced at Tas uncertainly— "claims that the Knight here on trial escorted him to Qualinesti, where they met Palin Majere at the home of Laurana, wife of the late Lord Tanis Half-Elven."

"Tasslehoff told me the same story, my lords. I have no reason to doubt it. If you mistrust his story or if you question my word, I suggest that there is an easy way to prove it. Contact Lord Warren in Solace and ask him."

"Of course, we do not question your word, First Master," the Lord Knight said, looking embarrassed.

"But you should, my lords," Lady Odila said. Rising to her feet, she faced Goldmoon. "How do we know you are what you claim to be? Your word alone. Why should we believe you?"

"You shouldn't," said Goldmoon. "You should question, Daughter. You should always question. Only by asking are we answered."

"My lords!" Starmaster Mikelis was shocked. "The First Master and I are old friends. I can testify that she is indeed Goldmoon, First Master of the Citadel of Light."

"Tell me what you are thinking, Daughter," Goldmoon said, ignoring the Starmaster. Her gaze fixed upon Lady Odila as if they were the only two in the room. "Speak your heart. Ask your question."

"Very well, I will do so." Lady Odila turned to face the Knights' Council. "My lords, the First Master Goldmoon is more than ninety years old! This woman is young, beautiful, strong. How is it possible, in the absence of the gods, that such miracles happen?"

"Yes, that is the question," Goldmoon said and sank back down in her chair.

"Do you have an answer, First Master?" asked Lord Tasgall.

Goldmoon looked at him steadily. "No, my lord, I do not. Except to say that, in the absence of the gods, what has happened to me is not possible."

The spectators began to whisper among themselves. The Knights exchanged doubtful glances. Starmaster Mikelis stared at her in helpless, baffled confusion. The Knight, Gerard, put his head in his hands.

Tasslehoff bounced to his feet. "I have the answer," he offered, but was quickly settled—and muffled—by the bailiff.

"*I* have something to say," said Conundrum in his thin and nasaly tones. He slid off his chair, nervously plucking at his beard.

Lord Tasgall gave the gnome gracious permission to speak. Solamnics have always felt a certain affinity for the gnomes.

"I just wanted to say that I had never seen any of these people before in my entire life until just a few weeks ago when this kender sabotaged my attempts to map the Hedge Maze and this human female stole my submersible. I have started a legal defense fund. If anyone would care to contribute?"

Conundrum glanced around hopefully. No one did, and so he sat back down. Lord Tasgall appeared considerably taken aback, but he nodded and indicated that the gnome's testimony was to be recorded.

"The Knight Gerard uth Mondar has already spoken in his own defense," said Lord Tasgall. "We have heard the testimony of the kender who claims to be Tasslehoff Burrfoot and that of Lady Odila Windlass and the . . . um . . . First Master. We will now withdraw to consider all of the testimony."

Everyone stood. The Knights withdrew. After they had departed, some people returned to their seats, but most hastened out of the room and into the corridor, where they discussed the matter in excited tones that could be heard clearly by those still inside the chamber.

Goldmoon rested her head against the wall and closed her eyes. She wanted nothing now but to be in a room by herself away from all this noise and commotion and confusion.

Feeling a touch on her hand, she saw Lady Odila standing before her.

"Why did you want me to ask that about the gods, First Master?" Lady Odila asked.

"Because it needed asking, Daughter," Goldmoon replied.

"Are you claiming there is a god?" Lady Odila frowned. "You spoke of a one—"

Goldmoon took hold of the woman's hand, wrapped her fingers around it, pressed it firmly. "I am saying to open your heart, Daughter. Open it to the world."

Lady Odila smiled wryly. "I opened my heart once, First Master. Someone came in and ransacked the place."

"So now you lock it with a quick wit and a glib tongue. Gerard uth Mondar is telling the truth, Lady Odila. Oh, they will send messengers to Solace and his homeland to verify his story, but you know as well as I do that this could take weeks. This will be too late. You believe him, don't you?"

"Corn bread and cornflowers," Lady Odila said, glancing at the prisoner as he stood patiently, but wearily, in the dock. She looked back at Goldmoon.

"Maybe I do, and maybe I don't. Still, as you say, only by asking are we answered. I will do what I can to either prove or disprove his claim."

The Knights returned. Goldmoon heard them speak their ruling, but their voices were distant, came to her from across a vast river.

"We have determined that we cannot pronounce judgment on the critical issues raised in the case until we have spoken to additional witnesses. Therefore we are sending messengers to the Citadel of Light and to Lord Warren in Solace. In the meantime, we will make inquiries throughout Solanthus to see if someone here knows the defendant's family and can verify this man's identity."

Goldmoon barely heard what was said. She had only a brief time left in this world, she felt. The youthful body could no longer contain the soul that yearned to be free of the burden of flesh and of feeling. She was living moment to moment. Heartbeat to heartbeat. Each beat grew a little weaker than the one before. Yet, there was something she still must do. Somewhere she still must go.

"In the meantime," Lord Tasgall was saying, concluding the proceedings, "the prisoner Gerard uth Mondar, the kender who goes by the name of Tasslehoff Burrfoot, and the gnome Conundrum are to be held in confinement. This council is adjourned—"

"My lords, I will speak!" Gerard cried, shaking loose the bailiff who was attempting to stop him. "Do what you will with me. Believe my story or not, as you see fit." He raised his voice to overcome the lord's repeated commands for him to be silent. "Please, I beg of you! Send aid and succor to the elves of Qualinesti. Do not allow the dragon Beryl to exterminate them with impunity. If you have no care for the elves as fellow beings, then at least you must see that once Beryl has destroyed the elves, she will next turn her attention northward to Solamnia—"

The bailiff summoned assistance. Several guards finally subdued Gerard. Lady Odila watched, said nothing, but glanced again at Goldmoon. She appeared to be asleep, her head slumped forward on her chest, her hands resting in her lap, much as an elderly woman might doze by the fire or in the warm sunshine, oblivious to what is now, dreaming of what will be.

"She *is* Goldmoon," Lady Odila murmured.

When order was restored, Lord Tasgall continued speaking. "The First Master is to be given into the care of Starmaster Mikelis. We ask that she not leave the city of Solanthus until such time as the messengers return."

"I will be honored if you would be a guest in my home, First Master," said Starmaster Mikelis, giving her a gentle shake.

"Thank you," said Goldmoon, waking suddenly. "But I will not be staying long."

The Starmaster blinked. "Forgive me, First Master, but you heard what the Knights said—"

Goldmoon had not in fact heard a word the Knights had said. She paid no heed to the living and no heed to the dead who came clustering around her.

"I am very tired," she told them all and, grasping her staff, she walked out the door.

24 PREPARING FOR THE END

Ever since their king had told them of their danger, the people of Qualinesti had been making preparations to stand against the dragon and her armies that were drawing near the elven capital. Beryl focused all her strength and her attention on capturing the elven city that had graced the world for so many years and on making that city her own. Soon humans would be moving into elven homes, chopping down the elves' beloved forests for lumber, turning hogs loose to forage in elven rose gardens.

The refugees were gone now. They had been evacuated through the dwarven tunnels, they had fled through the forests. With the refugees gone, those elves who had volunteered to remain behind to fight the dragon began to concentrate on the city's defenses. They were under no illusions. They knew that this was a battle they could win only by a miracle. At best, they were fighting a rearguard action. Every few hours they delayed the enemies' advance meant their families and friends were another few miles closer to safety. They had heard the news that the shield had fallen, and they spoke of the beauty of Silvanesti, of how their cousins would welcome the refugees, take them into their hearts and their houses. They spoke of the healing of the old wounds, of the future reunification of the elven kingdoms.

Their king, Gilthas, encouraged their hopes and their beliefs. Marshal Medan wondered when the young man found time to sleep. Gilthas was everywhere, it seemed. One moment he was underground, working alongside the dwarves and their burrowing worms, the next he was helping to set fire to a bridge across the White-rage River. The next time the Marshal saw the king, Gilthas was again in the underground tunnels, where most of the elves now lived. Down in these tunnels, built by the dwarves, the elves worked day and night forging and mending weapons and armor and braiding rope, miles and miles of thin, strong rope that would be needed to carry out the king's plan to destroy the dragon.

Every bit of cloth that could be spared had been given over to the production of the rope, from baby clothes to bridal gowns to shrouds. The elves took silken sheets from their beds, took woolen blankets from cribs, took tapestries that had hung for centuries in the Tower of the Sun. They tore them up without a second thought.

The work proceeded day and night. When one person grew too weary to continue braiding or cutting, when someone's hands grew too stiff or blistered, another would take over. After dark, the coils of rope that had been made during that day were smuggled out of the tunnels to be stowed away inside elven homes, inns, taverns, shops and warehouses. Elven mages went from place to place, placing enchantments on the rope. Sometimes the erratic magic worked, other times it did not. If one mage failed, another would come back and try later.

Above ground, the Dark Knights carried out the orders they had been given to rid the city of Qualinost of its inhabitants. They dragged elves out of their homes, beat them, and hauled them off to the prison camps that had been established outside the city. The soldiers threw furniture into the street, set homes ablaze, looted, and pillaged.

Beryl's spies, flying overhead, saw all this and reported back to Beryl that her orders were being faithfully followed. The spies did not know that the elves who huddled in terror in the prison camp by day were released by night, dispatched to different homes, there to be "arrested" again in the morning. If the spies had been careful observers, they might have noted that the furniture that was tossed in the streets blocked major thoroughfares and that the houses that were set ablaze were also strategically located throughout the elven city to impede the advance of troops.

The one person Medan had not seen during this busy time was Laurana. Since the day the Queen Mother had assisted him so ably in fooling Beryl's pet draconian, Medan had been occupied with planning the city's defenses and innumerable other tasks, and he knew that she must be busy, too. She was packing up her household and that of the king's, preparatory to traveling south, although, from what he had seen, she had little left to pack. She had given all her clothes except those on her back to be cut up for rope—even her wedding gown.

She had brought the gown herself, Medan heard, and when the elves had protested and told her she must keep that, if nothing else, she had taken up a pair of shears and cut the beautiful, silken fabric into strips with her own hands. All the while she told stories of her wedding to Tanis Half-Elven, making them laugh at the antics of the kender, Tasslehoff Burrfoot, who had wandered off with the wedding rings and been found upon the verge of trading them to a street urchin for a jar of tadpoles, and how Caramon

Majere, the best man, had been so flustered that when he rose to make the toast, he forgot Tanis's name.

Marshal Medan went to look at that particular coil of rope. He held the strand made up of the glistening silk that was the color of hyacinths in his hand and thought to himself that this length of rope needed no additional magical enchantment of strength, for it had been braided not with cord but with love.

The Marshal was himself extremely busy. He was able to snatch only a few hours of sleep every night, and these he forced himself to take, knowing well that he could not operate efficiently without them. He could have taken time to visit the Queen Mother, but he chose not to do so. Their former relationship—that of respectful enemies—had changed. Each knew, when they parted after that last meeting, that they would not be the same to each other as they had been in the past.

Medan felt a sense of loss. He was under no illusions. He had no right to her love. He was not ashamed of his past. He was a soldier, and he had done what a soldier must do, but that meant that he had the blood of her people on his hands and that therefore he could not touch her without staining her with that blood. He would never do that. Yet he sensed that they could not meet comfortably as old friends. Too much had happened between them for that. Their next meeting must be awkward and unhappy for both of them. He would bid her farewell, wish her luck in her journey south. When she was gone and he would never see her again, he would prepare himself to die as he had always known he would die—as a soldier, doing his duty.

At the precise moment when Gerard was eloquently but futilely pleading the cause of the elves before the Knights' Council in Solanthus, Marshal Medan was in the palace, making preparations to hold a final meeting of officers and commanders. He had invited the dwarf thane, Tarn Bellowsgranite; King Gilthas and his wife, the Lioness; and the elven commanders.

Medan had informed the king that tomorrow would be the last day the royal family could leave the city with any hope of escaping the enemy armies. He was concerned that the king had lingered too long as it was, but Gilthas had refused to leave earlier. This night, Medan would tell Laurana good-bye. Their farewells would be easier for both of them if they could do so when there were other people about.

"The meeting will begin at moonrise," Medan told Planchet, who would be carrying the messages to the elven commanders. "We will hold it in my garden."

His excuse was that the elves in attendance would not be comfortable in the thick-walled, stifling headquarters, but, in reality, he wanted a chance to show off his garden and to enjoy it himself for what would probably be the last time.

Naming off those who were to come, he said, almost offhandedly, "the Queen Mother—"

"No," said Gilthas.

The king had been pacing up and down the room, his head bowed, his hands clasped behind his back, so lost in meditation that Medan had not thought the king was paying any attention to him and was considerably startled when he spoke.

"I beg your pardon, Your Majesty?" Medan said.

Gilthas ceased pacing and came over to the desk that was now covered with large maps of the city of Qualinost and its environs.

"You will not tell my mother of this meeting," said Gilthas.

"This meeting is one of vital importance, Your Majesty," the Marshal argued. "We will be finalizing our plans for the city's defense and for your safe evacuation. Your mother is knowledgeable in such matters, and—"

"Yes," Gilthas interrupted, his voice grave. "She is knowledgeable. That is the very reason I do not want her to attend. Don't you understand, Marshal?" he added, bending over the desk, gazing intently into Medan's eyes. "If we invite her to this council of war, she will think we expect her to contribute that knowledge, to take part . . . "

He did not finish the sentence. He straightened abruptly, ran a hand through his hair, and stared unseeing out the window. The setting sun slanted through the crystal panes, shone full on the young king. Medan gazed at him expectantly, waiting for him to finish his sentence. He noted how the tension of the past few weeks had aged the young man. Gone was the languid poet, gazing listlessly around the dance floor. True, that mask had been put on to deceive the king's enemies. But they had been deceived because part of the mask was made of flesh and blood.

Gilthas was a gifted poet, a man of dreams, a man who taught himself to live much of his life internally, because he had come to believe he could not trust anyone. The face he showed the world—the face of the confident, strong and courageous king—was as much a mask as the other. Behind the mask was a man tormented by self-doubt, uncertainty, fear. He concealed it masterfully, but the sunlight on his face revealed the gray smudges beneath the eyes; the taut, tight-lipped smile that was no smile; the eyes that looked inward into shadows, not outward into sunlight.

He must be very like his father, Medan thought. It was too bad his father was not here to counsel him now, to put his hand upon his shoulder and assure him that his feelings were not a symptom of weakness, that they did him no discredit. Far from it, they would make him a better leader, a better king. Medan might have said these words himself, but he knew that coming from him they would be resented. Gilthas turned away from the window, and the moment passed.

"I understand," said Medan, when it became apparent from the uncomfortable silence that the king did not intend to finish his sentence, a sentence that presented a new and astonishing possibility to the Marshal. He had assumed Laurana intended to leave Qualinost. Perhaps he had assumed wrongly. "Very well. Planchet, we will say nothing about this meeting to the Queen Mother."

The moon rose and shone pale and sickly in the sky. Medan had never much liked this strange moon. Compared to the argent brilliance of Solinari or the red flame of Lunitari, this moon looked forlorn and meek. He could almost imagine it apologizing to the stars every time it appeared, as if ashamed to take its place among them. It did its duty now, and shed light enough that he did not have to bring the harsh glare of torches or lamps into his garden, lights that might reveal to any watcher flying overhead that there was a meeting in progress.

The elves expressed their admiration for his garden. Indeed, they were amazed that a human could create such beauty, and their amazement gave Medan as much satisfaction as their praise, for it meant the praise was genuine. His garden had never looked so hauntingly beautiful as it did by moonlight this night. Even the dwarf, who viewed plants as nothing more than food for cattle, looked about the garden with not quite a bored air and termed it "pretty," although he sneezed violently immediately afterward and constantly rubbed his itching nose throughout the meeting.

The Lioness was the first to give her report. She had nothing to say about the garden. She was cool, business-minded, obviously intending to end this quickly. She indicated where the enemy army was located, pointing to a map that had been spread out on a table near the fishpond.

"Our forces did what they could to slow the enemy's advance, but we were stinging flies to this behemoth. We annoyed him, we irritated him, we drew blood. We could impede him, but we could not stop him. We could slay a hundred men, and that was nothing but an irritant to him. Therefore, I ordered my people to pull back. We are now assisting the refugees."

Medan approved. "You will provide escort for the royal family. Of which you yourself are one," he added with a polite smile.

The Lioness did not return his smile. She had spent long years fighting him. She did not trust him, and for that he could not fault her. He did not trust her either. He had the feeling that if it had not been for Gilthas's intervention, the Marshal would have found the Lioness's knife sticking out of his ribcage.

Gilthas looked grim as he always did when his own departure was mentioned. Medan sympathized with the young king, understood how he felt. Most of the elves understood the reason for his departure. There were those who did not understand, who whispered that the elven king was abandoning Qualinost in its hour of need, leaving his people to die that he might live. Medan did not envy the young man the life that lay ahead of him: the life of the refugee, the life of the exile.

"I will personally escort His Majesty out through the tunnels," Bellowsgranite stated. "Then those of my people who have volunteered will remain in the tunnels beneath the city, ready to assist the battle. When the armies of darkness march into Qualinost"—the dwarf grinned broadly—"they will find more than woodchucks rising up out of holes to meet them."

As if to emphasize his words, the ground shook slightly beneath their feet, a sign that the giant dirt-devouring worms were at work.

"You and those coming with you must be in the tunnels first thing in the morning, Your Majesty," the Thane added. "We dare not wait longer."

"We will be there," said Gilthas, and he sighed and stared down at his hands, clasped tightly on the top of the table.

Medan cleared his throat and continued. "Speaking to the defense of the city of Qualinost: The spies sent to infiltrate Beryl's army report no change in her plan of attack. She will first order in the lesser dragons to scout the city, make certain all is well, and intimidate with their dragonfear any who may remain." The Marshal permitted himself a grim smile. "When Beryl has been assured that the city is deserted and her precious hide will be safe, she herself will enter Qualinost as leader of her armies.

Medan pointed to the map. "The city of Qualinost is protected from attack by a natural moat—the two arms of the White-rage River that encircle the city. We've received reports that Beryl's armies are already gathering along the banks of these streams. We have cut the bridges, but the water level is low this time of year and they will be able to ford the streams here, here, and here." He indicated three areas. "The crossing will slow them, for they will be forced to move through water that is swift-flowing and waist deep in some places. Our troops will be posted here and here and here"—more reference to the map—"with orders to allow a substantial number of troops to cross before they attack."

He looked around at the officers. "We must emphasize to the troops that they wait for the signal before they attack. We want the enemy forces split, with half on one side of the stream and half on the other. We want to create panic and disruption, so that those who are trying to cross are bottled up by those fighting for their lives on the bank. Elven archers stationed here and here will decimate their ranks with arrow fire. The dwarven army, under the leadership of the Thane's cousin"—Medan bowed to the dwarf—"will hit them here, drive them back into the water. The other elven forces will be posted here on the hillside to harry their flanks. Is this plan understood? Satisfactory to everyone?"

They had gone over this several times before. Everyone nodded.

"Finally, at our last meeting, we discussed sending for the Gray Robes who are stationed on the western border of Qualinesti and asking them for their assistance. It was decided that we would not seek their services, the feeling being that these gray-robed wizards cannot be trusted, a feeling in which I most heartily concurred. As it has turned out, it was well we did not count on them. It seems they have vanished. Not only have they disappeared without a trace, but the entire Forest of Wayreth has disappeared. I received a report that a strike force of draconians, one of Beryl's crack units, who had been diverted south with orders to slaughter the refugees, entered the forest and has not come out. We have heard nothing more of them, nor, I think, are we likely to.

"I suggest that we raise our glasses in a toast to the Master of the Tower of Wayreth."

Medan lifted a glass of elven wine from one of his last bottles. He was damned if he was going to leave any to be gulped by goblins. All shared in the toast, taking comfort in the fact that, for a change, a powerful force was on their side, mysterious and vagarious as it might be.

"I hear the sounds of laughter. I come upon you at a good time, it seems," said Laurana.

Medan had posted guards at the entrance, but he had given orders that if the Queen Mother arrived, she was to be admitted. He rose to do her honor, as did all of those present. The Lioness greeted her mother by marriage with an affectionate kiss. Gilthas kissed his mother, but he cast a rebuking glance at Medan.

"I took it upon myself to invite your honored mother," said the Marshal, bowing to the king. "I know that I went against Your Majesty's express wishes, but considering the extreme gravity of the situation, I deemed it best to exert my authority as military leader. As you yourself said, Your Majesty, the Queen Mother is knowledgeable in such matters."

"Please, be seated," said Laurana, taking a chair beside the Marshal, a chair he had made certain was left vacant. "I am sorry to be late, but an idea came to me, and I wanted time to think it through before I mentioned it. Tell me what I have missed."

He related the details of the meeting up to now, not knowing what he was saying, repeating by rote. Like his garden, Laurana was hauntingly beautiful that night. The moonlight stole away all color, so that the golden hair was silver, her skin white, her eyes luminous, her gown gray. She might have been a spirit, a spirit of his garden, for the scent of jasmine clung to her. He etched this image of her in his mind, planned to carry this image of her into death's realm, where, he hoped, it would serve to light the unending darkness.

The meeting continued. He asked for reports from the elven commanders. They reported that all was ready or nearly so. They needed more rope, but more rope was forthcoming, for those making it had not ceased their work, nor would they until the very final moments. The barricades were in place, trenches dug, traps set. The archers had been given their unusual assignment, and although they had found their work strange and difficult at first, they had soon accustomed themselves to the requirements and needed nothing but the signal to attack.

"It is imperative . . . imperative"—Medan repeated that firmly—"that no elf be seen by the dragon walking the streets. Beryl must think that the city has been cleared, that all the elves have either fled or are being held captive. The Knights will patrol the streets openly, accompanied by those elves disguised as Knights to fill out our ranks. Tomorrow night, once I have been assured the royal family is safely on their way"—he looked at the king as he spoke and received Gilthas's reluctant nod—"I will send a messenger to Beryl and tell her that the city of Qualinost surrenders to her might and that we have met all her demands. I will take my position at the top of the Tower of the Sun, and it is then that—"

"I beg your pardon, Marshal Medan," Laurana interrupted, "but you have not met the dragon's demands."

Medan had guessed this was coming. He knew by Gilthas's stiff rigidity and his sudden pallor that he had guessed it, as well.

"I beg *your* pardon, Madam," said Medan politely, "but I can think of nothing I have left undone."

"The dragon demanded that the members of the royal family be handed over to her. I believe that I was among those she specifically named."

"To my deep regret," said the Marshal with a wry smile, "the members of the royal family managed to escape. They are at this moment being pursued, and I am certain that they will be captured—"

Laurana was shaking her head. "That will not do, Marshal Medan. Beryl is no fool. She will be suspicious. All our carefully laid plans would be for naught."

"I will stay," said Gilthas firmly. "It is what I want to do anyhow. With myself as the Marshal's prisoner, standing with him on the tower, the dragon will have no suspicions. She will be eager to take me captive. You, Mother, will lead the people in exile. You will deal with the Silvanesti. You are the diplomat. The people trust you."

"The people trust their king," said Laurana quietly.

"Mother . . . " Gilthas's voice was agonized, pleading. "Mother, you cannot do this!"

"My son, you are king of the Qualinesti. You do not belong to me anymore. You do not belong to yourself. You belong to them."

Reaching across the table, Laurana took hold of her son's hand. "I understand how hard it is to accept the responsibility for thousands of lives. I know what you face. You will have to tell those who come to you for answers that all you have are questions. You will have to tell the despairing that you have hope, when despair is heavy in your own heart. You will bid the terrified to have courage when inside you are shivering with fear. It would take great courage to face the dragon, my son, and I admire and honor you for showing that courage, but such courage is paltry compared to the courage that will be required of you to lead your people into the future, a future of uncertainty and danger."

"What if I can't, Mother?" Gilthas had forgotten anyone else was there. These two spoke only to each other. "What if I fail them?"

"You will fail, my son. You will fail time and again. I failed those who followed me when I put my own wants over their needs. Your father failed his friends when he abandoned them while he pursued his love for the Dragon Highlord Kitiara."

Laurana smiled tremulously. Her eyes shimmered with tears. "You are the child of imperfect parents, my son. You will stumble and fall to your knees and lie bruised in the dust, as we did. You will only truly fail if you remain lying in the dust. If you regain your feet and continue, you will make of that failure a success."

Gilthas said nothing for long moments. He held fast to his mother's hand. Laurana held his hand, knowing that when she let go, she would let go of her son forever.

"I will not fail you, Mother," Gilthas said softly. He raised her hand to his lips, kissed it reverently. "I will not fail the memory of my father." Releasing her hand, he rose to his feet. "I will see you in the morning, Mother. Before I depart." He spoke the words without faltering.

"Yes, Gilthas," she said. "I will be waiting."

He nodded. The farewell they spoke then would last for all eternity. Blessed, heart-wrenching, those words were words to be spoken in private.

"If that is all, Marshal Medan," Gilthas said, keeping his eyes averted, "I have a great deal to do yet this night."

"I understand, Your Majesty," said the Marshal. "We have only small matters of no importance to clear up now. I thank you for coming."

"Small matters of no importance," Gilthas murmured. He looked back at his mother. He knew very well what they would be discussing. He drew in a deep breath. "Then I bid you good night, Marshal, and good luck to you and to all of you."

Medan rose to his feet, Lifting his glass of elven wine, he raised it. "I give you His Majesty, the King."

The elves raised their voices in unison. Bellowsgranite shouted out the toast in a hearty bellow that made the Marshal cringe and glance swiftly into the sky, hoping that none of Beryl's spies were in earshot.

Laurana raised her glass and pledged her son, her voice soft with love and pride.

Gilthas, overcome, gave a brief nod. He could not trust himself to speak. His wife put her arm around him. Planchet walked behind him. The king had no other guard. He had taken only a few steps when he looked back over his shoulder. His eyes sought out the Marshal.

Medan read the silent message and, excusing himself, accompanied the king through the darkened house. Gilthas said no word until he reached the door. Halting, he turned to face the Marshal.

"You know what my mother plans, Marshal Medan."

"I think I do, Your Majesty."

"Do you agree with her that such a sacrifice on her part is necessary?" Gilthas demanded, almost angrily. "Will you permit her to go through with this?"

"Your Majesty," the Marshal replied gravely, "you know your mother. Do you think there is any possible way to stop her?"

Gilthas stared at him, then he began to laugh. When the laughter came perilously close to tears, he fell silent until he could regain mastery over himself.

He drew in a deep breath, looked at the Marshal. "There is a chance that we will defeat Beryl, perhaps even destroy her. A chance that her armies will be stopped, forced to retreat. There is that chance, isn't there, Marshal?"

Medan hesitated, not wanting to offer hope where, in his opinion, there was none. Yet, which of them knew what the future would hold?

"There is an old Solamnic adage, Your Majesty, which I could quote just now, an adage that says there is about as much chance of that happening as of the moons falling out of the sky." Medan smiled. "As Your Majesty knows, the moons *did* fall out of the sky, so I will only tell you that, yes, there is a chance. There is always a chance."

"Believe it or not, Marshal Medan, you cheer me," Gilthas said. He held out his hand. "I regret that we have been enemies."

Medan took the king's hand, rested his other hand over it. He knew the fear that was in Gilthas's heart, and the Marshal honored him for not speaking it aloud, for not demeaning Laurana's sacrifice.

"Please rest assured, Your Majesty, that the Queen Mother will be a sacred trust for me," said Medan. "The most sacred of my life. I vow to you on my admiration and regard for her that I will be true to that trust to my last breath."

"Thank you, Marshal," Gilthas said softly. "Thank you."

Their handshake was brief, and the king departed. Medan stood a moment in the doorway, watching Gilthas walk down the path that gleamed silver-gray in the moonlight. The future the Marshal faced was grim and bleak. He could count the remaining days of his life upon the fingers of one hand. Yet, he thought, he would not trade it for the future faced by that young man.

Yes, Gilthas would live, but his life would never be his own. If he had no care for his people, it would be different. But he did care, and the caring would kill him.

25 ALONE TOGETHER

After a few more questions and some desultory discussion, the commanders departed. Medan and Laurana said nothing to each other, but between them words were no longer needed. She remained when the others had gone, and the two of them were alone together.

Alone together. Medan pondered that phrase. It was all two people could ever be to each other, he supposed. Alone. Together. For the dreams and secrets of our heart may be spoken, but words are poor handmaidens. Words can never fully say what we want them to say, for they fumble, stammer, and break the best porcelain. The best one can hope for is to find along the way someone to share the path, content to walk in silence, for the heart communes best when it does not try to speak.

The two sat in the garden beneath the moon that was strange and pale, as if it were the ghost of a moon.

"Beryl will come to Qualinost now," said the Marshal with satisfaction. "She will not pass up the opportunity to see you—the Golden General who defeated Queen Takhisis—shrink in terror before her bloated majesty. We will give Beryl what she wants. We will put on an excellent show."

"Indeed we will," said Laurana. "I have some ideas on that score, Marshal Medan. I spoke to you of them earlier in the evening." She cast a regretful look around the garden. "As beautiful as this place is, it seems a shame to leave it, yet what I have to show you should best be viewed under the cover of darkness. Will you accompany me back to Qualinost, Marshal?"

"I am yours to command, Madam," he replied. "The road is long and might be dangerous. Who knows if Beryl has assassins lurking about? We should ride, if that will be suitable to you."

They rode through the moonlit night. Their talk was of dragons.

"It is said of the Golden General that she was never daunted by dragonfear," Medan said, regarding Laurana admiringly. She sat a horse superbly, although she claimed it had been years since she last rode one.

Laurana laughed ruefully, shook her head. "Those who claimed that never knew me. The dragonfear was horrible. It never went away."

"Then how did you function?" he asked. "For certainly you fought dragons, and you fought them well."

"I was so afraid that the fear became a living part of me," Laurana replied, speaking softly, looking not at him, but into the night. "I could feel its pulse and beat inside me as if I had grown a terrible kind of heart, a heart that did not quite fit in my chest, for it always seemed to cut off my breathing."

She was silent a moment, communing with voices from the past. He no longer heard the voices from his past, but he remembered how they haunted a man or a woman, and he remained silent.

"I thought at first I could not continue on. I was too frightened, but then a wise man—his name was Elistan—taught me that I should not fear death. Death is inevitable, a part of life. It comes to all of us—humans, elves, even dragons. We defeat death by living, by doing something with our lives that will last beyond the grave. What I fear is fear, Marshal. I have never rid myself of that. I fight it constantly."

They rode in silence, alone together. Then she said, "I want to thank you, Marshal, for paying me the compliment of not trying to dissuade me from this course of action."

He bowed his head in acknowledgment but remained silent. She had more to say. She was thinking how to say it.

"I will use this opportunity to make reparation," she continued, speaking now not to him alone but to those voices in the past. "I was their general, their leader. I left them. Abandoned them. The War of the Lance was at a critical stage. The soldiers looked to me for guidance, and I let them down."

"You were faced with a choice between love and duty, and you chose love. A choice I, too, have made," he said with a glance at the aspen trees through which they rode.

"No, Marshal," she returned, "you choose duty. Duty to that which you love. There is a difference."

"At the beginning, perhaps," he said. "Not at the end."

She looked over at him and smiled.

They were nearing Qualinost. The city was empty, appeared abandoned. Medan drew up his horse. "Where are we bound, Madam? We should not ride openly through the streets. We might be seen."

"We are going to the Tower of the Sun," she said. "The implements of my plan are to be found inside. You look dubious, Marshal. Trust me." She regarded him with a mischievous smile, as he assisted her to dismount. "I cannot promise to make the moon fall from the sky. But I can give you the gift of a star."

The streets of Qualinost were empty, deserted. The two kept to the deep shadows, for they could feel the presence of watchers in the skies though they could not see them. Dragons would be difficult to see in the moonlight through the predawn mists that rose from the river, wound lovingly among the boles of the aspen trees.

The early morning was silent, eerily silent. The animals had gone to ground, the birds huddled hushed in the trees. The smell of burning, the smell of the dragon, the smell of death was in the air, and all creatures fled its coming.

"All those with sense," Medan said to himself. "Then there are the rest of us."

So deep was the silence that he thought if he listened closely he could hear the heartbeats of those hiding within the houses. Hearts that beat steadily, hearts that beat fast, hearts that trembled with fear. He could imagine lovers and friends sitting in the darkness in the silence, hands clasped, their touch conveying the words they could not speak and must be inadequate anyway.

They reached the Tower of the Sun just as the moon was dropping down from the sky. Located on the far eastern border of Qualinost, the tower graced the tallest hill. It provided a spectacular view of the city. The tower was made of burnished gold that shone as brilliantly as another sun when morning's first rays struck it, setting it aflame with warmth and life and the joy of a new day. So bright was the light that it dazzled the eyes. Approaching the tower in the daytime, Medan had often been forced to look away, lest it blind him.

At night, the tower reflected the stars, so that it was difficult to distinguish the tower—a myriad stars floating on its surface—from the night sky that was its backdrop.

They entered the tower through an entry hall whose doors were never locked and walked from there into the main chamber. Laurana had brought with her a small lantern to light their way. Torchlight would be too bright, too noticeable to anyone outside.

Medan had been inside the tower before for various ceremonies. Its beauty never failed to impress him. The tower rose hundreds of feet into the air with one central spire and two smaller ones jutting out to the sides. A person standing on the floor could see straight up to the top, to a wondrous mosaic. Windows placed in a spiral pattern in the tower's walls were positioned to capture the sunlight and reflect it downward upon the rostrum that stood in the center of the main chamber.

It was too dark for him to see the mosaic that portrayed the sky by day and the sky by night. Thus symbolically had the Qualinesti portrayed their relationship with their cousins, the Silvanesti. The creator of the mosaic had been optimistic, separating the two by a rainbow. He would have done better to separate them by jagged lightning.

"Perhaps this is the reason," Laurana said softly, looking upward to the mosaic not yet illuminated by the sunlight but hidden in darkness and in shadow. "Perhaps the sacrifice of my people is necessary for a new beginning—a beginning in which our two sundered people are finally one."

Medan could have told her that the reasons for the destruction of Qualinost had nothing to do with new beginnings. The reasons were evil and hideous, embedded in a dragon's hatred for all that she admired, the need to tear down that which she could never build and destroy that which she most desired to possess.

He kept his thoughts to himself. If her idea brought Laurana peace, he was more than willing to let her believe it. And, maybe, after all, their thoughts were but two sides to the same coin. Her side the light, his side the dark.

Leaving the main chamber, Laurana led the Marshal up one flight of stairs and onto a balcony that overlooked the main chamber. Doors made of silver and of gold lined the circular hallway. Laurana counted the doors as she went. When she came to the seventh door, counting from either direction, she drew a key from a blue velvet bag attached to her wrist. The key was also made of silver and of gold. The seventh door was decorated with an image of an aspen tree, its arms extended upward to the sun. Medan could see no lock.

"I know what is in this room," Medan said. "The Royal Treasury." He placed his hand over hers, stopped her from continuing. "Are you certain you want to reveal this to me, Madam? In there are secrets the elves have kept for a thousand years. Perhaps it would not be wise to betray them, even now."

"We would be like the miser in the story who hordes his money against the bad times and starves to death in the process. You would have me keep locked up that which well might save us?" Laurana asked.

"I honor you for your trust in me, Madam," said the Marshal, bowing.

Laurana counted seven tree limbs up from the bottom branch, counted seven leaves upon the trees and touched her key to the seventh leaf.

The door did not open. It vanished.

Medan stared into a vast hall that held the wealth of the elven kingdom of Qualinost. As Laurana lifted the lantern, the sight was more dazzling to the eyes than the sunlight striking the tower. Chests of steel coins, golden coins, and silver covered the floor. Weapons of fabulous make and design lined the walls. Casks of gems and pearls stood on the floor. The royal jewels—crowns and scepters and diadems, cloaks heavy with rubies and diamonds and emeralds—were displayed on velvet stands.

"Don't move, Marshal," Laurana warned him.

Medan had no intention of moving. He stood frozen inside the door. He gazed around and was angry. Coldly furious, he turned to Laurana.

"You speak of misers, Madam," he said, gesturing. "You have wealth enough here to buy the swords of every mercenary in Ansalon, and you horde gold while you spend the lives of your people!"

"Once, long ago, in the days of Kith-Kanan, such wealth was ours," said Laurana. "This is only its memory."

The moment she said the word, he understood. He saw through the illusion to the reality.

A large hole gaped at his feet. A single spiral staircase carved of stone led straight down into blackness. Anyone who did not know the secrets of that room would take no more than two steps across that illusory floor before plunging to his death.

Their only light was the single ray shining from the small lantern. By its steady and unwavering light, Medan followed Laurana down the stairs. At the bottom lay the true wealth of the elven kingdom of Qualinost: a single chest with a few bags of steel coins. Several empty chests, whose lids stood open, the homes of spiders and mice. Weapons had once been displayed on the walls, but these had long since been removed. All except one. Hanging on the wall was a footman's lance. The beam of light from her lantern struck it, caused it to shine silver as once had shone the silver moon of Solinari.

"A dragonlance," said Marshal Medan, his voice tinged with awe. "I have never seen one before, yet I would know it anywhere."

Laurana looked up at the lance with quiet pride. "I want you to have it, Marshal Medan." She glanced back at him. "Do you now understand what I have in mind?"

"Perhaps I do," he said slowly. He could not take his rapt gaze from the dragonlance. "Perhaps I am starting to."

"I wish I could tell you it had some heroic history," she said, "but if it does, we do not know it. The lance was given to Tanis shortly after we were married. A woman brought it to him. She said they had found it among her husband's possessions after his death. He had taken loving care of it, and he'd left a note saying that he wanted it given to someone who would understand. She knew he had fought in the war, but he never spoke of his deeds. He would say that he had done his duty, as did many others. He'd done nothing special."

"Yet, as I recall, only renowned and proven warriors were granted the honor of carrying the dragonlance," said Medan.

"I knew him, you see, Marshal. I remembered him. Oh, not him personally. But I remembered all those who gave up so much to join our cause and who were never honored with songs or immortalized with tombs or statues. They went back to their lives as butchers, seamstresses, farmers, or shepherds. What they did they did for no other reason than because they felt it was their duty. I thought it appropriate we should use this lance.

"As to the other weapons that were stored here, I sent many of them with those who departed Qualinost. I gave many more to those who remain to fight. In this casket"—Laurana ran her hand over a box carved plainly and simply of rosewood—"are the truly valuable jewels of antiquity. They will remain here, for they represent the past and its glory. Should a time come in the future when we are at peace, they will be recovered. If the time should come when no one lives who remembers us, perhaps these will be discovered and bring back the dreams of the elves to the world."

She turned from the rosewood casket, rested her hand on a tree limb. Odd, he thought, that a tree limb should be lying in the room. Kneeling beside it, she reached down and removed a piece of wood that was all but invisible in the center of the tree limb. Now Medan could see that the limb had been split lengthwise to form a case. Laurana lifted the lid.

Inside lay a sword. The weapon was enormous—a two-handed broadsword—and it would require two immensely large and strong hands to wield it. The blade was of shining steel, perfectly kept, with no spot of rust anywhere, no notches or scratches. The sword was plainly made, with none of the fancy ornamentation that sends the amateur into raptures but that veterans abhor. The sword had only a single decoration. Set into the pommel was a lustrous star sapphire, as big as a man's clenched fist.

The sword was lovely, a thing of deadly beauty. Medan reached out his hand in longing, then paused.

"Take it, Marshal," said Laurana. "The sword is yours."

Medan grasped the hilt, lifted the sword from its tree-limb case. He swung it gently, tested the balance. The sword might have been made for him. He was surprised to find that, although it appeared heavy, it was so well designed that he could wield it with ease.

"The sword's name is the Lost Star," said Laurana. "It was made for the elven paladin, Kalith Rian, who led the elves in the battle against Takhisis in the First Dragon War."

"How did the sword come by the name?" Medan asked.

"Legend has it that when the smith brought the sword to Kalith Rian, he told the elf lord this tale. While he was forging the sword, the smith saw a star flash across the heavens. The next morning, when he came to finish his work, he found this star sapphire lying amid the embers of his forge fire. He took it as a sign from the gods and placed the jewel in the sword's pommel. Rian named the sword the Lost Star. He slew the great red dragon Firefang with this sword, his final battle, for he himself was slain in the fight. The sword is said to be magical."

Medan frowned and handed the sword back hilt-first to Laurana. "I thank you, Madam, but I would much prefer to take my chances with an ordinary sword made of ordinary steel. I have no use for a sword that suddenly starts to sing an elven ditty in the midst of battle or one that transforms both me and it into a matched pair of serpents. Such occurrences tend to distract me."

"The sword will not start to sing, Marshal, I assure you," Laurana said with a ripple of laughter. "Hear me out before you refuse. It is said that those who look into the Lost Star when it is shining cannot look away, nor can they do anything else but stare at the jewel."

"That is even worse," he returned impatiently. "I become enamored of my own sword."

"Not you, Marshal. The dragon. And although I give the dragonlance to you, you will not wield the lance. I will."

"I see." Medan was thoughtful. He continued holding the sword, regarded it with new respect.

"This night as I was walking to the meeting in the darkness, I remembered this sword and its story, and I realized how it might be of use to us."

"Of use! This could make all the difference!" Medan exclaimed.

He took down the dragonlance from the wall and regarded it with interest, held it with respect. He was a tall man, yet the lance topped him by two feet. "I see one difficulty. This lance will be difficult to hide from Beryl. From what I recall, dragons are sensitive to the lance's magic."

"We will not hide it from her," Laurana replied. "As you say, she would sense its magic. We will keep it in the open, where she may see it plainly."

"Madam?" Medan was incredulous.

"Your gift to your overlord, Marshal. A powerful magical artifact from the Fourth Age."

Medan bowed. "I honor the wisdom of the Golden General."

"You will parade me, your hostage, before the dragon on top of the Tower of the Sun, as arranged. You will exhibit the dragonlance and offer that to her as a gift. If she tries to take hold of the lance—"

"She will," Medan interjected grimly. "She thirsts for magic as a drunkard his liquor."

"When she takes the lance," Laurana continued, "the lance—an artifact of light—will send a paralyzing shock through her. You will lift the sword and hold it before her eyes. Enthralled by the sword, she will be unable to defend herself. While the dragon stares mesmerized at the sword, I will take the lance and thrust it through the jaw and into her throat. I have some skill in the use of the lance," she added with quaint modesty.

Medan was approving, enthusiastic. "Your plan is an excellent one, General, and insures our success. I believe that, after all, I may yet live to walk my garden again."

"I hope so, Marshal," Laurana said, extending her hand to him. "I would miss my best enemy."

"And I mine," he replied, taking her hand and kissing it respectfully.

They climbed the stairs, leaving the treasure chamber to illusion. As they reached the door, Laurana turned and threw the velvet bag containing the key inside the room. They heard it strike the floor with a faint, muffled clink.

"My son now has the only key," she said softly.

26 PENALTY FOR BETRAYAL

The dragon Khellendros, whose common name among the lesser creatures of Krynn was Skie, had his current lair near the top of one of the smaller peaks of the Vingaard Mountains. Unlike the other dragon overlords, Malystryx and Sable, Skie had numerous lairs, all of them magnificent, none of them his home.

He was an enormous blue dragon, the largest of his kind by many times, an aberration of a blue dragon. Whereas most blues averaged forty feet in length, Skie had grown over the years until he was three hundred feet long from massive head to thrashing tail. He was not the same shade of blue as the other dragons of his type. Once his scales had gleamed sapphire. Over the past few years, however, the rich blue of his scales had faded, leaving him a dreary blue, as if he had acquired a fine coating of gray dust. He was aware that this color shift caused considerable comment among the smaller blues who served him. He knew they considered him a mutation, a freak, and although they deferred to him, deep inside they considered themselves better dragons because of it.

He didn't care what they thought. He didn't care where he lived, so long as it wasn't where he was. Restless, restive, he would move from one vast, serpentine tunnel gouged through the very heart of some immense mountain to an other on a whim, never remaining long in any of them.

A puny human might wander the wondrous labyrinths for a year and never find the ending. The blue's vast wealth was stashed in these lairs. Tribute came to him in a never-ending flood. Skie was overlord of the rich lord-city of Palanthas.

Skie cared nothing for the wealth. What need had he of steel coins? All the treasure chests of all the world overflowing with steel, gold, silver, and jewels could not buy him what he wanted. Even his own magical power—although it was inexplicably waning, it was still formidable—could not gain him his one desire.

Weaker dragons, such as the blue dragon Smalt, Skie's new lieutenant, might revel in such wealth and be glad to spend their paltry, pitiful lives in its gain. Skie had no care for the money. He never looked at it, he refused to listen to reports of it. He roamed the halls of his castle cavern until he could no longer stand the sight of them. Then he flew off to another lair, entered that one, only to soon sicken of it as well.

Skie had changed lairs four times since the night of the storm, the magical storm that had swept over Ansalon. He had heard a voice in that storm, a voice that he had recognized. He had not heard it since that night, and he searched for it, searched in anger. He had been tricked, betrayed, and he blamed the Speaker in the Storm for that betrayal. He made no secret of his rage. He spoke of it constantly to his minions, knowing that it would reach the right ears, trusting that someone would come to placate him.

"She had better placate me," Skie rumbled to Smalt. "She had better give me what I want. Thus far I have held my hand as I agreed. Thus far I have let her play her little game of conquest. I have not yet been recompensed, however, and I grow weary of waiting. If she does not give me what is my due, what I have been promised, I will end this little game of hers, break the board, and smash the pieces, be they pawn or Dark Knight."

Skie was kept apprised of Mina's movements. Some of his own subject blues had been among those who traveled to Silvanost to carry Mina and her forces into Nightlund. He was not surprised, therefore, when Smalt arrived to say that Mina wanted to arrange a meeting.

"How did she speak of me?" Skie demanded. "What did she say?"

"She spoke of you with great respect, O Storm Over Ansalon," Smalt replied. "She asks that you be the one to name the time and place for the meeting. She will come to you at your convenience, although it means leaving her army at a critical moment. Nevertheless, Mina deems this meeting with you important. She values you as an ally and is sorry to hear that you are in any way displeased or dissatisfied with the current arrangements. She is certain it is all a misunderstanding that can be smoothed over when the two of you come together."

Skie grunted, a sound that shook his enormous body—he was many times larger than the small blue dragon with the glistening sapphire scales who crouched humbly before him, wings drooping, tail curled submissively.

"In other words, you have fallen under her spell, Smalt, as they all do. Do not bother to deny it."

"I do not deny it, O Storm Over Ansalon," Smalt returned and there was an unusually defiant gleam in the blue's eyes. "She has conquered Silvanost. The wicked elves have fallen as grain to her scythe. Lord Targonne attempted to have her killed and instead was slain by her hand. She is now leader of the

Dark Knights of Neraka. Her troops are in Nightlund where she works on plans to lay siege to Solanthus—"

"Solanthus?" Skie growled.

Smalt's tail twitched nervously. He saw that he was in possession of news his master had not yet heard, and when a master is all knowing, to know something ahead of the master is never good.

"Undoubtedly she plans to discuss this with you first," Smalt faltered, "which is another reason why she is coming to meet with you, O Storm Over—"

"Oh, shut up and stop blathering, Smalt!" Skie snarled. "Get out."

"The meeting?" Smalt ventured.

"Tell her to meet me here at the eastern opening of this lair," Skie said glumly. "She may come to me whenever it suits her. Now leave me in peace."

Smalt was only too happy to do as he had been ordered.

Skie didn't give a damn about Solanthus. He had to do some hard thinking even to recall where the blasted city was located, and when he remembered, he thought his forces had already conquered Solanthus—he had a vague recollection of it. Perhaps that was some other city of humans. He didn't know, and he didn't care, or at least he hadn't cared until just now. Attacking Solanthus without asking his permission was another example of Mina's disdain for him, her lack of respect. This was a deliberate affront. She was showing him he was expendable, of no more use.

Skie was angered now, angry and, in spite of himself, afraid. He knew her of old, knew her vengeance, knew her wrath. It had never been turned on him. He had been a favorite. But then he had made a mistake. And now he was being made to pay.

His fear increased his anger. He had chosen the entrance of his lair as the meeting place because he could keep watch on all around him. He had no intention of being caught deep underground, trapped and ambushed. Once Smalt had departed, Skie paced about his lair and waited.

The blind beggar had reached his destination. He cast about with his staff until he located a large rock, sat down to rest himself and to consider what to do next. Since he could not see, he could not tell by sight exactly where he was. He knew from asking questions of people on the road that he was in Solamnia, somewhere in the foothills of the Vingaard Mountains. He had no real need to know his precise location, however, for he was not following a map. He was following his senses, and they had led him to this place. The fact that he knew the name of the place served merely to confirm in his mind what his soul already understood.

The silver dragon Mirror had traveled an immense distance in human form since the night of the magical storm—the storm that had wounded and scarred him, knocked him from the skies over Neraka, sent him plunging to the rocks below. Lying there, dazed and blind and bleeding, he had heard an immortal voice singing the Song of Death and he had been awed and appalled.

He had wandered aimlessly for a time, searching for and then finding Mina. He spoke with her. She was the one who sang the Song of Death.

The voice in the storm had been a summons. The voice had spoken the truth to him and, when he had refused to accept the truth, the Bringer of the Storm had punished him. Robbed of his sight, Mirror realized that he might be the only one in the world to see truly. He had recognized the voice, but he did not understand how it could be or why. So he had embarked on a quest to find out. In order to travel, he had been forced to take human form, because a blind dragon dare not fly, whereas a blind human can walk.

Trapped in this frail body, Mirror was helpless to act. He was frustrated in his search for answers, for the voice spoke to him constantly, taunted him, fed his fear, singing to him of the terrible events happening in the world: the fall of Silvanesti, the peril of Qualinost, the destruction of the Citadel of Light, the gathering of the dead in Nightlund. This was his punishment. Although he could not see, he was made to see all too clearly those he loved dying. He saw them stretch out their hands to him for help, and he was powerless to save them.

The voice sought to make despair his guide, and it had almost succeeded. He stumbled along the dark path, tapping out his way with his stick, and when he came to places where he cast about him with the stick and felt nothing ahead, he sometimes wondered if it would not be easier to keep walking, to fall off the edge of the precipice into the eternal silence that would close his ears to the voice, the darkness of death that could not be more dark than that in which he lived.

His search for others of his kind who had heard the voice, who might have heard the ancient words and understood them, had failed. He could find no other silver dragons. They had fled, disappeared. That gave him some indication that he had not been alone in recognizing the voice, but that was not much help if he were alone in the world—a blind dragon in human form—unable to do anything. In the moment of his despair Mirror formed a desperate resolution. One dragon would know the truth and might share it. But he was not a friend. He was a longtime enemy.

Skie, the immense blue dragon, had not arrived on Krynn as a stranger, as had Malys and the others. He had been in the world for years. True, Skie had changed much following the Chaos War. He had grown larger than any blue dragon was ever meant to grow. He had conquered Palanthas—the Dark Knights ruled that wealthy land in his name. He had gained the grudging respect of the great red Malystryx and her green cousin Beryl. Although rumor had it that he had turned upon his own kind and devoured them, as had Malys and Beryl, Mirror—for one—had not believed it.

Mirror would stake his life on that belief.

The silver dragon left Solace seeking Skie, tracking his enemy using the eyes of his soul to find the trail. His trek had led him here, to the foot of one of the blue dragon's mountain lairs. Mirror could not see the lair, but he could hear the enormous blue dragon roaming inside. He could feel the ground shake with every step Skie took, the mountains tremble as he lashed his tail. Mirror could smell the ozone of the blue's breath, feel the electricity tingle in the air.

Mirror rested for several hours, and when he felt his strength return, he began to climb. A dragon himself, he knew that Skie would have opened up many entrances to his lair. Mirror had only to find one of them.

Skie regarded the slight human female standing before him with barely concealed contempt. He had fostered a secret hope that in this female commander of armies he would find, once again, his lost Kitiara. He had relinquished that hope almost immediately. Here was no hot blood, no passion. Here was no love of battle for the sake of the challenge and the thrill of outwitting death. This female was as different from Kitiara as the ice floe differs from the frothing, crashing waves driven by the storm.

Skie might have been tempted to tell this girl to go away and send some responsible adult to deal with him, but he knew from the reports of his agents that she had flummoxed the Solamnics at Sanction, brought down the shield over Silvanost, and been the death of Lord Targonne—gone and quite easily forgotten.

She stood before him unafraid, even unimpressed, though he could have cracked the lithe, frail body with the flick of a claw. He had teeth that were bigger than this human.

"So you are the Healer, the Bringer of Death, the Conqueror of Elves," he grunted.

"No," she said. "I am Mina."

As she spoke, she lifted her gaze to meet his. He looked into the amber eyes and saw himself inside them. He saw himself small, shrunken, a lizard of a dragon. The sight was disquieting, made him ill at ease. He rumbled deep in his massive throat and arched his great neck and shifted the immense bulk of his body so that the mountain shook, and he felt reassured in his might and his strength. Still, in the amber eyes, he was very small.

"The One Who Heals, the One Who Brings Death, the One Who Conquers is the One God," Mina continued. "The One God I serve. The One God we both serve."

"Indeed I have served," Skie said, glowering. "I have served faithfully and well. I was promised my reward."

"You were given it. You were permitted to enter the Gray to search for her. If you have failed in your search, that is not the fault of the One God." Mina shrugged and slightly smiled. "You give up too easily, Skie. The Gray is a vast plane. You could not possibly have looked everywhere. After all, you did sense her spirit—"

"Did I?" Skie lowered his head so that his eyes could look directly into the amber eyes. He hoped to see himself grow large, but he failed. He was frustrated now, as well as angry. "Or was it a trick? A trick to get rid of me. A trick to cheat me of what I have earned."

He thrust forth his great head near her, exhaled a frustrated, sulfurous breath. "Two centuries ago, I was taken from my home world and brought in secret to the world known as Krynn. In return for my services it was promised that I would one day be granted the rulership of this world. I obeyed the commands given me. I traveled the Portals. I scouted out locations. I made all ready. I now claim the right to rule a world—this world. I could have done so thirty-eight years ago, but I was told that now was not the time.

"Then came the great red Malys and my cousins, and again I demanded my right to assert my authority. I could have stopped them, then. I could have cowed them, made them bow before me. Again, I was told, it is not the time. Now Beryl and Malystryx have grown in power that they gained by killing dragons of my own kin—"

"*Not* your kin," Mina corrected gently.

"My kin!" Skie thundered, his anger swelling to rage. Still, in the amber eyes, he remained small. "For over two hundred years I lived among blue dragons and fought alongside them. They are more my kin than those great bloated wyrms. Now the wyrms divide up the choicest parts between them. They extend their control. Be damned to the pact that was made. I—I am shunted off to the Gray on some wild kender chase.

"I say I was tricked!" the blue snarled. "I say I was deluded. Kitiara is not in the Gray. She was never in the Gray. I was sent there so that another could rule in my stead. Who is that other? You, girl? Or will it be Malys? Has another pact been made? A secret pact? That is why I came back—long before I was expected, seemingly, for I hear you are to now march upon Solanthus."

Mina was silent, considering.

Skie shifted his great bulk, lashed his tail so that it thumped against the walls of his lair, sending tremors through the mountain. Though the ground quaked beneath her feet, the human remained complacent. She gazed steadily at the dragon.

"The One God owes you nothing."

Skie drew in a seething breath. Lightning crackled between his teeth, sparked, and smoldered. The air was charged. Mina's cropped red hair rippled like that of a stalking panther. Ignoring his display of anger, she continued speaking, her voice calm.

"You abrogated your right to rule when you forgot your duties and forsook your oath of allegiance to the One to whom you owed everything, choosing instead to bestow your love and loyalty on a mortal. You rule the world!" Mina regarded the dragon with scorn and cool contempt. "You are not fit to rule a dung heap! Your services are no longer needed. Another has been chosen to rule. Your followers will serve me as they once served you. As to your precious Kitiara, you will never find her. She has passed far beyond your reach. But then, you knew that, didn't you, Skie?"

Mina's eyes fixed on him, unblinking. He found himself caught in them. He tried to look away, to break free, but he was held fast, the amber hardening around him.

"You refused to admit it," she went on, relentless, her voice digging deep beneath his scales. "Go back to the Gray, Skie. Go there to seek Kitiara. You can return anytime you want. You know that, don't you? The Gray is in your mind, Skie. You *were* deluded, but not by the One God. You deluded yourself."

Skie would send his answer to the One God—a charred lump. He unleashed his lethal breath, spat a gout of lightning at the girl. The bolt struck Mina on her black breastplate, over her heart. The fragile body crumpled to the cavern floor, frail limbs curled, contorted as those of a dead spider. She did not move.

Skie watched, cautious, wary. He did not trust her or the one she served. It had been too easy.

Mina lifted her head. A bolt of light flashed from her amber eyes and struck Skie in the center of his forehead.

The lightning burned his scales, jolted through his body. His heart clamored painfully in his chest, its rhythm knocked wildly askew. He could not breathe. Mist, gray mist, swirled before his eyes. His head sank to the stone floor of his lair. His eyes closed upon the gray mist that he knew so well. The gray mist where he heard Kitiara's voice calling to him. The gray mist that was empty . . .

Mina stood up. She had taken no hurt, seemingly, for her body was whole, her armor unblemished. She remained in the cave for several moments, watching the dragon, imprisoning his image behind her long lashes. Then she turned on her heel and walked from his lair.

The blind beggar remained crouched in the darkness of his hiding place while he tried to understand what had happened. He had arrived in Skie's lair at about the same time as Mina, only Mirror had come in by one of the back entrances, not by the front. His astonishment on hearing and recognizing Mina's voice had been immense. The last time he had seen her, he had met her on the road leading to Silvanost. Though he could not see her with his eyes, he had been able to see her through her voice. He had heard stories about her all along his road, and he had marveled that the orphan child he had known at the Citadel of Light, the child who had disappeared so mysteriously, had returned even more mysteriously. She had recognized him, known him for the silver dragon who had once guarded the citadel.

His astonishment at seeing her here, speaking to Skie, was not so great as his astonishment at their conversation. He was starting to understand, starting to find answers to his questions, but those answers were too astounding for him yet to comprehend them fully.

The silver dragon felt the Blue's fury building. Mirror trembled for Mina, not so much for her sake as for the sake of the orphan child she had been. Mirror would have to be the one to return to tell Goldmoon the horrible fate of the child she had once so loved. He heard the cracking of the lightning, bent beneath the shock wave of the thunder.

But it was not Mina who cried out in agony. The voice of pain was Skie's. Now the great blue dragon was quiet, except for a low, piteous moan.

Footsteps—booted, human footsteps—echoed in the lair and faded away.

Mirror felt more than heard the irregular thumping of Skie's heart, felt it pulse through the cavern so that it jarred his body. The giant heart was slowing. Mirror heard the soft moan of anger and despair.

Even a blind dragon was more at home in these twisting corridors than a human—sighted or not. A dragon could find his way through them faster.

Mirror had once, long ago, been larger than the Blue. That had changed. Skie had grown enormous, and now Mirror knew the reason why. Skie was not of Krynn.

Transforming himself into his true dragon form, Mirror was able to move without hindrance through the corridors of Skie's lair. The silver dragon glided along the passage, his wings folded tightly at his side, reaching out with his senses as a sightless human gropes with his hands. Sound and smell and a knowledge of how dragons build their lairs guided him, leading him in the direction of that last tortured cry of shock and pain.

Mirror advanced cautiously. There were other blue dragons in the vicinity of the lair. Mirror could hear their voices, though they were faint, and he could not understand what they said. He could smell their scent, a mixture of dragon and thunder, and he feared one or more of them might return to see what had befallen their leader. If the blues discovered Mirror, the blind silver would not stand a chance in battle against them.

The voices of the blue dragons died away. He heard the flapping of their wings. The lair stank of blue dragon, but instinct told Mirror the others were gone. They had left Skie to die. The other blues had deserted him to follow Mina.

Mirror was not surprised, nor did he blame them. He recalled vividly his own meeting with her. She had offered to heal him, and he had been tempted, sorely tempted, to let her. He had wished not so much that she would restore his sight but that she would restore to him something he had lost with the departure of the gods. He had found it, to his dismay. He had refused to allow her near him. The darkness that surrounded her was far deeper than the darkness that enveloped him.

Mirror reached the lair where Skie lay, gasping and choking. The Blue's immense tail twitched, back and forth, thumping the walls spasmodically. His body jerked, scraping against the floor, his wings flapped, his head thrashed. His claws scrabbled against the rock.

Mirror might be able to heal the body of the Blue, but that would avail Mirror little if he could not heal Skie's mind. Loyalty to Kitiara had turned to love, a hopeless love that had darkened to an obsession that had been fed and fostered so long as it served a useful purpose. When the purpose was complete, the obsession became a handy weapon.

It would be an act of mercy to let the tormented Skie die. Mirror could not afford to be merciful. He needed answers. He needed to know if what he feared was true.

Crouching in the cavern beside the body of his dying enemy, Mirror lifted his silver wings, spread them over Skie, and began to speak in the ancient language of the dragons.

27 THE CITY SLUMBERS

   Sitting in the dark on the wooden plank that was his bed in the cell, listening to his fourth Uncle Trapspringer tale in an hour, Gerard wondered if strangling a kender was punishable by death or if it would be considered a meritorious act, worthy of commendation.

   " . . . Uncle Trapspringer traveled to Flotsam in company with five other kender, a gnome, and a gully dwarf, whose name I can't remember. I think it was Phudge. No, that was a gully dwarf I met once. Rolf? Well, maybe. Anyway, let's say it was Rolf. Not that it matters because Uncle Trapspringer never saw the gully dwarf again. To go on with the story, Uncle Trapspringer had come across this pouch of steel coins. He couldn't remember where, he thought maybe someone had dropped it. If so, no one had come to claim it from him, so he decided that since possession is nine-tenths of a cat's lives he would spend some of the steel on magic artifacts, rings, charms, and a potion or two. Uncle Trapspringer was exceedingly fond of magic. He used to have a saying that you never knew when a good potion would come in handy, you just had to remember to hold your nose when you drank it. He went to this mage-ware shop, but the moment he walked in the door the most marvelous thing happened. The owner of the mage-ware shop happened to be a wizard, and the wizard told Uncle Trapspringer that not far from Flotsam was a cave where a black dragon lived, and the dragon had the most amazing collection of magical objects anywhere on Krynn, and the wizard just couldn't take Uncle Trapspringer's money when, with a little effort, Uncle Trapspringer could kill the black dragon and have all the magical objects he wanted. Now, Uncle Trapspringer thought this was an excellent idea. He asked directions to the cave, which the wizard most obligingly gave him, and he—"

"Shut up!" said Gerard through clenched teeth.

"I beg your pardon?" said Tasslehoff. "Did you say something?"

"I said 'shut up.' I'm trying to sleep."

"But I'm just coming to the good part. Where Uncle Trapspringer and the five other kender go to the cave and—"

"If you don't be quiet, I will come over there and quiet you," said Gerard in a tone that meant it. He rolled over on his side.

"Sleep is really a waste of time, if you ask me—"

"No one did. Be quiet."

"I—"

"Quiet."

He heard the sound of a small kender body squirming about on a hard wooden plank—the bed opposite where Gerard lay. In order to torture him, they had locked him in the same cell as the kender and had put the gnome in the next cell over.

" 'Thieves will fall out,' " the warden had remarked.

Gerard had never hated anyone in his life so much as he hated this warden.

The gnome, Conundrum, had spent a good twenty minutes yammering about writs and warrants and *Kleinhoffel* vs. *Mencklewink* and a good deal about someone named Miranda, until he had eventually talked himself into a stupor. At least Gerard supposed that was what had happened. There had been a gargle and a thump from the direction of the gnome's cell and then blessed silence.

Gerard had just been drifting off himself when Tasslehoff—who had fallen asleep the moment the gnome had opened his mouth—awakened the moment the gnome was quiet and launched into Uncle Trapspringer.

Gerard had put up with it for a long time, mostly due to the fact that the kender's stories had a numbing effect on him, rather like repeatedly hitting his head against a stone wall. Frustrated, angry—angry at the Knights, angry at himself, angry at fate that had forced him into this untenable position—he lay on the hard plank, unable to go back to sleep, and worried about what was happening in Qualinesti. He wondered what Medan and Laurana must think of him. He should have returned by now, and he feared they must have decided he was a coward who, when faced with battle, had run away.

As to his predicament here, the Lord Knight had said he would send a messenger to Lord Warren, but the gods knew how long that would take. Could they even find Lord Warren? He might have pulled out of Solace. Or he might be fighting for his life against Beryl. The Lord Knights said they would inquire around Solanthus to find someone who knew his family, but Gerard gave that long odds. First someone would actually have to inquire and in his cynical and pessimistic mood, he doubted if the Knights would trouble themselves. Second, if someone did know his father, that person might not know Gerard. In the past ten years, Gerard had done what he could to avoid going back home.

Gerard tossed and turned and, as one is prone to do during a restless, sleepless night, he let his fears and his worries grow completely out of proportion. The kender's voice had been a welcome distraction from his dark thoughts, but now it had turned into the constant and annoying drip of rain through a hole in the roof. Having fretted himself into exhaustion, Gerard turned his face to the wall. He ignored the kender's pathetic wrigglings and squirmings, intended, no doubt, to make him—Gerard—feel guilty and ask for another story.

He was floating on sleep's surface when he heard, or imagined he heard, someone singing a lullaby.

> Sleep, love; forever sleep.
> Your soul the night will keep.
> Embrace the darkness deep.
> Sleep, love; forever sleep.

The song was restful, soothing. Relaxing beneath the song's influence, Gerard was sinking beneath peaceful waves when a voice came out of the darkness, a woman's voice.

"Sir Knight?" the woman called.

Gerard woke, his heart pounding. He lay still. His first thought was that it was Lady Odila, come to torment him some more. He knew better almost at once, however. The voice had a different note, a more musical quality, and the accent was not Solamnic. Furthermore Lady Odila would have never referred to him as "Sir Knight."

Warm, yellow light chased away the darkness. He rolled over on his side so that he could see who it was who came to him in the middle of the night in prison.

He couldn't find her at first. The woman had paused at the bottom of the stairs to hear a reply, and the wall of the stairwell shielded her from his sight. The light she held wavered a moment, then began to move. The woman rounded the corner and he could see her clearly. White robes shimmered yellow-white in the candlelight. Her hair was spun silver and gold.

"Sir Knight?" she called again, looking searchingly about.

"Goldmoon!" cried out Tasslehoff. He waved his hand. "Over here!"

"Is that you, Tas? Keep your voice down. I'm looking for the Knight, Sir Gerard—"

"I am here, First Master," Gerard said.

Sliding off the plank, bewildered, he crossed the cell to stand near the iron bars, so that she could see him. The kender reached the bars in a single convulsive leap, thrust both arms out between the bars and most of his face. The gnome was awake, too, picking himself up off the floor. Conundrum looked groggy, bleary-eyed, and extremely suspicious.

Goldmoon held in her hand a long, white taper. Lifting the light close to Gerard's face, she studied him long and searchingly.

"Tasslehoff," she said, turning to the kender, "is this the Knight of Solamnia you told me about, the same Knight who took you to see Palin in Qualinesti?"

"Oh, yes, this is the same Knight, Goldmoon," said Tasslehoff.

Gerard flushed. "I know that you find this impossible to credit, First Master. But in this instance, the kender is telling the truth. The fact that I was found wearing the emblem of a Dark Knight—"

"Please say nothing more, Sir Knight," Goldmoon interrupted abruptly. "I do believe Tas. I know him. I have known him for many years. He told me that you were gallant and brave and that you were a good friend to him."

Gerard's flush deepened. Tas's "good friend" had been wondering, only moments earlier, how he might dispose of the kender's body.

"The best friend," Tasslehoff was saying. "The best friend I have in all the world. That's why I came looking for him. Now we've found each other, and we're locked up together, just like old times. I was telling Gerard all about Uncle Trapspringer—"

"Where am I?" the gnome asked suddenly. "Who are all of you?"

"First Master, I must explain—" Gerard began.

Goldmoon raised her hand, a commanding gesture that silenced all of them, including Tasslehoff. "I do not need explanations." Her eyes were again intent upon Gerard. "You flew here on a blue dragon."

"Yes, First Master. As I was about to tell you, I had no choice—"

"Yes, yes. It makes no difference. Haste is what counts. The Lady Knight said the dragon was still in the area, that they had searched for it but could not find it, yet they knew it was near. Is that true?"

"I . . . I have no way of knowing, First Master." Gerard was mystified. At first he thought she had come to accuse him, then maybe to pray for him or whatever Mystics did. Now he did know what she wanted. "I suppose it might be. The blue dragon promised to wait for me to return. I had planned to deliver my message to the Knights' Council, then fly back to Qualinesti, to do what I could to assist the elves in their battle."

"Take me there, Sir Knight."

Gerard stared at her blankly.

"I must go there," she continued, and her voice sounded frantic. "Don't you understand? I must find a way to go there, and you and your dragon will carry me. Tas, you remember how to get back, don't you?"

"To Qualinesti?" Tas said, excited. "Sure, I know the way! I have all these maps—"

"*Not* Qualinesti," Goldmoon said. "The Tower of High Sorcery. Dalamar's Tower in Nightlund. You said you were there, Tas. You will show me the way."

"First Master," Gerard faltered, "I am a prisoner. You heard the charges against me. I cannot go anywhere."

Goldmoon wrapped her hand around one of the bars of the cell. She tightened her grip until the knuckles on that hand grew as white as bare bone. "The warden sleeps under the enchantment I cast upon him. He will not stop me. No one will stop me. I must go to the Tower. I must speak with Dalamar and Palin. I could walk, and I will walk, if I have to, but the dragon is faster. You will take me, won't you, Sir Gerard?"

Goldmoon had been the ruler of her people. All her life, she had been a leader. She was accustomed to command and to being obeyed. Her beauty moved him. Her sorrow touched him. Beyond that, she offered him his freedom. Freedom to return to Qualinesti, to join the battle there, to live or die with those he had come to care for.

"The key to the cell is on the ring the warden carries—" he began.

"I have no need of it," Goldmoon said.

She closed her hand over the iron bars. The iron began to dissolve, melting like the wax of her candle. A hole formed in the center as the iron bars drooped, curled over.

Gerard stared. "How . . ." His voice was a hoarse croak.

"Hurry," Goldmoon said.

He did not move but continued to stare at her.

"I don't know how," she said and a note of desperation made her voice tremble. "I don't know how I have the power to do what I do. I don't know where I heard the words to the song of enchantment I sang. I know only that whatever I want I am given."

"Ah, now I remember who this woman is!" Conundrum heaved a sigh. "Dead people."

Gerard didn't understand, but then this was nothing new. He had not understood much of anything that had happened to him in the past month.

"Why start now?" Gerard muttered, as he stepped through the bars. He wondered where they had stashed his sword.

"Come along, Tas," Goldmoon said sternly. "This is no time to play games."

Instead of leaping joyously to freedom, the kender had suddenly and inexplicably retreated to the very farthest corner of the cell.

"Thank you for thinking of me, Goldmoon," Tasslehoff said, settling himself in the corner, "and thank you for melting the bars of the cell. That was wonderful and something you don't see everyday. Ordinarily I'd be glad to go with you, but it would be rude to leave my good friend Conundrum here. He's the best friend I have in all the world—"

Making a sound expressive of exasperation, Goldmoon touched the bars of the gnome's cell. The bars dissolved, as had the others. Conundrum climbed out the hole. Brow furrowed, he squatted with his hands on his knees, and began scraping up the iron meltings, muttering to himself something about smelting.

"I'll bring the gnome, Tas," Goldmoon said impatiently. "Now come out of there at once."

"We had better hurry, First Master," Gerard warned. He would have been quite happy to leave both gnome and kender behind. "The jailer's relief arrives two hours past midnight—"

"He will not come this night," Goldmoon said. "He will sleep past his time. But you are right. We must make haste, for I am called. Tas, come out of that cell this minute."

"Don't make me, Goldmoon!" Tasslehoff begged in pitiful tones. "Don't make me go back to the Tower. You don't know what they want to do to me. Dalamar and Palin mean to murder me."

"Don't be silly. Palin would never—" Goldmoon paused. Her severe expression softened. "Ah, I understand. I had forgotten. The Device of Time Journeying."

Tasslehoff nodded.

"I thought it was broken," he said. "Palin threw parts of it at the draconians, and it exploded, and I figured that's one thing I don't have to worry about anymore."

He gave a mournful sigh. "Then I reached into my pocket, and there it was. Still in pieces, but all the pieces were back in my pocket. I've thrown them away, time and again. I even tried giving them away, but they keep coming back to me. Even broken, they keep coming back." Tas looked at Goldmoon pleadingly. "If I go back to the Tower, they'll find it, and they'll fix it, and I'll have to be stepped on by a giant, and I'll die. I don't want to die, Goldmoon! I don't want to! Please don't make me."

Gerard almost suggested to Goldmoon that he hit the kender on the jaw and haul him out bodily, but on second thought, he kept silent. The kender looked so completely and utterly miserable that Gerard found himself feeling sorry for him. Goldmoon entered the cell and sat next to the kender.

"Tas," Goldmoon said gently, reaching out her hand and stroking back a lock of hair that had escaped his topknot and was straggling over his face, "I can't promise you that this will have a good and happy ending. Right now, to me it seems that it must end very badly. I have been following a river of souls, Tas. They gather at Nightlund. They do not go there of their own free will. They are prisoners, Tas. They are under some sort of terrible constraint. Caramon is with them, and Tika, Riverwind, and my daughter; perhaps all those we love. I want to find out why. I want to find out what is happening. You tell me that Dalamar is in Nightlund. I must see him, Tas. I must speak to him. Perhaps he is the cause. . . ."

Tasslehoff shook his head. "I don't think so. Dalamar's a prisoner, too, at least that's what he told Palin." The kender hung his head and plucked nervously at his shirt front. "There's something else, Goldmoon. Something I haven't told anyone. Something that happened to me in Nightlund."

"What is it, Tas?" Goldmoon looked concerned.

The kender had lost his jaunty gaiety. He was drooping and wan and shivering—shivering with fright. Gerard was amazed. He had often felt that a really good scare would be beneficial for a kender, would teach the rattle-brained little imps that life was not picnics by the tomb and taunting sheriffs and swiping gewgaws. Life was earnest and hard, and it was meant to be taken seriously. Now, seeing Tas dejected and fearful, Gerard looked away. He didn't know why, but he had the feeling that he had lost something, that he and the world had both lost something.

"Goldmoon," said Tas in an awful whisper, "I saw myself in that wood."

"What do you mean, Tas?" she asked gently.

"I saw my own ghost!" Tas said, and he shuddered. "It wasn't at all exciting. Not like I thought seeing one's own ghost would be. I was lost and alone, and

I was searching for someone or something. It may sound funny, I know, but I always thought that after I died, I'd meet up with Flint somewhere. Maybe we'd go off adventuring together, or maybe we'd just rest, and I'd tell him stories. But I wasn't adventuring. I was just alone . . . and lost . . . and unhappy."

He looked up at her, and Gerard was startled to see the track of a single tear trickle down through the grime on the kender's cheek.

"I don't want to be dead like that, Goldmoon. That's why I can't go back."

"Don't you see, Tas?" Goldmoon said. "That's why you *have* to go back. I can't explain it, but I am certain that what you and I have both seen is wrong. Life on this world is meant to be a way-stop on a longer journey. Our souls are supposed to move on to the next plane, to continue learning and growing. Perhaps we may linger, wait to join loved ones, as my dear Riverwind waits for me and somewhere, perhaps, Flint waits for you. But none of us can leave, apparently. You and I together must try to free these prisoner souls who are locked in the cell of the world as surely as you were locked in this cell. The only way we can do that is to go back to Nightlund. The heart of the mystery lies there."

She held out her hand to Tasslehoff. "Will you come?"

"You won't let them send me back?" he bargained, hesitating.

"I promise that the decision to go back or not will be yours," she said. "I won't let them send you back against your will."

"Very well," Tas said, standing up and dusting himself off and glancing about to see that he had all his pouches. "I'll take you to the Tower, Goldmoon. It just so happens that I have an extremely reliable body compass. . . ."

At this juncture, Conundrum, who had finished scraping up the melted iron, began to discourse on such things as compasses and binnacles and lode-stones and his great-great-uncle's theory on why north could be found in the north and not in the south, a theory that had proved to be quite controversial and was still being argued to this day.

Goldmoon paid no attention to the gnome's expostulations or Tasslehoff's desultory replies. She was imbued with a fixed purpose, and she went forward to achieve it. Unafraid, calm, and composed, she led them up the stairs, past the slumbering warden slumped over his desk, and out of the prison.

They hastened through Solanthus, a city of sleep and silence and half-light, for the sky was pearl gray with the coming of dawn. The gnome wound down like a spent spring. Tasslehoff was uncharacteristically quiet. Their footfalls made no sound. They might have been ghosts themselves as they roamed the empty streets. They saw no one, and no one saw them. They encountered no patrols. They met no farmer coming to market, no carousers stumbling home from the taverns. No dog barked, no baby cried.

Gerard had a strange impression of Goldmoon passing over the city streets, her cloak billowing out behind her, blanketing the city, closing eyes that were starting to open, lulling those who were waking back into sweet slumber.

They left Solanthus by the front gate, where no one was awake to stop them.

28 OVERSLEPT

Lady Odila woke to find the sun blazing in her eyes. She sat straight up in bed, irritated and annoyed. She was not generally a late sleeper; her usual time to rise being shortly before the gray light of dawn filtered through her window. She hated sleeping late. She was dull and listless, and her head ached. She felt as if she had spent the night carousing. True, after the Knights' Council, she had gone to the Dog and Duck, a tavern favored by members of the Knighthood, but not to drink. She had done what she had promised the First Master she would do: She had asked around to see if anyone knew or had ever met Gerard uth Mondar.

None of the Knights had, but one knew of someone who came from that part of Ansalon or thereabouts and another thought perhaps his wife's seamstress had a brother who had been a sailor and might have worked for Gerard's father. Not very satisfactory. Odila had lifted a mug of hard cider with her comrades and then gone to her bed.

She muttered imprecations to herself as she dressed, tugging on the padded leather tunic, linen shirt, and woolen socks she wore beneath her armor. She had intended to rise early to lead a patrol in search of the blue dragon, hoping to catch the beast while it was out hunting in the cool mists of early morning before it disappeared into its lair to sleep through the sunny part of the day. So much for that idea. Still, they might catch the beast napping.

Sliding the tunic, embroidered with the kingfisher and rose of the Solamnic Knighthood, over her head, Odila buckled on her sword, locked her door, and hurriedly left her quarters. She lived on the upper floor of a former inn that had been turned over to the Knighthood to house those who served in Solanthus. Clattering down the stairs, she noted that her fellow Knights appeared to be moving as slowly as she was this morning. She nearly collided with Sir Alfric, who was supposed to be in charge of the changing of the guard at the city's front gate and who would be late for his duty. Carrying his shirt and his sword belt in one hand, his helm in the other, he came dashing out of his room.

"And a good morning to you, too, my lord," said Odila, with a pointed stare at the front of his breeches.

Flushing deeply, Sir Alfric hastily laced himself into proper decorum and then fled out the door.

Chuckling at her jest, thankful she was not in for his reprimand, Odila walked briskly to the armorer. She had taken her breastplate to the armory yesterday to mend a torn leather strap and a bent buckle. They had promised to have it mended by this morning. Everyone she met looked sleepy and bedraggled or annoyed and put out. She passed by the man who was the relief for the night warden. The man was yawning and stumbling over his feet in his haste to report for work.

Had everyone in Solanthus overslept?

Odila pondered this disturbing question. What had seemed an odd and annoying occurrence was now starting to take on sinister significance. She had no reason to think this unusual bout of slothfulness on the part of Solanthus's inhabitants had anything to do with the prisoners, but, just to make certain, she altered her direction, headed for the prison.

She arrived to find everything peaceful. To be sure, the warden was sprawled over his desk, snoring blissfully, but the keys still hung from their hook on the wall. She woke the sleeping warden with a sharp rap of her knuckles on his bald pate. He sat straight up, wincing and blinking at her in confusion. While the warden rubbed his head, she made the rounds to find that the prison's inmates were all slumbering soundly in their cells. The prison had never been so quiet.

Relieved, Odila decided she would check on Gerard while she was here, to let him know that she knew people who might be able to swear to his identity. She walked down the stairs, rounded the corner and stopped and stared in amazement. Shaking her head, she turned on her heel and walked slowly up the stairs.

"And I had just decided he was telling the truth," she said to herself. "That will teach me to admire cornflower-blue eyes. Men! Born liars, every one of them.

"Sound the alarm!" she ordered the sleep-befuddled warden. "Turn out the guard. The prisoners have escaped."

She paused a moment, wondering what to do. First disappointed, she was now angry. She had trusted him, the absent gods knew why, and he had betrayed her. Not the first time this had happened to her, but she intended it should be the last. Turning, she headed for the stables. She knew where Gerard and his friends had gone, where they must go. He would head for his dragon. When she reached the stables, she checked to see if any horses were missing.

None were, and so she assumed that the Knight must be on foot. She was relieved. The gnome and kender, with their short legs, would slow him down.

Mounting her horse, she galloped through the streets of Solanthus that were slowly coming to life, as if the entire city was suffering from the ill effects of a wild drinking bout.

She passed through the numerous gates, pausing only long enough to determine if the guards had seen anything of the prisoners in the night. They hadn't, but then, by the looks of them, they hadn't seen anything except the insides of their eyelids. She arrived at the final gate to find Starmaster Mikelis there, as well.

The guards were red in the face, chagrined. Their superior was speaking to Mikelis.

"—caught sleeping on duty," he was saying irately.

Odila reigned in her horse. "What is the matter, Starmaster?" she asked.

Absorbed in his own troubles, he did not recognize her from the trial. "The First Master has gone missing. She did not sleep in her bed last night—"

"She was the *only* one in Solanthus who did not sleep, apparently," Lady Odila returned with a shrug. "Perhaps she went to visit a friend."

The Starmaster was shaking his head. "No, I have looked everywhere, spoken to everyone. No one has seen her since she left the Knights' Council."

Odila paused, considered this. "The Knights' Council. Where the First Master spoke in defense of Gerard uth Mondar. It might interest you to know, Starmaster, that last night the prisoner escaped from his cell."

The Starmaster looked shocked. "Surely, Lady Knight, you're not suggesting—"

"He had help," Odila said, frowning, "help that could have come only from someone who has mystical powers."

"I don't believe it!" Starmaster Mikelis cried heatedly. "First Master Goldmoon would never—"

Odila didn't wait to hear anymore about First Master Goldmoon. Spurring her horse to a gallop, she rode out of the gate and down the main road. As she rode, she tried to sort all this out. She had believed Gerard's story—strange and bizarre though it might be. She had been impressed by his eloquent plea at the end of the trial, a plea not for himself but for the elves of Qualinesti. She had been deeply impressed by the First Master, and that was odd, considering that Lady Odila did not put much stock in miracles of the heart or whatever it was clerics were peddling these days. She even believed the kender, and it was at that point that she wondered if she was running a fever.

Odila had ridden about two miles from the city when she saw a rider approaching her. He was riding fast, bent over his steed, kicking his horse in the flanks to urge it to even greater speed. Spittle whipped from the horse's mouth as it thundered past Odila. She recognized by his garb that the man was a scout and concluded that the news he brought must be urgent, judging from the breakneck pace he set. She was curious but continued on her way. Whatever news he brought, it would keep until she returned.

She had ridden another two miles when she heard the first horn call.

Odila reigned in her steed, turned in the saddle, stared back in consternation at the walls of the city. Horns and now drums were sounding the call to arms. An enemy had been sighted, approaching the city in force. To the west, a large cloud of dust obscured the horizon line. Odila stared at the dust cloud intently, trying to see what caused it, but she was too far away. She sat for a moment, irresolute. The horns called her back to duty behind the city walls. Her own sense of duty called her to continue on, to recapture the escaped prisoner.

Or, at least, to have a talk with him.

Odila cast a final glance at the dust cloud, noted that it appeared to be drawing nearer. She increased her speed down the road.

She kept close watch along the side of the highway, hoping to find the location where the group had left the road to go in search of their dragon. A few more miles brought her to the spot. She was surprised and oddly pleased to find that they had not even bothered to hide their tracks. An escaping felon—a cunning and hardened criminal—would have worked to throw pursuers off his trail. The party had cut a wide swath in the waving prairie grass. Here and there small excursions slanted off to the side as if someone—probably the kender—had wandered off, only to be hauled back.

Odila turned her horse's head and began following the clearly marked path. As she rode farther, drawing nearer to the stream, she came upon more evidence that she was on the right trail, sighting various objects that must have tumbled out of the kender's pouches: a bent spoon, a shining piece of mica, a silver ring, a tankard with Lord Tasgall's crest. She was among the trees now, riding along the bank of the stream where she had first caught Gerard.

The ground was damp from the morning mists, and she could see footprints: one pair of large booted feet, one pair of smaller feet wearing boots with soft soles, one pair of small kender feet—they were in front—and another pair of small feet straggling behind. Those must belong to the gnome.

Odila came to a place where three of them had halted and one had gone on ahead—the Knight, of course, going to seek out the dragon. She could see some signs that the kender had started to go with the Knight but had apparently been ordered back, because the small footprints, toes dragging, reversed themselves. She could see where the Knight had returned and the rest had gone forward with him.

Dismounting, Odila left her horse by the side of the river with a command to remain there until summoned. She proceeded forward on foot, moving silently, but with as much haste as she could. The footprints were fresh. The ground was just now starting to dry with the morning sun. She had no fear that she would be too late. She had kept watch on the skies to catch sight of a blue dragon, but she had seen no sign of one.

It would take some time, she reasoned, for the Knight to persuade a blue dragon—known to be extremely proud and wholly dedicated to the cause of evil—to carry a kender, a gnome, *and* a Mystic of the Citadel of Light. For that matter, Odila could not imagine the First Master, who had long ago risked her life to battle blue dragons and all they stood for, agreeing to come near a blue dragon, much less ride on one.

"Curiouser and curiouser," Odila said to herself.

The horn calls were distant, but she could still hear them. The city's bells were ringing now, too, warning the farmers and shepherds and those who lived outside the city to leave their homes and seek the safety of the city's walls. Odila strained her ears, focused on one sound, a sound apart from the horn calls and the wild clamoring of the bells. Voices.

Odila crept forward, listening. She recognized Gerard's voice and Goldmoon's. She loosened her sword in its sheath. Her plan was to rush in, knock down Gerard before he could react, and hold him hostage in order to prevent the dragon from attacking. Of course, depending on the relationship between dragon and Knight, the blue might well attack her with no regard for what happened to its master. That was a risk Odila was prepared to take. She was sick and tired of being lied to. Here was one man who was going to tell her the truth or die in the process.

Odila recognized this cavern. She had come across it in her earlier attempts to capture the dragon. She and her patrol had searched the cave but had found no trace of the beast. He must have moved here afterward, she concluded, venturing forward. Concentrating on her footing, taking care that she did not crack a stick beneath her boot, or tread on a pile of rustling leaves, she listened intently to what the voices were saying.

"Razor will carry you into Nightlund, First Master." Gerard was speaking, his voice low and deferential, respectful. "If, as the kender claims, the Tower of High Sorcery is located there, the dragon will find it. You need *not* rely on the kender's directions. But I beg you to reconsider, First Master." His voice grew more earnest, his tone more intense. "Nightlund has an evil reputation that, from all I have heard, is well deserved."

A pause, then, "Very well, First Master, if you are committed to this action—"

"I am, Sir Knight." Goldmoon's voice, clear and resolute, echoed in the cave.

Gerard spoke again. "Caramon's dying request was for me to take Tasslehoff to Dalamar. Perhaps I should reconsider and travel with you." He sounded reluctant. "Yet, you hear the horns. Solanthus is under attack. I should be back there. . . ."

"I know what Caramon intended, Sir Gerard," said Goldmoon, "and why he made that request. You have done more than enough to fulfill his last wishes. I absolve you of the responsibility. Your life and that of the kender have been intertwined, but the threads are now untangled. You are right to return to defend Solanthus. I will go forth on my own. What have you told the dragon about me?"

"I told Razor that you are a dark mystic, traveling in disguise. You have brought the kender because he claims to have found a way inside the Tower. The gnome is an accomplice of the kender who will not be separated from him. Razor believed me. Of course, he believed me." Gerard was bitter. "Everyone believes the lies I tell. No one believes the truth. What sort of strange, twisted world do we inhabit?"

He sighed heavily.

"You have the letter from King Gilthas," Goldmoon said. "They must believe that."

"Must they? You give them too much credit. You should make haste, First Master." Gerard paused, arguing with himself. "Yet, the more I think about it, the more I am loath to allow you to enter Nightlund alone—"

"I need no protection," Goldmoon assured him, her voice softening. "Nor do I think there is any protection you could offer me. Whoever summons me will see to it that I arrive safely at my destination. Do not lose faith in the truth, Sir Gerard," she added gently, "and do not fear the truth, no matter how awful it may seem."

Odila stood irresolute outside the cave, pondering what to do. Gerard had a chance to escape, and he was not taking it. He was planning to return to defend Solanthus. *Everyone believes the lies I tell. No one believes the truth.*

Drawing her sword, gripping the hilt tightly in her hand, Odila left the cover of the trees and walked boldly into the mouth of the cave. Gerard stood with his back to her, gazing into the darkness beyond. He wore the leathers of a dragonrider, the only clothes he had, the same that he'd worn in prison. He had recovered his sword and sword belt. In his hand he held the leather headgear of a dragonrider. He was alone.

Hearing Odila's footsteps, Gerard glanced around. He sighted her, rolled his eyes, shook his head.

"You!" he muttered. "All I need." He looked away into the darkness.

Odila thrust the tip of her sword into the back of his neck. She noted, as she did so, that he'd made a hasty job of putting on his leathers. Either that or he'd dressed in the dark. The tunic was on backward.

"You are my prisoner," she said, her voice harsh. "Make no move. Do not try to call out to the dragon. One word and I will—"

"You'll what?" Gerard demanded.

Whipping around, he shoved aside her sword with his hand and strode past her, out of the cave.

"Make haste, Lady, if you're coming," he said brusquely. "Or we will arrive back in Solanthus after the battle has ended."

Odila smiled, but only when his back was turned and he couldn't see her. Rearranging her face to look stern and severe, she hurried after him.

"Wait a minute!" she said. "Where do you think you are going?"

"Back to Solanthus," he said coolly. "Don't you hear the horns? The city is under attack."

"You are my prisoner—"

"Fine, I'm your prisoner," he said. Turning, he handed her his sword. "Where is your horse? I don't suppose you brought another one for me to ride. No, of course not: That would have required forethought, and you have all the brains of a newt. As I recall, however, your horse is a sturdy animal. The distance back to Solanthus is not far. He can carry us both."

Odila accepted the sword, used the hilt to rub her cheek. "Where did the Mystic go? And the others? The kender and the gnome. Your . . . um . . . accomplices."

"In there," Gerard said, waving his hand in the direction of the cave. "The dragon is in there, too, at the far end. They plan to wait until nightfall before they leave. Feel free to go back to confront the dragon. Especially since you brought only one horse."

Odila pressed her lips tightly together to keep from laughing.

"You really intend to go back to Solanthus?" she demanded, frowning darkly.

"I really do, Lady Knight."

"Then I guess you'll need this," she said and tossed him his sword.

He was so startled, he fumbled, nearly dropped it.

Odila walked past, giving him a wink and sly look from out the corner of her eye. "My horse can carry both of us, Cornbread. As you yourself said, we'd best hurry. Oh, and you better close your mouth. You might swallow a fly."

Gerard stared, dumbfounded, then sprang after her.

"You believe me?"

"*Now* I do," she said pointedly. "I don't want to hurt your feelings, Cornbread, but you're not clever enough to have put on an act like the one I just witnessed. Besides"—she sighed deeply—"your story is such a muddle, what with young ninety-year-old crones, a dead living kender, *and* a gnome. One has to believe it. No one could make up something like that." She looked at him over her shoulder. "So you really do have a letter from the elf king?"

"Would you like to see it?" he asked with a grudging smile.

Odila shook her head. "Not me. To be honest, I didn't even know the elves had a king. Nor do I much care. But it's good that someone does, I guess. What sort of a fighter are you, Cornbread? You don't look to have much in the way of muscle." She glanced disdainfully at his arms. "Maybe you're the small, wiry type."

"If Lord Tasgall will even let me fight," Gerard muttered. "I will offer my parole that I will not try to escape. If they will not accept it, I will do what I can to assist with the wounded or put out fires or however else I may serve—"

"I think they'll believe you," she said. "As I said, a story with a kender *and* a gnome . . ."

They reached the place where Odila had left her horse. Odila swung herself up into the saddle. She looked at Gerard, who looked up at her. He truly had the most startling blue eyes. She had never seen eyes that color before, never seen eyes of such clarity and brilliance. She reached out her hand to him.

Gerard grabbed hold, and she pulled him up to sit uncomfortably on the horse's rump behind her. Clucking her tongue, she commanded the horse forward.

"You had better put your arms around my waist, Cornbread," she said, "so that you don't fall off."

Gerard clasped his arms around her midriff, holding her firmly, sliding forward on the horse's rump so that he was pressed against her.

"Nothing personal, Lady Odila," he said.

"Ah, me," she returned with a gushy sigh. "And here I was going to go choose my wedding dress."

"Don't you ever take anything seriously, Lady?" Gerard asked, nettled.

"Not much," Odila answered, turning to grin at him. "Why should I, Cornbread?"

"My name is Gerard."

"I know," she replied.

"Then why don't you call me that?"

She shrugged. "The other suits you, that's all."

"I think it's because calling me by my name makes me a person, not a joke. I despise women, and I have the feeling you don't think much of men. We've both been hurt. Maybe both of us fear life more than we fear death. We can discuss that later over a cold pitcher of ale. But for now let's agree on this much: You will call me Gerard. Or Sir Gerard, if you prefer."

Odila thought she should have an answer to this, but she couldn't come up with one readily, one that was funny, at least. She urged her horse to a gallop.

"Stop!" Gerard said suddenly. "I thought I saw something."

Odila reined in the horse. The animal stood panting, flanks heaving. They had emerged from the tree line along the stream bank, were heading out into the open. The road lay before them, dipped down into a shallow depression before rising again to enter the city. She saw now what Gerard had seen. What she should have seen if she hadn't been so damn preoccupied with blue eyes.

Riders. Riders on horses. Hundreds of riders pouring across the plains, coming from the west. They rode in formation. Their flags fluttered in the wind. Sunlight gleamed off spear tips and flashed off steel helms.

"An army of Dark Knights," said Odila.

"And they are between us and the city," said Gerard.

29 CAPTOR CAPTIVE

"Q uick, before they see us!" said Gerard. "Turn this beast's head around. We can hide in the cave—"

"Hide!" Odila repeated, casting him a shocked glance over her shoulder. Then she grinned. "I like you, Corn—" She paused, then said, with a wry smile, "Sir Gerard. Any other Knight would have insisted we rush into battle." Sitting up straight and tall, she placed her hand on her sword hilt and declaimed, "I will stand and fight though the odds are a hundred to one. My honor is my life."

She turned her horse's head, began to ride back toward the cave.

Now it was Gerard who looked shocked. "Don't you believe that?"

"What good is your honor going to do you when you're dead? What good will it do anyone? I'll tell you what, Sir Gerard" she continued, "they'll make a song for you. Some damn stupid song they'll sing in the taverns, and all the fat shopkeepers will get misty-eyed and slobber in their beer about the brave Knight who fought odds of six hundred to one. But you know who *won't* be singing? Those Knights inside Solanthus. Our comrades. Our friends. The Knights who aren't going to have a chance to fight a glorious battle in the name of honor. Those Knights who have to fight to stay alive to protect people who have put their trust in them.

"So maybe our swords are only two swords, and two swords won't make a difference. What if every one of those Solamnic Knights in Solanthus decided to ride out onto the battlefield and challenge six hundred of the enemy to glorious combat? What would happen to the peasants who fled to the Knights for safety? Will the peasants die gloriously, or will they be spitted on the end of some soldier's spear? What will happen to the fat shopkeepers? Will they die gloriously, or will they be forced to watch while enemy soldiers rape their wives and daughters and burn their shops to the ground. The way I see it, Sir Gerard, we took an oath to protect these people. We didn't take an oath to die gloriously and selfishly in some hopeless, inane contest.

"The main objective of the enemy is to kill you. Every day you remain alive you defeat their main objective. Every day you stay alive you win and they lose—even if it's only skulking about, hiding in a cave until you can find a way to return to your comrades to fight alongside them. That, to me, is honor."

Odila paused for breath. Her body trembled with the intensity of her feeling.

"I never thought of it like that," Gerard admitted, regarding her in admiration. "I guess there is something you take seriously, after all, Lady Odila. Unfortunately, it all appears to have been for nothing." He raised his arm, pointed past her shoulder. "They've sent outriders to guard the flanks. They've seen us."

A group of horsemen, who had been patrolling the edge of the tree line, rode into view about a half mile away. The horse and riders standing alone amidst the prairie grass had been easily spotted. The patrol wheeled as one and was now galloping toward them to investigate.

"I have an idea. Unbuckle your sword belt and give it to me," Gerard said.

"What—" Frowning, Odila glanced around to see him pulling the leather helm over his head. "Oh!" Realizing what he meant to do, she began to unbuckle her sword. "You know, Sir Gerard, this ruse might work better if you weren't wearing your tunic backside-front. Hurry, shift it before they get a good look at us!"

Cursing, Gerard pulled his arms out of the sleeves and wriggled the tunic around until the emblem of the Dark Knights of Neraka was in the front.

"No, don't turn around," he ordered her. "Just do it. Be quick. Before they can get a good look at us."

Odila unbuckled her sword belt and slipped it into his hands. He thrust her sword, belt and all, inside his own swordbelt, then pulled on his helm. He did not fear he would be recognized, but the helm was excellent for concealing facial expressions.

"Hand me the reins and put your hands behind your back."

Odila did as he ordered. "You've no idea how exciting I find this, Sir Gerard," she murmured, breathing heavily.

"Oh, shut up," he muttered, fumbling with the knot. "Take *this* seriously, at least."

The patrol was drawing near. He could see details now, and he noted with astonishment that the leader was a minotaur. Gerard's hopes that they might get out of this alive increased. He had never met or even seen a minotaur before, but he had heard that they were thick-skulled and dim-witted. The remainder of the patrol were Knights of Neraka, experienced cavalrymen, judging by their skill in handling their mounts.

The enemy patrol galloped across the prairie, their horses sending up clouds of dust from the dry grass. A single gesture from the minotaur, who rode in the lead, sent the other members of the patrol out in a wide circle, surrounding Gerard and Odila.

Gerard had thought about riding forward to meet them but decided this might seem suspicious. He was a Dark Knight of Neraka near an enemy stronghold, encumbered with a prisoner, and he had good reason to react as warily to them as they did to him.

The minotaur raised his hand in salute. Gerard returned the salute, thanking whoever might be listening for his training under Marshal Medan. He sat his horse in silence, waited for the minotaur, who was his superior, to speak. Odila's cheeks were flushed. She glared at them all in stony silence. Gerard only hoped that silence would continue.

The minotaur eyed Gerard closely. The minotaur's eyes were not the dull eyes of a beast but were bright with intelligence.

"What is your name, your rank, and your commanding officer?" the minotaur demanded. His voice was gruff and growling, but Gerard had no difficulty understanding him.

"I am Gerard uth Mondar, aide to Marshal Medan."

He gave his real name because if, by some wild chance, they checked with Marshal Medan, he would recognize Gerard's name and know how to respond. He added the number of the unit serving in Qualinesti but nothing more. Like any good Knight of Neraka, he was suspicious of his comrades. He would answer only what he was asked, volunteering nothing.

The minotaur frowned. "You are a long way from home, dragonrider. What brings you this far north?"

"I was en route to Jelek on Marshal Medan's blue dragon with an urgent message from Marshal Medan to Lord of the Night Targonne," Gerard replied glibly.

"You are still a long way from home," the minotaur stated, the bestial eyes narrowing. "Jelek is a long way east of here."

"Yes, sir," said Gerard. "We flew into a storm and were blown off course. The dragon thought he could make it, but we were hit by a sudden gust of wind that flipped us over. I almost fell from the saddle, and the dragon tore a shoulder muscle. He continued to fly as long as he could, but it proved much too painful. We had no idea where we were. We thought we were near Neraka, but then we saw the towers of a city. Having grown up near here, I recognized Solanthus. At about the same time, we saw your army advancing on the city. Fearing to be noticed by the cursed Solamnics, the dragon landed in this forest and located a cave where he could rest and heal his shoulder.

"This Solamnic"—Gerard gave Odila a rough poke in the back—"saw us land. She tracked us to the cave. We fought, and I disarmed and captured her."

The minotaur looked with interest at Odila. "Is she from Solanthus?"

"She will not talk, sir, but I have no doubt that she is and can provide details about the number of troops stationed inside the city, its fortifications, and other information that will be of interest to your commander. Now, Talon

Leader," Gerard added, "I would like to know your name and the name of your commander."

This was bold, but he felt that he'd been interrogated enough, and to continue meekly answering questions without asking a few of his own would look out of character.

The minotaur's eyes flashed, and for a moment, Gerard thought he had overplayed his part. Then the minotaur answered. "My name is Galdar. Our commander is Mina." He spoke the odd name with a mixture of reverence and respect that Gerard found disconcerting. "What is the message you were carrying to Jelek?"

"My message is to Lord Targonne," Gerard replied and at the word *message*, his heart upended and slid down his gullet.

He remembered, suddenly, that he was carrying on his person a message that was not from Marshal Medan, but from Gilthas, king of the Qualinesti; a letter that would ruin him if it fell into the hands of the Dark Knights. Gerard could not believe his ill luck. The day when the letter might have done him some good, he'd left it with the dragon. The day when the letter could do him irreparable harm, it was tucked in his belt. What had he done in his lifetime to so outrage Fate?

"Lord Targonne is dead," responded the minotaur. "Mina is now Lord of the Night. I am her second-in-command. You may deliver the message to me, and I will relay it to her."

Gerard was not unduly surprised to hear that Targonne was dead. Promotion up the ranks of the Dark Knights often took place at night in the dark with a knife thrust to the ribs. This Mina had presumably taken command. He wrested his mind from dwelling on that blasted incriminating letter to dealing with the new turn of events. He could give his false message to this minotaur and be done with it. Then what would happen? They would take Odila from him and haul her off to be tortured while he would be thanked for his service and dismissed to return to his dragon.

"I was told to deliver the message to the Lord of the Night," returned Gerard stubbornly, playing the quintessential commander's aide—officious and self-important. "If that is not Lord Targonne, then my orders require me to deliver it to the person who has taken his place."

"As you will." The minotaur was in a hurry. He had more important things to do than bandy words with a marshal's aide. Galdar jerked a thumb in the direction of the dust cloud. "They'll be raising the command tent now. You'll find Mina there, directing the siege. I'll send a man with you to guide you."

"There is really no need, sir—" Gerard began, but the minotaur ignored him.

"As to your prisoner," the minotaur continued, "you can turn her over to the interrogator. He'll be setting up shop somewhere near the blacksmith's forge."

An image of red hot pokers and flesh-ripping iron tongs came unpleasantly to mind. The minotaur ordered one of his Knights to accompany them. Gerard would have liked to have dispensed with the company, but he didn't dare argue. Saluting the minotaur, Gerard urged the horse forward. For a moment he feared that the animal, feeling an unfamiliar hand on the reins, would balk, but Odila gave a slight kick with her heels, and the horse started moving. The minotaur stared intently at Gerard, during which the sweat trickled down the front of Gerard's breast. Then the minotaur wheeled his horse and galloped off. He and the rest of the patrol were soon lost to sight, entering the tree line. Gerard pulled up and peered back in the direction of the river.

"What is it?" their Dark Knight escort demanded.

"I'm concerned about my dragon," Gerard said. "Razor belongs to the Marshal. They've been comrades for years. It would mean my head if anything happened to the beast." He turned back to face the Knight. "I'd like to go check on the dragon, let Razor know what's going on."

"My orders are to take you to Mina," said the Knight.

"You don't have to come," said Gerard shortly. "Look, you don't seem to understand. Razor must have heard the horn calls. He's a blue. You know how blues are. They can *smell* battle. He probably thinks that the cursed Solamnics have turned out the city to search for him. If he feels threatened, he might mistakenly attack your army—"

"My orders are to take you to Mina," the Knight repeated with dull-witted stubborness. "When you have reported to her, you can return to the dragon. You need not be concerned about the beast. He will not attack us. Mina wouldn't let him. As to his wounds, Mina will heal him, and you both will be able to return to Qualinesti."

The Knight rode on, heading for the main body of the army. Gerard muttered imprecations at the Knight from the safety of the helm, but he had no choice except to ride after him.

"I'm sorry," he said under cover of the horse's hoofbeats. "I thought sure he'd fall for it. He gets rid of us, gets out of patrol duty, does what he wants for an hour or two, then reports back." Gerard shook his head. "Just my luck that I have to run into the only reliable Dark Knight who ever lived."

"You tried," said Odila and by twisting her hands, she managed to give him a pat on his knee. "You did the best you could."

Their guide rode on ahead, eager to do his duty. Annoyed that they weren't moving faster, he gestured with his arm for them to hasten their pace. Gerard ignored the Knight. He was thinking about what the minotaur had said, about the Dark Knights laying siege to Solanthus. If that was the case, he might well be riding into an army of ten thousand or more.

"What did you mean when you said I hated men?" Odila asked.

Jolted out of his thoughts, Gerard had no idea what she was talking about, and he said so.

"You said that you despised women and that I hated men. What did you mean?"

"When did I say that?"

"When we were talking about what to call you. You said that both of us feared life more than we did death."

Gerard felt his skin burn and was glad he was wearing the helm to cover his face. "I don't remember. Sometimes I say things without thinking—"

"I had the feeling you'd been thinking about this for a long time," Odila interrupted.

"Yes, well, maybe." Gerard was uncomfortable. He hadn't meant to lay himself wide open, and he certainly didn't want to talk to her about what was inside. "Don't you have other things to worry about?" he demanded irritably.

"Like having red-hot needles jabbed beneath my fingernails?" she asked coolly. "Or my joints dislocated on the rack? I have plenty to worry about. I'd rather talk about this."

Gerard fell silent a moment, then he said, awkwardly, "I'm not sure what I meant. Maybe it's just the fact that you don't seem to have much use for men. Not just me. That's understandable. But I saw how you reacted to the other Knights during the council meeting and to the warden and—"

"*How* do I react?" she demanded, shifting in the saddle to look back at him. "What's the matter with the way I react?"

"Don't turn around!" Gerard snapped. "You're my prisoner, remember? We're not supposed to be having a cozy chat."

She sniffed. "For your information, I adore men. I just happen to think they're all cheats and scoundrels and liars. Part of their charm."

Gerard opened his mouth to reply to this when the Knight escort dashed back toward them at a gallop.

"Blast!" Gerard muttered. "What does this great idiot want now?"

"You are dawdling," said the Knight accusingly. "Make haste. I must return to my duties."

"I've lost a dragon to injury," Gerard returned. "I don't plan to lose a horse."

There was no help for it, however. This Knight was apparently going to stick to them like a bloodsucking tick. Gerard increased the pace.

As they entered the outskirts of the camp, they saw the army that was beginning to dig in for the siege. The soldiers were setting up camp well outside the range of arrows from the city walls. A few Solanthus archers tried their luck, but their arrows fell well short, and eventually the firing ceased. Probably their officers told them to quit being fools and save their arrows.

No one in the enemy camp paid the archers any attention, beyond glancing now and then at the walls that were lined with soldiers. The glances were furtive and were often followed by an exchange of words with a comrade, both of whom would raise their eyebrows, shake their heads and return to work quickly before an officer noticed. The soldiers did not appear frightened at the daunting sight of the walled city, merely bemused.

Gerard indulged his curiosity, looked about intently. He was not part of this army and so his curiosity would appear justified.

He turned to his guide. "When do the rest of the troops arrive?"

The Knight's voice was calm, but Gerard noted that the man's eyes flickered behind his helm. "Reinforcements are on the way."

"A great number, I suppose," Gerard said.

"A vast number," said the Knight. "More than you can imagine."

"They're nearby?"

The Knight eyed Gerard narrowly. "Why do you want to know? What is it to you?"

Gerard shrugged. "I thought I might lend my sword to the cause, that's all."

"What did you say?" the Knight demanded.

Gerard raised his voice to be heard above the din of hammers pounding, officers shouting orders, and the general tumult that went along with setting up a field camp.

"Solanthus is the most well-fortified city on the continent. The mightiest siege engines on Krynn couldn't make a dent in those walls. There must be five thousand troops ready to defend the city. What do you have here? A few hundred? Of course, you're expecting reinforcements. It doesn't take a genius to figure that out."

The Knight shook his head. Rising in his stirrups, he pointed. "There is Mina's command tent. You can see the flag. I will leave you to find your own way."

"Wait a minute," Gerard shouted after the Knight. "I want to deliver my prisoner safely to the interrogator. There'll be a reward in this for me. I don't want her dragged off and lynched!"

The Knight cast him a scornful glance. "You are not in Neraka, sir," he said disdainfully and rode off.

Gerard dismounted, began leading the horse through the ordered confusion. The soldiers were working swiftly and with a will. The officers gave direction, but they were not haranguing, not threatening. No whips urged the men to work faster and smarter. Morale appeared high. The soldiers were laughing and joking with each other and singing songs to help ease their labor. Yet, all they had to do was to look up on the city walls to see ten times more than their own number.

"This is a joke," said Odila, keeping her voice low. They were surrounded by the enemy, and although the din was deafening, someone might overhear. "They have no army of reinforcements nearby. Our patrols go out daily. They would have seen such a massive buildup of troops."

"Apparently, they didn't," Gerard returned. "Solanthus was caught with its pants down."

Gerard kept his hand on his sword hilt, ready to fight should anyone decide to take it into his head to have a little fun with the Solamnic prisoner. The soldiers glanced at them with interest as they passed. A few halted to jeer at the Solamnic, but their officers quickly ordered the men back to work.

You're not in Neraka, the Knight had said. Gerard was impressed, also uneasy. This was not a mercenary army that fought for loot, for gain. This was a seasoned army, a disciplined army, one dedicated to its cause, whatever that cause might be.

The flag that fluttered on the spear driven into the ground beside the command was not really a flag, nothing more than a dirty scarf that looked as if it had been dipped in blood.

Two Knights posted guard outside the command tent that had been the first tent raised. Other tents were now going up around it. An officer stood in front of the tent, speaking with another Neraka Knight. The officer was an archer by his dress and the fact that he wore an enormous longbow slung over one shoulder. The Knight had his back to Gerard. He could not see the face. Judging by his slight build, this Knight was no more than a youth, eighteen, if that. He wondered if he was some Knight's son dressed up in his father's armor.

The archer spotted Gerard and Odila first. The archer's gaze was keen and appraising. He said something to the Knight, who turned to look at them. Gerard saw with a shock that the Knight was not a youth, as he had supposed, but a girl. A sheen of red hair, closely cropped, covered her head. Her eyes caught and held both of them in an amber gaze. He had never seen such extraordinary eyes. He felt uncomfortable under their scrutiny, as if he were a child again and she had caught him in some crime, perhaps stealing apples or teasing his little sister. She forgave him his offense because he did not know better. He was just a child. She might punish him, but the punishment would help him understand how to do right in the future.

Gerard was thankful for the helm, for he could avert his gaze and she wouldn't know it. But even as he tried, he couldn't keep his eyes from her. He stared at her, enthralled.

Pretty was not the word to describe her, nor beautiful. Her face was marked by its equanimity, its purity of thought. No line of doubt marred her smooth forehead. Her eyes were clear and saw far beyond what his eyes saw. Here was a person who would change the world for good or for evil. He recognized in that calm equanimity, Mina, commander of this army, whose name had been spoken with reverence and respect.

Gerard saluted.

"You are not one of my Knights, sir," Mina said. "I like to see faces. Remove your helm."

Gerard wondered how she knew he wasn't one of her Knights. No badge or emblem marked him as having come from Qualinesti, Sanction, or any other part of Ansalon. He removed his helm reluctantly, not because he thought she might recognize him, but because he had enjoyed its meager protection, shielded him from the intense scrutiny of her amber eyes.

He gave his name and related his story that had the advantage of being true for the most part. He spoke confidently enough, but the parts where he was forced to twist the truth or embellish it proved difficult. He had the strange feeling that she knew far more about him than he knew about himself.

"What is Marshal Medan's message?" Mina asked.

"Are you the new Lord of the Night, Lady?" Gerard asked. The question seemed expected of him, but he was uncomfortable. "Forgive me, but I was told that my message was to be delivered to the Lord of the Night."

"Such titles hold no meaning for the One God," she answered. "I am Mina, a servant of the One. You may deliver your message to me or not, as you choose."

Gerard stared, baffled and uncertain. He dared not look at Odila, although he wondered what she was thinking, how she was reacting. He had no idea what to do and realized that no matter what he did, he risked looking foolish. For some reason, he did not want to look foolish in those amber eyes.

"I choose to deliver my message to Mina," he said and was surprised to hear that same note of respect in his voice. "My message is this: Qualinesti is coming under attack from the green dragon Beryl. She has ordered Marshal Medan to destroy the city of Qualinost and threatens that if he does not, she will do so herself. She has ordered him to exterminate the elves."

Mina said nothing, indicated by a slight nod that she was listening and understood.

Gerard drew in a breath and continued. "Marshal Medan respectfully reminds the Lord of the Night that this attack on Qualinesti breaks the pact between the dragons. The Marshal fears that should Malys hear of it, all-out war will erupt among the dragons, a war that is likely to devastate much of Ansalon. Marshal Medan does not consider himself under the orders of Beryl. He is a loyal Knight of Neraka and therefore he requests orders from his superior, the Lord of the Night, on how to proceed. Marshal Medan also respectfully reminds his lordship that a city in ruins is worth very little and that dead elves pay no tribute."

Mina smiled slightly. The smile warmed the amber eyes, and they seemed to flow over Gerard like honey. "Lord Targonne would have been deeply moved by that sentiment. The *late* Lord Targonne."

"I am sorry to hear of his death." Gerard glanced somewhat helplessly at the archer, who was grinning at him as if he knew exactly what Gerard was thinking and feeling.

"Targonne is with the One God," Mina replied, her tone solemn and earnest. "He made mistakes, but he understands now and repents."

Gerard was thoroughly astounded by this. He had no idea what to say. Who was this One God, anyway? He dared not ask, thinking that as a Dark Knight, he might be supposed to know.

"I've heard of this One God," Odila said in dire tones. She ignored Gerard, who pinched her calf to warn her to keep her mouth shut. "Someone else spoke of a One God. One of those false Mystics from the Citadel of Light. Blasphemy! I tell you. All know that the gods are gone."

Mina lifted the amber eyes, fixed them on Odila.

"The gods may be gone to you, Solamnic," Mina said, "but not to me. Release the Knight's bindings. Let her dismount. Don't worry. She will not try to escape. After all, where could she go?"

Gerard did as he was told, helped Odila from the horse. "Are you trying to get us both killed?" he demanded under his breath as he undid the knot of the leather thong around her wrists. "This is no time to be discussing theology!"

"It got my hands untied, didn't it?" Odila returned, glancing at him from beneath her long lashes.

He gave her a rough shove toward Mina. Odila stumbled but caught herself and stood in front of the girl, who reached only to Odila's shoulder.

"There are no gods for anyone," Odila repeated with typical Solamnic stubbornness. "For you or me."

Gerard wondered what she had in mind. No way to tell. He would have to stay alert, be ready to pick up on her plan.

Mina was not angry or even annoyed. She regarded Odila with patience, rather like a parent watching a spoiled child throwing a temper tantrum. Mina reached out her hand.

"Take hold," she said to Odila.

Odila regarded her in blank astonishment.

"Take hold of my hand," Mina repeated, as if the child was rather a slow child.

"Do as she says, cursed Solamnic," Gerard ordered.

Odila cast him a glance. Whatever she had hoped would happen, this wasn't it. Gerard inwardly sighed, shook his head. Odila looked back at Mina and seemed on the point of refusing. Then her hand extended, reached out to Mina. Odila looked at the hand in amazement, as if the hand were acting of its own accord, against her will.

"What sorcery is this?" she cried, and she was in earnest. "What are you doing to me?"

"I am doing nothing," Mina said softly. "The part of you that seeks nourishment for your soul reaches out to me."

Mina took hold of Odila's hand in her own.

Odila gasped, as if in pain. She tried to break the hold, but could not, though Mina was not exerting any force that Gerard could see. Tears sprang to Odila's eyes, she bit her lip. Her arm shook, her body trembled. She gulped and seemed to try to bear the pain, but the next moment she sank to her knees. The tears spilled over, coursed down her cheeks. She bowed her head.

Mina moved close to Odila. She stroked Odila's long black hair.

"Now you see," said Mina softly. "Now you understand."

"No!" Odila cried in a choked voice. "No, I don't believe it."

"You do believe," Mina said. She put her hand beneath Odila's chin, lifted her head so that Odila was forced to look into the amber eyes. "I do not lie to you. You are lying to yourself. When you are dead, you will go to the One God, and there will be no more lies."

Odila stared at her wildly.

Gerard shuddered, chilled to the core of his being.

The archer leaned forward, said something to Mina. She listened and nodded.

"Captain Samuval says that you can undoubtedly provide us with valuable information about the defenses of Solanthus." Mina smiled, shrugged. "I do not require such information, but the captain believes that he does. Therefore you will be questioned first, before you are put to death."

"I won't tell you anything," Odila said thickly.

Mina regarded her with sorrow. "No, I don't suppose you will. Your suffering will be wasted, for, I assure you, you could not tell me anything that I do not already know. I do this only to humor Captain Samuval."

Bending down, Mina kissed Odila on the forehead. "I commend your soul to the One God," Mina said, and straightening, she turned to Gerard.

"I thank you for delivering your message. I would not advise you to return to Qualinost. Beryl would not permit you to enter that city. She launches her attack tomorrow at dawn. As for Marshal Medan, he is a traitor. He has fallen in love with the elves and their ways. His love finds shape and form in the Queen Mother, Lauralanthalasa. He has not evacuated the city as he was ordered. Qualinost is filled with elven soldiers, prepared to give their lives in defense of their city. The king, Gilthas, has laid a trap for Beryl and her armies—a cunning trap, I must admit."

Gerard gaped. His jaws went slack. His mouth hung open. He thought he should defend Medan, then knew he shouldn't, for doing so might implicate him. Or perhaps she already knew Gerard wasn't what he appeared and nothing that he did or didn't do would make any difference. He managed, at last, to ask the one thing that he had to know.

"Has Beryl . . . been warned?" Gerard's mouth was dry. He could barely speak the words.

"The dragon is in the keeping of the One God, as are we all," Mina replied. She turned away. Waiting officers moved forward to claim Mina's attention, badgered her with questions. She walked off to listen to them, answer them. Gerard was dismissed.

Odila stood up, staggering, and would have fallen if Gerard had not stepped forward and, under the guise of seizing her arm, supported her. He wondered, at that, who was leaning on whom. He was in need of some sort of support himself. Sweating profusely, he felt wrung out.

"I can't answer you," Captain Samuval said, although Gerard had not asked a question. The captain walked over to converse. "Is what Mina said about Medan true? Is he a traitor?"

"I don't . . . I don't . . ." Gerard's voice failed him. He was tired of lying, and it seemed pointless anyway. The battle for Qualinost would be held tomorrow at dawn, if he believed her, and he believed her, although he had no idea how or why. He shook his head wearily. "I guess it doesn't matter. Not now."

"We'd be glad if you joined our ranks," Captain Samuval offered. "Here, I'll show you where to take your prisoner. The interrogator's setting up, but he should be in business by tomorrow morning. We could use another sword." He glanced at the city, whose walls were dark with soldiers. "How many troops do you reckon are in there?"

"A lot," Gerard said with emphasis.

"Yes, I suppose you're right." Captain Samuval rubbed his grizzled chin. "I'll wager she knows, eh?" He jerked a thumb at Odila, who walked as if in a daze, hardly seeming to notice where she was going, hardly seeming to care.

"I don't know if she does or not," Gerard said glumly. "She hasn't said anything to me about it, and she won't say anything to that torturer of yours. She's stubborn, that one. Where do I put her? I'll be thankful to be rid of her."

Captain Samuval led Gerard to a tent that was close to where the blacksmith and his assistants were setting up his portable forge. Pausing at the smith's, Captain Samuval appropriated a pair of leg irons and manacles, assisted Gerard in attaching them to Odila's legs and wrists. He handed Gerard the key.

"She's your prisoner," he said.

Gerard thanked him, tucked the key into his boot.

The tent had no bedding, but the captain brought water and food for the prisoner. Odila refused to eat, but she drank some water and managed to sound grudgingly grateful for the attention. She lay down on the tent floor, her eyes wide open and staring.

Gerard left her, went outside, wondering what he was going to do now. He decided the best thing he could do was to eat. He had not realized how hungry he was until he saw the bread and dried meat in the captain's hand.

"I'll take that food," Gerard said, "since she doesn't want it."

Samuval handed it over. "No mess tent as yet, but there's more where this came from. I was headed that way myself. You want to join me?"

"No," said Gerard. "Thanks, but I'll keep an eye on her."

"She's not going anywhere," said the captain, amused.

"Still, she's my responsibility."

"Suit yourself," said Captain Samuval and strode off. He had sighted a friend apparently, for he began waving his hand. Gerard saw the minotaur who had been leading the patrol waving back.

Gerard squatted down outside the prison tent. He ate the meal without tasting it. Realizing that he'd left the waterskin inside with Odila, he entered the tent to retrieve it. He moved quietly, thinking she might be asleep.

She had not stirred since he had left her, except that now her eyes were closed. He was reaching quietly for the waterskin, when she spoke.

"I'm not asleep," she said.

"You should try to rest," he returned. "Nothing to do now except to wait for nightfall. I have the key to the leg irons. I'll try to find you some armor or a soldier's tunic—"

She shifted her gaze from him, looked away.

Gerard had to ask. "What did you see, Odila? What did you see when she touched you?"

Odila closed her eyes, shivered.

"I saw the mind of God!"

30 THE WAR
OF SOULS BEGINS

Galdar walked through the slumbering camp, yawning so wide he heard a distinct crack. A sharp pain in his jaw made him wince. Resolving not to do that again, he rubbed his jaw and continued on. The night was bright. The moon, within a sliver of being full, was large, lumpish, and vacuous. Galdar had the impression that it was a doltish moon. He'd never liked it much, but it would serve its purpose, if all went according to plan. Mina's plan. Mina's strange, bizarre plan. Galdar yawned again, but this time he took care not to crack his jaw.

The guards in front of Mina's tent recognized him—easy to spot the only minotaur in the entire army. They saluted and looked at him expectantly.

Her tent was dark. Not surprising, considering it was nearly dawn. He was loath to wake her, for she had been up before the sunrise the day before and had gone to bed well after midnight. He hesitated. After all, there wasn't anything she could do that he hadn't already done. Still, he felt she should know.

He thrust aside the flap and entered the command tent.

"What is it, Galdar?" she asked.

He was never certain if she was awake before he entered or if she woke on hearing him enter. Either way, she was always alert, responsive.

"The prisoner has escaped, Mina. The female Solamnic Knight. We can't find her captor, either. We believe they were in this together."

She slept in her clothes, woolen hose, and tunic. Her armor and her morning star stood at the foot of the bed. He could see her face, pale white, colder, more awful than the gibbous moon.

She evinced no surprise.

"Did you know of this, Mina? Did someone else come to tell you?" Galdar frowned. "I gave orders you were not to be disturbed."

"Yet now you disturb me, Galdar." Mina smiled.

"Only because all our efforts to find the Solamnic and this traitor Knight have failed."

"They are back in Solanthus now," Mina replied. Her eyes had no color in the darkness. He felt more comfortable with her in the darkness. He could not see himself in the amber. "They have been greeted as heroes. Both of them."

"How can you take this so calmly, Mina?" Galdar demanded. "They have been in our camp. They have tallied our numbers. They know how few of us there are."

"They can see that from the walls, Galdar."

"Not clearly," he argued. He had been opposed to this wild scheme from the beginning. "We have done what we could to deceive them. Put up empty tents, kept the men milling about so that they could not be easily counted. Our efforts have gone for naught."

Mina propped herself up on one elbow. "You remember that you wanted to poison their water supply, Galdar?"

"Yes," he said dourly.

"I counseled against it, for then the city would be useless to us."

He snorted. The city was useless to them right now and would remain so, for all he could see.

"You have no faith, Galdar," Mina said sadly.

Galdar sighed. His hand stole to his right arm, rubbed it involuntarily. It always seemed to ache now, as with rheumatism.

"I try, Mina. I truly do. I thought I had settled my doubts back in Silvanost, but now . . . I do not like our new allies, Mina," he stated abruptly. "And I am not alone."

"I understand," Mina said. "That is why I have been patient with you and with the others. Your eyes are clouded by fear, but the time will come when you will see clearly. Your eyes will be the only eyes that see clearly."

She smiled at her own jest.

Galdar did not smile. This was no laughing matter, as far as he was concerned.

She looked at him and very slightly shook her head. "As to the Solamnic, I have sent her into the city carrying a poison more destructive than the nightshade you wanted to dump in the city well."

He waited, suppressing a yawn. He had no idea what she was talking about. All he could think of was that it had all been for nothing. Hours of lost sleep sending out search parties, ransacking the camp, all for nothing.

"I have sent them the knowledge that there is a god," Mina continued, "and that the One God fights on our side."

Their escape had been ridiculously easy. So easy, Gerard would have said that it had been facilitated, if he could have thought of one single reason why the enemy would want them to return to Solanthus in possession of damning information about the enemy army camped outside their walls.

The only really tense moments came at Solanthus's outer gate, when there was some question as to whether or not the sentries were going to shoot them full of arrows. Gerard blessed Odila's strident voice and mocking tone, for she was immediately recognized and, on her word, they were both allowed admittance.

After that came hours of questioning from the officers of the Knighthood. The sun was rising now, and they were still at it.

Gerard had not had much sleep the night before. The day's strain and tension and the night's adventure had left him completely worn out. He'd told them everything he had seen or heard twice and was propping his eyelids open with his fingers when Odila's next words caused a minor explosion that jolted him into full wakefulness.

"I saw the mind of God," she said.

Gerard groaned and slumped back in his chair. He'd tried to warn her to keep quiet on that score, but, as usual, she had not listened to him. He'd been hoping for his bed, even if it was back in his cell, whose cool, quiet, and kenderless darkness was now strongly appealing. Now they were going to be here the rest of the day.

"What do you mean, exactly, Lady Odila?" Lord Tasgall asked carefully. He was thirty years Gerard's senior. His hair was iron gray and worn long, and he had the traditional mustaches of the Solamnic Knight. Unlike some Rose Knights Gerard had met, Lord Tasgall was not, as someone once disparagingly phrased it, a "solemnic" Knight. Although his face was suitably grave on this serious occasion, laugh lines around the mouth and eyes testified that he had a sense of humor. Obviously respected by those under his command, Lord Tasgall appeared to be a sensible, wise leader of men.

"The girl called Mina touched my hand, and I saw . . . eternity. There's no other way to describe it." Odila spoke in low tones, halting, obviously uncomfortable. "I saw a mind. A mind that could encompass the night sky and make it seem small and confining. A mind that could count the stars and know their exact number. A mind that is as small as a grain of sand and as large as the ocean. I saw the mind, and at first I knew joy, because I was not alone in the universe, and then I knew fear, terrible fear, because I was rebellious and disobedient and the mind was displeased. Unless I submitted, the mind would become angrier still. I . . . I could not understand. I did not understand. I still don't understand."

Odila looked helplessly at the Lord Knights as if expecting answers.

"What you saw must have been a trick, an illusion," Lord Ulrich replied soothingly. He was a Sword Knight, only a few years older than Gerard. Lord Ulrich was on the pudgy side, with a choleric face that indicated a love of spirits, perhaps more than was entirely good for him. He had a bright eye and a red nose and a broad smile. "We all know that the dark Mystics cause members of the Knighthood to experience false visions. Isn't that true, Starmaster Mikelis?"

The Starmaster nodded, agreed almost absently. The Mystic looked worn and haggard. He had spent the night searching for Goldmoon and had been amazed and bewildered when Gerard told him that she had left on the back of a blue dragon, flying to Nightlund in search of the wizard Dalamar.

"Alas," the Starmaster had said sadly. "She is mad. Quite mad. The miracle of her returned youth has overthrown her mentally. A lesson to us, I suppose, to be content with what we are."

Gerard would have been inclined to think so himself, except that her actions last night had been those of a sane person who is in command of the situation. He made no comment, kept his thoughts to himself. He had come to feel a great admiration and reverence for Goldmoon, although he had known her only one night. He wanted to keep the memory of their time together secret, sacred. Gerard closed his eyes.

The next moment, Odila elbowed him. Gerard jerked awake, sat up straight, blinking his eyes and wondering uneasily if anyone had noticed him napping.

"I tend to agree with Lord Ulrich," Lord Tasgall was saying. "What you saw, Lady Odila—or thought you saw—was not a miracle, but a trick of a dark mystic."

Odila was shaking her head, but she held her tongue, for which miracle Gerard was grateful.

"I realize we could debate the subject for days or even weeks and never reach a satisfactory conclusion," Lord Tasgall added. "However, we have much more serious matters that require our immediate attention. I also realize that you are both probably very tired after your ordeal." He smiled at Gerard, who flushed deeply and squirmed uncomfortably in his chair. "First, there is the matter of Sir Gerard uth Mondar. I will now see the letter from the elf king, Sir Knight."

Gerard produced the letter, somewhat crumpled, but quite legible.

"I am not familiar with the elf king's signature," said Lord Tasgall, reading the letter, "but I recognize the royal seal of Qualinesti. Alas," he added quietly, "I fear there is little we can do to help them in their hour of need."

Gerard bowed his head. He might have argued, but the presence of enemy troops camped outside Solanthus would render any argument he might make ineffective.

"He may have a letter from an elf," said Lord Nigel, Knight of the Crown, "but he was still apprehended in company with a dragon of evil. I cannot easily reconcile the two."

Lord Nigel was in his forties, one of those people who do not want to make a decision until he has ruminated on it long and hard and looked at every fact three times over from all possible angles.

"I believe his story," said Odila in her forthright manner. "I saw him and heard him in the cave with the First Master. He had the chance to leave, and he didn't take it. He heard the horns, knew we were under attack, and came back to help defend the city."

"Or betray it," said Lord Nigel, glowering.

"Gerard told me that if you would not let him wear his sword, as a true

Knight, he would do anything he could to help, from fighting fires to tending the wounded," Odila returned heatedly. "His quick thinking saved both our lives. He should be honored, not castigated."

"I agree," said Lord Tasgall. "I think we are all in agreement?" He looked at the other two. Lord Ulrich nodded at once and gave Gerard a grin and a wink. Lord Nigel frowned, but he had great respect for Lord Tasgall and so agreed to abide by his ruling.

Lord Tasgall smiled. "Sir Gerard uth Mondar, all charges against you are formally dropped. I regret that we have no time to publicly clear your name, but I will issue an edict to the effect that all may know of your innocence."

Odila rewarded Gerard with a grin and kicked his leg underneath the table, reminding him that he owed her one. This matter now dispensed with, the Knights could turn their attention to the problem of the enemy.

Despite the information they had received about the ridiculously small numbers of the enemy army currently besieging their city, the Solamnics did not take the situation lightly. Not after what Gerard told them about the expected reinforcements.

"Perhaps she means an enemy army marching out of Palanthas, my lord," Gerard suggested deferentially.

"No," said Lord Tasgall, shaking his head. "We have spies in Palanthas. They would have reported any massive troop movement, and there has been none. We have scouts watching the roads, and they have seen nothing."

"Begging your pardon, my lord," said Gerard, "but you didn't see this army coming."

"There was sorcery at work," said Lord Nigel grimly. "A magical sleep affected everyone in the city and its environs. The patrols reported that they were overcome with this fey sleep that affected man and beast alike. We thought the sleep had been cast upon us by the First Master Goldmoon, but Starmaster Mikelis has assured us that she could not possibly cast such a powerful spell."

He looked uneasily at Odila. Her words about the mind of God had brought a disquieting notion. "He tells us that no mortal could. Yet, we all slept."

I did not sleep, Gerard thought. Neither did the kender or the gnome. Goldmoon caused the iron bars to melt as if they were wax. What was it she said? *I don't know how I have the power to do what I do. I know only that whatever I want I am given.*

Who is the giver? Gerard glanced at Odila, troubled. None of the other Knights spoke. They were all sharing the same unwelcome thoughts, and no one wanted to give them voice. To go there was to walk the edge of a precipice blindfolded.

"Sir Gerard, Lady Odila, I thank you for your patience," Lord Tasgall said, rising to his feet. "We have information enough on which to act. If we have further need of you, we will summon you."

They were being dismissed. Gerard rose, saluted, thanked each Knight in turn. Odila waited for him, walked out with him. Looking back, Gerard saw the Knights already deep in discussion.

"It's not as if they have much choice," Odila said, shaking her head. "We can't just sit here and wait for them to bring in reinforcements. We'll have to attack."

"Damn strange way to run a siege," Gerard reflected. "I could understand it, their leader being hardly out of her baby clothes, but that captain looked to me to be a savvy officer. Why do they go along with her?"

"Perhaps she has touched their minds, as well," Odila muttered.

"What?" Gerard asked. She had spoken so softly he didn't think he'd heard right.

She shook her head glumly, and kept walking. "Never mind. It was a stupid thought."

"We'll be riding to battle soon," Gerard predicted, hoping to cheer her up.

"It can't be too soon for me. I'd like to meet that red-haired vixen with a sword in my hand. What about a drink?" she asked abruptly. "Or two or six or thirty?"

An odd tone in her voice caused Gerard to look at her sharply.

"What?" she demanded, defensive. "I want to drink that blasted God out of my mind, that's all. Come on. I'll buy."

"Not for me," he said. "I'm for my bed. Sleep. You should be, too."

"I don't know how you expect me to sleep with those eyes staring at me. Go to bed, then, if you're so tired."

He started to ask, "What eyes?" but Odila walked off, heading for a tavern whose signboard was a picture of a hunting dog holding a limp duck in its mouth.

Too exhausted to care, Gerard headed for a well-earned rest.

Gerard slept through the daylight and far into the night. He woke to the sounds of someone pounding on the door.

"Turn out! Turn out!" a voice called softly. "Muster in the courtyard in one hour. No lights, and keep the noise down."

Gerard sat up. The room was bright, but it was the white, eerie brightness of moonlight, not sunlight. Outside his door came the muffled sounds of Knights, their pages, squires, and servants up and about. So it was to be an attack by night. A surprise attack.

No noise. No lights. No drums calling the troops to muster. Nothing to give away the fact that the army of Solanthus was preparing to ride out and break the siege. Gerard approved. An excellent idea. They would catch the enemy asleep. With luck, perhaps they'd catch them sleeping off a night of carousing.

He had gone to bed in his clothes, so he had no need to dress, only to pull on his boots. Hastening down stairs crowded with servants and squires dashing about on errands for their masters, he shoved his way through the mob, pausing only to ask directions to the armory.

The streets were eerily silent, for most of the city was deep in slumber. Gerard found the armorer and his assistants scantily clad, for they had been yanked out of their beds at a moment's notice. The armorer was distraught that he could not outfit Gerard in proper Solamnic armor. There was no time to make any.

"Just give me the stuff you use in training," Gerard said.

The armorer was appalled. He couldn't think of sending a Knight to battle in armor that was dented, ill fitting, and scratched. Gerard would look like a scarecrow. Gerard didn't care. He was riding to his first battle, and he would have gone stark naked and not minded. He had his sword, the sword given to him by Marshal Medan, and that was what counted. The armorer protested, but Gerard was firm, and eventually the man brought what was required. His assistants—two pimple-faced, thirteen-year-old boys—were wild with excitement and bemoaned the fact that they could not ride out to fight. They acted as Gerard's squires.

He went from the armory to the stables where grooms were frantically saddling horses, trying to quiet the animals, excited by the unusual commotion. The stable master eyed Gerard dubiously in his borrowed armor, but Gerard gave the man to know in no uncertain terms that he intended to steal a horse if he wasn't provided one. The stable master still might not have gone along with Gerard's demand, but Lord Ulrich entered at that moment, and although he laughed uproariously at the sight of Gerard's shabby accouterments, he vouchsafed Gerard's credentials, giving orders that he was to be treated with the consideration due a Knight.

The stable master didn't go quite that far, but he did provide Gerard with a horse. The beast looked more suited to drawing a wagon than carrying a Knight. Gerard could only hope that it would head for the field of battle and not start morning milk deliveries.

His arguings and persuadings appeared to Gerard to take forever, and he was in a fever of impatience, afraid he would miss the battle. As it was he was already ahead of most of the other Knights. By the time he arrived in the courtyard, the foot soldiers were forming ranks. Well trained, they moved into position quickly, obeying soft-spoken commands. They had muffled the jingling of their chain mail with strips of cloth, and woe betide the spearman who dropped his spear with an awful rattle onto the cobblestones. Hissing curses, the officers pounced on the offender, promising all sorts of dire punishments.

The Knights began to assemble. They, too, had wrapped parts of their armor in cloth to reduce the noise. Squires stood by the side of each horse, ready to hand up weapon and shield and helm. The standard-bearers took their places. The officers took their places. Except for the normal sounds of the City Guard making their accustomed rounds, the remainder of the city was quiet. No one was shouting out, demanding to know what was going on. No crowds of gawkers had gathered. Gerard admired both the efficiency of the Knights' officers and the loyalty and common sense of the citizenry. Word must have been passed from household to household, warning everyone to stay indoors and douse their lights. The marvel was that everyone was obeying.

The Knights and soldiers—five thousand strong—were ready to march. Here and there the silence was broken by the muffled whinny of an excited steed, a nervous cough from one of the foot soldiers, or the rattle of a Knight putting on his helm.

Gerard sought out Odila. A Knight of the Crown, she took her place riding among the front ranks. She was accoutered in armor similar to that of the other Knights, but he picked her out immediately by the two long black braids that trailed down from the gleaming silver helm and her laughter that rang out for a brief moment, then was suitably stifled.

"Bless the woman, she'd clown at her own funeral," he said, laughing, and then, realizing the ill omen of his remark, he wished uneasily he hadn't made it.

Lord Tasgall, Knight of the Rose, rode at the head among his command staff, a white scarf fluttering from his hand. He raised it high, so that everyone could see, then let it fall. The officers started their men marching, the Knights rode forward. Gerard took his place in the very last ranks among the young-sters newly knighted. He didn't mind. He could have walked with the foot soldiers and wouldn't have minded. The army of Solanthus moved out with a shuffling, scraping sound like some huge wingless, moon-glittering dragon sliding over the ground. The inner gates, whose hinges had been well greased, were silently shoved open by silent men.

A series of bridges allowed access over the moat. After the last foot soldier had crossed the bridges, they were drawn up. The gates were closed and barred, the murder holes manned.

The army marched on to the outer gates that pierced the thick curtain wall surrounding the city. The hinges on these gates had also been well oiled. Gerard, riding underneath the walls, saw archers crouching down among the shadows of the crenellations to avoid being seen. He trusted the archers would have nothing to do this night. The Solamnic army should be able to wipe out the army of the Dark Knights almost before they knew what hit them. Still, the Lord Knights were wise to take no chances.

Once the foot soldiers and Knights were outside the last gate, and that gate had been shut, barred, and manned, the Lord Knight paused, looked back to see his command solid behind him. He raised another white scarf, let this one fall.

The Knights broke the silence. Lifting their voices in a song that was old when Huma was a boy, they urged their horses into a thundering gallop. The song sent the blood coursing through Gerard's veins. He found himself singing lustily, shouting whatever came to mind in the parts where he didn't remember the words. The order to the cavalry had been to split the ranks, to send half the Knights charging to the east, the other half to the west. The plan was to encircle the slumbering camp, drive the inhabitants into the center, where they would be attacked by the foot soldiers, who were to charge straight on down the center.

Gerard kept his eyes fixed on the enemy encampment. He expected, at the sound of thundering hooves, to see the camp roused. He expected torches to flare, sentries to cry out the alarm, officers to shout, and men to race for their weapons.

Strangely, the camp remained quiet. No sentry shouted a warning and, now that Gerard looked, he couldn't see a picket line. No movement, no sound came from the camp, and it began to look as if the camp had been abandoned in the night. But why would an army of several hundred troops walk off and leave tents and supplies behind?

Had the girl realized she'd bitten off more than she could chew? Had she decided to slink off in the night, save her own skin and that of her men? Thinking back to her, to her supreme faith in the One God, Gerard doubted it.

The Solamnic Knights continued their charge, sweeping around both sides of the camp in a great widening circle. They continued to sing, but the song had lost its charm, could not dispel the uneasiness creeping into their hearts. The silence was uncanny, and they didn't like it. They smelled a trap.

Lord Tasgall, leading the charge, was presented with a problem. Did he proceed as planned? How was he to react to this new and unexpected situation? A veteran of many campaigns, Lord Tasgall was well aware that the best-laid strategy never survives contact with the enemy. In this instance, however, the problem appeared to be the absence of contact with the enemy. Tasgall figured the girl had simply come to her senses and departed. If so, he and his forces had lost nothing but a few hours sleep. Lord Tasgall could not count on this, however. Quite possibly it was a trap. Better to error on the side of caution. Changing strategies now would only throw everyone into confusion. The Lord Knight would carry out his plan, but he did raise his hand to slow the progression of the cavalry, so that they were not riding heedlessly into whatever might await them.

He might have spared himself the trouble. The Knights were not prepared for what awaited them. They could never have been prepared for it.

Another song lifted into the air, a song that was a minor to their major, a song that ran counterpoint to theirs. One person sang the song, and Gerard, who had heard her voice, recognized Mina.

MARIONETTE

In bygone times and warmer climes
You Marionettes played.
Now restless, silent in a box,
Your scattered limbs are splayed.
Come feel the tug of dancing strings.
Your dust responds on shivering wings.
The Master Puppeteer now sings!
Rise up from where you're laid.

The Master calls you from the dark.
Your bones respond in haste.
Come act the part of living souls.
Their glory once more taste.
Connect again with warmer days,
And hearken to your former ways.
Out of that darkness you will raise
Up from your place of waste!

Now dance, you spirits gone before
The surging blood of old.
You sundered souls from times of yore
Play at a life once bold!
The Master heaves on strings of woe.
Torn from the dark your bones must go
To act once more that all may know
The Master's tale is told!

Soldiers on the right flanks began to shout and point. Gerard turned to look to see what was happening.

A thick fog rolled out of the west. The strange fog advanced swiftly, roiling over the grass, obliterating all it touched, blotted out the stars, swallowed the moon. Those watching it could see nothing within the fog, nothing behind it. Reaching the city's western walls, the fog boiled over them. The towers on the west side of Solanthus vanished from sight as thoroughly as if they had never been built. Faint cries came from that part of the city, but they were muffled, and no one could make out what was going on.

Watching the advance of this strange and unnatural fog, Lord Tasgall halted the charge and, with a wave of his hand, summoned his officers to him. Lord Ulrich and Lord Nigel left the ranks and galloped forward. Gerard edged near enough to overhear what they were saying.

"There is sorcery at work here." Lord Tasgall's voice was grim. "We've been duped. Lured out of the city. I say we sound the retreat."

"My lord," protested Lord Ulrich, chuckling, "it is a heavy dew, nothing more."

"Heavy dew!" repeated Lord Tasgall, with a snort of disgust. "Herald, sound the retreat!"

The herald lifted his horn to his lips, gave the signal to retreat. The Knights reacted with discipline, did not give way to panic. Rounding their horses, they began to ride in column toward the city. The foot soldiers wheeled about, headed in orderly march back to the walls. The Knights advanced to cover the footmen's retreat. The archers were now visible on the walls, arrows nocked.

Yet Gerard could see—everyone could see—that no matter how fast they moved, the strange fog would engulf them before the closest soldier could reach the safety of the sheltering walls. The fog slid over the ground with the rapidity of a cavalry charging at full gallop. Gerard stared at the fog as it drew nearer. Stared at it, blinked, rubbed his eyes. He must be seeing things.

This was not fog. This was not a "heavy dew." These were Mina's reinforcements.

An army of souls.

An army of conscripts, for the souls of the dead were trapped in the world, unable to depart. As each soul left its body that had bound it to this world, it knew an instant's elation and exultation and freedom. That feeling was quashed almost immediately. An Immortal Being seized the spirit of the dead and gave it to know an immense hunger, a hunger for magic.

"Bring me the magic, and you will be free," was the promise. A promise not kept. The hunger could never be satiated. The hunger grew in proportion to what it fed on. Those souls struggling to free themselves found there was nowhere to go.

Nowhere to go until they received the summons.

A voice, a human voice, a mortal voice, Mina's voice called to them. "Fight for the One God, and you will be rewarded. Serve the One God, and you will be free."

Desperate, suffering unending torments, the souls obeyed. They formed no ranks for their numbers were too great. The soul of the goblin, its hideous visage recreated from the soul's memory of its mortal shell, barred teeth of mist, grappled for a sword of gossamer and answered the call. The soul of a Solamnic Knight that had long ago lost all notions of honor and loyalty answered the call. The souls of goblin and Knight walked side by side and knew not what they attacked or what they fought. Their only thought was to please the Voice and, by pleasing, escape.

A fog it seemed at first to the mortals who faced it, but Mina called upon the One God to open mortal eyes to see what previously had been kept from their sight. The living were constrained to look upon the dead.

The fog had eyes and mouths. Hands reached out from the fog. Voices whispered from the fog that was not fog at all but a myriad souls, each holding a memory of what it had been, a memory traced in the ethers with the magical phosphoresence of moonlight and foxfire. The face of each soul bore the horror of its existence, an existence that knew no rest, knew only endless seeking and the hopeless desolation of not ever finding.

The souls held weapons, but the weapons were mist and moonglow and could not kill or maim. The souls wielded a single weapon, a most horrible weapon. Despair.

At the sight of the army of trapped souls, the foot soldiers threw down their weapons, heedless to the furious shouts of their officers. The knights guarding their flanks looked at the dead and shuddered in horror. Their instinct was to do the same as the soldiers, to give way to the feelings of terror and panic. Discipline held them for the moment, discipline and pride, but when each turned to look at the other, uncertain what to do, each saw his own fear reflected back to him in the faces of his comrades.

The ghostly army entered the enemy camp. The souls flitted restlessly among the tents and the wagons. Gerard heard the panicked neighing of horses and now, at last, sounds of movement from the camp—calls of officers, the clash of steel. Then all sound was swallowed up by the souls, as if jealous of sounds their dead mouths could not make. The enemy camp vanished from sight. The army of souls flowed toward the city of Solanthus.

Thousands of mouths cried out in silent torment, their whispered shouts a chill wind that froze the blood of the living. Thousands and thousands of dead hands reached out to grasp what they could never hold. Thousands upon thousands of dead feet marched across the ground and bent not a single blade of grass.

Officers fell prey to the same terror as their men, gave up trying to keep their men in order. The foot soldiers broke ranks and ran, panic-stricken, for the walls, the faster shoving aside or knocking down the slower in order to reach safety.

The walls afforded no sanctuary. A moat is no deterrent to those who are already dead, they have no fear of drowning. Arrows cannot halt the advance of those who have no flesh to pierce. The ghostly legions slid beneath the wicked points of the portcullis and swarmed over the closed gates, flitted through the murder holes and glided through the arrow slits.

Behind the army of souls came an army of the living. Soldiers of Mina's command had kept hidden inside their tents, waiting for the army of souls to advance, to terrify the enemy and drive him into panicked chaos. Under cover of this dread army, Mina's soldiers emerged from their tents and raced to battle. Their orders were to attack the Solamnic Knights when they were out in the open, isolated, cut-off, a prey to horror.

Gerard tried to halt the soldiers' flight as they trampled each other, fought to escape the ghost army. He rode after the men, yelling for them to stand their ground, but they ignored him, kept running. Everything disappeared. The souls of the dead surrounded him. Their incorporeal forms shimmered with an incandescent whiteness that outlined hands and arms, feet and fingers, clothing and armor, weapons or other objects that had been familiar to them in life. They closed in on him, and his horse screamed in terror. Rearing back on its hind legs, the horse dumped Gerard on the ground and dashed off, vanishing into a swirling fog of grasping, ghostly hands.

Gerard scrambled to his feet. He drew his sword out of instinct, for what was he going to kill? He had never been so terrified. The touch of the souls was like cold mist. He could not count the number of dead that encircled him. One, a hundred, twelve hundred. The souls were intertwined, one with another. Impossible to tell where one ended and another began. They flitted in and out of his vision so that he grew dizzy and confused watching them.

They did not threaten or attack him, not even those who might have done so in life. An enormous hobgoblin reached out hairy hands, which were suddenly the hands of a beautiful young elven woman, who became a fisherman, who shriveled into a frightened, whimpering dwarf child. The faces of the dead filled Gerard with a nameless horror, for he saw in all of them the misery and hopelessness of the prisoner who lies forgotten in the dungeon that is the grave.

The sight was so awful that Gerard feared he might go mad. He tried to remember the direction to take to reach Solanthus, where he could at least feel the touch of a warm hand as opposed to the caress of the dead, but the fall from the horse had disoriented him. He listened for sounds that might give him some indication which way to go. As in a fog, all sound was distorted. He heard steel clash and cries of pain and guessed that somewhere men fought the living, not the dead. But whether the sounds of battle came from in front of him or behind, he could not tell.

Then he heard a voice speaking coldly and dispassionately. "Here's another one."

Two soldiers, living men, wearing the emblem of Neraka, rushed at him, the ghostly figures parting like white silken scarves cut through by a cleaver. The soldiers fell on Gerard, attacking without skill, slashing and beating at him with their swords, hoping to overwhelm him with brute force before he could recover from his panicked horror. What they had not counted on was the fact that Gerard was so relieved to see a flesh-and-blood foe, one that could be punched and kicked and bloodied, that he defended himself with spirit.

He disarmed one man, sent his sword flying, and drove his fist into the jaw of the other. The two did not stick around to continue the fight. Finding their foe stronger than they had hoped, they ran off, leaving Gerard to his dread jailers, the souls of the dead.

Gerard's hand clenched spasmodically around his sword's hilt. Fearing another ambush, he looked constantly over his shoulder, afraid to stay where he was, more afraid to move. The souls watched him, surrounded him.

A horn call split the air like a scythe. The call came from within the city, sounding the retreat. The call was frantic and short-lived, ending in midnote, but it gave Gerard a sense of where he must go. He had to overcome his instincts, for the last time he'd seen the city walls, they were behind him. The horn call came from in front. He walked forward, slowly, unwilling to touch the souls, though he need not have worried, for though some reached out their hands to him with what seemed pitiful supplication and others reached out their hands in what seemed murderous intent, they were powerless to affect him, other than by the horror and fear they inspired. Still, that was bad enough.

When the sight became too awful for him to bear, he involuntarily shut his eyes, hoping to find some relief, but that proved even more harrowing, for then he could feel the touch of the ghostly fingers and hear the whispers of ghostly voices.

By this time the foot soldiers had reached the enormous iron gate that pierced the curtain wall. The panic-stricken men beat on the gate, shouted for it to open. The gate remained closed and barred against them. Angry and terrified, they cried out for their comrades within the city to open the gate and let them enter. The soldiers began to shove on the gate and shake it, cursing those within.

White light flared. A blast shook the ground, as a section of the wall near the gate exploded. Huge chunks of broken stone rained down on the soldiers massed in front of the closed gate. Hundreds died, crushed to death beneath the rubble. Those who survived lay pinned in the wreckage, begging for help, but no help came. From inside the city, the gates remained locked and barred. The enemy began to pour through the breech.

Hearing the blast, Gerard peered ahead, trying to see what had happened. The souls swirled around him, flitted past him, and he saw only white faces and grasping hands. Desperate, he plunged into the wavering figures, slashing at them wildly with his sword. He might have tried to skewer quicksilver, for the dead slid away from him, only to gather around him ever more thickly.

Realizing what he was doing, Gerard halted, tried to regain control of himself. He was sweating and shivering. The thought of his momentary madness appalled him. Feeling as if he were being smothered, he removed his helm and drew in several deep breaths. Now that he was calm, he could hear voices—living voices—and the sound of ringing steel. He paused another moment to orient himself and replace his helm, leaving the visor raised in order to hear and see better. As he ran toward the sound, the dead snatched at him with their chill hands. He had the skin-crawling sensation he was running through enormous cobwebs.

He came upon six enemy soldiers, who were very much alive, fighting a knight on horseback. He could not see the knight's face beneath the helm, but he saw two long black braids whipping around the knight's shoulders. The soldiers surrounded Odila, tried to drag her from her horse. She struck at them with her sword, kicked at them, fended off their blows with her shield. All the while, she kept the horse under control.

Gerard attacked the enemy from behind, taking them by surprise. He ran his sword through one. Yanking his weapon free of the corpse, Gerard elbowed another in the ribs. Doubling him over, he smashed his nose with a thrust of a knee.

Odila brought her sword down on a man's skull with such force that it split his helm and cleaved through his skull, splattering Gerard with blood and brains and bits of bone. He wiped the blood from his eyes and turned to a soldier who had hold of the horse's bridle, was trying to haul the animal down to the ground. Gerard slashed at the man's hands as Odila bashed another with her shield and struck again with her sword. Another man ducked beneath the horse's belly, came up behind Gerard. Before Gerard could turn from one foe to defend himself against the new one, the soldier struck Gerard a savage blow to the side of the head.

Gerard's helm saved him from a killing stroke. The blade glanced off the metal and cut open Gerard's cheek. He felt no pain and knew he'd been hit only because he could taste the warm blood that flooded his mouth. The man caught hold of Gerard's sword hand in a clench of iron, began trying to break his fingers to force him to drop his weapon. Gerard struck the man in the face, breaking his nose. Still the man hung on, grappled with Gerard. Flinging the man backward, Gerard kicked him in the gut, sent the man sprawling. Gerard moved to finish him, but the man scrambled to his feet and ran. Gerard was too exhausted to pursue him.

Gerard stood gasping for breath. His head hurt now, hurt abominably. Holding a sword was painful, and he shifted the weapon to his left hand, although what he would do with it there was open to question, since he'd never attained the skill to fight with both hands. He could at least use it as a club, he supposed.

Odila's armor was dented and blood-covered. He could not tell if she was hurt, and he lacked the breath to ask. She sat on her horse, looking around her, sword poised, waiting for the next assault.

Gerard realized suddenly that he could see trees silhouetted against the stars. He could see other knights, some mounted, some standing on the ground, some kneeling, some fallen. He could see stars, he could see the walls of

Solanthus, gleaming white in the bright moonlight, with one terrible exception. An enormous section of wall was missing, a section near the gate. A huge pile of blasted rock lay in front.

"What happened?" Odila gasped, snatching off her helm to see better. "Who did this? Why did the gates not open? Who barred them?" She stared at the walls that were silent and empty. "Where are our archers? Why have they left their posts?"

In an answer that seemed almost personal, so nearly did it coincide with Odila's question, a lone figure came to stand atop the city's outer walls above the gates that had had remained closed and barred against their own defenders.

The dead soldiers of Solanthus lay stacked in front of the city gate, an offering before an enormous altar. An offering to the girl Mina, whose black armor was sleek in the moonlight.

"Knights of Solamnia. Citizens of Solanthus." Mina addressed them, her voice ringing so that none on that bloody field had to strain to hear. "Through the might of the One God, the city of Solanthus has fallen. I hereby claim the city of Solanthus in the name of the One God."

Hoarse cries of shocked anger and disbelief rose from the battlefield. Lord Tasgall spurred his horse forward. His armor was dark with blood, his right arm hung limply, uselessly at his side.

"I do not believe you!" he shouted. "Perhaps you have won the outer walls, but you cannot fool me into thinking you have conquered the entire city!"

Archers appeared on the walls, archers wearing the emblems of Neraka. Arrows landed all around him; stuck, quivering, in the ground at his feet.

"Look to the heavens," said Mina.

Reluctantly, Lord Tasgall raised his head, his gaze searching the skies. He did not have to search long to see defeat.

Black wings slid over the stars, blotting them from view. Black wings sliced across the face of the moon. Dragons wheeled in the air, flying in low victorious circles over the city of Solanthus.

Dragonfear, awful and debilitating, shook Lord Tasgall and all the Solamnic Knights, caused more than one to quail and fling up his arm in terror or grip his weapon with hands that sweat and trembled.

No arrows from Solanthus fired at the dragons. No machines spewed forth flaming oil. One horn call alone had sounded the alarm at the start of battle, and that had been silenced in death.

Mina had spoken truly. The battle was over. While the Solamnic Knights had been held hostage by the dead and ambushed by the living, Mina and the remainder of her forces had flown on dragonback unimpeded into a city that had been emptied of most of its defenders.

"Knights of Solamnia," Mina continued, "you have witnessed the power of the One God, who rules the living and the dead. Go forth and carry word of the One God's return into the world with you. I have given the dragons orders not to attack you. You are free to leave. Go where you will." She waved her hand in a graceful, magnanimous gesture. "Even to Sanction. For that is where the gaze of the One God turns next. Tell the defenders of Sanction of the wonders you have seen this night. Tell them to fear the One God."

The Lord Knight sat unmoving in his saddle. He was in shock, stunned and overwhelmed by this unexpected turn of events. Other Knights rode or walked or limped to stand at his side. They gathered around him. Judging by their raised voices, some were demanding that they ride to the attack.

Gerard snorted in derision. Let them, he thought. Let this horde of dragons come down and snap off their fool heads. Idiots like that don't deserve to live and should certainly never father progeny. One had only to look up into the sky to see that there was nothing left for the Solamnic Knighthood in Solanthus.

Mina spoke one last time. "The night wanes. The dawn approaches. You have one hour to depart in safety. Any who remain within sight of the city walls by this day's dawning will be slain." Her voice grew gentle. "Have no fear for your dead. They will be honored, for they now serve the One God."

The bluster and the fury of the defeated Knights soon blew out. Those few foot soldiers who had escaped alive began to straggle off across the fields, many looking backward over their shoulders as if they could not believe what had happened and must constantly assure themselves by staring at the gruesome sight of their comrades crushed to death beneath the rubble of the once-mighty city.

The Knights managed to salvage what dignity they had left and returned to the field to pick up their fallen. They would not leave their dead behind, no matter what Mina or the One God promised. Lord Tasgall remained seated on his horse. He had removed his helm to wipe away the sweat. His face was grim and fixed, his complexion as white as that of the ghosts.

Gerard could not look at him, could not bear to see such suffering. He turned away.

Odila had not joined the rest of the Knights. She had not appeared even to see what was transpiring. She sat her horse, staring at the wall where the girl Mina had been standing.

Gerard had planned to go assist the other Knights with the wounded and dead, but he didn't like the expression on Odila's face. He grasped hold of her boot, jogged her foot to gain her attention.

She looked down at him and didn't seem to recognize him.

"The One God," Odila said. "The girl speaks the truth. A god has returned to the world. What can mortals do against such power?"

Gerard looked up to where the dragons danced in the heavens, flying triumphant amidst ragged wispy clouds that were not clouds, but the souls of the dead, still lingering.

"We do what she told us to do," Gerard said flatly, glancing back at the walls of the fallen city. He saw the minotaur standing there, watching the Solamnic Knights' retreat. "We ride to Sanction. We warn them of what is coming."

31 THE RED ROSE

In the dark hours before the dawn, on the day the dragon Beryl had appointed for the destruction of Qualinost, Marshal Medan took his breakfast in his garden. He ate well, for he would need the reserves of energy food provided later in the day. He had known men unable to swallow a mouthful before a fight or those who ate and then disgorged the contents of their stomachs shortly after. He had disciplined himself long ago to eat a large meal before a campaign and even to enjoy it.

He was able to accomplish this by focusing on each single minute as it happened, looking neither ahead to what must come or behind to what might have been. He had made his peace with the past last night before he slept—another discipline. As to what brief future might remain to him, he put his trust in himself. He knew his limits; he knew his strengths. He knew and trusted his comrades.

He dipped the last of the season's strawberries in the last of his elven wine. He ate olive bread and soft white cheese. The bread was hard and a week old, for the bakery fires had not been lighted these many days, the bakers either having left Qualinost or gone into hiding, working toward this day. Still, he relished the taste. He had always enjoyed olive bread. The cheese, spread on the bread, was excellent. A simple pleasure, one he would miss in death.

Medan did not believe in life beyond the grave. No rational mind could, as far as he was concerned. Death was oblivion. Each night's short sleep prepares us for the final night's long one. Yet he thought that even in oblivion, he would miss his garden and the soft cheese on the fragrant bread, he would miss moonlight shining on golden hair. He finished the cheese, scattered bread crumbs to the fish. He sat for another hour alone in the garden, listening to the sparrow sing her mournful song. His eyes misted for a moment, but that was for the birdsong that would for him be silenced, and for the beauty of the late-blooming flowers that he also would miss. When his eyes misted, he knew it was time to depart.

The Dark Knight Dumat was on hand to assist Medan into his armor. The Marshal would not wear full plate this day. Beryl would notice and find it suspicious. The elves had been killed, driven out, vanquished. The elven capital city was being delivered to her without a fight. Her Marshal was here to greet her in triumph. What use did he have for armor? Besides that, Medan needed to be free to move swiftly, and he was not going to be encumbered by heavy plate or chain mail. He wore his ceremonial armor—the highly polished breastplate with the lily and the skull, and his helm—but he dispensed with all the rest.

Dumat helped fasten the long, flowing cloak around Medan's shoulders. The cloak was made of wool that had been dipped in black dye and then in purple. Trimmed in gold braid, the cloak reached to the floor and weighed nearly as much as a chain-mail shirt. Medan despised it, never wore it except on those days when he had to make a show for the Senate. Today, though, the cloak would come in handy, for it covered a multitude of sins. Once he was attired, he experimented with the cloak to make certain it would perform as required.

Dumat assisted him to arrange the folds so that cloak fell over his left shoulder, concealing beneath those folds the sword he wore on his left hip. The sword he wore now was not the magical sword, not the Lost Star. For now, his customary sword would serve his purpose. He had to remember to make certain he held fast the cloak's edge with his left hand, so that the wind created by the dragon's fanning wings would not cause it to billow out. He practiced several times, while Dumat watched with a critical eye.

"Will it work, do you think?" the Marshal asked.

"Yes, my lord," Dumat replied. "If Beryl does catch a glimpse of steel, she will think it is only your sword, such as you always wear."

"Excellent." Medan let fall the cloak. He unbuckled his sword from its belt, started to set it aside. Then, thinking better of it, he handed the weapon to Dumat. "May it serve you well as it has served me."

Dumat rarely smiled, and he did not smile then. He removed his own sword—that was regulation issue—and buckled on the Marshal's, with its fine, tempered steel blade. He made no show of gratitude, other than a muttered thanks, but Medan saw that his gift had pleased and touched the soldier.

"You had better leave now," Medan said. "You have a long ride back to Qualinost and much to do this morning before the appointed time."

Dumat started to salute, but the Marshal extended his hand. Dumat hesitated, then grasped Medan's hand, shook it heartily in silence. Dumat took his leave. Mounting his horse, he headed at a gallop back to Qualinost.

Medan went over the plan again in his mind, checking and rechecking to see if he had missed anything. He was satisfied. No plan was perfect, of course, and events rarely went as one hoped, but he was confident he and

Laurana had anticipated most contingencies. He shut his house and locked it up. He wondered, idly, if he would be returning to unlock it or if they would carry his body back here to bury him in his garden as he had requested. In the afterdays when the elves came back to their homeland, would anyone live in this house? Would anyone remember?

"The house of the hated Marshal Medan," he said to himself with half a smile. "Perhaps they'll burn it to the ground. Humans would."

But elves were not like humans. Elves did not take satisfaction in such petty revenge, knowing that it would serve no purpose. Besides, they would not want to harm the garden. He could count on that.

He had one more task to perform before he left. He searched the garden until he found two perfect roses—one red, one white. He plucked them both and stripped the white one of its thorns. He placed the red rose, thorns and all, beneath his armor, against his breast.

The white rose in hand, he left his garden without a backward look. What need? He carried the sight and the fragrance in his mind, and he hoped, if death took him, that his last thought would wend its way back here, live forever in beauty and peace and solitude.

In her house, Laurana was doing much the same thing as the Marshal, with a few exceptions. She had managed to swallow only a few mouthfuls of food before putting aside the plate. She drank a glass of wine to give her heart, then retired to her room.

She had no one to assist her to dress and arm herself, for she had sent her maidservants away to safety in the south. They had gone reluctantly, separating from their mistress with tears. Now, only Kelevandros remained with her. She had urged him to leave, as well, but he had refused, and she had not pressed him. He wanted to stay, he said, to redeem his family's honor that had been besmirched by the treachery of his brother.

Laurana understood, but she was almost sorry he had done so. He was the perfect servant, anticipating her wants and needs, unobtrusive, a hard and diligent worker. But he no longer laughed or sang as he went about his tasks. He was quiet, distant, his thoughts turned inward, rebuffing any offers of sympathy.

Laurana wrapped around her waist the leather skirt that had been designed for her years ago when she was the Golden General. She had just enough feminine vanity to note that the skirt was a little tighter on her than it had been in her youth and just enough sense of the absurd to smile at herself for minding. The leather skirt was slit up the side for ease of movement and served well as protective armor whether standing or riding. When this was done, she started to summon Kelevandros, but he had been waiting outside and entered the room as his name formed on her lips.

Without speaking, he fastened on her the breastplate, blue with golden trim, she had worn those long years ago, then she draped a cloak around her shoulders. The cloak was oversized. She had made it specially for this occasion, working on it day and night so it would be ready in time. The cloak was white, of finely carded wool, and was fastened in the front by seven golden clasps. Slits had been placed in the side for her arms. She studied herself critically in the looking glass, moving, walking, standing still, making certain that no hint of leather or glint of metal gave her away. She had to look the part of the victim, not the predator.

Because the cloak restricted the movement of her arms, Kelevandros brushed and arranged her long hair around her shoulders. Marshal Medan had wanted her to wear her helm, arguing that she would need its protection. Laurana had refused. The helm would look out of place. The dragon would be suspicious.

"After all," she had said to him, half-teasing, wholly serious, "if she attacks, I don't suppose a helmet will make much difference."

Silver chimes rang outside the house.

"Marshal Medan is here," Laurana said. "It is time."

Lifting her gaze, she saw that Kelevandros's face had gone pale. His jaw tightened, his lips pressed tight. He looked at her, pleading.

"I must do this, Kelevandros," Laurana said, laying her hand gently on his arm. "The chance is a slim one, but it is our only hope."

He lowered his gaze, bowed his head.

"You should leave now," Laurana continued. "It is time you took your place in the tower."

"Yes, Madam," Kelevandros said in the same empty, toneless voice he had used since the day of his brother's death.

"Remember your instructions. When I say the words, *Ara Qualinesti* you will light the signal arrow and shoot it into the air. Fire it out over Qualinost, so that those watching for it can see it."

"Yes, Madam." Kelevandros bowed silently and turned to leave. "If you do not mind, I will depart through the garden."

"Kelevandros," Laurana said, halting him. "I am sorry. Truly sorry."

"Why should you be sorry, Madam?" he asked, not turning, keeping his back to her. "My brother tried to murder you. What he did was not your fault."

"I think perhaps it was," Laurana said, faltering. "If I had known how unhappy he was . . . If I had taken time to find out . . . If I had not assumed that . . . that . . ."

"That we were happy to have been born into servitude?" Kelevandros finished her sentence for her. "No, it never occurs to anyone, does it?" He looked at her with a strange smile. "It will from now on. The old ways end here. Whatever happens this day, the lives of the elves will never be the same. We can never go back to what we were. Perhaps we will all know, before the end, what it means to be born a slave. Even you, Madam. Even your son."

Bowing, Kelevandros picked up his bow and a quiver of arrows and started to take his leave. He was almost out the door when he turned to face her, yet he did not look at her.

"Oddly enough, Madam," he said, his voice rough, his eyes downcast. "I was happy here."

With another bow, he left.

"Was that Kelevandros I saw skulking through the garden?" Medan asked when Laurana opened the door to him. He looked at her intently.

"Yes," she said, glancing in that direction, though she could not see him for the thick foliage. "He has gone to take his place in the tower."

"You look troubled. Has he said or done something to upset you?"

"If he did, I must make allowances. He has not been himself since his brother's death. His grief overwhelms him."

"His grief is wasted," said the Marshal. "That wretched brother of his was not worth a snivel, let alone a tear."

"Perhaps," Laurana said, unconvinced. "And yet . . ." She paused, perplexed, and shook her head.

Medan regarded her earnestly. "You have only to say the word, Madam, and I will see to it that you escape safely from Qualinost this instant. You will be reunited with your son—"

"No, I thank you, Marshal," Laurana answered calmly, looking up at him. "Kelevandros must wrestle with his own demons, as I have wrestled with mine. I am resolved in this. I will do my part. You need me, I think, sir," she added with a hint of mischief, "unless you plan to dress up in one of my gowns and wear a blonde wig."

"I have no doubt that even Beryl, dense as she is, would see through that disguise," said Medan dryly. He was pleased to see Laurana smile. Another memory for him to keep. He handed her the white rose. "I brought this for you, Madam. From my garden. The roses will be lovely in Qualinost this fall."

"Yes," said Laurana, accepting the rose. Her hand trembled slightly. "They will be lovely."

"You will see them. If I die this day, you will tend my garden for me. Do you promise?"

"It is bad luck to speak of death before the battle, Marshal," Laurana warned, partly in jest, wholly in earnest. "Our plan will work. The dragon will be defeated and her army demoralized."

"I am a soldier. Death is in my contract. But you—"

"Marshal," Laurana interrupted with a smile, "every contract ever written ends in death."

"Not yours," he said softly. "Not so long as I am alive to prevent it."

They stood a moment in silence. He watched her, watched the moonlight gently touch her hair as he longed to touch it. She kept her gaze fixed upon the rose.

"The parting with your son Gilthas was difficult?" he asked at last.

She replied with a soft sigh. "Not in the way you imagine. Gilthas did not try to dissuade me from my chosen path. Nor did he try to free himself from walking his. We did not spend our last hours in fruitless argument, as I had feared. We remembered the past and talked of what he will do in the future. He has many hopes and dreams. They will serve to ease his journey over the dark, perilous road he must travel to reach that future. Even if we win this day, as Kelevandros said, the lives of the elves will never be the same. We can never go back to what we were." She was pensive, introspective.

In his heart Medan applauded Gilthas. The Marshal guessed how difficult it must have been for the young man to leave his mother to face the dragon while he departed safely out of harm's way. Gilthas had been wise enough to realize that attempting to dissuade her from her chosen course would have accomplished nothing and left him with only bitter recriminations. Gilthas would need all the wisdom he possessed to face what lay ahead of him. Medan knew the peril better than Laurana, for he had received reports of what was happening in Silvanesti. He said nothing to her, not wanting to worry her. Time enough to face that crisis when they had disposed of this one.

"If you are ready, Madam, we should leave now," he told her. "We'll steal through the city while night's shadows yet linger and enter the tower with the dawn."

"I am ready," Laurana said. She did not look behind her. As they walked down the path that led through the late-blooming lilacs, she said to him, "I want to thank you, Marshal, on behalf of the elven people, for what you do for us this day. Your courage will be long remembered and long honored among us."

Medan was embarrassed. "Perhaps it is not so much what I do this day, Madam," he said quietly, "as what I try to undo. Rest assured I will not fail you or your people."

"*Our* people, Marshal Medan," said Laurana. "Our people."

Her words were meant kindly, but they pierced his heart. He deserved the punishment, and he bore it in silence, unflinching, as a soldier. Thus he bore unflinching the sting of the rose's thorns against his breast.

Muffled sounds could be heard coming from the houses of the elves as Medan and Laurana passed swiftly through the streets on their way to the tower. Although no elf showed his face, the time for skulking in silence was gone. There were sounds of heavy objects being hauled up stairs, the rustlings of tree branches as the archers took their places. They heard orders given in calm voices both in Common and Elvish. Near the tower, they actually caught a glimpse of Dumat adding the finishing touches to a web of tree branches he had constructed over the roof of his house. Chosen to watch for Kelevandros's signal, Dumat would give the signal to the elves for the attack. He saluted the Marshal and bowed to the Queen Mother, then continued on about his work.

The morning sun rose, and by the time they reached the tower, the sun shone bright. Shading his eyes, Medan blessed the day for its clear visibility, although he caught himself thinking that his garden would have welcomed rain. He put the thought aside with a smile and concentrated on the task ahead.

The bright light streamed in through the myriad windows, sent rainbows dancing in dazzling array around the tower's interior, and lit the mosaic on the ceiling: the day and the night, separated by hope.

Laurana had locked away the sword and the dragonlance in one of the tower's many rooms. While she retrieved them, Medan looked out one of the windows, watching the preparations as Qualinost made ready for war. Like its Queen Mother, the city was transforming itself from lovely and demure maid into doughty warrior.

Laurana handed Medan the sword, Lost Star. He gravely saluted her with the sword, then buckled it around his waist. She helped him arrange the folds of the cloak to conceal it. Stepping back, she eyed him critically and pronounced his disguise successful. No gleam of metal could be seen.

"We climb this staircase." Laurana indicated a circular stair. "It leads to the balcony at the top of the tower. The climb is a long one, I fear, but there will be time to rest—"

Sudden night, strange and awful as that of an eclipse, quenched the sunlight. Medan hastened to look out the window, well knowing, yet dreading what he would see.

The sky was dark with dragons.

"Very little time, I fear," Medan said calmly, taking the dragonlance from her hand and shaking his head when she started to try to retrieve it. "The great green bitch has launched her attack early. No surprise there. We must make haste."

Opening the door, they began to climb the stairs that wound around and around a hollow shaft, a vortex of stone. A railing made of gold and of silver, twined together, spiraled upward. Formed in an imitation of a vine of ivy, the railing did not appear to have been built into the stone but seemed to have grown around it.

"Our people are ready," Laurana said. "When Kelevandros gives the signal, they will strike."

"I hope we can count on him to carry out his part," the Marshal said. "He has, as you say, been acting strange of late."

"I trust him," Laurana replied. "Look." She pointed at narrow booted footprints in the thick dust on the stairs. "He is here already, waiting for us."

They climbed as rapidly as possible, yet they dared not move too swiftly, lest they lose their strength before they had reached the top. "I am thankful . . . I did not wear full plate armor," the Marshal stated with what breath he had left. As it was, he had only reached what Laurana told him was the halfway mark and he was gasping for breath, his legs burned.

"I used to race . . . my brothers and Tanis up these stairs . . . when I was a girl," Laurana said, pressing her hand over her side to ease a jabbing pain. "We had better rest . . . a moment, or we're not going to make it."

She sank down on the staircase, wincing at the pain. Medan remained standing, staring out the window. He drew in deep breaths, flexed his legs to ease the cramped muscles.

"What can you see?" Laurana asked tensely. "What is happening?"

"Nothing yet," he reported. "Those are Beryl's minions in the skies. Probably scouting the city, making certain it is deserted. Beryl is a coward at heart. Without her magic, she feels naked, vulnerable. She won't come near Qualinost until she is assured nothing will harm her."

"When will her soldiers enter the city?"

Medan turned from the window to look down at her. "Afterward. The commanders won't send in the men until the dragons are gone. The dragonfear unsettles the troops, makes them difficult to manage. When the dragons are finished leveling the place, the soldiers will arrive. To 'mop up.'"

Laurana laughed shakily. "I hope they will not find much to 'mop.'"

"If all goes as planned," said Medan, returning her smile, "the floor will be wiped clean."

"Ready?" she asked.

"Ready," he replied and gallantly extended his hand to help her to her feet.

The stairs brought them to the top of the tower, to an entrance to a small alcove with an arched ceiling. Those passing through the alcove walked out onto a balcony that overlooked all of the city of Qualinost. The Speaker of the Suns and the clerics of Paladine had been accustomed to come to the top of the tower on holidays and feast days, to thank Paladine—or Eli, as the elves knew him—for his many blessings, the most glorious of which was the sun that gave life and light to all. That custom had ended after the Chaos War, and now no one came up here. What was the use?

Paladine was gone. The sun was a strange sun, and though it gave light and life, it seemed to do so grudgingly, not gloriously. The elves might have kept up the old tradition simply because it *was* tradition. Their Speaker, Solostaran, had kept up the custom during the years after the Cataclysm, when Paladine had not heeded their prayers. The young king, Gilthas, had not been able to make the arduous climb, however. He had pleaded ill health, and so the elves had abandoned tradition. The real reason Gilthas did not want to climb to the top of the Tower of the Sun was that he did not want to look out over a city that was captive, a city in chains.

"When Qualinost is no longer held in thrall," Gilthas had promised his mother during their last night together, "I will come back, and no matter if I am so old that my bones creak and I have lost every tooth in my head, I will run up those stairs like a child at play, for at the top I will look out over a country and a people who are free."

Laurana thought of him as she set her foot gratefully upon the last stair. She could see her son, young and strong—for he would be young and strong, not old and decrepit—bounding up the stairs joylessly to look out upon a land bathed in blessed sunlight.

She looked out the open archway leading to the balcony and saw only darkness. The wings of Beryl's subject dragons cut off the sunlight. The first tremors of dragonfear caused her throat to constrict, her palms to sweat, her hand involuntarily to tighten its grip around the slender railing. She had felt such fear before, and as had told Marshal Medan, she knew how to combat it. She walked across the landing, faced her enemy squarely, stared at the dragons long and hard until she had mentally conquered them. The fear did not leave her. It would always be there, but she was the master. The fear was under her control.

This settled, she looked around to find Kelevandros. She had expected to find him waiting for them on the landing, and she felt a twinge of worry that she did not see him. She had forgotten the effects of dragonfear, however. Perhaps he had been overcome by it and run away.

No, that could not have happened. There was only one way down. He would have passed them on the stairs.

Perhaps he had gone out on the balcony.

She was about to go in search of him when she heard the Marshal's footsteps behind her, heard him heave a great sigh of relief at finally reaching the top of the stairs. She turned to face him, to tell him that she could not find Kelevandros, when she saw Kelevandros emerging from the shadows of the arched entryway.

I must have walked right past him, she realized. Caught by the dragonfear, she had never noticed him. He stood crouched in the shadows, paralyzed, seeming unable to move.

"Kelevandros," Laurana said to the young elf in concern, "what you are feeling is the dragonfear—"

Marshal Medan rested the dragonlance against the wall. "And to think," he said, sucking in air, "we still have to make the climb down."

Kelevandros gave a convulsive leap. Steel flashed in his hand.

Laurana shouted a warning and lunged to stop him, but she was too late.

Kelevandros stabbed through the cloak the Marshal wore, aiming to strike beneath his upraised arm that had been holding the dragonlance, strike a part of the body the armor could not protect. The elf buried his knife to the hilt in Medan's ribcage, then jerked the knife free. His hand and the blade were stained with blood.

Medan gave a pain-filled cry. His body stiffened. He pressed his hand to his side and stumbled forward, fell to the floor on one knee.

"Ah!" He gasped for breath and found none. The blade had punctured his lung. "Ah!"

"Kelevandros . . ." Laurana whispered, overcome by shock. "What have you done?"

He had been staring at the Marshal, but now he turned his gaze to her. His eyes were wild and fevered, his face livid. He held up his hand to ward her off, raised the knife.

"Don't come near me, Madam!" he cried.

"Kelevandros," Laurana asked helplessly, "why? He was going to help us—"

"He killed my brother," Kelevandros gasped, his pallid lips quivering. "Killed him years ago with his filthy money and his foul promises. He used him, and all the while he despised him. Not dead yet, are you, you bastard?"

Kelevandros lunged to stab the Marshal again.

Swiftly, Laurana interposed her body between the elf and the human. For a moment she thought Kelevandros, in his rage, was going to stab her.

Laurana faced him, unafraid. Her death didn't matter. She would die now or later. Their plan lay in ruins.

"What have you done, Kelevandros?" she repeated sadly. "You have doomed us."

He glared at her. Froth bubbled on his lips. He raised the knife, but not to stab. With a wrenching sob, he threw the knife at the wall. She heard it hit with a clang.

"We were already doomed, Madam," he said, choking.

He fled the chamber, running blindly. Either he could not see where he was going or he did not care, for he crashed headlong into the railing of silver- and gold-twined ivy. The ancient railing shuddered, then gave way under the young elf's weight. Kelevandros plunged over the edge of the staircase. He made no attempt to catch himself. He fell to the floor below without a cry.

Laurana pressed her hands over her mouth and closed her eyes, aghast at the horror of the young elf's death. She stood shivering, trying desperately to banish the sickening feeling of numbness that paralyzed her.

"I won't give up," she said to herself. "I won't . . . Too much depends . . ."

"Madam . . ." Medan's voice was weak.

He lay on the floor, his hand still pressed against his side, as if he could halt the flow of blood that was draining away his life. His face was ashen, his lips gray.

Tears dimming her eyes, Laurana sank down on her knees beside him and began frantically to thrust aside the folds of the bloody cloak to find the wound, to see if there was anything she could do to stop the bleeding.

Medan caught her hand, held it fast, and shook his head.

"You weep for me," he said softly, astonished.

Laurana could not reply. Her tears fell on his face.

He smiled and made a move as if he would kiss her hand, but he lacked the strength. His grip on her hand tightened. He struggled to speak through the tremors of pain that shook his body.

"You must go now," he told her, using his remaining strength to force out each word. "Take the sword . . . and the lance. You are in command, Laurana."

Laurana shivered. *You are in command, Laurana.* The words had a familiar sound, harkened back to another time of darkness and death. She could not think why that should be so or where she had heard them before. She shook her head.

"No," she said brokenly. "I can't. . . ."

"The Golden General," Medan whispered. "I would have liked to have seen her. . . ."

He gave a sigh. The bloodstained hand loosed its grip, dropped limply to the floor. His eyes continued to look fixedly at her, and although no life was in them, she saw his faith in her, steadfast, unwavering.

He meant what he had said. She was in command. Except it was not his voice speaking those words. Another voice . . . far away.

You can command, Laurana. Farewell, elfmaid. Your light will shine in this world . . . It is time for mine to darken.

"No, Sturm, I can't do this," she cried wretchedly. "I am alone!"

As Sturm had been alone, standing by himself at the top of another tower in the bright sunshine of a new day. He had faced certain death, and he had not faltered.

Laurana wept for him. She wept for Medan and for Kelevandros. She wept for the hatred that had destroyed them both and would keep on destroying until someone somewhere had the courage to love. She wept for herself, for her weakness. When she had no more tears left, she lifted her head. She was calm now, in command of herself.

"Sturm Brightblade." Laurana clasped her hands together, praying to him, since there was no one else to hear her prayer. "True friend. I need your strength. I need your courage. Be with me, that I may save my people."

Laurana wiped away her tears. With hands that were firm and did not tremble, she closed the Marshal's eyes and kissed his cold forehead.

"You had the courage to love," she said to him softly. "That will be your salvation and my own."

Sunlight lit the alcove, gleamed on the dragonlance that stood against the wall, glistened in the splatters of blood on the floor. Laurana glanced out through the arched entrance to the blue sky, the empty blue sky. The minion dragons had departed. She did not rejoice. Their departure meant that Beryl was coming.

She thought despairingly of the plan she and the Marshal had made, then resolutely thrust aside both the thought and the despair. Kelevandros's bow and the pitch-covered signal arrow, his flint and tinderbox lay abandoned in the alcove where he had dropped them. She had no one to fire the signal arrow. She could not do it herself, not do that and face the dragon. She had no way now to send word to Dumat, who would be watching for the flare to give his order.

"No matter," she said to herself. "He will know when it is time. They will all know."

She unbuckled the sword belt from around the Marshal's waist. Trying to move hurriedly with fingers that were stiff and shaking, she fastened the belt with the heavy sword around her own waist and arranged the folds of her cloak over the sword. Her white cloak was stained red with the Marshal's blood. Nothing she could do about that. She would have to find some way to explain it to the dragon, explain not only the blood but why she was here atop the tower, a hostage without a captor. Beryl would be suspicious. She would be a fool not to be, and the dragon was no fool.

This is hopeless. There is no chance, Laurana told herself. She heard Beryl approaching, heard the creaking of enormous wings that obliterated the sun. Darkness descended. The air was tainted with the smell of the dragon's poisonous breath.

The dragonfear overwhelmed Laurana. She began to tremble, her hands were numb with cold. The Marshal was wrong. She couldn't do this. . . .

A ray of sunlight escaped from beneath the dragon's wings and shone bright on the dragonlance. The lance blazed with silver flame.

Moved by the beauty, Laurana remembered those who had wielded the lances so long ago. She remembered standing over Sturm's body, the lance in hand, defiantly facing his killer. She had been afraid then, too.

Laurana reached out her hand to touch the lance. She did not intend to take it with her. The lance was eight feet long. She could not hide it from the dragon. She wanted only to touch it, for memory's sake and in memory of Sturm.

Perhaps at this moment Sturm was with her. Perhaps the courage of those who wielded the lance was a part of the lance and now flowed through the metal and into her. Perhaps her own courage, the courage of the Golden General, the courage that had always been there, flowed from her into the dragonlance. All she knew was that when she touched the lance, her plan came to her. She knew what she would do.

Resolute, Laurana took hold of the dragonlance and carried it with her into the sunlight.

32 LOST STAR

Once, she had thought dragons beautiful.

The enemy dragons of Queen Takhisis. Beautiful they were, and deadly. The red dragons, whose scales flashed fire in the sunlight and whose breath was flame. The blue dragons with their swift and graceful flight, wheeling among the clouds, drifting with the thermals. White dragons, cold and glittering, and black dragons, shining, sinuous, and green dragons, emerald death. She feared them and hated them and loathed them, yet she never killed one but that she did not feel a flashing pang of remorse to see such a magnificent creature fall mortally wounded from the skies.

This dragon was not beautiful. Beryl was ugly, fat, and bloated—hideous. Her wings could barely support her hulking body. Her head was misshapen, the forehead jutting out over the eyes that were flat and opaque. Her lower jaw was underslung, the teeth snaggled and rotting. Her scales were not the shining green of emeralds but the green of putrid flesh, of maggot-ridden meat. Her eyes did not gleam with intelligence but flickered with the feeble flame of greed and low cunning. It was then Laurana knew with certainty that this dragon was not of Krynn. Beryl was not a dragon who had been touched by the minds of the gods. She worshiped nothing except her own brutish desire, reverenced nothing but herself.

The shadow of Beryl's wings slid over Qualinost, covering the city in darkness. Laurana stood proudly on the balcony, looked out over the city, and saw that the darkness could not wither the aspen trees or cause the roses to wilt. That might come later, but for now the elven people and the elven homeland stood defiant.

"We will rid the world of one monster, at least," Laurana said softly, as the first blast of wind from the dragon's wings tore at her hair. "You were wrong, Kelevandros. This hour is not our doom. This hour is our glory."

Beryl flew ponderously toward her, jaws gaping in a slavering grin of triumph. The dragonfear rolled off the dragon in waves but no longer affected Laurana. She had known the fear of a god. This mortal monster held no terror for her, no matter how hideous its visage.

The balcony of the Tower of the Sun was rimmed by a wall of burnished gold that came to her waist. The wall was thick and solid, for it had been shaped by ancient elven wizards from the bones of the tower itself. Flowing out from the tower, the balcony wrapped protectively around the people standing behind it. The balcony was large enough to hold a delegation of elves. A single elf standing alone in the center looked very small—almost lost. There should have been two people on the balcony. That had been the plan. Beryl would expect two: Marshal Medan and his prisoner, the Queen Mother.

Nothing Laurana could say or do, no lie she could tell, would alleviate Beryl's suspicions. Talk would only give the dragon time to think and to react.

Beryl's red gleaming eyes swept over the balcony. She was close enough now that she could see, and what she saw was apparently not sitting well with her, for the eyes swept back and forth several times. The lumpish forehead wrinkled, the wicked red eyes narrowed. The fanged mouth widened in a knowing sneer, as if she had foreseen something like this would happen.

That didn't matter now. Nothing mattered now except that this day the elves of Qualinesti and those who were their friends and allies would expend their last breaths to destroy this loathsome beast.

Laurana reached to the clasp of the white cloak and unfastened it. The cloak came off in her hands and fell to the balcony floor. Laurana's armor, the armor of the Golden General, shone in the sunlight. The wind of the dragon's wings blew back her hair that streamed out behind her, a gilded banner.

Beryl was perilously close to the tower now. A few more ungainly flaps of her wings would bring her hulking head so close to Laurana that she might have reached out to touch it. Laurana gagged on the fumes of the dragon's deadly, noxious gaseous breath. She choked, feared she must lose consciousness. The wind—a chill wind with a tinge of thunder in it—shifted directions to blow from the north, blow away the fumes.

Laurana grasped the hilt of the sword, Lost Star, clasped her hand around it. She drew the sword. The blade flashed in the sunlight, the jewel sparkled.

Beryl saw the sword in the hands of the lone elf woman and found the sight diverting. The dragon's jaws creaked apart in what might have been a horrible laugh, but then she sensed the magic. The red eyes flared, and a drool of saliva dribbled from between the fangs. The cruel eyes shifted to the dragonlance, a flame of argent in the sunlight. Beryl's eyes widened. She sucked in a breath of awe and desire.

The fabled dragonlance—bane of dragons. Forged by Theros Ironfeld of the Silver Arm, using the blessed Hammar of Kharas, the lances had the power to pierce a dragon's scales, penetrate through sinew, tissue, flesh, and bone. Dragons native to this wretched world spoke of the lance with fear and awe. Beryl had laughed in disdain. But she had been curious, eager to see one and, because the lances were magic, eager to possess one.

A magic sword, a magic lance, an elf queen, an elf city—rich reward for this day's work.

Clasping the sword beneath the hilt, Laurana walked to the very edge of the balcony and held the Lost Star high. She raised her voice and sang out in a rousing paean of defiance and pride.

Soliasi Arath!

Far below the balcony of the Tower of the Sun, Dumat crouched in the shadows of the rooftop of an elven house. Concealed by the camouflaging branches of the aspen trees, twenty elves watched him, awaiting the signal. At Dumat's side was his elven wife, Ailea, ready to translate should he need to give orders. Dumat spoke some Elvish, but when he did, Ailea always laughed at his accent. She had told him once it was like hearing a horse speak Elvish. He smiled at her, and she smiled at him, both confident, both ready. They had said their good-byes last night.

From his vantage point, Dumat could see the balcony of the tower. He could not gaze at the sunlit building too long, The light gleaming off the sides, made his eyes water. He looked, then, blinking, looked away, then looked again, waiting for Marshal Medan and Laurana to appear. The advent of the flight of minion dragons overhead had shaken Dumat, caused him momentarily to lose sight of the tower as the dragonfear cast a dimness over his eyesight and sent tremors through his body.

The elves on the roof were affected as well, but they, like Dumat, clenched their teeth on the fear. No one cried out, no one panicked. When Dumat was able to see again, he could see the tower clearly now. The shadow of the dragons' wings blotted out the sunlight.

The balcony was empty. No sign of Laurana or the Marshal.

Dumat began to worry. He did not know why, could not explain it. The instinct of a veteran soldier, perhaps. Something had gone wrong. Dumat considered for a brief moment making a dash for the tower, to see if there was anything he could do, but rejected the idea almost immediately. His orders were to remain here and wait for the signal. He would obey those orders.

The minion dragons departed and, like Laurana, Dumat realized that this was not a good sign. Beryl would be on her way. He tensed, staring at the tower that once again gleamed blindingly in the sunlight. He dared not look away for fear he might miss the signal, and he was forced to blink almost constantly to clear the tears from his eyes. When he saw Laurana, he let out a grateful whistle and watched for the Marshal.

Medan did not come.

Dumat gave the Marshal a count of ten, then a count of ten again, then gave up. He had known the truth before he started counting. Laurana would have never appeared on that balcony alone if Medan had been alive and able to stand beside her. Dumat said farewell to the Marshal, a soldier's farewell, brief and silent, but heartfelt. He crouched and waited, watching for the signal flare.

Those were the orders. Dumat and the rest of the elves and the few Dark Knights and dwarves who made up Qualinost's defense force were to watch for the flaming arrow and then launch the attack. Greatly daring, he lifted his head above the branches in order to gain a better view. Ailea pinched his leg to force him to duck back down, but he ignored her. He had to see.

Beryl came in sight, flying toward the tower. Dragonfear washed off her in great, billowing waves, but the fact that she had sent her followers first worked to her disadvantage. Those who were going to succumb to dragonfear had already done so and were recovering. Those who had not were not going to start now. Beryl's cunning eyes roved here and darted there, not trusting to Medan's reports the city was abandoned.

Search all you want, you great bitch, Dumat told her silently. You are here, you are right above us. There's no escape now.

Dumat ducked back down moments before the dragon's eyes might have seen him. Ailea gave him a look he knew well. It meant he was in for a scolding. He hoped against hope he'd live to receive it, but he wasn't counting on it. He stared back at the tower.

His eyesight was good, and he could see Laurana approach the edge of the balcony. He could not see her face, not from this distance—she was a small smear of white against the gold—but he could guess from the fact that she went to meet the dragon that she was not afraid.

"Good for you, Mum," he said quietly. "Good for you."

Beryl was close to the tower now. Dumat could see her underbelly and the underside of the wings, the hulking legs dangling beneath and the twitching tail. Her scaly hide was an evil green, mud-covered from her wallows.

When devising his plan, King Gilthas had first thought of trying to pierce her hide with arrows, but he had discarded the idea. Beryl's hide was thick, the scales strong. Arrows might bring her down but only if fired in massive numbers, and the elves did not have those numbers. Besides, she would expect such an attack and be prepared for it. They hoped she would not expect what she was about to get.

Dumat waited now only for the signal arrow that was to have been fired by the elf Kelevandros . . . Kelevandros . . . Dumat knew what had happened, knew it as well as if he had seen it himself. Kelevandros had avenged his brother. Medan was wounded . . . dead. Laurana was alone up there now. She had no one to fire the signal.

He saw her lift her arms.

The sun in this new sky might have seemed pale and strange to the people of Krynn, but perhaps they had managed to win its favor. As Dumat watched, the sun sent a ray of light, straight as an arrow to strike Laurana. In that moment, he thought she held a star.

White flame flared, a flame so brilliant and dazzling that Dumat had to squint his eyes against it and avert his gaze, as he might have done looking into the sun itself. This was the signal, he knew it more in his heart than his head.

With a wild shout, he reared up from among the tree branches and flung them aside. Around him, elves jumped to their feet, grabbed their slings and bows and took their places. Dumat looked to the other rooftops. He was not alone. He had no need to give another signal. Every one of the commanders had seen that flash of light and known it for what it was.

Dumat did not hear Laurana's shouted challenge because he was shouting a challenge of his own, as were the elves around him. Dumat gave the order, and the elves opened fire.

Soliasi Arath! Laurana shouted as she had shouted so many years before, challenging the dragons attacking the High Clerist's Tower to fly to their deaths. She held the sword with the Lost Star above her, held it with her left hand. If the jewel failed, if the legends were wrong, if the magic of the sword had dwindled as much of the magic in the world had dwindled during the Age of Mortals, their plans and hopes and dreams would end in death.

The sun pierced the jewel and the jewel burst in white fire. Laurana whispered a blessing on the soul of Kalith Rian and on the soul of that unknown elven smith who had found the lost star glittering in the ashes of the forge fire.

Beryl stared at the sword with intense longing, for its magic was powerful, and she wanted it desperately. The jewel in the hilt was the most fabulous she had ever seen. She could not take her eyes from it. She must have it. Malys had nothing this valuable in her treasure trove. Beryl could not take her eyes from it. . . .

Beryl was caught.

Laurana realized the spell had worked when she saw the glow of the jewel burn in the dragon's eyes, burn deep into the beast's brain. She held the sword steady, held it high.

Enthralled, Beryl hung almost motionless in the air above Qualinost, her wings fanning gently to keep her aloft, her rapt gaze fixed upon the Lost Star.

The sword was heavy, and Laurana held it in an awkward position in her left hand, but she dared not give way to weakness, dared not drop the sword. She feared even to move, afraid that she might break the spell. Once freed from the enchantment, Beryl would attack in a violent rage. Laurana knew a moment's despair as she waited in vain to hear some sign that the elves had launched the attack. Her plan had failed. Dumat was waiting for the signal arrow that would never come.

The cheering and shouted challenges rising up from the rooftops were sweeter than bards' songs to her, gave her tired arm muscles renewed strength. Elves appeared on the bridges that spanned the borders of Qualinost. Elves and Knights could be seen bursting out from the tree-branch rooftops, a blossom of deadly flowers. Ballistae that had been covered with vines were wheeled into position. The sling-throwers moved to the attack. A single shouted command begat hundreds of others. The elves launched the assault.

Spears fired from the ballistae streamed upward, flew in a graceful arc over Beryl's body. Trailing behind the spears were long lengths of rope—rope that had been formed of wedding gowns and baby clothes, cooks' aprons and senators' ceremonial robes. The hundreds of spears carried the ropes up and over Beryl. When the spears plummeted back down to the ground, the ropes settled over the dragon, falling across her body and her wings and her tail.

The sling-throwers launched their attack, sending lead missiles soaring into the air. Attached to the missiles were more ropes that sailed over the dragon. Reloaded, the ballistae fired again. The sling-throwers hurled their missiles again and yet again.

Elf wizards cast spells, not on the dragon, but on the ropes. They cast their spells not knowing if the erratic, wayward magic would work or not. They cast the spells more out of hope and despair than out of certainty. In some instances, the wizards cast spells as they had known them in the Fourth Age. In other instances they cast the spells of the wild magic of this new age. In all instances, the spells worked perfectly. The elf wizards were amazed—thrilled, but amazed.

Some spells strengthened the rope and made the cloth as strong as steel. Others caused the rope to burst into magical fire. The enchanted flames ran along the length of the cable, burning the dragon but not consuming the rope. Certain spells made the rope as sticky as cobweb. Adhering to the dragon's scales, the rope stuck fast. Still other spells caused the rope to loop and spiral as if it were alive. The living rope wrapped around and around the dragon's feet, trussed Beryl like a chicken going to market.

Now some of the elves dropped their weapons and grabbed hold of the ends of the ropes, waiting for the final command. More and more rope filled the air until Beryl looked like an enormous moth caught in a web spun by many thousands of spiders.

Beryl could do nothing. The dragon was aware of what was happening to her. Laurana looked directly into the reptilian eyes and saw first amusement at the feeble efforts of these puny beings to ensnare her, then annoyance, as Beryl realized her movements were becoming increasingly hampered by the ropes. The annoyance altered very rapidly to fury, when she realized she could do nothing to help herself. She could do nothing but stare at the jewel.

The dragon's body quivered in impotent rage. Saliva dripped from her jaws. Her neck muscles bulged and strained as she tried frantically to wrench her gaze from the jewel. Rope after rope fell over her body. Her wings were weighed down, her tail entangled. She could not move her hind feet. They were tied together. The horrid ropes were winding themselves around her forefeet. She could feel herself being hauled down out of the sky, and suddenly she was afraid. She was powerless to save herself.

It was at this moment, while Beryl was caught by the jewel and ensnared by the ropes, that Laurana had planned to attack with the dragonlance. She had intended to drive the lance into the dragon's throat, prevent her from breathing her deadly fumes. She was to have wielded the lance. Medan was to have wielded the sword, used it to slay the dragon.

A good plan, but Medan was dead. Laurana was alone. To wield the lance, she would have to drop the sword, free the dragon from the enchantment. This was the moment of peril.

Laurana began to edge backward, still holding the sword, still keeping it steady, though her tired arm muscles quivered with the strain. Step by step, she moved back to the wall where she had placed the dragonlance to have it ready within reach. She groped behind her with her right hand, feeling for the lance, for she did not dare take her eyes off Beryl. At first, Laurana could not find the lance, and fear seized her. Then her fingers touched the metal, warm in the sunshine. Her hand closed over it, and she sighed deeply.

Below Dumat was shrieking for those holding the ropes to pull hard. The elves and Knights who had been manning the ballistae and wielding the slings dropped their weapons and leaped to grab hold of the ropes, adding their weight to those already pulling. Slowly but inexorably, they began to drag the enmeshed dragon closer to the ground.

Laurana drew a deep breath, summoned all her strength. Silently speaking the name of Sturm, she sought inside herself for the courage and the will and the resolve that had been with him on the tower when death dived at him. Her one fear was that Beryl would attack her instantly upon being freed of the spell and breathe the deadly gas on her before Laurana could slay the dragon. If Beryl did that, if Laurana died before she could achieve her mission, the elves on the ground would die before they had accomplished their goal, for Beryl would breathe her poison on them, and they would fall where they stood.

Laurana had never felt so alone. There was no one to help her. Not Sturm, not Tanis, not the Marshal. Not the gods.

Yet at the end, we are all of us alone, she reminded herself. Those I have loved held my hand on the long journey, but when we came to the final parting, I released them, and they walked forward, leaving me behind. Now, it is my turn to walk forward. To walk alone.

Laurana lifted the sword with the Lost Star and flung it over the parapet. The spell was broken. Beryl's eyes blinked, then blazed with fury.

Beryl had two objectives. The first was to free herself from the infuriating snare. The second was to kill the elf who had tricked her, catching her in a magical trap that a hatchling might have had wit enough to avoid. Beryl could deal with one or the other. She was about to kill the elf, when a particularly violent pull of the ropes jerked her downward.

She heard laughter. The laughter came not from below her, not from the elves. The laughter came from the sky above.

Two of her minions, both reds, both dragons she had secretly suspected of plotting against her, wheeled among the clouds far, far above, and they were laughing. Beryl knew immediately the reds were laughing at her, watching and enjoying her humiliation.

She had never trusted them, these native dragons. She knew quite well they served her out of fear, not out of loyalty. Ascribing to them motives of treachery best suited to herself, Beryl concluded irrationally that the red dragons were in league with the elves. The reds were biding their time, waiting for her to become thoroughly ensnared, then they would close in for the kill.

Beryl dismissed Laurana from consideration. A lone elf—what harm could she do compared to two treacherous red dragons?

As Medan had said, Beryl was a coward at heart. She had never been trapped like this, rendered helpless, and she was terrified. She must free herself from this net, must return to the skies. Only there, where she could wheel and dive and use her enormous weight and strength to her advantage, would she be safe from her foes. Once in the heavens, she could destroy these wretched elves with a single breath. Once in the heavens, she could deal with her traitor servants.

Anger burned inside her. Beryl struggled to rid herself of the entangling ropes that hampered her flight. Heaving her shoulders, she lifted her wings and thrashed her tail, attempting to snap the ropes. She clawed at them with her sharp talons and turned her head to snap at them with her teeth. She had thought to break the puny ropes easily, but she had not counted on the strength of the magic or the will of those who had twined their love for their people and their homeland into the ropes.

A few strands broke, but most held. Her wild lashing and gyrations caused some elves to lose their grips. Some were dragged off rooftops or slammed into buildings.

Beryl cast a glance at the red dragons, saw that they had flown closer. Fear evolved into panic. Maddened, Beryl sucked in a huge breath, intending to destroy these insects who had so humbled her. Out of the corner of her eye, she caught sight of a flash of silver. . . .

Laurana watched in awe and terror as Beryl fought frantically to free herself. The dragon's head thrashed wildly. She shrieked curses and snapped at the ropes with her teeth. Appalled by the ferocity of the beast's rage, Laurana could not move. She stood trembling, clutching the lance in sweating hands. Her glance slid to the doorway that led to the arched alcove beyond, led to safety.

Beryl drew in a huge breath, drew it into lungs that would breathe out death on Laurana's people. Seizing the dragonlance with both hands, Laurana cried *Quisalan elevas!* to Tanis and Sturm and those who had gone before her. "Our loves-bond eternal." Aiming the lance at Beryl's lashing head, Laurana lunged at the dragon.

The dragonlance gleamed silver in the light of the strange sun. Putting all the strength of her body and soul and heart into her effort, Laurana plunged the dragonlance into Beryl's skull.

Blood spurted out in a great torrent, splashing over Laurana. Though her hands were wet and slippery with the dragon's blood, she held desperately to the lance, shoving it deeper into the dragon's head, as deep as it would go.

Pain—burning, flaring pain—exploded in Beryl's brain, as if someone had bored a hole through the bone, let in the blazing sun to set her soul on fire.

Beryl gagged on her own poison breath. Attempting to free herself from the horrible pain, she jerked her head.

The dragon's sudden, spasmodic movement lifted Laurana off the balcony. She hung suspended in the air, perilously close to the edge. Her hands lost their hold on the lance, and she fell to the balcony's floor, landing on her back. Bone snapped, pain flashed, but then, strangely, she could feel nothing. She tried to stand, but her limbs would not obey her brain's command. Unable to move, she stared into the dragon's gaping jaws.

Beryl's pain did not end. It grew worse. Half blinded by the blood that poured into her eyes, yet she could still see her attacker. She tried to breathe death on the elf woman, but the dragon failed, choked on her own poison.

Consumed by fear, maddened by pain, thinking only to avenge herself on the elf that had done her such terrible harm, Beryl brought her massive head crashing down on the Tower of the Sun.

The shadow of death fell over Laurana. She looked away from death, looked into the sun.

The strange sun, hanging in the sky. It seemed forlorn, bewildered . . . as though it were lost.

. . . a lost star . . .

Laurana closed her eyes against the darkening shadow.

"Our loves-bond . . ."

Hanging onto one of the ropes, pulling with all his strength, Dumat was not able to see what had happened on the tower, but he knew by Beryl's fearful shriek and the fact that they were not all dead of poison gas that Laurana must have dealt a blow to the creature. Dragon's blood and saliva splashed on him and around him, a hideous shower. The dragon was hurt. Now was the time to take advantage of her weakness.

"Pull, damn you! Pull!" Dumat yelled hoarsely, his voice rasping, almost gone. "She's not finished! Not by a long shot!"

Elves and humans who felt their strength ebbing in the battle with the dragon rallied and flung themselves with renewed energy on the ropes. Blood, running from their hands where the skin had been peeled off, stained the ropes. The pain of the raw nerves was intense, and some cried out even as they continued to tug, while others gritted their teeth and pulled.

Dumat watched in shock as Beryl attacked the tower, bashed her head into the building. His heart ached for Laurana, who must be trapped up there, and he hoped for her sake that she was already dead. Beryl's head struck the balcony, tore it free of the tower. The balcony plunged to the ground. Those people standing beneath it stared up in terror. Some had wits enough to flee. Others, bound up in fear, were unable to move. The balcony struck with a horrific crash, taking out buildings and cracking the paving stones. Debris flew through the air, killing and maiming. Dust rose in an immense cloud and rolled over them.

Dumat, coughing, turned to Ailea, to say some word of comfort, for his wife would be grieving the Queen Mother's death. The words of comfort were never spoken. Ailea lay staring up at Dumat with eyes that could no longer see him. A rock shard had pierced her breast. She had not lived long enough to scream.

Dumat stared at the dragon. She was down at treetop level now. Her forefeet touched the ground. Grim and empty, he redoubled his efforts on the rope.

"Pull, damn you!" he shouted. "Pull!"

Beryl's mad assault on the tower managed to slay her attacker, but that was all she accomplished. She was at last able to draw breath again, though it was wheezing and shallow, but the blow had not dislodged the dragonlance, as she had dimly hoped would happen. Far from shaking loose the splinter, the blow seemed to have driven it still deeper into her head. Her world was burning pain, and all she wanted to do was end it.

Beryl thrashed about, trying to free herself from the ropes, trying to dislodge the lance. Her flailings knocked down buildings, toppling trees. Her tail smashed into Dumat's house. He held onto the rope until the last possible moment. When the dragon crushed the house to tinder, Dumat fell through the broken roof. The house fell down on top of him. Buried alive, Dumat lay trapped in the rubble, pinned beneath a heavy tree limb, unable to move. He tasted blood in his mouth. Looking through the tangle of broken and twisted limbs and leaves, he saw the dragon above him. She had freed her wings, though ropes still dangled from them. She struggled to gain altitude, to rise above treetop level. But for every rope that snapped, two ropes held. More ropes fell across her. Elves and humans had died, but more had survived, and they continued the fight.

"Pull, damn you!" Dumat whispered. "Pull!"

The elves saw the Queen Mother die, they saw their loved ones die. They saw the dragon destroy the Tower of the Sun, the symbol of elven pride and hope. They used the strength lent them by grief and anger to drag down the dragon, drag her from the skies.

Beryl fought to free herself from the ropes and the horrible pain, but the more she struggled, the more she tangled herself in the elven cobweb. Her thrashing limbs and head and tail, her flailing wings crushed buildings and snapped trees. She struggled furiously to free herself, for she knew that when she hit the ground, she was vulnerable. The elves would move in with spear and arrow and finish the kill.

The elves saw that Beryl was starting to weaken. Her flailing grew less violent, her thrashing less destructive.

The dragon was dying.

Certain of that now, the elves pulled with a will and finally succeeded. They dragged Beryl's hulking body to the ground.

She landed with a shattering crash that crushed buildings and all those who had not been able to scramble out of the way. The force of the impact sent tremors rippling through the ground, shook the dwarves who waited in the tunnels below, sent rock and dust down on their heads, caused them to look in consternation at the beams that shored up the walls, kept the tunnels from collapsing.

When the tremors ceased and the dust settled, the elves grabbed their spears, moved in for the kill. After they had destroyed the dragon, they would be ready to fight her army.

The elves began to speak of victory. Qualinost had been grievously hurt, many had died, but the elven nation would live. They would bury their dead and weep for them. They would sing songs, grand songs about the death of the dragon.

But Beryl was not dead. Not by a long shot, as Dumat had said. The dragonlance had caused her great pain and disordered her thinking, but now the pain was starting to lessen. Her panic subsided and gave way to a fury that was cold and calculating and dangerous, far more dangerous than her tumultuous flailing. Her troops were massing on the banks of the two streams—offshoots of the White-rage River—that surrounded and protected Qualinost. Her troops were even now preparing to cross those streams. The elves had taken out the bridges, but Beryl's soldiers had brought hundreds of rafts and temporary bridges to carry her army across the one-hundred-foot-wide ravines.

Soon her soldiers would overrun Qualinost, put the elves to the sword. Elf blood would flow through the streets, sweeter to Beryl than May wine. The advent of her troops caused Beryl one difficulty: She could not use her poison gas to kill the elves, not without killing her troops as well. This was only a minor inconvenience, nothing to be concerned about. She would simply kill elves by the tens and not by the hundreds.

Relaxing, Beryl feigned weakness, lay sprawled ignominiously on the ground. She took a grim satisfaction in feeling the trees—so beloved of the elves—smash to splinters beneath her crushing body. Blinking her eyes free of blood, Beryl could see the damage she had wrought upon the once-beautiful city, and the sight was a boost to her spirits. She had never hated anyone or anything—not even her cousin Malys—more than she now hated these elves.

The elves were creeping out of their rat holes, coming to stare at her. They held spears and bows with arrows pointed at her. Beryl scorned them. The spear had not been made that could stay her, not even the fabled dragonlance. Nor could the arrows that were to her the size of bee stingers. She could see the elves all around her, puny, witless creatures, staring at her with their little squint eyes, gibbering in their greasy language.

Let them gibber. They would have something to chatter about shortly, that much was certain.

The pain in her head continued to ease. Resting on the ground, Beryl took careful stock of the situation. She had flung off or dislodged some of the ropes, and she could feel others starting to loosen. The magic spells were waning. Soon Beryl would be free to kill elves, slaying them one by one, stomping on them and snapping them in two. Her army would join her, and between them not one elf would remain alive in the world. Not one.

The dragonlance continued to be an irritant. Every once in a while, molten hot pain shot through her head, increased her rage. She lay on the ground, the elves at eye level, peering at them through squinted lids. In the distance, she heard horn calls, the sounds of her army advancing. They must have seen her fall. Perhaps they thought her dead. Perhaps her commanders were already spending in their feeble brains the loot that they would have been forced to share with her. They were in for a surprise. They were all in for a grand surprise. . . .

Bellowing a roar of defiance and triumph, Beryl lifted her head. Her huge clawed talons dug into the ground. With one push, one massive thrust of her gigantic legs, Beryl heaved herself to her feet.

The dwarven tunnels, a labyrinthine honeycomb built beneath Qualinost, buckled and collapsed under the dragon's weight. The ground gave way.

Beryl's roar changed to a startled shriek. She fought to save herself, scrabbling with her feet, frantically beating her wings to lift herself from the ruin. But her wings were still entangled with rope, her feet could find no purchase. An Immortal Hand cracked the bones of the world, split the ground asunder. Beryl plunged into the gaping fissure.

Torvold Bellowsgranite, cousin to the Thane of Thorbardin and leader of the dwarven army that had come to Qualinost to fight the Dark Knights of Neraka, heard the battle being fought above him, if he could not see it. Torvald stood at the foot of a ladder that led up to the surface, about twenty feet above him. He waited for the signal that meant the invading army had started to ford the river. His own army, comprised of a thousand dwarves, would then swarm up out of this tunnel and others dug beneath the city, march to attack.

The tunnel was as dark as deepest night, for the digging worms and their glowing larva had been dispatched back to Thorbardin. The darkness and the confined space and smell of freshly turned earth and worm leavings didn't bother the dwarves, who found the darkness and the smell familiar, comfortable. They were eager to depart the tunnels, however; eager to face their enemies, to do battle, and they fingered their axes and spoke of the coming glories with grim anticipation.

When the dwarves felt the first shudderings of the ground beneath their feet, they gave a cheer that echoed up and down the tunnels, for they hoped that meant that the elven strategy was working. The dragon had been hauled out of the skies and was lying helpless on the ground, emeshed in magical rope from which she could not escape.

"What's going on?" Torvald bellowed up at the scout, who was hunkered down near the entrance, his head poking up through the branches of a lilac bush.

"They got her," was the scout's laconic answer. "She's not moving. She's a goner."

The dwarves cheered again. Torvald nodded and was about to give the order for his men to start to climb the ladder when a fierce roar proved the scout wrong. The ground shook beneath Torvald's feet, the tremor so severe that the beams shoring up the walls creaked ominously. Dirt rained down on their heads.

"What the—" Torvald started to holler at the scout, then changed his mind. He began to climb the ladder to see for himself.

Another quake rumbled through the ground. The tunnel's ceiling split wide open. Dazzling sunlight streamed down through the gaping hole, half-blinding the dwarves. The horrified Torvald saw the blazing red eye of the infuriated dragon glaring down at him, and then the beams holding up the tunnel's roof cracked, the ladder splintered. The eye vanished amidst a huge cloud of dust and debris. The roof of the tunnel collapsed.

The world fell on top of Torvald, knocking him from the ladder. The horrifying screams of his dying comrades rose above the rending bones of Krynn, the last sounds he heard as tons of rock smashed down on him, crushing his skull and shattering his chest.

Stone, long trusted by the dwarves to shelter and to guard them against their enemies, became their enemy. Their killer. Their tomb.

Rangold of Balifor, now forty years old, had been a mercenary since he was fourteen. He fought for one reason and one alone—plunder. He had no other loyalties, knew nothing of politics, would switch sides in the middle of battle if someone made it worth his while. He had joined Beryl's army because he had heard they were going to be march on Qualinost. He had long anticipated the looting and sacking of the elven city. A man of foresight, Rangold had brought with him several large burlap bags in which he intended to carry home his fortune.

Rangold stood on the riverbank, eating stale bread and munching on dried beef, waiting his turn to cross the river. The blasted elves had cut the bridges. The ropes dangled far above them, for the banks were steep, the river low this time of year. Their scouts kept watch but reported seeing no elves. The first units had started across, some carrying their packs over their heads, others carrying their weapons. Those who could not swim were clearly uncomfortable as they waded deeper and deeper into the water that swirled around them. The water was cold, but ran calmly this time of year. In the spring, fed by the melting snows, the river would have been impassable.

Occasionally a red dragon could be seen circling high above the army, keeping watch. The men did not like the red dragons, did not trust them, even though they were on the same side, and kept glancing upward, hoping that the beast would fly away. Rangold didn't care anything about dragons. He shivered when the dragonfear was on him, shrugged it off when it was past and continued to eat his food. The thought of slaughtering elves and stealing their riches gave a fine, sharp edge to this appetite.

His first twinge of unease came when the ground suddenly lurched beneath his feet, throwing Rangold off balance and causing him to drop his sandwich. A limb fell with a shattering crash. A tree toppled. The river water heaved and surged, splashing up onto the bank. Rangold clung to the tree and stared around, trying to figure out what was happening. Overhead, the red dragon spread her wings and flew low over the woods, shouting out what sounded like warnings, but no one could make out what she was screaming.

The tremors continued, grew more severe. An enormous cloud of debris roiled into the air, so thick that it obliterated the light of the sun. Those crossing the river lost their footing, tumbled into the water. Those on the bank began hollering and running this way and that in confusion and panic, as the ground continued to heave and buckle beneath their feet.

"What are your orders?" a captain shouted.

"Hold your ground," his superior, a Knight of Neraka, answered tersely.

"That's easier said than done," the captain returned angrily, staggering to keep his balance. "I think we should get the hell out of here!"

"You have your orders, Captain," the Knight shouted. "This will stop in a—"

With an ear-splitting crack, an enormous tree limb broke loose and fell with a thundering crash, burying the Knight and the captain beneath its branches. Cries and moans came from the wreckage, pleas for help, pleas that Rangold ignored. He didn't know what the rest of the army planned to do, and he didn't care. As the captain had suggested, Rangold was going to get the hell out of here.

He started to scramble up the bank, but at that moment he heard an ominous, rolling, thunderous rumble. Turning to find the source of the sound, he saw a horrifying sight. A wall of water, bubbling and foaming, rushed down on them. The quakes caused the banks of the White-rage River to crumble. Fissures split open the rock ravines through which the river ran. Freed of its confinement, driven into tumult by the repeated tremors, the river went on a wild rampage.

The water uprooted trees, tore huge chunks of rock from the cliff faces through which it thundered, carried the rock and debris before it.

Rangold stared, appalled, and then turned and began to run. Behind him, those trapped in the water shrieked for help, but the rising river swiftly drowned their cries, as it swept them downstream. Rangold tried to clamber up the bank, but the sides were steep and slippery. He knew a moment's horrible fear, and then the water crashed into him with a force that shattered his breastbone and stopped his heartbeat. His body, limp and bloody, became just one more bit of debris the river carried downstream.

Bellowing and shrieking in rage, Beryl sank deeper and deeper as the ground gave way. The earth cracked beneath her weight. The cracks spread and radiated outward. Buildings, trees and homes collapsed and slid into the widening fissures. The headquarters of the Knights of Neraka, that squat, ugly building, fell in upon itself with booming crash. Debris rained down upon the dragon, striking her in the head, puncturing her wings. The castle of the king, built of living aspen trees, was destroyed, the trees uprooted, limbs shattered, huge trunks twisted and snapped.

The elves of Qualinost, who had remained to defend their homeland, died in the rubble of the homes they had wrought with such care, died in the gardens they had loved. Though they knew death was imminent and that there was no escape, they continued to fight their enemy, stabbing at Beryl with spear and sword until the pavement split asunder, gave way beneath their feet. The elves died with hope, for though they had perished, they believed that their city would survive and rise again from the ruins.

It was well they died, before they knew the truth.

Beryl realized suddenly that she was not going to survive, that she could not escape. The knowledge bewildered her. This wasn't the way it was supposed to end. She—the mightiest force to have ever been seen on Krynn—was going to die an ignominious death in a hole in the ground. How could this have happened? What had gone wrong? She didn't understand. . . .

Boulders rained down on her, cracking her skull and breaking her spine. Splintered trees ripped holes in her wings, falling rocks snapped the tendons. Sharp, jagged stones slashed open her belly. Blood spurted from beneath her scales. Pain wrenched her and twisted, her and she screamed for death to come to release her. The monster who had slain so many moaned and writhed in agony as rocks and trees and crumbling buildings pummeled her. The immense, misshapen head sank lower and lower. The red eyes rolled back. The broken wings, the thrashing tail grew still. With a last sigh, a bitter curse, Beryl died.

Tremors shook the ground around the elven city as the Immortal Hand pounded on it with a fist of hatred. The earth quaked and shattered. Cracks widened, fissures split the bedrock on which Qualinost had been built. The red dragons, looking down from the skies, saw an enormous, gaping hole where once had stood a beautiful city. The reds had no love for elves, for they had been enemies since the beginning of time, but so terrible was this sight, expressive of awful power, that the reds could not rejoice. They looked down upon the ruin and bowed their heads in reverence and respect.

The tremors ceased. The ground settled, no longer heaved and quivered. The White-rage River overflowed its banks, poured into the immense chasm where once had stood the elven city of Qualinost. Long after the quakes stopped, the water continued to boil and bubble and surge and heave, wave after wave crashing upon the newly created banks. Gradually, the river grew calm. The water lapped tremulously at the new banks that now surrounded it, hugged them close, as if shocked by its own fury and bewildered by the destruction it had wrought.

Night came without starlight or moonlight, a shroud drawn over the dead who rested far beneath the dark, quivering water.

33 NALIS AREN

Many miles away, Gilthas and his retinue parted with Tarn Bellowsgranite, the dwarven thane, then traveled south. They had ridden with what haste they could, the Lioness pushing them, for she feared that Beryl's army would split, send one force marching south to intercept the refugees while one force seized and held Qualinost. Despite her urging, their pace was slow, for their hearts were heavy and seemed to weigh them down. Whenever they came to the top of hill or ridge, Gilthas halted and turned in the saddle to stare at the horizon in some vain hope of seeing what was happening.

"We are too far away," his wife reminded him. "The trees block the view. I left runners, who will come after us swiftly to report. All will be well. We must move on, my love. We must move on."

They had stopped to rest and water their horses when they felt the ground shudder beneath their feet and heard a low rumble, as of a distant storm. The tremor was mild, but it caused Gilthas's hand to shake so that he dropped the water skin he had been filling. He rose and looked to the north.

"What was that? Did you feel that?" he demanded.

"Yes, I felt it," said the Lioness, coming to stand beside him. Her gaze joined his, and she was troubled. "I don't know what that was."

"There are sometimes quakes in the mountains, Your Majesty," Planchet suggested.

"Not like that. I've never felt anything like that. Something has gone wrong. Something terrible has happened."

"We don't know that," the Lioness said. "Perhaps it was nothing but a tremor, as Planchet says. We should keep going—"

"No," said Gilthas. "I'm staying here to wait for the runners. I'm not leaving until I find out what has happened."

He walked away, heading for a rock promontory that thrust up out of the ground. The Lioness and Planchet exchanged glances.

"Go with him," the Lioness said softly.

Planchet nodded and hurried after Gilthas. The Lioness instructed her troops to set up camp. She looked often to the north, and when she did, she sighed softly and shook her head.

Gilthas climbed with fevered energy; Planchet had difficulty keeping up with his king. Reaching the top, Gilthas stood long moments, staring intently to the north.

"Is that smoke, do you think, Planchet?" he asked anxiously.

"A cloud, Your Majesty," Planchet replied.

Gilthas continued to stare until he was forced to lower his gaze, wipe his eyes.

"It's the sun," he muttered. "It's too bright."

"Yes, Your Majesty," said Planchet softly, looking away. Imagining he could read the young king's thoughts, he added, "Your Majesty's decision to leave was the right—"

"I know, Planchet," Gilthas interrupted him. "I know my duty, and I will try to do it, as best as I am able. I wasn't thinking about that." He looked back to the north. "Our people have been forced to leave their ancient homeland. I was wondering what would happen to us if we could not go back."

"That will never come to pass, Your Majesty," said Planchet firmly.

"Why not?" Gilthas turned to look directly at him, curious to hear the answer.

Planchet was confounded. This was so simple, so elementary. "Qualinesti is ours, Your Majesty. The land belongs to the elves. It is ours by right."

Gilthas smiled sadly. "Some might say the only plot of land to which we mortals have an inherent right is the plot where we are finally laid to rest. Look down there. My dear wife paces like the giant cat for which she was named. She is nervous, worried. She does not want to stop. She wants to keep going. Why? Because our enemies pursue us. They hunt us—on our land."

"We will take it back—"

"Will we?" Gilthas asked quietly. "I wonder." He turned back to the north. "We are a people in exile. We have nowhere to go." He slightly turned his head. "I've heard the reports about Silvanesti, Planchet."

"Rumors, Your Majesty," Planchet returned, embarrassed and uncomfortable. "We cannot confirm them. We were going to tell you, but the Lioness said you were not to be troubled. Not until we knew something certain—"

"Certain." Gilthas shook his head. With the tip of his boot, he traced in the dust an outline of an oblong, six feet in length and three feet wide. "This is all that is certain, my friend."

"Your Majesty—" Planchet began, worried.

Gilthas turned to stare back to the north.

"Is that smoke, do you think?"

"Yes, Your Majesty," said Planchet. "That is smoke."

The runner caught up with them during the night. Accustomed to traveling under the cover of darkness, the Lioness and her rebel elves marked the trails as her Kagonesti ancestors had done long before her, using the petals of flowers that glowed in the darkness to indicate which fork to take, leaving glow worms trapped in bottles on a pile of rocks, or smearing a tree with phosphor. Thus the runner had been able to follow their trail even after night fell.

They had not lit a fire. The Lioness had counseled against it. They sat silently in the darkness, no one telling tales or singing a starsong, as they might have done in happier times.

Gilthas kept apart from the others, his thoughts straying back to his childhood as they had done often since his parting from his mother. He was remembering these times, thinking of his mother and his father, of their love and tender care for him, when he saw the guards jump to their feet. Their hands going to their swords, they ran to surround him.

Gilthas had not heard a sound, but that was not unusual. As his wife constantly teased him, he had "human ears." Sword drawn, Planchet came to stand by the side of his king. The Lioness remained in the center of the clearing, peering into the darkness. She whistled the notes of the song of the nightingale.

The answer came back. The Lioness whistled again. The elves relaxed, although they still kept up their guard. The runner entered the camp and, sighting the Lioness, approached her and began to speak to her in Kagonesti, the language of the Wilderelves.

Gilthas could speak some Kagonesti, but he could catch only fragments of the conversation, for the two kept their voices low, and the runner spoke too fast to be understood, his speech broken only by pauses for breath. Gilthas might have walked over and joined in the conversation, but he was suddenly unable to move. He could tell by the runner's tone that the news he was conveying was not good.

Then Gilthas saw his wife do something she had never before done. She fell to her knees and bowed her head. Her mane of hair covered her face like a veil of mourning. She lifted her hand to her eyes, and Gilthas saw that she wept.

Planchet gripped Gilthas's arm, but the king shook him off. Gilthas walked forward on feet that were numb. He could not feel the ground beneath them, and he stumbled once but caught himself. Hearing him approaching, the Lioness regained control of herself. Scrambling to rise, she hastened to meet him. She clasped his hands in hers. Her hands were as cold as death, and Gilthas shivered.

"What is it?" he demanded in a voice he did not recognize. "Tell me! My mother—" He could not speak it.

"Your mother is dead," the Lioness said softly, her voice trembling and husky with her tears.

Gilthas sighed deeply, but his grief was his own. He was king. He had his people to think about.

"What about the dragon?" he asked harshly. "What about Beryl?"

"Beryl is dead," the Lioness said. "There is more," she added quickly, when she saw Gilthas about to speak.

"The tremor we felt . . ." Her voice cracked. She moistened dry lips, then continued. "Something went wrong. Your mother fought alone. No one knows why or what happened. Beryl came and . . . your mother fought the dragon alone."

Gilthas lowered his head, unable to bear the pain.

"Laurana struck Beryl with the dragonlance but did not kill her. Furious, the dragon smashed the tower. . . . Your mother could not escape. . . . "

The Lioness was silent a moment, then went on. Her voice sounded dazed, as if she could not believe the words she was speaking. "The plan to snare the dragon worked. The people dragged her out of the skies. Your mother's attack kept Beryl from breathing her foul gas. The dragon was down on the ground, and it seemed she was dead. She was only shamming. Beryl heaved herself off the ground and was about to attack when the ground gave way beneath her."

Gilthas stared, appalled, unable to speak.

"The tunnels," said the Lioness, tears trailing down her cheeks. "The tunnels collapsed beneath the dragon. She fell in and . . . the city fell in on top of her."

Planchet gave a low cry. The elven guards, who had edged close to hear, gasped and cried out.

Gilthas could say nothing, could make no sound.

"Tell him," the Lioness ordered the runner in a choked voice, averting her face. "I can't."

The runner bowed to the king. The man's face was white. His eyes were wide. He was only now starting to recover his breath.

"Your Majesty," he said, speaking the Qualinesti tongue, "I grieve to tell you that the city of Qualinost is no more. Nothing remains."

"Survivors?" Gilthas asked without a voice.

"There could be no survivors, Your Majesty," the elf said. "Qualinost is now a lake. *Nalis Aren*. A lake of death."

Gilthas took his wife in his arms. She held him fast, murmuring incoherent words of comfort that could bring no comfort. Planchet wept openly, as did the elven guards, who began to whisper prayers for the spirits of the dead. Bewildered, overwhelmed, unable to comprehend the enormity of the disaster, Gilthas held fast to his wife and stared out into the darkness that was a lake of death washing over him.

34 THE PRESENCE

T he blue dragon circled over the treetops, searching for a place to land. The cypress trees grew thick, so thick that Razor talked of flying back to the east, to where grassy fields and low rolling hills provided more suitable sites. Goldmoon would not permit the dragon to turn back, however. She was nearing the end of her journey. Her strength waned with the passing seconds. Each beat of her heart was a little slower, a little weaker. What time she had left to her was precious, she could not waste a moment. Looking down from the dragon's back, she watched the river of souls flowing beneath her, and it seemed to her that she was not borne forward by the dragon's strong wings but by that mournful tide.

"There!" she said, pointing.

An outcropping of rock, gleaming chalk-white in the moonlight, thrust up from amid the cypress trees. The shape of the outcropping was strange. Seen from above, it had the look of a hand outstretched, palm upward, as if to receive something.

Razor regarded it intently and, after some thought, opined that he could land safely, although it would be their task to climb down the steep sides of the outcropping.

Goldmoon was not concerned. She had only to wade into the river to be carried to her destination.

Razor landed in the palm of the chalk-white hand, settling down as easily as possible, so as not to jar his passengers. Goldmoon dismounted, her strong youthful body carrying within it the faltering spirit.

She assisted Conundrum to slide down off the dragon's back. Her assistance was needed, for Razor rolled an eye, glared at the gnome balefully. Conundrum had spent the entire journey discoursing on the inefficiency of dragons for flight, the unreliability of scales and skin, bones and tendon. Steel and steam, said the gnome. Machines. That was the future. Razor flicked a wing, came very near knocking Conundrum off the cliff. The gnome, lost in a happy dream of hydraulics, never noticed.

Goldmoon looked up at Tasslehoff, who remained comfortably seated on the dragon's back.

"Here you are, Goldmoon," said Tas, waving his hand. "I hope you find whatever it is you're looking for. Well, come along, dragon. Let's get going. Can't waste time. We have cities to burn, maidens to devour, treasure to carry off. Good-bye, Goldmoon! Good-bye, Conund—"

Snapping his teeth, Razor arched his back, shook his mane. Tasslehoff's farewells were cut off in midsentence as the kender went flying heels over topknot, to land with uncomfortable finality on the rock.

"Bad enough I had to carry the little beast *this* far," Razor snarled. He shifted his gaze to Goldmoon. The dragon's red eye flickered. "You are not what the Knight Gerard claimed you to be, are you? You are not a dark mystic."

"No, I am not. But I thank you for bringing me to Nightlund," said Goldmoon absently. She was not afraid of the dragon's wrath. She felt a protective hand over her, as strong as the hand of rock that now supported her. No mortal being could harm her.

"I do not want your thanks," Razor returned. "Your thanks are nothing. I did this for her." His eyes clouded, his gaze lifted to the bright moon, the starlit heavens. "I hear her voice." He shifted the red eyes back to fix intently on Goldmoon. "You hear the voice, too, don't you? It speaks your name. Goldmoon, princess of the Qué-shu. You know the voice."

"I hear the voice," said Goldmoon, troubled. "But I do not know it. I do not recognize it."

"I do," said Razor restlessly. "I am called, and I will heed the call. But not without my master. We stand together, he and I."

The dragon spread his wings and soared off the rock, leaping straight up in order to clear the towering trees. He flew south, toward Qualinesti.

Tasslehoff picked himself up and collected all his pouches.

"I hope you know where we are, Burrfoot," said Conundrum in grim and accusing tones.

"No, I don't," said Tasslehoff cheerfully. "I don't recognize any of this." He added, with a heartfelt sigh of relief, "We're lost, Goldmoon. Most definitely lost."

"They know the way," said Goldmoon, looking down on the upturned faces of the dead.

Palin and Dalamar stood on the lowest floor of the Tower, staring intently into the darkness that lay thick and heavy beneath the cypress trees. Thick and heavy and empty. The roving, restless dead had vanished.

"We could leave now," Palin suggested.

He stood by the window, hands folded in his robes, for the Tower was chill and dank in the early morning and he was cold. Dalamar had mentioned something about mulled wine and a fire in the library, but although warmth for body and belly sounded good, neither man left to go in search of it.

"We could leave now, while the dead are not here to harass us. We could both leave."

"Yes," said Dalamar, standing, his hands in the sleeves of his robes, staring out the window. "We could leave." He cast a sidelong glance at Palin. "Or rather, you could leave, if you want. Search for the kender."

"You could leave, too," Palin returned. "Nothing's holding you here anymore." A sudden thought came to him. "Or perhaps since the dead have departed, so has your magic."

Dalamar smiled a dark smile. "You sound almost hopeful, Majere."

"You know I didn't mean it like that," Palin returned, nettled, although something deep inside him muttered that perhaps he had very much meant it like that.

Here am I, a middle-aged man, a spellcaster of considerable power and renown. I have not lost my abilities, as I had once feared. The dead have been stealing my magic. Yet, in the presence of Dalamar, I feel young and inferior and inadequate, as when I first came to the Tower to take my Test. Worse, perhaps, for youth by its nature is filled with confidence. I am constantly striving to prove my worth to Dalamar and always falling short of the mark.

And why should I? Palin demanded of himself. What does it matter what this dark elf thinks of me? Dalamar will never trust me, never respect me. Not because of anything I am, but because of what I am not. I am not my uncle. I am not Raistlin.

"I could leave, but I will not," Dalamar stated, his delicate brows drawing together as he continued to stare into the empty darkness. He shivered and withdrew more snuggly into his robes. "My thumbs prick. My hackles rise. There is a Presence here, Palin. I have felt it all this past night. A breath on the back of my neck. A whisper in my ear. The sound of distant laughter. An Immortal Presence, Majere."

Palin was uncomfortable. "That girl and her talk of her One God has gotten to you, my friend. That and an overactive imagination and the fact that you don't eat enough to keep my wife's canary bird alive."

Palin wished immediately he had not mentioned his wife, wished he had not thought about Usha. I should leave the Tower now if for no other reason than to return home. Usha will be worried about me. If she had heard of the attack on the Citadel of Light, perhaps she thinks I am dead.

"Let her think me dead," he said softly. "She will find more peace in the thought that I am dead than she knew when I was alive. If she thinks me dead, she will forgive me for hurting her. Her memories of me will be fond ones. . . ."

"Quit mumbling to yourself, Majere, and look outside. The dead have returned!"

Where before there had been stillness and quiet, the darkness was once again alive—alive with the dead. The restless spirits were back, roaming among the trees, prowling about the Tower, staring at it with eyes that were hungry and burning with desire.

Palin gave a sudden, hoarse cry and sprang to the window. He hit it with his hands so hard that he very nearly broke the glass.

"What?" Dalamar was alarmed. "What is it?"

"Laurana!" Palin gasped. He stared searchingly out into the shifting river of souls. "Laurana! I saw her! I swear! Look! Out there! No . . . She's gone. . . ."

Pushing away from the window, he walked resolutely toward the spell-bound door.

Dalamar sprang after him, laid a wresting hand on his arm. "Majere, this is madness—"

Palin shook him off. "I'm going out there. I have to find her."

"No, Palin." Dalamar stood in front of him, grasped hold of him tightly, fingers digging into the flesh of Palin's arms. "You don't want to find her. Believe me, Majere. She won't be Laurana. She won't be the Laurana you knew. She'll be . . . like the others."

"My father wasn't!" Palin retorted angrily, struggling to free himself. Who would have thought the emaciated elf could be so strong? "He tried to warn me—"

"He wasn't, at first," Dalamar said. "But he is now. He can't help himself. I know. I've used them. They have served me for years."

He paused, still retaining his grip on Palin, watching him warily.

Palin shook off Dalamar's grip. "Let go of me. I'm not going anywhere." Rubbing his arms, he returned to stand staring out the window.

"Are you certain it was Laurana?" Dalamar asked after a moment's silence.

"I am not certain of anything anymore." Palin was chilled through, worried, frustrated. "So much for your blasted hackles—"

"—we've come to the wrong place," a high, shrill voice cried plaintively from out of the darkness. "You don't want to go there, Goldmoon. Trust me. I know my Towers of High Sorcery, and this is not the right one."

"I seek the wizard, Dalamar!" another voice called. "If he is within, let him please open the doors of the Tower to me."

"I don't know how or why," Palin exclaimed, peering in astonishment through the glass, "but there's Tasslehoff, and he has brought Goldmoon with him."

"The other way round, from the sounds of it," Dalamar remarked, as he removed the magical spell from the door.

Tasslehoff continued to argue, as they stood outside the door of the Tower, that this was the wrong Tower. Goldmoon wanted Dalamar's Tower, the Tower of High Sorcery in Palanthas, and she could see quite obviously that this was not Palanthas. Therefore, she had the wrong Tower.

"You're not going to find anyone inside there," Tasslehoff was beginning to sound desperate. "You won't find Dalamar or Palin either, for that matter. Not that there's any reason to think Palin would be here," he added hastily. "I haven't seen Palin in the longest time. Not since Beryl attacked the Citadel of

Light. He went one way, and I went another. He had the magical Device of Time Journeying with him, except that he lost it. He tossed bits of it at the draconians. The device is lost, destroyed. No sign of it anywhere. So don't go looking for it, because you won't find it—"

"Dalamar," came Goldmoon's voice. "Please let me in!"

"I keep telling you," Tasslehoff argued, "Dalamar's not— Oh, hullo, Dalamar." The kender tried very hard to sound astonished. "What are you doing here in this *strange* Tower?" Tasslehoff winked several times and motioned with his head at Goldmoon.

"Welcome, Goldmoon, Healer, Priestess of Mishakal," said Dalamar in gracious tones, using her old title. "I am honored by your visit."

Ushering her into his dwelling with elven courtesy, Dalamar whispered a soft aside, "Majere! Don't let the kender get away!"

Palin seized hold of Tasslehoff, who was hovering on the threshold. Palin was about to haul him bodily inside the Tower, when he was considerably disconcerted to find a gnome planted on the threshold, as well. The gnome had his hands shoved into his pockets and was looking about. Apparently, from his expression, he was not much liking what he saw.

"Eh?" said Palin, staring at the gnome. "Who are you?"

"Short version: Conundrum. I'm with her." The gnome pointed a grimy finger at Goldmoon. "She stole my submersible. Cost a lot of money, submersibles. And who's going to pay? That's what I want to know. Are you going to pay for it? Is that why we're here?"

Conundrum held up a small fist. "Cold, hard steel. That's what I want. No wizard stuff. Bat's eyes." The gnome sniffed disdainfully. "We've got a vault full of them. Once you've ruled out ball bearings, what good are they?"

Keeping a firm grip on Tasslehoff's collar, Palin dragged the kender, kicking and squirming, over the doorstoop. Conundrum followed on his own, his small, quick eyes taking in everything and dismissing it all out of hand.

Goldmoon said nothing in response to Dalamar's greeting. She barely looked at him or at Palin. Her gaze went around the Tower. She stared at the spiraling staircase that went up into darkness. She glanced around at the chamber in which they stood. She looked, and her eyes grew wide. Her face, already pale, went ashen.

"What is this I feel?" she asked, her voice low and filled with dread. "Who is here?"

Dalamar shot Palin a glance that said *I told you so*. Aloud, he replied, "Palin Majere and I are the only two here, Healer."

Goldmoon looked at Palin and seemed not to recognize him, for almost immediately her gaze went around him, past him, beyond him.

"No," she said softly. "There is someone else. I am meeting someone here."

Dalamar's dark eyes flashed. He silenced Palin's startled exclamation with a glance.

"The person you are expecting has not yet arrived. Will you wait in my library, Healer? The room is warm, and there is spiced wine and food."

"Food?" The gnome perked up, then was immediately cast back into gloom. "Not bat's brains, is it? Monkey toes? I won't eat wizard food. Ruins the digestion. Pork rinds and tarbean tea. That's more like it."

"It has been nice seeing you again, Palin, and you, too, Dalamar," Tasslehoff said, wriggling in Palin's grip, "and I wish I could stay for dinner, because the monkey toes sound delicious, but I have to be running along—"

"I will show you to the library in just a moment, Healer," Dalamar said, "but first I must settle our other guests. If you will excuse me—"

Goldmoon didn't appear to hear. She continued to stare around the Tower, searching for something or someone. The sight was unnerving.

Dalamar glided over to Palin, plucked at his sleeve. "Regarding Tas—"

"What regarding me?" Tas asked, eyeing Dalamar suspiciously.

"You recall what Mina said to you, Majere? About the device?"

"Who said?" Tas demanded. "Said what? What device?"

"Yes," said Palin. "I remember."

"Take him and the gnome to one of the student rooms in the north wing. The first one in the corridor will do. It is a room that has *no* fireplace," Dalamar added with grim emphasis. "Search the kender. When you find the device, for mercy's sake, keep it safe. Don't go tossing bits of it around. Oh, and you might want to remain hidden in that wing of the building. Our guest should not find you here."

"Why be so mysterious?" Palin asked, irritated by Dalamar's smug tone. "Why not just tell Goldmoon that the person coming to see her is her foster daughter, Mina?"

"You humans," Dalamar returned disparagingly. "So quick to blurt out everything you know. Elves have learned the power of secrets. We have learned the value of keeping secrets."

"But what can you hope to gain—"

Dalamar shrugged. "I don't know. Maybe something. Maybe nothing. You tell me that the two of them were once close. Much may come out of the shock of a sudden reunion, the shock of recognition. People say things they never intended in such circumstances, especially humans, who are so swayed by wayward emotions."

Palin's expression hardened. "I want to be there. Goldmoon may appear young, but that is only a façade. You speak glibly of the shock to her to see this child that she once dearly loved, but such a shock might be fatal."

Dalamar was shaking his head. "Too dangerous—"

"You can arrange it," Palin said firmly. "I know you have ways."

Dalamar hesitated, then said ungraciously, "Very well. If you insist. But the responsibility is entirely yours. Remember that this Mina saw you though you were hidden behind a wall. If you are discovered, I can do nothing to save you."

"I wouldn't expect you to," Palin returned crisply.

"Meet us in the library, then, once you have those two locked up tight." Dalamar jerked a thumb at the kender and the gnome.

The dark elf turned away, then, pausing, glanced back over his shoulder. "I suppose, by the way, Majere, that the significance of the gnome has occurred to you?"

"The gnome?" Palin was taken aback. "No. What—"

"Recall your uncle's history," Dalamar said and his voice was grim.

Returning to Goldmoon, he led her up the winding stairs. He was gracious and charming, as he could be when he wanted. Goldmoon followed where he led, moving as one who walks in sleep, with no conscious awareness of where she was or where she might be going. The youthful, beautiful body walked and took her with it.

"Significance of the gnome," Palin repeated in disgust. "Gnomes . . . my uncle's history . . . what does he mean? Always so damn mysterious . . ."

Muttering to himself, Palin hauled the reluctant Tasslehoff up the stairs. Palin paid no attention to the kender's pleadings and excuses and lies, some of them quite original. His attention was focused on the small and wizened gnome who was trudging up the stairs alongside, complaining the entire way about the pains in his legs and extolling the virtues of gnome-flingers over stairs.

Palin couldn't find any significance to the gnome whatsoever. Not unless Dalamar intended to install gnome-flingers.

He escorted the two to the room mentioned, pried Tas's fingers loose when the kender tried to cling to the doorjamb, and shoved him bodily inside. The gnome clumped in after, talking of building code violations and asking about yearly inspections. Casting a wizard-lock spell on the door to keep his reluctant guests inside, Palin turned to confront Tasslehoff.

"Now, about the Device of Time Journeying—"

"I haven't got it, Palin," Tas said quickly. "I swear by the beard of my Uncle Trapspringer. You threw all the pieces at the draconians. You know you did. They are scattered all over the Hedge Maze—"

"Hah!" the gnome shouted and went to stand in a corner with his head pressed against the wall.

Tas was going on at a desperate pace. "—the pieces of the device were scattered all over the Hedge Maze, along with pieces of the draconians."

"Tas," Palin interrupted sternly, mindful of the passing time and wanting to hasten this along. "You have the device. It came back to you. It must come back to you, even if it is in pieces. I thought I had destroyed it, but the device can't be destroyed, any more than it can be lost."

"Palin, I—" Tas began, his lip quivering.

Palin steeled himself, expecting more lies. "What is it, Tas?"

"Palin . . . I saw myself!" Tas blurted out.

"Tas, really—"

"I was dead, Palin!" Tas whispered. His normally ruddy face was pale. "I was dead and I . . . I didn't like it! It was horrid, Palin. I was cold, so very cold. And I was lost, and I was frightened. I've never been lost, and I've never been frightened. Not like that, anyway.

"Don't send me back to die, Palin," Tas begged. "Don't turn me into a . . . a dead thing! Please, Palin. Promise me you won't!" Tasslehoff clutched at him. "Promise me!"

Palin had never seen the kender so upset. The sight moved him almost to tears himself. He stood perplexed, wondering what to do, all the time absently smoothing Tasslehoff's hair in an effort to calm him.

What can I do? Palin asked himself helplessly. Tasslehoff *must* go back to die. I have no choice in the matter. The kender must return to his own time and die beneath the heel of Chaos. I cannot make the promise he asks of me. No matter how much I want to.

What Palin found perplexing was that Tasslehoff had seen his own ghost. Palin might have thought this a ruse, an attempt by the kender to distract Palin from finding the device. But while Palin knew that Tas would never hesitate to tell a lie—either out of self-interest or for its entertainment value—Palin was convinced that this was the truth. Palin had seen fear in the kender's eyes, an uncommon sight, and one that Palin found heart-wrenching.

At least this answered one nagging question: Had Tasslehoff truly died or had he just been roaming about the world for all those years? The fact that he had seen his own ghost proved the answer conclusively. Tasslehoff Burrfoot had died in the final battle against Chaos. He was dead. Or at least, he should be dead.

The gnome left his corner, walked up and poked Palin in the ribs. "Didn't somebody mention food?"

The significance of the gnome. What was the significance of this irritating gnome?

Disengaging Tas's clutching hands, Palin knelt down in front of Tas. "Look at me, Tas," he said. "Yes, that's it. Look at me and listen to what I am saying. I don't understand what is going on. I don't understand what is happening in the world and neither does Dalamar. But I know this. The only way we can find out what has gone wrong and maybe fix it is if you are honest with us."

"If I am honest," said Tas, wiping away his tears, "will you still send me back?"

"I am afraid I have to, Tas," Palin said reluctantly. "You must understand. I don't want to. I would do anything or give anything not to have to. You've seen the dead souls, Tas. You've seen for yourself that they are desperately unhappy. They aren't supposed to be here in the world. Something or someone is keeping them prisoner."

"You mean *I'm* not supposed to be here?" Tas asked. "Not the live me. The dead me?"

"I don't know for sure, Tas. No one does. But I don't think so. Don't you remember what Lady Crysania used to say—that death was not the end but the beginning of a whole new life? That we would join our loved ones who have passed beyond, and we would be together and make new friends—"

"I always thought I'd be with Flint," Tas said. "I know he misses me." He was quiet a moment, then said, "Well . . . if you think it will help . . ."

He unhooked the strap of his pouch and, before Palin could stop him, upended the bag, spilling its contents onto the floor.

Amid the birds' eggs and the chicken feathers and ink pots and jam jars and apple cores and what appeared to be a peg someone had been using for an artificial leg, the gears and jewels and wheels and chain of the Device of Time Journeying winked and sparkled in the candlelight.

"Why, what's this?" said the gnome, squatting down and sorting through the pile. "Cogs, a widget and a whatsit and a thingamajig. Technical terms, you know," he added, glancing at Tas and Palin to see if they were impressed. "Not understandable to the amateur. I'm not sure what it was." He gathered up the pieces one by one, eyeing each in turn. "But it doesn't appear to be in proper working order. That's not a guess, mind you. That's the opinion of a professional."

Making a tray of his robe, the gnome carried the pieces of the device to a table. Bringing out the remarkable knife that was also a screwdriver, he settled down to work.

"You, there, boy," he said, waving his hand at Palin. "Bring us some lunch. Sandwiches. And a pot of tarbean tea. Strong as you can make it. Going to be an all-nighter."

And, then, of course, Palin remembered the device's history. He understood the significance of the gnome.

Apparently, so did Tasslehoff, who was staring at Conundrum with a hopeless and woebegone expression.

"Where have you been, Majere?" Dalamar demanded, confronting Palin as he came through the library door. The dark elf was nervous, on edge. He'd obviously been pacing the floor. "You took long enough! Did you find the Device?"

"Yes, and so did the gnome." Palin looked intently at Dalamar. "His coming here—"

"—completes the circle," Dalamar finished.

Palin shook his head, unconvinced. He glanced around the room. "Where is Goldmoon?"

"She asked to be taken to the old laboratory. She said she was given to know that the meeting would be held there."

"The laboratory? Is that safe?"

Dalamar shrugged. "Unless she's afraid of dust bunnies. They're the only danger I can see."

"Once a chamber of mystery and power, the laboratory is now a repository of dust, the refuge of two impotent old men," Palin said bitterly.

"Speak for yourself." Dalamar laid a hand on Palin's arm. "And keep your voice down. Mina is here. We must go. Bring the light."

"Here? But how—"

"Apparently she has free run of my Tower."

"Aren't you going to be there with them?"

"No," said Dalamar shortly. "I was dismissed to go about my business. Are you coming or not?" he demanded impatiently. "There's nothing we can do, either of us. Goldmoon is on her own."

Still Palin hesitated, but then he decided that he might best serve Goldmoon by keeping an eye on Dalamar. "Where are we going?"

"Through here," Dalamar said, halting Palin as he was continuing on down the stairs.

Making a turning, Dalamar passed his hand over the wall and whispered a word of magic. A single rune began to glow faintly on the stone. Dalamar put his hand over the rune, and a section of the wall slid to one side, revealing a staircase. As they entered, they could hear heavy footfalls echoing through the Tower. The minotaur, or so they guessed. The door slid shut after them, and they could hear nothing more.

"Where does this lead?" Palin whispered, holding up the lamp to illuminate the stairs.

"The Chamber of the Live Ones," Dalamar replied. "Hand me the lamp. I'll go first. I know the way." He descended the stairs rapidly, his robes fluttering around his ankles.

"I trust none of the 'Live Ones' are left alive," said Palin with a grimace, remembering what he had heard of some of his uncle's more gruesome experiments.

"No, they died a long time ago, poor wretches." Dalamar paused and looked up at Palin. His dark eyes glittered in the lamplight. "But the Chamber of Seeing remains."

"Ah!" Palin breathed, understanding.

When Raistlin Majere became Master of the Tower of High Sorcery of Palanthas, he also became a recluse. Rarely leaving his Tower, he spent his time concentrating on increasing his powers: magical, temporal, and political. In order to keep current on what was happening in the world, especially those events that might affect him, Raistlin used his magic to create a window onto the world. In the lowest regions of the Tower, he carved out a pool and filled it with enchanted water. Whoever looked into the pool could call to mind a location, and he would both see and hear what was transpiring in the location.

"Did you question the kender?" Dalamar asked, as they wound round and round down the hidden staircase.

"Yes. He has the device. He said something else that I found interesting, Dalamar"—Palin reached out his hand, touched the elf on the shoulder—"Tasslehoff saw his own ghost."

Dalamar swung the lamp around. "He did?" The elf was skeptical. "This isn't another of his swimming bird stories, is it?"

"No," said Palin. He could see again the fear and terror in the kender's bright eyes. "No, he was telling the truth. He's afraid, Dalamar. I've never see Tasslehoff afraid before."

"At least this proves he died," Dalamar said, offhandedly, and resumed his descent.

Palin sighed. "The gnome is trying to fix the device. That's what you meant, wasn't it? The significance of the gnome. A gnome fixed the device the last time it was broken. Gnimsh. The gnome my uncle murdered."

Dalamar said nothing. He continued hurrying down the stairs.

"Listen to me, Dalamar!" Palin said, moving so close to the elf that he had to be careful not to trip on the skirts of his robes. "How did the gnome come to be here? This is . . . this is not some simple coincidence, is it?"

"No," Dalamar murmured. "Not coincidence."

"Then what?" Palin demanded, exasperated.

Dalamar halted again, held up the light to illuminate Palin's face. He drew back, half-blinded.

"You don't understand?" Dalamar asked. "Not even now?"

"No," Palin retorted angrily. "And I don't think you do, either."

"Not entirely," Dalamar admitted. "Not entirely. This meeting should explain much, however."

Lowering the lamp, he turned back to the descent. He said nothing more, and neither did Palin, who had no intention of demeaning himself further by continuing to ask questions that would be answered only in riddles.

"I no longer keep the wizard-lock functional," Dalamar remarked. He gave the rune-covered door an impatient shove. "A waste of time and effort."

"You've obviously used this chamber once or twice yourself," Palin observed.

"Oh, yes," said Dalamar with a smile. "I keep close watch on all my friends."

He blew out the lamplight.

They stood on the edge of a pool of water that was as quiet and dark as the chamber in which they were standing. A jet of blue flame burned in the center of the pool. The flame gave no light. It seemed to exist in another place, another time, and at first Palin saw nothing except the reflection of the blue flame in the water. Then the two merged in his vision. The flame flared, and he could see the interior of the laboratory as clearly as if he had been inside.

Goldmoon stood by the long stone table. . . .

35 THE ONE GOD

Goldmoon stood by the long stone table, staring down unseeing at several books that had been left lying about. She heard voices coming nearer. The voice of the person she was meeting, the person she had been summoned by the dead to meet.

Shivering, Goldmoon clasped her hands tightly around her arms. The Tower was cold with a chill that could never be warmed. A place of darkness, a place of sorrow, a place of overreaching ambition, a place of suffering and of death. Her destination. The culmination of her strange journey.

Dalamar had given her a lamp, but its feeble light could not banish the immense darkness. The glow of the lamplight did nothing more than keep her company. Yet, for that she was grateful, and she kept near the lamp. She did not regret sending Dalamar away. She had never liked, never trusted the dark elf. His sudden reappearance here in this forest of death only increased her suspicions of him. He used the dead. . . .

"But then," said Goldmoon softly, "so do I."

Amazing power . . . for a person. A mere mortal.

Goldmoon began to tremble. She had stood before in the presence of a god, and her soul remembered. But something about this was not right. . . .

The door opened, thrust aside by an impatient hand.

"I can see nothing in this wizard's murk," said a girl's voice, a child's voice whose melody sang through Goldmoon's dreams. "We need more light."

The light grew brighter gradually. Soft and warm, at first, the flames of a few dozen candles. The light grew brighter still, until it seemed that the limbs of the cypress trees had parted, the top of the Tower had been lifted, and sunlight poured down into the chamber.

A girl stood in the doorway. She was tall and well-muscled. She wore a chain-mail shirt, a black tunic and black hose and over that a black tabard decorated with a white death lily, the symbol of a Dark Knight. Her head was covered with a light down of red. Goldmoon would not have recognized her but for the amber eyes and the voice that sent a thrill through her body.

So terrible and wonderful was the shock that she caught hold of the table and leaned against it to support herself.

"Mina?" Goldmoon faltered, not daring to believe.

The girl's face was suddenly illuminated, as if she were the sun, and the sun shone from within.

"You . . . you are so beautiful, Mother," Mina said softly, awed. "You look just as I imagined."

Sinking to her knees, the girl extended her hands. "Come, kiss me, Mother," she cried, tears falling. "Kiss me as you used to. For I am Mina. Your Mina."

Bewildered, her heart made whole by joy and riven by a strange and terrible fear, Goldmoon could feel nothing except the wild and painful beating of her heart. Unable to take her eyes from Mina, she stumbled forward and fell to her knees before her. She clasped the sobbing girl in her arms.

"Mina," Goldmoon whispered, rocking her as she used to rock her when Mina woke crying in the night. "Mina. Child . . . why did you leave us, when we all loved you so much?"

Mina raised her tearstained face. The amber eyes gleamed. "I left for love of you, Mother. I left to seek what you wanted so desperately. And I found it, Mother! I found it for you.

"Dearest Mother." Mina took hold of Goldmoon's cold and trembling hands and pressed them to her lips. "All that I am and all that I have done, I have done for you."

"I . . . don't understand, child." Goldmoon kept hold of Mina's hands, but her eyes went to the dark armor. "You wear the symbol of evil, of darkness. . . . Where did you go? Where have you been? What has happened to you?"

Mina laughed. She glittered with happiness and excitement. "Where I went and where I have been is not important. What happened to me along the way—that is what you must hear.

"Do you remember, Mother, the stories you used to tell me? The story about how you traveled into darkness to search for the gods? How you found the gods and brought faith in the gods back to the people of the world?"

"Yes," said Goldmoon, but the word was a breath, not spoken. She had ceased trembling and begun to shiver.

"You told me the gods were gone, Mother," said Mina, her eyes shining like those of a child who has a delightful surprise. "You told me that because the gods were gone we had to rely on ourselves to find our way in the world. But I didn't believe that story, Mother.

"Oh"—Mina placed her hand over Goldmoon's mouth, silencing her—"I don't think you lied to me. You were mistaken, that was all. You see, I knew better. I knew there was a god, for I heard the voice of the god when I was little and our boat sank and I was cast alone into the sea. You found me on the shore, do you remember, Mother? But you never knew how I came to be there, because I promised I would never tell. The others drowned, but I was saved. The god held me and supported me and sang to me when I was afraid of the loneliness and dark.

"You said there were no gods, Mother, but I knew you were wrong. And so I did what you did. I went to find God and bring God back to you. And I've done that, Mother." Mina was flushed with joy and pride in her achievement. The amber eyes were radiant. "The miracle of the storm. That is the One God. The miracle of your youth and beauty. That is the One God, Mother."

"You asked for this," Goldmoon cried, lifting her hand to touch her face, the face that had always seemed strange to her. "This is not me. It is your vision of me. . . ."

"Of course, Mother." Mina laughed delightedly. "Aren't you pleased? I have so much to tell you that will please you. I've brought the miracle of healing back into the world with the power of the One God. With the blessing of the One, I felled the shield the elves had raised over Silvanesti, and I killed the treacherous dragon Cyan Bloodbane. Another truly monstrous green dragon, Beryl, is dead by the power of the One God. The elven nations, which were corrupt and faithless, have both been destroyed. In death, the elves will find redemption. Death will lead them to the One God."

"Ah, child!" Goldmoon gasped. Casting off Mina's hands, which had been wrapped tightly around her own, Goldmoon stared at her in horror. "I see blood on these hands. The blood of thousands! This god you have found is a terrible god. A god of darkness and evil!"

"The One God told me you would feel this way, Mother," Mina said patiently. "When the other gods departed and you thought you were left alone, you were angry and afraid. You felt betrayed, and that was only natural. For you *had* been betrayed." Mina's voice hardened. "The gods in which you had so misguidedly placed your faith fled in fear. . . ."

"No!" Goldmoon rose unsteadily to her feet. She fell back, away from Mina, held out her hand in warding. "No, child, I don't believe it. I won't listen you."

Mina followed after her, seized hold of Goldmoon's hand. "You will listen, Mother. You must so that you will understand. The gods fled in fear of Chaos. All except one. One god remained loyal to the people she had helped to create. One only had the courage to face the terror of the Father of All and of Nothing. The battle left her weak. Too weak for her to make manifest her presence in the world. Too weak to fight the strange dragons who came to take her place. But although she could not be with her people, she gave gifts to her people to help them. The magic that they call the wild magic. The power of healing that you know as the power of the heart. . . . Those were her gifts. Her gifts to you.

"There is her sign." Mina pointed to the heads of the five dragons that guarded the Portal.

Shuddering, Goldmoon turned. Dark and lifeless, the heads began to glow with an eerie radiance, one red, one blue, one green, one white, one black.

She moaned and averted her eyes.

"Mother," said Mina, gently rebuking, "the One God does not ask you for thanks for these past gifts. Rest assured, she has more gifts to bestow on her faithful in the future. But she does require service, Mother. She wants you to serve her and to love her, as she has served you and loved you. Do this, Mother. Kneel down and offer your prayers of faith and thanksgiving to the One True God. The One God who remained faithful to her creation."

"No! I don't believe what you are telling me!" Goldmoon said through lips so stiff she could barely cause them to form the words. "You have been deceived, child. I know this One God. I know her of old. I know her tricks and her lies and deceits."

Goldmoon looked back at the five-headed dragon, whose terrible radiance shone undimmed, for no other opposing force existed that could cloud it.

"I do not believe your lies, Takhisis!" Goldmoon cried defiantly. "I will never believe that the blessed Paladine and Mishakal left us to your mercy! You are what you have always been—a God of Evil who does not want worshipers but slaves. I will never bow down to you. I will never serve you."

Fire flared from the eyes of the five dragons. The fire was white hot, and Goldmoon withered in the terrible heat. Her body shrank and shriveled. Her strength ebbed, and she collapsed to the floor. Her hands shook with palsy. The skin stretched tight over tendon and bone. Her arms grew thin and splotched with age. Her face wrinkled. Her beautiful silver-gold hair was white and wispy. She was an old woman, her pulse feeble, her heartbeat slowing.

"See, Mother," Mina said and her voice was sorrowful and afraid, "see what will happen if you continue to deny the One God what is due her?"

Kneeling beside Goldmoon, Mina took hold of the old woman's palsied hands and pressed them again to her lips. "Please, Mother. I can restore your youth. I can bring back your beauty. You can begin life all over again. You will walk with me, and together we will rule the world in the name of the One God. All you have to do is to come to the One God in humility and ask this favor of her, and it will be done."

Goldmoon closed her eyes. Her lips did not move.

Mina bent close. "Mother," she begged, and she sounded fearful. "Mother, do this for me if not for yourself. Do this for love of me!"

"I pray," said Goldmoon. "I pray to Paladine and Mishakal that they forgive me for my lack of faith. I should have known the truth," she said softly, her voice weakening as she spoke the words with her dying breath, "I pray that Paladine will hear my words, and he will come . . . for love of Mina . . . For love of all. . . ."

Goldmoon sank, lifeless, to the floor.

"Mother," said Mina, as bewildered as a lost child, "I did this for you. . . ."

EPILOGUE

That night, in the small port city of Dolphin View, in northern Abanasinia, a ship set sail across the Straits of Schallsea. The ship carried a single passenger, whose identity was known only to the captain. Heavily cloaked and hooded, the passenger boarded during the night, bringing with him nothing except his horse, a wild-eyed, short-tempered beast, who was housed below deck in a specially built stall.

The mysterious passenger was obviously a man of means, for he had hired the *Gull Wing* specially, and he had paid extra for his horse. The sailors, intensely curious about the passenger's identity, were envious of the cabin boy, who was granted permission to take the passenger his supper. They waited eagerly for the boy to return to tell them what he had seen and heard.

The cabin boy knocked on the door. No one answered and after a few more knocks, he trepidatiously tried the lock. The door opened.

A tall, slender man, wrapped in his cloak, stood staring out the porthole at the vast and glittering sea. He did not turn around, even after the cabin boy mentioned dinner several times. Shrugging, the cabin boy was about to withdraw when the mysterious passenger spoke. He used Common, but with a heavy accent. His voice quivered with impatience.

"Tell the captain I want this ship to go faster. Do you hear? We must go faster."

In her mountain lair, surrounded by the skulls of the dragons she had slain, the great red dragon Malystryx dreamed of water, inky black water, rising up over her red legs, her belly, her massive red tail. Rising to cover her red wings, her back. Rising to her mane. Rising to cover her head, her mouth and nostrils. She could not breathe. She fought to lift herself above the water, but her legs were pinned. She could not free herself. Her lungs were bursting. Stars exploded before her eyes. She gasped, opened her mouth. The water poured in, and she was drowning. . . .

Malystryx woke, suddenly, glared around, angry and uneasy. She had been dreaming, and she never dreamed. Never before had any dream disturbed her rest. She had heard voices in her dream, mocking, goading, and she heard them still. The voices came from the skull totem, and they sang a song about sleep. Forever sleep.

Malystryx lifted her enormous head and stared hard at the skull totem, at the white skulls of blue dragons piled on top of the skulls of silver dragons; at the skulls of red dragons lying atop of the skulls of gold dragons.

From out the empty eye sockets of all the dead dragons, eyes, living eyes, stared back at Malystryx.

Sleep. Forever sleep.

In the Tower of High Sorcery, Galdar waited for Mina, but she didn't return. At last, worried about her, not trusting this place or the wizards who inhabited it, he went in search of her.

He found her in the old laboratory.

Mina sat huddled on the floor beside the body of an old, old woman. Galdar approached, spoke to her. Mina did not look up. Bending down, Galdar saw that the old woman was dead.

Galdar lifted Mina, put his good strong right arm around her, and led her from the chamber.

The light of the dragons faded.

The laboratory was once more shrouded in darkness.

VOLUME
III

DRAGONS OF A
VANISHED
MOON

BOOK
I

LOST SOULS

In the dungeon of the Tower of High Sorcery, that had once been in Palanthas but now resided in Nightlund, the great archmagus Raistlin Majere had conjured a magical Pool of Seeing. By gazing into this pool, he was able to follow and sometimes shape events transpiring in the world. Although Raistlin Majere had been dead many long years, his magical Pool of Seeing remained in use. The wizard Dalamar, who had inherited the Tower from his *Shalafi*, maintained the magic of the pool. A veritable prisoner in the Tower that was an island in the river of the dead, Dalamar had often made use of the pool to visit in his mind those places he could not travel in his body.

Palin Majere stood now at the pool's edge, staring into the unwavering blue flame that burned in the center of the still water and was the chamber's only light. Dalamar was close beside him, his gaze fixed on the same unwavering fire. Although the mages could have seen events transpiring anywhere in the world, they watched intently an event that was happening quite close to them, an event taking place at the top of the very Tower in which they stood.

Goldmoon of the Citadel of Light, and Mina, Lord of the Night, leader of the Dark Knights of Neraka, were to meet in the laboratory that had once belonged to Raistlin Majere. Goldmoon had already arrived at the strange meeting place. The laboratory was cold and dark and shadowed. Dalamar had left her a lantern, but its light was feeble and served only to emphasize the darkness that could never truly be illuminated, not if every lantern and every candle on Krynn should burst into flame. The darkness that was the soul of this dread Tower had its heart here in this chamber, which in the past had been a scene of death and pain and suffering.

In this chamber, Raistlin Majere had sought to emulate the gods and create life, only to fail utterly, bringing into the world misbegotten, shambling, pathetic beings known as the Live Ones, who had lived out their wretched existence in the room where the two wizards now stood. In the chamber, the Blue Dragonlady Kitiara had died, her death as brutal and bloody as her life. Here stood the Portal to the Abyss, a link between the realm of the mortal and realm of the dead, a link that had long ago been severed and was nothing now but a home to mice and spiders.

Goldmoon knew the dark history of this room. She must be considering that now, Palin thought, watching her image that shimmered on the surface of the pool. She stood in the laboratory, her arms clasped about her. She shivered not with the cold, but with fear. Palin was concerned. He could not remember—in all the years that he had known her—seeing Goldmoon afraid.

Perhaps it was the strange body that Goldmoon's spirit inhabited. She was over ninety. Her true body was that of an elderly woman—still vigorous, still strong for her years, but with skin marked and marred with time, a back that was starting to stoop, fingers that were gnarled, but whose touch was gentle. She had been comfortable with that body. She had never feared or regretted the passage of the years that had brought the joy of love and birth, the sorrow of love and death. That body had been taken from her the night of the great storm, and she had been given another body, a stranger's body, one that was young and beautiful, healthful and vibrant. Only the eyes were the eyes of the woman Palin had known throughout his life.

She is right, he thought, this body doesn't belong to her. It's borrowed finery. Clothing that doesn't fit.

"I should be with her," Palin muttered. He stirred, shifted, began to pace restlessly along the water's edge. The chamber was made of stone and was dark and chill, the only light the unwavering flame that burned in the heart of the dark pool, and it illuminated little and gave no warmth. "Goldmoon looks strong, but she's not. Her body may be that of someone in her twenties, but her heart is the heart of a woman whose life has spanned nine decades. The shock of seeing Mina again—especially as she is—may kill her."

"In that case, the shock of seeing you beheaded by the Dark Knights would probably do very little for her either," returned Dalamar caustically. "Which is what she would see if you were to march up there now. The Tower is surrounded by soldiers. There must be at least thirty of them out there."

"I don't think they'd kill me," said Palin.

"No? And what would they do? Tell you to go stand in a corner with your face to the wall and think what a bad boy you've been?" Dalamar scoffed.

"Speaking of corners," he added suddenly, his voice altering, "did you see that?"

"What?" Palin jerked his head, looked around in alarm.

"Not here! There!" Dalamar pointed into the pool. "A flash in the eyes of dragons that guard the Portal."

"All I see is dust," Palin said after a moment's intense gaze, "and cobwebs and mouse dung. You're imagining things."

"Am I?" Dalamar asked. His sardonic tone had softened, was unusually somber. "I wonder."

"You wonder what?"

"A great many things," said Dalamar.

Palin eyed the dark elf closely but could not read on that gaunt and drawn face a single thought stirring behind the dark eyes. In his black robes, Dalamar was indistinguishable from the darkness of the chamber. Only his hands with their delicate fingers could be seen, and they appeared to be hands that lacked a body. The long-lived elf was presumably in the prime of life, but his wasted form, consumed by the fever of frustrated ambition, might have belonged to an elder of his race.

I shouldn't be casting aspersions. What does he see when he looks at me? Palin asked himself. A shabby, middle-aged man. My face wan and wasted. My hair graying, thin. My eyes the embittered eyes of one who has not found what he was promised.

I stand on the edge of wondrous magic created by my uncle, and what have I done, except fail everyone who ever expected anything of me. Including myself. Goldmoon is just the most recent. I should be with her. A hero like my father would be with her, no matter that it meant sacrificing his freedom, perhaps his life. Yet here I am, skulking in the basement of this Tower.

"Stop fidgeting, will you?" Dalamar said irritably. "You'll slip and fall in the pool. Look there." He pointed excitedly to the water. "Mina has arrived." Dalamar rubbed his thin hands. "Now we will see and hear something to our advantage."

Palin halted on the edge of the pool, wavering in his decision. If he left immediately, walked the corridors of magic, he might yet reach Goldmoon in time to protect her. Yet, he could not pull himself away. He stared down at the pool in dread fascination.

"I can see nothing in this wizard's murk," Mina was saying loudly. "We need more light."

The light in the chamber grew brighter, so bright that it dazzled eyes accustomed to the darkness.

"I didn't know Mina was a mage," said Palin, shading his eyes with his hand.

"She's not," said Dalamar shortly. He cast Palin a strange glance. "Doesn't that tell you something?"

Palin ignored the question, concentrated on the conversation.

"You . . . you are so beautiful, Mother," Mina said softly, awed. "You look just as I imagined."

Sinking to her knees, the girl extended her hands. "Come, kiss me, Mother," she cried, tears falling. "Kiss me as you used to. I am Mina. Your Mina."

"And so she was, for many years," murmured Palin, watching in sorrowful concern as Goldmoon advanced unsteadily to clasp her adopted child in her arms. "Goldmoon found Mina washed up on the shore, presumably the survivor of some terrible ship wreck, though no wreckage or bodies or any other survivors were ever discovered. They brought her to the Citadel's orphanage. Intelligent, bold, fearless, Mina charmed all, including Goldmoon, who took the child to her heart. And then, one day, at the age of fourteen, Mina ran away. We searched, but we could find no trace of her, nor could anyone say why she had gone, for she had seemed so happy. Goldmoon's heart broke, then."

"Of course, Goldmoon found her," Dalamar said. "She was meant to find her."

"What do you mean?" Palin glanced at Dalamar, but the elf's expression was enigmatic.

Dalamar shrugged, said nothing, gestured back to the dark pool.

"Mina!" Goldmoon whispered, rocking her adopted daughter. "Mina! Child . . . why did you leave us when we all loved you so much?"

"I left for love of you, Mother. I left to seek what you wanted so desperately. And I found it, Mother! I found it for you.

"Dearest Mother." Mina took hold of Goldmoon's hands and pressed them to her lips. "All that I am and all that I have done, I have done for you."

"I . . . don't understand, child," Goldmoon faltered. "You wear the symbol of evil, of darkness. . . . Where did you go? Where have you been? What has happened to you?"

Mina laughed. "Where I went and where I have been is not important. What happened to me along the way—that is what you must hear.

"Do you remember, Mother, the stories you used to tell me? The story about how you traveled into darkness to search for the gods? And how you found the gods and brought faith in the gods back to the people of the world?"

"Yes," said Goldmoon. She had gone so very pale that Palin determined to be with her, cost him what it might.

He began to chant the words of magic. The words that came out of his mouth, however, were not the words that had formed in his brain. Those words were rounded, smooth, flowed easily. The words he spoke were thick and square-sided, tumbled out like blocks dropped on the floor.

He halted, angry at himself, forced himself to calm down and try again. He knew the spell, could have said it backward. He might well have said it backward, for all the sense it made.

"You're doing this to me!" Palin said accusingly.

Dalamar was amused. "Me?" He waved his hand. "Go to Goldmoon, if you want. Die with her, if you want. I'm not stopping you."

"Then who is? This One God?"

Dalamar regarded him in silence a moment, then turned back to gaze down into the pool. He folded his hands in the sleeves of his robes. "There was no past, Majere. You went back in time. There was no past."

"You told me the gods were gone, Mother," Mina said. "You told me that because the gods were gone we had to rely on ourselves to find our way in the world. But I didn't believe that story, Mother.

"Oh"—Mina placed her hand over Goldmoon's mouth, silencing her—"I don't think you lied to me. You were mistaken, that was all. You see, I knew better. I knew there was a god for I heard the voice of the god when I was little and our boat sank and I was cast alone into the sea. You found me on the shore, do you remember, Mother? But you never knew how I came to be there, because I promised I would never tell. The others drowned, but I was saved. The god held me and supported me and sang to me when I was afraid of the loneliness and dark.

"You said there were no gods, Mother, but I knew you were wrong. So I did what you did. I went to find god and bring god back to you. And I've done that, Mother. The miracle of the storm. That is the One God. The miracle of your youth and beauty. That is the One God, Mother."

"Now do you understand, Majere?" Dalamar said softly.

"I think I am beginning to," said Palin. His broken hands clasped tightly together. The room was cold, his fingers ached with the chill. "I would add, 'the gods help us,' but that might be out of place."

"Hush!" Dalamar snapped. "I can't hear. What did she say?"

"You asked for this," Goldmoon demanded, indicating her altered body with a gesture. "This is not me. It is your vision of me. . . ."

"Aren't you pleased?" Mina continued, not hearing her or not wanting to hear. "I have so much to tell you that will please you. I've brought the miracle of healing back into the world with the power of the One God. With the blessing of the One, I felled the shield the elves had raised over Silvanesti and I killed the treacherous dragon Cyan Bloodbane. A truly monstrous green dragon, Beryl, is dead by the power of the One God. The elven nations that were corrupt and faithless have both been destroyed, their people dead."

"The elven nations destroyed!" Dalamar gasped, his eyes burning. "She lies! She cannot mean that!"

"Strange to say this, but I do not think Mina knows how to lie," Palin said.

"But in death, they will find redemption," Mina preached. "Death will lead them to the One God."

"I see blood on these hands," Goldmoon said, her voice tremulous. "The blood of thousands! This god you have found is terrible god. A god of darkness and evil!"

"The One God told me you would feel this way, Mother," Mina responded. "When the other gods departed and you thought you were left alone, you were angry and afraid. You felt betrayed, and that was only natural. For you *had* been betrayed. The gods in which you had so misguidedly placed your faith fled in fear. . . ."

"No!" Goldmoon cried out. She rose unsteadily to her feet and fell away from Mina, holding out her hand in warding. "No, Child, I don't believe it. I won't listen to you."

Mina seized Goldmoon's hand.

"You *will* listen, Mother. You must, so that you will understand. The gods fled in fear of Chaos, Mother. All except one. One god remained loyal to the people she had helped to create. One only had the courage to face the terror of the Father of All and of Nothing. The battle left her weak. Too weak to make manifest her presence in the world. Too weak to fight the strange dragons that came to take her place. But although she could not be with her people, she gave gifts to her people to help them fight the dragons. The magic that they called the wild magic, the power of healing that you know as the power of the heart . . . those were her gifts. Her gifts to you."

"If those were her gifts, then why did the dead need to steal them for her . . ." said Dalamar softly. "Look! Look there!" He pointed to the still water.

"I see." Palin breathed.

The heads of the five dragons that guarded what had once been the Portal to the Abyss began to glow with an eerie radiance, one red, one blue, one green, one white, one black.

"What fools we have been," Palin murmured.

"Kneel down," Mina commanded Goldmoon, "and offer your prayers of faith and thanksgiving to the One True God. The One God who remained faithful to her creation—"

"No, I don't believe what you are telling me!" Goldmoon said, standing fast. "You have been deceived, Child. I know this One God. I know her of old. I know her tricks and her lies and deceits."

Goldmoon looked at the five-headed dragon.

"I do not believe your lies, Takhisis!" Goldmoon said defiantly. "I will never believe that the blessed Paladine and Mishakal left us to your mercy!"

"They didn't leave, did they?" Palin said.

"No," Dalamar said. "They did not."

"You are what you have always been," Goldmoon cried. "A god of Evil who does not want worshipers, you want slaves! I will never bow down to you! I will never serve you!"

White fire flared from the eyes of the five dragons. Palin watched in horror to see Goldmoon begin to wither in the terrible heat.

"Too late," said Dalamar with terrible calm. "Too late. For her. And for us. They'll be coming for us soon. You know that."

"This chamber is hidden—" Palin began.

"From Takhisis?" Dalamar gave a mirthless laugh. "She knew of this chamber's existence long before your uncle showed it to me. How could anything be hidden from the 'One God'? The One God who stole away Krynn!"

"As I said, what fools we have been," said Palin.

"You yourself discovered the truth, Majere. You used the device to journey back to Krynn's past, yet you could go back only to the moment Chaos was defeated. Prior to that, there was no past. Why? Because in that moment, Takhisis stole the past, the present, and the future. She stole the world. The clues were there, if we'd had sense enough to read them."

"So the future Tasslehoff saw—"

"—will never come to pass. He leaped forward to the future that was supposed to have happened. He landed in the future that is now happening. Consider the facts: a strange-looking sun in the sky; one moon where there were once three; the patterns of the stars are vastly different; a red star burns in the heavens where one had never before been seen; strange dragons appear from out of nowhere. Takhisis brought the world here, to this part of the universe, wherever that may be. Thus the strange sun, the single moon, the alien dragons, and the One God, all-powerful, with no one to stop her."

"Except Tasslehoff," said Palin, thinking of the kender secreted in an upstairs chamber.

"Bah!" Dalamar snorted. "They've probably found him by now. Him and the gnome. When they do, Takhisis will do with him what we planned to do—she will send him back to die."

Palin glanced toward the door. From somewhere above came shouted orders and the sound of feet running to obey. "The fact Tasslehoff is here at all proves to me that the Dark Queen is not infallible. She could not have foreseen his coming."

"Cling to that if it makes you happy," said Dalamar. "I see no hope in any of this. Witness the evidence of the Dark Queen's power."

They continued to watch the reflections of time shimmering in the dark pool. In the laboratory, an elderly woman lay on the floor, her white hair loose and unbound around her shoulders. Youth, beauty, strength, life had all been snatched away by the vengeful goddess, angry that her generous gifts had been spurned.

Mina knelt beside the dying woman. Taking hold of Goldmoon's hands, Mina pressed them again to her lips. "Please, Mother. I can restore your youth. I can bring back your beauty. You can begin life all over again. You will walk with me, and together we will rule the world in the name of the One God. All you have to do is to come to the One God in humility and ask this favor of her, and it will be done."

Goldmoon closed her eyes. Her lips did not move.

Mina bent close. "Mother," she begged. "Mother, do this for me if not for yourself. Do this for love of me!"

"I pray," said Goldmoon in a voice so soft that Palin held his breath to hear, "I pray to Paladine and Mishakal that they forgive me for my lack of faith. I should have known the truth," she said softly, her voice weakening as she spoke the words with her dying breath. "I pray that Paladine will hear my prayer and he will come . . . for love of Mina . . . For love of all . . ."

Goldmoon sank, lifeless, to the floor.

"Mother," said Mina, bewildered as a lost child, "I did this for you. . . ."

Palin's eyes burned with tears, but he was not sure for whom it was he wept—for Goldmoon, who had brought light into the world, or for the orphan girl, whose loving heart had been snared, tricked, deceived by the darkness.

"May Paladine hear her dying prayer," Palin said quietly.

"May I be given bat wings to flap around this chamber," Dalamar retorted. "Her soul has gone to join the river of the dead, and I fancy that our souls will not be far behind."

Footsteps clattered down the stairs, steel swords banged against the sides of the stone walls. The footsteps halted outside their door.

"I don't suppose anyone found a key?" asked a deep, rumbling voice.

"I don't like this, Galdar," said another. "This place stinks of death and magic. Let's get out of here."

"We can't get in if there's no key, sir," said a third. "We tried. It wasn't our fault we failed."

A moment's pause, then the first voice spoke, his voice firm. "Mina gave us our orders. We will break down the door."

Blows began to rain on the wooden door. The Knights started to beat on it with their fists and the hilts of their swords, but none sounded very enthusiastic.

"How long will the spell of warding hold?" Palin asked.

"Indefinitely, against this lot," said Dalamar disparagingly. "Not long at all against Her Dark Majesty."

"You are very cool about this," said Palin. "Perhaps you are not overly sorry to hear that Takhisis has returned."

"Say, rather, that she never left," Dalamar corrected with fine irony.

Palin made an impatient gesture. "You wore the black robes. You worshiped her—"

"No, I did not," said Dalamar so quietly that Palin could barely hear him over the banging and the shouting and the thundering on the door. "I worshiped Nuitari, the son, not the mother. She could never forgive me for that."

"Yet, if we believe what Mina said, Takhisis gave us both the magic—me the wild magic and you the magic of the dead. Why would she do that?"

"To make fools of us," said Dalamar. "To laugh at us, as she is undoubtedly laughing now."

The sounds of fists beating at the door suddenly ceased. Quiet descended on those outside. For a hope-filled moment, Palin thought that perhaps they had given up and departed. Then came a shuffling sound, as of feet moving hastily to clear a path. More footsteps could be heard—lighter than those before.

A single voice called out. The voice was ragged, as if it were choked by tears.

"I speak to the wizard Dalamar," called Mina. "I know you are within. Remove the magical spell you have cast on the door that we may meet together and talk of matters of mutual interest."

Dalamar's lip curled slightly. He made no response, but stood silent, impassive.

"The One God has given you many gifts, Dalamar, made you powerful, more powerful than ever," Mina resumed, after a pause to hear an answer that did not come. "The One God does not ask for thanks, only that you serve her with all your heart and all your soul. The magic of the dead will be yours. A million million souls will come to you each day to do your bidding. You will be free of this Tower, free to roam the world. You may return to your homeland, to the forests that you love and for which you long. The elven people are lost, seeking. They will embrace you as their leader, bow down before you, and worship you in my name."

Dalamar's eyes closed, as if in pain.

He has been offered the dearest wish of his heart, Palin realized. Who could turn that down?

Still, Dalamar said nothing.

"I speak now to you, Palin Majere," Mina said, and it seemed to Palin that he could see her amber eyes shining through the closed and spell-bound door.

"Your uncle Raistlin Majere had the power and the courage to challenge the One God to battle. Look at you, his nephew. Hiding from the One God like a child who fears punishment. What a disappointment you have been. To your uncle, to your family, to yourself. The One God sees into your heart. The One God sees the hunger there. Serve the One God, Majere, and you will be greater than your uncle, more honored, more revered. Do you accept, Majere?"

"Had you come to me earlier, I might have believed you, Mina," Palin answered. "You have a way of speaking to the dark part of the soul. But the moment is passed. My uncle, wherever his spirit roams, is not ashamed of me. My family loves me, though I have done little to deserve it. I do thank this One God of yours for opening my eyes, for making me see that if I have done nothing else of value in this life, I have loved and been loved. And that is all that truly matters."

"A very pretty sentiment, Majere," Mina responded. "I will write that on your tomb. What of you, Dark Elf? Have you made your decision? I trust you will not be as foolish as your friend."

Dalamar spoke finally, but not to Mina. He spoke to the blue flame, burning in the center of the still pool of dark water.

"I have looked into the night sky and seen the dark moon, and I have thrilled to know that my eyes were among the few eyes that could see it. I have heard the voice of the god Nuitari and reveled in his blessed touch as I cast my spells. Long ago, the magic breathed and danced and sparkled in my blood. Now it crawls out of my fingers like maggots swarming from a carrion carcass. I would rather be that corpse than be a slave to one who so fears the living that she can trust only servants who are dead."

A single hand smote the door. The door and the spell that guarded it shattered.

Mina entered the chamber. She entered alone. The jet of flame that burned in the pool shone in her black armor, burned in her heart and in her amber eyes. Her shorn red hair glistened. She was might and power and majesty, but Palin saw that the amber eyes were red and swollen, tears stained her cheeks, grief for Goldmoon. Palin understood then the depth of the Dark Queen's perfidy, and he had never hated Takhisis so much as he hated her now. Not for what she had done or was about to do to him, but for what she had done to Mina and all the innocents like her.

Mina's Knights, fearful of the powerful wizards, hung back upon the shadowy stairs. Dalamar's voice raised in a chant, but the words were mumbled and inarticulate, and his voice faded slowly away. Palin tried desperately to summon the magic to him. The spell dissolved in his hands, ran through his fingers like grains of sand from a broken hourglass.

Mina regarded them both with a disdainful smile. "You are nothing without the magic. Look at you—two broken-down, impotent old men. Fall on your knees before the One God. Beg her to give you back the magic! She will grant your pleas."

Neither Palin nor Dalamar moved. Neither spoke.

"So be it," said Mina.

She raised her hand. Flames burned from the tips of her five fingers. Green fire, blue and red, white, and the red-black of embers lit the Chamber of Seeing. The flames merged together to form two spears forged of magic. The first spear she hurled at Dalamar.

The spear struck the elf in the breast, pinned him against the wall of the Chamber of Seeing. For a moment, he hung impaled upon the burning spear, his body writhing. Then his head sagged, his body went limp.

Mina paused. Holding the spear, she gazed at Palin.

"Beg," she said to him. "Beg the One God for your life."

Palin's lips tightened. He knew a moment's panicked fear, then pain sheared through his body. The pain was so horrific, so agonizing that it brought its own blessing. The pain made his last living thought a longing for death.

2 THE SIGNIFICANCE OF THE GNOME

Dalamar had said to Palin, "You do understand the significance of the gnome?"

Palin had not understood the significance at that moment, nor had Tasslehoff. The kender understood now. He sat in the small and boring room in the Tower of High Sorcery, a room that was pretty much devoid of anything interesting: sad-looking tables and some stern-backed chairs and a few knick-nacks that were too big to fit in a pouch. He had nothing to do except look out a window to see nothing more interesting than an immense number of cypress trees—more trees than were absolutely necessary, or so Tas thought—and the souls of the dead wandering around among them. It was either that or watch Conundrum sort through the various pieces of the shattered Device of Time Journeying. For now Tas understood all too well the significance of the gnome.

Long ago—just how long ago Tasslehoff couldn't remember, since time had become extremely muddled for him, what with leaping forward to one future that turned out wasn't the proper future and ending up in this future, where all anyone wanted to do was send him back to the past to die—anyhow, long ago, Tasslehoff Burrfoot had, through no fault of his own (well, maybe a little) ended up quite by accident in the Abyss.

Having assumed that the Abyss would be a hideous place where all manner of perfectly horrible things went on—demons eternally torturing people, for example—Tas had been most frightfully disappointed to discover that the Abyss was, in fact, boring. Boring in the extreme. Nothing of interest happened. Nothing of disinterest happened. Nothing at all happened to anyone, ever.

There was nothing to see, nothing to handle, nothing to do, nowhere to go. For a kender, it was pure hell.

Tas's one thought had been to get out. He had with him the Device of Time Journeying—this same Device of Time Journeying that he had with him now. The device had been broken—just as it was broken now. He had met a gnome—similar to the gnome now seated at the table across from him. The gnome had fixed the device—just as the gnome was busy fixing it now. The one big difference was that then Tasslehoff had *wanted* the gnome to fix the device, and now he didn't.

Because when the Device of Time Journeying was fixed, Palin and Dalamar would use it to send him—Tasslehoff Burrfoot—back in time to the point where the Father of All and of Nothing would squash him flat and turn him into the sad ghost of himself he'd seen wandering about Nightlund.

"What did you do with this device?" Conundrum muttered irritably. "Run it through a meat grinder?"

Tasslehoff closed his eyes so he wouldn't have to see the gnome, but he saw him anyway—his nut-brown face and his wispy hair that floated about his head as though he were perpetually poking his finger into one of his own inventions, perhaps the steam-powered preambulating hubble-bubble or the locomotive, self-winding rutabaga slicer. Worse, Tas could see the light of cleverness shining in the gnome's beady eyes. He'd seen that light before, and he was starting to feel dizzy. *What did you do with this device? Run it through a meat grinder?* were exactly the same words—or very close to them—that the previous gnome had said in the previous time.

To alleviate the dizzy feeling, Tasslehoff rested his head with its topknot of hair (going only a little gray here and there) on his hands on the table. Instead of going away, the uncomfortable dizzy feeling spiraled down from his head into his stomach, and spread from his stomach to the rest of his body.

A voice spoke. The same voice that he'd heard in a previous time, in a previous place, long ago. The voice was painful. The voice shriveled his insides and caused his brain to swell, so that it pressed on his skull, and made his head hurt horribly. He had heard the voice only once before, but he had never, ever wanted to hear it again. He tried to stop his ears with his hands, but the voice was inside him, so that didn't help.

You are not dead, said the voice, and the words were exactly the same words the voice had spoken so long ago, *nor were you sent here. You are not supposed to be here at all.*

"I know," said Tasslehoff, launching into his explanation. "I came from the past, and I'm supposed to be in a different future—"

A past that never was. A future that will never be.

"Is that . . . is that my fault?" Tas asked, faltering.

The voice laughed, and the laughter was horrible, for the sound was like a steel blade breaking, and the feel was of the slivers of the broken blade piercing his flesh.

Don't be a fool, kender. You are an insect. Less than an insect. A mote of dust, a speck of dirt to be flicked away with a brush of my hand. The future you are in is the future of Krynn as it was meant to be but for the meddlings of those who had neither the wit nor the vision to see how the world might be theirs. All that happened once will happen again, but this time to suit my purposes. Long ago, one died on a Tower, and his death rallied a Knighthood. Now, another dies on a Tower and her death plunges a nation into despair. Long ago, one was raised up by the miracle of the blue crystal staff. Now the one who wielded that staff will be raised up—to receive me.

"You mean Goldmoon!" Tasslehoff cried bleakly. "She used the blue crystal staff. Is Goldmoon dead?"

Laughter sliced through his flesh.

"Am I dead?" he cried. "I know you said I wasn't, but I saw my own spirit."

You are dead and you are not dead, replied the voice, *but that will soon be remedied.*

"Stop jabbering!" Conundrum demanded. "You're annoying me, and I can't work when I'm annoyed."

Tasslehoff's head came up from the table with a jerk. He stared at the gnome, who had turned from his work to glare at the kender.

"Can't you see I'm busy here? First you moan, then you groan, then you start to mumble to yourself. I find it most distracting."

"I'm sorry," said Tasslehoff.

Conundrum rolled his eyes, shook his head in disgust, and went back to his perusal of the Device of Time Journeying. "I think that goes here, not there," the gnome muttered. "Yes. See? And then the chain hooks on here and wraps around like so. No, that's not quite the way. It must go . . . Wait, I see. This has to fit in there first."

Conundrum picked up one of the jewels from the Device of Time Journeying and fixed it in place. "Now I need another of these red gizmos." He began sorting through the jewels. Sorting through them now, as the other gnome, Gnimsh, had sorted through them in the past, Tasslehoff noted sadly.

The past that never was. The future that was hers.

"Maybe it was all a dream," Tas said to himself. "That stuff about Goldmoon. I think I'd know if she was dead. I think I'd feel sort of smothery around the heart if she was dead, and I don't feel that. Although it is sort of hard to breathe in here."

Tasslehoff stood up. "Don't you think it's stuffy, Conundrum? I think it's stuffy," he answered, since Conundrum wasn't paying any attention to him.

"These Towers of High Sorcery are always stuffy," Tas added, continuing to talk. Even if he was only talking to himself, hearing his own voice was far, far better than hearing that other, terrible voice. "It's all those bat wings and rat's eyeballs and moldy, old books. You'd think that with the cracks in these walls, you'd get a nice breeze, but that doesn't seem to be the case. I wonder if Dalamar would mind very much if I broke one of his windows?"

Tasslehoff glanced about for something to chuck through the windowpane. A small bronze statue of an elf maiden, who didn't seem to be doing much with her time except holding a wreath of flowers in her hands, stood on a small table. Judging by the dust, she hadn't moved from the spot for half a century or so and therefore, Tas thought, she might like a change of scenery. He picked up the statue and was just about to send the elf maiden on her journey out the window, when he heard voices outside the Tower.

Feeling thankful that the voices were coming from outside the Tower and not inside him, Tas lowered the elf maiden and peered curiously out the window.

A troop of Dark Knights had arrived on horseback, bringing with them a horse-drawn wagon with an open bed filled with straw. The Knights did not dismount but remained on their horses, glancing uneasily at the circle of dark trees that surrounded them. The horses shifted restlessly. The souls of the dead crept around the boles of the trees like a pitiful fog. Tas wondered if the riders could see the souls. He was sorry he could, and he did not look at the souls too closely, afraid he'd see himself again.

Dead but not dead.

He looked over his shoulder at Conundrum, bent almost double over his work and still mumbling to himself.

"Whoo-boy, there are a lot of Dark Knights about," Tas said loudly. "I wonder what these Dark Knights are doing here? Don't you wonder about that, Conundrum?"

The gnome muttered, but did not look up from his work. The device was certainly going back together in a hurry.

"I'm sure your work could wait. Wouldn't you like to rest a bit and come see all these Dark Knights?" Tas asked.

"No," said Conundrum, establishing the record for the shortest gnome response in history.

Tas sighed. The kender and the gnome had arrived at the Tower of High Sorcery in company with Tas's former companion and longtime friend Goldmoon—a Goldmoon who was ninety years old if she was a day but had the body and face of a woman of twenty. Goldmoon told Dalamar that she was meeting someone at the Tower. Dalamar took Goldmoon away and told Palin to take Tasslehoff and the gnome away and put them in a room to wait—making this a waiting room. It was then Dalamar had said, *You do understand the significance of the gnome?*

Palin had left them here, after wizard-locking the door. Tas knew the door was wizard-locked, because he'd already used up his very best lockpicks without success in an effort to open it. The day lockpicks fail is a day wizards are involved, as his father had been wont to say.

Standing at the window, staring down at the Knights, who appeared to be waiting for something and not much enjoying the wait, Tasslehoff was struck by an idea. The idea struck so hard that he reached up with the hand that wasn't holding onto the bronze statue of the elf maiden to feel if he had a lump on his head. Not finding one, he glanced surreptitiously (he thought that was the word) back at the gnome. The device was almost back together. Only a few pieces remained, and those were fairly small and probably not terribly important.

Feeling much better now that he had a Plan, Tas went back to observing what was happening out the window, thinking that now he could properly enjoy it. He was rewarded by the sight of an immense minotaur emerging from the Tower of High Sorcery. Tas was about four stories up in the Tower, and he could look right down on the top of the minotaur's head. If he chucked the statue out the window now, he could bean the minotaur.

Clunking a minotaur over the head was a delightful thought, and Tas was tempted. At that moment, however, several Dark Knights trooped out of the Tower. They bore something between them—a body covered with a black cloth.

Tas stared down, pressing his nose so hard against the glass pane that he heard cartilage crunch. As the troop carrying the body moved out of the Tower, the wind sighed among the cypress trees, lifted the black cloth to reveal the face of the corpse.

Tasslehoff recognized Dalamar.

Tas's hands went numb. The statue fell to the floor with a crash.

Conundrum's head shot up. "What in the name of dual carburetors did you do that for?" he demanded. "You made me drop a screw!"

More Dark Knights appeared, carrying another body. The wind blew harder, and the black cloth that had been thrown carelessly over the corpse slid to the ground. Palin's dead face looked up at the kender. His eyes were wide open, fixed and staring. His robes were soaked in blood.

"This is my fault!" Tas cried, riven by guilt. "If I had gone back to die, like I was supposed to, Palin and Dalamar wouldn't be dead now."

"I smell smoke," said Conundrum suddenly. He sniffed the air. "Reminds me of home," he stated and went back to his work.

Tas stared bleakly out the window. The Dark Knights had started a bonfire at the base of the Tower, stoking it with dry branches and logs from the cypress forest. The wood crackled. The smoke curled up the stone side of the Tower like some noxious vine. The Knights were building a funeral pyre.

"Conundrum," said Tasslehoff in a quiet voice, "how are you coming with the Device of Time Journeying? Have you fixed it yet?"

"Devices? No time for devices now," Conundrum said importantly. "I have this contraption about fixed."

"Good," said Tasslehoff.

Another Dark Knight came out of the Tower. She had red hair, cropped close to her head, and Tasslehoff recognized her. He'd seen her before, although he couldn't recall where.

The woman carried a body in her arms, and she moved very slowly and solemnly. At a shouted command from the minotaur, the other Knights halted their work and stood with their heads bowed.

The woman walked slowly to the wagon. Tas tried to see who it was the woman carried, but his view was blocked by the minotaur. The woman lowered the person gently into the wagon. She backed away and Tasslehoff had a clear view.

He'd assumed that the person was another Dark Knight, maybe one who'd been wounded. He was astonished to see that the person in the wagon was an old, old woman, and Tas knew immediately that the old woman was dead. He felt very sorry and wondered who she was. Some relation of the Dark Knight with the red hair, for she arranged the folds of the woman's white gown around her and then brushed out with her fingers the woman's long, flowing, silver-white hair.

"So Goldmoon used to brush out my hair, Galdar," said the woman.

Her words carried clearly in the still air. Much too clearly, as far as Tas concerned.

"Goldmoon." Tas felt a lump of sadness rise up in his throat. "She *is* dead. Caramon, Palin . . . Everyone I love is dead. And it's my fault. I'm the one who *should* be dead."

The horses drawing the wagon shifted restlessly, as if anxious to leave. Tas glanced back at Conundrum. Only two tiny jewels remained to be stuck on somewhere.

"Why did we come here, Mina?" The minotaur's booming voice could be heard clearly. "You have captured Solanthus, given the Solamnics a sound spanking and sent them running home to mama. The entire Solamnic nation is yours now. You have done what no one else has been able to do in the entire history of the world—"

"Not quite, Galdar," Mina corrected him. "We must still take Sanction, and we must take it by the time of the Festival of the Eye."

"The . . . festival?" The minotaur's forehead wrinkled. "The Festival of the Eye. By my horns, I had almost forgotten that old celebration." He grinned. "You are such a youngling, Mina, I'm surprised you know of it at all. It hasn't been celebrated since the three moons vanished."

"Goldmoon told me about the festival," said Mina, gently stroking the dead woman's wrinkled cheek. "That it was held on the night when all three moons—the red, the white, and the black—converged, forming the image of a great staring eye in the heavens. I should like to have seen that sight."

"Among humans, it was a night for riot and revelry, or so I have heard. Among my people, the night was honored and reverenced," Galdar stated, "for we believed the Eye to be the eye of Sargas, our god—*former* god," he added hastily, with a sidelong glance at Mina. "Still, what has some old festival to do with capturing Sanction? The three moons are gone, and so is the eye of the gods."

"There will be a festival, Galdar," said Mina. "The Festival of the New Eye, the One Eye. We will celebrate the festival in the Temple of Huerzyd."

"But the Temple of Huerzyd is in Sanction," Galdar protested. "We are on the other side of the continent from Sanction, not to mention the fact that Sanction is firmly in control of the Solamnic Knights. When will the festival occur?"

"At the appointed time," said Mina. "When the totem is assembled. When the red dragon falls from the skies."

"Ugh," Galdar grunted. "Then we should be marching to Sanction now and bringing with us an army. Yet we waste our time at this fell place." He cast a glance of enmity at the Tower. "Our march will be further slowed if we must cart along the body of this old woman."

The bonfire roared and crackled. The flames leaped up the stone walls of the Tower, charring them. Smoke swirled about Galdar, who batted irritably at it, and drifted in through the window. Tas coughed, covered his mouth with his hand.

"I am commanded to bring the body of Goldmoon, princess of the Qué-shu, bearer of the blue crystal staff, to Sanction, to the Temple of Huerzyd on the night of the Festival of the New Eye. There a great miracle will be performed, Galdar. Our journey will not be slowed. All will move as has been ordered. The One God will see to that."

Mina raised her hands over the body of Goldmoon and lifted up her voice in prayer. Orangish-yellow light radiated from her hands. Tas tried to look into the light to see what was happening, but the light was like tiny pieces of glass in his eyes, made them burn and hurt so that he was forced to shut them tight. Even then he could see the glare right through them.

Mina's praying ceased. The bright light slowly faded. Tasslehoff opened his eyes.

The body of Goldmoon lay enshrined in a sarcophagus of golden amber. Encased in the amber, Goldmoon's body was once again youthful, beautiful. She wore the white robes she had worn in life. Feathers adorned her hair that was gold threaded with silver—yet all now held fast in amber.

Tas felt the sick feeling in his stomach rise up into his throat. He choked and clutched the window ledge for support.

"This coffin you've created is very grand, Mina," said Galdar, and the minotaur sounded exasperated, "but what do you plan to do with her? Cart her about as a monument to this One God? Exhibit her to the populace? We are not clerics. We are soldiers. We have a war to fight."

Mina stared at Galdar in silence, a silence so large and terrible that it absorbed into itself all sound, all light, snatched away the air they breathed. The awful silence of her fury withered Galdar, who shrank visibly before it.

"I'm sorry, Mina," he mumbled. "I didn't mean—"

"Be thankful that I know you, Galdar," said Mina. "I know that you speak from your heart, without thinking. But someday, you will go too far, and on that day I will no longer be able to protect you. This woman was more than mother to me. All I have done in the name of the One God, I have done for her."

Mina turned to the sarcophagus, placed her hands upon the amber, and bent near to look at Goldmoon's calm, still face. "You told me of the gods who had been but were no more. I went in search of them—for you!"

Mina's voice trembled. "I brought the One God to you, Mother. The One God gave you back your youth and your beauty. I thought you would be pleased. What did I do wrong? I don't understand." Mina's hands stroked the amber coffin, as if smoothing out a blanket. She sounded bewildered. "You will change your mind, dear Mother. You will come to understand. . . ."

"Mina . . ." Galdar said uneasily, "I'm sorry. I didn't know. Forgive me."

Mina nodded. She did not turn her head. .

Galdar cleared his throat. "What are your orders concerning the kender?"

"Kender?" Mina repeated, only half-hearing him.

"The kender and the magical artifact. You said they were in the Tower."

Mina lifted her head. Tears glistened on her cheeks. Her face was pale, the amber eyes wide. "The kender." Her lips formed the words, but she did not speak them aloud. She frowned. "Yes, of course, go fetch him. Quickly! Make haste!"

"Do you know where he is, Mina?" Galdar asked hesitantly. "The Tower is immense, and there are many rooms."

Mina raised her head, looked directly at Tas's window, looked directly at Tas, and pointed.

"Conundrum," said Tasslehoff in a voice that didn't sound to him like his own voice but belonged to some altogether different person, a person who was well and truly scared. "We have to get out of here. Now!"

He backed precipitously away from the window.

"There, it's finished," said Conundrum, proudly displaying the device.

"Are you sure it will work?" Tas asked anxiously. He could hear footsteps on the stairs, or at least he thought he could.

"Or course," Conundrum stated, scowling. "Good as new. By the way, what did it do when it *was* new?"

Tas's heart, which had leaped quite hopefully at the first part of the gnome's statement, now sank.

"How do you know it works if you don't know what it does?" Tas demanded. He could quite definitely hear footsteps. "Never mind. Just give it to me. Quickly!"

Palin had wizard-locked the door, but Palin was . . . wasn't here anymore. Tas guessed that the wizard-lock wasn't here either. He could hear footsteps and harsh breathing. He pictured the large and heavy minotaur, tromping up all those stairs.

"I thought at first it might be a potato peeler," Conundrum was saying. He gave the device a shake that made the chain rattle. "But it's a bit small, and there's no hydraulic lift. Then I thought—"

"It's a device that sends you traveling through time. That's what I'm going to do with it, Conundrum," Tasslehoff said. "Journey back through time. I'd take you with me, but I don't think you'd much like where I'm going, which is back to the Chaos War to be stepped on by a giant. You see, it's my fault that everyone I love is dead, and if I go back, they won't be dead. I'll be dead, but that doesn't matter because I'm already dead—"

"Cheese grater," said Conundrum, regarding the device thoughtfully. "Or it could be, with a few modifications, a meat grinder, maybe, and a—"

"Never mind," said Tasslehoff, and he drew in a deep breath to give himself courage. "Just hand me the device. Thank you for fixing it. I hate to leave you here in the Tower of High Sorcery with an angry minotaur and the Dark Knights, but once I'm stepped on, they might not be here anymore. Would you please hand me the device?"

The footsteps had stopped, but not the harsh breathing. The stairs were steep and treacherous. The minotaur had been forced to halt his climb to catch his breath.

"Combination fishing rod and shoe tree?" guessed the gnome.

The minotaur's footsteps started again.

Tas gave up. One could be polite for only so long. Especially to a gnome. Tas made a grab for the device. "Give it to me!"

"You're not going to break it again?" Conundrum asked, holding it just out of the kender's reach.

"I'm not going to break it!" Tasslehoff said firmly. With a another lunge, he succeeded in nabbing the device and wrenched it out of the gnome's hand. "If you'll watch closely, I'll show you how it works. I hope," he muttered to himself.

Holding the device, Tas said a little prayer in his heart. "I know you can't hear me, Fizban . . . Or maybe you can but you're so disappointed in me that you don't want to hear me. I'm truly sorry. Truly, truly sorry." Tears crept into his eyes. "I never meant to cause all this trouble. I only wanted to speak at Caramon's funeral, to tell everyone what a good friend he was to me. I never meant for this to happen. Never! So, if you'll help me just once to go back to die, I'll stay dead. I promise."

"It's not doing anything," Conundrum grumbled. "Are you sure it's plugged in?"

Hearing the footsteps growing louder and louder, Tas held the device over his head.

"Words to the spell. I have to say the words to the spell. I know the words," the kender said, gulping. "It goes . . . It goes . . . Thy time is thine . . . Around it you journey . . . No, that can't be right: Travel. Around it you travel . . . and something, something expanses . . ."

The footsteps were so close now that he could feel the floor shake.

Sweat beaded on the kender's forehead. He gulped again and looked at the device, as if it might help him. When it didn't, he shook it.

"Now I see how it got broken in the first place," said Conundrum severely. "Is this going to take long? I think hear someone coming."

"Grasp firmly the beginning and you'll end up at the end. No, that's wrong," Tas said miserably. "All of it's wrong. I can't remember the words! What's the matter with me? I used to know it by heart. I could recite it standing on my head. I know because Fizban made me do it. . . ."

There came a thundering crash on the door, as of a heavy minotaur shoulder bashing into it.

Tas shut his eyes, so that he wouldn't hear what was going on outside the door. "Fizban made me say the spell standing on my head backwards. It was a bright, sunny day. We were in a green meadow, and the sky was blue with these little puffy white clouds, and the birds were singing, and so was Fizban until I asked him politely not to. . . ."

Another resounding crash and a sound of wood splintering.

> *Thy time is thy own.*
> *Though across it you travel.*
> *Its expanses you see.*
> *Whirling across forever.*
> *Obstruct not its flow.*
> *Grasp firmly the end and the beginning.*
> *Turn them forward upon themselves.*
> *All that is loose shall be secure*
> *Destiny be over your own head.*

The words flooded Tasslehoff's being, as warm and bright as the sunshine on that spring day. He didn't know where they came from, and he didn't stick around to ask.

The device began to glow brightly, jewels gleaming.

The last sensation Tas felt was that of a hand clutching his. The last sound Tas heard was Conundrum's voice, crying out in panic, "Wait! There's a screw loose—"

And then all sound and sensation was lost in the wonderful and exciting rushing-wind noise of the magic.

3 THE PUNISHMENT
FOR FAILURE

"The kender is gone, Mina," Galdar reported, emerging from the Tower.

"Gone?" Mina turned away from the amber coffin that held the body of Goldmoon to stare at the minotaur. "What do you mean? That's impossible? How could he escape—"

Mina gave a cry of anguish. Doubling over in wrenching pain, she sank to her knees, her arms clasped around her, her nails digging into her bare flesh in transports of agony.

"Mina!" Galdar cried in alarm. He hovered over her, helpless, baffled. "What has happened? Are you wounded? Tell me!"

Mina moaned and writhed upon the ground, unable to answer.

Galdar glared around at her Knights. "You were supposed to be guarding her! What enemy has done this?"

"I swear, Galdar!" cried one. "No one came near her—"

"Mina," said Galdar, bending over her, "tell me where you are hurt!"

Shuddering, in answer, she placed her hand on the black hauberk she wore, placed her hand over her heart.

"My fault!" she gasped through lips that bled. She had bitten down on them in her torment. "My fault. This . . . my punishment."

Mina remained on her knees, her head bowed, her hands clenched. Rivulets of sweat ran down her face. She shivered with fevered chills. "Forgive me!" she gasped, the words were flecked with blood. "I failed you. I forgot my duty. It will not happen again, I swear on my soul!"

The spasms of wracking pain ceased. Mina sighed, shuddering. Her body relaxed. She drew in deep breaths and rose, unsteadily, to her feet.

Her Knights gathered around her, wondering and ill at ease.

"Alarm's over," Galdar told them. "Go back to your duties."

They went, but not without many backward looks. Galdar supported Mina's unsteady steps.

"What happened to you?" he asked, eyeing her anxiously. "You spoke of punishment. Who punished you and for what?"

"The One God," said Mina. Her face was streaked with sweat and drawn with remembered agony, the amber eyes gray. "I failed in my duty. The kender was of paramount importance. I should have retrieved him first. I . . ." She licked her bloodied lips, swallowed. "I was so eager to see my mother, I forgot about him. Now he is gone, and it is my fault."

"The One God did this to you?" Galdar repeated, appalled, his voice shaking with anger. "The One God hurt you like this?"

"I deserved it, Galdar," Mina replied. "I welcome it. The pain inflicted on me is nothing compared to the pain the One God bears because of my failure."

Galdar frowned, shook his head.

"Come, Galdar," she said, her tone chiding, "didn't your father whip you as a child? Didn't your battle master beat you when you made a mistake in training? Your father did not strike you out of malice. The battle master did not hit you out of spite. Such punishment was meant for your own good."

"It isn't the same," Galdar growled. He would never forget the sight of her, who had led armies to glorious conquest, on her knees in the dirt, writhing in pain.

"Of course, it is the same," Mina said gently. "We are all children of the One God. How else are we to learn our duty?"

Galdar had no reply. Mina took his silence for agreement.

"Take some of the men and search every room in the Tower. Make certain the kender is not hiding in any of them. While you are gone, we will burn these bodies."

"Must I go back in there, Mina?" said Galdar, his voice heavy with reluctance.

"Why? What do you fear?" she asked.

"Nothing living," he replied, with a dark scowl at the Tower.

"Don't be afraid, Galdar," said Mina. She cast a careless glance at the bodies of the wizards, being dragged to the funeral pyre. "Their spirits cannot harm you. They go to serve the One God."

A bright light shone in the heavens. Distant, ethereal, the light was more radiant than the sun, made that orb seem dim and tarnished by comparison. Dalamar's mortal eyes could not look long at the sun, lest he be blinded, but he could stare at this beautiful, pure light forever, or so he imagined. Stare at it with an aching longing that rendered all that he was, all that he had been, paltry and insignificant.

As a very small child, he had once looked up in the night sky above his homeland to see the silver moon. Thinking it a bauble, just out of his reach, he wanted it to play with. He demanded his parents fetch it for him, and when they did not, he wept in anger and frustration. He felt that way now. He could have wept, but he had no eyes to weep with, no tears to fall. The bright and beautiful light was out of reach. His way to it was blocked. A barrier as thin as gossamer and strong as adamant stretched in front of him. Try as he might, he could not move past that barrier, a prison wall that surrounded a world.

He was not alone. He was one prisoner among many. The souls of the dead roamed restlessly about the prison yard of their bleak existence, all of them looking with longing at the radiant light. None of them able to attain it.

"The light is very beautiful," said a voice that was soft and beguiling. "What you see is the light of a realm beyond, the next stage of your soul's long journey. I will release you, let you travel there, but first you must bring me what I need."

He would obey. He would bring the voice whatever it wanted, so long as he could escape this prison. He had only to bring the magic. He looked at the Tower of High Sorcery and recognized it as having something to do with what he was, what he had been, but all that was gone now, behind him. The Tower was a veritable storehouse for the magic. He could see the magic glistening like streams of gold dust among the barren sand that had been his life.

The other, restless souls streamed into the Tower, now bereft of the one who had been its master. Dalamar looked at the radiant light, and his heart ached with longing. He joined the river of souls that was flowing into the Tower.

He had almost reached the entrance when a hand reached out and seized hold of him, held him fast. The voice, angry and frustrated itself, hissed at him, "Stop."

"Stop!" Mina commanded. "Halt! Do not burn the bodies. I have changed my mind."

Startled, the Knights let loose their hold. The corpses flopped limply to the ground. The Knights exchanged glances. They had never seen Mina like this, irresolute and vacillating. They didn't like it, and they didn't like to see her punished, even by this One God. The One God was far away, had little to do with them. Mina was near, and they worshiped her, idolized her.

"A good idea, Mina," said Galdar, emerging from the Tower. He glared balefully at the dead wizards. "Leave the vultures to be eaten by vultures. The kender is not in the Tower. We've searched high, and we've searched low. Let's get out of this accursed place."

Fire crackled. Smoke curled about the Tower, as the mournful dead curled about the boles of the cypress trees. The living waited in hopeful expectation, longing to leave. The dead waited patiently, they had nowhere to go. All of them wondered what Mina meant to do.

She knelt beside Dalamar's body. Clasping one hand over the medallion she wore around her neck, she placed her other hand on the mage's mortal wounds. The staring eyes looked up vacantly.

Softly, Mina began to sing.

Wake, love, for this time wake.
Your soul, my hand does take.
Leave the darkness deep.
Leave your endless sleep.

Dalamar's flesh warmed beneath Mina's hand. Blood tinged the gray cheeks, warmed the chill limbs. His lips parted, drew in breath in a shivering gasp. He quivered and stirred at her touch. Life returned to the corpse, to all but the eyes. The eyes remained vacant, empty.

Galdar watched in scowling disapproval. The Knights stared in awe. Always before, Mina had prayed over the dead, but she had never brought them back to life. The dead serve the One God, she had told them.

"Stand up," Mina ordered.

The living body with the lifeless eyes obeyed, rose to its feet.

"Go to the wagon," Mina ordered. "There await my command."

The elf's eyelids shivered. His body jerked.

"Go to the wagon," Mina repeated.

Slowly, the mage's empty eyes shifted, looked at Mina.

"You will obey me in this," said Mina, "as you will obey me in all things, else I will destroy you. Not your body. The loss of this lump of flesh would be of little consequence to you now. I will destroy your soul."

The corpse shuddered and, after a moment's hesitation, shuffled off toward the wagon. The Knights fell back before it, gave it wide berth, although a few started to grin. The shambling thing looked grotesque. One of the Knights actually laughed aloud.

Horrified and repelled, Galdar saw nothing funny in this. He had spoken glibly of leaving the corpses to the vultures, and he could have done that without a qualm—they were wizards, after all—but he didn't like this. There was something wrong with this, although he couldn't quite say what or why it should so disturb him.

"Mina, is this wise?" he asked.

Mina ignored him. Singing the same song over the second wizard, she placed her hand upon his chest. The corpse sat up.

"Go join your fellow in the wagon," she commanded.

Palin's eyes blinked. A spasm contorted his features. Slowly, the hands with their broken fingers started to raise up, reach out, as if to grab and seize hold of something only he could see.

"I will destroy you," Mina said sternly. "You will obey me."

The hands clenched. The face contorted in agony, a pain that seemed far worse than the pain of death.

"Go," said Mina, pointing.

The corpse gave up the fight. Bowing its head, it walked to the wagon. This time, none of the Knights laughed.

Mina sat back, pale, wan, exhausted. This day had been a sad one for her. The death of the woman she loved as a mother, the anger of her god. She drooped, her shoulders sagged. She seemed scarcely able to stand under her own power. Galdar was moved to pity. He longed to comfort and support her, but his duty came first.

"Mina, is this wise?" he repeated in a low voice, for her ears alone. "Bad enough we must haul a coffin about Ansalon, but now we are further burdened by these two . . . things." He didn't know what name to call them. "Why have you done this? What purpose does it serve?" He frowned. "It unsettles the men."

The amber eyes regarded him. Her face was drawn with fatigue and grief, but the eyes shone clear, undimmed, and, as always, they saw right through him.

"It unsettles you, Galdar," she said.

He grunted. His mouth twisted.

Mina turned her gaze to the corpses, sitting on the end of the wagon, staring out at nothing.

"These two wizards are tied to the kender, Galdar."

"They are hostages, then?" said Galdar, cheering up. This was something he could understand.

"Yes, Galdar, if you want to think of it that way. They are hostages. When we recover the kender and the artifact, they will explain to me to how it works."

"I'll put an extra guard on them."

"That will not be necessary," Mina said, shrugging. "Think of them not so much as prisoners, but as animated slabs of meat."

She gazed at them, her expression thoughtful. "What would you say to an army of such as these, Galdar? An army of soldiers who obey commands without question, soldiers who fight without fear, who have inordinate strength, who fall, only to rise again. Isn't that the dream of every commander? We hold their souls in thrall," she continued, musing, "and send forth their bodies to do battle. What would you say to that, Galdar?"

Galdar could think of nothing to say. Rather, he could think of too much to say. He could imagine nothing more heinous, nothing more obscene.

"Fetch my horse, Galdar," Mina ordered. "It is time we left this place of sorrow."

Galdar did as he was told, obeyed that order eagerly.

Mounting her horse, Mina took her place at the head of the mournful caravan. The Knights fell in around the wagon, forming an honor guard for the dead. The wagon's driver cracked his whip, and the heavy draft horses heaved against the harness. The wagon and its strange burden lurched forward.

The souls of the dead parted for Mina, as did the trees. A trail opened up through the thick and tangled wood that surrounded the Tower of High Sorcery. The trail was smooth, for Mina would not have the coffin jostled. She turned often in her saddle to look back to the wagon, to the amber sarcophagus.

Galdar took his customary place at Mina's side.

The bodies of the two wizards sat on the back of the wagon, feet dangling, arms flaccid, hands resting in their laps. Their eyes stared straight ahead behind them. Once, Galdar glanced back at them. He saw two wispy entities trailing after the living corpses, like silken scarves caught in the wagon wheels.

Their souls.

He looked quickly away and did not look back again.

4 THE DEATH OF SKIE

The silver dragon had no idea how much time had passed since he had first entered the caverns of Skie, the mighty blue dragon. The blind silver, Mirror, had no way of judging time, for he could not see the sun. He had not seen it since the day of that strange and terrible storm, the day he'd heard the voice in the storm and recognized it, the day the voice had commanded that he bow down and worship, the day he'd been punished for his refusal, struck by the bolt that left him sightless and disfigured. That day was months past. He had wandered the world since, stumbling about in human form, because a blind human can walk, whereas a blind dragon, who cannot fly, is almost helpless.

Hidden away in this cave, Mirror knew nothing but night, felt nothing but night's cool shadows.

Mirror had no notion how long he had been here in the lair with the suffering blue dragon. It might have been a day or a year since Skie had sought to make demands of the One God. Mirror had been an unwitting witness to their encounter.

Having heard the voice in the storm and recognized it, Mirror had come seeking an answer to this strange riddle. If the voice was that of Takhisis, what was she doing in this world when all the other gods had departed? Thinking it over, Mirror had decided that Skie might be the one to provide him with information.

Mirror had always had questions about Skie. Supposedly a Krynn dragon like himself, Skie had grown larger and stronger and more powerful than any other blue dragon in the history of the world. Skie had purportedly turned on his own kind, slaying and devouring them as did the dragon overlords. Mirror had often wondered: Had Skie had truly turned upon his own kind? Or had Skie joined his own kind?

With great difficulty, Mirror had managed to find Skie's lair and enter it. He had arrived in time to witness Skie's punishment by Mina for his presumption, for his perceived disloyalty. Skie had sought to kill Mina, but the lightning bolt meant to slay her reflected off her armor, struck him. The immense blue dragon was mortally wounded.

Desperate to know the truth, Mirror had done what he could to heal Skie. He had been only partially successful. He was keeping the Blue alive, but the barbs of the gods are powerful weapons, and Mirror, though a dragon, was mortal.

Mirror left his charge only to fetch water for them both.

Skie drifted in and out of consciousness. During the times he was awake and lucid, Mirror was able to question the blue dragon about the One God, a god to whom Mirror was now able to give a name. These conversations took place over long periods of time, for Skie was rarely able to remain conscious long.

"She stole the world," Skie said at one point, shortly after he first regained his senses. "Stole it away and transported it to this part of the universe. She had long planned out her actions. All was in readiness. She awaited only the right moment."

"A moment that came during the Chaos War," Mirror said. He paused, asked quietly, "How are you feeling?"

"I am dying," Skie returned bluntly. "That's how I am feeling."

Had Mirror been human, he would have told some comforting falsehood intended to sooth the dying dragon's final moments. Mirror was not human, although he now walked in human form. Dragons are not given to telling falsehoods, not even those meant to comfort. Mirror was wise enough to know that such lies bring comfort only to the living.

Skie was a warrior dragon. A blue dragon, he had flown into battle countless times, had sent many of his foes plummeting to their deaths. He and his former rider, the infamous Kitiara uth Matar, had cut a swath of terror and destruction across half of Ansalon during the War of the Lance. After the Chaos War, Skie had been one of the few dragons in Ansalon to hold his own against the alien dragon overlords, Malys and Beryl, finally rising in power to take his place among them. He had slaughtered and gorged on other dragons, gaining in strength and power by devouring his own kind. He had built a hideous totem of the skulls of his victims.

Mirror could not see the totem, but he could sense it nearby. He heard the voices of the dead, accusing, angry, crying out for revenge. Mirror had no love for Skie. Had they met in battle, Mirror would have fought to defeat his foe and rejoiced in his destruction.

And Skie would have rejoiced in such a death. To die as a warrior, to fall from the skies with the blood of your foe wet on your talons, the taste of lightning on your tongue. That was the way Skie would have wanted to die. Not this way, not lying helpless, trapped in his lair, his life passing from him in labored, gasping breaths; his mighty wings stilled; his bloodied talons twitching and scrabbling on the rock floor.

No dragon should die this death, Mirror thought to himself. Not even my worst enemy. He regretted having used his magic to bring Skie back to life, but Mirror had to know more about this One God, he had to find out the truth. He inured himself against pity for his foe and continued asking questions. Skie did not have much time left to answer.

"You say Takhisis planned this removal," Mirror said, during another conversation. "You were part of her plan."

Skie grunted. Mirror could hear the massive body shift itself in an effort to ease the pain.

"I was the most important part, curse the eon I met the conniving bitch. I was the one who discovered the Portals. Our world, the world where I and others of my kind were born, is not like this world. We do not share our world with the short-lived, the soft-bodies. Ours is a world of dragons."

Skie was not able to say this without many pauses for breath and grunts of pain. He was determined to continue his tale. His voice was weak, but Mirror could still hear the anger, like a rumble of distant thunder.

"We roamed our world at will and fought ferocious battles for survival. These dragons you see here, this Beryl and this Malys, they seem to you enormous and powerful, but in comparison to those who ruled our world, they are small and pitiful creatures. That was one reason they came to this world. But I jump ahead of myself.

"I could see, as could others of our kind, that our world was growing stagnant. We had no future, our children had no future but to eat or be eaten. We were not advancing, we were regressing. I was not the only one to seek a way off the world, but I was the first to be successful. Using my magic, I discovered the roads that led through the ethers to worlds far beyond our own. I grew skilled at traveling these roads. Often the roads saved my life, for if I was threatened by one of the Elders, I had only to jump into the ethers to escape.

"It was while I was inside the ethers that I came upon Her Dark Majesty." Skie ground his teeth as he spoke, as if he would be glad to grind her between them. "I had never seen a god before. I had never before beheld anything so magnificent, never been in the presence of such power. I bowed before her and offered myself to her as her servant. She was fascinated by the roads through the ethers. I was not so enamored of her that I foolishly revealed their secrets to her, but I gave her enough information so that she could see how they might be of use to her.

"Takhisis brought me to her world that she called Krynn. She told me that on Krynn she was but one of many gods. She was the most powerful, she said, and because of that, the others feared her and were constantly conspiring against her. She would one day be triumphant over them, and on that day she would give me rich reward. I would rule Krynn and the soft-bodies who lived on it. This was to be my world in exchange for my services. Needless to say, she lied."

Anger stirred in Mirror, anger at the overweening ambition that gave no thought or care to any of those living on the world that was apparently little more than a bauble to Queen Takhisis. Mirror took care to keep his own anger hidden. He had to hear all that Skie had to tell. Mirror had to know what had happened. He could not change the past, but he might be able to affect the future.

"I was young then," Skie continued, "and the young of our species are the size of the blue dragons on Krynn. Queen Takhisis paired me with Kitiara—a favorite of the Dark Queen. Kitiara . . ."

Skie was silent, remembering. He gave a deep sigh, an aching sigh of longing. "Our battles together were glorious. For the first time, I learned that one could fight for more than survival—one could fight for honor, for the joy of the battle, for the glory in victory. At first, I despised the weaklings who inhabit this world: humans and the rest. I could not see why the gods permitted them to exist. Soon, I came to find them fascinating—Kitiara, especially. Courageous, bold, never doubting herself, knowing exactly what she wanted and reaching out to seize it. Ah, what a goddess *she* would have made."

Skie paused. His breath came with a painful catch. "I will see her again. I know I will. Together, we will fight . . . and ride once more to glory. . . ."

"And all this time," Mirror said, leading Skie back to the main topic, "you worked for Takhisis. You established the road that would take her here, to this part of the universe."

"I did. I made all ready for her. She had only to wait for the right time."

"But, surely, she could not have foreseen the Chaos War?" A terrible thought came to Mirror. "Or did that come about through her machinations?"

Skie snorted in disgust. "Clever Takhisis may be, but she is not that clever. Perhaps she had some inkling that Chaos was trapped inside the Graygem. If so, she had only to wait—for what is time to her, she is a god—for some fool to let him loose. If it had not been that, she would have found some other means. She was constantly watching for her chance. As it was, the Chaos War played right into her hands. All was in readiness. She made a show of fleeing the world, withdrawing her support and her power, leaving those who relied on her helpless. She had to do that, for she would need all her power for the enormous task that awaited her.

"The moment came. In the instant that Chaos was defeated, the energy released was immense. Takhisis harnessed that energy, combined it with her own power, and wrenched the world free of its moorings, brought it along the roads I had created with my magic, and set it here, in this part of the universe. All of this happened so fast that no one on the world was aware of the shift. The gods themselves, caught up in the desperate battle for survival, had no inkling of her plan, and once they realized what was happening, they were so depleted of their own power that they were helpless to stop her.

"Takhisis snatched the world away from them and hid it from their sight. All proceeded as she had planned. Bereft of the gods' blessing, stripped of their magic, the people of the world were thrown into turmoil and despair. She herself was exhausted, so weak that she was reduced to almost nothing. She needed time to heal herself, time to rest. But she wasn't worried. The longer the people were without a god, the greater their need. When she returned, they would be so thankful and relieved that they would be her abject slaves. She made one minor miscalculation."

"Malys," said Mirror. "Beryl and the rest."

"Yes. They were intrigued by this new toy that had suddenly dropped down among them. Weary of struggling to survive in their world, they were only too happy to take over this one. Takhisis was too weak to stop them. She could do nothing but watch in helpless frustration as they seized rulership of the world. Still, she lied to me and continued to promise me that someday, when she was again powerful, she would destroy the usurpers and give the world to me. I believed her for a while, but the years passed, and Malystryx and Beryl and the rest grew more powerful still. They killed the dragons of Krynn and feasted on them and built their totems, and I heard nothing from Takhisis.

"As for me, I could see this world degenerating into a world like the one I had left. I looked back with joy to my days of battle with Kitiara. I wanted nothing more to do with my kind, nothing more to do with the pathetic wretches who populated this place. I went to Takhisis and demanded payment.

"'Keep the world,' I said to her. 'I have no need of it. I do not want it. Restore Kitiara to me. We will travel the roads together. Together we will find a world where glory awaits us.'"

"She promised me she would. In a place called the Gray, I would find Kitiara's soul. I saw the Gray. I went there. Or thought I did." Skie rumbled deep in his chest. "You heard the rest. You heard Mina, the Dark Queen's new toady. You heard her tell me how I had been betrayed."

"Yet, others saw you depart. . . ."

"Others saw what she meant them to see, just as all saw what she meant them to see at the end of the Chaos War."

Skie fell silent, brooding over his wrongs. Mirror listened to the blue dragon's labored breathing. Skie might live for hours or days. Mirror had no way of knowing. He could not find out where Skie was wounded, and Skie himself would not tell him. Mirror wondered if the wound was not so much heart-deep as soul-deep.

Mirror changed the subject to turn Skie's thoughts. "Takhisis faced a new threat—the dragon overlords."

"The overlords." Skie grunted. "Yes, they were a problem. Takhisis had hoped that they would continue to fight and eventually slay each other, but the overlords agreed to a truce. Peace was declared. People began to grow complacent. Takhisis feared that soon people would start to worship the overlords, as some were already doing, and have no need of her. The Dark Queen was not yet strong enough to battle them. She had to find a way to increase her power. She had long recognized and lamented the waste of energy that passed out of the world with the souls of the dead. She conceived a way to imprison the dead within the world, and thus she was able to use them to steal away the wild magic and feed it to her. When she deemed she was strong enough to return, she came back, the night of the storm."

"Yes," said Mirror. "I heard her voice. She called to me to join her legions, to worship her as my god. I might have, but something stopped me. My heart knew that voice, if my head did not. And so I was punished. I—"

He halted. Skie had begun to stir, trying to lift his great bulk from the floor of the lair.

"What is it? What are you doing?"

"You had best hide yourself," said Skie, struggling desperately to regain his feet. "Malys is coming."

"Malys!" Mirror repeated, alarmed.

"She has heard I am dying. Those cowardly minions who used to serve me must have raced to her with the glad tidings. The great vulture comes to steal my totem. I should let her! Takhisis has usurped the totems for her own use. Malys takes her worst enemy to bed with her every night. Let the red monster come. I will fight her with my last breath—"

Skie might be raving, as Mirror truly thought he was, but the Blue's advice to hide was sound. Even had he not been blind, Mirror would have avoided a fight with the immense red dragon, much as he hated and loathed her. Mirror had seen too many of his kind caught and crushed in the mighty jaws, set ablaze by her horrific fire. Brute strength alone could not overcome this alien creature. The largest, strongest dragon ever to walk Krynn would be no match for Malystryx.

Not even a god had dared face her.

Mirror shifted back to human form. He felt very fragile and vulnerable in the soft skin, the thin and delicate bones, the paltry musculature. Yet, a blind human could manage in this world. Mirror began to grope his way around Skie's massive body. Mirror planned to retreat, move deeper into the twisting maze of corridors in the Blue's labyrinthine lair. Mirror was feeling his way about, when his hand touched something smooth and cold.

A shiver passed through his arm. Mirror could not see, but he knew immediately what he had touched—Skie's totem, made of skulls of his victims. Shuddering, Mirror snatched his hand away and almost lost his balance in his haste. He stumbled into the wall, steadied himself, used the wall to guide his steps.

"Wait," Skie's voice hissed through the dark corridors. "You did me a favor, Silver. You kept me from death by her foul hands. Because of you, I can die on my own terms, with what dignity I have left. I will do you a favor in return. The others of your kind—the Golds and Silvers—you've searched for them, and you cannot find them. True enough?"

Mirror was reluctant to admit this, even to a dying blue dragon. He made no reply but continued groping his way along the passage.

"They did not flee in fear," Skie continued. "They heard Takhisis's voice the night of the storm. Some of them recognized it, understood what it meant. They left the world to try to find the gods."

Mirror paused, turned his sightless face to the sound of Skie's voice. Outside, he could now hear what Skie had heard long before him—the beating of enormous wings.

"It was a trap," Skie said. "They left, and now they cannot return. Takhisis holds them prisoner, as she holds the souls of the dead prisoner."

"What can be done to free them?" Mirror asked.

"I have told you all I know," Skie replied. "My debt to you is paid, Silver. You had best make haste."

Moving as fast as possible, Mirror slipped and slid down the passage. He had no notion of where he was going, but guessed that he was traveling deeper into the lair. He kept his right hand on the wall, moved with the wall, never let go. Thus, he reasoned, he would be able to find his way out. When he heard Malys's voice, strident and high-pitched—an odd sound to come from such a massive creature—Mirror halted. Keeping his hand firmly against the wall, he hunkered down onto the smooth floor, shrouded in the lair's cool darkness. He quieted even his breathing, fearful that she might hear him and come seeking him.

Mirror crouched in the blue dragon's lair and awaited the outcome with dread.

Skie knew he was dying. His heart lurched and shivered in his rib cage. He fought for every breath. He longed to lie down and rest, to close his eyes, to lose himself in the past. To once more spread his wings that were the color of heaven and fly up among the clouds. To hear Kitiara's voice again, her firm commands, her mocking laughter. To feel her hands, sure and capable, on the reins, guiding him unerringly to the fiercest, hottest part of the battle. To revel again in the clash of arms and smell the blood, to feel the flesh rend beneath his talons and hear Kitiara's exultant battle cry, challenging all comers. To return to the stables, have his wounds dressed, and wait for her to come, as she always did, to sit down beside him and relive the battle. She would come to him, leaving behind those puny humans who sought to love her. Dragon and rider, they were a team—a deadly team.

"So, Skie," said a voice, a hated voice. Malys's head thrust inside the entrance to the lair, blotted out the sunlight. "I was misinformed. You're not dead yet, I see."

Skie roused himself. His dreams, his memories had been very real. This was unreality.

"No, I am not dead," he growled. His talons dug deep into the rock, fighting against the pain, forcing himself to remain standing.

Malys insinuated more of her great bulk inside his lair—her head and shoulders, front talons and neck. Her wings remained folded at her side, her hind feet and tail dangled down the cliff face. Her small, cruel eyes swept over him disdainfully. Discounting him, she searched for the reason she had come—his totem. She found it, elevated in the center of the lair, and her eyes glistened.

"Don't mind me," she said coolly. "You were dying, I believe. Please continue. I don't mean to interrupt. I just came to collect a few mementos of our time together."

Reaching out her talon, Malys began to weave a magical web around the skulls of his totem. Skie saw eyes in the skulls of the totem. He could sense his Queen's presence. Takhisis had no care for him. Not anymore. He was of no use to her now. She had eyes only for Malys. Fine. Skie wished them joy together. They deserved each other.

His legs trembled. They could not support his weight any longer, and he slumped to the floor of his lair. He was angry with himself, furious. He had to fight, to take a stand, to at least leave his mark upon Malys. He was so weak, shivering. His heart pounded as if it would burst in his chest.

"Skie, my lovely Blue!" Kitiara's voice came to him, mocking, laughing. "What, you sluggard, still asleep? Wake up! We have battles to fight this day. Death to deal. Our enemies do not slumber, you may be certain of that."

Skie opened his eyes. There she stood before him, her blue dragon armor shining in the sun. Kitiara smiled her crooked smile and, lifting her arm, she pointed.

"There stands your foe, Skie. You have one fight left in you. One more battle to go. Then you may rest."

Skie raised his head. He could not see Malys. His sight was going rapidly, draining away with his life. He could see Kitiara, though, could see where she pointed. He drew in a breath, his last breath. He had better make it a good one.

The breath mingled with the sulfur in his belly. He exhaled.

Lightning cracked and sizzled, split the air. Thunder boomed, shook the mountain. The sound was horrendous, but he could still hear Malys's shriek of rage and pain. He could not see what damage he had done to her, but he guessed it had been considerable.

Enraged, Malys attacked him. Her razor-sharp talons dug through his scales, ripped apart his flesh, tore a gaping hole in his flank.

Skie felt nothing, no more pain, no more fear.

Pleased, he let his head sink to the floor of his lair.

"Well done, my lovely Blue," came Kitiara's voice, and he was proud to feel the touch of her hand on the side of his neck. "Well done. . . ."

Skie's weak thunderbolt had caused Malys no real harm, beyond a jarring, tingling sensation that danced through her body and knocked a large chunk of scaly flesh off the joint of her upper left foreleg. She felt the pain more to her pride than to her great, bloated body, and she lashed out at the dying Skie, ripping and rending his flesh until the lair was awash with blood. Eventually, she realized she was doing nothing but maltreating an unfeeling corpse.

Her fury spent, Malys resumed her dismantling of his totem, prepared it for transport back to her lair in the new Goodlund Range, the Peak of Malys.

Gloating over her prize, eyeing with satisfaction the large number of skulls, Malys could feel her own power swell just handling them.

She had never had much use for Krynn dragons. In a world where they were the dominant species, Krynn dragons were feared and revered by the rest of the world's puny inhabitants and had thus become spoiled. Sometimes, it was true, Krynn's soft-skins had taken up arms against the dragons. Malys had heard accounts of these contests from Skie, heard him go on and on about some event known as the War of the Lance, about the thrill of battle and the bonds formed between dragonrider and dragon.

Clearly Skie had been away from his native world for too long, if he considered such childlike flailings to be true battles. Malys had gone up against a few of these dragonriders, and she'd never seen anything so amusing in her life. She thought back to her old world, where not a day went by but that some bloody fight erupted to establish hierarchy among the clan.

Survival had been a daily battle, then, one reason Malys and the others had been glad to find this fat and lazy world. She did not miss those cruel times, but she tended to look back upon them with nostalgia, like an old war veteran reliving his past. She and her kind had taught these weakling Krynn dragons a valuable lesson—those who survived. The Krynn dragons had bowed down before her, had promised to serve and worship her. And then came the night of that strange storm.

The Krynn dragons changed. Malys could not say exactly what was different. The Reds and Blacks and Blues continued to serve her, to come when summoned and answer her every beck and call, but she had the feeling they were up to something. She would often catch them in whispered conversations that broke off whenever she appeared. And, of late, several had gone missing. She'd received reports of Krynn dragons bearing dragonriders—Dark Knights of Neraka—into battle against the Solamnics at Solanthus.

Malys had no objections to the dragons killing Solamnics, but she should have been consulted first. Lord Targonne would have done so, but he had been slain, and it was in the reports of his death that Malys had first heard the most disturbing news of all—the appearance on Krynn of a god.

Malys had heard rumors of this god—the very god who had brought the world to this part of the universe. Malys had seen no signs of this god, however, and could only conclude that the god had been daunted by her arrival and had abandoned the field. The idea that the god might be lying low, building up her strength, never occurred to Malys—not surprising, for she came from a world devoid of guile, a world ruled by strength and might.

Malys began to hear reports of this One God and of the One God's champion—a human girl-child named Mina. Malys did not pay much attention to these, mainly because this Mina did nothing to annoy Malys. Mina's actions actually pleased Malys. Mina removed the shield from over Silvanesti and destroyed the sniveling, self-serving green dragon, Cyan Bloodbane. The Silvanesti elves were properly cowed, crushed beneath the boots of the Dark Knights.

Malys had not been pleased to hear that her cousin Beryl was about to attack the land of the Qualinesti elves. Not that Malys cared anything for the elves, but such actions broke the pact. Malys didn't trust Beryl, didn't trust her ambition and her greed. Malys might have been tempted to intervene and put a stop to this, but she had been assured by Lord Targonne, late leader of the Dark Knights, that he had the situation under control. Too late Malys found out that Targonne didn't even have his own situation under control.

Beryl flew off to attack and destroy Qualinesti, and she was successful. The Qualinesti elves were now fleeing the wreckage of their homeland like the vermin they were. True, Beryl managed to get herself killed in the process, but she had always been an impulsive, over-emotional, irrational nincompoop.

The green dragon's death was reported to Malys by two of Beryl's minions—red dragons, who cringed and groveled properly but who, Malys suspected, were chortling out of the sides of their mouths.

Malys did not like the way these reds gloated over her cousin's death. They didn't show the proper respect. Nor did Malys like what she heard of the reports of Beryl's death. It had the whiff of the god about it. Beryl might have been a braying donkey of a dragon, but she was an immense and powerful beast, and Malys could not envision any circumstances under which a band of elves could have taken her down without divine assistance.

One of the Krynn dragons gave Malys the idea of seizing Beryl's totem. He had happened to mention the totem, wondered what they were going to do with it. Power radiated from the totem still, even after Beryl's death. There was some talk among her surviving human generals that they might make use of it themselves, if they could figure out how to harness the magic.

Appalled by the idea of humans laying their filthy hands on something so powerful and sacred as the totem, Malys flew immediately to claim it for herself. She used her magic to transport it to her lair, added the skulls of Beryl's victims to the skulls of her own. She drew upon the magic and felt it well up inside her, making her stronger, more powerful than ever. Then came the report from Mina that she had slain the mighty Skie.

Malys wasted no time. So much for this god. She had best creep back into whatever hole she had crawled out of. Malys wrapped Skie's totem in magic and prepared to carry it off. Pausing, she glanced at the mangled remains of the great blue dragon, and wondered if she should add his head to the totem.

"He does not deserve such distinction," Malys said, shoving aside a bit of Skie's bone and flesh with a disdainful toe. "Mad, that's what he was. Insane. His skull would likely be a curse."

She glowered at the wound on her shoulder. The bleeding had stopped, but the burned flesh stung and ached, the damage to the muscle was causing her front foreleg to stiffen. The wound would not impede her flying, however, and that was all that mattered.

Gathering up the skulls in her magical web, Malys prepared to depart. Before leaving, she sniffed the air, took one last look around. She had noticed something strange on her arrival—an odd smell. At first she'd been unable to determine the nature of the smell, but now she recognized it. Dragon. One of those Krynn dragons and, unless Malys was much mistaken, a Krynn metallic dragon.

Malys searched the chamber of Skie's lair in which his body lay, but found no trace of a metallic dragon: no golden scales lying about, no silver scrapings on the walls. At length, Malys gave up. Her wound pained her. She wanted to return to the dark and restful sanctuary of her lair and build up her totem.

Holding fast to the web-encased skulls of the totem and favoring her wounded leg, Malys wormed her massive body out of the lair of the dead Blue and flapped off eastward.

5 THE SILVER DRAGON AND THE BLUE

Mirror remained in hiding until he was certain beyond doubt that Malys was gone and that she would not return. He had heard the battle, and he'd even felt pride in Skie for standing up to the heinous red dragon, experienced a twinge of pity at Skie's death. Mirror heard Malys's furious roar of pain, heard her rip apart Skie's body. When he felt a trickle of warm liquid flow past his hand, Mirror guessed that it was Skie's blood.

Yet now that Malys was gone, Mirror wondered what he would do. He put his hand to his maimed eyes, cursed his handicap. He was in possession of important information about the true nature of the One God. He knew what had become of the metallic dragons, and he could do nothing about any of it.

Mirror realized he was going to have to do something—go in search of food and water. The odor of dragon blood was strong, but through it he could just barely detect the scent of water. He used his magic to shift back to his dragon form, for his sense of smell was better in that form than this puny human body. He invariably looked forward to the shifting, for he felt cramped and vulnerable in the frail, wingless human form, with its soft skin and fragile bones.

He flowed into the dragon's body, enjoying the sensation as a human enjoys a long, luxurious stretch. He felt more secure with his armored scales, felt better balanced on four legs than on two. He could see far more clearly, could spot a deer running through a field miles below him.

Or, rather, I could have once seen more clearly, he amended.

His sense of smell now much more acute, he was soon able to find a stream that flowed through the cavernous lair.

Mirror drank his fill and then, his thirst slaked, he next considered easing his hunger pangs. He smelled goat. Skie had brought down a mountain goat and not yet had a chance to eat it. Once he quieted the rumblings of his belly, Mirror would be able to think more clearly.

He hoped to avoid returning to the main chamber where the remnants of Skie's body lay, but his senses told him that the goat meat he sought was in that chamber. Hunger drove Mirror back.

The floor was wet and slippery with blood. The stench of blood and death hung heavy in the air. Perhaps it was this that dulled Mirror's senses or perhaps the hunger made him careless. Whatever the reason, he was startled beyond measure to hear a voice, dire and cold, echo in the chamber.

"I thought at first you must be responsible for this," said the dragon, speaking in the language of dragons. "But now I realize that I was wrong. You could not have brought down the mighty Skie. You can barely move about this cavern without bumping into things."

Calling defensive magical spells to mind, Mirror turned his sightless head to face the unknown speaker—a blue dragon, by the sound of his voice and the faint scent of brimstone that hung about him. The blue must have flown in the main entrance to Skie's lair. Mirror had been so preoccupied with his hunger that he had not heard him.

"I did not slay Skie," said Mirror.

"Who did, then? Takhisis?"

Mirror was surprised to hear her name, then realized that he shouldn't be. He was not the only one to have recognized that voice in the storm.

"You might say that. The girl called Mina wielded the magical bolt that brought about his death. She acted in self-defense. Skie attacked her first, claiming that she had betrayed him."

"Of course she betrayed him," said the Blue. "When did she ever do anything else?"

"I am confused," said Mirror. "Are we speaking of Mina or Takhisis?"

"They are one and the same, to all intents and purposes. So what are you doing here, Silver, and why is the stench of Malys heavy about the place?"

"Malys took away Skie's totem. Skie was mortally wounded, yet he still managed to defy her. He wounded her, I think, though probably not severely. He was too weak. She did this to him in retaliation."

"Good for him," growled the Blue. "I hope gangrene sets in and she rots. But you didn't answer my first question, Silver. Why are you here?"

"I had questions," said Mirror.

"Did you receive answers?"

"I did," said Mirror.

"Were you surprised to hear these answers?"

"No, not really," Mirror admitted. "What is your name? I am called Mirror."

"Ah, the Guardian of the Citadel of Light. I am called Razor. I am"—the Blue paused and when he next spoke, his voice was heavy and tinged with grief—"I was the partner of Marshal Medan of Qualinesti. He is dead, and I am on my own now. You, being a Silver, might be interested to hear that

Qualinesti has been destroyed," Razor added. "The Lake of Death, the elves call it. That is all that is left of the once-beautiful city."

Mirror was suspicious, wary. "I can't believe this!"

"Believe it," said Razor grimly. "I saw the destruction with my own eyes. I was too late to save the Marshal, but I did see the great, green dragon Beryl meet her death." His tone held grim satisfaction.

"I would be interested to hear the account," said Mirror.

The Blue chuckled. "I imagine you would. The elves of Qualinesti were warned of her coming, and they were ready for her. They stood on their rooftops and fired thousands of arrows at her. Attached to each arrow was cord that someone had strengthened with magic. The elves thought it was their magic, naturally. It wasn't. It was her magic."

"Takhisis?"

"Simply ridding herself of another rival and the elves at the same time. The thousands of strands of magical cord formed a net over Beryl, dragged her down from the skies. The elves planned to kill her as she lay helpless on the ground, but their plans went awry. The elves had worked with the dwarves, you see, to dig tunnels beneath the ground of Qualinost. Many elves managed to escape through these tunnels, but, in the end, they proved to be Qualinost's undoing. When Beryl landed on the ground, her great weight caused the tunnels to collapse, forming a huge chasm. She sank deep into the ground. The waters of the White-Rage River left their banks and flowed into the chasm, flooding Qualinost and turning it into a gigantic lake. A Lake of Death."

"Beryl dead," Mirror murmured. "Skie dead. The Qualinesti lands destroyed. One by one, Takhisis rids herself of her enemies."

"Your enemies, too, Silver," said Razor. "And mine. These overlords, as they call themselves, have slain many of our kind. You should rejoice in our Queen's victory over them. Whatever you may think of her, she is the goddess of our world, and she fights for us."

"She fights for no one but herself," Mirror retorted. "As she has always done. This is all her fault. If Takhisis had not stolen away the world, these overlords would have never found us. Those who have died would be alive today: dragons, elves, humans, kender. The great dragons murdered them, but Takhisis herself is ultimately responsible for their deaths, for she brought us here."

"Stole the world . . ." Razor repeated. His claws scratched against the rock. He shifted his tail slowly back and forth, his wings stirred restlessly. "So that is what she did."

"According to Skie, yes. So he told me."

"And why would he tell you, Silver?" Razor asked, sneering.

"Because I tried to save his life."

"He a blue dragon, your most hated enemy! And you tried to save his life!" Razor scoffed. "I am not some hatchling to swallow this kender tale."

Mirror couldn't see the Blue, but he could guess what he looked like. A veteran warrior, his blue scales would be shining clean, perhaps with a few scars of his prowess on his chest and head.

"My reasons for saving him were cold-blooded enough to satisfy even you," Mirror returned. "I came to Skie seeking answers to my questions. I could not let him die and take those answers to the grave with him. I used him. I admit it. I am not proud of myself, but at least, because of my aid, he managed to live long enough to strike a blow against Malys. For that, he thanked me."

The Blue was silent. Mirror could not tell what Razor was thinking. His claws scraped the rock, his wings brushed the blood-tainted air of the lair, his tail swished back and forth. Mirror had spells ready, should Razor decide to fight. The contest would not be equal—a seasoned, veteran Blue against a blind Silver. But at least, like Skie, Mirror would leave his mark upon his enemy.

"Takhisis stole the world." Razor spoke in thoughtful tones. "She brought us here. She is, as you say, responsible. Yet, she is our goddess as of old, and she fights to avenge us against our enemies."

"Her enemies," said Mirror coldly. "Else she would not bother."

"Tell me, Silver," Razor challenged, "what did you feel when you first heard her voice. Did you feel a stirring in your heart, in your soul? Did you feel nothing of this?"

"I felt it," Mirror admitted. "When I first heard the voice in the storm, I knew it to be the voice of a god, and I thrilled to hear it. The child whose father beats him will yet cling to that parent, not because he is a good or wise parent, but because he is the only parent the child knows. But then I began to ask questions, and my questions led me here."

"Questions," Razor said dismissively. "A good soldier never questions. He obeys."

"Then why haven't you joined her armies?" Mirror demanded. "Why are you here in Skie's lair, if not to ask questions of him?"

Razor had no response. Was he brooding, thinking things over or was he angry, planning to attack? Mirror couldn't tell, and he was suddenly tired of this conversation, tired and hungry. At the thought of food, his stomach rumbled.

"If we are going to battle," Mirror said, "I ask that we do it after I have eaten. I am famished, and unless I am mistaken, I smell fresh goat meat in the lair."

"I am not going to fight you," said Razor impatiently. "What honor is there in fighting a blind foe? The goat you seek is over to your left, about two talon-lengths away. My mate's skull is in one of those totems. Perhaps, if we had not been brought to this place, she would be alive today. Still," the Blue added moodily, slashing his tail, "Takhisis *is* my goddess."

Mirror had no help to offer the Blue. Mirror had solved his own crisis of faith. His had been relatively easy, for none of his kind had ever worshiped Takhisis. Their love and their loyalty belonged to Paladine, God of Light.

Was Paladine out there somewhere searching for his lost children? After the storm, the metallic dragons left to find the gods, or so Skie had said. They must have failed, for Takhisis remained unrivaled. Yet, Mirror believed, Paladine still exists. Somewhere the God of Light is looking for us. Takhisis shrouds us in darkness, hides us from his sight. Like castaways lost at sea, we must find a way to signal those who search the vast ocean that is the universe.

Mirror settled down to devour the goat. He did not offer to share. The Blue would be well fed, for he could see his prey. When Mirror walked the land in human form, he carried a begging bowl, lived off scraps. This was the first fresh meat he'd eaten in a long time and he meant to enjoy it. He had some notion now of what he could do, if he could only find the means to do it. First, though, he had to rid himself of this Blue, who appeared to think he had found a friend.

Blues are social dragons, and Razor was in no hurry to leave. He settled down to chat. He had seemed initially a dragon of few words, but now they poured out of him, as though he was relieved to be able to tell someone what was in his heart. He described the death of his mate, he spoke with sorrow and pride of Marshal Medan, he talked about a Dark Knight dragonrider named Gerard. Mirror listened with half his brain, the other half toying with an idea.

Fortunately, eating saved him from the necessity of replying beyond a grunt or two. By the time Mirror's hunger was assuaged, Razor had once more fallen silent. Mirror heard the dragon stir and hoped that finally the Blue was ready to leave.

Mirror was mistaken. Razor was merely shifting his bulk to obtain a more comfortable position.

If I can't get rid of him, Mirror decided dourly, I'll make use of him.

"What do you know of the dragon-skull totems?" Mirror asked cautiously.

"Enough." Razor growled. "As I said, my mate's skull adorns one of them. Why do you ask?"

"Skie said something about the totems. He said"—Mirror had to do some fancy mental shuffling to keep from revealing all Skie had said about the totems and the missing metallic dragons—"something about Takhisis having taken them over, subverted them to her own use."

"What does that mean? It's all very vague," Razor stated.

"Sorry, but he didn't say anything more. He sounded half crazy when he said it. He may have been raving."

"From what I have heard, one person alone knows the mind of Takhisis, and that is the girl Mina, the leader of the One God's armies. I have spoken to many dragons who have joined her. They say that this Mina is beloved of Takhisis and that she carries with her the goddess's blessing. If anyone knows the mystery of the totems, it would be Mina. Not that this means much to you, Silver."

"On the contrary," Mirror said thoughtfully, "it might mean more than you imagine. I knew Mina as a child."

Razor snorted, skeptical.

"I am Guardian of the Citadel, remember?" Mirror said. "She was a foundling of the Citadel. I knew her."

"Perhaps you did, but she would consider you her enemy now."

"So one would think," Mirror agreed. "But she came upon me only a few months ago. I was in human shape, blind, weak, and alone. She knew me then and spared my life. Perhaps she remembered our experiences together when she was a child. She was always asking questions—"

"She spared you out of sentimental weakness." Razor snorted. "Humans, even the best of them, all have this failing."

Mirror said nothing, carefully hid his smile. Here was a blue dragon who could grieve for his dead rider and still chide a human for being sentimentally attached to people from her youth.

"Still, in this instance, the failing could prove useful to us," Razor continued. He gave a refreshing shake, from his head to the tip of his tail, and flexed his wings. "Very well. We will confront this Mina, find out what is going on."

"Did you say 'we'?" Mirror asked, astounded. He truly thought he hadn't heard correctly, although the words "we" and "I" in the language of dragons are very distinct and easily distinguished.

"I said"—Razor lifted his voice, as though Mirror were deaf, as well as blind—"that we will go together to confront this Mina and demand to know our Queen's plans—"

"Impossible," said Mirror shortly. Whatever he himself planned, it did not involve partnering with a Blue. "You see my handicap."

"I see it," said Razor. "A grievous injury, yet it does not seem to have stopped you from doing what you needed to do. You came here, didn't you?"

Mirror couldn't very well deny that. "I travel on foot, slowly. I am forced to beg for food and shelter—"

"We don't have time for such nonsense. Begging! Of humans!" Razor shook his head so that his scales rattled. "I would think you would have much rather died of starvation. You must ride with me. Time is short. Momentous events are happening in the world. We don't have time to waste trudging along at a human's pace."

Mirror didn't know what to say. The idea of a blind silver dragon riding on the back of a Blue was so utterly ludicrous as to make him sorely tempted to laugh out loud.

"If you do not come with me," Razor added, seeing that Mirror was apparently having trouble making up his mind, "I will be forced to slay you. You speak very glibly about certain information Skie gave you, yet you are vague and evasive when it comes to the rest. I think Skie told you more than you are willing to admit to me. Therefore you will either come with me where I can keep an eye on you, or I will see to it that the information dies with you."

Mirror had never more bitterly regretted his blindness than at this moment. He supposed that the noble thing to do would be to defy the Blue and die in a brief and brutal battle. Such a death would be honorable, but not very sensible. Mirror was, so far as he knew, one of two beings on Krynn who were aware of the departure of his fellow gold and silver dragons, who had flown off on the wings of magic to find the gods, only to be trapped and imprisoned by the One God. Mina was the other being who knew this, and although Mirror did not think that she would tell him anything, he would never know for certain until he had spoken to her.

"You leave me little choice," said Mirror.

"Such was my intent," Razor replied, not smug, merely matter-of-fact.

Mirror altered his form, abandoning his strong, powerful dragon body for the weak, fragile body of a human. He took on the aspect of a young man with silver hair, wearing the white robes of a mystic of the Citadel. He wore a black cloth around his hideously injured eyes.

Moving slowly on his human feet, he groped about with his human hands. His shuffling footsteps stumbled over every rock in the lair. He slipped in Skie's blood and fell to his knees, cutting the weak flesh. Mirror was thankful for one blessing—he did not have to see the look of pity on Razor's face.

The Blue was a soldier, and he made no gibes at Mirror's expense. Razor even guided Mirror's steps with a steadying talon, assisted him to crawl upon the Blue's broad back.

The stench of death was strong in the lair where lay Skie's maltreated corpse. Both Blue and Silver were glad to leave. Perched on the ledge of the cavern, Razor drew in a breath of fresh air, spread his wings and took to the clouds. Mirror held on tightly to the Blue's mane, pressed his legs into Razor's flanks.

"Hold on," Razor warned. He soared high into the air, wheeled about in a huge arc. Mirror guessed what Razor planned and held on tightly, as he'd been ordered.

Mirror felt Razor's lungs expand, felt the expulsion of breath. He smelt the brimstone and heard the sizzle and crackle of lightning. A blast and the sound of rock splitting and shattering, then the sound of tons of rock sliding down the cliff face, rumbling and roaring amidst the thunder of the lightning bolt. Razor unleashed another blast, and this time it sounded to Mirror as if the entire mountain was falling into rubble.

"Thus passes Khellendros, known as Skie," said Razor. "He was a courageous warrior and loyal to his rider, as his rider was loyal to him. Let this might be said of all of us when it comes our time to depart this world."

His duty done to the dead, Razor dipped his wings in a final salute, then wheeled and headed off in a different direction. Mirror judged by the warmth of the sun on the back of his neck that they were flying east. He held fast to Razor's mane, feeling the rush of wind strong against his face. He envisioned the trees, red and gold with the coming of autumn, like jewels set against the green velvet cloth of the grasslands. He saw in his mind the purple-gray mountains, capped by the first snows of the seasons. Far below, the blue lakes and snaking rivers with the golden blot of a village, bringing in the autumn wheat, or the gray dot of a manor house with all its fields around it.

"Why do you weep, Silver?" Razor asked.

Mirror had no answer, and Razor, after a moment's thought, did not repeat the question.

6 THE STONE FORTRESS OF THE MIND

The Wilder elf known as the Lioness watched her husband with growing concern. Two weeks had passed since they had heard the terrible news of the Queen Mother's death and the destruction of the elven capital of Qualinost. Since that time, Gilthas, the Qualinesti's young king, had barely spoken a word to anyone—not to her, not to Planchet, not to the members of their escort. He slept by himself, covering himself in his blanket and rolling away from her when she tried to offer him the comfort of her presence. He ate by himself, what small amount he ate. His flesh seemed to melt from his bones, and he'd not had that much to spare. He rode by himself, silent, brooding.

His face was pale, set in grim, tight lines. He did not mourn. He had not wept since the night they'd first heard the dreadful tidings. When he spoke, it was only to ask a single question: how much farther until they reached the meeting place?

The Lioness feared that Gilthas might be slipping back into the old sickness that had plagued him during those early years of his enforced rulership of the Qualinesti people. King by title and prisoner by circumstance, he had fallen into a deep depression that left him lethargic and uncaring. He had often spent days sleeping in his bed, preferring the terrors of the dream world to those of reality. He had come out of it, fighting his way back from the dark waters in which he'd nearly drowned. He'd been a good king, using his power to aid the rebels, led by his wife, who fought the tyranny of the Dark Knights. All that he had gained seemed to have been lost, however. Lost with the news of his beloved mother's death and the destruction of the elven capital.

Planchet feared the same. His Majesty's bodyguard and valet-de-chamber, Planchet had been responsible, along with the Lioness, for luring Gilthas away from his nightmare world back to those who loved and needed him.

"He blames himself," said the Lioness, riding alongside Planchet, both gazing with concern on the lonely figure, who rode alone amidst his bodyguards, his eyes fixed unseeing on the road ahead. "He blames himself for leaving his mother there to die. He blames himself for the plan that ended up destroying the city and costing so many hundreds of lives. He cannot see that because of his plan Beryl is dead."

"But at a terrible cost," said Planchet. "He knows that his people can never return to Qualinost. Beryl may be dead, but her armies are not destroyed. True, many were lost, but according to the reports, those who remain continue to burn and ravage our beautiful land."

"What is burned can be restored. What is destroyed can be rebuilt. The Silvanesti went back to their homes to fight the dream," said the Lioness. "They took back their homeland. We can do the same."

"I'm not so sure," Planchet returned, his eyes fixed on his king. "The Silvanesti fought the dream, but look where it led them—to even greater fear of the outside world and an attempt to isolate themselves inside the shield. That proved disastrous."

"The Qualinesti have more sense," insisted the Lioness.

Planchet shook his head. Not wanting to argue with her, he let the subject drop. They rode several miles in silence, then Planchet said quietly, "You know what is truly wrong with Gilthas, don't you?"

The Lioness said nothing for long moments, then replied softly, "I think I do, yes."

"He blames himself for not being among the dead," said Planchet.

Her eyes filling with tears, the Lioness nodded.

Much as he now loathed this life, Gilthas was forced to live it. Not for his sake, for the sake of his people. Lately he began to wonder if that was reason enough to go on enduring this pain. He saw no hope for anyone, anywhere in this world. Only one thin strand tethered him to this life: the promise he had made to his mother. He had promised Laurana that he would lead the refugees, those who had managed to escape Qualinesti and who were waiting for him on the edges of the Plains of Dust. A promise made to the dead is a promise that must be fulfilled.

Still, they never rode past a river but he looked into it and imagined the peace he would find as the waters closed over his head.

Gilthas knew his wife grieved for him and worried about him. He knew or suspected that she was hurt that he had withdrawn from her, retreated to the stone-walled fortress in which he hid from the world. He would have liked to open the gates and let her come inside, but that required effort. He would have to leave the sheltered corner in which he'd taken refuge, advance into the sunlight, cross the courtyard of memory, unlock the gate to admit her sympathy, a sympathy he did not deserve. He couldn't bear it. Not yet. Maybe not ever.

Gilthas blamed himself. His plan had proven disastrous. His plan had brought destruction to Qualinesti and its defenders. His plan had caused his mother's death. He shrank from facing the refugees. They would think him a murderer—and rightly so. They would think him a coward—and rightly so. He had run away and left his people to die. Perhaps they would accuse him of having deliberately plotted the Qualinesti's downfall. He was part human, after all. In his depression, nothing was too outrageous or fantastic for him to believe.

He toyed with the idea of sending an intermediary, of avoiding facing the refugees directly.

"How very like the coward you are," Gilthas said to himself with a sneer. "Shirk that responsibility, as you've shirked others."

He would face them. He would suffer their anger and pain in silence as his due. He would relinquish the throne, would hand over everything to the Senate. They could choose another ruler. He would return to the Lake of Death, where lay the bodies of his mother and his people, and the pain would end.

Thus were the dark thoughts of the young elven king as he rode, day after day, by himself. He looked straight ahead toward a single destination—the gathering place for the refugees of Qualinost, those who had, through the gallant efforts of the dwarves of Thorbardin, escaped through tunnels that the dwarves had dug deep beneath the elven lands. There to do what he had to do. He would fulfill his promise, then he would be free to leave . . . forever.

Sunk in these musings, he heard his wife's voice speak his name.

The Lioness had two voices—one her wifely voice, as Gilthas termed it, and the other her military commander voice. She made the shift unconsciously, not aware of the difference until Gilthas had pointed it out to her long ago. The wife's voice was gentle and loving. The commander's voice could have cut down small trees, or so he teasingly claimed.

He closed his ears to the gentle and loving wife's voice, for he did not feel he deserved love, anyone's love. But he was king, and he could not shut out the voice of the military commander. He knew by the sound she brought bad news.

"Yes, what is it?" he said, turning to face her, steeling himself.

"I have received a report . . . several reports." The Lioness paused, drew in a deep breath. She dreaded telling him this, but she had no choice. He was king. "The armies of Beryl that we thought were scattered and destroyed have regrouped and reformed. We did not think this was possible, but it seems they have a new leader, a man named Samuval. He is a Dark Knight, and he follows a new Lord of the Night, a human girl called Mina."

Gilthas gazed at his wife in silence. Some part of him heard and understood and absorbed the information. Another part crawled farther into the dark corner of his prison cell.

"This Samuval claims he serves a god known as the One God. The message he brings his soldiers is this: The One God has wrenched Qualinesti from the elves and means to give it back to the humans, to whom this land rightly belongs. Now, all who want free land have only to sign on to serve with this Captain Samuval. His army is immense, as you can imagine. Every derelict and ne'er-do-well in the human race is eager to claim his share of our beautiful land. They are on the march, Gilthas," the Lioness said in conclusion. "They are well armed and well supplied and moving swiftly to seize and secure Qualinesti. We don't have much time. We have to warn our people."

"And then do what?" he asked.

The Lioness didn't recognize his voice. It sounded muffled, as if he were speaking from behind a closed door.

"We follow our original plan," she said. "We march through the Plains of Dust to Silvanesti. Only, we must move faster than we had anticipated. I will send riders on ahead to alert the refugees—"

"No," said Gilthas. "I must be the one to tell them. I will ride day and night if need be."

"My husband . . ." The Lioness shifted to the wife voice, gentle, loving. "Your health—"

He cast her a look that silenced the words on her lips, then turned and spurred his horse. His sudden departure took his bodyguard by surprise. They were forced to race their horses to catch up with him.

Sighing deeply, the Lioness followed.

The place Gilthas had chosen for the gathering of the elven refugees was located on the coast of New Sea, close enough to Thorbardin so that the dwarves could assist in the defense of the refugees, if they were attacked, but not near enough to make the dwarves nervous. The dwarves knew in their heads that the forest-loving elves would never think of living in the mighty underground fortress of Thorbardin, but in their hearts the dwarves were certain that everyone on Ansalon must secretly envy them their stronghold and would claim Thorbardin for themselves, if they could.

The elves had also to be careful not to draw the ire of the great dragon Onysablet, who had taken over what had once been New Coast. The land was now known as New Swamp, for she had used her foul magicks to alter the landscape into a treacherous bog. To avoid traveling through her territory, Gilthas was going to attempt to cross the Plains of Dust. A vast no-man's land, the plains were inhabited by tribes of barbarians, who lived in the desert and kept to themselves, taking no interest in the world outside their borders, a world that took very little interest in them.

Slowly, over several weeks, the refugees straggled into the meeting place. Some traveled in groups, streaming through the tunnels built by the dwarves and their giant dirt-devouring worms. Others came singly or by twos, escaping through the forests with the help of the Lioness's rebel forces. They left behind their homes, their possessions, their farmland, their crops, their lush forests and fragrant gardens, their beautiful city of Qualinost with its gleaming Tower of the Sun.

The elves were confident they would be able to return to their beloved homeland. The Qualinesti had always owned this land, or so it seemed to them. Looking back throughout history, they could not find a time when they had not claimed this land. Even after the elven kingdoms had split in twain following the bitter Kinslayer Wars, creating the two great elven nations,

Qualinesti and Silvanesti, the Qualinesti continued to rule and inhabit land that had already been theirs.

This uprooting was temporary. Many among them still remembered how they had been forced to flee their homeland during the War of the Lance. They had survived that and returned to make their homes stronger than before. Human armies might come and go. Dragons might come and go, but the Qualinesti nation would remain. The choking smoke of burning would soon be blown away. The green shoots would shove up from underneath the black ash. They would rebuild, replant. They had done it before, they would do it again.

So confident were the elves of this, so confident were they in the defenders of their beautiful city of Qualinost, that the mood in the refugee camps, which had been dark at first, became almost merry.

True, there were losses to mourn, for Beryl had taken delight in slaughtering any elves she caught out in the open. Some of the refugees had been killed by the dragon. Others had run afoul of rampaging humans or been caught by the Dark Knights of Neraka and beaten and tortured. But the numbers of dead were surprisingly few, considering that the elves had been facing destruction and annihilation. Through the planning of their young king and the help of the dwarven nation, the Qualinesti had survived. They began to look toward the future and that future was in Qualinesti. They could not picture anything else.

The wise among the elves remained worried and troubled, for they could see certain signs that all was not well. Why had they not heard any news from the defenders of Qualinesti? Wildrunners had been stationed in the city, ready to speed swiftly to the refugee camps. They should have been here by now with either good news or bad. The fact that they had not come at all was deeply disturbing to some, shrugged off by others.

"No news is good news," was how the humans put it, or "No explosion is a step in the right direction," as the gnomes would say.

The elves pitched their tents on the sandy beaches of New Sea. Their children played in the gently lapping waters and made castles in the sand. At night they built fires of driftwood, watching the ever-changing colors of the flames and telling stories of other times the elves had been forced to flee their homeland—stories that always had a happy ending.

The weather had been beautiful, with unusually warm days for this late in the year. The seawater was the deep, blue-black color that is seen only in the autumn months and presages the coming of the winter storms. The trees were heavily laden with their harvest gifts, and food was plentiful. The elves found streams of fresh water for drinking and bathing. Elven soldiers stood guard over the people by day and by night, dwarven soldiers watched from the forests, keeping one eye alert for invading armies and one eye on the elves. The refugees waited for Gilthas, waited for him to come tell them that the dragon was defeated, that they could all go home.

"Sire," said one of the elven body guards, riding up to Gilthas, "you asked me to tell you when we were within a few hours' ride of the refugee camp. The campsite is up ahead." The elf pointed. "Beyond those foothills."

"Then we will stop here," said Gilthas, reigning in his horse. He glanced up at the sky, where the pale sun shone almost directly overhead. "We will ride again when dusk falls."

"Why do we halt, my husband?" the Lioness asked, cantering up in time to hear Gilthas give his instructions. "We have nearly broken our necks to reach our people, and, now that we are near, we stop?"

"The news I have to tell should be told only in darkness," he said, dismounting, not looking at her. "The light of neither sun nor moon will shine on our grief. I resent even the cold light of the stars. I would pry them from the skies, if I could."

"Gilthas—" she began, but he turned his face from her and walked away, vanishing into the woods.

At a sign from the Lioness, his guard accompanied him, maintaining a discreet distance, yet close enough to protect him.

"I am losing him, Planchet," she said, her voice aching with pain and sorrow, "and I don't know what to do, how to reclaim him."

"Keep loving him," Planchet advised. "That is all you can do. The rest he must do himself."

Gilthas and his retinue entered the elven refugee encampment in the early hours of darkness. Fires burned on the beach. Elven children were sprightly shadows dancing amidst the flames. To them, this was a holiday, a grand adventure. The nights spent in the dark tunnels with the gruff-voiced and fearsome looking dwarves were now distant memories. School lessons were suspended, their daily chores remitted. Gilthas watched them dance and thought of what he must tell them. The holiday would end this night. In the morning, they would begin a bitter struggle, a struggle for their very lives.

How many of these children who danced so gaily around the fire would be lost to the desert, succumbing to the heat and the lack of water, or falling prey to the evil creatures reputed to roam the Plains of Dust? How many more of his people would die? Would they survive as a race at all, or would this be forever known as the last march of the Qualinesti?

He entered the camp on foot without fanfare. Those who saw him as he passed were startled to see their king—those who recognized him as their king. Gilthas was so altered that many did not know him.

Thin and gaunt, pale and wan, Gilthas had lost almost any trace of his human heritage. His delicate elven bone-structure was more visible, more pronounced. He was, some whispered in awe, the very image of the great elven kings of antiquity, of Silvanos and Kith-Kanan.

He walked through the camp, heading for the center, where blazed a large bonfire. His retinue stayed behind, at a command from the Lioness. What Gilthas had to say, he had to say alone.

At the sight of his face, the elves silenced their laughter, ceased their story-telling, halted the dancing, and hushed their children. As word spread that the king had come among them, silent and alone, the elves gathered around him. The leaders of the Senate came hastily to greet him, clucking to themselves in irritation that he had robbed them of a chance to welcome him with proper ceremony. When they saw his face—deathlike in the firelight—they ceased their cluckings, forgot their welcoming speeches, and waited with dire foreboding to hear his words.

Against the music of the waves, rolling in one after the other, chasing each other to shore and falling back, Gilthas told the story of the downfall of Qualinesti. He told it clearly, calmly, dispassionately. He spoke of the death of his mother. He spoke of the heroism of the city's defenders. He lauded the heroism of the dwarves and humans who had died defending a land and a people not their own. He spoke of the death of the dragon.

The elves wept for their Queen Mother and for loved ones now surely dead. Their tears slid silently down their faces. They did not sob aloud lest they miss hearing what came next.

What came next was dreadful.

Gilthas spoke of the armies under this new leader. He spoke of a new god, who claimed credit for ousting the elves from their homeland and who was handing that land over to humans, already pouring into Qualinesti from the north. Hearing of the refugees, the army was moving rapidly to try to catch them and destroy them.

He told them that their only hope was to try to reach Silvanesti. The shield had fallen. Their cousins would welcome them to their land. To reach Silvanesti, however, the elves would have to march through the Plains of Dust.

"For now," Gilthas was forced to tell them, "there will be no homecoming. Perhaps, with the help of our cousins, we can form an army that will be powerful enough to sweep into our beloved land and drive the enemy from it, take back what they have stolen. But although that must be our hope, that hope is far in the future. Our first thought must be the survival of our race. The road we walk will be a hard one. We must walk that road together with one goal and one purpose in our hearts. If one of us falls out, all will perish.

"I was made your king by trickery and treachery. You know the truth of that by now. The story has been whispered among you for years. The Puppet King, you called me."

He cast a glance at Prefect Palthainon as he spoke. The prefect's face was set in a sorrowful mask, but his eyes darted this way and that, trying to see how the people were reacting.

"It would have been best if I had remained in that role," Gilthas continued, looking away from the senator and back to his people. "I tried to be your ruler, and I failed. It was my plan that destroyed Qualinesti, my plan that left our land open to invasion."

He raised his hand for silence, for the elves had begun to murmur among themselves.

"You need a strong king," Gilthas said, raising his voice that was growing hoarse from shouting. "A ruler who has the courage and the wisdom to lead you into peril and see you safely through it. I am not that person. As of now, I abdicate the throne and renounce all my rights and claims to it. I leave the succession in the hands of the Senate. I thank you for all the kindness and love that you have shown me over the years. I wish I had done better by you. I wish I was more deserving."

He wanted to leave, but the people had pressed close about him and, much as he needed to escape, he did not want to force a path through the crowd. He was forced to wait to hear what the Senate had to say. He kept his head lowered, did not look into the faces of his people, not wanting to see their hostility, their anger, their blame. He stood waiting until he was dismissed.

The elves had been shocked into silence. Too much had happened too suddenly to absorb. A lake of death where once stood their city. An enemy army behind them, a perilous journey to an uncertain future ahead of them. The king abdicating. The senators thrown into confusion. Dismayed and appalled, they stared at each other, waited for someone to speak the first word.

That word belonged to Palthainon. Cunning and conniving, he saw this disaster as a means to further his own ambition. Ordering some elves to drag up a large log, he mounted it and, clapping his hands, called the elves loudly to silence, a command that was completely unnecessary, for not even a baby's cry broke the hushed stillness.

"I know what you are feeling, my brethren," the prefect stated in sonorous tones. "I, too, am shocked and grieved to hear of the tragedy that has befallen our people. Do not be fearful. You are in good hands. I will take over the reins of leadership until such time as a new king is named."

Palthainon pointed his bony finger at Gilthas. "It is right that this young man has stepped down, for he brought this tragedy upon us—he and those who pulled his strings. Puppet King. Yes, that best describes him. Once Gilthas allowed himself to be guided by my wisdom and experience. He came to me for advice, and I was proud and happy to provide it. But there were those of his own family who worked against me. I do not name them, for it is wrong to speak ill of the dead, even though they sought continuously to reduce my influence."

Palthainon warmed to his topic. "Among those who pulled the puppet's strings was the hated and detested Marshal Medan—the true engineer of our destruction, for he seduced the son as he seduced the mother—"

Rage—white-hot—struck the fortress prison in which Gilthas had locked himself, struck it like the fiery bolt of a blue dragon. Leaping upon the log on which Palthainon stood, Gilthas hit the elf a blow on the jaw that sent him reeling. The prefect landed on his backside in the sand, his fine speech knocked clean out of his head.

Gilthas said nothing. He did not look around. He jumped off the log and started to shove his way through the crowd.

Palthainon sat up. Shaking his muzzy head, he spat out a tooth and started to sputter and point. "There! There! Did you see what he did! Arrest him! Arrest—"

"Gilthas," spoke a voice out of the crowd.

"Gilthas," spoke another voice and another and another.

They did not chant. They did not thunder his name. Each elf spoke his name calmly, quietly, as if being asked a question and giving an answer. But the name was repeated over and over throughout the crowd, so that it carried with it the quiet force of the waves breaking on the shore. The elderly spoke his name, the young spoke his name. Two senators spoke it as they assisted Palthainon to his feet.

Astonished and bewildered, Gilthas raised his head, looked around.

"You don't understand—" he began.

"We do understand," said one of the elves. His face was drawn, marked with traces of recent grief. "So do you, Your Majesty. You understand our pain and our heartache. That is why you are our king."

"That is why you have always been our king," said another, a woman, holding a baby in her arms. "Our true king. We know of the work you have done in secret for us."

"If not for you, Beryl would be wallowing in our beautiful city," said a third. "We would be dead, those of us who stand here before you."

"Our enemies have triumphed for the moment," said yet another, "but so long as we keep fast the memory of our loved nation, that nation will never perish. Some day, we will return to claim it. On that day, you will lead us, Your Majesty."

Gilthas could not speak. He looked at his people who shared his loss, and he was ashamed and chastened and humbled. He did not feel he had earned their regard—not yet. But he would try. He would spend the rest of his life trying.

Prefect Palthainon spluttered and huffed and tried to make himself heard, but no one paid any attention to him. The other senators crowded around Gilthas.

Palthainon glared at them grimly, then, seizing hold of the arm of an elf, he whispered softly, "The plan to defeat Beryl was my plan all along. Of course, I allowed His Majesty to take credit for it. As for this little dust-up between us, it was all just a misunderstanding, such as often happens between father and son. For he is like a son to me, dear to my heart."

The Lioness remained on the outskirts of the camp, her own heart too full to see or speak to him. She knew he would seek her out. Lying on the pallet she spread for both of them, on the edge of the water, near the sea, she heard his footsteps in the sand, felt his hand brush her cheek.

She put her arm around him, drew him beside her.

"Can you forgive me, beloved?" he asked, lying down with a sigh.

"Isn't that the definition of being a wife?" she asked him, smiling.

Gilthas made no answer. His eyes were closed. He was already fast asleep.

The Lioness drew the blanket over him, rested her head on his chest, listened to his beating heart until she, too, slept.

The sun would rise early, and it would rise blood red.

7 AN UNEXPECTED JOURNEY

Following the activation of the Device of Time Journeying, Tasslehoff Burrfoot was aware of two things: impenetrable darkness and Conundrum shrieking in his left ear, all the while clutching his (Tasslehoff's) left hand so tightly that he completely lost all sense of feeling in his fingers and his thumb. The rest of Tas could feel nothing either, nothing under him, nothing over him, nothing next to him—except Conundrum. Tas couldn't tell if he was on his head or his heels or an interesting combination of both.

This entertaining state of affairs lasted an extremely long time, so long that Tas began to get a bit bored by it all. A person can stare into impenetrable darkness only so long before he thinks he might like a change. Even tumbling about in time and space (if that's what they were doing, Tas wasn't at all sure at this point) grows old after you've been doing it a long while. Eventually you decide that being stepped on by a giant is preferable to having a gnome shrieking continuously in your ear (remarkable lung capacity, gnomes) and nearly pinching your hand off at the wrist.

This state of affairs continued for a good long while until Tasslehoff and Conundrum slammed down, bump, into something that was soft and squishy and smelled strongly of mud and pine needles. The fall was not a gentle one and knocked the boredom out of the kender and the shrieks out of the gnome.

Tasslehoff lay on his back, making gasping attempts to catch what would probably be the last few breaths he would ever take. He looked up, expecting to see Chaos's enormous foot poised above him. Tas had just a few seconds in which to explain matters to Conundrum, who was about to be inadvertently squished.

"We're going to die a hero's death," said Tasslehoff with his first mouthful of air.

"What?" Conundrum shrieked with his first mouthful of air.

"We're going to die a hero's death," Tasslehoff repeated.

Then he suddenly realized that they weren't.

Absorbed in preparing both himself and the gnome for an imminent demise, Tasslehoff had not taken a close look at their surroundings. He assumed that all he would be seeing was the ugly underside of Chaos's foot. Now that he had time to notice, he saw above him not a foot, but the dripping needles of a pine tree in a rain storm.

Tasslehoff felt his head to see if he had received a severe bump, for he knew from past experience that severe bumps to the head can cause you to see the most remarkable things, although those were generally starbursts, not dripping pine needles. He could find no signs of a bump, however.

Hearing Conundrum drawing in another large breath, undoubtedly preparatory to letting loose another ear-piercing shriek, Tasslehoff raised his hand in a commanding gesture.

"Hush," he whispered tensely, "I thought I heard something."

Now, if truth be told, Tasslehoff had not heard something. Well, he had. He'd heard the rain falling off the pine needles, but he hadn't heard anything dire, which is what his tone implied. He'd only pretended that in order to shut off the gnome's shrieks. Unfortunately, as is often the way with transgressors, he was immediately punished for his sin, for the moment he pretended to hear something dire, he *did* hear something dire—the clash of steel on steel, followed by a crackling blast.

In Tas's experience as a hero, only two things made sounds like that: swords beating against swords and fireballs exploding against just about anything.

The next thing he heard was more shrieking, only this time it was not, blessedly, Conundrum. The shrieking was some distance away and had the distinct sound of dying goblin to it, a notion that was reinforced by the sickening smell of burnt goblin hair. The shrieking ended summarily, then came a crashing, as of large bodies running through a forest of dripping wet pine needles. Thinking these might be more goblins and realizing that this was an inopportune time to be running into goblins, especially those who have just been fireball-blasted, Tasslehoff squirmed his way on his belly underneath a sheltering, low-hanging pine bough and dragged Conundrum in after him.

"Where are we?" Conundrum demanded, lifting up his head out of the mud in which they were lying. "How did we get here? When are we going back?"

All perfectly sound, logical questions. Trust a gnome, thought Tas, to go right to the heart of the matter.

"I'm sorry," said Tas, peering out through the wet pine needles, trying to see what was going on. The crashing sounds were growing louder, which meant they were coming closer. "But I don't know. Any of it."

Conundrum gaped. His chin fell so far it came back up with mud on it. "What do you mean you don't know?" he gasped, swelling with indignation. "You brought us here."

"No," said Tas with dignity, "I didn't. *This* brought us here." He indicated the Device of Time Journeying that he was holding in his hand. "When it wasn't supposed to."

Seeing Conundrum sucking in another huge breath, Tas fixed the gnome with a withering stare. "So I guess you didn't fix it, after all."

The breath wheezed out of Conundrum. He stared at the device, muttered something about missing schematics and lack of internal directives, and held out his mud-covered hand. "Give it to me. I'll take a look at it."

"No, thank you," said Tasslehoff, shoving the device into a pouch and closing the flap. "I think I should hold onto it. Now hush!" Turning back to stare out from under the pine bough, Tas put his fingers to his lips. "Don't let on we're here."

Contrary to most gnomes, who never see anything outside of the inside of Mount Nevermind, Conundrum was a well-traveled gnome who'd had his share of adventures, most of which he hadn't enjoyed in the slightest. Nasty, bothersome things, adventures. Interrupted a fellow's work. But he had learned an important lesson—the best way to survive adventures was to lie hidden in some dark and uncomfortable place and keep your mouth shut. This he was good at doing.

Conundrum was so good at hiding that when Tasslehoff, who was not at all good at this sort of thing, started to get up with a glad and joyful cry to go to meet two humans who had just run out of the forest, the gnome grabbed hold of the kender with a strength borne of terror and dragged him back down.

"What in the name of all that's combustible do you think you're doing?" Conundrum gasped.

"They're not burnt goblins, like I first thought," Tas argued, pointing. "That man is a Solamnic Knight. I can tell by his armor. And the other man is a mage. I can tell by his robes. I'm just going to go say hello and introduce myself."

"If there is one thing that I have learned in my travels," said Conundrum in a smothered whisper, "it is that you never introduce yourself to anyone carrying a sword or wearing wizard's robes. Let them go their way, and you go your way."

"Did you say something?" said the strange mage, turning to his companion.

"No," said the Knight, raising his sword and looking keenly about.

"Well, somebody did," said the mage grimly. "I distinctly heard voices."

"I can't hear anything for the sound of my own heart beating." The Knight paused, listening, then shook his head. "No, I can't hear a thing. What did it sound like? Goblins?"

"No," the mage said, peering into the shadows.

The man was a Solamnic by his looks, for he had long, blond hair that he wore braided to keep out of his way. His eyes were blue, keen, and intense. He wore robes that might have started out red but were now so stained with mud, charred with smoke, and smeared with blood that their color was indistinguishable in the gray light of the rainy day. A glint of golden trim could be seen at the cuffs and on the hem.

"Look at that!" gasped Tasslehoff, agog with amazement, "He's carrying Raistlin's staff!"

"Oddly enough," the mage was saying, "it sounded like a kender."

Tasslehoff clapped his hand over his mouth. Conundrum shook his head bleakly.

"What would a kender be doing here in the middle of a battle field?" asked the Knight with a smile.

"What does a kender do anywhere?" the mage returned archly, "except cause trouble for those who have the misfortune to encounter him."

"How true," sighed Conundrum gloomily.

"How rude," muttered Tasslehoff. "Maybe I won't go introduce myself to them, after all."

"So long as it was not goblins you heard," the Knight said. He cast a glance over his shoulder. "Do you think we've stopped them?"

The Knight wore the armor of a Knight of the Crown. Tas had first taken him to be an older man, for the Knight's hair had gone quite gray, but after watching him awhile, Tas realized that the Knight was far younger than he appeared at first glance. It was his eyes that made him look older—they had a sadness about them and a weariness that should not have been seen in one so young.

"We've stopped them for the time being," the mage said. Sinking down at the foot of the tree, he cradled the staff protectively in his arms.

The staff was Raistlin's, all right. Tasslehoff knew that staff well, with its crystal ball clutched in the golden dragon's claw. He remembered the many times he'd reached out to touch it, only to have his hand smacked.

"And many times I've seen Raistlin hold the staff just like that," Tas said softly to himself. "Yet that mage is most certainly *not* Raistlin. Maybe he's stolen Raistlin's staff. If so, Raistlin will want to know who the thief is."

Tas listened with all his ears, as the old kender saying went.

"Our enemy now has a healthy fear of your sword and my magic," the mage was saying. "Unfortunately, goblins have an even healthier fear of their own commanders. The whip will soon convince them to come after us."

"It will take them time to regroup." The Knight squatted down beneath the tree. Picking up a handful of wet pine needles, he began to clean the blood off his sword. "Time enough for us to rest, then try to find our way back to our company. Or time for them to find us. They are undoubtedly out searching for us even now."

"Searching for *you*, Huma," said the mage with a wry smile. He leaned back against the tree and wearily closed his eyes. "They will not be looking very hard for me."

The Knight appeared disturbed by this. His expression grave, he concentrated on his cleaning, rubbing hard at a stubborn speck. "You have to understand them, Magius—" he began.

"Huma . . ." Tas repeated. "Magius . . ." He stared at the two, blinked in wonder. Then he stared down at the Device of Time Journeying. "Do you suppose . . . ?"

"I understand them quite well, Huma," Magius returned. "The average Solamnic Knight is an ignorant, superstitious dolt, who believes all the dark tales about wizards told to him by his nursery maid in order to frighten him into keeping quiet at night, in consequence of which he expects me to start leaping through camp naked, gibbering and ranting and transforming him into a newt with a wave of my staff. Not that I couldn't do it, mind you," Magius continued with a quirk of his brow and the twist of an infectious smile. "And don't think I haven't considered it. Spending five minutes as a newt would be an interesting change for most of them. Expand their minds, if nothing else."

"I don't think I'd much care for life as a newt," said Huma.

"You, alone, are different, my friend," Magius said, his tone softening. Reaching out his hand, he rested it on the Knight's wrist. "You are not afraid of new ideas. You are not afraid of that which you do not understand. Even as a child, you did not fear to be my friend."

"You will teach them to think better of wizards, Magius," said Huma, resting his hand over his friend's. "You will teach them to view magic and those who wield it with respect."

"*I* will not," said Magius coolly, "for I really have no care what they think of me. If anyone can change their obsolete, outdated and outmoded views, you are the one to do it. And you had best do it quickly, Huma," he added, his mocking tone now serious. "The Dark Queen's power grows daily. She is raising vast armies. Countless thousands of evil creatures flock to her standard. These goblins would never before have dared to attack a company of Knights, but you saw with what ferocity they struck us this morning. I begin to think that it is not the whip they fear, but the wrath of the Dark Queen should they fail."

"Yet she will fail. She must fail, Magius," said Huma. "She and her evil dragons must be driven from the world, sent back to the Abyss. For if she is not defeated, we will live as do these wretched goblins, live our lives in fear." Huma sighed, shook his head. "Although, I admit to you, dear friend, I do not see how that is possible. The numbers of her minions are countless, their power immense—"

"But you do defeat her!" Tasslehoff cried, unable to restrain himself any longer. Freeing himself from Conundrum's frantic grasp, Tas scrambled to his feet and burst out from underneath the pine trees.

Huma jumped up, drawing his sword in one, swift movement. Magius extended the staff with the crystal held fast in the dragon's claw, aimed the staff at the kender, and began to speak words that Tas recognized by their spidery sound as being words of magic.

Knowing that perhaps he didn't have much time before *he* was turned into a newt, Tasslehoff accelerated his conversation.

"You raise an army of heroes, and you fight the Queen of Darkness herself, and while you die, Huma, and you die, too, Magius—I'm really very sorry about that, by the way—you do send all the evil dragons back to— ulp"

Several things happened simultaneously with that "ulp." Two large, hairy, and foul-smelling goblin hands grabbed hold Conundrum, while another yellow-skinned, slavering-jawed goblin seized hold of Tasslehoff.

Before the kender had time to draw his blade, before Conundrum had time to draw his breath, a blazing arc of lightning flared from the staff and struck the goblin who had hold of Conundrum. Huma ran his sword through the goblin trying to drag off Tas.

"There are more goblins coming," said Huma grimly. "You had best take to your heels, Kender."

Flapping goblin feet could be heard crashing through the trees, their guttural voices raised in hideous howls, promising death. Huma and Magius stood back to back, Huma with his sword drawn, Magius wielding his staff.

"Don't worry!" Tasslehoff cried. "I have my knife. It's called Rabbit-slayer." Opening a pouch, he began searching among his things. "Caramon named it. You don't know him—"

"Are you mad?" Conundrum screamed, sounding like the noon whistle at Mount Nevermind, a whistle that never, on any account, goes off at noon.

A hand touched Tasslehoff on the shoulder. A voice in his ear whispered, "Not now. It is not yet time."

"I beg your pardon?" Tasslehoff turned to see who was talking.

And kept turning. And turning.

Then he was still, and the world was turning, and it was all a mass of swirling color, and he didn't know if he was on his head or his heels, and Conundrum was at his side, shrieking, and then it was all very, very dark.

In the midst of the darkness and the turning and the shrieking, Tasslehoff had one thought, one important thought, a thought so important that he made sure to hang onto it with all his brain.

"I found the past. . . ."

8 THE COMING OF THE GOD

Rain fell on the Solamnic plains. The rain had been falling without letup since the Knights' crushing defeat by Mina's force at the city of Solanthus. Following the loss of the city, Mina had warned the surviving Knights that she meant next to take the city of Sanction. She had also told them to think on the power of the One God, who was responsible for the Solamnics' defeat. This done, she had bidden them ride off in safety, to spread the word of the One God.

The Knights didn't have much choice but to glumly obey the command of their conqueror. They rode for days through the rain, heading for Lord Ulrich's manor house, located about fifty miles east of Solanthus. The rain was chill and soaked everything. The Knights and what remained of their meager force were wet through, coated with mud, and shivering from the cold. The wounded they brought with them soon grew feverish, and many of them died.

Lord Nigel, Knight of the Crown, was one of the dead. He was buried beneath a rock cairn, in the hopes that at some future date his relatives would be able to remove the body and give him proper burial in his family's vault. As Gerard helped place the heavy stones over the corpse, he couldn't help but wonder if Lord Nigel's soul had gone to join the army that had defeated the Solamnic Knights—the army of the dead. In life, Lord Nigel would have shed his last drop of blood before he betrayed the Knighthood. In death, he might become their enemy.

Gerard had seen the souls of other Solamnic Knights drifting on the fearful tide of the river of souls. He guessed that the dead had no choice, they were conscripts, constrained to serve. But who or what did they serve? The girl, Mina? Or someone or something more powerful?

Lord Ulrich's manor house was constructed along simple lines. Built of stone quarried from the land on which the house stood, it was solid, massive, with square towers and thick walls. Lord Ulrich had sent his squire ahead to warn his lady wife of their coming, and there were roaring fires, fresh rushes on the floors, hot bread and mulled wine waiting for them on their arrival. The Knights ate and drank, warmed themselves and dried out their clothes. Then they met in council to try to determine what to do next.

Their first move was obvious—they sent messengers riding in haste to Sanction to warn the city that the Knights of Neraka had taken Solanthus and that they were threatening to march next on Sanction. Before the loss of Solanthus, the Knights would have scoffed at this notion. The Dark Knights of Neraka had been laying siege to Sanction for months without any success. Solamnic Knights insured that the port remained open and that supplies flowed into the city, so that while the besieged citizens didn't live well, they didn't starve either. The Solamnics had once almost broken the siege, but had been driven back by strange mischance. The siege continued, the balance held, neither side making any headway against the other.

But that had been before Solanthus had fallen to an army of dead souls, living dragons, a girl called Mina, and the One God.

These all figured large in the discussions and arguments that rang throughout the great hall of the manor house. A large, rectangular room, the hall had walls of gray stone covered with a few splendid tapestries depicting scenes illustrative of texts from the Measure. Thick, beeswax candles filled the hall with light. There were not enough chairs, so the Knights stood gathered around their leaders, who sat behind a large, ornately carved wooden table.

Every Knight was permitted his say. Lord Tasgall, Lord of the Rose and head of the Knights' Council, listened to them all in patient silence—including Odila, whose say was extremely uncomfortable to hear.

"We were defeated by a god," she told them, as they shifted and muttered and glanced askance at each other. "What other power on Krynn could hurl the souls of the dead against us?"

"Necromancers," suggested Lord Ulrich.

"Necromancers raise the bodies of the dead," Odila stated. "They drag skeletons from the ground to fight against the living. They have never had power over the souls of the dead."

The other Knights were glum, bedraggled, dour. They looked and felt defeated. By contrast, Odila was invigorated, exalted. Her wet, black hair gleamed in the firelight, her eyes sparked as she spoke of the god.

"What of death knights such as Lord Soth?" Lord Ulrich argued. The pudgy Lord Ulrich had lost considerable weight during the long, dispirited journey. Loose skin sagged around his mouth. His usually cheerful face was solemn, his bright eyes shadowed.

"You prove my point, my lord," Odila replied coolly. "Soth was cursed by the gods. Only a god has such power. And this god is powerful."

She raised her voice to be heard among the angry cries and denunciations. "You have seen that for yourself! What other force could create legions of souls and claim the loyalty of the dragons. You saw them! You saw them on the walls of Solanthus—red and white, black and green and blue. They were not there in the service of Beryl. They were not there in the service of Malys or any other of the dragon overlords. They were there in the service of Mina. And Mina is there in the service of the One God."

Odila's words were drowned out by jeers and boos, but that meant only that she'd struck a weak point in their armor. None could deny a word she said.

Lord Tasgall, the elder Knight, graying, upright, stern of bearing and countenance, shouted repeatedly for order and banged his sword hilt upon the table. Eventually order was restored. He looked at Odila, who remained standing, her head with its two thick, black braids thrown back in defiance, her face flushed.

"What is your proposal—" he began, and when one of the Knights hissed, the Lord Knight silenced him with a withering glance.

"We are a people of faith," said Odila. "We have always been people of faith. I believe that this god is trying to speak to us and that we should listen—"

The Knights thundered in anger, many shaking their fists.

"A god who brings death!" cried one, who had lost his brother in the battle.

"What of the old gods?" Odila shouted back. "*They* dropped a fiery mountain on Krynn!"

Some of the Knights were silenced by this, had no argument. Others continued to rant and rage.

"Many Solamnics lost their faith after the Cataclysm," Odila continued. "They claimed that the gods had abandoned us. Then we came to find out during the War of the Lance that we were the ones who had abandoned the gods. And after the Chaos War, when we woke to find the gods missing, we cried out again that they had left us. Perhaps again that is not the case. Perhaps this Mina is a second Goldmoon, coming to bring us the truth. How do we know until we investigate? Ask questions?"

How, indeed? Gerard asked himself, the seeds of a plan starting to take root in his mind. He couldn't help but admire Odila, even as he wanted to grab her by the shoulders and shake her until her teeth rattled. She alone had the courage to say aloud what needed to be said. Too bad she lacked the tact to say it in such a way that didn't start fistfights.

The hall erupted into chaos with people arguing for and against and Lord Tasgall banging his sword hilt with such force that chips flew from the wooden table. The wrangling continued far into the night, and eventually two resolutions were presented for consideration. A small but vocal group wanted to ride to Ergoth, where the Knights still held firm, there to lick their wounds and build up their strength. This plan was favored by many until someone sourly pointed out that if Sanction fell they might build up their strength from now until the end of forever and they wouldn't be strong enough to retake all that they had lost.

The other resolution urged the Knights to march to Sanction, there to reinforce the Knights already defending that disputed city. But, argued the minority, how do we even know they mean to go to Sanction? Why would this girl give away her plans? It is a trick, a trap. Thus they argued, back and forth. No one mentioned anything about the One God.

The council itself was divided. Lord Ulrich was in favor of riding to Sanction. Lord Siegfried, who replaced the late Lord Nigel on the council, was from Ergoth and argued that the Knights would do better to retreat.

Gerard glanced at Odila, who stood near him. She was thoughtful and very quiet, her eyes dark and shadowed. She apparently had no more arguments to present, nothing more to say. Gerard should have realized silence was a bad sign for the glib-tongued young woman. As it was, he was too absorbed in his own thoughts and plans to pay much attention to her beyond wondering what she'd expected to accomplish in the first place. When next he looked around at her, to ask her if she wanted to go get something to eat, he found that she had gone.

Lord Tasgall rose to his feet. He announced that the council would take both matters under advisement. The three retired to discuss the matter in private.

Thinking that his own proposed plan of action might aid their decision making, Gerard left his fellows, who were still arguing, and went in search of the Lord Knights. He found them closeted in what had once been an old chapel dedicated to the worship of Kiri-Jolith, one of the old gods and one favored by the Solamnic Knights.

Retainers in the service of Lord Ulrich stood guard at the door. Gerard told them he had a matter of urgency to bring before the council and then, having been standing for hours, he sank thankfully onto a bench outside the chapel to await the Lord Knights' pleasure. While he waited, he went over his plans once more, searching for any flaw. He could find none. Confident and excited, he waited impatiently for the Knights to summon him.

At length, the guard came to him and said that they would see him now. As Gerard entered the old chapel, he realized that the council had already reached a decision. He guessed, by the way Lord Ulrich was smiling, that the decision was to march to Sanction.

Gerard was kept waiting a moment longer while Lord Siegfried conferred in a low voice with Lord Tasgall. Gerard glanced with interest around the old chapel. The walls were made of rough-hewn stone, the floor lined with wooden benches, worn smooth by years of use. The chapel was small, for it was a private chapel, intended for the family and servants. An altar stood at the front. Gerard could just barely make out the symbol of Kiri-Jolith—the head of a buffalo—carved in relief.

Gerard tried to picture in his mind what the chapel had been like all those many years ago, when the Lord Knight and his lady wife and their children, their retinue and their servants, had come to this place to worship their god. The ceiling would have been hung with bright banners. The priest—probably a stern, warrior-type—would have taken his place at the front as he prepared to read from the Measure or relate some tale of Vinas Solamnus, the founder of the Knighthood. The presence of the god would have been felt in this chapel. His people would have been comforted by that presence and would have left to go about their daily lives strengthened and renewed.

His presence was lacking now, when it was sorely needed.

"We will hear you now, Sir Gerard," said Lord Tasgall with a touch of impatience, and Gerard realized with a start that this was the second time he'd been addressed.

"I beg your pardon, my lords," said Gerard, bowing.

Receiving an invitation to advance and speak, he did so, outlining his plan. The three Knights listened in silence, giving no hint of their feelings. In conclusion, Gerard stated, "I could provide you with the answer to one question, at least, my lords—whether in truth this Mina does intend to march to Sanction or if that was a ruse to divert us from her true goal. If so, I might be able to discover the nature of that goal."

"The risk you run is very great," observed Lord Siegfried, frowning.

" 'The greater the risk, the greater the glory,' " quoted Lord Ulrich, with a smile.

"I would it were so, my lord," said Gerard with a shrug, "but, in truth, I will not be in all that much danger. I am known to the Dark Knights, you see. They would have little reason to question my story."

"I do not approve of the use of spies," stated Lord Siegfried, "much less one of our own Knights acting in such a demeaning capacity. The Measure forbids it."

"The Measure forbids a lot of things," said Lord Tasgall dryly. "I, for one, tend to choose common sense over rules that have been handed down in the distant past. I do not command you to do this, Sir Gerard, but if you volunteer—"

"I do, my lord," said Gerard eagerly.

"—then I believe that you can be of inestimable help to us. The council has determined that the Knights will ride to the support of Sanction. I am convinced that this Mina does mean to attack and therefore we cannot delay. However, I would be glad to receive confirmation of this and to learn of any plans she has for the capture of the city. Even with dragons, she will find her way difficult, for there are many underground structures where armies can be safely concealed from attack."

"Then, too, her own armies may be susceptible to the dragonfear," stated Lord Ulrich. "She may use dragons against us, only to watch helplessly as her own troops flee the field in terror."

The dead won't flee in terror, thought Gerard, but he kept that thought to himself. He knew by their grim expressions and grimmer faces that the Knights understood that as well as he did.

"Good luck to you, Sir Gerard," said Lord Tasgall, rising to his feet to shake hands.

Lord Ulrich also shook hands heartily. Lord Siegfried was stiff and solemn and clearly disapproving, but he made no further argument and actually wished Gerard luck, although he did not shake hands.

"We'll say nothing of this plan to anyone, gentlemen," said Lord Tasgall, glancing around at the others.

This agreed to, Gerard was about to take his departure when the retainer entered to say that a messenger had arrived with urgent news.

Since this might have some impact on Gerard's plan, Lord Tasgall gave a sign that he was to remain. The messenger entered. Gerard was alarmed to recognize a young squire from the household of Lord Warren, commander of the outpost of Solamnic Knights that protected Solace, location of Gerard's last posting. Gerard tensed, sensing dire news. The young man was mud-spattered, his clothes travel-worn. He strode forward, came to stand in front of Lord Tasgall. Bowing, he held out a sealed scrollcase.

Lord Tasgall opened the scrollcase, drew out the scroll, and began to read. His countenance changed markedly, his eyebrows raised. He looked up, amazed.

"Do you know what this contains?" Lord Tasgall asked.

"Yes, my lord," answered the squire. "In case the message was lost, I committed it to memory to relate to you."

"Then do so," said Lord Tasgall, leaning on the table. "I want these gentlemen to hear. I want to hear myself," he added in a low voice, "for I can scarce believe what I have read."

"My lords," said the squire, facing them, "three weeks ago, the dragon Beryl launched an attack against the elven nation of Qualinesti."

The Knights nodded. None were surprised. Such an attack had been long foreseen. The messenger paused to draw breath and consider what he would say next. Gerard, in a fever of impatience to hear news of his friends in Qualinesti, was forced to clench his fists to keep from dragging the information out of the man's throat.

"My lord Warren regrets to report that the city of Qualinost was completely destroyed in the attack. If the reports we have received are to be believed, Qualinost has disappeared off the face of Ansalon. A great body of water covers the city."

The Knights stared, astounded.

"The elves did manage to take their enemy down with them. The dragon overlord, Beryl, is dead."

"Excellent news!" said Lord Ulrich.

"Perhaps there is a god, after all," said Lord Siegfried, making a weak joke at which no one laughed.

Gerard bounded across the room. Grasping the startled messenger by the collar, Gerard nearly lifted the young man off the floor. "What of the elves, damn you? The Queen Mother, the young king? What of them? What has happened to them?"

"Please, sir—" the messenger exclaimed, rattled.

Gerard dropped the gasping young man. "I beg your pardon, sir, my lords," he said, lowering his strident tones, "but I have recently been in Qualinesti, as you know, and I came to care deeply for these people."

"Certainly, we understand, Sir Gerard," said Lord Tasgall. "What news do you have of the king and the royal family?"

"According to the survivors who managed to reach Solace, the Queen Mother was killed in the battle with the dragon," said the messenger, eyeing Gerard distrustfully and keeping out of his reach. "She is being proclaimed a hero. The king is reported to have escaped safely and is said to be joining the rest of his people, who fled the dragon's wrath."

"At least with the dragon dead, the elves can now go back to Qualinesti," said Gerard, his heart heavy.

"I am afraid that is not the case, my lord," the messenger replied grimly. "For although the dragon is dead and her armies dispersed, a new commander arrived very shortly afterward to take control. He is a Knight of Neraka and claims he was present during the attack on Solanthus. He has rallied what was left of Beryl's armies and overrun Qualinesti. Thousands flock to his standard for he has promised wealth and free land to all who join him."

"What of Solace?" asked Lord Tasgall anxiously.

"For the moment, we are safe. Haven is free. Beryl's forces who held control of that city abandoned their posts and traveled south to be in on the looting of the elven nation. But my lord believes that once this Lord Samuval, as he calls himself, has a firm grip on Qualinesti, he will next turn his gaze upon Abanasinia. Thus does my lord request reinforcements. . . ."

The messenger paused, looked from one lord Knight to another. None met the man's pleading gaze. They looked at each other and then looked away. There were no reinforcements to send.

Gerard was so shaken that he did not immediately recognize the name Samuval and call to mind the man who had escorted him through Mina's camp. He would remember that only when he was on the road to Solanthus. For now, all he could think about was Laurana, dying in battle against the great dragon, and his friend and enemy, the Dark Knight commander, Marshal Medan. True, the Solamnics would never mention him or name Medan a hero, but Gerard guessed that if Laurana had died, the gallant Marshal had preceded her in death.

Gerard's heart went out to the young king, who must now lead his people in exile. Gilthas was so young to have such terrible responsibility thrust upon him, young and untried. Would he be up to the task? Could anyone, no matter how old and experienced, be up to that task?

"Sir Gerard . . ."

"Yes, my lord."

"You have leave to go. I suggest that you depart tonight. In all the turmoil, no one will think to question your disappearance. Do you have everything you need?"

"I need to make arrangements with the one who is to carry my messages, my lord." Gerard had no more luxury for sorrow. Someday, he hoped to have the chance to avenge the dead. But, for now, he had to make certain that he did not join them. "Once that is accomplished, I am ready to depart on the instant."

"My squire, Richard Kent, is young, but sensible, and an expert horseman," said Lord Tasgall. "I will appoint him to be your messenger. Would that be satisfactory?"

"Yes, my lord," said Gerard.

Richard was summoned. Gerard had seen the young man before and been impressed with him. The two soon settled where Richard was to wait to hear from Gerard and how they were going to communicate. Gerard saluted the Knights of the council, then departed.

Leaving the chapel of Kiri-Jolith, Gerard entered the sodden wet courtyard, ducked his head to keep the rain out of his eyes. His first thought was to find Odila, to see how she was faring. His second and better thought convinced him to leave her alone. She would ask questions about where he was going and what he was planning, and he'd been ordered to tell no one. Rather than lie to her, he decided it would be easier to not speak to her at all.

Taking a circuitous route to avoid the possibility of bumping into her or anyone else, he went to gather up what he needed. He did not take his armor, nor even his sword. Going to the kitchen, he packed some food in a saddlebag, snagged some water, and a thick cape that had been hung in front of the fire to dry. The cape was still damp in places and smelled strongly of wet sheep that had been baked in an oven, but it was ideal for his purpose. Clad only in his shirt and breeches, he wrapped himself in the cape and headed for the stables.

He had a long ride ahead of him—long, wet, and lonely.

9 THE PLAINS OF DUST

The rain that drenched the northlands of Ansalon and was such a misery to the Solamnic Knights would have been welcome to the elves in the south, who were just starting their journey through the Plains of Dust. The Qualinesti elves had always gloried in the sun. Their Tower was the Tower of the Sun; their king, the Speaker of the Sun. The sun's light banished the darkness and terrors of the night, brought life to the roses and warmth to their houses. The elves had loved even the new sun, that had appeared after the Chaos War, for though its light seemed feeble, pale, and sickly at times, it continued to bring life to their land.

In the Plains of Dust, the sun did not bring life. The sun brought death.

Never before had any elf cursed the sun. Now, after only a few days' travel through the empty, harsh land under the strange, glaring eye of this sun—an eye that was no longer pale and sickly but fierce and unforgiving as the eye of a vengeful goddess—the elves grew to hate the sun and cursed it bleakly as it rose with malevolent vindictiveness every morning.

The elves had done what they could to prepare for their journey, but none, except the runners, had ever traveled so far from their homeland, and they had no idea what to expect. Not even the runners, who maintained contact with Alhana Starbreeze of the Silvanesti, had ever crossed the Plains of Dust. Their routes took them north through the swamp land of the dragon overlord Onysablet. Gilthas had actually considered trying to travel these routes, but rejected the idea almost immediately. While one or two could creep through the swamps undetected by the dragon or the evil creatures who served her, an entire populace could not escape her notice. The runners reported that the swamp grew darker and more dangerous, as the dragon extended her control over the land, so that few who ventured into it these days came out alive.

The rebel elves—most of them Wilder elves, who were accustomed to living out-of-doors—had a better idea of what the people would face. Although none of them had ever ventured out into the desert, they knew that their lives might well depend on being able to flee at a moment's notice, and they knew better than to burden themselves with objects that are precious in life, but have no value to the dead.

The majority of the refugees had yet to learn this hard lesson. The Qualinesti elves had fled their homes, made a dangerous journey through dwarven tunnels or traveled by night under the shelter of the trees. Even so, many had managed to bring along bags and boxes filled with silken gowns, thick woolen robes, jewels and jewel boxes, books containing family histories, toys and dolls for the children, heirlooms of all types and varieties. Such objects held sweet remembrances of their past, represented their hope for the future.

Acting on the advice of his wife, Gilthas tried to convince the people that they should leave their heirlooms and jewels and family histories behind. He insisted that every person carry as much water as he or she could possibly manage, along with food enough for a week's journey. If that meant an elf maiden could no longer carry her dancing shoes, so be it. Most thought this stricture harsh in the extreme and grumbled incessantly. Someone came up with the idea of building a litter that could be dragged along behind and soon many of the elves began lashing together tree limbs to haul their goods. Gilthas watched and shook his head.

"You will never force them to abandon their treasures, my love," said the Lioness. "Do not try, lest they come to hate you."

"But they will never make it alive through the desert!" Gilthas gestured to an elven lord who had brought along most of his household possessions, including a small striking clock. "Don't they understand that?"

"No," the Lioness said bluntly, "but they will. Each person must make the decision to leave his past behind or die with it hanging about his neck. Not even his king can make that decision for him." Reaching out, she rested her hand over his. "Remember this, Gilthas, there are some who would *rather* die. You must steel yourself to face that."

Gilthas thought of her words as he trudged over the windswept rock that flowed like a harsh, hard, and barren red-orange sea to the blue horizon. Looking back across the land that shimmered in the hot sun, he saw his people straggling along behind. Distorted by the waves of heat rising from the rock, they appeared to waver in his vision, to lengthen and recede as he watched. He had placed the strongest at the rear of the group to assist those who were having difficulty, and he set the Wilder elves to keep watch along the flanks.

The first few days of their march, he had feared being attacked by the human armies rampaging through Qualinesti, but after traveling in the desert, he soon realized that here they were safe—safe because no one in his right mind would ever waste his energy chasing after them. Let the desert kill them, his enemies would say. Indeed, that seemed likely.

"We're not going to make it," Gilthas realized.

The elves did not know how to dress for the desert. They discarded their clothes in the heat and many were terribly burned by the sun. The litters now served a useful purpose—carrying those too burned or sick to walk. The heat sapped strength and energy, so that feet stumbled and heads bowed. As the Lioness had predicted, the elves began to divest themselves of their past. Although they left no mark on the rock, the tale of their passage could be read in the abandoned sacks and broken chests dumped off the litters or thrown down by weary arms.

Their pace was slow—heartbreakingly slow. According to the maps, they would have to cross two hundred and fifty miles of desert before they reached the remnants of the old King's Highway that led into Silvanesti. Managing only a few miles a day, they would run out of both food and water long before they reached the midpoint. Gilthas had heard that there were places in the desert where one could find water, but these were not marked on the maps, and he didn't know how to locate them.

He had one hope—the hope that had led him to dare to make this treacherous journey. He must try to find the Plainspeople who made their homes in this forbidding, desolate land. Without their help, the Qualinesti nation would perish.

Gilthas had naively supposed that traveling the Plains of Dust was similar to traveling in other parts of Ansalon, where one could find villages or towns within a day's journey along the route. He had been told that there was a village of Plainspeople at a place called Duntol. The map showed Duntol to be due east from Thorbardin. The elves traveled east, walking straight into the morning sun, but they saw no signs of a village. Gazing across the empty expanse of glistening red rock, Gilthas could see for miles in all directions and in all directions he saw no sign of anything except more rock.

The people were drinking too much water. He ordered that waterskins be collected by the Wilder elves and rationed. The same with the food.

At the loss of their precious water, the elves became angry and afraid. Some fought, others pleaded with tears in their eyes. Gilthas had to be harsh and stern, and some of the elves turned from cursing the sun to cursing their king. Fortunately for Gilthas—his one single stroke of luck—Prefect Palthainon was so badly sunburned that he was too sick to cause trouble.

"When the water runs out, we can bleed the horses and live off their blood for a few days," said the Lioness.

"What happens when the horses die?" he asked.

She shrugged.

The next day, two of the sunburn victims died. The elves could not bury them, for no tool they owned would break through the solid rock. They could find no stones on the windswept plains to cover the bodies. They finally wrapped them in woolen capes and lowered the bodies with ropes into deep crevices in the rock.

Light-headed from walking in the blazing sun, Gilthas listened to the keening of those who mourned the dead. He stared down into the crevice and thought dazedly how blissfully cool it must be at the bottom. He felt a touch on his arm.

"We have company," said the Lioness, pointing north.

Gilthas shaded his eyes, tried to see against the harsh glare. In the distance, wavering in the heat, he could make out three riders on horseback. He could not discern any details—they were shapeless lumps of darkness. He stared until his eyes watered, hoping to see the riders approaching, but they did not move. He waved his arms and shouted until his parched throat was hoarse, but the riders simply stood there.

Unwilling to lose any more time, Gilthas gave the order for the people to start walking.

"Now the watchers are on the move," said the Lioness.

"But not toward us," said Gilthas, sick with disappointment.

The riders traveled parallel to the elves, sometimes vanishing from sight among the rocks, but always reappearing. They made their presence known, made the elves aware that they were being watched. The strange riders did not appear threatening, but they had no need to threaten. If they viewed the elves as an enemy, the blazing sun was the only weapon they required.

Hearing the wailing of children in his ears and the moans of the ill and dying, Gilthas could bear it no longer.

"You're going to talk to them," the Lioness said, her voice cracking from lack of water.

He nodded. His mouth was too parched to waste words.

"If they are Plainspeople, they have no love for strangers trespassing in their territory," she warned. "They might kill you."

He nodded again and took hold of her hand, raised it to his lips, kissed it. Turning his horse's head, he rode off toward the north, toward the strange riders. The Lioness called a halt to the march. The elves sank down on the burning rock. Some watched their young king ride off, but most were too tired and dispirited to care what happened to him or them.

The strange riders did not gallop forth to meet Gilthas, nor did they gallop off. They waited for him to come to them. He could still make out very few details, and as he drew closer, he could see why. The strangers were enveloped in white garments that covered them from head to toe, protecting them from the sun and the heat. He could also see that they carried swords at their sides.

Dark eyes, narrowed against the sun, stared at him from the shadows cast by the folds of cloth swathed around their heads. The eyes were cold, dispassionate, gave no indication of the thoughts behind them.

One rider urged his horse forward, putting himself forth as the leader. Gilthas took note of him, but he kept glancing at a rider who kept slightly apart from the rest. This rider was extremely tall, towered over the heads of the others, and, although Gilthas could not say why, instinct led him to believe that the tall man was the person in charge.

The lead rider drew his sword, held it out before him and shouted out a command.

Gilthas did not understand the words. The gesture spoke for itself, and he halted. He raised his own sunburned hands to show that he carried no weapons.

"*Bin'on du'auth,*" he said, as best he could talk for his cracked lips. "I give you greeting."

The stranger answered with a swarm of unfamiliar words that buzzed about the king's ears, all of them sounding alike, none making any sense.

"I am sorry," Gilthas said, flushing and shifting to Common, "but that is all I know of your language." Speaking was painful. His throat was raw.

Waving the sword, the stranger spurred his horse and rode straight at Gilthas. The king did not move, did not flinch. The sword whistled harmlessly past his head. The stranger wheeled, galloped back, bringing his horse to a halt in a flurry of sand and a fine display of riding skill.

He was about to speak, but the tall man raised his hand in a gesture of command. Riding forward, he eyed Gilthas approvingly.

"You have courage," he said, speaking Common.

"No," Gilthas returned. "I am simply too tired to move."

The tall man laughed aloud at this, but his laughter was short and abrupt. He motioned for his comrade to sheathe his sword, then turned back to Gilthas.

"Why do the elves, who should be living on their fat land, leave their fat land to invade ours?"

Gilthas found himself staring at the waterskin the man carried, a waterskin that was swollen and beaded with drops of cool water. He tore his gaze away and looked back at the stranger.

"We do not invade your land," he said, licking his dry lips. "We are trying to cross it. We are bound for the land of our cousins, the Silvanesti."

"You do not plan to take up residence in the Plains of Dust?" the tall man asked. He was not wasteful of his words, spoke only what was needful, no more, no less. Gilthas guessed that he was not one to waste anything on anyone, including sympathy.

"Trust me, no, we do not," said Gilthas fervently. "We are a people of green trees and cold, rushing water." As he spoke these words, a homesickness welled up inside him so that he could have wept. He had no tears. They had been burned away by the sun. "We must return to our forests, or else we will die."

"Why do you flee your green land and cold water?" the tall man asked.

Gilthas swayed in the saddle. He had to pause to try to gather enough moisture in his throat to continue speaking. He failed. His words came out a harsh whisper.

"The dragon, Beryl, attacked our land. The dragon is dead, but the capital city, Qualinost, was destroyed in the battle. The lives of many elves, humans, and dwarves were lost defending it. The Dark Knights now overrun our land. They seek our total annihilation. We are not strong enough to fight them, so we must—"

The next thing Gilthas knew, he was flat on his back on the ground, staring up at the unwinking eye of the vengeful sun. The tall man, wrapped in his robes, squatted comfortably at his side, while one of his comrades dribbled water into Gilthas's lips.

The tall man shook his head. "I do not know which is greater—the courage of the elves or their ignorance. Traveling in the heat of the day, without the proper clothing . . ." He shook his head again.

Gilthas struggled to sit up. The man giving him water shoved him back down.

"Unless I am much mistaken," the tall man continued, "you are Gilthas, son of Lauralanthalasa and Tanis Half-elven."

Gilthas stared, amazed. "How did you know?"

"I am Wanderer," said the tall man, "son of Riverwind and Goldmoon. These are my comrades." He did not name them, apparently leaving it up to them to introduce themselves, something they did not seem disposed to do. Obviously a people of few words. "We will help you," he added, "if only to speed you through our land."

The offer was not very gracious, but Gilthas took what he could get and was grateful for it.

"If you must know," Wanderer continued, "you have my mother to thank for your salvation. She sent me to search for you."

Gilthas could not understand this in the slightest, could only suppose that Goldmoon had received a vision of their plight.

"How is . . . your mother?" he asked, savoring the cool drops of tepid water that tasted of goat, yet were better to him than the finest wine.

"Dead," said Wanderer, gazing far off over the plains.

Gilthas was taken aback by his matter-of-fact tone. He was about to mumble something consoling, but the tall man interrupted him.

"My mother's spirit came to me the night before last, and told me to travel south. I did not know why, and she did not say. I thought perhaps I might find her body on this journey, for she told me that she lies unburied, but her spirit disappeared before she could tell me where."

Gilthas again began to stammer his regrets, but Wanderer paid no heed to his words.

"Instead," Wanderer said quietly, "I find you and your people. Perhaps you know how to find my mother?"

Before Gilthas could answer, Wanderer continued on. "I was told she fled the Citadel before it was attacked by the dragon, but no one knows where she went. They said that she was in the grip of some sort of madness, perhaps the scattered wits that come to the very old. She did not seem mad to me when I saw her spirit. She seemed a prisoner."

Gilthas thought privately that if Goldmoon was not mad, her son certainly was—all this talk of spirits and unburied bodies. Still, Wanderer's vision had saved their lives, and Gilthas could not very well argue against it. He answered only that he had no idea where Goldmoon was, or if she was dead or alive. His heart ached, for he thought of his own mother, lying unburied at the bottom of a new-formed lake. A great weariness and lethargy came over him. He wished he could lie here for days, with the taste of cool water on his lips. He had his people to think of, however. Resisting all admonitions to remain prone, Gilthas staggered to his feet.

"We are trying to reach Duntol," he said.

Wanderer rose with him. "You are too far south. You will find an oasis near here. There your people may rest for a few days and build up their strength before you continue your journey. I will send my comrades to Duntol for food and supplies."

"We have money to pay for it," Gilthas began. He swallowed the words when he saw Wanderer's face darken in anger. "We will find some way to repay you," he amended lamely.

"Leave our land," Wanderer reiterated sternly. "With the dragon seizing ever more land to the north, our resources are stretched as it is."

"We intend to," said Gilthas, wearily. "As I have said, we travel to Silvanesti."

Wanderer gazed long at him, seemed about to say more, but then apparently thought better of it. He turned to his companions and spoke to them in the language of the Plainspeople. Gilthas wondered what Wanderer had been about to say, but his curiosity evaporated as he concentrated on just remaining upright. He was glad to find that they had given his horse water.

Wanderer's two companions galloped off. Wanderer offered to ride with Gilthas.

"I will show you how to dress yourselves to protect your fair skin from the sun and to keep out the heat," Wanderer said. "You must travel in the cool of the night and the early morning, sleep during the heat of the day. My people will treat your sick and show you how to build shelters from the sun. I will guide you as far as the old King's Highway, which you will be able to follow to Silvanesti. You will take that road and leave our land and not return."

"Why do you keep harping on this?" Gilthas demanded. "I mean no offense, Wanderer, but I cannot imagine anyone in his right mind wanting to live in a place like this. Not even the Abyss could be more empty and desolate."

Gilthas feared his outburst might have angered the Plainsman and was about to apologize, when he heard what sounded like a smothered chuckle come from behind the cloth that covered Wanderer's face. Gilthas remembered Riverwind only dimly, when he and Goldmoon had visited his parents long ago, but he was suddenly reminded of the tall, stern-faced hunter.

"The desert has its own beauty," said Wanderer. "After a rain, flowers burst into life, scenting the air with their sweetness. The red of the rock against the blue of the sky, the flow of the cloud shadows over the rippling sand, the swirling dustdevils and the rolling tumbleweed, the sharp scent of sage. I miss these when I am gone from them, as you miss the thick canopy of incessantly dripping leaves, the continuous rain, the vines that tangle the feet, and the smell of mildew that clogs the lungs."

"One man's Abyss is another man's Paradise, it seems," said Gilthas, smiling. "You may keep your Paradise, Wanderer, and you are welcome to it. I will keep my trees and cool water."

"I hope you will," said Wanderer, "but I would not count upon it."

"Why?" Gilthas asked, alarmed. "What do you know?"

"Nothing for certain," said Wanderer. Checking his horse, he turned to face Gilthas. "I was of two minds whether to tell you this or not. These days, rumors drift upon the wind like the cottonwood seeds."

"Yet, obviously, you give this rumor credence," Gilthas said.

When Wanderer still did not speak, Gilthas added, "We intend to go to Silvanesti no matter what has happened. I assure you, we have no plans to remain any longer in the desert than is necessary for us to cross it."

Wanderer gazed out across the sand to the mass of elves, bright spots of color that had blossomed among the rocks without benefit of life-giving rain.

"The rumors say that Silvanesti has fallen to the Dark Knights." Wanderer turned his dark eyes to Gilthas. "You've heard nothing of this?"

"No," replied Gilthas. "I have not."

"I wish I could give you more details, but, needless to say, your people do not confide in us. Do you believe it?"

Even as Gilthas shook his head firmly in the negative, his heart sank. He might speak confidently before this stranger and before his people, but the truth was that he had heard nothing from the exiled Silvanesti queen, Alhana Starbreeze, in many weeks, not since before the fall of Qualinost. Alhana Starbreeze had been waging a concerted fight to reenter Silvanesti, to destroy the shield that surrounded it. The last Gilthas had heard, the shield had fallen and she and her forces were poised on the border, ready to enter her former homeland. One might argue that Alhana's messengers would have a difficult time finding him, since he'd been on the move, but the Silvanesti Wildrunners were friends with the eagles and the hawks and all whose sight was keen. If they had wanted to find him, they could have. Alhana had sent no runners, and perhaps this explained why.

Here was yet another burden to bear. If this was true, they were not fleeing danger, they were running headlong toward it. Yet, they could not stay in the desert.

At least if I have to die, let it be under a shade tree, Gilthas thought.

He straightened in the saddle. "I thank you for this information, Wanderer. Forewarned is forearmed. Now I should no longer delay telling my people that help is coming. How many days will take us to reach the King's Highway?"

"That depends on your courage," said Wanderer. Gilthas could not see the man's lips, due to the folds of cloth that swathed his face, but he saw the dark eyes warm with a smile. "If all your people are like you, I should not think the journey will take long at all."

Gilthas was grateful for the compliment. He wished he had earned it. What is taken for courage might only be exhaustion, after all.

10 BREAKING INTO PRISON

Gerard planned to enter Solanthus on foot. He stabled the animal at a roadhouse about two miles from the city—a roadhouse recommended by young Richard. Taking the opportunity to eat a hot meal (about the best that could be said for it), Gerard caught up on the local gossip. He put out that he was a sell-sword, wondered if there might be work in the great city.

He was immediately told all he needed and more than he wanted to know about the disastrous rout of the Solamnic Knights and the takeover of the city by the Dark Knights of Neraka. There had not been many travelers after the fall of Solanthus several weeks ago, but the inn's mistress was hopeful that business would soon improve. Reports coming from Solanthus indicated that the citizens were not being tortured and slaughtered in droves as many had feared, but that they were well treated and encouraged to go about their daily lives as though nothing had happened.

Oh, certainly, a few people had been hauled off to prison, but they had probably deserved it. The person in charge of the Knights, who was said to be a slip of a girl, was not lopping off heads, but was preaching to the people of a new god, who had come to take care of them. She had gone so far as to order an old temple of Paladine cleaned out and restored, to be dedicated to this new god. She went about the city healing the sick and performing other miracles. The people of Solanthus were becoming enamored of her.

Trade routes between Solanthus and Palanthas, long closed, had now been reopened, which made the merchants happy. All in all, the innkeeper stated, things could be worse.

"I heard there were evil dragons about," Gerard said, dunking his stale bread in the congealing gravy, the only way to make either palatable. "And worse than that." He lowered his voice. "I heard that the dead walked in Solanthus!"

The woman sniffed. She'd heard something along these lines, but she'd seen nothing of any dragons herself, and no ghost had come to the roadhouse asking for food. Chuckling at her own humor, she went bustling off to provide indigestion to some other unsuspecting guest, leaving Gerard to feed the rest of his meal to the roadhouse dog and ponder what he'd heard.

He knew the truth of the matter. He'd seen the red and blue dragons flying above the city, and he'd seen the souls of the dead surrounding the city's walls. The hair still rose on the back of his neck whenever he thought about that army of empty eyes and gaping mouths, wispy hands with ragged fingers that stretched out to him over the gulf of death. No, that had been very real. Inexplicable, but real.

He was startled to hear that the people of Solanthus were being so well treated, but not much surprised to hear that they had apparently taken Mina to their hearts. He'd had only a brief talk with the charismatic leader of the Dark Knights, and yet he retained a vivid picture of her: he could see the fell, amber eyes, hear the timbre of her voice, recall every word she'd spoken. Did the fact that she was treating the Solanthians well make his job easier or more difficult? He argued one way and the other and at length came to the conclusion that the only way to find out was to go there and see for himself.

Paying for his meal and for the stabling of the horse for a week, Gerard set out for Solanthus on foot.

Coming within sight of the city walls, he did not immediately enter. He sat down in a grove of trees, where he could see but not be seen. He needed more information on the city, and he needed that information from a certain type of person. He had been sitting there for about thirty minutes when a wicket at the main gate opened up and several small bodies shot out, as though forcibly propelled from behind.

The small bodies picked themselves up, dusted themselves off as though this were nothing out of the ordinary, and, after shaking hands all round, set off upon their separate ways.

One of the small bodies happened to pass quite close to Gerard. He called out, accompanying his call with a friendly gesture, and the small body, which belonged to a kender, immediately came over to chat.

Reminding himself that this was for a worthy cause, Gerard braced himself, smiled in a friendly manner at the kender, and invited him to be seated.

"Goatweed Tangleknot," said the kender, by way of introduction. "My goodness, but you're ugly," he added cheerfully, peering up into Gerard's pockmarked face, admiring his corn-yellow and recalcitrant hair. "You're probably one of the ugliest humans I've ever met."

The Measure promised that all who made the supreme sacrifice for the sake of their country would be rewarded in the afterlife. Gerard figured that this particular experience should gain him a suite of rooms in some celestial palace. Gritting his teeth, he said he knew he wouldn't win any prizes as queen of the May dance.

"And you have *very* blue eyes," said Goatweed. "Uncomfortably blue, if you don't mind my saying so. Would you like to see what I have in my pouches?"

Before Gerard could answer, the kender dumped out the contents of several pouches and began happily to sort through them.

"You just left Solanthus," Gerard said, interrupting Goatweed in the middle of a story about how he'd come by a hammer that had once belonged to some unfortunate tinker. "What's it like inside there? I heard that it had been taken over by Dark Knights?"

Goatweed nodded vigorously. "It's about the same as usual. The guards round us up and throw us out. Except that now they take us first to this place that used to belong to the Mystics, and before that it was a temple of some old god or other. They brought in a group of Mystics from the Citadel of Light and talked to them. That was fun to watch, I tell you! A girl stood up in front of them, dressed up like a knight. She had very strange eyes. Very strange. Stranger than your eyes. She stood in front of the Mystics and told them all about the One God, and she showed them a pretty lady stored up in an amber box and told them that the One God had already performed one miracle and given the pretty lady her youth and beauty and the One God was going to perform another miracle and bring the pretty lady back to life.

"The Mystics stared at the pretty lady, and some of them began to cry. The girl asked the Mystics if they wanted to know more about this One God, and those who said they did were marched off one way, and those who said that they didn't were marched off another, including some old man called the Starmaster or something like that. And then the girl came to us and asked us lots of questions, and then she told *us* all about this new god who has come to Krynn. And then she asked us if we'd like to worship this new god and serve the new god."

"And what did you say?" Gerard was curious.

"Why, I said 'yes,' of course," said Goatweed, astonished that he could suppose otherwise. "It would be rude *not* to, don't you think? Since this new god has taken all this trouble to come here and everything, shouldn't we do what we can to be encouraging?"

"Don't you think it might be dangerous to worship a god you don't know anything about?"

"Oh, I know a lot about this god," Goatweed assured him. "At least, as much as seems important. This god has a great liking for kender, the girl told us. A very great liking. So great that this god is searching for one very special kender in particular. If any of us find this kender, we're supposed to bring him to the girl and she'll give us a huge reward. We all promised we would, and that's the very thing I'm off to do. Find this kender. You haven't seen him, by any chance?"

"You're the first kender I've seen in days," said Gerard. And hopefully the last, he added mentally. "How do you manage to get into the city without—"

"His name," said Goatweed, fixated on his quest, "is The Tasslehoff Burrfoot, and he—"

"Eh?" Gerard exclaimed, astonished. "What did you say?"

"Which time? There was what I said about Solanthus and what I said about the girl and what I said about the new god—"

"The kender. The special kender. You said his name was Burrfoot? Tasslehoff Burrfoot?"

"*The* Tasslehoff Burrfoot," Goatweed corrected. "The 'The' is very important because he can't be just any Tasslehoff Burrfoot."

"No, I guess he couldn't be," said Gerard, thinking back to the kender who had started this entire adventure by managing to get himself locked inside the Tomb of Heroes in Solace.

"Although, to make sure," Goatweed continued, "we're supposed to bring any Tasslehoff Burrfoot we find to Sanction for the girl to have a look at."

"You mean Solanthus," said Gerard.

Goatweed was absorbed in examining with interest a bit of broken blue glass. Holding it up, he asked eagerly, "Do you think that's a sapphire?"

"No," said Gerard. "It's a piece of broken blue glass. You said you were supposed to take this Burrfoot to Sanction. You mean Solanthus. The girl and her army are in Solanthus, not Sanction."

"Did I say Sanction?" Goatweed scratched his head. After some thought, he nodded. "Yes, I said Sanction, and I meant Sanction. The girl told us that she wasn't going to be in Solanthus long. She and her army were all heading off to Sanction, where the new god was going to establish a huge temple, and it was in Sanction where she wanted to see Burrfoot."

That answers one of my questions, Gerard thought to himself.

"*I* think it's a sapphire," Goatweed added, and slid the broken glass back into his pouch.

"I once knew a Tasslehoff Burrfoot—" Gerard began hesitantly.

"Did you?" Goatweed leaped to his feet and began to skip around Gerard in excitement. "Where is he? How do I find him?"

"I haven't seen him for a long time," Gerard said, motioning the kender to calm down. "It's just that I was wondering what makes this Burrfoot so special."

"I don't think the girl said, but I may be mistaken. I'm afraid I dozed off for a bit at about that point. The girl kept us sitting there a very long time, and when one of us tried to get up to leave, a soldier stuck us with a sword, which isn't as exciting as it sounds like it might be. What was the question?"

Patiently, Gerard repeated it.

Goatweed frowned, a practice that is commonly known to aid the mental process, then said, "All I can remember is that he is very special to the One God. If you see this Tasslehoff friend of yours, will you be sure to tell him the One God is looking for him? And please mention my name."

"I promise," said Gerard. "And now, you can do me a favor. Say that a fellow had a very good reason for *not* entering Solanthus through the front gate, what's another way a fellow could get inside?"

Goatweed eyed Gerard shrewdly. "A fellow about your size?"

"About," said Gerard, shrugging.

"What would this information be worth to a fellow about your size?" Goatweed asked.

Gerard had foreseen this, and he brought forth a pouch containing an assortment of interesting and curious objects he'd appropriated from the manor house of Lord Ulrich.

"Take your pick," he said.

Gerard regretted this immediately, for Goatweed was thrown into an agony of indecision, dithering over the lot, finally ending up torn between a rusty caltrop and an old boot missing its heel.

"Take them both," Gerard said.

Struck by such generosity, Goatweed described a great many places whereby one could sneak unnoticed into Solanthus. Unfortunately, the kender's descriptions were more confusing than helpful, for he often jumped forward to add details about one he hadn't described yet or fell backward to correct information about one he'd described fifteen minutes earlier.

Eventually, Gerard pinned Goatweed down and made him go over each in detail—a time-consuming and frustrating process, during which Gerard came perilously close to strangling Goatweed. At length, Gerard had three locations in mind: one he deemed most suitable to his needs and the other two as back-up. Goatweed required Gerard to swear on his yellow hair that he would never, never divulge the location of the sites to anyone. Gerard did so, wondering if Goatweed himself had taken that very same vow and considering it highly likely.

After this came the hard part. Gerard had to rid himself of the kender, who had by now decided that they were best friends, if not brothers or maybe cousins. The loyal Goatweed was quite prepared to travel with Gerard for the rest of his days. Gerard said that was fine with him, he was going to lounge about here for a good long while. Maybe take a nap. Goatweed was free to wait.

Fifteen minutes passed, during which the kender developed the fidgets and Gerard snoozed with one eye open to see that he didn't lose anything of value. Finally Goatweed could stand the strain no longer. He packed up his treasure and departed, coming back several times to remind Gerard that if he saw The Tasslehoff Burrfoot, he was to send him straight to the One God and mention that his friend Goatweed was to receive the reward. Gerard promised and finally managed to rid himself of the kender. He had several hours to wait until darkness, and he whiled away his time trying to figure out what Mina wanted with Tasslehoff Burrfoot.

Gerard couldn't imagine that Mina had any great love for kender. The magical Device of Time Journeying the kender carried was probably the prize the girl was after.

"Which means," said Gerard to himself, "that if the kender can be found, we should be the ones to find him."

He made a mental note to tell the Solamnic Knights to be on the lookout for any kender calling himself Tasslehoff Burrfoot and to seize and hold said kender for safekeeping and, above all, not let him fall into the hands of the Dark Knights. This settled, Gerard waited for nightfall.

THE PRISON HOUSE
OF DEATH

Gerard had no difficulty slipping unobserved into the city. Although his first choice had been blocked up—showing that the Dark Knights were working to stop up all the "rat holes"—they had not yet found the second. True to his vow, Gerard never revealed the location of the entrance site.

The streets of Solanthus were dark and empty. According to the innkeeper, a curfew had been imposed on the city. Patrols marched through the streets, forcing Gerard to duck and dodge to avoid them, sliding into a shadowed doorway, ducking behind piles of rubbish in an alleyway.

What with hiding from the patrols and an imperfect knowledge of the streets, Gerard spent a good two hours roaming about the city before he finally saw what he'd been looking for—the walls of the prison house.

He huddled inside a doorway, keeping watch and wondering how he was going to manage to sneak inside. This had always been the weak point of his plan. Breaking into a prison was proving just as difficult as breaking out.

A patrol marched into the courtyard, escorting several curfew violators. Listening as the guard made his report, Gerard found out that all the taverns had been shut down by order of the Dark Knights. A tavern owner, trying to cut his losses, had secretly opened his doors to a few regular customers. The private party had turned rowdy, drawing the attention of the patrols, and now the customers and the proprietor were all being incarcerated.

One of the prisoners was singing at the top of his lungs. The proprietor wrung his hands and demanded to know how he was supposed to feed his family if they took away his livelihood. Another prisoner was sick on the pavement. The patrol wanted to rid themselves of their onerous burden as quickly as possible, and they beat on the door, yelling for the gaoler.

He arrived, but he didn't look pleased. He protested that the jail cells were filled to overflowing, and he didn't have room for any more. While he and the patrol leader argued, Gerard slid out of his doorway, darted across the street, and took his place at the back of the group of prisoners.

He pulled the hood of his cloak over his head, hunched his shoulders, and crowded as close to the others as possible. One of the prisoners glanced at him, and his eyes blinked. Gerard held his breath, but after staring at him a moment, the man broke into a drunken grin, leaned his head on Gerard's shoulder, and burst into tears.

The patrol leader threatened to march away and leave the prisoners in the street, adding that he would most certainly report this obstruction of his duty to his superiors. Cowed, the gaoler flung open the door of the prison and shouted for the prison guards. The prisoners were handed over, and the patrol marched off.

The guards herded Gerard and the others into the cell block.

The moment the gaoler came in sight, the prisoners began shouting. The gaoler paid no attention to them. Shoving his prisoners into any cell that could accommodate them, the gaoler and his guards left with all haste.

The cell in which they stuffed Gerard was already so packed that he didn't dare sit down for fear of being trampled. Adjoining cells were just as bad, some filled with men, others with women, all of them clamoring to be set free. The stench of unwashed bodies, vomit, and waste was intolerable. Gerard retched and clamped his hand over his nose and mouth, trying desperately and unsuccessfully to filter the smell through his fingers.

Gerard shoved his way through the mass of bodies toward the back of the cell, as far from the overflowing slop bucket as he could manage. He had feared he and his clothes might look too clean for what he planned, but he no longer had to worry about that. A few hours in here and the stench would cling to him so that he doubted if he could ever be free of it. After a brief time spent convincing himself that he was not going to throw up, he noticed that a neighboring cell—one that was large and spacious—appeared to be empty.

Nudging one of his cellmates in the ribs, Gerard jerked a thumb in that direction.

"Why don't they put some of us in there?" he asked.

"You can go in there if you want to," said the prisoner, with a dark glance. "Me, I'll stay here."

"But it's empty," Gerard protested.

"No, it ain't. You just can't see 'em. Good thing, too." The man grimaced. "Bad enough lookin' at 'em by daylight."

"What are they?" asked Gerard, curious.

"Wizards," the man grunted. "At least, that's what they was. I ain't sure what they are now."

"Why? What's wrong with them?"

"You'll see," the man predicted dourly. "Now let me get some sleep, will you?"

Squatting down on the floor, the man closed his eyes. Gerard figured he should try to rest, too, although he guessed gloomily it would be impossible.

He was pleasantly amazed to wake up some hours later to find daylight struggling to make its way inside the slit windows. Rubbing the sleep from his eyes, he looked with interest at the occupants of the neighboring cell, wondering what made the wizards so very formidable.

Startled, Gerard pressed his face against the bars that separated the two cells.

"Palin?" Gerard called out in a low voice. "Is that you?"

He honestly wasn't certain. The mage looked like Palin. But if this was Palin, the usually conscientious mage had not bathed or shaved or combed his hair or taken any care of his appearance for weeks. He sat on a cot, staring at nothing, eyes empty, his face expressionless.

Another mage sat on another cot. This mage was an elf, so emaciated that he might have been a corpse. He had dark hair, unusual in the elves, who tended to be fair, and his skin was the color of bleached bone. He wore robes that might have started out black in color, but grime and dust had turned them gray. The elf sat still and lifeless as Palin, the same expression that was no expression on his face.

Gerard called Palin's name again, this time slightly louder so that it could be heard over the coughing, hacking, wheezing, shouting, and complaining of his fellow prisoners. He was about to call again when he was distracted by a tickling sensation on his neck.

"Damn fleas," he muttered, slapping at it.

The mage lifted his head, looked up.

"Palin! What are you doing here? What's happened to you? Are you hurt? Drat these fleas!" Gerard scrubbed viciously at his neck, wriggled about in his clothes.

Palin stared vacantly at Gerard for long moments, as if waiting for him to do something or say something more. When Gerard only repeated his earlier questions, Palin shifted his eyes away and once more stared at nothing.

Gerard tried several more times but finally gave up and concentrated on ridding himself of the itching vermin. He managed to do so at last, or so he assumed, for the tickling sensation ceased.

"What happened to those two?" Gerard asked his cellmate.

"Dunno," was the answer. "They were like that when I was brought here, and that was three days ago. Every day, someone comes in and gives 'em food and water and sees that they eat it. All day, they just sit like that. Gives a fellow the horrors, don't it."

Yes, Gerard thought, indeed it did. He wondered what had happened to Palin. Seeing splotches of what appeared to be dried blood on his robes, Gerard concluded that the mage had been beaten or tortured so much that his wits had left him. His heart heavy with pity, Gerard scratched absently at his neck, then turned away. He couldn't do anything to help Palin now, but, if all went as he planned, he might be able to do something in the future.

He squatted down in the cell, keeping his distance from a loathsome-looking straw mattress. He had no doubt that's where he'd picked up the fleas.

"Well, that was a waste of time," remarked Dalamar.

The elf's spirit lingered near the prison's single window. Even in this twilight world that he was forced to inhabit—neither dead nor alive—he felt as if he were suffocating inside the stone walls. He found it comforting at least to imagine he was breathing fresh air.

"What were you trying to accomplish?" he asked. "I take it you weren't indulging in a practical joke."

"No, no joke," said Palin's spirit quietly. "If you must know, I was hoping to be able to contact the man, to speak to him."

"Bah!" Dalamar snorted. "I would have thought you had more sense. He cares nothing for us. None of them do. Who is he, anyhow?"

"His name is Gerard. He's a Solamnic Knight. I knew him in Qualinesti. We were friends . . . well, maybe not friends. I don't think he liked me. You know how Solamnics feel about mages, and I wasn't very pleasant company, I have to admit. Still"—Palin remembered what it was to sigh—"I thought perhaps I might be able to communicate with him, just as my father was able to communicate with me."

"Your father loved you, and he had something of importance to relate to you," said Dalamar. "Besides, Caramon was quite thoroughly dead. We are not, at least I must suppose we are not. Perhaps that has something to do with it. What were you hoping he could do for you, anyhow?"

Palin was silent.

"Come now," said Dalamar. "We are hardly in a position to keep secrets from one another."

If that is true, Palin thought, then what do you do on those solitary rambles of yours? And don't tell me you are lingering beneath the pine trees to enjoy nature. Where do *you* go and why?

For a long time after their return from death, the mages' spirits remained tethered to the bodies they had once inhabited, as a prisoner is chained to a wall. Dalamar, restless, searching for a way back to life, was the first to discover that their bonds were self-created. Perhaps because they were not wholly dead, their spirits were not enslaved to Takhisis, as were the souls caught up in the river of the dead. Dalamar was able to sever the link that bound body and soul together. His spirit left its jail, left Solanthus, or so he told Palin, although he didn't say where he had gone. Yet, even though he could leave, the mage was always forced to return.

Their spirits tended to be as jealous of their bodies as any miser of the chest that holds his wealth. Palin had tried venturing out into the sad world of the other imprisoned souls only to be consumed by fear that something might happen to his body in his absence. He flitted back to find it still sitting there, staring at nothing. He knew he should feel glad, and part of him was, but another part was bitterly disappointed. After that, he did not leave his body. He could not join with the dead souls, who neither saw nor heard him. He did not like to be around the living for the same reason.

Dalamar was often away from his body, though never for long. Palin was convinced that Dalamar was meeting with Mina, trying to bargain with her for the return of his life. He could not prove it, but he was certain it was so.

"If you must know," said Palin, "I was hoping to persuade Gerard to kill me."

"It would never work," said Dalamar. "Don't you think I've already considered it?"

"It might," Palin insisted. "The body lives. The wounds we suffered are healed. Killing the body again might sever the cord that binds us."

"And once again, Takhisis would bring us back to this charade of life. Haven't you figured out why? Why does our Queen feed us and watch over us as the *Shalafi* once fed and cared for those poor wretches he termed the Live Ones? We are her experiment, as they were his. The time will come when she will determine if her experiment has succeeded or failed. *She* will determine it. We will not. Don't you think I've tried?"

He spoke the last bitterly, confirming Palin's suspicions.

"First," Palin said, "Takhisis is not my queen, so don't include me in your thinking. Second, what do you mean—experiment? She's obviously keeping us around to make use of the magical Device of Time Journeying, should she ever get hold of it."

"In the beginning that was true. But now that we've done so well—thrived, so to speak—she's starting to have other ideas. Why waste good flesh and bone by letting it rot in the ground when it could be animated and put to use? She already has an army of souls. She plans to augment her forces by creating an army of corpses to go along with it."

"You sound very certain."

"I am," said Dalamar. "One might say I've heard it from the horse's mouth."

"All the more reason for us to end this," said Palin firmly. "I—"

Dalamar's spirit made a sudden move, darted quickly back to be near the body.

"We are about to have visitors," he warned.

Guards entered the cells, dragging along several kender, tied together with ropes around their waists. The guards marched the kender through the cells to the clamorous amusement of the other prisoners. Then jeering and insults ceased abruptly. The prison grew hushed, quiet.

Mina walked along the rows of cells. She glanced neither to the right nor the left, took no interest in those behind the bars. Some of the prisoners looked at her with fear, some shrank from her. Others reached out their hands in wordless pleading. She ignored them all.

Halting in front of the cell in which the bodies of the two mages were incarcerated, Mina took hold the rope and dragged the assorted kender forward.

"Every one of them claims to be Tasslehoff Burrfoot," she said, speaking to the corpses. "Is one of these the kender I seek? Do either of you recognize him?"

Dalamar's corpse responded with a shake of the head.

"Palin Majere?" she asked. "Do you recognize any of these kender?"

Palin could tell at a glance that none of them were Tasslehoff, but he refused to answer. If Mina imagined she had the kender, let her waste her time finding out otherwise. He sat there, did nothing.

Mina was not been pleased at his show of defiance.

"Answer me," she commanded. "You see the shining light, the realms beyond?"

Palin saw them. They were his constant hope, his constant torment.

"If you have any thought of freedom, of obtaining your soul's wish to leave this world, you will answer me."

When he did not, she clasped her hand around the medallion she wore at her throat.

"Just tell her!" Dalamar hissed at him. "What does it matter? A simple search of the kender will reveal that they don't have the device. Save your defiance for something truly important."

Palin's corpse shook its head.

Mina released her hold on the medallion. The kender, most of them protesting that they were too The Tasslehoff Burrfoot, were marched away.

Watching them go, Palin wondered how Tasslehoff—the real one—had managed to evade capture for so long. Mina and her God were both growing increasingly frustrated.

Tasslehoff and his device were the bedbugs keeping the Queen from having a really good night's sleep. The knowledge of her vulnerability must nip at her constantly, for no matter how powerful she grew, the kender was out there when and where he should not be.

If anything happened to him—and what kender ever lived to a ripe old age?—Her Dark Majesty's grand schemes and plans would come to naught. That might be a comforting thought, but for the fact that Krynn and its people would come to naught, as well.

"All the more reason to remain alive," Dalamar stated with vehemence, speaking to Palin's thoughts. "Once you join that river of death, you will drown and be forever at the mercy of the tide, as are those poor souls who are out there now. We still have a modicum of free will, as you just discovered. That is the flaw in the experiment, the flaw that Takhisis has yet to correct. She has never liked the concept of freedom, you know. Our ability to think and act for ourselves has always been her greatest enemy. Unless she somehow finds a way to deprive us of that, we must cling to our one strength, keep fast hold of it. Our chance will come, and we must be ready to seize it."

Our chance or yours? Palin wondered. He was half-amused by Dalamar, half-angry at him, and on reflection, wholly ashamed of himself.

As usual, he thought, I've been sitting around feeling sorry for myself while my self-serving, ambitious colleague has been out and doing. No more. I will be just as selfish, just as ambitious as any two Dalamars. I may be lost in a foreign country, hobbled hand and foot, where no one speaks my language and they are all deaf, dumb, and blind to boot. Yet, some way, some how, I will find someone who sees me, who hears me, who understands me.

Your experiment will fail, Takhisis, Palin vowed. The experiment itself will see to that.

12 IN THE PRESENCE OF THE GOD

The day Gerard spent in the cell was the worst day of his life. He hoped he would grow used to the smell, but that proved impossible, and he caught himself seriously wondering if breathing was actually worth it. The guards tossed food inside and brought buckets of water for drinking, but the water tasted like the smell, and he gagged as he swallowed. He was gloomily pleased to note that the day gaoler, who appeared none too intelligent, was, if possible, more harassed and confused than the night man.

Late in the afternoon, Gerard began to think that he'd miscalculated, that his plan wasn't as good as he'd thought and that there was every possibility he would spend the rest of his life in this cell. He'd been caught by surprise when Mina had entered the cells, accompanying the kender. She was the last person he wanted to see. He kept his face hidden, remained crouched on the floor until she had gone.

After a few more hours, when it appeared that no one else was likely to come, Gerard was beginning to have second thoughts about this mission. Suppose no one came? He was reflecting that he wasn't nearly as smart as he'd thought he was, when he heard a sound that improved his spirits immensely—the rattle of steel, the clank of a sword.

Prison guards carried clubs, not swords. Gerard leaped to his feet. Two members of the Dark Knights of Neraka entered the prison cells. They wore their helmets with the visors lowered (probably to keep out the smell), cuirasses over woolen shirts, leather breeches, and boots. They kept their swords sheathed but their hands on the hilts.

Immediately the prisoners set up a clamor, some demanding to be freed, others pleading to be able to talk to someone about the terrible mistake that had been made. The Dark Knights ignored them. They headed for the cell where the two mages sat staring at the walls, oblivious to the uproar.

Lunging forward, Gerard managed to thrust his arm between the bars and seize hold of the sleeve of one of the Dark Knights. The man whipped around. His companion drew his sword, and Gerard might have lost his hand had he not snatched it away.

"Captain Samuval!" Gerard shouted. "I must see Captain Samuval."

The Knight's eyes were glints of light in the shadow of his helm. He lifted his visor to get a better view of Gerard.

"How do you know Captain Samuval?" he demanded.

"I'm one of you!" Gerard said desperately. "The Solamnics captured me and locked me up in here. I've been trying to convince the great oaf who runs this place to set me free, but he won't listen. Just bring Captain Samuval here, will you? He'll recognize me."

The Knight stared at Gerard a moment longer, then snapped his visor shut and walked over to the cell that held the mages. Gerard could do nothing more but hope that the man would tell someone, would not leave him here to die of the stink.

The Dark Knights escorted Palin and his fellow mage out of the cellblock. The prisoners fell back as the mages shuffled past, not wanting anything to do with them. The mages were gone for more than an hour. Gerard spent the time wondering if the Knight would tell someone. Hopefully, the name of Captain Samuval would spur the Knight to action.

The clanking of swords announced the Knights' return. They deposited their catatonic charges back on their cots. Gerard hastened forward to try to talk to the Dark Knight again. The prisoners were banging on the cell bars and shrieking for the guards when the commotion suddenly ceased, some swallowing their cries so fast that they choked.

A minotaur entered the cells. The beast-man, who had the face of a bull made even more ferocious by the intelligent eyes that looked out of the mass of shaggy brown fur, was so tall that he was forced to walk with his head bowed to avoid raking his sharp horns against the low ceiling. He wore a leather harness that left bare his muscular torso. He was armed with numerous weapons, among them a heavy sword that Gerard doubted he could have lifted with two hands. Gerard guessed rightly that the minotaur was coming to see him, and he didn't know whether to be worried or thankful.

As the minotaur approached his cell, the other prisoners scrambled to see who could reach the back fastest. Gerard had the front of the cell all to himself. He tried desperately to remember the minotaur's name, but it eluded him.

"Thank goodness, sir," he said, making do. "I was beginning to think I'd rot in here. Where's Captain Samuval?"

"He is where he is," the minotaur rumbled. His small, bovine eyes fixed on Gerard. "What do you want with him?"

"I want him to vouch for me," said Gerard. "He'll remember me, I'm sure. You might remember me, too, sir. I was in your camp just prior to the attack on Solanthus. I had a prisoner—a female Solamnic Knight."

"I remember," said the minotaur. The eyes narrowed. "The Solamnic escaped. She had help. Yours."

"No, sir, no!" Gerard protested indignantly. "You've got it all wrong! Whoever helped her, it wasn't me. When I found out she was gone, I chased after her. I caught her, too, but we were close to the Solamnic lines. She shouted, and before I could shut her up"—he drew his hand across his throat—"the Solamnics came to her rescue. They took me prisoner, and I've been locked here ever since."

"Our people checked to see if there were any Knights being held prisoner after the battle," said the minotaur.

"I tried to tell them then," said Gerard, aggrieved. "I've been telling them ever since! No one believes me!"

The minotaur said nothing in reply, just stood staring. Gerard had no way of knowing what the beast-man was thinking beneath those horns.

"Look, sir," said Gerard, exasperated, "would I be in this stinking hole if my story wasn't true?"

The minotaur stared at Gerard a moment longer. Turning on his heel, he stalked off to the end of the corridor to confer with the gaoler. Gerard saw the jailer peer at him and then shake his head and fling up his hands helplessly.

"Let him out," ordered the minotaur.

The gaoler hurried to obey. Fitting the key in the lock, he opened the cell door. Gerard walked out to the tune of muttered curses and threats from his fellow prisoners. He didn't care. At that moment, he could have hugged the minotaur, but he thought his reaction should be one of indignation, not relief. He flung a few curses himself and glowered at the gaoler.

The minotaur laid a heavy hand on Gerard's shoulder. The hand was not there in the spirit of friendship. The minotaur's nails dug painfully into Gerard's shoulder.

"I will take you to Mina," said the minotaur.

"I plan to pay my respects to Lord of the Night Mina," said Gerard, "but I can't appear before her like this. Give me some time to wash up and find some decent clothes—"

"She will see you as you are," said the minotaur, adding, as an afterthought, "She sees all of us as we are."

This being precisely what he feared, Gerard was not in the least eager to be interviewed by Mina. He had hoped to be able to retrieve his knightly accoutrements (he knew the storehouse where the Solamnics had stashed them) and blend in with the crowd, hang about the barracks with the other Knights and soldiers, pick up the latest gossip, discover who'd been given orders to do what, then leave to make his report.

There was no help for it, however. The minotaur (whose name was Galdar, Gerard finally remembered), marched Gerard out of the prison. Gerard cast a last glance at Palin as he left. The mage had not moved.

Shaking his head, feeling a shiver run through him, Gerard accompanied the minotaur through the streets of Solanthus.

If anyone would know Mina's plans, it was Galdar. The minotaur was not the talkative type, however. Gerard mentioned Sanction a couple of times, but the minotaur answered only with a cold, dark glower. Gerard gave up and concentrated on seeing what he could of life in Solanthus. People were out in the streets, going about their daily routine, but they did so in a fearful and hurried manner, keeping their heads down, not wanting to meet the eyes of the numerous patrols.

All the taverns were closed, their doors ceremoniously sealed by a band of black cloth that had been stretched across them. Gerard had always heard the saying about courage being found at the bottom of a jug of dwarf spirits, and he supposed that was why the taverns had been shut down. The black cloth was stretched across other shops, as well—most notably mageware shops and shops that sold weapons.

They came within sight of the Great Hall, where Gerard had been brought to trial. Memories came back to him forcibly, particularly memories of Odila. She was his closest friend, his only friend, really, for he was not the type to make friends easily. He was sorry now that he hadn't said good-bye to her and at least given her some hint of what he planned.

Galdar steered Gerard past the Great Hall. The building teemed with soldiers and Knights, for it had apparently been taken over as a barracks. Gerard thought they might stop here, but Galdar led him to the old temples that stood near the hall.

These temples had been formerly dedicated to the gods most favored by the Knights—Paladine and Kiri-Jolith. The temple of Kiri-Jolith was the older of the two and slightly larger, for Kiri-Jolith was considered the Solamnics' special patron. Paladine's temple, constructed of white marble, drew the eye with its simple but elegant design. Four white columns adorned the front. Marble steps, rounded so that they resembled waves, flowed down from the portico.

The two temples were attached by a courtyard and a rose garden. Here grew the white roses, the symbol of the Knighthood. Even after the departure of the gods and, subsequently, the priests, the Solamnics had kept up the temples and tended the rose gardens. The Knights had used the temples for study or for meditation. The citizens of Solanthus found them havens of peace and tranquility and could often be seen walking here with their families.

"Not surprising this One God looks on them with covetous eyes," Gerard said to himself. "I'd move here in a minute if I were out wandering the universe, searching for a home."

A large number of the citizens stood gathered around the outer doors of the temple of Paladine. The doors were closed, and the crowd appeared to be awaiting admittance.

"What's going on, sir?" Gerard asked. "What are all these people doing here? They aren't threatening to attack, are they?"

A tiny smile creased the minotaur's muzzle. He almost chuckled. "These people have come to hear about the One God. Mina speaks to crowds like this every day. She heals the sick and performs other miracles. You will find many residents of Solanthus worshiping in the temple."

Gerard had no idea what to say to this. Anything that came to mind would only land him in trouble and so he kept his mouth shut. They were walking past the rose garden when a brilliant flash of sunlight reflecting off amber caught his eye. He blinked, stared, then stopped so suddenly that Galdar, irritated, almost yanked off his arm.

"Wait!" Gerard cried, appalled. "Wait a minute." He pointed. "What is that?"

"The sarcophagus of Goldmoon," said Galdar. "She was once the head of the Mystics of the Citadel of Light. She was also the mother of Mina—her adopted mother," he felt compelled to add. "She was an old, old woman. Over ninety, so they say. Look at her. She is young and beautiful again. Thus does the One God grant favor to the faithful."

"A lot of good that does her if she's dead," Gerard muttered, his heart aching, as he looked at the body encased in amber. He remembered Goldmoon vividly, remembered her beautiful, golden hair that seemed spun with silver moonbeams, remembered her face, strong and compassionate and lost, searching. He couldn't find the Goldmoon he had known, though. Her face, seen beneath the amber, was the face of no one, anyone. Her gold and silver hair was amber-colored. Her white robes amber. She'd been caught in the resin, like all the rest of the insects.

"She will be granted life again," said Galdar. "The One God has promised to perform a great miracle."

Gerard heard an odd tone in Galdar's voice and he glanced, startled, at the minotaur. Disapproving? That was hard to be believe. Still, as Gerard thought back over what he knew of the minotaur race, he had always heard them described as devout followers of their former god, Sargonnas, who was himself a minotaur. Perhaps Galdar was having second thoughts about this One God. Gerard marked that down as a hunch he might be able to make use of later.

The minotaur gave Gerard a shove, and he had to continue walking. He looked back at the sarcophagus. Many of the citizenry were standing around the amber coffin, gaping at the body inside and sighing and ooohing and aahing. Some were on their knees in prayer. Gerard kept twisting his head to look around, forgot to watch where he was going, and tripped over the temple stairs. Galdar growled at him, and Gerard realized he had better keep his mind on his own business or he'd end up in a coffin himself. And the One God wasn't likely to perform any miracle on him.

The temple doors opened for Galdar, then shut behind him, to the great disappointment of those waiting outside.

"Mina!" they called out, chanting her name. "Mina! Mina!"

Inside, the temple was shadowed and cool. The pale light of the sun, that seemed to have to work hard to shine through the stained glass windows, formed weak and watery patterns of blue, white, green, and red on the floor, criss-crossed with black bars. The altar had been covered with a cloth of white velvet. A single person knelt there. At the sound of their footfalls in the still temple, the girl raised her head and glanced over her shoulder.

"I am sorry to disturb you in your prayers, Mina," said Galdar in a subdued voice that echoed eerily in the still temple, "but this is a matter of importance. I found this man in the prison cells. You may remember him. He—"

"Sir Gerard," said Mina. Rising, she moved away from the altar, walked down the central aisle. "Gerard uth Mondar. You brought that young Solamnic Knight to us. Odila was her name. She escaped."

Gerard had his story all ready, but his tongue stuck firmly to the roof of his mouth. He had not thought he could ever forget those amber eyes, but he had forgotten the powerful spell they could cast over any person caught in their depths. He had the feeling that she knew all about him, knew everything he had done since they last parted, knew exactly why he was here. He could lie to her, but he would be wasting his time.

Still, he had to try, futile as it might be. He stumbled through his tale, thinking all the while that he sounded exactly like a guilty child lying to avoid the strap and the woodshed.

Mina listened to him with grave attention. He ended by saying that he hoped that he would be permitted to serve her, since he understood that his former commander, Marshal Medan, had died in the battle of Qualinesti.

"You grieve for the Marshal and for the Queen Mother, Laurana," said Mina.

Gerard stared at her, dumbfounded.

She smiled, the amber eyes shone. "Do not grieve for them. They serve the One God in death as they both unwittingly served the One God in life. So do we all serve the One God, whether we will or no. The rewards are greater for those who serve the One God knowingly, however. Do you serve the One God, Gerard?"

Mina came nearer to him. He saw himself small and insignificant in her amber eyes, and he suddenly wanted very much to do something to make her proud of him, to win her favor.

He could do so by swearing to serve the One God, yet in this, if in nothing else, he must speak the truth. He looked at the altar, and he listened to the stillness, and it was then he knew for a certainty that he was in the presence of a god and that this god saw through to his very heart.

"I . . . I know so little of this One God," he stammered evasively. "I cannot give you the answer you want, Lady. I am sorry."

"Would you be willing to learn?" she asked him.

"Yes" was all he needed to say to remain in her service, yet the truth was that he didn't want to know anything at all about this One God. Gerard had always done very well without the gods. He didn't feel comfortable in the presence of this one.

He mumbled something unintelligible, even to himself. Mina seemed to hear what she wanted to hear from him, however. She smiled.

"Very well. I take you into my service, Gerard uth Mondar. The One God takes you into service, as well."

At this, the minotaur made a disgruntled rumbling sound.

"Galdar thinks you are a spy," said Mina. "He wants to kill you. If you are a spy, I have nothing to hide. I will tell you my plans freely. In two days time, an army of soldiers and Knights from Palanthas will join us, adding another five thousand to our number. With that army and the army of souls, we will march on Sanction. And we will take it. Then we will rule all of the northern part of Ansalon, well on our way to ruling all of this continent. Do you have any questions?"

Gerard ventured a feeble protest. "Lady, I am not—"

Mina turned from him. "Open the doors, Galdar," she ordered. "I will speak to the people now." Glancing back at Gerard, she added, "You should stay to hear the sermon, Sir Gerard. You might find my words instructive."

Gerard could do nothing but acquiesce. He glanced sidelong at Galdar, caught the minotaur glowering back at him. Clearly, Galdar knew him for what he was. Gerard must take care to keep out of the minotaur's way. He supposed he should be thankful, for he'd accomplished his mission. He knew Mina's plans—always provided she was telling the truth—and he had only to hang about for a couple of days to see if the army from Palanthas showed up to confirm it. His heart was no longer in his mission, however. Mina had killed his spirit, as effectively as she might have killed his body.

We fight against a god. What does it matter what we do?

Galdar flung wide the temple doors. The people streamed inside. Kneeling before Mina, they pleaded with her to touch them, to heal them, to heal their children, to take away their pain. Gerard kept an eye on Galdar. The minotaur watched a moment, then walked out.

Gerard was about to sidle out the door when he saw a troop of Knights marching up the stairs. They had with them a prisoner, a Solamnic, to judge by the armor. The prisoner's arms were bound with bowstrings, but she walked with her head held high, her face set in grim determination.

Gerard knew that face, knew the expression on that face. He groaned softly, swore vehemently, and hastily drew back into the deepest shadows, covering his face with his hands as though overcome by reverence.

"We captured this Solamnic trying to enter the city, Mina," said one of the Knights.

"She's a bold one," said another. "Walked right in the front gate wearing her armor and carrying her sword."

"Surrendered her sword without a fight," added the first. "A fool and a coward, like all of them."

"I am no coward," said Odila with dignity. "I chose not to fight. I came here of my own accord."

"Free her," said Mina, and her voice was cold and stern. "She may be our enemy, but she is a Knight and deserves to be treated with dignity, not like a common thief!"

Chastened, the Knights swiftly removed the bindings from Odila's arms. Gerard had stepped into the shadows, afraid that if she looked around and saw him, she might give him away. He soon realized he could spare himself the worry. Odila had no eyes for anyone except Mina.

"Why have you come all this way and risked so much to see me, Odila?" Mina asked gently.

Odila sank to her knees, clasped her hands.

"I want to serve the One God," she said.

Mina bent down, kissed Odila on the forehead.

"The One God is pleased with you."

Mina removed the medallion she wore on her breast, fastened the medallion around Odila's neck.

"You are my cleric, Odila," said Mina. "Rise and know the blessings of the One God."

Odila rose, her eyes shining with exaltation. Walking to the altar, she joined the other worshipers, knelt in prayer to the One God. Gerard, a bitter taste in his mouth, walked out.

"Now what in the Abyss do I do?" he wondered.

13 THE CONVERT

Absorbed into the main body of the Dark Knights of Neraka, Gerard was assigned to patrol duty. Every day, he and his small band of soldiers marched through their assigned portion of Solanthus, keeping the populace in check. His task was not difficult. The Dark Knights under Mina's command had acted swiftly to round up any members of the community who might have given them trouble. Gerard had seen most of them inside the prison.

As for the rest, the people of Solanthus appeared to be in a state of shock, stunned by the recent, disastrous turn of events. One day they were living in the only free city in Solamnia, and the next day their city was occupied by their most hated enemy. Too much had happened too quickly for them to comprehend. Given time, they might organize and become dangerous.

Or they might not.

Always a devout people, the Solamnics had grieved over the absence of their gods. Feeling an absence and a lacking in their lives, they were interested in hearing about this One God, even if they didn't plan on believing what they heard. The adage goes that while elves strive to be worthy of their gods, humans require that their gods be worthy of them. The citizens of Solanthus were naturally skeptical.

Every day, the sick and the wounded came or were carried to the former temple of Paladine, now the temple of the One God. The lines for miracles were long and the lines waiting to view the miracle maker were longer still. The elves of far-off Silvanesti, so Mina had told them, had bowed down to the One God and proclaimed their devotion. By contrast, the humans of Solanthus started fistfights, as those who believed in the miracles took umbrage with those who claimed they were tricks. After two days of patrol duty, Gerard was ordered to cease walking the streets (where nothing happened) and to start breaking up fights in the temple.

Gerard didn't know if he was glad for this change in assignment or not. He'd spent the last two days trying to decide if he should confront Odila and try to talk some sense into her or if he should continue to avoid her. He didn't think she'd give him away, but he wasn't certain. He couldn't understand her sudden religious fervor and therefore no longer trusted her.

Gerard had never really been given the choice of worshiping the gods, so he hadn't wasted much thought on the matter. The presence or absence of the gods had never made much difference to his parents. The only change that had occurred in their lives when the gods left was that one day they said prayers at the table and the next day they didn't. Now Gerard was being forced to think about it, and in his heart he could sympathize with those who started the fights. He wanted to punch someone, too.

Gerard sent off his report to Richard, who was waiting for it at the roadhouse. He gave the Knights' Council all the information he'd gleaned, confirming that Mina planned to march to Sanction.

Counting the reinforcements expected to arrive from Palanthas, Mina had over five thousand soldiers and Knights under her command. A small force, yet with this force she planned to take the walled city that had held out against double that number of troops for over a year. Gerard might have laughed at the notion, except that she'd taken Solanthus—a city considered impregnable—with far fewer troops than that. She'd taken Solanthus using dragons and the army of souls, and she spoke of using dragons and the army of souls to take Sanction. Recalling the terror of that night he'd fought the dead, Gerard was convinced that nothing could withstand them. He said as much to the Knights' Council, although they hadn't asked for his opinion.

His assignment now completed, he could have left Solanthus, returned to the bosom of the Solamnic Knighthood. He stayed on, however, at risk of his life, he supposed, for Galdar considered him a spy. If that was true, no one paid much attention to him. No one watched him. He was not restricted in his movements. He could go anywhere, talk to anyone. He was not admitted to Mina's inner circle, but he didn't lose by that, for apparently Mina had no secrets. She freely told everyone who asked what she and the One God meant to do. Gerard was forced to concede that such supreme confidence was impressive.

He stayed in Solanthus, telling himself that he would remain to see if Mina and her troops actually marched out, headed east. In truth, he was staying because of Odila, and the day he took up his duties at the temple was the day he finally admitted as much to himself.

Gerard stationed himself at the foot of the temple steps, where he could keep a watchful eye on the crowd, who had gathered to hear Mina speak. He posted his men at intervals around the courtyard, trusting that the sight of armed soldiers would intimidate most of the troublemakers. He wore his helmet, for there were those in Solanthus who might recognize him.

Mina's own Knights, under the command of the minotaur, surrounded her, kept watch over her, guarding her not so much from those who would do her harm, but from those who would have adored her to death. Her speech concluded, Mina walked among the crowd, lifting up children in her arms, curing the sick, telling them all of the One God. The skeptical watched and jeered, the faithful wept and tried to fling themselves at Mina's feet. Gerard's men broke up a few fights, hauled the combatants off to the already crowded prisons.

When Mina's steps began to falter, the minotaur stepped in and called a halt. The people still waiting for their share of the miracles groaned and wailed, but he told them to come back tomorrow.

"Wait a moment, Galdar," said Mina, her voice carrying clearly over the tumult. "I have good news to tell the people of Solanthus."

"Silence!" Galdar shouted, but the effort was needless. The crowd immediately hushed, leaned forward eagerly to hear her words.

"People of Solanthus," Mina cried. "I have just received word that the dragon overlord, Khellendros, also known as Skie, is dead. Only a few days earlier, I told you that the dragon overlord, Beryl, was dead, as well as the wicked dragon known as Cyan Bloodbane."

Mina raised her arms and her eyes to the heavens. "Behold, in their defeat, the power of the One God!"

"Khellendros dead?" The whisper went through the crowd, as each person turned to his neighbors to see what their reaction was to such astonishing news.

Khellendros had long ruled over much of the old nation of Solamnia, exacting tribute from the citizens of Palanthas, using the Dark Knights to keep the people in line and the steel flowing into the dragon's coffers. Now Khellendros was dead.

"So when does this One God go after Malys?" someone yelled.

Gerard was appalled to find that the someone was himself.

He'd had no idea he was going to shout those words. They'd burst out before he could stop them. He cursed himself for a fool, for the last thing he wanted to do was draw attention to himself. Snapping shut the visor of his helm, he glared around, as if searching for the person who had spoken. He did not fool Mina, however. Her amber gaze pierced the eyeslits of his helmet with unerring accuracy.

"After I have taken Sanction," Mina said coolly, "then I will deal with Malys."

She acknowledged the cheers of the crowd with a gesture toward heaven, indicating that their praise belonged to the One God, not to her. Turning, she disappeared inside the temple.

Gerard's skin burned so hot it was a wonder that his steel helm didn't melt around his ears. He expected to feel the heavy hand of the minotaur close around his neck any moment, and when someone touched his shoulder, he nearly crawled out of his armor.

"Gerard?" came a puzzled voice. "Is that you in there?"

"Odila!" he gasped in relief, uncertain whether to hug her or hit her.

"So now you're back to being a Dark Knight," she said. "I must concede that drawing your pay from two coffers is a good way to make a living, but don't you find yourself getting confused? Do you flip a coin? 'Which armor do I put on this morning? Heads Dark Knight, tails Solamnic—'"

"Just shut up, will you," Gerard growled. Grabbing her by the arm, he glanced around to see if anyone had been listening, then hauled her off to a secluded part of the rose garden. "Apparently finding religion hasn't caused you to lose your twisted sense of humor."

He yanked off his helm, glared at her. "You know perfectly well why I'm here."

She eyed him, frowning. "You didn't come after me, did you?"

"No," he answered, which was truth enough.

"Good," she said, her face clearing.

"But now that you mention it—" Gerard began.

Her frown returned.

"Listen to me, Odila," he said earnestly, "I came at the behest of the Knights' Council. They sent me to find out if Mina's threat to attack Sanction is real—"

"It is," said Odila coolly.

"I know that now," said Gerard. "I'm on an intelligence-gathering mission—"

"So am I," she said, interrupting, "and my mission is far more important than yours. You are here to gain information about the enemy. You are here to listen at keyholes and count the numbers of troops and how many siege engines they have."

She paused. Her gaze shifted to the temple. "I am here to find out about this god."

Gerard made a sound.

She looked back at him. "We Solamnics can't ignore this, Gerard, just because it makes us uncomfortable. We can't deny this god because the god came to an orphan girl and not to the Lord of the Rose. We have to ask questions. It is only in the asking that we find answers."

"And what have you found out?" Gerard asked unwillingly.

"Mina was raised by Goldmoon at the Citadel of Light. Yes, I was surprised to hear that myself. Goldmoon told Mina stories of the old gods, how she—Goldmoon—brought knowledge of the gods back to the people of Ansalon when everyone thought the gods had left the world in anger. Goldmoon showed them that it was not the gods who had left mankind but mankind who had left the gods. Mina asked if that might be what was happening now, but Goldmoon told her no, that this time the gods had gone, for there were those who spoke to Paladine and the other gods before they left and who were told that the gods departed the world to spare the world the wrath of Chaos.

"Mina didn't believe this. She knew in her heart that Goldmoon was wrong, that there was a god on this world. It was up to Mina to find the god, as Goldmoon had once found the gods. Mina ran away. She searched for the gods, always keeping her heart open to hear the voice of the gods. And, one day, she heard it.

"Three years, Mina spent in the presence of the One God, learning the One God's plans for the world, plans for us, learning how to put those plans in motion. When the time was right and Mina was strong enough to bear the burden of the task given to her, she was sent to lead us and tell us of the One God."

"That answers some of the questions about Mina," said Gerard, "but what about this One God? So far all I've seen is that this god is a sort of press-gang for the dead."

"I asked Mina about that," Odila said, her face growing solemn at the memory of that terrible night she and Gerard had fought the dead souls. "Mina says that the souls of the dead serve the One God willingly, joyfully. They are glad to remain among the living in the world they love."

Gerard snorted. "They didn't look glad to me."

"The dead do no harm to the living," Odila said sharply. "If they seem threatening, it is only because they are so eager to bring the knowledge of the One God to us."

"So that was proselytizing?" Gerard said. "While the souls preach to us of the One God, Mina and her soldiers fly red dragons into Solanthus. They kill a few hundred people in the process, but I suppose that's just more evangelical work. More souls for the One God."

"You saw the miracles of healing Mina performed," said Odila, her gaze clear and level. "You heard her tell of the deaths of two of the dragon overlords who have long terrorized this world. There *is* a god in this world, and all your gibes and snide comments won't change that."

She thrust a finger accusingly into his chest. "You're afraid. You're afraid to find out that maybe you're *not* in control of your own destiny. That maybe the One God has a plan for you and for all of us."

"If you're saying I'm afraid to find out I'm a slave to this One God, then you're right!" Gerard returned. "I make my own decisions. I don't want any god making them for me."

"You've done so well so far," Odila said caustically.

"Do you know what *I* think?" Gerard returned, jabbing his finger in her chest with a force that shoved her backward a step. "I think you made a mess of your life, and now you're hoping this god will come along and fix everything."

Odila stared at him, then she rounded on her heel, started to walk away. Gerard leaped after her, caught hold of her by the arm.

"I'm sorry, Odila. I had no right to say that. I was just angry because I don't understand this. Any of it. And, well, you're right. It does frighten me."

Odila kept her head turned away, her face averted, but she didn't try to break loose from his grip.

"We're both in a tough situation here," Gerard said, lowering his voice. "We're both in danger. We can't afford to quarrel. Friends?"

He let go her arm, held out his hand.

"Friends," Odila said grudgingly, turning around to shake hands. "But I don't think we're in any danger. I honestly believe that the entire Solamnic army could walk in here and Mina would welcome them with open arms."

"And a sword in each hand," Gerard muttered beneath his breath.

"What did you say?"

"Nothing important. Listen, there's something you can do for me. A favor—"

"I won't spy on Mina," Odila stated firmly.

"No, no, nothing like that," Gerard said. "I saw a friend of mine in the dungeon. His name is Palin Majere. He's a wizard. He doesn't look well, and I was wondering if maybe Mina could . . . er . . . heal him. Don't tell her I said anything," he added hurriedly. "Just say that you saw him and you were thinking . . . I mean, it should sound like your idea. . . ."

"I understand," Odila said, smiling. "You really do believe that Mina has god-given powers. This proves it."

"Yes, well, maybe," said Gerard, not wanting to start another argument. "Oh, and one thing more. I hear that Mina is searching for Tasslehoff Burrfoot, the kender who was with me. You remember him?"

"Of course." Odila's eyes were suddenly alert and focused, intent on Gerard's face. "Why? Have you seen him?"

"Look, I have to ask—what does this One God want with Tasslehoff Burrfoot. Is this some sort of joke?"

"Far from it," said Odila. "This kender is not supposed to be here."

"Since when is a kender supposed to be anywhere?"

"I'm serious. This is very important, Gerard. Have you seen him?"

"No," said Gerard, thankful he didn't have to lie to her. "Remember about Palin, will you? Palin Majere? In the prison?"

"I'll remember. And you keep watch for the kender."

"I will. Where can we meet?"

"I am always here," Odila said, gesturing toward the Temple.

"Yeah, I guess you are. Do you . . . um . . . pray to this One God?" Gerard asked uncomfortably.

"Yes," said Odila.

"Have your prayers been answered?"

"You're here, aren't you?" Odila said. She wasn't being glib. She was serious. With a smile and a wave, she walked back toward the temple.

Gerard gaped at her, speechless. Finally, he found his tongue. "I'm not . . ." he shouted after her. "I didn't . . . You didn't . . . Your god didn't . . . Oh, what's the use!"

Figuring that he was confused enough for one day, Gerard turned on his heel and stalked off.

The minotaur, Galdar, saw the two Solamnics deep in discussion. Convinced that both of them were spies, he sauntered their direction in hopes of hearing something of their conversation. One drawback to being a minotaur in a city of humans was that he could never blend in with his surroundings. The two stood near the amber sarcophagus of Goldmoon, and using that as cover, he edged near. All he could hear was a low murmur, until at one point they forgot themselves and their voices rose.

"You're afraid," he heard the the female Solamnic say in accusing tones. "You're afraid to find out that maybe you're *not* in control of your own destiny. That maybe the One God has a plan for you and for all of us."

"If you're saying I'm afraid to find out I'm a slave to this One God, then you're right!" the Knight returned angrily. "I make my own decisions. I don't want any god making them for me."

At that point their voices dropped again. Even though they were talking theology, not sedition, Galdar was still troubled. He remained standing in the shadow of the sarcophagus until long after they had both gone, one returning to the temple and the other heading back to his quarters. The Knight's face was red with anger and frustration. He muttered to himself as he walked and was so absorbed in his thoughts that he passed within a foot of the enormous minotaur and never noticed him.

Solamnics and minotaurs have always had much in common—more in common than not, although, throughout history, it was the "not" that divided them. Both the Solamnics and the minotaurs place high emphasis on personal honor. Both value duty and loyalty. Both admire courage. Both reverenced their gods when they had gods to worship. Both gods were gods of honor, loyalty and courage, albeit one god fought for the side of light and the other for the side of darkness.

Or was it truly that? Might not it be said that one god, Kiri-Jolith, fought for the side of the humans and that Sargonnas fought for the minotaurs? Was it race that divided them, not daylight and night shadow? Humans and minotaurs both told tales of the famous Kaz, a minotaur who had been a friend of the great Solamnic Knight, Huma.

But because one had horns and a snout and was covered with fur and the other had soft skin and a puny lump of a nose, the friendship between Kaz and Huma was considered an anomaly. The two races had been taught to hate and distrust each other for centuries. Now the gulf between them was so deep and wide and ugly that neither could cross.

In the absence of the gods, both races were deteriorating. Galdar had heard rumors of strange doings in the minotaur homeland—rumors of murder, treachery, deceit. As for the Solamnics, few young men and women in this modern age wanted to endure the rigors and constraints and responsibilities of the Knighthood. Their numbers were dwindling, their backs were to the wall. And they had a new enemy—a new god.

Galdar had seen in Mina the end of his quest. He had seen in Mina a sense of duty, honor, loyalty, and courage—the ways of old. Yet, certain things Mina had said and done had begun to trouble Galdar. The foremost of these was the horrible rebirth of the two wizards.

Galdar had no use for wizards. He could have watched these two being tortured without a qualm, could have slain them with his own hand and never given the matter another thought. But the sight of their lifeless bodies being used as mindless slaves gave him a sick feeling in the pit of his stomach. He could not look at the two shambling corpses without feeling his gorge rise.

Worst was the One God's punishment of Mina for losing the kender. Recalling the sacrifices Mina had made, the physical pain she had endured, the torment, the exhaustion, thirst, and starvation, all in the name of the One God, then to see her suffering like that, Galdar was outraged.

Galdar honored Mina. He was loyal to Mina. His duty lay with Mina. But he was beginning to have doubts about this One God.

The Solamnic's words echoed in Galdar's mind. *If you're saying I'm afraid to find out I'm a slave to this One God, then you're right! I make my own decisions. I don't want any god making them for me.*

Galdar did not like thinking of himself as a slave to the will of this One God or any god. More important, he didn't like seeing Mina as a slave to this One God, a slave to be whipped if she failed to do the god's bidding.

Galdar decided to do what he should have done long ago. He needed to find out more about this One God. He could not speak of this to Mina, but he could speak of it to this Solamnic female.

And perhaps kill two with one blow, as the saying went among minotaurs, in reference to the well-known tale of the thieving kender and the minotaur blacksmith.

14 FAITH IN THE ONE GOD

Over a thousand Knights and soldiers from Palanthas entered the city of Solanthus. Their entry was triumphant. Flags bearing the emblems of the Dark Knights as well as flags belonging to individual Knights whipped in the wind. The Dark Knights who served in Palanthas had grown wealthy, for although much of the tribute had gone to the late dragon Khellendros and still more had been sent to the late Lord of the Night Targonne, the high-ranking Knights of Palanthas had done all right for themselves. They were in a good mood, albeit a bit concerned over rumors that had reached them concerning the new, self-proclaimed Lord of the Night—a teen-age girl.

These officers could not imagine how any right-thinking veteran soldier could take orders from a chit who should be dreaming of dancing around the Maypole, not leading men into battle. They had discussed this on the march to Solanthus and had privately agreed among themselves that there must be some shadowy figure working behind the scenes—this minotaur, who was said never to stir far from Mina's side. He must be the true leader. The girl was a front, for humans would never follow a minotaur. There were some who pointed out that few men would follow a slip of a girl into battle, either, but others replied knowingly that she performed tricks and illusions to entertain the ignorant, dupe them into fighting for her.

No one could argue with her success, and so long as it worked, they had no intention of destroying those illusions. Of course, as intelligent men, they would not be fooled.

As had others before them, the officers of the Palanthas Knighthood met Mina with boisterous bravado, preparing to hear her with outward composure, inward chuckles. They came away pale and shaken, quiet and subdued, every one them trapped in the resin of the amber eyes.

Gerard faithfully recorded their numbers in a coded message to the Knighthood. This was his most important missive yet, for this confirmed that Mina meant to attack Sanction and she meant to march soon. Every blacksmith and weaponsmith in the city was pressed into duty, working day and night, making repairs on old weapons and armor and turning out new ones.

Her army would move slowly. It would take weeks, maybe months, to march through the woods and trek across the grasslands and into the mountains that surrounded Sanction. Watching the preparations and thinking of this prolonged march, Gerard developed a plan of attack that he included along with his report. He had little hope that the plan would be adopted, for it involved fighting by stealth, hitting the flanks of the army as it crawled across the ground, striking their supply trains, attacking swiftly, then disappearing, only to strike again when least expected.

Thus, he wrote, *did the Wilder elves of Qualinesti succeed in doing great damage to the Dark Knights who occupied that land. I realize that this is not an accepted means of fighting for the Knighthood, for it is certainly not chivalric nor honorable nor even particularly fair. However, it is effective, not only in reducing the numbers of the enemy but in destroying the morale of the troops.*

Lord Tasgall was a sensible man, and Gerard actually thought that he might toss aside the Measure and act upon it. Unfortunately, Gerard couldn't find any way of delivering the message to Richard, who'd been instructed to return to the roadhouse on a weekly basis to see if Gerard had more information.

Gerard was now being watched day and night, and he had a good idea who was to blame. Not Mina. The minotaur, Galdar.

Too late Gerard had noticed the minotaur eavesdropping on his conversation with Odila. That night, Gerard discovered Galdar was having him watched.

No matter where Gerard went, he was certain to see the horns of the minotaur looming over the crowd. When he left his lodging, he found one of Mina's Knights loitering about in the street outside. The next day, one of his patrol members fell mysteriously ill and was replaced. Gerard had no doubt that the replacement was one of Galdar's spies.

He had no one to blame but himself. He should have left Solanthus days ago instead of hanging about. Now he had not only placed himself in danger, he'd imperiled the very mission he'd been sent to accomplish.

During the next two days, Gerard continued to perform his duties. He went to the temple as usual. He had not seen Odila since the day they'd spoken and was startled to see her standing alongside Mina today. Odila searched the crowd until she found Gerard. She made a small gesture, a slight beckoning motion. When Mina left, and the supplicants and idlers had departed, Gerard hung around outside, waiting.

Odila emerged from the temple. She shook her head slightly, indicating he was not to speak to her, and walked past him without a glance.

As she passed, she whispered, "Come to the temple tonight an hour before midnight."

Gerard sat gloomily on his bed, waiting for the hour Odila had set. He whiled away the time, by staring in frustration at the scrollcase containing the message that should have been in the hands of his superiors by now. Gerard's quarters were in the same hall once used to house the Solamnic Knights. He had at first been assigned a room already occupied by two other Knights, but he'd used some of the money he'd earned from the Dark Knights to buy his way into a private chamber. The chamber was, in reality, little more than a windowless storage room located on the first level. By the lingering smell, it had once been used to store onions.

Restless, he was glad to leave it. He walked openly into the streets, pausing only long enough to lace up his boot and to catch a glimpse of a shadow detaching itself from a nearby doorway. Resuming his pace, he heard light footfalls behind him.

Gerard had a momentary impulse to whirl around and confront his shadow. He resisted the impulse, kept walking. Going straight to the temple, he entered and found a seat on a stone bench in a corner of the building.

The temple's interior was dark, lit by five candles that stood on the altar. Outside, the sky was clouded over. Gerard could smell rain in the air, and within a few moments, the first drops began to fall. He hoped his shadow got soaked to the skin.

The flames of the candles wavered in a sudden gust stirred up by the storm. A robed figure entered the temple from a door in the rear. Pausing at the altar, she fussed with the candles for a moment, then, turning, walked down the aisle. Gerard could see her silhouetted against the candlelight, and although he could not see her face, he knew Odila by her upright bearing and the tilt of her head.

She sat down beside him, slid closer to him. He shifted on the stone bench, moved nearer to her. They were the only two in the temple, but they kept their voices low.

"Just so you know, I'm being followed," he whispered.

Alarmed, Odila turned to stare at him. Her face was pale against the candle-lit darkness. Her eyes were smudges of shadow. Reaching out her hand, she fumbled for Gerard's, found it, and clasped hold tightly. He was astonished, both at the fact that she was seeking comfort and by the fact that her hand was cold and trembling.

"Odila, what is it? What's wrong?" he asked.

"I found out about your wizard friend, Palin," she said in a smothered voice, as if she found it hard to draw breath. "Galdar told me."

Odila's shoulders straightened. She turned to him, looked him in the eyes. "Gerard, I've been a fool! Such a fool!"

"We're a pair of them, then," he said, patting her hand clumsily.

He felt her stiff and shivering, not comforted by his touch. She didn't seem to hear his words. When she spoke, her voice was muffled.

"I came here hoping to find a god who could guide me, care for me, comfort me. Instead I've found—" She broke off, said abruptly. "Gerard, Palin's dead."

"I'm not surprised," Gerard said, with a sigh. "He didn't look well—"

"No, Gerard!" Odila shook her head. "He was dead when you saw him."

"He wasn't dead," Gerard protested. "He was sitting on his cot. After that, I saw him get up and walk out."

"And I'm telling you that he was dead," she said, turning to face him. "I don't blame you for not believing me. I didn't believe it myself. But I . . . Galdar took me to see him. . . ."

He eyed her suspiciously.

"Are you drunk?"

"I wish I were!" Odila returned, but with sudden, savage vehemence. "I don't think there's enough dwarf spirits in the world to make me forget what I've seen. I'm cold sober, Gerard. I swear it."

He looked at her closely. Her eyes were focused, her voice shaking but clear, her words coherent.

"I believe you," he said slowly, "but I don't understand. How could Palin be dead when I saw him sitting and standing and walking?"

"He and the other wizard were both killed in the Tower of High Sorcery. Galdar was there. He told me the whole story. They died, and then Mina and Galdar found out that this kender they were searching for was in the Tower. They went to find him, only they lost him. The One God punished Mina for losing the kender. Mina said that she needed the wizards' help to find him, and . . . and she . . . she gave them back their lives."

"If she did, they didn't look any too pleased by it," Gerard said, thinking of Palin's empty eyes, his vacant stare.

"There's a reason for that," Odila returned, her voice hollow. "She gave them their lives, but she didn't give them their souls. The One God holds their souls in thrall. They have no will to think or act on their own. They are nothing more than puppets, and the One God holds the strings. Galdar says that when the kender is captured, the wizards will know how to deal with him and the device he carries."

"And you think he's telling the truth?"

"I know he is. I went to see your friend, Palin. His body lives, but there is no life in his eyes. They're both corpses, Gerard. Walking corpses. They have no will of their own. They do whatever Mina tells them to do. Didn't you think it was strange the way they both just sit there, staring at nothing?"

"They're wizards," Gerard said lamely, by way of excuse.

Now that he looked back, he wondered he hadn't guessed something was wrong. He felt sickened at the thought.

Odila moistened her lips. "There's something else," she said, dropping her voice so that it was little more than a breath. Gerard had to strain to hear her. "Galdar told me that the One God is so pleased by this that she has ordered Mina to use the dead in battle. Not just the souls, Gerard. She is supposed to give life back to the bodies."

Gerard stared at her, aghast.

"It doesn't matter that Mina plans to attack Sanction with a ridiculously small army," Odila continued relentlessly. "None of her soldiers will ever die. If they do, Mina will just raise them up and send them right back into battle—"

"Odila," said Gerard, his voice urgent, "we have to leave here. Both of us. You don't want to stay, do you?" he asked suddenly, uncertain.

"No," she answered emphatically. "No, not after this. I am sorry I ever sought out this One God."

"Why did you?" Gerard asked.

She shook her head. "You wouldn't understand."

"I might. Why do you think I wouldn't?"

"You're so . . . self-reliant. You don't need anyone or anything. You know your own mind. You know who you are."

"Cornbread," he said, recalling her disparaging nickname for him. He had hoped to make her smile, but she didn't even seem to have heard him. Speaking of his feelings like this wasn't easy for him. "I'm looking for answers," he said awkwardly, "just like you. Just like everyone. Like you said, in order to find the answers, you have to ask questions." He gestured outside the temple, to the steps where the worshipers congregated every day. "That's what's the matter with half these people around here. They're like starving dogs. They are so hungry to believe in something that they take the first handout that's offered and gulp it down, never dreaming that the meat might be poisoned."

"I gulped," said Odila, sighing. "I wanted what everyone claimed they had in the old days. You were right when you said I hoped that the One God would fix my life. Make everything better. Take away the loneliness and the fear—" She halted, embarrassed to have revealed so much.

"I don't think even the old gods did that, at least from what I've been told," Gerard said. "Paladine certainly didn't solve all Huma's problems. If anything, he heaped more on him."

"Unless you believe that Huma chose to do what he did," said Odila softly, "and that Paladine gave him strength to do it." She paused, then added, in bleak despair, "We can't do anything to this god, Gerard. I've seen the mind of this god! I've seen the immense power this god wields. How can such a powerful god be stopped?"

Odila covered her face with her hands.

"I've made such a mess of things. I've dragged you into danger. I know the reason you've stayed around Solanthus, so don't try to deny it. You could have left days ago. You *should* have. You stayed around because you were worried about me."

"Nothing matters now because both of us are going to leave," Gerard said firmly. "Tomorrow, when the troops march out, Mina and Galdar will be preoccupied with their own duties. There will be such confusion that no one will miss us."

"I want to get out of here," Odila said emphatically. She jumped to her feet. "Let's leave now. I don't want to spend another minute in this terrible place. Everyone's asleep. No one will miss me. We'll go back to your quarters—"

"We'll have to leave separately. I'm being followed. You go first. I'll keep watch."

Reaching out impulsively, Odila took hold of his hand, clasped it tightly. "I appreciate all you've done for me, Gerard. You are a true and loyal friend."

"Go on," he said. "Quickly. I'll keep watch."

Releasing his hand with a parting squeeze, she started walking toward the temple doors, which were never locked, for worshipers of the One God were encouraged to come to the temple at any time, day or night. Odila gave the doors an impatient push and they opened silently on well-oiled hinges. Gerard was about to follow when he heard a noise by the altar. He glanced swiftly in that direction, saw nothing. The candle flames burned steadily. No one had entered. Yet he was positive he'd heard something. He was still staring at the altar, when he heard Odila give a strangled gasp.

Gerard whipped around, his hand on his sword. Expecting to find that she had been accosted by some guard, he was surprised to see her standing in the open doorway, alone.

"Now what's the matter?" He didn't dare go to her. The person following him would be watching for him. "Just walk out the damn door, will you?"

Odila turned to stare at him. Her face glimmered so white in the darkness, that he was reminded uncomfortably of the souls of the dead.

She spoke in a harsh whisper that carried clearly in the still night. "I can't leave!"

Gerard swore beneath his breath. Keeping a tight grip on his sword, he sidled over to the wall, hoping to remain unseen. Reaching a point near the door, he glared at Odila.

"What do you mean you won't leave?" he demanded in low and angry tones. "I risked my neck coming here, and I'll be damned if I'm going to leave without you. If I have to carry you—"

"I didn't say I won't leave!" Odila said, her breath coming in gasps. "I said I *can't!*"

She took a step toward the door, her hands outstretched. As she came nearer the door, her movements grew sluggish, as if she were wading into a river, trying to move against a swift-flowing current. Finally, she came to a halt and shook her head.

"I . . . can't!" she said, her voice choked.

Gerard stared in perplexity. Odila was trying her best, that much was clear. Something was obviously preventing her from leaving.

His gaze went from her terrified face to the medallion she wore around her neck.

He pointed at it. "The medallion! Take it off!"

Odila raised her hand to the medallion. She snatched back her fingers with a pain-filled cry.

Gerard grabbed the medallion, intending to rip it off her.

A jolting shock sent him staggering back against the doors. His hand burned and throbbed. He stared helplessly at Odila. She stared just as helplessly back.

"I don't understand—" she began.

"And yet," said a gentle voice, "the answer is simplicity itself."

Hand on his sword hilt, Gerard turned to find Mina standing in the doorway.

"I want to leave," Odila said, managing with a great effort to keep her voice firm and steady. "You have to let me go. You can't keep me here against my will."

"I am not keeping you here, Odila," said Mina.

Odila tried again to walk through the door. Her jaw clenched, and she strained every muscle. "You are lying!" she cried. "You have cast some sort of evil spell on me!"

"I am no wizard," said Mina, spreading her hands. "You know that. You know, too, what binds you to this place."

Odila shook her head in violent negation.

"Your faith," said Mina.

Odila stared, baffled. "I don't—"

"But you do. You believe in the One God. You said so yourself. 'I've seen the mind of this god! I've seen the immense power this god wields.' You have placed your faith in the One God, Odila, and in return, the One God claims your service."

"Faith shouldn't make anyone a prisoner," Gerard said angrily.

Mina turned her eyes on him, and he saw with dismay the images of thousands of people frozen in their amber depths. He had the terrible feeling that if he looked long enough, he would see himself there.

"Describe to me a faithful servant," said Mina, "or, better yet, a faithful knight. One who is faithful to his Order. What must he do to be termed 'faithful'?"

Gerard stubbornly kept silent, but that didn't matter, because Mina answered her own question.

Her tone was fervent, her eyes glowed with an inner light. "A faithful servant performs loyally and without question all the duties his master asks of him. In return, the master clothes him and feeds him and protects him from harm. If the servant is disloyal, if he rebels against his master, he is punished. Just so the faithful knight who is duty-bound to obey his superior. If he fails in his duty or rebels against authority, what happens to him? He is punished for his oath breaking. Even the Solamnics would punish such a knight, wouldn't they, Sir Gerard?"

She is the faithful servant, Gerard realized. She is the faithful knight. And this makes her dangerous, perhaps the most dangerous person to have ever lived on Krynn.

Her argument was flawed. He knew that, in some deep part of him, but he couldn't think why. Not while staring into those amber eyes.

Mina smiled gently at him. Because he had no answer, she assumed she had won. She turned the amber eyes back to Odila.

"Deny your belief in the One God, Odila," Mina said to her, "and you will be free to go."

"You know I cannot," Odila said.

"Then the One God's faithful servant will remain here to perform her duties. Return to your quarters, Odila. The hour is late. You will need your rest, for we have much to do tomorrow to prepare for the battle that will see the fall of Sanction."

Odila bowed her head, started to obey.

"Odila!" Gerard risked calling.

She kept walking. She did not look back at him.

Mina watched her depart, then turned to Gerard. "Will we see you among the ranks of our Knights as we march in triumph to Sanction, Sir Gerard? Or do you have other duties that call you away? If you do, you may go. You have my blessing and that of the One God."

She knows! Gerard realized. She knows I'm a spy, yet she does nothing. She even offers me the chance to leave! Why doesn't she have me arrested? Tortured? Killed? He wished suddenly that she would. Even death would be better than the notion in the back of his mind that she was using him, allowing him to think he was acting of his own free will, when all the time, whatever he did, he was carrying out the will of the One God.

"I'll ride with you," Gerard said grimly and stalked past her through the door.

On the steps of the temple he halted, stared in the darkness, and announced in a loud voice, "I'm going back to my quarters! Try to keep up, will you?"

Entering his room, Gerard lit a candle, then went to his desk and stood staring for long moments at the scrollcase. He opened it, removed the paper that detailed his plans to defeat Mina's army. Deliberately, grimly, he ripped the paper into small pieces. That done, he fed the pieces, one by one, to the candle's flame.

15 THE LAME AND THE BLIND

Mina's army left Solanthus the next day. Not all the army marched, for she was forced to leave behind troops enough to occupy what was presumably a hostile city. Its hostility was largely a myth, judging by the number of Solanthians who turned out to cheer her and wish her well and press gifts upon her—so many that they would have filled the wagon that contained the amber sarcophagus, had Mina permitted it. She told them instead to give the gifts to the poor in the name of the One God. Weeping, the people of Solanthus blessed her name.

Gerard could have wept, too, but for different reasons. He'd spent the night wondering what to do, whether to go or stay. He decided finally to remain with the army, ride with them to Sanction. He told himself it was because of Odila.

She rode with the army. She sat in the wagon with the corpse of Goldmoon, imprisoned in amber, and the corpses of the two wizards, imprisoned in their own flesh. Viewing the wretched, ambulating corpses, Gerard wondered that he had not known the truth the moment he saw Palin, with his staring, vacant eyes. Odila did not glance at Gerard as the wagon rumbled past.

Galdar looked at him, dark eyes baleful. Gerard stared back. The minotaur's displeasure gave Gerard one consolation. The fact that he was accompanying Mina's army so obviously angered the minotaur that Gerard felt he must be doing something right.

As he cantered out the gates, taking up a position in the rear, as far from Mina as he could get and still be part of her army, his horse nearly ran down two beggars, who scrambled hastily to get out of his way.

"I'm sorry, gentlemen," said Gerard, reigning in his horse. "Are you hurt, either of you?"

One beggar was an older man, human, with gray hair and a gray, grizzled beard. His face was seamed with wrinkles and browned from the sun. His eyes were a keen, glittering blue, the color of new-made steel. Although he limped and leaned upon a crutch, he had the air and bearing of a military man. This was borne out by the fact that he wore what appeared to be the faded, tattered remnants of some sort of military uniform.

The other beggar was blind, his wounded eyes wrapped in a black bandage. He walked with one hand resting on the shoulder of his comrade, who guided him along his way. This man had white hair that shone silver in the sun. He was young, much younger than the other beggar, and he lifted his sightless head at the sound of Gerard's voice.

"No, sir," said the first beggar gruffly. "You did but startle us, that is all."

"Where is this army bound?" the second beggar asked.

"Sanction," said Gerard. "Take my advice, sirs, keep clear of the temple of the One God. Even though they could heal you, I doubt it's worth the price."

Tossing each beggar a few coins, he turned his horse's head, galloped off down the road, and was soon enveloped in a cloud of dust raised by the army.

The citizens of Solanthus watched until Mina was long out of sight, then they turned back to their city, which seemed bleak and empty now that she was gone.

"Mina marches on Sanction," said the blind beggar.

"This confirms the information we received last night," said the lame beggar. "Everywhere we go, we hear the same thing. Mina marches on Sanction. Are you satisfied now, at last?"

"Yes, Razor, I am satisfied," the blind man replied.

"About time," Razor muttered. He hurled the coins Gerard had given him at the blind man's feet. "No more begging! I have never been so humiliated."

"Yet, as you have seen, this disguise permits us to go where we will and talk to whom we want, from thief to knight to nobleman," Mirror said mildly. "No one has any clue that we are more than we seem. The question now is, what do we do? Do we confront Mina now?"

"And what would you say to her, Silver?" Razor raised his voice to a mocking lilt. " 'Where, oh where, are the pretty gold dragons? Where, oh where, can they be?' "

Mirror kept silent, not liking how close Razor had come to the mark.

"I say we wait," Razor continued. "Confront her in Sanction."

"Wait until Sanction has fallen to your Queen, you mean," Mirror stated coldly.

"And I suppose you're going to stop her, Silver? Alone, blind?" Razor snorted.

"You would have me walk into Sanction, alone and blind," said Mirror.

"Don't worry, I won't let anything happen to you. Skie told you more than you've let on. I intend to be there when you have your conversation with Mina."

"Then I suggest you pick up that money, for we will need it," said Mirror. "These disguises that have worked well thus far will aid us all the more in

Sanction. What better excuse to speak to Mina than to come before her as two seeking miracles?"

Mirror could not see the expression on Razor's face, but he could imagine it—defiant at first, then glum, as he realized that what Mirror said made sense.

He heard the scrape of the coins being snatched irritably from the ground.

"I believe you are enjoying this, Silver," Razor said.

"You're right," Mirror returned. "I can't think when I've had this much fun."

16 AN UNEXPECTED MEETING

Like leaves flung from out the center of the cyclone, the gnome and the kender fluttered to the ground. That is, the kender—with his gaily colored clothes—fluttered. The gnome landed heavily, resulting in a subsequent cessation of breathing for a few heart-stopping minutes. Lack of breath also resulted in a cessation of the gnome's shrieking, which, considering where they found themselves, was undeniably a good thing.

Not that they knew right away where they were. All Tasslehoff knew, as he looked about, was where he wasn't, which was anywhere he'd been up to this point in his life. He was standing—and Conundrum was lying—in a corridor made of enormous blocks of black marble that had been polished to a high gloss. The corridor was lit sporadically with torches, whose orange light gave a soft and eerie glow to the corridor. The torches burned clean, for no whisper of air stirred. The light did nothing to remove the gloom from the corridor. The light only made the shadows all that much darker by contrast.

No whisper, no sound at all came from anywhere, though Tas listened with all his might. Tas made no sound either, and he hushed Conundrum as he helped the gnome to his feet. Tas had been adventuring most of his life, and he knew his corridors, and without doubt, this corridor had the smothery feeling of a place where you want to be quiet, very quiet.

"Goblins!" was the first word Conundrum gasped.

"No, not goblins," said Tasslehoff in a quiet tone that was meant to be reassuring. He rather spoiled by it by adding cheerfully, "Probably worse things than goblins down here."

"What do you mean?" Conundrum wheezed and clutched at his hair distractedly. "Worse than goblins! What could be worse than goblins? Where are we anyway?"

"Well, there's lots worse than goblins," whispered Tas upon reflection. "Draconians, for instance. And dragons. And owlbears. Did I ever tell you the story about the Uncle Trapspringer and the owlbear? It all began—"

It all ended when Conundrum doubled up his fist and punched Tasslehoff in the stomach.

"Owlbears! Who cares about owlbears or your blasted relations? I could tell you stories about my cousin Strontiumninety that would make your hair fall out. Your teeth, too. Why did you bring us here, and where is here, anyway?"

"*I* didn't bring us anywhere," returned Tasslehoff in irritable tones when he could speak again. Being struck soundly and unexpectedly in the stomach tended to make a fellow irritable. "The device brought us here. And I don't know where 'here' is anymore than you do. I— Hush! Someone's coming."

When in a dark and smothery feeling corridor, it is always a good idea to see who is coming before giving them a chance to see you. That's the maxim Uncle Trapspringer had always taught his nephew, and Tas had found that, in general, it was a good plan. For one thing, it allowed you to leap out of the darkness and give the person a grand surprise. Tasslehoff took hold of the collar of Conundrum's shirt and dragged the gnome behind a black, marble pillar.

A single figure walked the corridor. The figure was robed in black and was not easily distinguishable from either the darkness of the corridor or the black, marble walls. Tasslehoff had his first good view of the figure as it passed beneath one of the torches. Even in the darkness, able to see only the dimmest, shadowiest outline of the figure, Tasslehoff had the strange and squirmy feeling in his stomach (probably left over from being struck) that he knew this person. There was something about the walk that was slow and halting, something about the way the person leaned upon the staff he was carrying, something about the staff that gave off a very soft, white light.

"Raistlin!" Tasslehoff breathed, awed.

He was about to repeat the name in a much louder voice, accompanied by a whoop and a shout and a rushing forward to give his friend, whom he hadn't seen in a long time and presumed to be dead, an enormous hug.

A hand grasped his shoulder, and a voice said softly, "No. Leave him be."

"But he's my friend," Tas said to Conundrum. "Not counting the time he murdered another friend of mine, who was a gnome, by the way."

Conundrum's eyes opened wide. He clutched at Tas nervously. "This friend of yours. He doesn't make it a practice of . . . of m-m-murdering gnomes, does he?"

Tas missed this because he was staring at Conundrum, noting that the gnome had hold of Tasslehoff's sleeve with one hand and his shirt front with the other. This accounted for two hands and, so far as Tas knew, gnomes came with only two hands. Which meant there was a hand left over, and that hand was holding Tasslehoff firmly by the shoulder. Tasslehoff twisted and squirmed to see who had hold of him, but the pillar behind which they were standing cast a dark shadow, and all he could see behind him was more darkness.

Tas looked round at the other hand—the hand that was on his shoulder—but the hand wasn't there. Or at least, it was there because he could feel it, but it wasn't there because he couldn't see it.

Finding this all very strange, Tasslehoff looked back at Raistlin. Knowing Raistlin as he did, Tas was forced to admit that there were times when the mage had not been at all friendly to the kender. And there was the fact that Raistlin *did* murder gnomes. Or at least, he had murdered one gnome for fixing the Device of Time Journeying. This very device, although not this very gnome. Raistlin wore the black robes now, and he had been wearing black robes then, and while Tasslehoff found Conundrum extremely annoying at times, he didn't want to see the gnome murdered. Tasslehoff decided that for Conundrum's sake he would keep silent and not jump out at Raistlin, and he would forgo the big hug.

Raistlin passed very near the kender and the gnome. Conundrum was, thank goodness, speechless with terror. Through a heroic effort on his part, Tasslehoff kept silent, though the absent gods alone knew what this cost him. He was rewarded with an approving squeeze by the hand on his shoulder that wasn't there, which, all in all, didn't make him feel as good as it might have under the circumstances.

Raistlin was apparently deep in thought, for his head was bowed, his walk slow and abstracted. He stopped once to cough, a racking cough that so weakened him he was forced to lean against the wall. He choked and gagged, his face grew deathly pale. Blood flecked his lips. Tas was alarmed, for he'd seen Raistlin have these attacks before but never one this bad.

"Caramon had a tea he used to fix for him," Tas said, starting forward.

The hand pressed him back.

Raistlin raised his head. His golden eyes shone in the torchlight. He looked about, up and down the corridor.

"Who spoke?" he said in his whispering voice. "Who spoke that name? Caramon? Who spoke, I say?"

The hand dug into Tasslehoff's shoulder. He had no need of its caution, however. Raistlin looked so very strange and his expression was so very terrible that the kender would have kept silent, regardless.

"No one," said Raistlin, at last able to draw a ragged breath. "I am imagining things." He mopped his brow with the hem of his black velvet sleeve, then smiled sardonically. "Perhaps it was my own guilty conscience. Caramon is dead. They are all dead, drowned in the Blood Sea. And they were all so shocked when I used the dragon orb and departed, leaving them to their fate. Amazed that I would not meekly share in their doom."

Recovering his strength, Raistlin drew away from the wall. He steadied himself with the staff, but did not immediately resume his walk. Perhaps he was still too weak.

"I can see the look on Caramon's face now. I can hear his blubbering." Raistlin pitched his voice high, spoke through his nose. " 'But . . . Raist—' " He ground his teeth, then smiled again, a most unpleasant smile. "And Tanis, that self-righteous hypocrite! His illicit love for my dear sister led him to betray his friends, and yet he has the temerity to accuse *me* of being faithless! I can see them all—Goldmoon, Riverwind, Tanis, my brother—all staring at me with great cow eyes."

Again, his voice rose to mimic. " 'At least save your brother . . .' " The voice resumed its bitter monologue. "Save him for what? A lawn ornament? His ambition takes him no further than the bed of his latest conquest. All my life, he has been the manacles that bound my hands and shackled my feet. You might as well ask me to leave my prison but take along my chains. . . ."

He resumed his walk, moving slowly down the corridor.

"You know, Conundrum," whispered Tasslehoff, "I said he was my friend, but it takes a lot of work to like Raistlin. Sometimes I'm not sure it's worth the effort. He's talking about Caramon and the rest drowning in the Blood Sea, but they didn't drown. They were rescued by sea elves. I know because Caramon told me the whole story. And Raistlin knows they weren't drowned because he saw them again. But if he thinks that they're drowned, then obviously he doesn't yet know that they weren't, which means that he must be somewhere between the time he thought they drowned and the time he finds that they didn't. Which means," Tas continued, awed and excited, "that I've found another part of the past."

Hearing this, Conundrum eyed the kender suspiciously and backed up a few steps. "You haven't *met* my cousin, Stroniumninety, have you?"

Tas was about to say that he hadn't had the pleasure when the sound of footsteps rang through the corridor. The footsteps were not those of the mage, who barely made any noise at all beyond the occasional rasping cough and the rustle of his robes. These footsteps were large and imposing, thunderous, filling the corridor with noise.

The hand that wasn't on Tasslehoff's shoulder pulled him back deeper into the shadows, cautioning him with renewed pressure to keep quiet. The gnome, with finely honed instincts for survival so long as steam-powered pistons weren't in the offing, had already pressed himself so far into the wall that he might have been taken for the artistic renderings of some primitive tribe.

A man as large as his footfalls filled the corridor with sound and motion and life. He was tall and brawny, wore heavy, ornately designed armor that seemed a part of his anatomy for all that it slowed him down. He carried under his arm the horned helm of a Dragon Highlord. An enormous sword clanked at his side. He was obviously on his way somewhere with a purpose in mind, for he walked rapidly and with intent, looking neither to the right nor the left. Thus he very nearly ran down Raistlin, who was forced to fall back against the wall at the man's coming or be crushed.

The Dragon Highlord saw the mage, acknowledged his presence with no more than a sharp glance. Raistlin bowed. The Dragon Highlord continued on his way. Raistlin started to go his, when suddenly the Highlord halted, spun round on his heel.

"Majere," boomed the voice.

Raistlin halted, turned. "My Lord Ariakas."

"How do you find things here in Neraka? Your quarters comfortable?"

"Yes, my lord. Quite adequate for my simple needs," Raistlin replied. The light of the crystal ball atop his staff glimmered ever so slightly. "Thank you for asking."

Ariakas frowned. Raistlin's response was polite, servile, as the Dragon Highlord had a right to respect. Ariakas was not a man to note subtleties, but apparently even he had heard the sardonic tone in the mage's raspy voice. The Highlord could not very well rebuke a man for a tone, however, so he continued.

"Your sister Kitiara says that I am to treat you well," said Ariakas gruffly. "You have her to thank for your post here."

"I owe my sister a great deal," Raistlin replied.

"You owe me more," said Ariakas grimly.

"Indeed," said Raistlin with another bow.

Ariakas was plainly not pleased. "You are a cool one. Most men cringe and cower when I speak to them. Does nothing impress you?"

"*Should* anything impress me, my lord?" Raistlin returned.

"By our Queen," Ariakas cried, laying his hand on the hilt of his sword, "I could strike off your head for that remark!"

"You could try, my lord," said Raistlin. He bowed again, this time more deeply than before. "Forgive me, sir, I did not mean the words the way they sounded. Of course, I find you impressive. I find the magnificence of this city impressive. But just because I am impressed does not mean I am fearful. You do not admire fearful men, do you, my lord?"

"No," said Ariakas. He stared at Raistlin intently. "You are right. I do not."

"I would have you admire me, my lord," said Raistlin.

Ariakas continued to stare at the mage. Then, suddenly, the Highlord burst out laughing. His laughter was enormous. It rolled and crashed through the corridor, smashed the gnome up against the wall. Tasslehoff felt dazed by it, as though he'd been struck in the head by a large rock. Raistlin winced slightly, but held his ground.

"I don't admire you yet, mage," said Ariakas, when he had regained control of himself. "But someday, Majere, when you have proven yourself, maybe I will."

Turning on his heel, still chuckling, he continued on his way down the corridor.

When his footfalls had died away and all was once again silent, Raistlin said softly, "Someday, when I have proven myself, my lord, you will do more than admire me. You will fear me."

Raistlin turned and walked away, and Tasslehoff turned to try to see who it was who didn't have hold of his shoulder, and he turned and turned and kept on turning. : . .

BOOK
II

1 MEETING OF THE GODS

The gods of Krynn met in council, as they had done many times since the world had been stolen away from them. The gods of light stood opposite the gods of darkness, as day stands opposite night, with the gods of neutrality divided evenly in between. The children of the gods stood together, as they always did.

These council sessions had accomplished little in the past except to sometimes soothe raging tempers and cheer crushed spirits. One by one, each of the gods came forth to tell of searching that had been done in vain. Many were the journeys taken by each god and goddess to try to find what was lost. Long and dangerous were some of these treks through the planes of existence, but one and all ended in failure. Not even Zivilyn, the all-seeing, who existed in all times and in all lands, had been able to find the world. He could see the path Krynn and its people would have taken into the future, but that path was populated now by the ghosts of might-have-beens. The gods were close to concluding sorrowfully that the world was lost to them forever.

When each had spoken, Paladine appeared to them in his radiance.

"I bring glad tidings," he said. "I have heard a voice cry out to me, the voice of one of the children of the world. Her prayer rang through the heavens, and its music was sweet to hear. Our people need us, for as we had suspected, Queen Takhisis now rules the world unchallenged."

"Where is the world?" Sargonnas demanded. Of all the gods of darkness, he was the most enraged, the most embittered, for Queen Takhisis had been his consort, and he felt doubly betrayed. "Tell us and we will go there immediately and give her the punishment she so richly deserves."

"I do not know," Paladine replied. "Goldmoon's voice was cut off. Death took her and Takhisis holds her soul in thrall. Yet, we now know the world exists. We must continue to search for it."

Nuitari stepped forth. The god of the magic of darkness, he was clad all in black. His face, that of a gibbous moon, was white as wax.

"I have a soul who begs an audience," he said.

"Do you sponsor this?" Paladine asked.

"I do," Nuitari answered.

"And so do I." Lunitari came forward in her red robes.

"And so do I." Solinari came forth in his silver robes.

"Very well, we will hear this soul," Paladine agreed. "Let this soul come forward."

The soul entered and took his place among them. Paladine frowned at the sight, as did most of the other gods, light and darkness alike, for none trusted this soul, who had once tried to become a god himself.

"Raistlin Majere has nothing to say that I want to hear," Sargonnas stated with a snarl and turned to depart.

The others grumbled their agreement—all but one.

"I think we should listen to him," Mishakal said.

The other gods turned to look at her in surprise, for she was the consort of Paladine, a loving goddess of healing and compassion. She knew better than most the harm and suffering and sorrow that this man had brought upon those who loved and trusted him.

"He made reparation for his crimes," Mishakal continued, "and he was forgiven."

"Then why has his soul not departed with the rest?" Sargonnas demanded. "Why does he linger here, except to take advantage of our weakness?"

"Why does your soul remain, Raistlin Majere," Paladine asked sternly, "when you were free to move on?"

"Because half of me is missing," returned Raistlin, facing the god, meeting his eyes. "Together, my brother and I came into this world. Together, we will leave it. We walked apart for much of our lives. The fault was mine. If I can help it, we will not be separated in death."

"Your loyalty is commendable," said Paladine dryly, "if a bit belated. But I do not understand what business you have with us."

"I have found the world," said Raistlin.

Sargonnas snorted. The other gods stared at Raistlin in troubled silence.

"Did you hear Goldmoon's prayer as well?" Paladine asked.

"No," Raistlin responded. "I could hardly be expected to, could I? I did hear something else, though—a voice chanting words of magic. Words I recognized, as perhaps none other could. I recognized, as well, the voice that spoke them. It belonged to a kender, Tasslehoff Burrfoot."

"That is impossible," said Paladine. "Tasslehoff Burrfoot is dead."

"He is and he isn't, but I will come to that later," Raistlin said. "His soul remains unaccounted for." He turned to Zivilyn. "In the future that was, where did the kender's soul go after his death?"

"He joined his friend Flint Fireforge," said Zivilyn readily.

"Is his soul there now? Or does the grumbling dwarf wait for him still?"

Zivilyn hesitated, then said, "Flint is alone."

"A pity you did not notice this earlier," Sargonnas growled at Zivilyn. The minotaur god turned his glare at Raistlin. "Suppose this blasted kender *is* alive. What was he doing speaking words of magic? I never had much use for you mages, but at least you had sense enough to keep kender from using magic. This story of yours smells of yesterday's fish to me."

"As for the magic words he spoke," Raistlin replied, unperturbed by the minotaur god's gibe, "they were taught to him by an old friend of his, Fizban, when he gave into his hands the Device of Time Journeying."

The gods of darkness raised a clamor. The gods of magic looked grave.

"It has long been decreed that none of the Gray Gemstone races should ever be given the opportunity to travel through time," said Lunitari accusingly. "We should have been consulted in this matter."

"In truth, I gave him the device," said Paladine with a fond smile. "He wanted to attend the funeral of his friend Caramon Majere to do him honor. Quite logically assuming that he would die long before Caramon, Tasslehoff asked for the device so that he could go forward into the future to speak at the funeral. I thought this a noble and generous impulse, and thus I permitted it."

"Whether that was wise or not, you know best, Great One," Raistlin said. "I can affirm that Tasslehoff did travel forward in time once, but he missed, arriving at the funeral too late. He came back, thinking he would go again. As for what happened after that, the following is surmise, but since we know kender, I believe we can all agree that the premise I put forth is logical.

"One thing came up, then another, and Tasslehoff forgot all about traveling to Caramon's funeral until he was just about to be crushed by Chaos. At that moment, with only a few seconds of life left, Tas happened to recall this piece of unfinished business. He activated the device, which carried him forward in time. He arrived in the future, as he intended, except that it was a different future. Quite by mischance, the kender found the world. And I have found the kender."

For long moments, no one spoke. The gods of magic glanced at one another, their thoughts in perfect accord.

"Then take us there," said Gilean, the keeper of the book of knowledge.

"I would not advise it," Raistlin returned. "Queen Takhisis is extraordinarily powerful now. She is watchful. She would be aware of your coming far in advance, and she has made preparations to receive you. Should you return now, weak and unprepared to face her, she might well destroy you."

Sargonnas rumbled deep in his chest. The thunder of his ire echoed through the heavens. The other gods were scornful, suspicious, or solemn, depending on the nature of each.

"You have another problem," Raistlin continued. "The people of the world believe that you abandoned them in their hour of greatest need. If you enter the world now, you will not find many who will welcome you."

"My people know I did not abandon them!" Sargonnas cried, clenching his fist.

Raistlin bowed, made no reply. He kept his gaze upon Paladine, who looked troubled.

"There is something in what you say," said Paladine at last. "We know how the people turned against us after the Cataclysm. Two hundred years passed before they were ready to accept us back. Takhisis knows this, and she would gladly use the distrust and anger of the people against us. We must proceed slowly and cautiously, as we did then."

"If I might suggest a plan," Raistlin said.

He detailed his idea. The gods listened, most of them. When he concluded, Paladine glanced around the circle.

"What say you all?"

"We approve," said the gods of magic, speaking together with one voice.

"I do not," said Sargonnas in anger.

The other gods remained silent, some doubtful, others disapproving.

Raistlin looked at each of them in turn, then said quietly, "You do not have an eternity to mull this over and debate among yourselves. You may not even have one second. Is it possible that you do not see the danger?"

"From a kender?" Sargonnas laughed.

"From a kender," said Nuitari. "Because Burrfoot did not die when he was supposed to have died, the moment of his death hangs suspended in time."

Solinari caught up his cousin's words, so that they seemed to come from the same throat. "If the kender dies in a time and place that is not his own, Tasslehoff will not defeat Chaos. The Father of All and Nothing will be victorious, and he will carry out his threat to destroy us *and* the world."

"The kender must be discovered and returned to the time and place of his death," Lunitari added, her voice stern. "Tasslehoff Burrfoot must die when and where he was supposed to die or we all face annhilation."

The three voices that were distinct and separate and yet seemed one voice fell silent.

Raistlin glanced around again. "I take it I have leave to go?"

Sargonnas muttered and grumbled, but in the end he fell silent.

The other gods looked to Paladine.

At length, he nodded.

"Then I bid you farewell," said Raistlin.

When the mage had departed, Sargonnas confronted Paladine. "You heap folly upon folly," the minotaur stated accusingly. "First you give a powerful magical artifact into the hands of a kender, then you send this twisted mage to fight Takhisis. If we are doomed, you have doomed us."

"Nothing done out of love is ever folly," Paladine returned. "If we face great peril, we now do so with hope." He turned to Zivilyn. "What do you see?"

Zivilyn looked into eternity.

"Nothing," he replied. "Nothing but darkness."

2 THE SONG OF THE DESERT

Mina's army moved east, heading for Sanction. The army traveled rapidly, for the skies were clear, the air cool and crisp, and they met no opposition. Blue dragons flew above them, guarding their march and scouting out the lands ahead. Rumor of their coming spread. Those along their route of march quaked in fear when they heard that they lay in the path of this conquering army. Many fled into the hills. Those who could not flee or had nowhere to go waited fearfully for destruction.

Their fears proved groundless. The army marched through villages and past farms, camped outside of towns. Mina kept her soldiers under strict control. Supplies they could have taken by force, they paid for. In some cases, when they came to an impoverished house or village, the army gave of what they had. Manor houses and castles they could have razed, they let stand. Everywhere along their route, Mina spoke to the people of the One God. All they did, they did in the name of the One God.

Mina spoke to the high born and the low, to the peasant and the farmer, the blacksmith and the innkeeper, the bard and the tinker, the noble lord and lady. She brought healing to the sick, food to the hungry, comfort to the unhappy. She told them how the old gods had abandoned them, left them to the scourge of these alien dragons. But this new god, the One God, was here to take care of them.

Odila was often at Mina's side. She took no part in the proceedings, but she watched and listened and fingered the amulet around her neck. The touch no longer seemed to cause her pain.

Gerard rode in the rear, as far as possible from the minotaur, who was always in the front ranks with Mina. Gerard guessed that Galdar had been ordered to leave him alone. Still, there was always the possibility of an "accident." Galdar could not be faulted if a poisonous snake happened to crawl into Gerard's bedroll or a broken tree branch came crashing down on his head. Those few times when the two were forced by circumstance to meet, Gerard saw by the look in the minotaur's eyes that Gerard was alive only because Mina willed it.

Unfortunately, riding in the rear meant that Gerard was back among those who guarded the wagon carrying the sarcophagus of Goldmoon and the two wizards. The phrase, "More dead than alive" came to Gerard's mind as he looked at them, and he looked at them often. He didn't like to. He couldn't stand the sight of them, sitting on the end of the wagon, bodies swaying to and fro with the motion of the bumpy ride, feet and arms dangling, heads drooping. Every time he watched them, he rode away sickened, vowing that was the last time he would have anything to do with them. The next day he was drawn to stare at them, fascinated, repulsed.

Mina's army marched toward Sanction, leaving behind not fire and smoke and blood, but cheering crowds, who tossed garlands at Mina's feet and sang praises of the One God.

Another group marched east, traveling almost parallel to Mina's army, separated by only a few hundred miles. Their march was slower because it was not as organized and the land through which they traveled was not as hospitable. The same sun that shone brightly on Mina seared the elves of Qualinesti as they struggled across the Plains of Dust, heading for what they hoped would be safe sanctuary in the land of their kin, the Silvanesti. Every day, Gilthas blessed Wanderer and the people of the plains, for without their help, not a single elf would have crossed the desert alive.

The Plainspeople gave the elves enveloping, protective clothing that kept out the heat of the day and held body warmth for the cold nights. The Plainspeople gave the elves food, which Gilthas suspected they could ill afford to share. Whenever he questioned them about this, the proud Plainspeople would either ignore him or cast him such cold glances that he knew that to continue to ask questions would offend them. They taught the elves that they should march during the cool parts of the morning and night and seek shelter against the sweltering heat of the afternoon. Finally, Wanderer and his comrades offered to accompany the elves and serve as guides. Gilthas knew, if the rest of the elves did not, that Wanderer had a twofold purpose. One was beneficent—to make certain the elves survived the crossing of the desert. The other was self-serving—to make certain the elves crossed.

The elves had come to look very much like the Plainspeople, dressing in baggy trousers and long tunics and wrapping themselves in many layers of soft wool that protected them from the desert sun by day and the desert chill by night. They kept their faces muffled against the stinging sand, kept delicate skin shielded from exposure. Having lived close to nature, with a respect for nature, the elves soon adapted to the desert and lost no more of their people. They could never love the desert, but they came to understand it and to honor its ways.

Gilthas could tell that Wanderer was uneasy at how swiftly the elves were adapting to this hard life. Gilthas tried his best to convince the Plainsman that the elves were a people of forests and gardens, a people who could look on the red and orange striated rock formations that broke the miles of endless sand dunes and see no beauty, as did the Plainspeople, but only death.

One night, when they were nearing the end of their long journey, the elves arrived at an oasis in the dark hours before the dawn. Wanderer had decreed that here the elves could rest this night and throughout the day tomorrow, drinking their fill and renewing their strength before they once more took up their weary journey. The elves made camp, set the watch, then gave themselves to sleep.

Gilthas tried to sleep. He was weary from the long walk, but sleep would not come. He had fought his way out of the depression that had plagued him. The need to be active and responsible for his people had been beneficial. He had a great many cares and worries still, not the least of which was the reception they might receive in Silvanesti. He was thinking of these matters, and restless, he left his bedroll, taking care not to wake his slumbering wife. He walked into the night to stare up at the myriad stars. He had not known there were so many. He was awed and even dismayed by their number. He was staring thus, when Wanderer found him.

"You should be sleeping," said Wanderer.

His voice was stern, he was giving a command, not making idle conversation. He had not changed from the day Gilthas had first met him. Taciturn, quiet, he never spoke when a gesture would serve him instead. His face was like the desert rock, formed of sharp angles marred by dark creases. He smiled, never laughed, and his smile was only in his dark eyes.

Gilthas shook his head. "My body yearns for sleep, but my mind prevents it."

"Perhaps the voices keep you awake," said Wanderer.

"I've heard you speak of them before," Gilthas replied, intrigued. "The voices of the desert. I have listened, but I cannot hear them."

"I hear them now," said Wanderer. "The sighing of the wind among the rocks, the whispering of the sand floes. Even in the silence of the night, there is a voice that we know to be the voice of the stars. You cannot see the stars in your land or, if you can, they are caught and held prisoner by the tree branches. Here"—Wanderer waved his hand to the vast vault of star-studded sky that stretched from horizon to horizon—"the stars are free, and their song is loud."

"I hear the wind among the rocks," said Gilthas, "but to me it is the sound of a dying breath whistling through gaping teeth. Yet," he added, pausing to look around him, "now that I have traveled through this land, I must admit that there is a beauty to your night. The stars are so close and so numerous that sometimes I *do* think I might hear them sing." He shrugged. "If I did not feel so small and insignificant among them, that is."

"That is what truly bothers you, Gilthas," said Wanderer, reaching out his hand and touching Gilthas on his breast, above his heart. "You elves rule the land in which you live. The trees form the walls of your houses and provide you shelter. The orchids and the roses grow at your behest. The desert will not be ruled. The desert will not be subjugated. The desert cares nothing about you, will do nothing for you except one thing. The desert will always be here. Your land changes. Trees die and forests burn, but the desert is eternal. Our home has always been, and it will always be. That is the gift it gives us, the gift of surety."

"We thought our world would never change," said Gilthas quietly. "We were wrong. I wish you a better fate."

Returning to his tent, Gilthas felt exhaustion overcome him. His wife did not waken, but she was sleepily aware of his return, for she reached out her arms and drew him close. He listened to the voice of her heart beating steadily against his. Comforted, he slept.

Wanderer did not sleep. He looked up at the stars and thought over the words of the young elf. And it seemed to Wanderer that the song of the stars was, for the first time since he'd heard it, mournful and off-key.

The elves continued their trek, their progress slow but steady. Then came the morning the Lioness shook her husband awake.

"What?" Gilthas asked, fear jolting him from sleep. "What is it? What is wrong?"

"For a change, nothing," she said, smiling at him through her rampant, golden curls. She sniffed the air. "What do you smell?"

"Sand," said Gilthas, rubbing his nose, that always seemed clogged with grit. "Why? What do you smell?"

"Water," said the Lioness. "Not the muddy water of some oasis but water that runs swift and fast and cold. There is a river nearby. . . ." Her eyes filled with tears, her voice failed her. "We have done it, my husband. We have crossed the Plains of Dust!"

A river it was, yet no river such as the Qualinesti had ever before seen. The elves gathered on its banks and stared in some dismay at the water, that flowed red as blood. The Plainspeople assured them that the water was fresh and untainted, the red color came from the rocks through which the river ran. The elves might have still hesitated, but the children broke free of their parents' grasp and rushed forward to splash in the water that bubbled around the roots of giant cottonwood and willow trees. Soon what remained of the Qualinesti nation was laughing and splashing and rollicking in the River Torath.

"Here we leave you," said Wanderer. "You can ford the river at this point. Beyond, only a few miles distant, you will come upon the remains of the King's Highway that will take you to Silvanesti. The river runs along the highway for many miles, so you will have water in abundance. The foraging is good, for the trees that grow along the river give of their fruits at this time of year."

Wanderer held out his hand to Gilthas. "I wish you good fortune and success at your journey's end. And I wish for you that someday you will hear the song of the stars."

"May their song never fall silent for you, my friend," said Gilthas, pressing the man's hand warmly. "I can never thank you enough for what you and your people have done—"

He stopped speaking, for he was talking to Wanderer's back. Having said all that was needed, the Plainsman motioned to his comrades, led them back into the desert.

"A strange people," said the Lioness. "They are rude and uncouth and in love with rocks, which is something I will never understand, but I find that I admire them."

"I admire them, too," said Gilthas. "They saved our lives, saved the Qualinesti nation. I hope that they never have reason to regret what they have done for us."

"Why should they?" the Lioness asked, startled.

"I don't know, my love," Gilthas replied. "I can't say. Just a feeling I have."

He walked away, heading for the river, leaving his wife to gaze after him with a look of concern and consternation.

3 THE LIE

Alhana Starbreeze sat alone in the shelter that had been shaped for her by those elves who still had some magical power remaining to them, at least enough to command the trees to provide a safe haven for the exiled elven queen. As it turned out, the elves did not need their magic, for the trees, which have always loved the elves, seeing their queen sorrowful and weary to the point of collapse, bent their branches of their own accord. Their limbs hung protectively over her, their leaves twined together to keep out the rain and the wind. The grass formed a thick, soft carpet for her bed. The birds sang softly to ease her pain.

The time was evening, one of the few quiet times in Alhana's unquiet life. These were busy times, for she and her forces were living in the wilderness, fighting a hit-and-run war against the Dark Knights: raiding prison camps, attacking supply ships, making daring forays into the city itself to rescue elves in peril. For the moment, though, all was peaceful. The evening meal had been served. The Silvanesti elves under her command were settling down for the night. For the moment, no one needed her, no one demanded that she make decisions that would cost more elven lives, shed more elven blood. Alhana sometimes dreamed of swimming in a river of blood, a dream from which she could never escape, except by drowning.

Some might say—and some elves did—that the Dark Knights of Neraka had done Alhana Starbreeze a favor. She had once been deemed a dark elf, exiled from her homeland for daring to try to bring about peace between the

868 THE WAR OF SOULS

Silvanesti and their Qualinesti cousins, for daring to marry a Qualinesti in order to unite their two squabbling realms.

Now, in their time of greatest trouble, Alhana Starbreeze had been accepted back by her people. The sentence of exile had been lifted from her formally by the Heads of House who remained alive after the Dark Knights had completed their occupation of the capital, Silvanost. Alhana's people now embraced her. Kneeling at her feet, they were loud in their lamentations for the "misunderstanding." Never mind that they had tried to have her assassinated. In the very next breath, they cried to her, "Save us! Queen Alhana, save us!"

Samar was furious with her, with her people. The Silvanesti had invited the Dark Knights into their city and turned away Alhana Starbreeze. Not so many weeks before, they had fallen on their knees before the leader of the Dark Knights, a human girl called Mina. The Silvanesti had been warned of Mina's treachery, but they had been blinded by the miracles she performed in the name of the One God. Samar had been among those who had warned them that they were fools to put their trust in humans—miracles or not. The elves had been all astonishment and shock and horror when the Dark Knights had turned on them, set up their slave camps and prisons, killed any who opposed them.

Samar was grimly pleased that the Silvanesti had at last come to revere Alhana Starbreeze, the one person who had remained loyal to them and fought for them when they had reviled her. He was less pleased with his queen's response, which was forgiving, magnanimous, patient. He would have seen them cringe and grovel to obtain her favor.

"I cannot punish them, Samar," Alhana said to him on the evening on which the sentence of exile had been lifted. She was now free to return to her homeland—a homeland ruled over by the Dark Knights of Neraka, a homeland she was going to have to fight to reclaim. "You know why."

He knew why: All she did was for her son, Silvanoshei, who was the king of Silvanesti. An unworthy son, as far as Samar was concerned. Silvanoshei had been the person responsible for admitting the Knights of Neraka into the city of Silvanost. Enamored of the human girl, Mina, Silvanoshei was the cause of the downfall of the Silvanesti people.

Yet the people adored him and still claimed him as their king. Because of him, they followed his mother. Because of Silvanoshei, Samar was on a perilous journey, forced to leave his queen at the most desperate time in the ancient history of Silvanesti, forced to go chasing over Ansalon after this very son. Although few knew it, Silvanoshei, the king of the Silvanesti, had run away the very night Samar and other elves had risked their lives to rescue him from the Dark Knights.

Few knew he was gone, because Alhana refused to admit it, either to her people or to herself. Those elves who had been with them the night of his departure knew, but she had sworn them to secrecy. Long loyal to her, loving her, they had readily agreed. Now Alhana kept up the pretense that Silvanoshei was ill and that he was forced to remain in seclusion until he had healed.

Meantime, Alhana was confident he would return. "He is off sulking somewhere," she told Samar. "He will get over this infatuation and come to his senses. He will come back to me, to his people."

Samar did not believe it. He tried to point out to Alhana the evidence of the tracks of horse's hooves. The elves had brought no horses with them. This animal was magical, had been sent for Silvanoshei. He wasn't coming back. Not then, not ever. At first Alhana had refused even to listen to him. She had forbidden him to speak of it. But as the days passed and Silvanoshei did not return, she was forced to admit, with a breaking heart, that Samar might be right.

Samar had been gone long weeks now. During this time, Alhana had kept up the pretense that Silvanoshei was with them, sick and confined to his tent. She even went so far as to maintain his tent, pretend to go visit him. She would sit on his empty bed and talk to him, as if he were there. He would come back, and when he did, he would find her waiting for him, with all in readiness as if he had never left.

Alone in her bower, Alhana read and reread her latest message from Samar, a message carried by a hawk, for these birds had long served as messengers between the two. The message was brief—Samar not being one to waste words—and it brought both joy and sorrow to the anxious mother, dismay and despair to the queen.

> *I have picked up his trail at last. He took a ship from Abanasinia, sailed north to Solamnia. There he traveled to Solanthus in search of this female, but she had already marched eastward with her army. Silvanoshei followed her.*
>
> *Other news I have heard. The city of Qualinost has been utterly destroyed. A lake of death now covers what remains of Qualinost. The Dark Knights now ravage the countryside, seizing land and making it their own. It is rumored that many Qualinesti escaped, including Laurana's son, Gilthas, but where they are or what has happened to them is unknown. I spoke to a survivor, who said that it is certain that Lauranalanthalasa was slain in the battle, along with many hundreds of Qualinesti, as well as dwarves of Thorbardin and some humans who fought alongside them. They died heroes. The evil dragon Beryl was killed.*
>
> *I am on the trail of your son. I will report when I can.*
> *Your faithful servant,*
> *Samar*

Alhana whispered a prayer for the soul of Laurana and the souls of all those who had perished in the battle. The prayer was to the old gods, the departed gods, who were no longer there to heed it. The beautiful words eased her grief, even if she knew in her heart that they held no meaning. She prayed, too, for the Qualinesti exiles, hoping that the rumor of their escape was true. Then, concern for her son banished all other thoughts from her mind.

"What witchery has this girl worked on you, my son?" she said softly, absently smoothing the vellum on which Samar had written his note. "What foul witchery . . ."

A voice spoke from outside her shelter, calling her name. The voice belonged to one of her elite guard, a woman who had served her long, through many difficult and dangerous times. She was known to Alhana to be stoic, reserved, never showing any emotion, and the queen was startled and alarmed now to hear a tremor in the woman's voice.

Fears of all kinds and sorts crowded around Alhana. She had to steel herself to react calmly. Crumpling the vellum in her hand, she thrust it into the bosom of her chemise, then ducked out of the sheltering vines and branches to face the woman. She saw with her a strange elf, someone unknown to her.

Or was he unknown? Or simply forgotten? Alhana stared at him closely. She knew this young man, she realized. Knew the lines of his face, knew the eyes that held in them a sadness and care and crushing responsibility to mirror her own. She could not place him, probably due to the foreign garb he wore—the long and enveloping robes of the barbarians who roamed the desert.

She looked to her guard for answers.

"The scouts came across him, my queen," said the woman. "He will not give his name, but he claims to be related to you through your honored husband, Porthios. He is Qualinesti, beneath all these layers of wool. He does not come armed into our lands. Since he may be what he claimed, we brought him to you."

"I know you, sir," Alhana said. "Forgive me, I cannot give you a name."

"That is understandable," he replied with a smile. "Many years and many trials separate us. Yet"—his voice softened, his eyes were warm with admiration—"I remember you, the great lady so wrongfully imprisoned by her people—"

Alhana gave a glad cry, flung herself into his arms. Even as she embraced him, she remembered the mother he had lost, who would never more put her arms around her son. Alhana kissed him tenderly, for her sake and that of Laurana's, then she stepped back to look at him.

"Those trials of which you speak have aged you more than the corresponding years. Gilthas of the House of Solostaran, I am pleased beyond measure to see you safe and well, for I just heard the sad news concerning your people. I hoped that what I heard was rumor and gossip and that it would prove false, but, alas, I see the truth in your eyes."

"If you have heard that my mother is dead and that Qualinost is destroyed, then you have heard the truth," Gilthas said.

"I am sorry beyond measure," Alhana said, taking his hand in her own and holding it fast. "Please, come inside, where you may be comfortable, for I see the weariness of many weeks of travel lie on you. I will have food and water brought to you."

Gilthas accompanied Alhana into the shelter. He ate the food that was offered, though Alhana could see he did so out of politeness rather than hunger. He drank the water with a relish he could not disguise, drank long and deep, as if he could never get enough.

"You have no idea how good this water tastes to me," he said, smiling. He glanced around. "But when am I going to have a chance to greet my cousin, Silvanoshei? We have never met, he and I. We heard the sad rumor that he had been slain by ogres and were glad to receive news that this was not true. I am eager to embrace him."

"I regret to say that Silvanoshei is not well, Gilthas," said Alhana. "He was brutally beaten by the Dark Knights when they seized Silvanost and barely escaped with his life. He keeps to his tent on the order of the healers and is not permitted to have any company."

She had told this lie so often that she was able to tell it now without a break in her voice. She could meet the young man's eyes and never falter. He believed her, for his face took on a look of concern.

"I am sorry to hear this. Please accept my wishes for his swift recovery."

Alhana smiled and changed the subject. "You have traveled far and on dangerous roads. Your journey must have been a hard and perilous one. What can I do for you, Nephew? May I call you that, although I am only your aunt by marriage?"

"I would be honored," said Gilthas, his voice warm. "You are all the family I have left now. You and Silvanoshei."

Alhana's eyes filled with sudden tears. He was all the family she had, at this moment, with Silvanoshei lost to her. She clasped his hand, and he held fast to hers. She was reminded of his father, Tanis Half-Elven. The memory was heartening, for the times in which they had known each other had been fraught with peril, yet they had overcome their foes and gone on to find peace, even if only for a short while.

"I come to ask a great boon of you, Aunt Alhana," he said. He gazed at her steadfastly. "I ask that you receive my people."

Alhana stared at him, bewildered, not understanding.

Gilthas gestured to the west. "Three days' ride from here, on the border of Silvanesti, a thousand exiles from Qualinesti wait to receive your permission to enter the land of our cousins. Our home is destroyed. The enemy occupies it. We lack the numbers to fight them. Someday," he said, his chin lifting and pride lighting his eyes, "we will return and drive the Dark Knights from our land and reclaim what is ours.

"But that day is not today," he continued, the light fading, darkened by shadow. "Nor is it tomorrow. We have traveled across the Plains of Dust. We would have died there but for the help of the people who call that terrible land home. We are weary and desperate. Our children look to us for comfort, and we have none to give them. We are exiles. We have nowhere to go. Humbly we come to you, who left so long ago, and humbly we ask that you take us in."

Alhana looked long at him. The tears that had burned in her eyes now slid unchecked down her cheeks.

"You weep for us," he said brokenly. "I am sorry to have brought this trouble to you."

"I weep for us all, Gilthas," Alhana said. "For the Qualinesti people, who have lost their homeland, and for the Silvanesti, who are fighting for ours. You will not find peace and sanctuary here in these forests, my poor nephew. You find us at war, battling for our very survival. You did not know this when you set out, did you?"

Gilthas shook his head.

"You know this now?" she asked.

"I know," he said. "I heard the news from the Plainspeople. I had hoped they exaggerated—"

"I doubt it. They are a people who see far and speak bluntly. I will tell you what is happening, and then you can decide if you want to join us."

Gilthas would have spoken, but Alhana raised her hand, silenced him. "Hear me out, Nephew." She hesitated a moment, underwent some inward struggle, then said, "You will hear from some of our people that my son was bewitched by this human girl, Mina, the leader of the Dark Knights. He was not the only Silvanesti to fall under her fatal spell. Our people sang songs of praise to her as she walked through the streets. She performed miracles of healing, but there was a price—not in coin but in souls. The One God wanted the souls of the elves to torment and enslave and devour. This One God is not a loving god, as some of our people mistakenly thought, but a god of deceit and vengeance and pain. Those elves who served the One God were taken away. We have no idea where. Those elves who refuse to serve the One God were killed outright or enslaved by the Dark Knights.

"The city of Silvanost is completely under the control of the Dark Knights. Their forces are not yet large enough to extend that control, and so we are able to maintain our existence here in the forests. We do what we can to fight against this dread foe, and we have saved many hundreds of our people from torture and death. We raid the prison camps and free the slaves. We harass the patrols. They fear our archers so much that no Dark Knight now dares set foot outside the city walls. All this we do, but it is not enough. We lack the forces needed to retake the city, and every day the Dark Knights add to its fortifications."

"Then our warriors will be a welcome addition," said Gilthas quietly.

Alhana lowered her eyes, shook her head. "No," she said, ashamed. "How could we ask that of you? The Silvanesti have treated you and your people with contempt and disdain all these years? How could we ask you to give your lives for our country?"

"You forget," said Gilthas, "that our people have no country. Our city lies in ruins. The same foe that rules your land rules ours." His fist clenched, his eyes flashed. "We are eager to take retribution. We will take back your land, then combine our forces to take back our own."

He leaned forward, his face alight. "Don't you see, Alhana? This may be the impetus we need to heal the old wounds, to once more unite our two nations."

"You are so young," Alhana said. "Too young to know that old wounds can fester so that the infection strikes to the very heart, turning it sick and putrid. You do not know that there are some who would see all of us fall rather than one of us rise. I tried to unite our people. I failed and this is what has come of my failure. I think it is too late. I think that nothing can save our people."

He gazed at her in consternation, clearly disturbed by her words.

Alhana rested her hand on his. "Maybe I am wrong. Perhaps your young eyes see more clearly. Bring your people into the safety of the forest. Then you must go before the Silvanesti and tell them of your plight and ask them to admit you into their lands."

"Ask them? Or do you mean beg them?" Gilthas rose, his expression cool. "We do not come before the Silvanesti as beggars."

"There, you see," Alhana said sadly. "You have been infected. Already, you jump to conclusions. You should ask the Silvanesti because it is politic to ask. That is all I meant." She sighed. "We corrupt our young, and thus perishes hope for anything better."

"You are sorrowful and weary and worried for your son. When he is well, he and I— Alhana," Gilthas said, alarmed, for she had sunk down upon a cushion and begun weeping bitterly. "What is wrong? Should I call someone? One of your ladies?"

"Kiryn," Alhana said in a choked voice. "Send for Kiryn."

Gilthas had no notion who this Kiryn was, but he ducked outside the shelter and informed one of the guards, who dispatched a runner. Gilthas went back inside the shelter, stood ill at ease, not knowing what to do or say to ease such wrenching grief.

A young elf entered the dwelling. He looked first at Alhana, who was struggling to regain her composure, then at Gilthas. Kiryn's face flushed with anger.

"Who are you? What have you said—"

"No, Kiryn!" Alhana raised her tearstained face. "He has done nothing. This is my nephew, Gilthas, Speaker of the Sun of the Qualinesti."

"I beg your pardon, Your Majesty," said Kiryn, bowing low. "I had no way of knowing. When I saw my queen—"

"I understand," said Gilthas. "Aunt Alhana, if I inadvertently said or did anything to cause you such pain—"

"Tell him, Kiryn," Alhana ordered in a tone that was low and terrible to hear. "Tell him the truth. He has a right . . . a need to know."

"My queen," said Kiryn, glancing at Gilthas uncertainly, "are you certain?"

Alhana closed her eyes, as if she would thankfully close them upon this world. "He has brought his people across the desert. They came to us for succor, for their capital city is destroyed, their land ravaged by the Dark Knights."

"Blessed E'li!" exclaimed Kiryn, calling, in his astonishment, upon the absent god Paladine or E'li, as the elves know him.

"Tell him," said Alhana, sitting with her face averted from them, hidden behind her hand.

Kiryn motioned Gilthas to draw near. "I tell you, Your Majesty, what only a few others know, and they have taken vows of secrecy. My cousin, Silvanoshei, is not wounded. He does not lie in his tent. He is gone."

".Gone?" Gilthas was puzzled. "Where has he gone? Has he been captured? Taken prisoner?"

"Yes," said Kiryn gravely, "but not the way you mean. He has become obsessed with a human girl, a leader of the Dark Knights called Mina. We believe that he has run off to join her."

"You *believe?*" Gilthas repeated. "You do not know for sure?"

Kiryn shrugged, helpless. "We know nothing for certain. We rescued him from the Dark Knights, who were going to put him to death. We were escaping into the wilderness when a magical sleep came over us. When we awoke, Silvanoshei was gone. We found the tracks of a horse's hooves. We tried to follow the hoofprints, but they entered the Than-Thalas River, and although we searched upstream and down, we could not find any more tracks. It was as if the horse had wings."

Alhana spoke, her voice muffled. "I have sent my most trusted friend and advisor after my son, to bring him back. I have told the Silvanesti people nothing about this. I ask you to say nothing of this to anyone."

Gilthas was troubled. "I don't understand. Why do you keep his disappearance secret?"

Alhana lifted her head. Her eyes were swollen with her grief, red-rimmed. "Because the Silvanesti people have taken him to their hearts. He is their king, and they follow him, when they would not willingly follow me. All I do, I do in his name."

"You mean you make the hard decisions and face the danger, while your son, who should be sharing your burden, chases after a petticoat," Gilthas began sternly.

"Do not criticize him!" Alhana flared. "What do you know of what he has endured? This female is a witch. She has ensorcelled him. He does not know what he is doing."

"Silvanoshei was a good king until he had the misfortune to meet Mina," said Kiryn defensively. "The people came to love and respect him. He will be a good king when this spell is broken."

"I thought you should know the truth, Gilthas," Alhana said stiffly, "since you have responsibilities of your own you must bear, decisions you must make. I ask only that you do as Kiryn does, respect my wishes and say nothing of this to anyone. Pretend, as we pretend, that Silvanoshei is here with us."

Her tone was cold, her eyes beseeching. Gilthas would have given much to have been able to ease her pain, to lift her burdens. But, as she said, he bore burdens himself. He had responsibilities, and they were to his people.

"I have never yet lied to the Qualinesti, Aunt Alhana," he said, as gently as he could. "I will not start now. They left their homeland on my word, they followed me into the desert. They have given their lives and the lives of their children into my hands. They trust me, and I will not betray that trust. Not even for you, whom I love and honor."

Alhana rose to her feet, her fists clenched at her sides. "If you do this, you will destroy all that I have worked for. We might as well surrender to the Dark Knights now." Her fists unclenched, and he saw that her hands trembled. "Give me some time, Nephew. That is all I ask. My son will return soon. I know it!"

Gilthas shifted his gaze from her to Kiryn, looked long and intently at the young elf. Kiryn said nothing, but his eyes flickered. He was clearly uncomfortable.

Alhana saw Gilthas's dilemma.

"He is too kind, too polite, too mindful of my pain to speak the words that must be burning on his tongue," she said herself. "If he could, he would say to me, *This is not my doing. I am not at fault. This is your son's doing. Silvanoshei has failed his people. I will not follow in those same footsteps."*

Alhana was angry with Gilthas, jealous of him and proud of him, all in the same scalding moment. She envied Laurana suddenly, envied her death that brought blessed silence to the turmoil, an end to pain, an end to despair. Laurana had died a hero's death, fighting to save her people and her country. She had left behind a legacy of which she could be proud, a son she could honor.

"I tried to do what was right," Alhana said to herself in misery, "but it all has ended up so terribly wrong."

Her loved husband Porthios had vanished and was presumed to be dead. Her son, her hope for the future, had run away to leave her to face that future alone. She might tell herself he had been ensorcelled, but deep in her heart, she knew better. He was spoiled, selfish, too easily swayed by passions she had never had the heart to check. She had failed her husband, she had failed her son. Her pride refused to let her admit it.

Pride would be her downfall. Her pride had been wounded when her people turned against her. Her pride had caused her to attack the shield, to try to reenter a land that didn't want her. Now her pride forced her to lie to her people.

Samar and Kiryn had both counseled against it. Both had urged her to tell the truth, but her pride could not stomach it. Not her pride as a queen, but her pride as a mother. She had failed as a mother and now all would see that failure. She could not bear for people to regard her with pity. That, more than anything else, was the true reason she had lied.

She had hoped that Silvanoshei would come back, admit that he had been wrong, ask to be forgiven. If that had happened, she could have overlooked his downfall. She knew now after reading Samar's letter that Silvanoshei would never come back to her, not of his own free will. Samar would have to drag him back like an errant schoolboy.

She looked up to find Gilthas looking at her, his expression sympathetic, grave. In that moment, he was his father. Tanis Half-Elven had often looked at her with that same expression as she underwent some inward battle, fought against her pride.

"I will keep your secret, Aunt Alhana," Gilthas said. His voice was cool, he was clearly unhappy with what he was doing. "As long as I can."

"Thank you, Gilthas," she said, grateful and ashamed for having to be grateful. Her pride! Her damnable pride. "Silvanoshei will return. He will hear of our plight and come back. Perhaps he is already on his way."

She pressed her hand over her bosom, over Samar's letter that said entirely the opposite. Lying had become so easy, so very easy.

"I hope so," said Gilthas somberly.

He took her hand in his own, kissed it respectfully. "I am sorry for your trouble, Aunt Alhana. I am sorry to have added to your trouble. But if this brings about the reunification of our two nations, then someday we will look back upon the heartbreak and turmoil and say that it was worth it."

She tried to smile, but the stiffness of her lips made her mouth twitch. She said nothing, and so in silence they parted.

"Go with him," she told Kiryn, who remained behind. "See to it that he and his people are made welcome."

"Your Majesty—" Kiryn began uneasily.

"I know what you are going to say, Kiryn. Do not say it. All will be well. You will see."

After both had left, she stood in the doorway of the shelter, thinking of Gilthas.

"Such pretty dreams," she said softly. "The dreams of youth. Once I had pretty dreams. Now, like my pretty gowns, they hang about me in rags and in tatters. May yours fit better, Gilthas, and last longer."

4 WAITING AND WAITING

General Dogah, leader of the Dark Knights in Silvanost, was having his own problems. The Dark Knights used blue dragons as scouts, patrolling the skies above the thick and tangled forests. If the dragons caught sight of movement on the ground, they swooped down and, with their lightning breath, laid waste to entire tracts of forest land.

These dragon scouts saw the large gathering of people in the desert but had no idea they were Qualinesti. The scouts thought them the barbarians, the Plainspeople, fleeing the onslaught of the dragon overlord Sable. General Dogah wondered what to do about this migration. He had no orders concerning the Plainspeople. His forces were limited, his hold on Silvanost tenuous at best. He did not want to start war on another front. He dispatched a courier on dragonback with an urgent message for Mina, telling her about the situation and asking for orders.

The courier had some difficulty locating Mina, for he flew first to Solanthus, only to find that her army had left there and was on the march for Sanction.

After another day's flying, the courier located her. He sped back with this reply, short and terse.

General Dogah
These are not Plainspeople. They are Qualinesti exiles. Destroy them.

In the name of the One God,
Mina

Dogah sent off his dragonriders to do just that, only to find that in the interim the Qualinesti had disappeared. No trace of them could be found anywhere. He received this report with a bitter curse, for he knew what it meant. The Qualinesti had managed to escape into the forests of Silvanesti and were now beyond his reach.

Here were yet more elves to attack his patrols and fire flaming arrows at his supply ships. To add to his woes, the dragons began bringing reports that the ogres, long enraged at the Knights for stealing their land, were massing on the northern Silvanesti border that adjoined Blöde, undoubtedly hoping to seize some elven land in return.

And to make matters worse, Dogah was having morale trouble. So long as Mina had been around to enchant them and entrance them, the soldiers were committed to her cause, dedicated and enthusiastic followers. But Mina had been gone many long weeks now. The soldiers and the Knights who commanded them were isolated in the middle of a strange and unfriendly realm, where enemies lurked in every shadow—and Silvanesti was a land of shadows. Arrows came out of the skies to slay them. Even the vegetation seemed intent on trying to kill them. Tree roots tripped them, dead limbs dropped on their heads, forests lured them into tangles from which few ever returned.

Not a single supply ship had sailed down the river in the past week. The elves set fire to those that made the attempt. The soldiers had no food other than what the elves ate, and no human could subsist on leaves and grass for long. The meat-hungry humans dared not enter the woods to hunt, for, as they soon discovered, every creature in the forest was a spy for the elves.

The elves of the city of Silvanost, seemingly cowed by the might of the Dark Knights, were growing bolder. None of Dogah's men dared venture into the city alone lest they risk being found dead in an alley. The men began to grouse and grumble.

Dogah issued orders to torture more elves, but such entertainment could keep his troops occupied for only so long. He was fortunate in that there were no desertions. This was not due to loyalty, as he well knew, but to the fact that the men were too terrified of the elves and the forest that sheltered them to flee.

Now, with the knowledge that a thousand more elves had joined those already in the forest, the mutinous rumblings grew loud as thunder, so that Dogah could not remain deaf to them. He himself began to doubt. When he could not see himself reassuringly reflected in her amber eyes, his trust in Mina started to wane.

He dispatched another urgent message to Mina, telling her that the Qualinesti had escaped his best efforts to destroy them, that morale was in the privies, and that unless something happened to change the situation, he would have no choice but to pull out of Silvanesti or face mutiny.

Dark-bearded and, these days, dark-faced and gloomy, the short, stocky Dogah sat alone (he had very little trust even in his own bodyguards these days) in his quarters, drank elven wine that he wished mightily was a liquor far stronger, and waited for Mina's reply.

The Qualinesti entered the forest to be coolly welcomed by their long-estranged cousins, the Silvanesti. A polite cousinly kiss of greeting was exchanged, and then spears and arrows were thrust into Qualinesti hands. If they were going to relocate to Silvanesti, they had better be prepared to fight for it.

The Qualinesti were only too happy to oblige. They saw this as a chance to avenge themselves on those who had seized their own realm and were now laying waste to it.

"When do we attack?" they demanded eagerly.

"Any day now," was the response from the Silvanesti. "We are waiting for the right time."

"Waiting for the right time?" the Lioness asked her husband. "For what 'right time' do we wait? I have talked to the scouts and spies. We outnumber the Dark Knights who are bottled up in Silvanost. Their morale sinks faster than a shipwrecked dwarf in full battle armor. Now is the opportune time to attack them!"

The two spoke in the shelter that had been provided for them—a hutch made of woven willow branches on the side of a bubbling stream. The space was small and cramped, but they were luckier than most of the elves, for they had a place of their own (due to Gilthas's royal rank) and some privacy. Most of the elves slept in the boughs of living trees or the hollowed-out boles of dead ones, inside caves or simply lying in the grass under the stars. The Qualinesti had no complaints. After their trek through the desert, they asked for nothing more than to sleep on crisp-smelling pine needles, lulled by the gentle murmur of the falling rain.

"You tell me nothing that I don't already know," said Gilthas morosely. He had taken to wearing clothing more typical of his people—the long, belted tunic, woollen shirt, and stockings in woodland colors. But he had folded neatly and put away safely the coverings of the desert.

"There are problems, however. The Silvanesti are spread out all over the land. Some are stationed along the river to disrupt the Dark Knights' supply lines. Others hide near the city of Silvanost, to make certain that any patrol that has nerve enough to leave the city does not return intact. Still others are scattered along the borders . . ."

"The wind, the hawk, the squirrel carry messages," returned the Lioness. "If the orders were sent now, most of the Silvanesti could be gathered outside Silvanost in a week's time. Days go by, and the orders are not given. We must skulk about in the forest and wait. Wait for what?"

Gilthas knew, but he could not answer. He kept silent, was forced let his wife fume.

"We know what will happen if the opportunity is missed! Thus did the Dark Knights take over our homeland during the Chaos War. The same will be true of the Silvanesti, if we don't act now. Is it your cousin, Silvanoshei, who holds back? He is young. Probably he doesn't understand. You must speak to him, Gilthas, explain to him—"

She knew her husband well. At the look on her face, the words clotted on her tongue.

The Lioness eyed him narrowly. "What is it, Gilthas? What's wrong? Something about Silvanoshei, isn't it?"

Gilthas looked at her ruefully. "Am I so transparent? Kings should be cloaked in inscrutability and mystery."

"My husband," said the Lioness, unable to keep from laughing, "you are inscrutable and mysterious as a crystal goblet. The truth inside you is plain for all the world to see."

"The truth . . ." Gilthas made a wry face. "The truth is, my dear, that Silvanoshei could not lead his people in a three-legged race, much less lead them to war. He is nowhere near here, nowhere near Silvanesti. I promised Alhana I would say nothing, but now a fortnight has passed and it seems to me that the time for lying has come to an end. Although"—Gilthas shook his head—"I fear that the truth will do more harm than good. The Silvanesti follow Alhana now only because she speaks in the name of her son. Some still view her with suspicion, see her as a 'dark elf.' If they find out the truth, that she has been lying to them, I fear they will never believe her again, never listen to her."

The Lioness looked into her husband's eyes. "That leaves you, Gilthas."

Now it was his turn to laugh. "I am everything that they despise, my dear. A Qualinesti with human blood thrown in. They will not follow me."

"Then you must persuade Alhana to tell her people the truth."

"I don't believe she can. She has told the lie so long that, for her, the lie has become the truth."

"So what do we do?" the Lioness demanded. "Live here in the forest until we take root along with the trees? We Qualinesti could attack the Dark Knights—"

"No, my dear," said Gilthas firmly. "The Silvanesti have permitted us to enter their homeland, that much is true, but they view us with suspicion, nonetheless. There are those who think we are here to usurp their homeland. For the Qualinesti to attack Silvanost—"

"The Qualinesti are *not* attacking Silvanost. The Qualinesti are attacking the Dark Knights *in* Silvanost," argued the Lioness.

"That is not how the Silvanesti will view it. You know that as well as I do."

"So we sit and do nothing."

"I do not know what else we can do," said Gilthas somberly. "The one person who could have united and rallied his people has been lured away. Now the only people left to lead the elves are a dark elf queen and a half-human king."

"Yet sooner or later someone must take the lead," the Lioness said. "We must follow someone."

"And where would that someone lead them?" Gilthas asked somberly, "except to our own destruction."

General Dogah drank his way through several barrels of wine. His problems increased daily. Six soldiers ordered to stand guard on the battlements refused to obey. Their officer threatened them with the lash. They attacked him, beat him severely, and ran off, hoping to lose themselves in the streets of Silvanost.

Dogah sent his troops after the deserters, intending to string them up to serve as examples to the rest.

The elves saved him the cost of rope. The bodies of the six were delivered to the castle. Each had died in some gruesome, grotesque manner. A note found on one, scrawled in Common, read, *A gift for the One God.*

That night, Dogah sent another messenger to Mina, pleading for either reinforcements or permission to withdraw. Although, he thought glumly, he had no idea where he would withdraw to. Everywhere he looked, he saw enemies.

Two days later, the messenger finally returned.

General Dogah
Hold your ground. Help is on the way.

In the name of the One God.
Mina

That wasn't much comfort.

Every day, Dogah cautiously mounted the walls of Silvanost, peered out to the north, the south, the east, and the west. The elves were out there. They had him surrounded. Every day, he expected the elves to attack.

Days passed, and the elves did nothing.

5 THE HEDGE MAZE

Tasslehoff Burrfoot was, at that moment in time feeling extremely put-out, put-upon, dizzy, and sick to his stomach. Of the three feelings, the dizzy feeling predominated, so that he was finding it hard to think clearly. Plain, wooden floors and good, hard ground had once seemed mundane objects as far as he was concerned, but now Tasslehoff thought fondly, wistfully, longingly of ground or floor or any solid surface beneath his feet.

He also thought longingly of his feet returning to their proper place as feet and not thinking themselves his head, which they were continually doing, for he always looked for them below and found them above. The only good thing to happen to Tasslehoff was that Conundrum had screamed himself hoarse and could now make only feeble croaking sounds.

Tas blamed everything on the Device of Time Journeying. He wondered sadly if this whirling and turning and dropping in on various points of time was going to go on eternally, and he was a bit daunted at the prospect. Then it occurred to him that sooner or later, the device was bound to land him back in the time where he'd be stepped on by Chaos. All in all, not a bright prospect.

Such thoughts ran through his head, which was constantly whirling and twirling through time. He thought them through as best he could, given the dizzy feeling, and suddenly a fresh thought popped in. Perhaps the owner of the voice that he heard in his ear and the hand that he felt on his shoulder could do something about this endless whirling. He made up his mind that the moment they landed again, he would do everything in his power to see the hand's owner.

Which he did. The very minute he felt firm ground (blessed ground!) beneath his feet, he stumbled around (rather wobbly) to look behind him.

He saw Conundrum and Conundrum's hand, but that was the wrong hand. No one else was about, and Tas immediately knew why. He and the gnome were standing in what appeared to be a field blackened by fire. Some distance away, crystal buildings caught the last glow of evening, glimmered orange or purple or gold as the dying rays of the sun painted them. The air was still tainted with the smell of burning, although the fire that had consumed the vegetation had been put out some time ago. He could hear voices, but they were far distant. From somewhere came the sweet and piercing music of a flute.

Tasslehoff had the vague notion that he'd been here before. Or maybe he'd been here after before. What with all the time jumping, he wasn't certain about anything anymore. The place looked familiar, and he was about to set off in search of someone who could tell him where he was, when Conundrum gave a wheezing gasp.

"The Hedge Maze!"

Tas looked down and looked sideways, and he realized that Conundrum was right. They were standing in what remained of the Hedge Maze after the red dragons had destroyed it with their fiery breath. The walls of leaves were burnt down to the ground. The paths that wound and twisted between them—leading those who walked the paths deeper into the maze—were laid bare. The maze was a maze no longer. Tas could see the pattern clearly, the white paths standing out starkly against the black. He could see every twist, every turning, every whorl, every jog, every dead end. He saw the way to the heart of the Hedge Maze and he saw the way out. The silver stair stood naked, exposed. He could see plainly now that it led up and up to nowhere, and with a queasy flutter of the stomach, he remembered his leap off the top and his dive into the smoke and the flame.

"Oh, my!" whispered Conundrum, and Tas remembered that mapping the Hedge Maze had been the gnome's Life Quest.

"Conundrum," said Tas somberly. "I—"

"You can see everything," said the gnome.

"I know," said Tas, patting the gnome's hand. "And I—"

"I could walk from one end to the other," said Conundrum, "and never get lost."

"Maybe you could find some other line of work," Tas suggested, wanting to be helpful. "Although I'd stay away from the repair of magical devices—"

"It's perfect!" Conundrum breathed. His eyes filled with happy tears.

"What?" Tas asked, startled. "What's perfect?"

"Where's my parchment?" Conundrum demanded. "Where's my ink bottle and my brush?"

"I don't have an ink bottle—"

Conundrum glared at him. "Then what good are you? Never mind," he added huffily. "Ah ha! Charcoal! That'll do."

He plopped down on the burnt ground. Spreading out the hem of his brown robes, he picked up a charred stick and began slowly and laboriously tracing the route of the burnt Hedge Maze on the fabric.

"This is so much easier," he muttered to himself. "I don't know why I didn't think of it sooner."

Tasslehoff felt the familiar touch of the hand on his shoulder. The jewels of the Device of Time Journeying began to sparkle and glitter with golden and purple light, a reflection of the setting sun.

"Goodbye, Conundrum," Tas called, as the paths of the Hedge Maze began to swirl in his vision.

The gnome didn't look up. He was concentrating on his map.

6 THE STRANGE PASSENGER

At a small port in southern Estwilde, the strange passenger disembarked from the ship on which he had sailed across New Sea. The captain was relieved to be rid of his mysterious passenger and more relieved to be rid of the passenger's fiery-tempered horse. Neither the captain nor any of the crew knew anything about the passenger. No one ever saw his face, which he kept hidden beneath the hood of his cloak.

Such seclusion had raised much speculation among the crew about the nature of their passenger, most of it wild and all of it wrong. Some guessed the passenger was a woman, disguised as a man, for the cabin boy had once caught a glimpse of a hand that, according to him, was slender and delicate in appearance. Others suspected him to be a wizard of some sort for no other reason than that wizards were known to wear hooded cloaks and that they were always mysterious and never to be trusted. Only one sailor stated that he believed the passenger to be an elf, hiding his face because he knew that the humans aboard ship would not take kindly to one of his race.

The other sailors scoffed at this notion and, since the conversation was being held at dinner, they threw weevily biscuits at the head of the man who made it. He offered his hunch as a wager, and everyone took him up on it. He became a wealthy man, relatively speaking, at the end of the voyage, when a gust of wind blew back the passenger's hood as he was leading his horse down the gangplank to reveal that he was, indeed, an elf.

No one bothered to ask the elf what brought him to this part of Ansalon. The sailors didn't care where the elf had been or where he was going. They were only too happy to have him off their ship, it being well known among seafarers that the sea elves—those who purportedly make their homes in the watery deeps—will try to scuttle any ship carrying one of their land-bound brethren in order to persuade them to live the remainder of their lives below the sea.

As for Silvanoshei, he never looked back, once he had set foot on land. He had no care for the ship or the sailors, although both had sped him across New Sea at a truly remarkable rate of speed. The wind had blown fair from the day they set forth, never ceasing. There had been no storms—a miracle this late in the season. Yet no matter how fast the ship sailed, it had not sailed fast enough for Silvanoshei.

He was overjoyed when he first set foot on land, for this was the land on which Mina walked. Every step brought him closer to that loved face, that adored voice. He had no idea where she was, but the horse knew. Her horse, which she had sent for him. The moment he set foot on shore, Silvanoshei mounted Foxfire, and they galloped off so fast that he never knew the name of the small port in which they'd landed.

They traveled northwest. Silvanoshei would have ridden day and night, if he could, but the horse (miraculous animal though it was) was a mortal horse and required food and rest, as did Silvanoshei himself. At first he bitterly grudged the time they must spend resting, but he was rewarded for his sacrifice. The very first night away from the ship, Silvanoshei fell in with a merchant caravan bound for the very same port town he'd recently left.

Many humans would have shunned a lone elf met by chance on the road, but merchants view every person as a potential customer and thus they tend not to be prejudiced against any race (except kender). Elven coin being just as good (or oftentimes better) than human, they cordially invited the young elf, whose clothing, though travel-stained, was of fine quality, to share their repast. Silvanoshei was on the verge of loftily refusing—he wanted to do nothing but sit by himself and dream of amber eyes—when he heard one of them speak the name, "Mina."

"I thank you gentlemen and ladies for your hospitality," said Silvanoshei, hurrying over to sit by their roaring fire. He even accepted the tin plate of dubious stew they offered him, although he didn't eat it, but surreptitiously dumped it in the bushes behind him.

He still wore the cloak he had worn on board ship, for the weather this time of year was cool. He removed the hood, however, and the humans were lost in admiration for this handsome youth, with his wine-colored eyes, charming smile and a voice that was sweet and melodious. Seeing that he'd eaten his stew quickly, one of the women offered him more.

"You're as thin as last year's mattress," she said, filling a plate, which he politely declined.

"You mentioned the name 'Mina,'" Silvanoshei said, trying to sound casual, though his heart beat wildly. "I know someone of that name. She wouldn't be an elf maid, by chance?"

At this they all laughed heartily. "Not unless elf maids wear armor these days," said one.

"I heard tell of an elf maid who wore armor," protested another, who seemed of an argumentative nature. "I recall my grandfather singing a song about her. Back in the days of the War of the Lance, it was."

"Bah! Your grandfather was an old souse," said a third. "He never went anywhere, but lived and died in the bars of Flotsam."

"Still, he's right," said one of the merchant's wives. "There was an elf maid who fought in the great war. Her name was Loony-tarry."

"Lunitari was the old goddess of magic, my dear," said her friend, another one of the wives, with a nudge of her elbow. "The ones who went away and left us to the mercy of these huge, monstrous dragons."

"No, I'm sure it wasn't," said the first wife, offended. "It was Loony-tarry, and she slew one of the foul beasts with a gnomish device called a dragonlunch. So called because she rammed it down the beast's gullet. And I wish another such would come and do the same to these new dragons."

"Well, from what we hear, this Mina plans to do just that," said the first merchant, trying to make peace between the two women, who were muttering huffily at each other.

"Have you seen her?" Silvanoshei asked, his heart on his lips. "Have you seen this Mina?"

"No, but she's all anyone's talking about in the towns we've passed through."

"Where is she?" Silvanoshei asked. "Is she close by?"

"She's marching along the road to Sanction. You can't miss her. She rides with an army of Dark Knights," answered the argumentative man dourly.

"Don't you take that amiss, young sir," said one of the wives. "Mina may wear black armor, but from what we hear, she has a heart of pure gold."

"Everywhere we go, we see some child she's healed or some cripple she's made to walk," said her friend.

"She's going to break the siege of Sanction," added the merchant, "and give us our port back. Then we can quit trekking halfway across the continent to sell our wares."

"And none of you think this is wrong?" said the argumentative man angrily. "Our own Solamnic Knights are in Sanction, trying to hang onto it, and you're cheering on this leader of our enemies."

This precipitated a lively discussion, which led at last to the majority of the group being in favor of whichever side would at last open up the ports to shipping once again. The Solamnics had tried to break out of Sanction and failed. Let this Mina and her Dark Knights see what they could do.

Shocked and horrified to think of Mina placing herself in such danger, Silvanoshei slipped away to lie awake half the night sick with fear for her. She must not attack Sanction! She must be dissuaded from such a dangerous course of action.

He was up and away with the first light of dawn. He had no need to urge the horse. Foxfire was as anxious to return to his mistress as was his rider. The two pushed themselves to the limit, the name "Mina" sounding with every hoofbeat, every beat of Silvanoshei's heart.

Several days after their encounter with Silvanoshei, the merchant caravan arrived in a port town. Leaving their husbands to set up camp, the two women went to visit the marketplace, where they were stopped by another elf, who was loitering about the stalls, accosting all new-comers.

This elf was an "uppity" elf, as one of the wives stated. He spoke to them, as one said, "like we were a bit of something that dropped in the dog's dish."

Still, they took the elf's money readily enough and told him what he wanted to know in exchange for it.

Yes, they had run into a young elf dressed like a fine gentleman on the road. A polite, well-spoken young man. Not like *some,* said the merchant's wife with a telling look. She could not recall where he said he'd been going, but she did remember that they had talked about Sanction. Yes, she supposed it was possible that he might be going to Sanction, but she thought it just as possible he might be going to the moon, for all she knew of the matter.

The older elf, whose face was grim and manner chill, paid them off and left them, traveling the same road as Silvanoshei.

The two wives knew immediately what to make of it.

"That young man was his son and has run away from home," said the first, nodding sagely.

"I don't blame him," said the second, looking after the elf irately. "Such a sour-faced old puss as that."

"I wish now I'd thrown him off the trail," said the first. "It would have served him right."

"You did what you thought was best, my dear," said her friend, craning her neck to see how many silver coins had been taken in. "It's not up to us to get involved in the affairs of the likes of such outlandish folk."

Linking arms, the two headed for the nearest tavern to spend the elf's money.

7 FAITH'S CONVICTS

Mina's forces moved relentlessly, inexorably toward Sanction. They continued to march unopposed, met no resistance on the way. Mina did not ride with her legions but traveled on ahead of them, entering cities, villages, and towns to work her miracles, spread the word of the One God, and round up all the kender. Many wondered at this last. Most assumed she meant to slay the kender (and few would have been sorry), but she only questioned them, each and every one, asking about a particular kender who called himself Tasslehoff Burrfoot.

Many Tasslehoffs presented themselves to her, but none was ever The Tasslehoff Burrfoot. Once they had all been questioned, Mina would then release the kender and send them on their way, with promise of rich reward should they find this Burrfoot.

Every day, kender arrived at the camp in droves, bringing with them Tasslehoff Burrfoots of every shape and description in hopes of receiving the reward. These Tasslehoffs included not only kender but dogs, pigs, a donkey, a goat, and once an extremely irate and hung-over dwarf. Trussed and bound, he was dragged into camp by ten kender, who proclaimed he was The Tasslehoff Burrfoot trying to disguise himself in a false beard.

The humans and the kender of Solamnia and Throt and Eastwilde were as enchanted with Mina as the elves of Silvanesti had been. They viewed her with deep suspicion when she rode in and followed after her with prayers and songs when she left. Castle after castle, town after town fell to Mina's charm, not her might.

Gerard had long ago given up hoping that the Solamnic Knights would attack. He guessed that Lord Tasgall intended to concentrate his efforts in Sanction rather than try to halt Mina along the way. Gerard could have told them they were wasting their time. Every day, Mina's army grew larger, as more and more men and women flocked to her standard and the worship of the One God. Although the pace her officers set was fast and the troops were forced to be up with the dawn and march until nightfall, morale was high. The march had more the feeling of a wedding procession, hastening forward to joyous celebration, rather than marching toward battle, carnage, and death.

Gerard still did not see much of Odila. She traveled in Mina's retinue and was often away from the main body of the force. Either she went by consent or she was forced to go, Gerard could not be sure, for she carefully avoided any contact with him. He knew that she did this for his own safety, but he had no one else to talk to, and he felt he would have risked the danger just for the chance to share his thoughts—dark and pessimistic as they were—with someone who would understand.

One day Gerard's contemplations were interrupted by the minotaur, Galdar. Discovering Gerard riding in the rear, the minotaur tersely ordered him to take his place at the front with the rest of the Knights. Gerard had no choice but to obey, and he spent the rest of the march traveling under the minotaur's watchful eye.

Why Galdar didn't kill him was a mystery to Gerard, but then Galdar himself was a mystery. Gerard felt Galdar's beady eyes on him often, but the look in them was not so much sinister as it was speculative.

Gerard kept to himself, rebuffing the attempts by his "comrades" to make friends. He could not very well share the cheerful mood of the Dark Knights nor participate in discussions of how many Solamnics they were going to gut or how many Solamnic heads they were going to mount on pikes.

Because of his morose silence and perverse nature, Gerard soon acquired the reputation as a dour, unsociable man, who was little liked by his "fellow" Knights. He didn't care. He was glad to be left alone.

Or perhaps not so alone. Whenever he roamed off by himself, he would often look up to find Galdar shadowing him.

The days stretched into weeks. The army traveled through Estwilde, wound north through Throt, entered the Khalkist Mountains through the Throtyl Gap, then headed due south for Sanction. As they left the more populated lands behind, Mina returned to the army, riding in the vanguard with Galdar, who now paid far more attention to Mina than he did to Gerard, for which Gerard was grateful.

Odila also returned, but she rode in the rear, in the wagon carrying the amber sarcophagus. Gerard would have liked to have found a way to talk to her, but the one time he lagged behind, hoping he wouldn't be missed, Galdar sought him out and ordered him to maintain his position in the ranks.

Then the day came that a mountain range appeared on the horizon. They saw it first as a dark blue smudge, which Gerard mistook for a bank of dark blue storm clouds. As the army drew closer, he could see plumes of smoke drifting from the summits. He looked upon the active volcanoes known as the Lords of Doom—the guardians of Sanction.

"Not long now," he thought, and his heart ached for the defenders of Sanction, watching and waiting. They would be confident, certain their defenses would hold. They had held for over a year now; why should they expect anything different?

He wondered if they'd heard rumors about the horrific army of the dead that had attacked Solanthus. Even if they had, would they believe what they heard? Gerard doubted it. He would not have believed such tales himself. He wasn't certain, thinking back on it, that he believed it even now. The entire battle had the unreal disconnection of a fever dream. Did the army of the dead march with Mina? Gerard sometimes tried to catch a glimpse of them, but, if the dead were with them, this fell ally traveled silently and unseen.

Mina's army entered the foothills of the Khalkists and began the climb that would lead them to the pass through the Lords of Doom. In a valley, Mina halted their march, telling them they would remain here for several days. She had a journey to make, she said, and, in her absence, the army would prepare for the push through the mountains. Everyone was ordered to have armor and weapons in good condition, ready for battle. The blacksmith set up his forge, and he and his assistants spent the days mending and making. Hunting parties were sent out to bring in fresh meat.

They had only just set up camp on the first day when the elf prisoner was captured.

He was dragged into camp by several of the outriders who patrolled the army's flanks, scouring the area for any sign of the enemy.

Gerard was at the smith's, having his sword mended and finding it strange to think that the very enemy who might soon be spitted on that sword was now working hard to fix it. He had determined that he would take the opportunity of Mina's absence to try to convince Odila to escape with him. If she refused, he would ride off for Sanction alone, to take the news to them of the approaching enemy. He had no idea how he was going to manage this, how he was going to elude Galdar or, once he reached Sanction, how he was going to pass through the hordes of the enemy who had the city surrounded, but he figured he would deal with all that later.

Bored with waiting, tired of his own gloomy thoughts, he heard a commotion and walked over to see what was going on.

The elf was mounted on a red horse of fiery temper and disposition, for no one was able to get near the beast. The elf himself seemed uneasy on his mount, for when he reached down a hand to try to sooth the animal, the horse flung his head about and bit at him. The elf snatched his hand back and made no further move to touch the horse.

A crowd had gathered around the elf. Some knew him, apparently, for they began to jeer, bowing before him mockingly, saluting the "king of Silvanesti" with raucous laughter. Gerard eyed the elf curiously. He was dressed in finery that might have suited a king, though his cloak of fine wool was travel-stained and his silken hose were torn, his gold-embroidered doublet worn and frayed. He paid no attention to his detractors. He searched the camp for someone, as did the horse.

The crowd parted, as it always did whenever Mina walked among them. At the sight of her, the eyes of both horse and rider fixed on her with rapt attention.

The horse whinnied and shook his head. Mina came to Foxfire, laid her head against his, ran her hand over his muzzle. He draped his head over her shoulder and closed his eyes. His journey ended, his duty done, he was home, and he was content. Mina patted the horse and looked up at the elf.

"Mina," said the young man, and her name, as he spoke it, was red with his heart's blood. He slid down off the horse's back, stood before her. "Mina, you sent for me. I am here."

Such aching pain and love was in the elf's voice that Gerard was embarrassed for the young man. That his love was not reciprocated was obvious. Mina paid no attention to the elf, continued to lavished her attention on the horse. Her disregard for the young man did not go unnoticed. Mina's Knights grinned at one another. Bawdy jests were whispered about. One man laughed out loud, but his laughter ceased abruptly when Mina shifted her amber eyes to him. Ducking his head, his face red, he slunk away.

Mina finally acknowledged the elf's presence. "You are welcome, Your Majesty. All is in readiness for your arrival. A tent for you has been prepared next to mine. You have come in good time. Soon we march on Sanction to lay claim to that sacred city in the name of the One God. You will be witness to our triumph."

"You can't go to Sanction, Mina!" said the elf. "It's too dangerous . . ." His words faltered. Glancing around the crowd of black-armored humans, he seemed to have only just now realized that he had ridden into a camp of his enemies.

Mina saw and understood his unease. She cast a stern look around the crowd, quelled the jokes and silenced the laughter.

"Let it be known throughout the army that the king of the elves of the land of Silvanesti is my guest. He is to be treated with the same respect with which you treat me. I make each and every one of you responsible for his safety and well being."

Mina's gaze went searchingly about the camp and, to Gerard's great discomfiture, halted when it reached him.

"Sir Gerard, come forward," Mina ordered.

Aware that every man and woman in camp was staring at him, Gerard felt the hot blood suffuse his face, even as a cold qualm gripped his gut. He had no idea why he was being singled out. He had no choice but to obey.

Saluting, he kept quiet, waited.

"Sir Gerard," said Mina gravely, "I appoint you as special bodyguard for the elven king. His care and comfort are your responsibility. I choose you because you have had considerable experience dealing with elves. As I recall, you served in Qualinesti before coming to us."

Gerard could not speak, he was so astonished, primarily at Mina's cursed cleverness. He was her avowed enemy, a Solamnic Knight come to spy on her.

She knew that. And because he was a Solamnic Knight, he was the only person in her army to whom she could entrust the life of the young elven king. Set a prisoner to guard a prisoner. A unique concept, yet one that must work in Gerard's case.

"I am sorry, but I fear that this duty will keep you out of the battle for Sanction, Sir Gerard," Mina continued. "It would never do for His Majesty to be exposed to that danger, and so you will remain with him in the rear, with the baggage train. But there will be other battles for you, Sir Gerard. Of that, I am certain."

Gerard could do nothing but salute again. Mina turned her back, walked away. The elf stood staring after her, his face bleak and pale. Many in the army remained to stare and, now that Mina had departed, resume their gibes at the elf's expense. Some started to grow downright nasty.

"Come on," said Gerard and, seeing that the elf was not going to move unless prompted, he grabbed hold of the elf's arm and hauled him off bodily. Gerard marched the elf through the camp toward the area where Mina had raised her tent. Sure enough, another tent had been set up a short distance from hers. The tent was empty, awaiting the arrival of this strange guest.

"What is your name?" Gerard asked grumpily, not feeling kindly disposed toward this elf, who had further complicated his life.

The elf didn't hear at first. He kept looking about, trying to find Mina.

Gerard asked again, this time raising his voice.

"My name is Silvanoshei," the elf replied. He spoke Common fluently, though his accent was so thick it was hard to understand him. The elf looked directly at Gerard, the first time he'd done so since Gerard had been put in charge of him.

"I don't recognize you. You weren't with her in Silvanesti, were you?"

No need to specify which "her" he was talking about. Gerard could see plainly that for this young man, there was only one "her" in the world.

"No," said Gerard shortly. "I wasn't."

"Where has she gone now? What is she doing?" Silvanoshei asked, looking about again. "When will she come back?"

Mina's tent and those of her bodyguards stood apart from the main camp, off to themselves. The noise of the camp faded behind them. The show was over. The Knights and soldiers went back to the business of making ready for war.

"Are you really king of the Silvanesti elves?" Gerard asked.

"Yes," said Silvanoshei absently, preoccupied by his search, "I am."

"Then what in the Abyss are you doing here?" Gerard demanded bluntly.

At that moment, Silvanoshei saw Mina. She was far distant, galloping on Foxfire across the valley. The two were alone, happy together, racing the wind with wild abandon. Seeing the pain in the young man's eyes, Gerard answered his own question.

"What did you say?" Silvanoshei asked, sighing and turning around. Mina had ranged out of sight. "I didn't hear you."

"Who's ruling your people in your absence, Your Majesty?" Gerard asked accusingly. He was thinking of another elven king—Gilthas—who had sacrificed so much to save his people. Not run away from them.

"My mother," said Silvanoshei. He shrugged. "It's what she's always wanted."

"Your mother rules," said Gerard skeptically. "Or the Dark Knights of Neraka? I hear they've taken over Silvanesti."

"Mother will fight them," said Silvanoshei. "She enjoys fighting. She has always enjoyed it, you know. The battle and the danger. It's what she lives for. I hate it. Our people, dying and suffering. Dying for her. Always dying for her. She drinks their blood, and it keeps her beautiful. But it poisoned me."

Gerard stared at him in perplexity. Even though the elf had been speaking Common, Gerard had no idea what he was talking about. He might have asked, but at that moment, Odila emerged from a tent that was set up next to Mina's. She stopped at the sight of Gerard, flushed self-consciously, then turned swiftly and walked off.

"I will fetch you some hot water, Your Majesty," Gerard offered, keeping an eye on her. "You'll want to freshen up and clean away the dust of the road. And I'll bring food and drink. You look as if you could use it."

That much was true. Elves were always thin, but this young elf was emaciated. Apparently he was trying to live on love. Gerard's anger started to fade. He was beginning to feel sorry for this young man, who was as much a prisoner as any of them.

"As you wish," said Silvanoshei, not caring. "When do you think Mina will return?"

"Soon, Your Majesty," said Gerard, almost shoving the young man into the tent. "Soon. You should be rested."

Having rid himself of his responsibility, at least for the moment, he hurried after Odila, who was walking through the camp.

"You've been avoiding me," he said in an undertone, catching up to her.

"For your own good," she replied, still walking. "You should leave, take word to the Knights in Sanction."

"I was planning to." He jerked his thumb back over his shoulder. "Now I have this besotted young elf king on my hands. I've been assigned duty as his bodyguard."

Odila halted, stared at him. "Truly?"

"Truly."

"Mina's idea?"

"Who else?"

"How clever," Odila remarked, continuing on.

"My thoughts exactly," said Gerard. "You don't happen to know what she plans to do with him, do you? I can't think she's romantically inclined."

"Of course not," said Odila. "She told me all about him. He may not look it at the moment, but he has the potential to be a strong and charismatic leader of the elven nation. Mina saw the threat and acted to remove it. I don't know much about elven politics, but I gather that the Silvanesti will not willingly follow anyone but him."

"Why doesn't she just kill him?" Gerard asked. "Death would be more merciful that what she's doing to him now."

"His death makes him a martyr, gives his people a cause for which they would fight. Now they do nothing but sit and twiddle their thumbs, waiting for him to come back. There's Galdar watching us," she said suddenly. "I should go on alone. Don't come with me."

"But where are you going?"

She did not look at him. "It is my task to take food to the two wizards. Force them to eat."

"Odila," said Gerard, holding her back, "you still believe in the power of this One God, don't you?"

"Yes," she said, casting him a swift and defiant glance.

"Even though you know it's an evil power?"

"An evil power that heals the sick and brings peace and comfort to hundreds," Odila returned.

"And restores hideous life to the dead!"

"Something only a god could do." Odila faced him squarely. "I believe in this god, Gerard, and, what's more, so do you. That's the real reason you're here."

Gerard tried to come up with a glib rejoinder, but found he couldn't. Was this what the voice in his heart was trying to tell him? Was he here of his own free will, or was he just one more prisoner?

Seeing he had no response, Odila turned and left him.

Gerard stood in troubled silence, watched her make her way through the bustling camp.

8 KNIGHT OF
THE BLACK ROSE

The journey this time was brief. Tas had barely started to
grow annoyed with the tumbling about when he was suddenly right side up
and standing solidly on his own two feet. Time, once again, stopped.

He exhaled in relief and looked around.

The Hedge Maze was gone. Conundrum was gone. Tas stood alone in
what must have once been a beautiful rose garden. The garden was beautiful
no longer, for everything in it had died. Dried rose blossoms, that had once
been red, were now dark as sorrow. Their heads hung drooping on the stems
that were brown and withered. Dead leaves from years that knew nothing but
winter lay in piles beneath a crumbling stone wall. A path made of broken
flagstones led from the dead garden into a manor house, its walls charred and
blackened by long-dead flames. Tall cypress trees surrounded the manor house,
their enormous limbs cutting off any vestige of sunlight, so that if night fell,
it came only as a deepening of day's shadows.

Tasslehoff thought that he had never in his life seen any place that made
him feel so unutterably sad.

"What are you doing here?"

A shadow fell over the kender. A voice spoke, a voice that was fell and cold.
A knight, clad in ancient armor, stood over him. The knight was dead. He
had been dead for many centuries. The body inside the armor had long ago
rotted away. The armor was the body now, flesh and bone, muscle and sinew,
tarnished and blackened with age, charred by the fires of war, stained with
the blood of his victims. Red eyes, the only light in an eternal darkness, were

visible through the slit visor of the helm. The red eyes flicked like flame over Tasslehoff. Their gaze was painful, and the kender flinched.

Tasslehoff stared at the apparition before him, and a most unpleasant feeling stole over him, a feeling he had forgotten because it was such a horrible feeling that he didn't like to remember it. His mouth filled with a bitter taste that stung his tongue. His heart lurched about in his chest as though it were trying to run away, but couldn't. His stomach curled up in a ball and searched for some place to hide.

He tried to answer the question, but the words wouldn't come out. He knew this knight. A death knight, Lord Soth had taught the kender fear, a sensation that Tasslehoff had not liked in the least. The thought came that perhaps Lord Soth might not remember him, and it occurred to Tas that it might be a good thing if Lord Soth didn't, for their last meeting hadn't been all that friendly. That notion was quickly dispelled by the words that bit at the kender like winter's bitter wind.

"I don't like to repeat myself. What are you doing here?"

Tas had been asked that question a lot in his long life, although never quite with this shade of meaning. Most of the time the question was: "What are you doing *here?*" said in tones that implied the questioner would be glad if whatever he was doing *here* he would do it someplace else. Other times, the question was: "What are you *doing* here?" which really meant stop *doing* that immediately. Lord Soth had placed the emphasis on the "you" making it "What are *you* doing here?" which meant that he was referring to Tasslehoff Burrfoot directly. Which meant that he recognized him.

Tasslehoff made several attempts to answer, none of which were successful, for all that came out of his mouth was a gargle, not words.

"Twice I asked you a question," said the death knight. "And while my time in this world is eternal, my patience is not."

"I'm trying to answer, sir," returned Tas meekly, "but you cause the words to get all squeezed up inside of me. I know that this is impolite, but I'm going to have to ask you a question before I can answer yours. When you say 'here', what exactly do you mean by that?" He mopped sweat from his forehead with the sleeve of his hand and tried to look anywhere except into those red eyes. "I've been to lots of 'heres,' and I'm a bit muddled as to where your 'here' is."

Soth's red eyes shifted from Tasslehoff to the Device of Time Journeying, clutched in the kender's stiff fingers. Tas followed the death knight's gaze.

"Oh, uh, this," Tas said, gulping. "Pretty, isn't it? I came across it on my . . . er . . . last trip. Someone dropped it. I plan on returning it. Isn't it lucky I found it? If you don't mind, I'll just put it away—" He tried to open one of his pouches, but his hands wouldn't quit shaking.

"Don't worry," said Soth. "I won't take it from you. I have no desire for a device that would carry me backward in time. Unless"—he paused, the red eyes grew shadowed—"unless it would take me back to undo what I did. Perhaps then I might make use of it."

Tas knew full well that he could never stop Lord Soth from taking the device if he wanted it, but he meant to give it a good try. The courage that is true courage and not merely the absence of fear rose up in Tasslehoff, and he fumbled for the knife, Rabbit Slayer, that he wore on his belt. He didn't know what good his little knife could do against a death knight, but Tas was a Hero of the Lance. He had to try.

Fortunately, his courage was not tested.

"But what would be the use?" said Lord Soth. "If I had it to do over again, the outcome would be the same. I would make the same decisions, commit the same heinous acts. For that was the man I was."

The red eyes flickered. "If I could go back, knowing what I know, maybe then my actions would be different. But our souls can never go back. They can only go forward. And some of us are not even permitted to do that. Not until we have learned the hard lessons life—and death—teach us."

His voice, already cold, grew colder still, so that Tas stopped sweating and began to shiver.

"And now we are no longer given the chance to do that."

The red eyes flared again. "To answer your question, kender, you are in the Fifth Age, the so-called 'Age of Mortals'." The helmed head shifted. He lifted his hand. The tattered cape he wore stirred with his motion. "You stand in the garden of what was once my dwelling place and is now my prison."

"Are you going to kill me?" Tas asked, more because it was a question he might be expected to ask than because he felt threatened. A person has to take notice of you in order to threaten you, and Tas had the distinct impression that he was of less interest to this undead lord than the withered stems or the dried-up rose petals.

"Why should I kill you, kender?" Soth asked. "Why should I bother?"

Tas gave the matter considerable thought. In truth, he could find no real reason why Soth should kill him, other than one.

"You're a death knight, my lord," Tas said. "Isn't killing people your job?"

"Death was not my job," Soth replied tonelessly. "Death was my joy. And death was my torment. My body has died, but my soul remains alive. As the torture victim suffers in agony when he feels the red-hot brand sear his flesh, so I suffer daily, my soul seared with my rage, my shame, my guilt. I have sought to end it, sought to drown the pain in blood, ease the pain with ambition. I was promised that the pain would end. I was promised that if I helped my goddess achieve her reward, I would be given my reward. My pain would end, and my soul would be freed. These promises were not kept."

The red eyes flicked over Tasslehoff, then roved restlessly to the withered and blackened roses.

"Once I killed out of ambition, for pleasure and for spite. No more. None of that has any meaning to me now. None of that drowned the pain.

"Besides," Soth added off-handedly, "in your case, why should I bother to kill you? You are already dead. You died in the Fourth Age, in the last second of the Fourth Age. That is why I ask, why are you here? How did you find this place, when even the gods cannot see where it is hidden?"

"So I *am* dead," Tas said to himself with a little sigh. "I guess that settles it."

He was thinking it strange that he and Lord Soth should have something in common, when a voice, a living voice, called out, "My lord! Lord Soth! I seek an audience with you!"

A hand closed over the kender's mouth. Another strong hand wrapped around him, and he was suddenly enveloped in the folds of soft black robes, as if night had taken on shape and form and dropped over his head. He could see nothing. He could not speak, could barely breathe, for the hand was positioned right over his nose and mouth. All he could smell—oddly enough—was rose-petals.

Tas might have strongly protested this rude behavior, but he recognized the living voice that had called out to Lord Soth, and he was suddenly quite glad that he had the strange hand to help him keep quiet, for even though sometimes he meant to be very quiet, words had a tendency to leap out of his throat before he could stop them.

Tas wriggled a bit to try to free up his nose for breathing, which—dead or not—his body required him to do. This accomplished, he held perfectly still.

Lord Soth did not immediately answer the call. He, too, recognized the person who had called out, although he had never before met her or seen her. He knew her because the two of them were bound together by the same chain, served the same master. He knew why she had come to him, knew what she meant to ask of him. He did not know what his answer would be, however. He knew what he wanted it to be, yet doubted if he had the courage.

Courage. He smiled bitterly. Once he'd imagined himself afraid of nothing. Over time, he'd come to realize he'd been afraid of everything. He had lived his life in fear: fear of failure, fear of weakness, fear that people would despise him if they truly knew him. Most of all, he had feared she would despise him, once she found out that the man she adored was just an ordinary man, not the paragon of virtue and courage she believed him.

He had been given knowledge by the gods that might have prevented the Cataclysm. He had been riding to Istar when he had been confronted by a group of elven women, misguided followers of the Kingpriest. They told him lies about his wife, told him she had been unfaithful to him and that the child she carried was not his. His fear caused him to believe their stories, and he had turned back from the path that might have been his salvation. Fear had stopped his ears to his wife's protestations of innocence. Fear had made him murder that which he truly loved.

He stood thinking of this, remembering it all yet again, as he had been doomed to remember so many, many times.

Once more he stood in the blooming garden where she tended the roses with her own hands, not trusting the gardener he had hired to do the work for her. He looked with concern at her hands, her fair skin torn and scratched, marred with drops of blood.

"Is it worth it?" he asked her. "The roses cause you so much pain."

"The pain lasts for but a moment," she told her. "The joy of their beauty lasts for days."

"Yet with winter's chill breath, they wither and die."

"But I have the memory of them, my love, and that brings me joy."

Not joy, he thought. Not joy, but torment. Memory of her smile, her laughter. Memory of the sorrow in her eyes as the life faded from them, taken by my hand. Memory of her curse.

Or was it a curse? I thought so then, but now I wonder. Perhaps it was, in truth, her blessing on me.

Leaving the garden of dead roses, he entered the manor house that had stood for centuries, a monument to death and fear. He took his seat in the chair that was covered with the dust of ages, dust that his incorporeal body never disturbed. He sat in that chair and stared, as he had stared for hour after hour after hour, at the bloodstain upon the floor.

There she fell.

There she died.

For eons he had been doomed to hear the recital of his wrongs sung to him by the spirits of those elven women who had been his undoing and who were cursed to live a life that was no life, an existence of torment and regret. He had not heard their voices since the Fifth Age began. How many years that was he did not know, for time had no meaning to him. The voices were part of the Fourth Age, and they had remained with the Fourth Age.

Forgiven, at last. Granted permission to leave.

He sought forgiveness, but it was denied him. He was angry at the denial, as his queen had known he would be. His anger snared him. Thus Takhisis caught him in her trap and bound him fast and carried him here to continue on his wretched existence, waiting for her call.

The call had come. Finally.

Footsteps of the living brought him out of his dark reverie. He looked up to see this representative of Her Dark Majesty and saw a child clad in armor, or so he first thought. Then he saw that what he had mistaken for a child was a girl on the edge of womanhood. He was reminded of Kitiara, the only being who had, for a brief time, been able to ease his torment. Kitiara, who never knew fear except once, at the very end of her life, when she looked up to see him coming for her. It was then, when he gazed into her terror-stricken eyes, that he understood himself. She had given him that much, at least.

Kitiara was gone now, too, her soul moving on to wherever it needed to go. Was this to be another? Another Kitiara, sent to seduce him?

No, he realized, looking into the amber eyes of the girl who stood before him. This was not Kitiara, who had done what she did for her own reasons, who had served no one but herself. This girl did all for glory—the glory of the god. Kitiara had never willingly sacrificed anything in order to achieve her goals. This girl had sacrificed everything, emptied herself, left herself a vessel to be filled by the god.

Soth saw the tiny figures of thousands of beings held fast in the amber eyes. He felt the warm amber slide over him, try to capture and hold him, just another insect.

He shook his helmed head. "Don't bother, Mina," he told the girl. "I know too much. I know the truth."

"And what is that truth?" Mina asked. The amber eyes tried again to seize hold of him. She was not one to give up, this woman-child.

"That your mistress will use you and then abandon you," Soth said. "She will betray you, as she has betrayed everyone who ever served her. I know her of old, you see."

He felt the stirrings of his queen's anger, but he chose to ignore it. Not now, he told her. You cannot use that against me now.

Mina was not angry. She seemed saddened by his response. "How can you say that of her when she went to such trouble to bring you with her? You are the only one so honored. All the rest . . ." She waved her hand to indicate the chamber, empty of its ghosts, or so it must seem to her. To him, the chamber was crowded. "All the rest were banished to oblivion. You alone were granted the privilege of remaining with this world."

"Oblivion is it? Once I believed that. Once I feared the darkness, and thus she kept her hold on me. Now I know differently. Death is not oblivion. Death frees the soul to travel onward."

Mina smiled, pitying his ignorance. "You are the one who has been deceived. The souls of the dead went nowhere. They vanished into the mist, wasted, forgotten. The One God now takes the souls of the dead unto her and gives them the opportunity to remain in this world and continue to act for the good of the world."

"For the good of the god, you mean," said Soth. He stirred in his chair, which gave him no comfort. "Let us say I find myself grateful to this god for the privilege of remaining in the world. Knowing this god as I do of old, I know that she expects my gratitude to take on a tangible form. What is it she requires of me?"

"Within a few days time, armies of both the living and the dead will sweep down on Sanction. The city will fall to my might." Mina did not speak with bravado. She stated a fact, nothing more. "At that time, the One God will perform a great miracle. She will enter the world as she was long meant to do, join the realms of the mortal and the immortal. When she exists in both realms, she will conquer the world, rid it of such vermin as the elves, and establish herself as the ruler of Krynn. I am to be made captain of the army of the living. The One God offers you the captaincy of the army of the dead."

"She 'offers' me this?" Soth asked.

"Offers it. Yes, of course," said Mina.

"Then she will not be offended if I turn down her offer," said Soth.

"She would not be offended," Mina replied, "but she would be deeply grieved at your ingratitude, after all that she has done for you."

"All she has done for me." Soth smiled. "So this is why she brought me here. I am to be a slave leading an army of slaves. My answer to this generous offer is 'no.'

"You made a mistake, my queen," called Soth, speaking to the shadows, where he knew she lay coiled, waiting. "You used my anger to keep your talons in me, and you dragged me here so that you could make use of me still. But you left me alone too long. You left me to the silence in which I could once more hear my wife's beloved voice. You left me to the darkness that became my light, for I could once more see my wife's beloved face. I could see myself, and I saw a man consumed by his fear. And it was then I saw you for what you are.

"I fought for you, Queen Takhisis. I believed your cause was mine. The silence taught me that it was you who fed my fear, raising around me a ring of fire from which I could never escape. The fire has gone out now, my queen. All around me is nothing but ashes."

"Beware, my lord," said Mina, and her tone was dire. "If you refuse this, you risk the god's anger."

Lord Soth rose to his feet. He pointed to a stain upon the stone floor.

"Do you see that?"

"I see nothing," said Mina, with an indifferent glance, "nothing except the cold, gray rock."

"I see a pool of blood," said Lord Soth. "I see my beloved wife lying in her blood. I see the blood of all those who perished because my fear kept me from accepting the blessing the gods offered to me. Long have I been forced to stare at that stain, and long have I loathed the very sight of it. Now, I kneel on it," he said, bending his knees on the stone, "I kneel in her blood and the blood of all who died because I was afraid. I beg her to forgive me for the wrong I did to her. I beg them all to forgive me."

"There can be no forgiveness," said Mina sternly. "You are cursed. The One God will cast your soul into the darkness of unending pain and torment. Is this what you choose?"

"Death is what I choose," said Lord Soth. Reaching beneath the breast plate of his armor, he drew forth a rose. The rose was long dead, but its vibrant color had not faded. The rose was red as her lips, red as her blood. "If death brings unending torment, then I accept that as my fitting punishment."

Lord Soth saw Mina reflected in the red fire of his soul. "Your god has lost her hold on me. I am no longer afraid."

Mina's amber eyes hardened in anger. Turning on her heel, she left him kneeling on the cold stone, his head bowed, his hands clasped over the thorns and dried leaves and crumpled petals of the red rose. Mina's footfalls reverberated through the manor house, shook the floor on which he knelt, shook the charred and broken walls, shook the blackened beams.

He felt pain, physical pain, and he looked in wonder at his hand. The accursed armor was gone. The thorns of the dead rose pierced his flesh. A tiny drop of blood gleamed on his skin, more red than the petals.

A beam above him gave way and crashed down beside him. Shards of splintered wood flew from the shattered beam, punctured his flesh. He gritted his teeth against the pain of his wounds. This was the Dark Queen's last, desperate attempt to keep her hold on him. He had been given back his mortal body.

She would never know, but she had, in her ignorance, granted him a final blessing.

She lay coiled in the shadows, certain of her triumph, waiting for his fear to once more bind him to her, waiting for him to cry out that he had been wrong, waiting for him to plead and grovel for her to spare him.

Lord Soth lifted the rose to his lips. He kissed the petals, then scattered them over the blood that stained the gray stone red. He cast off the helm that had been his flesh and bone for so many empty years. He tore off the breastplate and hurled it far from him, so that it struck the wall with a clank and a clatter.

Another beam fell, hurled by a vengeful hand. The beam struck him, crushed his body, drove him to the floor. His blood flowed freely, mingled with his dear wife's blood. He did not cry out. The pain of dying was agony, but it was an agony that would soon end. He could bear the pain for her sake, for the pain her soul had born for him.

She would not be waiting for him. She had long ago made her own journey, carrying in her arms their son. He would make his solitary way after them, lost, alone, seeking.

He might never find them, the two he had so wronged, but he would dedicate eternity to the search.

In that search, he would be redeemed.

Mina stalked through the rose garden. Her face was livid and cold as a face carved of marble. She did not look back to see the final destruction of Dargaard Keep.

Tasslehoff, peeping out from behind a fold of blackness, saw her leave. He did not see where she went, for at that moment the massive structure collapsed, falling in upon itself with a thunderous crash that sent clouds of dust and debris roiling up into the air.

A gigantic block of stone smashed down into the rose garden. He was extremely surprised to find that he wasn't underneath it, for it fell right where he'd been standing, but, like thistledown, he floated on the winds of ruin and death and was lifted above them into the pure, chill blue of a cloudless, sunlit sky.

9 THE ATTACK ON SANCTION

The city of Sanction had been besieged for months. The Dark Knights threw everything they had against it. Countless numbers died in the shadows of Sanction's walls, on both sides of Sanction's walls, died for no reason, for the siege could not be broken. When Mina's army marched into view, Sanction's defenders laughed to see it, for how could such pitifully small numbers of men make any difference?

They did not laugh long. The city of Sanction fell to the army of souls in a single day.

Nothing could halt the advance of the dead. The moats of sluggish, hot lava flowing from the Lords of Doom that kept the living at bay, were no barrier to the souls. The newly built and strengthened earthwork fortifications against which the army of the Dark Knights had thrown themselves time and again without success now stood as monuments to futility. The thick, gray mist of hapless souls flowed down the sides of the mountains, filled the valleys like a rising tide, and boiled up and over the fortifications. Besieger and besieged alike fled before the terrifying dead.

Mina's sappers had no need to batter down the gates that led into the city or breach the walls. Her troops had only to wait until the gates were flung open from within by the panic-stricken defenders. Fleeing the army of the dead, they soon joined their ranks. Mina's Knights, hidden among the ghastly mist, cut down the living without mercy. Led by Galdar, the army stormed through the gates to do battle in the city.

Mina fought her battles in the foothills around Sanction, doing what she could to quell the panic of the army of besiegers, who were just as terrified as their enemy. She rode among them, halting their flight, urging them back to battle.

She seemed to be everywhere upon the battlefield, galloping swiftly on her red horse to wherever she was needed. She rode without care for her own safety, often leaving her bodyguards far behind, spurring their steeds frantically to keep up.

Gerard did not take part in the battle. True to her word, Mina posted him and his prisoner, the elf king, atop a ridgeline overlooking the city.

Along with the elf, Gerard and four other Dark Knights guarded the wagon carrying the amber sarcophagus of Goldmoon and the two dead wizards. Odila rode with the wagon. Like Gerard, her gaze was fixed on the battle in which she could take no part. Frustrated, helpless to do anything to aid his fellow Knights, Gerard followed the battle from his detested safe vantage point. Mina shone with a pale, fey light that made her a rallying point anywhere on the field.

"What is that strange fog that fills the valley?" Silvanoshei asked, staring down from his horse in wonder.

"That strange fog is not fog, Your Majesty. That is an army of dead souls," Gerard answered grimly.

"Even the dead adore her," Silvanoshei said. "They come to fight for her."

Gerard glanced at the wagon, carrying the bodies of the two dead mages. He wondered if Palin's soul was on that battlefield, fighting for Mina. He guessed how much Palin "adored" her. He could have pointed this out to the besotted young elf, but he kept quiet. The young man wouldn't listen, anyway. Gerard sat his horse in grim silence.

The din of battle, the cries of the dying, rose up from the mist of souls that grew thicker by the moment. Gerard suddenly saw it all in a blood-drenched haze, and he determined to ride down to join that desperate battle, though he knew from the outset that he could do no good and would only die in the attempt.

"Gerard!" Odila called out.

"You can't stop me!" he cried angrily, and then, when the red haze cleared a bit, he saw she wasn't trying to stop him. She was trying to warn him.

Four of Mina's Knights, who were supposed to be guarding the elf, spurred their horses, surrounded him.

He had no idea how they had divined his intention, but he drew his sword, fiercely glad to have this chance to do battle. Their first words astonished him.

"Ride off, Gerard," said one, a man named Clorant. "This is not your fight. We mean you no harm."

"It is my fight, you bloody bastards—" Gerard began. His words of defiance sputtered out.

They were not staring at him. Their hate-filled eyes stared behind him, at the elf. Gerard remembered the jeers and catcalls he'd heard when the elven king rode into camp. He glanced over his shoulder. Silvanoshei was not armed. He would be defenseless against these four.

"What happens to the pointy-ear is none of your concern, Gerard," Clorant said. His tone was dire. He was in deadly earnest. "Ride on, and don't look back."

Gerard had to grapple with himself, squelch his rage, force himself to think calmly and rationally. All the while, he cursed Mina for seeing into his heart.

"You boys have got yourselves all turned around," Gerard said. Trying his best to sound casual, he edged his horse so that it was between Clorant and the young elf. Gerard pointed. "The fight's in that direction. Behind you."

"You won't get into trouble with Mina, Gerard," Clorant promised. "We have our story all thought out. We're going to tell her we were attacked by an enemy patrol that had been lurking up in the mountains. We drove them off, but in the confusion the elf was killed."

"We'll drag a couple of bodies up here," added another. "Bloody ourselves up some. Make it look real."

"I'll be happy to bloody any one of you," said Gerard, "but it's not going to come to that. This elf's not worth it. He's no threat to anybody."

"He's a threat to Mina," said Clorant. "He tried to kill her when we were in Silvanesti. The One God brought her back to us, but the next time the bastard might succeed."

"If he did try to kill her, let Mina deal with him," said Gerard.

"She can't see through his tricks and deceits," said Clorant. "We have to protect her from herself."

He's a jealous lover, Gerard realized. Clorant is in love with Mina himself. Every one of them is in love with her. That's the real reason they want to kill this elf.

"Give me a sword. I can fight my own battles," declared Silvanoshei, riding up alongside Gerard. The elf cast him a proud and scornful glance. "I don't need you to fight them for me."

"You young fool," Gerard growled out of the side of his mouth. "Shut up, and let me handle this!"

Aloud he said, "Mina ordered me to guard him, and I'm bound to obey. I took an oath to obey, the same as you. There's a concept floating around called honor. Maybe you boys have heard of it?"

"Honor!" Clorant spat on the ground. "You talk like a cursed Solamnic. You have a choice, Gerard. You can either ride off and let us deal with the elf, in which case we'll see to it that you don't get into trouble, or you can be one of the corpses we leave on the field to prove our story. Don't worry," he sneered. "We'll tell Mina that you died 'with honor.' "

Gerard didn't wait for them to come at him. He didn't even wait for Clorant to finish his speech but spurred his horse toward him. Their swords clanged together on the word, "honor."

"I'll deal with this bastard," shouted Clorant. "The rest of you kill the elf!"

Leaving Clorant to take care of Gerard, the other three galloped toward the elf. Gerard heard Silvanoshei shout in Elvish, heard one of the Knights curse, and then a thud and a clatter of metal. Risking a glance, Gerard saw to his amazement that Silvanoshei, with no weapon but his own hands, had thrown himself bodily on one of the armored Knights, carried him off his horse and onto the ground. The two floundered, grappling for the Knight's loose sword.

The Knight's comrades circled around the combatants, waiting a chance to strike the elf, not wanting to risk hitting their friend.

Gerard had his own problems. Fighting an armed foe on horseback is not so much a matter of skilled thrust and parry between two swordsmen as a bludgeoning, slashing battle to try to unseat your foe.

Their horses snorted and churned up the ground with their hooves. Clorant and Gerard circled each other, swords swinging wildly, striking any part of the body that came into view, neither making much headway. Gerard's fist smashed into Clorant's jaw, his sword sliced through the chain mail of the man's upper arm. Gerard himself was not wounded, but he was the one at a disadvantage. Clorant had only to defend himself, keep Gerard occupied so that he could not save the elf.

Another glance showed Gerard that Silvanoshei had managed to grab the fallen Knight's sword. Taking up a defensive position, Silvanoshei grimly eyed his foes, two of whom were still mounted and still armed. The fallen Knight was staggering to his feet.

Raising his sword, one Knight sent his horse at a gallop straight at Silvanoshei, intending to behead him with a slashing downward stroke. Desperate, Gerard turned his back on Clorant. Gerard was leaving himself wide open, but he had no other recourse if he wanted to save the elf's life. Gerard spurred his horse, so that the startled animal leaped ahead, his intent being to gallop between the two combatants, putting himself between the elf and his attacker.

Clorant struck Gerard from behind. His sword thunked against Gerard's helm, setting his ears to ringing and scattering his wits. Then Clorant was at Gerard's side. A sword flashed in the sunlight.

"Stop this!" a woman shouted, her voice shaking with fury. "In the name of the One God, stop this madness!"

The Knight galloping down on the elf pulled so hard on the reins that his horse reared and practically upended both of them. Gerard had to rein in his steed swiftly or crash into the floundering animal. He heard Clorant suck in his breath, heard him try to check his horse.

Gerard lowered his sword, looked about to see who had spoken. He could tell by Clorant's wild-eyed stare and guilty expression that he thought the voice was Mina's. Gerard knew it wasn't. He recognized the voice. He could only hope that Odila had the nerve to pull this off.

Her face livid, her robes whipping about her ankles, Odila marched into the midst of the sweating, bleeding, deadly fray. She thrust aside a sword with her bare hand.

Glaring around at them, her eyes burning, she looked directly at Clorant. "What is the meaning of this? Did you not hear Mina's command that this elf was to be treated with the same respect you show her?" Odila sent a flashing glance at each one of them in turn, not excluding Gerard. "Put away your weapons! All of you!"

She was taking a great risk. Did these men view her as a true cleric, a representative of the One God, someone as sacred as Mina herself? Or did they see her as nothing more than a follower, no different from themselves?

The men hesitated, glanced uncertainly at each other. Gerard kept quiet, tried to look as guilty and dismayed at the rest. He cast one warning glance at the elf, but Silvanoshei had the sense to keep his mouth shut. He panted, gasping for breath, kept wary watch on his enemies.

Odila's gaze hardened, her eyes narrowed. "In the name of the One God put down your weapons," she ordered again, and this time she pointed at Clorant, "lest your sword hand wither with my displeasure and fall from your arm!"

"Will you tell Mina about this?" Clorant asked sullenly.

"I know that you did what you did out of misguided care for Mina," said Odila, her voice softening. "You have no need to protect her. The One God holds Mina in the palm of her hand. The One God knows what is best for Mina and for us all. This elf lives only because the One God wills it." Odila pointed in the direction of Sanction. "Return to the battle. Your true foe lies down there."

"Will you tell Mina?" Clorant persisted, and there was fear in his voice.

"I won't," said Odila, "but you will. You will confess to her what you have done and seek her forgiveness."

Clorant lowered his sword and, after a moment's hesitation, thrust it into his sheath. He made a motion for his comrades to do the same. Then, casting a final, loathing glance at the elf, he turned his horse's head and galloped down the hill, heading for Sanction. His friends rode after him.

Exhaling a great sigh of relief, Gerard slid down from his horse.

"Are you all right?" he asked Silvanoshei, looking him over. He saw a few splashes of blood on his clothes but nothing serious.

Silvanoshei drew away from him, stared at him suspiciously. "You—a Dark Knight—risked your life to save mine. You fought your own comrades. Why?"

Gerard could not very well tell him the truth. "I didn't do it for you," he said gruffly. "I did it for Mina. She ordered me to guard you, remember?"

Silvanoshei's face smoothed. "That makes sense. Thank you."

"Thank Mina," muttered Gerard ungraciously.

His movements stiff and painful, he limped over to Odila. "Well acted," he said in low tone. "That was quite a performance. Though, I'm curious—what would have happened if Clorant had called your bluff? I thought he was going to for a minute there. What would you have done then?"

"It's strange," Odila said. Her gaze was abstracted, her voice soft and introspective. "At the moment I made the threat, I knew I had the power to carry it out. I could have withered his hand. I could have."

"Odila—" he began to remonstrate with her.

"It doesn't matter if you believe me or not," Odila said bleakly. "Nothing can stop the One God."

Clasping the medallion she wore around her neck, she walked back to the wagon.

"Nothing can stop the One," Odila repeated. "Nothing."

10 CITY OF GHOSTS

Riding in the vanguard of the triumphant army as they entered, unopposed, Sanction's West Gate and marched victorious along the famous Shipmaker's Road, Gerard looked at the city and saw nothing but ghosts: ghosts of the past, ghosts of the present, ghosts of prosperity, ghosts of war.

He remembered what he'd heard of Sanction, remembered—as if it had happened to someone else and not to him—talking to Caramon Majere about hoping to be sent to Sanction. *Someplace where there is real fighting going on,* he had said or, if he had not said it, he had thought it. He looked back on that ghost of himself and saw a callow youth who didn't have sense enough to know when he was well off.

What must Caramon have thought of me? Gerard flushed as he remembered some of his foolish spoutings. Caramon Majere had fought in many wars. He knew the truth about glory—that it was nothing more than a bloodstained and rusted old sword hanging on the wall of an old man's memory. Riding past the bodies of those who had defended Sanction, Gerard saw the true glory of war: the carrion birds flapping down to pluck out eyeballs, the flies that filled the air with their horrid buzzing, the burial crews laughing and joking as they filled wheelbarrows with bodies and dumped them into mass graves.

War was a thief who dared accost Death, robbing that majestic noble of his dignity, stripping him bare, tossing him in a pit, and covering him with lime to stop the stench.

Gerard was grateful for one blessing: The dead were laid to rest. At the end of the battle, Mina—her armor covered with blood, herself unscathed—knelt beside the first of the hastily dug trenches meant to receive the dead and prayed over them. Gerard watched in stomach-clenching horror, more than half expecting the bloodied corpses to rise up, seize their weapons, and fall into ranks at Mina's command.

Fortunately, that did not happen. Mina commended the spirits to the One God, urged them all to serve the One God well. Gerard glanced at Odila, who stood not far from him. Her head was bowed, her hands clasped.

Gerard was angry at her and angry at himself for being angry. Odila had done nothing more than speak the truth. This One God was all-seeing, all-knowing, all-powerful. There was nothing they could do to stop the One. He was loath to face the truth. That was all. Loath to admit defeat.

After the ceremony for the dead ended, Mina mounted her horse and rode into the city, which was, for the most part, deserted.

During the War of the Lance, Sanction had been an armed camp dedicated to the Queen of Darkness, headquarters for her armies. The draconians had been born in the temple of Luerkhisis. Lord Ariakas had his headquarters in Sanction, trained his troops here, kept his slaves here, tortured his prisoners here.

The Chaos War and the departure of the gods that brought devastation to many parts of Ansalon delivered prosperity to Sanction. At first, it seemed that Sanction must be destroyed and that no one would rule it, for the lava flows spilling from the Lords of Doom threatened to bury the city. A man called Hogan Bight arrived to save Sanction from the mountains' wrath. Using powerful magicks that he never explained, he diverted the flow of lava, drove out the evil people who had long ruled the city. Merchants and others seeking to better their lives were invited in and, almost overnight, Sanction grew prosperous, as goods flowed into its wharves and docks.

Seeing its wealth, needing access to its ports, the Dark Knights had wanted Sanction back under their control, and now they had it.

With Qualinost destroyed, Silvanesti occupied, and Solamnia under her rulership, it might be truly said that those parts of Ansalon that were not under Mina's control were not worth controlling. She had come full circle, back to Sanction where her legend had begun.

Having been warned of Mina's march on their city, the citizens of Sanction, who had weathered the siege without any great hardship, heard the rumors of the advancing army of Dark Knights, and fearing that they would be enslaved, their homes looted, their daughters raped, their sons slain by their cruel conquerers, they took to their boats or their horse carts, putting out to sea or heading for the mountains.

Only a few remained behind: the poor who did not have the means to leave; the infirm, the elderly, the sick who could not leave; kender (a fact of nature); and those entrepreneurs who had no care for any god, who owed no allegiance to any government or cause except their own. These people lined the streets to watch the entry of the army, their expressions ranging from dull apathy to eager anticipation.

In the case of the poor, their lives were already so miserable that they had nothing to fear. In the case of the entrepreneurs, their eyes fixed greedily on two enormous, wooden, iron-bound chests that had been transported under heavy guard from Palanthas. Here was much of the wealth of the Dark Knights, wealth that the late Lord Targonne had so covetously amassed. The wealth was now to be shared with all those who had fought for Mina, or so the rumor ran.

Reinforce religious fervor with bags of steel coins—a wise move, Gerard thought, and one guaranteed to win her the hearts, as well as the souls, of her soldiers.

The army advanced along Shipbuilder's Road into a large marketplace. One of Gerard's fellow Knights, who had once visited Sanction, stated that this was known as the Souk Bazaar, and that it was usually so crowded with people that one scarcely had room enough to draw a breath, let alone walk. That was not true now. The only people around were a few enterprising hoodlums taking advantage of the commotion to raid the abandoned stalls.

Calling a halt at this central location, Mina proceeded to take control of the city. She dispatched guards under trustworthy officers to seize the warehouses, the taverns, the mageware shops, and the shops of the money-lenders. She sent another group of guards, led by the minotaur Galdar, to the impressive palace where lived the city's governor, the mysterious Hogan Bight. The guards had orders to arrest him, take him alive if he cooperated, kill him if he didn't. Hogan Bight continued to be a mystery, however, for Galdar returned to report that the man was nowhere to be found and no one could tell when they'd last seen him.

"The palace is empty and would make an ideal dwelling place for you, Mina," said Galdar. "Shall I order the troops to make it ready for your arrival?"

"The palace will be military headquarters," said Mina, "but not my dwelling place. The One God does not reside in grand palaces, and neither will I."

She glanced at the wagon carrying the body of Goldmoon in the amber coffin. Goldmoon's body had not withered, had not decayed. Frozen in the amber, she seemed forever young, forever beautiful. The wagon had been given an honored place in the procession, following directly after Mina, surrounded by an honor guard of her Knights.

"I will dwell in what was once called the Temple of Huerzyd but is now known as the Temple of the Heart. Detain any of the Mystics who remain in the temple. Put them somewhere secure, for their own safety. Treat them with respect and tell them that I look forward to meeting with them. You will escort the body of Goldmoon to the temple and carry the sarcophagus inside to be placed before the altar. You will feel at home, Mother," said Mina, speaking softly to the still, cold face of the woman imprisoned in amber.

Galdar did not appear particularly pleased at his assignment. He did not question Mina, however. The wagon and its guard of honor rolled out of the bazaar, heading for the temple, which was located in the northern part of the city.

Seated astride her irritable horse, Mina proceeded to issue commands. Her Knights crowded around her, eager to serve, hoping for a look, a word, a smile. Gerard held back, not wanting to get caught in the crush of men and horses. He needed to know what he was to do with the elf, but he wasn't in any hurry. He was glad to have this time to think, determine what his next move was going to be. He didn't like at all what was happening to Odila. Her talk of withering hands frightened him. Medallion or no medallion, he was going to find a way to get her out of here, if he had to bash her over the head and haul her out bodily.

Gerard suddenly felt a fierce determination to do something—anything—to fight this One God, even if he caused the One God less harm than a bee sting. One bee might not do much damage, but if there were hundreds of bees, thousands . . . He'd heard stories of dragons fleeing such swarms. There had to be—

"Hey, Gerard," called someone. "You've lost your prisoner."

Gerard came to himself with a jolt. The elf was no longer at his side. Gerard had no fear—or hope—that Silvanoshei would try to escape. He knew right where to look for him. Silvanoshei was urging his horse forward, trying to force his way through the armed circle of Knights surrounding Mina.

Cursing them both beneath his breath, Gerard spurred his horse. The Knights around Mina were aware of the elf and were deliberately blocking his passage. Silvanoshei set his jaw and continued to determinedly and stubbornly pursue his course. One of the Knights, whose horse was jostled by Silvanoshei's horse, turned to stare at him. The Knight was Clorant, his face bruised and swollen, his lip bloodied. The split lip pulled back in a grimace. Silvanoshei hesitated, then pushed ahead. Clorant tugged sharply on the reins, jerking his horse's head. The animal, annoyed, took a nip at Silvanoshei's horse, which bared its teeth. In the confusion, Clorant gave Silvanoshei a shove, trying to unseat him. Silvanoshei managed to cling to the saddle. He shoved back.

Gerard guided his steed through the melee and caught up with the elf, jostling Clorant's arm in passing.

"This is not a good time to interrupt Mina, Your Majesty," Gerard said in an undertone to the elf. "Maybe later." He reached for the reins of Silvanoshei's horse.

"Sir Gerard," called Mina. "Attend me. Bring His Majesty with you. The rest of you, make way."

At Mina's command, Clorant was forced to edge his horse backward, so that Gerard and Silvanoshei could ride past. Clorant's dark, grim gaze followed them. Gerard could feel it tickle the back of his neck as he rode to receive his orders.

Removing his helm, Gerard saluted Mina. Due to his fight with Clorant, Gerard's face was bruised, dried blood matted his hair. Most of the other Knights looked the same or worse, though, after the battle. Gerard was hoping Mina wouldn't notice.

She might not have noticed him, but she gazed intently at Silvanoshei, whose shirt was sliced open and stained with blood, his traveling cloak covered with dirt.

"Sir Gerard," Mina said gravely, "I entrusted His Majesty to you, to keep him safely out of the affray. I see you both bruised and bloodied. Did either of you take serious harm?"

"No, Madam," replied Gerard.

He refused to call her Mina, as did her other Knights. Like a medicine made of alum and honey, her name, sweet at first, left a bitter taste on his tongue.

He said nothing more about the fight with Clorant and his fellow Knights. Neither did Silvanoshei. After assuring her that he was not injured, the elf fell silent. No one in the crowd of waiting Knights spoke. Here and there, a horse shifted beneath a restless rider. By now all Mina's Knights knew about the affray. Perhaps they had even been in on the conspiracy.

"What are your orders, Madam?" Gerard asked, hoping to let the matter drop.

"That can wait. What happened?" Mina persisted.

"A Solamnic patrol came out of nowhere, Madam," said Gerard evenly. He looked straight into the amber eyes. "I think they hoped to seize our supply wagon. We drove them away."

"His Majesty fought them, too?" asked Mina, with a half smile.

"When they saw he was an elf, they sought to rescue him, Madam."

"I didn't want to be rescued," Silvanoshei added.

Gerard's lips tightened. That statement was true enough.

Mina cast the young elf a cool glance, then turned her attention back to Gerard.

"I saw no bodies."

"You know Solamnics, Madam," he replied evenly. "You know what cowards they are. We rattled our swords at them, and they ran away."

"I *do* know Solamnics," Mina replied, "and contrary to what you believe, Sir Gerard, I have a great respect for them."

Mina's amber gaze swept over the line of Knights, unerringly picked out the four who had been involved. Her gaze fixed longest on Clorant, who tried to defy it, but ended up squirming and cringing. Finally, she turned her amber eyes back to Silvanoshei, another insect caught in the warm resin.

"Sir Gerard," said Mina, "do you know where to find the City Guard Headquarters?"

"No, Madam," said Gerard. "I have never been in Sanction. But I have no doubt I can locate it."

"There you will find secure prison cells. You will escort His Majesty to these cells and make certain that he is locked in one of them. See to his comfort. This is for your own protection, Your Majesty," Mina added. "Someone might try to 'rescue' you again, and the next time you might not have such a valiant defender."

Gerard glanced at Silvanoshei, then looked away. The sight was too painful. Her words might have been a dagger thrust in the elf's gut. His face drained of life. Even the lips lost their color. In the young man's livid face, the burning eyes were the only life.

"Mina," he said quietly, desperately. "I have to know one thing. Did you ever love me? Or have you just been using me?"

"Sir Gerard," said Mina, turning away. "You have your orders."

"Yes, Madam," he said. Taking the reins from the elf's hand, he started to lead his horse away.

"Mina," pleaded Silvanoshei. "I deserve at least that much. To know the truth."

Mina glanced back at him, over her shoulder.

"My love, my life is the One God."

Gerard led the elf's horse away.

The City Guard Headquarters turned out to be south of the West Gate by a few blocks. The two rode in silence through the streets that had been deserted when the army marched in, but were now filling rapidly with the soldiers of the army of the One God. Gerard had to watch where they were going to avoid riding down anyone, and their progress was slow. He glanced back in concern for Silvanoshei, saw his face set, his jaw clenched, his eyes staring down at the hands that gripped the pommel so tightly the knuckles were chalk white.

"Women." Gerard grunted. "It happens to all of us."

Silvanoshei smiled bitterly and shook his head.

Well, he's right, Gerard admitted. None of the rest of us had a god involved in our love-making.

They rode past the West Gate. Gerard had been harboring a vague notion that he and the elf might be able to escape during the confusion, but he discarded that idea immediately. The road was clogged with Mina's troops, and more remained on the field outside the city. Every man they passed cast Silvanoshei a dark, frowning glance. More than one muttered threats.

Mina is right, Gerard decided. Prison is probably the safest place for the young man. If any place is safe for Silvanoshei in Sanction.

The city guards had either fled the guardhouse or been killed. Mina had placed one of her Knights in charge. The Knight glanced without interest at Silvanoshei, listened with impatience to Gerard's insistence that the young man be placed under special guard. The Knight jerked a thumb in the direction of the cell block. A brief search turned up the keys.

Gerard escorted his prisoner to a cell in darkest corner of the block, hoping he would escape notice.

"I'm sorry about this, Your Majesty," said Gerard.

Silvanoshei shrugged, sat down on the stone block that passed for a bed. Gerard shut the cell door, locked it.

At the sound of key turning, Silvanoshei raised his head. "I should thank you for saving my life."

"I'll bet now you wished I'd let them kill you," said Gerard, sympathetic.

"*Their* swords would have been less painful," Silvanoshei agreed with a pale flicker of a smile.

Gerard glanced around. They were the only two in the cellblocks. "Your Majesty," he said quietly. "I can help you escape. Not now—there's something else I have to do first. But soon."

"Thank you, sir. But you'd be putting yourself in danger for nothing. I can't escape."

"Your Majesty," said Gerard, his voice hardening, "you saw her, you heard her. You have no chance with her! She doesn't love you. She's all wrapped up in this . . . this god of hers."

"Not only hers. My god, too," he said, speaking with an eerie calm. "The One God promised me that Mina and I would be together."

"Do you still believe that?"

"No," Silvanoshei said, after a moment. The word seemed wrenched from him. "No, I don't."

"Then be ready. I'll come back for you."

Silvansoshei shook his head.

"Your Majesty," said Gerard, exasperated, "do you know the reason Mina lured you here away from your kingdom? Because she knows that your people will not follow anyone but you. The Silvanesti are sitting around waiting for you to return to them. Go back and be their king, the king she fears!"

"Go back to be their king." Silvanoshei's mouth twisted. "Go back to my mother, you mean. Go back to ignominy and shame, tears and rebukes. I would sit in this prison cell the rest of my life—and we elves live a long, long time—rather than face that."

"Look, damn it, if it was just you, I'd let you rot here," Gerard said grimly. "But you're their king, like it or not. You have to think about your people."

"I am," said Silvanoshei. "I will."

Rising to his feet, he walked over to Gerard, tugging on a ring as he came. "You're a Solamnic Knight, as Mina said, aren't you? Why are you here? To spy on Mina?"

Gerard glowered, shrugged, didn't answer.

"You don't have to admit it," said Silvanoshei. "Mina saw into your heart. That's why she set you to guard me. If you're serious about wanting to help me—"

"I am, Your Majesty," said Gerard.

"Then take this." Silvanoshei handed through the cell bars a blue, glittering ring. "Somewhere out there—close by, I'm certain—you will find an elven warrior. His name is Samar. He has been sent by my mother to bring me back home. Give him this ring. He will recognize it. I've worn it since I was a child. When he asks you how you came by it, tell him you took it from my corpse."

"Your Majesty—"

Silvanoshei thrust the ring at him. "Take it. Tell him I am dead."

"Why would I lie? And why would he believe me?" Gerard asked, hesitating.

"Because he will want to believe you," said Silvanoshei. "And by this action, you will free me."

Gerard took the ring, which was a circlet of sapphires, small enough to fit a child's hand.

"How will I find this Samar?"

"I will teach you a song," said Silvanoshei. "An old elven children's song. My mother used it as a signal if ever she needed to warn me of danger. Sing the song as you ride. Samar will hear it, and he will be intensely curious as to how you—a human—would know this song. He will find you."

"And then slit my throat—"

"He'll want to interrogate you first," said Silvanoshei. "Samar is a man of honor. If you tell him the truth, he'll know you for a man of honor, as well."

"I wish you'd reconsider, Your Majesty," Gerard said. He was starting to like this young man, even as he deeply pitied him.

Silvanoshei shook his head.

"Very well," said Gerard, sighing. "How does this song go?"

Silvanoshei taught the song to Gerard. The words were simple, the melody melancholy. It was a song meant to teach a child to count. "'*Five for the fingers on each hand. Four for the legs upon a horse.*'"

The last line he knew he would never forget.

"'*One is one and all alone and evermore shall be so.*'"

Silvanoshei went to the stone bed, lay down upon it, turned away his face.

"Tell Samar I am dead," he reiterated softly. "If it's any comfort to you, Sir Knight, you won't be telling a lie. You'll be telling him the truth."

11

TO FREE THE
SNARED BIRD

Gerard emerged from the prison to find that night had fallen. He looked up the street and down, even took a casual saunter behind the prison, and saw no one lurking in a doorway or hiding in the shadows.

"This is my chance," he muttered. "I can ride out of the gate, lose myself in the confusion of the troops setting up camp, find this Samar, and start over from there. That's what I'll do. Leaving now is logical. It makes sense. Yes, that's definitely what I'm going to do."

But even as he said this to himself, even as he told himself repeatedly that this was his best course of action, he knew very well that he wouldn't. He would go find Samar, he had to go—he had promised Silvanoshei he would, and that was a promise he planned to keep, even if he didn't plan to keep any of the rest of the promises he'd made to the young man.

First, he had to talk to Odila. The reason was, of course, that he hoped to persuade her to come with him. He had thought up some very fine arguments against this One God and he planned to use them.

The Temple of the Heart was an ancient building that predated the Cataclysm. Dedicated to the worship of the old gods of Light, the temple had been built at the foot of Mount Grishnor and was reputed to be the oldest structure in Sanction, probably built when Sanction was little more than a fishing village. Various rumors and legends surrounded the temple, including one that the foundation stone had been laid by one of the Kingpriests, who'd had the misfortune to be shipwrecked. Washing up on this shore, the Kingpriest had given thanks to Paladine for his survival. To show his gratitude, he built a temple to the gods.

After the Cataclysm, the temple might have suffered the same fate as many other temples during that time, when people took out their anger on the gods by attacking and destroying their temples. This temple remained standing, unscathed, mostly due to the rumor that the spirit of that same Kingpriest lingered here, refusing to allow anyone to harm his tribute to the gods. The temple suffered from neglect, but that was all.

Following the Chaos War, the vengeful spirit must have departed, for the Mystics of the Citadel of Light moved into the temple without encountering any ghosts.

A small, square, unimposing structure of white marble, the temple had a steeply pitched roof that soared up among the trees. Beneath the roof was a central altar chamber—the largest and most important room in the temple. Other rooms surrounded the altar and were there to support it: sleeping quarters for the priests, a library, and so forth. Two sets of double doors led into the temple from the front.

Deciding that he would make faster time in the crowded streets on foot, Gerard stabled his horse in a hostelry near the West Gate and walked north to where the temple stood on a hill, somewhat isolated from the city, overlooking it.

He found a few people gathered in front of the temple, listening to Mina telling them of the miracles of the One God. An elderly man frowned exceedingly, but most of the others appeared interested.

The temple flared with lights, both inside and out. Huge double doors were propped open. Under Galdar's command, the Knights were carrying Goldmoon's amber sarcophagus into the altar room. The head of the minotaur was easily seen, his horns and snout silhouetted against the flames of torches that had been placed in sconces on the walls. Mina kept close watch on the procedure, glancing often in the direction of the procession to make certain that the sarcophagus was being handled carefully, that her Knights were behaving with dignity and respect.

Pausing in the deep shadows of a night-shrouded tree to reconnoiter, and, hopefully, try to catch a glimpse of Odila, Gerard watched the amber sarcophagus move slowly and with stately formality into the temple. He heard Galdar issue a sharp rebuke at one point, saw Mina turn her head swiftly to look. She was so concerned that she lost the thread of her exhortation and was forced to think a moment to remember where she'd left off.

Gerard could never ask for a better time to talk to Odila than this, while Galdar was supervising the funeral detail and Mina was proselytizing. When a group of Knights walked toward the temple, carrying Mina's baggage, Gerard fell in behind them.

The Knights were in a good mood, talking and laughing over what a fine joke it was on the do-gooder Mystics that Mina had taken over their temple. Gerard couldn't see the humor himself, and he doubted very much if Mina would have been pleased had she overheard them.

The Knights entered through another set of double doors, heading for Mina's living quarters. Looking through an open door on his left into a blaze of candle light, Gerard saw Odila standing beside the altar, directing the placement of the amber sarcophagus on several wooden trestles.

Gerard hung back in the shadows, hoping for a chance to catch Odila alone. The Knights lumbered in with their burden, deposited it with much grunting and groaning and a yelp and a curse, as one of the men dropped his end of the coffin prematurely, causing it to pinch the fingers of another man's hand. Odila issued a sharp rebuke. Galdar growled a threat. The men pushed and shoved, and soon the crystal sarcophagus was in place.

Hundreds of white candles burned on the altar, probably placed there by Odila's hands. The reflection of the candles burned in the amber, so that it seemed Goldmoon lay in the midst of a myriad tiny flames. The light illuminated her waxen face. She looked more peaceful than Gerard remembered, if such a thing were possible. Perhaps, as Mina had said, Goldmoon was pleased to be home.

Gerard wiped his sleeve across his forehead. The candles gave off a surprising amount of heat. Gerard found a seat on a bench in the back of the altar room. He moved as quietly as he could, holding his sword to keep it from knocking against the wall. He couldn't see very well, having stared into the candle flames, and he bumped into someone. Gerard was about to make his excuses when he saw, with a shudder, that his companion was Palin. The mage sat unmoving on the bench, stared unblinking into the candle flames.

Touching the mage's flaccid arm was like touching a warm corpse. Feeling his gorge rise, Gerard moved hastily to another bench. He sat down, waited impatiently for the minotaur to leave.

"I will post a guard around the sarcophagus," Galdar stated.

Gerard muttered a curse. He hadn't counted on that.

"No need," Odila said. "Mina is coming to worship at the altar, and she has given orders that she is to be left alone."

Gerard breathed more freely, then his breathing stopped altogether. The minotaur was half-way out the door when he paused, sent a searching gaze throughout the altar room. Gerard froze in place, trying desperately to remember whether or not minotaurs have good night vision. It seemed to him that Galdar saw him, for the beady, bovine eyes stared straight at him. He waited tensely for Galdar to call to him, but, after a moment's scrutiny, the minotaur walked out.

Gerard wiped away the sweat that was now running down his face and dripping off his chin. Slowly and cautiously, he edged out from the rows of benches and walked toward the front of the altar. He tried to be quiet, but leather creaked, metal rattled.

Odila was swathed in candlelight. Her face was partially turned toward him, and he was alarmed to see how thin and wasted she had grown. Riding for weeks in the wagon, doing nothing but listening to Mina's harangues and force-feeding the mages had caused her fine muscle tone to diminish. She could probably still wield her sword, but she wouldn't last two rounds with a healthy, battle-hardened opponent.

She no longer laughed or spoke much, but went about her duties in silence. Gerard hadn't liked this god before. Now he was starting to actively hate the One God. What sort of god stamped out joy and was offended by laughter? No sort of god he wanted to have anything to do with. He was glad he'd come to talk to her, hoped to be able to convince her to abandon this and come away with him.

But even as the hope was born, it died within him. One look at her face as she bent over the candles and he knew he was wasting his time.

He was suddenly reminded of an old poacher's trick for snaring a bird. You attach berries at intervals to a long, thin cord tied to a stake. The bird eats the berries, one by one, ingesting the cord at the same time. When the bird reaches the end of the cord, it tries to fly away, but by now the cord is wound up inside its vitals, and it cannot escape.

One by one, Odila had consumed the berries attached to the lethal cord. The last was the power to work miracles. She was tied to the One God, and only a miracle—a reverse miracle—would cut her free.

Well, perhaps friendship was that sort of miracle.

"Odila—" he began.

"What do you want, Gerard?" she asked, without turning around.

"I have to talk to you," he said. "Please, just a moment. It won't take long."

Odila sat down on a bench near the amber sarcophagus. Gerard would have been happier sitting farther back, out of the light and the heat, but Odila wouldn't move. Tense and preoccupied, she cast frequent glances at the door, glances that were half-nervous, half-expectant.

"Odila, listen to me," said Gerard. "I'm leaving Sanction. Tonight. I came to tell you that and to try to convince you to leave with me."

"No," she said, glancing at the door. "I can't leave now. I have too much to do here before Mina comes."

"I'm not asking you to go on a picnic!" he said, exasperated. "I'm asking you to escape this place with me, tonight! The city is in confusion, what with soldiers marching in and out. No one knows what's going on. It'll be hours before some sort of order is established. Now's the perfect time to leave."

"Then go," she said, shrugging. "I don't want you around anyway."

She started to rise. He grabbed her arm, gripped her wrist tightly, and saw her wince with pain.

"You don't want me around because I remind you of what you used to be. You don't like this One God. You don't like the change that's come over you anymore than I do. Why are you doing this to yourself?"

"Because, Gerard," Odila said wearily, as if she'd gone over the same argument again and again, "the One God is a god. A god who came to this world to care for us and guide us."

"Where? Off the edge of a precipice?" Gerard demanded. "After the Chaos War, Goldmoon found her guide in her own heart. Love and caring, compassion, truth, and honor did not leave with gods of light. They are inside each of us. Those are our guides or they should be."

"At her death, Goldmoon turned to the One God," said Odila, glancing at the still, calm face entombed in amber.

"Did she?" Gerard demanded harshly. "I wonder about that. If she really did embrace the One God, why didn't the One God keep her alive to go around shouting her miracle to the world? Why did the One God feel it necessary to stop her mouth in death and lock her up in an amber prison?"

"She will be freed, Mina says," said Odila defensively. "On the Night of the New Eye, the One God will raise Goldmoon from the dead, and she will come forth to rule the world."

Gerard released her hand, let go of her. "So you won't come with me?"

Odila shook her head. "No, Gerard, I won't. I know you don't understand. I'm not as strong as you are. I'm all by myself in the dark forest, and I'm afraid. I'm glad to have a guide, and if the guide is not perfect, neither am I. Goodbye, Gerard. Thank you for your friendship and your caring. Go on your journey safely in the name of the—"

"One God?" he said grimly. "No, thanks."

Turning, he walked out of the altar room.

The first place Gerard went was to the army's central command post, located in the former Souk Bazaar, whose stalls and shops had been replaced by a small city of tents. Here, the contents of the strongboxes were being distributed.

Taking his place in line, Gerard felt a certain satisfaction in taking the Dark Knights' steel. He'd earned it, no question about that, and he would need money for his journey back to Lord Ulrich's manor or wherever the Knights were consolidating their forces.

After receiving his pay, he headed for the West Gate and freedom. He put Odila out of his mind, refused to let himself think about her. He removed most of his armor—the braces and greaves and his chain mail, but continued to wear the cuirass and helm. Both were uncomfortable, but he had to consider the possibility that sooner or later Galdar might grow tired of shadowing Gerard and just stab him in the back.

The bulk of the two towers of the West Gate loomed black against the red light that shone from the lava moat surrounding the city. The gates had been shut. The gate guards weren't about to open them until they'd had a good look at Gerard and heard his story—that he was a messenger dispatched to Jelek with word of their victory. The guards wished him a good journey and opened a wicket gate to let him ride through.

Glancing back to see the walls of Sanction lined with men, Gerard was once more profoundly and grudgingly impressed with Mina's leadership and her ability to impose discipline and order on her troops.

"She will grow in strength and in power every day she remains here," he remarked gloomily to himself as his horse cantered through the gate. Ahead of him was the harbor and beyond that the black expanse of New Sea. A whiff of salt air was a welcome relief from the continuous smell of sulfur and brimstone that lingered in the air of Sanction. "And how are we to fight her?"

"You can't."

A hulking figure blocked his path. Gerard recognized the voice, as his horse recognized the stench of minotaur. The horse snorted and reared, and Gerard had his hands full trying to remain on the animal's back, during which frantic few moments he lost any opportunity he might have had to either run the minotaur down or gallop away and leave him standing in the dust.

The minotaur drew closer, his bestial face faintly illuminated by the red glow of the lava that made Sanction's night perpetual twilight. Galdar grabbed hold of the horse's bridle.

Gerard drew his sword. He had no doubt that this was going to be their final confrontation, and he was not in much doubt about how it would end. He'd heard tales of how Galdar had once cut a man in two with a single stroke of his massive sword. One glance at the knotty muscles of the arms and the smooth, sleek muscles of the minotaur's hairy chest attested to the veracity of the storyteller.

"Look, Galdar," Gerard said, interrupting the minotaur as he was about to speak, "I've had a bellyful of sermons, and I'm fed up with being watched day and night. You know that I'm a Solamnic Knight sent here to spy on Mina. I know you know, so let's just end this right now—"

"I would like to fight you, Solamnic," said Galdar, and his voice was cold. "I would like to kill you, but I am forbidden."

"I figured as much," said Gerard, lowering his sword. "May I ask why?"

"You serve her. You do her bidding."

"Now, see here, Galdar, you and I both know that I'm not riding to do Mina's bidding—" Gerard began, then stopped, growing confused. Here he was, arguing for his own death.

"By *her*, I do not mean Mina," said Galdar. "I mean the One God. Have you never thought to find out the name?"

"Of the One God?" Gerard was becoming increasingly annoyed by this conversation. "No. To be honest, I never really gave a rat's—"

"Takhisis," said Galdar.

"—ass," said Gerard, and then fell silent.

He sat on his horse in the road in the darkness, thinking, it all makes sense. It all makes bloody, horrible, awful sense. No need to ask him if he believed the minotaur. Deep inside, Gerard had suspected this truth all along.

"Why are you telling me this?" he demanded.

"I am not allowed to kill you," Galdar said dourly, "but I can kill your spirit. I know your plans. You carry a message from that wretched elf king to his people, begging them to come save him. Why do you think Mina chose you to take the elf to prison, if not to be his 'messenger'? She *wants* you to bring his people here. Bring the entire elven nation. Bring the Knights of Solamnia—what is left of them. Bring them all here to witness the glory of Queen Takhisis on the Night of the New Eye."

The minotaur released the horse's bridle. "Ride off, Solamnic. Ride to whatever dreams of victory and glory you have in your heart and know, as you ride, that they are nothing but ash. Takhisis controls your destiny. All you do, you do in her name. As do I."

Giving Gerard an ironic salute, the minotaur turned and walked back to the walls of Sanction.

Gerard looked up at the sky. Clouds of smoke rolling from the Lords of Doom obliterated the stars and the moon. The night was dark above, fire-tinged below. Was it true that somewhere out there, Takhisis watched him? Knew all he thought and planned?

"I have to go back," Gerard thought, chilled. "Warn Odila." He started to turn his horse's head, then halted. "Maybe that's what Takhisis *wants* me to do. If I go back, perhaps she'll see to it that I lose my chance to talk with Samar. I can't do anything to help Odila. I'll ride on."

He turned his horse's head the other way, then stopped. "Takhisis wants me to talk to the elf. Galdar said as much. So maybe I shouldn't! How can I know what to do? Or does it even make any difference?"

Gerard stopped dead in his tracks.

"Galdar was right," he said bitterly. "He would have done me a favor by sticking a plain, ordinary, everyday sword in my gut. The blade he's left there now is poisoned, and I can never rid myself of it. What do I do? What *can* I do?"

He had only one answer, and it was the one he'd given Odila.

He had to follow what was in his heart.

12 THE NEW EYE

As he stalked back toward the West Gate, Galdar was disappointed to find that he didn't feel as pleased with himself as he should have. He had hoped to infect the confident and self-assured Solamnic with the same sickness that infected him. He'd done what he'd set out to accomplish—the angry, frustrated expression on the Solamnic's face had proven that. But Galdar found he couldn't take any satisfaction from his victory.

What had he hoped? That the Solamnic would prove him wrong?

"Bah!" Galdar snorted. "He's caught in the same coil as the rest of us, and there's no way out. Not now. Not ever. Not even in death."

He rubbed his right arm, which had begun to ache persistently, and found himself wishing he could lose it again, so much did it pain him. Once he'd been proud of that arm, the arm that Mina had restored to him, the first miracle she'd ever performed in the name of the One God. Now he caught himself fingering his sword with some vague notion of hacking off the arm himself. He wouldn't, of course. Mina would be angry with him and, worse, she would be hurt and saddened. He could endure her anger, he'd felt its lash before. He could never do anything to hurt her. Most of the pent-up fury and resentment he felt toward Takhisis was based not on her treatment of him but the way she treated Mina, who had sacrificed everything, even her life, for her goddess.

Mina had been rewarded. She'd been given victory over her enemies, given the power to perform miracles. But Galdar knew Takhisis of old. The minotaur race had never thought very highly of the goddess, who was the consort of the minotaur god, Sargas, or Sargonnas, as the other races called him. Sargas had remained with his people to fight Chaos until the bitter end, when—so legend had it—he had sacrificed himself to save the minotaur race. Takhisis would never dream of sacrificing herself for anything. She expected sacrifices to be made to her, demanded them in return for her dubious blessings.

Perhaps that is what she has in mind for Mina. Galdar grew uneasy listening to Mina's constant talk of this "great miracle" Takhisis was going to perform on the Night of the New Eye. Takhisis never gave something for nothing. Galdar had only to feel the throbbing pain of the goddess's displeasure with him to know that. Mina was so trusting, so guileless. She could never understand Takhisis's deceitfulness, her treacherous and vindictive nature.

That, of course, was why Mina had been chosen. That and because she was beloved of Goldmoon. Takhisis would not pass up a chance to inflict pain on anyone, most especially on Goldmoon, who had thwarted her in the past.

I could tell all this to Mina, Galdar thought as he entered the temple. I could tell her, but she wouldn't hear me. She hears only one voice these days.

The Temple of the Heart, now the Temple of the One God. How Takhisis must revel in that appellation! After an eternity of being one of many, now she was one and all powerful.

He shook his horned head gloomily.

The temple grounds were empty. Galdar went first to Mina's quarters. He did not truly expect to find her there, although she must be exhausted after the day's battle. He knew where she would be. He wanted to check to make certain that everything was prepared for her when she finally chose to go to bed.

He glanced into the room that had once been the room for the head of the Order, probably that old fool who'd scowled all through Mina's sermon. Galdar found all in readiness. Everything had been arranged for her comfort. Her weapons were here, as was her armor, carefully arranged on a stand. Her morning star had been polished, the blood cleaned from it and from her armor. Her boots were free of dirt and blood. A tray of food stood on a desk near the bed. A candle burned to light her way in the darkness. Someone had even thought of placing some late-blooming wildflowers in a pewter cup. Everything in the room attested to the love and devotion her troops felt for her.

For her. Galdar wondered if she realized that. The men fought for her, for Mina. They shouted her name when she led them forth to battle. They shouted her name in victory.

Mina . . . Mina . . .

They did not shout, "For the One God." They did not shout, "For Takhisis." "And I'll wager you don't like that," Galdar said to the darkness.

Could a god be jealous of a mortal?

This god could, Galdar thought, and he was suddenly filled with fear.

Galdar entered the altar room, stood blinking painfully while his eyes became accustomed to the light of the candles blazing on the altar. Mina was alone, kneeling before the altar in prayer. He could hear her voice, murmuring, halting, then murmuring again, as if she were receiving instructions.

The other Solamnic, the female Knight turned priestess, lay stretched out on a bench, asleep. She slept soundly on her hard bed. Mina's own cloak covered the female. Galdar could never remember her name.

Goldmoon, in her amber coffin, slept as well. The two mages sat in the back of the chamber, where'd they'd been planted. He could see their forms, shadowy in the candlelight. His gaze flicked over them quickly, went back to Mina. The sight of the wretched mages gave him the horrors, made the hair rise on his spine, ripple down his back.

Someday perhaps his own corpse would sit there quietly, staring at nothing, doing nothing, waiting for Takhisis's orders.

Galdar walked toward the altar. He tried to move quietly, out of respect for Mina, but minotaurs are not made for stealthy movement. His knee bumped a bench, his sword clanked and clattered at his side, his footfalls boomed, or so it seemed to him.

The female Solamnic stirred uneasily, but she was too deeply drowned in sleep to waken.

Mina did not hear him.

Walking up to stand behind her, he spoke to her quietly, "Mina."

She did not lift her head.

Galdar waited a moment, then said, "Mina" again and placed his hand gently on her shoulder.

Now she turned, now she looked around. Her face was pale and drawn with fatigue. Smudged circles of weariness surrounded her amber eyes, whose bright gleam was dimmed.

"You should go to bed," he told her.

"Not yet," she said.

"You were all over the battlefield," he persisted. "I couldn't keep up with you. Everywhere I looked, there you were. Fighting, praying. You need your rest. We have much to do tomorrow and in the days following to fortify the city. The Solamnics will attack us. Their spy rides to alert them even now. I let him go," Galdar growled, "as you commanded. I think it was a mistake. He's in league with the elf king. The Solamnics will make some deal with the elves, bring the might of both nations down on us."

"Most likely," said Mina.

She held out her hand to Galdar. He was privileged to help her rise to her feet. She retained his hand—his right hand—in her own, looked up into his eyes.

"All is well, Galdar. I know what I am doing. Have faith."

"I have faith in you, Mina," Galdar said.

Mina cast him a disappointed glance. Releasing his hand, she turned away from him to face the altar. Her look and her silence were her rebuke, that and the sudden gut-twisting pain in his arm. He clamped his lips shut, massaged his arm, and stubbornly waited.

"I have no more need of you, Galdar," Mina said. "Go to your bed."

"I do not sleep until you sleep, Mina. You know that. Or you should, after all this time together."

Her head bowed. He was astonished to see two tears glitter in the candlelight, slide down her cheeks. She whisked them both swiftly away.

"I know, Galdar," she said in muffled voice that tried to be gruff but failed, "and I do appreciate your loyalty. If only . . ." She paused, then, glancing back at him, she said, almost shyly, "Will you wait here with me?"

"Wait for what, Mina?"

"For a miracle."

Mina lifted her hands in a commanding gesture. The flames leaped and swelled, burning brighter and hotter. A wave of searing heat smote Galdar in the face, causing him to gasp for breath and lift his hand to shield himself.

A breath filled the chamber, blew on the flames, caused them to grow stronger, burn higher. Banners and tapestries graced with emblems sacred to the Mystics hung behind the altar. The flames licked the fringe of the tapestries. The fabric caught fire.

The heat grew in intensity. Smoke coiled around the altar and around Goldmoon's amber sarcophagus. The Solamnic female began to cough and choke and woke herself up. She stared in fearful amazement, jumped to her feet.

"Mina!" she cried. "We must get out of here!"

The flames spread rapidly from the banners to the wooden beams that supported the steep ceiling. Galdar had never seen fire move so fast, as if the wood and the walls had been soaked with oil.

"If your miracle is to burn down this temple, then the Solamnic is right," Galdar bellowed over the roar of the fire. "We must get out of here now, before the ceiling collapses."

"We are in no danger," Mina said calmly. "The hand of the One God protects us. Watch and wonder and glory in her power."

The gigantic wooden ceiling beams were now ablaze. At any moment, they would start to crumble and break apart, come crashing down on top of them. Galdar was just about to grab hold of Mina and carry her out bodily, when he saw, to his utter confusion, that the flames consumed the beams entirely. Nothing was left of them. No cinders fell, no fiery timbers came thundering down in a rush of sparks. The holy fire devoured the wood, devoured the ceiling, devoured whatever materials had been used to build the roof. The flames consumed and then went out.

Nothing was left of the temple roof, not even ashes. Galdar stared into the night sky that glittered with stars.

The corpses of the two mages sat on their bench, unseeing, uncaring. They could have perished in the flames and never made a sound, spoken no word of protest, done nothing to save themselves. At a sharply spoken command from Mina, the bodies of the mages rose to their feet and moved toward the altar. Walking without seeing where they were going, they came to a halt when Mina ordered them to stop—near Goldmoon's amber sarcophagus—and stood once more staring at nothing.

"Watch!" said Mina softly. "The miracle begins."

Galdar had seen many wondrous and terrible sights in his long life, particularly that part of it that revolved around Mina. He had never seen anything like this, and he stared, thunderstruck.

A hundred thousand souls filled the night sky. The ghostly mist of their hands, their faces, their diaphanous limbs blotted out the stars. Galdar stared, aghast, amazed, to see that in their ephemeral hands, the dead carried the skulls of dragons.

Reverently, gently, the souls of the dead lowered the first skull through the charred opening where the roof had been and placed the skull on the floor, before the altar.

The skull was enormous, that of a gold dragon—Galdar could tell by the few golden scales that clung to the bone and gleamed pathetically in the flickering candlelight. Though the altar room was large, the skull filled it.

The dead brought down another skull, that of a red dragon. The dead placed the skull of the red dragon down beside that of the gold.

Shouts and cries rose up from outside. Seeing the flames, people came running to the Temple. The shouts ceased as they gazed in shock at the wondrous and fearful sight of dragon skulls, hundreds of them, spiraling down out of the dark night, cradled in the arms of the dead.

Methodically, the dead piled the skulls one on top of the other, the largest skulls on the bottom to form a secure base, the skulls of smaller dragons piled on top of that. The mound of skulls rose higher and higher, stacking up well above what would have been the height of the steep-pitched roof.

Galdar's mouth went dry. His eyes burned, his throat constricted so that he had difficulty speaking.

"This is a skull totem from one of the dragon overlords!" he cried.

"*Three* of the dragon overlords to be precise," Mina corrected.

The totem increased in height, now taller than the tallest trees, and still the dead continued to bring more skulls to add to it.

"This is the totem of Beryllinthranox the Green and of Khellendros the Blue and of Malystryx the Red. As Malystryx stole the totems of the other two, so the dead steal hers."

Galdar's stomach shriveled. His knees weakened. He was forced to grab hold of the altar to remain standing. He was terrified, and he was not ashamed to admit to his terror.

"You have stolen Malys's totem? The dragon will be furious, Mina. She will find out who has taken the totem, and she will come here after you!"

"I know," said Mina calmly. "That is the plan."

"She will kill you, Mina!" Galdar gasped. "She will kill us all. I know this foul dragon. No one can stand up to her. Even her own kind are terrified of her."

"Look, Galdar," said Mina softly.

Galdar turned his reluctant gaze back to the pile of skulls that was now almost complete. One last skull, that of a small white dragon, was laid upon the top. The dead lingered for a moment, as if admiring their handiwork. A chill wind blew down from the mountainside, shredded the souls into wisps of fog, and dispersed them with a puff.

The eyes of dead dragons began to shine from their hollow eye sockets. It seemed to Galdar that he could hear voices, hundreds of voices, raised in a triumphant paean. A shadowy form took shape above the totem, coiled around it covetously. The shadowy form became clearer, more distinct. Scales of many colors gleamed in the candlelight. An enormous tail curled around the totem's base, the body of a giant dragon circled it. Five heads rose over the totem. Five heads attached to one body and that body attached to the totem.

The body lacked substance, however. The five heads were daunting, but they were not real heads, not as real as the skulls of the dead over which they hovered. The eyes of the dead dragons gleamed bright. Their light was almost blinding, and suddenly it lanced straight into the heavens.

The light of the totem blazed through the sky, and there, looking down upon them, was a single eye. The eye of the goddess.

White, staring, the eye gazed down at them, unblinking.

The body of the five-headed dragon grew more distinct, gained in substance and in strength.

"The power of the totem feeds the One God as the totem once fed Malys," Mina said. "With each passing moment, the One God comes closer to entering the world, joining the mortal and immortal. On the Night of the Festival of the New Eye, the One God will become the paradox, she will take a mortal form and imbue it with immortality. In that moment, she will rule over all that is in the heavens and all that is below. She will rule over the living and the dead. Her victory will be assured, her triumph complete."

She will take a mortal form. Galdar knew then why they'd been forced to cart the body of Goldmoon across Ansalon, haul it up mountains, and hoist it out of valleys.

Takhisis's final revenge. She would enter the body of the one person who had fought life-long against her, and she would use that body to seduce and enthrall and entrap the trusting, the innocent, the guileless.

He could hear outside the temple a hubbub of voices, raised in excitement, babbling and clamoring at the sight of this new moon in the heavens. The cry raised, "Mina! Mina!"

She would go out to them, bask in the light and warmth of their affection, far different from that chill, cold light. She would tell them that this was the work of the One God, but no one would pay any attention.

"Mina . . . Mina . . ."

She walked out the door of the ruined temple. Galdar heard the swelling cheer raised when she appeared, heard it reverberate off the sides of the mountains, echo to the heavens.

To the heavens.

Galdar looked up at the five heads of the ethereal dragon, swaying over the totem, consuming its power. The single eye burned, and he realized in that moment that he was closer to this goddess than Mina was or ever could be.

The trusting, the innocent, the guileless.

Galdar wanted his bed, wanted to sleep and forget all this in dark oblivion. He would break his own rule this night. Mina was with those who adored her. She had no need of him. He was about to depart, when he heard a moan.

The Solamnic female crouched on the floor, huddled within herself, staring up, appalled, at the monster that writhed and coiled above her.

She, too, had seen the truth.

"Too late," he said to her as he passed by on his way to his bed. "Too late. For all of us."

13 RESTLESS SPIRITS

The bodies of the two mages stood where they had been told to stand, near the amber sarcophagus in the Temple of the Heart, now the Temple of the One God. The spirit of only one of the mages was there to watch the building of the totem. Dalamar's spirit had departed with the arrival of the skull-bearing dead. Palin continued to watch the totem grow, a monument to the strengthening power of Queen Takhisis. He had no idea where Dalamar had gone. The spirit of the dark elf was often absent, gone more than he was around.

Palin still found it disconcerting to be away from his body for any period of time, but had been venturing farther these past few days. He was growing increasingly alarmed, for he realized—as did all the dead—that Takhisis was very close to the time when she would make her triumphant entry into the world.

Palin watched the totem grow and, with it, Takhisis's power. Takhisis could take many forms, but when dealing with dragons, she preferred her dragon form. Five heads, each of a different color and species of dragon, emerged from a body of massive power and strength. The head of the red dragon was brutal, vicious. Flames flickered in the nostrils. The head of the blue was sleek, elegant, and deadly. Lightning crackled from between the razor-sharp fangs. The head of the black was cunning, sly, and dripped poison acid. The head of the white was cruel, calculating, and radiated a bone-numbing chill. The head of the green was devious and clever. Noxious fumes spewed from the gaping jaws.

This was Takhisis on the immortal plane, the Takhisis the dead served in dread terror, the Takhisis whom Palin hated and loathed and, despite himself, felt moved to worship. For in the eyes of the five dragons was the mind of the god, a mind that could span the vastness of eternity and see and understand the limitless possibilities and, at the same time, number all the drops in the swelling seas and count the grains of sand in the barren desert.

The sight of the Dark Queen hovering around the skulls of the dead dragons, receiving the accolades of the dead dragons, was too much for him to bear. Palin tore his spirit from his body and flitted restlessly out into the darkness.

He found it difficult to give up the habits of the living, and so he roamed the streets of Sanction in his spirit form as he might have done in his living form. He walked around buildings, when he might have passed through them. Physical objects were no barrier to a spirit, yet they blocked him. To walk through walls—to do something that was so completely against the laws of nature—would be to admit that he had lost any connection to life, to the physical part of life. He could not do that, not yet.

His spirit form did allow him easy passage through the streets that were clogged with people, everyone running to the newly proclaimed Temple of the One God to see the miracle. If he had been alive and breathing, Palin would have been swept up in the mob or run down, just as were two beggars floundering in the street. One, a lame man, had his crutch knocked out from under him. The other, a blind man, had lost his cane and was groping about helplessly with his hands, trying to find it.

Instinctively, Palin started to offer them help, only to remember what he was, remember there was no help he could give. Drifting nearer, Palin noted that the blind man looked familiar—the silver hair, the white robes. . . . The silver hair especially. He couldn't see the man's face, which was covered by bandages to hide the hideous wound that had robbed him of his sight. Palin knew the blind man, but he couldn't place him. The man was out of context, not where he was supposed to be. The Citadel of Light came to Palin's mind, and he suddenly recalled where he had seen this man before. This man, who was no man.

Using the eyes of the spirit world, Palin saw the true forms of the two beggars, forms that existed on the immortal plane and thus could not be banished, although they had taken other shapes in the mortal world. A silver dragon—Mirror—former guardian of the Citadel of Light stood side by side, wing-tip to wing-tip with a blue dragon.

Palin remembered then what it was to hope.

Dalamar's spirit was also abroad this night. The dark elf ventured much farther afield than Palin. Unlike Palin, Dalamar let no physical barrier impede him. Mountains were for him as insubstantial as clouds. He passed through the solid rock walls of Malys's lair, penetrated its labyrinthine chambers with the ease of blinking an eye or drawing a breath.

He found the great, red dragon sleeping, as he had been accustomed to finding her on previous occasions. Yet, this time, there was a difference. On his earlier visits, she'd slept deeply and peacefully, secure in the knowledge that she was supreme ruler of this world and there were none strong enough to challenge her. Now, her sleep was troubled. Her huge feet twitched, her eyes roved behind closed lids, her nostrils inflated. Saliva drooled from her jaw, and a growl rumbled deep in her chest. She dreamed—an unpleasant dream, seemingly.

That would be nothing, compared to her waking.

"Most Great and Gracious Majesty," Dalamar said.

Malys opened one eye, another sign that her slumber was not restful. Usually Dalamar had to speak to her several times or even summon one of her minions to come wake her.

"What do you want?" she growled.

"To make you aware of what is transpiring in the world while you sleep."

"Yes, go on," Malys said, opening the other eye.

"Where is your totem, Majesty?" Dalamar asked coolly.

Malys turned her massive head to look reassuringly upon her collection of skulls, trophies of her many victories, including those over Beryl and Khellendros.

Her eyes widened. Her breath escaped in a sizzling hiss. Rearing up with such force that she caused the mountain to quiver, she turned her head this way and that.

"Where is it?" she bellowed, lashing out with her tail. Granite walls cracked at the blows, stalactites crashed down from the ceiling, shattered on her red scales. She paid them no attention. "Where is the thief? Who has stolen it? Tell me!"

"I will tell you," Dalamar said, ignoring her fury, for she could do him no harm. "But I want something in exchange."

"Always the shrewd bargainer!" she hissed with a flicker of flame from out her teeth.

"You are aware of my present lamentable condition," said Dalamar, extending his hands to exhibit his ghostly form. "If you recover the totem and defeat the person who has unlawfully taken it, I ask that you use your magic to restore my soul to my living body."

"Granted," said Malys with a twitch of her clawed foot. Her head leaned forward. "Who has it?"

"Mina."

"Mina?" Malys repeated, baffled. "Who is this Mina and why has she taken my totem? *How* has she taken it? I smell no thief! No one has been in my lair! No thief could transport it!"

"Not even an army of thieves," Dalamar agreed. "An army of the dead could. And did."

"Mina . . ." Malys breathed the name with loathing. "Now I remember. I heard it said that she commanded an army of souls. What rubbish!"

"The 'rubbish' stole away the totem while you slept, Majesty, and they have rebuilt it in Sanction, in what was once known as the Temple of the Heart, but is now known as the Temple of the One God."

"This so-called One God again," snarled Malys. "This One God is starting to annoy me."

"The One God could do far more than annoy you, Majesty," said Dalamar coolly. "This One God was responsible for the destruction of Cyan Bloodbane, your cousin Beryl, and Khellendros the Blue—next to yourself, the three mightiest dragons in Krynn. This One God has encompassed the fall of

Silvanesti, the destruction of Qualinost, the defeat of the Solamnic Knights in Solanthus, and now she has been victorious in Sanction. You alone stand in the way of her absolute triumph."

Malys glowered, silent, brooding. He had spoken harshly, and although she didn't like to hear it, she couldn't deny the truth.

"She steals my totem. Why?" Malys asked sullenly.

"It has not been your totem for a long time," Dalamar replied. "The One God has been subverting the souls of the dead dragons who once worshiped her. She has been using the power of their souls to fuel her own power. By stealing the totems of your cousin and Khellendros, you played into the One God's hands. You made the souls of the dead dragons more powerful still. Do not underestimate this goddess. Although she was weakened and near destruction when first she came to this world, she has recovered her strength, and she is now poised to lay claim to a prize she has long coveted."

"You speak as if you know this goddess," said Malys, eyeing Dalamar with contempt.

"I do know her," said Dalamar, "and so do you—by reputation. Her name is Takhisis."

"Yes, I've heard of her," said Malys, with a dismissive flick of a claw. "I heard she abandoned this world during the war with Father Chaos."

"She did not abandon it," said Dalamar. "She stole it and brought it here, as she had long planned to do with the aid of Khellendros. Did you never stop to think how this world suddenly came into being in this part of the universe? Did you never wonder?"

"No, why should I?" Malys returned angrily. "If food falls into the hands of a starving man, he does not question, he eats!"

"You dined exceedingly well, Majesty," Dalamar agreed. "It is a shame that afterward you did not take out the garbage. The souls of the dead dragons have recognized their queen, and they will do anything she requires. You are sadly outnumbered, Your Majesty."

"Dead dragons have no fangs." Malys sneered. "I face a puny god who has a child for a champion and who must rely on expired souls for her might. I will recover my totem and deal a death blow to this god."

"When does Your Majesty plan to attack Sanction?" Dalamar asked.

"When I am ready," Malys growled. "Leave me now."

Dalamar bowed low. "Your Majesty will not forget her promise—to restore my soul to my body. I could be of so much more use to you as one whole person."

Malys waved a claw. "I do not forget my promises. Now go."

Closing her eyes, she let her massive head sink to the floor.

Dalamar was not fooled. For all her appearance of nonchalance, Malys had been shaken to the core of her being. She might sham sleep, but inside the fires of her rage burned bright and hot.

Satisfied that he had done all he could—here, at least—Dalamar departed.

The totem grew inside the fire-ravaged Temple. Mina's Knights and soldiers cheered her and called her name. Takhisis's shadow hovered over the totem, but few could see her. They did not look for her. They saw Mina, and that was all they cared about.

In Sanction's streets, now almost completely emptied, the silver dragon Mirror groped about for his beggar's staff, that had been knocked out of his hands.

"What is happening?" he asked his companion, who silently handed him his staff. "What is going on? I hear a tumult and a great cry."

"It is Takhisis," said Razor. "I can see her. She has revealed herself. Many of my brethren circle in the heavens, shouting her name. The dead dragons cry out to her. I hear the voice of my mate among them. Red, blue, white, black, green, living, dead—all swear their loyalty to her. She grows in power as I speak."

"Will you join them?" Mirror asked.

"I have been thinking long on what you said back in the cave of the mighty Skie," said Razor slowly. "How none of the calamities that have befallen this world would have happened if it had not been for Takhisis. I hated and detested Paladine and the other so-called gods of light. I cursed his name, and if I had a chance to kill one of his champions, I took that chance and gloried in it. I longed for the day when our queen might rule uncontested.

"Now that day has come, and I am sorry for it. She has no care for us." Razor paused, then said, "I see you smiling, Silver. You think 'care' is the wrong word. I agree. Those of us who followed the Dark Queen are not noted for being caring individuals. Respect. That is the word I want. Takhisis has no respect for those who serve her. She uses them until they are no longer of value to her, then she casts them aside. No, I will not serve Takhisis."

"But will he work actively against her?" a familiar voice whispered in Mirror's ear. "If you will vouch for him, I can use his help, as well as yours."

"Palin?" Mirror turned gladly in the direction of the voice. He reached out his hand toward the source of the voice, but felt no warm hand clasp his in return.

"I cannot see you or touch you, but I hear you, Palin," Mirror said. "And even your voice seems far away and distant, as though you speak from across a wide vale."

"So I do," said Palin. "Yet, together, perhaps we can cross it. I want you to help me destroy this totem."

Dalamar's spirit joined the river of souls flowing toward the Temple of the One, as other rivers flow toward the sea. His spirit paid no heed to the rest, but concentrated on his next objective. The other souls ignored him. They would not have heard him if he had spoken. They did not see him. They heard only one voice, saw only one face.

On arriving, Dalamar broke free of the torrent that spiraled around and around the totem of dragon skulls. The immense monument towered high in the air, visible for miles, or so said some of the thousands who stood staring at it in awe and admiration, exulting in Mina's victory over the hated red dragon, Malys.

Dalamar flicked the totem a glance. It was impressive, he had to admit. He then shifted his mind to more urgent matters. Guards stood posted at the temple doors. None with substantial bodies were being admitted inside the temple. His spirit flowed past the guards and into the altar room. He made certain that his body was safe, noted with some suprise that Palin's spirit was abroad this night.

Palin's departure was such an unusual occurrence that, despite the urgency of his errand, Dalamar paused to ponder where he might be, what the mage's soul could be up to. Dalamar wasn't concerned. He considered Palin as devious as a bowl of porridge.

"Still," Dalamar reminded himself, "he is Raistlin's nephew. And while porridge may be pale and lumpy, it is also thick and viscous. Much can be concealed beneath that bland surface."

The souls whirled in frenetic ecstasy around the totem, as thick as smoke rising from water-soaked wood. Millions of faces streamed past Dalamar any instant he chose to look. He continued on his way, moved ahead with the next stage of his plan.

Mina stood alone at the candle-lit altar. Her back to the totem, she stared, rapt, into the flames. The big minotaur was nearby. Where Mina was, the minotaur was.

"Mina, you are exhausted," Galdar pleaded. "You can barely stand. You must come to your bed. Tomorrow . . . who knows what tomorrow will bring? You should be rested."

"I thought you went to bed, Galdar," said Mina.

"I did," the minotaur growled. "I could not sleep. I knew I would find you here."

"I like to be here," said Mina in a dreamy voice. "Close to the One God. I can feel her holy presence. She folds me in her arms and lifts me up with her."

Mina raised her gaze upward into the night sky, now visible since the roof of the temple had been destroyed. "I am warm when I am with her, Galdar. I am warm and loved and fed and clothed and safe in her arms. When I come back to this world, I am cold and starving and thirsty. It is a punishment to be here, Galdar, when I would so much rather be up there."

Galdar made a rumbling sound in his throat. If he had doubts, he knew better than to speak them. He said only, "Yet, while you are down here, Mina, you have a job to do for the One God. You will not be able to do that job if you are sick with fatigue."

Mina reached out her hand, placed it on the minotaur's arm. "You are right, Galdar. I am being selfish. I will come to bed, and I will even sleep late in the morning."

Mina turned to look at the totem. Her amber eyes shone as if she still stared into the flames. "Isn't it magnificent?"

She might have said more, but Dalamar took care to enter her line of sight. He bowed low.

"I seek but a moment of your time, Mina," said Dalamar, bowing again.

"Go on ahead and make certain that my chamber is prepared, Galdar," Mina ordered. "Don't worry. I will come shortly."

Galdar's bestial eyes passed over the place where Dalamar's spirit hovered. Dalamar could never decide if the minotaur saw him or not. He didn't think so, but he had the feeling that Galdar knew his spirit was there. The minotaur's nose wrinkled, as though he smelled something rotten. Then with a grunting snort, Galdar turned away and left the altar room.

"What do you want?" Mina asked Dalamar. Her tone was calm, composed. "Have you word of the magical device carried by the kender?"

"Alas, no, Mina," said Dalamar, "but I do have other information. I have dire news. Malys is aware that you are the one who has stolen her totem."

"Indeed," said Mina, smiling slightly.

"Malys will come to take it back, Mina. The dragon is furious. She sees you now as a threat to her power."

"Why are you telling me all this, wizard?" Mina asked. "Surely, you are not fearful for my safety."

"No, Mina, I am not," said Dalamar coolly. "But I am fearful for my own if something should happen to you. I will help you defeat Malys. You will need a wizard's help to fight against this dragon."

"How will you, in your sorry state, help me?" Mina asked, amused.

"Restore my soul to my body. I am one of the most powerful wizards in the history of Krynn. My help to you could be invaluable. You have no leader for the dead. You tried to recruit Lord Soth and failed."

The amber eyes flickered. She was displeased.

"Yes, I heard about that," Dalamar said. "My spirit travels the world. I know a great deal about what is transpiring. I could be of use to you. I could be the one to lead the dead. I could seek out the kender and bring him and the device to you. Burrfoot knows me, he trusts me. I have made a study of the Device of Time Journeying. I could teach you to use it. I could use my magic to help you fight the dragon's magic. All this I could do for you—but only as living man."

Dalamar saw himself reflected in the amber eyes—a wisp, more insubstantial than spider's silk.

"All this you will do for me and more, if I require it," Mina said, "not as living man but as living corpse." She lifted her head proudly. "As for your help against Malys, I have no need of your aid. The One God supports me and fights at my side. I need no other."

"Listen to me, Mina, before you go," insisted Dalamar, as she was turning away. "In my youth, I came to your One God as a lover comes to his mistress. She embraced me and caressed me and promised me that one day we would rule the world, she and I. I believed her, I trusted in her. My trust was betrayed. When I was no longer of use to her, she cast me to my enemies. She will do the same to you, Mina. When that day comes, you will need an ally of my strength and power. A living ally, not a corpse."

Mina paused, glanced back at him. She wore a thoughtful look. "Perhaps there is something in what you say, wizard."

Dalamar watched her warily, not trusting this sudden about-face. "There is, I assure you."

"Your faith in the One God was betrayed. She might say the same of you, Dalamar the Dark. Lovers often quarrel, a silly quarrel, soon forgotten, neither of them remembering."

"I remember," said Dalamar. "Because of her betrayal, I lost everything I ever loved and valued. Do you think I would so readily forget?"

"She might say that you put all that you loved and valued above her," Mina said, "that she was the one forsaken. Still, after all this time, it doesn't matter who was at fault. She values your affection. She would like to prove she still loves you by restoring to you everything you lost and more."

"In return for what?" Dalamar asked warily.

"A pledge of your affection."

"And? . . ."

"A small favor."

"And what is this 'small' favor?"

"Your friend, Palin Majere—"

"He is not my friend."

"That makes this easier, then," Mina said. "Your fellow wizard conspires against the One God. She is aware of his plots and schemings, of course. She would have no trouble thwarting them, but she has much on her mind these days, and she would appreciate your help."

"What must I do?" Dalamar asked.

Mina shrugged. "Nothing much. Simply alert her when he is about to act. That is all. She will take care of the matter from there."

"And in return?"

"You will be restored to life. You will be given all you ask for, including the leadership of the army of souls, if that is what you want. In addition . . ." Mina smiled at him. The amber eyes smiled.

"Yes? In addition?"

"Your magic will be restored to you."

"*My* magic," Dalamar emphasized. "I do not want the magic she borrowed from the dead and then loaned to me. I want the magic that once lived inside me!"

"You want the god's magic. She promises."

Dalamar thought back to all the promises Takhisis had made him, all the promises she had broken. He wanted this so much. He wanted to believe.

"I will," he said softly.

14 THE RING AND THE CLOAK

Days, weeks, had passed since the Qualinesti elves had arrived in Silvanesti. How long they had been here, Gilthas could not say, for one day blended into another in the timeless woods. And though his people were content to allow one day to slide off time's silken strand and fall into the soft green grass, Gilthas was not. He grew increasingly frustrated. Alhana kept up the pretense that Silvanoshei was recovering inside his tent. She spoke of him to her people, giving details of what he said and what he ate and how he was slowly mending. Gilthas listened in shock to these lies, but, after a time, he came to the conclusion that Alhana actually believed them. She had woven the threads of falsehood into a warm blanket and was using that blanket to shield herself from the cold truth.

The Silvanesti listened to her and asked no questions—something else that was incomprehensible to Gilthas.

"We Silvanesti do not like change," explained Kiryn in response to Gilthas's frustration. "Our mages halted the changing of the seasons, for we could not bear to see the green of spring wither and die. I know you cannot understand this, Gilthas. Your human blood runs hot, will not let you sit still. You count the seconds because they are so short and slip away so fast. The human side of you revels in change."

"Yet change comes!" said Gilthas, pacing back and forth, "whether the Silvanesti will it or not."

"Yes, change has come to us," said Kiryn with a sad smile. "Its raging torrent has washed away much of what we loved. Now the waters are calmer, we are content to float on the surface. Perhaps we will wash up on some quiet shore, where no one will find us or touch us or harm us ever again."

"The Dark Knights are desperate," said Gilthas. "They are outnumbered, they have no food. Their morale is low. We should attack now!"

"What would be the outcome?" asked Kiryn, shrugging. "The Dark Knights are desperate, as you say. They will not go down without a fight. Many of our people would die."

"And many of the enemy would die," said Gilthas impatiently.

"The death of one human is as the crushing of an ant—there are so many left and so many more to come. The death of a single elf is like the falling of a mighty oak. None will grow up to take his place for hundreds of years, if then. So many of us have died already. We have so little left to us, and it is all precious. How can we waste it?"

"What if the Silvanesti knew the truth about Silvanoshei?" Gilthas asked grimly. "What would happen then?"

Kiryn looked out into the green leaves of the never changing forest. "They know, Gilthas," he said quietly. "They know. As I said, they do not like change. It easier to pretend that it is always springtime."

Eventually, Gilthas had to quit worrying about the Silvanesti and start worrying about his own people. The Qualinesti were beginning to splinter into factions. One was led, unfortunately, by his wife. The Lioness sought revenge, no matter what the cost. She and those like her wanted to fight the humans in Silvanost, drive them out, whether the Silvanesti would join them or not. It fell to Gilthas to argue time and again that under no circumstances could the Qualinesti launch an attack against the lord city of their cousins. No good could come of this, he argued. It would lead to more years of bitter division between the two nations. He could see this so clearly that he wondered how others could be so blind.

"You are the one who is blind," said the Lioness angrily. "No wonder. You stare constantly into the darkness of your own mind!"

She left him, moved out of their tent, going to live among her Wilder elf troops. Gilthas grieved at this quarrel—the first since their marriage—but he was king first, not loving husband. Much as he longed to give in, he could not, in good conscience, permit her to have her way.

Another faction of Qualinesti was being seduced by the Silvanesti way of life. Their hearts bruised and aching, they were content to live in the dreamlike state in the beautiful forest that reminded them of the forests of their homeland. Senator Palthainon, the leader of this faction, slavishly flattered the Silvanesti, dropping hints into their ears that Gilthas, because he was part human, was not the right ruler of the Qualinesti and could never be. Gilthas was erratic and wayward, as are all humans, and not to be trusted. If it had not been for the staunch and steadfast courage of Senator Palthainon, the Qualinesti would have never made it across the desert alive, and so on and so forth.

Some of the Qualinesti knew this to be untrue, and many argued in favor of their king, but the rest, while they applauded Gilthas's courage, would not have been sorry to see him go. He was the past, the pain, the gaping wound. They wanted to start to heal. As for the Silvanesti, they did not trust Gilthas to begin with, and Palthainon's whispers did not help.

Gilthas felt as though he had walked into a quagmire. Relentlessly, inch by agonizing inch, he was being sucked down into some nameless doom. His struggles caused him to sink further, his cries went unheeded. The end was approaching so slowly that no one else seemed to be aware of it. Only he could see it.

The stalemate continued. The Dark Knights hid in Silvanost, afraid to come out. The elves hid in the forest, unwilling to move.

Gilthas had taken to walking the forests alone these days. He wanted no company for his gloom-ridden thoughts, had even banished Planchet. Hearing a bestial cry from the air, he looked up, and his blood thrilled. A griffin, bearing a rider, circled above the trees, searching for a safe place to land. Change, for good or ill, was coming.

Gilthas hastened through the forest to where Alhana had established her camp, about thirty miles south of the border between Silvanesti and Blöde. The majority of the Silvanesti force was in this location, along with the refugees who had fled or been rescued from the capital city of Silvanost, and the Qualinesti refugees. Other elven forces were located along the Thon-Thalas River, with more lurking in the Bleeding Woods that surrounded Silvanost. Although scattered, the elven forces were in constant contact, using the wind, the creatures of woods and air, and runners to speed messages from one group to another.

Gilthas had wandered far from the campsite, and he was some time retracing his steps. When he arrived, he found Alhana in company with an elf who was a stranger to him. The elf was dressed as a warrior, and by the looks of his weathered face and travel-stained clothing, he had been on the road for many long months. Gilthas could tell by the warmth in Alhana's voice and the agitation in her manner that this elf was someone special to her. Alhana and the strange elf disappeared inside her shelter before Gilthas had a chance to make himself known.

Seeing Gilthas, Kiryn waved him over.

"Samar has returned."

"Samar . . . the warrior who went in search of Silvanoshei?"

Kiryn nodded.

"And what of Silvanoshei?" Gilthas looked in the direction of Alhana's tent.

"Samar came back alone," said Kiryn.

An agonized cry came from Alhana's shelter. The cry was quickly smothered and was not repeated. Those waiting tensely outside glanced at each other and shook their heads. A sizeable crowd had formed in the small clearing. The elves waited in respectful silence, but they waited, determined to hear the news for themselves.

Alhana came out to speak to them, accompanied by Samar, who stood protectively at her side. Samar reminded Gilthas of Marshal Medan, a resemblance that would not have been appreciated by either one. Samar was an older elf, probably near the same age as Alhana's husband, Porthios. Years of exile and warfare had etched the delicate bone structure of the elven face into granite, sharp and hard. He had learned to bank the fire of his emotions so that he gave away nothing of what he was thinking or feeling. Only when he looked at Alhana did warmth flicker in his dark eyes.

Alhana's face, surrounded by the mass of black hair, was normally pale, the pure white of the lily. Now her skin was completely without color, seemed translucent. She started to speak, but could not. She shuddered, pain wracked her as if it might rend her bone by bone. Samar reached out a supportive arm. Alhana thrust him aside. Her face hardened into firm resolve. Mastering herself, she looked out upon the silent watchers.

"I give my words to the wind and to the rushing water," said Alhana. "Let them carry the words to my people. I give my words to the beasts of the forests and the birds of the air. Let them carry my words to my people. All of you here, go forth and carry my words to my people and to our cousins, the Qualinesti." Her gaze touched on Gilthas but only for an instant.

"You know this man—Samar, my most trusted commander and loyal friend. Many long weeks ago, I sent him on a mission. He has returned from that mission with news of importance." Alhana paused, moistened her lips. "In telling you what Samar has told me, I must make an admission to you. When I claimed that Silvanoshei, your king, was ill inside his tent, I lied. If you want to know why I told this lie, you have only to look about you. I told the lie in order keep our people together, to keep us unified and to keep our cousins united beside us. Because of the lie, we are strong, when we might have been terribly weakened. We will need to be strong for what lies ahead."

Alhana paused, drew in a shivering breath.

"What I tell you now is the truth. Shortly after the battle of Silvanost, Silvanoshei was captured by the Dark Knights. We tried to rescue him, but he was taken away from us in the night. I sent Samar to try to find out what had become of him. Samar has found him. Silvanoshei, our king, is being held prisoner in Sanction."

The elves made soft sounds, as of a breath of wind blowing through the branches of the willow, but said nothing.

"I will let Samar tell you his tale."

Even as Samar spoke to the people, he had a care for Alhana. He stood near her, ready to assist her if her strength failed.

"I met a Knight of Solamnia, a brave and honorable man." Samar's dark eyes swept the crowd. "For those who know me, this is high praise. This Knight saw Silvanoshei in prison and spoke to him, at peril of his own life. The Knight bore Silvanoshei's cloak and this ring."

Alhana held up the ring for all to see. "The ring is my son's. I know it. His father gave it to him when he was a child. Samar also recognized it."

The elves looked from the ring to Alhana, their expressions troubled. Several officers, standing near Kiryn, nudged him and urged him forward.

Kiryn advanced. "May I have permission to speak, gracious Queen?"

"You may, Cousin," said Alhana, regarding him with an air of defiance as if to say, "You may speak, but I do not promise to listen."

"Forgive me, Alhana Starbreeze," Kiryn said respectfully, "for doubting the word of such a great and renowned warrior as Samar, but how do we know we can trust this human Knight? Perhaps it is a trap."

Alhana relaxed. Apparently this wasn't the question she had been anticipating.

"Let Gilthas, ruler of the Qualinesti, son of the House of Solostaran, come forward."

Wondering what this had to do with him, Gilthas walked out of the crowd to make his bow to Alhana. Samar's stern gaze flicked over Gilthas, who had the impression of being weighed in the balance. Whether he came out the winner or the loser in Samar's estimation, the young king had no way of judging.

"Your Majesty," said Samar, "when you were in Qualinesti, did you know a Solamnic by the name of Gerard uth Mondar?"

"Yes, I did," said Gilthas, startled.

"You consider him a man of courage, of honor?"

"I do," said Gilthas. "He is all that and more. Is this the Knight of whom you spoke?"

"Sir Gerard said he heard that the king of the Qualinesti and survivors of that land were going to try to reach safe haven in our land. He expressed deep sorrow for your loss but rejoiced that you are safe. He asked to be remembered to you."

"I know this Knight. I know of his courage, and I can attest to his honor. You are right to trust his word. Gerard uth Mondar came to Qualinesti under strange circumstances, but he left that land a true friend carrying with him the blessing of our beloved Queen Mother Lauranalanthalasa. His was one of the last blessings my mother ever bestowed."

"If both Samar and Gilthas attest to the honor of this Knight, then I have no more to say against him," said Kiryn. Bowing, he returned to his place within the circle.

Over a hundred elves had gathered. They were quiet, said nothing, but exchanged glances. Their silence was eloquent. Alhana could proceed, and she did so.

"Samar has brought other information. We can now give a name to this One God. The One God came to us in the name of peace and love, but that turned out to be part of her despicable plan to ensnare and destroy us. And now we know why. The name of the One God is an ancient one. The One God is Takhisis."

Like a pebble dropped into still water, the ripples of this astounding news spread among the elves.

"I cannot explain to you how this terrible miracle came about," Alhana continued, her voice growing stronger and more majestic with every word. The elves were with her now. She had their full support. All questions about the human Knight were forgotten, overshadowed by the dark wings of an ancient foe. "But we do not need to know. At last, we can put a name to our enemy and it is an enemy that we can defeat, for we have defeated her in the past.

"The Solamnic Knight, Gerard, carries word of this to the Knights' Council," Samar added. "The Solamnics are forming an army to attack Sanction. He urges the elves to be part of this force, to rescue our king. What say you?"

The elves gave a cheer that caused the branches of the trees to shake. Hearing the commotion, more and more elves came running to the site, and they raised their voices. The Lioness arrived, her Wilder elves behind her. Her face was aglow, her eyes alight.

"What is this I hear?" she cried, sliding from her horse and racing to Gilthas. "Is it true? Are we going to war at last?"

He did not answer her, but she was too excited to notice. Turning from him, she sought out those soldiers among the Silvanesti. Before this, they would have never deigned to speak to a Wilder elf, but now they answered her eager questions with joy.

Alhana's officers clustered around her and around Samar, offering suggestions, making plans, discussing what routes that they would take and how fast they could possibly reach Sanction and who would be permitted to go and who would be left behind.

Gilthas alone stood silent, listening to the tumult. When he finally spoke, he heard his own voice, heard the human sound to it, deeper and harsher than the voices of the elves.

"We must attack," he said, "but our target should not be Sanction. Our target is Silvanost. When that city is secure, then we turn our eyes to the north. Not before."

The elves stared at him in shocked disapproval, as if he were a guest at a wedding who had gone berserk and smashed all the gifts. The only elf who paid any heed to him was Samar.

"Let us hear the Qualinesti king," he orderd, raising his voice over the angry rumblings.

"It is true that we have defeated Takhisis in the past," Gilthas told his glowering audience, "but we had the help of Paladine and Mishakal and the other gods of light. Now Takhisis is the One God, alone and supreme. Her defeat will not be easy.

"We will have to march hundreds of miles from our homeland, leaving our own land in the hands of the enemy. We will join a fight with humans to attack and try to win a human city. We will make sacrifices for which we will never be rewarded. I do not say that we should *not* join this battle against Takhisis," Gilthas added. "My mother, as all of you know, fought among humans. She fought to save human cities and human lives. She made sacrifices for which no one ever thanked her. This battle against Takhisis and her forces is a battle that I believe is worth fighting. I counsel only that we make certain we have a homeland to which to return. We have lost Qualinesti. Let us not lose Silvanesti."

Hearing his impassioned words, the Lioness's expression softened. She came to stand at his side.

"My husband is right," she said. "We should attack Silvanost and hold it secure before we send a force to rescue the young king."

The Silvanesti looked at them with hostile eyes. A half-human and a Wilder elf. Outsiders, aliens. Who were they to tell the Silvanesti and even the Qualinesti what to do? Prefect Palthainon stood beside Alhana, whispering in her ear, undoutedly urging her to pay no attention to the "puppet king." Gilthas found one ally among them—Samar.

"The king of our cousins speaks wisely, Your Majesty," said Samar. "I think we should heed his words. If we march to Sanction, we leave behind us an enemy who may well attack and slay us when our backs are turned."

"The Dark Knights are trapped in Silvanost like bees caught in a jar," replied Alhana. "They bumble about, unable to escape. Mina has no intention of sending reinforcements to the Dark Knights in Silvanost. If she was going to, she would have done so by now. I will leave a small force behind to keep up the illusion that a larger force has them surrounded. When we return, triumphant, we will deal with these Dark Knights, my son and I," she added proudly.

"Alhana," Samar began.

She cast him a glance, her violet eyes wine-dark and chill.

Samar said nothing more. Bowing, he took up his stance behind his queen. He did not look at Gilthas, nor did Alhana. The decision had been made, the matter closed.

Silvanesti and Qualinesti gathered eagerly around her, awaiting her commands. The two nations were united at last, united in their determination to march to Sanction. After a moment's worried look at her husband, the Lioness squeezed his hand for comfort, then she, too, hastened over to confer with Alhana Starbreeze.

Why couldn't they see? What blinded them?

Takhisis. This is her doing, Gilthas said to himself. Now free to rule the world unchallenged, she has seized hold of love's sweet elixir, stirred it with poison, and fed it to both the mother and her son. Silvanoshei's love for Mina turns to obsession. Alhana's love for her son muddles her thoughts. And how can we fight this? How can we fight a god when even love—our best weapon against her—is tainted?

15 THE RESCUE OF A KING

Elves could be dreamy and lethargic, spend all their daylight hours watching the unfolding of the petals of a rose or sit hushed and rapt beneath the stars for nights on end. But when they are stirred to action, the elves astonish their humans observers with their quickness of thought and of movement, their ability to make swift decisions and carry them through, their resolve and determination to overcome any and all obstacles.

If either Alhana or Samar slept in the next few days, Gilthas had no idea when. Day and night, the stream of people coming and going from her tree shelter never ceased. He himself was one of them, for as ruler of his people, he was included in all important decisions. He said very little, however, although Alhana graciously took pains to invite him to share his opinion. He knew quite well that his opinion was not valued. In addition, he had such small knowledge of the lands through which they must pass that he was not much help anyway.

He was surprised to see how readily the Silvanesti and Qualinesti looked to Alhana, once an outcast, a dark elf, for leadership. His surprise ended when he heard her detail the outlines of her plan. She knew the mountainous lands through which they must march, for she had hidden her forces there for many years. She knew every road, every deer path, every cave. She knew war, and she knew the hardships and terrors of war.

No Silvanesti commander had such extensive knowledge of the lands they would traverse, the forces they might have to fight, and soon the most obdurate of them deferred to Alhana's superior knowledge and swore loyalty to her. Even the Lioness, who would lead her Wilder elves, was impressed.

Alhana's plan for the march was brilliant. The elves would travel north into into Blöde, land of their enemies, the ogres. This might appear to be suicidal, but many years ago, Porthios had discovered that the Khalkist mountain range split in two, hiding with its tall peaks a series of valleys and gorges nestled in the center. By marching in the valleys, the elves could use the mountains to guard their flanks. The route would be long and arduous, but the elven army would travel light and swift. They hoped to be safely through Blöde before the ogres knew they were there.

Unlike human armies, who must cart about blacksmith forges and heavily laden supply wagons, the elves wore no plate or chain armor, carried no heavy swords or shields. The elves relied on the bow and arrow, making good use of the skill for which elven archers are renowned. Thus the elven army could cover far greater distances than their human counterparts. The elves would have to travel swiftly, for within only a few short weeks the winter snows would start to fall in the mountains, sealing off the passes.

Much as he admired Alhana's plan of battle, every fiber in Gilthas's body cried out that it was wrong. As Samar had said, they should not march ahead, leaving the enemy in control behind. Gilthas grew so despondent and frustrated that he knew he must stop going to the meetings. Yet, the Qualinesti needed to be represented. He turned to the man who had been his friend for many years, a man who had, along with his wife, helped to lift Gilthas from the debilitating depression that had once sought to claim him.

"Planchet," said Gilthas, early one morning, "I am dismissing you from my service."

"Your Majesty!" Planchet stared, aghast and dismayed. "Have I done anything or said anything to displease you? If so, I am truly sorry—"

"No, my friend," said Gilthas, smiling a smile that came from the heart, not from diplomacy. He rested his arm on the shoulder of the man who had stood by his side for so long. "Do not protest the use of that word. I say 'friend,' and I mean it. I say adviser and mentor, and I mean that, too. I say father and councilor, and I mean those, as well. All these you have been to me, Planchet. I do not exaggerate when I say that I would not be standing here today if it were not for your strength and your wise guidance."

"Your Majesty," Planchet protested, his voice husky. "I do not deserve such praise. I have been but the gardener. Yours is the tree that has grown strong and tall—"

"—from your careful nurturing."

"And this is the reason I must leave His Majesty?" Planchet asked quietly.

"Yes, because now it is your time to nurture and watch over others. The Qualinesti need a military leader. Our people clamor to march to Sanction. You must be their general. The Lioness leads the Kagonesti. You will lead the Qualinesti. Will you do this for me?"

Planchet hesitated, troubled.

"Planchet," said Gilthas, "Prefect Palthainon is already trying to squirm his way into this position. If I appoint you, he will grumble and gripe, but he will not be able to stop me. He knows nothing of military matters, and you are a veteran with years of experience. You are liked and trusted by the Silvanesti. Please, for the sake of our people, do this for me."

"Yes, Your Majesty," Planchet replied at once. "Of course. I thank you for your faith in me, and I will try to be worthy of it. I know that Your Majesty is not in favor of this course of action, but I believe that it is the right one. Once we defeat Takhisis and drive her from the world, the shadow of dark wings will be lifted, the light will shine on us, and we will remove the enemy from both our lands."

"Do you truly think so, Planchet?" Gilthas asked in somber tones. "I have my doubts. We may defeat Takhisis, but we will not defeat that on which she thrives—the darkness in men's hearts. Thus I think we would be wise to drive out the enemy that holds our homes, secure our homeland and make it strong, then march out into the world."

Planchet said nothing, appeared embarrassed.

"Speak your thoughts, my friend," said Gilthas, smiling. "You are now my general. You have an obligation to tell me if I am wrong."

"I would say only this, Your Majesty. It is these very isolationist policies that have brought great harm to the elves in the past, causing us to be mistrusted and misunderstood by even those who might have been our allies. If we fight alongside the humans in this battle, it will prove to them that we are part of the larger world. We will gain their respect and perhaps even their friendship."

"In other words," said Gilthas, smiling wryly, "I have always been one to languish in my bed and write poetry—"

"No, Your Majesty," said Planchet, shocked. "I never meant—"

"I know what you meant, dear friend, and I hope you are right. Now, you'll be wanted in the next military conference that is convening shortly. I have told Alhana Starbreeze of my decision to name you general, and she approves of it. Whatever decisions you make, you make them in my name."

"I thank you for your trust, Your Majesty," said Planchet. "But what will you do? Will you march with us or remain behind?"

"I am no warrior, as you well know, dear friend. What small skill I have with the sword I have you to thank for it. Some of our people cannot travel, those with children to care for, the infirm and the elderly. I am considering remaining behind with them."

"Yet, think, Your Majesty, Prefect Palthainon marches with us. Consider that he will attempt to insinuate himself into Alhana's trust. He will demand a part in any negotiations with humans, a race he detests and despises."

"Yes," said Gilthas wearily. "I know. You had best go now, Planchet. The meeting will convene shortly, and Alhana requires that everyone be prompt in their attendance."

"Yes, Your Majesty," said Planchet, and with one final, troubled glance at his young king, he departed.

Within a far shorter time than anyone could have imagined, the elves were prepared to march. They left behind a force as the home guard to watch over those who could not make the long trek north, but the force was small, for the land itself was their best defender—the trees that loved the elves would shelter them, the animals would warn them and carry messages for them, the caverns would hide them.

They left behind another small force to maintain the illusion that an elven army had the city of Silvanost surrounded. So well did this small force play its part that General Dogah, shut up in the walls of a city he'd come to loathe, had no idea that his enemy had marched away. The Dark Knights remained imprisoned inside their victory and cursed Mina, who had left them to this fate.

The kirath remained to guard the borders. Long had they walked within the gray desolation left behind by the shield. Now they rejoiced to see small green shoots thrusting up defiantly through the gray dust and decay. The kirath took this as a hopeful sign for their homeland and their people, who had themselves almost withered and died, first beneath the shield, then beneath the crushing boot of the Dark Knights.

Gilthas had made up his mind to stay behind. Two days before the march, Kiryn sought him out.

Seeing the elf's troubled face, Gilthas sighed inwardly.

"I hear you plan to remain in Silvanesti," Kiryn said. "I think you should change your mind and come with us."

"Why?" asked Gilthas.

"To guard the interests of your people."

Gilthas said nothing, interrogated him with a look.

Kiryn flushed. "I was given this information in confidence."

"I do not want you to break a vow," said Gilthas. "I have no use for spies."

"I took no vow. I think Samar wanted me to tell you," said Kiryn. "You know that we march through the Khalkist Mountains, but do you know how we plan to make our way into Sanction?"

"I know so little of the territory—" Gilthas began.

"We will ally ourselves with the dark dwarves. March our army through their underground tunnels. They are to be well-paid."

"With what?" Gilthas asked.

Kiryn stared down at the leaf-strewn forest floor. "With the money you have brought with you from Qualinesti."

"That wealth is not mine," Gilthas said sharply. "It is the wealth of the Qualinesti people. All that we have left."

"Prefect Palthainon offered it to Alhana, and she accepted."

"If I protest, there will be trouble. My attendance on this ill-fated venture will not change that."

"No, but now Palthainon, as highest-ranking official, has charge of the wealth. If you come, you take your people's trust into your keeping. You may be forced to use it. There may not be another way. But the decision would be yours to make."

"So now it comes to this," Gilthas muttered when Kiryn had gone. "We pay off the darkness to save us. How far do we sink into darkness before we become the darkness?"

On the day the march began, the Silvanesti left their beloved woods with dry eyes that looked to the north. They marched in silence, with no songs, no blaring horns, no crashing cymbals, for the Dark Knights must never know that they were leaving, the ogres must not be warned of their coming. The elves marched in the shadows of the trees to avoid the eyes of watchful blue dragons, circling above.

When they crossed the border of Silvanesti, Gilthas paused to look behind him at the rippling leaves that flashed silver in the sunlight, a brilliant contrast to the gray line of decay that was the forest's boundary, the shield's legacy. He gazed long, with the oppressive feeling in his heart that once he crossed, he could never go back.

A week after the Silvanesti army had departed, Rolan of the kirath walked his regular patrol along the border. He kept his gaze fixed on the ground, noting with joy in his heart a small sign that nature was fighting a battle against the evil caused by the shield.

Although the shield's deadly magic was gone, the destruction wrought by its evil magic remained. Whatever plant or tree the shield had touched had died, so the borders of Silvanesti were marked by a gray, grim line of death.

Yet now, beneath the gray shroud of desiccated leaves and withered sticks, Rolan found tiny stalks of green emerging triumphantly from the soil. He could not tell yet what they were: blades of grass or delicate wildflowers or perhaps the first brave shoot of what would become a towering oak or a flame-colored maple. Maybe, he thought with a smile, this was some common, humble plant he tended—dandelion or catnip or spiderwort. Rolan loved this, whatever it might turn out to be. The green of life sprouting amidst death was an omen of hope for him and for his people.

Carefully, gently he replaced the shroud, which he now thought of as a blanket, to protect the frail young shoots from the harsh sunlight. He was about to move on when he caught whiff of a strange scent.

Rolan rose to his feet, alarmed. He sniffed the air, trying hard to place the peculiar odor. He had never smelled anything like it: acrid, animal. He heard distant sounds that he recognized as the crackling of breaking tree limbs, the trampling of vegetation. The sounds grew louder and more distinct, and above them came sounds more ominous: the warning cry of the hawk, the scream of the timid rabbit, the panicked bleat of fleeing deer.

The foul animal scent grew strong, overwhelming, sickening. The smell of meat-eaters. Drawing his sword, Rolan put his fingers to his lips to give the shrill, penetrating whistle that would alert his fellow kirath to danger.

Three enormous minotaurs emerged from the forest. Their horns tore the leaves, their axes left gashes in the tree limbs as they impatiently hacked at the underbrush that blocked their way. The minotaurs halted when they saw Rolan, stood staring him, their bestial eyes dark, without expression.

He lifted his sword, made ready to attack.

A bovine smell engulfed him. Strong arms grabbed him. He felt the prick of the knife just below his ear; swift, bitter pain as the knife slashed across his throat . . .

The minotaur who slew the elf dumped the body onto the ground, wiped the blood from his dagger. The minotaur's companions nodded. Another job well done. They proceeded through the forest, clearing a path for those who came behind.

For the hundreds who came behind. For the thousands.

Minotaur forces tramped across the border. Minotaur ships with their painted sails and galleys manned by slaves sailed the waters of the Thon-Thalas, traveling south to the capital of Silvanost, bringing General Dogah the reinforcements he had been promised.

Many kirath died that day, died as did Rolan. Some had the chance to fight their attackers, most did not. Most were taken completely by surprise.

The body of Rolan of the kirath lay in the forest he had loved. His blood seeped below the gray mantle of death, drowned the tiny green shoots.

16 ODILA'S PRAYER, MINA'S GIFT

In the night, the eyes of the dead dragons within the skulls that made up the totem gleamed bright. The phantom of the five-headed dragon floated above the totem, causing those who saw it to marvel. In the night, in the darkness that she ruled, Queen Takhisis was powerful and reigned supreme. But, with the light of the sun, her image faded away. The eyes of the dead dragons flickered and went out, as did the candles on the altar, so that only wisps of smoke, blackened wicks, and melted wax remained.

The totem that appeared so magnificent and invulnerable in the darkness was by daylight a pile of skulls—a loathsome sight, for bits of scales or rotted flesh still clung to the bones. By day, the totem was a stark reminder to all who saw it of the immense power of Malys, the dragon overlord who had built it.

The question on everyone's lips was not *if* Malys would attack, but when. Fear of her coming spread through the city. Fearing massive desertions, Galdar ordered the West Gate closed. Although publicly Mina's Knights maintained a show of nonchalance, they were afraid.

When Mina walked the streets every day, she lifted fear from the hearts of all who saw her. When she spoke every night of the power of the One God, the people listened and cheered, certain that the One God would save them from the dragon. But when Mina departed, when the sound of her voice could no longer be heard, the shadow of red wings spread a chill over Sanction. People looked to the skies with dread.

Mina was not afraid. Galdar marveled at her courage, even as it worried him. Her courage stemmed from her faith in Takhisis, and he knew the goddess was not worthy of such faith. His one hope was that Takhisis needed Mina and would thus be loath to sacrifice her. One moment he had convinced himself she would be safe, the next he was convinced that Takhisis might use this means to rid herself of a rival who had outlasted her usefulness.

Compounding Galdar's fears was the fact that Mina refused to tell him her strategy for defeating Malys. He tried to talk to her about it. He reminded her of Qualinost. The dragon had been destroyed, but so had a city.

Mina rested her hand reassuringly on the minotaur's arm. "What happened to Qualinost will not happen to Sanction, Galdar. The One God hated the elves and their nation. She wanted to see them destroyed. The One God is pleased with Sanction. Here she plans to enter the world, to inhabit both the physical plane and the spiritual. Sanction and its people will be safe, the One God will see to that."

"But then what is your strategy, Mina?" Galdar persisted. "What is your plan?"

"To have faith in the One God, Galdar," said Mina, and with that, he had to be content, for she would say no more.

Odila was also worried about the future, worried and confused and distraught. Ever since the souls had built the totem and she had recognized the One God as Queen Takhisis, Odila had felt very much like one of the living dead mages. Her body ate and drank and walked and performed its duties, but she was absent from that body. She seemed to stand apart, staring at it uncaring, while mentally she groped in the storm-ridden darkness of her soul for answers, for understanding.

She could not bring herself to pray to the One God. Not any longer. Not since she knew who and what the One God was. Yet, she missed her prayers. She missed the sweet solace of giving her life into the hands of Another, some Wise Being who would guide Odila's steps and lead her away from pain to blissful peace. The One God had guided Odila's steps but not to peace. The One God had led her to turmoil and fear and dismay.

More than once Odila clasped the medallion at her throat and was prepared to rip it off. Every time her fingers closed around the medallion, she felt the metal's warmth. She remembered the power of the One God that had flowed through her veins, the power to halt those who had wanted to slay the elven king. Her hand fell away, fell limp at her side. One morning, watching the sun's red rays give a sullen glow to the clouds that hung perpetually over the Lords of Doom, Odila decided to put her faith to the test.

Odila knelt before the altar that was near the totem of dragon skulls. The room smelled of death and decay and warm, melting wax. The heat of the candles was a contrast to the cold draught that blew in from the gaping hole in the roof, whistled eerily through the teeth of the skulls. Sweat from the heat chilled on Odila's body. She wanted very much to flee this terrible place, but the medallion was warm against her cold skin.

"Queen Takhisis, help me," she prayed, and she could not repress a shudder at speaking that name. "I have been taught all my life that you are a cruel god who has no care for any living being, who sees us all as slaves meant to obey your commands. I have been taught that you are ambitious and self-serving, that you mock and denigrate those principles that I hold dear: honor, compassion, mercy, love. Because of what you are, I should not believe in you, I should not serve you. And yet . . ."

Odila lifted her eyes, gazed up into the heavens. "You are a god. I have witnessed your power. I have felt it thrill inside me. How can I choose *not* to believe in you? Perhaps . . ." Odila hesitated, uncertain. "Perhaps you have been maligned. Misjudged. Perhaps you *do* care for us. I ask this not for myself, but for someone who has served you faithfully and loyally. Mina faces terrible danger. I am certain that she intends to try to fight Malys alone. She has faith that you will fight at her side. She has put her trust in you. I fear for her, Queen Takhisis. Show me that my fears are unfounded and that you care for her, if you care for no one else."

She waited tensely, but no voice spoke. No vision came. The candle flames wavered in the chill wind that flowed through the altar room. The bodies of the mages sat upon their benches, staring unblinking into the flames. Yet, Odila's heart lightened, her burden of doubt eased. She did not know why and was pondering this when she became aware of someone standing near the altar.

Her eyes dazzled by the bright light of hundreds of candles, she couldn't see who was there.

"Galdar?" she said, at last making out the minotaur's hulking form. "I didn't hear you or see you enter. I was preoccupied with my prayers."

She wondered uneasily if he had overheard her, if he was going to berate her for her lack of faith.

He said nothing, just stood there.

"Is there something you want from me, Galdar?" Odila asked. He'd never wanted anything of her before, had always seemed to distrust and resent her.

"I want you to see this," he said.

In his hands, he carried an object bound in strips of linen, tied up with rope. The linen had once been white, but was now so stained by water and mud, grass and dirt that the color was a dull and dingy brown. The ropes had been cut, the cloth removed, but both appeared to have been clumsily replaced.

Galdar placed the object on the altar. It was long and did not seem particularly heavy. The cloth concealed whatever was inside.

"This came for Mina," he continued. "Captain Samuval sent it. Unwrap it. Look inside."

Odila did not touch it. "If it is a gift for Mina, it is not for me to—"

"Open it!" ordered Galdar, his voice harsh. "I want to know if it is suitable."

Odila might have continued to refuse, but she was certain now that Galdar had heard her prayer, and she feared that unless she agreed to this, he might tell Mina. Gingerly, her fingers trembling from her nervousness, Odila tugged at the knots, removed the strips of cloth. She was unpleasantly reminded of the winding cloths used to bind the bodies of the dead.

Her wonder grew as she saw what lay beneath, her wonder and her awe.

"Is it what Samuval claims it to be?" Galdar demanded. "Is it a dragonlance?"

Odila nodded wordlessly, unable to speak.

"Are you certain? Have you ever seen one before?" Galdar asked.

"No, I haven't," she admitted, finding her voice. "But I have heard stories of the fabled lances from the time I was a little girl. I always loved those stories. They led me to become a Knight."

Odila reached out her hand, ran her fingers along the cold, smooth metal. The lance gleamed with a silver radiance that seemed apart and separate from the yellow flames of the candles.

If all the lights in the universe were snuffed out, Odila thought, even the light of sun and moon and stars, the light of this lance would still shine bright.

"Where did Captain Samuval find such a treasure?" she asked.

"In some old tomb somewhere," said Galdar. "Solace, I think."

"Not the Tomb of the Heroes?" Odila gasped.

Snatching her hand back from the lance, she stared at Galdar in horror.

"I don't know," said Galdar, shrugging. "He didn't say what the tomb was called. He said the tomb brought him bad luck, for when the locals caught him and his men inside, they attacked in such numbers that he barely escaped with his life. He was even set upon by a mob of kender. This was one of the treasures he managed to bring along with him. He sent it to Mina with his regards and respect."

Odila sighed and looked back at the lance.

"He stole it from the dead," said Galdar, frowning. "He said himself it was bad luck. I do not think we should give it to Mina."

Before Odila could answer, another voice spoke from out of the darkness.

"Do the dead have need of this lance anymore, Galdar?"

"No, Mina," he said, turning to face her. "They do not."

The light of the lance shone bright in Mina's amber eyes. She took hold of it, her hand closing over it. Odila flinched when she saw Mina touch it, for there were some who claimed that the fabled dragonlances could be used only by those who fought on the side of light and that any others who touched them would be punished by the gods.

Mina's hand grasped the lance firmly. She lifted the lance from the altar, hefted it, regarded it with admiration.

"A lovely weapon," she said. "It seems almost to have been made for me." Her gaze turned to Odila. The amber eyes were warm as the medallion around Odila's throat. "An answer to a prayer."

Placing the lance upon the altar, Mina reverently knelt before it.

"We will thank the One God for this great blessing."

Galdar remained standing, looking stern. Odila sank down before the altar. Tears flowed down Odila's cheeks. She was grateful for Mina's sake that her prayer had been answered. Her tears were not for something found, however, but for something lost. Mina had been able to grip the lance, to lift it from the altar, to hold it in her hand.

Odila looked down at her own hands through her tears. The tips of the fingers that had touched the dragonlance were blistered and burned, and they hurt so that she wondered if she would ever again be free of the pain.

17 THE VOLUNTEER

Light had come again to Sanction. Night was always a relief to the inhabitants, for it meant that they'd survived another day. Night brought Mina out to speak them of the One God, speeches in which she lent them some of her courage, for when in her presence they were emboldened and ready for battle against the dragon overlord.

Having lived for centuries within the shadows of the Lords of Doom, the city of Sanction was essentially fireproof. Buildings were made of stone, including the roofs, for any other material, such as thatch, would have long ago burned away. True, it was said that the breath of dragons had the power to melt granite, but there was no defense against that, except to hope desperately that whoever spread the rumor was exaggerating.

Every soldier was being hastily trained in archery, for with a target this large, even the rankest amateur could hardly miss. They hauled catapults up onto the wall, hoping to fling boulders at Malys, and they trained their ballistae to shoot into the sky. These tasks accomplished, they felt they were ready, and some of the boldest called upon Malys to come and have done with it. Still, all were relieved when night fell and they'd lived through another day, never mind that dread came again with morning.

The blue dragon Razor, still forced to rove about Sanction in human guise, watched the preparations with the keen interest of a veteran soldier and told Mirror about them in detail, adding his own disapproval or approval, whichever seemed warranted. Mirror was more interested in the totem, in what it looked like, where it was positioned in the city. Razor had been supposed to reconnoiter, but he'd been wasting time among the soldiers.

"I know what you're thinking," Razor said suddenly, stopping himself in the midst of describing the precise workings of a catapult. "You're thinking that none of this will make any difference. None will have any effect on that great, red bitch. Well, you're right. And," he added, "you're wrong."

"How am I wrong?" Mirror asked. "Cities have used catapults before to defend against Malys. They've used archers and arrows, heroes and fools, and none have survived."

"But they have never had a god on their side," stated Razor.

Mirror tensed. A silver dragon, loyal to Paladine, he had long feared that Razor would revert to his old loyalties, to Queen Takhisis. Mirror had to proceed carefully. "So you are saying we should abandon our plan to help Palin destroy the totem?"

"Not necessarily," said Razor evasively. "Perhaps, reconsider, that is all. Where are you going?"

"To the temple," said Mirror. Shrugging off Razor's guiding hand, the blind silver dragon in human guise started off on his own, tapping his way with his staff. "To view the totem for myself, since you will not be my eyes."

"This is madness!" Razor protested, following after him with his fake limp. Mirror could hear the pounding of the crutch on the bricks. "You said before that Mina saw you in your beggar form on the road and immediately recognized you as the guardian of the Citadel of Light. She knows you by sight, both as a human and in your true form."

Mirror began to rearrange the bandages he wore wrapped about his damaged eyes, tugging them down so that they covered his face.

"It is a risk I must take. Especially if you are wavering in your decision."

Razor said nothing. Mirror could no longer hear the crutch thumping along beside him and assumed that he was going alone. He had only the vaguest idea where the temple was located. He knew only that it was on a hill overlooking the city.

So, he calculated, if I walk uphill, I am bound to find it.

He was startled to hear Razor's rasping breath in his ear. "Wait, stop. You've blundered into a cul-de-sac. I'll guide you, if you insist on going."

"Will you help me destroy the totem?" Mirror demanded.

"That I must think about," said Razor. "If we are going, we should go now, for the temple is most likely to be empty."

The two wended their way through the mazelike streets. Mirror was thankful for Razor's guidance, for the blind silver could have never found his way on his own.

What will Palin and I do if Razor decides to shift his allegiance? Mirror wondered. A blind dragon and a dead wizard out to defeat a goddess. Well, if nothing else, maybe Takhisis will get a bellyache from laughing.

The noise made by the crowds told Mirror they were close to the temple. And there was Mina, telling them of the wonders and magnificence of the One God. She was persuasive, Mirror had to admit. He had always liked Mina's voice. Even as a child, her tone had been mellow and low and sweet to hear.

As he listened, he was taken back to those days in the Citadel, watching Mina and Goldmoon together—the elderly woman in the sunset of her life, the child bright with the dawn. Now Mirror could not see Mina for the darkness, and not the darkness of his own blind eyes.

Razor led him past the crowd. The two proceeded quietly, not to draw attention to themselves, and entered the ruined temple that now stood as a monument to the dragon skull totem.

"Are we alone?" Mirror asked.

"The bodies of the two wizards sit in a corner."

"Tell me about them," said Mirror, his heart aching. "What are they like?"

"Like corpses propped up at their own funerals," said Razor dourly. "That is all I will say. Be thankful you cannot see them."

"What of their spirits?"

"I see no signs of them. All to the good. I have no use for wizards, living or dead. We don't need their meddling. Here, now. You stand before the totem. You can reach out and touch the skulls, if you want."

Mirror had no intention of touching anything. He had no need to be told he stood before the totem. Its magic was powerful, potent—the magic of a god. Mirror was both drawn to it and repelled by it.

"What does the totem look like?" he asked softly.

"The skulls of our brethren, stacked one on top of the other in a grotesque pyramid," Razor answered. "The skulls of the larger support the smaller. The eyes of the dead burn in the sockets. Somewhere in that pile is the skull of my mate. I can feel the fire of her life blaze in the darkness."

"And I feel the god's power residing within the totem," said Mirror. "Palin was right. This is the doorway. This is the Portal through which Takhisis will walk into the world at last."

"I say, let her," said Razor. "Now that I see this, I say let Takhisis come, if her help is needed to slay Malystryx."

Mirror could smell the flickering candles, if he could not see them. He could feel their heat. He could feel, as Razor felt, the heat of his own anger and his longing for revenge. Mirror had his own reasons for hating Malys. She had destroyed Kendermore, killed Goldmoon's dearly loved husband Riverwind and their daughter. Malys had murdered hundreds of people and displaced thousands more, driving them from their homes, terrorizing them as they fled for her own cruel amusement. Standing before the totem that Malys had built of the bones of those she had devoured, Mirror began to wonder if Razor might not be right.

Razor leaned near, whispered in his ear. "Takhisis has her faults, I admit that freely. But she is a god, and she is our god, of our world, and she's all we've got. You have to concede that."

Mirror conceded nothing.

"You can't see them," Razor continued relentlessly, "but there are the skulls of silver dragons in that totem. A good many of them. Don't you want to avenge their deaths?"

"I don't need to see them," said Mirror. "I hear their voices. I hear their death cries, every one of them. I hear the cries of their mates who loved them and the cries of the children who will never be born to them. My hatred for Malys is as strong as yours. To rid the world of this terrible scourge, you say I must choke down the bitter medicine of Takhisis's triumph."

Razor shrugged. "She is our god," he repeated. "Of our world."

A terrible choice. Mirror sat on the hard bench, trying to decide what to do. Lost in his thoughts, he forgot where he was, forgot he was in the camp of his enemies. Razor's elbow dug into his side.

"We have company," the blue warned softly.

"Who is it? Mina?" Mirror asked.

"No, the minotaur who is never far from her side. I told you this was a bad idea. No, don't move. It's too late now. We're in the shadows. Perhaps they won't take notice of us. Besides," the Blue added coolly, "we might learn something."

Indeed, Galdar did not notice the two beggars as he entered the altar room. At least, not immediately. He was preoccupied with his own worries. Galdar knew Mina's plan, or he thought he did. He hoped he was wrong, but his hope wasn't very strong, probably because he knew Mina so well.

Knew Mina and loved her.

All his life, Galdar had heard legends of a famous minotaur hero known as Kaz, who had been a friend of the famous Solamnic hero, Huma. Kaz had ridden with Huma in his battle against Queen Takhisis. The minotaur had risked his life for Huma many times, and Kaz's grief at Huma's death had been lifelong. Although Kaz had been on the wrong side of the war, as far as the minotaur were concerned, he was honored among his people to this day for his courage and valor in warfare. A minotaur admires a valiant warrior no matter which side he fights on.

As for his friendship with a human, few minotaurs could understand that. True, Huma had been a valiant warrior—for a human. Always that qualification was added. In minotaur legends, Kaz was the hero, saving Huma's life time and again, at the end of which, Huma is always humbly grateful to the gallant minotaur, who accepts the human's thanks with patronizing dignity.

Galdar had always believed these legends, but now he was starting to think differently. Perhaps, in truth, Kaz had fought with Huma because he loved Huma, just as Galdar loved Mina. There was something about these humans. They wormed their way into your heart.

Their puny bodies were so frail and fragile, and yet they could be tough and enduring as the last hero standing in the bloodstained arena of the minotaur circus.

They never knew when they were defeated, these humans, but fought on when they should have laid down and died. They led such pitifully short lives, but they were always ready to throw away these lives for a cause or a belief, or doing something as foolish and noble as rushing into a burning tower to save the life of a total stranger.

Minotaurs have their share of courage, but they are more cautious, always counting the cost before spending their coin. Galdar knew what Mina planned, and he loved her for it, even as his heart ached to think of it. Kneeling beside the altar, he vowed that she would not go into battle alone if there was any way he could stop her. He did not pray to the One God. Galdar no longer prayed to the One God, ever since he'd found out who she was. He never said a word to Mina about this—he would take his secret to the grave with him—but he would not pray to Queen Takhisis, a goddess whom he considered treacherous and completely without honor. The vow he made, he made within himself.

His prayer concluded, he rose stiffly from the altar. Outside, he could hear Mina telling the admiring crowds that they had no need to fear Malys. The One God would surely save them. Galdar had heard it all before. He no longer heard it now. He heard Mina's voice, her loved voice, but that was all. He guessed that was all most of those listening heard.

Galdar fidgeted near the altar, waiting for Mina, and it was then he saw the beggars. The altar room was crowded during the day, for the inhabitants of Sanction, mostly soldiers, came to make offerings to the One God or to gape at the totem or to try to catch a glimpse of Mina and touch her or beg her blessing. At night, they went to hear her, to hide themselves beneath the blanket of her courage. After that, they went to their posts or to their beds. Few worshipers came to the altar room at night, one reason Galdar was here.

This night, a blind man and a lame beggar sat on a bench near the altar. Galdar had no use for mendicants. No minotaur does. A minotaur would starve to death before he would dream of begging for even a crust. Galdar could not imagine what these two were doing in Sanction and wondered why they hadn't fled, as had many of their kind.

He eyed them more closely. There was something about them that made them different from other beggars. He couldn't quite think what it was—a quiet confidence, capability. He had the feeling that these were no ordinary beggars and he was about to ask them a few questions when Mina returned.

She was exalted, god-touched. Her amber eyes shone. Approaching the altar, she sank down, almost too tired to stand, for during these public meetings, she poured forth her whole soul, giving everything to those who listened, leaving nothing for herself. Galdar forgot the strange beggars, went immediately to Mina.

"Let me bring you some wine, something to eat," he offered.

"No, Galdar, I need nothing, thank you," Mina replied. She sighed deeply. She looked exhausted.

Clasping her hands, she said a prayer to the One God, giving thanks. Then, appearing refreshed and renewed, she rose to her feet. "I am only a little tired, that is all. There was a great crowd tonight. The One God is gaining many followers."

They follow you, Mina, not the One God, Galdar might have said to her, but he kept silent. He had said such things to her in the past, and she had been extremely angry. He did not want to risk her ire, not now.

"You have something to say to me, Galdar?" Mina asked. She reached out to remove a candle whose wick had been drowned in molten wax.

Galdar arranged his thoughts. He had to say this carefully, for he did not want to offend her.

"Speak what is in your heart," she urged. "You have been troubled for a long time. Ease your burden by allowing me to share it."

"You are my burden, Mina," said Galdar, deciding to do as she said and open his heart. "I know how you plan to fight Malys on dragonback. You have the dragonlance, and I assume that the One God will provide you with a dragon. You plan to go up alone to face her. I cannot allow you to do that, Mina. I know what you are about to say." He raised his hand, to forestall her protest. "You will not be alone. You will have the One God to fight at your side. But let there be another at your side, Mina. Let me be at your side."

"I have been practicing with the lance," Mina said. Opening her hand, she exhibited her palm, that was red and blistered. "I can hit the bull's-eye nine times out of ten."

"Hitting a target that stands still is much different from hitting a moving dragon," Galdar growled. "Two dragonriders are most effective in fighting aerial battles, one to the keep the dragon occupied from the front while the other attacks from the rear. You must see the wisdom in this?"

"I do, Galdar," said Mina. "True, I have been studying the combat in my mind, and I know that two riders would be good." She smiled, an impish smile that reminded him of how young she was. "A thousand riders would be even better, Galdar, don't you think?"

He said nothing, scowled at the flames. He knew where she was leading him, and he could not stop her from going there.

"A thousand would be better, but where would we find these thousand? Men or dragons?" Mina gestured to the totem. "Do you remember all the dragons who celebrated when the One God consecrated this totem? Do you remember them circling the totem and singing anthems to the One God? Do you remember, Galdar?"

"I remember."

"Where are they now? Where are the Reds and the Greens, the Blues and the Blacks? Gone. Fled. Hiding. They fear I will ask them to fly against Malys. And I can't blame them."

"Bah! They are all cowards," said Galdar.

He heard a sound behind him and glanced around. He'd forgotten the beggars. He eyed them closely, but if either of them had spoken neither seemed inclined to do so now. The lame beggar stared down at the floor. As for the blind beggar, his face was so swathed in bandages that it was difficult to tell if he had a mouth, much less whether he had used it. The only other two beings in the room were the wizards, and Galdar had no need to look at them. They never moved unless someone prodded them.

"I'll make you a bargain, Galdar," Mina said. "If you can find a dragon who will voluntarily carry you into battle, you can fly at my side."

Galdar grunted. "You know that is impossible, Mina."

"Nothing is impossible for the One God, Galdar," Mina told him, gently rebuking. She knelt down again before the altar, clasped her hands. Glancing up at Galdar, she added, "Join me in my prayers."

"I have already made my prayer, Mina," said Galdar heavily. "I have duties to attend to. Try to get some rest, will you?"

"I will," she said. "Tomorrow will be a momentous day."

Galdar looked at her, startled. "Will Malys come tomorrow, Mina?"

"She will come tomorrow."

Galdar sighed and walked out into the night. The night may bring comfort to others but not to him. The night brought only morning.

Mirror felt Razor's human body shift restlessly on the bench beside him. Mirror sat with his head lowered, taking care that Mina did not see him, although he suspected he could have leaped up and done a dance with bells and tambour and she would have been oblivious to him. She was with her One God. For now, she had no care or concern for what transpired on this mortal plane. Still, Mirror kept his head down.

He was troubled and at the same time relieved. Perhaps this was the answer.

"You would like to be the dragon that Galdar seeks, is that right?" Mirror asked in a quiet undertone.

"I would," Razor said.

"You know the risk you take," said Mirror. "Malys's weapons are formidable. Fear of her alone drove a nation of kender mad, so it is claimed by the wise. Her flaming breath is said to be hotter than the fires of the Lords of the Doom."

"I know all this," Razor returned, "and more. The minotaur will find no other dragon. Craven cowards, all of them. No discipline. No training. Not like the old days."

Mirror smiled, thankful that his smile was hidden beneath the bandages.

"Go, then," he said. "Go after the minotaur and tell him that you will fight by his side."

Razor was silent. Mirror could feel his astonishment.

"I cannot leave you," Razor said, after a pause. "What would you do without me?"

"I will manage. Your impulse is brave, noble, and generous. Such weapons are our strongest weapons against her." By *her*, Mirror did not mean Malys, but he saw no reason to clarify his pronoun.

"Are you certain?" Razor asked, clearly tempted. "You will have no one to guard you, protect you."

"I am not a hatchling," Mirror retorted. "I may not be able to see, but lack of sight does not hamper my magic. You have done your part and more. I am glad to have known you, Razor, and I honor you for your decision. You had best go after the minotaur. You two will need to make plans, and you will not have much time to make them."

Razor rose to his feet. Mirror could hear him, feel him moving at his side. The Blue's hand rested on Mirror's shoulder, perhaps for the last time.

"I have always hated your kind, Silver. I am sorry for that, for I have discovered that we have more in common than I realized."

"We are dragons," said Mirror simply. "Dragons of Krynn."

"Yes," said Razor. "If only we had remembered that sooner."

The hand lifted. Its warm pressure gone, Mirror felt the lack. He heard footsteps walking swiftly away, and he smiled and shook his head. Reaching out his hand, groping about, he found Razor's crutch, tossed aside.

"Another miracle for the One God," said Mirror wryly. Taking the crutch, he secreted it beneath the bench.

As he did so, Mina's voice rose.

"Be with me, my god," she prayed fervently, "and lead me and all who fight with me to glorious victory against this evil foe."

"How can I refuse to echo that prayer?" Mirror asked himself silently. "We are dragons of Krynn, and though we fought against her, Takhisis was our goddess. How can I do what Palin asks of me? Especially now that I am alone."

Galdar made the rounds, checking on the city's defenses and the state of Sanction's defenders. He found all as he expected. The defenses were as good as they were going to get, and the defenders were nervous and gloomy. Galdar said what he could to raise their spirits, but he wasn't Mina. He couldn't lift their hearts, especially when his own was crawling in the dust.

Brave words he'd spoken to Mina about fighting at her side against Malys. Brave words, when he knew perfectly well that when Malys came he'd be among those watching helplessly from the ground. Tilting his head, he scanned the skies. The night air was clear, except for the perpetual cloud that roiled out of the Lords of Doom.

"How I would love to astonish her," he said to the stars. "How I long to be there with her."

But he was asking the impossible. Asking a miracle of a goddess he didn't like, didn't trust, couldn't pray to.

So preoccupied was Galdar that it took him some time—longer than it should have—for him to realize he was being followed. This was such a strange occurrence that he was momentarily taken aback. Who could be following him and why? He would have suspected Gerard, but the Solamnic Knight had left Sanction long ago, was probably even now urging the Knights to rise up against them. Everyone else in Sanction, including the Solamnic female, was loyal to Mina. He wondered, suddenly, if Mina was having him followed, if she no longer trusted him. The thought made him sick to his stomach. He determined to know the truth.

Muttering aloud something about needing fresh air, Galdar headed for the temple gardens that would be dark and quiet and secluded this time of night.

Whoever was following him either wasn't very good at it or wanted Galdar to notice him. The footfalls were not stealthy, not padded, as would be those of a thief or assassin. They had a martial ring to them—bold, measured, firm.

Reaching a wooded area, Galdar stepped swiftly to one side, concealed himself behind the bole of a large tree. The footsteps came to a halt. Galdar was certain that the person must have lost him, was astonished beyond measure to see the man walk right up to him.

The man raised his hand, saluted.

Galdar started instinctively to return the salute. He halted, glowering, and rested his hand on his sword's hilt.

"What do you want? Why do you sneak after me like a thief?" Peering more closely at the person, Galdar recognized him and was disgusted. "You filthy beggar! Get away from me, scum. I have no money—"

The minotaur paused. His gaze narrowed. His hand tightened its grasp on the hilt, half-drew the sword from its sheath. "Weren't you lame before? Where is your crutch?"

"I left it behind," said the beggar, "because I no longer need it. I want nothing of you, sir," he added, his tone respectful. "I have something to give you."

"Whatever it is, I don't want it. I have no use for your kind. Begone and trouble me no more or I'll have you thrown in prison." Galdar reached out his hand, intending to shove the man aside.

The night shadows began to shimmer and distort. Tree branches cracked. Leaves and twigs and small limbs rained down around him. Galdar's hand touched a surface hard and solid as armor, but this armor wasn't cold steel. It was warm, living.

Gasping, Galdar staggered backward, lifted his astounded gaze. His eyes met the eyes of a blue dragon.

Galdar stammered something, he wasn't sure what.

The blue dragon drew in a huge breath and expelled it in satisfaction and immense relief. Fanning his wings, he luxuriated in a stretch and sighed again. "How I hate that cramped human form."

"Where . . . ? What . . . ?" Galdar continued to stammer.

"Irrelevant," said the dragon. "My name is Razor. I happened to overhear your conversation with your commander in the temple. She said that if you could find a dragon that would carry you into battle against Malys, you could fight at her side. If you truly meant what you said, warrior; if you have the courage of your convictions, then I will be your mount."

"I meant what I said," Galdar growled, still trying to recover from the shock. "But why would you do this? All your brethren have fled, and they are the sensible ones."

"I am"—the dragon paused, corrected himself with grave dignity—"I *was* the dragon attached to Marshal Medan. Did you know him?"

"I did," said Galdar. "I met him when he came to visit Lord Targonne in Jelek. I was impressed. He was a man of sense, a man of courage and of honor. A valiant Knight of the old school."

"Then you know why I do this," said Razor, with a proud toss of his head. "I fight in his name, in his memory. Let's be clear about that from the outset."

"I accept your offer, Razor," said Galdar, joy filling his soul. "I fight for the glory of my commander. You fight for the memory of yours. We will make this battle one of which they will sing for centuries!"

"I was never much for singing," said Razor dourly. "Neither was the Marshal. So long as we kill that red monstrosity, that is all I care about. When do you think she will attack us?"

"Mina says tomorrow," said Galdar.

"Then tomorrow I will be ready," said Razor.

18 DAY'S DAWNING

A tremor shook the city of Sanction in the early hours before the dawn. The rippling ground dumped sleepers from their beds, sent the crockery spilling to floor, and set all the dogs in the city to barking. The quake jarred nerves that were already taut.

Almost before the ground had ceased to tremble, crowds began to gather outside the temple. Although no official word had been given or orders gone out, rumors had spread, and by now every soldier and Knight in Sanction knew that this was the day Malys would attack. Those not on duty (and even some who were) left their billets and their posts and flocked to the temple. They came out of a hunger to see Mina and hear her voice, hear her reassurance that all would be well, that victory would be theirs this day.

As the sun lifted over the mountains, Mina emerged from the temple. Customarily at her appearance a resounding cheer went up from the crowd. Not this day. Everyone stared, hushed and awed.

Mina was clad in glistening armor black as the frozen seas. The helm she wore was horned, the visor black, rimed with gold. On the breastplate was etched the image of a five-headed dragon. As the first rays of the sun struck the armor, the dragon began to shimmer eerily, shifting colors, so that some who saw it thought it was red, while others thought it was blue, and still others swore it was green.

Some in the audience whispered in excited voices that this was armor once worn by the Dragon Highlords, who had fought for Takhisis during the fabled War of the Lance.

In her gloved hand, Mina held a weapon whose metal burned like flame as it caught the rays of the rising sun. She lifted the weapon high above her head in a gesture of triumph.

At this, the crowd raised a cheer. They cheered long and loud, crying, "Mina, Mina!" The cheers rebounded off the mountains and thundered over the plains, shaking the ground like another tremor.

Mina knelt upon one knee, the lance in her hand. The cheering ceased as people joined her in prayer, some calling upon the One God, many more calling upon Mina.

Rising to her feet, Mina turned to face the totem. She handed the lance to a priestess of the One God, who stood beside her. The priestess was clad in white robes, and whispers went about that she was a former Solamnic Knight who had prayed to the One God and been given the dragonlance, which she had in turn given to Mina. The Solamnic held the lance steady, but her face was contorted by pain, and she often bit her lip as if to keep from crying out.

Mina placed her hands upon two of the enormous dragon skulls that formed the totem's base. She cried out words that no one could understand, then stepped back and raised her arms to the heavens.

A being rose from the totem. The being had the shape and form of an enormous dragon, and those standing near the totem tumbled back in terror.

The dragon's brown-colored scaly skin stretched taut over its skull, neck, and body. The skeleton could be seen clearly through the parchmentlike skin: the round disks of the neck and spine, the large bones of the massive rib cage, the thick and heavy bones of the gigantic legs, the more delicate bones of the wings and tail and feet. Sinews were visible and tendons that held the bones together. Missing were the heart and blood vessels, for magic was the blood of this dragon, vengeance and hatred formed the beating heart. The dragon was a mummified dragon, a corpse.

The wing membranes were dried and tough as leather, their span massive. The shadow of the wings spread over Sanction, doused the rays of the sun, turned dawning day to sudden night.

So horrible and loathsome was the sight of the putrid corpse hanging over their heads that the cheers for Mina died, strangled, in the throats of those who had raised them. The stench of death flowed from the creature, and with the stench came despair that was worse than the dragonfear, for fear can act as a spur to courage, while despair drains the heart of hope. Most could not bear to look at it, but lowered their heads, envisioning their own deaths, all of which were pain-filled and terrifying.

Hearing their cries, Mina took pity on them and gave to them from her own strength.

She began to sing, the same song they'd heard many times, but now with new meaning.

The gathering darkness takes our souls,
Embracing us in chilling folds,

Deep in a Mistress's void that holds
Our fate within her hands.

Dream, warriors, of the dark above
And feel the sweet redemption of
The Night's Consort, and of her love
For those within her bands.

Her song helped quell their fears, eased their despair. The soldiers called her name again, vowed that they would make her proud of them. Dismissing them, she sent them to do their duties with courage and with faith in the One God. The crowd left, Mina's name on their lips.

Mina turned to the priestess, who had been holding the lance all this time. Mina took the lance from her.

Odila snatched her hand away, hid her hand behind her back.

Mina raised the visor of her helm. "Let me see," she said.

"No, Mina," Odila mumbled, blinking back tears. "I would not burden you—"

Mina grabbed hold of Odila's hand, brought it forth to the light. The palm was bloodied and blackened, as if it had been thrust into a pit of fire.

Holding Odila's hand, Mina pressed her lips to it. The flesh healed, though the wound left terrible scars. Odila kissed Mina and bade her good fortune in a soundless voice.

Holding the lance, Mina looked up to the death dragon. "I am ready," she said.

The image of an immortal hand reached out of the totem. Mina stepped upon the palm and the hand lifted her gently from the ground, carried her safely through the air. The hand of the goddess raised her higher than the treetops, higher than the skulls of the dragons stacked one atop the other. The hand halted at the side of the death dragon. Mina stepped off the hand, mounted the dragon's back. The corpse had no saddle, no reins that anyone could see.

Another dragon appeared on the eastern horizon, speeding toward Sanction. People cried out in fear, thinking that this must be Malys. Mina sat astride the death dragon, watched and waited.

As the dragon came in sight, cries of fear changed to wild cheering. The name "Galdar" flew from mouth to mouth. His horned head, silhouetted against the rising sun, was unmistakable.

Galdar held in his hand an enormous pike of the kind usually thrust into the ground to protect against cavalry charges. The pike's heavy weight was nothing to him. He wielded it with as much ease as Mina wielded the slender dragon-lance. In his other hand, he held the reins of his mount, the blue dragon, Razor.

Galdar lifted the pike and shook it in defiance, then raised his voice and gave a mighty roar, a minotaur battle cry. An ancient cry, the words called upon the god Sargas to fight at the warrior's side, to take his body if he fell in the fray, and to smite him if he faltered. Galdar had no idea where the words came from as he shouted them. He supposed he must have heard this cry when he was a child. He was astonished to hear the words come from his mouth, but they were appropriate, and he was pleased with them.

Mina raised her visor to greet him. Her skin, in stark contrast to the black of the helm, was bone white. Her eyes shone with her own excitement. He saw himself in the amber mirror, and for the first time he was not a bug trapped in their molten gold. He was himself, her friend, her loyal comrade. He could have wept. Perhaps he did weep. If so, his battle lust burned away the tears before they could shame him.

"You will not go alone into battle this day, Mina!" Galdar roared.

"The sight of you gladdens my heart, Galdar," Mina shouted. "This is a miracle of the One God. It is among the first we will see this day, but not the last."

The blue dragon bared his teeth, a sparkle of lightning flickered from his clenched jaws.

Perhaps Mina was right. Truly, this did feel miraculous to Galdar, as wonderful a miracle as the tales of heroes of old.

Mina lowered her visor. A touch of her hand upon the corpse dragon caused it to lift its head, spread its wings, and soar into the sky, carrying her high above the clouds. The Blue glanced back at Galdar to ascertain his orders. Galdar indicated they were to follow.

The city of Sanction dwindled in size. The people were tiny black dots, then they disappeared. Higher the Blue climbed into the cold, clear air, and the world itself grew small beneath him. All was quiet, profoundly quiet and peaceful. Galdar could hear only the creak of the dragon's wings, then even that stopped as the beast took advantage of a thermal to soar effortlessly among the clouds.

All sounds of the world ceased, so that it seemed to Galdar that he and Mina were the only two left in it.

On the ground below, the people watched until they could no longer catch sight of Mina. Many still continued to watch, staring into the sky until their necks ached and their eyes burned. Officers began shouting orders, and the crowd started to disperse. Those on duty went to their posts, to take up positions on the walls. A vast number of people continued to crowd around the temple, talking excitedly of what they had seen, speaking of Malys's easy defeat and how from this day forth Mina and the Knights of the One God would be the rulers of Ansalon.

Mirror lingered near the totem, waiting for Palin's spirit to join him. The Silver did not wait long.

"Where is the blue dragon?" Palin asked immediately, alarmed by his absence.

Palin's words came to the Silver clearly, so clearly that Mirror could almost believe they were spoken by the living, except that they had a strange feel to them, a spidery feel that brushed across his skin.

"You have only to look in the sky above you to see where Razor has gone," said Mirror. "He fights his own battle in his own way. He leaves us to fight ours—whatever that may be."

"What do you mean? Are you having second thoughts?"

"That is the nature of dragons," said Mirror. "We do not rush into things headlong like you humans. Yes, I have been having second thoughts and third and fourth thoughts as well."

"This is nothing to joke about," said Palin.

"Too true," said Mirror. "Have you considered the consequences of your proposed actions? Do you know what destroying the totem will do? Especially destroying it as Malys attacks?"

"I know that this is the only opportunity we will have to destroy the totem," said Palin. "Takhisis has all her attention focused on Malys, as does everyone else in Sanction. If we miss this chance, we will not have another."

"What if, in destroying the totem, we give the victory to Malys?"

"Malys is mortal. She will not live forever. Takhisis will. I admit," Palin continued, "that I do not know what will be the consequences of the destruction of the totem. But I do know this. Every day, every hour, every second I am surrounded by the souls of the dead of Krynn. Their numbers are countless. Their torment is unspeakable, for they are driven by a hunger that can never be assuaged. She makes them promises she has no intention of keeping, and they know this, and yet they do her bidding in the pitiful hope that one day she will free them. That day will never come, Mirror. You know that, and I know it. If there is a chance that the totem's destruction will stop her from entering the world, then that is a chance we must take."

"Even if it means that we are all burned alive by Malys?" Mirror asked.

"Even if it means that," said Palin.

"Leave me a while," said Mirror. "I need to think this over."

"Do not think too long," Palin cautioned. "For while dragons think, the world moves under them."

Mirror stood alone, wrestling with his problem. Palin's words were meant to remind Mirror of the old days when the dragons of light lay complacent and sleepy in their lairs, ignoring the wars raging in the world. The dragons of light spoke smugly and learnedly of evil: evil destroys its own, good redeems its own, they said. Thus they spoke and thus they had slept and thus the Dark Queen stole their eggs and destroyed their children.

The wind shifted, blowing from the west. Mirror sniffed, caught the scent of blood and brimstone, faint, but distinct.

Malys.

She was far distant still, but she was coming.

Locked in his prison house of darkness, he heard the people around him talking glibly of the approaching battle. He could find it in his heart to pity them. They had no idea of the horror that was winging toward them. No idea at all.

Mirror groped his way past the totem, heading for the temple. He moved slowly, forced to tap out a clear path with his staff, bumping it into people's shins, knocking against trees, stumbling off the path and bumbling into flower gardens. The soldiers swore at him. Someone kicked him. He kept the rising sun on his left cheek and knew he was heading in the direction of the temple, but he should have reached it by now. He feared that he had veered off course. For all he knew, he could be headed up the mountain—or off it.

He cursed his own helplessness and came to a standstill, listening for voices and the clues they might give. Then a hand touched his outstretched hand.

"Sir, you appear to be lost and confused. Can I be of aid?"

The voice was a woman's, and it had a muffled, choked sound to it, as though she had been weeping. Her touch on his hand was firm and strong, he was startled to feel calluses on her palm, the same that could be felt on the hands of those who wielded a sword. Some female Dark Knight. Odd that she should trouble herself with him. He detected a Solamnic accent, though. Perhaps that was the reason. Old virtues are comfortable, like old clothes, and hard to part with.

"I thank you, Daughter," he said humbly, playing his role of beggar. "If you could lead me into the temple, I seek counsel."

"There we are alike, sir," said the woman. Linking her arm in his, she slowly guided his steps. "For I, too, am troubled."

Mirror could hear the anguish in her voice, feel it in the trembling of her hand.

"A burden shared is a burden halved," he said gently. "I can listen, if I cannot see."

Even as he spoke, he could hear, with his dragon soul, the beating of immense wings. The stench of Malys grew stronger. He had to make his decision.

He should break off this conversation and go about his own urgent business, but he chose not to. The silver dragon had lived long in the world. He did not believe in accidents. This chance meeting was no chance. The woman had been drawn to him out of compassion. He was touched by her sadness and pain.

They entered the Temple. He groped about with his hand, until he found what he sought.

"Stop here," he said.

"We have not reached the altar," said the woman. "What you touch is a sarcophagus. Only a little farther."

"I know," Mirror said, "but I would rather remain here. She was an old friend of mine, you see."

"Goldmoon?" The woman was startled, wary. "A friend of yours?"

"I came a long way to see her," he said.

Palin's voice whispered to him, soft and urgent. "Mirror, what are you doing? You cannot trust this woman. Her name is Odila. She was once a Solamnic Knight, but she has been consumed by darkness."

"A few moments with her. That's all I ask," Mirror replied softly.

"You may take all the time you want with her, sir," said Odila, mistaking his words. "Although the time we have is short before Malys arrives."

"Do you believe in the One God?" Mirror asked.

"Yes," said Odila, defiantly. "Don't you?"

"I believe in Takhisis," said Mirror. "I revere her, but I do not serve her."

"How is that possible?" Odila demanded. "If you believe in Takhisis and revere her, it follows that you must serve her."

"My reply takes the form of a story. Were you with Goldmoon when she died?"

"No," Odila said. Her voice softened. "No one but Mina was with her."

"Yet there were witnesses. A wizard named Palin Majere saw and heard their conversation, during which Takhisis revealed her true nature to Goldmoon. That was a moment of triumph for Takhisis. Goldmoon had long been her bitter enemy. How sweet it must have been for Takhisis to tell Goldmoon that it was she who gave Goldmoon the power of the heart, the power to heal and to build and to create. Takhisis told Goldmoon that this power of the heart stemmed not from the light but from the darkness. Takhisis hoped to convince Goldmoon to follow her. The goddess promised Goldmoon life, youth, beauty. All in return for her service, her worship.

"Goldmoon refused to accept. She refused to worship the goddess who had brought such pain and sorrow to the world. Takhisis was angry. She inflicted on Goldmoon the burden of her years, made her old and feeble and near death. The goddess hoped Goldmoon would die in despair, knowing that Takhisis had won the battle, that she would be the 'one god' for now and forever. Goldmoon's dying words were a prayer."

"To Takhisis?" Odila faltered.

"To Paladine," said Mirror. "A prayer asking for his forgiveness for having lost her faith, a prayer reaffirming her belief."

"But why did she pray to Paladine when she knew he could not answer?" Odila asked.

"Goldmoon did not pray for answers. She knew the answers. She had long carried the truth of his wisdom and his teachings in her soul. Thus, even though she might never again see Paladine or hear his voice or receive his blessings, he was with her, as he had always been. Goldmoon understood that Takhisis had lied. The good that Goldmoon had done came from her heart, and that good could never be claimed by darkness. The miracles would always come from Paladine, because he had never left her. He was always with her, always a part of her."

"It is too late for me," said Odila, despairing. "I am beyond redemption. See? Feel this." Grasping his hand, she placed his fingers on her palm. "Scars. Fresh scars. Made by the blessed dragonlance. I am being punished."

"Who punishes you, Daughter?" Mirror asked gently. "Queen Takhisis? Or the truth that is in your heart?"

Odila had no answer.

Mirror sighed deeply, his own mind at ease. He had his answer. He knew now what he must do.

"I am ready," he said to Palin.

19 MALYS

Galdar and Mina flew together, though not side by side. The blue dragon, Razor, kept his distance from the death dragon. He would not come near the foul corpse, did nothing to hide his disgust. Galdar feared that Mina might be offended by the Blue's reaction, but she did not seem to notice, and he came at last to realize that she saw nothing except the battle that lay ahead. All else, she had shut out of her mind.

As for Galdar, even though he was certain that his own death lay ahead of him, he had never been so happy, never been so much at peace. He thought back to the days when he'd been a one-armed cripple, forced to lick the boots of such scum as his former talon leader, the late and unlamented Ernst Magit. Galdar looked back along the path of time that had brought him to this proud moment, fighting alongside her, the one who had saved him from that bitter fate, the one who had restored his arm and, in so doing, restored his life. If he could give that life for her, to save her, that was all he cared about.

They flew high into the air, higher than Galdar had ever flown on dragon-back before. Fortunately, he was not one of those who are cursed with vertigo. He did not enjoy flying on dragonback—the minotaur has not been born who enjoys it—but he did not fear it. The two dragons soared above the peaks of the Lords of Doom. Galdar looked down, fascinated, to see the fiery red innards of the mountains boiling and bubbling inside deep cavities of rock. The dragons flew in and out of the clouds of steam spewing from the mountains, keeping watch for Malys, hoping to see her first, hoping for the advantage of surprise.

The surprise came, but it was on them. Galdar and Mina and the dragons were keeping watch on the horizon when Mina gave a sudden shout and pointed downward. Malys had used the clouds herself to evade their watchfulness. She was almost directly below them and flying fast for Sanction.

Galdar had seen red dragons before and been awed by their size and their might. The red dragons of Krynn were dwarf dragons, compared to Malystrx. Her massive head could have swallowed him and his Blue in one snap of the jaws. Her talons were large enough to uproot mountains, and sharp as the mountain peaks. Her tail could flatten those peaks, obliterate them, make of them piles of dust. He stared at the dragon in dry-mouthed wonder, his hand clutching the pike so that his fingers ached.

Galdar had a sudden vision of the fire belching from Malys's belly, the dragon-fire that could melt stone, consume flesh and bone in an instant, set the seas to boiling. He was about to order Razor to chase after her, but the dragon was an old campaigner and knew his business, probably better than Galdar. Swift and silent, Razor folded his wings to his sides and dived down upon his foe.

The death dragon matched Razor's speed, then outdid him. Mina lowered her visor. Galdar could not see her face, but he knew her so well that he had no need to. He could envision her: pale, fey. She and the death dragon were far ahead of him now. Galdar cursed and kicked at the Blue as if he were a horse, urging him to keep up. Razor did not feel the minotaur's kicks, nor did he need any urging. He was not going to be left behind.

The dragon flew so fast that the stinging wind brought tears to Galdar's eyes, forced his eyelids shut. Try as he might, he could not keep them open except for quick peeks now and then. Malys was a red blur through the tears that never had a chance to fall, for the wind whipped them away.

Razor did not slacken his speed. Despite the wind in Galdar's eyes, this maddened flight was exhilarating, just as the first wild charge in battle was exhilarating. Galdar gripped his pike, leveled it. The notion came to him that Razor meant to crash headlong into Malys, ram her as one ship rams another, and though that would mean Galdar's death, he had no care about that, no care for himself at all. A strange calm came over him. He had no fear. He wanted to deal death, to kill this beast. Nothing else mattered.

He wondered if Mina, gripping the dragonlance, had the same idea. He envisioned the two of them, dying together in blood and in fire, and he was exalted.

Malystryx's target was Sanction. She had the city in sight. She could see its buglike inhabitants, who were just now starting to feel the terror of her might. Malys did not fear attack from the air, for she never imagined that anyone—not even this Mina—would be so crazed as to fight her from dragon-back. Happening to glance up for no other reason than to enjoy the prospect of the bright blue sky, Malys was shocked to the depth of her soul to see two dragonriders plummeting down on her.

She was so startled that for a moment she doubted her senses. That moment almost proved to be her last, for her foes were on her with a suddenness that took away her breath. An instinctive, banking move saved her, carried her out of their path. The attacking dragons were flying too fast to be able to halt. They sailed past her and began to pull up, both of them circling around for another attack.

Malys kept her eye on them, but she did not immediately fly to annihilate them. She held back, wary, watchful, waiting to see what they would do next. No need to exert herself. She had only to wait until the dragonfear, which she knew how to wield better than any other dragon who had ever existed on Krynn, caused these pitiful, lesser dragons to blanch and break, turn tail and flee. Once they had their backs to her, then she would slay them.

Malys waited, watched in glee to see the blue dragon falter in his flight, while his minotaur rider cowered on his back. Certain those two were not a threat, Malys turned her attention to the other dragon and its rider. She was annoyed to note that the other dragon had not halted in its banking turn, but was coming straight for her. Malys suddenly understood why her fear did not work on this one. She had seen enough dragon corpses to recognize one more.

So this One God could raise the dead. Malys was more irritated than impressed, for now she would have to rethink her battle strategy. This creaking, worm-eaten, grotesque monstrosity could not be defeated by terror and would not succumb to pain. It was already dead, so how could she kill it? This was going to be more work than she'd anticipated.

"First you use the souls of the dead to rob me," Malys roared. "Now you bring a moldering, mummified relic to fight me. What do you and this small and desperate god of yours expect me to do? Scream? Faint? I have no fear of the living or the dead. I have fed upon both. And I will soon feed upon you!"

Malys watched her enemies carefully, trying to guess what they would do, even as she plotted her next attack. She discounted the blue dragon. The creature was in a sad state. She could smell the reek of his dread and his rider was not much better. The rider of the dead dragon was different. Malys hovered before Mina, letting the human get a good look at the power of her foe. She could not possibly win. No god could save her.

Malys knew the impression she must make upon the human. The largest living being on all of Krynn, the red dragon was enormous, dwarfing all native dragons. A snap of Malys's massive jaws could sever the spine of the mummy dragon. A single claw was as large as this human who dared to challenge her. Beyond that, Malys wielded a magical power that had raised up mountains.

She opened her jaws, let the molten fire drool from her mouth, pool around her sharp fangs. She flexed the claws that were stained brown with blood, claws that had once pierced the scales of a gold dragon and ripped out the still-beating heart. She twitched the huge tail that could crack a red dragon's skull or break its neck, sending it plummeting to the ground while its hapless rider could do nothing but scream to see obliteration rushing up at him.

Few mortals had ever been able to withstand the horror of Malys's coming, and it seemed that Mina could not. She froze on the back of the mummified beast. She tried to keep her head up, but the terror of what she saw seemed to crush her, for she drooped and shrank, then lowered her head as if she knew death was coming and could not bear to look at it.

Malys was pleased and relieved. Opening her mouth, she drew in a breath of air that would mix with the brimstone in her belly and be unleashed in a gout of flame, cremating what was left of the corpse dragon and turn this minion of the so-called One God into a living torch.

Mina did not lower her head in fear. She lowered her head in prayer, and her god did not abandon her. Mina raised her head, looked directly at Malys. In her hand she held the dragonlance.

Silver light shone from the lance, light as sharp as the lance itself. The stabbing light struck Malys full in the eyes, for she'd been staring straight at it. Momentarily blinded, she choked upon the flaming breath, swallowed most of it. Thwarted in her attack she blinked her eyes, tried to rid them of the dazzling light.

"For the One God!" Mina cried.

Galdar knew they were finished. He hoped that they were finished. He longed for easeful death to end the fear that dissolved his organs so that he was literally drowning in his own terror. Beneath him, he could feel Razor shivering, hear the clicking of his teeth and feel tremor after tremor shake the Blue's body.

Then Mina called upon Takhisis, and the goddess answered. The dragonlance flared like a bursting star. Silver light shot through Galdar's darkness, channeled the fear into his muscles and his sinews and his brain. Razor let out a roar of defiance, and Galdar lifted his voice to match.

Mina gestured with the lance, and Galdar understood. They were not going to charge again, but would try another dive, attacking Malys from above. The red dragon, in her arrogance, had slowed her flight. They would wheel and attack her before she could recover.

The two dragons banked and began their dive. Malys gave one flap of her mighty wings, then another, and suddenly she was speeding straight at them with deadly intent. Her jaws gaped wide.

Razor anticipated the Red's attack. The Blue veered off, flipping over backward to avoid the blast of flame that came so close it singed the scales on his belly.

The world reeled beneath Galdar's horns. The minotaur's stomach rolled. Dangling upside down in the harness that held him to the saddle, he clung frantically to the pommel with one hand, his weapon with the other. The harness had been built for human dragonriders, not for a minotaur. Galdar could only hope that the straps held his weight.

Razor rolled out of his turn. Galdar was upright again, the world was back where it was supposed to be. He looked hastily about to see what had become of Mina. For a moment, he could not find her, and his heart nearly burst with fear.

"Mina!" he shouted.

"Below us!" Razor called out.

She was very far below them, flying close to the ground, flying underneath Malys, who was now caught between the two of them.

Malys's attention fixed on the Blue. A lazy flap of her wings and suddenly she was driving straight for them. Razor turned tail, beat his wings frantically.

"Fly, damn you!" Galdar snarled, although he could see that Razor was using every ounce of strength to try to outdistance the large red dragon.

Galdar looked back over his shoulder to see that the race was hopeless, lost before it could be won. Razor gasped for breath. His wings pumped. The muscles of the dragon's body flexed and heaved. Malys was barely even puffing. She seemed to fly effortlessly. Her jaws parted, fangs gleamed. She meant to snap the Blue's spine, dislodge his rider, send Galdar falling thousands of feet to his death on the rocks below.

Galdar gripped his pike.

"We're not going to make it!" he shouted at Razor. "Turn and close with her!"

The blue dragon wheeled. Galdar looked into Malys's eyes. He gripped the pike, prepared to launch it down her throat.

Malys opened her jaws, but instead of snapping at the Blue, she gave a gasp.

Mina had flown up underneath Malys. Wielding the dragonlance, Mina struck the Red in the belly. The lance sliced through the outer layer of red scales, ripped open a gash in the dragon's gut.

Malys's gasp was more astonishment than pain, for the lance had not done her serious damage. The shock and, worse than that, the insult angered her. She flipped in mid-air, tail over head, claws reaching and teeth gnashing.

The death dragon proved itself adept at maneuvering. Flying rapidly, ducking and dodging, it scrambled to keep clear of the red dragon's wild flailings. The death dragon dived. Galdar and his Blue rose and then banked for another attack.

Malys was growing weary of this battle, which was no longer fun for her. She could exert herself to some purpose when she tried, and now she stretched her wings and sought speed. She would catch this corpse and rend it bone from rotting bone, peel off its flesh and crush it into dust. And she would do the same to its rider.

Galdar had never seen anything move so fast. He and Razor flew after Malys, but they could not hope to catch up with her, not before she had slain Mina.

Malys breathed out a blast of flame.

Galdar screamed in defiance and kicked the flanks of the Blue. He might not be able to save Mina but he would avenge her.

Hearing the flame belch forth, the dead dragon lowered its head, nose down, and spread its leather wings. The ball of fire burst on its belly, spread along the wings. Galdar roared in rage, a roar that changed to a howl of glee.

The dragonlance gleamed in the flames. Mina lifted the lance, waved it to show Galdar she was safe. The death dragon's leathery wings and body shielded her from the fire. The maneuver was not without cost. The corpse's leather wings were ablaze. Tendrils of smoke snaked into the air. No matter that the corpse could neither feel pain nor die. Without the membrane of its wings, it could not remain airborne.

The death dragon began to lose altitude, flame dancing along the skeletal remains of its wings.

"Mina!" Galdar shouted in wrenching agony. He was helpless to save her. Its wings consumed by the fire, the death dragon spiraled downward.

Certain that one foe was doomed, Malys turned her attention back to Galdar. The minotaur cared nothing about himself. Not anymore.

"Takhisis," he prayed. "I do not matter. Save Mina. Save her. She has given her all for you. Spare her life!"

In answer to his prayer, a third dragon appeared. This dragon was neither dead nor living. Shadowy, without substance, the five heads of this dragon flowed into the body of the dead dragon. The goddess herself had come to join in the battle.

The dead dragon's leathery wings began to shimmer with an eerie light. Even as flames continued to burn, the corpse pulled out of its death spiral only a short distance above the ground.

Galdar raised a mighty cheer and brandished his pike, hoping to draw Malys's attention from Mina.

"Attack!" he roared.

Razor needed no urging. He was already in a steep dive. The blue dragon bared his teeth. Galdar felt a rumbling in the dragon's belly. A bolt of lightning shot forth from the Blue's jaws. Crackling and sizzling, the lightning bolt struck Malys on the head. The concussive blast that followed nearly knocked Galdar from the saddle.

Malys jerked spasmodically as the electricity surged through her body. Galdar thought for a moment that the jolt had finished her, and his heart leaped in his chest. The lightning dissipated. Malys shook her head groggily, like a fighter who has received a blow to the nose, then she reared back, opened her jaws and came at them.

"Take me close!" Galdar cried.

Razor did as commanded. He swept in low over Malys's head. Galdar flung the pike with all his strength into the dragon's eye. He saw the pike pierce the eyeball, saw the eye redden and the dragon blink frantically.

Nothing more. And that blow had cost him dearly.

Razor's move had carried them too close to the dragon to be able to escape her reach. Galdar's strike had not taken Malys out of the battle, as he hoped. The huge pike looked puny, sticking out of Malys's eye. She felt it no more than he might feel an eyelash.

Her head reared up. She lunged at them, jaws snapping.

Galdar had one chance to save himself. He flung himself from the saddle, grabbed hold of Razor around the neck and held on. Malys drove her teeth into the blue dragon's body. The saddle disappeared in her maw.

Blood poured down Razor's flanks. The blue dragon cried out in pain and in fury as he struggled desperately to fight his attacker, lashing out with his forelegs and his hind legs, slapping at her with his tail. Galdar could do nothing but hang on. Splashed with the Blue's warm blood, Galdar clung to Razor's neck.

Malys shook the blue dragon like a dog shakes a rat to break its spine. Galdar heard a sickening crunch of bone, and Razor gave a horrifying scream.

Mina looked up to see the blue dragon clasped in Malys's jaws. She could not see Galdar and assumed that he was dead. Her heart ached. Among all those who served her, he was most dear to her. Mina could see clearly the wound on the dragon's belly. A trail of glistening, dark red marred the fire-orange red of the scales. Yet, the wound was not mortal.

The dead dragon's wings were sheets of flame, and the flames were spreading to the body. Soon Mina would be sitting on a dragon made of fire. She felt the heat, but it was an annoyance, nothing more. She saw only her enemy. She saw what she must do to defeat the enemy.

"Takhisis, fight with me!" she cried and, raising her lance, she pointed upward.

Mina heard a voice, the same voice she had heard call to her at the age of fourteen. She had run away from home to seek out that voice.

"I am with you," said Takhisis.

The goddess spread her arms, and they became dragon wings. The burning wings of the death dragon lifted into the air, propelled by the wings of the goddess. Faster and faster they flew, the air fanning the flames on the dragon, whipping them so that the fire swirled about Mina. Her armor protected her from the flames but not from the heat. Imbued with the spirit of the god, she did not feel the burning, hot metal start to sear her skin. She saw clearly that victory must be theirs. The wounded underbelly of the red dragon came closer and closer. Malys's blood dripped down on Mina's upturned face.

And then, suddenly, Takhisis was gone.

Mina felt the absence of the goddess as a rush of chill air that snatched away her breath, left her suffocating, gasping. She was alone now, alone on a dragon that was disintegrating in fire. Her goddess had left her, and Mina did not know why.

Perhaps, Mina thought frantically, this is a test.

Takhisis had administered such tests before when Mina had first found the One God and offered to be her servant. Those tests had been hard, demanding that she prove her loyalty in blood, word, and deed. She had not failed one of them. None had been as hard as this one, though. She would not survive this one, but that made no difference, because, in death, she would be with her goddess.

Mina willed the death dragon that was now a dragon of fire to keep going, and either her will or the dragon's own momentum carried it up those last few feet.

The blazing dragon crashed into Malys's body with tremendous force. The blood dripping from the wound began to bubble and boil, so hot were the flames.

Lifting the dragonlance, Mina drove it with all her strength into the dragon's belly. The lance pierced through the weakened scales, opened a gaping wound in the flesh.

Engulfed in blood and in fire, Mina held fast to the lance and prayed to the goddess that she might now be found worthy.

Malys felt pain, a pain such as she'd never before experienced. The pain was so dreadful that she released her hold on the blue dragon. Her bellowings were horrible to hear. Galdar wished he could cover his ears so that he could blot out the sound. He had to endure it, though, for he dared not move or he would lose his hold and fall to his death. He and Razor were spiralling downward. The Lords of Doom that had been small beneath Galdar now towered over him. The jagged rocks of the mountainous terrain would make for a bone-crunching landing.

Razor had taken a mortal wound, but the dragon was still alive and with unbelievable courage was struggling desperately to remain in control. Although Razor knew he was doomed, he was fighting to save his rider. Galdar did what he could to help, hanging on and trying not move. Every flap of the dragon's wings must be agony, for Razor gasped and shuddered with the pain, but he was slowly descending. He searched with his dimming vision for a clear spot on which to land.

Clinging to the neck of the dying dragon, Galdar looked up to see Mina sitting astride wings of fire. The dragon's entire body was in flames. Flames raced up the dragonlance. The fiery dragon rammed Malys, struck her in the belly. Mina jabbed the dragonlance straight into the wound she'd already made. Malys's belly split wide open. A great, gushing rush of black blood poured out of the dragon.

"Mina!" Galdar cried out in anguish and despair, as a terrifying roar from Malys obliterated his words.

Malys screamed her death scream. She knew that death scream. She'd heard it often. She'd heard it from the Blue as she shattered his spine. Now it was her turn. The death scream rose, bubbling with agony and fury, from her throat.

Blinded by the dragon's blood, abandoned by her god, Mina yet held fast to the dragonlance. She thrust the lance up into the dreadful wound, guided the lance to pierce Malys's heart.

The red dragon died in that moment, died in midair. Her body plunged from the sky, smashed onto the rocks of the Lords of Doom below. She carried her slayer down with her.

20 BLINDING LIGHT

So pent up and excited were the defenders of Sanction that they gave a cheer when Malys's huge, red body emerged from shredded clouds.

The cheers sank, as did their courage, when the dragonfear washed over Sanction in a tidal wave that crushed hope and severed dreams and brought every person in the city face to face with the dread image of his own doom. The archers who were supposed to fire arrows at the gleaming red scales threw down their bows and fell to their bellies and lay there shivering and whimpering. The men at the catapults turned and fled their posts.

The stairs leading up to the battlements were clogged with the terrified troops so that none could go up and none could go down. Fights broke out as desperate men sought to save themselves at the expense of their fellows. Some were so maddened by the fear that they flung themselves off the walls. Those who managed to control their fear tried to calm the rest, but they were so few in number that they made little difference. One officer who tried to halt the flight of his panic-stricken men was struck down with his own sword, his body trampled in the rush.

Stone walls and iron bars were no barrier. A prisoner in the guard house near the West Gate, Silvanoshei felt the fear twist inside him as he lay on his hard bed in his dark cell, dreaming of Mina. He knew he was forgotten, but he could never forget her and he spent entire nights in hopeless dreams that she would walk through that cell door, walk with him again the dark and tangled path of his life.

The jailer had come to the cells to give Silvanoshei his daily food ration, when Malys's dragonfear washed over the city. The jailer's duty was onerous and boring, and he liked to brighten it by tormenting the prisoners. The elf was an easy target, and, although the jailer was forbidden to harm Silvanoshei physically, he could and did torment him verbally. The fact that Silvanoshei never reacted or responded did not faze the jailer, who imagined that he was having a devastating effect on the elf. In reality, Silvanoshei rarely even heard what the man said. His voice was one of many: his mother's, Samar's, his lost father's, and the voice that had made him so many promises and kept none. Real voices, such as the jailer's, were not as loud as these voices of his soul, were no more than the chattering of the rodents that infested his cell.

The dragonfear twisted inside Silvanoshei, caught in his throat, strangling and suffocating. Terror jolted him out of the nether world in which he existed, flung him onto the hard floor of reality. He crouched there, afraid to move.

"Mina save us!" moaned the jailer, shivering in the doorway. He made a lunge at Silvanoshei, caught hold of his arm with a grip that nearly paralyzed the elf.

The jailer broke into slobbering tears and clung to Silvanoshei as if he'd found an elder brother.

"What is it?" Silvanoshei cried.

"The dragon! Malys," the jailer managed to blurt out. His teeth clicked together so he could barely talk. "She's come. We're all going to die! Mina save us!"

"Mina!" Silvanoshei whispered. The word broke the shackling fear. "What has Mina to do with this?"

"She's going to fight the dragon," the jailer burbled, wringing his hands.

The prison erupted into chaos as the guards fled and the prisoners screamed and shouted and flung themselves against the bars in frantic efforts to escape the horror.

Silvanoshei pushed away the quivering, blubbering mound that had once been the jailer. The cell door stood open. He ran down the corridor. Men pleaded with him to free them, but he paid no heed to them.

Emerging outside, he drew in a deep breath of air that was not tainted with the stink of unwashed bodies and rat dung. Looking into the blue sky, he glimpsed the red dragon—a huge, bloated monster hanging in the heavens. His eager, searching gaze flicked past Malys without interest. Silvanoshei scanned the heavens and at last found Mina. His sharp elven eyesight could see better than most. He could see the tiny speck that gleamed silver in the sunlight.

Silvanoshei stood in the middle of the street, staring upward. People ran past him, dashed into him, shoved him and jostled him in their mindless panic. He paid no attention, fended off hands, fought to keep his feet, and fought to keep his gaze fixed upon that small sparkle of light.

When Malys appeared, Palin discovered that there was one advantage to being dead. The dragonfear that plunged Sanction's populace into chaos had no effect upon him. He could look upon the great red dragon and feel nothing.

His spirit hovered near the totem. He saw the fire blaze in the eyes of the dead dragons. He heard their cries for revenge rise up to the heavens, rise up to Takhisis. Palin never doubted himself. His duty was clear before him. Takhisis must be stopped or at least slowed, her power diminished. She had invested much of that power into the totem, planning to use it as a doorway into the world, to merge the physical realm and the spiritual. If she succeeded she would reign supreme. No one—spirit or mortal—would be strong enough to fight her.

"You were right," said Mirror, who stood by Palin's side. "The city has gone mad with terror."

"It will wear off soon—" Palin began. He broke off abruptly.

Dalamar's spirit emerged from among the dragon skulls.

"The view of the battle is better from the box seats," Dalamar said. "You do not have feet, you know, Majere. You are not bound to the ground. Together you and I can sit at our ease among the clouds, watch every thrust and parry, see the blood fall like rain. Why don't you join me?"

"I have very little interest in the outcome," said Palin. "Whoever wins, we are bound to lose."

"Speak for yourself," Dalamar said.

To Palin's discomfiture, Dalamar's spirit was taking an unusual interest in Mirror.

Could Dalamar see both the man and the silver dragon? Could Dalamar have guessed their plan? If he knew, would he attempt to thwart them, or was he preoccupied with his own schemes? That Dalamar had schemes of his own, Palin did not doubt. Palin had never fully trusted Dalamar, and he had grown more wary of him these past few days.

"The battle goes well," Dalamar continued, his soul's gaze fixed on Mirror. "Malys is fully occupied, that much is certain. People are calming down. The dragonfear is starting to abate. Speaking of which, your blind beggar friend appears to be remarkably immune to dragonfear. Why is that, I wonder?"

What Dalamar said was true. The dragonfear was fading away. Soldiers who had been hugging the ground and screaming that they were all going to die were sitting up, looking sheepish and embarrassed.

If we are going to do this, we have to act now, realized Palin. What danger can Dalamar be to us? He can do nothing to stop them. Like me, he has no magic.

A roaring bellow boomed among the mountains. People in the street stared upward, began to shout and point to the sky.

"A dragon has drawn blood," said Mirror, peering upward. "Hard to say which, though."

Dalamar's spirit hung in the air. The eyes of his soul stared at them as if he would delve the depths of theirs. Then, suddenly, he vanished.

"The outcome of this fight means something to him, that is certain," said Palin. "I wonder which horse he is backing."

"Both, if he can find a way," said Mirror.

"Could he see your true form, do you think?" Palin asked.

"I believe that I was able to hide from him," said Mirror. "But when I begin to cast my magic, I can no longer do so. He will see me for what I am."

"Then let us hope the battle proves interesting enough to keep him occupied," said Palin. "Do you have fur and amber . . . ? Ah, sorry, I forgot," he added, seeing Mirror smile. "Dragons have no need of such tools for their spell casting."

Now that the battle had begun, the totem's magic intensified. Eyes in the skulls burned and glittered with a fury so potent it shone from ground to heaven. The single eye, the New Eye, gleamed white, even in the daylight. The magic of the totem was strong, drew the dead to it. The souls of the dead circled the totem in a pitiful vortex, their yearning a torment fed by the goddess.

Palin felt the pain of longing, a longing for what is lost beyond redemption.

"When you cast your spell," he said to Mirror, the longing for the magic an aching inside him, "the dead will swarm around you, for yours is a magic they can steal. The sight of them is a terrible one, unnerving—"

"So there is at least one advantage to being blind," Mirror remarked, and he began to cast the spell.

Dragons, of all the mortal beings on Krynn, are born with the ability to use magic. Magic is inherent to them, a part of them like their blood and their shining scales. The magic comes from within.

Mirror spoke the words of magic in the ancient language of dragons. Coming from a human throat, the words lacked the rich resonance and rolling majesty that the silver dragon was accustomed to hearing, sounded thin and weak. Small or large, the words would accomplish the goal. The first prickles of magic began to sparkle in his blood.

Wispy hands plucked at his scales, tore at his wings, brushed across his face. The souls of the dead now saw him for what he was—a silver dragon—and they surged around him, frantic for the magic that they could feel pulsing inside his body. The souls reached out to him with their wispy hands and pleaded with him. The souls clung to him and hung from him like tattered scarves. The dead could do him no harm. They were an annoyance, like scale mites. But scale mites did nothing more than raise an irritating itch. Scale mites did not have voices that cried out in desperation, begging, beseeching. Hearing the despair in the voices, Mirror realized he had spoken truly. There was an advantage to being blind. He did not have to see their faces.

Even though the magic was inherent to him, he still had to concentrate to cast the spell, and he found this difficult. The fingers of the souls raked his scales, their voices buzzed in his ears.

Mirror tried to concentrate on one voice—his voice. He concentrated on the words of his own language, and their music was comforting and reassuring. The magic burned within him, bubbled in his blood. He sang the words and opened his hands and cast the magic forth.

Although Dalamar guessed that his fellow mage was up to something, he had discounted Palin as a threat. How could he be? Palin was as impotent as Dalamar when it came to magic. True, Dalamar would not let that stop him. He had schemed and connived so that whichever way the bread landed, he'd still have the butter side up.

Yet, there was something strange about that blind beggar. Probably the fellow was or fancied himself a wizard. Probably Palin had concocted some idea that they could work together, although what sort of magical rabbit they would be able to pull out of their joint hats was open to debate. If they were able to come up with a rabbit at all, the souls of the dead would grab it and rip it apart.

Satisfied, Dalamar felt it safe to leave Palin and his blind beggar to bumble about in the darkness while he went to witness first hand the gladiatorial contest between Malys and Mina. Dalamar was not overly interested in which one won. He viewed the battle with the cold, dispassionate interest of the gambler who has all his bets covered.

Malys breathed blazing fire on the corpse dragon, the leather wings erupted into flames. Malys chortled, thinking she was the victor.

"Don't count your winnings yet," Dalamar advised the red dragon, and he was proven right.

Takhisis advanced onto the field of battle. Reaching out her hand, she touched the death dragon. Her spirit flowed into the body of the burning corpse, saving Mina, her champion.

At that moment, Dalamar's soul heard the sound of a voice chanting. He could not understand the words, but he recognized the language of dragons, and he was alarmed to realize by the cadence and the rhythm that the words were magic. His spirit fled the battle, soared back to the temple. He saw a spark of bright light and realized immediately that he had made a mistake—perhaps a fatal mistake.

As Dalamar the Dark had misjudged the uncle, so had he misjudged the nephew. Dalamar saw in an instant what Palin planned.

Dalamar recognized the blind beggar as Mirror, guardian of the Citadel of Light, one of the few silver dragons who had dared remain in the world after all the others had so mysteriously fled. He saw the dead surrounding Mirror, trying to feed off the magic he was casting, but the dragon would be poor pickings. The dead might leech some of the magic, but they would not seriously impede Mirror's spellcasting. Dalamar knew immediately what the two were doing, knew it as well as if he had plotted it with them.

Dalamar looked back to the battle. This was Takhisis's moment of victory, the moment she would avenge herself on this dragon who had dared moved in to take over her world. The Dark Queen had been forced to endure Malys's taunts and gibes in seething silence. She had been forced to watch Malys slay her minions and use their power—that should have been her power.

At last, Takhisis had grown strong enough to challenge Malys, to wrench away the souls of the dead dragons, who now worshiped their queen and gave their power to their queen. Dragons of Krynn, their souls were hers to command.

Long had Takhisis watched and worked and waited for this moment when she would remove the last obstacle to stand in her way of taking full and absolute control of her world. Concentrating on the foe in front, Takhisis was oblivious to the danger creeping up on her from behind.

Dalamar could warn Takhisis. He had but to say one word and she would run to protect her totem. She could not afford to do otherwise. She had worked hard to create the door for her entry and she was not about to have it slammed shut in her face. There would be other days to fight Malys, other champions to fight Malys if she lost Mina.

Dalamar hesitated.

True, Takhisis had offered him rich reward—a return to his body and the gifting of the magic to go with it.

Dalamar reached out with his soul and touched the past, touched the memory that was all that was left to him: the memory of the magic. He would do anything, say anything, betray, destroy anyone for the sake of the magic.

The thought that he must abase himself before Takhisis was galling to him. Once years ago, when the magic had been his to command, he had been open in his defiance of the Dark Queen. Nuitari, her son, had no love for his mother and could always be counted upon to defend his worshipers against her. Nuitari was gone now. The power the dark god of magic had lavished on his servant was gone.

Dalamar must now abase himself before the Dark Queen, and he knew that Takhisis would not be generous in her victory over him. Yet, for the magic, he could do even this.

Takhisis straddled the world, watching the battle in which she took such a keen interest. Her champion was winning. Mina flew straight up at Malys, the gleaming dragonlance in her hand.

Dalamar knelt in the dust and bowed his head low and said humbly, "Your Majesty . . ."

Mirror could not see the magic, but he could feel it and hear it. The spell flowed from his fingers as bolts of jagged, blue lightning that crackled and sizzled. The air smelled of brimstone. He could see the blazing bolts in his mind's eye, see them striking a skull, dancing from that skull to another, from the skull of a gold to the skull of a red, from that skull to the skull touching it, and round and round, jumping from one to the next, in a blazing, fiery chain.

"Is the spell cast?" Mirror cried.

"It is cast," said Palin, watching in awe.

He wished Mirror could see this sight. The lightning sizzled and danced. Blue-white, the bolts jumped from one skull to the next, so fast that the eye could not follow them. As the lightning struck each skull, that skull began to glow blue-white, as though dipped in phosphorus. Thunder boomed and blasted, shaking the ground, shaking the totem.

Power built in the totem, the magic shuddered in the air. The voices of the dead fell silent as the voices of the living raised in a terrible clamor, screaming and crying out. Feet pounded, some running toward the totem, others running away.

Watching Mirror cast the spell, Palin recited to himself the words of magic that for him held no meaning, but which were imprinted on his soul. His body sat unmoved, uncaring, on a bench in the temple. Exultant, his soul watched lightning leap from skull to skull, setting each afire.

The magic reverberated, hummed, grew stronger and stronger. The white-hot fire burned bright. The intense heat drove back those gathered around the totem. The skulls of the dragons now had eyes of white flame.

In the heavens, thunder rolled. The New Eye glared down on them.

Dark clouds, thick and black, shot through with bolts of orange and red, bubbled and boiled and frothed. Tendrils of destruction twisted down from the storm, raising dust clouds and uprooting trees. Hail pelted, smashed into the ground.

"Do your damndest, Takhisis," cried Palin to the thundering, angry voice of the storm. "You are too late."

The black clouds blanketed Sanction with darkness and rain and hail. A gust of wind blew on the totem. Torrential rains deluged the city, trying desperately to douse the magic.

The rain was like oil on the fire. The wind fanned the flames. Mirror could not see the fire, but he could feel the searing heat. He staggered backward, stumbling over benches, backed into the altar. His groping hands found purchase, cool and smooth. He recognized by touch the sarcophagus of Goldmoon, and it seemed to him that he could hear her voice calm and reassuring. Mirror crouched beside the sarcophagus, though the heat grew ever more intense. He kept his hand upon it protectively.

A ball of fire formed in the center of the totem, shining bright as a lost star fallen to the ground. Light, bright and white as starlight, began to shine within the eyes of the dragons. The light grew brighter and brighter until none of the living could look at it, but were forced to cover their eyes.

The fire grew in strength and intensity, burning purely and radiantly, its luminous brilliance so dazzling that Mirror could see it through his blindness, saw bursting, blue-white flame and the petals of flame drifting up into the heavens. The rain had no effect on the magical fire. The wind of the goddess's fury could not diminish it.

The light shone pure white at its heart. The skulls of the dragons shattered, burst apart. The totem teetered and swayed, then fell in upon itself, dissolving, disintegrating.

The New Eye stared into the white heart of the blaze. Blood-red, the Eye fought to maintain its gaze, but the pain proved too much.

The Eye blinked.

The Eye vanished.

Darkness closed over Mirror, but he no longer cursed it, for the darkness was blessed, safe and comforting as the darkness from which he'd been born. His trembling hand ran over the smooth, cool surface of the sarcophagus. There came a ringing sound as of shattering glass, and he felt cracks in the surface, felt them spread through the amber like winter ice melting in the spring sun.

The sarcophagus broke apart, the bits and pieces falling around him. He felt a soft touch on his hand that was like ashes drifting on the wind.

"Goodbye, dear friend," he said.

"The blind beggar!" a voice like thunder rumbled. "Slay the blind beggar. He has destroyed the totem! Malys will kill us! Malys will kill us all."

Voices cried out in anger. Footsteps pounded. Fists began to pummel him. A rock struck Mirror and another.

Palin watched, exultant, as the totem fell. He saw the sarcophagus destroyed and, though he could not find Goldmoon's spirit, he rejoiced that her body would no longer be held in thrall, that she would no longer be a slave of Takhisis.

He would be called to account. He would be made to pay. He could not avoid it, could not hide, for though her eye might have been blinded, Takhisis was still master. Her presence in the world had not been banished, merely diminished. He remained a slave, and there was nowhere he could hide that her dogs would not sniff him out, hunt him down.

He waited to accept his fate, waited near the crumbling ruins of the totem, waited beside the pitiful shell of flesh that was his body. The dogs were not long in coming.

Dalamar appeared, materializing out of the smoking ruins of the burning skulls.

"You should not have done this, Palin. You should not have interfered. Your soul faces oblivion. Darkness eternal."

"What is to be your reward for your service to her?" Palin asked. "Your life? No"—he answered his own question—"you cared little for your life. She gave you back the magic."

"The magic is life," said Dalamar. "The magic is love. The magic is family. The magic is wife. The magic is child."

Inside the temple, Palin's body sat on the hard bench, stared unseeing at the candle flames that wavered, fearful and helpless, in the storm winds that swept through the room.

"How sad," he said, as his spirit started to ebb, water receding from the shoreline, "that only at the end do I know what I should have known from the start."

"Darkness eternal," Dalamar echoed.

"No," said Palin softly, "for beyond the clouds, the sun shines."

Rough hands seized hold of Mirror. Angry, panicked voices clamored in his ear, so many at once that he could not possibly understand them. They mauled him, pulled him this way and that, as they screeched and argued between themselves about what to do with him. Some wanted to hang him. Others wanted to rend him apart where he stood.

The silver dragon could always slough off this puny human guise and transform into his true shape. Even blind, he could defend himself against a mob. He spread his arms that would become his silver wings and lifted his head. Joy filled him even as danger closed in on him. In a moment, he would be himself, shining silver in the darkness, riding the winds of the storm.

Shackles clamped over his wrists. He almost laughed, for no iron forged of man could hold him. He tried to shake them off, but the shackles would not fall, and he realized that they were not forged of iron, but of fear. Takhisis made them and she clamped them on him. Strive as he might, he could not transform himself. He was chained to his human body, shackled to this two-legged form, and in that form, blind and alone, he would die.

Mirror fought to escape his captors, but his thrashings only goaded them to further torment. Rocks and fists struck him. Pain shot through him. Blow after blow rained down on him. He slumped to the ground.

He heard, as in a dream of pain, a strong, commanding voice speak out. The voice was powerful, and it quelled the clamor.

"Back away!" Odila ordered. Her voice was cold and stern and accustomed to being obeyed. "Leave him alone or know the wrath of the One God!"

"He used some sort of magic to destroy the totem!" a man cried. "I saw him!"

"He's done away with the moon!" cried another. "Done something foul and unnatural that will curse us all!"

Other voices joined in the accusing clamor, demanded his death.

"The magic he used is the magic of the One God," Odila told them. "You should be down on your knees, praying for the One God to save us from the dragon, not maltreating a poor beggar!"

Her strong, scarred hands took firm hold of him, lifted him up.

"Can you walk?" she whispered to him, low and urgent. "If so, you must try."

"I can walk," he told her.

A trickle of warm blood seeped down into the bandages he wore around his eyes. The pain in his head eased, but he felt cold and clammy and nauseous. He staggered to his feet. Her arms wrapped around him, supported his faltering steps.

"Good," Odila whispered in his ear. "We're going to walk backward." Taking a firm grip on him, she suited her action to her words. He stumbled with her, leaning on her.

"What is happening?" he asked.

"The mob is holding back for the moment. They feel my power, and they fear it. I speak for the One God, after all." Odila sounded amused, reckless, joyful. "I want to thank you," she said, her voice softening. "I was the one who was blind. You opened my eyes."

"Let's go after him," someone shouted. "What's stopping us? She's not Mina! She's just some traitor Solamnic."

Odila let go of Mirror, moved to stand defensively in front of him. He heard a roar as the mob surged forward.

"A traitor Solamnic with a club, not a sword," Odila said to him. He heard the splintering of wood, guessed that she had smashed up one of the benches. "I'll hold them off as long as I can. Make your way behind the altar. You'll find a trapdoor—"

"I have no need for trapdoors," Mirror said. "You will be my eyes, Odila. I will be your wings."

"What the—" she began, then she gasped. He heard her drop the club.

Mirror spread his arms. Fear was gone. The Dark Queen had no power over him. He could see, once again, the radiant light. As it had destroyed the totem, so it burned away the shackles that bound him. His human body, so frail and fragile, small and cramped, was transformed. His heart grew and expanded, blood pulsed through massive veins, fed his strong taloned legs and an enormous silver-scaled body. His tail struck the altar, smashed it, sent the candles tumbling to the floor in a river of melted wax.

The mob that had surged forward to kill a blind beggar fell all over itself trying to escape a blind dragon.

"No saddle, Sir Knight," he told Odila. "You'll have to hang on tight. Grasp my mane. You'll need to lean close to my head to be able to tell me where we are going. What of Palin?" he asked, as she caught hold of his mane and pulled herself up on his back. "Can we take him with us?"

"His body is not there," Odila reported.

"I feared as much," said Mirror quietly. "And the other one? Dalamar."

"He is there," said Odila. "He sits alone. His hands are stained with blood." Mirror spread his wings.

"Hold on!" he shouted.

"I'm holding," said Odila. "Holding fast."

In her hand was the medallion that bore on it the image of the five-headed dragon. The medallion burned her scarred fingers. The pain was minor compared to the pain that seared her when she touched the dragonlance. Clasping the medallion, Odila tore it off.

The silver dragon gave a great leap. His wings caught the winds of the storm, used them to carry him aloft.

Odila brought the medallion to her lips. She kissed it, then, opening her fingers, she let the medallion fall. The medallion spiraled down into the pile of dust that was now all that remained of Malys's monument to death.

Mina's followers witnessed the breathtaking battle. They cheered to see Malys fall, gasped in horror as Mina fell in flames along with her foe.

Desperately they waited to see her rise again from the fire, as she had done once before. Smoke drifted up from the mountain, but it brought no Mina with it.

Silvanoshei had watched with the rest. He started walking. He would go to the temple. Someone there would have news. As he walked, as the blood flowed and his stiff muscles warmed, he came gradually to realize that not only was he still alive, he was free.

People milled about in the streets, shocked and confused. Some wept openly. Some simply wandered aimlessly, not knowing what to do next, waiting for someone to come and tell them. Some spoke of the battle, reliving it, relating over and over what they had seen, trying to make it real. People jabbered about the moon and that it was gone and so was the One God, if the One God had ever been, and that now Mina was gone too. No one paid any attention to Silvanoshei. Everyone was too caught up in his own despair to care about an elf.

I could walk out of Sanction, Silvanoshei said to himself, and no one would lift a finger to stop me.

He had no thought of leaving Sanction, however. He could not leave, not until he knew for certain what had become of Mina. Arriving at the temple, he found a huge throng of people gathered around the totem and he joined them, staring in dismay at the pile of ashes that had once been the glory of Queen Takhisis.

Silvanoshei stared into the ashes and he saw what he had been, saw what he might have been.

He saw the events that had led him to this point, saw them with his soul that never sleeps, always watches. He saw the terrible night the ogres attacked. He saw himself— consumed with hatred for his mother and for the life she had forced him to lead, consumed with fear and guilt when it seemed that she might die at the hands of the ogres. He saw himself running through the darkness to save her, and he saw himself proud to think that he would be the one to save his people. He saw the lightning bolt that sent him tumbling into unconsciousness. He saw himself falling down the hill to land at the base of the shield and then he saw what he had not been able to see with mortal eyes. He saw the dark hand of the goddess lift the shield so that he could enter.

Staring into the darkness, he saw the darkness staring back at him, and he realized that he had looked into the Dark Queen's eyes many times before, looked into them without blinking or turning away.

He heard again words that Mina had said to him on that first night they had come together. Words that he had tossed aside as nonsense, meaningless, without importance.

You do not love me. You love the god you see in me.

Everything his mother yearned for, he had been given. She had wanted to rule Silvanesti. He was the king of Silvanesti. She had longed to be loved by the people. They loved him. That.was his revenge, and it had been sweet. But that was only part of the revenge. The best part was that he had thrown it all away. Nothing he could have done had the power to hurt his mother more.

If the goddess had used him, it was because Takhisis had gazed deeply into the eyes of his soul and had seen one eye wink.

21   THE DEAD AND DYING

Razor's strength gave out while they were still airborne. He could no longer move his wings, and he began to twist downward in an uncontrolled dive. Galdar had the terrifying image of sheer-sided, jagged rocks stabbing upward. Razor crashed headlong into a small grove of pine trees.

For a heart-stopping moment, all Galdar could see was a blur of orange rocks and green trees, blue dragon scales and red blood. He squinched his eyes tight shut, gripped the dragon with all the strength of his massive body, buried his head in the dragon's neck. Buffeted and jolted, he heard the rending and snapping of limbs and bones, smelled and tasted the sharp odor of pine needles and the iron-tinged smell of fresh blood. A branch struck him on the head, nearly ripping off his horn. Another smote him on the back of his shoulder. Shattered branches tore at his legs and arms.

Suddenly, abruptly, they slammed to a halt.

Galdar spent a long moment doing nothing except gasping for breath and marveling that he was still alive. Every part of him hurt. He had no idea if he was seriously wounded or not. He moved, gingerly. Feeling no sharp, searing pain, he concluded that no bones were broken. Blood dribbled down his nose. His ears rang, and his head throbbed. He felt Razor give a shuddering sigh.

The dragon's head and upper portion of his shattered body rested in the pine trees that had broken beneath his weight. Disentangling himself from a nest of twisted, snapped branches, Galdar slid down off the dragon's back. He had the woozy impression that the blue dragon was resting in a cradle of pine boughs. The lower half of the dragon's body—the broken wings and tail—trailed behind him onto the rocks, leaving a smear of blood.

Galdar looked swiftly about for Malys's carcass. He saw it, off in the distance. Her corpse was easy to located. In death, she made her final mountain—a glistening, red mound of bloody flesh. Smoke and flame drew his eye. Fire consumed the death dragon, the flames spreading to the scrub pine. Farther down in the valley lay Sanction, but he couldn't see the city. Dark thunderclouds swirled beneath him. Where he stood, the sun shone brightly, so brightly that it had apparently eclipsed that New Eye, for he could not see it.

He did not take time to search for it. His main concern was Mina. He was frantic with worry about her and wanted nothing more than to go off immediately to search for her. But the minotaur owed his life to the heroics of the blue dragon. The least Galdar could do was to stay with him. No one, minotaur or dragon, should die alone.

Razor was still alive, still breathing, but his breaths were pain-filled and shallow. Blood flowed from his mouth. His eyes were starting to grow dim, but they brightened at the sight of Galdar.

"Is she . . ." The blue dragon choked on his own blood, could not continue.

"Malys is dead," Galdar said, deep and rumbling. "Thank you for the battle. A glorious victory that will be long remembered. You die a hero. I will honor your memory, as will my children and my children's children and their children after."

Galdar had no children, nor was there any likelihood he would ever have any. His words were the ancient tribute given to a warrior who has fought valiantly and died with honor. Yet Galdar spoke them from the depth of his soul, for he could only imagine what terrible agony these last few moments were for the dying dragon.

The blue dragon gave another shudder. His body went limp.

"I did my duty," he breathed, and died.

Galdar lifted his head and gave a howl of grief that echoed among the mountains—a final, fitting tribute. This done, he was free at last to follow his aching heart, to find out what had happened to Mina.

I should not be worried, he told himself. I have seen Mina survive poisoning, emerge whole and unscarred from her own flaming funeral pyre. The One God loves Mina, loves her as perhaps she has never before loved a mortal. Takhisis will protect her darling, watch over her.

Galdar told himself that, told himself repeatedly, but still he worried.

He scanned the rugged rocks around the carcass of the dragon. Chunks of flesh and gore were splattered about a wide area, the rocks were slippery with the mess. He hoped to see Mina come striding toward him, that exalted glow in her eyes. But nothing moved on the rocky outcropping where the dragon had fallen. The birds of the air had fled at her coming, the animals gone to ground. All was silent, except for a fierce and angry wind that hissed among the rocks with an eerie, whistling sound.

The rocks were difficult enough to navigate without the blood and blubber. Climbing was slow going, especially when every movement brought the pain of some newly discovered injury. Galdar found his pike. The weapon was covered with blood, and the blade was broken. Galdar was pleased to retrieve it. He would give it to Mina as a memento.

Search as he might, he could not find her. Time and again, he roared out, "Mina!" The name came back a hundredfold, careening off the sides of the mountains, but there was no answering call. The echoes faded away into silence. Climbing up and over a jumble of boulders, Galdar came at last to Malys's carcass.

Looking at the wreckage of the gigantic red dragon, Galdar felt nothing, not elation, not triumph, nothing except weariness and grief and a wonder that any of them had come out of this confrontation alive.

"Perhaps Mina didn't," said a voice inside him, a voice that sent shudders through him.

"Mina!" He called again, and he heard, in answer, a groan.

Malys's red-scaled and blood-smeared flank moved.

Alarmed, Galdar lifted the broken pike. He looked hard at the dragon's head, that lay sideways on the rocks, so that only one eye was visible. That eye stared, unseeing, at the sky. The neck was twisted and broken. Malys could not be alive.

The groan was repeated and a weak voice called out, "Galdar!"

With a cry of joy, Galdar flung down the pike and bounded forward. Beneath the belly of the dragon he saw a hand, covered with blood and moving feebly. The dragon had fallen on top of Mina, pinning her beneath.

Galdar put his shoulder to the fast cooling mass of blubber and heaved. The dragon's carcass was heavy, weighing several hundred tons. He might as well have tried to shift the mountain.

He was frantic with worry now, for Mina's voice sounded weak. He put his hands on the belly that had been slit wide open. Entrails spewed out; the stench was horrible. He gagged, tried to stop breathing.

"I can barely lift this, Mina," he called to her. "You must crawl out. Make haste. I can't hold it for long."

He heard something in reply but could not understand, for her voice was muffled. He gritted his teeth and bent his knees and, sucking in a great breath of air, he gave a grunt and heaved upward with all his might. He heard a scrabbling sound, a pain-filled gasping for breath, and a muffled cry. His muscles ached and burned, his arms grew wobbly. He could hold on no longer. With a loud shout of warning, he dropped the mass of flesh and stood gasping for breath amid the putrid remains. He looked down to find Mina lying at his feet.

Galdar was reminded of a time when Mina had been invited to bless a birthing. Galdar hadn't wanted to be there, but Mina had insisted and, of course, he'd obeyed. Looking down at Mina, Galdar remembered vividly the tiny child, so frail and fragile, covered in blood. He knelt by Mina's side.

"Mina," he said, helpless, afraid to touch her, "where are you hurt? I cannot tell if this is your blood or the dragon's."

Her eyes opened. The amber was bloodshot, rimmed with red. She reached out her hand, grasped Galdar's arm. The move caused her pain. She gasped and shivered but still managed to cling to him.

"Pray to the One God, Galdar," she said, her voice no more than a whisper. "I have done something . . . to displease her . . . Ask her . . . to forgive . . ."

Her eyes closed. Her head lolled to one side. Her hand slipped from his arm. His own heart stopping in fear, Galdar put his hand on her neck to feel for her pulse. Finding it, he gave a great sigh of relief.

He lifted Mina in his arms. She was light as he remembered that newborn babe to have been.

"You great bitch!" Galdar snarled. He was not referring to the dead dragon.

Galdar found a small cave, snug and dry. The cave was so small that the minotaur could not stand to his full height, but was forced to crouch low to enter. Carrying Mina inside, he laid her down gently. She had not regained consciousness, and although this scared him, he told himself this was good, for otherwise she would die of the pain.

Once in the cave, he had time to examine her. He stripped away her armor, tossed it outside to lie in the dust. The wounds she had sustained were terrible. The end of her leg bone protruded from the flesh, that was bloody, purple, and grotesquely swollen. One arm no longer looked like an arm, but like something hanging in a butcher's stall. Her breathing was ragged and caught in her throat. Every breath was a struggle, and more than once he feared she lacked the strength to take another. Her skin was burning hot to the touch. She shivered with the cold that brings death.

He no longer felt the pain of his own wounds. Whenever he made a sudden move and a sharp jab reminded him, he was surprised, wondered vaguely where it came from. He lived only for Mina, thought only of her. Finding a stream a short distance from the cave, he rinsed out his helm, filled it with water, carried it back to her.

He laved her face and touched her lips with the cool liquid, but she could not drink. The water trickled down her blood-covered chin. Up here in these rocks he would find no herbs to treat her pain or bring down her fever. He had no bandages. He had a rough sort of battlefield training in healing, but that was all, and it was not much help. He should amputate that shattered leg, but he could not bring himself to do it. He knew what it was for a warrior to live as a cripple.

Better she should die. Die in the glorious moment with the defeat of the dragon. Die as a warrior victorious over her foe. She was going to die. Galdar could do nothing to save her. He could do nothing but watch her life bleed away. He could do nothing but be by her side so that she would not die alone.

Darkness crept into the cave. Galdar built a fire inside the cavern's entrance to keep her warm. He did not leave the cavern again. Mina was delirious, fevered, murmuring incoherent words, crying out, moaning. Galdar could not bear to see her suffer, and more than once, his hand stole to his dagger to end this swiftly, but he held back. She might yet regain consciousness, and he wanted her to know, before she died, that she died a hero and that he would always love and honor her.

Mina's breathing grew erratic, yet she struggled on. She fought very hard to live. Sometimes her eyes opened and he saw the agony in them and his heart wrenched. Her eyes closed again without showing any signs of recognition, and she battled on.

He reached out his hand, wiped the chill sweat from her forehead.

"Let go, Mina," he said to her, tears glimmering on his eyelids. "You brought down your enemy—the largest, most powerful dragon ever to inhabit Krynn. All nations and people will honor you. They will sing songs of your victory down through the ages. Your tomb will be the finest ever built in Ansalon. People will travel from all over the world to pay homage. I will lay the dragonlance at your side and the put the monstrous skull of the dragon at your feet."

He could see it all so clearly. The tale of her courage would touch the hearts of all who heard it. Young men and women would come to her tomb to pledge themselves to lives of service to mankind, be it as warrior or healer. That she had walked in darkness would be forgotten. In death, she was redeemed.

Still, Mina fought on. Her body twitched and jerked. Her throat was ragged and raw from her screams.

Galdar could not bear it. "Release her," he prayed, not thinking what he was doing or saying, his only thought of her. "You've done with her! Release her!"

"So this is where you have her hidden," said a voice.

Galdar drew his dagger, twisted to his feet, and emerged from the cave all in one motion. The fire stole away his night vision. Beyond the crackling flames, all was darkness. He was a perfect target, standing there in the firelight, and he moved swiftly. Not too far away. He would never leave Mina, let them do what they might to him.

He blinked his eyes, tried to pierce the shadows. He had not heard the sound of footfalls or the chink of armor or the ring of steel. Whoever it was had come upon him by stealth, and that boded no good. He made certain to hold his dagger so it did not reflect the firelight.

"She is dying," he said to whoever was out there. "She has not long to live. Honor her dying and allow me to remain with her to the end. Whatever is between us, we can settle that afterward. I pledge my word."

"You are right, Galdar," said the voice. "Whatever is between us, we will settle at a later date. I gave you a great gift, and you returned my favor with treachery."

Galdar's throat constricted. The dagger slid from the suddenly nerveless right hand, landed on the rocks at his feet with a clash and a clatter. A woman stood at the mouth of the cave. Her figure blotted out the light of the fire, obliterated the light of the stars. He could not see her face with his eyes, for she had yet to enter the world in her physical form, but he saw her with the eyes of his soul. She was beautiful, the most beautiful thing he had ever seen in his life. Yet her beauty did not touch him, for it was cold and sharp as a scythe. She turned away from him. She walked toward the entrance to the cave.

Galdar managed with great effort to move his shaking limbs. He dared not look into that face, dared not meet those eyes that held in them eternity. He had no weapon that could fight her. No such weapon existed in this world.

He had only his love for Mina, and perhaps that was what gave him courage to place his own body between Queen Takhisis and the cave.

"You will not pass," he said, the words squeezed out of him. "Leave her alone! Let go of her! She did what you wanted and without your help. You abandoned her. Leave it that way."

"She deserves to be punished," Takhisis returned, cold, disdainful. "She should have known the wizard Palin was treacherous, secretly plotting to destroy me. He nearly succeeded. He destroyed the totem. He destroyed the mortal body that I had chosen for my residence while in the world. Because of Mina's negligence, I came close to losing everything I have worked for. She deserves to punished! She deserves death and worse than death! Still—" Takhisis's voice softened— "I will be merciful. I will be generous."

Galdar's heart almost stopped with fear. He was panting and shaking, yet he did not move.

"You need her," said Galdar harshly. "That's the only reason you're saving her." He shook his horned head. "She's at peace now, or soon will be. I won't let you have her."

Takhisis moved closer.

"I keep you alive, minotaur, for only one reason. Mina asks me to do so. Even now, as her spirit is wrenched from its shell of flesh, she begs me to be merciful toward you. I indulge her whim, for now. The day will come, however, when she will see that she no longer has need of you. Then, what lies between you and me will be settled."

Her hand lifted him up by the scruff of his neck and tossed him carelessly aside. He landed heavily among the sharp rocks and lay there, sobbing in anger and frustration. He pounded his left hand into the rocks, pounded it again and again so that it was bruised and bloody.

Queen Takhisis entered the cavern, and he could hear her crooning softly, sweetly, "My child . . . My beloved child . . . I do forgive you. . . ."

22 LOST IN THE MAZE

Gerard was determined to reach the Knights' Council with the urgent news of the return of Queen Takhisis as quickly as possible. He guessed that once she had built her totem and secured Sanction, the Dark Queen would move swiftly to secure the world. Gerard had no time to waste.

Gerard had found the elf, Samar, without difficulty. As Silvanoshei had predicted, the two men, though of different races, were experienced warriors and, after a few tense moments, suspicion and mistrust were both allayed. Gerard had delivered the ring and the message from Silvanoshei, though the Knight had not been exactly honest in relating the young king's words. Gerard had not told Samar that Silvanoshei was captive of his own heart. Gerard had made Silvanoshei a hero who had defied Mina and been punished for it. Gerard's plan was for the elves to join the Solamnics in the attempt to seize Sanction and halt the rise of Takhisis.

Gerard trusted that the elves would want to free their young king, and although Gerard had received the distinct impression that Samar did not much like Silvanoshei, Gerard had managed to impress the dour warrior with the true story of Silvanoshei's courage in the fight with Clorant and his fellow Knights. Samar had promised that he would carry the matter to Alhana Starbreeze. He had little doubt that she would agree to the plan. The two had parted, vowing to meet each other again as allies on the field of battle.

After bidding farewell to Samar, Gerard rode to the sea coast. Standing on a cliff that overlooked the crashing waves, he stripped off the black armor that marked him as a Knight of Takhisis, and one by one he hurled the pieces into the ocean. He had the distinct satisfaction of seeing, in the pre-dawn light, the waves lift the black armor and slam it against the jutting rocks.

"Take that and be damned to you," Gerard said. Mounting his horse, clad only in leather breeches and a well-worn woolen shirt, he set off west.

He hoped that with fair weather and good roads he might reach Lord Ulrich's manor in ten days. Gerard soon glumly revised his plan, hoped to reach the manor house in ten years, for at that point everything began to go strangely wrong. His horse threw a shoe in a region where no one had ever heard of a blacksmith. Gerard had to travel miles out of his way, leading his lame horse, to find one. When he did come across a blacksmith, the man worked so slowly that Gerard wondered if he was mining the iron and then forging it.

Days passed before his horse was shod and he was back in the saddle, only to discover that he was lost. The sky was cloudy and overcast. He could see neither sun nor stars, had no idea which direction he was heading. The land was sparsely populated. He rode for hours without seeing a soul. When he did come upon someone to ask directions, everyone in the land appeared to have suddenly gone stupid, for no matter what route he was told to take, the road always landed him in the middle of some impenetrable forest or stranded him on the banks of some impassable river.

Gerard began to feel as if he were in one of those terrible dreams, where you know the destination you are trying to reach, but you can never quite seem to reach it. At first he was annoyed and frustrated, but after days and days of wandering he began to feel uneasy.

Galdar's poisoned sword lodged in Gerard's gut.

"Am I making the decisions or is Takhisis?" he asked himself. "Is she determining my every move? Am I dancing to her piping?"

Constant rain soaked him. Cold winds chilled him. He had been forced to sleep outdoors for the past few nights, and he was just asking himself drearily what was the use of going on, when he saw the lights of a small town shining in the distance. Gerard came upon a road house. Not much to look at, it would provide a roof over his head, hot food and cold drink and, hopefully, information.

He led his horse to the stable, rubbed the animal down and saw to it that the beast was fed and resting comfortably. This done, he entered the road house. The hour was late, the innkeeper had gone to bed and was in a foul mood at being wakened. He showed Gerard to the common room, indicated a place on the floor. As the Knight spread out his blanket, he asked the innkeeper for the name of the town.

The man yawned, scratched himself, muttered irritably, "The town is Tyburn. On the road to Palanthas."

Gerard slept fitfully. In his dreams, he wandered about inside a house, searching for the door and never finding it. Waking long before morning, he stared at the ceiling and realized that he was now completely and thoroughly lost. He had the feeling the innkeeper was lying about the town's name and location, although why he should lie was a mystery to Gerard, except that he now suspected everyone he met of lying.

He went down to breakfast. Sitting in a rickety chair, he poked at a nameless mass that a scullery maid termed porridge. Gerard had lost his appetite. His head ached with a dull, throbbing pain. He had no energy, although he'd done nothing but ride about aimlessly the day before. He had the choice of doing that again today or going back to his blanket. Shoving aside the porridge, he walked over to the dirty window, rubbed off a portion of soot with his hand, and peered out. The drizzling rain continued to fall.

"The sun has to shine again sometime," Gerard muttered.

"Don't count on it," said a voice.

Gerard glanced around. The only other person in the inn was a mage, or at least that's what Gerard presumed, for the man was clad in reddish brown robes—the color of dried blood—and a black, hooded cloak. The mage sat in a small alcove as near the fire burning in the large stone hearth as he could manage. He was ill, or so Gerard assumed, for the mage coughed frequently, a bad-sounding cough that seemed to come from his gut. Gerard had noticed him when he first entered, but because he was a mage, Gerard had left his fellow traveler to himself.

Gerard hadn't thought he'd spoken loudly enough to be heard on the other side of the room, but apparently what this inn lacked in amenities it made up for in acoustics.

He could make some polite rejoinder or he could pretend he hadn't heard. He decided on the latter. He was in no mood for companionship, especially companionship that appeared to be in the last stages of consumption. He turned back to continue staring out the window.

"She rules the sun," the mage said. His voice was weak, with a whispering quality to it that Gerard found eerily compelling. "Although she no longer rules the moon." He gave what might have been a laugh, but it was interrupted by a fit of coughing. "She will soon rule the stars if she is not stopped."

Finding this conversation disturbing, Gerard turned around. "Are you speaking to me, sir?"

The mage opened his mouth, but was halted by another fit of coughing. He pressed a handkerchief to his lips, drew in a shuddering breath. "No," he rasped, irritated, "I am speaking for the joy of spitting up blood. Talking is not so easy for me that I waste my breath on it."

The shadow of the hood concealed the mage's face. Gerard glanced about. The maid had vanished back into a smoke-filled kitchen. Gerard and the mage were the only two in the room. Gerard moved closer, determined to see the man's face.

"I refer, of course, to Takhisis," the mage continued. He fumbled in the pocket of his robes. Drawing out a small, cloth pouch, he placed it on the hob. A pungent smell filled the room.

"Takhisis!" Gerard was astounded. "How did you know?" he asked in a low voice, coming to stand beside the mage.

"I have known her long," said the mage in his whispering voice, soft as velvet. "Very long, indeed." He coughed again briefly and motioned with his hand. "Fetch the kettle and pour some hot water into that mug."

Gerard didn't move. He stared at the hand. The skin had a gold tint to it, so that it glistened in the firelight like sunlit fish scales.

"Are you deaf as well as doltish, Sir Knight?" the mage demanded.

Gerard frowned, not liking to be insulted and not liking to be ordered about, especially by a total stranger. He was tempted to bid this mage a cold good morning and walk out. The mage's conversation interested him, however. He could always walk out later.

Lifting the kettle with a pair of tongs, Gerard poured out the hot water. The mage dumped the contents of the pouch into the mug. The smell of the mixture was noxious, caused Gerard to wrinkle his nose in disgust. The mage allowed the tea to steep and the water to cool before he drank it.

Gerard found a chair, dragged it over.

"Do you know where I am, sir? I've been riding for days without benefit of sun or stars or compass to guide me. Everyone I ask tells me something different. This innkeeper tells me that this road leads to Palanthas. Is that right?"

The mage sipped at his drink before he answered. He kept his hood pulled low over his head, so that his face was in shadow. Gerard had the impression of keen, bright eyes, with something a bit wrong with them. He couldn't make out what.

"He is telling the truth as far as it goes," said the mage. "The road leads to Palanthas—eventually. One might say that all roads that run east and west lead to Palanthas—eventually. What you should be more concerned with now is that the road leads to Jelek."

"Jelek!" Gerard exclaimed. Jelek—the headquarters of the Dark Knights. Realizing that his alarm might give him away, he tried to pass it off with a shrug. "So it leads to Jelek. Why should that concern me?"

"Because at this moment twenty Dark Knights and a few hundred foot soldiers are bivouacked outside of Tyburn. They march to Sanction, answering Mina's call."

"Let them camp out where they will," said Gerard coolly. "I have nothing to fear from them."

"When they find you here, they will arrest you," said the mage, continuing to sip at his tea.

"Arrest me? Why?"

The mage lifted his head, glanced at him. Again, Gerard had the impression there was something wrong with the man's eyes.

"Why? Because you might as well have 'Solamnic Knight' stamped in gold letters on your forehead."

"Nonsense," said Gerard with a laugh, "I am but a traveling merchant—"

"A merchant without goods to sell. A merchant who has a military bearing and close-cropped hair. A merchant who wears a sword in the military manner, counts cadence when he walks, and rides a trained war-horse." The mage snorted. "You couldn't fool a six-year-old girlchild."

He went back to drinking his tea.

"Still, why should they come here?" Gerard asked lightly, though his nervousness was increasing.

"The innkeeper knew you for a Solamnic Knight the moment he saw you." The mage finished his tea, placed the empty mug upon the hob. His cough had noticeably improved. "Note the silence from the kitchen? The Dark Knights frequent this place. The innkeeper is in their pay. He left to tell them you were here. He will gain a rich reward for turning you in."

Gerard looked uneasily toward the kitchen that had grown strangely quiet. He shouted out loudly for the innkeeper.

There was no response.

Gerard crossed the room and flung open the wooden door that led to the cooking area. He startled the scullery maid, who confirmed his fears by giving a shriek and fleeing out the back door.

Gerard returned to the common room.

"You are right," said Gerard. "The bastard has run off, and the maid screamed as though I was likely to slit her throat. I had best be going." He held out his hand. "I want to thank you, sir. I'm sorry, but I never asked your name or gave you mine. . . ."

The mage ignored the outstretched hand. He took hold of a wooden staff that had been resting against the chimney and used it to support himself as he regained his feet.

"Come with me," the mage ordered.

"I thank you for your warning, sir," said Gerard firmly, "but I must depart and swiftly—"

"You will not escape," said the mage. "They are too close. They rode out with the dawn, and they will be here in minutes. You have only one chance. Come with me."

Leaning on the staff, which was decorated with a gold dragon claw holding a crystal, the mage led the way to stairs that went to the upper floor. His motions were quick and fluid, belying his frail appearance. His nondescript robes rustled around his ankles. Gerard hesitated another moment, his gaze going to the window. The road was empty. He could hear no sounds of an army, no drums, no stamp of marching feet.

Who is this mage that I should trust him? Just because he seems to know what I am thinking, just because he spoke of Takhisis . . .

The mage paused at the foot of the staircase. He turned to face Gerard. The strange eyes glittered from the shadows.

"You spoke once of following your heart. What is in your heart now, Sir Knight?"

Gerard stared, his tongue stuck to the roof of his mouth.

"Well?" said the mage impatiently. "What is in your heart?"

"Despair and doubt," said Gerard at last, his voice faltering, "suspicion, fear . . ."

"Her doing," said the mage. "So long as these shadows remain, you will never see the sun." He turned, continued walking up the stairs.

Gerard heard sounds now, sounds of men shouting orders, sounds of jingling harness and the clash of steel. He ran for the stairs.

The lower level contained the kitchen, an eating room, and a large common room where Gerard had passed the night. The upper level contained separate rooms for the convenience of better-paying guests, as well as the innkeeper's private quarters, protected by a door that was locked and bolted.

The mage walked straight up to this door. He tried the handle, which wouldn't budge, then touched the lock with the crystal of his staff. Light flared, half blinding Gerard, who stood blinking and staring at blue stars for long moments. When he could see, the mage had pushed open the door. Tendrils of smoke curled out from the lock.

"Hey, you can't go in there—" Gerard began.

The mage cast him a cold glance. "You are starting to remind me of my brother, Sir Knight. While I loved my brother, I can truthfully say of him that there were times he irritated me to death. Speaking of death, yours is not far off." The mage pointed with his staff into the room. "Open that wooden chest. No, not that one. The one in the corner. It is not locked."

Gerard gave up. In for a copper, in for a steel as the saying went. Entering the innkeeper's room, he knelt beside the large wooden chest the mage had indicated. He lifted the lid, stared down at an assortment of knives and daggers, the odd boot, a pair of gloves, and pieces of armor: bracers, grieves, epaulets, a cuirass, helms. All of the armor was black, some stamped with the emblem of the Dark Knights.

"Our landlord is not above stealing from his guests," said the mage. "Take what you need."

Gerard dropped the lid of the chest with a bang. He stood up, backed off. "No," he said.

"Disguising yourself as one of them is your only chance. There is not much there, to be sure, but you can cobble something together, enough to pass."

"I just rid myself of an entire suit of that accursed stuff—"

"Only a sentimental fool would be that stupid," the mage retorted, "and thus I am not surprised to hear that you did it. Put on what armor you can. I'll loan you my black cloak. It covers a multitude of sins, as I have come to know."

"Even if I am disguised, it won't matter anyway," Gerard said. He was tired of running, tired of disguises, tired of lying. "You said the innkeeper told them about me."

"He is an idiot. You have a quick wit and a glib tongue." The mage shrugged. "The ruse may not work. You may still hang. But it seems to me to be worth the risk."

Gerard hesitated a moment longer. He may have been tired of running, but he wasn't yet tired of living. The mage's plan seemed a good one. Gerard's sword, a gift from Marshal Medan, would be recognized. His horse still bore the trappings of a Dark Knight, and his boots were like those worn by the Dark Knights.

Feeling more and more as if he were caught in a terrible trap in which he was continually running out the back only to find himself walking in the front, he grabbed up what parts of the armor he thought might fit him, began hastily buckling them onto various parts of his body. Some were too big and others painfully small. He looked, when he finished, like an armored harlequin. Still, with the black cloak to cover him, he might just pull it off.

"There," he said, turning around. "How do I—"

The mage was gone. The black cloak he had promised lay on the floor.

Gerard stared about the room. He hadn't heard the mage depart, but then he recalled that the man moved quietly. Suspicion crept into Gerard's mind, but he shrugged it off. Whether the strange mage was for him or against him didn't much matter now. He was committed.

Gerard picked up the black cloak, tossed it over his shoulder, and hastened from the landlord's room. Reaching the stairs, he looked out a window, saw a troop of soldiers drawn up outside. He resisted the urge to run and hide. Clattering down the stairs, he walked out door to the road house. Two soldiers, bearing halberds, shoved him rudely in their haste to enter.

"Hey!" Gerard called out angrily. "You damn near knocked me down. What is the meaning of this?"

Abashed, the two halted. One touched his hand to his forehead. "I beg pardon, Sir Knight, but we're in a hurry. We've been sent to arrest a Solamnic who is hiding in this inn. Perhaps you have seen him. He is wearing a shirt and leather breeches, tries to pass himself off as a merchant."

"Is that all you know of him?" Gerard demanded. "What does he look like? How tall is he? What color hair does he have?"

The soldiers shrugged, impatient. "What does that matter, sir. He's inside. The innkeeper told us we would find him here."

"He *was* in there," said Gerard. "You just missed him." He nodded his head. "He rode off that way not fifteen minutes ago."

"Rode off!" The soldier gaped. "Why didn't you stop him?"

"I had no orders to stop him," said Gerard coldly. "The bastard is none of my concern. If you make haste, you can catch him. Oh, and by the way, he's a tall, handsome man, about twenty-five years old, with jet-black hair and a long black mustache. What are you standing there staring at me for like a pair of oafs? Be off with you."

Muttering to themselves, the soldiers dashed out the door and down the street, not even bothering to salute. Gerard sighed, gnawed his lip in frustration. He supposed he should be grateful to the mage who had saved his life, but he wasn't. At the thought of yet more lying, dissembling, deceiving, of being always on his guard, always fearful of discovery, his spirits sank. He honestly wondered if he could do it. Hanging might be easier, after all.

Removing his helm, he ran his fingers through his yellow hair. The black cloak was heavy. He was sweating profusely, but dared not discard it. In addition, the cloak had a peculiar smell—reminding him of rose petals combined with something else not nearly as sweet or as pleasant. Gerard stood in the doorway, wondering what to do next.

The soldiers were escorting a group of prisoners. Gerard paid little attention to the poor wretches, beyond thinking he might have been one of them.

The best course of action, he decided, would be to ride away during the confusion. If anyone stops me, I can always claim to be a messenger heading somewhere with something important.

He stepped out into the street. Glancing up in the sky, he noted with pleasurable astonishment that the rain had ceased, the clouds departed. The sun shone brightly.

A very strange sound, like the bleat of a pleased goat, caused him to turn around.

Two pairs of gleaming eyes stared at him over the top of a gag. The eyes were the eyes of Tasslehoff Burrfoot, and the bleat was the glad and cheerful bleat of Tasslehoff Burrfoot.

The Tasslehoff Burrfoot.

23

IN WHICH IT IS PROVEN THAT NOT ALL KENDER LOOK ALIKE

The sight of Tasslehoff there, right in front of him, affected Gerard like a lightning blast from a blue dragon, left him dazed, paralyzed, incapable of thought or action. He was so amazed he simply stared. Everyone in the world was searching for Tasslehoff Burrfoot—including a goddess—and Gerard had found him.

Or rather, more precisely, this troop of Dark Knights had found the kender. Tasslehoff was among several dozen kender who were being herded to Sanction. Every single one of them probably claimed to be Tasslehoff Burrfoot. Unfortunately, one of them really was.

Tasslehoff continued to bleat through the gag, and now he was trying his best to wave. One of the guards, hearing the unusual sound, turned around. Gerard quickly clapped his helm over his head, nearly slicing off his nose in the process, for the helm was too small.

"Whoever's making that noise, stop it!" the guard shouted. He bore down on Tasslehoff, who—not watching where he was going—stumbled over his manacles and tumbled to the street. His fall jerked two of the kender who were chained to him off their feet. Finding this a welcome interlude in an otherwise dull and boring march, the other kender jerked themselves off their feet, with the result that the entire line of some forty kender was cast into immediate confusion.

Two guards, wielding flails, waded in to sort things out. Gerard strode swiftly away, almost running in his eagerness to leave the vicinity before something worse happened. His brain hummed with a confusion of thoughts, so that he moved in a kind of daze without any real idea of where he was going. He blundered into people, muttered excuses. Stepping into a hole, he wrenched his ankle and almost fell into a water trough. At last, spotting a shadowy alley, he ducked into it. He drew in several deep breaths. The cool air soothed his sweat-covered brow, and he was at last able to catch his breath and sort out the tangle.

Takhisis wanted Tasslehoff, she wanted the kender in Sanction. Gerard had a chance to thwart her, and in this, Gerard knew he followed the dictates of his own heart. The shadow lifted. The seeds of a plan were already sprouting in his mind.

Giving a mental salute to the wizard and wishing him well, Gerard headed off to put his plan, which involved finding a knight Gerard's own height and weight and, hopefully, head size, into action.

The Dark Knights and their foot soldiers set up camp in and around the town of Tyburn, bedded down for the night. The commander and his officers took over the road house, not much of a triumph, for its food was inedible and its accommodations squalid. The only good thing that could be said of the ale was that it made a man pleasantly light-headed and helped him forget his problems.

The commander of the Dark Knights drank deeply of the ale. He had a great many problems he was glad to drown, first and foremost of which was Mina, his new superior.

The commander had never liked nor trusted Lord Targonne, a small-minded man who cared more for a bent copper than he did for any of the troops under his command. Targonne did nothing to advance the cause of the Dark Knights but concentrated instead on filling his own coffers. No one in Jelek had mourned Targonne's death, but neither did they rejoice at Mina's ascension.

True, she was advancing the cause of the Dark Knights, but she was advancing at such a rapid pace that she had left most of them behind to eat her dust. The commander had been shocked to hear that she had conquered Solanthus. He wasn't sure that he approved. How were the Dark Knights to hold both that city and Solanthus and the Solamnic lord city of Palanthas?

This blasted Mina never gave a thought to guarding what she'd taken. She never gave a thought to supply lines stretched too thin, men overworked, the dangers of the populace rising in revolt.

The commander sent letters explaining all this to Mina, urging her to slow down, build up her forces, consolidate her winnings. Mina had forgotten someone else, too—the dragon overlord Malys. The commander had been sending conciliatory messages to the dragon, maintaining that the Dark Knights had no designs on her rulership. All this new territory they were conquering was being taken in her name, and so forth. He'd heard nothing in response.

Then, a few days ago, he had received orders from Mina to pull out of Jelek and march his forces south to help reinforce Sanction against a probable attack by a combined army of elves and Solamnics. He was to set forth immediately, and while he was at it, he was to round up and bring along any kender he happened to come across.

Oh, and Mina thought it quite likely that Malys was also going to attack Sanction. So he was to be prepared for that eventuality, as well.

Even now, rereading the orders, the commander felt the same shock and outrage he'd experienced reading them the first two dozen times. He had been tempted to disobey, but the messenger who had delivered the message made it quite clear to the commander that Mina and this One God of hers had a long reach. The messenger provided several examples of what had happened to commanders who thought they knew better than Mina what course of action to take, starting with the late Lord Targonne himself. Thus the commander now found himself on the road to Sanction, sitting in this wretched inn, drinking tepid ale, of which to say it tasted like horse piss was to give it a compliment it didn't deserve.

This day had gone from bad to worse. Not only had the kender slowed up their progress by tangling themselves in their chains—a tangle that had taken hours to sort out—the commander had lost a Solamnic spy, who'd been tipped off to their coming. Fortunately, they now had a good description of him. With his long black hair and black mustache, he should be easy to apprehend.

The commander was drowning his problems in ale when he looked up to see yet another messenger from Mina come walking through the door. The commander would have given all of his wealth to hurl the mug of ale at the man's head.

The messenger came to stand before him. The commander glowered balefully and did not invite him to be seated.

Like most messengers, who needed to travel light, this one was clad in black leather armor covered by a thick black cloak. He removed his helm, placed it under his arm, and saluted.

"I come in the name of the One God."

The commander snorted in his ale. "What does the One God want with me now? Has Mina captured Ice Wall? Am I supposed to march there next?"

The messenger was an ugly fellow with yellow hair, a pockmarked face, and startling, blue eyes. The blue eyes stared at the commander, obviously baffled.

"Never mind." The commander sighed. "Deliver your message and be done with it."

"Mina has received word that you have captured several kender prisoners. As you may know, she is searching for one kender in particular."

"Burrfoot. I know," said the commander. "I have forty or so Burrfoots out there. Take your pick."

"I will do that, with your permission, sir," said the messenger respectfully. "I know this Burrfoot by sight. Because the matter of his capture is so very urgent, Mina has sent me to look over your prisoners to see if I can find him among them. If he is, I'm to carry him to Sanction immediately."

The commander looked up in hope. "You wouldn't like to take all forty, would you?"

The messenger shook his head.

"No, I didn't think so. Very well. Go look for the blasted thief." A thought occurred to him. "If you do find him, what am I supposed to do with the rest?"

"I have no orders regarding that, sir," said the messenger, "but I would think you might as well release them."

"Release them . . ." The commander stared more closely at the messenger. "Is that blood on your sleeve? Are you wounded?"

"No, sir," said the messenger. "I was attacked by bandits on the road."

"Where? I'll send out a patrol," said the commander.

"No need to bother, sir," said the messenger. "I resolved the matter."

"I see," said the commander, who thought he noted blood on the leather armor, too. He shrugged. None of his concern. "Go search for this Burrfoot, then. You, there. Escort this man immediately to the pen where we keep the kender. Give him any assistance he requires." Raising his mug, he added, "I drink to your success, sir."

The messenger thanked the commander and departed.

The commander ordered another ale. He mulled over what to do with the kender. He was considering lining them all up and using them for target practice, when he heard a commotion at the door, saw yet another messenger.

Groaning inwardly, the commander was about to tell this latest nuisance to go roast himself in the Abyss, when the man shoved back his hat, and the commander recognized one of his most trusted spies. He motioned him forward.

"What news?" he asked. "Keep your voice down."

"Sir, I've just come from Sanction!"

"I said keep your voice down. No need to let everyone know our business," the commander growled.

"It won't matter, sir. Rumor follows fast on my heels. By morning, everyone will know. Malys is dead. Mina killed the dragon."

The crowd in the alehouse fell silent, everyone too stunned to speak, each trying to digest this news and think what it might mean to him.

"There's more," said the spy, filling the vacuum with his voice. "It is reported that Mina is dead, too."

"Then who is in charge?" the commander demanded, rising to his feet, his ale forgotten.

"No one, sir," said the spy. "The city is in chaos."

"Well, well." The commander chuckled. "Perhaps Mina was right, and prayers are answered after all. Gentlemen," he said, looking around at his officers and staff, "no sleep for us tonight. We ride to Sanction."

One down, thought Gerard to himself, tramping off behind the commander's aide. One to go.

Not the easiest, either, he thought gloomily. Hoodwinking a half-drunken commander of the Dark Knights had been goblin-play compared to what lay ahead—extricating one kender from the herd. Gerard could only hope that the Dark Knights, in their infinite wisdom, had seen fit to keep the kender gagged.

"Here they are," said the aide, holding up a lantern. "We have them penned up. Makes it easier."

The kender, huddled together like puppies for warmth, were asleep. The night air was cold, and few had cloaks or other protection from the chill. Those who did shared with their fellows. In repose, their faces looked pinched and wan. Obviously the commander wasn't wasting food on them, and he certainly wasn't concerned about their comfort.

The kenders' manacles were still attached, as were their leg irons and—Gerard breathed a hefty sigh of relief—their gags were still in place. Several soldiers stood guard. Gerard counted five, and he suspected there might be more he couldn't see.

At the bright light, the kender lifted their heads and blinked sleepily, yawning around the gags.

"On your feet, vermin," order the Knight. Two of the soldiers waded into the pen to kick the kender into wakefulness. "Stand up and look smart. Turn toward the light. This gentleman wants to see your dirty faces."

Gerard spotted Tasslehoff right away. He was about three-quarters of the way down the line, gaping and peering about and scratching his head with a manacled hand. Gerard had to make a show of inspecting every single kender, however, and this he did, all the while keeping one eye on Tas.

He looks old, Gerard realized suddenly. I never noticed that before.

Tas's jaunty topknot was still thick and long. Gray streaks were noticeable here and there, however, and the wrinkles on his face were starkly etched in the strong light. Still, his eyes were bright, his bearing bouncy, and he was watching the proceedings with his usual interest and intense curiosity.

Gerard walked down the line of kender, forcing himself to take his time. He wore a leather helm to conceal his face, afraid that Tas would recognize him again and make a glad outcry. His scheme did not work, however, for Tasslehoff shot one inquisitive look through the eyeslits of the helm, saw Gerard's bright blue eyes, and beamed all over. He couldn't speak, due to the gag, but he gave a wriggle expressive of his pleasure.

Coming to a halt, Gerard stared hard at Tas, who—to Gerard's dismay—gave a broad wink and grinned as wide as the gag would permit. Gerard grabbed hold of the kender's topknot and gave it a good yank.

"You don't know me," he hissed out from behind the helm.

"OfcourseIdont," mumbled the gagged Tas, adding excitedly, "Iwassosurprisedtoseeyouwherehaveyoubeen—"

Gerard straightened. "This is the kender," he said loudly, giving the topknot another yank.

"This one?" The aide was surprised. "Are you sure?"

"Positive," said Gerard. "Your commander has done an outstanding job. You may be certain that Mina will be most pleased. Release the kender immediately into my custody. I'll take full responsibility for him."

"I don't know . . ." The aide hesitated.

"Your commander said I was to have him if I found him," Gerard reminded the man. "I've found him. Now release him."

"I'm going to go bring back the commander," said the aide.

"Very well, if you want to disturb him. He looked pretty relaxed to me," Gerard said with a shrug.

His ploy didn't work. The aide was one of those loyal, dedicated types who would not take a crap without asking for permission. The aide marched off. Gerard stood in the pen with the kender, wondering what to do.

"I overplayed my hand," Gerard muttered. "The commander could decide that the kender is so valuable he'll want to take him himself to claim the reward! Blast! Why didn't I think of that?"

Tasslehoff had, meanwhile, managed to work the gag loose, dislodging it with such ease that Gerard could only conclude he'd kept it on for the novelty.

"*I don't know you,*" said Tasslehoff loudly and gave another conspiratorial wink that was guaranteed to get them both hung. "What's your name?"

"Shut up," Gerard shot out of the corner of his mouth.

"I had a cousin by that name," observed Tas reflectively.

Gerard tied the gag firmly in place.

He eyed the two guards, who were eyeing him back. He'd have to act quickly, couldn't give them a chance to cry out or start a racket. The old ruse of pretending to find scattered steel coins on the ground might work. He was just about to gasp and stare and point in astonishment, readying himself to whack the two in the head when they came over to look, when a commotion broke out behind him.

Torchlight flared up and down the road. People began shouting and rushing about. Doors slammed and banged. Gerard's first panicked thought was that he'd been discovered and that the entire army was turning out to seize him. He drew his sword, then realized that the soldiers weren't running toward him. They were running away from him, heading for the road house. The two guards had lost interest in him entirely, were staring and muttering, trying to figure out what was going on.

Gerard heaved a sigh. This alarm had nothing to do with him. He forced himself to stand still and wait.

The aide did not return. Gerard muttered in impatience.

"Go find out what's going on," he ordered.

One guard ran off immediately. He stopped the first person he came to, then turned and pounded back their direction.

"Malys is dead!" he shouted. "And so is that Mina girl! Sanction is in turmoil. We're marching there straight away."

"Malys dead?" Gerard gaped. "*And* Mina?"

"That's the word."

Gerard stood dazed, then came to his senses. He'd served in the army a good many years, and he knew that rumors were a copper a dozen. This might be true—he hoped it was—but it might not be. He had to act under the assumption that it wasn't.

"That's all very well, but I still need the kender," he said stubbornly. "Where's the commander's aide?"

"It was him I talked to." The guard fumbled at his belt. Producing a ring of keys, he tossed them to Gerard. "You want the kender? Here, take 'em all."

"I don't want them all!" Gerard cried, aghast, but by that time, the two guards had dashed off to join the throng of troops massing in the road.

Gerard looked back to find every single kender grinning at him.

Freeing the kender did not prove easy. When they saw that Gerard had the keys, the kender set up a yell that must have been heard in Flotsam and surged around him, raising their manacled hands, each kender demanding that Gerard unlock him or her first. Such was the tumult that Gerard was nearly knocked over backward and lost sight of Tasslehoff in the mix.

Bleating and waving his hand, Tasslehoff battled his way to the front of the pack. Gerard got a good grip on Tas's shirt and began to work at the locks on the chains on his hands and feet. The other kender milled about, trying to see what was going on, and more than once jerked the chains out of Gerard's grip. He cursed and shouted and threatened and was even forced to shove a few, who took it all in good humor. Eventually—he was never to know how—he managed to set Tasslehoff free. This done, he tossed the keys into the midst of the remaining kender, who pounced on them gleefully.

Gerard grabbed the bedraggled, disheveled, straw-covered Tasslehoff and hurried him off, keeping one eye on Tas and the other on the turmoil among the troops.

Tas ripped off his gag. "You forgot to remove it," he pointed out.

"No, I didn't," said Gerard.

"I am so glad to see you!" Tas said, squeezing Gerard's hand and stealing his knife. "What have you been doing? Where have you been? You'll have to tell me everything, but not now. We don't have time."

He came to a halt, began fumbling about for something in his pouch. "We have to leave."

"You're right, we don't have time for talk." Gerard retrieved his knife, grabbed Tas by the arm and hustled him along. "My horse is in the stable—"

"Oh, we don't have time for the horse either," said Tasslehoff, wriggling out of Gerard's grasp with the ease of an eel. "Not if we're going to reach the Knights' Council in time. The elves are marching, you see, and they're about to get into terrible trouble and—well, things are happening that would take too long to explain. You'll have to leave your horse behind. I'm sure he'll be all right, though."

Tas pulled out an object, held it to the moonlight. Jewels sparkled on its surface, and Gerard recognized the Device of Time Journeying.

"What are you doing with that?" he asked uneasily.

"We're going to use it to travel to the Knights' Council. At least, I *think* that's where it's going to take us. It's been acting funny these past few days. You wouldn't believe the places I've been—"

"Not me," said Gerard, retreating.

"Oh, yes, you," said Tasslehoff, nodding his head so vigorously that his topknot flipped over and struck him in the nose. "You have to come with me because they won't believe *me*. I'm just a kender. Raistlin says they'll believe you, though. When you tell them about Takhisis and the elves and all—"

"Raistlin?" Gerard repeated, trying desperately to keep up. "Raistlin who?"

"Raistlin Majere. Caramon's brother. You met him in the road house this morning. He was probably mean and sarcastic to you, wasn't he? I knew it."

Tas sighed and shook his head. "Don't pay any attention. Raistlin always talks like that to people. It's just his way. You'll get used to it. We all have."

The hair on Gerard's arms prickled. A chill crept up his back. He remembered hearing Caramon's stories about his brother—the red robes, the tea, the staff with the crystal, the mage's barbed tongue . . .

"Stop talking nonsense," said Gerard in a decided tone. "Raistlin Majere is dead!"

"So am I," said Tasslehoff Burrfoot. He smiled up at Gerard. "You can't let a little thing like that stop you."

Reaching out, Tas took hold of the Knight's hand. Jewels flashed, and the world dropped out from under Gerard's feet.

24 THE DECISION

When Gerard was young, a friend of his had concocted a swing for their entertainment. His friend suspended a wooden board, planed smooth, between two ropes and tied the ropes to a high tree branch. The lad then persuaded Gerard to sit in the swing while he turned him round and round, causing the ropes to twist together. At that point, his friend gave the swing a powerful shove and let loose. Gerard went spinning in a wildly gyrating circle that ended only when he pitched out of the swing and landed facedown on the grass.

Gerard experienced exactly the same sensation with the Device of Time Journeying, with the notable exception that it didn't dump him facedown. It might as well have, though, for when his feet touched the blessed grass, he didn't know if he was up or down, on his head or his heels. He staggered about like a drunken gnome, blinking, gasping, and trying to get his bearings. Wobbling about beside him, the kender also looked rattled.

"As many times as I've done that," said Tasslehoff, mopping his forehead with a grimy sleeve, "I never seem to get used to it."

"Where are we?" Gerard demanded, when the world had ceased to spin.

"We *should* be attending a Knights' Council," said Tasslehoff, dubious. "That's where we wanted to go, and that's the thought I thought in my head. But whether we're at the *right* Knights' Council is another question. We might be at Huma's Knights' Council, for all I know. The device has been acting very oddly." He shook his head, glanced about. "Does anything look familiar?"

The two had been deposited in a heavily forested tract of land on the edge of a stubbly wheat field that had long since been harvested. The thought came to Gerard that he was lost yet again, and this time a kender had lost him. He had no hope that he would ever be found and was just about to say so when he caught a glimpse of a large stone building reminiscent of a fortress or a manor. Gerard squinted, trying to bring the flag fluttering from the battlements into focus.

"It looks like the flag of Lord Ulrich," said Gerard, astonished. He looked all around him more closely now and thought that he recognized the landscape. "This *could* be Ulrich manor," he said cautiously.

"Is that where we're supposed to be?" Tas asked.

"It's where they were holding the Knights' Council the last time I was here," said Gerard.

"Well done," said Tasslehoff, giving the device a pat. He dropped it back carelessly into his pouch and stared expectantly at Gerard.

"We should hurry," he said. "Things are happening."

"Yes, I know," said Gerard, "but we can't just say we dropped out of the sky." He cast an uneasy glance upward.

"Why not?" Tas was disappointed. "It makes a great story."

"Because no one will believe us," Gerard stated. "I'm not sure I believe us." He gave the matter some thought. "We'll say that we rode from Sanction and my horse went lame and we had to walk. Got that?"

"It's not nearly as exciting as dropping out of the sky," Tas said. "But if you say so," he added hurriedly, seeing Gerard's eyebrows meet together in the middle of his forehead.

"What is the horse's name?" he asked, as they started off across the field, the stubble crunching beneath their feet.

"What horse?" Gerard muttered, absorbed in his thoughts that continued to whirl, even though he was, thankfully, on solid ground.

"Your horse," said Tas. "The one that went lame."

"I don't have a horse that went lame . . . Oh, that horse. It doesn't have a name."

"It *has* to have a name," said Tas severely. "All horses have names. I'll name it, may I?"

"Yes," said Gerard in a rash moment, thinking only to shut the kender up so he could try to sort out the puzzle of the strange mage and the extremely fortuitous and highly coincidental discovery of the kender in exactly the right place, in exactly the right time.

A walk of about a mile brought them to the manor house. The Knights had transformed it into an armed camp. Sunlight glinted off the steel heads of pikes. The smoke of cook fires and forge fires smudged the sky. The green grass was trampled with hundreds of feet and dotted with the colorful striped tents of the Knights. Flags representing holdings from Palanthas to Estwilde flapped in the brisk autumn wind. The sounds of hammering, metal on metal, rang through the air. The Knights were preparing to go to war.

After the fall of Solanthus, the Knights had sent out the call to defend their homeland. The call was answered. Knights and their retainers marched from as far as Southern Ergoth. Some impoverished Knights arrived on foot, bringing with them nothing but their honor and their desire to serve their country. Wealthy Knights brought their own troops, and treasure boxes filled with steel to hire more.

"We're going to see Lord Tasgall, Knight of the Rose and head of the Knights' Council," said Gerard. "Be on your best behavior, Burrfoot. Lord Tasgall doesn't tolerate any nonsense."

"So few people do," said Tas sadly. "I really think it might be a better world all the way around if more people did. Oh, I've thought of your horse's name."

"Have you?" Gerard asked absently, not paying attention.

"Buttercup," said Tasslehoff.

"That is my report," said Gerard. "The One God has a name and a face. Five faces. Queen Takhisis. How she managed to achieve this miracle, I cannot say."

"I can," Tasslehoff interrupted, leaping to his feet.

Gerard shoved the kender back into his chair.

"Not now," he said, for the fortieth time. He continued speaking. "Our ancient enemy has returned. In the heavens, she stands alone and unchallenged. In this world, though, there are those who are willing to give their lives to defeat her."

Gerard went on to tell of his meeting with Samar, spoke of the promise of that warrior that the elves would ally themselves with the Knights to attack Sanction.

The three lords glanced at each other. There had been much heated debate among the leadership as to whether the Knights should try to recapture Solanthus before marching to Sanction. Now, with Gerard's news, the decision was almost certainly going to be made to launch a major assault on Sanction.

"We received a communiqué stating that the elves have already begun their march," said Lord Tasgall. "The road from Silvanesti is long and fraught with peril—"

"The elves are going to be attacked!" Tasslehoff sprang out of his chair again.

"Remember what I said about the nonsense!" Gerard said sternly, shoving the kender back down.

"Does your friend have something to say, Gerard?" asked Lord Ulrich.

"Yes," said Tasslehoff, standing up.

"No," said Gerard. "That is, he always has something to say, but not anything we need to listen to."

"We have no guarantee that the elves will even arrive in Sanction," Lord Tasgall continued, "nor can we say *when* they will arrive. Meanwhile, according to reports we have been receiving from Sanction, all is in confusion there. Our spies confirm the rumor that Mina has vanished and that the Dark Knights are engaged in a leadership struggle. If we judge by events of the past, someone will rise to take her place, if that has not happened already. They will not be leaderless for long."

"At least," said Lord Ulrich, "We don't have to worry about Malys. This Mina managed to do what none of us had the guts to do. She fought Malys and killed her." He raised a silver goblet. "I drink to her. To Mina! To courage."

He gulped down the wine noisily. No one else raised a glass. The others appeared embarrassed. The Lord of the Rose fixed a stern gaze upon Lord Ulrich, who—by his flushed features and slurred words—had taken too much wine already.

"Mina had help, my lord," said Gerard gravely.

"You might as well call the goddess by name," said Lord Siegfried in dire tones. "Takhisis."

Lord Tasgall looked troubled. "It is not that I doubt the veracity of Sir Gerard, but I cannot believe—"

"Believe it, my lord," called Odila, entering the hall.

She was thin and pale, her white robes covered in mud and stained with blood. By her appearance, she had traveled far and slept and eaten little.

Gerard's gaze went to her breast, where the medallion of her faith had once hung. Its place was empty.

Gerard smiled at her, relieved. She smiled back. Her smile was her own, he was thankful to see. A bit tremulous, perhaps, and not quite as self-assured or self-confident as when he had first met her, but her own.

"My lords," she said, "I bring someone who can verify the information presented to you by Sir Gerard. His name is Mirror, and he helped rescue me from Sanction."

The lords looked in considerable astonishment at the man Odila brought forward. His eyes were wrapped in bandages that only partially concealed a terrible wound that had left him blind. He walked with a staff, to help him feel his way. Despite his handicap, he had an air of quiet confidence about him. Gerard had the feeling he'd seen this man somewhere before.

The Lord of the Rose made a stiff bow to the blind man, who, of course, could not see it. Odila whispered something to Mirror, who bowed his head. Lord Tasgall turned his complete attention to Odila. He regarded her sternly, his face impassive.

"You come to us a deserter, Sir Knight," he said. "It has been reported you joined with this Mina and served her, did her bidding. You worshiped the One God and performed miracles in the name of the One God, a god we now learn is our ancient foe, Queen Takhisis. Are you here because you have recanted? Do you claim to have discarded your faith in the god you once served? Why should we believe you? Why should we think that you are anything more than a spy?"

Gerard started to speak up in her defense. Odila rested her hand on his arm, and he fell silent. Nothing he could say would do any good, he realized, and it might do much harm.

Odila bent down on one knee before the lords. Although she knelt before them, she did not bow her head. She looked at all of them directly.

"If you expect shame or contrition from me, my lords, you will be disappointed. I am a deserter. That I do not deny. Death is the punishment for desertion, and I accept that punishment as my due. I offer only in my defense that I went in search of what we all are seeking. I went in search of a power greater than my own, a power to guide me and comfort me and give me the knowledge that I was not alone in this vast universe. I found such a power, my lords. Queen Takhisis, our god, has returned to us. I say 'our' god, because she is that. We cannot deny it.

"Yet I say to you that you must go forth and fight her, my lords. You must fight to halt the spread of darkness that is fast overtaking our world. But in order to fight her, you must arm yourselves with your faith. Reverence her, even as you oppose her. Those who follow the light must also acknowledge the darkness, or else there is no light."

Lord Tasgall gazed at her, his expression troubled. Lord Siegfried and Lord Ulrich spoke softly together, their eyes on Odila.

"Had you made a show of contrition, Lady, I would not have believed you," said Lord Tasgall at last. "As it is, I must consider what you say and think about it. Rise, Odila. As to your punishment, that will be determined by the council. In the meantime, I am afraid that you must be confined—"

"Do not lock her away, my lord," urged Gerard. "If we are going to attack Sanction, we are going to need all the experienced warriors we can muster. Release her into my care. I guarantee that I will bring her safely to trial, as she did me when I was on trial before you in Solanthus."

"Will this suit you, Odila?" asked the Lord of the Rose.

"Yes, my lord." She smiled at Gerard, whispered to him in an undertone. "It seems our destiny to be shackled together."

"My lords, if you're going to attack Sanction, you could probably use the help of some gold and silver dragons," Tasslehoff stated, jumping to his feet. "Now that Malys is dead, all the red dragons and the blue dragons and the black and the green will come to Sanction's defense—"

"I think you had better remove the kender, Sir Gerard," said the Lord of the Rose.

"Because the gold and silver dragons *would* come," Tasslehoff shouted over his shoulder, squirming in Gerard's grasp. "Now that the totem is destroyed, you see. I'd be glad to go fetch them myself. I have this magical device—"

"Tas, be quiet!" said Gerard, his face flushed with the exertion of trying to retain a grip on the slippery kender.

"Wait!" the blind man called out, the first words he'd spoken. He had been standing so quietly that everyone in the hall had forgotten his presence.

Mirror walked toward the sound of the kender's voice, his staff impatiently striking and knocking aside anything that got in his way. "Don't remove him. Let me talk to him."

The Lord of the Rose frowned at this interruption, but the man was blind, and the Measure was strict in its admonition that the blind, the lame, the deaf, and the dumb were to be treated with the utmost respect and courtesy.

"You may speak to this person, of course, sir. Seeing that you are sadly afflicted and lack sight, I think it only right to tell you, however, that he is naught but a kender."

"I am well aware that he is a kender, my lord," said Mirror, smiling. "That makes me all the more eager to speak to him. In my opinion, kender are the wisest people on Krynn."

Lord Ulrich laughed heartily at this odd statement, to receive another reproving glance from Lord Tasgall. The blind man reached out a groping hand.

"I'm here, sir," said Tas, catching hold of Mirror's hand and shaking it. "I'm Tasslehoff Burrfoot. *The* Tasslehoff Burrfoot. I tell you that because there's a lot of me going around these days, but I'm the only real one. That is, the others are real, they're just not really me. They're themselves, if you take my meaning, and I'm myself."

"I understand," said blind man solemnly. "I am called Mirror and *I* am, in reality, a silver dragon."

Lord Tasgall's eyebrows shot up to his receding hairline. Lord Ulrich sputtered in his wine. Lord Siegfried snorted. Odila smiled reassuringly at Gerard and nodded complacently.

"You say that you know where the silver and gold dragons are being held prisoner?" Mirror asked, ignoring the Knights.

"Yes, I know," Tasslehoff began, then he halted. Having been termed one of "the wisest people on Krynn," he felt called upon to tell the truth. "That is, the device knows." He patted his pouch where the Device of Time Journeying was secreted. "I could take you there, if you wanted," he offered, without much hope.

"I would like to go with you very much," said Mirror.

"You would?" Tasslehoff was astonished, then excited. "You would! That's wonderful. Let's go! Right now!" He fumbled about in his pouch. "Could I ride on your back? I love flying on dragons. I knew this dragon once. His name was Khirsah, I think, or something like that. He took Flint and I riding, and we fought a battle, and it was glorious."

Tas halted his fumbling, lost in reminiscences. "I'll tell you the whole story. It was during the War of the Lance—"

"Some other time," Mirror interrupted politely. "Speed is imperative. As you say, the elves are in danger."

"Oh, yes." Tas brightened. "I'd forgotten about that." He began once again to fumble in his pouch. Retrieving the device, Tas took hold of Mirror by the hand. The kender held the device up over his head and began to recite the spell.

Waving to the astonished Knights, Tas cried, "See you in Sanction!"

He and Mirror began to shimmer, as if they were oil portraits that someone had left out in the rain. At the last moment, before he had disappeared completely, Mirror reached out, seized hold of Odila, who reached out to take hold of Gerard.

In an eyeblink, all four of them vanished.

"Good grief!" exclaimed the Lord of the Rose.

"Good riddance," sniffed Lord Siegfried.

25 INTO THE VALLEY

The elven army marched north, made good time. The warriors rose early and slept late, speeding their march with songs and tales of the old days that lightened their burdens and gladdened their hearts.

Many of the Silvanesti songs and stories were new to Gilthas, and he delighted in them. In turn, the stories and songs of the Qualinesti were new to their cousins, who did not take so much delight in them, since most were concerned with the Qualinesti's dealing with lesser races such as humans and dwarves. The Silvanesti listened politely and praised the singer if they could not praise the song. The one song the Silvanesti did not sing was the song of Lorac and the dream.

When the Lioness traveled among them, she sang the songs of the Wilder elves, and these, with their stories of floating the dead down rivers and living wild and half-naked in the treetops, succeeded in shocking the sensibilities of both Qualinesti and Silvanesti, much to the amusement of the Wilder elves. The Lioness and her people were rarely among them, however. She and her Wilder elves acted as outriders, guarding the army's flanks from surprise attacks, and riding in advance of the main body to scout out the best routes.

Alhana seemed to have shed years. Gilthas had thought her beautiful when he'd first met her, but her beauty had a frost upon it, as a late-blooming rose. Now, she walked in autumn's bright sunshine. She was riding to save her son, and she could ride with honor, for she believed that Silvanoshei had redeemed himself. He was being held prisoner, and if he had landed himself in this predicament by his near fatal obsession with this human girl, her mother's heart could conveniently forget that part of the tale.

Samar could not forget it, but he kept silent. If what Sir Gerard had told him about Silvanoshei proved true, then perhaps this hard experience would help the young fool grow into a wise man, worthy of being king. For Alhana's sake, Samar hoped so.

Gilthas marched with his own misgivings. He had hoped that once they were on the road, he could cast off his dark fears and forebodings. During the day he was able to do so. The singing helped. Songs of valor and courage reminded him that there had been heroes of old, who had overcome terrible odds to drive back the darkness, that the elven people had undergone greater trials than this and had not only survived, but thrived. In the night, however, trying to sleep while missing the comfort of his wife's arms around him, dark wings hovered over him, blotted out the stars.

One matter worried him. They heard no news from Silvanesti. Admittedly, their route would be difficult for a runner to follow, for Alhana had not been able to tell the runners exactly where to find them. She had sent back runners of her own to act as guides, however, while every chipmunk would be able to give news of their passing. Time passed without word. No new runners came, and their own runners did not return.

Gilthas mentioned this to Alhana. She said sharply that the runners would come when they came and not before and it was not worth losing sleep and wasting one's energy worrying about it.

The elves traveled north at a prodigious pace, eating up the miles, and soon they had entered the southern portion of the Khalkist Mountains. They had long ago crossed the border into ogre lands, but they saw no signs of the ancient enemy, and it seemed that their strategy—to march along the backbone of the mountains, hiding themselves in the valleys—was working. The weather was fine, with cool days that were cloudless and sunny. Winter held back her heavy snow and frost. There were no mishaps on the trail, none fell seriously ill.

If there had been gods, it might have been said that they smiled upon the elves, so easy was this portion of their march. Gilthas began to relax, let the warm sun melt his worries as it melted the light dusting of snowflakes that sometimes fell in the night. Exhaustion from the long day's march and the crisp mountain air forced sleep upon him. He slept long and deeply and woke refreshed. He could even remind himself of the old human adage, "No news is good news," and find some comfort in that.

Then came the day that Gilthas would remember for the rest of his life, remember every small detail, for on that day life changed forever for the elves of Ansalon.

It began as any other. The elves woke with the first gray light of dawn. Packing up their bedrolls with practiced haste, they were on the march before the sun had yet lifted up over the mountaintops. They ate as they walked. Food was harder to come by in the mountains where vegetation was sparse, but the elves had foreseen this and filled their packs with dried berries and nutmeats.

They were still many hundred miles from Sanction, but all spoke confidently of their journey's end, which seemed no more than a few weeks away. The dawn was glorious. The Qualinesti elves sang their ritual song to welcome the sun, and this morning the Silvanesti joined in. The sun and the marching burned away night's chill. Gilthas marveled at the beauty of the day and of the mountains. He could never feel at home among mountains, no elf could, but he could be moved and awed by their stark grandeur.

Then, behind him came the pounding of horse's hooves. Ever after, when he heard that sound, he was swept back in time to this fateful day. A rider was pushing the horse to the limit, something unusual on the narrow, rocky trails. The elves continued to march, but many cast wondering glances over their shoulders.

The Lioness rode into view, the sun lighting her golden hair so that it seemed she was bathed in fire. Gilthas would remember that, too.

He reined in his horse, his heart filled suddenly with dread. He knew her, knew the grim expression on her face. She rode past him, heading for the front of the column. She said nothing to him, but cast him a single glance as she galloped by, a glance that sent him spurring after her. He saw now that there were two people on the horse. A woman sat behind the Lioness, a woman clad in the green, mottled clothing of a Silvanesti runner. That was all Gilthas noticed about her before the Lioness's mad charge carried her around a bend in the narrow trail and out of his sight.

He rode after her. Elves were forced to scatter in all directions or be ridden down. Gilthas had a brief glimpse of staring eyes and concerned faces. Voices cried out, asking what was going on, but the words whipped past him and he did not respond. He rode recklessly, fear driving him.

He arrived in time to see Alhana turn her horse's head, stare back in astonishment at the Lioness, who was shouting in her crude Silvanesti for the queen to halt. The runner dismounted, sliding off the back of the horse before the Lioness could stop the plunging animal. The runner took a step, then collapsed onto the ground. The Lioness slid off her horse, knelt beside the fallen runner. Alhana hastened to her, accompanied by Samar. Gilthas joined them, gesturing to Planchet, who marched at the head of the column with the Silvanesti commanders.

"Water," Alhana commanded. "Bring water."

The runner tried to speak, but the Lioness wouldn't permit her, not until she had drunk something. Gilthas was close enough now to see that the runner was not wounded, as he had feared, but weak from exhaustion and dehydration. Samar offered his own waterskin, and the Lioness gave the runner small sips, encouraging her with soothing words. After a draught or two, the runner shook her head.

"Let me speak!" she gasped. "Hear me, Queen Alhana! My news is . . . dire. . . ."

Among humans, a crowd would have gathered around the fallen, ears stretched, anxious to see and hear what they could. The elves were more respectful. They guessed by the commotion and the hurry that the news this runner bore was probably bad news, but they kept their distance, patiently waiting to be told whatever they needed to know.

"Silvanesti has been invaded," said the runner. She spoke weakly, dazedly. "Their numbers are countless. They came down the river in boats, burning and looting the fishing villages. So many boats. None could stop them. They entered Silvanesti, and even the Dark Knights feared them, and some fled. But they are allies now. . . ."

"Ogres?" Alhana asked in disbelief.

"Minotaurs, Your Majesty," said the runner. "Minotaurs have allied with the Dark Knights. The numbers of our enemies are vast as the dead leaves in autumn."

Alhana cast Gilthas one burning-eyed glance, a glance that seared through flesh and bone and struck him in the heart.

You were right, the glance said to him. *And I was wrong.*

She turned her back on him, on them all, and walked away. She repulsed even Samar, who would have gone to her.

"Leave me," she commanded.

The Lioness bent over the runner, giving her more water. Gilthas was numb. He felt nothing. The news was too enormous to comprehend. Standing there, trying to make sense of this, he noticed that the runner's feet were bruised and bloody. She had worn out her boots, run the last miles barefoot. He could feel nothing for his people, but her pain and heroism moved him to tears. Angrily, he blinked them away. He could not give in to grief, not now. He strode forward, determined to talk to Alhana.

Samar saw Gilthas coming and made a move as if to intercept him. Gilthas gave Samar a look that plainly said the man could try, but he might have a tough time doing it. After a moment's hesitation, Samar backed off.

"Queen Alhana," said Gilthas.

She lifted her face, that was streaked with tears. "Spare me your gloating," she said, her voice low and wretched.

"This is no time to speak of who was right and who was wrong," Gilthas said quietly. "If we had stayed to lay siege to Silvanesti, as I counseled, we would all probably be dead right now or slaves in the belly of a minotaur galley." He rested his hand gently on her arm, was shocked to feel her cold and shivering. "As it is, our army is strong and intact. It will take some time for the armies of our enemies to entrench themselves. We can return and attack, take them by surprise—"

"No," said Alhana. She clasped her arms around her body, set her teeth and, through sheer effort of will, forced herself to stop shaking. "No, we will continue on to Sanction. Don't you see? If we help the human armies conquer Sanction, they will be honor-bound to help us free our homeland, drive out the invaders."

"Why should they?" he asked sharply. "What reason would humans have to die for us?"

"Because we will help them fight for Sanction!" Alhana stated.

"Would we be doing that if your son were not being held prisoner inside Sanction's walls?" Gilthas demanded.

Alhana's skin, cheeks, lips were all one, all ashen. Her dark eyes seemed the only living part of her, and they were smudged with shadow.

"We Silvanesti will march to Sanction," she said. She did not look at him. She stared southward, as if she could see through the mountains and into her lost homeland. "You Qualinesti may do what you like."

Turning from him, she said to Samar. "Summon our people. I must speak to them."

She walked away, tall, straight-backed, shoulders squared.

"Do you agree with this?" Gilthas demanded of Samar as he started to follow her.

Samar cast Gilthas a look that might have been a backhanded blow across the face, and Gilthas realized he had been wrong to ask. Alhana was Samar's queen and his commander. He would die before he questioned any decision she made. Gilthas had never before felt so utterly frustrated, so helpless. He was filled with raging anger that had no outlet.

"We have no homeland," he said, turning to Planchet. "No homeland at all. We are exiles, people without a country. Why can't she see that? Why can't she understand?"

"I think she does," said Planchet. "For her, attacking Sanction is the answer."

"The wrong answer," said Gilthas.

Elven healers came to tend to the runner, treating her wounds with herbs and potions, and they shooed the Wilder elf away. The Lioness walked over to join him.

"What are we doing?"

"Marching to Sanction," Gilthas said grimly. "Did the runner have any news of our people?"

"She said that there were rumors they had managed to escape Silvanesti, flee back into the Plains of Dust."

"Where they will most certainly *not* be welcome." Gilthas sighed deeply. "The Plainspeople warned us of that."

He stood, troubled. He wanted desperately to return to his people, and he realized now that the anger he was feeling was aimed at himself. He should have followed his instincts, remained with his people, not marched off on this ill-fated campaign.

"I was wrong, as well. I opposed you. I am sorry, my husband," said the Lioness remorsefully. "But don't punish yourself. You could not have stopped the invasion."

"At least I could be with our people now," he said bitterly. "Sharing their trouble, if nothing else."

He wondered what he should do. He longed to go back, but the way would be hard and dangerous, and the odds were he would never make it alone. If he took away Qualinesti warrriors, he would leave Alhana's force sadly depleted. He might cause dissension in the ranks, for some Silvanesti would certainly want to return to their homes. At this time, more than any other, the elves needed to be united.

A shout rang from the rear, then another and another, all up and down the line. Alhana stopped in the midst of her speech, turned to look. The cries were coming from every direction now, thundering down on them like the rocks of an avalanche.

"Ogres!"

"What direction?" the Lioness called out to one of her scouts.

"All directions!" he cried and pointed.

Their line of march had carried the elves into a small, narrow valley, surrounded by high cliffs. Now, as they looked, the cliffs came alive. Thousands of huge, hulking figures appeared along the heights, stared down at the elves, and waited in silence for the order to start the killing.

26 THE JUDGMENT

The gods of Krynn met once again in council. The gods of light stood opposite the gods of darkness, as day stands opposite night, with the gods of neutrality divided evenly in between. The gods of magic stood together, and in their midst was Raistlin Majere.

Paladine nodded, and the mage stepped forward.

Bowing, he said simply, "I have been successful."

The gods stared in wordless astonishment, all except the gods of magic, who exchanged smiles, their thoughts in perfect accord.

"How was this accomplished?" Paladine asked at last.

"My task was not easy," Raistlin said. "The currents of chaos swirl about the universe. The magic is wayward and unwieldy. I no more set my hand upon it than it slides through my fingers. When the kender used the device, I managed to seize hold of him and wrench him back into the past, where the winds of chaos blow less fiercely. I was able to keep Tas there long enough for him to have a sense of where he was before the magic whipped away from me and I lost him. I knew where to look for him, however, and thus, when next he used the device, I was ready. I took him to a time we both recognized, and he began to know me. Finally, I carried him to the present. Past and present are now linked. You have only to follow the one, and it will lead you to the other."

"What do you see?" Paladine asked Zivilyn.

"I see the world," said Zivilyn softly, tears misting his eyes. "I see the past, and I see the present, and I see the future."

"Which future?" asked Mishakal.

"The path the world walks now," Zivilyn replied.

"Then it is not possible to alter it?" Mishakal asked.

"Of course, it is possible," said Raistlin caustically. "We may all yet cease to exist."

"You mean that the blasted kender is not yet dead?" Sargonnas growled.

"He is not. The power of Queen Takhisis has grown immense. If you are to have any hope of defeating her, Tasslehoff has yet one important task to accomplish with the Device of Time Journeying. If he accomplishes this task—"

"—he must be sent back to die," said Sargonnas.

"He will be given the choice," Paladine corrected. "He will not be forced back or sent against his wishes. He has freedom of will, as do all living beings upon Krynn. We cannot deny that to him, just because it suits our convenience."

"Suits our convenience!" Sargonnas roared. "He could destroy us all!"

"If that is the risk we run for our beliefs," said Paladine, "then so be it. Your queen, Sargonnas, disdained free will. She found it easier to rule slaves. You opposed her in that. Would your minotaurs worship a god who made them slaves? A god who denied them their right to determine their own fate, a right to find honor and glory?"

"No, but then my minotaurs have sense. They are not brainless kender," muttered Sargonnas, but he muttered it into his fur. "That brings us to the next question, however. Providing this kender does not yet get us all killed"—he cast a baleful glance at Paladine—"what punishment do we mete out to the goddess whose name I will never more speak? The goddess who betrayed us?"

"There can be only one punishment," said Gilean, resting his hand upon the book.

Paladine looked around. "Are we all agreed?"

"So long as the balance is maintained," said Hiddukel, the keeper of the scales.

Paladine looked at each of the gods. Each, in turn, nodded. Last, he looked at his mate, his beloved Mishakal. She did not nod. She stood with her head bowed.

"It must be," said Paladine gently.

Mishakal lifted up her eyes, looked long and lovingly into his. Then, through her tears, she nodded.

Paladine rested his hand upon the book. "So be it," he said.

27 TASSLEHOFF BURRFOOT

Tasslehoff's life had been made up of glorious moments. Admittedly, there had been some bad moments, too, but the glorious moments shone so very brightly that their radiance overwhelmed the unhappy moments, causing them to fade back into the inner recesses of his memory. He would never forget the bad times, but they no longer had the power to hurt him. They only made him a little sad.

This moment was one of the glorious moments, more glorious than any moment that had come before, and it kept improving, with each coming moment shining more gloriously than the next.

Tas was now growing accustomed to traveling through space and time, and while he continued to feel giddy and disoriented every time the device dumped him out at a destination, he decided that such a sensation, while not suited to everyday use, made for an exhilarating change. This time, after landing and stumbling about a bit and wondering for an exciting instant if he was going to throw up, the wooziness receded, and he was able to look around and take note of his surroundings.

The first thing he saw was an immense silver dragon, standing right beside him. The dragon's eyes were horribly wounded by a jagged scar that slashed across them, and Tas recognized the blind man who had spoken to him in the Knights' Council. The dragon, like Tas, appeared to have taken the journey through time in stride, for he was fanning his wings gently and turning his head this way and that, sniffing the air and listening. Either traveling through time did not bother dragons, or being blind kept one from getting dizzy. Tas wondered which it was and made a mental note to ask during a lull in the proceedings.

His other two companions were not faring quite as well. Gerard had not liked the journey the first time, so he could be excused for really not liking it the second time. He swayed on his feet and breathed heavily.

Odila was wide-eyed and gasping and reminded Tas of a poor fish he'd once found in his pocket. He had no idea how the fish had come to be there, although he did have a dim sort of memory that someone had lost it. He'd managed to restore the fish to water, where, after a dazed moment, it had swum off. The fish had the same look that Odila had now.

"Where are we?" she gasped, clinging to Gerard with a white-knuckled grip.

He looked grimly at the kender. One and all, they looked grimly at the kender.

"Right were we're supposed to be," Tas said confidently. "Where the Dark Queen has kept the gold and silver dragons prisoners." Gripping the device tightly in his hand, he added a soft, "I hope!" that didn't come out all that softly and rather spoiled matters.

Tas had never been anywhere like this before. All around him was gray rock and nothing except gray rock as far as the eye could see. Sharp gray rocks, smooth gray rocks, enormous gray rocks, and small gray rocks. Mountains of gray rock, and valleys of the same gray rock. The sky above him was black as the blackest thing he'd ever seen, without a single star, and yet he was bathed in a cold white light. Beyond the gray rock, on the horizon, shimmered a wall of ice.

"I feel stone beneath my feet," said Mirror, "and I do not smell vegetation, so I assume the land in which we have arrived is bleak and barren. I hear no sounds of any kind: not the waves breaking on the shore, not the wind rushing through the trees, no sound of bird or animal. I sense that this place is desolate, forbidding."

"That about sums it up," said Gerard, wiping sweat from his forehead with the back of his hand. "Add to that description the fact that the sky above us is pitch black, there is no sun, yet there is light; the air is colder than a troll's backside, and this place appears to be surrounded by what looks like a wall made of icicles, and you have said all there is to say about it."

"What he didn't say," Tas felt called upon to point out, "is that the light makes the wall of ice shimmer with all sorts of different colors—"

"Rather like the scales of a many-colored dragon?" Mirror asked.

"That's it!" Tas cried, enthused. "Now that you come to mention it, it does look like that. It's lovely in a sort of cold and unlovely way. Especially how the colors shift whenever you look at them, dancing all along the icy surface . . ."

"Oh, shut up!" ordered Gerard.

Tas sighed inwardly. As much he liked humans, traveling with them certainly took a lot of joy out of the journey.

The cold was biting. Odila shivered, wrapped her robes around her more closely. Gerard stalked over to the ice wall. He did not touch it. He looked it up and down. Drawing his dagger, he jabbed the weapon's point into the wall.

The blade shattered. Gerard dropped the knife with an oath, wrung his hand in pain, then slid his hand beneath his armpit.

"It's so damn cold it broke the blade! I could feel the chill travel through the metal and strike deep into my bone. My hand is still numb."

"We can't survive long in this," Odila said. "We humans will perish of the cold, as will the kender. I can't speak for the dragon."

Tas smiled at her to thank her for including him.

"As for me," said Mirror, "my species is cold-blooded. My blood will thicken and grow sluggish. I will soon lose my ability to fly or even to think clearly."

"And except for you," said Gerard grumpily, looking around the barren wasteland on which they stood, "I don't see a single dragon."

Tasslehoff was forced to admit that he was feeling the chill himself and that it was causing very unpleasant sensations in his toes and the tips of his fingers. He thought with regret back to a fur-lined vest he'd once owned, and he wondered whatever became of it. He wondered also what had become of the dragons, for he was absolutely positive—well, relatively certain—that this was the place where he'd been told he would find them. He peered under a few gray rocks with no luck.

"You better take us back, Tas," said Odila, as best she could for her teeth clicking together.

"He can't take us back," said Mirror, and the dragon was oddly complacent. "This place was constructed as a prison for dragons. It has frozen the magic in my blood. I doubt if the magic of the device will work either."

"We're trapped here!" Gerard said grimly. "To freeze to death!"

Tasslehoff drew himself up. This was a glorious moment, and while admittedly it didn't look or feel very glorious (he'd lost all feeling in his toes), he knew what he was doing.

"Now, see here," he said sternly, eyeing Gerard. "We've been through a lot together, you and I. If it wasn't for me, you wouldn't be where you are today. That being the case," he added hurriedly, before Gerard could reply, "follow me."

He turned around, bravely confident, ready to proceed forward, without having the least idea where he was going.

A voice said softly, distinctly, in his ear, "Over the ridge."

"Over the ridge," said Tasslehoff. Pointing at the first ridge of gray rock that he saw, he marched off that direction.

"Should we go after him?" Odila asked.

"We don't dare lose him," said Gerard.

Tas clamored among the gray stones, dislodging small rocks that slid and slithered out from under him and went clattering and bounding down behind him, seriously impeding Odila and Gerard, who were attempting to climb up after him. Glancing back, Tas saw that Mirror had not moved. The silver dragon continued to stand where he had landed, fanning his wings and twitching his tail, probably to try to keep his blood stirring.

"He can't see," said Tasslehoff, stung by guilt. "And we've left him behind, all alone. Don't worry, Mirror!" he called out. "We'll come back for you."

Mirror said something in response, something that Tas couldn't quite hear clearly, what with all the noise that Odila and Gerard were making dodging rocks, but it seemed to him that he heard, "The glory of this moment is yours, kender. I will be waiting."

"That's the great thing about dragons," Tas said to himself, feeling warm all over. "They always understand."

Topping the ridge, he looked down, and his breath caught in his throat.

As far as the eye could see were dragons. Tasslehoff had never seen so many dragons in one place at one time. He had never imagined that there were so many gold and silver dragons in the world.

The dragons slumbered in a cold-induced torpor. They pressed together for warmth, heads and necks entwined, bodies lying side by side, wings folded, tails wrapped around themselves or their brother dragons. The strange light that caused rainbows to dance mockingly in the ice wall stole the colors from the dragons, left them gray as the rocky peaks that surrounded them.

"Are they dead?" Tas asked, his heart in his throat.

"No," said the voice in his ear, "they are deeply asleep. Their slumber keeps them from dying."

"How do I wake them?"

"You must bring down the ice wall."

"How do I do that? Gerard's knife broke when he tried it."

"A weapon is not what is needed."

Tas thought this over, then said doubtfully, "Can I do it?"

"I don't know," the voice said. "Can you?"

"By all that is wonderful!" Gerard exclaimed. Pulling himself up to the top of the ridge, he now stood beside Tasslehoff. "Would you look at that!"

Odila said nothing. She stood long moments, gazing down at the dragons, then she turned and ran back down the ridge. "I will go tell Mirror."

"I think he knows," said Tasslehoff, then he added, politely, "Excuse me. I have something to do."

"Oh, no. You're not going anywhere!" Gerard cried and made a snatch at Tasslehoff's collar.

He missed.

Tasslehoff began running full tilt, as fast as he could run. The climb had warmed his feet. He could feel his toes—essential for running—and he ran as he had never run before. His feet skimmed over the ground. If he stepped on a loose rock that might have sent him tumbling, he didn't touch it long enough to matter. He fairly flew down the side of the ridge.

He gave himself to the running. The wind buffeted his face and stung his eyes. His mouth opened wide. He sucked in great mouthfuls of cold air that sparkled in his blood. He heard shouts, but their words meant nothing in the wind of his running. He ran without thought of stopping, without the means of stopping. He ran straight at the ice wall.

Wildly excited, Tas threw back his head. He opened his mouth and cried out a loud "Yaaaa" that had absolutely no meaning but just felt good. Arms spread wide, mouth open wide, he crashed headlong into the wall of shimmering ice.

Rainbow droplets fell all around him. Sparkling in a radiant silver light, the droplets plopped down on his upturned face. He raced through the curtain of water that had once been a wall of ice, and he continued to run, out of control, running, madly running, and then he saw that just ahead of him, almost at his feet, the gray rock ended abruptly and there was nothing below it except black.

Tas flailed his arms, trying to stop. He struggled with his feet, but they seemed to have minds of their own, and he knew with certainty that he was going to sail right off the edge.

My last moment, but a glorious one, he thought.

He was falling, and silver wings flew above him. He felt a claw seize hold of his collar (not a new sensation, for it seemed that someone was always seizing hold of his collar), except that this was different. This was a most welcome seize.

Tas hung suspended over eternity.

He gasped for breath that he couldn't seem to find. He was dizzy and light-headed. Tilting back his head, he saw that he dangled from the claw of a silver dragon, a silver dragon who turned his sightless eyes in the general direction of the kender.

"Thank goodness you kept yelling," said Mirror, "and thank goodness Gerard saw your peril in time to warn me."

"Are they free?" Tasslehoff asked anxiously. "The other dragons?"

"They are free," said Mirror, veering slowly about, returning to what Tas could see now was nothing more than an enormous island of gray rock adrift in the darkness.

"What are you and the other dragons going to do?" Tas asked, starting to feel better now that he was over solid ground.

"Talk," said Mirror.

"Talk!" Tasslehoff groaned.

"Don't worry," said Mirror. "We are keenly aware of the passing of time. But there are questions to be asked and answered before we can make any decision." His voice softened. "Too many have sacrificed too much for us to ruin it all by acting rashly."

Tas didn't like the sound of that. It made him feel extremely sad, and he was about to ask Mirror what he meant, but the dragon was now lowering the kender to the ground. Gerard caught hold of Tasslehoff in his arms. Giving him a hug, he set him on his feet. Tas concentrated on trying to breathe. The air was warmer, now that the ice wall was gone. He could hear wings beating and the dragons' voices, deep and resonant, calling out to each other in their ancient language.

Tas sat on the gray rocks and waited for his breathing to catch up with him and for his heart to realize that he'd quit running and that it didn't need to beat so frantically. Odila went off with Mirror to serve as his guide, and he soon heard the silver dragon's voice rising in joy at finding his fellows. Gerard remained behind. He didn't tromp about, as usual, peering into this and investigating that. He stood looking down at Tas with a most peculiar expression on his face.

Maybe he has a stomach ache, Tas thought.

As for Tasslehoff, since he didn't have breath enough to talk, he spent some time thinking.

"I never quite looked at it that way," he thought to himself.

"What did you say?" Gerard asked, squatting down to be level with the kender.

Tas made up his mind. He could talk now and he knew what he had to say. "I'm going back."

"We're all going back," Gerard stated, adding, with an exasperated glance in the direction of the dragons, "eventually."

"No, I don't mean that," said Tas, having trouble with a lump in his throat. "I mean I'm going back to die." He managed a smile and a shrug. "I'm already dead, you know, so it won't be such a huge change."

"Are you sure about this, Tas?" Gerard asked, regarding the kender with quiet gravity.

Tas nodded. "'Too many have sacrificed too much . . .' that's what Mirror said. I thought about that when I ran off the edge of the world. If I die here, I said to myself, where I'm not supposed to, everything dies with me. And then, do you know what happened, Gerard? I felt scared! I've never been scared before." He shook his head. "Not like that."

"The fall would be enough to scare anyone," said Gerard.

"It wasn't the fall," Tas said. "I was scared because I knew if everything died, it would all be my fault. All the sacrifices that everybody has made down through history: Huma, Magius, Sturm Brightblade, Laurana, Raistlin . . ." He paused, then said softly, "Even Lord Soth. And countless others I'll never know. All their suffering would be wasted. Their joys and triumphs would be forgotten."

Tasslehoff pointed. "Do you see that red star? The one there?"

"Yes," said Gerard. "I see it."

"The kender tell me that people in the Fifth Age believe Flint Fireforge lives in that star. He keeps his forge blazing so that people will remember the glory of the old days and that they will have hope. Do you think that's true?"

Gerard started to say that he thought the star was just a star and that a dwarf could never possibly live in a star, but then, seeing Tas's face, the Knight changed his mind.

"Yes, I think it's true."

Tas smiled. Rising to his feet, he dusted himself off, looked himself over, twitched his clothes and his pouches into place. After all, if he was going to be stepped on by Chaos, he had to look presentable.

"That red star is the very first star I'm going to visit. Flint will be glad to see me. I expect he's been lonely."

"Are you going now?" Gerard asked.

"'No time like the present,'" Tas said cheerfully. "That's a time-travel joke," he added, eyeing Gerard. "All us time travelers make time-travel jokes. You're supposed to laugh."

"I guess I don't feel much like laughing," Gerard said. He rested his hand on Tas's shoulder. "Mirror was right. You are wise, perhaps the very wisest person I know, and certainly the most courageous. I honor you, Tasslehoff Burrfoot."

Drawing his sword, Gerard saluted the kender, the salute one true Knight gives to another.

A glorious moment.

"Goodbye," Tasslehoff said. "May your pouches never be empty."

Reaching into his pouch, he found the Device of Time Journeying. He looked at it, admired it, ran his fingers over the jewels that sparkled more brightly than he ever remembered seeing them sparkle before. He caressed it lovingly, then, looking out at the red star, he said, "I'm ready."

"The dragons have finally reached a decision. They're about ready to return to Krynn," said Odila. "And they want us to go with them." She glanced about. "Where's the kender? Have you lost him again?"

Gerard wiped his nose and his eyes and thought, smiling, of all the times he'd wished he could have lost Tasslehoff Burrfoot.

"He's not lost," Gerard said, reaching out to take hold of Odila's hand. "Not anymore."

At that moment, a shrill voice spoke from the darkness.

"Hey, Gerard, I almost forgot! When you get back to Solace, be sure to fix the lock on my tomb. It's broken."

28 THE VALLEY OF FIRE AND ICE

The ogres did not attack immediately. They had laid their ambush well. The elves were trapped in the valley, their advance blocked, their retreat cut off. They weren't going anywhere. The ogres could start the assault at a time of their own choosing, and they chose to wait.

The elves were prepared to do battle now, the ogres reasoned. Courage pumped in their veins. Their enemy had come upon them so suddenly and unexpectedly that the elves had no time for fear. But let the day linger on, let the night come. Let them lie sleepless on their blankets and stare at the bonfires ringed around them. Let them count the numbers of their enemies, and let fear multiply those numbers, and by next day's dawning, elf stomachs would shrivel and elf hands shake, and they would puke up their courage on the ground.

The elves moved immediately to repel the enemy attack, moved with discipline, without panic, taking cover in stands of pine trees and brush, behind boulders. Elven archers sought higher ground, picked out their targets, took careful aim and waited for the order to fire. Each archer had an adequate store of arrows, but those would soon be spent, and there would be no more. They had to make every shot count, although the archers could see for themselves that they might spend every arrow they possessed and still not make a dent in the numbers of the enemy.

The elves were ready. The ogres did not attack. Understanding their strategy, Samar ordered the elves to stand down. The elves tried to eat and sleep, but without much success. The stench of the ogres, that was like rotting meat, tainted their food. The light of their fires crept beneath closed eyelids. Alhana walked among them, speaking to them, telling them stories of old to banish their fears and lift their hearts. Gilthas did the same thing, talking to his people, bolstering their spirits, speaking words of hope that he did not himself believe, that no rational person could believe. Yet, it seemed to bring comfort to the people and, oddly, to Gilthas himself. He couldn't understand it, for he had only to look all around to see the fires of his enemies outnumbering the stars. He supposed, cynically, that hope was always the last man standing.

The person Gilthas most sought to comfort refused to be comforted. The Lioness disappeared shortly after bringing the elven runner into camp. She galloped away on her horse, ignoring Gilthas's shout. He searched the camp for her, but no one who had seen her, not even among her own people. He found her at last, long after darkness. She sat on a boulder, far from the main camp. She stared out into the night, and although Gilthas knew that she must have heard him approach, for she could hear a sparrow moving in the woods twenty feet away, she did not turn to look at him.

No need to tell her that she was placing herself in danger of being picked off by some ogre raider. She knew that better than he.

"How many of your scouts are missing?" he asked.

"My fault!" she said bitterly. "My failure! I should have seen something, heard something to keep us from this peril!" She gestured toward the mountain peaks. "Look at that. Thousands of them! Ogres, who shake the ground with their feet and splinter trees and stink like warm cow dung. And I did not see them or hear them! I might as well be blind, deaf, and dumb with my nose cut off for all the good I am!"

After a pause, she added harshly. "Twenty are missing. All of them friends, loyal and dear to me."

"No one blames you," said Gilthas.

"I blame myself!" the Lioness said, her voice choked.

"Samar says that the some of the ogres have grown powerful in magic. Whatever force blocks our magic and causes it to go awry works in the ogres' favor. Their movements were cloaked by sorcery. You could not possibly be faulted for failing to detect that."

The Lioness turned to face him. Her hair was wild and disheveled, hung ragged about her face. The tracks of her tears left streaks of dirt on her cheeks. Her eyes burned.

"I thank you for trying to comfort me, my husband, but my only comfort is the knowledge that my failure will die with me."

His heart broke. He had no words to say. He held out his arms to her, and she lunged into them, kissed him fiercely.

"I love you!" she whispered brokenly. "I love you so much!"

"And I love you," he said. "You are my life, and if that life ends this moment, I count it blessed for having you in it."

He stayed with her, far from camp, all through the night, waiting for those who would never return.

The ogres attacked before dawn, when the sky was pale with the coming of morning. The elves were ready. None had been able to sleep. Each knew in his heart that he would not survive to see the noontide.

The hulking ogres began the assault by rolling boulders down the sides of the cliffs. The boulders were enormous, the size of houses, and here was proof of a goddess's magic, for although ogres are huge, averaging over nine feet in height, and massively built, not even the most powerful ogre was strong enough to wrench those gigantic rocks out of the ground and fling them down the mountainside. The voices of the ogre mages could be heard chanting the magic that was a gift from Queen Takhisis. .

The boulders careened into the valley, forcing the elves who had taken refuge among the rocks to flee and sending elven archers leaping for the lives. The dying screams of those crushed by the rocks echoed among the mountains, to be answered with gleeful hoots by the ogres.

A few angry or panicked elven archers wasted arrows, shooting before the enemy was in range. Samar angrily rebuked those who did, reiterated the command to wait for his orders. Gilthas was no archer. He gripped his sword and waited grimly for the charge. He wasn't very good with his weapon, but he'd been improving—so Planchet told him—and he hoped he would be good enough to at least take a few of the enemy with him and make the spirit of his father and mother proud.

Gilthas was strangely conscious of his mother this morning. He had the feeling that she was beside him, and once he thought he heard her voice and felt her touch. The feeling was so intense that he actually turned to look to see if she stood near him. What he saw was the Lioness, who smiled at him. They would fight together, here at the end, and lie together in death as they had lain together in life.

The ogres were black upon the mountain tops. They raised their spears and shook them, giving the elves a clear view of their fate, and then the ogres gave a cheer that rebounded down the mountain.

The elves gripped their weapons and waited for the onslaught. Gilthas and the Lioness stood among the command group, gathered around Queen Alhana and the elven standards of both the Qualinesti and the Silvanesti.

Finally we are united, only when we face annihilation and it is too late. Gilthas quickly put the bitter thought out of his mind. What was done was done.

Having cleared their way, the ogres began to move inexorably down the mountain, their numbers so great that they blackened the mountain side. The entire ogre nation must be here, Gilthas realized.

He reached out, clasped hold of the Lioness's hand. He would fill his soul with love and let that love carry him to wherever it was souls went.

Samar gave the order to prepare to fire. The elven archers nocked their arrows and took aim. Samar raised his hand, but he did not drop it.

"Wait!" he cried. His eyes squinted as he tried to see more clearly. "What is that, my queen? Am I seeing things?"

Alhana stood on a knoll, from which she could have a view of the battlefield and direct the battle, such as it would be. She was calm, beautiful as ever.

More beautiful, if that were possible, fell and deadly. She shaded her eyes with her hands, stared into the east and the sun that had just now lifted above the mountaintops. "The forces near the mountaintop have slowed," she reported coolly, no emotion in her voice, neither elation nor despair. "Some are actually turning around."

"Something has them frightened," cried the Lioness. Lifting her gaze skyward, she pointed. "There! Blessed *E'li*! There!"

Light flared above them, light so brilliant that it seemed to catch the sun and drag its bright rays into the valley, banishing the shadows. At first, Gilthas thought that some miracle had brought the sun to the elves, but then he realized that the light was reflected light—the sun's rays shining off the scales of the belly of a golden dragon.

The Gold dived low, aiming for the side of the mountain that was thick with ogres. At the sight of the resplendent dragon, the marching ranks of the enemy dissolved into a jumbled mess. Mad with terror, the ogres ran up the mountainside and down and even sideways in their panicked effort to escape.

The dragon blasted the hillside with a fiery breath. Jammed together in knots of fear, the ogres died by the hundreds. Their agonized screams echoed among the rocks, screams so horrible that some of the elves covered their ears to blot out the sound.

The Gold sailed up and over the mountain. Smaller silver dragons flew in behind, breathing killing hoarfrost that froze the fleeing ogres, froze their blood, froze their hearts and their flesh. Hard and cold as rock, the bodies toppled over, rolled down into the valley. More golden dragons flew to the attack, so that the sky was aflame with the glitter of their scales. The ogre army that had been racing down gleefully upon their trapped enemy was now in full retreat. The dragons followed them, hunted them down wherever they tried to hide.

The ogres had sent thousands of their people into this fight that was supposed to lop off the head of the elven army and rip out its heart. United under the command of the ogre titans, trained into a disciplined fighting force, the ogres had tracked the elven march with cunning patience, waited for them to enter this valley.

The ogres lost a great many in the battle that day, but their nation was not destroyed, as some elves and humans would later claim. The ogres knew the land, they knew where to find caves in which to hide until the dragons departed. Skulking in the darkness, they licked their wounds and cursed the elves and vowed revenge. The ogres were now firmly allied with the minotaur nation. Penned up on northern islands, its burgeoning population spilling out into the ocean, the minotaurs had long eyed the continent of Ansalon as an area ripe for expansion. Although the ogres had been defeated this day, they would remain firm in their alliance with the minotaurs. A day of reckoning was yet to come.

Those ogres who dashed into the valley and accosted the elves were mad with fury, forgot their training, sought only to kill. The elves dispatched these with ease, and soon the battle was over. The ogres named the battlefield the Valley of Fire and Ice and proclaimed it accursed. No ogre would set foot there ever after.

The tide of battle had turned so swiftly that Gilthas could not comprehend they were safe, could not adjust to the fact that death was not advancing on him with club and spear. The elves were cheering now and singing anthems of joy to welcome the dragons, who wheeled overhead, the sun blazing off their glistening scales.

Two silver dragons broke free of the pack. They circled low, searching for a smooth and level patch of ground on which to land. Alhana and Samar advanced to meet them, as did Gilthas. He marveled at Alhana. He was shaking with the reaction of the sudden release of fear, the sudden return of life and of hope. She faced this reversal in fortune with the same cool aplomb that she had faced certain destruction.

The silver dragons settled to the ground—one of them with swooping, graceful movements, and the other landing as awkwardly as a young dragon fresh from the egg. Gilthas wondered at that, until he saw that this second dragon was maimed, his eyes disfigured and destroyed.

The dragon flew blind, under the guidance of his rider, a Solamnic Knight. Long black braids streamed down from beneath her shining helm. She saluted the queen, but did not dismount. She remained seated on the dragon, her sword drawn, keeping watch as other dragons hunted down and destroyed the remnants of the ogre army. The rider of the second dragon waved his hand.

"Samar!" he shouted.

"It is the Knight, Gerard!" exclaimed Samar, shocked out of his usual stoic complacency. "I would know him anywhere," he added, as Gerard ran toward them. "He is the ugliest human you are ever likely to see, Your Majesty."

"He looks very beautiful to me," said Alhana.

Gilthas heard tears in her voice, if he did not see them on her face, and he began to understand her better. She was frost without, fire within.

Gerard's face brightened when he saw Gilthas, and he came hastening forward to greet the Qualinesti king. Gilthas gestured obliquely with his head. Gerard took the hint and looked to Alhana. He halted dead in his tracks, stared at her, rapt. Too awestruck by beauty to remember his manners, he gaped, his mouth wide open.

"Sir Gerard," she said. "You are a most welcome sight.

Only then, at the sound of her voice, did he recall that he was in the presence of royalty. He sank down on one knee, his head bowed.

"Your servant, Madam."

Alhana extended her hand. "Rise, please, Sir Gerard. I am the one who should kneel to you, for you have saved my people from certain destruction."

"No, Madam, not me," said Gerard, flushing red, looking about as ugly as it was possible for a human to look. "The dragons came to your aid. I just went along for the ride and . . ." He seemed about to add something, but changed his mind.

Turning to Gilthas, Gerard bowed deeply. "I am overjoyed to see that you are alive and well, Your Majesty." His voice softened. "I was deeply grieved to hear of the death of your honored mother."

"Thank you, Sir Gerard," said Gilthas, clasping the Knight by the hand. "I find it strange that the paths of our lives cross once again—strange, yet fortuitous."

Gerard stood awkwardly, his keen blue eyes going from one to the other, searching, seeking.

"Sir Gerard," said Alhana, "you have something else to say. Please, speak without fear. We are deeply in your debt."

"No, you're not, Your Majesty," he said. His speech and manner were clumsy and awkward, as humans must always look to elves, but his voice was earnest and sincere. "I don't want you to think that. It's for this very reason I hesitate to speak, yet"—he glanced toward the sun—"time advances and we stand still. I have dire news to impart, and I dread to speak it."

"If you refer to the minotaur seizure of our homeland, we have been made aware of that," said Alhana.

Gerard stared at her. His mouth opened, shut again.

"Perhaps I can help," she said. "You want us to fulfill the promise Samar made and ride with you to attack Sanction. You fear that we will feel pressured into doing this by the fact that you came to our rescue."

"Lord Tasgall wants me to assure you that the Knights will understand if you feel the need to return to fight for your homeland, Madam," said Gerard. "I can say only that our need is very great. Sanction is guarded by armies of both the dead and the living. We fear that Queen Takhisis plans to try to rule both the mortal world and the immortal. If that happens, if she succeeds, darkness will encompass all of us. We need your help, Madam, and that of your brave warriors if we are to stop her. The dragons have offered to carry you there, for they will also join the battle."

"Have you had news? Is my son Silvanoshei still alive?" Alhana asked, her facing paling.

"I do not know, Madam," Gerard replied evasively. "I hope and trust so, but I have no way of knowing."

Alhana nodded, and then she did something unexpected. She turned to Gilthas. "You know what my answer must be, Nephew. My son is a prisoner. I would do all in my power to free him." Her cheeks stained with a faint flush. "But, as king of your people, you have the right to speak your thoughts."

Gilthas might have felt pleased. He might have felt vindicated. But he had been awake all night. He felt only bone tired.

"Sir Gerard, if we aid the Knights in the capture of Sanction, can we expect the Knights to aid us in the retaking of our homeland?"

"That is up to the Knights' Council, Your Majesty," Gerard replied, uncomfortable. As if aware that his answer was a poor one, he added with conviction, "I do not know what the other Knights would do, Your Majesty, but I willingly pledge myself to your cause."

"I thank you for that, sir," said Gilthas. He turned to Alhana. "I was opposed to this march at the beginning. I made no secret of that. The doom I foresaw has fallen. We are exiles now, without a homeland. Yet as this gallant Knight states, if we foreswear the promise Samar made to aid the Knights in their fight,

Queen Takhisis will triumph. Her first act would be to destroy us utterly, to annihilate us as a people. I agree. We must march on Sanction."

"You have our answer, Sir Gerard," Alhana declared. "We are one—the Qualinesti and the Silvanesti—and we will join with the other free people of Ansalon to fight and destroy the Queen of Darkness and her armies."

Gerard said what was proper. He was obviously relieved and now eager to be gone. The dragons circled above them, the shadows of their wings sliding gracefully over the ground. The elves greeted the dragons with glad cries and tears and blessings, and the dragons dipped their proud heads in response to the salutes.

The silver dragons and the gold began to swoop down into the valley, one or two at a time. The elven warriors mounted on the backs of the dragons, crowding as many on as possible. Thus had the elves ridden into battle during the days of Huma. Thus had they ridden to battle during the War of the Lance. The air was charged with a sense of history. The elves began to sing again, songs of glory, songs of victory.

Alhana, mounted on a golden dragon, took the lead. Raising her sword into the air, she shouted an elven battle cry. Samar lifted his sword, joined in. The Gold carried the queen of the Silvanesti into the air and flew off over the mountains toward the west, toward Sanction. The blind silver dragon departed, guided by his human rider.

Gilthas volunteered to remain to the last, to make certain that the dead were given proper rites, their bodies cremated in dragonfire, since there was no time to bury them and no way they could be returned to their homeland. His wife stayed with him.

"The Knights will not come to our aid, will they?" said the Lioness abruptly, as the last dragon stood ready to bear them away.

"The Knights will not come," Gilthas said. "We will die for them, and they will sing our praises, but when the battle is won, they will return to their homes. They will not come to die for us."

Together, he and the Lioness and the last of the Qualinesti warriors took to the skies. The songs of the elves were loud and joyful and filled the valley with music.

Then all that was left was the echoes.

Then those faded away, leaving only silence and smoke.

29 THE TEMPLE OF DUERGHAST

Galdar had not seen Mina since her triumphant return to Sanction. His heart was sore as his body, and he used his wounds as an excuse to remain in his tent, refusing to see or speak to anyone. He was considerably surprised that he was still alive, for Takhisis had good reason to hate him, and she was not merciful to those who had turned on her. He guessed that Mina had much to do with the fact that he was not lying in a charred lump alongside Malys's carcass.

Galdar had not stayed to listen to the conversation between Takhisis and Mina. His fury was such that he could have torn down the mountain, stone by stone, with his bare hands, and fearing that his fury would hurt Mina, not help her, he stalked away to rage in solitude. He returned to the cave only when he heard Mina call for him.

He found her well, whole. He was not surprised. He expected nothing less. Nursing his bruised and bloodied hand—he had taken out his anger on the rocks—he regarded her in silence, waited for her to speak.

Her amber eyes were cold and hard. He could still see himself frozen inside them, a tiny figure, trapped.

"You would have let me die," she said, accusing.

"Yes," he replied steadily. "Better that you should have died with your glory fresh upon you than live a slave."

"She is our god, Galdar. If you serve me, you serve her."

"I serve you, Mina," Galdar said, and that was the end of the conversation.

Mina might have dismissed him. She might have slain him. Instead, she started off on the long trek down the Lords of Doom. He went with her. She spoke to him only once more, and that was an offer to heal his injuries. He declined. They walked to Sanction in silence and they had not talked since.

The joy at Mina's return was tumultuous. There had been those who were sure she was dead and those who were sure she lived, and so high was the level of anxiety and fear that these two factions came to blows. Mina's Knights argued among themselves, her commanders bickered and quarreled. Rumors flew about the streets, lies became truth, and truth degenerated into lies. Mina returned to find a city of anarchy and chaos. The sound of her name was all that it took to restore order.

"Mina!" was the jubilant cry at the gate as she appeared. "Mina!"

The name rang wildly throughout the city like the joyous sound of wedding bells, and she was very nearly overrun and smothered by those who cried out how thankful they were to see her alive. If Galdar had not wordlessly swept her up in his arms and mounted her on his strong shoulders for everyone to see, she might well have been killed by love.

Galdar could have pointed out that it was Mina they cheered, Mina they followed, Mina they obeyed. He said nothing, however, and she said nothing either. Galdar heard the tales of the destruction of the totem, of the appearance of a silver dragon who had attacked the totem and who had, in turn, been attacked and blinded by Mina's valiant troops. He heard of the perfidy and treachery of the Solamnic priestess who had joined forces with the silver dragon and how they had flown off together.

Lying on his cot, nursing his injuries, Galdar recalled the first time he'd seen the lame beggar, who had turned out to be a blue dragon. He had been in company with a blind man with silver hair. Galdar pondered this and wondered.

He went to view the wreckage. The pile of ash that had been the skulls of hundreds of dragons remained untouched, undisturbed. Mina would not go near it. She did not return to the altar room. She did not return to her room in the temple, but moved her things to some unknown location.

In the altar room, the candles had all melted into a large pool of wax colored dirty gray by the swirling ashes. Benches were overturned, some blackened from the fire. The odor of smoke and magic was all pervasive. The floor was covered with shards of amber, sharp enough to puncture the sole of a boot. No one dared enter the temple, which was said to be imbued with the spirit of the woman whose body had been imprisoned in the amber sarcophagus and was now a pile of ashes.

"At least one of us managed to escape," Galdar told the ashes, and he gave a soldier's salute.

The body of one of the wizards was gone, as well. No one could tell Galdar what had happened to Palin Majere. Some claimed to have seen a figure cloaked all in black carry it off, while others swore that they had seen the wizard Dalamar tear it apart with his bare hands. At Mina's command, a search was made for Palin, but the body could not be found, and finally Mina ordered the search ended.

The body of the wizard Dalamar remained in the abandoned temple, staring into the darkness, apparently forgotten, his hands stained with blood.

There was one other piece of news. The jailer was forced to admit that during the confusion of Malys's attack, the elf lord Silvanoshei had escaped his prison cell and had not been recaptured. The elf was thought to be still in the city, for they had posted look-outs for him at the exits, and no one had seen him.

"He is in Sanction," Mina said. "Of that, you may be certain."

"I will find him," said the jailer with an oath. "And when I do, I will bring him straight to you, Mina."

"I am too busy to deal with him," said Mina sharply. "If you find him, kill him. He has served his purpose."

Days passed. Order was restored. The elf was not found, nor did anyone really bother to look for him. Rumors were now whispered that Mina was having the ancient Temple of Duerghast, that had long been left to lie in ruins, reconstructed and refurbished. In a month's time, she would be holding a grand ceremony in the temple, the nature of which was secret. It would be the greatest moment in the history of Krynn, one that would be long celebrated and remembered. Soon, everyone in Sanction was saying that Mina was going to be rewarded with godhood.

The day Galdar first heard this, he sighed deeply. On that day, Mina came to see him.

"Galdar," she called outside his tent post. "May I come in?"

He gave a growl of acquiescence, and she entered.

Mina had lost weight—with Galdar not around, no one was there to persuade her to eat. Nor was anyone urging her to sleep, apparently, for she looked worn, exhausted. Her eyes blinked too often, her fingers plucked aimlessly at the buckles of her leather armor. Her skin was pale, except for a hectic, fevered stain on her cheeks. Her red hair was longer than he had ever known her to wear it, curled fretfully about her ears and straggled down her forehead. He did not rise to greet her, but remained sitting on his bed.

"They say you keep to your quarters because you are unwell," Mina said, regarding him intently.

"I am doing better," he said, refusing to meet her amber eyes.

"Are you able to return to your duties?"

"If *you* want me." He laid emphasis on the word.

"I do." Mina began to pace the tent, and he was startled to see her nervous, uneasy. "You've heard the talk that is going around. About my becoming a god."

"I've heard it. Let me guess, Her Dark Majesty isn't pleased."

"When she enters the world in triumph, Galdar, then there will be no question of whom the people will worship. It's just that . . ." Mina paused, helpless to explain, or perhaps loath to admit to the explanation.

"You are not to blame, Mina," said Galdar, relenting and taking pity on her. "You are here in the world. You are something the people can see and hear and touch. You perform the miracles."

"Always in her name," Mina insisted.

"Yet you never stopped them from calling out *your* name," Galdar observed. "You never told them to shout for the One God. It is always 'Mina, Mina.'"

She was silent a moment, then said quietly, "I do not stop it because I enjoy it, Galdar. I cannot help it. I hear the love in their voices. I see the love in their eyes. Their love makes me feel that I can accomplish anything, that I can work miracles . . ."

Her voice died away. She seemed to suddenly realize what she had said. *That I can work miracles.*

"I understand," Mina said softly. "I see now why I was punished. I am amazed the One God forgave me. Yet, I will make it up to her."

She abandoned you, Mina! Galdar wanted to shout at her. If you had died, she would have found someone else to do her bidding. But you didn't die, and so she came running back with her lying tale of "testing" and "punishing."

The words burned on his tongue, but he kept his mouth shut on them, for if he spoke them, Mina would be furious. She would turn from him, perhaps forever, and he was the only friend she had now, the only one who could see clearly the path that lay ahead of her. He swallowed the words, though they came nigh to choking him.

"What is this I hear of you restoring the old Temple of Duerghast?" Galdar asked, changing the subject.

Mina's face cleared. Her amber eyes glimmered with a glint of her former spirit. "That is where the ceremony will be held, Galdar. That is where the One God will make manifest her power. The ceremony will be held in the arena, and it will be magnificent, Galdar! Everyone will be there to worship the One God—her foes included."

Galdar's choked-down words were giving him a bellyache. He felt sick again, and he remained sitting on the bed, saying nothing. He couldn't look at her, couldn't return her gaze, couldn't bear to see himself, that tiny being, held fast in the amber. Mina came to him, touched his hand. He kept his face averted.

"Galdar, I know that I hurt you. I know that your anger was really fear—fear for me." Her fingers closed fast over his hand. "You are the only one who ever cared about me, Galdar. About *me*, about Mina. The others care only for what I can do for them. They depend on me like children, and like children I must lead them and guide them.

"I cannot depend on them. But I can depend on you, Galdar. You flew into certain death with me, and you were not afraid. I need you now. I need your strength and your courage. Don't be angry with me anymore." She paused, then said, "Don't be angry with *her.*"

His thoughts went back to the night he'd seen Mina emerge from the storm, heralded by thunder, born of fire. He remembered the thrill when she touched his hand, this hand, the hand that was her gift. He had so many memories of her, each one linked with another to form a golden chain that bound them together. He lifted his head and looked at her, saw her human, small and fragile, and he was suddenly very much afraid for her.

He was so afraid that he could even lie for her.

"I am sorry, Mina," he said gruffly. "I was angry at—"

He paused. He had been going to say "Takhïsis," but he was loath to speak her name. He temporized. "I was angry at the One God. I understand now, Mina. Accept my apology."

She smiled, released his hand. "Thank you, Galdar. You must come with me to see the temple. There is still much work to be done to make ready for the ceremony, but I have lighted the altar and—"

Horns blared. Rumbling drumbeats rolled over her words.

"What is this?" Mina asked, walking to the tent flap and peering out, irritated. "What do they think they are doing?"

"That is the call to arms, Mina," said Galdar, alarmed. He hastily grabbed up his sword. "We must be under attack."

"That cannot be," she returned. "The One God sees all and hears all and knows all. I would have been warned. . . ."

"Nevertheless," Galdar pointed out, exasperated, "that *is* the call to arms."

"I don't have time for this," she said, annoyed. "There is too much work to be done in the temple."

The drumbeat grew louder, more insistent.

"I suppose I will have to deal with it." She stalked out of the tent, walking with haste, her irritation plain to be seen.

Galdar strapped on his sword, snatched up the padded leather vest that served him for armor, and hastened after her, fastening buckles as he ran.

The streets were awash in confusion, with some people staring stupidly in the direction of the walls, as if they could divine what was going on by just looking, while others were loudly demanding answers from people who were just as confused as they were. The levelheaded raced to their quarters to grab their weapons, reasoning that they'd arm themselves first and find out who they were fighting later.

Galdar opened up a path through the panic-clogged streets. His voice bellowed for people to make way. His strong arms picked up and tossed aside those who didn't heed his command. Mina followed closely behind him, and at the sight of her, the people cheered and called her name.

"Mina! Mina!"

Glancing back, Galdar saw her still annoyed by the interruption, still determined that this was nothing. They reached the West Gate. Just as the huge doors were thundering shut, Galdar caught a glimpse of one of their scouts—a blue dragon, who had landed outside the walls. The dragon's rider was talking to the Knight commanding the gate.

"What is going on? What is happening?" Mina demanded, shoving her way through the crowd to reach the officer. "Why did you sound the alarm? Who gave the order?"

Knight and rider both swung toward Mina. Both began talking at once. Soldiers and Knights crowded around her, adding to the chaos by trying to make their own voices heard.

"An army led by Solamnic Knights is on its way to Sanction, Mina," said the dragonrider, gasping for breath. "Accompanying the Knights is an army of elves, flying the standards of both Qualinesti and Silvanesti."

Mina cast an irate glance at the Knight in charge of the gate. "And for this you sound the alarm and start a panic? You are relieved of your command. Galdar, see that this man is flogged." Mina turned back to the dragonrider. Her lip curled. "How far away is this army? How many weeks' march?"

"Mina," the rider said, swallowing. "They are not marching. They ride dragons. Gold and silver dragons. Hundreds of them—"

"Gold dragons!" a man cried out, and before Galdar could stop him, the fool had dashed off, shouting out the news in a panicked voice. It would be all over the city in minutes.

Mina stared at the rider. Blood drained from her face, seemed to drain from her body. She had looked more alive when she was dying. Fearing she might collapse, Galdar put his hand out to steady her. She pushed him away.

"Impossible," she said through pale lips. "The gold and silver dragons have departed this world, never to return."

"I am sorry to contradict you, Mina," the rider said hesitantly, "but I saw them myself. We"—he gestured outside the walls, where his Blue stood, her flanks heaving, her wings and head drooping with exhaustion—"we were caught off-guard, nearly killed. We barely made it here alive."

Mina's Knights gathered tensely around her.

"Mina, what are your orders?"

"What is your command, Mina?"

Her pale lips moved, but she spoke to herself. "I must act now. The ceremony cannot wait."

"How far away are the dragons?" Galdar asked the rider.

The man glanced up fearfully at the sky. "They were right behind me. I am surprised you cannot see them yet—"

"Mina," said Galdar, "send out an order. Summon the red dragons and the blue. Many of Malys's old minions still remain close by. Summon them to fight!"

"They won't come," said the dragonrider.

Mina shifted her gaze to him. "Why not?"

He gestured with a jerk of his thumb over his shoulder to his own blue dragon. "They won't fight their own kind. Maybe later, the old animosities will return, but not now. We're on our own."

"What do we do, Mina?" her Knights demanded, their voices harsh and filled with fear. "What are your orders?"

Mina did not reply. She stood silent, her gaze abstracted. She did not hear them. She listened to another voice.

Galdar knew well whose voice she heard, and he meant that this time she should hear his. Grabbing her arm, Galdar gave her a shake.

"I know what you're thinking, and we can't do it, Mina," Galdar said. "We can't hold out against this assault! Dragonfear alone will unman most of our troops, make them unfit for battle. The walls, the moat of fire—these won't stop dragons."

"We have the army of the dead—"

"Bah!" Galdar snorted. "Golden dragons have no fear of the souls of dead humans or dead goblins or any of these other poor wretches whose spirits the

One God has imprisoned. As for the Solamnics, they have fought the dead before, and this time they will be prepared to face the terror."

"Then what do you advise, Galdar?" Mina asked, her voice cold. "Since you are so certain we cannot win."

"I advise we get the hell out of here," Galdar said bluntly, and her Knights loudly echoed his opinion. "If we leave now, we can evacuate the city, escape into the mountains. This place is honeycombed with tunnels. The Lords of Doom have protected us before, they'll protect us again. We can retreat back to Jelek or Neraka."

"Retreat?" Mina glared at him, tried to wrench her arm from his grasp. "You are a traitor to even speak those words!"

He held onto her with grim determination. "Let the Solamnics have Sanction, Mina. We took it away from them once. We can take it away from them again. We still own Solamnia. Solanthus is ours, as is Palanthas."

"No, we don't," Mina said, struggling to free herself. "I ordered most of our forces to march here, to come to Sanction to be witness to the glory of the One God."

Galdar opened his mouth, snapped it shut.

"I did not think there would be dragons!" Mina cried out.

He saw the image of himself in her eyes growing smaller and smaller. He loosed his hold on her.

"We will not retreat," she stated.

"Mina—"

"Listen to me, every one of you." She gathered them together with a glance, all the tiny figures frozen in the amber eyes. "We must hold this city at all costs. When the ceremony is complete and the One God enters this world, no force on Krynn will be able to stand against her. She will destroy them all."

The officers stared at her, not moving. Some flinched and cast glances skyward. Galdar felt a twinge of fear twist his gut—the dragonfear, distant yet, but fast approaching.

"Well, what do wait for?" Mina demanded. "Return to your posts."

No one moved. No one cheered. No one spoke her name.

"You have your orders!" Mina shouted, her voice ragged. "Galdar, come with me."

She turned to leave. Her Knights did not move. They blocked her path with their bodies. She bore no weapon. She had not thought to bring one.

"Galdar," said Mina. "Kill any man who tries to stop me."

Galdar laid his hand on the hilt of his sword.

One by one, the Knights stepped aside, cleared a path.

Mina walked among them, her face cold as death.

"Where are you going?" Galdar demanded, following after her.

"To the temple. We have much to do and little time to do it."

"Mina," he said, his voice low and urgent in her ear, "you can't leave them to face this alone. For love of you, they will find the courage to stand and fight even golden dragons, but if you are not here—"

Mina halted.

"They do not fight for love of me!" Her voice trembled. "They fight for the One God!" She turned around to face her Knights. "Hear my words. You fight this battle for the One God. You must hold this city in the name of the One God. Any man who flees before the enemy will know the wrath of the One God."

Her Knights lowered their heads, turned away. They did not march proudly back to their posts, as they might once have done. They slunk back sullenly.

"What is the matter with them?" Mina asked, dismayed, confused.

"Once they followed you for love, Mina. Now they obey you as the whipped dog obeys—in fear of the lash," said Galdar. "Is this what you want?"

Mina bit her lip, seemed to waver in her decision, and Galdar hoped that she might refuse to heed the voice. That she would do what she knew to be honorable, knew to be right. She would remain loyal to her men, who had remained loyal to her through so much.

Mina's jaw set. The amber eyes hardened. "Let the curs run. I don't need them. I have the One God. I am going to the temple to prepare for the ceremony. Are you coming?" she demanded of Galdar. "Or are you going to run away, too?"

He looked into the amber eyes and could no longer see himself. He could no longer see anyone. Her eyes were empty.

She did not wait for his answer. She stalked off. She did not look to see if he was following. She didn't care, one way or the other.

Galdar hesitated. Looking back at the West Gate, he saw the Knights gathered in knots, talking in low voices. He doubted very much if they were determining a strategy for battle. A babble of screams and cries rose from the streets as word spread that hundreds of golden and silver dragons were bearing down on Sanction. No one was acting to quell the terror. Each man thought only of himself now, and he had only one thought in his mind—to survive. Soon there would be rioting, as men and women devolved into wild beasts, bit and clawed and fought to save their own hides. In their miserable panic, they might well destroy themselves before the armies of their enemies ever arrived.

If I stay here on the walls, I might rally a few, Galdar thought. I might find some who would brave the horror and fight alongside me. I would die well. I would die with honor.

He watched Mina walking away, walking alone, except for that shadowy five-headed figure that hovered over her, surrounded her, cut her off from everyone who had ever loved her or admired her or cared about her.

"You great bitch!" Galdar muttered. "You won't get rid of me that easily."

Gripping his sword, he hastened after Mina.

Mina was wrong when she told Galdar that he was the only one who had ever cared for her. Another cared, cared deeply. Silvanoshei hurried after her, shoving and pushing his way through the crowds that now milled about in panic in the streets, trying to keep her in sight.

He had stayed in Sanction to hear some word of Mina. Silvanoshei's joy when he heard she was alive was heartfelt, even as her return plunged him once more into danger. People suddenly remembered having seen an elf walking about Sanction.

He was forced to go into hiding. A kender obligingly introduced Silvanoshei to the system of tunnels that criss-crossed beneath Sanction. Elves abhor living beneath the ground, and Silvanoshei could remain in the tunnels for only short periods of time before he was driven to the surface by a desperate need for air. He stole food to keep himself alive, stole a cloak with a hood and a scarf to wrap around his face, hide his elven features.

He lurked about the ruins of the totem, hoping to find a chance to talk to Mina, but he never saw her there. He grew fearful, wondered if she'd left the city or if she had fallen ill. Then he overheard a chance bit of gossip to the effect that she had moved out of the Temple of the Heart and had taken up residence in another temple, the ruined Temple of Duerghast that stood on the outskirts of Sanction.

Built to honor some false god dreamed up by a demented cult, the temple was notorious for having an arena where human sacrifices were sent to die for the entertainment of a cheering crowd. During the War of the Lance, Lord Ariakas had appropriated the temple, using its dungeons to torture and torment his prisoners.

The temple had an evil reputation, and there had been talk in recent days, during the reign of Hogan Bight, of razing it. Tremors had caused gigantic cracks to open in the walls, weakening the structure to the point where no one felt safe even going near it. The citizens of Sanction had decided to let the Lords of Doom complete the destruction.

Then came the news that Mina was planning to rebuild the temple, transform it into a place of worship of the One God.

The Temple of Duerghast lay on the other side of the moat of lava that surrounded Sanction. The temple could not be reached overland, not without bridging the moat. Therefore, Silvanoshei reasoned, Mina would be forced to enter the temple via one of the tunnels. He traipsed about the tunnel system, losing himself more than once, and at last found what he was searching for—a tunnel that ran beneath the curtain wall on the southern side of the city.

Silvanoshei had been planning to explore this tunnel when the alarm was raised. He saw the dragonrider fly overhead and land outside the West Gate. Guessing that Mina would come to take charge of the situation, Silvanoshei concealed himself in the crowds of people who were eager to see Mina. He pressed as close as he dared, hoping against hope just to catch a glimpse of her.

Then he saw her, surrounded by her Knights, speaking to the dragonrider. Suddenly one man broke from the group and raced into the crowd, shouting out that silver and gold dragons were coming, dragons ridden by Solamnic Knights. People swore and cursed and started to push and shove. Silvanoshei was jostled and nearly knocked down. Through it all, he fought to keep his eyes on her.

The news of dragons and Knights meant little to Silvanoshei. He thought of it only in terms of how this would affect Mina. He was certain she would lead the battle, and he feared that he would have no opportunity to talk to her. He was astonished beyond measure to see her turn around and walk off, abandoning her troops.

Their loss was his blessing.

Her voice carried to him clearly. "I am going to the temple to prepare for the ceremony."

At last, maybe he could find a way to speak to her.

Silvanoshei entered the tunnel he had found, hoping that his calculations were correct and that it led beneath the moat of fire to the Temple of Duerghast. Hope almost died when he found that the tunnel roof had partially collapsed. He made his way past the chunks of rock and soil, continued on, and eventually found a ladder that led to the surface.

He climbed swiftly, had sense enough to slow as he neared the top. A wooden trapdoor kept the tunnel opening concealed from those above. As he pushed against the door, his hand broke through the rotting wood. A cascade of dirt and splinters fell down around him. Cautiously, he peered out of the hole in the trapdoor. Bright sunshine half-blinded him. He blinked his eyes, waited for them to become accustomed to the light.

The Temple of Duerghast stood only a short distance away.

To reach the temple, he would have to cross a space of open ground. He would be visible from the walls of Sanction. Silvanoshei doubted if anyone would see him or pay attention to him. All eyes would be turned skyward.

Silvanoshei wormed his way out of the hole and ran across the open patch of ground, hid himself in a shadow cast by the temple's outer wall. Constructed of black granite blocks, the temple's curtain wall was built in the shape of a square. Two towers guarded the front entrance. Circling around the wall, hugging the building, he searched for some way inside. He came to one of the towers, and here he found two doors, one at either end of the wall.

Heavy slabs of iron controlled by winches served for gates. Although they were covered with rust, the iron gates remained in place and would probably still be standing when the rest of the temple fell down around them. He could not enter there, but he could enter through a part of the outer wall that had collapsed into a pile of rubble. The climb would be difficult, but he was nimble. He was certain he could manage.

He started toward the wall, then halted, frozen in the shadows. He had caught movement out of the corner of his eye.

Someone else had come to the Temple of Duerghast. A man stood before it, gazing at it. The man stood in the open, the sunshine pouring down on him. Silvanoshei must have been blind to have missed seeing him. Yet, he could have sworn that there had been no one there when he came around the corner.

Judging by his looks, the man was not a warrior. He was quite tall, above average height. He wore no sword, carried no bow slung across his shoulder. He was clad in brown woolen hose, a green and brown tunic, and tall leather boots. A cowl, brown in color, covered his head and shoulders. Silvanoshei could not see the man's face.

Silvanoshei fumed. What was this simpleton doing here? Nothing, by the looks of it, except gawking at the temple like a kender on holiday. He had no weapon, he wasn't a threat, yet Silvanoshei was reluctant to have the man see him. Silvanoshei was determined to talk to Mina, and for all he knew this man might be some sort of guard. Or perhaps this stranger was also waiting to speak to her. He had the look of someone waiting.

Silvanoshei wished the man away. Time was passing. He had to get inside. He had to talk to Mina. Still the man did not move.

At last, Silvanoshei decided he could wait no longer. He was a swift runner. He could outdistance the man, if the stranger gave chase, lose himself in the temple confines before the man figured out what had happened. Silvanoshei drew in a breath, ready to run.

The man turned his head. Drawing back his cowl, he looked straight at Silvanoshei.

The man was an elf.

Silvanoshei stared, riveted, unmoving. For a petrifying moment, he feared that Samar had tracked him down, but he recognized immediately that this was not Samar.

At first glance, the elf appeared young, as young as Silvanoshei. His body had the strength, the lithesome grace of youth. A second glance caused Silvanoshei to rethink his first. The elf's face was unmarred by time, yet in his expression held a gravity that was not youthful, had nothing to do with youth's hope and high spirits and joyful expectations. The eyes were bright as the eyes of youth, but their brilliance was shadowed, tempered by sorrow. Silvanoshei had the odd impression that this man knew him, but he could not place the strange elf at all.

The elf looked at Silvanoshei, then he looked away, turned his gaze back to the temple.

Silvanoshei took advantage of the elf's shift in attention to sprint to the opening in the wall. He climbed swiftly, one eye on the strange elf, who never moved. Silvanoshei dropped down over the side of the wall. He peered back through the rubble to see the elf still standing there, waiting.

Putting the stranger from his mind, Silvanoshei entered the ruined temple and set off in search of Mina.

30 FOR LOVE OF MINA

Mina fought her way through the crowded streets of Sanction. Her movement was hampered by the people who, at the sight of her, surged forward to touch her. They cried out to her in fear of the coming dragons. They begged her to save them.

"Mina, Mina!" they shouted, and the din was hateful to her.

She tried to block it out, tried to ignore them, tried to free herself from their clutching, clinging hands, but with every step she took, they gathered around her more thickly, calling out her name, repeating it over and over as a frantic litany against fear.

Another called her name. The voice of Takhisis, loud and insistent, urging her to make haste. Once the ceremony was complete, once Takhisis had entered the world and united the spiritual realm with the physical, the Dark Queen could take any form she chose, and in that form she would fight her enemies.

Let the foul Golds and the craven Silvers go up against the five-headed monster that she could become. Let the puny armies of the Knights and the elves battle the hordes of the dead that would rise up at her command.

Takhisis was glad that the wretched mage and his tool, the blind Silver, had freed the metallic dragons. She had been furious at the time, but now, in her calmer moments, she remembered that she was the only god on Krynn. Everything worked to her own ends, even the plots of her enemies.

Do what they might, they could never harm her. Every arrow they fired would turn to their own destruction, target their own hearts. Let them attack. This time she would destroy them all—knights, elves, dragons—destroy them utterly, wipe them out, crush them so that they would never rise up against her again. Then she would seize their souls, enslave them. Those who had fought her in life would serve her in death, serve her forever.

To accomplish this, Takhisis needed to be in the world. She controlled the door on the spiritual realm, but she could not open the door on the physical. She needed Mina for that. She had chosen Mina and prepared her for this one task. Takhisis had smoothed Mina's way, had removed Mina's enemies. Takhisis was so close to achieving her overweening ambition. She had no fear that the world might be snatched from her at the last moment. She was in control. No other challenged her. She was impatient, however. Impatient to begin the battle that would end in her final triumph.

She urged Mina to make haste. Kill these wretches, she commanded, if they will not get out of your way.

Mina grabbed a sword and raised it in the air. She no longer saw people. She saw open mouths, felt clutching hands. The living surrounded her, plucking at her, shrieking and gibbering, pressing their lips against her skin.

"Mina, Mina!" they cried, and their cries changed to screams and the hands fell away.

The street emptied, and it was only when she heard Galdar's horrified roar and saw the blood on her sword and on her hands and the bleeding bodies lying in the street that she realized what she had done.

"She commands me to hurry," Mina said, "and they wouldn't get out of my way."

"They are out of your way now," Galdar said.

Mina looked down at the bodies. Some she knew. Here was a soldier who had been with her since the siege of Sanction. He lay in a pool of blood. Her sword had run him through. She had some dim memory of him pleading with her to spare him.

Stepping over the dead, she continued on. She kept hold of the sword, though she had no skill in the use of such a weapon and she grasped it awkwardly, her hand gummed with blood.

"Walk ahead of me, Galdar," she ordered. "Clear the way."

"I don't know where we're going, Mina. The temple ruins lie outside the wall on the other side of the moat of fire. How do you get there from here?"

Mina pointed with the sword. "Stay on this street, follow the curtain wall. Directly across from the Temple of Duerghast is a tower. Inside the tower, a tunnel leads beneath the wall and underneath the moat to the temple."

They proceeded on, moving at a dead run.

"Make haste," Takhisis commanded.

Mina obeyed.

The first enemy dragons came into view, flying high over the mountains. The first waves of dragonfear began to affect Sanction's defenders. Sunlight glittered on gold and silver scales, glinted off the armor of the dragonriders. Only in the great wars of the past had this many dragons of light come together to aid humans and elves in their cause. The dragons flew in long lines—the swift-flying Silvers in the lead, the more ponderous Golds in the rear.

A strange sort of mist began to flow up over the walls, seep into the streets and alleyways. Galdar thought it odd that fog should arise suddenly on a sunny day, and then he saw suddenly that the mist had eyes and mouths and hands. The souls of the dead had been summoned to do battle. Galdar looked up through the chill mist, looked up into the blue sky. Sunlight flashed off the belly of a silver dragon, argent light so bright that it burned through the mists like sunshine on a hot summer day.

The souls fled the light, sought the shadows, slunk down alleyways or sought shelter in the shade cast by the towering walls.

Dragons do not fear the souls of dead humans, dead goblins, dead elves.

Galdar envisioned the blasts of fire breathed by the gold dragons incinerating all those who manned the walls, melting armor, fusing it to the living flesh as the men inside screamed out their lives in agony. The image was vivid and filled his mind, so that he could almost smell the stench of burning flesh and hear the death cries. His hands began to shake, his mouth grew dry.

"Dragonfear," he told himself over and over. "Dragonfear. It will pass. Let it pass."

He looked back at Mina to see how she was faring. She was pale, but composed. The empty amber eyes stared straight ahead, did not look up to the skies or to the walls from which men were starting to jump out of sheer panic.

The Silvers flew overhead, flying rapidly, flying low. These were the first wave and they did not attack. They were spreading fear, evoking panic, doing reconnaissance. The shadows of the gleaming wings sliced through the streets, sending people running mad with terror. Here and there, some mastered their fear, overcame it. A lone ballista fired. A couple of archers sent arrows arcing upward in a vain attempt at a lucky shot. For the most part, men huddled in the shadows of the walls and drew in shivering breaths and waited for it all to go away, just please go away.

The fear that descended on the population worked in Mina's favor. Those who had been clogging the streets ran terrified into their homes or shops, seeking shelter where no shelter existed, for the fire of the Golds could melt stone. But at least they left the streets. Mina and Galdar made swift progress.

Arriving at one of the guard towers that stood along Sanction's curtain wall, Mina yanked open a door at the tower's base. The tower was sparsely inhabited, most of its defenders had fled. Those who were left, hearing the door bang open, peered fearfully down the spiral stairs. One called out in a cracked voice, "Who goes there?"

Mina did not deign to answer, and the soldiers did not dare come down to find out. Galdar heard their footsteps retreat farther down the battlements.

He grabbed a torch, fumbled to light it from a slowmatch burning in a tub. Mina took the torch from him and led the way down a series of dank stone stairs to what appeared to be a blank wall, through which she walked without hesitation. Either the wall was illusion, or the Dark Queen had caused the solid stone to dissolve. Galdar didn't know, and he had no intention of asking.

He gritted his teeth and barged in after her, fully expecting to dash his brains out against the rock.

He entered a dark tunnel that smelled strongly of brimstone. The walls were warm to the touch. Mina had ranged far ahead of him, and he had to hurry to catch up. The tunnel was built for humans, not minotaurs. He was forced to run with his shoulders hunched and his horns lowered. The heat increased. He guessed that they were passing directly under the moat of fire. The tunnel looked to be ancient. He wondered who had built it and why, more questions he was never going to have answered.

The tunnel ended at yet another wall. Galdar was relieved to see that Mina did not walk through this wall. She entered a small door. He squeezed in after her, a tight fit, to find himself in a prison cell.

Rats screeched and chittered at the light, scrambled to escape. The floor was alive with some sort of crawling insects that swarmed into the nooks and crevices of the crumbing stone walls. The cell door hung on a single rusted hinge.

Mina left the cell, that opened up into a corridor. Galdar caught a glimpse of other rooms extending off the main hall and he knew where he was—the Temple of Duerghast.

Thinking back to what he had heard about this temple, he guessed that these were the torture chambers where once the prisoners of the dragonarmy were "questioned." The light of his torch did not penetrate far into the shadows, for which he was grateful.

He hated this place, wished himself away from it, wished himself anywhere but here, even in the city above, though that city might be crawling with gold dragons. The screams of the dying echoed in these dark corridors, the walls were wet with tears and blood.

Mina looked neither to the right nor the left. The light of her torch illuminated a flight of stairs, leading upward. Climbing those stairs, Galdar had the feeling he was clawing his way back from death. They reached ground level, the main part of the temple.

Cracks had opened in the walls, and Galdar was able to catch a whiff of fresh air. Though it smelled strongly of sulfur from the moat of fire, the smell up here was better than what he'd smelled below. He drew in a deep breath.

Rays of dust-clouded sunlight filtered through the cracks. Galdar started to douse the torch, but Mina stopped him.

"Keep it lit," she told him. "We will need it where we are going."

"Where are we going?" he asked, fearing she would say the altar room.

"To the arena."

She led the way through the ruins, moving swiftly and without hesitation. He noted that piles of rubble had been cleared aside, opening up previously clogged corridors.

"Did you do this work yourself, Mina?" Galdar asked, marveling.

"I had help," she replied.

He guessed the nature of that help and was sorry he'd asked.

Unlike humans, Galdar was not disgusted to hear a temple had an open-air arena where people would come to witness blood sports. Such contests are a part of a minotaur's heritage, used to settle everything from family feuds to marital disputes to the choosing of a new emperor. He had been surprised to find that humans considered such contests barbaric. To him, the malicious, backstabbing political intrigue in which humans indulged was barbaric.

The arena was open to the air and was visible from the highest walls of Sanction. Galdar had noted it before with some interest as being the only arena he'd ever seen in human lands. The arena was built into the side of the mountain. The floor was below ground level and filled with sand. Rows of benches, carved into the mountain's slope, formed a semicircle around the floor. The arena was small by minotaur standards, and was in a state of ruin and decay. Wide cracks had opened up among the benches, holes gaped in the floor.

Galdar followed Mina through dusty corridors until they came to a large entryway that opened out onto the arena. Mina walked through the entryway. Galdar followed and went from dusty daylight to darkest night.

He stopped dead, blinking his eyes, suddenly afraid that he'd been struck blind. He could smell the familiar odors of the outdoors, including the sulfur of the moat of fire. He could feel the wind upon his face. He should be feeling the warmth of the sun on his face, as well, for only seconds before he had been able to see sunshine and blue sky through the cracks in the ceiling. Looking up, he saw a black sky, starless, cloudless. He shuddered all over, took an involuntary step backward.

Mina grabbed hold of his hand. "Don't be afraid," she said softly. "You stand in the presence of the One God."

Considering their last meeting together, Galdar did not find reassuring the knowledge that he was in Takhisis's presence. He was more determined than ever to leave. He had made a mistake in coming here. He had come out of love for Mina, not love for Takhisis. He did not belong here, he was not welcome.

Stairs led from the ground floor into the arena.

Mina let go of his hand. She was in haste, already hurrying down the stairs, certain he would follow. The words to say goodbye to her clogged in his throat. Not that there were any words that would make a difference. She would hate him for what he was going to do, detest him. Nothing he could say would change that. He turned to leave, turned to go back into the sunlight, even though that meant the dragons and death, when he heard Mina give a startled cry.

Acting instinctively, fearing for her life, Galdar drew his sword and clattered down the stairs.

"What are you doing here, Silvanoshei? Skulking about in the shadows like an assassin?" Mina demanded.

Her tone was cold, but her voice trembled. The light of the torch she held wavered in her shaking hand. She'd been caught off-guard, taken unawares.

Galdar recognized Mina's besotted lover, the elf king. The elf's face was deadly pale. He was thin and wan, his fine clothes tattered, ragged. He no longer had that wasted, desperate look about him, however. He was calm and composed, more composed than Mina.

The word "assassin" and the young man's strange composure caused Galdar to lift his sword. He would have brought it down upon the young elf's head, splitting him in two, but Mina stopped him.

"No, Galdar," she said, and her voice was filled with contempt. "He is no threat to me. He can do nothing to harm me. His foul blood would only defile the sacred soil on which we stand."

"Be gone then, scum," said Galdar, reluctantly lowering his weapon. "Mina gives you your wretched life. Take it and leave."

"Not before I say something," said Silvanoshei with quiet dignity. "I am sorry, Mina. Sorry for what has happened to you."

"Sorry for me?" Mina regarded him with scorn. "Be sorry for yourself. You fell into the One God's trap. The elves will be annihilated, utterly, finally, completely. Thousands have already fallen to my might, and thousands more will follow until all who oppose me have perished. Because of you, because of your weakness, your people will be wiped out. And *you* feel sorry for *me?*"

"Yes," Silvanoshei said. "I was not the only one to fall into the trap. If I had been stronger, I might have been able to save you, but I was not. For that, I am sorry."

Mina stared at him, the amber of her eyes hardening around him, as if she would squeeze the life out of him.

He stood steadfast, his eyes filled with sorrow.

Mina turned away in contempt. "Bring him," she ordered Galdar. "He will be witness to the end of all that he holds dear."

"Mina, let me slay him—" Galdar began.

"Must you always oppose me?" Mina demanded, rounding on him angrily. "I said bring him. Have no fear. He will not be the only witness. All the enemies of the One God will be here to see her triumph. Including you, Galdar."

Turning, she entered the door that led into the arena.

The hackles rose on the back of Galdar's neck. His hands were wet with sweat.

"Run," he said abruptly to the elf. "I will not stop you. Go on, get out of here."

Silvanoshei shook his head. "I stay as do you. We both stay for the same reason."

Galdar grunted. He stood in the doorway, debating, though he already knew what he would do. The elf was right. They both stayed for the same reason.

Gritting his teeth, Galdar stalked through the door and entered the arena. Glancing back to see if the elf king was following, Galdar was astonished to see another elf standing behind Silvanoshei.

Ye gods, the place is crawling with them! Galdar thought.

The elf looked fixedly at Galdar, who had the sudden uneasy feeling that this elf with the young face and the old eyes could read the thoughts of his head and of his heart.

Galdar didn't like this. He didn't trust this new elf, and he hesitated, wondering if he should go back to deal with him.

The elf stood calmly, waiting.

All the enemies of the One God will be here to witness her triumph.

Assuming that this was just one more, Galdar shrugged and entered the arena. He was forced to follow the light of Mina's torch, for he could not see her in the darkness.

31 THE BATTLE OF SANCTION

The silver dragons flew low over Sanction, not bothering to use their lethal breath weapons, relying on fear alone to drive away the enemy. Gerard had flown on dragonback before, but he'd never flown into battle, and he had often wondered why any person would risk his neck fighting in the air when he could be standing on solid ground. Now, experiencing the exhilaration of a diving rush upon Sanction's defenses, Gerard realized that he could never again go back to the heave and crush and heat of battle on land.

He yelled a Solamnic war cry as he and his Silver dived down upon the hapless defenders, not because he thought they would hear him, but for the sheer joy of the flight and the sight of his enemy fleeing before him in screaming panic. All around him, the other Knights yelled and shouted. Elven archers seated on the backs of golden dragons loosed their arrows into the throngs of soldiers trying desperately to escape the glittering death that circled above them.

The river of souls swirled around Gerard, seeking to stop him, seeking to wrap their chill arms around him, submerge him, blind him. But the army of the dead was leaderless now. They had no one to give them orders, no one to direct them. The wings of the golden and silver dragons sliced through the river of souls, shredding them like the rays of the sun shred the morning mists that drift along the riverbank. Gerard saw the clutching hands and pleading mouths of the souls whirl about him. They no longer inspired terror. Only pity.

He looked away, looked back to the task at hand, and the dead vanished.

When most of the defenders had been swept from the walls, the dragons landed in the valleys that surrounded Sanction. The elven and human warriors who had been riding on their backs dismounted. They formed into ranks, began to march upon the city, while Gerard and the other dragonriders continued to patrol the skies.

The Silvanesti and Qualinesti placed their flags on a small knoll in the center of the valley. Alhana would have liked to lead the assault on Sanction, but she was the titular ruler of the Silvanesti nation and reluctantly agreed with Samar that her place was in the rear, there to give orders and guide the attack.

"I will be the one to rescue my son," she said to Samar. "I will be the one to free him from his prison."

"My Queen—" he began, his expression grave.

"Do not say it, Samar," Alhana commanded. "We will find Silvanoshei alive and well. We will."

"Yes, Your Majesty."

He left her, standing on the hill, the colors of their tattered flag forming a faded rainbow above her head.

Gilthas stood beside her. Like Alhana, he would have liked to be among the warriors, but he knew that an inept and unpracticed swordsman is a danger to himself and everyone unfortunate enough to be near him. Gilthas watched his wife race to battle. He could pick her out of a crowd of thousands by her wild, curling mass of hair and by the fact that she would always be in the vanguard along with her Kagonesti warriors, shouting their ancient war cries and brandishing their weapons, challenging the enemy to quit skulking behind the walls and come out and fight.

He feared for her. He always feared for her, but he knew better than to express that fear to her or to try to keep her safe by his side. She would take that as an insult and rightly so. She was a warrior with a warrior's heart and a warrior's instincts and a warrior's courage. She would not be easy to kill. His heart reached out to her, and as if she felt his love touch her, she turned her head, lifted her sword, and saluted him.

He waved back, but she did not see him. She had turned her face toward battle. Gilthas could do nothing now but await the outcome.

Lord Tasgall led the Knights of Solamnia from the back of a silver dragon. He still smarted from the defeat of Solanthus. Remembering Mina's taunts from the walls as she stood victorious in the city, he was looking forward to seeing her once again upon a wall—her head on a pike on that wall.

A few of the enemy had managed to overcome the dragonfear and were mounting a defense. Archers regained the battlements, launched a volley of arrows at the silver dragon carrying Lord Tasgall. A golden dragon spotted the volley, breathed on it, and the arrows burst into flame. Lord Tasgall guided his silver dragon into the heart of Sanction.

The armies in the valley marched up to the moat of fire that guarded the city. The silver dragons breathed their frost-breath on the moat, cooling the lava and causing it to harden into black rock. Steam rose into the air, providing cover for the advancing armies as a few staunch defenders began to fire at them from the towers.

Elven archers halted to fire, sending wave after wave of arrows at the enemy. Under cover of the fire, Lord Ulrich led his men-at-arms in a rush upon the walls. A few catapults were still in operation, sent a boulder or two crashing down, but they were fired in panicked haste. Their aim was off. The boulders bounded harmlessly away. The soldiers flung grappling hooks up over the walls, began to scale them.

A few daring bands of elven archers dropped down off the backs of the low-circling dragons, landing on the roofs of the houses inside Sanction. From this vantage point, they fired their arrows into the backs of the defenders, wreaking further havoc.

They had not been able to bring with them a battering ram to smash open the gates, but as it turned out, they had no need. A golden dragon settled in front of the West Gate and, paying small heed to the arrows being fired at her from the battlements, breathed a jet of flame on the gates. The gates disintegrated into flaming cinders. With a triumphant cry, the humans and elves stormed into Sanction.

Once inside the city, the battle became more intense, for the defenders, faced now with certain death, lost their fear of the dragons and fought grimly. The dragons could do little to assist, afraid of harming their own forces.

Still, Gerard guessed that it would not be long before the day was theirs. He was about to order his dragon to set him down, so that he could join the fighting when he heard Odila shout his name.

As the blind silver dragon, Mirror, could not join in the assault, he and Odila had volunteered to act as scouts, directing the attackers to places they were needed. Calling out to Gerard, she pointed northward. A large force of black-armored Knights of Neraka and foot soldiers had managed to escape the city and were retreating toward the Lords of Doom. They were not in panicked flight but marched in ragged ranks.

Loath to let them escape, knowing that once they were in the mountains, they would be impossible to ferret out, Gerard urged his own dragon to fly to intercept them. A flash of metal from one of the mountain passes caught his eye.

Another army was marching out of the mountains to the east. These soldiers marched in rigid order, moving swiftly down the mountainside like some enormous, deadly, shining-scaled snake.

Even from this distance, Gerard recognized the force for what it was—an army of draconians. He could see the wings on their backs, wings that lifted them up and carried them easily over any obstacle in their way. Sunlight shone on their heavy armor, gleamed off their helms and their scaled skin.

Draconians were coming to Sanction's rescue. A thousand or more. The army of escaping Dark Knights saw the draconians heading in their direction and broke into cheers so loud that Gerard could hear them from the air. The retreating army of Dark Knights shifted about, intending to regroup and return to the attack with their new allies.

The draconians moved rapidly, racing down the sides of the mountains. They would soon be over Sanction's walls, and once they were in the city, the dragons could do nothing to stop them for fear of harming the Knights and elves fighting in the streets.

Gerard's Silver was preparing to dive to the attack, when, staring in astonishment, Gerard bellowed an order for his dragon to halt.

Wheeling smartly, the draconians smashed into the astonished ranks of Dark Knights that had, only moments before, been hailing the draconians as friends.

The draconians made short work of the beleaguered Knights. The force crumbled under the attack, and as Gerard watched, it disintegrated. The job done, the draconians reformed again into orderly ranks and marched on toward Sanction.

Gerard had no idea what was going on. How was it possible that draconians should be allies of Solamnics and elves? He wondered if he should try to halt their march, or if he should allow the draconians to enter the city. Common sense voted for one, his heart held out for the other.

The decision was taken out of his hands, for the next instant, the city of Sanction, the snaking lines of marching draconians, the silver wings, head, and mane of the dragon on which he rode dissolved before his eyes.

Once again, he experienced the dizzying, stomach-turning motion of a journey through the corridors of magic.

Gerard found himself seated on a hard stone bench under a night-black sky, staring down into an arena that was illuminated by a chill, white light. The light had no source that he could see at first, but then he realized with a shudder that it emanated from the souls of the countless dead who overflowed the arena, so that it seemed to him that he and the arena and everyone in it floated upon a vast, unquiet ocean of death.

Gerard looked around to see Odila, staring, open-mouthed. He saw Lord Tasgall and Lord Ulrich seated together, with Lord Siegfried some distance off. Alhana Starbreeze occupied a seat, as did Samar, both staring about in anger and bewilderment. Gilthas was present, with his wife, the Lioness, and Planchet.

Friend and foe alike were here. Captain Samuval sat in the stands, looking dismayed and baffled. Two draconians sat there, one a large bozak wearing a golden chain around his neck, the other a sivak in full battle regalia. The bozak looked stern, the sivak uneasy. More than one person in that crowd had been snatched bodily from the fray. Their faces flushed and hot, spattered with blood, they stared about in amazed confusion. The body of the wizard Dalamar was here, sitting on a bench, staring at nothing.

The dead made no sound, and neither did the living. Gerard opened his mouth and tried to call out to Odila, only to discover that he had no voice. An unseen hand stopped his tongue, pressed him down into his seat so that he could not move except as the hand guided him. He could see only what he was meant to see and nothing more.

The thought came to him that he was dead, that he'd been struck down by an arrow in the back, perhaps, and that he'd been taken to this place where the dead congregated. His fear subsided. He could feel his heart beating, hear the blood pounding in his ears. He could clench his hands into fists, dig his nails into his flesh and feel pain. He could shuffle his feet. He could feel terror, and he knew then that he wasn't dead. He was a prisoner, brought here against his will for some purpose that he could only assume was a horrible one.

Silent and unmoving as the dead, the living were constrained to stare down into the eerily lit arena.

The figure of a dragon appeared. Ephemeral, insubstantial, five heads thrust hideously from a single neck. Immense wings formed a canopy that covered the arena, blotting out hope. The huge tail coiled around all who sat in the dread shadow of the wings. Ten eyes stared in all directions, looking forward and behind, seeing into every heart, searching for the darkness within. Five mouths gnawed hungrily, finding the darkness and feeding upon it.

The five mouths opened and gave forth a silent call that split the eardrums of all listening, so that they gritted their teeth against the pain and fought back tears.

At the call, Mina entered the arena.

She wore the black armor of the Knights of Neraka. The armor did not shine in the eerie light but was one with the darkness of the dragon's wings. She wore no helm, and her face glimmered ghostly white. She carried in her hand a dragonlance. Behind her, almost lost in the shadows, stood the minotaur, faithful guard at her back.

Mina faced the silent crowd in the stands. Her gaze encompassed both the dead and the living.

"I am Mina," she called out. "The chosen of the One God."

She paused, as if waiting for the cheers to which she'd become accustomed. None spoke, not the living, not the dead. Their voices stolen, they watched in silence.

"Know this," Mina resumed, and her voice was cold and commanding. "The One God is the One God for now and forever. No others will come after. You will worship the One God now and forever. You will serve the One God now and forever, in death as in life. Those who serve faithfully will be rewarded. Those who rebel will be punished. This day, the One God makes manifest her power. This day, the One God enters the world in physical form and thus joins together the immortal with the mortal. Free to move between both of them at will, the One God will rule both."

Mina lifted up the dragonlance. Once lovely to look upon, the shining silver lance glimmered cold and bleak, its point stained black with blood.

"I give this as proof of the One God's power. I hold in my hand the fabled dragonlance. Once a weapon of the enemies of the One God, the dragonlance has become her weapon. The dragon Malystryx died on the point of the dragon-lance, died by the will of the One God. The One God fears nothing. In token of this, I shatter the dragonlance."

Grasping the lance in both hands, Mina brought it down upon her bent knee. The lance snapped as if it were a long-dead and dried-up stick, broken in twain. Mina tossed the pieces contemptuously over her shoulder. The pieces landed on the sandy floor of the arena. Their silver light flickered briefly, valiantly.

The dragon's five heads spat upon them, the dragon's breath smothered them. Their light diminished and died.

The living and the dead watched in silence.

Galdar watched in silence.

He stood behind Mina, guarding her back, for somewhere in the darkness lurked that strange elf, not to mention the wretch, Silvanoshei. Galdar had not much fear of the latter, but he was determined that no one should get past him. No one would accost Mina in this, her hour of triumph.

This will be her hour, Galdar told himself. She will be honored. Takhisis can do no less for her. He told himself that repeatedly, yet fear gnawed at him.

For the first time, Galdar witnessed the true power of Queen Takhisis. He watched in awe to see the stadium fill with people, taken prisoner in the midst of their lives and brought here to watch her victorious entry into the mortal realm. He looked in awe at her dragon form, her vast wingspan blotting out the light of hope, bringing eternal night to the world.

He realized then that he had discounted her, and his soul sank to its knees before her. He was a rebellious slave, one who had tried foolishly to rise above his place. He had learned his lesson. He would be a slave always, even after death. He could accept his fate because here, in the presence of the Dark Queen's full might and majesty, he understood that he deserved nothing else.

But not Mina. Mina was not born to be a slave. Mina was born to rule. She had proven herself, proven her loyalty. She had walked through blood and fire and never blanched, never swerved in her unwavering belief. Let Takhisis do with him what she would, let her devour his very soul. So long as Mina was honored and rewarded, Galdar would be content.

"The foes of the One God are vanquished," Mina cried. "Their weapons are destroyed. None can stop her triumphant entry into the world."

Mina raised up her hands, her amber eyes lifted to the dragon. "Your Majesty, I have always adored you, worshiped you. I pledged my life to your service, and I stand ready to honor that pledge. Through my fault, you lost the body of Goldmoon, the body you would have inhabited. I offer my own. Take my life. Use me as your vessel. Thus, I prove my faith!"

Galdar gasped, appalled. He wanted to stop this madness, wanted to stop Mina, but though he roared his protest, his words came out a silent scream that no one heard.

The five heads gazed down on Mina.

"I accept your sacrifice," said Queen Takhisis.

Galdar lunged forward and stood still. He raised his arm and it didn't move. Bound by darkness, he could do nothing but watch to see all he had ever loved and honored destroyed.

Clouds, black and ghastly and shot with lightning, rolled down from the Lords of Doom. The clouds boiled around the Dragon Queen, obscuring her from view. The clouds swirled and churned, raised a whipping wind that buffeted Galdar with bruising force, drove him to his knees.

Mina's prayer, Mina's faith unlocked the prison door.

The storm clouds transformed into a chariot, drawn by five dragons. Standing in the chariot, her hand on the reins, was Queen Takhisis, in woman's form.

She was beautiful, her beauty fell and terrible to look upon. Her face was cold as the vast, frozen wastelands to the south, where a man perishes in an instant, his breath turning to ice in his lungs. Her eyes were the flames of the funeral pyre. Her nails were talons, her hair the long and ragged hair of the corpse. Her armor was black fire. At her side, she wore a sword perpetually stained with blood, a sword used to sever the souls from their bodies.

Her chariot hung in the air, the wings of the five dragons fanning, keeping it aloft. Takhisis left the chariot, descended to the arena floor. She trod on the lightning bolts, the storm clouds were her cloak, trailing behind her.

Takhisis walked toward Mina. The five dragons lifted their heads, cried out a paean of triumph.

Galdar could not move, he could not save her. The wind beat at him with such force that he could not even lift his head. He cried out to Mina, but his voice was whipped away by the raging wind, and his cry went unheard.

Mina smiled a tremulous smile. "My Queen," she whispered.

Takhisis stretched out her taloned hand.

Mina stood, unflinching.

Takhisis reached for Mina's heart, to make that heart her own. Takhisis reached for Mina's soul, to snatch it from her body and cast it into oblivion. Takhisis reached out to fill Mina's body with her own immortal essence.

Takhisis reached out, but her hand could not touch Mina.

Mina looked startled, confused. Her body began to tremble. She reached out her hand to her Queen, but could not touch her.

Takhisis glared. The eyes of flame filled the arena with the hideous light of her anger.

"Disobedient child!" she cried. "How dare you oppose me?"

"I do not!" Mina gasped, shivering. "I swear to you—"

"She does not oppose you. I do," said a voice.

The strange elf walked past Galdar.

The wind of the Dark Queen's fury howled around the elf and struck at him. Her lightning flared over him and sought to burn him. Her thunder boomed and tried to crush him. The elf was bowed by the winds, but he kept walking. He was knocked down by the lightning, but he rose again and kept walking. Undaunted, unafraid, he came to stand before the Queen of Darkness.

"Paladine! My dear brother!" Takhisis spat the words. "So you have found your misplaced world." She shrugged. "You are too late. You cannot stop me."

Amused, she waved her hand toward the gallery. "Find a seat. Be my guest. I am glad you came. Now you can witness my triumph."

"You are wrong, Sister," the elf said, his voice silver, ringing. "We can stop you. You know how we can stop you. It is written in the book. We all agreed."

The flame of the Dark Queen's eyes wavered. The taloned fingers twitched. For an instant, her crystalline beauty was marred with doubt, anxiety. Only for an instant. Her doubts vanished. Her beauty was restored.

She smiled.

"You would not do that to me, Brother," Takhisis said, regarding him with scorn. "The great and puissant Paladine would never make the sacrifice."

"You misjudge me, Sister. I already have."

The elf thrust his hand into a pouch he wore at his side and drew out a small knife, a knife that had once belonged to a kender of his acquaintance.

Paladine drew the knife across the palm of his hand.

Blood oozed from the wound, dripped onto the floor of the arena.

"The balance must be maintained," he said. "I am mortal. As are you."

Storm clouds, dragons, lightning, chariot, all disappeared. The sun shone bright in the blue sky. The seats in the gallery were suddenly empty, except for the gods.

They sat in judgment, five on the side of light: Mishakal, gentle goddess of healing; Kiri-Jolith, beloved of the Solamnic Knights; Majere, friend of Paladine, who came from Beyond; Habbakuk, god of the sea; Branchala, whose music soothes the heart.

Five took the side of darkness: Sargonnas, god of vengeance, who looked unmoved on the fall of his consort; Morgion, god of disease; Chemosh, lord of the undead, angered at her intrusion in what had once been his province; Zeboim, who blamed Takhisis for the death of her loved son, Ariakan; Hiddukel, who cared only that the balance be maintained.

Six stood between: Gilean, who held the book; Sirrion, god of nature; Shinare, his mate, god of commerce; Reorx, the forger of the world; Chislev, goddess of the woodland; Zivilyn, who once more saw past, present and future.

The three children, Solinari, Nuitari, Lunitari, stood together, as always.

One place, on the side of light, was empty.

One place, on the side of darkness, was empty.

Takhisis cursed them. She screamed in rage, crying out with one voice now, not five, and her voice was the voice of a mortal. The fire of her eyes that had once scorched the sun dwindled to the flicker of the candle flame that may be blown out with a breath. The weight of her flesh and bone dragged her down from the ethers. The thudding of her heart sounded loud in her ears, every beat telling her that some day that beating would stop and death would come. She had to breathe or suffocate. She had to work to draw one breath after the other. She felt the pangs of hunger that she had never known and all the other pains of this weak and fragile body. She, who had traversed the heavens and roamed among the stars, stared down with loathing at the two feet on which she now must plod.

Lifting her eyes, that were gritty with sand and burning with fury, Takhisis saw Mina, standing before her, young, strong, beautiful.

"You did this," Takhisis raved. "You connived with them to bring about my downfall. You wanted them to sing your name, not my own!"

Takhisis drew her sword and lunged at Mina. "I may be mortal, but I can still deal death!"

Galdar gave a bellowing roar. He leaped to stop the blow, jumped in front of Mina to shield her with his body, raised his sword to defend her.

The Dark Queen's blade swept down in a slashing arc. The blade severed Galdar's sword arm, hacked it off below the shoulder.

Arm, hand, sword fell at his feet, lay there in a widening pool of his own blood. He fell to his knees, fought the pain and shock that were trying to rob him of his senses.

The Dark Queen lifted her sword and held it poised above Mina's head.

Mina said softly, "Forgive me," and stood braced for the blow.

His own life ebbing away, Galdar was about to make a desperate lunge, when something smote him from behind. Galdar looked up with dimming eyes to see Silvanoshei standing over him.

The elf king held in his hand the broken fragment of the dragonlance. He threw the lance, threw it with the strength of his anguish and his guilt, threw it with the strength of his fear and his love.

The lance struck Takhisis, lodged in her breast.

She stared down in shock to see the lance protruding from her flesh. Her fingers moved to touch the bright, dark blood welling from the terrible wound. She staggered, started to fall.

Mina sprang forward with a wild cry of grief and love. She clasped the dying queen in her arms.

"Don't leave me, Mother," Mina cried. "Don't leave me here alone!"

Takhisis ignored her. Her eyes fixed upon Paladine, and in them her hatred burned, endless, eternal.

"If I have lost everything, so have you. The world in which you took such delight can never go back to the way it was. I have done that much, at least."

Blood frothed upon the queen's lips. She coughed, struggled to draw a final breath. "Someday you will know the pain of death. Worse than that, Brother"—Takhisis smiled, grimly, derisively, as the shadows clouded her eyes—"you will know the pain of life."

Her breath bubbled with blood. Her body shuddered, and her hands fell limp. Her head lolled back on Mina's cradling arm. The eyes fixed, stared into the night she had ruled so long and that she would rule no more.

Mina clasped the dead queen to her breast, rocked her, weeping. The rest, Galdar, the strange elf, the gods, were silent, stunned. The only sound was Mina's harsh sobs. Silvanoshei, white-lipped and ashen-faced, laid a hand upon her shoulder.

"Mina, she was going to kill you. I couldn't let her. . . ."

Mina lifted her tear-ravaged face. Her amber eyes were hot, liquid, burned when they touched his flesh.

"I wanted to die. I would have died happily, gratefully, for I would have died serving her. Now, I live and she is gone and I have no one. No one!"

Her hand, wet with the blood of her queen, grasped Takhisis's sword.

Paladine sought to intercede, to stop her. An unseen hand shoved him off balance, sent him tumbling into the sand. A voice thundered from the heavens.

"We will have our revenge, Mortal," said Sargonnas.

Mina plunged the sword into Silvanoshei's stomach.

The young elf gasped, stared at her in astonishment.

"Mina . . ." His pallid lips formed the word. He had no voice to speak it. His face contorted in pain.

Furious, grim-faced, Mina thrust harder, drove the sword deeper. She let him hang, impaled on the blade, for a long moment, while she looked at him, let the amber eyes harden over him. Satisfied that he was dying, she yanked the sword free.

Silvanoshei slid down the blade that was smeared with his blood and crumpled into the sand.

Clutching the bloody sword, Mina walked over to Paladine, who was slowly picking himself up off the floor of the arena. Mina gazed at him, absorbed him into the amber. She tossed the sword of Takhisis at his feet.

"You *will* feel the pain of death. But not yet. Not now. So my Queen wished it, and I obey her last wishes. But know this, wretch. In the face of every elf I meet, I will see your face. The life of every elf I take will be your life. And I will take many . . . to pay for the one."

She spat at him, spat into his face. She turned to the gods, regarded them in defiance. Then Mina knelt beside the body of her queen. She kissed the cold forehead. Lifting the body in her arms, Mina carried her dead from the Temple of Duerghast.

All was silent in the arena, silent except for Mina's departing footfalls. Galdar laid down his head in the sand that was warm from the sunshine. He was very tired. He could rest now, though, for Mina was safe. She was safe at last.

Galdar closed his eyes and began the long journey into darkness. He had not gone far, when he found his path blocked.

Galdar looked up to see an enormous minotaur. The minotaur stood tall as the mountain on which the red dragon had perished. His horns brushed the stars, his fur was jet black. He wore a leather harness, trimmed in pure, cold silver.

"Sargas!" Galdar whispered. Clutching his bleeding stump, he stumbled to his knees and bowed his head. His horns touched the ground.

"Rise, Galdar," said the god, his voice booming across the heavens. "I am pleased with you. In your need, you turned to me."

"Thank you, great Sargas," said Galdar, not daring to rise, tentatively lifting his head.

"In return for your faith, I restore your life," said Sargas. "I give you your life and your sword arm."

"Not my arm, great Sargas," Galdar pleaded, the pain burning hot in his breast. "I accept my life, and I will live it to honor you, but the arm is gone and I do not want it back."

Sargas was displeased. "The minotaur nation has at last thrown off the fetters that have bound us for so many centuries. We are breaking out of the islands where we have long been imprisoned and moving to take our rightful place upon this continent. I need gallant warriors such as yourself, Galdar. I need them whole, not maimed."

"I thank you, great Sargas," said Galdar humbly, "but, if it is all the same to you, I will learn to fight with my left hand."

Galdar tensed, waited in fear of the god's wrath. Hearing nothing, Galdar risked a peep.

Sargas smiled. His smile was grudging, but it was a smile. "Have it your way, Galdar. You are free to determine your own fate."

Galdar gave a long, deep sigh. "For that, great Sargas," he said, "I do truly thank you."

Galdar blinked his eyes, lifted his muzzle from the wet sand. He couldn't remember where he was, couldn't imagine what he was doing lying here, taking a nap, in the middle of the day. Mina would need him. She would be angry to find him lazing about. He jumped to his feet and reached instinctively for the sword that hung at his waist.

He had no sword. No hand to grasp it. His severed arm lay in the sand at his feet. He looked at where the arm had been, looked at the blood in the sand, and memory returned.

Galdar was healthy, except for his missing right arm. The stump was healed. He turned to thank the god, but the god was gone. All the gods were gone. No one remained in the arena except the body of the elf king and the strange elf with the young face and the ancient eyes.

Slowly, clumsily, fumbling with his left hand, Galdar picked up his sword. He shifted the sword belt so that he wore it now on his right hip, and, after many clumsy tries, he finally managed to return the sword to its sheath. The weapon didn't feel natural there, wasn't comfortable. He'd get used to it, though. This time, he'd get used to it.

The air was not as warm as he had remembered it. The sun dipped down behind the mountain, casting shadows of coming night. He would have to hurry, if he was going to find her. He would have to leave now, while there was still daylight left.

"You are a loyal friend, Galdar," said Paladine, as the minotaur stalked past him.

Galdar grunted and trudged on, following the trail of her footprints, the trail of her queen's blood.

For love of Mina.

32 THE AGE OF MORTALS

The fight for the city of Sanction did not last long. By nightfall, the city had surrendered. It would have probably surrendered much sooner, but there was no one willing to make the decision.

In vain, the Dark Knights and their soldiers called out Mina's name. She did not answer, she did not come, and they realized at last that she was not going to come. Some were bitter, some were angry. All felt betrayed. Knowing that they if they survived the battle they would be executed or imprisoned, a few Knights fought on. Most fought because they were trapped or cornered by the advancing enemy.

Some had decided to act on Galdar's advice and tried to find refuge in the caves of the Lords of Doom. These formed the force that had run into the army of draconians. Thinking that they had found an ally, the Dark Knights had been prepared to halt their retreat, turn around to try to retake the city. Their shock when the draconians smashed into them had been immense but short-lived.

Who these strange draconians were and why they came to the aid of elves and Solamnics would never be known. The draconian army did not enter Sanction. They held their position outside the city until they saw the flag of the Dark Knights torn down and the banners of the Qualinesti, the Silvanesti, and the Solamnic nation raised in its stead.

A large bozak draconian, wearing armor and a golden chain around his neck, marched forward, together with a sivak, wearing the trappings of a draconian high commander. The sivak called the draconian troops to attention. He and the bozak saluted the banners. The draconian troops clashed their swords against their shields in salute. The sivak gave the order to march, and the draconians wheeled and departed, heading back into the mountains.

Someone recalled hearing of a group of draconians who had taken control of the city of Teyr. It was said that these draconians had no love for the Dark Knights. Even if this was true, Teyr was a long march from Sanction, and no one could say how the draconians had managed to arrive at the critical time. Since no one ever saw the draconians again, this mystery was never solved.

When the victory in Sanction had been achieved, many of the golden and silver dragons departed, heading for the Dragon Isles or wherever they made their homes. Before they left, each dragon lifted up and carried away a portion of the ashes from the totem, taking them for a proper burial on the Dragon Isles. The Golds and Silver took all the remains, even though mingled among them were the ashes of Reds and Blues, Whites, Greens, and Blacks. For they were all dragons of Krynn.

"And what about you, sir?" Gerard asked Mirror. "Will you go back to the Citadel of Light?"

Gerard, Odila, and Mirror stood outside the West Gate of Sanction, watching the sunrise on the day after the battle. The sunrise was glorious, with bands of vibrant reds and oranges darkening to purple and deeper into black as day touched the departing night. The silver dragon faced the sun as if he could see it—and perhaps, in his soul, he could. He turned his blind head toward the sound of Gerard's voice.

"The Citadel will have no more need of my protection. Mishakal will make the temple her own. As for me, my guide and I have decided to join forces."

Gerard stared blankly at Odila, who nodded.

"I am leaving the Knighthood," she said. "Lord Tasgall has accepted my resignation. It is best this way, Gerard. The Knights would not have felt comfortable having me among their ranks."

"What will you do?" Gerard asked. They had been through so much, he had not expected to part with her so soon.

"Queen Takhisis may be gone," Odila said somberly, "but darkness remains. The minotaurs have seized Silvanesti. They will not be content with that land and may threaten others. Mirror and I have decided to join forces." She patted the silver dragon's neck. "A dragon who is blind and a human who was once blind—quite a team, don't you think?"

Gerard smiled. "If you're headed for Silvanesti, we may run into each other. I'm going to try to establish an alliance between the Knighthood and the elves."

"Do you truly believe the Knights' Council will agree to help the elves recover their land?" Odila asked skeptically.

"I don't know," Gerard said, shrugging, "but I'm damn sure going to make them think about it. First, though, I have a duty to perform. There's a broken lock on a tomb in Solace. I promised to go fix it."

An uncomfortable silence fell between them. Too much was left to say to be said now. Mirror fanned his wings, clearly eager to be gone. Odila took the hint.

"Goodbye, Cornbread," she said, grinning.

"Good riddance," said Gerard, grinning back.

Odila leaned close, kissed him on the cheek. "If you ever again take a bath naked in a creek, be sure and let me know."

She mounted the silver dragon. He dipped his sightless head in salute, spread his wings, and lifted gracefully into the air. Odila waved.

Gerard waved back. He watched them as they dwindled in size, remained watching until long after they had vanished from his sight.

Another goodbye was said that day. A farewell that would last for all eternity.

In the arena, Paladine knelt over the body of Silvanoshei. Paladine closed the staring eyes. He cleansed the blood from the young elf's face, composed the limbs. Paladine was tired. He was not accustomed to this mortal body, to its pains and aches and needs, to the range and intensity of emotions: of pity and sorrow, anger and fear. Looking into the face of the dead elven king, Paladine saw youth and promise, all lost, all wasted. He paused in his labor, wiped the sweat from his forehead, and wondered how, with such sorrow and heaviness in his heart, he could go on. He wondered how he could go on alone.

Feeling a gentle touch upon his shoulder, he looked to see a goddess, beautiful, radiant. She smiled down upon him, but there was sadness in her smile and the rainbows of unshed tears in her eyes.

"I will carry the young man's body to his mother," Mishakal offered.

"She was not witness to his death, was she?" Paladine asked.

"She was spared that much, at least. We freed all those who had been brought here forcibly by Takhisis to view her triumph. Alhana did not see her son die.

"Tell her," said Paladine quietly, "that he died a hero."

"I will do that, my beloved."

A kiss as soft as a white feather brushed the elf's lips.

"You are not alone," Mishakal said to him. "I will be with you always, my husband, my own."

He wanted very much for this to be so, willed that it should be so. But there was a gulf between them, and he saw that gulf grow wider with every passing moment. She stood upon the shore, and he floundered among the waves, and every wave washed him farther and farther away.

"What has become of the souls of the dead?" he asked.

"They are free," she said and her voice was distant. He could barely hear her. "Free to continue their journey."

"Someday, I will join them, my love."

"On that day, I will be waiting," she promised.

The body of Silvanoshei vanished, born away on a cloud of silvery light.

Paladine stood for a long time alone, stood in the darkness. Then he made his solitary way out of the arena, walked alone into the world.

The children of the gods, Nuitari, Lunitari, Solinari, entered the former Temple of the Heart. The body of the wizard Dalamar sat upon a bench, staring at nothing.

The gods of magic took their places before the dark and abandoned altar.

"Let the wizard, Raistlin Majere, come forth."

Raistlin emerged from the darkness and ruins of the temple. The hem of his black velvet robe scattered the amber shards that still lay upon the floor of this temple, for no one could be found who dared touch the accursed remnants of the sarcophogus that had imprisoned the body of Goldmoon. He trod upon them, crushed the amber beneath his feet.

In his arms, Raistlin held a body, shrouded in white.

"Your spirit is freed," said Solinari sternly. "Your twin brother awaits you. You promised to leave the world. You must keep that promise."

"I have no intention of remaining here," Raistlin returned. "My brother awaits, as do my former companions."

"They have forgiven you?"

"Or I have forgiven them," Raistlin returned smoothly. "The matter is between friends and none of your concern." He looked down at the body he held in his arms. "But this is."

Raistlin laid the body of his nephew at the feet of the gods. Then, drawing back his hood, he faced the three siblings.

"I ask one last boon of you, of all of you," said Raistlin. "Restore Palin to life. Restore him to his family."

"And why should we do this?" Lunitari demanded.

"His steps strayed onto the path that I once walked," said Raistlin. "He saw his mistake at the end, but he could not live to redeem it. If you give him back his life, he will be able to retrace his wandering footsteps and find the way home."

"As you could not," said Lunitari gently.

"As I could not," said Raistlin.

"Brothers?" Lunitari turned to Solinari and Nuitari. "What do you say to this?"

"I say that there is another matter to be decided, as well," said Nuitari. "Let the wizard Dalamar come forth.

The elf's body sat unmoving on the bench. The spirit of the wizard stood behind the body. Wary, tense, Dalamar approached the gods.

"You betrayed us," said Nuitari, accusing.

"You sided with Takhisis," said Lunitari, "and we nearly lost the one chance we had to return to the world."

"You betrayed our worshiper Palin," said Solinari sternly. "By her command, you murdered him."

Dalamar looked from one shining god to the next and when he spoke, his soul's voice was soft and bitter. "How could you possibly understand? How would you know what it feels like to lose everything?"

"Perhaps," said Lunitari, "we understand better than you think."

Dalamar kept silent, made no response.

"What is to be done with him?" Lunitari asked. "Is he to be given back his life?"

"Unless you give me back the magic," Dalamar interposed, "don't bother."

"I say we do not," said Solinari. "He used the dead to work his black arts. He does not deserve our mercy."

"I say we do," said Nuitari coolly. "If you restore Palin to life and offer him the magic, you must do the same for Dalamar. The balance must be maintained."

"What do you say, Cousin?" Solinari asked Lunitari.

"Will you accept my judgment?" she asked.

Solinari and Nuitari eyed each other, then both nodded.

"This is my decree. Dalamar shall be restored to life and the magic, but he must leave the Tower of High Sorcery he once occupied. He will henceforth be barred from entry there. He must return to the world of the living and be forced to make his way among them. Palin Majere will also be restored to life. We will grant him the magic, if he wants it. Are these terms satisfactory to you both, Cousins?"

"They are to me," said Nuitari.

"And to me," said Solinari.

"And are they satisfactory to you, Dalamar?" Lunitari asked.

Dalamar had what he wanted, and that was all he cared about. As for the rest, he would return to the world. Someday, perhaps, he would rule the world.

"They are, Lady," he said.

"Are these satisfactory to you, Raistlin Majere?" Lunitari asked.

Raistlin bowed his hooded head.

"Then both requests are granted. We grant life, and we gift you with the magic."

"I thank you, lords and lady," Dalamar said, bowing again. His gaze lingered for a moment on Nuitari, who understood perfectly.

Raistlin knelt beside the body of his nephew. He drew back the white shroud. Palin's eyes opened. He gazed around in shocked bewilderment, then his gaze fixed on his uncle. Palin's shock deepened.

"Uncle!" he gasped. Sitting up, he tried to reach out to take his uncle's hand. His fingers, flesh and bone and blood, slid through Raistlin's hand that was the ephemeral hand of the dead.

Palin stared at his hand, and the realization came to him that he was alive. He looked at his hands, so like the hands of his uncle, with their long, delicate fingers, and he could move those fingers, and they would obey his commands.

"I thank you," Palin said, lifting his head to see the gods in their radiance around him. "I thank you, Uncle." He paused, then said, "Once you foretold that I would be the greatest mage ever to live upon Krynn. I do not think that will come to pass."

"We had much to learn, Nephew," Raistlin replied. "Much to learn about what was truly important. Farewell. My brother and our friends await." He smiled. "Tanis, as usual, is impatient to be gone."

Palin saw before him a river of souls, a river that flowed placidly, slowly among the banks of the living. Sunlight shone upon the river, starlight sparkled in its fathomless depths. The souls of the dead looked ahead of them into a sea whose waves lapped upon the shores of eternity, a sea that would carry each on new journeys. Standing on the shore, waiting for his twin, was Caramon Majere.

Raistlin joined his twin. The brothers raised their hands in farewell, then both stepped into the river and rode upon its silvery waters that flow into the endless sea.

Dalamar's spirit flowed into his body. The magic flowed into his spirit. The blood burned in his veins, the magic burned in his blood, and his joy was deep and profound. Lifting his head, he looked up into the sky.

The one pale moon had vanished. Two moons lit the sky, one with silver fire, the other with red. As he watched in awe and thankfulness, the two converged into a radiant eye. The black moon stared out from the center.

"So they gave you back your life, as well," said Palin, emerging from the shadows.

"And the magic," Dalamar returned.

Palin smiled. "Where will you go?"

"I do not know," said Dalamar carelessly. "The wide world is open to me. I intend to move out of the Tower of High Sorcery. I was prisoner there long enough. Where do you go?" His lip curled slightly. "Back to your loving wife?"

"If Usha will have me," said Palin, his tone and look somber. "I have much to make up to her."

"Do not be too long about it. We must meet soon to discuss the reconvening of the Orders," said Dalamar briskly. "There is work to be done."

"And there will be other hands to do it," said Palin.

Dalamar stared at him, now suddenly aware of the truth. "Solinari offered you the magic. And you refused it!"

"I threw away too much of value because of it," said Palin. "My marriage. My life. I came to realize it wasn't worth it."

You fool! The words were on Dalamar's lips, but he did not say them aloud, kept them to himself. He had no idea where he was going, and there would be no one to welcome him when he got there.

Dalamar looked up at the three moons. "Perhaps I will come to visit you and Usha sometime," he said, knowing he never would.

"We would be honored to have you," Palin replied, knowing he would never see the dark elf again.

"I had best be going," Dalamar said.

"I should be going, too," said Palin. "It is a long walk back to Solace."

"I could speed you through the corridors of magic," Dalamar offered.

"No, thank you," said Palin with a wry smile. "I had best get used to walking. Farewell, Dalamar the Dark."

"Farewell, Palin Majere."

Dalamar spoke the words of magic, felt them bubble and sparkle on his lips like fine wine, drank deeply of them. In an instant, he was gone.

Palin stood alone, thoughtful, silent. Then he looked up at the moons, which were for him now nothing but moons, one silver and one red.

Smiling, his thoughts turning to home, he matched his feet to the same direction.

The Solamnic Knights deployed their forces on Sanction's battlements, started hasty work repairing the West Gate and shoring up the holes that had been made in Sanction's walls. Scouts from the ranks of the Knights and those of the elves were sent to search for Mina. Silver dragons flying the skies kept watch for her, but no one found her. Dragons brought word of enemy forces marching toward Sanction, coming from Jelek and from Palanthas. Sooner or later, they would hear word that Sanction had fallen, but how would they react? Would they turn and flee for home, or would they march on to try to retake it? And would Mina, bereft of her god-given power, return to lead them, or would she remain in hiding somewhere, licking her wounds?

None would ever know where the body of Queen Takhisis lay buried—if she had been buried at all. Down through the years, those who walked on the side of darkness would search for the tomb, for the legend sprang up that her unquiet spirit would grant gifts to those who found her final resting place.

The most enduring mystery was what became known as the Miracle of the Temple of Duerghast. People from all parts of Sanction, all parts of Ansalon, all parts of the world, had been snatched abruptly from their lives by the Dark Queen and brought to the arena in the Temple of Duerghast to witness her triumphant entry into the world. Instead, they witnessed an epoch.

Those who saw firsthand the death of Queen Takhisis retained the images of what they saw and heard forever, feeling it branded into their souls as the brand burns the flesh. The shock and pain were searing, at first, but eventually the pain faded away, as the body and mind worked to heal themselves.

At first, some missed the pain, for without it, what proof was there that this had all been real? To make it real, to insure that it had been real, some talked of what they had seen, talked volubly. Others kept their thoughts locked away inside and would never speak of the event.

As with those on Krynn who had witnessed other epochs—the chaotic travels of the Gray Gem, the fall of Istar, the Cataclysm—they passed their stories of the Miracle from one generation to the next. To future generations living on Krynn, the Fifth Age would begin with the theft of the world at the moment of Chaos's defeat. But the Fifth Age would only come to be widely called the Age of Mortals on the day when the Judgment of the Book took away the godhood of one god and accepted the sacrifice of the other.

Silvanoshei was to be laid to rest in the Tomb of the Heroes in Solace. This was not to be his final burial place. His grieving mother, Alhana Starbreeze, hoped to one day take him home to Silvanesti, but that day would be long in coming. The minotaur nation poured in troops and supplies and were firmly entrenched in that formerly fair land.

Captain Samuval and his mercenaries continued to raid throughout the elven lands of Qualinesti. The Dark Knights drove out or killed the few elves who remained and claimed the land of Qualinesti as their own. The elves were exiles now. The remnants of the two nations argued over where to go, what to do.

The elven exiles camped in the valley outside of Sanction, but they were not at home there, and the Solamnic Knights, now the rulers of Sanction, urged them politely to consider moving somewhere else. The Knights' Council discussed allying with the elves to drive the minotaurs out of Silvanesti, but there was some question in regard to the Measure, and the matter was referred to scholars to settle, which they might confidently be expected to do in ten or twenty years.

Alhana Starbreeze had been offered the rulership of the Silvanesti, but, her heart broken, she had refused. She suggested that Gilthas rule in her stead. The Qualinesti wanted this, most of them. The Silvanesti did not, though they had no one else to recommend. The two quarreling nations came together once more, their representatives traveling together to the funeral of Silvanoshei.

A golden dragon bore the body of Silvanoshei to the Tomb of the Heroes. Solamnic Knights, riding silver dragons, formed a guard of honor, led by Gerard uth Mondar. Alhana accompanied the body of her son, as did his cousin Gilthas.

He was not sorry to leave the quarrels and intrigues behind. He wondered if he had the strength to go back. He did not want the kingship of the elven nations. He did not feel he was the right person. He did not want the responsibility of leading a people in exile, a people without a home.

Standing outside the tomb, Gilthas watched as a procession of elves carried the body of Silvanoshei, covered in a shroud of golden cloth, to its temporary resting place. His body was laid in a marble coffin, covered over with flowers. The shards of the broken dragonlance were placed in his hands.

The tomb would be the final resting place of Goldmoon. Her ashes were mingled with the ashes of Riverwind. The two of them together at last.

An elf dressed in travel-stained clothes of brown and green came to stand beside Gilthas. He said nothing but watched in solemn reverence as the ashes of Goldmoon and Riverwind were carried inside.

"Farewell, dear and faithful friends," he said softly.

Gilthas turned to him:

"I am glad to have this chance to speak to you, E'li—" he began.

The elf halted him. "That is my name no longer."

"What, then, should we call you, sir?" Gilthas asked.

"So many names I have had," said the elf. "E'li among the elves, Paladine among the humans. Even Fizban. That one, I must admit, was my favorite. None of them serve me now. I have chosen a new name."

"And that is—" Gilthas paused.

"Valthonis," said the elf.

"'The exile?'" Gilthas translated, puzzled. Sudden understanding rushed upon him. He tried to speak but could not manage beyond saying brokenly, "So you will share our fate."

Valthonis laid his hand upon Gilthas's shoulder. "Go back to your people, Gilthas. They are both your people, the Silvanesti and the Qualinesti. Make them one people again, and though they are a people in exile, though you have no land to call your own, you will be a nation."

Gilthas shook his head.

"The task before you is not an easy one," Valthonis said. "You will work hard and painstakingly to join together what others will endeavor to tear apart. You will be beset with failure, but never give up hope. If that happens, you will know defeat."

"Will you be with me?" Gilthas asked.

Valthonis shook his head. "I have my own road to walk, as do you, as does each of us. Yet, at times, our paths may cross."

"Thank you, sir," said Gilthas, clasping the elf's hand. "I will do as you say. I will return to my people. All my people." He sighed deeply, smiled ruefully. "Even Senator Palthainon."

Gerard stood at the entrance to the tomb, waiting for the last of the mourners to leave. The ceremony was over. Night had fallen. The crowds who had gathered to watch began to drift away, some going to the Inn of the Last Home, where Palin and Usha joined with his sisters, Laura and Dezra, to comfort all who mourned, giving them smiles and good food and the best ale in Ansalon.

As Gerard stood there, he thought back to all that had happened since that day, so long ago, when he had first heard Tasslehoff's voice shouting from inside the tomb. The world had changed, and yet it had not.

There were now three moons in the sky instead of one. Yet the sun that rose every morning was the same sun that had ushered in the Fifth Age. The people could look up into the sky again and find the constellations of the gods and point them out to their children. But the constellations were not the same as they had once been. They were made up of different stars, held different places in the heavens. Two could not be found, would never be found, would never be seen above Krynn again.

"The Age of Mortals," Gerard said to himself. The term had a new significance, a new meaning.

He looked inside the tomb to see one last person still within—the strange elf he had first seen in the arena. Gerard waited respectfully, patiently, fully prepared to give this mourner all the time he needed.

The elf said his prayers in silence, then, with a final loving farewell, he walked over to Gerard.

"Did you fix the lock?" he asked, smiling.

"I did, sir," said Gerard. He shut the door to the tomb behind him. He heard the lock click. He did not immediately leave. He was also loath to say goodbye.

"Sir, I was wondering." Gerard paused, then plunged ahead. "I don't know how to say this, but did Tasslehoff—Did he . . . did he do what he meant to do?"

"Did he die when and where he was meant to die?" the elf asked. "Did he defeat Chaos? Is that what you mean?"

"Yes, sir," said Gerard. "That's what I mean."

In answer, the elf lifted his head, looked into the night sky. "There once used to be a red star in the heavens. Do you remember it?"

"Yes, sir."

"Look for it now. Do you see it?"

"No, sir," said Gerard, searching the heavens. "What happened to it?"

"The forge fire has gone out. Flint doused the flame, for he knew he was no longer needed."

"So Tasslehoff found him," said Gerard.

"Tasslehoff found him. He and Flint and their companions are all together again," said the elf. "Flint and Tanis and Tasslehoff, Tika, Sturm, Goldmoon and Riverwind. They wait only for Raistlin, and he will join them soon, for Caramon, his twin, would not think of leaving without him."

"Where are they bound, sir?" Gerard asked.

"On the next stage of their souls' journey," said the elf.

"I wish them well," said Gerard.

He left the Tomb of the Last Heroes, bade the elf farewell, and, pocketing the key, turned his steps toward the Inn of the Last Home. The warm glow that streamed from its windows lit his way.

DUNGEONS & DRAGONS®

FROM THE RUINS OF FALLEN EMPIRES, A NEW AGE OF HEROES ARISES

It is a time of magic and monsters, a time when the world struggles against a rising tide of shadow. Only a few scattered points of light glow with stubborn determination in the deepening darkness.

It is a time where everything is new in an ancient and mysterious world.

BE THERE AS THE FIRST ADVENTURES UNFOLD.

THE MARK OF NERATH
Bill Slavicsek
August 2010

THE SEAL OF KARGA KUL
Alex Irvine
December 2010

The first two novels in a new line set in the evolving world of the DUNGEONS & DRAGONS® game setting. If you haven't played . . . or read D&D® in a while, your reintroduction starts in August!

ALSO AVAILABLE AS E-BOOKS!
Follow us on Twitter @WotC_Novels